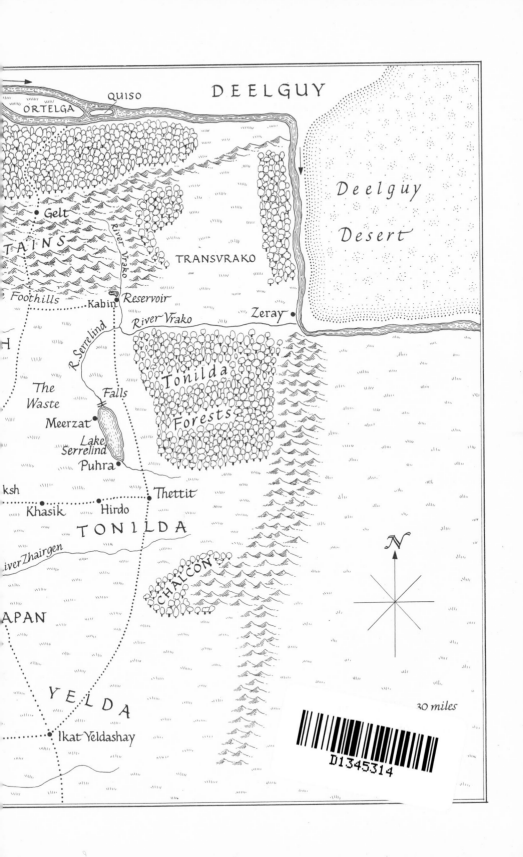

: MAIA :
Richard Adams

VIKING

VIKING

Penguin Books, Harmondsworth, Middlesex, England
Viking Penguin Inc., 40 West 23rd Street, New York, New York 10010, U.S.A.
Penguin Books Australia Ltd, Ringwood, Victoria, Australia
Penguin Books Canada Ltd, 2801 John Street, Markham, Ontario, Canada L3R 1B4
Penguin Books (N.Z.) Ltd, 182–190 Wairau Road, Auckland 10, New Zealand

First published 1984

Set in 9/11 pt Monophoto Sabon
Printed in Great Britain by
Richard Clay (The Chaucer Press) Ltd,
Bungay, Suffolk

BRITISH LIBRARY CATALOGUING IN PUBLICATION DATA

Adams, Richard, 1920–
    Maia.
    I. Title
    823'.914 [F]   PR6051.D345

ISBN 0–670–80033–3

To
Peter Johnson and Michael Mahony,
my sons-in-law,
in whom I count myself fortunate

Ὑγιαίνειν μὲν ἄριστον ἀνδρὶ θνατῷ,
δεύτερον δὲ φυὰν καλὸν γενέσθαι,
τὸ τρίτον δὲ πλουτεῖν ἀδόλως,
καὶ τὸ τέταρτον ἡβᾶν μετὰ τῶν φίλων.

(Anon., 6th–5th centuries B.C.)

οὔτε γὰρ ἐν τοῖς ἄλλοις ζῴοις οὔτ' ἐπὶ τῶν ἐθνῶν ὁρῶμεν τὴν ἀνδρίαν ἀκολουθοῦσαν τοῖς ἀγριωτάτοις, ἀλλὰ μᾶλλον τοῖς ἡμερωτέροις καὶ λεοντώδεσιν ἤθεσιν.

Aristotle, Politics, VIII

('Among the barbarians, and among animals, we find courage associated not with the greatest ferocity, but with a gentle and lion-like temper.')

CONTENTS

: PART III :

THE SERRELINDA

ACKNOWLEDGEMENTS

I acknowledge with gratitude the help I have received from Peter Carson, Bob Gottlieb and John Guest, who read the book before publication and made valuable criticisms and suggestions.

The manuscript was typed by Mrs Elizabeth Aydon, Mrs Janice Kneale, Mrs A.-M. Sjöwall-Nilsson and Mrs Janice Watterson. I thank them all most warmly. In addition, Mrs Aydon gave invaluable help as a sort of 'continuity girl', picking up several inconsistencies, lacunae and points for correction. She deserves special thanks on this account.

NOTE

Readers of *Shardik* will observe that the maps, included in this story, of the Beklan Empire and of Bekla itself differ from those in the earlier book. These maps are not, however, inconsistent with those. Certain places, e.g., Lak and Tissarn, shown on the *Shardik* maps have been omitted here, since they form no part of Maia's story. Conversely, other features, e.g., Lake Serrelind, Nybril and Suba, played no part in *Shardik*, and accordingly were not shown on those maps.

The events in this story ante-date *Shardik* by a few years.

'Maia' rhymes with 'higher' (not with 'layer').

LIST OF CHARACTERS

This list is in alphabetical order (not in order of appearance or importance) and is intended for the convenience of anyone wishing to be reminded, while reading, of the identity of this or that character. Minor characters appearing in a single episode are omitted. On the other hand, several characters are included (e.g., Drigga, Senda-na-Say) who, while they do not appear directly, are recurrently mentioned and relevant to the story.

Anda-Nokomis: ('The Dragonfly's Son') See *Bayub-Otal*.

Ashaktis: A Palteshi woman, attendant upon Fornis.

Astara: See *Nokomis*.

Bayub-Otal: (otherwise known as 'Anda-Nokomis') The dispossessed Ban of Suba: natural son of Nokomis by the High Baron of Urtah: half-brother of Eud-Ecachlon.

Bel-ka-Trazet: High Baron of Ortelga.

Berialtis: An Ortelgan girl: Ta-Kominion's mistress.

Blarda: A farm lad, brother of Clystis.

Brero: A soldier, attendant upon Maia in Bekla.

Chia: An Urtan girl, enslaved in Bekla.

Clystis: Kerkol's wife.

Domris: Proprietress of the Lily Pool in Thettit-Tonilda.

Drigga: An old woman, neighbour to Morca during Maia's childhood: a village story-teller, ballad-singer, etc.

Durakkon: High Baron of Bekla and nominal head of the Leopards.

Dyphna: A concubine of Sencho, later a Beklan courtesan or 'shearna'.

Elleroth: Son and heir of the Ban of Sarkid: commander of a force of irregulars with Santil-kè-Erketlis.

Elvair-ka-Virrion: Son of Kembri-B'sai, Lord General of Bekla.

Enka-Mordet: A baron in Chalcon: father of Milvushina.

Eud-Ecachlon: Son and heir of the High Baron of Urtah: half-brother of Bayub-Otal.

Fleitil: A master-sculptor of Bekla (grandson of 'the great Fleitil').

Fordil: A master-musician of Bekla.

Fornis: Daughter of Kephialtar-ka-Voro, High Baron of Paltesh: Sacred Queen of Airtha in Bekla.

Frarnli: Proprietress of 'The Safe Moorings', a tavern at Meerzat.

Fravak: A Beklan metal-merchant; at one time Sencho's master.

Gehta: A girl working on a farm north-west of Bekla.

Genshed: A slave-trader employed by Lalloc.

Han-Glat: The Leopards' Controller of Fortifications: designer of the fortress at Dari-Paltesh.

Jarvil: Sencho's door-keeper or porter: later, Maia's porter.

Jejjereth: A half-crazy orator and self-styled prophet in Bekla.

Kapparah: A Beklan captain.

Karnat: King of Terekenalt.

Kelsi: The eldest of Maia's three younger sisters.

Kembri-B'sai: Lord General of Bekla: father of Elvair-ka-Virrion.

Kephialtar-ka-Voro: High Baron of Paltesh: father of Fornis.

Kerith-a-Thrain: A Beklan general.

Kerkol: A small farmer.

Kram: A Suban youth.

Lalloc: A Deelguy slave-dealer in Bekla.

Lenkrit-Duhl: Baron of Upper Suba.

Lirrit: An infant, youngest of Maia's three sisters.

Lokris: Milvushina's maid in Bekla.

Luma: A Suban girl.

Maia: A Tonildan girl.

Makron: A Suban village elder, husband of Penyanis.

Malendik: A man employed by N'Kasit.

Megdon: A slave-trader employed by Lalloc.

Mendel-el-Ekna: A Lapanese captain, adherent of Randronoth.

Meris: A Belishban, concubine of Sencho.

Milvushina: A Chalcon girl, daughter of Enka-Mordet.

Mollo: Elleroth's captain of pioneers.

Morca: Tharrin's wife.

Nala: The second of Maia's three younger sisters.

Nasada: A Suban doctor.

Nennaunir: A Beklan courtesan or 'shearna'.

N'Kasit: A Kabinese merchant dealing in hides, leather, etc., in Bekla.

Nokomis: ('The Dragonfly'; originally named Astara) A Suban dancing-girl, mother of Bayub-Otal by the High Baron of Urtah.

Occula: A black girl.

Ogma: A lame slave-girl.

Otavis: A Beklan slave-girl, later a courtesan or 'shearna'.

Penyanis: A Suban lady, wife of Makron.

Perdan: A slave-trader employed by Lalloc.

Pillan: Servant to Bayub-Otal.

Pokada: Prison governor in Bekla.

Randronoth: Governor of Lapan.

Santil-kè-Erketlis: A baron in Chalcon.

Sarget: A wealthy Beklan wine-merchant.

Sednil: A young Palteshi: lover of Nennaunir.

Seekron: A Lapanese nobleman, adherent of Randronoth.

Selperron: A Kabinese merchant, friend of N'Kasit.

Sencho-bè-L'vandor: High Counsellor of Bekla: the Leopards' Chief of Intelligence.

Senda-na-Say: The former High Baron of Bekla, killed by Durakkon.

Sendekar: A Beklan general.

Sessendris: Housekeeper (or 'säiyett') to Kembri.

Shend-Lador: A young Leopard, son of the castellan of the Beklan citadel.

Sphelthon: A young Tonildan soldier.

Ta-Kominion: A young Ortelgan noble.

Terebinthia: Housekeeper (or 'säiyett') to Sencho.

Tescon: A young Suban, adherent of Lenkrit.

Tharrin: Maia's step-father.

Thel: A young Suban, adherent of Lenkrit.

Tolis: A junior officer in Elleroth's force: lieutenant to Mollo.

'Zai': Occula's name for her father (actually named Baru): a jewel-merchant.

Zen-Kurel: A Katrian staff officer of King Karnat.

Zirek: A pedlar.

Zuno: A young man in Lalloc's, later in Fornis's employ.

: PART I :
THE PEASANT

I

THE FALLS

Three hundred yards downstream the noise of the falls, muffled by inter-vening trees and undergrowth in the crook of the bend, was reduced to a quiet murmur of pouring water, a natural sound more smoothly continuous than any other—than wind, insects or even night frogs in the marshes. In winter it might increase to the heavy roar of spate: in summer drought, diminish to a mere splashing among fern at lip and weed at base. It never ceased.

Below the bend the river ran strongly under the further bank, where its uneven bed of stones, gravel and sunken logs made the surface ripple and undulate, so that the tilted planes glittered in the late afternoon sun. Under the overgrown, nearer bank it was deeper and stiller, dully re-flecting sky and trees. All about, on either side, masses of plants were in vivid bloom; some forming wide beds in the shallows, others lining the banks waist-high or trailing from the trees in festoons of saffron, crimson and greenish-white. Their honey-sweet or citrous scents filled the air, as did the hum of insects hovering and gliding, hunting prey or themselves darting in flight. Here and there a fish rose, gulped down a floating fly and vanished, leaving widening circles that died away on the surface.

Taller than the rushes and swamp-grass filling a marshy inlet on the further bank, a *keriot*—the green, frog-hunting heron of the Tonildan Waste—stood motionless, watching the few feet of slow-moving water around it with alert, voracious eyes. From time to time it would bend its long neck and stab, gobbling quickly before resuming its still posture.

At length, as the sun, declining, dipped behind the tops of the trees, throwing their shadows across the river, the keriot became restless. Wary even beyond the common run of wild creatures, it was alerted and made uneasy by such slight intrusions as the change of light, the movement of shadows and the breeze now sprung up among the creepers. Having taken a few restless steps this way and that through the plumed reeds, it rose into the air and flew upstream, its long legs trailing behind the slow beat of its wings. Flying directly up the line of the river, it was making for the still-sunlit falls.

The big bird was high enough above the river to see, over the lip of the falls, the lake beyond lying calm in the sun, its blue expanse contrasting with the tumult and white water of the twenty-foot-high outfall. There were in fact two falls, each about fifteen yards wide, separated by a little, green island bordered, at this time of year, with forget-me-not and golden water-lilies, some nodding and dipping upon the very edge, as though peering down into the welter below.

The keriot had circled twice and was just about to glide down to the flat stones at the foot of the falls when suddenly it rose again, turned and made heavily off across the near-by thickets of scrub willow, disappearing at length into the recesses of the swamp. Something had evidently decided it to go elsewhere.

Here, at close quarters, the noise of the falls was made up of all manner of sounds: boomings, gurglings, patterings of spray, sudden spurts and bubblings here and gone above the steady beat of water falling into water and the higher, smacking note of water falling upon flat stones. And amongst this tumult a girl was singing, her voice rising clearly above the plunging boil.

'Why was I born? Ah, tell me, tell me, Lord Cran!
Isthar, isthal a steer.
Thou wast born, my daughter, to bear the weight of a man.
Isthar a steer, na ro, isthal a rondu.'

The singer was nowhere to be seen. Though her song had alarmed the keriot, a human listener (supposing there to be one at hand) must surely have been affected otherwise, for it possessed not only youthful gladness, but also a kind of tentative, wondering quality of which the singer herself could hardly have been conscious, just as no bird or animal can be aware of its own beauty. Her voice, common and beautiful as any of the flowers by the pool, fell silent, leaving only the water-noises, but still there was no one to be seen along the verge or on the stones beneath the green-and-white stretch of the falls. Then, as though a spirit's, the song resumed from a different place, close to the further bank.

'"Fill thou my purse, great Cran; my purse is cut."
Isthar, isthal a steer.
"Seek, daughter, that horn of plenty with which men butt."
Isthar a steer, na ro, isthal a rondu.'

Out through the curtain of falling water stepped a girl, perhaps fifteen years old: sturdy and well-made, the very picture of youthful energy and health, her naked body glistening as the cascade beat down upon it, pouring in streams from her shoulders, her out-thrust breasts and the firm curve of her buttocks. Laughing, she flung back her head and for a moment took the full force of the fall in her face; then, spluttering, she threw up her arms and spread her open hands to shield herself from the water. In this posture she rocked on her heels, swaying back and forth, now disappearing behind the water-curtain, now covered with it as by a bright, translucent cloak and again leaning forward to leave the torrent unbroken at her back.

22

Despite the bloom and opulence of her body and the words of her song, both her face and a certain ingenuous quality in her bearing suggested the child rather than the woman. Her absorbed, joyous movements as she played her game (not far removed from hide-and-seek or peep-bo), in and out of the water-curtain; her impulsive, unself-conscious delight, like that of a creature unreflectingly happy in the immediate moment; her very nakedness in this open (if lonely) spot—all denoted a girl who, while she might have learned already to know the world as a place where one could be tired, hungry or even ill, had never yet found it perilous or cruel, or become aware (except perhaps in stories or songs) of the kind of danger which would certainly have been present to the mind of an older girl bathing alone in this wilderness. Not that she was unconscious of her early maturity and beauty: indeed, standing under the fall, deliberately moving so that the inexhaustible water deluged and caressed in turn her shoulders, her belly, thighs and rump, she appeared sensible of nothing else.

Longing for the future, dwelling on it, even enacting it in imagination— such blending of syrupy concoctions never includes the sharper ingredients infused by experience. These would be as unpalatable to the immature taste of young girls (who are free to exclude them from their dreams) as they often are to the taste of grown women (who are not free to exclude them from their lives).

At length, tiring of picking her way back and forth along the cool, slippery recesses behind the fall and looking out—like a sentry from a castle—through rifts in the falling water, the girl burst through it once more, hop, skip and jump on the stones, plunged headlong into the pool and swam swiftly down to the shallow water at its foot. Here, as the sand and small gravel of the bed brushed her prone length, she came to rest, turned on her back and lay spread-eagled, legs apart, her head resting on a convenient, flat stump just above the surface.

> "'The flowers of spring, Lord Cran, they cannot be counted.'
> *Isthar, isthal a steer.*
> "They bloom in the green field where the mare was mounted."
> *Isthar a steer, na ro, isthal a rondu.*
>
> "I will tell thee, my daughter —"'

She giggled, sinking a few moments below the surface, so that the words were lost in bubbling. Then, standing up, she began wandering here and there through the shallows, pulling the long-stalked lilies, gold and pink, piercing their fibrous, dripping stems with her thumb-nail and threading them into a wreath. A tangle of scarlet *trepsis* hung over the opposite bank, and she waded across and wrenched out half a dozen strands, twining them into the lily-garland until it was nearly as thick as her arm.

Hanging it round her neck, she stood dabbling her feet, picking up sticks between her toes and bending her head this way and that to smell the great collar of bloom that covered her shoulders. Then, off again like a child who cannot remain still but must find some outlet for its energy, she began gathering more flowers—pulling tufted heads off the clustering *hellias*, plucking daisies out of the grass, campions, orange ladies' cups— whatever came to hand. She made a belt, bracelets of flowers and a lop-sided, fragile crown that would not hold together until she had bound it with another strand of trepsis. She put a crimson flower behind each ear and another in the hollow of her navel—whence it almost at once fell out. Then, smiling—for in imagination she was teasing an outraged, invisible companion—she tore up a sheaf of forget-me-nots and, pinching the thin stems one by one from the plant, threaded them in and out of the fleece of hair at her groin, until it was first speckled and then almost completely hidden beneath a close mat of small, sky-blue flowers.

'I am the Queen of Bekla!'

Raising open arms, she began pacing with measured dignity across the shallows, but unluckily trod on a pointed stone, cried 'Ow!' and stood wobbling on one leg. Petulantly, she kicked the water, sending up a shower of drops; then bent down, pulled up the offending stone, spat on it and tossed it away among the trees. Another impulse coming upon her, she climbed out on the bank, ran to the head of the pool, took three steps into the deeper water, turned on her back and slowly drifted, flowers and all, out towards the centre. Here she floated, arms at her sides, only her breasts and face above the surface, gazing up at the sinking disc of the sun.

'You dazzle me—reckon I'll dazzle you!' she whispered. 'Go on, try and burn me, then—yah, I'm in the wa-ter!'

As she remained floating, the current, rippling over and past her, gently soaked and pulled at her frail finery, gradually loosening and untwining it, so that the flowers began to drift away piecemeal from her body; here a lily, there a daisy carried away on the stream, some vanishing swiftly, some twirling in slow eddies under the bank, until at length, save for a bloom or two, she was naked as at first. Last of all, she allowed herself to drift downstream until she was standing once more at the tail of the pool, the water to her knees.

The sun had dropped lower and now the falls lay in shadow, their multifoliate white faded to a single, smooth grey. The girl—a strong swimmer, continually in and out of the water all her short life—had swum far out into the lake that afternoon before returning to laze by the pool. Now she felt weary; hungry, too, and a little cold. Wading to the bank she paused, straddling her thighs to make water in the stream. Then, putting

24

one knee on the short grass of the bank to clamber up, she wrung out her long, wet hair with quick, impatient twistings, pulled her shift and worn, homespun smock over her still-wet shoulders, scrambled up the slope to one side of the falls and, barefoot, sauntered away down the lakeside in the light of the sunset.

She had neither seen nor heard anything to suggest to her that she was observed. In fact, however, she had been watched for some time by a man hidden among the trees, the sound of whose approach and later occasional movements to keep her in view had been covered by the noise of the falls. As soon as she had gone he stepped out of hiding, hastened along the bank, flung himself down on the turf and in a matter of seconds gratified himself, panting with closed eyes and in his transport pressing his face into the grass where her naked body had lain.

He was her step-father.

: 2 :

THE CABIN

It was already dusk as the girl strolled through the hamlet near the upper end of the lake and on a few hundred yards, down a high-banked, narrow track leading to a timber cabin. The cabin, fairly large but in poor repair, stood beside a fenced grazing-field with an old shed in one corner. Between it and the surrounding wasteland lay three or four cultivated patches of millet and close by, the greener, conical sprouts of a late crop of *brillions*.

A younger girl, perhaps eleven or twelve years old, came running down the track, her bare feet sending up little clouds of dust. In one hand she was clutching a hunk of black bread from which, as she came to a stop, she took a quick bite.

The older girl also stopped, facing her.

'What's up then, Kelsi?'

'Mother's that cross with you, Maia, for bein' away so long.'

'I don't care,' replied the girl. 'Let her be!'

'I saw you was coming: I come to let you know. She told me to go and get the cows in, 'cos Tharrin's not come home yet either. I'll have to go back now, 'fore she starts wonderin' where I got to.'

'Give me a bit of that bread,' said the girl.

'Oh, Maia, it's all she give me!'

'Just a bite, Kelsi, come on: I'm starving! She'll give me mine: then I'll give it back to you.'

'I know your bites,' said Kelsi. She broke off a small piece between a dirty finger and thumb. Maia took it, chewing slowly before swallowing.

'She'd better not try to do anything to me,' she said at length. 'Supper—she'd just better give me some, that's all.'

'She don't like you, does she?' said Kelsi, with childish candour. 'Oh, not for a while now. What you done?'

Maia shrugged. 'Dunno; I don't like *her* much, either.'

'She was sayin' this evening as you was big enough to do half the work, but you left it all to her. She said—'

'I don't care what she said. Tharrin wasn't there, was he?'

'No, he's been out all day. I'll have to go now,' said Kelsi, swallowing the last of the bread. She set off up the track, running.

Maia followed with the idling pace of reluctance. Before approaching the door of the cabin she stopped and, on impulse, scrambled up the bank and tugged down a branch of orange-flowering *sanchel*. Plucking a bloom, she stuck it behind her left ear, pulling back her hair to make sure that it was not hidden among the wet tresses.

Just as she entered, a chubby little girl, no more than three years old, came running through the doorway and full-tilt against her knee. Maia, stooping, snatched her up and kissed her before she could begin to cry.

'Where were you running to, Lirrit, m'm? Running away, little *banzi*? Going to run all the way to Thettit, were you?' The little girl laughed and Maia began tossing her in her arms, singing as she did so.

> '*Bring* me my *dagger* and *bring* me my *sword*.
> *Lir*rit's the *la*dy to *go* by my *side*.
> *I'm* off to *Bek*la to *meet* the great *lord*—'

'Are you going to stand there all night squalling your head off, you lazy, good-for-nothing slut?'

The woman who spoke was looking backwards over her shoulder as she stirred a pot hanging over the fire. She was thin and sharp-eyed, with a lean, shrewd face retaining traces of youth and beauty much as the sky outside retained the last light of day. Her eyes were red-rimmed with smoke and a powder of wood-ash discoloured her black hair.

The fire and the twilight together gave enough light to show the squalor of the room. The earth floor was littered with rubbish—fish-bones, fruit rinds and vegetable peelings, a broken pail, a dirty fragment of blanket, some sticks that Lirrit, playing, had dragged out of the wood-pile and left lying where they fell. An odour of rancid fat mingled with the faint, sweet-sour smell of infant's urine. A long oar, cracked a foot above the blade, was standing upright against the farther wall and in the firelight its shadow danced back and forth with irregular monotony.

Before Maia could answer, the woman, dropping her iron ladle into the

26

pot, turned round and faced her, hands on hips. She stood leaning back-ward, for she was pregnant. One of her front teeth was broken short, giving her voice a sibilant, hissing sound.

'Kelsi's driving in the cows, and a fine time she's taking over it, too. Nala's supposed to be bringing the clothes in off the hedge—that's if no one's pinched them. Where your step-father's got to nobody knows—'

'I'm done bringing in the clothes,' said a cheerful, dirty-faced nine-year-old, sprawled on a pile of wattle hurdles in the shadows. 'Can I have some bread now, mum?'

'Oh, there you are!' replied the woman. 'Well, you can just make yourself a bit more useful first, my girl. You can pick all this muck up off the floor and put it on the fire, and after that you can go out and bring in some water. We'll see about bread when you're done.' She came over to Maia, who had not moved and was still dandling the little girl in her arms.

'And where in Cran's name have you been, miss, eh? Leaving us all to break our backs until you choose to come trapesing back half out of your clothes, like a Beklan *shearna* looking for a night's work!' Her voice cracked with rage. 'What's that behind your ear, you trollop?'

'Flower,' said Maia. Her mother snatched the bloom and threw it on the floor.

'I know it's a flower, miss! And p'raps you're going to tell me you don't know what it means to go about wearing a sanchel behind your left ear?'

'I know what it means,' said Maia, smiling sidelong at the floor.

'So you stroll about like that while I'm slaving here—a great, dirty baggage, strong as an ox—'

'I'm not dirty,' said Maia. 'I've been swimming in the lake. You're dirty. You smell.'

Her mother struck at her face, but as her arm swung forward Maia, still holding the child on one arm, caught and twisted it sideways, so that she stumbled and half-fell, cursing. The little girl began to scream and Maia, hushing her as she went, walked across to the fire and began ladling soup from the pot into a bowl standing on the hearth.

'You just let that alone!' shouted her mother. 'That's for your step-father when he gets back. And if there's any left it'll go to your sisters, as have done some honest work. Do you hear me?' she went on as Maia, taking no notice, put down the little girl, carried the bowl over to the table and seated herself on a rickety bench. She snatched up a stick from behind the door. 'You do as I say or I'll have the skin off that fat back of yours, you see if I don't!'

Maia, gulping soup, looked up at her over the rim of the bowl.

'You'd best let me alone. Might get hurt else.'

Her mother paused a second, glaring. Then, holding the stick out in front of her, stiff-armed and striking clumsily from side to side, she rushed at Maia. The girl, springing to her feet and overturning the bench on the floor, threw the bowl at her. It struck her on the neck and fell to the ground, covering her with the spilt soup. At the same time the point of the stick caught and scratched Maia's forearm, drawing blood. Kelsi, coming in from the cowshed, found her mother and sister grappling across the table, panting as they tugged at each other's hair and aimed slapping blows at heads and shoulders. At this moment the pale sky of nightfall in the open doorway was darkened by a man's figure stooping under the lintel.

'Cran and Airtha!' said the man. 'What the devil's going on, eh? D'you want them to hear you down the other end of the lane? Here, leave off, now, will you?'

The woman happening to be the nearest, he took her by the forearms and pulled her back against him. She stood panting, still clutching the stick. He took it from her and then, glancing slowly round as his eyes became accustomed to the smoky half-light, took in the overturned bench, the spilt soup and the blood along Maia's arm.

'Having a bit of a row, were you?' he said, as though not unused to such things or inclined to attach much weight to them. 'Well, you can stop it now, both of you, and get me some supper—that's if there's any left. I'd have been here sooner, only for carrying in the nets. What were you doing, Maia? Come on, pick up that bowl and get me something to eat in it, there's a good lass.'

In the scuffle Maia's worn, flimsy smock had been torn across the bodice. As she bent to pick up the bowl one of her breasts fell out.

Her step-father laughed. 'Going to give us all a treat, eh? Better leave it till I'm not so damned hungry. Come on, Morca my lass, what was all the row about, eh?'

Morca, silent, dipped a rag in the water-jar to wipe her sweating face.

Maia, straightening up with the bowl in one hand, held the ripped cloth in place with the other as she answered her step-father.

'I come in from swimming. I wanted something to eat. Mother said as I wasn't to have any, that's all.'

At this Morca broke in shrilly, bringing up one thing after another, emptying the whole pail of grievance and resentment in a deluge about the man's ears. 'House-full of good-for-nothing brats—soon be another and whose fault's that?—never enough to go round—tell us you're going to market—drinking half the day in Meerzat—some Deelguy drab—oh, yes, don't think I don't know—daughters growing up as lazy as you—Maia never does a hand's turn, takes no notice of me or anyone else—she'll end in Zeray, mark my words—place'll fall round our ears one of these days—don't know why I ever took up with you—'

28

Tharrin, apparently quite untroubled by this tirade, sat at the table eating bread, soup and fish as Maia brought them to him. He had something of the look of a man who has been caught out in a heavy shower—a slight air of bravado, mingled with resignation and the hope that the rain will not last much longer.

He was not himself a Tonildan, having been born, some thirty-nine years before, the fourth son of a miller in Yelda. He had grown up footloose and happy-go-lucky, seldom much concerned about work as long as he had the price of a meal and a drink, yet able, when driven by need, to buckle down well enough; so that he soon acquired the reputation of a decent enough casual worker. He was a pleasant companion, largely because he never troubled about the morrow, never argued and had no principles to defend. If ever there was a man who took life entirely as it came it was Tharrin. Once, having joined an iron-trading expedition to the Gelt mountains, he had shown himself exceptionally useful and energetic. Yet when news of his capacities came to the ears of a Beklan officer, who offered him the rank of *tryzatt* at higher pay than he had ever earned or was ever likely to earn in any other way, he unhesitatingly declined between one drink and the next; and a month later took an ill-paid job helping to build huts at a farm in Tonilda, his fancy having been taken by a girl in the near-by village.

For girls also he took as they came; and since he was a presentable young fellow and open-handed whenever he happened to have any money, they came easily enough. He had never been known to ill-use or even to lose his temper with a girl. However the girls, in the long run, customarily lost theirs, for Tharrin, good-humoured as always, would laugh and shrug his shoulders at outraged accusations of absence or proven infidelity, merely waiting for anger to give way to tears and reconciliation. If it did not, he would simply transfer his favours with no hard feelings whatever.

Since the only provocation he ever gave was by what he did not do rather than by anything he did; and since almost the only retaliation to which he ever resorted was his own departure, he was largely successful, at all events during his youth and early manhood, in persuading the world to take him on his own terms, or at any rate to grin indulgently and acquiesce. He got away with a great deal.

Such accomplishments, however, are very much a gift of the prime, and tend to wane with it. There came a time when people began to feel unconsciously and then, after a few more years, to say in so many words that Tharrin's ways were hardly fitting for a fellow of his age. The part of the roving blade no longer suited him. It was time he learnt some sense and settled down.

Such remarks, however, did nothing to change Tharrin, who had no enemies and always seemed as content with empty pockets as full ones. He was about thirty when, having taken service for a year in the household of Ploron, head forester to the Ban of Sarkid, he met his daughter Keremnis at the spring festival and, without the least thought of bettering himself but simply in the course of his own pleasure, got her with child.

Had Tharrin's motive been deliberate Ploron, himself a shrewd, calculating man who had risen step by step through keeping a continual eye on the main chance and marrying to his advantage, would almost certainly have accepted the situation with grudging respect for a kindred spirit. In short, he would have put a good face on it and given him the girl and her dowry. That Tharrin had been nothing but impulsive was bad enough: but that he should then make it plain that he did not particularly want the girl and all that would go with her was unforgivable, a deadly insult to hard-won rank and standing. For Tharrin to remain anywhere in the southern provinces of the empire was no longer healthy or practicable. He disappeared north for three years, scratching a living first by rope-making on Ortelga, the remote, despised island in the Telthearna, and then as a drover in Terekenalt.

And indeed he might well have remained in Terekenalt for the rest of his life, had it not been for the so-called Leopard revolution which took place in Bekla during the third year after his flight from Sarkid. This, which culminated in the murder of the High Baron Senda-na-Say, the accession of Durakkon and of the notorious Sacred Queen Fornis, had been to some extent abetted for his own gain by Karnat, King of Terekenalt—Karnat the Tall, as he was called. Since Terekenalt was in a state of more or less permanent hostility to the Beklan Empire, it contained a number of exiles and fugitives from Senda-na-Say's régime, several of whom now felt it safe to return. Tharrin, too, also felt that it might be safe to return; though he judged it prudent to remain in the north of the empire.

For a time he settled in Kabin of the Waters but then, having travelled one spring the fifty miles south to Thettit as drover to a Deelguy cattle trader, left him there and wandered as far as the shores of Lake Serrelind. It was here that he met with Morca, not long widowed and desperate to know what to do for herself and her three fatherless girls; and took up with her as easily as he had taken up with eight or nine other women during the past twenty years.

Her husband's death had not left Morca a beggar. She had the cabin, a fishing boat and nets and a few cows. Yet in a lonely, country place; and in such times, with the Leopard régime exploiting the peasantry and virtually encouraging gangs of itinerant slave-traders, there could be little peace of mind for a widow living alone with a young family. For Morca Tharrin, improvident and loose-living though he might be, meant the difference between some sort of security and a life of continual fear and anxiety on the edge of the Tonildan Waste. She was content to take him for bed-mate and protector and when, three years later, Lirrit was born, she was not ill-pleased.

Tharrin, for his part, found himself, as first the months and then the years went by, settling into the life of a Tonildan small-holder much as a chance-flung stone settles into mud. He fished the lake and taught the two older girls to help him in the boat; he did a certain amount of work on Morca's land but rather more (since this paid ready money) on the land of her better-off neighbours; loafed in the Meerzat taverns and from time to time disappeared to Thettit. As will be seen, he discharged some unusual commissions. Yet somehow he always drifted back. For the truth was (though he would never have admitted it) that he was beginning to need, more and more, to settle for what he could get without too much hard work and fatigue. For him it was the first breath of autumn. With little reflection (to which he had, in any case, always been a stranger) he found himself staying on with Morca and her girls. The girls made it easy for him to do so, for while their mother, soured by work and worry, was often shrewish, Tharrin was uncritical, kindly and good-natured, and on this account they liked him and usually banded together to take his part after news of one or another of his escapades had filtered back to the cabin. In return he allowed them to pamper him with what meagre luxuries were to be had, let them do much as they pleased and filled their heads with half-understood bawdy jokes and tall stories of former drinking-bouts and girls in Sarkid and Terekenalt. Like many another seedy adventurer drifting into middle age, he had come down to representing himself as a devil of a fellow to youngsters not yet possessed of sufficient experience to see him with eyes other than his own.

His unspoken, but probably strongest, reason for remaining was Maia. Tharrin followed whims and inclinations, not trains of thought. Any notion of fatherly responsibility towards Maia was the last thing that ever entered his head, let alone any consideration of her future or her best interests. He simply enjoyed seeing her about the place, finding her there when he got home, smacking her buttocks and telling her to bring his supper. He liked to tease her and sit laughing as she stared out of her great blue eyes when he had told her some indecent anecdote beyond her comprehension. Girls, to be sure, were—or had once been—two a *meld* to Tharrin, but for all that, his palate was not so jaded but he could still be stirred by an exceptionally pretty one. During the past six months—much as a man might begin by casually approving a good-looking colt in a neighbour's field and end with an almost obsessive longing to own it for himself—he had become more and more engrossed by the thought of delicious, ripening Maia—

31

Maia laughing, Maia insolent and defiant to Morca, Maia picking flowers, Maia stripping herself to wash with a child's heedlessness of who might be by. Two things had so far held him back. The first was Morca's sharp, un-hoodwinked jealousy. Though nothing was said, he sensed that she knew very well what he was feeling. Probably it had even occurred to her that he might exchange mother for daughter and vanish one night down the road to Thettit—to Kabin—to anywhere. The other was the girl's own inno-cence. Short of rape, it is difficult to seduce someone who simply does not know what it is all about; who has not yet even begun to be aware of carnal feelings in her own body—burgeoning though it may be. So Tharrin, as he clutched Morca in the darkness behind the curtain screening their bed from the rest of the room, fixed his thoughts on Maia, imagining in his mind's eye her glowing cheeks and downcast eyes as he undressed her, hearing her begging him to be gentle, her mounting cries at the onset of a pleasure never before known: and other delightful fancies, borrowed from memories of years before; for it was many a day since he had had the opportunity to instruct an ingénue, and hearts that he had broken long ago had long been breaking others.

As Morca's next pregnancy advanced, she grew daily more irritable, nervous and moody; flying into tempers with the girls, taking less and less care either of her appearance or of the cleanliness of the cabin, re-lapsing into fits of lassitude and, increasingly, denying her body to Tharrin with a kind of bitter satisfaction, so that often even his good-nature (which in any case was composed of indolence and weakness rather than of any real charity) was strained. She, like him but more comfortlessly, had now begun, with the years, to see ahead down a long and ever-darkening slope. Sometimes, her anxiety and chagrin gnawing while she waited for Tharrin to return from the tavern—or else-where—the fancy would come upon her that not only her beauty, but her very capacity to contend with life was being drained away into Maia's sleek, firm young body, her rosy cheeks and golden hair. Her former husband had been thrifty and hard-working. If he had lived, they would probably have been well-off in a few more years. Maia—so it seemed to Morca—had become, with her selfish, wayward intractability, nothing but a dead weight and a useless mouth.

Not far from the cabin a great ash-tree stood beside the lake, and here, during the summer afternoons, Morca would often catch sight of Maia sprawled along a branch, chewing grass and gazing down at her reflection in the green water, indolent and luxurious as a cat on a bench. Then she would scream at her to come down and sweep the floor or peel the vegetables; and the girl would comply with a lazy, shoulder-shrugging grace which only increased Morca's resentment. After a time, however,

Maia, tired of predictable interruption, forsook the ash-tree and took to straying further afield, to the marshes or the waterfall: or she would swim out more than half a mile, to an island near the centre of the lake, there to bask away the afternoon before returning for a supper to the preparation of which she had contributed nothing.

There was never quite enough to go round—never enough, that is, for satisfaction. They were not starving, or even in serious want; yet throughout the past year, as the girls had grown, there seemed to Morca to be less and less than in days gone by—less variety and quality and less prospect of making provision for the future. Often it was all she could do to feed Tharrin as a man ought to be fed and to fend off, with bread, apples and porridge, the continual hunger of the rest. Once, Maia had sat down by the road and eaten half the butter she was supposed to be taking to market at Meerzat.

'But she won't do it again,' Morca had said in relating the matter to Tharrin, who roared with laughter and invited Maia to show him her weals. There were only two, for after the second blow Maia had torn the stick out of her mother's hand and snapped it across her knee.

Perhaps it was the recollection of this which now caused Morca to cut short her tirade. Taking down a wooden tub from where it hung on two nails by the door, she carried it over to the hearth and began to fill it with warm water for Tharrin to wash. Her back being turned, he winked at Maia, holding a finger to his lips. The girl smiled back and, having gone so far as to turn away before stripping to her shift, wrapped herself in an old blanket, sat down on a stool and began mending her torn bodice with needle and thread.

Tharrin, wiping his mouth and spitting raisin stones on the floor, followed Morca across to the hearth, sat down on a stool and bent to unwind his muddy leggings.

'Come on, old girl,' he said, as she set the steaming tub at his feet. 'What's the use of a house full of caterwauling, eh? Life's too short. Look here'—pulling her reluctantly down on his knee—'this'll put a smile on your face. You didn't know I was a silver diviner, did you?'

'What you talking about?' replied Morca sulkily, yet making no move to get up.

'I can find silver anywhere. Look!' And, suddenly thrusting his hand down the front of her smock, before she could grab his wrist he drew it out with a coin held up between his fingers. 'Fifty meld! And all for you, my pretty Morca! You just take that to market tomorrow along with the cheese and butter, and buy yourself something nice. And don't you dare go telling me anything about taverns and Deelguy girls again. It's you I love; and you ought to know that by this time.'

Morca stared; then took the coin between her finger and thumb and bit it.

'Where'd you find this?'

'In between your *deldas*!'

On the other side of the hearth Maia, holding her stitching up to the light from the fire, suppressed a gurgle of laughter.

'Go on, take it!' persisted Tharrin. 'It's not stolen, I'll tell you that much. It's yours, fair and square. Come on, now, give us a kiss!'

'Well—' Morca paused, only half-appeased. 'What's all this leading up to? You're off to Thettit, I suppose, and see you back when we do?'

'Never in the world! Why, I'm taking the boat out tomorrow, soon as young Maia's mended that hole in the net. When you come back from market the place'll be stacked with carp, perch, trout—anything you like. Make another eighty meld, easy. Come on, Nala,' he called to the nine-year-old, 'just you get that banzi laid down to sleep, now! And you, Kelsi, see to covering down the fire: you can pull out that big log and dip it in the tub here; I'm done with the water. I don't know about the rest of you, but I'm tired out. Give over stitching, now, Maia; you'll only spoil those big blue eyes! You can finish it tomorrow! Come on, my lass,' he said, putting his arm round Morca's waist and fondling her, 'just you be getting that big belly into bed, and I'll be along to remind you how you came by it.'

Fifty meld was more money than the house had seen for weeks. But impulse and unpredictability were Tharrin's hallmarks, and Morca had learned better than to provoke further absurd replies by pressing him to tell how the windfall had been come by. All the same, she would have given half of it to know where he had been that day.

: 3 :

THE NET

The setting moon, shining through a crack in the shutters, fell upon the dirty, ragged bedclothes and on the one bare leg which Maia, asleep in her shift, had thrust out to lie along a bench beside the bed. The bed had become too narrow for both herself and Nala, and Maia, who, however bitterly she might quarrel with Morca, was for the most part generous and kindly towards her sisters, had taken to sleeping with one leg out on the bench so that Nala could be more at ease. On summer nights such as this the arrangement was not really troublesome, except that turning over was tricky. However, Maia usually fell asleep quickly and slept sound.

In the foetid air behind the closed wooden shutters, flies buzzed and droned about the room, and from time to time the gnawing of a mouse sounded from somewhere along the wall by the hearth. Tharrin, awake beside the sleeping Morca, drew the curtain a crack and lay watching the shaft of moonlight as it slowly travelled across Maia's bare shoulders and tumbled curls.

Moonlight is commonly believed to induce dreams, and certainly Maia was dreaming. Tharrin could hear her murmuring in her sleep. Yet into the world within her solitary head he could not follow.

At first her dream was formless, possessed of no images from the waking world; there was only an awareness of shining, misty distance; an empty place of opalescent light. Then, looking down, she saw that she was clothed all in flowers; not merely hung about with them, as on the waterfall the evening before, but clad in a long robe made entirely of scented, brilliant blooms such as she had never seen in her life.

'I am the Queen of Bekla!' she pronounced; yet without speaking; for miraculously, her every thought was a royal utterance automatically heard by multitudes waiting silently round her. Slowly, magnificently, she paced between them towards her carriage; for, as she knew, she was to ride through the city to some sacred destination, there to fulfil her rôle of queen.

The carriage, curved and faintly lustrous like a shell, stood waiting. To either side of its red-painted pole was harnessed a white, long-horned goat. Each, scarlet-plumed and gold-tasselled, was hung about, as though for market, with all manner of fruit and vegetables—beans in their long pods, bunches of carrots; marrows and pendent green cucumbers. Some shadowy, half-seen person was waiting to lead them, but she waved him aside.

'I will drive them: they are mine.' And, grasping the shaft of a cloven-headed goad which stood in a holster beside her seat, she pricked and urged them forward.

Now, as though swimming in choppy water, she was rocking on through unseen crowds like waves, swaying, moving up and down as her goats bore her through an applauding city all tumult. Between her legs she was holding a hollowed gourd full of ripe figs, and these she tossed in handfuls to either side.

'They're for everyone! Everyone is to have them!' she cried. There was scrambling, tussling and a smell of crushed figs, but of all this she was aware without discerning anyone out of a concourse formless as lake-mist. Yet she knew that even in the midst of their admiration she was in deadly danger. A great, fat man was guzzling and stuffing himself with her figs. He had the power to kill her, yet she drove past him unharmed, for a black girl was holding him back.

Amid the cheering crowds she reached her destination. It was the ash-tree by the lake. Reining in her goats she scrambled out, climbed to the bough over the water and lay along it, looking down. Yet it was not her own face she saw below her, but that of an old, grey man, gazing kindly yet gravely up at her from the green depths. He was himself a denizen of water-ways and water; that much she knew. She wondered whether he was actually lying stretched beneath the surface, or whether what she saw was only a reflection and he behind her. Yet as she turned her head to look, the boughs began to sway and rustle, a bright light dazzled her and she woke to find the moonlight in her eyes.

For some time she lay still, recalling the dream and repeating in her mind a proverb once told to her by her father.

> If you want your dream made real,
> Then to none that dream reveal.
> If you want your dream to die,
> Tell it ere the sun is high.

She remembered the dream vividly; not merely what she had seen, but chiefly what she had felt—the all-informing atmosphere of a splendour composed of brilliant yet come-by trappings, their bizarre nature unques-tioned while the dream held sway. The splendour—and the danger. And the strange old man in the water. She could not tell whether or not she wanted that dream to come true. Anyway, how could it?

Ah, but suppose she took no steps to *stop* it coming true? Then it might come true in its own way—in some unexpected, unbeautiful way—like the disregarded prophecies in the hero-tales that Tharrin sometimes told, or the ballads sung by Drigga, the kindly old woman who lived up the lane. And if it *were* to come true, would she know at the time, or only after-wards?

She felt hungry. Listening intently and holding her breath, she could just catch the sound of Morca's regular breathing from behind the curtain. The girls were forbidden to help themselves to food. Morca would have liked to be able to lock the cupboard-like recess that served for a larder, but a Gelt lock was a luxury far beyond the household's means. Maia had never even seen one.

She slipped out of bed, pulled on her half-mended smock and tiptoed across to the larder. The door was fastened with a length of cord, and this she untied with scarcely a sound. Groping, her hand found a lump of bread and some cold fish left over from Tharrin's supper. Taking them, she tied the cord again, stole to the door, raised the bar and stepped out into the clear, grey twilight of the early summer morning.

Bird song was growing all around her, and from the lake came a harsh, vibrating cry and a watery scuttering. She crouched, clasping her knees, and made water in the grass; then, picking fragments of fish off the bone as she went, she wandered slowly down to the ash-tree and climbed to her accustomed branch.

Resting her arms before her as she lay prone along the branch, she laid her forehead on them and breathed the air thus imprisoned in the cave between bosom and forearms. The bread was hard, and she held it for a little while in her armpit before biting and gulping it down. Just as she finished it, a brilliant shaft of light shot all across the lake and the rim of the sun appeared above the further shore three miles away.

The glittering water, dazzling her, reminded her once more of her dream. 'If you want your dream made real—' Suddenly an idea occurred to her. Dreams, as everyone knew, came from Lespa of the Stars, the beautiful consort of the god Shakkarn. Lespa had sent this dream, and therefore Lespa must know all about it. She, Maia, would give it back to her, confess her own incomprehension and beg the goddess to do as she thought best. In this way she would both have told and not have told her dream.

Pulling off her clothes, she laid them across the branch and then, swinging a moment on her arms, lightly dropped the ten feet to the water. A quick shock of cold, to which she was well-accustomed, a blowing of her nose and sluicing of her eyes, and she was swimming easily, on her back, out into the lake lying smoother than snakeskin in the sun.

Now she was resting still on the surface, more alone than in the grass, more easy than in bed, gazing up into the early-morning, pale-blue dome of the sky.

'Hear me, sweet Lespa, thou who from thy silver stars dost sprinkle the world with dreams. Behold, I give thee back thy dream, not ungratefully, but in bewilderment. Do for me as may be best, I humbly pray thee.'

'Maia! Ma—ia!'

Maia dropped her legs, treading water, pushed back her hair and looked quickly round towards the shore. It was Morca's voice, strident and sharp, and now she could see Morca herself standing by the door of the cowshed, shading her eyes and staring out across the lake.

She could see Morca. Why could Morca not see her? Then she realized why. Morca was looking straight into the risen sun, and her own head—all of her that was above water—must appear as a mere dot in the path of light streaming across the lake. Turning, she began swimming away, directly into the sun, taking care to leave scarcely a ripple on the surface.

It was nearly two hours before she returned, wading ashore near the ash-tree and pausing a few moments to brush the water from her body and limbs before climbing up to her clothes. As she strolled up towards the cabin, Nala came running down to meet her.

'Where've you been, Mai?'

'Where d'you think? In the lake.'

'Mother's been looking for you everywhere. She was that angry!'

'That's a change. Where is she now?'

'Gone to market in Meerzat. She's taken Kelsi with her. She was going to tell you all the things you had to do while she's gone, but she's told them to me instead and I'm to tell you.'

'Well, for a start I'm going to mend the net for Tharrin. He said so last night. Where's *he* got to, anyway?'

'I don't know. He went up the lane. Let me tell you what mother said, otherwise I'll never remember.'

'All right, but I shan't do no more 'n what I want.'

She was lying near the shore in the warm sun. All around her were spread the folds of the big net, and through her smock she could feel its knotted mesh against her back. She had piled up part of the mass behind her like a couch, and was now reclining at ease, the rent she was mending opened across her lap. Tar, cord, wax, twine and knife lay about her, conveniently to hand. Her fingers were covered with streaks of tar and felt sore from all the knotting and pulling tight.

The flies buzzed, the water glittered and from somewhere behind her a bluefinch repeated its song over and over. Dropping a handful of the net, she fell into a day-dream. 'Queen of Bekla'—she knew what the Sacred Queen in Bekla had to do, for Tharrin had once told her, with much sniggering detail, about the great craftsman Fleitil's brazen image of Cran, that marvel of dedicated artistry; which, in answer to her abashed but fascinated questioning, he was forced to admit he had never seen for himself. 'And if she didn't do it, lass, the crops wouldn't grow—nothing would grow.'

'You mean, not any longer at all?' she had asked.

He chuckled. 'Nothing would grow any longer. Not mine or anyone else's. Wouldn't that be terrible?'

'I don't understand.'

'Ah, well, there's plenty of time. Every apple falls in time, you know.' And, pinching her arm and laughing, he was off to the tavern.

She settled herself more comfortably in the net, stretched and yawned. The job was nearly finished. There would be about another half-hour's work. Once she had taken on a task for Tharrin she liked to take pains to please him: but this had been a long, dull, careful job and now she felt weary of it. She was overcome by a sudden, depressing sense of the monotony of her life; dull food, rough, dirty clothes, too much work and tedious, unvarying companionship. Save for her solitary escapes to the lake it was

38

seldom enough, she reflected, that she got away. Last year Tharrin had taken them all to the wine festival at Meerzat—a piffling enough sort of affair, he'd called it, compared with those he had known in Ikat and Thettit. And yet, she thought resentfully, it was the best she was ever likely to see. 'Queen of Bekla'—She felt herself to be beautiful, she felt confidence in her beauty—oh, ah, she thought, beautiful in dirt and rags, in a hovel on the Tonildan Waste. Mend the nets, gather the firewood, mind the banzi, don't eat so much, there isn't enough to go round. If only there could be something *sweet* to eat, she thought—and swallowed the saliva that filled her mouth at the longing.

She felt drowsy. Her deft fingers recommenced their work, then faltered and paused, lying still as she leant back in the soft, resilient thickness of the piled net and closed her eyes. The breeze, the wavelets lapping on the shore, the leaves of the ash-tree, the flies darting in the bright air—all these were in motion above and around her, so that she herself seemed like a still centre, a sleeping princess, motionless save for the gentle rise and fall of her bosom under the half-mended dress.

She woke with a start, conscious that someone was standing beside her. She half-sprang up, then lay back, laughing with relief as she realized that it was only Tharrin.

'Oh—Tharrin—oh, you give me such a turn! I'd dropped off for a moment. Don't matter, I've done most of it, look. It's done proper, too—won't go again in 'urry.'

He lay down beside her, leaning on his elbow and gazing up at her intently. As he still said nothing she felt a touch of nervousness.

'What's up, then, Tharrin? Nothin' wrong, is there?'

At this he smiled. 'No, nothing,' he answered, laying a hand on her bare forearm. 'Nothing at all.'

'Well, go on, *look* at it, then! I've made a good job of it, you c'n see that.'

He began picking over the mended places, lifting the net in his two hands and idly testing the knotting between his fingers. She saw that they were trembling slightly and felt still more puzzled.

'You all right? What's matter then?'

Suddenly he flung one entire fold of the net over her from head to foot and, as she struggled beneath the mesh, pushed her back into the piled folds, laughing and pressing his hands down on her shoulders. She laughed, too, for she had often romped with him before; but then quickly shook her head, throwing one hand up to her face.

'Ow! You caught me in the eye, Tharrin—do look out—'

'I've caught a fish! A golden fish! What a beauty!'

'No, honest, Tharrin, it hurts! Look, does it show?' And, still lying

39

under the net, she turned her face towards the light, pulling down her lower eyelid as the water ran down her cheek.

'I'm sorry, Maia fish! Oh, I didn't mean to hurt you! Here, let me kiss it better.'

He took her head, wrapped in the net, between his hands and kissed her eyelid through the mesh.

'Want to come out, pretty fish? Ask nicely!'

She pouted. 'I'm not bothered. I'll come out when I please!'

'Well, I'm in no hurry either, come to that.' And with this he pulled aside the fold, lay down beside her and drew it back over both of them.

'You've caught me too, you know, golden Maia. Look, here's something nice. I brought it specially for you.'

Fumbling a moment, he held out to her a lump of something brown and glistening, about half as big as his fist. At the smell, at once sweet and nutty-sharp, she began to salivate once more.

'Go on; try it! You'll like it. Look!' He bit off a piece and lay nibbling, crackling the brittle stuff between his teeth.

Maia copied him. The taste was delicious, filling her mouth and throat, suffusing her with the luxury of its sweetness. With closed eyes she bit, chewed, swallowed and bit again, her smarting eye quite forgotten.

'M'mm! Oh, it's gorgeous, Tharrin! What is it?'

'Nut *thrilsa*. Nuts baked in honey and butter.'

'But these aren't ordinary nuts. Where do they come from? Oh, do give me some more!'

'No, these are *serrardoes*. The black traders bring them to Ikat from heaven knows where—far away to the south. Want some more?'

'Yes! Yes!'

'Come and get it, then!' Very deliberately, and holding her gaze, he put a piece lightly between his front teeth, then took each of her hands in one of his own, fingers interlocked, and held them back against the net.

Slowly, realizing what he meant and why he had done it, Maia raised her head and placed her mouth against his. His arms came gently round her shoulders, clasping her to him, and as she drew the sweetmeat into her mouth his tongue followed it, licking and caressing. She offered no resistance, only breathing hard and trembling.

Releasing her, he smiled into her eyes. 'Was *that* nice, too?'

'I don't—I don't know!'

'And this?' He slid his hand beneath her torn dress, fondling one breast.

'Oh, you shouldn't; don't!' But her hands made no move to pluck his away.

Pressing himself against her from head to foot, lithe and strong, he once more took her hand and drew it downward between his legs.

40

And now indeed she cried out in earnest, suddenly realizing what before she had only half-understood. Feeling, with a kind of panic, what he had meant her to feel, she thought—like a young soldier for the first time face to face with the enemy—'This isn't a game any more—this is what really happens—and it's happening to me.' For long moments she lay tense in his arms; yet she did not struggle.

Suddenly her body felt full and smooth and sufficient—like a new boat pushed down into the water. It was as though she were standing back, regarding it with satisfaction. It was sound: it floated. Her body, her beautiful body, which could swim miles in the lake—her body would take care of everything. She had only to allow it to do what it had been created for. Sighing, she pressed herself against Tharrin and waited, shuddering as he caressed her.

The moment he entered her, Maia was filled from head to foot with a complete, assenting knowledge that this was what she had been born for. All her previous, childish life seemed to fall away beneath her like broken fragments of shell from the kernel of a cracked nut. Tharrin's weight upon her, Tharrin's thrusting, his arms about her, were like the opening of a pair of great, bronze doors to disclose some awesome and marvellous treasure within. Only, she herself was at one and the same time the doors, the portress and the treasure. Catching her breath, moaning, struggling not against but with him, as though they had both been hauling on a sail, she clutched him about, crying incoherently, 'Oh, don't—don't—'

At this, he held back for a moment.

'Don't what, my darling?'

'Don't *stop*! Oh, Cran and Airtha, don't stop!'

Laughing with delight, he took her once more in a close embrace and entirely at her word.

When she came to herself she was lying in the net and he was smiling down at her.

'I've landed my fish! It *is* a beauty! Don't you agree?'

She answered nothing; only panting up at him, a child caught at the end of some hide-and-seek game.

'Are you all right, pretty Maia?'

She nodded. The unshed tears in her blue eyes made them seem even bigger.

'Like some more thrilsa?' He put a piece to her lips: she bit into it with relish.

'You like that?'

'Oh, it's simply lovely! I've never had it before!'

He roared with laughter. 'What are you talking about—thrilsa?'

Realizing what she had said, Maia laughed too.

41

'Tharrin, did you mean to come and do this when you told me to mend the net?'

'No, not just like that, fish: but I've wanted to do it for a long time. You didn't know?'

'Well—p'raps I did, really. Leastways, I c'n see it now.'

'Yes, you can see it now. There!'

She bit her lip, looking away.

'Never seen a man's *zard* before, pretty girl? Come on, you're a woman now!'

'It's soft, and—and smaller. Oh, Tharrin, I've just remembered—' and since it never occurred to Maia to think of the words of a song separately from their tune, she sang ' "Seek, daughter, that horn of plenty with which men butt"—that what that means, then?'

'Yes, of course. If you didn't know, where did you learn that song?'

'I was with mother one day in Meerzat. It was that hot in the market and I got a headache. She told me to wait for her with the tavern-keeper's wife at "The Safe Moorings"—you know, Frarnli, the big woman with the cast in her eye.'

'I know.'

'Frarnli let me lie down on her bed. There was men drinking and singing in the next room: I just thought it was a pretty song. I remembered the tune and some of the words and what I couldn't remember later I made up: but I never knew what it meant. When mother heard me singin' it she got angry and said I wasn't to sing it n' more.'

'I'm not surprised.'

'So I used to sing it out on the waterfall, by myself. Oh, Tharrin, Tharrin! Look! Blood! What's happened?'

'Out of your *tairth*? That's nothing. That's only the first time. Just wash it off in the lake, that's all.'

'My—what did you say?—tairth?'

Gently, he touched her. 'That's your tairth. And you've been basted— you know *that* word, don't you?'

'Oh, yes; I've heard the drovers saying that. "Get that damned cow through the basting gate"—you know how they talk.'

'Yes, I know, but I don't like to use it for swearing. Love-words shouldn't be used like that, fish.'

'I'm your fish now. What sort of fish am I?'

He paused, considering. 'A carp. Yes, round and golden. I must say, you're a fine girl for your age, Maia. You're really lovely—do you know that? I mean, anyone, anywhere, would think you were lovely—in Ikat or Thettit—or Bekla, come to that: though I've never been to Bekla. You're just about the prettiest girl I've ever seen in my life. Lespa can't be more beautiful than you are.'

She made no reply, lying easy in the delicious warmth of the sun, feeling the cords and knots of the net all about her. She felt content.

After a time he said, 'Come on, let's take the boat out now. After all, we'd better have a few fish to show when Morca gets back, don't you think?'

He got to his feet, stretched out a hand and pulled her up.

'Maia?'

'M'm-h'm?'

'Take care of our secrets, darling. I've heard you talk in your sleep before now.'

This was typical of Tharrin. How do you take care not to talk in your sleep?

: 4 :

VISITORS

Like most men of his sort, Tharrin was kind-hearted (as long as it did not involve taking too much trouble), and quite good company in his own superficial way. No less than a soldier, a poet or a mountaineer, a philanderer needs certain natural qualities, and Tharrin had made a reasonably good job of seducing Maia. That is to say, he had not forced, frightened or hurt her, he had given her pleasure and satisfaction and left her with no regrets and the conviction that this was the most exciting thing that had ever happened to her and that she had crossed a great threshold—as indeed she had. The harm, of course, lay not in what Tharrin had actually done, but in what he was and the situation in which he had placed himself and Maia. He might have disappeared one dark night, taking Maia with him—though for her the outlook would have been a poor one indeed. He might have stressed yet again the need for, and then gone on to instruct her in, the strictest secrecy, continuing to make love to her only at safe opportunities. Or he might even have told her firmly that the matter must end where it had begun—and stuck to that.

He did none of these things. To have become once more, at his time of life, the lover of an exceptionally pretty, ardent young girl, whom no one else had ever enjoyed, went to Tharrin's unstable head like Yeldashay wine. He showed attentions to Maia. He called her by pet-names. He bought her a glass necklace from a pedlar, though it was weeks since he had given Morca any trinket. Giving out implausibly that he wanted her opinion about a new fishing-boat he was thinking of buying (there was not so much money in the household as would have bought a pair of oars) he took her with him to Meerzat and gave her a couple of drinks and a meal at 'The Safe Moorings'. On that occasion he certainly took pains to see that she enjoyed herself, but his real motive—even though he was perhaps unaware of it himself—was to show her off; and in this he was most successful, for he was no stranger to the place and Frarnli, the proprietress, who had had the measure of him for some time, was not one to fail to draw conclusions. Irresponsibility and indiscretion are two lovely berries moulded on one stem, so it is hardly surprising that Tharrin, having begun his pleasure with the one, should continue it with the other.

Children are quick to sense any change in domestic atmosphere, and it was not long before nine-year-old Nala perceived—and remarked to Maia upon—something new in the relationship between her and Tharrin. Maia's response was first to threaten and then to cajole her, and sharp little Nala began to turn the situation to her own advantage with a kind of petty blackmail.

But the biggest give-away was Maia herself—her bearing and the impression she made on everyone around her. Unless what has happened is altogether against her own wishes—intimidation or rape—any normal girl is bound to feel herself in love with the first man who possesses her. And while to a man love-making is an end in itself and primarily a matter of recreation, to a girl it appears in the nature of a foundation on which she wants to build. Maia began to make herself useful. She cooked for Tharrin, washed his clothes and went through his implements and other possessions to see whether there was anything she could do to improve them. When Tharrin was at home she was like a sea-anemone with its brilliantly-coloured, frond-like tentacles extended. When he was absent she was still happy enough—closing in on herself like a scarlet pimpernel in wet weather. Her behaviour to Morca was much improved, and displayed a kind of joyous and quite unconscious condescension, which could hardly have failed to strike any woman, let alone Morca.

Meanwhile, she had taken to love-making like a good dog to work, and in response to Tharrin's experienced, if rather facile instruction, was gaining in reciprocity, confidence and pleasure. Enthusiasm she possessed in abundance, and if she had unthinkingly formed a somewhat mechanical notion of physical love as a matter of method and sensation rather than warmth and feeling, it was scarcely any blame to her, for Tharrin was not really capable of deep emotion. That which he was capable of, however, he performed as genially as a tapster broaches a cask.

It scarcely matters in precisely what way the secret of two illicit lovers leaks out. If it did not happen in one way then it would happen in another, and if not on Tuesday then on Wednesday. Lovers are greatly inclined to the assumption that no one can wish them ill, and that as long as they do not actually utter anything revealing, their looks, gestures and mutual behaviour convey nothing to anybody else. Even illiterate lovers are almost invariably careless. Did Morca set a trap—return unexpectedly from borrowing a spool of thread from old Drigga up the lane, and glimpse, through a chink, Tharrin fondling Maia's thighs? Did she need to do even so much as that? Did Frarnli, perhaps, hint to her enough to make it unnecessary? *Did* Maia talk in her sleep—or merely expose, when washing, a shoulder displaying the marks of teeth, or something of a similar nature which Morca herself, of course, would already have experienced? It is unimportant compared with Morca's bitter, secret and revengeful resentment. Despite her outburst in the cabin on the evening of Maia's return from the waterfall, Morca was by nature inarticulate and little given to overt self-expression. Her way (developed during long years of childhood with a brutal and unpredictable father in whom it had never even occurred to her to confide) was to nurse an injury, like a boil, until it burst; and then to act alone; often with excessive, disproportionate savagery, in a situation which another woman would have resolved by simply having everything out in a good row. Poverty, together with a sour sense of desertion and of her own lost youth, had done nothing to modify or soften this dismal wont.

One fine morning, a few weeks after the mending of the net, Tharrin, slinging over his shoulder the bundle which Maia had put together for him, set off on the twenty-five-mile journey to Thettit-Tonilda, whence he would not be returning for several days. His ostensible purpose was to buy some new tackle for the boat, since it was the time of year when the annual consignment of rope arrived in Thettit from Ortelga. During his time on that island (the time when he had been lying low from Ploron) he had made a friend, an Ortelgan named Vassek, who was usually ready to let him have a fair amount at less than the going price. What he did not need for himself he was able, on his return, to sell locally at a profit. As a result, this particular season had come to be the annual occasion for a little spree. He would walk to Meerzat, beg a lift in a boat bound across the lake and then, as often as not, talk his way on to some merchant's tilt going to Thettit. The journey back, laden with coils of rope, was harder, but Tharrin had always been a resourceful opportunist.

Maia went with him to see him off at Meerzat, carrying his bundle on one arm. After a mile or so, with no need of more than a glance and a nod between them, he took her hand and led her across a dry ditch and so into a copse, through the midst of which a rill still flowed among the weeds in the bed of the shrunken stream. It was far too shallow to swim but nevertheless Maia, always drawn to any water, pulled off her smock and splashed into the one pool she could find. Watching from the shade, Tharrin—largely for his own anticipatory enjoyment—contained himself for a time before sliding down to lift her out bodily and lay her on the green bank.

Half an hour later she stirred drowsily, one hand fondling the length of his body.

'Oh, Tharrin, whatever shall I do while you're away?'

'It's not for long.'

'How long?'

'Six days—seven days. All depends.'

'What on?'

'Aha! Pretty goldfish mustn't ask too many questions. I'm a very mysterious man, you know!'

He waited, grinning sideways at her, clearly pleased with himself. Then, as she did not speak, 'Don't you think so? Look!'

She stared in astonishment at the big coin held up between his finger and thumb.

'Whatever's that, then? A hundred meld? Must be!'

He laughed, gratified by her surprise. 'Never seen one before?'

'Dunno as I have.'

'Can now, then.'

He flipped it across to her. She caught it and, turning it one way and the other, examined the stylized design of leopards and the obverse image of Frella-Tiltheh the Inscrutable, hand outstretched above the sprouting *tamarrik* seed. After a minute she made to give it back, but he shook his head.

'It's yours, goldfish.'

'Oh, Tharrin, I can't take that! 'Sides, anyone I was to give it to'd reckon I must 'a pinched it—a girl like me.'

He chuckled. 'Or earned it, perhaps; such a pretty girl. And haven't you?'

She coloured. 'That's worse, anyone go thinkin' that. Oh, Tharrin, don't tease *that* way. I don't like it. I'd never, *never* do it for money!'

Seeing that she was on the verge of serious vexation, he hurriedly pulled the subject back on course.

'You can have five twenty-meld pieces if you'd rather. Here they are, look.'

'Tharrin! However much you got, then?'

He jingled the coins, tossing them up and down before her eyes.

'That and more.'

'But how?' Then, sharply, 'You never stole it, did you? Oh, Tharrin—'

He laid a quick hand on her wrist. 'No, fish, no; you can think better of me than that.'

46

She, carefree and pretty as a butterfly in the sunshine, waited silently before at length asking, 'Well?'

'I'm a patriot.'

'What's that, then?'

'Well, you see, I'm the sort of man who's not afraid to take risks, so I'm rewarded accordingly. They don't take on just anyone to do the kind of work I do, I'll tell you.'

She knew that he was serious, yet she felt no alarm on his account; her half-childish thoughts ran all on excitement, not on danger.

'Oh, Tharrin! Risks? Who for? Does mother know?'

'Ah! That'd be telling. No, 'course she doesn't: only you. And you just keep it quiet, too. I don't want to be sorry I told you.'

''Course I will. But what's it all about, then?'

'And *that'd* be telling, too. But I'm a secret messenger; and I'm paid what I'm worth.'

'But darling, surely you'll need the money for this trip, won't you?'

'What's a hundred meld to a man like me? Come on, you just put them away safe now, else they'll get scattered all over 'fore we're done.'

Obediently Maia put them away before returning to more immediate things.

She left him in high spirits on the jetty at Meerzat, chatting with an acquaintance who was taking his boat out as soon as he had got the cargo aboard; and strolled home at her leisure, stopping more than once to pick flowers or chase butterflies; for it was Maia's way to pursue pleasure quite spontaneously in anything that might happen to take her fancy.

It was a little after noon when she came up the lane towards the cabin. The sanchel on the bank had almost finished flowering, its orange blossoms turned to soft, fluffy seeds like long sprays of thistledown, which the first winds of autumn would send floating across the waste. There were three blooms left at the end of a long, out-thrust branch. Maia climbed up the bank to reach them, clutching the branch and almost overbalancing as she leant outwards.

Suddenly she stopped trying to reach the blooms and released the bent branch, staring towards the cabin and the patch of rough grass where the chopping-block stood beside the hen-coops.

Under a clump of sycamores on the edge of the patch, a cart was standing in the shade. Two bullocks, side by side, were in the shafts, shaking and tossing their heads under a cloud of flies. It was not they, however, which arrested her attention, but the cart itself. She had never seen one like it. It was unusually solid, rectangular, narrow and entirely covered not by any sort of tilt or hood, but by a timber roof as stout as its sides. It was unpainted and bound about with four iron hoops bolted to the timber. Unless there was some window or opening at the front (which from where she was standing she could not see) it had none; but near the top of the one side half-facing her was a long, narrow slit. At the back was a door, closed and fitted with a hasp and staple, in which a heavy padlock was hanging open.

Maia was mystified and much intrigued. She could imagine neither the use of such a vehicle—for some special use it must obviously have—nor why it should be visiting their home. Who owned it? Why had he come? Obviously, whoever he was, Morca must know, and presumably he was indoors with her now, unless they were out looking at cattle or something like that. To dwellers in remote places, any visitor or unexpected event brings welcome variety to the monotony of the day's routine. Maia felt excited. Jumping down from the bank, she ran across the lane and in at the door.

The only person to be seen in the room, however, was Morca, sitting on a stool by the fire, plucking a fowl. Handfuls of feathers, brown and white, lay round her feet. Some had found their way into the fire, and Maia wrinkled her nose at the acrid smell.

Morca rose clumsily, smoothing her sacking apron over her belly, laid the fowl on one side and stood looking at her daughter with a smile.

'Well—you got back all right, then?' she asked. 'You're not too tired? Did Tharrin catch the boat? On his way now, is he?'

Something in her manner puzzled Maia and made her hesitate before replying. Morca was no more—indeed, was even less—given than most peasant mothers to asking her daughters polite questions about their welfare, and Maia—just as unused to receiving them—hardly knew how to answer.

'Tired? Oh, no, I'm fine, no danger,' she said after a moment. 'Mum, what's that cart—'

'And he got the boat all right, did he?' interrupted Morca. 'He's gone off?'

'Well, 'course he did,' answered Maia with a touch of impatience. 'Why wouldn't he?' Then, impudently, 'Hadn't, I shouldn't be here. The cart, mum, what's that queer-looking cart outside? Who's brought it?'

'Ah!' said Morca, still smiling. 'Strikes me some people's left their eyes outside in the sun, or maybe they're just not very bright today. Haven't you seen—'

'What's up with that curtain, then?' asked Maia suddenly, looking across at the screened-off sleeping place on the other side of the room. 'Hens got in behind it or something?'

'Oh, cat's been asleep in there all morning,' answered Morca quickly. 'But never you mind that now, Miss Maia; just look behind you at what's laying on the table. Walked right past it, didn't you?'

'On the table? Oh!' Maia, having turned about, stood staring, fingers on either side of her open mouth.

Lying across the table—otherwise bare and unusually clean—was a cream-coloured dress made of some smooth, softly-shining material, its bodice embroidered with blue and green flowers. Displayed thus in the centre of the squalid, smoky room it appeared marvellously beautiful and so inexplicably out of place as almost to seem unreal—a vision or an illusion. Maia, gazing at it speechlessly, felt a kind of alarm. If something like this could materialize out of nowhere, then almost anything could happen. But what?

Walking over to the table, she looked at the dress more closely. Of course, she thought with some chagrin, she could hardly expect to be much of a judge of such things. The effect of its beauty was to subdue her, making her feel grubby and ignorant.

'D'you like it?' asked Morca from behind her.

'Like it?' echoed Maia abstractedly. The question seemed to have no meaning. It was rather as though her mother had asked her whether she liked the lake or the stars. Tentatively, she put out a hand towards the thick, creamy material of the skirt.

'Better not touch it just yet, Maia dear,' said Morca. 'Not until you've had a wash. There's some nice hot water ready for you on the fire, look.'

Her mother's unusually amiable and coaxing manner—certainly she did not normally go out of her way to encourage the girls to wash—following upon the apparition of the strange cart and the dress, completed Maia's bewilderment. She sat down on the bench beside the table.

'What's it all mean, then, mum? Who's brought that cart and what for? Where is he now? Did he bring this dress and all?'

Morca waddled to the hearth, took up the pannikin and began ladling hot water into the tub.

'Well, it's good news for you right enough,' she said. 'There's two of 'em. They sell fine clothes to rich people, that's what. Clothes the like of that over there.'

'Sell fine clothes?' Maia, ceasing for a moment her contemplation of the dress, turned, frowning in puzzlement, and looked at her mother. 'I don't understand. What are they doing here? They can't think to be selling such things to the likes of us. Anyway, where are they?'

'Oh—I reckon they're gone down to the lake for a bit of a cool-off,' said Morca. 'They'll be back soon, I expect, so you'd best just hurry, hadn't you?'

'Hurry? What d'you mean, hurry?' Then, petulantly, 'Why can't you explain so's I c'n understand?'

'Yes, I should do, shouldn't I?' answered Morca. 'Well, I said it was good news for you—all depending on whether you fancy it, I suppose. These men have come from Thettit, that's where, and their work's selling clothes the like of that to the sort of folk who can afford to buy them—the Governor and his captains and their ladies, I dare say. Seems they were in "The Safe Moorings" yesterday and Frarnli told them you were near enough the prettiest girl in these parts. So they've just come out this morning to see for themselves, haven't they?'

'Come from Meerzat this morning? I never saw them on the road.'

'Very like they might have gone by while you just happened to be *off* the road,' replied Morca, putting down the pannikin and looking up at her sharply. Maia bit her lip and made no reply.

'You never heard tell the way fine clothes are sold?' went on her mother. 'Dresses like that aren't sold in shops or markets, you know, like the sort of things *we* buy—raisins and pitch and that. Oh dear, no! The merchants who deal in these things take them to rich folks' houses in special covered carts like that one outside, and then show them privately, that's what they do.'

'Well, what if they do?' retorted Maia, resentful of this instruction.

'When they go to the rich folks' houses, miss, they take a pretty girl with them, and the way of it is, she puts on the dresses so the rich folks and their wives—or maybe their shearnas, for all I know—can see the way they look when they're on, and whether they fancy them. Well,' she added, as Maia stood staring at her with dawning comprehension, 'd'you like the idea? There may be good pickings, I dare say. Anyway, they've waited a goodish time now to have a look at you.'

'You mean—you mean they want *me* to do that kind of work?'

'Well, I'm telling you, aren't I?' snapped Morca. 'That's if they like the look of you, of course. Do it right and I dare say you might make more money than me or your step-father ever did—that's if you can keep yourself out of trouble. You'd best get stripped off and washed, my girl, that's what; and then into that dress—there's a silk shift goes with it, look, laid on the bed there—and then I'll call them in and you can ask them all your silly questions for yourself.'

'But—but would I go on living here, or what? Does Tharrin know? He can't do, else he'd have said something—'

'All I know is they spoke to Frarnli and then they came out here. If you don't fancy it, don't do it, Miss Particular. I dare say there's plenty of other girls'll jump at the chance; and the money, too.' And thereupon Morca, shrugging her shoulders, sat down again, picked up the half-plucked fowl and began pulling out handfuls of feathers with an air of detachment.

Filled with nervous excitement and perplexity, Maia stood looking at the dress with its pattern of big flowers like open, gazing eyes. In her fancy they became the eyes of the rich lords and their ladies, all staring at her as she paced slowly down the length of some great, stone hall—she'd heard tell of such places—in Thettit or Ikat Yeldashay. There would be food and drink in plenty, no doubt—admiration—money—how was she to know? How would Tharrin come into it?—as of course he must, somehow. One question after another rose in her mind. One thing was certain, however. She, Maia, could not simply say no and thereupon forget the matter and go out with the buckets to the lake—her usual chore at this time of day. Here, clearly, was a wonderful opportunity; yet a disturbing one too—to step into the unknown. No doubt the men themselves would be better able than Morca to answer her questions.

At this moment a happy thought came to her. Of course, she need agree to nothing now; she could merely find out from the men as much as possible, ask them to give her a few days to think it over, and get Tharrin's advice when he came home!

Walking over to the tub by the fire, she stepped into the warm water and then, raising her arms, pulled both smock and shift over her head and tossed them aside.

'I'll just give you a hand, dear,' said Morca. 'There's a nice little keech of tallow here and I'll mix some ashes into it for you.'

Maia, naked, stooped for the pannikin and poured warm water pleasurably over her shoulders.

'Where's Kelsi and Nala, then?' she asked. 'Isn't it just about time for dinner?'

'Ah, I dare say they won't be long now,' answered Morca comfortably. 'Just turn round, dear, and I'll soap your back down. My, you *are* getting a fine big girl, aren't you? Turn a few heads in Thettit, I wouldn't wonder.'

She certainly seemed to have recovered her good humour, adding hot water from the cauldron, soaping each of Maia's feet, as she lifted them, with a handful of tallow and wood-ash, and making her turn this way and that until at length she stepped out to towel herself dry, back and front, in the mid-day sunshine pouring through the open door. When she was ready Morca, having washed her own hands, helped her into the silk shift and the amazing dress.

It felt strange; heavy and enveloping. Maia's sensation was of being altogether encumbered and swathed in the thick, smooth material falling from shoulders to ankles. Awkwardly, and filled now with a certain sense of self-doubt, she tried a turn across the room and stumbled as the skirt swung against her knees like a half-full sack—or so it felt. Looking down, she saw the blue and green flowers curving outward over her bosom, while their stems seemed gathered again at her waist by the corded girdle binding them together. 'Oh, that's clever!' she thought. 'That's pretty! Who'd ever 'a thought of that, now?' Clearly, there was more in this clothes business than she had ever imagined.

'It feels sort of heavy, mum,' she said. 'I dunno as I'm going to be able to manage this—not without they show me.'

'Oh, they'll show you, no danger,' replied Morca. 'There now, drat! We've got no salt, look! What's left's all damped out! Slip the dress off, Maia dear, and just run up to old Drigga and borrow a handful, will you?'

Maia stared. 'Damp? At this time of year?'

Morca shrugged. 'I must have left it too near the steam or something, I suppose. Never mind. Won't take you more than a minute or two, will it?'

'That's a job for Nala, more like,' said Maia. 'Running errands.'

'Well, she's not here, is she?' retorted Morca. 'Sooner you're gone, sooner you'll be back again, won't you? Come on, now, I'll just help you out of the dress.'

When Maia returned a quarter of an hour later with half a cupful of old Drigga's salt, the visitors had evidently returned from the lake. While still some little distance up the lane she could hear their voices raised in conversation with Morca, but as she came in at the door they stopped talking and turned to look at her.

They were certainly not at all what she was expecting. In her mind's eye she had unconsciously formed a picture of tall, dignified men—she was not sure how old they would be—but certainly well-dressed and -groomed; exotic, perhaps—dark-skinned, with pointed beards and gold rings in their ears, like the merchants in tales and ballads. Looking at these men, however, her first thought was that they would have appeared rough in a crowd of drovers at Meerzat market. One, certainly, was tall, and looked strong as a wrestler: his long, black hair, however, was lank and dirty, the bridge of his nose was broken, and down one of his cheeks ran a ragged, white scar. His hands looked like those of a man accustomed to rough work. His companion, younger, and hardly taller than Maia herself, was standing a little behind him, his back to the fire, picking his blackened teeth with a splinter of wood. He had sandy hair and a slight cast in one eye. He leered at Maia, but then at once looked away, dropping the splinter. A length of thin cord was wound round his waist like a belt and in this was stuck an iron spike. His feet, in metal-toed wooden clogs, fidgeted with a shuffling sound on the earth floor.

Her mother, seated on the stool, had finished plucking the fowl and was now drawing it, flinging the guts into the fire as she worked. Maia looked about for the dress, but it was nowhere to be seen.

52

'Here she is back, then, your fine young lady,' said Morca, standing up and wiping her hands on her apron. 'What d'you think, then; will she do for you?'

'Here's the salt, mum,' said Maia, embarrassed and not knowing what else to say.

'The salt? Oh, ah, to be sure, the salt,' answered Morca. 'Right; well, put it down on the side there, Maia, that's a good girl. These are the gentlemen, then, as are ready to make your fortune if you want.'

'Oh, yer, that's right, that's right,' said the sandy-haired man, speaking in a kind of quick, low gabble. 'Make y' fortune, that's right.'

Maia waited for one or the other to say more, but neither did so. A silence fell, the tall man merely glowering bleakly down at her, while the other continued his shuffling from side to side.

'Well, then, we'll just have a drink on it,' said the shorter man at length. 'D'you want to step outside for a minute or two, missus, or how d'you want to settle?'

Maia now realized even more clearly that she must talk to Tharrin before agreeing to anything. Little as she knew about the ways of the world, it was plain that these men must be—could only be—the servants or underlings of the real dress-merchants themselves. She had not known her mother was such a fool. Obviously, she would have to find out for herself who and where their master was and tell them to say that Tharrin would take her to see him in a few days' time.

Lucky I've got a bit of a head on my shoulders, she thought. Mother's no help; I'll just have to handle this myself. I've got to show them I'm a smart girl, that's what.

'Do you want me to put the dress on now?' she asked, speaking directly to the taller man.

'What? The dress? No!' he answered in a kind of growl; and resumed his silence.

'Oh, no; no, no,' said the other, withdrawing one hand from beneath his clothes. 'Nice girl like you, do very well, very well. Yer, yer.'

'You understand, of course,' said Maia, assuming an air and feeling very self-possessed and business-like as she recalled the words of a cattle-dealer who had come to see Tharrin a week or two before, 'you understand that I can't just rightly conclude the matter at this moment? I shall need to have a word with my partner—I mean my step-father—and see you again. Where shall I be able to find you?' That was good, she thought—'be able to find you.'

The shorter man burst into a high-pitched laugh, but made no reply.

'That's all right, dear,' said Morca. 'The gentlemen understand very well. They've just asked us to have a drink with them before they go back to Meerzat, so let's all sit down nice and comfortable, shall we, and take it easy?'

For the first time Maia noticed that four battered pewter goblets were standing on the table, already filled. They certainly did not belong to the house. Suddenly it occurred to her that this might be some sort of custom, like striking hands, or earnest money (she knew about that), which might later be held to have committed her. Ah, but I've got my wits about me, she thought. Mother's only thinking of the money, but there's a lot more to it than that. I'm not going to lose my head or rush into anything.

'Very pleased, I'm sure,' she said primly. 'But this is quite without any— er—without any promising, of course. A drink, but not to say a bargain yet: that's right, isn't it?' She smiled graciously at the sandy-haired man— the other seemed just a grumpy fool, she thought—and sat down on the bench.

'Oh, no, no,' he gabbled, seating himself beside her. 'Oh, no bargain, no!' The tall man remained standing, but Morca sat down opposite, picking up a cup in each hand. Maia noticed that she was sweating heavily and that her hands were trembling. The sultry weather, she thought; she had seen enough of pregnancy to know that it sometimes had this kind of effect.

'Feeling a bit queer, mum?' she asked. 'You all right?'

'Oh, well, this'll put me right,' answered Morca with a laugh. 'It'll pass off quick enough. Now here's yours, sir, and this one's for you, Maia—'

Stooping, the tall man, without a word, leant over and took out of her hand the goblet she was offering to Maia. Morca bit her lip—and no wonder, thought Maia; we may be poor, but at least we've got better manners than that—and then gave her one of the remaining two goblets which the sandy-haired man pushed across the table.

'Well, here's good health to us all!' said Morca rather shrilly.

Maia took a sip of the tepid, yellow wine. The taste was strong and strange to her, though perhaps a little like the liquorice sweetmeats she had once or twice tasted at Meerzat. It was not altogether pleasant, but it was certainly heady; of course (she told herself), as Tharrin had once said, girls of her age had to be at it for a while before they could really enjoy the taste of certain wines; but it would not do, before these men, to appear childishly inexperienced.

'It's very nice,' she said, making herself take a longer draught. 'Yelda-shay, isn't it?'

'Oh, you're very nice, yer, very nice girl,' said the sandy-haired man, touching his goblet to hers. Raising one hand, he stroked Maia's shoulder; then dropped his arm, laughed and looked away. Maia, to cover her confusion, took another mouthful of the wine. At least that was better than the man's breath, which had quite disgusted her. And no wonder, she thought, with those teeth. I wonder whether his employer knows he behaves like this when he's out working for him? Still, I'd better not risk offending him, I suppose—he might say something against me when he gets back. She edged a foot or two away along the bench.

'That's a lovely dress you brought with you, isn't it?' she said, to resume the conversation. 'The flowers are beautifully embroidered. Do you carry the dresses round in that cart? I suppose that's what it's for, is it—so they can lie unfolded, and it's shut-in on top to keep out the dust an' that?'

'Oh, yer, that's the way, that's the way,' answered the man. 'There's lots in the cart now, plenty of others—prettier than that, too.'

'Prettier than that?' asked Maia. 'Really?'

'Oh, yer, yer,' he said, draining his goblet. 'Want to come and see? Finish up what you got left, and I'll show y' if you like.'

'I'll finish it when I come back,' said Maia. 'I'd like to see the dresses.'

'Go on, you can drink up that little drop, dear,' urged Morca.

'Too strong for you, is it?' laughed the man. 'Not had any the like of that before, eh? Like it when you're older, when you're older, that's it.'

'I like it now!' retorted Maia indignantly.

With this she finished the wine, swallowing with an effort which she did her best to conceal. Then, standing up, she led the way across to the door.

The tall man followed her closely, stooping under the lintel as he came out. The leaves hung unmoving in the hot, noonday air and the lake, level to the horizon, reflected a cloudless sky. The birds had fallen silent. Even the oxen under the trees seemed to have ceased their restless stamping and tossing. The stillness was so deep that Maia's ears could just catch, far off, the sound of the falls. I'll go down there and cool off this afternoon, she thought. Where's Kelsi and Nala got to, anyway? Reckon it must be well past dinner-time. Like to see the dresses, though.

Crossing the waste patch, she caught her foot in a tangle of bindweed, stumbled and almost fell. Recovering herself, she realized that she was feeling dizzy. That wine had certainly gone to her head. She wished the dealers had not come while Tharrin was away. The sandy-haired man had quite upset her with his wretched fidgeting and pawing. Still, I suppose I'll have to learn, now, how to deal with that sort of nonsense, she thought. Bound to come across the likes of him now and again, I dare say.

Coming up to the cart she swayed, closing her eyes and biting on her thumb to bring herself round. Unspeaking, the tall man lifted her bodily, turned her round and sat her down on the iron step below the cart door.

The sycamore leaves had become a green, mottled blur flowing up and over her head. She tried shutting her eyes, but at once opened them again, sickened by the sensation of turning a kind of floating somersault.

'I'm—I'm—trying to—' she said gravely to the sandy-haired man, who had taken the padlock out of the staple and was opening the door. She bent forward, head between her knees, and as she did so the door swung outwards behind her, its corner just brushing her left shoulder.

'All right, Perdan?' said the sandy-haired man. The other nodded and pulled Maia to her feet.

'Right, miss,' said the sandy-haired man. 'Now you just have a look, have a look inside now, and tell us what you can see. Out loud, now, so's we can all hear.'

Maia, finding herself facing the cart, stared into the sliding, trickling gloom of its interior. She could see nothing—neither dresses nor anything else. The oblong space, insofar as she was capable of perceiving it, looked completely empty. She began to speak, but then found that for some reason she could only do so very slowly, word by word.

'I—come—over—funny,' she said. 'Want—mother—tell—her—'

As her surroundings misted and dissolved, she felt herself lifted once more and pushed forward supine into the long, narrow body of the cart. Before the door had shut upon her she was already lying senseless, stretched full length on the floor.

: 5 :

A JOURNEY

Just as light before dawn increases gradually and without, at first, any obvious source, so that it is impossible to tell the precise instant at which darkness has ceased and daylight begun, so Maia's consciousness returned. In the midst of a confused dream she became sensible first of discomfort and then of a continuous, afflictive motion from which there was no relief. As though in a fever she tossed and turned, trying but failing to be comfortable. Little by little she became aware that she was awake. Her body, from head to foot, was being jolted and shaken, not roughly but without pause. Next, through another gate of her senses, came a fusty, mucid smell, not strong but pervasive. And at last, like a terrible sunrise completing the destruction of twilight, came the recollection of the men, the cart and her own fainting-fit. Immediately she opened her eyes, sat up and looked about her.

For a few moments she could neither focus her sight nor make any sense of what little she could see. Then she realized that she was sitting on a soft, padded surface—as soft as her own bed or softer. The place she found herself in was like a little, oblong cell, perhaps seven feet long and about two or three feet wide and high. It was dim, for the only openings were two slits, one on either side, immediately below the roof. The whole interior—all six surfaces—was covered with a kind of coarse quilting. It was from this that the musty smell came. Here and there the quilting was torn and tufts of coarse hair protruded like stuffing from a burst mattress.

The whole kennel was in continual movement, gently bumping and swaying, with now and then a sharper jolt; and with this went a creaking, trundling sound. There could be no doubt where she was. She was inside the strange cart, which was going slowly but steadily along.

Her head ached, her mouth was dry and she felt frowzy and sweaty. What had happened after she had fainted? Why wasn't she at home? All of a sudden the answer occurred to her. Her mother must have been so keen for her to take the wonderful job and make the family's fortune that rather than lose the opportunity she had sent her off with the dress-dealers then and there. The more she thought about this, the more stupid she felt her mother had been; and she would tell her so, too, the moment she got back. To let her be driven away in a closed cart, without her tidy clothes (such as they were), without her own agreement and without telling her where she was going or when she'd be coming back; probably spoiling the bargain, too (whatever it might be), by showing such eagerness to clinch it at any price! Maia fairly gritted her teeth with annoyance. Tharrin should hear all about it the moment he came home—which was where she herself must set about returning immediately, even if she had to walk every step of the way. Where was she, anyway? On the Meerzat road, presumably, which she would therefore, by nightfall, have covered four times that day.

Turning on her stomach, she thumped her fist on the quilting in front of her, shouting 'Stop! Stop at once!' There was no reply and no alteration of the slow, uneven movement. Quickly she turned head-to-tail and pushed hard on the door at the back. It gave a fraction before being checked against the padlock and staple. She was locked in.

No sooner had Maia grasped this than she flung herself once more at the front of the quilted box, battering and shouting in a frenzy. When at length she paused for breath she became aware that the cart had stopped. There followed the click and squeak of the opening padlock and a moment later the door swung open to reveal the tall man peering in at her.

With a keen sense of her tousled, undignified appearance, Maia slid forward, lowered her feet to the ground and stood up.

It was early evening: the air was cooling and the sun sinking behind the trees. They were halted on the edge of a dusty, rutted track. The bullocks, having pulled the cart at an angle to the verge, were cropping the dry grass and heat-withered flowers. On her left was a belt of trees, on her right a few fields among wasteland stretching away to the lake in the distance. This was nowhere she knew. The cart was pointing southward, certainly, but the road and surroundings were strange to her. They must, therefore, now be beyond Meerzat and further along the shore of the lake than she had ever been.

Turning to face the tall man, she saw that he was holding in one hand a kind of thin, leather leash, like those used for hounds. He rather resembled a large, unpredictable hound himself, she thought: though there was nothing amusing in the comparison. His scowling silence was frightening but, as with a hound, it was important not to show fear.

'There's been a mistake,' she said. 'I don't know what my mother's told you, but I can't go with you now, or start the work yet. I never said as I would, you know. You'll just have to take me back home.'

The man snapped his fingers and pointed into the back of the cart.

'Well, if you won't take me back,' said Maia, 'reckon I'll just have to walk back myself.'

She took a step past the man, who immediately caught her by the wrist and, with a kind of snarl, flung her back against the cart so violently that she cried out with fear and pain.

'Steady, Perdan, steady!' said the sandy-haired fellow, appearing round the end of the cart. 'Mustn't damage the goods, y'know. Might lose commission, yer, yer.' He turned to Maia. 'Come on, now, miss. No good crying over a broken pot, you know. What you want? You want to shit or just piss, which is it now?'

Maia choked back her tears. A cunning thought had come to her. Once she had got a little way clear of them she would run. She might or might not be a match for the tall man, but it was worth trying.

'The first,' she answered, avoiding the coarse word.

The sandy-haired man took the leather leash from his companion, fastened it round her neck and gave it a gentle tug.

'Come on, then,' he said, sniggering. 'Good doggie! No, don't try to undo it, miss, else I'll only have to get rough. Don't want that, do we?' He patted her cheek.

'How *dare* you treat me like this?' blazed Maia. 'You just wait till my step-father hears of it! I'll be damned if I'll work for you, or your master either; no, not for a fortune I won't!'

The tall man seemed about to speak, but the other cut in quickly.

'Don't tell her, Perdan. Makes it easier, yer, long as possible. Come on now, miss, d'you want to shit or not?'

Holding the leash, he led her across the road and a few yards in among the trees. Here he stopped.

'Well, go away!' she said, pointing. 'Right away, too! Back there!'

'We better get this straight,' replied the sandy-haired man. 'I can't leave you; got no chains, see? But it'll be a good two hours to Puhra, so if you want to do anything you'd better get on with it, yer, else you'll only be laying in there in your own muck.'

'You mean you're taking me to Puhra by force? How *can* you s'pose I'd work for your master after that? Does he know what you're doing?'

The man made no reply but, still holding the leash, turned his back on her.

'Go on if you're going.'

Weeping with shame and humiliation, she crouched and relieved herself; then allowed him to lead her back to the cart and lock her in.

The creaking and rumbling began again, but soon afterwards the cart stopped once more. From the murmur of voices and the bovine stamping and blowing, Maia realized that they must be changing the bullocks. Probably they had already been changed once earlier in the afternoon, while she still lay asleep. Evidently these men had standing arrangements along the roads they used.

It occurred to her to call out for help from whomever might be talking to the men. Yet instinctively she sensed that this would be useless. Besides, she had conceived a terror of the man with the broken nose. Though born poor, Maia had never experienced any violence worse than her mother's fits of temper, and unconsciously she had grown up not to expect it. The tall man's unhesitant use of force had frightened her badly, leaving her with the flinching realization that here was someone to whom terror and the infliction of pain were all in a day's work.

She was still unshaken in her determination to go home at the first opportunity, but clearly there could be no attempting anything for the time being. She would have to wait until they reached Puhra. She had never been to Puhra in her life, and knew of it only as a small fishing town, presumably much like Meerzat, at the southern end of Lake Serrelind; though of a trifle more consequence on account of lying not far from the high road between Thettit and Bekla. No doubt there would be ordinary, decent folk there who would help her to get away from these disgusting men.

The time dragged on. Her headache, as she lay in the stuffy, musty-smelling box, grew worse, until she felt near-feverish and too much confused to think clearly. At last, from sheer exhaustion, she dozed off again, and woke to feel the cart rumbling over a paved surface.

A minute or two later it stopped and she heard the men talking together as they got down. She waited for the door to be opened, but instead the voices receded and vanished. Listening, she could hear various sounds from outside: clattering pots, the shutting of a door, a thudding noise like someone beating something soft and heavy—bedding, perhaps—against a hard surface. There was a smell of wood-smoke and cooking, but no bustle, cries or other normal sounds of a frequented place. Wherever they were, it was evidently neither a tavern nor any sort of big house full of servants.

After some time she heard footsteps returning; the lock clicked and the door opened. The sandy-haired man, holding up a lantern, was grinning in at her, his face a half-and-half mask of light and shadow. As she was about to slide out of the cart he put down the lantern, grasped her ankles, pulled her towards him and began to stroke her thighs.

Maia, struggling, kicked him in the stomach, and he staggered back, cursing. A moment later her satisfaction turned to terror as she realized that there was no escaping him, confined as she was in the box. She lay cowering like a rabbit, staring and waiting.

The man, winded but recovering his breath, leant forward, his hands on the sill of the opening. She realized that she had excited rather than deterred him.

'Steady, missy, steady now,' he said at length, smirking and showing his horrible teeth. 'I might go and fetch Perdan; wouldn't like that, would you? He's apt to forget himself, y'know, is Perdan. Now *I* just want to be nice.'

Maia once more burst into tears. 'O gods, can't you let me alone? I'm tired out, I'm took bad. Surely to Cran you can understand that much?' She scrambled out onto the cobblestones.

Plainly her anguish had no more effect on him than that of a snared animal on a trapper, who has seen the like many times and in the circumstances would be surprised not to see it. For some seconds he stood in silence, looking her up and down. Then he raised a dirty hand to her cheek.

'Well, y'can just make yerself comfortable now, yer,' he said. 'I'll take y' in where yer going, that's right.'

Grasping her firmly by the arm, he led her across the cobblestones, the lantern swinging from his other hand.

The twilight was not yet so deep as to prevent her from taking in her immediate surroundings. She was walking up a long, rather narrow yard, its paving overgrown with rank grass and edged with clumps of dock and nettle. In places the stones were gone altogether, leaving only patches of dusty soil. In one corner lay a pile of refuse—rags, vegetable peelings, bones, fragments of broken harness. As she looked, a rat scuttled out of it. Behind her the bullocks, still in the shafts, had been hitched to a post beside a pair of high, spiked gates fastened with a bar and a locked chain. On one side of the yard stood an open-fronted shed containing three or four more beasts, while along the other extended a high wall which abutted, at its further end, on a stone-faced building. This, though solidly built and clearly old, was dilapidated. Weeds were growing among the broken roof-tiles, and in several places the stone had fallen away, revealing the brick-work behind. The ugly door, however, was new and very solid, and the windows (through two of which candlelight was shining) were barred. The whole place had an air of having seen better days, and also, in some indefinable way, of having been turned over to a use other than that for which it had originally been built.

Maia thought that it might perhaps be—or once have been—the ser-vants' quarters of some big house, but could not see, in the gathering darkness, whether there was any other building beyond. The surrounding silence, unbroken save for a late bellbird drowsily calling somewhere out of sight, hardly suggested it. One thing was clear: there was no hope of getting out of such a place on the sly—not even by night.

Looking up, she could see the stars beginning to twinkle in a clear sky. 'O sweet Lespa,' she prayed silently, 'you see me from those stars. Send me help, great queen, for I'm alone, in trouble and afraid.'

Her prayer was indeed to be answered, yet in no way she could have foreseen.

The sandy-haired man, pushing the door open with a thrust of his foot, led her into a candle-lit room. Before Maia's eyes had taken in anything, she felt on the soles of her bare feet a kind of cool smoothness and, looking down, saw that the floor was made of slate flags—a luxury entirely out of her experience. Earth and rushes were what she was used to. Then, glancing round in the candlelight, she saw that the room, though dirty and untidy, was better appointed than any she had seen before. To Maia a room was the same thing as a dwelling, consisting of stick or mud-and-wattle walls and a plank door, enclosing an area of hard earth, a brick or stone hearth and chimney and a thatched roof. The room she was now in, however, was evidently one of several in the house. Its windows—two of them—were both set in the wall fronting on the courtyard. At each side were hinged shutters, left open on this night of late summer. Opposite was a second door which must lead into the rest of the house. The walls were wooden-panelled and the flat ceiling, darkened with smoke, was of close-fitting planks supported by cross-beams. The hearth, where a fire was burning, had a wide, iron fire-basket and beside it, in a recess, lay a pile of sawn logs and broken sticks. In the middle of the room was a heavy table which, though scratched and dirty, retained here and there a few faint traces of polish.

The general air of the room, even to Maia's inexperienced eyes, was of a once-handsome place fallen on shabby times. It smelt; not of clean pros-perity, but of grime and neglect. The floor, plainly, was seldom swept. There were cobwebs round the windows and the table was covered with candle-droppings.

The broken-nosed man, Perdan, was already seated at supper. His two knives were stuck into the table beside him and he was now eating, with his fingers, the ham, eggs and onions which he had already cut up. At his elbow, beside one of the candles, lay a wineskin, its neck tied with twine.

As Maia entered with her guide, an old, black-clad woman, stooping and red-eyed, looked up from the fire. She seemed about to speak, but the sandy-haired man forestalled her.

'Come on, y' basting old bitch, where's my supper, then, supper, eh?'

Opening one of the horn panels in the lantern, he blew it out and then shut the door. He was about to bar it when the old woman stopped him with a gesture.

'There's another to come yet, U-Genshed,' she said, coughing as she spoke. 'Megdon's bringin' another from Thettit; special one, coming alone. Be in later tonight, he said.'

'All right, all right,' answered Genshed, putting down the door-bar. 'The basting supper, I said! And after that you can get out to those bullocks. I left 'em for yer special.' He laughed, loosened the string of the wineskin, filled a clay cup and drank.

The old woman, however, remained staring at Maia where she stood dishevelled and haggard in the candlelight.

'Oh, that's a pretty one, isn't it?' she said quaveringly. 'That's a beauty! She going up with this lot, then? 'Nother for Lalloc, is it?'

'Yer, and he don't know yet,' answered Genshed. 'We just happened to come by her, acting on information received, yer, yer. So she's still off the record, in't she?' Closing his fingers round Maia's upper arm, he led her to the bench opposite Perdan and sat down beside her.

The old woman, without replying, turned back to her cooking-pots and filled two wooden dishes, which she carried over and set down on the table.

'Bread,' said Genshed, pulling one of them towards him. 'And why don't you give her some basting knives, you old cow? Think she can cut it up without?'

The old woman obeyed him and then, wiping her hands on her skirt, muttered 'See to the beasts, then,' and went out into the yard.

Worn out and frightened to the point of collapse, Maia could scarcely have collected herself sufficiently to tell anyone even her name or where she came from. She tried to eat, but the food tasted like straw and she could not swallow. Every few seconds she shut her eyes, breathing in gasps and feeling her pulse pounding. She was now long past thinking about how to get out of the house. She was an exhausted, terrified child; and the worst of her fear was that while she now knew that her situation could not be as she had supposed, she had no idea what it might really be, or what was likely to befall her. Yet it was bad; of that she felt sure. Each time she opened her eyes it was to see the baleful face and hunched shoulders of Perdan opposite. Each time she closed them, she felt Genshed's hands groping at her back, her neck or her arms.

Suddenly, just as the old woman reappeared, she rose to her feet, swayed, clutched the edge of the table and then, before Genshed could catch her, slid to the floor unconscious.

Perdan stooped and lifted her bodily in his arms.

'Open the basting door, then,' he said to Genshed, nodding across the room, 'and bring a candle.'

'Top room on the right, Perdan,' said the old woman over her shoulder. 'The left-hand room's for the other one—the one Megdon's bringing. There's blankets up there already, and the lock and chain's hanging on the wall inside.'

: 6 :

THE BLACK GIRL

Waking in an instant, Maia started up in bed with alarm sharp as the snapping of a stick. Looking round her in the darkness, she could make out only a square of deep-blue sky, pricked with a star or two and crossed by the black lines of the window-bars. She was still dressed in her clothes, but covered by one or two coarse blankets. Some insect had bitten her right ankle and the place was itching. She scratched it quickly with the rough skin of her other heel.

After a moment she became aware of what must have woken her; a sound of stealthy movement somewhere close by. Simultaneously, she perceived the shape of a door facing her, a few feet beyond the foot of the bed—an ill-fitting door, with chinks between its planks and a chain passing through two holes, one in the edge of the door and the other beside it in the jamb. And this she could see because there was light outside; a flickering light which, throwing glimmers through the chinks, showed her that she was in a small room—no more than a cell—containing her bed, a stool and a bench against the wall under the window.

Someone outside the door had released the chain and was pulling it through the holes.

Sitting on the bed, her knees drawn up, and biting her finger-tips in her terror, she watched as the chain was slowly drawn out. To scream did not even occur to her, so complete was her unthinking conviction of the hostility—or at best the indifference—of anyone likely to hear her.

Creaking slightly, the door opened inwards, just clearing the foot of the bed, to reveal Genshed holding up a candle. As their eyes met he smiled, as though pleased to find her awake. His hand, shaking slightly, sent shadows wavering along the walls.

'Y'all right, then?' he said in a whisper, stepping into the room and putting the candle down on the stool.

Maia made no reply, only shrinking back against the wall as Genshed sat down on the edge of the bed.

'Oh, y'needn't be frightened of me,' he went on, staring at her with his mouth slightly open. 'Just come to see if y'all right, that's all. You fainted, y'know—fell on the floor downstairs, remember?'

She nodded.

'Did y'hurt y'self? Any bruises, eh, nice bruises?'

She shook her head.

'Well, better have a look, hadn't we?' said Genshed in a thicker, more intense whisper. His spittle, as he spoke, fell on the back of Maia's hands clutching the blankets to her chin. She turned them over, wiping them quickly, and as she did so he suddenly leant forward, plucked them aside and dragged the blankets to the foot of the bed.

'No!' she cried desperately, and instantly one of his hands was over her mouth, while the other ripped her smock from throat to waist. Panting, he forced her down and flung himself on top of her, tugging at her shift, his knees forcing her legs apart. Feeling him pressed against her as she had once felt Tharrin, she was filled with unspeakable horror and loathing. Struggling, she jerked her head forward and her forehead struck him violently in the face.

Genshed, blood pouring from his nose, knelt back on his heels.

'You dirty little tairth!' he whispered. 'Cran, you'll just about wish you hadn't—'

Very deliberately, he drew a knife from his belt, turning it in his hand so that it glittered a moment, paralysing her with fear. Then, holding the hilt loosely, he began jabbing the point here and there, lightly pricking her wrists, her arms and shoulders. As she whimpered, cringing one way and another and vainly trying to avoid the thrusts, his enjoyment plainly increased and the bloody mask of his face grinned in the candlelight.

At length he laid the knife aside and rose to his feet beside the bed.

'Now, my pretty little pet,' he said, and pulled his leather jerkin over his head.

At this moment, just as his head came clear of the garment, a dark presence, like an apparition, appeared in the doorway, took a step forward and dealt him a swinging blow on the side of the neck. He stumbled against the wall, and as he did so the figure kicked him in the stomach, so that he fell to the floor.

Everything had happened so fast that Maia had had no time even to feel relief. Utterly bewildered, she stared up from where she lay, by no means sure whether her rescuer might be human or supernatural: and for this uncertainty she had some reason, since the figure before her was like no one she had ever seen in her life.

Standing at the foot of the bed was a girl a few years older and a little taller than herself, with a broad nose and short, curling black hair. Completely naked, her lithe, slim body was dark brown—almost black. She was wearing a necklace of curved teeth; and thrown back from its fastening round her neck, so that it hung behind her from shoulders to knees, was a scarlet cloak. As she blinked, Maia saw in the candlelight that her eyelids were painted silver.

Meeting Maia's eyes, the girl smiled briefly. Then she picked up Genshed's knife and tried it in her hand with the air of one not unused to such things.

At the same moment Genshed turned over, sat up on the floor and set his back against the rough, lime-washed wall.

'Stay there, you blasted pig,' said the black girl quietly. 'Doan' try to get up, or I'll cut your zard off and stuff it up your *venda*.'

Her voice, smooth and unusually low, had a curious, exotic quality, as though she were speaking—albeit with complete fluency—a language to which her lips and palate were not entirely suited. Her words were not elided in the manner of common utterance and her accent was not Tonildan.

Genshed, staring up at her, wiped the back of one hand across his blood-smeared face and spat.

'Who the hell are you?' he said. 'What d' y' think you're doing, comin' in here? Give me that knife and get back to your room.'

'You mother-bastin' little tairth of a slave-trader,' replied the girl evenly, without raising her voice, '*I* doan' have to ask what *you* were doin'. You work for Lalloc, doan' you? and I suppose you'll tell me you doan' know it's a strict rule that stock-in-trade's not to be raped or interfered with by the likes of you? You zard-suckin' little swine, this is goin' to cost you your job before I've done.'

'Not so much of your basting lip!' cried Genshed. 'You just give me that knife, now!'

'Yes, you can have the knife,' replied the girl. 'That poor little banzi's bleedin' along of you, you filthy bastard; I *could* make *you* bleed: but I'm not goin' to waste any time on you. For now, I'm just goin' to get you out of here and later, back into the gutter you came from: or even into Zeray, I wouldn' wonder. Here's your knife.'

On the instant she threw it by the blade across the few feet between them. The point pierced Genshed's calf to a depth of a good inch, and as he grabbed the hilt with a cry of pain, dark blood welled out and flowed down his leg.

The black girl, with a quick movement, drew one wing of her scarlet cloak across her body and stood coolly looking down at him.

'I'm val'able merchandise,' she said. 'You know that, doan' you? *I'm* to arrive at Bekla in perfect condition. And *you're* just a dirty little nit-pickin', venda-crawlin' menial; there's any number like you. You try an' touch me and I'll cut your balls off. Now put that lousy jerkin on again and get out of here.' She kicked it into his lap.

'All right, all right, less of it now,' said Genshed, in the tone of one who feels himself beaten but is trying not to show it. 'Who d'you think you are, anyway?' Pulling a dirty rag from somewhere under his clothes, he began dabbing at his bleeding leg.

A small, dark man, with the look of an Ortelgan, whom Maia had not seen before, appeared in the doorway and stood staring at the scene before him.

'Who am I, Megdon?' said the black girl. 'You better tell him.'

The dark man smiled. It seemed to Maia that he did not like Genshed. 'Her name's Occula,' he said, 'from Thettit-Tonilda.'

'Yes!' cried the girl, raising her voice for the first time. 'I am—the *Lady* Occula, you stinkin' little tairth-trader. Have you ever heard of Madam Domris?'

'Runs a knocking-shop in Thettit, Thettit, don't she?' muttered Genshed, without meeting her eye.

'Runs a knockin'-shop in Thett, Thett, Thettit!' mimicked Occula, spitting on him where he sat slumped on the floor. 'I'll give you knockin'-shop, you leakin' little piss-bucket! You wait till she hears you said that! Madam Domris's shearnas are famous all over the empire! And *I'm* one of her girls, you shit-faced maggot! Do you know what I'm worth? Well over ten thousand meld, that's how much—more than you'll see in a lifetime!'

'Well, I never touched you, did I?' replied Genshed sullenly.

'No, and you wouldn' dare, you squitterin' cockroach; but you thought you'd get away with havin' a bit of fun on the side, didn' you, with this poor little banzi, on account of you picked her up by chance, I suppose, and she's not on a list yet—Lalloc's or anyone else's. Think I doan' know your cunnin' little ways, you pox-faced rat? But worse, you woke *me* up! Just when I'd managed to get to sleep in this crawlin' pigsty—I'm bitten like a dog already—I'm woken up by snivellin' cesspits like you, tryin' to rape helpless little girls. You crawlin' lump of offal, I suppose you think Lalloc's goin' to think that's the way for his shearnas to make a good start—to be terrified and force-basted by menstrual turds like you?' She paused. 'Well, do you? 'Cos I'm goin' to tell him, no danger.'

Her voice, easy and controlled, dominated the room as a curlew's a hillside. It was as though Genshed had inadvertently opened a tap, thereby causing her foul language to come pouring over himself in a smooth, mephitic stream.

A silence fell. Occula, having waited for Genshed's reply long enough to make it clear that there would be none, turned her back on him. The candle, already burned low, began to gutter.

'Right,' said the girl at length, 'Megdon, will you please bring two fresh candles into my room? As for you—whatever your name is—I *could* make you wash this girl and clean her up, only she wouldn' care to be touched by a disgustin' worm like you; so I'll just oblige you and do it myself. Go and get me some hot water with herbs in it, and a clean towel. And doan' be long, either.'

'Fire's out,' muttered Genshed. 'Middle middle of the night, ennit?'

'Then light it again, baste you,' replied the black girl, without turning round. 'And you, banzi,' she said, turning to Maia with a sudden flash of white teeth, 'you'd better come in next door with me; come on!'

She held out a pale-palmed hand. Maia, hardly knowing what she did, grasped it and went where she was led.

: 7 :

A FRIEND IN NEED

The room across the passage—what little Maia could see of it in the candlelight and her own shocked and exhausted condition—was larger than the one she had left, as was the bed. There were two or three stools, and near the door a small wooden chest with two bronze handles and some lettering branded across the lid. Occula, releasing Maia's hand, ran her own fore-finger over the first two or three characters.

'Can you read, banzi?' she asked.

Maia shook her head. 'Precious little. Can you?'

'Sort of,' answered the black girl. 'Anyway, that's my name. Old Domris gave me this, for my clothes an' things, 'fore I left Thettit-Tonilda. You can put your own things in it if you like. There's enough room.'

Before Maia could reply, Megdon came in with two fresh candles, a towel and a wooden pail, the steam from which gave off a pleasantly herbal smell.

'Didn' I tell that other bastard *he* was to bring the hot water?' asked Occula.

Megdon, lighting the new candles from the other burning by the bed, shrugged his shoulders.

'I shouldn't push it too far, Occula, if I were you. He's a very funny lad, is Genshed. You get them in this business, you know.'

The girl shrugged her shoulders. 'He'll be a lot funnier when I've finished, tell you that. I'm goin' to speak to Lalloc as soon as I get to Bekla.'

'D'you know Lalloc?' replied Megdon, grinning. 'Ever met him?'

Occula, without replying, opened the chest and took out a sheet of reed-paper, which she held up for a moment before putting it back and closing the lid.

'See that?' she said. 'That's a letter from Domris to Lalloc; as well as her bill for me. Doan' you start thinkin' Lalloc woan' listen to me, because he will. Your friend Genshed's as good as out.'

'But why, Occula?' asked Megdon. 'This young girl doesn't belong to anyone yet. Far as I can make out she's some sort of lucky dip. I didn't even know she was here until you started the row.'

'*I* started the row?' retorted Occula, rising to her feet and turning to face him. 'Some lout of yours goes in for rapin' stock-in-trade and you say *I* started the row? I doan' give a baste how you came by her: once the likes of him start rapin' stock, there's not a girl's goin' to be safe. You know Lalloc's rules as well as I do. A little banzi like that, knows nothin', never seen anythin'—what good's she goin' to be to Lalloc or anyone else when your friend Genshed's finished with her? You're a damn' fool, Megdon. Go back to bed. And doan' wake me in the mornin'. I'll come down when I'm ready.'

As soon as the man had gone Occula threw back her cloak, knelt beside the pail and dipped one end of the towel in the steaming water.

'Come on, banzi,' she said. 'Sit on this stool; and lean forward, so I can get at those shoulders and arms. Who knows where that bastard's filthy knife has been?'

Her hands were surprisingly gentle. None of the scratches and pricks was deep, though one continued to bleed despite repeated staunching with the towel.

'Leave it,' said Occula at length. 'It'll clean out the cut, and we can see to it in the mornin'. Doesn' hurt much, does it?'

Maia smiled faintly. 'Not now. You've been—oh, thank you for what you've done! I don't know what I—'

'So now we can both get back to sleep,' interrupted the black girl, carrying the pail into the further corner of the room. 'This bed's big enough for two.' She grinned. 'You used to someone else in bed?'

Maia grinned back. 'My little sister.'

'What a shame!' replied Occula unexpectedly. 'You poor banzi! Well, you can tell me all about it tomorrow.'

She waited as Maia climbed into the bed and then, blowing out the candles, got in on the other side. Maia was asleep almost as soon as her companion had settled herself beside her.

Often, when we have fallen asleep in an unaccustomed place, we wake in the momentary belief that we are back at home, or wherever we have recently been used to sleeping, so that we have to suffer the initial grief of disillusion even before trying to face up to whatever trouble, known or unknown, the coming day may have in store. This, however, Maia was spared. Waking smoothly from several hours of profound sleep, the first thing she saw was Occula's brown arm lying across the pillow. At once she recalled where she was and all that had happened the previous day.

For a little while she lay still, watching the black girl's face and the rise and fall of her breathing. Her lashes, under the silvered lids, were very long and thick and her hair, like none that Maia had ever seen, curled close about her head like some miraculous cap. Seeing her now, in repose and daylight, Maia felt that although she was certainly not what most people would have called beautiful, her appearance was so unusual and striking that the question scarcely applied. Suppose, she thought, that somewhere in the world there was a race of people who'd never seen a cat. Then if a cat was to appear, they wouldn't hardly stop to argue about whether or not it was beautiful, would they? Everyone would want to look at it and touch it—yes, and keep it for themselves, too, if they could.

Who was this strange girl, and what was she doing here? Was *she* going to sell fine clothes in rich Tonildan houses? Yet she had spoken of arriving in Bekla. Little as Maia had really taken in of her scalding words to Genshed, she remembered that. The girl had been very kind. Perhaps she would help her to return home?

It was still early—not long after dawn, as she could tell by the strength and lie of the light. Slipping quietly out of bed, she stole across to the barred window.

The sun was out of sight to her left, but the late summer wilderness below her was already full of light; the tangled, dew-drenched grass glittering, the trees looped and netted with shadow, spiders' webs iridescent among the brambles. In the silence she could hear the intermittent murmuring of a pigeon. The place, she could see, had once been a garden, for there were fruit-trees and rose-bushes half-buried in undergrowth, while further off a broken fountain stood in the centre of its empty basin.

Half out of sight, beyond a grove of *zoans*, she could make out the ruins of a big house. Roofless it was, its stone walls streaked black with fire, weeds trailing from window-spaces that framed only the sky. Why then, she thought, this place where she had spent the night must indeed be the servants' quarters, or some such, of that house. She wondered how it had come to grief, and what might have befallen its lord and his followers when the flames roared up and the roof fell in. How long ago had it happened? Some time, by the look of the place.

How far was she from home? If it were not for these bars on the windows she would have risked jumping down into the long grass, found some way out and been off before anyone knew she was gone. She bent forward, trying to see what lay on either side of the window.

A hand fell on her shoulder and she started. Occula, wrapped in her red cloak, was standing behind her, yawning like a cat and rubbing the sleep out of her eyes together with what remained of the silver paint on her eyelids.

'Oh! You frightened me!' said Maia. 'I didn' know you were awake.'

'I'm not,' replied the black girl, stretching her arms above her head. 'Just walkin' in m' sleep.' Again she put her hand on Maia's shoulder, caressing and stroking. 'Want to come back to bed?'

Maia laughed. 'I just want to get out of here, that's all. What's more, I'm going to, soon as I can: this very morning.'

Occula frowned a moment, as though puzzled: then she looked up sharply. 'You doan' mean—kill yourself? It's never that bad, you know, banzi. That little bastard woan' try anythin' again, believe you me.'

'Kill myself?' answered Maia, puzzled in her turn. ''Course not; why should you think that? I just mean I don't want to work for these people and I'm going back home.'

'But how?'

'Well, very like I'll have to walk, but it can't be more than ten or twelve miles, I suppose.'

Occula sat down on the nearest stool. For about a quarter of a minute she remained looking down at the floor, tapping her knee with the fingers of one hand. At length she asked, 'Banzi, do you know where you are and who these people are?'

'No, I don't,' answered Maia, ''ceptin' I don't like 'em.'

'You'd better tell me how you come to be here. You talk and I'll listen.'

Maia gave an account of what had happened the previous day, omitting only any mention of what had passed between herself and Tharrin.

'—so then, last night, I got up from the table, 'cos I was going to go straight out and start off back in the dark, see?' she concluded. 'Only I was that done up, what with being in that cart and everything, I must 'a gone right off on the floor, 'cos next thing I remember's being woken up by that man and then you coming in.'

Occula, taking both her hands in her own, looked gravely up at her from the stool.

'How old are you?'

'Fifteen.'

'Just a banzi. What's your name?'

'Maia. My mother's Morca. We live near Meerzat, up along the lake.'

'Well, listen, Maia. I've got to tell you somethin' you doan' know—somethin' very bad, too. Are you ready for it?'

Maia stared. 'What you mean, then?'

'Tell you what I mean. These men are slave-traders. They're employed by dealers in Bekla—mostly by a man called Lalloc. He buys and sells girls—and little boys too. And from what you've just told me, I'm certain as I can be that your mother sold you to them yesterday.'

Like a great work of art, really bad news—enormous loss, ruin, disaster—takes time to make its full impact. Our first reaction is often almost idle, as though by trifling with the business we could reduce it, too, to triviality.

'What would she do that for?' asked Maia.

'You tell me,' replied the black girl. ''Cos that's what she did, and it's no good pretendin' she didn'; not if what you've told me's right. So what have you left out?'

Suddenly it dawned on Maia why Morca should have done it. Thereupon she felt like one who, having woken from sleep but still half-awake, realizes that the dully-perceived object swaying a foot or two from her head is in fact a deadly snake. All was clear on the instant: everything fitted. There was no way in which what had happened could be otherwise explained. Shuddering, she sank to the floor, burying her face in her hands and moaning.

'The pretty dress—that's an old trick to get a sight of a girl naked,' went on Occula matter-of-factly. 'They'd have been hidin' somewhere, of course, where they could watch you. And then she sent you off on some errand or other while they worked out the price. And what was in the wine, I wonder?—yours, of course; no one else's. *Tessik*, most likely. They'd not risk *theltocarna* on a banzi like you—might 'a killed you. And the padded cart—well, some girls throw themselves about, you know, when they realize what's happened—bang their heads and so on.'

Maia lay sobbing hysterically on the wooden boards. There was a knock and the door opened.

'Get out, Megdon,' said Occula. 'Go on, piss off.'

'Brought your breakfast,' said the man, in an injured tone. 'Hot water, too. Don't you want it?'

'Yes, when I say,' replied the girl. 'Just leave the hot water and get out.' The door closed.

Taking her stool over to the window, she sat looking out through the bars. At last she said, 'Banzi, listen to me. I've seen a lot of girls this has happened to. I know what I'm talkin' about.'

As Maia, prone on the floor, continued sobbing, she went across to her, turned her over bodily and then, sitting down beside her, took her head in her lap. 'Listen to me; because this may very well save your life, and I'm not jokin'. *Save* your *life*! Understand this—from now on you're in danger; as much as a soldier on a battlefield. But if your mate—that's me—stands by you and if you can keep your head and make good use of what you've been taught—that's to say, what I'll teach you—you've got a good chance of stayin' alive.'

Maia, with another burst of tears, tried to struggle from her arms.

'O Kantza-Merada give me patience!' cried the black girl, holding her down by force. 'All right, you're *not* a bastin' soldier, then! But I've got to make you see it, banzi! How? How? Here—answer me—can you swim?'

The simple question penetrated Maia's hysteria.

'Yes.'

'In the lake? You've always swum, have you? You swim well?'

When we are plunged in desperate trouble, often it affords some slight relief to give what we know to be the right answer to a question—any question—even one that seems to have no bearing on our misery. Perhaps this is due to superstition—in some unforeseeable way the answer, being correct, may help. Certainly it can do no harm, and the mere giving of it grants a little respite.

'I've swum three miles before now. Anything an otter can do, I can do it.'

'Good,' said Occula. 'Well, now, banzi, understand this. You're out in deep water, and it's a bastin' long way to the land. Never mind how you got there. No good thinkin' about that now; that woan' keep you afloat. You're there, in the water, got it? What you goin' to do? Tell me, because I'm no swimmer.'

'Take it steady,' replied Maia without hesitation. 'No good losing your head, start splashin' about; only wear yourself out, start swallowing water an' then very likely that's it.'

'Anythin' else?'

'Well, say you're making for somewhere as you can see, you got to watch ahead—make out if you're drifting one way or t'other. Then you can alter according, see, with the drift.'

'Fine! You've just given yourself better advice than ever I could. Now you just keep afloat and stop strugglin', because I'm goin' to tell you where we are. Right?'

Maia, biting her lip, stared at her.

'You're a *slave* now,' said Occula deliberately. 'A slave bought and sold. You can't go home. If you try to escape, they've got ways of hurtin' you that doan' show. Now go on listenin' to me, because it's important. Tell me, where is this place, d'you know?'

'Puhra, isn't it?'

'Yes, about a mile outside Puhra. Ever heard of Senda-na-Say?'

Maia nodded. 'He used to be High Baron of Bekla. He's dead, isn't he?'

'He was murdered by the Leopards nearly seven years ago. That out there—' she nodded towards the window—'that's what's left of one of his great houses. They burnt it, and most of his household, too. This used to be the grooms' quarters, but after the big house was burned, Lalloc and Mortuga and one or two more of the big slave-dealers in Bekla turned it into a sort of depôt. They've got their agents out all over the eastern provinces, you see, and this makes a convenient collectin'-place for slaves being sent up to Bekla.

'The big money's in girls; girls and little boys, that is. As far as I can make out, they're even hotter for girls in Bekla than they are in Thettit, and that's sayin' somethin'. That's why I'm goin' there. Still, there'll be plenty of time later on to tell you about me.

'Now listen, Maia, and try not to get upset any more, because that woan' help you. But *I'll* help you: I'm your big sister. Got it?'

Maia nodded again.

'They're goin' to take us up to Bekla, to this man Lalloc, to be sold for bed-girls. And now I'm goin' to tell you two bits of sense that may very well make all the difference to you. First, a bed-girl's got to be cunnin' and tough, even if she never shows it. Other people have fathers, mothers, families, homes, money, social standin', Cran knows what. We've got *nothin'*. We just have to rely on ourselves. A bed-girl who isn't tough and cunnin', or starts feelin' sorry for herself, just goes down and down until she dies young. And I mean *dies*, banzi! Have you got that?'

Her eyes, brown-irised and slightly bloodshot, gazed earnestly into the younger girl's.

'Yes,' whispered Maia faintly.

'Now the second thing is this. People value a girl as she values herself. Behave like a queen and you may even end up by convincin' some of the bastards that you really are one. Never ask a favour or tell them what's really in your heart. Somehow or other, you've got to keep your authority. Never act as if you wanted anyone to feel sorry for you. Do you understand?'

Maia smiled faintly, returning the squeeze of her hand.

'Good,' said the black girl. 'Now understand: *I'll* stick by you, because

I've taken a fancy to you. Aren't you bastin' lucky? Doan' cry in front of those swine out there. Cry when you're alone with me and I'll wipe your eyes. Right?'

'Best's I can,' replied Maia, choking back a sob.

'Then you can start bein' tough now, this very minute. We'll wash and dress—is that all you've got, what you've slept in? I'll make them give you better than that—and go downstairs and eat breakfast as if there was nothin' the matter. But doan' start chatterin' in front of them, d'you see? You've got to keep your dignity, else they'll despise you and start treatin' you *worse* than a slave. How hot's that water? Has it gone cold?'

Maia went over to the pail.

'No; reckon it's about right.'

'Then you have it first. Properly, too; head to foot.'

Obediently, Maia stripped and stood in the pail, stooping and rinsing. The warm water was refreshing. As once before, a sudden feeling came upon her that the only thing to do was to refrain from thought or deliberation and simply leave her body to carry on.

Looking round, she was startled to see the black girl staring at her with an air of astonishment.

'What's up?' she asked nervously.

'Oh, banzi,' whispered Occula, 'you're *nice*, aren't you? Turn round: let's have a proper look!' Maia turned and faced her. 'Oh, Cran and Airtha, what a figure! You'll be worth a fortune, my girl! Just keep your head screwed on right and doan' make a fool of yourself, and you can' go wrong! This may even turn out to be the best thing that's ever happened to you—a lot better than a hut on the Tonildan Waste, I wouldn' wonder. Stick with me, banzi, and before we're done we'll turn Bekla upside-down!'

: 8 :

KANTZA-MERADA

Occula spent some time in dressing and preparing herself to go downstairs. Maia, despite the misery and anxiety flooding her mind, watched with involuntary fascination as the black girl selected from her chest a Yelda-shay-style *metlan* of brilliant orange, over which she belted on a kind of leather hunting-jacket trimmed with scarlet bows. The whole effect, bizarre and incongruous, was nevertheless most arresting, as though the wearer were a kind of incarnation of fantasy and extravaganza, exempt from all normal sartorial conventions.

Looking up from a battered metal mirror as she finished painting a crimson streak along the outer edge of each eye, Occula winked.

'Interestin', aren't I? Start as you mean to go on. Doan' worry, banzi, you'll be gettin' plenty of nice clothes before you're much older; that's one consolation.'

Picking up a shining, golden stud, she fitted it into place through the side of one nostril.

'For now, you'll have to wear the dress that bastard ripped, but put my cloak on over the top. No, not like that, banzi: here, let me help you. Cran! What a shame to cover up a pair of deldas like those!'

When the girls came down into the stone-floored kitchen, it was empty except for the old woman, who was sitting by the fire slicing a pile of brillions. By daylight she looked still more sleazy. Even by Maia's standards she was dirty, and had on one cheek a weeping sore. Occula stood looking her up and down without a word, until at length the old woman, plainly annoyed but apparently wary of provoking the black girl, made shift to save her face by looking briefly at the remaining brillions and remarking, 'Well, that's enough o' them, I reckon. And I suppose now you want something to eat, miss, is that it, after sending back what Megdon took you up earlier?'

'This place is filthy,' said Occula, 'and so are you. We'll stick to boiled eggs and fruit, and boiled milk to drink.'

'Why, you little bitch,' retorted the old woman, 'you just wait till they sell you up in Bekla! They'll soon teach you to mind your tongue there, you black-faced tart—'

'You were a tart once,' replied Occula calmly. 'But you mustn' judge me by yourself, you know. I'm goin' to be much more successful and finish up a lot better off. When I'm your age *I* shan' be crawlin' about in a pile of shit, slicin' brillions for slave-traders.'

'Basting hell!' shouted the old woman, rushing at her and swinging back her arm. Occula caught her by the wrist, gripped it for a few moments and then pushed it gently back to her side.

'It's no good, grandma,' she said, not unkindly. 'Just do as I ask you and let's have no trouble, shall we? Come on, now; eggs, milk and fruit.'

'There's no fruit,' snapped the old woman, turning away.

'The garden's full of it,' said Occula. 'Ripe, too. Banzi, go out and pick some, will you?'

'No, she won't!' cried the old woman. 'Think we let you little whores go wandering about outside just as you like? D'you know what "slave" means, miss, eh?'

'You'd better go yourself, then,' said Occula. 'You used to be a whore— and a slave. I'm goin' to be a shearna—and in the upper city, too.'

'D'you think I'm running your errands, miss?' screamed the old woman. 'You'll eat what you're given or else go without, you black cow—'

In a flash Occula had snatched up the peeling-knife. At the same moment Megdon, entering the room, reached her in three strides, plucked it out of her hand and threw it into a corner.

'Easy now, Occula,' said the slave-trader. 'You're getting a lot too handy with knives, you know. What's the row?'

Occula stood impassively beside the table as the old woman began a shrill tirade of explanation and abuse. It was plain, however, that Megdon was only half-listening. At length, shrugging his shoulders, he said, 'Well, if she wants some fruit you'd better go and get her some. I'll stay here with them till you come back.'

The old woman seemed about to argue: then, muttering, she took up a basket and shuffled out of the room.

Megdon turned back to Occula, who had flung back her leather jacket and, her hands behind her on the table, was leaning backwards, her body arched from the hips. As he took a step towards her she said, 'Do you want this little girl to watch? Is that what you like?'

'It would be easier to go upstairs, wouldn't it?' answered Megdon. 'What are you charging this time, Occula? Too much, if I know anything about it.'

'You bugger, I haven' charged you a meld yet,' said Occula.

'Not money, no,' replied Megdon, never taking his eyes off her. 'But a slap-up dinner—and it *was* slap-up, Occula; you can't say it wasn't—and two bottles of Yeldashay at the best place between here and Thettit. *And* that gold stud in your nose.'

'Which you took off some other poor girl,' said Occula. 'You're lucky, you know. Six months from now and you woan' be able to get me for five times that. In fact, you woan' be able to get me at all, so you'd better make the most of it while you can.'

'Well, for your own sake, I hope you're right, Occula,' answered Megdon. 'To tell you the truth, I wish we had to handle more girls like you: life would be a lot easier.'

'There's no one like me. What's happened to that little bastard I sorted out last night?'

'Gone to Zalamea on a collecting job. Won't be back till tonight. There's only Perdan, and he's still asleep.'

'All right; you want to know the price,' said Occula. 'I'll tell you. You'll send us on to Hirdo today; me and this banzi here. And you'll fit her out with some decent clothes. And that's all: cheap, isn't it?'

'I can't do it, Occula,' answered Megdon. 'I can give the girl a dress; three, if you like. That's easy enough. But I can't send you on to Hirdo today, because there's no one to take you.'

'There's you.'

'Genshed's bringing five girls on foot from Zalamea. They'll have done fourteen miles. I've no idea what they'll be like. You know how it is: some may be violent, some may even try to kill themselves. Me and Perdan have both got to be here. You'll go up to Hirdo tomorrow, on foot, with the rest of them. You're part of Lalloc's consignment, you see: I can't alter that. Sorry.'

To Maia's surprise Occula made no retort whatever, merely turning away and sitting down on the bench on the opposite side of the table. Megdon, coming round behind her, fondled her shoulders and then, bending his head, murmured, 'All right, then, Occula? Not my fault, you know. Anything else—'

'When I've had some breakfast you can baste yourself silly if you want to,' interrupted the black girl. 'For now, jus' let me be.' And thereupon, the old woman at this moment returning with her basket full of plums and apricots, the talk broke off.

At least the old woman did not stint them. Maia, in spite of everything, made a hearty meal and, as is often the way in trouble, began to feel the better for it. Also, it raised her spirits a little to perceive that Megdon at least seemed to show some consideration in dealing with Occula and herself. He spoke a few kindly words to her, said he was sorry about Genshed, assured her that nothing of the kind would happen again and told her to ask him for anything she needed.

'Just because I'm a slave-trader you mustn't think I'm a brute,' he concluded.

'Who are you foolin'?' asked Occula. 'Besides yourself, I mean?'

'No, honest, I won't let her come to any harm,' said Megdon. 'Not if she's a friend of yours, Occula. Let her go and choose herself some clothes. Come on, Shirrin,' he said to the old woman. 'Wash your hands and show her what's in those cupboards down the passage.'

If the old woman had shown her any warmth or kindness while they were alone together, no doubt Maia would have given way to more tears. Her surly indifference, however, only went to prove the soundness of Occula's advice. Maia, to the best of her ability, preserved her detachment and said as little as possible. The clothes were fully as good as any she had ever been used to, and anyway she was too much upset to be hard to satisfy. Twenty minutes later she returned to Occula's room, which she found empty.

She had just taken off the scarlet cloak and folded it across the bed when the black girl strolled through the open door, wearing her shift and carrying the rest of her clothes over one arm.

'Just doan' talk to me, banzi,' she said, flinging herself prone across the bed. 'O Cran, I'm just about ready to throw up! That dirty little stinker—I thought when it came to the big moment I'd get what we want out of him, but did I hell? He's *still* sayin' it can' be done. I've just given him a baste for nothin', that's what it comes to.'

'You mean, about going to Hirdo today?' said Maia. Occula made no reply and after a moment Maia asked rather hesitantly, 'Why's it so important? I don't want to go to Hirdo—I don't want to go anywhere—'ceptin' home.'

Occula rolled over, looking up at her with half-closed eyes and compressed lips.

'D'you think I'm goin' to go trampin' to Hirdo in a slave-gang—three-quarters of them pot-drabs and scullery-girls—very likely chained—and that bastard Perdan in charge, probably with a whip? And who's goin' to carry this box of mine? D'you suppose I'm goin' to arrive in Bekla in a herd, lookin' like some Deelguy drover's ten-meld bang-bargain? Banzi, you just doan' know what it's all about, do you? We've got to try to arrive at Bekla in *style*, my girl! This blasted man Lalloc's got to feel we're the biggest catch this side of the Telthearna—the sort of girls he can sell into some really wealthy household. You doan' want to be flogged off to some bloody knockin'-shop in the lower city, do you, where you start bad and go right on down? We've got to start four or five rungs up the ladder, and go up another three before next year. Now doan' interrup' me. Jus' let me think.'

She turned on her belly and for some time lay unmoving, her face buried in her arms. Maia went across to the window and resumed her silent contemplation of the overgrown garden. There came back to her the words of an old song her father had sometimes sung.

> Would to Cran we were the geese,
> For they live and die at peace—

She choked back a sob, and in a few moments would have been crying in earnest, had not Occula at that instant suddenly sprung up like a hare from the fern, clapped her hands and cried, 'Banzi!' so sharply that Maia jumped.

'This is risky and it may not work,' said the black girl, kneeling in front of her chest and rummaging under a jumble of gaudy clothes and brightly-coloured knick-knacks, 'but we'll try it. Stands to reason a slave-trader's agents in a place like this have got to be bone-stupid. Now, listen, banzi—ah, here it is!—you got to get this right, 'cos we can't do it twice and anyway I've only got one of these bastin' things. A Deelguy from up north gave it me last year, after I'd made sure he'd really enjoyed himself. I've never seen it used yet, but he said for Cran's sake doan' use it unless you mean business, because it's god-awful. Let's hope it is!'

She handed to Maia a grey-coloured object about as big as an apple, the covering of which was a kind of coarse canvas. It was not entirely firm, but gave slightly under the fingers. Maia could feel, inside, a gravel-like sliding and crunching of granules.

'Hide this somewhere under your clothes, where you can get it out quickly,' said Occula. 'All right? Now: this is Kantza-Merada. Take a good look at her.'

Drawing the strings of a cloth bag, she took out of it a figure carved in polished black wood. It was about nine inches high, squat, big-bellied, the conical breasts pointed like weapons, the slit-mouthed face a level, tilted plane broken only by nostrils and by slant, black-pupilled eyes of white bone. Meeting their gaze Maia shuddered, making the sign against evil. Indeed, the figure seemed to manifest overpoweringly something far beyond the mere image of a woman. It was not like a work of art created by the carver from experience and imagination, but rather a kind of revelation—for those who could endure it—of the true nature of the world; transcendentally malevolent, pitiless and savage.

'Doan' you start thinkin' *this* is Kantza-Merada,' said Occula, observing with satisfaction the undisguised fear and horror of the younger girl. 'This is only jus' to put anyone in mind of Kantza-Merada, that's all. You ought to be in the Govig at night, banzi, with the sand-wind blowin', and hear the drums beatin' when you know there's no one around for hundreds of miles. That's when you pray to Kantza-Merada—not when you're safe in bed in Thettit. Where I come from, they pray to a *real* goddess; one with power—not to Cran and Airtha. Still, never min' that now. We're goin' back down, and I'm goin' to kick up a real bastin' racket, understand? You keep out of the way, but whatever you do stay close to the fire. Once I start in they'll forget about you. When you hear me call on Kantza-Merada, and not before, put that ball in the fire—only doan' let anyone see you doin' it—and then run straight over to me and act like you're frightened. Go mad—call out "No, no, doan'!"—anythin' you like. And *doan'* get it wrong, see? because everythin' depends on that ball burnin'. If that dirty little Megdon thinks he can baste me for nothin' and get away with it, I'm goin' to hit him with everythin' I've got. Now *doan'* start askin' questions, banzi, or we'll never get to Hirdo tonight. Come on down, and min' you get it right.'

Megdon, with a look of satisfied contentment, was drowsing on a bench, while the old woman crouched on the floor, scouring a pot with sharp sand. Occula, who was still wearing nothing but her shift, walked up to her and kicked the pot out of her hands. At the clatter Megdon sat up quickly.

'Baste you!' said the black girl. 'I'm goin' to Hirdo—now! Understand?'

'Now don't go too far, Occula!' said Megdon sharply. 'Enough's enough! I can have you whipped, d'you realize that? Just you go and pick that pot up, go on!'

Occula spat in her hand and slapped his face. At the same moment the old woman, coming up behind her, grabbed her by the hair. Occula turned quickly, clenched her fist and knocked her down.

'Perdan!' shouted Megdon at the top of his voice. 'Perdan! Here! Quick!'

Running across to the door leading into the courtyard, Occula beat on it frenziedly.

'Open this damned, bastin' door!' she screamed. 'I'm goin' to Hirdo! I'm goin' to Hirdo!'

Perdan, stooping under the lintel, strode quickly into the room holding a length of cord in one hand.

'Now, miss, now!' yelled the old woman, picking herself up and following him across to the door. 'You'll just find out—'

'Don't damage her, Perdan!' said Megdon quickly. 'Just tie her up!'

'Kantza-Merada!' cried Occula. 'Kantza-Merada, blot this damn' place off the face of the earth!' Kneeling, flinging back her head and raising both arms, she burst into a torrent of speech in a snarling, foreign tongue.

Maia, standing close beside the hearth, dropped the canvas ball into the red heart of the fire.

'Kantza-Merada!' cried Occula again. 'Fire and smoke! Fire and smoke come down!'

Maia rushed across the room.

'Don't, Occula, don't! Not that! No, not that! You'll kill us all! You'll *kill* us!'

'Belch smoke and fall roof!' screamed Occula at the top of her voice. 'Kantza-Merada, smoke and smother this filthy house!'

On the instant there leapt up on the hearth a quick, brilliant flash. As it vanished, masses of dense, black smoke began to pour into the room. Perdan, cursing, let go his hold of Occula. Megdon and the old woman, choking and gasping, were blotted out in an all-enveloping, acrid smother. Maia, terrified, felt Occula grab her wrist.

'Keep it up, banzi,' whispered the black girl. 'Go on!'

'Take it away, Occula!' screamed Maia. 'Call it back! Don't kill them! Oh, no! not like that last time—' She could get no further. Her throat was full of the smoke, which seemed almost palpable, thick as wool and bitter. She felt herself suffocating, her head reeling, eyes burning under tight-shut lids. The invisible room seemed turning upside-down. She fell forward into Occula's arms.

At the same instant one or other of the two men contrived to get the door open. A few moments later Occula, stumbling through the swirling blackness, half-dragged and half-supported Maia outside. In the doorway she almost fell over the prostrate body of the old woman but, recovering herself, groped forward into the open courtyard and lowered Maia into a sitting position on the edge of a stone cattle-trough. Both girls were covered with a thick grime which clung in greasy, cobweb-like streaks to their faces, hair and clothes.

'Well done, banzi!' panted Occula. 'Do you reckon it'll burn the damned house down?'

'That old woman, Occula!' gasped Maia. 'We'll have to get her out or she'll die!'

'Hope so,' answered the black girl. 'No; no such luck: here she comes, look!'

The smoke was still pouring thickly both out of the windows and the door, but in the courtyard had dispersed into a somewhat thinner cloud. Through this, as they watched, Megdon and Perdan appeared, dragging the old woman between them. They laid her down on the cobbles and Megdon, kneeling beside her, raised her head with one hand and slapped her cheeks with the other.

'It's stoppin', look!' whispered Occula. 'You wait here, banzi: I've got to be quick, now.'

With this she ran up the courtyard towards the house. At her approach both men backed away in obvious fear, leaving the old woman lying where she was. Occula, spreading her arms, faced about and stood in the doorway. For several seconds she waited. Then, bowing her head and folding her hands at her waist she called, 'O Kantza-Merada, take back thy fire! If it be thy will, spare this vile house at thy servant's plea!' Then once more she spoke in the unknown tongue; and at length fell silent, standing motionless as the smoke slowly thinned about her.

Meanwhile the old woman had come to her senses, sitting up on the stones and weakly clutching here and there at her fouled clothes. So forlorn and bedraggled did she appear, like some wretched old hen not worth the killing, that Maia could not help pitying her. She stood up, intending to go and help her if she could; but at this the old woman gave a screech, got to her feet and hobbled across to the men on the other side of the courtyard.

Occula continued to stand in the doorway, gazing at the ground as though in a trance. The men were plainly at a loss, afraid to go near or even speak to her. So for a while they remained as they were, the black girl still a statue; the men muttering to each other in low voices; the old woman moaning and rocking herself from side to side; and Maia, a little distance away, sitting down once more on the edge of the trough.

At length Megdon, with the air of one compelling himself to act, went

81

across to Occula. He seemed about to speak when the girl—taller than he—raised her head and stared at him. His words died on his lips and after a moment she, as though giving a command to some animal—an ox in the shafts, perhaps, or a dog—uttered the one word 'Hirdo!'

Megdon seemed about to reply when suddenly Perdan forestalled him. 'Let her go, the damned black witch, before she kills us all with her sorcery!'

'Ay, ay! In Cran's name!' whimpered the old woman.

Megdon said nothing. Occula turned and walked slowly back into the kitchen; and here the others, following one by one—Maia a little behind the rest—found her leaning, with folded arms, against the side of the hearth. The fire was burning normally, but the entire room and everything in it was coated with a foul soot clinging alike to walls and furniture. There was a disgusting, vellicative reek, as of burnt bones.

The old woman began to weep—from fear, it seemed, as much as from dismay.

Megdon turned to Perdan. 'The girls Genshed's bringing'll have to clean this up tonight. It'll take hours. Shirrin can't do it on her own.'

Perdan made no reply.

'Go and get one of the carts ready,' said Megdon.

Perdan looked up. 'I'm not taking her!'

'I'll drive it,' replied Megdon. 'Just go and get the damned cart ready, Perdan, that's all!'

Occula spoke from the fireside. 'Food.' She jerked her thumb towards Maia. 'Get her some hot water. Fresh clothes.'

Half an hour later Maia, washed and changed, but still feeling as un- steady as though she had escaped from drowning, carried a pail of hot water up to Occula's room. The black girl was lying naked on the bed, her fouled shift crumpled across one of the stools. She had vomited into an old earthenware pot, and one arm was hanging down from the bed as though to grab it again at need. She looked up and grinned weakly at Maia.

'Cran! I thought we'd done for ourselves, banzi, didn' you? I just hope they felt as bad as we did, that's all. Think you can clear this away without anyone seein' you? Oh, chuck the lot out the damned window—what's it matter? When they're ready to go, call me, and send that lout up to fetch my chest.'

: 9 :

OCCULA'S COMFORT

At Hirdo the track ran into the paved road between Thettit and Bekla. In this town the slave-dealers had no private quarters, as at Puhra, but paid the keeper of one of the inns to provide accommodation as often as they might require it.

The journey from Puhra, in the heat of the day, took more than four hours, and by the time they arrived both the girls—whom Megdon had been content merely to chain together by one ankle—were weary, less with actual fatigue than with that general sense of bodily discomfort peculiar to prolonged travelling. Maia, unable, during the afternoon, to keep from brooding on her betrayal and misery, would more than once have wept, but the black girl would not suffer it, scolding her fiercely in whispers and more than once threatening to abandon her altogether if she gave way in front of Megdon. (Megdon himself, leading the bullocks and obviously preferring to keep as far away from Occula as possible, was out of hearing.) Maia, knowing now what Occula was capable of and more than anxious not to antagonize her only friend, choked back her tears as best she could.

On reaching the inn Megdon had a stroke of luck, finding there a young man named Zuno, a kind of steward whom Lalloc employed as an agent, a travelling auditor of slave quotas and the like. Zuno was on his way back to Bekla, having just completed an errand to Thettit. Megdon at once insisted on handing the girls over to him (making use of the innkeeper as a witness) and forthwith departed precipitately, not even stopping to eat.

To Maia this young Zuno, with his quiet, authoritative drawl, seemed the finest gentleman she had ever set eyes on. Not only his dandified clothes but his aloof air intensified her already dismal sense of being altogether out of her depth among contemptuous strangers to whom she was nothing but a little hoyden—a body for sale. She could not imagine herself conversing with him on any level at all, so cold and superior was his manner. And his appearance reinforced it. His long hair and curled beard were scented with sandalwood. The large bone buttons—eight in number—decorating his sky-blue *abshay* were each carved in a different likeness; one of a fish, another of a lizard, a third of a naked boy, and so on. His breeches of soft, thin leather clung close to his hips and thighs and were gathered into green, gold-tasselled half-boots. With him, in a wicker basket, he carried a long-haired, white cat; and to this, in his quiet, mincing voice, he talked a good deal, while saying little to anyone else.

Apart from all this magnificence, she intuitively sensed about Zuno a novel and (to her) puzzlingly strange kind of detachment—a detachment,

83

as it were, of inward inclination as well as of outward manner—which daunted her because it lay outside her experience and she could not understand it. During the past year or so Maia had unconsciously become used to being looked at and spoken to by men in a certain way. The way, while it might take this form or that, always implied—as she very well knew—that they found her attractive and were in no hurry to get out of her company. The behaviour of neither Perdan nor the vile Genshed had been out of accord with this: that is to say, while hating and fearing them, she had known only too well what they were feeling about her.

There was, however, something inexplicable about Zuno; something which confused her in a way that Genshed had not. He was like another order of being—a feathered reptile or a three-legged bird. His manner towards Occula and herself was one of detachment, and this stemmed—or so she sensed—less from superiority or social distance than from some curious absence of natural inclination. At first she could only suppose that the unexpected task thrust upon him by Megdon—a task which he could not very well refuse, since he was in Lalloc's employment and travelling to Bekla—was extremely unwelcome to him. But then it occurred to her that perhaps this might be what everyone was like in Bekla, for she had less idea of what people were like in Bekla than of what it might be like at the bottom of Lake Serrelind.

Worst of all, the man seemed to subdue even Occula. Upon their arrival the black girl had at once adopted an entirely different bearing from that with which Maia had watched her dominate the household at Puhra. As Zuno—looking up from stroking the cat and picking his teeth with a carved splinter of bone which he took out of a leather case—gave them his instructions, the black girl stood with downcast eyes, murmuring only 'Yes, sir' or 'Very well, sir,' and at length, as he turned back to his meal, raising her palm to her forehead and leaving the room without a word.

The innkeeper, though under orders to lock the girls into one of the rooms used for slaves in transit, affably brought them half a jar of wine with their supper and remained chatting for some little while, until tartly called by his wife to resume the evening's duties. Later a shy, smiling wench brought up hot water, but they were allowed no lamp. 'Dare say they're afraid we might try to burn the damn' place down and run away,' said Occula, climbing into bed. 'How d'you fancy goin' up to Bekla with that sonsy little wafter and his pussy-cat, banzi?'

'I can't make him out,' replied Maia dolefully. 'I don't fancy him at all!'

The black girl chuckled. 'Be terrible if you did, wouldn' it? But banzi, if you start lettin' fairies like that get you down, you're not the girl I took you for. Anyway, let's get to sleep. I'm worn out, aren't you?'

Maia fell asleep to the sounds of the tavern below—murmurs of conversation, the clink of pots and vessels, footsteps, closing doors, an occasional raised voice calling to a servant. Despite these, she slept heavily and did not stir for several hours.

When she woke the room was in darkness. Was it still early in the night, she wondered, or near dawn? She got up and went across to the barred window. The stars shone bright. There was not a trace of dawn in the sky, and no sound either from the inn or the road below. It must be well after midnight. Everyone, everything was asleep but she. She was alone with her personal loss of all that had once made life familiar and secure, of her home and of all those upon whom she had ever relied for comfort and affection. She would never again make her way home, with the old, familiar hunger in her belly and the certainty of what tomorrow would bring. One of her mother's mordant sayings returned to her mind most bitterly: 'Never's a long time.'

What will become of me? she thought. What does it mean, to be a slave? How will the days be spent—what sort of people will be around me? And then, like the half-child she still was, 'Is there anything nice at all to look forward to?' No, there was nothing—nothing. The future was a black pit: and Maia, leaning her forehead on the window-sill, covered it with hopeless tears.

'Banzi!'

Maia jumped, for once again the black girl had made no sound. Turning Maia away from the window, she clasped her in her arms and rocked her gently, stroking her hair as she continued to weep with great, shuddering sobs. At length Occula whispered, 'Come back to bed, banzi. No sense standin' here. Least you got a bed. And you got me—'less you doan' fancy.'

Leading Maia to her own bed, she got in beside her. For some little time they lay unspeaking. Slowly, Maia's weeping ceased, her tears though not her misery exhausted. At length Occula said 'Why didn' you wake me?'

'I—I didn't think—you said—tough and cunning—'

'Oh, but not to each *other*, banzi! Only to *men*! Cran and the stars, how I despise men! I'm hard as stone—I hope. I wouldn' have given a baste if we'd choked one of those swine to death this morning. But a girl's got to be soft to *someone*. I can't be a brute to the whole world. For my own self-respect I've got to love somebody, else I'd soon be as big a bastard as Genshed or Perdan—and wretched into the bargain. Listen, Maia, I meant what I told you. I'll be your true friend, I'll stand by you and look after you. I'll *never* let you down! If you like I'll swear it by Kantza-Merada. You may be up to the neck in shit, but for what it's worth, you got me.'

'Reckon that makes it a lot better,' answered Maia, less because she felt it than because it seemed to her that she could not decently say anything else. Occula's flesh smelt pleasantly strange—light and sharp, something like clean coal.

Drawing Maia's head onto her shoulder, the black girl stroked her hair. 'You haven' really told me about yourself yet, have you? Not properly. Why *did* your mother sell you? What's it all about?'

At this, the recollection of Tharrin shot up in Maia's heart with a vividness which the horror of the past two days had obliterated. Tharrin smiling at her as she lay in the net; Tharrin laughing over the wine at Meerzat; Tharrin panting in pleasure; Tharrin kissing her good-bye on the jetty before he went on board the boat.

'Tharrin,' she said. 'Tharrin—'

'Tharrin! Who's he? He loved you?'

'Loved me? Well—I suppose so, yes. He made everything a lot of fun. *I* loved *him*, anyway.'

'One of those, eh?' said Occula. 'Come on then, tell me.'

Hesitantly at first, then more freely as the memories came flooding, Maia talked of Tharrin. At last she said, 'So that's why she must've done it, see? She must've found out. And that'd be like her, too. Mother was always one to bottle it up, like, when anything made her mad, and then go too far.'

'And d'you think he'll come and look for you?' asked Occula.

Maia considered this for a moment, then choked back a fresh sob. 'I *know* he won't! 'Twouldn't be—well, it just wouldn't be like him. Not Tharrin.'

'You poor little beast!' whispered Occula, putting her arms round her once more. '*I'd* look for you—that I would—from here to Zeray and back.'

From somewhere in the distance outside sounded the barking of a dog. A voice shouted to it; it ceased and the silence returned, empty and remote.

'Do *you* like *me*?' asked Occula.

'Like you?' answered Maia, surprised. 'Well, 'course I do! You ask me that—after all you've done to help me?'

'Oh, that little bastard last night? That's nothin'—that was just a bit of sport. I didn't mean are you grateful. I meant do you *fancy* me?'

'How couldn't I?' Maia was all bewilderment.

Occula embraced her more closely, kissing her neck and shoulders. Her lips, in the dark, felt thick, pliant and soft.

'You had some nice times with Tharrin, then?' she asked.

'Oh, yes, it was lovely.' Maia, accustomed to having someone else in bed with her and comforted by the warmth and quiet, felt her misery abating. Youth and health possess almost unbelievable resilience.

'Did he do it nicely?'

'M'mm.' She felt drowsy again now, at ease in the soft bed. It might almost have been Nala lying beside her.

'What sort of things did he do? Did he ever do this?'

'Ah! Oh, Occula!'

A moment later the black girl's lips were pressed to her own, the tip of her tongue slipping between them into Maia's mouth. One hand gently stroked her thigh beneath her shift.

'But *he* let you down, didn' he, banzi?' whispered Occula. 'Men—who wants men? Liars, cowards, baste-and-run, the lot of them. We'll make our fortune out of those fools, you wait and see! But *I* woan' let you down, banzi. I need you: I need you to be good to. Kiss me! Come on, kiss me like I kissed you!'

For a long moment Maia hesitated. The fascination of this extraordinary, exotic girl, her apparent omniscience, her domination and self-sufficiency seemed extending all about her, enveloping her like a protective cloak. *Here* was a refuge from loneliness and from dread of the future. One need only surrender everything to Occula to be shielded, defended. Just as the lake had once been her own place, just as she had felt safe in its deep water, which everyone else thought dangerous because it was not dry land, so Occula—cunning and violent; black devotee of some appalling goddess of vengeance and sorcery—must have been vouchsafed to her for a retreat and refuge in the terrible misfortune which had befallen her. Occula was her own and no one else's. Clipping her about, running her fingers through her crisp, amazing hair, she kissed her passionately—her mouth, her cheeks, her eyelids—kissed her until she lay back, laughing and breathless.

'Take off your shift,' whispered the black girl, her hands already busy. 'No, wait: let me. There, that's nice, isn't it? And is *that* nice? D'you fancy me, banzi—really?'

: 10 :

NIGHT TALK

They lay together under a single blanket, perspiring, relaxed and easy.

'Occula! Oh, I wouldn't never have thought—'

'Sh!'

'I don't want to go to sleep now.'

'I didn' say go to sleep. I said sh!'

'Well, so I will. You talk, then. Tell me who you are—where you come from. Are they all black, there, like you? Where is it?'

'Head on my shoulder, then; that's right. Well, where shall I start?'

'Where you were born.'

'Where I was born? Ah! do you want to make me cry like you? I've buried that under a great rock, banzi, like Deparioth in the ballad—oh, years past—since I was a lot younger than you are now. Yes, buried— except in dreams. I remember some man tellin' me once that he knew all shearnas had one thing in common; they came from bad homes. But this one didn'.' She paused. 'Well, what lies out beyond Belishba, banzi, do you know?'

'Belishba? Where's that, then?'

'Where's Belishba? Oh, banzi, my pretty little net-mender, didn' anyone ever teach you pig's arse is pork? Belishba lies out beyond Sarkid—far away. Herl-Belishba must be more than a hundred miles from here; south— oh, yes, a long way south—from Dari-Paltesh. But it's not Herl-Belishba I come from, nor nowhere near.'

'Where, then?'

'On the furthest south-western edge of Belishba, far out, the country gets dry and stony, until in the end you come to the desert—the desert the Belishbans call the Harridan. But when I was a little girl I never knew that name, 'cos I was born on the other side—yes, on the other side of the most terrible desert in the world. We called it by its right name, and I still do. It's the Govig. The Govig, banzi—five hundred miles of stony slopes and dry sand. Five hundred miles of nothing—of ghosts and the wind that talks. Five hundred miles of sky and red clouds, and never a drop of water out of them by day or night.'

Maia, pleasantly intrigued and not really distinguishing in her mind between Occula's talk and one of old Drigga's tales, waited for her to go on.

'And then, beyond the Govig again—ah, that's where my home was, banzi; that's where men are men and women have hearts like the sun— honest and decent and nothin' hidden, nothin' but what you can feel shinin' warm all over you.'

'What's the country like?' asked Maia.

'Fertile. Flat. The water was slow and brown—it ran in long ditches up and down the fields.'

'For the beasts?'

'For rice. But *we* didn' use the fields—my family, I mean. My father was a merchant. We lived in Tedzhek. Silver Tedzhek, they call it, 'cos the river runs round it on three sides. The sand-spits are all silver along the water, and the women wash the clothes there, and twice a year there's a fair on the Long Spit and they act plays in honour of Kantza-Merada. I was three when Zai first took me to the Long Spit. I sat on his shoulders, right up above the crowds of people swayin' like long grass in a field. He was a fine, big man, you see, my father was.

'Zai was a jewel-merchant. And I doan' mean one of those fat, greasy old twisters with a house all bolts and bars and guards with clubs. Zai was a merchant-venturer, and Kantza-Merada only knows where he didn' get to. He'd been to the Great Sea—'

'What's that?'

'Never mind. He'd been there, anyway, and to Sellion-Rabat in the clouds, where the air's so thin that you can hardly breathe until you get used to it, he said; and out beyond the Usakos—that's where he nearly died of frostbite and had to fight his way back through bandits who tried to steal his stock. That's the trouble with jewels, you see; they're so terribly easy to steal. Zai used to disguise himself as a crazy pilgrim, sometimes, or even a drover, complete with bullocks. Once he was a lame beggar, with the jewels hidden in his false wooden leg.

'We never knew when he was goin' to get home again. Sometimes he was away for months and months. Once Ekundayo—that was mother's maid—came and said there was a pedlar at the door sellin' shells and carved toys, and did mother want to see what he'd got or should she send him away. But it was Zai come back: he hadn' let on, for a joke, and Ekundayo hadn' recognized him. But I did. I did!

'Oh, banzi, I could tell you all night, but I'd only be cryin' my eyes out. What's the good? I must have been nine—yes, it was nine—when Zai made his first crossin' of the Govig. I remember mother beggin' him not to try it. No one had ever done it, you see, and no one knew how far it was or what was on the other side. All we knew was that people had died tryin' to cross the Govig—or at any rate they'd never been heard of again.

'But Zai came back—he always came back. He'd taken sixty-two days to cross the Govig and he'd discovered the Beklan Empire. He'd sold his opals and emeralds and sapphires in Bekla for really big' money— more than he'd ever made in his life—even though he'd had to give a lot of it to the High Baron in return for protection. That was Lord Senda-na-Say—him whose stables we were in last night. He had a great house in Bekla, of course, in the upper city, and that was where Zai put himself under his protection. A foreigner on his own's not safe, you see, offerin' jewels for sale. How Zai learned Beklan to begin with I never knew. Our tongue's quite different—well, you've heard me speak it, haven' you? So you know.

'Zai hadn' been back long before he began plannin' to go again. "There's a fortune there, just waitin' to be picked up," he told mother. "Now I know what they want to buy and who to go to, I can come back with twice as much. Risk? Yes, of course there's risk. Life's a risk, come to that."

That was Zai all over—I believe he did it for the risk—the sport—not just the money—'

'Strikes me as I know his daughter,' whispered Maia.

'Oh, yes? Well, he reckoned one more trip to Bekla would set us all up for the rest of our lives. He planned to take four or five stout lads along with him, then he wouldn' need to buy so much protection—'

'All black people?'

'Of course. In my country, banzi, *you'd* be the queer one. In the real world, proper people are *black*: got it? Only he had the devil's own job findin' them, you see. The Govig—it was a name of terror. He had a job to convince anyone that he'd really crossed it twice, there and back.

'After nearly a year he was ready to go—provisions, stock, stout fellows, everythin'. I was gettin' on for eleven by then. I remember it all so well.

'And then the sickness came to Tedzhek. O Kantza-Merada, didn' they die? No one could bury them all—they threw the bodies out on the spits for the wild dogs and the birds. I wasn' allowed out of the house for weeks on end.

'After two months mother took the sickness. I remember her sayin' to Zai, "Oh, Baru, the air—how sweet it smells!" He burst into tears. He knew what that meant.'

'And she died?' Maia shivered, and drew up the blanket.

'She died. We watched her die. Ekundayo—she died, too. Pray—only pray you never see the sickness, banzi. There was a song—how did it go?' Occula paused a few moments, then sang, very low, in her own tongue. 'Oh, I forget it. It means

> '"My mother sleeps for ever,
> My father weeps for ever,
> And still the goddess reaps for ever."

'When it ended—after six months, it must have been—there was no one left at home but Zai and me. All the servants who weren' dead had run away. And one night he took me on his knee—we were all alone and I remember the wind blowin' outside—and said he was still goin' to cross the Govig.

'"It's not the money, 'Cula," he said. "What does that matter to me, now? Though it might be some use to you one day, I suppose. But I can' stay here. What's a man to do while he walks under the sun? There's three of my lads left and they'll come, I know. But what am I to do with you, my beautiful girl? Where do you want to live till I come back?"

'"I'm goin' with you," I said.

'He laughed. "That you aren't. You'd only die."

'"If you doan' take me, Zai," I said, "I'll drown myself in the river."

90

'And the long and short of it was that he did take me. Everyone said his grief must've turned his wits, to take an eleven-year-old girl into the Govig. And I dare say he *wasn'* himself, come to that. He'd loved mother very deeply, you see, and he was all to pieces—desperate, really. That was why he was determined to go. He felt it was the only thing that could make him forget.

'When we set out I was proud as a pheasant. He'd rigged me out as well as any of the men. I even had my own knife, and he made me learn how to use it, too. "You never know what might happen," he said. I was absolutely determined that no one was goin' to be put to extra trouble or hardship on my account. I could keep up all right if I held on to Zai's hand; *and* I carried my own gear. At least it was soft goin'—most of it, anyway—and walkin's like anythin' else—you get better by doin' it. Sometimes Zai carried me on his shoulders for a bit, but no one else ever did. And I could cook and mend, and I could catch insects and lizards. You eat them in the Govig, you see. You eat anythin' you can get.

'We walked by night—always by night. In that heat there's no movin' by day. We went by the stars. That was one of the tricks Zai had taught himself that no one before him had ever properly understood. Most people doan' take enough trouble. They think they're goin' in one direction, but really they're goin' in circles, so they die. We were goin' east. You picked a star as it rose and then went on it for a little while before pickin' another one risin' from the same place. Whatever star we were goin' on, one or other of us watched it all the time—never took his eyes off it. You might not be able to pick it out again, you see. As soon as daylight began to show at all, Zai used to stop us. We had to make a thorn fire and cook (while we had anythin' left to cook, that was) and then be in shelter before the sun hit us.

'Sometimes there might be natural shelter from the sun—a cave, or a dry cleft—*tibas*, they call them. Sometimes, banzi, we used to hold our water for hours, and then piss on skins, wrap up in them and bury ourselves in the sand. Anythin' to keep moisture in the body.

'That was Zai's other trick—he'd found out how to spot water. There are a few—a very few—holes and wells out there, and those you can spot by the scrub—by the plants; and sometimes by birds. But then—and this was the trick—there are patches of water—or sometimes just patches of moisture—underground: and those you have to tell by insects, or by huntin' with a forked stick in your two hands. That's a kind of witchcraft, though—I can't explain. There were times when we had to scoop up mud and suck it. And I never complained, not once.

'I doan' know how far we went every night. Usually about ten miles, I should guess. The ground—it's soft goin', but it's very difficult and slow.

Zai used to mark the days on a notched stick. We crossed the Govig in fifty-five days; quicker than either of his other two crossin's. He'd learned the tricks, you see, and learned the way, too. Some of the places we came to he recognized. And he was always cheerful: he kept us all in heart. I knew he'd get us through. I suffered—oh, yes!—and often I was frightened half crazy—the drums!—but I never once thought really I was goin' to die. Not with Zai there.'

'The drums?' said Maia.

'You hear things that aren't real, banzi, and sometimes you even *see* things that aren't real. I've lain petrified with fear and listened to the drums; and not by night, either—in broad, still daylight. There's a power out there that wants to kill you—doesn' want you to cross the Govig—and we'd challenged that power. It was Kantza-Merada that saved us. I saw her once, walkin' in a great, whirlin' column of sand, taller than the Red Tower in Tedzhek, and that was the most frightenin' thing of all. Only her face was turned away; else we'd all have died, Zai said.

'When we came out of the Govig we were nothin' but skin and bone, and there were only four of us. One of the men, M'Tesu, had been stung by a *kreptoor* in his blanket. You have to shake your blankets, always, and he'd forgotten; just once. That was enough.

'Where we came out, it's hardly twenty miles to Herl-Belishba from the edge of the desert. Zai had friends in Herl—people who'd helped him when he came before. They were timber merchants. We stayed with them until we'd got our strength back, and they gave us clothes, too. They weren't new clothes, but at least they weren't in tatters, like ours. And of course they were the sort of clothes people wear here. Made us look less conspicuous, black or no. Zai promised to pay them in Beklan money on the way back. They trusted him, you see.

'And then we went up to Bekla. It's six days' journey, and half-way you have to cross the Zhairgen on the Renda-Narboi—the Bridge of Islands. The Zhairgen's all of a hundred and fifty yards wide at the Renda-Narboi.

'But when we got to Bekla, banzi, we found the city full of fear—fear and uncertainty. There was civil war. No one knew who the rulers were from one day to the next, and there was no countin' on law and order. That was the Leopard revolution—we'd walked right into the middle of it: Fornis, Kembri and the others; those that set up Durakkon.

'Zai went straight to the big house of Senda-na-Say in the upper city, but we never saw Senda-na-Say. They told us he'd gone east, into Tonilda. His steward told us we were welcome to stay in the servants' quarters until things were quieter and Lord Senda-na-Say had time to spare for us. He said things would get better soon; but they never did.

'There was no open fightin' in the city—only murder behind closed doors: and no one knew who was still alive from day to day, let alone who was in power. Zai said it was the worst possible luck for a trader, and we must just lie low and hope for the best.

'It was Senda-na-Say the Leopards were really after. The queen—the Sacred Queen of Airtha, as they call her—she didn' matter. The Leopards could deal with her later, if only they could kill Senda-na-Say and his people. I didn' understand all that till much later, of course. But I remember the fear—the horrible fear all over the city. When you're a banzi you can often see grown-up men and women clearer 'n they can see themselves.'

'Ah, that you can,' said Maia.

'That devils' wind—it blew down the peace and happiness of the peasants—what little they'd ever had. It blew down the right rulers of Bekla, and it caught us up and threw us down along with them; it threw us down for ever. Wait, and I'll tell you.

'One afternoon I was sittin' in the window-seat in the servants' big hall, watchin' the sparrows peckin' about in the dust outside. It was very hot, and the lattice-blinds were all drawn against the glare of the sun. I was supposed to be mendin' my clothes, but I was just idlin' really, a bit drowsy with the heat. And then suddenly the big double doors at the far end of the hall were thrown wide open, both of them, and in came a woman like a goddess come down from the sky—or that's what she looked like to me then. She might have been—oh, I doan' know—about twenty-six, I suppose—with a great mane of red hair. You've never seen anythin' like it. It glowed, as though there was light in it, and it was fine as gossamer, blazin' over her neck and all down her shoulders; and her shoulders—they were sort of creamy, the skin shinin' like pearls. She was wearin' a loose robe of light green—I can see it now—held in at the waist and wrists with a gold girdle and gold bracelets, and embroidered back and front with all manner of birds and beasts in gold thread; and you could see right through it—you could see her body underneath. There were four or five girls with her, one to hold her fan, and another to carry her cloak and so on; and a great, tall soldier behind her, with a sword at his belt. I stared and stared: but of course no one took any notice of me. I just sat in the window-seat and watched.

'There were only a few of the lower servants about in the hall at the time. They stood up, of course, and Zai and his men stood up too. The lady looked round, and as soon as she saw Zai—naturally, you could pick him out anywhere—she walked over to him and said "Are you the jewel-merchant from beyond the Harridan?"

'I could see Zai wonderin' what to answer, because he hadn' told anyone except the steward. And while he was hesitatin', this princess said, "Oh, you can trust me, U-Baru. I'm a close friend of Lord Senda-na-Say. In case you doubt it, here's his seal-ring, which he's lent me to show that you can trust me. He'll be here himself tomorrow; but you know the seal, doan' you?"

'Well, Zai did know it, of course: so then he showed her all the jewels he'd got with him—the opals and sapphires and the rest. And she purred over them like a great cat and held them against her white skin, and one of her girls held up a silver mirror so that she could admire herself.

'I was afraid of her: I was afraid of her because I could see that her girls were afraid of her; and because I could see what Zai was feelin' and what all the men were feelin'. They were—well, bewitched, really. A woman like that can turn men into fools, you know—yes, even my father. But he was—well, like a starvin' man, wasn' he? I can see that now. She'd have stiffened the zard on a stone statue, that one.

'At last she said very graciously, "U-Baru, I'll buy your jewels and pay you well for them. Wait until tomorrow, when Lord Senda-na-Say will return. Then he and I will see you together." And then she and her girls left the hall, and the soldier with them.

'We supposed—well, you know—Zai and the men supposed that she must be some marvellous shearna that Senda-na-Say was keepin'. But the only puzzlin' thing about that, according to Zai, was that she'd spoken of seein' him again together with Senda-na-Say, and the last time Zai had been in Bekla Senda-na-Say had always seen him together with his wife. Still, said Zai, who was to tell? That might have changed.

'We didn' know who she was, and there were a few other things we didn' know, too. We didn' know that Senda-na-Say had already been murdered, and that his steward—Zai's friend—was in the hands of the Leopards: he'd told them everythin' he could think of, in the hope of savin' his own life: and amongst other things he'd told them about Zai and the jewels. The woman—she was Fornis of Paltesh; her that the Leopards set up to be Sacred Queen of Airtha, after they'd killed the rightful one.'

'Her that's Queen now?' said Maia.

'Yes; her that's Queen now. Six and a half years she's been Sacred Queen of Airtha—the mortal consort of your god Cran. What have you heard of her?'

'The god's in love with her, Tharrin used to say. That's why the crops thrive and the empire's safe. She's the sacred luck of the empire, and that's why she can do anything she pleases and take anything she wants.'

'Yes, well, she did that all right. Listen. Zai and his men had been lodged to sleep in the hall with the men-servants: but I used to sleep with the women, of course. The buttery-maid had taken a likin' to me and I used to sleep in her room, along with two other girls a bit older than I was. Before I went to sleep the girls used to leave me and Zai together for a bit,

94

so that we could pray to Kantza-Merada. That's what they did that night. We prayed, and then he kissed me and left me to go to sleep.

'I never saw Zai again. That night the Leopards seized the house, and Queen Fornis's men murdered Zai and the others, and took the jewels.'

'But weren't they hidden?' asked Maia. 'Like you said?'

Occula was silent. At length she said, 'Yes; but they—found them: in the end. Any man talks—in the end.'

'And—and you?' said Maia.

'I've often wished they'd killed me too. Next mornin' it was all over. Just the girls cryin' and sobbin' and each of them tryin' not to be the one who had to tell me.

'They'd only killed Zai and his men. There wasn't anyone else worth killin', you see. The Leopards took over the palace, servants and all. I might have become a slave there, I suppose; but someone or other—the new steward, perhaps—decided that it would be best if I was sold. I dare say they didn' want a slave—even a child—who knew they'd murdered her father. Or perhaps the new steward just saw a way to make a bit of easy money.

'I wasn' sold in the market. It was a private sale. Domris bought me. She was on one of her trips from Thettit-Tonilda to buy girls for her house— the Lily Pool, it's called. It wasn' her house then, actually, though it is now: but she was helpin' to run it. She liked to buy girls very young and train them. I was a curiosity, of course—a black girl. Hardly anybody'd ever seen one. I might as well have been blue or green.

'Domris was kind enough as long as you did what you were told. "It's bad luck for you, dear," she said to me, "but seein' it's happened, let's jus' try to make the best of it, shall we? It's a hard world for most women, you know—for me as much as you. I doan' like it any more than you do, but you be a good girl and do as I say and I woan' cheat you."

'And to do her justice she didn', the old cow. She was hard as rock and she's made me as hard as rock, but at least she didn' cheat me.

'At the start I thought I'd never be done cryin'. I doan' know why I didn' die of grief. But there were three or four little girls about my age who all had more than enough to cry about, same as me. And none of *them* had come alive through the Govig, so I decided I was better than them and I was still Zai's daughter even if he *was* dead; so *I'd* be the one that didn' cry.

'I learnt the trade; and banzi, I turned myself into a one-girl fortress. The men were outside, and I was inside, with Kantza-Merada. They could get into me but they couldn' get into *me*, if you see what I mean. I learnt to play the *hinnari*, to sing, to dance the Silver Zard and Goat in the Circle. They all told Domris I was the spiciest little piece they'd ever known in their lives—the dirty fools! You can build a wall round yourself, banzi, and live untouched inside it, believe me you can. You do as I tell you and you'll be all right.

'Domris let me keep quite a nice little bit. She liked me: I took good care to see she did—and I laid it out carefully; you know, clothes and make-up and whatever bits of jewellery I could afford. I had plans, you see. I didn' mean to go on being the mainstay of the Lily Pool until I'd been basted to bits before my time. Well over six years' hard work and I reckoned it was time for a change.'

'She let you go?' asked Maia wonderingly.

'Ah, it wasn' *that* easy, banzi. I had to make a bargain with Domris—talk her into it. It was one night about three months ago.

' "Ever thought of sendin' me to Bekla, *säiyett?*" I said. "It'd pay you hands down in the long run."

'She looked puzzled and stuffed another sweet in her mouth. "How can it—m'm, m'm—do that, dear?" she asked.

' "Why," I said, "all sorts of ways. I could be your eyes and ears in Bekla, and the times are so uncertain that that might make a lot of difference one day—swift news in a pinch, you know. But better than that, I could buy for you. You lose the best of the Beklan market now, jus' through not bein' on the spot. You come up to Bekla once or twice a year and have to take what's to be had when you're there. I could save you all that trouble, and you'd do better into the bargain." '

'But how could you do all that?' asked Maia, 'just being a slave in someone's house?'

'Oh, banzi, did you think I was aimin' no higher than that? I was tryin' to persuade Domris to set me up as a shearna in Bekla—a free woman. But she wouldn'. Well, it was flyin' too high, really—I can see that. Anyway, she wasn' havin' it. But finally she agreed to sell me to a well-connected dealer in Bekla, on his promise that he'd dispose of me only to some wealthy house where I'd have a good chance of gettin' on.

' "I'll speak to Lalloc next time I go up," she said. "He knows the market and he sells to all the wealthiest Leopard houses in the upper city. And that's the best I can do for you, my dear. But if you manage to get your own head above water—and if anyone can I should think it's you—let me know, and I'll certainly engage you to buy for me—on commission, too."

'So that was how it was arranged. Lalloc agreed to pay Domris ten thousand down and another two thousand if he was able to sell me for more than fourteen. And out of that two thousand, if it comes off, I'm to have five hundred for myself. It's not much, but it may make a lot of difference to us, banzi, if only we can hide it safe, wherever we get to.

That's what all this damned fuss has been for, this last two days—*now* do you see? I've got a position to keep up. Lalloc told that Megdon fellow to take me over from Domris at Thettit and see me up to Bekla, but of course if you let yourself in for being carted about by bastards like that, *they're* not goin' to take the trouble to help you to stand out from a bunch of ten-meld sluts. You've got to see to that sort of thing for yourself. And so I did.'

'And U-Zuno—you reckon *he* will?' asked Maia. 'Don't mind me sayin' it, but struck me as you were kind of quiet in front of him.'

'Well, but he's a wafter, banzi, for Cran's sake! Wouldn' be any good offerin' *him* anything, would it? Never, never try to put anythin' across a wafter!'

'Whatever's a wafter?'

'You mean to say—oh, banzi!' And forthwith Occula—with many wondering interjections and questions from the uninitiated Maia—explained.

'So we've got no sort of grip on him, have we?' concluded the black girl. 'And 'twouldn' be any good tryin' any old smoky tricks on the likes of *him*. That's a clever young man, if I'm any judge; a man on the way up. All he's concerned with at present are the future fortunes of U-Zuno.'

They lay quiet for a time.

'Sleepy?' asked the black girl at length.

'M'mm. Dearest Occula.'

'Listen! Did you hear that? Long way off.'

'What?'

'Cocks are crowin'.'

'I never heard.'

'Yes; and it's gettin' light, look.'

Maia, rubbing her eyes, slipped out of bed for the second time and crossed to the window. The eastern sky was full of smooth, cloudless light and now she could indeed hear a cock crowing in the distance. A cold breeze was blowing and she shivered, hunching her shoulders.

'Another jolly day all ready for the spoilin',' said Occula. 'But they woan' be comin' to unlock us just yet. Come back here, pretty banzi. I remember what misery feels like all right. Oh, I've *got* to be nice to you, haven' I?'

II

ON THE ROAD

It soon became clear that Occula's assessment of Zuno had been as shrewd as most of her judgements. He was certainly a good cut above Megdon: fastidious, detached and (as the girl had guessed) prepared to treat Maia and herself reasonably well provided they fell in with what he wanted; which, in a word, was deference. Having become part of his equipage, it was necessary that they (like the cat) should reflect his own conception of his personal elegance and style. Occula, by her docility and readiness not only to comply with but plainly to appreciate the wisdom of his every decision, contrived to convince him that she was an intelligent girl who could be trusted to behave sensibly.

The authority flowing naturally from a man who is well-dressed, constrained in manner but clear and confident in his instructions, ensured that the girls were adequately fed and treated with consideration, despite the innkeeper's wife's obvious wish to see the back of them as soon as possible. (She was hardly to be blamed, for Occula's sense of mischief had led her first to beg the innkeeper—who needed little pressing—to be so good as to look for a fly in her eye and then to take a thorn—which was not there— out of Maia's foot.) They were certainly not hurried into an early start, for it was not until some three hours before noon that Zuno had them summoned to join him outside the tavern.

He himself (with the cat) was travelling in a *jekzha*—a light, wicker-sided cart with two high wheels and an awning to keep off the sun. This was actually the property of Lalloc (a fact of which Occula took good care to seem ignorant), as were the two Deelguy slaves pulling it. These men, who understood only a little Beklan, clearly expected no attention apart from their orders, but conversed together—and even laughed and joked— in their own language throughout the day's journey.

As the party was about to leave, Occula asked Zuno whether he might feel able graciously to permit her companion and herself to walk beside the jekzha without actually being tied to it.

'I'm sure you will already be aware, sir,' she said, standing before him with folded hands and eyes on the ground, 'that it's at my own request that I've been so fortunate as to be purchased from Madam Domris by U-Lalloc. There's no question of *my* not wishing to go to Bekla. As for this girl, you'll already have perceived that she's barely more than a child. If you'll be graciously pleased to accept my assurance, I'll answer entirely for her good behaviour.'

'Very well,' replied Zuno, yawning. 'What have you got in that box? Is it heavy?'

'No, sir. Only a few poor clothes and trinkets of my own.'

'Then you may put it in here, next to mine,' said Zuno. 'Now, you are both to keep a steady pace, remain close behind and bear yourselves quietly and properly throughout the day. Otherwise you will be chained. Understand that, for I shan't repeat it.'

'There'll be no need for you to do so, sir.'

From Hirdo to Bekla was some thirty-five miles, over which Zuno planned to take two-and-a-half days. He was in no hurry, for a leisurely progress consorted best with his own idea of his standing. In any case, their progress was more or less imposed by the location of such inns along the road as could offer reasonable lodgings; at Khasik, thirteen miles from Hirdo, and at Naksh, some fourteen miles beyond that. Paradoxically, it was the girls themselves who would have preferred a swifter journey. Maia, despite further intermittent pangs of homesickness and loss, was in better spirits than the day before—largely on account of Occula's protective affection. Also, something of the black girl's pluck and self-sufficiency was beginning to rub off on her. There were even moments when she found herself excited by the prospect of Bekla. 'Why, even Tharrin's never been *there*!' she thought. 'Reckon if I can only stick with Occula, might p'raps work out all right one way or t'other. Anyhow, no good worrying 'fore it's time.' And with this she settled herself to the day's journey.

The cool breeze which had sent her back to bed at dawn was pleasant enough as the sun rose higher. The leaves fluttered, gazefinches and grey cracker-birds darted in and out of the bushes beside the road, and the long spokes of the jekzha turned rhythmically at her elbow. She could have walked faster, and twice Occula had to warn her, silently, to maintain the demure pace that Zuno's consequence required.

The country into which they were journeying was lonely and uncultivated. On either side of the road was nothing but rough, dried-up grass, patches of woodland and tall scrub. At one time, in the days of Senda-na-Say, the highway had been policed, and parties travelling in convoy had been able to rely upon armed escorts. Now, after six and a half years of Leopard rule, the road was in poor repair, and travellers perforce made their own plans for safety. Lalloc's arrangements, somewhat expensive but at any rate reliable, extended to the protection not only of his servants, but also of whatever human goods they might happen to be conveying on his behalf.

Before mid-day the girls experienced a signal instance of Zuno's detachment from and contempt for the tedious vulgarity of mere danger. They had reached the foot of a long, gradual slope, up which the road wound through brake and tall trees, and the Deelguy, having slackened their pace, were leaning well forward, hands raised to the bar, when suddenly three ragged, villainous-looking men, each armed with a cudgel, stepped out from the undergrowth and stood silently barring the way. The slaves came to a halt. Occula, reaching out a hand to Maia, drew her against her.

'This could mean a whole lot of trouble, banzi,' she whispered. 'Whatever you do, doan' act frightened; but if I say so, run like buggery.'

For several seconds not a word was spoken on either side. The Deelguy, as though aware that if anyone were going to be attacked it would not be them, simply stood like bullocks, waiting. Then Zuno, speaking coldly and displaying no trace of agitation, said, 'Would you very much mind standing out of the way, please?'

'Ah, when we've done what we come for,' replied one of the ruffians: and at this all three moved forward, pressing round the offside wheel. Occula, her arm still round Maia, moved back a pace.

'Stay where you are, will you?' drawled Zuno to the girls over his shoulder: and then, turning back to the men, 'May I enquire whether you work for Shion?'

'What's that to you?' replied another. The first, however, as though to establish his authority, silenced him with a gesture and then, sneering up at Zuno, said, 'You can *enquire* what you like, milord. We're not here to answer your basting questions.'

'Are you not?' said Zuno equably. 'Then pray allow me at least to show you something which may be of interest to you.' His air of disdainful indifference seemed already to have thrown the footpads into some uncertainty, for none made any further move as he bent down to search under the seat.

'Ah! This,' he continued at length, straightening up and extending one arm over the side of the jekzha with an air of detached distaste, 'is Shion's token of safe-conduct, issued personally to U-Lalloc at Bekla. If you *do* in fact work for Shion, you will no doubt recognize it. If you do *not*, I would strongly advise you to remove yourselves altogether from this length of road, which Shion regards as his territory.'

The leader looked at the token, but whether he recognized it neither Occula nor Maia could tell. It was plain, however, that both he and his mates were disconcerted. Muttering, they drew together on one side of the road. As they did so, Zuno very deliberately returned the token to his scrip, put the scrip back under the seat, snapped his fingers to the two slaves and then, settling himself comfortably, said, 'Go on! And be careful to keep clear of those pot-holes in front.'

Maia, who was on the side nearest to the three men, followed the jekzha without daring even to glance in their direction, expecting at any moment to feel a blow on her neck or a hand clutching her shoulder. Even Occula was breathing hard. But nothing happened; and when at length they plucked up courage to look behind, the men had disappeared.

'I'd never have thought I *could* feel grateful to a man, banzi, let alone to a wafter,' whispered the black girl, wiping the sweat from her forehead. 'You've got to admit he's got his wits about him. 'Course, it was us they were after; you realize that, doan' you? Did you see the way they were lookin' at you? Cran and Airtha, I'm glad we didn' have to settle for a jolly-baste with that lot, aren't you?'

'You mean we'd—?' Maia stared.

'Well, better than gettin' our throats cut, perhaps,' said Occula cheerfully. 'But we'd never have got to Bekla, would we? Flat on our backs in some damned cave. I'll do him a good turn, this boy, if ever I get the chance, damned if I doan'.'

About noon they turned off the road and halted in the shade of a grove of ilex trees, where a little stream wound among clumps of rushes and purple-flowering water-thelm. There was a glitter of flies and a warm, herbal smell of peppermint. Zuno, after feeding the cat, gave the girls some bread and cheese and waved them away, spreading his cloak on the grass and settling himself for a nap. When they had gone about twenty or thirty yards, however, he raised himself on one elbow and called, 'You are not to go out of earshot. I don't want to have to call you twice.'

'We shall be ready whenever it may suit you, sir,' replied Occula.

The girls wandered down to the stream. Shrunken by summer drought, it was hardly more than a chain of pools—the biggest barely four feet deep—divided by narrow bars of gravel, through and over which the water trickled in glistening films. Dragonflies hovered and darted over the reeds, and from somewhere among the trees a *damazin* was calling. The heat was intense.

'Come on, let's go in the water,' said Maia. 'We can eat later.'

'Yes, you go on in, banzi,' said Occula. 'I'll come and join you a bit later. The Deelguy woan' come peepin'; they wouldn' dare. But if anyone else comes—like those bastards this mornin'—doan' try to hide or anythin' like that. Make as much noise as you can and run back to Lord Pussy-cat like shit from a goose. Understand?'

Kissing Maia on both cheeks, she strolled away along the bank and was lost to sight among the reeds.

Maia, comforted by the familiarity of solitude and clear water, slipped out of her clothes and into the deepest of the pools. Although there was barely depth to swim, she made a stroke or two across and then drew herself up onto the opposite bank. For some time she lay prone, easy and almost content—for Maia was a girl who lived, if not from moment to moment, yet certainly from hour to hour—simply to listen for the call of the damazin and to feel the flow of the calid water round her body.

'They think I'm beautiful!' she murmured aloud. 'Well, happen I might just be lucky an' all.' And for the moment it really did seem to her that she was lucky, and that her future, dark, uncertain and inauspicious as it must have appeared to anyone else, could not but turn out right in the end.

After a little it occurred to her to wonder what had become of Occula. 'Whatever she wanted to do, she's had time enough to do it,' she thought. Idly, she splashed some of the water up between her breasts, pressing them together to hold it in a miniature pool and bending her head to sip. 'I'll go and look for her. I must get her to come in too.' She waded out through the reeds, slipped on her clothes and walked upstream in the direction which the black girl had taken.

After a minute or two she stopped, for a moment alarmed, then merely puzzled. Although she could recognize Occula's voice a little way off, it did not sound as though she were in conversation with anybody. Not only was there no other voice to be heard, but there was a certain evenness of flow and cadence, unquestioning and unhesitating, rather as though Occula might be telling a story or delivering a speech. Clearly she was not in danger or even in haste.

Maia stole closer. It seemed strange that she could not see Occula, for wherever she might be concealed her voice was quite near-by. And now Maia could catch words, uttered in a rhythmic, liturgical measure.

'Then, as she entered the fifth gate,
The gold rings were taken from her fingers.
  "Pray what is this that now you do to me?"
  "Most strangely, Kantza-Merada, are the laws of the dark world effected.
  O Kantza-Merada, do not question the laws of the nether world."'

As she uttered the last two lines Occula rose suddenly into view, standing, with outspread, open arms, among the bushes. She was facing away from Maia and so did not see her. After a moment or two of silence she knelt again, prostrating herself in an obeisance with palms and forehead low among the clumps of grass.

'Then, as she entered the sixth gate,
The jewelled breastplate was taken from her bosom.
  "Pray what is this that now you do to me?"'

Once more Occula rose and stood, gazing sternly into the trees as though answering a living questioner hidden among them.

'"Most strangely, Kantza-Merada, are the laws of the dark world effected.
O Kantza-Merada, do not question the laws of the nether world."'

Despite the harsh voice in which she was speaking—evidently in a rôle—Maia could see that her face was wet with tears, and as she knelt yet again there came the sound of a sob, cut short as she spoke the next words.

'Then, as she entered the seventh gate,
All the fine garments of her body were taken from her.
"Pray what is this that now you do to me?"'

Occula stood again, her whole body shaken with weeping.

'"Most strangely, Kantza-Merada, are the laws of the dark world effected.
O Kantza-Merada, do not question the laws of the nether world."

At the word of the dark judges, that word which tortures the spirit,
Kantza-Merada, even the goddess, was turned to a dead body,
Defiled, polluted, a corpse hangin' from a stake—'

Real or not, Occula's grief now appeared so extreme that Maia could no longer bear to stand by and do nothing. Hastening forward as though she had only that moment come upon her friend by chance, she took her hand.

Occula turned upon her with blazing eyes.

'What the bastin' hell are you doin' here? Didn' I say I'd come back when I was ready?'

'Oh, Occula, don't be angry! I didn't mean any harm, honest I never! I came to look for you and you seemed so unhappy. Is it real trouble, or—or some kind of prayer, is it? I heard you say "Kantza-Merada—"'

For some moments Occula made no reply, only looking round her as though returning slowly from some inward country of trance. At length she said, 'I'm sorry, banzi. It's no fault of yours. Anyway, I'm not alone, am I, as long as I've got you to look after? So the goddess must have *sent* you, mustn' she?'

Maia burst out laughing. 'Oh, I'm not laughing at *you*, Occula. Only it just seems so funny, the idea of your goddess sending *me*.'

Occula said nothing, and Maia went on quickly, 'What was it, then, that happened to Kantza-Merada—what you were saying about the—the dark world? It sounded—well, very sad, like.'

'It's the wrong time of year, really,' replied Occula rather absently. 'That—what you heard me sayin'—that's part of the midwinter ritual. I ought to be sayin' it in Tedzheki, of course, but after all these years I've forgotten a lot of the words; it comes easier in Beklan nowadays.

'Kantza-Merada, from the great above she descended to the great below.
The goddess abandoned heaven, abandoned earth,
Abandoned dominion, abandoned ladyship,
To the nether world of darkness she descended.'

'But you said—just now—you said as she was turned to a dead body. What happened?'

'Why, she died for *us*, of course! She resigned herself to every foul thing that could happen to her.'

'And then?' Instinctively Maia knew that there must be more.

'After three days and nights had passed away—

'Oh, I can't tell you all of it now, banzi. How does it go—

'Upon her defiled body,
Sixty times the food of life,
Sixty times the water of life they sprinkled,
And Kantza-Merada, Kantza-Merada arose.
When Kantza-Merada ascended from the dark world,
The little demons like reeds walked by her side—

'And after that, it says, she wandered through all the cities of the world—oh, I can' tell you all of it, but she was saved, banzi; restored! And d'you think she woan' save *me*? I'll do it! I'll succeed, and *she'll* save me! She'll save me!'

'Succeed?'

'Yes! Whatever the odds! However it's to be done—'

Clasping Maia's hands, Occula gazed into her eyes with an air of such passionate desperation that Maia, used as she had become to the older girl's customary air of cynical worldly-wisdom, was almost frightened.

'I—I'm sure you will,' she stammered. 'Occula, yes, of *course* you will! But what is it that you have to do?'

At that moment Zuno's voice called, 'Will you please come at once? I'm starting!'

'Get the rest of that bread and cheese stuffed down you quick, banzi,' said Occula. 'You'll be glad enough of it before ever we get to Khasik.'

12

AN OFFER DECLINED

The inn at Khasik, called 'The Bow and Quiver', stood on a little rise at the western end of the village, where the road from Hirdo came out onto the Beklan plain. Here, a bare twenty-two miles from the capital, there was more traffic, for lesser roads ran into the highway both from north and south. During the last mile or two of the day's journey the girls found themselves walking through (and breathing) clouds of the white, powdery dust of summer, stirred up by all manner of other travellers—a detachment of soldiers marching down to Thettit, three or four uniformed pedlars plodding together for company; a lean, threadbare minstrel, his cased hinnari slung on his back; a gang of Urtan drovers, shouting to one another in their own dialect across the backs of their brown-woolled sheep; a priest of Cran, travelling alone and doubtless trusting for safety to his robe and the other signs of his sacred calling; and six Belishban slaves carrying a curtained litter, in which, as it passed, Maia glimpsed a portly, half-naked occupant sleeping—or affecting to sleep—through all the heat and commotion.

Outside 'The Bow and Quiver' a fair crowd—perhaps thirty or forty people—were scattered on the grassy slope. Most were busy drinking, and among them a potman was hurrying to and fro: others were simply lounging and talking as they waited for supper, a few of them checking over ox-harness, pack straps and such-like gear. Away to one side a group of ten or twelve were listening to a grey-haired story-teller—one who evidently knew his job, for when he paused to pass round his cup the quarter- and half-melds fairly rattled in to make him go on. The setting sun, shining full in the girls' faces, lit up the whole tranquil scene and threw long shadows across the grass.

The Deelguy slaves helped Zuno down and handed him the basket containing the cat. After brushing off his clothes and telling them to see to stabling the jekzha, he nodded to Occula to follow him and proceeded up the slope towards the smarter-looking of the two entrances.

There were several women among the crowd, and as they passed one of these called out a friendly greeting. Maia, who was carrying Occula's box, acknowledged this with a quick nod and smile but, mindful of Zuno's dignity, made no other response.

It soon became clear, however, that Zuno was in an expansive mood—partly, no doubt, at the thought that he was now nearer to Bekla than to Thettit, and also, perhaps, on account of being not altogether displeased with his handling of the situation that morning. Having reminded the innkeeper of who he was and who his employer was, he insisted on a secure room for the two girls. Occula thanked him very properly for his solicitude, whereupon he went so far as to tell her that he was not dissatisfied with their conduct and behaviour during the day. They seemed, he thought, obedient and reliable girls, who might do well in Bekla once they had learned their business. Occula, giving no indication that she had been learning her business for the past six or seven years, replied that she felt his good opinion to be most encouraging. 'From someone so knowledgeable as yourself, sir—one, I mean, who is familiar with good society at first hand—such kind words are very welcome.'

'Well—' Zuno paused. 'Well—you may both take supper with me this evening.'

Occula drew in her breath and looked at Maia round-eyed, as though scarcely able to credit such an honour.

'When you have *washed*,' went on Zuno emphatically, 'and made yourselves as tidy as you can, I will meet you in the refectory: the upper refectory; that is to say, the better one. It's through there, do you see? Don't be long. What is your name?' he added to Maia.

'Maia, sir. From Lake Serrelind.'

Zuno, nodding rather curtly by way of implying that she had presumed to tell him more than he had asked, motioned them to be off to their room.

Once there, Occula, having looked through her box, selected a half-sleeved, dark-red *pellard*, its tubular skirt pleated in the Lapanese style, with a low bodice which left her neck and shoulders bare. To this she added a broad, black belt, intensifying the dusky, smouldering effect and strikingly offsetting her necklace of teeth. Maia watched her with wistful envy but without resentment.

'Like me to rub your back, banzi?' asked the black girl, at length looking up from her mirror. A few minutes later, as Maia lay sighing pleasurably under her hands, she said, 'I wish you'd do me a favour: put on that powder-blue robe-thing I've left out over there. Some bastin' idiot gave it to me in Thettit. I ask you—can you see *me* in soft blue? But then he was the sort of man who'd put his own zard down somewhere and forget it: probably has by now. Anyone pinch it be doin' him a favour—save him a lot of money, too.'

As she brushed Maia's hair and helped her to dress, her ribaldry continued, until both of them were tittering and giggling together about everything and nothing.

'So then this man said—'

'Oh, he never!'

'—so then, you see, I said all right, I'd cut his toe-nails for him. And Cran knows they needed it! They'd have taken a baboon's balls off. So he went and fetched a stool and said he'd be all ready when I came back with the file and the knife. But when I came back I said "That's not a foot!" and he said, "Well, maybe not, but it's a good eight inches—"'

'Oh, Occula! You are awful! Hee-hee! Hee-hee!'

'Feelin' better?' said the black girl. 'Come on, we'd best be gettin' downstairs now, or Pussy'll be havin' kittens.'

When they came into the refectory, however, Zuno was nowhere to be seen. The room was not crowded, for supper was not yet ready, though a pleasant smell of cooking suggested that it would not be much longer.

The two girls, having hesitated a few moments, decided—or at all events Occula decided—that they had better wait for Zuno where they were.

'Lucky he likes to do himself well, isn' it?' said Occula. 'We might have found ourselves havin' to hang around in the monkey-house down the other end. All the same, we mustn' stand about here lookin' as if we were up for offers. Let's sit down somewhere out of the way and hope he woan' be much longer.'

Well-scrubbed tables with benches took up most of the length of the room. Occula led the way to the nearest corner and they sat down side by side, facing the wall and continuing to talk quietly together.

In the corner furthest from them a group of four or five middle-aged men were also waiting, and at intervals from their direction came a raised voice or a burst of laughter.

'What's that talk they're on with, then?' whispered Maia. 'That's never Beklan.'

'No, they're Ortelgans,' said Occula, 'Telthearna frogs, like that damned Megdon. I was beginnin' to think he'd baste like a frog if he could—you know, hang on for two or three days.'

'There's one of them keeps looking this way,' said Maia. 'Oh, Occula, he's getting up, look!'

'I thought the wasps'd be round the blasted jam-pot soon,' answered Occula. 'Leave this to me, banzi, and for goodness' sake remember Zuno's comin' in any moment. If he were to tell Lalloc he'd found us chattin' up a bunch of Ortelgans—well, anyway, just you sit still, that's all.'

A moment later the man, about forty, stocky and dark-bearded, edged his way between the benches and sat down next to Occula. His clothes were of good quality and he had the self-confident air of a prosperous man.

'Good evening, young ladies,' he said, speaking Beklan with a marked Ortelgan accent. 'Are you dining by yourselves? Will you let me buy you some wine, you and your pretty friend?'

'No, sir,' answered Occula, looking fixedly at the table in front of her.

'We're expectin' our patron at any moment. I must beg you to leave us. We're respectable girls and our patron will—'

'Well, I'm respectable myself,' returned the man. 'My friends here and I, we're dealers in rope, from Ortelga. Just been to Bekla, you know.' He settled himself more comfortably, putting his elbows on the table and leaning forward to smile past Occula at Maia—'and now we're going back by way of Thettit and Kabin. I've done pretty well this trip and I enjoy spending money on nice girls. In fact, you could call me a generous man.'

Occula said nothing.

'I've never seen a girl like you in my life,' went on the man, quite unperturbed. 'Now I'd say the chief advantage of such a striking appearance as yours is that you can't blush. Your friend's blushing, though. It suits her very well, too.'

At this, poor Maia coloured still more deeply: and she was on the point of bursting into nervous giggling when Occula, no doubt anticipating the danger, trod painfully on her toe.

'I saw you arrive this evening,' said the man, laying a plump fore-finger in the bend of Occula's elbow, 'and I saw the fellow you call your patron riding and you walking. Your patron—he keeps pussy-cats, doesn't he? Does he ever sell them? Do *you* ever sell pussy-cats, eh?'

A voice from the far end of the room called out, 'How you getting on, Tephil? Want any help?'

The man, ignoring the interruption, pulled a leather scrip out of his pocket, drew the strings and dropped it on the table. Some of the contents spilled out; several twenty- and fifty-meld pieces, a sparkling pupil-diamond, a heavy silver ring and a little figure, rather smaller than a man's thumb, in the likeness of a bear, modelled in gold, with dark-red garnets for eyes.

'You see?' said the man complacently. 'I'm well set-up. In fact, in my own country, I may tell you, I'm personally acquainted with the young High Baron, Bel-ka-Trazet—the famous hunter, you know. I'll be perfectly honest with you. I've taken a great fancy to your pretty friend, and I'm in a position to put a lot of money in *both* your pockets—'

At this moment Zuno walked hurriedly into the room, looked round, saw the girls and stood weighing the situation with obvious distaste. Occula at once rose, turned towards him and, putting her head on one side and slightly opening her mouth, spread out her hands in a gesture implying 'What could I do?'

Zuno, approaching to within ten paces—which he evidently thought close enough—said quietly, 'A word with you, sir, if you please.'

After a moment's hesitation the man stood up and went across to him, while two of the other Ortelgans, scenting trouble, left their corner and joined their friend. Occula also took a few steps in their direction, but remained a little apart, letting it be seen that she was ready to speak if Zuno should call upon her. Maia remained where she was.

At first the conversation reached her only in fragments. 'Quite out of the question, my good man—' '—no, no; certainly not; not molesting at all, sir. Perfectly civil, I assure you.' '—entirely inappropriate. You must see for yourself—'

'But, sir,' said the Ortelgan, raising his voice, which now reached Maia clearly, 'these girls are slaves, surely? I saw them arrive this evening at your cart-tail. Aren't you a man of business? I'll pay you three hundred meld to spend the night with the younger girl. Upon my word, I never saw such a—'

'The matter is not within my power,' answered Zuno firmly. 'The girls are the property of the noted dealer U-Lalloc, in Bekla. For all I know they have already been promised to some important client in the upper city. If you were taking a consignment of rope to Bekla for which you already had a customer, I would not—would I?—expect you to let me hire it or make use of it.'

At length the man, shrugging, turned away and picked up his crip from the table, quickly and carelessly shovelling in the spilled contents with his free hand; after which he and his friends strolled away up the length of the room. Zuno sat down.

'That was no fault of yours,' he said to Occula. 'I should have been here before you. Er—' he hesitated slightly—'it might perhaps be better not to mention this matter to Lalloc. Ah! Here's supper at last. I expect we should all enjoy some wine with it.'

An hour later Maia, slightly tipsy, was helping Occula to undress and fold her clothes.

'See what I mean, banzi?' said the black girl.

'About authority? Oh, yes, Occula, you were wonderful! I couldn't never have—'

'No, you dimwit; I meant *you*! That Ortelgan bastard offered—great gods!—he offered *three hundred meld* to spend the night with you! That's more than old Domris used to charge for a night with any girl in the place, d'you realize that? You've got a great future, my lass, so cheer up. Better than wearin' sackin' and herdin' cattle on the Tonildan Waste, believe you me.'

'I believe you. Oh, Occula, I feel real *safe* with you, that I do!'

'Safe? You're *never* safe, banzi, in this game.'

'Well, I reckon I've made at *least* three hundred meld, anyway, and no more work to it than's needed to shut the door.' Maia held out her closed fist. 'Kiss and don't tell goes halves.'

'Three hundred meld? What d'you—oh—Maia!'

Maia, smiling broadly, was displaying on her palm the golden bear with garnet eyes.

Occula stared at it speechlessly. Then she sat down on her box, looking up at Maia in bewilderment.

'I doan' understand, banzi. Why on earth did he give you that?'

'He didn't,' answered Maia complacently. 'He opened his purse—on the table—remember? Then when Zuno came in he went over to talk to him, and so did you. That was when I took it, when no one was looking.'

Occula, without replying, sat staring fixedly at the floor. After a few moments Maia realized that her silence was due to fear. Her hands were trembling and beads of sweat were standing on her forehead. At last she whispered, 'Banzi, do you realize we can both hang upside-down for this? O gods, what's to be done? You blasted little fool—'

'But—but why?' stammered Maia. 'You said we was to be tough—stand on our own feet. What's wrong?'

'Every damn' thing's wrong!' cried the black girl desperately. 'Can' you see? You're not a banzi stealin' apples now! This is the real world, where slaves are thieves and thieves are hanged! O Cran and Airtha, why did I ever get mixed up with a little goat like you! That's an *Ortelgan*, Maia, for pity's sake! They *worship* a bear; didn' you know? They believe the sun shines out of its damn' venda! They believe it's goin' to return from God-knows-where and lead them all to Buggery-in-the-Sky or somewhere. That man probably *prays* to this! Once he's missed it he's liable to raise the damn' roof! And the first people he'll suspect is *us*—that's for sure. He'll go to Zuno; he's bound to. And if they find it—'

She bit her lip, breathing hard and beating her fist into her palm.

'What's to be done? What's to be done? I suppose there's just a chance he may not have missed it yet. We might have given it back to him and told him some damn' nonsense or other. But we're locked in! And they may be here any moment!'

She stood up. 'Give it to me, banzi!'

In the very moment that she took the bear out of Maia's hand they heard footsteps outside, followed by the rattling of the chain and the turning of the key in the lock.

The door opened and Zuno came in alone. Maia, who was wearing nothing but her shift, threw a blanket round her shoulders. This, though she did not know it, was impertinence on her part, for she had neither right nor business to be covering her nakedness from Zuno. As a slave, she had no privacy and it was of no importance whether he saw her clothed or naked. Occula, naked to the waist and knowing better, merely faced him with lowered eyes.

Zuno, perceiving at once that both the girls seemed tense and frightened, looked at them for a moment in some surprise. Then, shrugging his shoulders, he said, 'I have been giving some further thought to the offer made by this Ortelgan rope-dealer. The man and his friends are leaving tomorrow. I have decided that as long as the matter is not mentioned anywhere else—you follow me?—perhaps I need not stand in your way if one or other of you wishes to take the opportunity of making this rather large sum of money by giving the man what he wants.'

He paused, but as neither girl replied asked abruptly, 'Well?'

'I'm greatly obliged to you, sir,' replied Occula. 'It's most kind and generous—it is indeed. Speakin' for myself, I'd have been glad to gratify the man, but unfortunately it happens to be the wrong time of the month. As for Maia—'

'Can't she speak for herself?' asked Zuno rather sharply.

'She's extremely young, sir,' went on Occula, 'and knows nothin' whatever of this work as yet. Speakin' from my own experience, I think it would be better for her not to take this offer, invitin' as it appears.'

'And you? What do *you* think, young woman?' asked Zuno, turning to Maia where she stood beside the bed.

'It jus' seemed to me, sir,' continued Occula, in her low, smooth voice, 'that Maia is well above the ordinary run, and will command a high price in Bekla. This Ortelgan—we know nothin' about him, after all; and for so young a girl, first experiences are very important—'

'What is that to do with you?' replied Zuno.

For the briefest of moments Occula raised her head and looked him in the eye.

'I am U-Lalloc's property, sir. His wish is my wish. I'm only tryin' to guess, as I'm sure you are, what that wish might be.'

It took Zuno no more than a few seconds to grasp her meaning and also that there was no getting round it. 'I thought,' he said coldly, 'that you would have been glad of the opportunity to make so much money. You and the girl might have kept it for yourselves.'

'You are so good-hearted, sir,' murmured Occula. 'What a great pity that it's not possible!'

Zuno had already turned on his heel when she added quickly, 'But I'm very glad you came here, sir. Indeed, it's providential. This trinket—after the Ortelgan had left us this evenin' I found it lyin' on the floor. It can only be his: I meant to return it at once, of course, but I'm afraid it slipped my mind.'

Zuno glanced at the bear and took it from her.

'Well,' he said, 'he evidently hasn't missed it as yet. The men are still drinking downstairs; so I'll return it to him myself.' He paused. 'I don't pretend to understand your attitude in this business, Occula, but it's ended now. You understand me, don't you?'

'Yes, sir.'

As soon as the sound of Zuno's footsteps had died away, Occula took Maia in her arms, kissed her and then pushed her back until her shoulders were pressed against the wall.

'And that's that!' she said. 'Now you listen to me, banzi. I've jus' saved your bastin' life—I should think. Whether you realize it or not, that was the silliest damn' thing you've ever done. When Pussy came in I was just goin' to throw the blasted bear out of the window, but even *that* probably wouldn' have saved us. Just look out there; see? A flat, bare yard. They'd have found it all right, *and* they'd have guessed how it got there. Slaves can be tortured on mere suspicion of crime, you know. Still, that doan' matter now. But what I'm goin' to say does.

'Understand this once and for all: only ten-meld tarts steal from men. A girl who steals from men is a fool. I'm not talkin' about good and bad, or right and wrong, or any rubbish like that. I know it's a hard, unfair world full of rich, selfish bastards. But there are far cleverer and safer ways to take their money off them than stealin' it.'

'Can't see that,' answered Maia sulkily. 'Strikes me as you—'

'*Doan'* speak to me like that!' blazed Occula, slapping her hard across the face. 'Now that's for your own good! I've saved your fartin' little life and now I'm talkin' to you seriously, so you damn' well listen! Everybody's certain sure that all bed-girls are liars and thieves. So they are. We tell men the lies they pay to be told, and we steal men's great stiff zards off their wives for money. That's business! But suppose you steal a man's money, or his rings, or his silver knives, or any damn' thing he's got when you're with him, you're just diggin' your own grave. A stupid girl says to herself, "Oh, I wasn' caught, and what's more he daren' accuse me: his wife might get to hear, or he wouldn' like So-and-so to know where he'd been." But none of that matters a baste. He'll know when he misses it, and so will the next fellow she steals from, *and* the next. They woan' come back—and worse than that, she'll get a reputation, and likely enough a knife in her back one night. I knew a real, live girl it happened to! Stealin' becomes a habit, you see, and then one day you go too far. Every time's a big success until the last one. Believe me, a good girl can get far, far more out of a man's pocket *without* pickin' it. And they're so surprised to find you're what they call honest that you get one hell of a reputation—"Coo, an honest shearna!"—as if you were a god-damn' talkin' monkey or somethin'. So *then* you can take even more off them. And you doan' have to be afraid all the time, or wonder when you're goin' to be caught.'

112

Maia digested this straight-from-the-shoulder advice in silence. At length she said, 'When you gave it to him just now—the bear, I mean—weren't you afraid he'd think *you* might have stolen it?'

''Course not!' said Occula contemptuously. 'He'd know perfectly well *I'd* never try and do anythin' so bastin' stupid.'

'And why did you tell him that we wouldn't do what the man—'

'Did you want to do it?'

'Well, I don't know, really. I—I can't tell. But three hundred meld! I can't hardly believe it! We never saw that much in three months at home! I—'

'Well, to start with he wouldn' have paid *you*; he'd have paid Zuno, and I wouldn' mind bettin' the reason Zuno came here was because he'd been talkin' to the man after we'd gone, and quite likely been offered even more than three hundred. Some men go crazy when they can' get somethin' they want—you, in this case. But how much of it d'you think *we'd* have seen? Not a lot, if I'm any judge. And then, an Ortelgan—those squitterin' Telthearna turds! He might have wanted you to—oh, I doan' know— some beastly thing or other would have made you sick. And he might easily be diseased—though I admit he didn' look it. I wasn' goin' to see you packed off to a man like that, just to put dishonest money in Zuno's pocket. Besides, just think! We'd have had a guilty secret from Lalloc. A nice way to start! And you'd never know when Zuno might not come out with it some other time, just to put the squeeze on us for some reason or other. Whereas now, *we've* got somethin' on *him*. He knows damned well Lalloc would have been dead against it. If you were some little drover's drab, 'twould have been different; but a girl like you, banzi? Oh dear, no! You're set for the top, my lass, and now U-Pussy knows we know it. With any luck you'll be in a position to piss on *him* one day.'

'But won't he take it out on us tomorrow?'

'I doan' reckon so. In fact, *we* can use it a little bit on *him*, as long as we take care not to rub his nose in it. He wouldn' like us to mention it to Lalloc, you see. He couldn' possibly deny it; there's two of us, and we know the Ortelgan's name as well. But we doan' want to make an enemy of him. Jus' let him think about what we know, and that *he* tried to do wrong and we didn'.'

She smiled. 'That's tomorrow. But tonight, let's jus' forget the damned lot of them and have a bit of a nice time! Come here, banzi, so that I can forgive you! Oh, aren't you jus' the prettiest thing this side of a rainbow? How couldn' I be good to you? You make me feel like a nice girl again. I can stop cheatin' with you. Isn' it lovely to be able to give somethin' for nothin'?'

Maia shivered deliciously as the black girl's hands caressed her from her forgiven shoulders to her pardoned thighs. Blowing out the candle, she drew Occula down on the bed.

13

THE GIBBET

Next day they travelled fourteen miles and spent the night uneventfully at Naksh. Zuno having determined on a late start to cover the last seven miles of their journey, they set off an hour before noon in a blinding glare.

The white, dusty road across the plain lay empty in the mid-day heat. Zuno dozed where he sat. Soon the Deelguy had slackened their pace to a mere dawdle, now and then surreptitiously passing a flask between them.

'They're not going to offer us any, the lice,' whispered Occula.

'It's enough to make anyone take on bad,' panted Maia, for the twentieth time wiping the sweat from the back of her neck. Her body, under her clothes, felt covered with a kind of paste of sweat and road-dust. Her hair was full of dust and every now and then she spat a mouthful of gritty saliva into the road.

'Doan' keep doin' that,' said Occula. 'Just throwin' away moisture: you need it.'

'Well, I'm blest if I'm going to swallow it,' replied Maia.

'Gettin' particular?' panted the black girl. 'I wouldn' say no to a pint of cold piss, myself. Never mind, banzi. We'll soon be there now—less than two hours, I'd say.'

The girls had gradually edged away from behind the jekzha and were now trudging a little in front of it, on the opposite side of the road. Here, although there was no shade—for the baked, cracked plain, covered with sun-dried grass and withered flowers, was treeless for miles—they were at least out of the dust raised by the slaves and the wheels.

'Am I dreamin',' said Occula, 'or is this soddin' road goin' uphill *again?*'

'Ah, that it is,' answered Maia. 'Funny, isn't it? You don't notice the slopes till you come to them. It looks flat in front, but then you find—oh, I say, Occula, what's that, look, up there on the top?'

'Jus' doan' talk to me, banzi, while I finish meltin',' grunted the black girl, lowering her head like a straining bullock as the slope grew steeper.

Maia, tottering and closing her eyes against the dust, felt ready to fling herself down by the roadside and be hanged to what might follow. She watched a grasshopper leap out of the weeds and travel twenty feet, gliding on brown-edged, rosy wings. 'Wish I could do that,' she thought. 'S'pose they don't need to drink, else they couldn't live here.'

Reaching at length the top of the long rise, the Deelguy halted, support-ing the shafts on their backs as they leaned forward, drawing deep breaths. There was still no shade, but the girls, past waiting for permission, flung themselves down on the verge. Occula's face looked as though it had been chalked in long, uneven smears.

Maia grinned. 'You look like you was got up for the mumming.'

Suddenly she broke off, staring in speechless horror at the rising ground on the opposite side of the road.

About fifty yards away, in front of a clump of sage bushes, stood a narrow, wooden platform, from which rose two stout posts, about ten feet high and as far apart. The top of the square was completed by a cross-bar, deeply notched in four places. From each notch hung a short length of chain ending in a fetter.

The fetters were secured round the ankles of what had once been two men. The dried bodies, hanging motionless in the still heat, were indescribably ghastly, so dreadful as to seem unreal, like spectres encountered in nightmare or some drug-induced trance. The expressions of agony and despair on their crumbled, lip-retracted faces were no less appalling for being inverted, eyeless and half-flayed by insects and birds. Their lank hair was bleached almost white by the sun. The three arms still hanging below the heads were nothing but bundles of grey sticks, to which, here and there, adhered rags and fragments of flesh. One still ended in a fist of tight-clutched fingers: below the others, small, white bones lay scattered on the turf.

Maia, with an inarticulate cry, buried her face in her hands. At this moment, as though the abomination had power to pursue her and pierce whatever feeble barrier she could raise against it, the ghost of a breeze stole down the slope, bringing with it a vile, carrion odour.

Occula, after one brief glance, turned back to Maia, shaking her gently by the shoulder.

'Never seen a crows' picnic before, banzi? Come on, they woan' bite you, poor bastards. They might have once.'

'Oh—' Maia lay retching and shuddering in the grass. 'I never—'

'Gives you a turn the first time, doan' it?' said the black girl. 'That's why they do it, of course. "Come all you jolly highway rogues, this warnin' take by me. The crows have pecked my bollocks off, as you can plainly see. But once when I was young and gay, I used to—"'

'Oh, Occula, can't we go away from here?' Maia was weeping. 'Whatever can they have done?'

'How the hell d'you expect me to know?' replied Occula. 'Dropped a plate on a Leopard's toe, I expect, or made Queen Fornis's bath too hot.'

'Or possibly even made indiscreet jokes about the Sacred Queen,' cut in Zuno from the jekzha. 'But,' he resumed after a few moments, 'if *all* of us were to repeat everything we heard, it would give rise to too much awkwardness altogether, wouldn't it?'

Occula, who, as soon as he spoke, had stood up and turned towards him, made no reply, merely standing acquiescently as though awaiting an order. Unexpectedly, it was one of the Deelguy who next spoke, jerking his thumb towards the gallows.

'Make—onnemies. No good. Too monny, finish.'

'Certainly there is seldom anything to be gained by making enemies,' said Zuno. 'We'll stop here for a few minutes,' he added, extending a hand to show that he wished to be helped down from the jekzha. 'Since there is no shade for miles, this place will do as well as anywhere else.'

Having alighted, he sauntered away in the opposite direction from the gallows, while the Deelguy crawled under the wheels and began playing some game with tossed sticks in the dust.

'They're a nasty, cruel lot, these Leopards, by all I ever heard,' said Occula, as soon as she was sure that Zuno was out of hearing. 'Never mind, banzi; we'll take bastin' good care they never hang *us* up, woan' we?'

None the less, despite her indifferent manner and air of flippancy, she appeared by no means unaffected by the spectacle on the slope. Her smile, as Maia pulled her to her feet, seemed forced and unnatural, as did the four or five little dancing steps she took across the grass by way of beginning their stroll. When Maia caught up with her she was biting her lip and staring pensively at the ground.

'Yes, a nasty lot,' she repeated. 'And if you go to bed with a murderer, banzi, how sound can you sleep?'

'What?' asked Maia, frowning. 'I don't understand.'

'No; I'm the one who understands; may all the gods help me!' But thereupon she broke off and, drawing Maia round, pointed towards the purple-rimmed horizon.

'Look, banzi! Take a damn' good look! We've come far enough to see it, doan' you reckon?'

Half-closing her eyes against the glare, Maia gazed westward across the plain. Four miles away, a high, irregular mass cutting the skyline, stood the solitary peak of Mount Crandor, the mid-day brilliance throwing its ridges and gullies into sharp contrasts of sunlight and purple shadow. Encircling it, she could just make out a thin, darker streak— the line of the city walls, broken at intervals by the points of the watch-turrets.

To Crandor's right, immediately below the heat-hazed slopes, lay Bekla itself. Maia, who had never seen even Kabin or Thettit-Tonilda, stared incredulously at the mile-wide drift of smoke above the tilted roofs, through which rose the slender columns of towers taller than any trees; clustered together, as it seemed from this distance, like reeds in a pool.

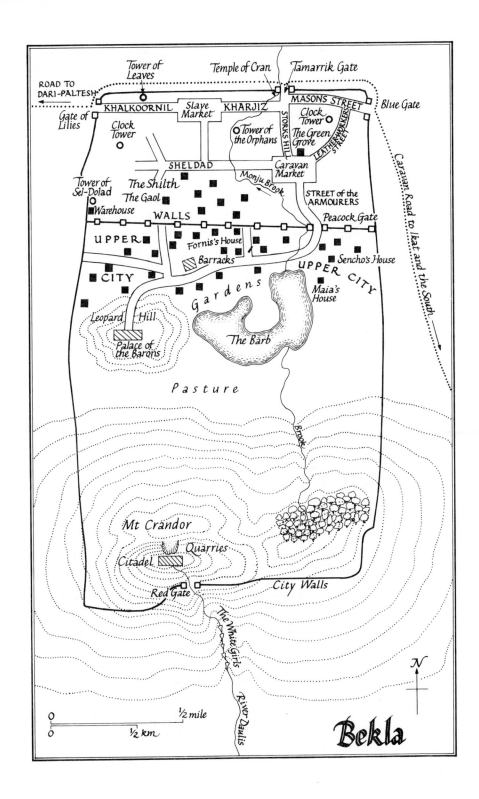

Tower of Leaves

Temple of Cran

Tamarrik Gate

ROAD TO DARI-PALTESH

KHALKOORNIL

Slave Market

KHARJIZ

MASONS STREET

Blue Gate

Gate of Lilies

Clock Tower

Tower of the Orphans

STORKS HILL

Clock Tower

The Green Grove

LEATHERWORKERS STREET

SHELDAD

Caravan Market

Caravan Road to Ikat and the South

Tower of Sel-Dolad

The Shilth

Monju Brook

STREET OF THE ARMOURERS

The Gaol

WALLS

Peacock Gate

Warehouse

UPPER

Fornis's House

Sencho's House

CITY

Barracks

UPPER CITY

Gardens

Maia's House

Leopard Hill

The Barb

Palace of the Barons

Pasture

Brook

Mt Crändor

Quarries

Citadel

City Walls

Red Gate

The White Girls

River Davlis

N

0   ½ mile

0   ½ km

Bekla

Above the city, between it and the lower slopes of Crandor itself, the Palace of the Barons crowned the Leopard Hill, its ranges of polished marble balconies catching the noon-day sun and flashing gleams of light across the intervening plain. Even at this distance—or so, at all events, she thought—Maia's ears could catch, far-off and faint, a hum and murmur like that of bees about a hive.

'Turn Bekla upside-down?' she breathed at last. 'Why, we'll just be goin' in there like—like coal to the blacksmith's, no danger!'

'Now stop it, banzi!' said the black girl quickly. 'All right, I admit it's enough to poke your eyes out, sure enough; but stands to reason, doan' it, it's got to be like anywhere else—bung-full of randy sods with standin' rods? Get that into your head and keep on rememberin' it. You're not like a confectioner or a silk-merchant—someone people can do without at a pinch. You're like a baker or a midwife: life just can't go on without the likes of us. Whoever they are, they've got to be born, they've got to eat, they've got to baste and they've got to die.'

'But I never imagined; it's so big!' Maia stared once more at the distant city with its array of tapering spires.

'Well, that's what the priestess said to the drover, but she found she could manage it all right after a bit. Look, there's old Puss-arse coming, see? Let's get back down before he starts calling us. And for Cran's sake doan' let him think you've got the wind-up about the mighty city of Bekla. You've got to learn to shrug your shoulders and spit, banzi. Go on, do it now.'

Smiling in spite of herself, Maia obeyed; whereupon Occula took her hand and ran with her down the slope. Maia noticed, however, that she still kept her eyes averted from the opposite rise.

: 14 :

BEKLA

A little less than two hours later they found themselves on the north-eastern outskirts of Bekla and approaching the Blue Gate. The mid-day heat was beginning to lessen. Behind its walls the city, stirring like some great, prostrate animal, was awakening from its sun-drenched torpor. Yawning shopkeepers with poles were pushing up the heavy, top-hung shutters they had let fall at noon. A few street cries could be heard, and here and there women, with baskets on their arms, were venturing forth from doors and passage-ways. The cripples and beggars sleeping along the alleys woke, brushed the flies from their suppurating eyelids and once more set about the task of keeping alive. As the Deelguy slaves joined other carts and wayfarers jostling between the walls of the outer precinct leading to the gate itself, the city's two water-clocks struck the third hour of the afternoon, first one and then the other releasing an iron ball to fall into a resonant copper basin. The nearer clock tower stood a bare two hundred yards from the Blue Gate and at the sudden, reverberant clang Maia started, looking up quickly towards the gold-painted grilles below the tapering spire.

Although their journey had been only half as long as those of the two previous days, both girls were spent with the heat. Maia's left ankle was swollen and she winced at every step. As they followed the jekzha under the arch of the gate she suddenly stumbled and clutched at Occula's arm, leaning her head against the wall and panting.

Five or six passers-by, attracted by the sight of such a pretty girl in obvious distress, formed a small crowd, chattering to one another and proffering advice, until a respectable-looking, elderly woman, attended by a slave carrying her basket, stepped forward and helped Maia to a stone bench recessed in the wall.

Whether Zuno felt some slight twinge of conscience; whether he thought that it might look better if the girls did not arrive at Lalloc's in a state of sweating and bedraggled exhaustion; or whether he simply wished to avoid a street-row (for some of the crowd were beginning to mutter and point at him), there can be no telling. At all events he got down from the jekzha, went across to one of the soldiers on guard-duty and asked to see the tryzatt in the guard-room (which was also situated in the thickness of the wall). Here, having shown Lalloc's token (which was stamped with the Leopard seal), he obtained leave to bring his property into the guard-room. Then he despatched one of the Deelguy to hire a second jekzha, while he himself, having told the other to come and let him know as soon as it arrived, went across the street to the nearest wine-shop.

The soldiers off-duty were sympathetic to the girls, as most common people, themselves all-too-familiar with hardship and adversity, usually are towards anyone whom they perceive to be in genuine distress. When Occula had explained the reason for Maia's exhaustion there was a good deal of indignation.

'Made 'em walk from Naksh, tryze, since this morning,' said one of the soldiers to the guard-commander, who had just returned from a quick and illicit drink with Zuno across the road. 'And that fancy bastard of Lalloc's riding along in the shade.'

'Rotten sod!' replied the tryzatt, his eyes taking in Maia from head to foot as she lay on a bench against the further wall. 'Mean 'e never give 'em no water nor nothing? Well, Cran knows a soldier's life's nothing to shout about, but I'd rather that than yours, y' poor lass,' he said to Occula.

'Oh, you jus' wait a bit,' replied Occula, grinning up at him through her mask of dust. 'Give it a year and we might both be on our backs—you on a battlefield and me in a Leopard's bed.'

There was a general laugh, but the tryzatt, unhooking the wine-skin from the wall and tilting it to her mouth, put a fatherly hand on her shoulder.

'Well, just you be careful how you *do* go jumping into Leopards' beds, my girl—that's if you ever get that far. There's plenty don't come so well out of that game as they reckon they're going to.'

'Ah, that's right,' said another soldier. 'You don't have to shake the *melikon* for the berries to fall.'

'Oh, bugger the melikon!' said Occula. 'This banzi's not sixteen and you start talkin' about berries fallin'! As you're all bein' so kind,' she went on, 'I wonder whether there's any water we could wash in, if it's not too much trouble?'

The guard-quarters boasted a small, brick-floored bath-house, with a piped supply from the Monju Brook—the outfall stream of the lake called the Barb. Here the girls stripped and sluiced each other down. When Zuno reappeared a quarter of an hour later they were both feeling—and look-ing—in much better shape; Occula in her orange metlan and Maia in the powder-blue robe, with a scarlet trepsis bloom, given her by one of the soldiers, stuck behind her ear. The guard-commander, having civilly but firmly refused a tip from Zuno, helped the girls into the hired jekzha, which thereupon set off, following the two Deelguy down Masons Street towards the Kharjiz.

Simply to be sitting down, moving effortlessly along, instead of trudging in the heat and dust, was enough to fill Maia with a delightful sense of luxury. The pleasure—which she had very seldom known before—of being carried on wheels, and the swift succession of sights and sounds pressing from all directions upon her fatigued senses, were bemusing, and imparted to her surroundings a rather dream-like quality. She had never seen so many, and such different kinds of people, all intent upon their various affairs. She watched two men—evidently, from their uniform clothes, some kind of public servants—laying the dust in the street by sprinkling water from a metal tank on wheels; a hawker selling eggs and bread; an old woman haggling with a stall-keeper over a scale-full of brillions; two lads who were having difficulty in carrying a rolled-up carpet through the crowds; a man whose shop was itself a huge cage, full of brilliant-plumaged birds; a hard-faced, painted girl, little older than herself, standing watch-fully on a corner with a studied air of being at a loose end; and a leather-aproned harness-maker at his bench, surrounded by his wares as he plied his heavy needle. The air was full of all manner of smells, some familiar, others entirely unknown to her—incense drifting through an open door at the top of a flight of stone steps; a medley of spicy odours from an open-fronted cookshop, inside which charcoal braziers were glowing in a shady, welcoming gloom; and, again and again, the languorous, citrous fragrances of flowers and blossoming shrubs—big, glowing blooms of kinds she had never seen—thriving in well-watered beds beside the street and allaying with their greenery the oppression of summer's end. All about her—so that she had to raise her voice even to talk to Occula beside her—rang the multifoliate clamour of the city; the crying of wares, the shouting of children at play, the gabbling of bargainers and quarrellers, the tappings and hammerings peculiar to tinkers, carpenters, smiths, cobblers, masons, wheelwrights. Once, as the jekzha went by, she caught for a few moments the voice of someone singing a Tonildan ballad she recognized. At a crossing, a scarlet-liveried slave strode across their front, staff in hand, crying 'Make way! Make way!', followed by a curtained litter adorned, behind and before, with the cognizance of a crowned leopard. Across the roof-tops sounded from the upper city the wavering, gong-like notes of copper bells.

Most of all, Maia was amazed by the size and grandeur of the buildings. Bekla, growing up upon a natural site for a city, with a virtually impregnable hilltop citadel; watered by a lake and standing at the convergence of five roads traversing a wide plain, had been built almost entirely from the stone quarries of Mount Crandor. Time out of mind it had been renowned for its builders, masons and stone-carvers. Almost every house, from the Palace of the Barons to the lodgings for the itinerant herdsmen, was of stone. The market-colonnades, the temples, the graceful towers and other public buildings were of a beauty and magnificence unparalleled in any other city throughout the empire. The very fact that the old ceremonial name, Bekla-lo-Senguel-Cerith ('The Garden of Dancing Stone'), was still commonly used in poems, songs and ballads testified to the universal pride and veneration felt for the capital.

All this Maia, like everyone else, had heard from infancy. But there is a world of difference between hearing tell and seeing for oneself. Staring up at rows of decorated corbels supporting overhanging upper storeys, at innumerable foliate chamfers and casement mouldings, at delicate inter-penetrations of stone executed with almost incredible craftsmanship and skill, the spontaneous Maia, hitherto entirely ignorant of such things, was entranced by what seemed to her little short of a miracle—of hundreds of miracles. How could *stone* be made to float like lilies, curl like waves, drift like clouds? Who had raised these stones, piling them up to stand firm, one upon another, far above the heads of mortals walking safe and unconcerned below: and then, not content with that, carved them into flowers and foliage, snarling beasts, armed men, naked girls?

Why, 'tis past all believing! she thought. If ever I see Tharrin again, reckon *I'll* be the one as does the talking. Occula might be right after all— if only things turn out lucky, I could find myself better off than ever I was back home. She sighed. All same, I'd like to see the old lake again, and have a swim under the falls, that I would.

Their progress was slow, for as the afternoon cooled the streets grew ever more busy. Several times their jekzha was forced to a halt and Zuno, ahead, was obliged to stop and wait until they could catch him up. Their journey, though only a little over three-quarters of a mile, lasted a full half-hour.

Amid all the excitement and activity, Occula had entirely recovered her spirits, and was highly tickled by the prospect of arriving at their destination on wheels rather than on foot. Furthermore, it was flattering to have beside her the ingenuous Maia, full of wonder and curiosity and hanging upon her every word. For a time she was content simply to rest her feet on the rail in front of them and reply to Maia's questions. Soon, however, her natural energy and unsleeping sense of self-interest began to take over.

'Come on, banzi,' she said, putting an arm round Maia's shoulders and impelling her forward on to the edge of the seat. 'Bugger the bells, and the carvin' too! *They* woan' do anythin' for you! You've got to show off a bit, my lass! This is no time to be starin' round at other people and forgettin' all about yourself. *They're* the ones who've got to be doin' the starin'. Our job's to put on some style!'

'Whatever for?' asked Maia. 'We're going to this Lalloc man, aren't we?'

'Yes, but you never know who may happen to see you and take a fancy: that's the way a good shearna works—never misses casual opportunities. Lean forward, pull your dress down a bit. Get those deldas out—no, right down to the strawberries, come on—'

'Here, steady on!' Maia turned scarlet as the black girl pulled down her bodice.

'That Ortelgan stiff was right—blushin' *does* suit you,' replied Occula. 'I doan' know about the men, banzi, but *I* could eat you up.'

'Hey, girls, any room for a little one?' called a young fellow in a carter's smock and leggings, cracking his whip to attract their attention.

'I like big ones,' answered Occula, holding her hands up about a foot apart.

'And *I* like willing ones,' said the carter. 'I like that black skin of yours, too. Where d'you come from, lass?'

'The finest country in the world,' replied Occula.

'Then what are you doing here?'

'Well, where I come from, you see, the girls give so much pleasure that the men have all died of it, so I've had to look elsewhere.'

'Fancy that, now!' said the carter. 'And who's your pretty friend?'

'One you can' afford,' answered Occula.

'By Lespa, and I reckon that's true enough for now!' called the young fellow after them, as the jekzha began to move on. 'Might see you again one day, though. Where you going?'

'Time you've made your fortune,' replied Occula, 'we'll be so famous you woan' have any trouble findin' us!'

At the western end of Masons Street the jekzha turned left into the foot of Storks Hill, but the girls had scarcely time to glimpse, behind them, the breath-taking Tamarrik Gate before they turned again, this time to the right, down the broad thoroughfare of the Kharjiz and so on into the Slave Market.

Since this was not a market day the big square was not crowded. A gang of municipal slaves was at work clearing and sweeping, while two masons were repairing one of the raised sale platforms on the north side. Here, too, all was built of stone and beautified with flowers—beds of golden lilies and scarlet askinnias dividing the various rostra and barracoons one from another. Each roofed and pillared rostrum was decorated with a carved relief, depicting scenes appropriate to the kind of slaves sold on it. This was recent work, commissioned by Queen Fornis herself—a great promoter of the slave trade.

'Oh, look at the men fighting!' cried Maia, pointing at a battle scene which ran down one entire side of a rostrum forty feet long.

'That must be where they sell the soldiers,' replied Occula.

'They *sell* soldiers?' Maia was puzzled.

'Well, some kinds, yes,' answered the black girl. 'Prisoners taken in war—you know, Katrians and Terries—fellows from Terekenalt—if they're not badly wounded or disabled, and if no one ransoms them, they're often sold. They wouldn' be any good for the regular army, you see—not former enemy wouldn'—but provincial barons buy them for their household companies, and often people from other countries buy them, too. The further off a man comes from, the more useful he is to a baron's local bunch of bastards, you see.'

'Oh, and that platform there, look! That must be for the roadmakers, I suppose. What wonderful pictures! I've never seen anything like them!'

In fact, of course, Maia had never seen any graphic or sculptural art whatever, except for crude peasant work at Meerzat and round about: and although, often, that was not lacking in a certain power and beauty, it had not prepared her for the art of such great Beklan craftsmen as Fleitil,

Sandruhlet and those others whose names, still known today, can only make us regret that virtually all their work is lost to us for ever. Gazing at Sandruhlet's frieze—of which only a fragment survives—of the pioneer gang driving the Gelt road into the foothills, all newly painted in brilliant, stylized colours intensifying its half-barbaric impact, Maia felt herself actually tingling at the sight of the straining, muscular young men, the rain glistening on their half-naked bodies as they heaved on the sledge-ropes.

'Clever work, isn' it?' said Occula. 'You've got to admit these Beklans do know how to slice up a bit of stone. The whole city's full of that sort of thing. I remember Zai took me to the upper city once, to see the Barons' Palace close to. We couldn' go into the Palace, of course, but I've never forgotten it. There's a carved—'

'Oh—!' interrupted Maia suddenly, staring and putting a hand up to her mouth in an involuntary, startled gesture. Turning her head away, she looked at Occula in confusion, but then, despite herself, looked back again. 'What—whatever—?'

Occula chuckled. 'That's where they sell the girls. I've never seen it before, but someone in Thettit told me the carvers spent four years on that. They *did* rather let themselves go, didn' they? All good for trade, banzi, you know. Didn' leave much to the imagination, did they?'

'Oh, and three or four together, look—and there—' Maia became speechless. Then 'And right out in the open, where everyone can see— you'd wonder who ever thought of such things, wouldn't you?'

'Fellows who think of nothin' else, that's who,' said Occula, enjoying her confusion. 'It just shows you, doesn' it, what a lot of silly sods there are who've got it on the brain? See what I mean? With a bit of luck we can' go wrong. But we've got to be sharp, banzi. What it comes down to is that they want figs for nothin', but somehow or other we've got to sell figs dear. And what *that* comes down to, really, is bein' better than the competition.'

'But will *we* have to—you know—stand up there with no clothes on—?'

The black girl shook her head. 'Shouldn' think so. I told you, Lalloc said to Domris he'd sell me privately, into a wealthy household. Of course I can' tell them straight out that where I go you're comin' too. You're worth a lot of money—so am I—and even a rich man who buys one girl may not be able to afford two—or not two at once. But you can be sure of one thing: Lalloc'll be out to sell you to his own best advantage, whatever that is; and I doan' think a girl like you'll be thrown in with a lot of others.'

As the jekzha was about to leave the market and enter the long slope of the Khalkoornil—the Street of Leaves—it was once again forced to a halt by a heavy wagon loaded with a single block of stone, which was coming slowly up the hill towards them. This was surrounded by a noisy crowd, many of whom were helping the carters and their bullocks to drag and push it the final few yards uphill into the Slave Market.

'Oh, look, Occula, it's carved in the shape of a woman, d'you see? Wonder where they're taking it?'

'That's the new statue of Airtha,' said their jekzha-man over his shoulder. 'Fleitil and his lads have been working on it all summer up in the quarries. Only the big statues, they always start them up there and then finish them when they've been brought down. There's hundreds been waiting down at the Gate of Lilies to give them a hand. They reckon that's lucky, see, to touch it as it comes in.'

'Where's it to go?' asked Occula.

'Outside the Temple of Cran. That's U-Fleitil, look, just over there; see him?'

Maia looked over the heads of the crowd towards where the man was pointing. Before she could pick out Fleitil, however, she became aware of someone else—a young man standing quite close by on the opposite side of the road.

He was certainly of striking appearance. Taking no part in the turmoil round the wagon, he was leaning, with a relaxed yet alert air, against the doorpost of a wine shop, eating grapes—or at any rate holding a bunch in one hand—and staring directly at her. Everything about him suggested self-confidence, wealth and aristocracy. He was tall, with long, dark hair and a short, neatly-trimmed beard; and not so much handsome in any conventional way as having an aspect and air of gallantry which made one forget to consider whether he was or not. He was wearing a close-fitting abshay of rose-coloured silk, with a silver belt at the waist. Its puffed sleeves, the inverted pleats of which were inset with silver, were gathered a little below the elbow. Both this and his pale-yellow, damasked breeches were overspread with small, semi-precious stones, lustrous and blue-green in colour. His sword was sheathed in a scabbard jewelled with larger stones of the same sort, while slung at his back, on a crimson-tasselled cord, was a large hat adorned with coloured plumes of red and blue. On his left shoulder, worked in silver thread, was the cognizance of a leopard.

Despite his elegance and flamboyant dress, his bearing suggested not so much the fop as the courtier and nobleman capable of turning soldier at need. He was plainly quite unconcerned to conceal his interest in Maia. She, abashed and self-conscious, looked quickly away, pulling up the bodice which Occula had disarranged. Yet when she looked round it was only to meet once more the young man's unwavering gaze.

'Smile, you fool,' whispered Occula out of the side of her mouth.

Maia, feeling as awkward as a ploughboy called to the side of a lady's carriage to tell her the way, tried to smile but found she seemed to have lost the trick. However, at this moment the young man smiled at her, tossed his grapes into the lap of a near-by beggar and strolled across the street, the crowd seeming to part before him as undergrowth parts before a hound on the scent.

Putting one hand on the rail at the girls' feet and looking up at Maia with an air expressive of admiration both given and received (as though to say 'It's pleasant to be beautiful—don't you agree?'), he said, 'To my own great surprise, I don't seem to know your name. Still, I dare say you can put that right for me, can't you?'

'Oh—sir—I—that's to say—'

Maia's confusion was so clearly unfeigned that the young man, for a moment at all events, appeared to lose his own self-possession. With a slightly puzzled look he said, 'I hope I've not embarrassed you or made a mistake. But if you're not shearnas—and very pretty ones at that—why are you riding through the lower city in an open jekzha, with no escort?'

'We're here from Thettit-Tonilda, sir,' said Occula, smiling at him and leaning forward to put her hand for a moment on his, 'with a recommendation to U-Lalloc.'

'Oh, I see,' said the young man, with an air of disappointment. 'You mean he's going to sell you?'

'I'm very sorry; I'm afraid not, sir,' answered Occula, as though he had made a request which she was obliged to decline with regret. 'We're already promised to a noble house.'

'I'm not at all surprised to hear it,' said the young man. 'Well, perhaps we may meet again. If that—er—*noble house*—' he smiled, giving an ironical emphasis to the words—'should ever wish to part with you, perhaps you'll contrive to let me know, will you?'

With this he pressed a kiss on Maia's bare foot, turned on his heel and was gone across the market-place, his feathered hat tossing on his shoulders.

As the jekzha moved on, neither girl spoke for a minute or two. Then Maia, still bewildered by the encounter, said 'But he never told us who he was.'

'You're supposed to know who he is,' answered Occula. 'It wouldn' occur to him that you didn'. He's a Leopard, obviously.'

'Do *you* know?'

'No, 'course I doan'. But it might be a good idea to find out, doan' you think?'

'Oh, I felt so terrible—'

'You doan' know your own strength, banzi, that's your trouble,' said the black girl, smacking at a fly on her forearm. 'You did fine. He woan' forget us in a hurry. Cran! I'm hungry, aren't you? Surely it can' be much further now.'

126

In fact it was no distance at all. Hardly had they passed, on their right, the dark column of the Tower of Leaves, with its foliated, circular balcony projecting a hundred feet above their heads, when Zuno's jekzha turned off under a low stone arch. Following him, they found themselves in a narrow lane, which made a turn and opened into a paved courtyard. Here Zuno had already got down, and motioned to them to do the same. Together they unloaded Occula's box and stood waiting while he settled with the jekzha-man. His raised-eyebrow technique was no less effective than it had been with the footpads. After a short conversation, and assuming a slightly pained manner, he murmured, 'Nonsense, my good man; you're well paid,' walked across to a door on the courtyard's further side and unlocked it with a key taken from his pocket.

About to enter, however, he suddenly stopped and, turning to Occula, said, 'The—er—young nobleman who spoke to you just now: what might he have said to you?'

'He paid us compliments, sir.'

'Did he express any interest in purchase?'

'Not seriously, sir: I think he was just amusin' himself. I simply told him that if he was interested he'd better speak to U-Lalloc.'

Zuno paused. 'Do you know who he is?'

'No, sir.'

'That is Elvair-ka-Virrion, only son of the Lord General Kembri-B'sai.'

Thereupon, without waiting for an answer from Occula, he went indoors.

: 15 :

AT LALLOC'S

Occula and Maia, carrying the box between them, stepped through the doorway into a kind of cloister about twenty yards square. Its centre, open to the sky, was a rough garden—a grassed area with a few flowers and a pool on one side. This was surrounded by a low wall, from which rose plain stone columns supporting the roof of a covered way running round the four sides of the enclosure. At intervals along this ambulatory were various doors—and windows also, for the rooms behind the doors had no openings except those looking inwards onto the covered way. The whole place, secure as any prison, comprised Lalloc's premises, where he kept his stock and from which he carried on his business.

Maia had caught no more than a glimpse of four or five rather rough-looking girls playing with a ball near the pool, before Zuno conducted them both into a small room off the ambulatory. This was furnished with a heavy table, two or three benches, a closet and a bed covered with two or three cushions and a thick rug. On the bed was lounging a big, brawny-looking woman of about thirty, who climbed heavily to her feet as Zuno came in.

'Ah; Vartou,' said Zuno, sitting down on one of the benches and helping himself to wine from a jug on the table. 'Is U-Lalloc here?'

'No, he isn't, U-Zuno,' replied the woman. 'He's gone to the upper city on business, but he said he'd be in again early tomorrow. Did you have a good journey from Thettit?'

'Oh—quite uneventful, thank you,' replied Zuno with an air of slight impatience. 'Well, in that case I suppose *you* had better take delivery of these two girls. I received them from Megdon at Hirdo.'

'At *Hirdo*?' asked the woman.

'Yes—yes.' Zuno closed his eyes wearily. 'Perdan will be bringing the normal quota on foot, as usual. I imagine he will be here tomorrow or the day after. The young black woman is here at her own request—an arranged sale—from the Lily Pool at Thettit. This is a letter, which she's brought with her, from the Säiyett Domris to U-Lalloc.' He handed it over.

'Oh, I see; Säiyett Domris's girl. Yes, she's expected. U-Lalloc knows about her.'

'The other girl, I understand, is not part of Megdon's quota at all. Apparently she is in the nature of a fortuitous acquisition. Megdon told me he gave a considerable sum for her. Since I gather he was dealing with a peasant woman—a totally inexperienced vendor—he may well be lying, but at all events there is his receipt. It means very little, since the woman was evidently illiterate—a thumb-print, as you can see. U-Lalloc may want to go further into the matter, but Megdon could reasonably argue, I suppose, that it's all clear profit. Anyway, that will be a matter for U-Lalloc when Megdon renders his accounts next month. And now I must be going. Good evening!'

As soon as he had gone, the woman turned to Occula and Maia with an air of truculence.

'Well, and why were you sent here ahead of Megdon's quota? Some trouble, was there? What's the rights of it, eh?'

'U-Megdon thought we were both a little out of the ordinary, säiyett,' replied Occula, 'and wished U-Lalloc to see us as soon as possible.'

'Huh!' said the woman. 'So you think you're out of the ordinary, do you, with your black skin?'

'*I* think nothin', säiyett. I'm simply tellin' you what U-Megdon said.'

'And why were *you* sold to Megdon?' asked the woman, turning to Maia. 'Some baron basted you and then got tired of you, did he?'

At her coarse, unfriendly manner Maia, hungry and tired out, felt the tears starting to her eyes.

'With respect, säiyett,' said Occula, 'my friend will be ready to tell U-Lalloc everythin' that he may want to know tomorrow. Perhaps we could leave it at that. You see a great many slaves, I'm sure. They're not usually over-anxious to talk about their bad luck, are they?'

'Hoity-toity, miss!' cried the woman, 'and who do you think you're talking to, hey?'

'Merely a suggestion, säiyett.' Occula, looking her calmly in the eye, said no more.

The woman, opening the closet behind her, took out a pliant ash-stick. 'D'you see this?' she said. 'It's for girls who give trouble. Any more impudence and you'll be making its closer acquaintance.'

Occula remained impassive and silent and the woman, after glaring at her for a few more moments, put the stick down on the table.

'Well,' she said, 'you can both come with me now and I'll show you your quarters. Bring that box along with you.'

She led the way out of the room and along the ambulatory. Maia, limping on her swollen ankle as she helped to carry the box, could hardly keep up. Coming, at the corner, to a door standing open in the wall, Vartou, who was unusually tall, stooped under it and then stood to one side as they followed her through.

The two girls found themselves in a stone-floored room, perhaps fifty feet long, with three barred windows opening inwards on the covered way and a hearth in the opposite wall, where a fire was burning. All round were beds, separated by wooden partitions, and in the centre stood a long, rough table with benches. The floor was clean and the whole place looked a good deal tidier than anything Maia was used to.

'This is the room for women and grown girls,' said Vartou, 'but there's only five other girls in here just now, so you can more or less suit yourselves for beds. The bath-house is next door; and damned well *use* it, d'you see? There's soap and there's sulphur. If you've got lice, get rid of them. Any girl found with lice on her gets whipped—and soundly, too. Your ankle's swollen,' she went on unexpectedly, turning to Maia. 'Does it hurt?'

'Yes, säiyett.'

'Come to me when you've bathed and I'll strap it up for you. Any kind of cut or ailment, you tell me and I treat it, do you understand? That's a strict rule. Except for children, rations are given out mornings and evenings and you cook them for yourselves. That's what the fire's for.'

She paused; then said emphatically, 'Now understand this once and for all. This is a high-class establishment. You're lucky. Girls who come here are valuable property and treated accordingly. They're always surprised to find it's better than the homes they've left. Good food, comfortable beds, fresh clothes for those who need them, plenty of towels, soap and water. Do either of you have fits or wet the bed?'

'No, säiyett.'

'Anyone who fouls or smashes anything is severely punished, and anyone who isn't clean is punished. U-Lalloc will want to see you both tomorrow.'

And with this she was gone.

Occula thumbed her nose after her. 'Lice who come here are lucky and val'able, banzi. They're so surprised, they have fits and wet the bed. Bastin' old bitch! Lice, indeed! Come on, let's pitch camp over here, away from the fire. These two beds'll do.' She punched one of them tentatively, then flung herself down on it. 'Airtha tairtha! She was right enough, though; they *are* comfortable! If the rations are as good, we're well away. Can you cook?'

'Sort of,' said Maia. ''Pends what it is.'

'More 'n I can. Never had to—not since the Govig, anyway. Look, banzi, we'd better not both go and bath at once. We doan' know what sort may be here: one of us had better stay with this box. Would you like to go first?'

'No, darling,' said Maia. 'I'm all right. We had a bath with the soldiers, remember?'

'Sounds marvellous! How long ago was that? Did I enjoy it? Anyway, I'm ready for another. Why doan' you have a nice little rest till I come back? I suppose the towels must be in the bath-house.'

Left to herself, Maia lay down on her bed. The wooden partition at her elbow was incised all over with names and other rough scrawls. 'Maydis of Dari' she spelt out slowly; and a date five years earlier. Then—and here she had the help of a crude but remarkably graphic illustration—'Thylla bastes like a sow.'

Having dozed for a time, she had just begun studying a third inscription when a big-built, rough-looking girl of about seventeen, with dark hair and a noticeable squint, walked into the room gnawing an apple. At the sight of Maia she stopped short, looked her up and down for a few moments and then said, unsmilingly and with a kind of wary belligerence, 'Hullo; who are you?'

Maia sat up on the edge of her bed and smiled at her. 'My name's Maia: I come from Tonilda.'

'Come from Delda, did you say?' answered the girl. 'Great Cran, you look like it, too! Stack 'em on the shelf at night, do you?'

Her disagreeable, sneering manner made it impossible to take this as either a joke or a compliment. Still, I'd better be careful, thought Maia.

She's too big for me. Besides, for all I know her friends may be in any minute.

'What d'you want to quarrel for?' she said. 'Aren't we both in enough trouble as it is?'

'*You* may be,' returned the girl. 'Speak for yourself. Going to have a big belly as well, are you?'

'I didn't mean that—'

'What's in that box?' interrupted the girl, walking up to the bed and looking down at it.

'You let that alone!' said Maia sharply. 'That's Occula's box—my friend's. She'll be back directly.'

'Boccula's ox?' said the girl, mimicking her Tonildan accent and blowing three or four apple pips over her. 'Well, then, dear, I'm afraid darling Shockula's in for a bit of an ock.' She laughed briefly at this witticism, stooped and flung back the lid.

Maia grasped her wrist. 'I said, let it alone!'

The girl, easily twisting her wrist free, stuffed her apple core down Maia's neck just as Occula, a towel round her waist, came back into the room carrying her orange metlan and an iron frying-pan.

'Banzi,' she said, 'I found this outside. Why doan' we—' Seeing the girl standing over her opened box, she stopped. 'What's goin' on? Did you open that or did she?'

'She did,' panted Maia. 'I tried to stop her—'

'This'll stop her,' said Occula, and without a moment's hesitation hit the girl over the head with the frying-pan, which rang like a gong.

The girl staggered and went down on the floor, but was up again in a moment, spittle dribbling down her chin. Occula, having quickly tossed her metlan and the frying-pan to Maia, was waiting as she rushed at her. They closed and Maia was horrified to see her friend go down under the girl's much heavier weight. While they lay struggling on the floor, three or four more girls came running into the room and gathered round, shouting excitedly.

Occula, lying beneath the girl, clutched her tightly about with her arms and legs. 'Now *hit* her, banzi, hard!'

Maia, swinging back the frying-pan in both hands, hit the back of the girl's head as hard as she could. The girl collapsed across Occula's body just as Vartou came rushing into the hall.

'What's all this basting row?'

There was instant silence. It was plain that all the girls were afraid of her.

Vartou stooped and without the least effort lifted Occula's assailant bodily, threw her across Maia's bed and slapped her face. She would probably have gone on to deal with Occula in the same way, but the black girl was already up, shutting her box and getting dressed as though nothing had happened.

'And what the hell d'you think *you're* doing?' said Vartou, turning towards her.

'Gettin' dressed, säiyett.'

'I'll give you getting dressed, you black trollop!'

Standing over Occula, she fixed her with a terrifying stare, which the black girl met unwaveringly.

'Get up!' said Vartou at length, turning back to the other girl, who instantly obeyed her, albeit in a somewhat dazed manner. 'Now, listen. I don't want to hear anything from either of you about who started this: you can save your damned breath. If you weren't both due to be seen by U-Lalloc tomorrow I'd thrash you both within an inch of your dirty little lives. But there are ways of hurting girls without leaving any mark on them, and if there's any more trouble that's what'll happen, d'you see?'

'Yes, säiyett,' replied Occula. 'May I please be allowed to put my box in a safe place? Then I dare say you woan' be put to the trouble of havin' to defend me again.'

'You've got a blasted sight too much to say for yourself,' said Vartou. 'Since you're so particular, you can take it back to my room now, you and your precious friend; and you can draw the rations as well. Time you did some work, both of you.'

Both girls were astonished by the issued rations. There was about half a pound of lean meat for each girl in the hall; fresh vegetables, milk, bread, cheese and fruit. They had to make two trips.

'Perhaps you see now, do you,' said Vartou sourly, 'how much better you're treated here than you deserve? Everything's to be cleared away and clean by the time I come round; if it's not, there'll be trouble.' Then, suddenly, to Occula, 'You seem to have your wits about you, black or not. That's a rough lot of girls—rougher than most. You'd better help to keep them in order, d'you see?'

'Very well, säiyett.'

An hour and a half later Maia, bathed and dressed, her ankle tightly bandaged over a cold compress, was lying on her bed digesting a heavy meal in a state as close to satisfaction as she had known since the commencement of her misfortunes five days before. As not infrequently happens when two tough characters have had a scrap and cooled off, Occula and the cast-eyed girl had become guardedly friendly. The latter, while helping Maia to cook the supper, had unbent to the extent of telling her that her name was Chia and that she had arrived, two weeks before, in a slave quota from Urtah.

'And the curse of the Streels on that bastard of an elder who picked on me,' she added. 'He had a down on my father, Surdad did. I wasn't well when we started and it was all of sixty miles. Once we got here I went down delirious—didn't know where I was for four or five days. That's why I haven't been sold yet, see? I'm supposed to be getting my health back. You'll be all right,' she said, looking enviously at Maia. 'Don't know why you're here, really. Girls like you don't become slaves as a rule—not where I come from, anyway. Who d'you think's going to want me? Washing-up girl in some pot-house'll be about the size of it, I dare say.'

Maia had felt sorry for her and invited her to sit down and eat with Occula and herself, which she seemed glad enough to do.

Now they had all three dragged their beds side by side and were chatting in the fading evening light.

'You know, dearest,' said Maia to Occula, 'I thought you were going to say some more to Zuno 'bout that young prince—nobleman—whatever he was. Don't you think he might buy us, if Lalloc was to put it to him?'

'Well, he might,' said Occula, 'but I'm not goin' to, all the same. If Lalloc's already got his own ideas for sellin' us, it woan' do us any good to start havin' our own. And then again, that's only a young man, even if he is a high-up Leopard. Young men like that doan' usually buy girls. In a city like this they doan' need to. And s'pose he did, then p'raps he suddenly goes off to a war or somethin'—decides to cut down on his household while he's gone and sells you off. Oh, no, he's not at all the sort of man we ought to be hopin' for.'

'Then what is?'

'Well—if we're lucky—an older man's house, where girls are kept as part of the household—you know, for style as much as for pleasure: that's often the way in a rich house; I've seen it. Then we know where we are and what's expected of us, and once we've found our feet we can start lookin' round for friends and opportunities to better ourselves. Tell you the truth, banzi, I can tell you what I doan' like the idea of, even if I can't tell you 'zactly what I do: and I just didn' altogether fancy your prince. Bit too good to be true, somehow. Sort of—I doan' know—well, unreliable. I could be wrong. It's only a hunch. But one thing's for sure—it's no good actin' as if we weren't Lalloc's property, because we are.'

She turned to Chia. 'What was that you said before supper—somethin' about the curse of the Streels?'

Chia coloured. 'I shouldn't have said it.'

'What is the curse of the Streels?'

'I can't tell you. No Urtan can tell you. Forget I said it.'

'Can you put it on people?'

'Great Shakkarn, no! It's something far, far more dreadful. But don't worry, Occula; you'll never come to the Streels.'

Occula received this in silence. At length, shrugging her shoulders as though to dismiss the subject, she said, 'By the way, banzi, I doan' want anyone else to know where I come from or to hear the story I told you the other night. All right?'

Maia nodded.

'Oh, can you tell stories?' asked Chia. 'You're a sort of trained entertainer, aren't you? You've worked in a pleasure-house, haven't you? Did you tell stories there?'

Occula laughed, as though relieved by the change of subject brought about through what she had said to Maia being taken up in this way. 'Oh, Cran! I know plenty of stories.'

'Come on, then, tell us one now! Tell us about Lespa, or one of the other goddesses.' And thereupon, without waiting for Occula's assent, Chia called out to the rest of the room, 'Occula's going to tell a story!'

Most of the other girls gathered round. It was plain that Occula was already regarded as an exotic character, possessed of style and magnetism.

For a few moments she remained silent, looking round the little group and tantalizing their eagerness and expectancy. At length she said, 'Looks as if I'll have to, doan' it? What did you say—Lespa?'

'Yes, tell us about Lespa,' said Chia. 'The time when she was just a village girl on earth, same as we are. Or same as we *used* to be,' she added bitterly.

At this there were murmurs of sympathy and fellow-feeling from the others, and as they died away Occula began.

: 16 :
THE TALE OF LESPA'S SACRIFICE

'Well, as you all know, there was a time long ago when Lespa—she that dwells among the glitterin' stars and sends us her precious gift of dreams— was a mortal girl on this earth. Where she lived none knows for certain, but everyone claims her for their own. Men from Kabin—and I've been with a few—will tell you that it was near Kabin that she dwelt: yet a man from Ikat will tell you that Lespa was a Yeldashay girl. But as I've always understood, she was born in a village of lower Suba, near where the Valderra runs into the Zhairgen.'

'Why, so she was!' cried one of the girls. 'My mother was from those parts, and anyone will tell you that's where Lespa grew up.'

'It's a lie!' said a second girl, furiously. 'Lespa came from Sarkid of the Sheaves. My mother told me—'

'Doan' that just show you?' intervened Occula equably. 'Well, wherever it was she came from it wasn' *my* country; so perhaps I'd better just leave this story until you've had time to sort it out among yourselves.'

'No, no! Go on, Occula,' said Chia, 'and you other banzis just shut up and listen!'

'Well, wherever 'twas,' resumed Occula, 'they were luckier than if one end of a rainbow had come down in the village street, for Lespa was just the prettiest girl that's ever been seen in this world. When she was fourteen or fifteen, she had only to walk through the fields in hay-time to take her father his dinner, for every lad to be driven half out of his mind. They'd gather round, and keep her talkin' through the dinner-hour, and then they'd fight over who should get into trouble for cuttin' his work to walk along with her, back to her home.

'Now of all the young fellows in the village there was one, and his name was Baltis, who could scarcely sleep by night or work by day for the mischief that Lespa quite innocently wrought in his heart. He was a fine, big lad, apprenticed to a smith; and as you know, Baltis is still a general name for smiths all over the empire. If you a meet a lad named Baltis, chances are he's often a smith.

'Baltis never lost the least chance of seein' Lespa. He fought three or four other young chaps and beat them, simply to keep them away from her: and even at that he was none too successful, for however badly he beat them they'd come limpin' back for more of what had brought it on them, just like moths to a candle. He came near to losin' his place in the forge, even though he'd always worked well and was nearly out of his time, simply because he'd down his hammer and be off if he so much as saw Lespa comin' out of her mother's door.

'Now Baltis—he knew very well what he wanted; but you must understand that as yet Lespa didn'. She was as unversed in the ways of love as a new-hatched butterfly dryin' its wings in the sun. All she knew was that she must be beautiful, for she had only to walk down the street for five or six lads to appear from nowhere and start tellin' her so; and after a time she had to give up bathin' in the river altogether—unless she could persuade her mother to come along with her and keep a look-out. All the same, in spite of bein' ignorant of what it was they were after, she enjoyed—well, which of us doesn'?—the attention of the lads, and used to show it plainly enough when they pleased her. For even in those days of her maidenhood, Lespa had pretty ways and knew—well, just as a mare or a partridge knows—how to give the right answers to those who pleased her, and how to keep them by her side as long as she wanted.

135

'Well, when a queen bee flies, the swarm follows—right? But she flies high, and only the strongest gets her. And the strongest—well, it often costs him all he's got. Young Baltis, so the tales tell, was simply not his own master in those days, for he gave all he had. Every minute of his time, every meld he could scrape together went on Lespa. And so it came about that after a time Lespa, even though she couldn' have told just what it was she wanted from him, nevertheless came to feel that she'd like to be alone with him, to be in his arms and let him teach her whatever it was that she still had to learn.

'Yet even when she'd come to this resolve, to find the least chance proved altogether beyond her. For the truth was that her father, who was a prosperous man, with a farm of his own and money comin' in from a half-share in a fishin'-boat on the Zhairgen, considered Baltis beneath the family. He wanted to freeze him off, that's what. So after a bit poor old Baltis gave up comin' to the door, for no one was glad to see him but Lespa, and she'd only get a flea in her ear if she showed as much. But you know how it is: this only made her long all the more for a chance to find out what it was that Baltis wanted so desperately; for she felt it stirrin' in her body as a kind of riddle. She felt as though she must know the answer very well, but couldn' quite see it; somethin' like as though she'd dreamt it and forgotten, perhaps—but of course those were the days before there were dreams.'

'Before there were *dreams*?' asked Chia.

'Certainly,' replied Occula. 'How the hell could there be dreams before Lespa's palace came to be raised among the stars?'

'Before there were dreams?' muttered another girl. 'There was a hard world, then.'

'Now in that village where sweet Lespa lived,' went on Occula, 'the god they worshipped in those days of long ago was Shakkarn. And as you lot come from all over everywhere, and I doan' know how much or how little you know, I'd better tell you that as I've always understood— ever since I came to the empire, that is—Shakkarn's a god older than either Cran or Airtha. He was god of this land long, long ago; before the Ortelgans brought their bear to Bekla, even; and it must be all of five hundred years now since they were driven out to their island in the Telthearna. You can tell who are the oldest peoples in the empire, so they say, by how much honour they pay to Shakkarn. Shakkarn's a god of country places, where he's been able to survive. And Cran or no Cran, when Shakkarn leaves the empire—which he will if ever people cease to honour him altogether—the empire will fall, and a good job too. He's a god of simple folk and rough old village temples—not a god of rich priests suckin' up to richer tyrants.'

136

'Oh, be careful, Occula!' whispered Chia, squinting up at her and putting a quick, restraining hand on her arm.

'You needn' look like that, with one eye on me and the other on the north end of south Belishba,' replied Occula. 'I'm worth far too much money to get into trouble in a dump like this. If we were in the upper city, now, that might be another matter. But anyway, just in case anyone doan' know, Shakkarn's big festival is held during the first days of autumn. And then every village that has a temple of Shakkarn decorates it with flowers and woven hangin's. Very often the women work half a year or more, weavin' them. And on the festival day the men all bring somethin' from their work or their trade: lambs or goats or calves if they're farmers, ironwork if they're smiths, leather if they're cobblers and so on. These are all called Shakkarn's sacrifices, whether they're livin' things or just things the men have made. And every unmarried girl over thirteen lets her hair grow all the year, cuts it off on the day of the festival and offers it to Shakkarn. And those are called the girls' sacrifices, but what use they are I'll be hanged if I ever heard.'

'Why, don't you know? They stuff quilts and pillows with them,' said Chia. 'Then anyone gets married, they spend their bridal night in the temple, soft and warm as you like. Makes the babies come; well, stands to reason, doesn't it?'

'Well, now I know, doan' I?' said Occula, rolling over comfortably to smile at her. 'Maybe I ought to try it myself, d'you think? Sounds like a bit of good stuffin', anyway. But I'm right, aren't I, that Shakkarn has no priests? His rites vary from one village to another, or so I've always been told. They're handed down from one generation to the next and just carried out by the village folk themselves.

'Well, to come back to Lespa. This autumn, in her village, Shakkarn's temple was being decorated from top to bottom and everythin' put to rights for the big festival. Masses of flowers had been brought in—wreaths of trepsis to make a splash, bunches of *planella* to scent the place, and so on—and the actual decoratin' was bein' done, on the day before the festival itself, by two old village wives who'd done the job for years and meant to go on doin' it every year until they were carried out kickin' and screamin'.'

'Ah, we had one or two like that round our way,' said Maia.

'Where haven' they? Well, that mornin' this precious two were hard at it, tyin' wreaths and flowers round all the pillars and pilin' green branches under the windows and so on. And then, after a time, they came to have a look at the altar itself.

'Now the altar had a beautiful, thick, fringed and embroidered cloth, which covered it all over and right down to the floor. It had been made years before, by about twenty of the village women workin' together for months, and it was reckoned to be just about the finest thing in the temple. People comin' from other parts were often invited to step in and admire it. But this mornin', when these two old dears came to decorate the altar, they were really upset to see somethin' they hadn't previously noticed. Somehow or other—probably mice—the fringe along the bottom of the altar cloth was hangin' off in several places; and just above the fringe, on one side, there were one or two little rents in the material as well.

'"Oh, just look at that, now!" says one of them. "That doan' look very nice at all, does it? That's got to be put right before tomorrow, that it has."

'"Yes, it certainly has," says the other. "But we haven' really got the time to be doin' it ourselves, have we? what with all these flowers and things still to get done."

'"Well, but we doan' want to be askin' any favours of other people," says the first one. "Not when everybody knows that it's us as decorates the temple and we've always told them we doan' need any help from anybody." So then they just sat down and had a bit of a think about it.

'"I'll tell you what," says the second one. "Come to look at it, we doan' really have to take the cloth off the altar to mend it, do we? I think it'd be too heavy for us to lift or carry, anyway. But if anyone didn' mind workin' sittin' or lyin' on the floor, they could mend it where it is, without havin' to move it at all."

'"That's a job for a young girl, then," says the first one. "And it would be easier to *ask* a young girl too, wouldn' it? A young girl wouldn' start sayin' 'Oh, fancy you needin' help! I thought you said you could do it all by yourselves'—same as some of the older ones might. Who do we know as'd do?"

'"Why, there's Lespa," says the other. "Very nice, obligin' girl; only lives just up the road, and her people are well off, they've probably got all the coloured thread she'd need as well. Then we wouldn' have to pay for it, even."

'"Fine, fine," says the first old tabby. So off they go up the road to knock on Lespa's door.

'Now young Baltis hardly ever stopped keepin' an eye on Lespa's door, even while he might be hammerin' out a bolt or fittin' a grate together. So it's not really surprisin' that he saw them come to the door, and he saw Lespa's mother answer it; and then after a bit Lespa gets called to the door too, and there she is noddin' and smilin', and then she runs back in and comes out with a work-box and she's holdin' up bits of this coloured thread and that, and there they all are clackin' away like rooks on a fine evenin'.

'Young Baltis doan' have to be a genius to work out that Lespa's goin' off to the temple to oblige the old girls with a bit of needlework. And the very notion of being able to meet her there fairly filled his heart to thumpin'. It so happened that the smith had gone off to talk to a farmer about a new well-head and chain, so Baltis, he just downs tools and slips out of the forge while they're still yammerin' away in the sunshine on the doorstep, and up the street he goes and into the empty temple.

'Well, when he got inside he was still supposin', you see, that he'd find himself alone with Lespa—for you know how often we let ourselves believe that what we'd like to happen is what's going to happen. And findin' the flowers lyin' in heaps all round the temple, he put together a posy, all different kinds—selvon and jennet and whitebells and so on—to give to Lespa when she arrived. And he was still sittin' there, imaginin' how he'd give them to her and what he'd say, when suddenly, just outside, he heard the voices of the two old girls as they came back, bringin' Lespa with them.

'Baltis knew that if they found him in there they'd know very well why he'd come, and he didn' fancy being made to look a fool in front of Lespa; but there seemed to be nowhere to hide. I suppose the temple wasn't all that big and hadn't got much in the way of odd corners. Anyway, just as he was at his wits' end, he realized that there was only one place out of sight, and that was under the altar-coverin'; and he just had time to slip in underneath it before Lespa and the others came in.

'The altar was just a big, solid table, really, and Baltis was crouchin' under it, with the thick cloth hangin' right down to the floor all round him, when he heard the three of them come up and stop right beside him— just the cloth between them, not three feet apart.

' "Do you think you can do it, dear, without takin' the cloth off?" asks one of the old dears: and Lespa says, "Oh, yes, säiyett, I'm sure I can do that—just stitch up the fringe and mend those few rents, is it? I've got some matchin' thread here. I doan' think it'll show at all."

'So after a bit more talk the two old things went back to their decoratin' at the other end of the temple, leavin' Lespa to get down to work.

'Lespa went down on one knee, put on her thimble and picked up the hem of the altar cloth in her left hand to get a closer look at it. She'd just put it down again and was holdin' her needle up to the light, when she felt somethin' ticklin' her foot, looked down and saw it was a yellow bloom of cassia. She thought it must have fallen off the altar, so she picked it up and put it to one side. She'd just threaded the needle when she felt the ticklin' again, and she looked down and there was another bloom on her foot; and this time she saw the hand that had put it there, and she recognized it by a scar on one of the fingers. She peeped under the altar cloth and there was Baltis, smilin', with his finger on his lips. The next moment he'd drawn

139

her in under the cloth and was kissin' her so hard that she couldn' draw breath to utter a word.

'He was still kissin' her when one of the old women called out from the other end of the temple, "Why, wherever have you got to, Lespa dear? Are you all right?"

'Baltis let her go then, and she put out her head and said, "Oh, fine, säiyett, thank you! I was just havin' a look from inside, to see if the light would show any little holes I hadn't noticed. I'm just goin' to make a start now."

'And then she tried to come out, but she couldn', or not altogether, because Baltis had his hands round her two ankles.

'"Let me go! Baltis, sweetheart, let me go!" she whispered: and then she suddenly realized that she didn' want him to let her go. She was sick of always being made to send Baltis away, and of havin' him sent away just when she wanted to keep him with her; and now here he was, cracklin' like a summer fire in the gorse. Besides, pretty Lespa had a great sense of mischief even then—though as you know she's got an even bigger one now—and the situation amused her.

'"I think the best way I can tackle this will be to get right down to it and make myself comfortable, säiyett, if that'll be all right," she called. "The cloth's rather too heavy to hold up for long, you see." And the old girl called back, "Yes, of course, dear, just do it in any comfortable position that suits you."'

'Oo hoo! Oo hoo! I know what's coming!' bubbled Chia.

'Well, don't *tell* us, will you?' said Maia. 'We simply can't imagine! Go on, Occula: never mind her.'

'So then pretty Lespa rolls up her cloak and puts it behind her head, lies down with her head and shoulders just clear of the altar cloth and begins stitchin' the fringe back on the hem. But soon it was as much as she could do to stop herself cryin' out from—well, I suppose from—er—agitation: or it might be, disturbance. And perhaps she might have stood up and put an end to it, only that was no longer possible, you see, because by now the ladies had worked their way rather further up the temple towards her; and under the altar cloth she was all disarranged—to say the least—and they'd have seen. Besides, she was very much in two minds, for that's fishin' country, is Suba, and Baltis had been ticklin' trout almost since he could walk. It's no good startlin' them, you know. They've got to be sort of hypnotized, so that they enjoy it.

'And then, all in a moment, she went "Ah!" so loud that the two old ladies fairly jumped.

'"Why, whatever's the matter, dear?" called one of them. "Have you hurt yourself?"

'"Oh, no, no, säiyett—thank you!" answered Lespa, as well as she could for the delicious agony. "I—er—I just caught my finger with the needle, that's all."

'"Oh, poor thing! I'm so sorry!" said the old lady. "It gives you such a shock, doesn't it? to get a sudden prick like that: but it woan' go on hurtin' very long, you know. Is it bleedin'?"

'"Well, no, only just a little, säiyett," gasped Lespa. "It feels better already, thank you."'

At this point the story-teller was obliged to pause, sitting unsmiling in the midst of her convulsed audience.

'Same old tripe, banzi,' muttered the black girl under her breath to the hysterical Maia. 'You'd really wonder, wouldn', you, sometimes? Do you want me to go on?' she enquired of the others in freezing tones.

'Yes! Yes!'

'Just as well I'm not down in the market, isn't it?' said Occula. 'Then it'd be half-melds in the cup all round. You're gettin' this for free—same as Baltis did. All right, shut up then and I'll go on.

'And now, indeed, sweet Lespa could scarcely tell whether she was stitchin' for the god or the god was stitchin' her, for such exquisitely fine stitchin' was altogether outside her experience and quite carried her away. And indeed, we must believe that the god had lent Baltis some of his miraculous powers, for you'll agree that a young man that could eat strawberries and angle in a pool at one and the same time, and never make a sound either, must have had somethin' god-like in him. At all events, Lespa felt that she had something god-like in her, and more than she could well endure for pleasure; and she clasped the hem of the altar cloth close before her face and drew the thread back and forth, back and forth, all ways at once and any way but the right one, and fairly bit her lip over the delicate task she'd undertaken.

'And then, suddenly, she cried aloud in all earnest, writhin' and moanin' where she lay under the altar, for she no longer knew where she was or what she was doin'.

'Now it so happened that at this moment the two good old souls were busy fastenin' some long strands of green ivy to hang right across the temple aisle from one column to another. One of them was up a ladder tyin' the ivy-trail as high as she could, while the other was steadyin' the foot of the ladder and makin' useless suggestions. And suddenly, in the middle of their labours, they heard Lespa cry out, and turned round to see her writhin' like a snake under a farmer's hoe.

'"Oh, good gracious! Oh, dear Shakkarn!" they shrieked. "Oh, the poor girl's been taken with a fit! What shall we do?"

'"Help me down, dear, quick!" cried the one up the ladder. "Doan' stop holdin' it till I'm down or it'll slip! I'll be as quick as I can, but I daren' risk a fall!"

'But Lespa's thrashin' and crowin' had thrown them into such a state that in fact it was a good half-minute before they'd got themselves into marchin' order and come up to the altar, where she was still lyin' on the floor. And by this time she was feelin' a little calmer, and so contented with herself and the world that she felt equal to anythin'.

'"What is it, dear?" asked the first old lady. "Have you been taken ill? Where do you feel the pain?"

'"I'm so sorry, säiyett," gasped Lespa, hurriedly pulling the altar-cloth tighter round her shoulders. "It's the cramp! I've been taken with the cramp!"

'"Oh, you poor thing! Give me your hands, dear, and I'll pull you up."

'But they couldn' pull her up, and this was hardly surprisin', for Baltis was holdin' on to her legs and tryin' to put her clothes straight at the same time.

'"I'll run and get the smith, or else that nice young Baltis who works for him," said the second old girl. "You stay here with her, dear, and I'll be back directly." And off she ran.

'When she'd gone, Lespa said to the other one, "Dear säiyett, would you be so very kind as to bring me a drink of water? I'm sure that would make me feel much better."

'"Yes, yes, of course, dear," says she, and hurried away to the stream outside. And when she came back with the water, there was sweet Lespa sittin' quietly on the steps in front of the altar, a little dishevelled but otherwise none the worse.

'"Oh, it seems to have passed off, säiyett, thank goodness," says she. "I wonder, would you be so good as just to give me your arm into the fresh air for a few minutes? I'm sure I'll be quite all right then."

'And while they were takin' a turn, young Baltis slipped out and got back to the forge unmissed, for the smith hadn' yet returned from his trip to the farm.

'As for Lespa, she was right as rain in no time, wouldn' you just know, and mended the altar cloth in half an hour. And that evenin', when she'd shorn her hair for the sacrifice, she went singin' about the kitchen and made a huge game pie to take to the feast the next day.

'Everyone swore it was a pie in a thousand, but then Lespa was so pretty that they'd have said as much if it had been made of pebbles topped off with a sheet of lead. And when the feast was finished and before the dancin' began, she told her parents to stay where they were and slipped back home again, like the good girl she was, to see to her old granny, who was too rheumaticky to do more than sit at the door and listen to the music.

142

'"Well, dearest child," quavered the old granny, "did you make your sacrifice to Shakkarn?"

'"Yes, that I did," says she. "The finest sacrifice that ever a girl made to Shakkarn."

'"And did they like your pie?"

'"Indeed they did, granny. And now I'm such a fine pastry-cook, believe me, I'll never be without a good rollin'-pin as long as I live."'

'Now then, you girls,' said Vartou, appearing in the doorway. 'Off to bed with you, and if anyone disturbs me in the night without some very good reason, she'll just wish she hadn't, that's all. You, Chia, make sure the fire's out, too.'

'Come on, banzi,' said Occula, putting her arm round Maia as the woman shut and locked the heavy door behind her, 'these beds are narrower than a bloody drain, but you can go back to your own later.'

Maia hesitated. 'Here? With all of them—'

'Nothin' wrong with sharin' a bed,' said the black girl. 'And from all I can see, we're not the only ones. 'Sides, you doan' know where you might be tomorrow night, do you?'

: 17 :

LALLOC

After returning to her own bed Maia slept soundly and, waking an hour or two after dawn, found the fire already lit and three or four of the girls cooking breakfast. Occula, however, was still asleep and, when Maia brought her breakfast to her bed and woke her, showed no particular inclination to be up and stirring.

'I doan' think there's any particular hurry for us, banzi,' she said, lying back and letting Maia feed her with new bread dipped in honey. 'They'll send for us all right, but it woan' be for a while.'

'How d'you know?' asked Maia.

'Oh, I just know. Try goin' in the bath-house and tell me what happens.'

Maia, puzzled, followed her advice, and was immediately stopped in the cloister by Vartou, who sent her back with orders to wash up the breakfast plates and sweep the floor. About an hour later she called Maia and Occula and told them to bath.

The stone trough in the bath-house had already been refilled with clean, scented water and Maia, trying it with her foot, found that it was delightfully warm—just right. After two of the best meals she had ever had in her life, separated by a long sleep in a comfortable bed, her normal appetite for pleasure was beginning, despite her troubles, to return. Without more ado she unrolled the bandage from her ankle, stripped and gave herself up to the water. After soaking for some time, she and Occula proceeded to amuse themselves by making use of every brush, vessel and unguent they could find in the room, soaping, scrubbing and rinsing each other until at length Vartou, flouncing in, ordered them to dry and get dressed.

'Do you girls mean to keep U-Lalloc waiting half the morning?' she snapped, pulling the wooden plug out of the trough. 'A fine way to start off on the right foot, I'm sure!'

'But *have* we been keepin' him waitin', säiyett?' asked Occula, smiling at her rather slyly. 'I rather thought we'd been obligin' him.'

'Your tongue's too long by half, miss,' answered Vartou. 'Just you get on and do as I say, now, else you'll soon wish you had.'

Maia had entirely forgotten about their impending inspection by Lalloc. Now, as she sat on her bed combing her hair, her hands began to tremble with apprehension and she could hardly restrain her tears. Occula came across the room, knelt on the floor in front of her and, reaching up, took her chin between her hands.

'Take it easy, banzi. They're not goin' to hurt us and there's plenty worse things—toothache, for instance. I'd rather this than toothache, wouldn' you?'

'But—but he'll want to see us naked—'

''Course not,' replied Occula. 'He's done that already, you goat!'

'When has he?'

'Why, in the damn' bath-house, of course! Didn' you notice that muslin panel in the wall, by the corner? Of course, you've never been in a pleasure-house, have you? They nearly always have them in one or two of the rooms. Some people like to watch other people, you know. Made me feel quite at home to see a muslin panel again.'

'But did you *see* him there?'

'No, 'course not; you can't; that's what the muslin's for. But I didn' *need* to. I just showed off for all I was worth. Come to think of it, it's rather lucky I *didn'* tell you, isn' it? Poor pet, you'd have been all elbows and knees, wouldn' you? What d'you think all that scented water and stuff were for? You doan' suppose they get all that ready for Urtan cows who squint, do you? That was for us—special. Cheer up, you woan' have to strip again—not jus' yet, anyway. And whatever happens, I'll be there.'

When they came into Vartou's room, Maia immediately got another surprise. Insofar as she had thought about Lalloc, she had imagined someone middle-aged and stout, bearded and wearing a robe. The man sitting at Vartou's table, however, was no more than twenty-eight or thirty, heavily-built certainly, but clean-shaven, fair-haired, and (to the eyes of a peasant girl if not to those of a lady) smartly turned out, in the gaudy style of the Deelguy—a sort of blend of gipsy and flash magsman. He was wearing gold earrings, a crimson-and-blue scarf, a yellow jerkin with a large brooch of Telthearna aquamarines, and leather breeches dyed dark-red. Various papers were lying before him, including the letter brought by Occula, and as the girls entered he concluded his perusal of one of these before looking up and motioning them to sit down on the bench in front of the table. Zuno, standing behind him, nodded coldly to Occula and then whispered to Vartou behind his hand.

'Ah!' said Lalloc, smiling at Occula and speaking with a strong Deelguy accent. 'You're the black girl from Modom Domris? She toll me all about you, said you're a good girl, fully trained.'

'I hope so, sir,' answered Occula.

'Well, you been soveral years with Domris, you'll be good enoff in bed, she say so.' He tapped the letter. 'What about wait at table—she don't say about thot?'

'I've had plenty of trainin' and experience, sir.'

'You rockon you're fit to go to household of a rich man in the opper city?'

'Yes, sir, I do.'

'But thot's high-class work, now,' said Lalloc, staring at her shrewdly. 'All kinds of work, too. No good if you don't foncy it. You don't foncy it, you say now, not later. Then I soll you somewhere else, what you foncy—jost to oblige Domris, you know.'

'Thank you, sir. I'd like a rich household in the upper city. I'm talented, and I can assure you that your reputation as a dealer woan' suffer through me.'

Lalloc picked up the letter and rapidly re-read it. 'I soll you on approval, we hope you don't come bock, eh? But I suppose Domris don't be solling you to me onless she think you're good.'

Putting the letter back on the table, he picked up an abacus and began making calculations. At length Occula said, 'May I ask you about the money, sir?'

'Monny?' replied Lalloc, looking up at once.

'Yes, sir. Madam Domris promised me five hundred meld for myself out of the purchase money.'

'Ah,' replied Lalloc, 'thot's if we're gotting what we hope for.'

'Sir, may I beg you very respectfully to put yourself in my position? I've come here at my own request, to do you credit and make my fortune, if I can. I haven' any money at all. A little of my own, for minor expenses, will make a lot of difference to the amount of credit I can do you.'

'Well—well—' Lalloc made an impatient gesture—'likely we monage something, if thot's what Domris say. Now this other girl—' he turned towards Maia, who blushed and looked down at the floor—'we don't know nothing about her. She's surplus to the Tonilda quota, Zuno, thot's it?'

'Yes, sir. I gather Megdon—'

'Vorry nice—*vorry* nice,' said Lalloc, regarding Maia with a smile and rubbing his hands together. 'How you say Megdon gotting her?'

'I—er—gather, sir,' drawled Zuno, 'that Megdon—or Perdan—one of our men in Tonilda, anyway—was in the neighbourhood of a place called Meerzat, when he was approached by a woman who said she wanted to sell the girl. He went and inspected her; and not unnaturally he bought her.'

'How moch he pay?'

'You have his receipt, sir: I gave it to Vartou last night.'

'And *I* say, how moch he *pay*? You trost Megdon?' said Lalloc.

'I trust no one, sir, in the trade—except yourself, of course. Megdon bought the girl from an illiterate peasant woman, and there is his receipt. As you can see, it's for much less than we can hope to get for a girl like this: that's all I can say. Megdon will no doubt be rendering his accounts next month as usual.'

There was a pause.

'Who's this who soll you?' said Lalloc to Maia.

'My—my mother, sir,' whispered poor Maia almost inaudibly.

'Step-mother?'

'No, sir.'

'Your *real* mother soll you? Why?'

'I don't—I don't know, sir.'

Lalloc leant across the table and gripped Maia's chin so that she was forced to meet his eye. 'You been on a game, hov you? Hovving baby? Or maybe you try to kill her, eh? Come on, you toll us now.'

Maia, jerking away from him and burying her face in her hands, began to weep uncontrollably. Occula bent over her, doing her best to calm her. Vartou clicked her tongue impatiently. Lalloc sat back, drumming his fingers on the table.

'Shall I bring her to her senses, sir?' asked Vartou.

'No,' said Lalloc. 'Dozzn't motter—not thot moch. I jost want to know she's not sick and she's not hovving baby, that's all. If not, we soll her straightaway: soll her good, too.'

'Will you be selling her to the same house as me, sir?' asked Occula.

'Don't be fool,' said Lalloc. 'We soll you fourteen, maybe fifteen thousand; you think the man pay two lots like that, one time, eh?'

Maia, clutching at Occula and crying hysterically, was jerked to her feet by Vartou, who held her upright and put a hand over her mouth.

'You botter take her outside, Vartou,' said Lalloc. 'Calm her down; but don't mark or bruise her, you see? Not like thot one last month you knock her teeth out. Thot's jost waste of monny. You jost see you can find out she's not sick, thot's all.'

'I think I can tell you all you want to know, sir,' said Occula, as the door closed behind Maia and the woman. 'The girl's told me her story, and I'm sure it's true. While she was at home she became the mistress of her step-father, but she's never had anyone else in her life. They're a poor family—hardly food enough to go round, she told me, and the mother pregnant herself. She found out what was goin' on and sold the girl out of resentment and jealousy, while the step-father was away on some business or other. She's not diseased and I'm good as certain she's not pregnant.'

'Why you ask me soll her with you?' asked Lalloc.

'Well, chiefly because I like her, sir, and she likes me: I admit that. But I can see advantages for yourself. She's very young and completely inexperienced, and I can train her better than anyone else because she trusts me and isn' afraid of me. I think, with her looks and mine—you know, the contrast—we could come to work very well together. She'll do much better and be more of a credit to your fine reputation as a dealer if I can look after her and make her less nervous—which I'm sure I can.' Her eye flickered towards Zuno. 'Doan' you agree, sir? Didn' you think, for instance, that she seemed rather nervous at—well, at *Khasik*? You recall the night at Khasik?'

Zuno paused. 'Well—er—well, we need hardly talk about Khasik now; but perhaps there may be something in what you say. I'm inclined to agree, sir, with what this girl suggests. Always provided, of course, that it's possible to sell them together for a good total figure.'

Lalloc considered. From what Domris had told him this black girl, apart from her unusual and striking looks, was sharp and able—a girl out of the ordinary. She was likely to go far—indeed, in the present state of Bekla, no one could say how far. A rich voluptuary's pet concubine; a baron's favourite shearna—there was no telling. One of the built-in features of the bed-girl trade (and he had known others come unstuck through it) was that while there were big profits to be made out of such girls while they were young and starting out, it might later prove important—you could never tell—not to have antagonized them. Conversely, if they retained not-too-unpleasant memories of the way you had treated them, they could in time become influential friends and valuable sources of information. Indeed, he recalled that Hosein, a former dealer at the time of the Leopard

147

rising six or seven years ago, had been able to cut and run just in time, following a word from a girl who owed him a good turn.

'Well,' he said at length, 'we try it, Occula. But it's expocting something, I toll you. This is roch man all right, oh, yes, but I don't think he spond thot moch—and if he don't, thot's it and nobody making trobble, right?'

'Yes, sir.'

'Maybe I give you your monny now, then no one olse see. You got where you can put it?'

'Yes, sir.'

'We going opper city this morning. You—well, you don't need hair-drosser; only the other girl. You need clothes?'

'I have some clothes with me, sir, which suit me very well, I think. You'll judge for yourself. But my friend will need some.'

'You botter go now, talk to her. She got to look nice: no good we gotting there she's making a foss, look like she been crying.'

'She woan', sir. Leave it to me.'

An hour later Maia, dressed in a close-fitting, low-cut, green-and-white robe, her golden hair combed smooth and falling over her bare shoulders, was being carried with Occula in a curtained litter up the Street of the Armourers to the Peacock Gate, the only entrance from the lower to the upper city. Here Lalloc, the girls, litter-bearers and all were conducted to the enclosed chamber known as the Moon Room, searched and their identities noted; for even a dealer of Lalloc's standing was not immune from the strict and vigilant surveillance imposed by the Leopard régime. Finally the litter itself was also searched. Thereupon the porter operated the counter-poise that opened the postern and Lalloc, followed by his wares, proceeded towards the group of wealthy houses east of the Barb, one of which was that of Sencho-bè-L'vandor, High Counsellor of the Beklan Empire.

: PART II :

THE SLAVE-GIRL

SENCHO

His Worthiness Sencho-bè-L'vandor, High Counsellor of Bekla, was, in this seventh year of the reign of Durakkon, forty-five years of age, a leading member of the Leopard faction and one of the wealthiest and most powerful men in the empire.

He had been born in the lower city of Bekla, the bastard of a common prostitute. By the age of ten he had already been trained both to tout and to steal and, being a very personable child when clean, had also learned a good deal on his own account about turning to profit the sexual propensities of grown men and women. At this time his mother, having taken up with a gang of thieves and realizing that her life was in danger through knowing too much about a murder, fled across the Vrako and ended in Zeray, leaving Sencho to fend for himself. A certain steward who pandered to his master's proclivities, catching sight one day of the handsome child begging at the back door, gave him a place in the kitchen; and a week or two later, having satisfied himself that his judgement had been correct and that the lad would do, brought him before his master, the prosperous iron-merchant Fravak.

Fravak, sitting in his courtyard after dinner on an afternoon of early summer, thrust a hand tipsily under the boy's tunic and, fondling and pinching, questioned him about his past experience, concluding by requiring him to demonstrate one or two of his claims. Some time later, before settling himself comfortably to sleep, he instructed the steward to take Sencho away and prepare him for his future rôle in the household.

For the next ten or twelve weeks the boy was confined to a luxuriously-furnished room on the upper floor of Fravak's mansion. Here he had a private balcony and bathroom and his own personal slave, a girl from Gelt who said little but carried out conscientiously her duties of attending to his health, of oiling and massaging his body and above all, of compelling him to eat.

He was required to eat almost from morning to night—quantities of rich, delicious food, gradually increased as the weeks went by. Whenever he would not or could not eat more he was beaten with a pliant cane, until he lay screaming on the thickly-carpeted floor. When he succeeded in eating even more than was demanded of him he was rewarded with gifts; pretty boxes, combs and necklaces, or with money which he was encouraged to send the slave-girl out to spend on his behalf. When not eating or sleeping he lay in the sun, in order that his smooth, oiled flesh might not grow pallid with confinement; learned to read, write and sing; and practised certain other skills in which his master wished him to become adept.

After some three months he had acquired an almost insatiable capacity for rich food and become, in his upstairs boudoir, as plump as a quail ready for the pot. His cunning was no less but his well-being and energy had much increased. At once firm and soft, his buttocks, arms and legs dimpled with chubby, rosy flesh, his belly round and smooth as a gourd, he was again presented to the merchant to take up the duties for which he had been so assiduously prepared.

At first, however, he had relatively little to do by day. When his master returned from business in the evening, Sencho would prepare his bath and then join him in it to soap and oil him; and later, would dry and massage him, either on the balcony or, if it were the rainy season, in the warmth of the bedroom. After this he would accompany him to dinner and wait upon him. The boy learned to carve, to serve vegetables and cheeses, to pour wine and to mix all manner of liquors and syllabubs. Watching him as he went about his duties, the merchant would sigh with contentment and, when the other servants had been dismissed from the room, would call him to stand beside his couch, loosen his clothes and caress his limbs and body. Then, shuddering with pleasure and drawing the boy down beside him in the cushions, he would sodomize him.

Sencho's sharp wits did not desert him, and neither did his constant awareness of where his own best interests lay. The merchant, as he grew older and still more wealthy, acquired other boys and these Sencho, so far from treating with jealousy or malice (which would only have precipitated his own return to the gutter or the slave market), took care to encourage and to praise to his master, at the same time making sure that Fravak appreciated that he himself had played a large part in preparing and training them for his enjoyment. By imperceptible degrees his function in the household changed from that of a catamite to a procurer and supervisor of the iron-merchant's pleasures. No boy could hope to remain long in Fravak's favour unless he cultivated Sencho's as well, but a boy who showed that he was ready to accept Sencho's instructions was given them in full measure, since it suited Sencho to be relieved of the tedious task of simulating enjoyment in order to flatter and gratify the merchant. Besides, he was now beginning to take more than a little interest in women and accordingly preferred to avoid wasting nights in his master's bed. By the time he was sixteen, though he sometimes, at the merchant's bidding, used to amuse him by bringing girls to his room and there doing with them as he wished, he played almost no other direct part in his pleasures.

Next—watching every opportunity to run errands to and from those with whom Fravak did business, and to accompany him to the metal-market and his warehouses—he set himself to learn all that he could about the iron trade and Fravak's interests in it. Making himself agreeable to other dealers, who knew his influence with Fravak and wished to make use of him if they could, he kept his ear close to the ground. One day, having slipped away to the house of a copper-merchant who had more than once importuned him, he was refreshing himself in the bath after the strenuous activities required of him, when a friend of his new patron called on business. Having been hospitably offered them by the copper-merchant, this friend also availed himself of the boy's pleasant services. Afterwards the two men, relaxing contentedly over their wine, spoke frankly and unguardedly together of certain business plans, while Sencho lay in bed pretending slumber. What he heard that afternoon, duly related to Fravak, saved his master from becoming the victim of a scheme which would almost certainly have ruined him.

Understanding from henceforth what a pearl he had in Sencho—for the matter was complicated, and not every youth would have comprehended the significance of what he had overheard—Fravak henceforth gave him every opportunity to educate himself in the business. Once, having been entrusted with an important mission to Gelt itself, he returned with not only the problem untangled but also a pretty little boy whom he had spotted in an iron-master's household and bought for Fravak on his own initiative. This was characteristic of his cunning, for while building up his own grasp of the business he also took care to see that Fravak, as he aged, became more and more indolent and addicted to luxury. After a time his dependence upon Sencho became virtually complete.

Sencho, however, was too clever to cheat his master, knowing that the merchant, who was (or had once been) no fool, would be expecting and watching for him to do just this. He was after a far bigger prize. The accounts he rendered were honest and accurate. The reports and news which he brought to Fravak were reliable. He himself lived plainly and took care that his sprees were intermittent and indulged away from the household. Except when bidden, for his master's titillation and amusement, he never touched any girl about the place. Over the years he was successful in convincing the lonely and ageing merchant of what he wanted to believe; namely, that here at least was one friend who felt genuine affection and loyalty towards him, one whom he could trust and deserved his gratitude. For the merchant (like Occula) felt a need for someone towards whom he could honestly feel he had behaved generously.

One spring day, when Sencho was in his twenty-fifth year, the elderly Fravak revealed to him that he had made him his heir and intended him, as the reward of his faithful services, to succeed to the control of the iron business. Sencho, who did not mean to remain buying and selling metal all his life, now realized that it was vital that he should take the next step before anything might happen to cause Fravak to change his mind.

The murder was astonishingly easy. At this particular time the merchant had two favourites, one a merry, lewd-minded little Yeldashay boy, ten years old and shaping well; the other, who had been longer in the household, a dark, handsome, thirteen-year-old Katrian, taken in a raid across the Zhairgen north of Dari-Paltesh, not popular in the household on account of speaking little or no Beklan and all too plainly regarding himself as still an enemy of Bekla. At first Fravak had greatly enjoyed this boy, but of late had begun to prefer the Yeldashay lad as being more ingenious and reciprocal. Sencho, who of course had a key to his master's room, simply went to it in the middle of the night when Fravak and the lad were asleep, stabbed them both and then left the knife and his key in the Katrian boy's bed. As Fravak's heir and representative at law he gained credit for earnestly begging the authorities that the boy, on account of his youth, should receive a quick and merciful death. The last thing he wanted was for the boy to be tortured, for those *in extremis* speak the truth, and an experienced examiner is adept at perceiving when they are doing so. The boy's continued insistence on his innocence might have given rise to speculation.

At first Sencho was content to use Fravak's money in pitting his wits against other iron-merchants, in entering new areas of trade—cloth, rope and precious stones—and in indulging his greed and lust more fully and pleasantly than had been possible before. Fravak had been a sound rather than an enterprising merchant and, despite the fact that he traded a great deal in iron required for weapons and armour, had never felt any inclination, in his dealings with the Beklan military commanders, to advance himself other than financially. By contrast, Sencho was consumed with the desire for real and actual power.

At this period of the empire's history—inevitably, in a semi-barbaric country where roads and transport were still rudimentary—the scope of the central authority was limited. Bekla itself, of course, was a natural focal point or hub for communications and trade. Centuries before, the barons of Bekla, able to exercise control over this important cross-roads and commercial centre, had turned the city's position to advantage by collecting dues from those who came to trade in or travel through it. These had been Senda-na-Say's ancestors—controllers of an asset which the provinces around them could not well do without, and for the benefit of which they were accordingly ready to pay. Later, as Bekla's prestige, wealth and strength gradually grew, they also became prepared to bid against one another for its support. Lapan would ask for protection against Yelda, Urtah against Paltesh, and so on. It became Bekla's policy to exploit a rudimentary balance of power. Sometimes payment was made in money, cattle or slaves; sometimes by way of a pact which further extended Beklan authority.

Gradually a hegemony emerged, centring on Bekla and extending from Belishba to the Vrako and from Yelda to the Telthearna. But although Bekla now collected taxes and controlled a standing army made up of contingents from the provinces, the autonomy of the provincial barons was certainly not at an end. Once, for example, when the army had been ordered to Sarkid to enforce a Beklan tax decree, the Sarkid contingent deserted at the frontier, the army encountered strong local resistance and the end of the business was a very nominal and face-saving enforcement of the decree for a year, after which it was conveniently forgotten. Sarkid, of course, with its ruling line descended from the legendary hero U-Deparioth, had always been an exceptionally proud and independent province, but the incident exemplified clearly enough that the provinces and their baronial rulers were by no means entirely under Beklan control.

The provincial barons met yearly, in the great Palace on the Leopard Hill, at the time of the spring festival held to celebrate the Sacred Queen's ceremonial union with the god Cran. At these meetings oaths of loyalty were sworn, the empire's affairs-in-common were discussed and policy more-or-less agreed upon; but the house of na-Say had learned, over many years, that the continuance of its power was only partly dependent upon intimidation. Equally important were first, the benefits it could grant or withhold—namely, help in emergency, assistance with civil works and enforcement of law and order—and secondly, the exercise of a prudent discretion in ignoring provincial quarrels unless and until they went too far.

The empire's intermittent war with Terekenalt, on its western borders, had lasted longer than living memory. The kingdom of Terekenalt was a relatively small country, no bigger than two Beklan provinces put together, but its people were hardy, warlike and almost entirely loyal to an able monarchy. The war, conducted in difficult country between armies able to campaign effectively only during the summer months, was for the most part an affair of personal exploits, skirmishes, raids, burnings and lootings. Every now and then, however, under the leadership of some determined captain on one side or the other, it would flare up into a more serious business. The Zhairgen, down the last fifty miles of its length, represented a considerable obstacle between the contestants. Nevertheless, it was crossed again and again by commanders of both sides eager to prove their worth and to take booty.

The principal contested area was Suba, the watery region lying between the Zhairgen on the west and its tributary, the Valderra, on the east. This, somewhat tenuously owing allegiance to Urtah, was (as Occula described it in her story) marsh and fishing country, full of lakes, criss-crossed by tributaries of both rivers and inhabited from time immemorial by men

155

inured to swamps and mists, accustomed to building their dwellings on islands or even on stilts above the water, and expert in the use of rafts, boats and nets. To the Beklans it was unarguable that the natural frontier between Terekenalt and the empire was the River Zhairgen. The kings of Terekenalt considered that it should be the River Valderra. From time to time Terekenalt would invade Suba—insofar as anyone could effectively invade such a country—until the empire, goaded into concerted action, would mount an expedition to repulse so serious a threat to Urtah and Paltesh.

Immediately to the west of the Zhairgen lay the Terekenalt province of Katria, the northern part of which comprised the wild and dangerous Blue Forest. Keril, the principal town of Katria, had more than once been menaced by a Beklan raiding force, but never as yet taken.

So matters stood some two or three years after Sencho's inheritance of the wealth of Fravak. About this time there appeared two figures—one on each side—whose respective effects were to strengthen Terekenalt's ambition to take Suba; and to weaken the resistant power of Paltesh and hence of the empire itself.

On the one hand, King Karnat succeeded to the throne of Terekenalt. Even in a long line of warlike kings, Karnat was egregious. In the first place he was, physically, almost a giant—immensely tall, and well-made in proportion. The very sight of him was enough to inspire his subjects and followers with admiration and confidence. Secondly, he soon showed himself an active leader, aggressive and daring—the kind of man whose latest exploit is related from mouth to mouth. Finally he was, in a rudimentary way, a diplomat, taking pains to conciliate local nobility in outlying parts of the Beklan Empire. It was rumoured that his agents had even travelled as far as Chalcon, the wild and mountainous country lying between Tonilda and Yelda, though of this there was no real proof. What was clear, however, was that Karnat the Tall was hell-bent on an effort, more determined than any made by his predecessors, to conquer and integrate Suba.

On the other hand, upon the sudden death of her father, the High Baron Kephialtar-ka-Voro, a young woman named Fornis became, at seventeen, the eristic ruler of Paltesh. Fornis was Kephialtar's only child and he, foreseeing disputes following his death without a male heir (for he had lived many years in the shadow of this virtually certain eventuality), had already made two attempts to marry her to suitable young men, either of whom he would have been glad to regard as his successor. That Fornis should have succeeded personally in bringing both matches to nothing was matter for head-shaking in a country where daughters commonly did as they were told. At fifteen she had effectively subverted her father's choice of Renva-Lorvil, the eldest son of his most trusted commander—a young man, as everyone knew, ready to live and die for Paltesh. What had finally tipped the scale had been the puzzled, half-incredulous realization of the suitor himself—a likeable, straightforward youth—that in some odd way he was afraid of the girl and unmanned in her presence. She, for her part, while never saying or doing anything which could be singled out for rebuke, contrived to convince everyone that she despised Renva and found him ludicrous—and this even while seeming to obey her father's injunction to encourage and be pleasant to him. In time the sound of her detached, mocking laughter, simulating courteous reciprocity, became almost more than her father could bear. It was the young man himself who finally told Kephialtar, almost with tears, that he felt unable to go through with the business. Fornis's sustained front of self-possessed mordancy and contempt had defeated him. Frankly, he had no wish to spend the rest of his life with her.

The second rejection was a far more dramatic affair. Fornis was formally betrothed to Eud-Ecachlon, heir of the High Baron of Urtah—a less attractive young man than Renva, but politically an even better match from the point of view of her father and of Paltesh as a whole, since in time it would unite the two provinces and thus strengthen both against Terekenalt. Eud-Ecachlon, though not a fool, was a rather stolid and insensitive young man; not at all the sort to be either thrown off balance, like Renva, by a cold and malicious girl or, conversely, unduly enflamed if he had happened to be offered a warm and passionate one. Fornis's father—by the standards of his own society kindly and humane—thinking that the girl's unenthusiastic attitude might be due to a secret fear of marriage or of sex, and half-expecting some sort of trouble similar to that with Renva, talked seriously to her about her duty as his sole heiress and about the desperate need of Paltesh for political security. Fornis, seeming to acquiesce, met her bridegroom and complied with all the customary formalities.

A week before the wedding day, during a night of full moon, she vanished, taking with her her personal maid, Ashaktis, and two young men from the crew of her father's boat on the Zhairgen. These lads had happened to be the watch on the High Baron's moorings for the first part of that night, but whether they were secretly in Fornis's pay and had already agreed to come with her, or whether she had suborned them on the spot, no one ever knew. By the time they were missed it was reckoned that the light, swift boat they had taken must have had a start of a good thirty miles. Another was at once despatched to follow and find them, but everyone knew that unless they had come to grief, any serious hope of overtaking them—wherever they might be bound—was out of the question. Kephialtar's anxiety was greater than his anger, for he loved Fornis dearly and knew that she must be sailing straight down the lower Zhair-gen—several hours in full view from the Katrian bank.

Fornis, however, did not come to grief. Six days later, having sailed nearly two hundred miles down the Zhairgen and then the Telthearna, she landed at the Ortelgans' sacred island of Quiso and sought sanctuary of the Tuginda and her priestesses—a request never denied to any fugitive woman not guilty of a grave crime. And here she remained for two months, while the scandalous news of her exploit was bruited from Ortelga to Urtah, Dari and all over the empire.

Before the end of those two months, Kephialtar was killed in a brush with the Katrians.

Fornis, an exceptionally strong, energetic girl, returned to Dari on foot by way of Gelt and Bekla; a journey lasting three weeks. She was escorted by Ortelgans, for although Ashaktis was still with her, the two young sailormen were not. Indeed, where they went no one ever found out; but it was commonly supposed that they must be afraid of the probable conse-quences of showing their faces again in Paltesh. A few days after her arrival, having summoned her father's barons and commanders—all those who were not in the field against Karnat—she told them that she, the indisputable successor to her father, intended to rule Paltesh in her own right: she called upon them all for loyal allegiance and support.

Her announcement fell upon the province like hail in harvest. Everyone had hitherto supposed that if the girl had fled from her bridegroom and her wedding, it could only be because she had secretly promised herself to some other lover—an affair of the heart. Her tomboy reputation—though nothing scandalous was known against her—tended to support the notion. There were those who, unenthusiastic about Eud-Ecachlon, were ready to take her part, despite the appalling effect of what she had done on relations between Paltesh and Urtah. Ah, well, but she'd shown herself a fine, spirited girl, now, hadn't she?—too good by half for that thick Urtan fellow. She'd displayed dash and courage: she was her father's daughter all right. Depend upon it, her heart was already fixed on some young blade of lower birth than her father would have welcomed. Good luck to him, whoever he was! But who *was* he? It took them some time to become convinced that nothing like this was involved at all.

That the people in general were ready to condone and support her if they possibly could was in large measure due to Fornis's appearance and style. From the age of thirteen or fourteen the girl had been strikingly—almost magically—beautiful, the talk and pride of the province, her fame extending to Bekla and far beyond. Her exquisite, rather pale face and wide, green eyes were framed by a great mane of auburn hair which actually seemed to glow with a kind of incandescence so intense as almost to transcend nature. People stood and stared at her as they might have stared at some magnificent summer sunset, or the migrant purple *kynat* returned in spring. Beauty of this order (which again and again had blunted the edge of her father's anger) conferred on Fornis a power beyond her years. It was very difficult to resist her. Doors opened easily and objections tended to dissolve.

Together with this, however, she had tastes and leanings over which her uncles—her mother's family—had often expressed misgiving among themselves. Kephialtar had been much engaged in campaigning and all the other affairs of a border province. His wife was a placid, indolent woman, not given to taking a long view or considering consequences. As a child Fornis, lacking brothers and sisters, had been left a great deal with the servants. From their company she had acquired a racy élan, a sly and cunning opportunism in getting her own way, a great belief in the value of intimidation, an appetite for material possessions and a general conviction that principle and responsibility were so much pretentious rubbish. Whatever else she might have acquired was as yet uncertain; but there had been a whispered rumour, never allowed to reach the ears of her father, that once, when she was fourteen, she had been seen with her maid on the balcony of a room overlooking her private garden, pointing and laughing as though at a play, while below her, on the grass, her groom supervised the serving of a sow by a boar.

In company she was free and bold and from an early age well able to converse and hold her own with her father's subjects of all degrees; but particularly with soldiers, huntsmen, tradesmen and the like. Peasants on the whole she despised, preferring sharper performers and quicker wits.

When her father's barons had at length realized that in fact there had never been anyone whom Fornis wanted to marry, that she had no intention of marrying and seriously intended them to regard her as the actual ruler of Paltesh, there was grave disquiet. Inheritance by a female in her own right was unknown to Beklan tradition and custom. No female had ever attempted it. Yet since there was no written code of law, Fornis's design could not simply be declared invalid. If a man had daughters but no sons, then by custom the inheritance passed to his eldest daughter's husband. If his daughters were unmarried, then the male next of kin—his brother or cousin—had prior claim. As her maternal uncles were not slow to point out, there was no precedent for what Fornis meant to do. But among those with no personal interest the disquiet was scarcely less. For a girl of seventeen to rule a province herself, let alone a province at war, was of course out of the question. Who then was to be the real and actual ruler?

Fornis might, of course, have chosen a small executive council of five or six nobles and governed in her own name with their advice and support. If she had done this, she would probably (dependent upon results) have had sufficient baronial backing, despite her immodest audacity. But a responsible approach of this kind was altogether foreign to her character. Wayward, domineering and headstrong by nature, she enjoyed risk and excitement for their own sake. She also enjoyed provoking her father's former friends and flouting propriety and custom. At this time in her life she placed a high value on luxury and frivolous pleasure, and delighted in exploiting her appearance. Regarding this last, however, she was shrewd enough to realize that if once she gave herself to any man—whether in marriage or otherwise—its general power would diminish; and accordingly she took care that whatever older people might say about her behaviour, no one could credibly allege that she had ever been loose in the hilts. Here, however—as will be seen later—her natural propensities helped rather than hindered her.

By the customs of the society in which she lived, she should have been reprehended and brought to comply with what was expected of her and of womanhood. This her uncles attempted, but what Fornis had realized was that while she might be advised, browbeaten, importuned, even entreated to act in a conventional manner, she could not be compelled. The province was hers and this could not be gainsaid or altered. At one point an attempt was made to keep her under house arrest until she saw reason, but this failed on account of her widespread popularity among the common people who, as soon as they knew what was going on, demanded her release.

Gradually a *modus vivendi* evolved. The truth was that Fornis, in asserting her own right to Paltesh, had never intended actually to govern— a task far too tedious and demanding for her taste. What she wanted was simply to do as she pleased and have the spending of as much money as she could get her hands on. Left to herself, she would probably have beggared the province in five years and then sold it to the highest bidder. Her uncles, understanding the risk, finally made the best of a bad job. What this came down to was that they paid her a large allowance and governed the province in her name.

With this Fornis at first appeared content. But her uncles had under-rated her. If they had known what she was capable of they would certainly, despite the unforeseeable consequences, have had her assassinated. For a time she amused herself with various extravagances in Dari, spending not only her own money but also that of any young noble or rich man's son sufficiently infatuated to give her more. Her personal daring and bravado added greatly to her popularity among those with no responsibility in the province, and stories were always circulating of her audacious exploits; how she had joined in following up a wounded leopard in close country; scaled a sheer cliff for a wager; or plunged forty feet from a promontory into the Zhairgen.

After a time, however, beginning to tire of Dari, she started making trips to Bekla. Here, naturally enough, she soon became all the rage among the younger men in the upper city, where she bought a house and entertained lavishly. In reply to those who condemned the shameless freedom of her behaviour—nothing like it had been seen before in the empire, where women of good family lived in relative seclusion—her adherents pointed out that at all events her chastity was indisputable and beyond question; she was just a fine, spirited girl. And since she spent much time in the company not only of young nobles but of influential and well-connected men such as senior army officers, most people assumed that her real intention must be to find herself a husband, one who could rule Paltesh with her or for her. In this, however, they were mistaken.

At this time the empire was enjoying greater prosperity than ever before, due partly to increasing exploitation of its natural resources and partly to the growth of trade to the southward, beyond Yelda. The landed nobility were ceasing to be the only wealthy class. Fortunes were being made, particularly by those dealing in luxuries—builders, stone-masons, purveyors of slaves, and merchants buying and selling metals and jewels. Among the foremost of these was Sencho, who was seizing every opportunity to advance money and gain influence in the upper city. Needy and unscrupulous aristocrats were very much up his street, for what he was really seeking was the practical means to power.

Sencho had been in the same company as Fornis on at least six or seven occasions before she even became aware of him as an individual. When she did, she naturally despised him, since apart from being a merchant and a man of no birth—to say the least—he had never been a soldier, was neither a hunter nor an athlete and appeared to have no recreations apart from gluttony and loose women. Sencho, however, endured her contempt with the kind of indifference that a general on campaign might show towards severe weather. He simply took it in his stride. 'You can despise and insult me as much as you like,' his manner seemed to imply. 'Spit in my face if you want to. That's quite immaterial to what you do not as yet realize to be our mutual interest; to what I have to seek and to offer.'

Fornis became intrigued. She could perceive well enough—she had had sufficient experience for twenty girls—that whatever his designs might be, they were not sexual. She knew also that he was rich and cunning, while she herself was a feckless spendthrift with few ideas beyond luxury and the easy admiration of unprincipled people. (She received none, for example, from the High Baron Senda-na-Say, who pointedly ignored her and on public matters dealt direct with her uncles in Paltesh.)

In the end she decided to give Sencho an opportunity to talk to her freely, and with characteristic effrontery invited him to supper with her on the Bramba Tower of the Barons' Palace, dismissing her maids at the end of the meal. Nevertheless, she learned nothing of importance that evening, nor for several meetings after. At this stage Sencho wished only to gain more of her interest and confidence while he made preparations in other quarters. He would speak out in his own time, when he was ready. He lent her, however, a large sum of money.

He was ready in about ten months, towards the end of Fornis's next visit to the capital. She had run through twice as much as her uncles were prepared to give her for the following year, and was in debt both in Paltesh and Bekla. This she told Sencho in his own dining-room, but did not suggest another loan. That—or something—she knew he would offer un-solicited if it formed part of his scheme; and else not. Sencho, stuffing himself with peach pie and almonds, watched her closely as he listened; and then, perceiving that the time was ripe, at last spoke without reserve.

What he outlined—once it had become clear to her—made the blood beat in Fornis's head and aroused her so powerfully with its mixture of deadly risk, cruelty, wickedness and great gain that she almost offered herself to him on the spot. She realized, however, that this would merely earn his contempt. In the real world, appreciated by only a perceptive few, the enjoyment of bodies—zard and tairth—was a superficial matter. Anyone physically attractive was good enough for that. What lay between her and Sencho was something far colder and deeper. This real world she had now been invited to enter; if she chose. If not, she was free to decline, and know for ever after that her show of audacity and ruthlessness had been a mere act, a bluff which Sencho had called.

Sencho's proposition was that they should destroy the *de facto* government in Dari-Paltesh by first suborning the soldiery and then deliberately murdering her uncles and anyone else in their entourage sufficiently powerful to merit it. Thereafter Fornis would be able to live entirely as she wished and make use of as much of the provincial revenue as she liked. He himself would finance the preparations and provide the necessary bribes, which would need to be large. He also had, ready and willing to discuss the matter further, two suitable and resolute men—soldiers of fortune—who, with the co-operation of some of her own intimates in Paltesh, he felt would be equal to pulling off the necessary mutiny and bloodshed.

Fornis was fascinated by his contempt for humanity and his cold zest for gain through treachery and destruction. This, she now realized, was what she had unknowingly been seeking in flouting her family and outraging the orthodox. Those, though mere games of a child, had nevertheless served their turn by leading her to this present, clear vision. She had thought herself a hedonist; she had been wrong. She had been born for a more demanding, worthwhile vocation—the seizure and exercise of power.

Meeting Sencho's fellow-conspirators, her confidence grew. Han-Glat, aged about thirty, was a former slave promoted and freed after more than ten years' valuable service in the army, during which he had distinguished himself by showing remarkable ability in the sphere of fortifications and similar military works. Nothing would appear more natural than that he, now his own master, should seek still further advancement by active service in Paltesh.

The second man, Kembri-B'sai, was a compelling figure; the embittered younger son of an impoverished baron in Lapan. Huge, black-bearded and taciturn, he looked a warrior capable of wading through oceans of blood without turning a hair. A professional soldier with a good record, for some unknown reason he had nevertheless been disappointed in his hopes of advancement under Senda-na-Say, against whom he entertained a brooding hatred.

The plot took two years to come to fruition and was entirely successful. Fornis showed herself a model of cunning and duplicity. Having completely regained the confidence of both her uncles by a convincingly sustained show of contrition and reformed ways, she was able with little difficulty, on the night of the coup, to poison them both, at the very time when Kembri and Han-Glat, having brought their mutiny to the boil, were killing the Palteshi commanders in Dari.

In such affairs, one step tends to compel the next. Sencho and Kembri had foreseen this, though Fornis had not. Senda-na-Say in Bekla could seem to ignore much of the internecine quarrelling of the provinces, but this he could not ignore. The conspirators' night's work had seriously weakened the effective strength of the empire to resist Terekenalt, and in all probability only the onset of the rains (Kembri had timed the business with this in mind), putting an end to campaigning for that year, had averted an immediate invasion of Suba by King Karnat. Fornis was summoned to Bekla to give an account of herself and of the death of her uncles.

She declined to go, pleading at first illness and then, with some plausibility, the impossibility of travelling seventy miles over roads more than ankle-deep in rain and mud (though her secret messengers continued to reach Sencho throughout the winter). Nor was Senda-na-Say prepared to travel then, being beset nearer home with difficulties of a nature and gravity which his predecessors had never encountered.

The truth was that Senda-na-Say had first failed to grasp and then completely under-rated the profound social change in Bekla brought about by the growth of trade and wealth. Years before, he had inherited a realm based on aristocracy and land tenure, but these were now of diminishing importance in a society increasingly full of moneyed commoners—many

163

richer than nobles and actually able to buy them up—impatient for re-cognition and influence commensurate to their wealth and the taxes they paid. Not surprisingly, he and his associates had little time for people like Sencho and Lalloc; but less excusably, they were not ready to listen to more acceptable representatives of the merchant and craftsman class—men such as Fleitil, for instance. Whether they pretended or whether they genuinely thought that there was nothing to discuss, the effect was the same. They lost the confidence of their most affluent subjects, men well able to bribe servants to spy and soldiers to desert. Also turning against them was the newly-formed clique of Beklan nobles calling themselves the Leopards, several of whom had friends (and creditors) among the mer-chants.

With the return of the spring, envoys were once more sent to Dari-Paltesh, with a mandate that Fornis should return with them at once. For three weeks nothing was heard. Then came news more disturbing than any received by a ruler of Bekla in living memory. Fornis, having agreed with King Karnat of Terekenalt to offer no resistance to his occupation and annexation of Suba, in return for his promise to desist from further attacks on Paltesh, had publicly declared herself Sacred Queen of Airtha and, with Kembri and Han-Glat at the head of a considerable force, was about to advance on Bekla.

The office of Sacred Queen was a religious, not a political one. Tradi-tionally, the Queen's rôle was to officiate as chief priestess in the temple of Cran and in particular, at the great spring festival held each year as soon as the rains had ended, to perform her ceremonial coupling with the god in the presence of the rulers, nobility, priests and chief dignitaries of Bekla. Nine months later, at the winter solstice, she gave symbolic birth to the new year in a ceremony attended only by her own priestesses and certain noblewomen of the city. A new Sacred Queen of Airtha was chosen by popular acclaim every fourth year, immediately after the ritual birth. Al-though the people usually acclaimed a well-born and beautiful girl of good family, and although the office conferred great honour, it had never involved any political influence, even for the Queen's male relatives. Very often, in practice, the Queen was content to leave the esoteric work and ritual of the temple to the professional priesthood, herself simply playing her appointed part on ceremonial occasions and notably at the two fes-tivals.

Fornis's claim to be Sacred Queen, in a year when a new Queen fell to be chosen, was a most adroit move which had, of course, originated with Sencho and already been agreed by Han-Glat and Kembri. Whatever her reputation, Fornis's beauty and nobility were incontestable. These she now turned to account. Having known in her heart for years—so ran her proclamation—that the god intended her for his Sacred Queen, she had abstained from marriage; and on this account had suffered injustice and slander for his sake. Now her hour had come, and she called upon all true devotees of Cran and Airtha to support her in her holy vocation.

Thanks largely to Sencho, Lalloc and others, there were many in Bekla ready to uphold her. As in Dari, the common people tended to idolize Fornis for her beauty and audacity. Several of the Leopards supported her, having already become her adherents in the upper city. What possible objection could there be, said these young men, to Fornis becoming Sacred Queen? The Sacred Queen, whoever she had been, had never harmed anyone, and anyway the temple and its priests could do with gingering up a bit. Gradually it was borne in upon Senda-na-Say first, that there were regiments in the army upon which he could place no more than doubtful reliance, and secondly that his only practicable strategy was to try to defeat Fornis before ever she reached Bekla. If she were to succeed in entering the city, her very presence would split it apart.

In the event, however, there was no fighting. Senda-na-Say, learning that Fornis had only just set out, concluded that provided he acted with the greatest despatch he would have time to raise an auxiliary force in Tonilda sufficient to tip the scale. For generations past his family had had a large country estate at Puhra, on Lake Serrelind, and their personal influence and standing in Tonilda were stronger than in any other province. If he could cover the fifty miles to Puhra and lead three thousand men back before Fornis had reached Bekla, he would be able to add them to the loyal part of the army and with luck bring her to battle well out on the plain to the west of the city.

Kembri and Sencho had foreseen that Tonilda was a rope to which Senda-na-Say would cling when the storm got up, but to ensure that it would break in his hand proved almost beyond them. In the end they were able to do so only by paying more than they really wanted to give—though not in money. A high-ranking baron named Durakkon—by nature neither opportunist nor conspirator, but an idealist, critical of Senda-na-Say's régime—was persuaded to risk his life and all that he possessed to prevent Senda-na-Say's return from Puhra, on the promise of nothing less than the succession of the high barony of Bekla and hence the rule of the empire. In the event of his success it would not be practicable to break this promise, for he stood well among the aristocratic Leopards and was popular with the soldiery.

Senda-na-Say left Bekla in a forced march for Puhra on the third day of the month Prahn. On the night of the 6th Prahn Durakkon, setting out from Thettit with no more than thirty men, fired his house about his ears and, as chance would have it, brought about his death beneath a falling beam.

(It was at about this time that the child Occula, her father and his men reached Bekla from Herl-Belishba.)

For several days Bekla remained in a state of general fear, suspicion and uncertainty. There was murder done on both sides, but lacking Senda-na-Say the army did no more than send out a half-hearted force which fell slowly back before the determined Kembri and Han-Glat, finally declining to give battle altogether.

Fornis, to her own surprise, reached Bekla unopposed, before the rumour of Senda-na-Say's death had been confirmed there; for Durakkon had closed the road from Thettit, sending word to her only. Once arrived in the city she published the news and at once sent for Durakkon to authenticate it.

Two of the army regiments—those of Urtah and of Tonilda—refused to serve under the new régime and, in the general confusion of the first days, left Bekla unopposed and returned to their home provinces. The other six were taken over without resistance by the Leopards. Before the end of Prahn, Durakkon had been confirmed as High Baron of Bekla and ruler of the empire, Kembri-B'sai and Han-Glat being appointed Lord General and Controller of Fortifications respectively. Immediately upon the spring festival (which had been delayed) Fornis was acclaimed Sacred Queen of Airtha. On the same day Sencho-bè-L'vandor, now appointed High Counsellor of Bekla and the Leopards' Chief of Secret Intelligence, took up residence in his new house in the upper city, formerly that of Senda-na-Say's brother.

The Leopard victory was complete. In time both Urtah and Tonilda renewed their allegiance to Bekla, once more paying dues and providing contingents for the army. Their entire reliability, however, remained open to grave doubt, and consequently it was upon these provinces that Sencho and his intelligence agents chiefly concentrated during the ensuing years.

: 19 :

THE VIEWING

As might be expected, the Leopard régime was characterized from the outset by opportunism and corruption. It was soon clear that the would-be liberal Durakkon was ineffective and possessed no dominance or personal ascendancy over those who had brought him to power. The majority of appointments and nominations were in effect sold to the highest bidder and it was common knowledge that those who held them were venal. Taxation, on the other hand, was lower than under Senda-na-Say, partly because Bekla was no longer for the time being at war with Karnat of Terekenalt and partly because certain activities connected with law and order, such as the regular patrolling of the highways by troops, were no longer carried out. Those using the roads either travelled together in parties, hiring their own armed guards, or else, like Lalloc, bribed the brigands not to molest them and theirs.

The strength of the régime, despite the rapacity and profligacy of its real leaders, in whose hands Durakkon found himself virtually powerless, lay in the merchants and their wealth. Traders were enabled by law to buy raw materials—for instance, wool and leather—from provincial peasants and small farmers at fixed prices; and if the peasants refused to sell at these rates, the traders could buy armed force to compel them. Many of the landed aristocracy, who might once have resisted this, were encouraged or influenced to leave their estates in the hands of bailiffs and live in Bekla, where pleasure and luxury were more widespread than ever before. Those who bought office under the Leopards usually found that they were able to make a better thing of it than ever they had of seigneurial life in the provinces.

Changes such as these were what underlay the poverty of thousands of country small-holders like Morca, who could not sell what they produced for more than the prices fixed by the Leopards.

The growth of large households and luxurious ostentation among the wealthy increased the demand for slaves, until it became worthwhile for men to become professional dealers and cater for it. One means of supply was direct purchase from village elders, but kidnapping (sometimes with payment, as in the case of Maia, but often without) also became widespread. At length a number of the Leopards, foreseeing a steady, long-term demand, set up slave-breeding farms in certain provinces of the empire. Lacking protection from absentee overlords, the remoter villages came to live in continual fear of slave-raiders. On the River Telthearna, north of Gelt, the young High Baron Bel-ka-Trazet was said to be turning his island of Ortelga into what was in effect a moated fortress. The slave-dealers, of course, were prosperous enough to pay heavy taxes to the Leopard rulers, to whom they were also acceptable on account of the additional trade they brought to such craftsmen as clothiers, shoemakers, blacksmiths and innkeepers.

The support of the common people of Bekla and other principal cities was ensured by cheap food and high expenditure on public entertainment. Most ordinary citizens, whether of middle or low degree, felt—not altogether without justification—that Queen Fornis, by giving Suba to Karnat and so ending the war with Terekenalt, had shown herself shrewd and benefited Bekla, and accordingly that she deserved to be where she was. The barons of Urtah, however, refusing to stomach what they regarded as her treachery (for Suba had been a dependency owing allegiance to the High Baron of Urtah), maintained along the Valderra a bitter hostility towards Karnat's outposts holding the western bank. Raids and clashes were frequent.

From the time when, as High Counsellor, he took up residence in the upper city, Sencho's life became one of the most delightful luxury. Enjoying the support of Queen Fornis and General Kembri-B'sai he was soon able, through seizure, extortion and various confiscations, to regain and more than regain the large sums which he had paid out in bribes and silence-money during the three or four years preceding the fall of Senda-na-Say. Having acquired a virtual monopoly of the metal trade, he appointed (for money) others to carry it on for him. The function which he now fulfilled personally—and for which he quickly showed himself to possess a remarkable aptitude—was that of controlling the Leopards' extensive network of spies and of advising Kembri, Han-Glat and Fornis not only upon their reports but also upon all information obtained from political prisoners and suspects. This work, however, in the course of which he gradually made himself universally feared and attained to a most extensive knowledge of almost everything being plotted or discussed (some even said thought) throughout the empire, was not permitted to interfere with his full indulgence of those appetites he had acquired as a boy in the service of Fravak.

To the gratification of his gluttony he was now able to devote as much money and time as he pleased. His cooks, whom he bought for very large sums, were among the most skilled in the empire, while his cellarer was a former merchant-vintner, for whom it was actually more profitable to cater for Sencho's needs alone. From Yelda to Kabin the High Counsellor's personal agents spent lavishly, not only on the best game, fruit and other produce, but also on ensuring that it reached him in perfect condition.

The daily planning of his greed, in consultation with his cooks, occupied him for a considerable time each morning. Upon its conclusion he would retire to the bath, or to an arbour on the terrace, there to hear reports and interview spies, as well as to meditate pleasurably upon what he would eat throughout the day. About noon would commence the dinner so delightfully anticipated, which usually continued for some two or three hours, or until such time as he was obliged to desist, less from satisfaction than from the sheer inability to contain more.

Throughout the latter part of the afternoon he would sleep—the satisfying sleep of one compelled to abstain for a time from enjoyment, yet knowing that it is to be resumed as soon as rest and ease have restored his capacities. As the evening became cool his slaves, awakening him, would refresh and prepare him for the renewed felicity of supper; upon the conclusion of which, swollen and stupefied, he would once more fall asleep in a contentment far beyond the range of such coarse and unrefined persons as those among whom he had once been compelled to live.

Now, after several years of this delectable life, he was beginning from time to time to consider whether it would be safe for him to delegate his intelligence work for the Leopards and retire altogether into private life. He had become so fat that he was almost incapable, and could not even gratify his greed without the continual help of his slaves. His eyes were nearly buried in the flesh of his face, his arms and legs were shapeless under great rolls of flesh and even in repose he grunted continually, scarcely able to draw his breath for corpulence. The weight of his enormous belly was more than he could bear, so that he had grown accustomed to gorge himself lying upon a couch beside the table, and naked for his greater ease. When the huge mound was fully distended he could neither stand nor sit, could not endure the least disturbance and, as soon as his slaves had attended to his bodily needs, would fall asleep in the cushions where he had dined; while they, tiptoeing about the hall, removed from around him the débris of his luxury.

These cultivated pleasures occupied him fully. But in addition, time must necessarily be devoted to gratifying the lust naturally induced by such gluttony; and for this too he made ample provision. A year or so after the accession of Queen Fornis, he compelled an ageing epicure in Bekla to sell him a Belishban woman named Terebinthia, already of great repute in the upper city for her skill in ministering to the specialized requirements of extreme obesity.

Terebinthia was plump, silent-moving and misleadingly indolent in manner; an expert in massage and in the preparation of herbal baths, sedatives and stomach-soothing drinks and medicines. She soon showed herself adept in ministering to her master's tastes, in alleviating the discomforts following upon excess, and in training young women to perform those attentions which he most enjoyed. Although a strict disciplinarian in the household, she was by no means above surreptitiously lending the young women in her charge to other wealthy inhabitants of the upper city: she took her cut of the gratuities they brought back, but seldom troubled the High Counsellor by informing him of such trifling matters.

Summoned early by Zuno, acting on his employer's instructions, Terebinthia had come down to Lalloc's premises in the lower city and been present in concealment while Occula and Maia were disporting themselves in the bath. Soon after, she had returned to Sencho's house, having agreed with Lalloc that he should bring the black girl to be shown to the High Counsellor later that morning. The slave-dealer had said nothing about Maia, and Terebinthia had assumed that he must have other plans for selling her. Since she had already left before Lalloc's talk with Occula in Vartou's room, she was somewhat taken by surprise when, the litter having been carried into the courtyard of Sencho's house and the gates closed behind it, Lalloc opened the curtains to disclose both the girls.

Sitting on the coping of the fountain basin and fanning herself—for it was already very hot—Terebinthia turned slowly to Lalloc, looking up at him through eyes half-closed against the glare.

'You didn't say—you were bringing both the girls?'

'Well, only so the High Counsellor hov a look at them, you know,' answered Lalloc. 'Then he please himself, of course, yoss, yoss.'

Terebinthia gazed down into the pool, slowly stirring the tepid water with one hand. 'But you didn't say so before?'

Lalloc spread out his hands. 'We talk last week, I toll you this black girl coming from Thettit, you say U-Sencho like to see her. Then after you go this morning I think "Well, show them both, where's the harm? If he don't like the other, I take her away again." But *you* don't like we show her, then she stay here.'

Terebinthia paused; and at length shrugged. 'Very well. I'll take them both in. If he wants to see you personally I'll let you know.'

Sencho had been roused late that morning, following an especially excellent supper the previous night and a sound sleep from which he had woken without the least indigestion or discomfort. Lying in the bath, groaning and farting as his bath-slave pressed and kneaded his belly, he allowed his thoughts to revert to two separate matters which had occupied him the day before. The first of these was altogether satisfying. As Controller of Mines and Metals throughout the empire he had, some months before, given audience to two prospectors arrived from some distant country south of Yelda. In response to their request he had granted them permission to search for metal in Chalcon—the mountainous, afforested region comprising south-eastern Tonilda—on condition that they duly reported and registered any veins which they might discover. Recently returned, they had given details of what sounded like an excellent lode of copper and asked his permission to work it. This he had naturally withheld and, having decided that it might not be altogether prudent to kill them (since this might have the undesirable effect of discouraging trade with the south), had ordered an armed guard to conduct them over the border beyond Ikat Yeldashay. Meanwhile, one of his own men, with six or seven pioneers, had been despatched to locate the lode and start work on it. Knowing a good deal about such matters and able as a rule to tell a good thing when he heard of it, Sencho had little doubt that the affair was likely to turn out most profitably.

In his own household, however, he had just suffered an unexpected vexation. His most adroit and valuable girl, a Lapanese named Yunsaymis, had been found to be infected with the *marjil*—a sexual disease. He had been lucky to escape himself, and only the conscientious vigilance of Terebinthia had protected him. She must have picked it up at one or other of the parties he had recently been to in the upper city, to which he generally took a couple of his girls to attend upon him. There could never be any telling, of course, what they might get up to after one had done with them and fallen asleep. If the girl herself had told Terebinthia, there might have been some prospect of retaining her, especially as she was skilful and naturally lubricious. As things were, however, an example had been made of her—a good whipping, followed by her removal to Lalloc's together with another young woman, Tuisto, whom he was selling on account of her age. Sencho never retained women beyond the age of twenty-three or twenty-four. To do so would have been unstylish, like keeping an old watchdog or old wall-hangings. His establishment normally comprised three or four concubines of outstanding appearance and quality, but this was in part for show and style, and for the entertainment of his guests. Being so fat, he had come to detest exertion, preferring the ministrations of girls who had been taught to do what he liked. Yunsaymis had been expert: he could hardly have felt more annoyed if one of his cooks had become unserviceable. It was a pity that he had already packed her off: she might well have been whipped a second time. This might quite possibly, of course, have lowered her selling price, but he would have enjoyed it.

From these meditations he was roused by Terebinthia, come to tell him that Lalloc had brought a pair of girls for him to look at, one being the black girl expected up from Thettit-Tonilda, whom she had mentioned to him a few days ago. In her view both were at least worth inspecting. Sencho, whose immediate desire was for massage and excretion, enquired whether she was sure that the girls were healthy. Reassured on this point, he agreed to see them in the small dining-hall in about an hour's time.

At this season of the year the small hall, facing north, with an outlook over the roofs and towers of the lower city and thence across the sunlit plain to the Gelt mountains fifty miles away, was refreshingly cool. A malachite basin, designed by Fleitil himself, caught with a light, plashing sound two streams of water gushing from the breasts of a marble nymph half-hidden among translucent, jade reeds. Here Sencho was helped to a couch and settled comfortably in the cushions, while Meris, another of his girls, took up her place beside him to attend to any needs or inclinations which he might feel. Since only slaves were to be present, it was unnecessary for him to be clothed, and the girl, knowing what he liked, gently rubbed his loins while he discussed the day's meals with two of his cooks. This important business at length concluded, he told Terebinthia that he was ready to see what Lalloc had brought. Even lying down to view fresh slaves, however, he must be eating, and accordingly a second girl, Dyphna, was summoned to kneel beside the couch with a silver tray of saffron cakes, preserved ginger and sesame biscuits.

Sencho had never seen a black girl before and this one, as Terebinthia conducted her into the hall and drew her scarlet cloak off her shoulders, aroused in him an immediate and titillating piquancy of excitement. Having called her over to stand beside the couch, he spent some little time in examining her smooth, dark limbs and in handling the various parts of her body. She was arresting. As far as he could see there was no contrivance: her flesh had not been stained or dyed; she was a healthy, natural girl. Sencho, his childhood spent in the slums of the lower city, detested freaks, regarding them as he regarded cripples and hunchbacks. This girl, however, was no freak. He felt himself aroused. She struck him as being of a buoyant, energetic temperament, experienced without being hardened, and showed not the least aversion or embarrassment as he stroked her thighs and buttocks. He questioned her about her origin, but of this she could tell nothing except that she had come as a child from somewhere far beyond the empire—north of the Telthearna, she thought.

Lying back in the cushions, Sencho considered. Lalloc's price for a novelty like this would be high. The girl would certainly make an original addition to his household and no doubt attract a good deal of attention; but unless she possessed aptitude, mere novelty for its own sake would afford little real satisfaction. Like a child in a bazaar, he would merely have spent money on a showy trinket which had caught his fancy at first glance. Calling for cooled wine to rinse the ginger from his mouth, he told Meris to spread cushions on the floor and fetch in the youth who looked after the water-garden.

At this, to his surprise, the black girl spoke directly to him of her own accord. Nothing would delight her more, she said, than to oblige the High Counsellor in any way he pleased. She hoped she would soon have every opportunity to prove this to him. He would not have forgotten, however, that she was still U-Lalloc's property. Might she be graciously allowed to ask his consent before doing as the High Counsellor wished?

Sencho, far from being angry, approved of this, which suggested to him first, that the girl possessed spirit and sense and secondly, that if she could show this sort of responsibility to Lalloc she might show it to him. So many girls turned out to be too timid, submissive and docile to impart zest to their work. As long as she did not get above herself, a sharp girl would suit him very well.

Lalloc having replied by Terebinthia that he had no objection as long as the girl was not scratched, bitten or otherwise marked, the youth was summoned.

Five minutes were enough to convince Sencho that he would at any rate make an offer: and he was about to indulge with Meris the very natural inclinations induced by what he had been watching, when Terebinthia, bending over him, enquired in a whisper whether he wished to see the second girl. Being in haste to do as he wished, he had already declined when the black girl, slipping quickly out of the room, herself led in her companion and removed her pleated, green-and-white robe.

Sencho, his lust already enflamed, stared at her in astonishment. Living in the debauchery of the upper city like a shark enclosed in a lagoon, it was a long time since he had even seen a girl like this. She was very young—no more than fifteen—and startlingly beautiful, with an air of naïveté and a child-like, unspoilt bloom; golden hair falling about her shoulders and a firm, opulent figure glowing with health and vitality. More delightfully still, she was blushing, trembling and trying to cover herself with her hands; he could see the tears standing in her eyes. The very sight of her roused him beyond endurance. He found himself consumed with the desire to clutch her, to feel her struggling, to hear her begging for mercy as he forced himself upon her. His huge bulk quivered in an access of delicious, intoxicating concupiscence.

Scarcely knowing what he did, he attempted to rise from the cushions but, far too fat, sank back, helpless and panting. A moment later the girl had broken free from Terebinthia's restraining arm and run out of the room. Sencho, however, had seen enough to realize that there was nothing further to be gained by questioning or testing an innocent like this. He must either buy her as she was, or else let be. As things had turned out, with the loss of Yunsaymis he needed two fresh girls. He recalled the large sum which he would undoubtedly gain from the new Tonildan copper mine: he could well afford a little extravagance.

Having finished with Meris, he sent word to Lalloc that he would be ready to discuss terms of purchase that evening, and thereupon told Terebinthia to order dinner to be served early.

MERIS

'Thirty thousand!' said Occula with satisfaction. 'Thirty thousand meld, banzi, for the two of us! That means you'd probably have fetched at least fifteen thousand on your own. What about that?'

'I can't see why you're so pleased,' said Maia, who was rubbing Occula's back with pumice as she lay on a couch in the women's quarters at the High Counsellor's house. '*We* don't see a meld of it—well, only five hundred. Anyway, how d'you know?'

'That Terebinthia woman told me,' answered Occula. 'She was there when they did the deal. "Well, I hope you're pleased with yourselves," she said. "You ought to be. This is the richest house in Bekla, next to Durakkon and the Sacred Queen." All the same, I wouldn't trust her a yard, banzi, if I were you. You can be quite sure she tells him everythin'.'

'We could have fetched a hundred thousand, come to that,' said Maia. 'Wouldn't have made any difference to us, would it?'

'Oh, you really make me cross! Lower down, banzi! That's lovely! Go on doin' that! Doan' you see, pet, we're *really* val'able now? They doan' damage or waste beautiful things like you—not unless you go and make some sort of fool of yourself. You're like that fountain in his hall; he's paid for it—he's not goin' to see it spoilt or messed up.'

Maia burst into tears. 'I think he's *horrible*! I can't *bear* him! He makes me feel—oh!' Pulling Occula over on her back, she flung herself into her arms. 'Oh, I was so excited to be going to Bekla with you; and to think it's all come to this! That dreadful—'

Occula sat up quickly, holding her at arm's length by the shoulders.

'Are you crazy? Banzi, it couldn' have turned out better! All my good advice, and you haven' understood the first thing! You think that fat brute's supposed to be in exchange for your Tharrin, doan' you? You think you're expected to have a nice time, as if it was Tharrin, or me? Can' you see that's a totally wrong idea of the business altogether?' She stroked Maia's shoulders and arms. 'Oh, there's a lovely body, if ever a girl had one! Now listen: you used to use that body for swimmin' in your lake, didn' you, and that was effort and pleasure, right? And you used to use it for choppin' wood and carryin' pails of water, and that was effort and work. Well, this is the same. Where *he's* concerned, you use it for work. It's not *supposed* to be pleasure—that's the secret. But it's *easy* work, banzi—easy! That randy old pig—Terebinthia was sayin' half the time he's gorged himself until he can' even do anythin'. Any girl who knows what she's doin', take about half a minute to make him piss his tallow and go to sleep. But you take the trouble to please him and keep your wits about you and Cran only knows where you might end up.'

She stared seriously into Maia's blue eyes.

'And you *mustn*', banzi—you must *not* let him think you're frightened of him. Tell you why. He's a cruel bastard: he mus' be, or he wouldn' be where he is. If he thinks you're frightened or disgusted he'll set out to have some fun with you. He'll have you buggered, or basted by a goat or somethin', jus' so's he can enjoy watchin' it. It all comes down to what I told you in Puhra, remember? You've got to keep some kind of authority, even if you're underneath a Deelguy cattle-dealer. That's accomplishment, that is!'

'But I've *got* no accomplishments!' cried Maia desperately.

'You told me you could swim.'

'So I can; but what good's that going to be?'

'You never know. Girls who can swim well look nice when they're doin' it, same as girls who can dance well. Ah, that's an idea! Why didn' I think of that before? If you're a good girl I'll teach you the *senguela*. You're made for it!'

'What's the senguela?'

'It's a dance about Shakkarn and Lespa. The way *I* do it, it's just sort of Come and get me: but the way *you* might learn to do it, it could be like Lespa come down to earth. Ah, well! plenty of time.'

'Fifteen thousand meld!' said Maia. 'That's far more than my mother'll see in her whole life!'

'And if I know anythin' about it, most of it's peasants' taxes,' said Occula, drawing up a stool to a large mirror fixed to the wall. 'That's a laugh, isn't it? Your mother takes Lalloc's money for *you*, pays her taxes to Sencho and Sencho pays it back to Lalloc. She might as well have blown it out of her venda, mightn' she?'

'But Occula, you said you were going to tell Lalloc about Genshed— what he got up to that night in Puhra: but you never.'

'Oh, not *yet*, banzi! That'll come later, when we've become the bounciest girls in Bekla—thousand meld a bounce. But I shan' forget, believe you me. He'll come to bits like a turd in the rain, you see if he doesn'.' She put on her necklace of teeth and arranged it carefully. 'For Lespa's sake, do count your blessin's. Look at that bath—this mirror—your clothes! We're wallowin' in luxury! There's others outside beggin' their bread; and all you've got to do is learn a few bed-tricks and look as if you were enjoyin' yourself. With *your* looks you can' go wrong.'

At this moment the Belishban girl, Meris, quite naked, entered quickly from the corridor leading to the bedrooms and, ignoring Occula and Maia, stepped down into the pool. Occula broke off and for a time there was silence, broken only by Meris's ripplings and splashes as she moved restlessly in the water. At length she looked up and said to Occula, 'Where the hell are you from, anyway?'

'We're from Tonilda, both of us,' answered Occula placidly.

'First I heard the people in Tonilda were black. Anyway, you can damn' well go back there for me.'

She struck the surface hard with the flat of her hand, but the splash did not reach Occula and Maia.

The black girl got up, went to the edge of the pool and stood over her. 'What the hell's the matter? D'you want a row or somethin'? It'll only bring Terebinthia in, and then we'll all be in the shit.'

'I don't care!' said Meris. 'She can do what she likes: she's done enough already.'

She was a very pretty girl, with dark eyes and a full, sensual mouth, but now her face was peaked and sharp with anger and latent violence. One could see what she might look like in ten years' time.

'What's happened, then?' asked Occula. 'P'raps we ought to know, ought we?'

She put out a hand, drew Meris to her feet and began rubbing her down with a dry towel.

'Oh, it's Yunsaymis,' replied Meris after a time. 'One day I'm going to stick a knife into that fat bastard and hang upside-down for it. Yunsaymis was the only friend I had.'

'Why, is she dead, then, or what?'

'No, she picked up a dose of the marjil: someone at a party where Sencho'd taken her. We might have put it right, the two of us, and no one any the wiser, only that bitch Terebinthia found out and told him. Terebinthia always hated Yunsaymis, only she never dared say so to Sencho, 'cos he had such a fancy for her; but she told me once that she meant to get Yunsaymis out of here one way or another. The moment she found out she'd got the marjil, she was off to Sencho like a scalded cat. I had to stay beside him and do what he wanted while he watched Yunsaymis being whipped.'

'Where is she now?' asked Maia.

'Sold—her and Tuisto together. Tuisto was expecting it: she was well over twenty-four. Girls here are always sold about that age.'

'How old are you?' said Occula.

'Nineteen.'

'Been at it long?'

Meris smiled wryly. 'Depends what you call "it". You want to take a good look at me, black girl: I'm an awful warning; or I shall be in a few years.'

'Get away?' said Occula. 'When did it all start, then?'

'Oh, when I was thirteen,' said Meris. 'That's not too young in Belishba, you know. I could have been married at thirteen, down there. I never wanted to get married, though; I just liked basting. Didn't much matter who it was. I wore out every boy for miles around, until my father turned me out of doors. He said I was a whore, but I never took a damned meld, and that's the truth!'

She crashed her clenched fist hard against the woodwork of the wall. Maia and Occula exchanged glances. 'What happened then?' asked Occula.

'Well, I couldn't starve, so I set off to walk to Herl. But on the way I took up with Latto—this lad I met. He was on the run.'

'A slave?'

'What else? Belishba's always full of slaves on the run—or it was, five years ago. But Latto—he never would tell me a word about himself. "I'm your gift from Shakkarn," he used to say. "That's good enough for you." It was, too: that boy had a zard could have broken a door down! He used to—' And here Meris grew quite remarkably obscene, until it became clear to both the girls that she was talking to herself as much as to them.

'You *are* in a state, aren' you?' interrupted Occula at length.

'Oh, shut up!' said Meris. 'Where was I? Oh, yes; well, we joined a band of fellows—all runaways—they were on the game along the Herl-Dari highway, a bit south of the Zhairgen ferry. Latto had to fight to get taken into the gang—they wouldn't take just anyone. Even then I don't think they'd have had him, but the thing was they wanted *me*, and I wouldn't join unless they took him as well, you see.'

'You mean they *all* basted you?' asked Maia.

'Oh, Cran, no! They'd have liked to, but Latto would have killed me. He'd have killed anyone who tried, too. No, I was there as live bait— worth my weight in gold to them. I used to pick men up on the road— anyone who looked as if he might be worth a bit. Then we'd go into the bushes and as soon as the fellow'd got stripped off and started, the lads'd get started, too. Gods, it was funny to see their faces when they realized! You'd have *roared* laughing! D'you know, one day I got three fellows— Lapanese, they were—and made them think I was longing to have them all three at once. They were armed, you see, so I had to get them all stripped and off their guard at the same time. The funny thing was, I *would* have liked to have had them all three at once! I s'pose that's why they fell for it. Anyway, they all got undressed, right there in the trees. The boys had a bit of fun with them; *and* about four thousand meld as well.'

'See what I mean, banzi?' asked Occula. 'Sometimes it's play. Sometimes it's work. When you're lucky it's both. Have fun and make a ton.'

'But what happened in the end?' asked Maia.

'What d'you think? The soldiers came, of course. *They* set a trap for *us*, and I fell right into it. I *thought* the fellow didn't look much like a merchant. Still, I got started and then before I knew what was happening the soldiers were into the lads. They killed four or five then and there, and Latto and two others they hung upside-down by the road. They'd have killed me, too, but the tryzatt said I was too pretty and he'd take and sell me in Dari. And so he did—once he'd finished with me himself.'

'How d'you come to be here, then?' asked Occula.

'Why, that tryzatt sold me to General Han-Glat,' said Meris. 'He happened to be in Dari, you see, working on the new fortress. Ever seen it? No? Oh, it's unbelievable! He used to take me along with him and baste me on the battlements when he'd finished in the evenings. That was the best time I ever had, while I was with Han-Glat. He'd got two other girls, but he liked me best.'

'How did you come to leave him?' asked Maia.

'Well, once when he was back in Bekla, you see, reporting to Kembri, he saw a girl of Sencho's he fancied, so he offered Sencho his pick of the three of us. Sencho fancied me, worse luck, and we were exchanged.'

'What's wrong with this, then?' asked Occula. 'Or is it jus' that you've lost Yunsaymis?'

'What's wrong?' answered Meris. 'Cran and Airtha! You never get a man, that's what's wrong.'

'But you say Yunsaymis got the marjil?'

'Yunsaymis was the same as me—she wanted a man. Sencho doesn't baste, you see—or very seldom. He's so fat he can hardly walk. You have to lie there and do what he wants—drives you half-crazy and then you don't get anything yourself. But when he goes to a party or a banquet, he always takes one or two girls with him. Only you're not supposed to have anything to do with another guest, of course, unless your master offers you. Sencho was very jealous of Yunsaymis—men were always after her, you see. Well, at this party he'd eaten till he couldn't move and she had to sit there and watch the whole room basting, she said. So in the end she told him she needed five minutes' fresh air, and she went outside and got laid by one of the house-slaves; and *he* had the marjil all right. He didn't have the whipping, though: Yunsaymis had that all to herself.'

At this moment Terebinthia came silently into the room, her bare feet noiseless on the red-and-blue tiled floor. Slowly waving a great semi-circle of white plumes before her face, she looked round at the girls one by one.

'What did U-Lalloc say your name was?' she murmured at length, looking at Occula.

'Occula, säiyett.'

'And yours?'

'Maia, säiyett.'

'Well, Occula, you're lucky. The High Counsellor wishes to play with his new toy. After what we saw this morning I'm sure you'll be able to please him.'

'Am I to go to him now, säiyett?'

'I'll take you,' said Terebinthia. 'No, you needn't get dressed: you'll do very well as you are.'

: 21 :

THE PEDLAR

Upon the city the heat lay like a thick, soft filling between one building and the next. In the half-deserted Caravan Market the porters sat idle on their haunches. The very dogs lay panting along the shady flanks of the fly-buzzing, tinder-dry laystalls. The level of the Barb had dropped six feet and more, and the cracked mud looked like a huge, meshed net spread to dry by the waterside. The leaves hung limp and motionless and not a bird was singing in the gardens beside the northern bank.

The highest room in the Barons' Palace, which overlooked the Barb, caught, as the sun sank, the faintest of breezes—barely enough to stir the muslin screens fixed across the window embrasures. The door had been left open and below, at the foot of the spiral stair, one of Kembri-B'sai's personal bodyguard stood posted to ensure that no chance servant or other passer-by should come within earshot.

Durakkon, High Baron of Bekla, having filled his cup from a porous, moisture-beaded wine-jar standing behind the open door, carried it across to the window and, drinking, stood looking out towards the brown, motionless water three hundred yards away at the foot of the Leopard Hill. Kembri was seated at the table. Sencho lay sweating on a couch, fanned by a deaf-mute slave whose eyes never wandered from the floor.

'What it comes to is this,' said Durakkon at length. 'We can tell Karnat as often as we like that Suba's his and that the Leopards have never been at war with him: but as long as the Urtans are continually sending raiding-parties over the Valderra to cut up his men, he can call us liars. Suppose he were to make that a pretext to cross the Valderra himself and try for Dari, what's to stop him?'

'That's what the fortress was built for,' said Kembri. 'It's impregnable, and Karnat knows that as well as we do. Anyway, the rains are coming any day now, so even Karnat won't be able to move for at least two months.'

'I know that,' answered Durakkon. 'I was thinking of next spring; but I suppose it'll have to wait.' He turned, facing into the room as the faint clangour of the clocks' gongs came up from the lower city. 'There are more urgent matters. According to Sencho, we've got difficulties that *won't* keep through the rains.'

Sencho began to speak of the latest reports from his spies in Tonilda. Even after nearly seven years of Leopard rule, several parts of that province had by no means lost their sense of allegiance to the fallen house of Senda-na-Say. The former High Baron's estates had, of course, been sequestered by the Leopards, and Enka-Mordet, Senda-na-Say's nephew, now farming an estate in northern Chalcon, south-east of Thettit, was kept under constant surveillance. Though he had, to all outward appearances, always taken care to avoid becoming a focus for local disaffection, he had recently gone so far as to protest on behalf of his tenants against the increasing incidence of kidnapping and slaving raids in the neighbourhood. Similar protests had come in from other parts of Tonilda. Sencho was apprehensive of collusion and the possibility of a concerted insurrection.

'But if we arrest half-a-dozen landowners,' said Kembri, 'that may only lead to worse trouble. It's only smouldering now. Why not tell the dealers to go easy on Tonilda for a year or two?'

Sencho, motioning impatiently to the slave to place fresh cushions under his belly, pointed out that the problem would be solved when the new farms began to supply the market, thereby enabling the provincial quotas to be diminished. This, however, could not take place for another few years, since as yet the children born on the farms were not old enough to be sold.

'There are too many slaves, that's the truth of it,' said Durakkon shortly. 'There never used to be these armies of slaves in rich households, eating their heads off, most of them doing far too little, retained for nothing but show—'

'Turning *heldro*, are you?' asked Kembri, smiling up at him, chin on hands. (*Heldril*, meaning 'old-fashioned people', was a colloquial term for those in the provinces—particularly nobility—not in agreement with the Leopard régime.)

'I'm well aware there's money in the slave-trade,' said Durakkon. 'It's made fortunes and Bekla's profited by it; but you can't deny that in some ways it's turned the empire into a marsh where there used to be firm ground. The whole place is becoming lawless and dangerous. Every lonely stretch of road's infested with gangs of escaped slaves preying on travellers, terrifying villagers, even fighting each other—'

'Districts with troubles like that know their remedy,' said Kembri. 'If they're ready to pay for soldiers we'll supply them. And they only have to pay by results, too. You may remember how we cleared the highway between Herl and Dari three or four years ago. That cost Paltesh and Belishba far less than they used to have to pay in taxes for the upkeep of regular highway patrols.'

'It cost them less in money, I dare say,' said Durakkon.

Sencho broke in. The merchants were not complaining, and they were the class who made most use of the highways. The general principle of Leopard rule was an excellent one: provinces, like citizens, paid Bekla on the nail for whatever they needed. The Leopards had ended the war with Terekenalt, reduced taxation and enabled hundreds, if not thousands, to enrich themselves by trade and merchandise.

'I dare say,' said Durakkon again, stepping round the High Counsellor's panting bulk as he crossed the room to fill his wine-cup once more. 'And you, as a merchant yourself, ought to be able to tell a high price when you see it. The price is that the peasants hate us; and that nobody dares to travel alone along any lonely road in the empire.' He paused a few moments and then said deliberately, 'I've often felt myself to be nothing but the Leopards' hired assassin. Senda-na-Say may have been an antiquated blockhead, but at least he knew the most important thing was public safety: law and order.'

'But he couldn't keep it,' sighed Sencho, his hand disappearing to the wrist as he scratched his sweating buttocks. 'That's why we're ruling now. We—'

'No point in talking like this,' broke in Kembri. 'You sent for us, sir, as I understand it, to discuss three things. First, stopping Urtah from continuing to provoke Karnat: secondly the state of affairs in Tonilda; and finally the problem of escaped slaves turned outlaw. I'll tell you my answers. As to Urtah, I think we should do nothing until after the rains. We could demand hostages from them now, but as there'll be half a dozen Urtan nobles staying in Bekla during the rains—including Eud-Ecachlon, the High Baron's heir, as well as that Bayub-Otal fellow—that hardly seems necessary. Let it wait for two months, and then warn Urtah that if there's any more raiding across the Valderra they'll be in trouble with *us*—not just with Karnat. As for Tonilda, I'll tell the governor that we'll lower the slave quota if the province will pay the difference in money. And I'll confirm once again, to every governor and baron throughout the empire, that the army's ready to rid any area of outlaws upon request—at the usual rates, of course. And now if that's all, sir, I must ask you to excuse me. I'm asked to supper with the Sacred Queen, and as you know she doesn't like to be kept waiting. Shall I send up your slaves to carry you down?' he added to Sencho.

Durakkon, his hand clenching on his wine-cup at the disrespect in the Lord General's voice and manner, placed himself in the open doorway, impeding him in the act of departing. 'The Sacred Queen?' he said quietly; then looked down at the floor, pretending reflection. 'That's another matter I wish to mention before I give you *leave* to go.' Kembri said nothing and he went on, 'As you know, it's over two and a half years now since Fornis began her second term as Sacred Queen. In less than eighteen months that second term will end. She'll be thirty-four. Apart from anything else, for a woman of that age to be Sacred Queen would be an insult to the god. What's to be done with Fornis when she ceases to be Sacred Queen?'

Kembri, who had been listening with his eyes on the ground, looked up. 'I think it may very well be, sir,' he replied, 'that when the time comes, that's one matter on which you and I will find ourselves in complete agreement. I have certain ideas; we'll discuss them later.' Craning past the High Baron towards the stairhead outside, he called down to the sentry, 'Karval! Send up the High Counsellor's slaves!'

'No, no, banzi! Doan' try to take it all at once like that. Take a little at a time, and get used to that before you try to take any more.'

'It keeps choking me. I'll never do it!'

'Yes, you will. It's like the hinnari. You think you'll never be able to hold six strings down with one finger, and then one day you find you can. Come on, now, try again.'

'M'm—m'm—m'm!'

'Fine! Now just rock your head. That's right! You'll find you can take the whole lot just for a moment before you come up again. Once more! Right, that'll do for now. There, that wasn't so bad, was it?'

'But when there's someone else pushing too?'

'Then you have to close down a bit tighter. You're the one in control, remember, even if you never say a word. It's astonishin' how they accept what you do if only you do it the right way. If you doan' like whatever he's doin', you can pretend you're simply dyin' for him to do somethin' else and get him to go on to that—oh, yes, he will, if he thinks he's making *you* enjoy yourself. It plays on a man's vanity, you see. Flattery gets you everywhere, as long as they doan' realize what it is.'

'You'll have to open a school, Occula.' Both girls looked round to see Terebinthia leaning against one of the columns near the entrance. They wondered how long she had been there.

'Is there anything I can have the pleasure of doing for you, säiyett?' asked Occula.

'Not at the moment,' replied Terebinthia, yawning and stretching her arms above her head. 'There's a pedlar here, selling perfumes—soaps—jewellery—things like that. He's been talking with the High Counsellor;

but he's finished now. If you'd like him to come in here and show you what he's got, I have no objection.'

'Shall we, banzi?' asked Occula. 'It'll pass the time and we might pick up some gossip and news, even if we doan' buy anythin'. Where's he from, säiyett, do you know?'

'From Tonilda, I think,' replied Terebinthia.

'Oh, well, that settles it,' said Occula. 'Have you got any money, Meris?'

'Some: but Dyphna's got more,' said Meris, sliding off the couch where she had been dozing in the heat. 'I'll go and ask her whether she's interested.'

Dyphna, the fourth girl in Sencho's household, was a tall, graceful, rather superior girl from Yelda, whom Sencho occasionally made use of himself, but really kept by way of trying to convince Beklan aristocrats that his enjoyment of women was capable of going beyond the merely physical. So far, Occula and Maia had seen little of her except at meals, when she spoke seldom but seemed friendly enough. As the senior concubine she had her own, larger room, where she spent most of her time. Maia had become nervous of her upon discovering that she could read and write and apparently—according to Meris—possessed all manner of other accomplishments; but as Occula pointed out, she had done nothing by way of pushing these down their throats or trying to make them feel small.

She came in now, following Meris and fastening a cloak over her transparent muslin shift. The airless heat in the women's quarters was hard enough to bear even without clothes, and Maia, who felt little interest either in the pedlar or in any news there might be from Tonilda, hoped Occula and the others would not keep him long. She had just slipped into her robe and was running a comb through her hair when Terebinthia returned, holding the bead curtains aside for a tall young man who ducked his head as he came through the doorway.

Pedlars licensed to travel throughout the empire under the protection of Bekla wore a traditional costume to denote their occupation. Maia had often seen such men as this in the streets of Meerzat or tramping the lakeside road. His round, hard hat of scarlet leather, too hot to wear at this time of year, hung at his back by a loop, and the sleeves of his green shirt, dark with sweat, were rolled above the elbow. His jerkin, with its white stripe back and front and coloured ribbons at each shoulder, was slung over one arm, while on the other he was carrying by its straps his canvas pack, from the top of which protruded three or four coloured feather dusters on sticks. Coming to a halt in the middle of the room, he pulled out one of these and tickled Meris under the chin.

'Well, well, well,' said the pedlar cheerfully. 'Keeping nice and warm, young ladies, are we, this weather? Not too cold in bed, I hope?'

The eye with which he winked at Maia was sharp and bright as a jackdaw's. He looked about twenty-three or -four, and everything about him, from his sunburned face to the dust on his shoes, suggested a life spent out of doors and a man used to give-and-take with all comers.

'Is that all you've come to sell us?' asked Meris, grabbing for his hand and missing it. 'Feather dusters?' She had let her cloak slide down from her shoulders, exposing as much as she dared with Terebinthia in the room.

'Oh, no, no!' said the pedlar, tickling her again. 'By no means! But I always begin by tickling—that's the style, don't you think, to get things going? I'm sure she knows more about tickling than I do,' he remarked to Maia.

Meris squealed with laughter. The young man unslung his pack, put it down on the floor and then turned to look more closely at Maia. 'Where you from, lass?'

'Lake Serrelind,' said Maia, her eyes pricking in spite of herself.

'Then you ought to be back there, that's all I can say,' answered he, in a more serious tone. 'You're far too young to be here. How did they come to steal you?'

Terebinthia spoke languidly from the opposite side of the room.

'Do you know where you are, my good man? You're in the upper city, in the house of the High Counsellor. If you have any goods fit to show these girls, you'd better get on with it, and stop wasting their time and mine.'

'Why, certainly, säiyett,' replied he. 'But I was waiting until all the young ladies were present. Isn't there one more somewhere?'

Maia, looking round, realized that Occula was not in the room. She had not seen her leave it.

'What do *you* know—?' Terebinthia was beginning, when Occula came in from the corridor leading to the bedrooms wearing her gold nose-stud, orange metlan and hunting-jacket. The pedlar, who had been crouching beside his pack to open it, stood up again.

'Hello, Zirek,' said Occula. 'Did you know I was here?'

'I heard at Lalloc's,' answered he. 'I knew you'd gone to Bekla, of course, for Domris told me: to better yourself, she said. I hope you will. They miss you at the Lily Pool, I'm told.'

'Oh, do get on and open your pack!' cried Meris. 'I mean, if you're both from Thettit that's wonderful, I'm sure, but I want to see what you've brought.'

'Why, I've got rolls of silk,' said the pedlar, 'and veils, all fine *tartua*-work—see, here—if that's your style. And just try this perfume, now. That's real *kepris*, that is, from up the Vrako. Let me put a drop on the back of your hand. The whole flask's only a hundred meld to you. Well, say ninety, but I couldn't let it go for less.'

Meris's face fell. 'I can't manage that much.'

'Well, here's a nice soap, now, scented with roses, and that's only four meld for a big one like this; and the same in scent, only that's thirty meld. And then I've these necklaces, see: topaz this one; and this one's onyx. Only they're dear. I don't really know why I risk my life carrying them about, but one day some lady'll put up the money, I dare say.'

'Got any ornaments?' asked Occula suddenly. 'My room's as bare as a cell.'

The pedlar turned and looked at her for a moment.

'Why, yes, quite a few. They're all just pottery, animals and birds, you know, but they're nicely painted.'

He laid out a couple of dozen bulls, bears and leopards; pigeons and terracotta cockerels—all the same size and painted in gaudy colours. 'How about this cat, now? She's Yeldashay, she is. It's one of their tales down that way, you know—the Cat Colonna.'

'I thought they called her—*Bakris?*' replied Occula, with a certain emphasis.

'Why, so they may, perhaps,' said the pedlar. 'I see she's got a bit chipped, so you can have her for nothing, if you like.' He handed her the rather clumsy little figure with its curving, erect tail. Occula took it from him with a curtsey and a flash of her white teeth.

'Oh, she'll brighten up the place no end: I like a bit of plain pottery. Everythin's gold and silver here—'cept me, of course—you get tired of it.'

'And what are you?' asked the pedlar.

'Black marble,' said Occula. 'Polished, too. Can' you tell?'

At this moment Dyphna entered into the conversation by enquiring the price of a carnelian ring laid out beside the necklaces. The pedlar, having told her rather shortly that it was eighty-five meld, was turning back to Occula when Dyphna quietly offered him seventy in ready money. Clearly surprised, he suggested seventy-five, but the girl merely smiled, shrugged her shoulders and seemed about to go when he accepted her offer, remarking that it would be a pleasure to be ruined by such a beautiful girl. Thereupon Dyphna, fetching from her room a bronze casket, unlocked it and paid him on the spot.

'I'll bet she's got a damned sight more than that, too, banzi,' whispered Occula as Dyphna, having evidently concluded business for the day, smiled graciously at the pedlar and left the room. 'Makes you realize the possibilities, doesn't it? How long's she been at it, d'you suppose? Five years? Six?'

'Oh, it's the noblemen who fancy *her*,' said Meris, glancing round to make sure that Terebinthia, who was examining the necklaces, was out of earshot. 'You've only got to see the way she lays it out at one of these banquets. She can sing and tell stories and play the hinnari and dance and—oh, she's got a lot of style, has Dyphna. She can make herself very good company. And as for business, she's got it all arranged. Terebinthia takes a good, big cut, but Dyphna'll have enough to buy herself out soon and set up as a shearna. Or she might even get married, I suppose.'

'But would Sencho let her go?' asked Maia.

'He'll *have* to, if she offers the price: that's the law, you see. If a girl can put up twelve thousand meld five years or more after she was first bought, her master has to let her go. But that's nearly always to his own advantage, anyway. He's had the girl for five years, you see. She must have lost value, but he can always get another for twelve thousand or less.'

'Not one like me he can', said Occula. 'I'll wipe her eye, you see if I doan'.'

At this moment Ogma, the club-footed servant-girl who looked after the women's quarters, came in, raised her palm to her forehead and stood silently by the entrance, waiting for Terebinthia to give her leave to speak. It pleased the säiyett to keep her waiting for some little while. When at length she beckoned her over, it was to be told that Sencho wished to see her at once. She left hastily and with none-too-well-concealed apprehension.

'Ah, well,' said Zirek, returning his wares one by one to the pack. 'It's always nice to have a chat with a bunch of pretty girls, even if you don't sell much. I'll have to be getting along now, though. I'm glad we met, Occula: I'll see you again.' He paused a moment. 'Tell us what you can, won't you? There's various ways, as I dare say you know; but I'll be back myself as soon as I can.'

'I'll buy your flask of kepris, if you like,' said Meris suddenly. 'I'll give you a damn' good price, too. Here it is.'

Placing herself squarely in front of him, she unclasped her cloak and let it fall to the floor. Except for her shoes and a silver bracelet on one arm she was naked, and in the warm, still room her body gave off a faint perfume of lilies. As she held out her arms to him, smiling, the young man stared at her without a word.

'There's a room through there,' she said, 'but we'll have to be quick. She'll be back soon.'

Occula, stepping forward, picked up her cloak.

'I'm only new roun' here,' she said to Meris, 'and Cran knows I hate to spoil a bit of fun. But even more would I hate to see you both hangin' upside-down: and make no mistake, that's what it'll be if she comes back and catches you. Come on, Zirek, get your pack in one hand and your zard in the other and get out of here.'

'Damn you, Occula!' shouted Meris. 'What the basting hell's it got to do with you?'

As Occula held her by the shoulders she struggled fiercely, twisting her head round and trying to bite her hand. 'Why can't you get her off me?' she cried to the pedlar, stamping her foot. 'Don't you want to baste me? There's plenty'd like to who can't, I'll tell you that!'

'O Cran preserve us!' said Occula. 'Meris, haven' you got any blasted sense at all? She'll be back any minute, you little hot-tairth idiot! Zirek, get out, go on, or I'll go and fetch the porter myself, damned if I doan'!'

At this moment Meris, who seemed completely beside herself, swung back one of her shod heels and kicked Occula on the shin. Occula, cursing with pain, slapped her as hard as she could, and as the girl sank to her knees once more gripped her under the shoulders.

'It's the heat,' said the black girl, rubbing her bleeding shin against her other calf. 'Come on, banzi, help me get her into her bedroom. For the last time, Zirek, will you *get out?*'

The two girls carried Meris bodily out of the room. Once they had put her on her bed she lay there quietly, her head thrust between two cushions. When they returned the pedlar had gone.

'Now that just shows you, banzi,' said Occula, 'how easy it is to go on your ruin just because you itch and mustn' scratch. That girl's pretty enough to make a fortune, but she'll come to a bad end, you mark my words! Can you imagine what would have happened if old Terebinthia had come back just in time for a nice, private *kura?*'

'What's a kura?' asked Maia.

'Oh, give me patience!' said Occula. 'A kura's when boys and girls are set to do it openly, at a party or a banquet, to amuse the ladies and gentlemen and get them going. Doan' worry, you'll see plenty before long. But if *we'd* had to admit that we knew what Meris was doin' and hadn' tried to stop her, we'd have been lucky to get off with a whippin'; and as for Meris herself—'

The beads clicked: Terebinthia was once more in the room. As the girls turned to face her she picked up a towel to wipe her sweating face and neck.

'The pedlar's gone?' she asked at length.

'Yes, säiyett.'

'And where is Meris?' Terebinthia's tone was rather sharper.

'Gone to lie down, säiyett: the heat, you know.'

Terebinthia paused. Her silence exuded a kind of suspicion and menace. Maia, realizing that very little escaped her and that that was one reason why she had risen to her position in this world where she herself must now live, felt afraid.

187

'Well,' said Terebinthia, with a certain air of deciding on balance to leave something unsaid, 'that will be—quieter, I dare say.'

She paused again: the girls waited silently.

'I've just been talking with the High Counsellor,' she resumed at length. 'He tells me he has been advised from the temple that the rains are almost certainly going to set in before morning.'

'Good news, säiyett,' said Occula.

'And if they do,' continued Terebinthia, ignoring her, 'the Lord General will be holding his customary banquet tomorrow night. The High Counsellor will be attending, of course. He wishes Meris to accompany him, and also you, Maia, so that you can gain some experience.'

'*Me*, säiyett? But—'

'And now I wish to see Meris,' said Terebinthia. 'No, Occula, you needn't bring her here: I'll go and talk to her in the bedroom. Perhaps by this time she'll be finding the—er—*heat* less troublesome.'

'Oh, we'll take good care to keep on the right side of *her*, banzi!' said the black girl, holding the pottery cat up to the light and turning it this way and that. 'If she was jus' to take a dislike to one of us, I doan' believe she'd stop at anythin', do you?'

: 22 :

THE RAINS BANQUET

In the midst of the dry, tawny plain Bekla, at the foot of Crandor's slope, lay like a tilted stone on the bed of a pool. For weeks the pool had been land-locked; the air inert, unstirring, so that no flow (one might imagine), even the most sluggish, could take place above its towers or across the long walls. Sometimes, indeed, it seemed to move a little, back and forth, with a turgid languor caused by no wind; perhaps by the jostling of sweating bodies or the babel of voices, just as still water round a stone might momentarily be troubled, before settling once more, by the passing of some weary, trapped fish.

Beyond the city, harvest was ended and summer hung dry and empty as a husk. The little herd-boys lay in the shade, paying no heed to cattle too listless to stray from the banks of shrunken rivers where the baked mud could afford them no relief. The work of the world was to wait for rain, and weary work it was—heavier even than the thundery cloud-banks piling up, day after day, above the Tonildan mountains a hundred miles to the east.

Slowly, as though their mass were too great for even the gods to move without exertion, these clouds began to advance westward above the plain; and below them went a mist white as wool, creeping through the treetops of the Tonildan forest, moving silently on across the expanse of Lake Serrelind, thickening among the hovels of Puhra and Hirdo. And behind the mist, at first indistinguishable from it, came rain; a rain that joined the mist to the clouds, so that everything—villages, roads, huts in fields, boats on rivers—was isolated first by mist, then by rain, and at last by mud. Yet villagers, travellers, farmers, fishermen—all were prepared, forewarned by the fleecy mist, its approach visible for miles as it billowed up and over the low saddles between the ridges of the plain and flowed down to fill the hollows below. This isolation was relief, deliverance at last from the arid remnant of summer, a warrant to sit idle and cool under a roof while outside, far and wide, further than the eye could see, the gods went about their share of the world's work so that in time man might return to plough, sow and graze cattle once more.

The rain, advancing out of the mist, fell with a quiet hissing upon dried grass, trees and dusty roads. At last the soft, slow wind which bore it reached and flowed over Bekla itself, spilling currents of cool air through its streets and alleys. Everywhere sounded pattering and trickling. Soon the gutters were flowing, the winking surface of the Barb was almost visibly rising and fountains which had stood dry for weeks began to spout water. Householders, opening their windows, sat by them silently, watching and smelling the rain in rapt contentment, while the homeless beggars, gathering in the colonnades, spat and nodded together, their sores and scabs eased by the moist coolness. Sencho, drowsing in the bath, woke at the long-awaited sound and, erecting with pleasure, sent for Occula and Meris to join him. Fleitil and his journeymen-assistants, having made their wedges and blocks firm round the base of the new statue of Airtha by the Tamarrik Gate, covered it with a canvas tarpaulin, packed their tools and set off for the nearest tavern, there to drink to the prospect of two months' profitable studio work under cover.

As evening began to fall Durakkon, standing at one of the east-facing windows of the Barons' Palace, watched the mist top the low ridge four miles away and inch down the slope, obliterating yard by yard the highway to Thettit. He could make out no single traveller on the road, but this was not surprising. Travellers would be unlikely to have delayed leaving Naksh for Bekla as late as the afternoon, for they too would have seen the mist, which often advanced faster than a man could walk; and as the roads were now, a wayfarer overtaken by it might well find himself at the mercy of worse than rain. Just as Senda-na-Say, waking by night at Puhra in the crackling fume, had encountered not only smoke but the death that lay within it.

189

Senda-na-Say had been a fool, thought Durakkon. He had unthinkingly assumed that the empire should and could be governed in the light of traditional, unchanging principles. He had never appreciated that new social forces had emerged within its society's complex structure; or if he had, had believed that concepts like honour, duty and the hereditary authority of the High Barons of Bekla could be stretched indefinitely, to embrace and control them. He himself, Durakkon, had known seven years ago that he and not Senda-na-Say was the man to move with the times and guide the empire along new paths. That was why he had taken the opportunity offered to him by Kembri and Sencho. They had needed a real and indisputable nobleman, a man of high rank, to lend respectability to the Leopards' seizure of power. He had seen the chance to fulfil his ideals, to give the empire enlightened, modern rule and greater prosperity; to sail with the irresistible current and not against it, to bring about the beneficial changes which Senda-na-Say would never have effected in a hundred years. Senda-na-Say had been a foolish, honourable man. The days of honourable men were past.

And his own ideals—what had become of them, those ambitions? He thought of the unspeakable Sencho, spinning his spy-nets, subsidizing delators and peculating the revenues as he lay stuffing and rutting among his trulls; of Kembri bargaining with the highest bidder for the use of Beklan soldiers to sustain the internecine feuds of the provinces. They, of course, remained untroubled by recurrent dreams of smoke and fire by night and the screaming of women from upper storeys.

Prosperity, he thought: yes, there was certainly plenty of that for those— and they were not a few—in whose power it lay to attain it. Standing at the window, looking out across the upper city, he saw a green-shirted pedlar emerge from the gate of Sencho's house and trudge quickly away towards the Peacock Gate, clearly in a hurry to get back to his lodgings before the rain could reach him. That pedlar, enjoying the protection of the law—only a month before, two men found guilty of waylaying a licensed pedlar had been sentenced to hang upside-down on the ridge between Naksh and Bekla—would certainly, since he had judged it worth his while to call at Sencho's, be carrying goods of higher price and quality than those to be found in a pack eight years before. As the man disappeared under the arch of the Peacock Gate, the oncoming streamers of mist began creeping across the Thettit highway, a mile beyond the eastern walls.

Durakkon turned from the window, hearing outside the room the voice of the soldier on duty. In accordance with his own orders, someone was being denied access. Nevertheless, he thought, he might as well deal with the matter now—whatever it might be—rather than later. He went across to the doorway.

'What is it, Harpax?'

'My lord, a messenger from the Sacred Queen; one of her attendants.'

'Admit her.'

He recognized the woman who entered; Ashaktis, Fornis's personal maid, a Palteshi who had come with her from Dari and remained with her ever since. Fornis, feeling, like himself, the need to be continually on her guard against assassination, restricted her personal entourage largely to Palteshis.

'So the rains are here at last, Ashaktis,' said Durakkon, by way of greeting.

'Yes, my lord, Cran be blest for them! The Sacred Queen commends herself to you, my lord. She is unwell—'

'I am sorry to hear it,' said Durakkon perfunctorily.

'It is not serious, my lord, but she thinks it best not to leave her house for the time being. She has asked me to say that nevertheless, she needs to speak with you and accordingly begs that you will be so good as to visit her this evening. Naturally, she hopes that her request will not put you to inconvenience and that you will be at liberty to have supper with her.'

He had better go, thought Durakkon. It was quite probable that Fornis had in all earnest come across something of which he ought to learn without delay. Calling in Harpax, he ordered an armed bodyguard to be ready in half an hour. Seven years ago, he reflected, he could have walked alone and unarmed through any part of the upper and most parts of the lower city.

Before the rain began to fall that evening and washed on through the night, drumming on roofs and shutters, running in brown rivulets down the steep streets below the central walls—the Street of the Armourers, Storks Hill and the Street of Leaves—turning the outfall of the Barb to a chattering torrent racing past the Tamarrik Gate through all three open sluices, calling a two months' halt to trade and war alike, not only the powerful and wealthy but also those who catered for or pandered to them had already been preparing for the weeks ahead. In many respects life in Bekla during the rains was anything but inactive. In Beklan idiom the season was called 'Melekril'; a word meaning, literally, the disappearance into cover of a hunted animal. Although supplies of fresh food were diminished, a certain amount still reached the markets and was bought by the rich, who traditionally passed the time in entertaining one another, often on a lavish scale. Vintners, grocers and bakers commonly laid in large stocks well before the onset of the rains, while herds of cattle were driven into the covered pounds outside the Gate of Lilies, there to be fed on roots and hay, for slaughter as required. The well-paved and -drained stone streets of the city made social intercourse easy enough for ladies carried in their litters. Among men, the customary practice was to walk through the warm rain with a stout cloak and overshoes.

The household of Kembri-B'sai had for some days past been fettled against the coming of the rains, for the Lord General customarily entertained freely during Melekril, partly because, like many successful soldiers of fortune, he enjoyed the display of wealth and the flattery and admiration of lesser personages; but also because he found this an excellent way of keeping his ear to the ground, of hearing rumours and assessing the undercurrents running through the life of the city.

For several years past he had given a banquet on the evening after the rains began, and this had now become something of an institution. Even as Durakkon was setting out for the house of the Sacred Queen, Kembri's servants were already on errands about the upper city, carrying his invitations for the following night. Meanwhile, slaves were preparing the great hall, polishing, sweeping, filling and trimming lamps, ensuring the flow of water to the pools and fountains and setting up the extra benches, couches and tables necessary for so large a number of guests. Several smaller rooms off the hall were also made ready, some for privacy and conversation, others for gambling or for still more pleasant diversion. The housekeeper, plate-master, chief cook and butler, themselves dignitaries in their own right in a household numbering over two hundred servants and slaves, held last-minute conferences and issued final instructions to their underlings. Great masses of fresh flowers from the gardens, kept shaded and watered for cutting at the last possible moment, were brought in and banked in the pools, ready to be made next day into wreaths, garlands and decorations. Kembri, as was his custom, had already instructed two of his army doctors to be in attendance; for experience had taught him that it would be unusual if the night's entertainment did not give rise to some illnesses, to say nothing of quarrels and injuries. Then, having supped, he betook himself—again by custom—to sleep at the house of one of his senior officers, for his own would be full of disturbance throughout the night.

'Banzi, have you used that stuff Terebinthia gave you?'

'Oh, Cran, yes! It felt horrible. I couldn't hardly do it!'

'But you *did* do it? Properly? You stuffed it right up?'

'Yes. Well, she saw to that.'

'Good! Only whatever happens you must *not* go and let some bastin' idiot make you pregnant. That'd ruin everythin', that would.'

'Oh, Occula, I wish you were coming too! I feel so nervous—'

'Well, it's bad luck in a way, but it can' be helped. Old Piggy-wig wants you and Meris and that's the end of it. Cran knows why! A big feast like this, he'd do much better to take two reliable, experienced girls like me and Dyphna, but there you are. Let's have a look at you. Oh, my goodness, banzi, it's lucky all the girls doan' look like you! There'd be rape every day!'

In spite of her agitation Maia could not help smiling. One glance in the wall-mirror had already been enough to tell her that no barefoot, hungry, cow-herding lass on the shores of Lake Serrelind had ever looked like this. The toes of her white leather slippers were stitched with crimson beads which matched the pleats of her full, Yeldashay-style skirt. A close-fitting, ribbed but flexible silk bodice both supported her bosom and left it almost completely uncovered, except by the tumble of well-brushed, golden hair falling two-thirds of the way to her waist. On one side of her head was fastened a spray of crimson *keranda*, the tiny, nacreous blooms of which gave off a fragrance perceptible five feet away. After much consultation, Terebinthia and Occula had agreed that she should wear no jewels at all, but that her eyelids and nipples should be gilded. The effect was startling and even Terebinthia, by glances if not in so many words, had shown herself not unimpressed.

'Now you listen to me carefully, banzi,' said Occula, drawing her down to sit beside her on a bench by the pool. 'You look good enough to eat—every lustful Leopard's little lump of loveliness. A few jaded palates are goin' to be tickled up no end, I wouldn' wonder. You look exactly what you are, my dearest—the pretty peasant-girl the goddess took a fancy to immortalize. Now for Cran's sake—no, for Kantza-Merada's sake, for I'm serious—remember this and doan' forget it! You're not goin' to a country dance or a festival in Meerzat to find yourself a nice boy. You're *workin*'! You're Piggy-wig's personal property, got it? You're there to do whatever he wants, and so that he can show you off same as that damn' fountain of his. If you forget that and let some rich man take you off into a corner without his permission—in fact, if you treat your master disrespectfully in any way at all—he can have you whipped or sold or anything he likes. And from what I've seen of this fat brute he'd be quite likely to. Now, do you under*stand*?'

'Yes, Occula. But what do I do if another man—some powerful man—comes and asks—well, you know—'

'You answer, "That's for my master to say." No one's more powerful than Sencho, anyway. Now this is the other thing. If you get any chance to oblige him or please him or do somethin' of your own accord before he tells you, *take* it. Whatever you think he wants, do it. Now you do *see*, banzi, do you?'

'What does she see?' asked Meris, coming into the room in a cloud of lime perfume. 'Her deldas sticking out? Occula, can you fix these blasted earrings for me? I can't get the pins out on the other side of the lobes.'

The Belishban girl's shining, black hair was coiled round her head in thick braids fastened with gold combs, leaving her olive-skinned, dark-eyed face to speak, as it were, for itself. It certainly did that, thought Maia. Her striking beauty had a sulky, lascivious quality, as though, sated with luxury, she were now determined to refuse herself to everyone, except to a man who could make her feel differently about it. She was wearing a thin necklace of plaited gold, gold bracelets on her bare arms, and a close-fitting robe of jade-green, gathered at the waist with a gold belt and falling to her ankles. The general effect was provocative in the last degree.

'You look like a trap ready to go off any minute,' said Occula. 'Jus' keep still while I slip 'em in.'

'Are you girls ready?' called Terebinthia from the other side of the bead curtains. 'Remember, you have to get everything prepared and be waiting by the High Counsellor's couch when he arrives. Meris, by this time you ought to know everything that has to be done. Mind you tell Maia, and see she doesn't make any mistakes.'

'Very well, säiyett,' answered Meris. 'Have you seen my cloak anywhere?'

'I have it here,' replied Terebinthia, 'and Maia's too.'

No other Beklan noble left his house so rarely as Sencho. Detesting exertion, or any interruption of his pleasures beyond what was necessary for the maintenance of his power and influence, he never visited the premises of merchants or craftsmen, but made them—as he had made Lalloc—bring their wares to him. When summoned by Durakkon he was obliged to obey, if only for the sake of appearance, but otherwise—and this seclusion was an important constituent of his power and of the fear he inspired—he attended only the greater religious ceremonies and perhaps half a dozen parties and banquets a year—those of the Sacred Queen and the other principal rulers.

Accordingly he did not keep litter-slaves, having little employment for them, but was accustomed, when he went abroad, to make use of soldiers. This evening he had ordered no fewer than twenty, under a tryzatt. Six of these, with two more for torch-bearers, were to carry the girls in a closed litter, arriving at the Lord General's house half an hour before Sencho himself.

Terebinthia, as mindful as any good huntsman or shepherd of her responsibility for her master's property, had ordered the big litter to be set down in the outer lobby of the women's quarters and left there. Once the girls had got into it, she closed and pinned the curtains and then called the soldiers back. Having reminded them of their orders not to speak to the girls and to take every care to carry them smoothly despite the mud, rain and falling dusk, she accompanied them as far as the gate, where old Jarvil, the porter, was waiting with the torch-bearers.

The distance to Kembri-B'sai's house was about three-quarters of a mile. Nevertheless, the journey lasted half an hour, for as they approached the gates they fell in with any number of other litters, the bearers jostling and pressing forward upon one another in the gathering darkness, all eager to get out of the rain.

'Silly bastards!' said Meris, holding on to a strut of the litter and peering out through a chink in the curtains. 'Why isn't there someone to keep all these damn' turds in order and let them in one or two at a time? Look, there's two lots actually come to blows over there! Thank Cran we've got soldiers! That's one consolation for belonging to Sencho, anyway.'

' 'Tis awful stuffy, isn't it?' said Maia. ' 'Nough to make anyone take on bad. Hope it isn't much further.'

'When the barons and the big shearnas start arriving later, *their* litter-bearers'll all be properly directed,' said Meris, 'but of course that'd be too much trouble to take over the likes of us. Oh, look! One of those torch-bearers isn't half a fine, big fellow, can you see?'

At this moment the tryzatt, standing outside, apologized to them for the delay and inconvenience, which he was now, he said, going to cut short. Thereupon, raising a cry of 'Way for the High Counsellor's girls!' he strode ahead of them, the litter following through the surrounding darkness and hubbub. The close air, their own exhaled breath in the confined space, the continual dipping and lurching as the soldiers lost their step in the crowd and the incessant drumming of the rain on the roof were beginning to make Maia turn sick and faint, when suddenly the noise subsided and she saw the glow of lamplight between the curtains. A moment later the litter was put down and she heard the orders of the tryzatt as he collected his men and left.

'Can we get out now?' she asked Meris, her curiosity and eagerness mounting as she realized that they must have arrived.

'Not yet,' replied the Belishban girl. 'You have to wait till the head steward or the säiyett comes and opens your litter. There'll be someone like Terebinthia, only not such a bitch—well, she couldn't be, could she? It isn't very long, as a rule.'

A minute later the curtains were drawn apart by a smiling, fair-haired woman of about thirty-five, dressed in a sky-blue robe fastened with two emerald brooches.

'You must be U-Sencho's girls?' asked this lady, on whose shoulder Maia now saw the cognizance of a chained leopard in gold.

'Yes, säiyett,' replied Meris, taking the hand extended to help her out of the litter.

195

'It's nice to see the High Counsellor's doing himself as well as usual,' smiled the other, evidently wishing to say something hospitable and pleasant. 'Have you been to the Lord General's Rains banquet before?'

'Yes, once; with General Han-Glat, säiyett,' said Meris, 'before I joined U-Sencho's household.'

'Oh, you've been with General Han-Glat?' said she, with a rather knowing smile. 'I see. And what about this lass?' she went on, giving her hand to Maia in turn. Then, as Maia stepped out and the lamplight fell on her, 'Oh, what a pretty girl! But you're only a *child*! How old are you?'

'Fifteen, säiyett.'

'And of course *you* haven't been here before, have you?'

'I've only been in Bekla just a short time, säiyett: I don't know a great lot about anything much.'

'Oh, you're charming! From Tonilda, aren't you? What's your name?'

'Maia, säiyett. Yes, from Lake Serrelind.'

'How nice! Well, I've got a lot to see to, so I can't stay talking any longer now, I'm afraid. Will you both be making your way upstairs?'

'Told you she'd be better than Terebinthia, didn't I?' said Meris, as they picked their way to the foot of the staircase between the litters filling the covered courtyard.

'No one's ever spoke to me like that before,' answered Maia. 'I mean, 's if I was a young lady. I thought we was slaves?'

'We are,' said Meris, 'and I shouldn't forget it if I were you. But we're the High Counsellor's bed-slaves. For all *she* knows we might have influence with him, you see, and she's not taking any chances.'

Maia made no further reply, being so much startled by their surroundings that she had scarcely heard what Meris had said. It was not her way to think ahead or try to imagine what a place would be like before she saw it, but she had always had a very lively apprehension of what was before her eyes. Looking round now, she felt sheer astonishment, mingled with something not unlike fear. Although darkness had fallen, the staircase was brilliant—brighter than day, or so it seemed to her, for the sources of light were so close. There were innumerable lamps—more, thought Maia, than she could possibly have seen before in all her days. Some, suspended by silver chains, were hanging in clusters from the high ceiling; others, all the way up the staircase, projected from the wall on copper brackets. At the top of the flight stood two bronze candelabra, fashioned to resemble *sestuaga* trees with their white spikes of bloom. The blooms were lighted candles—more than a hundred to each tree—and beside them stood two pretty girls, costumed as leopards in golden silk embroidered with black spots, whose tasks were to tend and replace the candles, welcome guests and—probably most important—simply to look beautiful. One of these, catching Maia's eye, gave her a friendly smile, which made her feel a little less nervous.

The staircase itself was of green-veined marble, with broad, shallow steps and a balustrade made of some gleaming, black wood unknown to Maia, which had been polished with a resinous oil, sharp and fresh to the smell. Putting one hand on this, she felt its glossy smoothness, with never a hint of a splinter, and saw her forearm reflected in a surface dark as a forest pool.

There were any number of girls both above and below them; blonde, fair-skinned Yeldashay; a little group of Ortelgans, talking together in their own tongue; two Belishbans, distinguishable by their accent like Meris's; an arrestingly lovely girl in a robe of pale grey, embroidered with the corn-sheaves of Sarkid; two broad-nosed, plaited-black-haired Deelguy, dressed in characteristically bright-coloured style, with necklaces of coins and gold hoops in their ears. All these and many more were climbing the stairs with a kind of leisurely eagerness. Suddenly Maia realized what underlay this poised, controlled yet confident excitement. 'Every single one of them's here,' she thought, 'because she's so out-of-ordinary beautiful that she belongs to a rich man in the upper city; and she knows it.' And then, with a kind of incredulous jolt to her thoughts, 'And—I'm one of them!'

The spacious landing on the first storey was laid out to represent a glade. The greensward was a carpet of thick pile, varying from level, smooth expanses to clumps and patches three or four inches high, all inter-woven with clusters of flowers; some from the life—primulas, white anemones and purple trails of vetch—others fancifully imagined. Upon this stood bushes and shrubs of bronze and green copper, their flowers and fruit carved from quartz, beryl and many other kinds of semi-precious stones, which sparkled in the lamplight. Among them, here and there, were life-size silver pheasants, quails, partridges and hares, watched from a little distance by a crafty, golden fox and a white marble ermine half-concealed in the undergrowth.

Through the midst of this make-believe game-park a path speckled with embroidered daisies led to a pool in which real goldfish were swimming among lilies and scented rushes. The fountain group at its centre repre-sented a naked couple, almost life-size. The boy, his head thrown back ecstatically, reclined on his side among the reeds, while the caressive hand of the laughing girl kneeling beside him appeared to be causing the fountain to play in spurting, intermittent jets. Maia, blushing, and equally unable either to gaze naturally at the fountain or to look away from it, noticed that most of the girls around her hardly spared it a glance.

Passing the pool, she unexpectedly saw that beyond, at the far end of the hall, rose a second staircase. It had never entered Maia's head that any house could consist of more than two storeys. Yet so it was. They were now going to ascend again; and it must be safe, for the stairs were crowded not only with girls but with male slaves in crimson uniform, one on each side all the way up, facing inward and holding silver candelabra. There were no lamps here, so that the candles formed a kind of tunnel of light leading upward through the lofty dimness above and around. Peering through this, Maia could glimpse expanses of painted walls—beasts and hunters, forests and falling water—all lying in shadowy gloom beyond the slaves' extended arms and the lambent, yellow flames.

At the top of the staircase stood a brazier of charcoal, tended by two more leopard-maids. From time to time one of these threw a pinch of incense on the glowing fuel, so that a thin cloud of scented smoke filled the landing and drifted down towards the girls as they came up. But indeed there was such a confusion of perfumes, both from the girls themselves and from the masses of lilies, jasmine, trepsis, planella and tiare banked about the staircase, that Maia felt quite overcome, and stopped for a moment, leaning on the balustrade. Meris, a step or two above her, looked round impatiently. 'What's the matter?'

'Nothing!' answered Maia, laughing. 'Just lucky it's my nose and not my eyes; reckon I'd be blinded else!'

Beyond the brazier, she and Meris found themselves in a broad corridor. This was open along its inner side, being flanked only by fluted, gilded columns. Within and a little below these lay the dining-hall itself which, passing through the colonnade and descending two or three shallow steps, they now entered.

After the flamboyance and display below, the hall at once impressed Maia with its calmer, restrained atmosphere; as though here, decoration and the delight of the eye were intended to become adjunct, subordinate to other pleasures. Over eighty feet long—by far the largest room Maia had ever been in—it contained no pictorial or statuary decoration whatever, being beautified almost solely by the quality and variety of its woodwork. The smooth, narrow planks of the floor were a light tan colour, waxed and polished, while the long steps by which the girls had descended from the outer corridor were of the same black, gleaming wood as the balustrades on the lower staircase. The colonnade extended along only two sides of the hall, the other two being panelled with five or six kinds of wood differing not only in colour but in grain: one resembling concentric ripples and maculate with knots; another brown, regular and close as honeycomb; and yet another very dark, but with a polished surface which, like starlings' wings, revealed its damascene intricacies only when seen in a strong light. All these were contrasted in bold patterns: lightning-like zigzags of pale against dark; luteous chevrons recessed in bevelled surfaces of chestnut; showers of dark stars minutely inlaid with patterned slips of white bone, so that they seemed to twinkle along the hollow-chamfered cornices. Above the lamps, the transoms spanning the vault were encrusted with fragments of fluorspar fine as gravel, which from the high dusk of the roof returned a faint glitter, like an echo of the light below.

The illumination here was more subdued than that on the staircases, for while there were indeed a great many lamps, all were in baskets of silver filigree, the effect of which was to perforate the light, so that it fell like petals over the tables and couches. Here and there, but particularly round the Lord General's table, this was augmented by foliated candelabra, forming pools of greater luminescence to emphasize the grandeur of the chief dignitaries.

In the centre of the hall, within a low, curving marble surround, lay another lily pool—the work of Fleitil. This had no central fountain, but more than fifty tiny jets, arranged symmetrically over the surface and barely clear of it, kept the water in continual, light movement with a rippling and pattering as of raindrops. From the bed a copper cylinder, in the form of an erect, swaying serpent, rose through the pool and on up to its outlet in the vault of the roof. This was in fact a flue, for the pool was floored with glass (the lilies being potted), and below it was a chamber in which lamps had been placed to illuminate the water from below and make it sparkle among the lily-leaves.

Along the shorter wall, three doors led to the kitchens. These had been wedged open, and through them slaves were coming and going, putting their finishing touches to the preparations for the banquet. The long, oak tables and benches were interspersed with couches, for throughout the empire at this time it remained a matter of local custom—or simply of personal choice—whether one ate sitting or reclining, and a particularly prolonged and enjoyable dinner might well begin with the first and conclude with the second. Upon a dais at one end stood the Lord General's table, surrounded with ferns and scented shrubs in leaden troughs. All the tables were scattered with fresh flowers, which two slaves were sprinkling with water. Silver cauldrons filled with different kinds of wine stood at the foot of the steps below the shorter colonnade, and a steward was inspecting these and removing any motes or flies which he found before covering them with muslin and placing beside each a bronze dipper and jug.

A great many girls were now entering, and Maia noticed that almost all, as they came through the colonnade and down the steps, made their way towards a tall, grave man wearing a Leopard cognizance on a crimson uniform like that of the slaves on the staircase. This, she guessed, must be the chief steward, for as each girl spoke to him, presumably giving her master's name, he would consult some sort of list or plan which he was holding, before directing her to one or another of the tables.

Meris plucked her sleeve. 'Come on, Maia! We haven't got much time.'

'D'you want me to—to ask him where we're to go?' asked Maia rather hesitantly; she felt timid of the authoritative, unsmiling figure, having just watched him snub with glacial propriety a little, merry-faced, black-eyed lass, rather like a nubile squirrel, whose manner he had evidently considered pert.

'Great Cran, no!' said Meris. 'We don't have to *ask* where the High Counsellor's couch is!'

They threaded their way among the girls and slaves, Meris leading. Maia, stopping to gaze with wonder at the coruscating pool, grew absorbed and came to herself to find that she was alone. A moment later, however, she caught sight of Meris stepping up on to the dais, and hurried to rejoin her. Stumbling against a lad carrying a tray full of silver salt-cellars, she clutched at his shoulder to save herself from falling.

'Oh—I'm so sorry—I—'

The boy turned towards her, the oath that he had been about to utter dying on his lips. ' 'S all right,' he answered, smiling. 'You can bump me with those as much as you want. Like some salt on them?'

He seemed about to oblige her without waiting for a reply, but Maia—who in Meerzat would have been well up to a little banter of this sort—only hastened quickly away.

On the dais, Meris was already engaged in altercation with an elderly slave lugging a wheeled basket full of cushions, some of which he had just given her.

'Come on, *far* more than that, damn you!' she said, stamping her foot.

'There's no more to spare,' answered the man gruffly. 'I must go and do—'

'You must do—' Meris gripped him by the shoulder—'what I *tell* you to do! Either you put ten more cushions on that couch at once, or I'm going to the chief steward.'

'There's others—' began the man.

'I don't give a baste for the others,' snapped Meris. 'I'm here to see the High Counsellor has what he needs. Now get *on* with it, unless you want a whipping!'

They were both standing beside a huge, upholstered couch, measuring something like ten feet by five, placed close to the Lord General's table. This was already thickly strewn with cushions and two or three leopard-skins, while beside it stood an array of basins, ewers, towels, two urns of water and a tray covered with bunches of herbs and jars of oil and ointment. As the slave, still grumbling, began taking more cushions from his basket and putting them on the couch, Meris turned away to inspect these various items.

'I only wish to Cran Terebinthia was here,' she said to Maia, whose brief absence she had apparently not noticed. 'Tell you the truth, I don't know as much as I ought to about all this stuff. Let's only hope the chief steward does. He must have looked after Sencho plenty of times before now.'

'But what's it all for?' asked Maia, as Meris dipped her finger in a jar of ointment, rubbed her forearm and smelt it.

'Why, to help him to stuff himself silly, of course,' answered Meris. 'You've never done this before, have you? Never mind. Long as we've got all we need, I can tell you what to do. For a start, you can bank those extra cushions up so that they overlap each other. No, not like that! They have to curve out and round, to support his belly; and we'll keep a few back, so that we can add more when he wants them.'

She continued their preparations energetically, twice sending Maia with fresh demands to the household slaves. At length, standing back, she said, 'Well, that's all I can think of. And we sit on these stools here. I should think the guests'll be up any minute.'

All the girls were waiting, now, in their places; some seated on stools, like Meris and Maia, others standing behind the benches. The slaves were ranged along the walls and the carvers behind their tables. The hall had fallen quiet and there was a general air of expectancy.

After about a minute a soldier, dressed in black and gold, appeared between the central columns and sounded four notes on a long, slender trumpet. This done, he made his way to the dais, taking up a position not far from Maia and Meris. Behind him the guests began entering the hall in groups, talking and laughing together as they came.

Back in Tonilda, Maia's path had very seldom crossed that of rich men. Once, when she was no more than nine and swimming in the lake, some noble of Serrelind, sailing his boat, had shouted to her to get out of the way as the bow came gliding swiftly down upon her. Frightened, she had had time to stare up a moment into his intent, elsewhere-gazing face as the boat swept past, leaving her bobbing in its wash. And again, during a festival in Meerzat, she had watched as two roistering young blades, in great boots and feathered hunting-caps, set upon a fisherman and then carried off his pretty young wife, laughing at her screams and shouting that it was all in sport.

Now the room was full of such voices and such men, dressed in splendid robes or brilliant, open-weave shirts and silken breeches, carrying silver goblets and tooled leather knife-cases, conversing with confident indifference to everything but themselves and their own affairs. They made her so nervous that as a group approached the dais it was all she could do to remain seated on her stool. 'Keep still!' whispered Meris. 'Stop fidgeting!'

Among the guests walked several shearnas, and at these Maia looked with some surprise. She had been expecting a galaxy of outstanding beauty, and at first felt puzzled and rather disappointed that while some were certainly beyond argument beautiful, as well as being magnificently robed and jewelled, many struck her as nothing out of the ordinary. Suddenly (and thereupon feeling even more acutely her own lack of experience and maturity) she recalled what Occula had said about authority and style. These girls were strolling, talking and laughing among the nobles with assurance, treating them as equals and giving every appearance of being entirely at ease.

In that moment it dawned upon her that a girl like Meris was nothing but a pretty face one end and a hot tairth the other, and that this was Sencho's compass—all he could rise to. She realized intuitively that for all his wealth and power, few of the girls sauntering among these nobles would care to consort with the High Counsellor, any more than an intrepid hunter would want to go ratting. They fairly emanated style, accomplishment and wit. Whom they would they encouraged and whom they would they teased or brushed aside. What they were offering to their admirers, she grasped with some awe, was their company; just that; as much out of bed as in. Occula, she remembered, had remarked that they themselves had got to be better than the others. Well, here were the others. She felt disheartened. 'S'pose they feel like I do when I'm swimming,' she thought. And then, 'But where do such girls come from, I wonder, and how do they get to be—'

Suddenly her thoughts were interrupted and she started. Through the colonnade, not forty feet away from her, appeared the young man who had spoken to Occula and herself in their jekzha at the top of the Khalkoornil. Dressed in a saffron-coloured robe embroidered across the breast with a snarling, crimson leopard, he was talking animatedly to a brown-haired, demure-looking girl who, as Maia watched, smiled at him sidelong and then said something which made him turn towards her with a quick burst of laughter, laying one hand on her wrist.

A moment later he glanced towards the Lord General's table, caught sight of Maia, stared for a moment and then, murmuring a few words to his companion, came across to the foot of the dais and smiled up at her. Maia, uncertain what to do, got to her feet; whereupon the young man raised his palm to his forehead, at which her colour rose.

'Well, well, the princess with the golden hair!' said the young man. 'We met in the Khalkoornil, didn't we, the day they were bringing in the new statue of Airtha? Do you recall?'

'Yes, my lord,' replied Maia, forcing herself to smile and look him in the eye.

'But I didn't introduce myself, did I?' said he.

Maia felt a sudden access of courage. If he wanted to tease, well, she might as well try her hand, seeing as he seemed so friendly.

'No, my lord, you must have forgot; but you're that notorious, see, I know who you are; only that's part of my business, that is.'

The young man laughed, apparently delighted. 'The devil it is! And is business good? You got yourself sold all right, then? Who to?'

'To the High Counsellor U-Sencho, my lord.'

His face fell. 'Oh. Oh, well; I suppose you had no choice in the matter, had you? And your pretty black friend?'

'The same. But she's not here tonight.'

'I'll hope to see more of you later on: I must get back now, or *my* friend'll be wondering what on earth I'm up to. Come to that, she could be right, you know.' Thereupon, with a quick wave of the hand, he was gone.

'Bloody basting Cran!' said Meris. 'Wasn't that Lord Elvair-ka-Virrion?'

'M'm-h'm.'

'You've met him before?'

'Oh, ah.'

But Meris had no chance to pursue her enquiries, for now all the guests had taken their places and were awaiting the Lord General and his party, who could be seen assembling in the colonnade outside.

The heavy, broad-shouldered figure of Kembri preceded his guests into the hall. Having ascended the dais, however, he turned and, in accordance with custom, gave his hand to each, himself conducting him to his place and putting on his head the flower-crown lying ready on the table. If one did not seem to him to suit a guest as well as it should, he laid it aside and chose another, taking his time until he and all the guests were content. While this ceremony was proceeding, ten soldiers carried Sencho on a litter down the steps, into the hall and up to his couch.

The High Counsellor was not clothed, for he meant to enjoy himself, but for decency's sake was partly covered with a length of white-and-gold fabric, already clinging with sweat to his monstrous body. Torques of jewelled silver were half-buried in the flesh of his arms and a great ruby ring, which he could no longer wear on any finger, hung by a chain among the rolls of fat at his neck. Maia wondered by what means he could have been brought up the stairs. The soldiers, halting, held the litter beside and on a level with the couch, while four slaves lifted him bodily from one to the other. At the same time Meris, standing ready with a towel wrung out in tepid water, wiped his face and shoulders, gesturing to Maia to place more cushions under his belly and beneath his legs. At length, sighing with pleasant anticipation and indicating that all was now to his satisfaction, the High Counsellor waved the girls back to their places.

In all this he displayed no embarrassment or any sign that he felt in the least self-conscious or singular among the guests. Most, indeed, as he well knew, envied and feared him and, so far from being disgusted, were rather disposed to admire the wealth and luxury of a court where a man could become so fat that he could not walk ten steps across a room. Nor did it trouble him that every other guest on the dais was either alone, like Durakkon, or accompanied by some well-known shearna. His slave-girls had cost a great deal of money, showed to advantage and suited his personal inclinations and needs better than any free woman.

When Kembri had concluded his ritual of welcome, his guests all turned towards the body of the hall, extending their arms and acknowledging the applause and cries of congratulation from below. Then the Lord General greeted the company, wishing them a happy and profitable Melekril and conveying the regret of the Sacred Queen that she was unable to be present on account of an indisposition, which fortunately was not serious. Finally, he welcomed Durakkon as High Baron of Bekla, and formally asked his consent for the feast to begin.

An hour later, Maia was feeling completely bewildered. Once or twice, indeed, she had found herself wondering in all earnest whether she might not be dreaming. She would not have believed such gluttony to be physically possible; yet the banquet was not half-finished. She was not to know, of course, that greed is largely a matter of practice, that most of these nobles were well accustomed to eating to excess and that the whole feast had been carefully planned to make it easy and pleasant for them to do so. Commencing with little, savoury delicacies—biscuits baked with spices, fish-flavoured pancakes and fowls' livers with peppers and mushrooms— they had, after a time, continued by mingling these with several sorts of soup; hare with artichoke; thick broth of fish; chilled, mint-flavoured cucumber, and eggs beaten together with lemons. Next, whole baked *bramba*, bred in enclosed pools of the Barb, were carried in, smothered in savoury butter and surrounded by poached trout and crayfish covered in a sharp, green *seriabre* sauce. Then, since even these Beklans were obliged to pause for a time in their luxury, there ensued an interval, while slaves opened the windows on the cool, rain-hissing night and carried round damp towels and bowls of lemon-water.

Maia, who as one of Sencho's attendant girls had been told by the chief steward to eat as much as she wished, was by now more than satisfied. She could not have continued for a bag of gold. Although Meris had warned her against drinking more than half a goblet of wine, she was so much excited and so little used to it that this alone had made her slightly tipsy. How long was it now, she wondered, since the evening when she had begged Kelsi for a mouthful of bread in the lane? Had Morca had the baby yet, and might it have been a boy? What was Tharrin doing for pleasure, now she was gone? These thoughts made her feel anything but homesick. Full-fed girls with exquisite clothes did not eke out their existence on the Tonildan Waste. Sitting demurely on her stool, she watched a plump, half-naked shearna with soft, white shoulders lean back on her couch while a big man in a purple tunic fed her with morsels of trout held in his fingers, and then supported her head on one arm as he tilted his goblet to her lips. The mere sight made her feel that she herself was no longer the same girl.

At length the windows were again closed round the cooled room and the trumpeter recalled those who had gone out to stroll in the colonnade. When all had returned, a procession of thirty slaves entered amidst cheers and applause, each pair holding between them an immense silver dish of venison. A second procession followed, carrying joints of beef; then a third with roast pigs and a fourth with pheasants and turkeys. The carvers set about their work, while bowls of vegetables and spices were placed on the tables for all to share as they pleased. At this point several of the men left the benches for couches near-by, their companions following to feed them where they lay.

Up to this point the High Counsellor had required little or no help from either Meris or Maia, the household slaves having brought him food and drink in the same way as they had waited upon the rest of Kembri's guests. Now, however, with gestures and impatient gruntings, he conveyed to Meris wishes which she evidently understood for, having once more wiped his face and body (opening each crease between her fingers with sedulous care), she crushed a handful of pungent, sharp-scented herbs and held it for him to smell, at the same time pushing towards Maia a tubular, silver vessel with a bulbous base and pointing towards the foot of the couch. Maia, uncomprehending, stood looking uncertainly at the vessel, which was engraved all round with a stylized pattern of chubby little boys making water on each other's buttocks. Meris, fuming with impatience, had to tell her what to do. Thrusting her trembling hands under the gold-embroidered cloth, she groped among the folds of sweating fat and at length, having achieved what was required of her, felt the High Counsellor respond with shuddering relief to the sensation of the cool rim. A household slave, attracting her attention with a touch on the elbow, passed her a clean cloth for the conclusion of her task, took the vessel from her, covered it with a towel and carried it away.

She had already turned to go back to her stool when Meris, snapping her fingers to attract her attention, picked up one of the bowls filled with perfumed oil. Thereupon she nodded to Maia to stand opposite her on the other side of the couch and draw back the cloth to bare the High Counsellor's belly. As the Belishban girl held the bowl towards her, Maia understood that she was to rub her master with the oil.

After some moments, however, Sencho began to stir and shake his head in irritation. Meris, giving the bowl to Maia, herself undertook the task of rubbing, working smoothly with her finger-tips as the High Counsellor relaxed pleasurably under her more practised ministrations.

'What does it do?' whispered Maia.

'Helps his belly to distend and hold still more,' answered Meris. 'Now wipe off what's left with that towel there—no, gently, Maia!—and put some fresh cushions that side while I help him to turn over.'

Sencho, however, now wished to be supported into a half-sitting posture, and in this position gave instructions to a slave who had brought to the couch a small carving-table. Maia supposed that he would carve and then retire, but instead the High Counsellor ordered him to cut up all the meat on the board—fowls, pork, beef and venison—and then to remain standing by the couch while he ate, Meris holding at his elbow a tray of sauces and vegetables.

During the next half-hour several guests, well aware of the power and wealth of the High Counsellor, left their places below and made their way up to the dais to speak a few words to Sencho and—insofar as it was possible to pierce his preoccupation—ingratiate themselves. Receiving little response some of these, to keep themselves in countenance, began chatting with the girls and paying them compliments. Maia, praised and flattered by one man after another—and even by two or three of the shearnas, who were rather taken with her child-like beauty and ingenuous replies—began to feel admiration for her master and, for the first time, pride in belonging to a man whom rich nobles went out of their way to propitiate and whom she had seen, with her own eyes, consume more rich food than her entire family could have eaten in a week, as well as having drunk over half a gallon of wine.

'Will he be sick?' she whispered to Meris, seeing the Belishban girl bend down for a pottery basin as Sencho, gulping the last of the meat, lay back, clutching his belly, over which he could barely clasp his hands.

'The High Counsellor very seldom cares to vomit,' replied Meris in a matter-of-fact tone, as though Maia had asked her whether he liked to sleep after dinner. 'If he needs to he'll tell you.' Thereupon she began picking fragments of meat and vegetables out of the cushions and putting them in the basin, which she handed to a slave to be removed.

A second interlude had now begun. The windows were again opened for a time, but fewer guests left the hall, since most felt little inclination—or, indeed, ability—to move from where they lay. Ten or twelve slaves carried round silver vessels like that used by Sencho, while others followed with incense-burning censers and aspergills for sprinkling rose-water. Here and there men had already fallen asleep, and one or two of these, whom ·their girls knew from experience were unlikely to revive for some hours, were carried out, lying on their couches.

After about half an hour eating was resumed, but now the intensity of greed was succeeded by a kind of frivolous toying with sugared delicacies and sweet things. The formal seating broke up. Many of the guests formed small groups, joining friends at other tables or gathering about some shearna whom they admired. Round the flat-topped, marble parapet of the pool the servants placed trays of little cakes, syllabubs, custards, fruit, cream pancakes, jellies, junkets, caramels and the like. To these the slave-girls went and helped themselves, bringing back to their masters whatever they fancied. Meanwhile Durakkon and Kembri left the dais and began to wander among the company, making themselves agreeable and receiving congratulations and praise.

Sencho, having sent Meris to fetch a bowl of peaches in sweet wine, allowed her to feed him for a time, but then became petulant, pushing the bowl aside and sending her back several times for other delicacies, none of which served to revive the all-absorbing ardour of greed which had engrossed him hitherto. Having rinsed his mouth and called for fresh cushions, he ordered Meris once more to pull the cloth off his body in order that he might drowse at greater ease; for torpor and indolence, following upon satiety, formed a very real and conscious part of the High Counsellor's pleasure. Now that he was fully glutted, to lie naked in the presence of nobles and free women who thought it more prudent to hide whatever distaste they might feel—or who might even feel admiration—afforded him peculiar satisfaction; him who had once begged for scraps outside a merchant's back door and subsequently, knowing what was good for him, pretended to enjoy gratifying that merchant and his greasy, foul-breathed friends. He thrust a hand under Meris's skirt but then, reflecting that perhaps even he had better, in accordance with custom, wait until after the kura, closed his eyes and in a minute or two had fallen asleep.

Maia, relieved to have carried out her duties so far without any serious blunder, felt free to relax. Meris, she noticed, seemed now to have become possessed by a kind of panting animation and excitement. The detached professionalism with which she had concentrated on ministering to Sencho had been replaced by a quick-glancing alertness and response to everyone around them. She sat smiling boldly at each guest who strolled past; and when a tall young man, wearing the Fortress cognizance of Paltesh, offered her his goblet, she almost snatched it from him, drained it dry, flung her arms round his neck and kissed him warmly on the lips. Emboldened by this example, Maia called a passing slave-boy and asked him to bring her some more wine. It was of beautiful quality, cool and deliciously refreshing—'Wonder what Tharrin'd say to this?' she thought—and as it mounted to her head she stood up, walked over to one side of the dais and stood looking out over the lamp-lit hall, from the centre of which the rippling pool glittered up at her like an open eye.

The scent of jasmine and lilies was now stronger still on the warmed air. On impulse she picked up a crown of tiare blossom, four inches deep, which one of Kembri's guests had left lying on the table, and placed it on her own head. Mingled with the perfumes filling the hall were smells of wine, of lamps, of the sweating slaves and the resinous polish in the warmed panelling, and beyond all these the fresh, cool smell of the rain outside—that same rain which she knew was falling, mile after mile, across the solitude of Lake Serrelind. 'Only I'm not there now, see?' she remarked happily to a passing noble with a slim, graceful shearna on his arm. The girl glared haughtily at her, but the young man, obviously in a mood to be delighted by everything and especially by such a pretty lass, replied 'Well, wherever it is, I should think you soon will be, if you go on looking like that,' and gave her hand a quick squeeze before passing on.

Maia, still staring at the sparkling water and remembering the flocks of white ibis wading in the lake shallows on a summer morning, was recalled to her surroundings as the trumpeter sounded yet again. Indeed he made her jump, for he was only a few yards away. Sencho, however, did not even stir. Not knowing what might be to follow, she hurried back to her stool. Half a dozen musicians had entered the hall—three hinnari players, a drummer, a flautist and a man with a kind of wooden xylophone called a *derlanzel*—and taken up their places in the open space round the pool. Meanwhile slaves, using hooked poles, lowered and extinguished several of the clusters of lamps. The outer parts of the hall grew dimmer, so that the centre appeared brighter by contrast. The musicians, after tuning for a few moments, began to play a minor-harmonized refrain—no more than four bars—varied only by the changing rhythms of the drummer and the derlanzist. After they had repeated this several times, twenty young women in gauzy, transparent robes of grey, brown, green and white came running gracefully into the hall, took up their positions round the pool and then, at a signal from their leader, began to dance.

Maia had always taken a natural delight in dancing, and back in Tonilda had been reckoned a good hand at clapping, stamping and twirling in the ring. But she had never seen anything like this, the goddess Airtha's sacred

Thlela; an age-old institution of Bekla, famous throughout the empire. All the girls, trained from childhood, were dedicated to the service of the goddess. They were neither free women nor slaves, but imperial property (like state jewels or a household guard), their function being to enhance and beautify the public occasions of the city, both religious and secular. Like soldiers, they lived together, were subject to the rule of their order and enjoyed the public respect and status proper to their vocation (though ordinary citizens perhaps honoured rather than envied their restricted, exacting lives). Some, as they grew older, might, with the Sacred Queen's approval, leave the Thlela and marry, but others, having the dance and its way of life in their blood, spent their latter days as teachers, wardrobe-mistresses or such-like hangers-on of one kind and another. The entire business of the Thlela—recruiting, training, costuming and so on—was state-financed and it was universally regarded as one of the great glories of the city. Sencho himself, attempting a few years before to remove from it a girl he fancied—for such was his way when so inclined—had been met with an incredulous, outraged hauteur which had made even him think better of the idea.

Their dance now—as Maia, after a minute or two, grasped with growing delight and elation—represented the turbulence, flow and changes of a great river throughout the weathers and seasons of the year. This dance, the 'Telthearna', had become a favourite at the Rains banquet, and many of those present, familiar with every sequence and movement, watched with discriminating eyes and appraising connoisseurship. What Maia felt, however, was the even greater, unrepeatable pleasure of a completely new experience, to which she responded with nothing apart from her own natural ardour and native wit. The look and behaviour of wide expanses of water was something she knew everything about at first hand. She almost wept to recognize—and to realize that she recognized—the grey waves lapping at morning under a light wind, the sand-bars bared by summer drought and then a storm coming down upon the turbid, brown floods of the rain season. Luckily for her, the High Counsellor's sleep remained unbroken, for the dance had reft her out of herself so completely that she would certainly have bungled any duties that might have been required of her. Indeed, the memory of that Telthearna, danced in Kembri-B'sai's great hall, remained with Maia all her life.

It came to an end at last in a gradual drifting away of the waters into distance and starlight, with a remote thrumming and vibration of the muted hinnaris, the girls sinking down to lie prone and at last motionless upon the floor. The Thlela never sought or received applause, which would have been regarded as impious and profane. A deep silence of admiration, however, lasted for a full minute; after which conversation gradually resumed.

At this point Durakkon, together with a small group of nobles from the older aristocratic families, left the banquet. Others began strolling out—some to gamble in the private rooms; others with their slave-girls or shearnas, waving to their friends and promising to return later.

More lamps were quenched and the hall became dimmer still, save for the central window embrasure in the longer wall. This, the sill of which stood about five feet from the floor, was so wide and deep as to resemble a small, open-fronted room, the shuttered window forming a wall at the back. Here the lamplight remained bright, so that the recess looked not unlike a stage.

First the dancing-girls of the Thlela and then the serving-slaves left the hall (among them Maia's salt-boy, who grinned at her as he passed). The last to go drew a mesh of thin, gold-tinted curtains between the columns of the colonnade. The musicians, however, remained in their places, playing a quiet improvisation of chords which did no more, as it were, than lightly to colour the air with sound.

For a while the murmur of talk and laughter continued, but Maia could sense behind it an expectancy and tension, as though some fresh excitement were now awaited. Suddenly the tall young man from Paltesh, who had offered his goblet to Meris, appeared in the lamplight at the foot of the window embrasure. In one hand he was holding a cushion and this, waving it over his head, he tossed up into the embrasure with a cry of 'Otavis!'

At this there was some cheering and several other men echoed 'Otavis! Otavis!' But at once another young man strode up to the embrasure, threw in a second cushion and cried 'Melthrea!' at which there were further cries of support and approval.

Other men followed, one by one adding cushions to the growing pile now beginning to form a bed in the embrasure. Each, as he threw his cushion upward, called out a name—Otavis, Melthrea, Nyctenthis, Pensika and so on—while one of Kembri's girls, a slim Lapanese with dark hair falling to her waist and ruby bracelets on her bare arms, made marks with chalk on one of the tables.

Watching, Maia became aware that Meris was breathing hard and uttering low cries of excitement. 'Eighteen!' she exclaimed at length, as Elvair-ka-Virrion himself, tossing up his cushion, called 'Otavis!' and paused to refill his goblet from one of the cauldrons before returning to his place.

'I don't think she'll be beaten now!' she added, glancing round at Maia, 'Fat lot of chance we'll ever have! That bitch Terebinthia hardly ever allows us out.'

'But what's it all about?' asked Maia.

'Why, they're voting to elect the Kura Queen, of course,' answered

Meris. 'First they decide how many cushions are going to be thrown altogether, and then the men draw lots for who's to throw them. It's always fifty at the Rains banquet, and the girl who gets most cushions is the Kura Queen.'

'A shearna?'

'Oh, Maia, don't be damn' silly; shearnas don't perform the kura! The Kura Queen's always a slave-girl, but the thing is she gets a prize of a thousand meld, and very often she's freed afterwards. It's the one bit of luck every girl hopes for: I might have got it if only I'd stayed with Han-Glat. He always lends his girls very freely, you know, so they have plenty of chances to make friends and become popular. But you're making me lose count. How many's that, Ravana?' she called to a girl near-by, who was watching as closely and excitedly as herself.

'Twenty-one for Otavis now!' answered the girl. 'Good luck to her! She lent me forty meld last year and never asked for it back.'

A few moments later a cheer went up as it became clear that Otavis's total number of cushions could not now be beaten. The few remaining to make up the fifty were flung into the embrasure and two girls, climbing up, spread them evenly over the sill. As they slid down again a brief silence fell. Then, into the pool of lamplight stepped the strikingly beautiful girl in the pale-grey robe embroidered with corn-sheaves, whom Maia had noticed on the staircase. She was smiling, but Maia could see tears glistening in her eyes and it was plain that she was half-overcome with excitement and delight. Amidst cries of acclamation and a hammering of goblets she raised her arms to the company, placed both hands on the window-sill and vaulted up into it as lightly as a leaf, turning, as she did so, to sit facing the hall. In this position, while the music became louder and its rhythm more marked and insistent, she slowly and deliberately loosened her robe at the throat and, drawing up her shoulders in a kind of smooth, graceful shrug, caused it to subside like grey foam about her, until she was sitting naked to the thighs. Then, as she held out one slim foot, a broad-shouldered young man, clad only in a pair of leather breeches, came forward, drew off her sandals and laid them side by side on the floor.

'Spelta-Narthè!' whispered Meris. 'I wondered who she'd have lined up.'

'Who's he?' asked Maia.

'Well, he *is* a slave—strictly speaking—but a very privileged and senior one. He's Elvair-ka-Virrion's huntsman. He's well-known to be able to do it anywhere. He's been invited into quite a few Leopard ladies' beds, so they say.'

Otavis, now completely naked and so beautiful that the sight drew fresh murmurs of admiration from every man in the hall, rose slowly to her feet, stepping out of the tumble of gauze about her ankles and letting it fall to the floor. Then, laughing as she bent down and gave him her hand, she helped her partner up into the embrasure and, kneeling before him in the posture with which a kura customarily began, swiftly and deftly made him as naked as herself.

Ever since Occula had told her what a kura was, Maia had had at the back of her mind a feeling of distaste and aversion. She had, she now realized, unconsciously been imagining other people watching herself and Tharrin forced against their will to exhibit that which they would have wished to keep private between themselves. What she saw now, however, was altogether different in mood. The beauty and her partner, who knew very well what they were doing and were obviously proud of it, went about their business with a light-hearted, jocund gaiety and entire lack of shame which, she realized after a minute or two, had already brought to her own lips a smile of complicit enjoyment. This outrageous behaviour, pursued with a kind of sportive warmth which involved and was meant to involve the watchers, was marked by the one quality essential to prevent it from being sordid or disgusting: it was frivolously playful. The tone of the love-making was very light, the emphasis all on provocation, amusement and ingenuity rather than on any pretended depth of passion which, by being plainly insincere, would have struck a false note. 'This is *not* passion,' the participants seemed to be saying. 'This is sport—bird-song to awaken you in the garden of pleasure.' Maia's response was unforced and spontaneous. Indeed, at one point, when Otavis, facing the company and leaning back in her partner's arms as she sat astride his lap, looked down for a moment, feigning shocked astonishment, and then once more opened her arms to the onlookers with a dazzling smile, as though delighted to find herself thus flagrantly displayed, Maia felt so deeply excited that she could only stand gazing silently amid the general laughter and acclamation.

After some six or seven minutes it became clear that most of the watchers no longer needed any further stimulation or example, even of so expert and charming a nature. In the dim light, men lay in the arms of their girls, who openly caressed them in front of others similarly engaged and too much preoccupied to pay heed. From all sides came cries of tension and excitement, with here and there a quick squeal of protest or half-hearted remonstration. Otavis and her huntsman, their task complete, slipped down unnoticed from the window embrasure, picked up their clothes and stole away together.

As the sport intensified, Meris sprang suddenly to her feet.

'Baste it!' she cried, turning to Maia and speaking with such fury that Maia jumped, supposing for a moment that she must have done something wrong. 'What are we sodding well supposed to be made of—cream cheese?'

In an instant she had loosened the neck-cord and belt of her robe and stepped out of it even more swiftly than Otavis. Rather as a flowering shrub may look somewhat the worse for wilting in strong sunshine yet still strikingly beautiful, so Meris, plainly off-balance with wine and enflamed lust, was none the less a sumptuous sight, standing in nothing but her sandals and bracelets. Even Maia, who had of course seen her naked more than once, found herself looking with admiration at the lithe, taut flow of her limbs and body, informed now with a kind of questing voracity. No wonder, she thought, that all those wayfarers had gone to their grief on the Herl-Dari highway; and no wonder, either, that the tryzatt had spared the girl to blame for it.

'Maia,' said Meris with lofty dignity, 'jus' look aft' that till I get back!'

Picking up her robe from the floor, she folded it, with a kind of lunatic precision, across the High Counsellor's belly, stepped down from the dais and was immediately lost to view in the shadowy hall, which to Maia now resembled nothing so much as Lake Serrelind at windy nightfall—a blurred, tossing expanse, noisy with fluid babbling and cries not unlike those of unseen birds. Reckon this must be one bit as got left out of that dance, she thought.

She had just retrieved Meris's robe and laid it by her stool when she felt a touch on her shoulder. Turning, she caught her breath to recognize Elvair-ka-Virrion. He was alone and plainly sober. She stood up, palm to forehead. 'My lord!'

Without hesitation Elvair-ka-Virrion drew her to him and kissed her.

'I'm not a lord, I'm a man. Maia, do you know you're by far the most beautiful girl in the room? I've never forgotten you from the moment I saw you in the Khalkoornil that day. You've conquered me, Maia! Come and make love with me! You'll make me the happiest man in Bekla—and the luckiest!'

Maia, thrown for the moment into utter confusion, shrank back as though scorched from this blaze of ardour. As Elvair-ka-Virrion waited for her reply, gazing passionately into her eyes, she recalled what Occula had impressed so emphatically upon her.

'I can't, my lord: I'm attending on the High Counsellor.'

Elvair-ka-Virrion gave the sleeping Sencho a brief glance of contempt and turned back to her. 'That pig? He won't stir. Maia, do you know what it is that's made it impossible for me to forget you? You're *real*—you're unspoiled—you're like some marvellous lily out on the plain that no one knows about, no one's picked; that no one had even seen until I found it. You're natural, you're honest.' He waved his hand towards the hall. 'You feel disgusted by all this, don't you? I don't like it, either. Let me take you to my own rooms. I only want to be good to you! You've stolen my heart, Maia!' Then, as she made no reply, 'It's true! Don't you believe me?'

Maia's eyes filled with tears. 'I'm a slave-girl, my lord! My master—'

'Oh, I'll make it all right with him,' said Elvair-ka-Virrion. Yet this was spoken with less conviction than anything he had yet said: even Maia could perceive that it was bravado. The High Counsellor, as Occula had already pointed out to her, had all the touchy, humourless pride of a parvenu. A young gallant like Elvair-ka-Virrion would no more be able to placate his vindictive anger, if it were aroused, than a child could hold a bull. In her mind's eye she seemed to see Occula silently shaking her head.

'I can't, my lord: not without my master's consent. Another time, p'raps—'

'No, now!' cried Elvair-ka-Virrion, dashing his fist into his palm and laughing at his own frustration.

Maia's self-possession collapsed. 'Oh, my lord, please don't make it so hard for me! If you really want to be good to me, as you say you do, then go!'

For a long moment Elvair-ka-Virrion gazed at her; at her trembling lips and the tears in her eyes. Then he answered shortly, 'Very well,' turned on his heel and strode quickly down from the dais and away into the shadows.

Left to herself once more, Maia sat down. The encounter had upset her: she felt afraid. She had grown up in a simple world, where the worst troubles were empty bellies and toothache—bad enough in all conscience, but at least one knew what was what. Here, all was strange; it was like walking in the dark. She had duly done as Occula had said. But was that really the best—the safest—thing she could have done? Suppose Elvair-ka-Virrion were now to make himself her enemy? 'Lespa!' she whispered. 'Goddess Lespa!' But the stars outside were hidden behind clouds and rain: Lespa seemed far away. Her head was beginning to ache. She wished they could go home to bed.

She had altogether forgotten her master, lying inert on his couch like some bloated alligator on a mudbank. But now, licking his thick lips and fluttering his eyelids, he began to stir and, struggling to turn on his side, reached out one arm towards a cloth lying at the head of the couch. Maia, jumping up, wrung out a fresh towel and wiped his face and body as she had seen Meris do. Then, supporting his head, she offered him wine and held crushed herbs to his nostrils.

Sencho, having rinsed his mouth with the wine, spat it back into the goblet, which Maia put down on the floor. As she once more bent over him, he put a groping arm round her neck and sucked one of her breasts, at the same time drawing her hand down to his loins. Clearly he was still not fully woken from his stupor, for after a few moments his lips released her nipple and his head sank back upon the cushions. Yet what he wanted was plain enough: if it had been Tharrin, she would have known very well what to do. She paused, uncertain. At this moment the High Counsellor, without opening his eyes, belched and then panted urgently, 'Meris! Meris!' As Maia, now at a complete loss, remained unmoving beside the couch, he repeated, more forcefully and with a kind of snarling impatience, 'Meris!'

In panic Maia turned and plunged down into the crowded hall, calling 'Meris! Meris!' She tripped in a heap of yellow lilies and almost fell as her sandalled feet crushed the stems into a slippery pulp. Racing on towards the pool, she measured her length over a girl's buttocks and, picking herself up, heard behind her an oath and a male cry of anger. 'Meris!' she called. 'Meris!'

Suddenly, in the flickering half-light, there was Meris, lying in a scatter of cushions on the floor. It was as though Maia herself had conjured her up from some subterranean obscurity. Her shadow-dappled body was half-covered by a man's, round which her raised legs were locked, clutching and pressing. Her mouth was open, her eyes half-closed, her breath coming hard as though she were climbing a hill.

'Meris!' cried Maia, bending over her. 'Meris!'

'What the hell?' murmured the Belishban girl dazedly. 'Oh, Cran, Maia, it's you! Let us alone, damn you!'

Maia, reaching across the man's heaving shoulders, shook her roughly. 'Meris! He's awake! He's calling for you! For *you*, Meris! D'you hear me?'

'Sod off!' hissed Meris, baring her teeth like a cat. 'Baste the High Counsellor! Baste everything!' Seizing the lobe of her partner's ear between her teeth, she bit it so that he cried out. 'Oh, you're marvellous!' she babbled, her biting turning to frantic kisses. 'Go on! Go on! I'll *kill* you if you stop!'

For a moment Maia stood irresolute in the throbbing gloom around her, alone in the tumult as though under the waterfall of Lake Serrelind. Then she turned and ran back towards the dais.

During the past few days Sencho's thoughts had reverted several times to the young Tonildan—whose name he had forgotten, if he had ever known it. Buying her from Lalloc had been an impulsive extravagance about which he was now rather in two minds. The sight of the lovely girl, naked and frightened before his couch, had reminded him of his young manhood, reviving that delicious, brutal rapacity which in those days he had now and then had a chance to gratify. She had, in fact, put him in mind of a certain lass, more than twenty years before, in Kabin, whither he had gone on business for Fravak. He had never known *her* name, either. A servant in the inn where he was staying, she was, he had suddenly realized at the time, entirely innocent and inexperienced, having left her parents' home only a few days before. That evening he had settled up with the landlord, over-paying him a little, and then unobtrusively carried his baggage-roll to one of the outhouses. Twenty minutes later, calling the girl out on some pretext, he had thrown her down, raped her and then simply walked away and put up elsewhere, trusting—successfully, as it turned out—to the unlikelihood of the landlord going to undue trouble over a simple and very young woman's unsubstantiated word against an open-handed customer who was now nowhere to be found. He could still hear, and relish in memory, the girl's shuddering sobs as he spent himself in her.

Similarly to have ravished this Tonildan child would have been delightful; but unfortunately he was no longer capable of forcing himself upon any girl. Perhaps, after all, he had better ask Lalloc to take her back and refund the money, for an innocent like her would take far too much training; and nowadays the hesitancy and clumsiness of an inept, nervous girl, however pretty, was more than he could endure.

He had consulted the sleek, self-possessed Terebinthia as she fanned him, lying in the vine-shaded verandah one afternoon of still, thundery heat before the rains. Her advice was to keep the girl, at all events for the time being. In the first place, she felt, they needed to maintain a degree of continuity in the women's quarters. Yunsaymis and Tuisto had just gone and it seemed likely that Dyphna—who in any case lacked the salacity so much valued by the High Counsellor—would soon be putting up the money to buy her freedom. Her departure would be perfectly acceptable: she had always behaved well and done everything required of her. About Meris, naturally licentious though she was, Terebinthia had always had grave reservations, for the girl was difficult and intractable, with a criminal record of violence. This young Tonildan, on the other hand, might turn out very well in time. In the first place she was physically splendid— exactly what the High Counsellor liked. But also, she had shown certain promising signs. She had a sexual relationship with the black girl (Terebinthia missed very little), to whom she seemed devoted, and through this was learning fast. Given the chance, the black girl would no doubt teach her a lot. She had shown herself compliant, ready to learn and anxious to please. Being so young, she could probably be taught to do what the High Counsellor liked without feeling the sort of resentment all too regrettably shown by Meris and other girls accustomed to straightforward basting. Sencho, well-fed and somnolent in the heat, had agreed to keep her for the moment and see how she developed.

It was in fact her beauty, together with her biddable docility, which had made him decide upon her as one of the two girls he would take to the Rains banquet, where he always liked to appear with something new and conspicuous. He would, of course, need an experienced girl as well. For an unconstrained occasion like this Meris would be better than the rather fastidious Dyphna. Nothing whatever disgusted Meris. She, like himself, was a born guttersnipe, and besides, would be better than Dyphna at ordering the Tonildan child about and teaching her how to attend to his needs. Of course it was possible that the Tonildan would be overcome with timidity, but on balance this might be rather enjoyable. Other people's distress was always pleasant.

In the event his judgement had proved correct. The two girls had attracted notice and favourable comment and several people, including Kembri, had complimented him on them. They had also attended him smoothly and on the whole competently, with the result that he had been able to enjoy the excellent dinner to the full. In the normal way he would have remained awake afterwards, watched the kura and then gratified himself, but so pleasantly excessive had been the meal that he had been quite unable to desist from sleeping for a time.

Waking slowly and while still half-stupefied, he felt himself consumed by an overwhelming ruttishness. Dimly he was aware of a girl's soft, perfumed flesh and felt her supporting his head and wiping his body. Clutching and mouthing, he found her breasts and, in a perfect madness of lust, pulled her hand down to his loins. Yet this, since she did nothing, only added to his frustration. Remembering now where he was and that Meris was in attendance upon him, he called for her, unable to understand why she was not instantly there. Then, to his outraged amazement, he suddenly found himself alone.

Helpless, and afflicted with his lust to the exclusion of all else, like a dog kept from a bitch in heat, he groaned, wallowing in the cushions. His torment became unbearable, for at such times he was quite unused to the least frustration or delay. Now fully conscious, he could see and hear all around him a frenzy of licentious enjoyment. He tried to raise himself on the couch and for a few moments actually succeeded. A slim, dark-haired girl was running towards him, laughing over her shoulder at someone out of sight behind her. Stretching out one hand, he contrived to clutch her thigh before, with a little shriek of amusement, she freed herself and fell across a near-by couch, where—as though on purpose to add to Sencho's torture—she was instantly mounted by the young man who had been pursuing her. Choking with rage, the High Counsellor fell back, slavering down his chin and snorting like a tethered boar.

All in a moment his agony vanished, extinguished like a candle-flame, to be instantly succeeded by an exquisite sensation of moist, lubricious luxury. Within moments he was beside himself with pleasure, rendered all the more intense by reason of his sudden deliverance from the horrible thwarting he had undergone. Gasping, neither knowing nor caring what had happened, aware of nothing except that he was doing what he wanted, he gave himself wholly up to his gratification, concluding what needed to be little more than the briefest of effort with a roaring, bellowing flux such as he had not experienced for years.

Dazed, and dripping sweat from every pore, Sencho came slowly to himself and opened his eyes. The Tonildan girl, kneeling beside the couch, was rinsing her mouth from Meris's goblet and groping on the floor for the spray of keranda bloom which had fallen out of her hair. Looking up, she caught his eye for a moment and smiled shyly. The High Counsellor, drowsy now but filled with a supreme sense of his own shrewdness in having recognized such an excellent thing when he saw it, fondled her shoulders for a moment, grunted with satisfaction and once more fell asleep.

: 23 :

MERIS WHIPPED

'Couldn' be better,' said Occula, filling a pink palm with oil and bending over Maia's shoulders. 'Couldn' be better! Banzi, I never thought you had it in you!'

'I didn't,' said Maia.

'Oh, and witty too! The girl's all talent! Can you sing as well?'

'I want to learn to dance, Occula. What was that dance you said?'

'The *senguela*. All in good time, my lass, all in good time. Just keep still while I finish rubbin' you down. You do me credit, banzi, that you do.'

Even Terebinthia was smiling. On the day following the banquet, after leaving the High Counsellor to sleep until the afternoon, she had woken him to a light meal, during which he had first told her of Meris's iniquitous dereliction of duty and then warmly congratulated her upon her advice about the Tonildan girl. No praise, it seemed, was too high for the way in which Maia had acquitted herself. Finally Sencho, his lust renewed by his own account to Terebinthia, ordered her to fetch the girl then and there, in order that she might personally witness her remarkable talent. Alone with the High Counsellor and Terebinthia, Maia at first felt nervous, but then, with peasant shrewdness, realized that, short of smashing a plate over his head, there was virtually nothing she could do which her master, in his present mood, would not find entirely pleasing. Having once more gratified him—while Terebinthia held a mirror to add to his enjoyment—she and the säiyett had left the High Counsellor to sleep and returned to the women's quarters.

The weather, after two days of rain, had turned colder. The stove had been lit and the murmur and movement of the flames, together with the steady, gentle sibilance of the rain outside, made a pleasant background for conversation.

Maia turned over on her back. 'Oh, 'twas just lucky, honest,' she answered. 'Tell you the truth, I was frightened half silly. But I mean, someone had to do something.'

'Or you could have been where Meris is now.' Terebinthia, seated near-by, was looking over the clothes and jewels which the girls had worn the night before. '*She's* the one to blame, the little fool: an experienced girl, and simply couldn't control herself. Let that be a warning to you.'

'But, banzi,' said Occula, 'you say Elvair-ka-Virrion came and pressed you, and you sent him away?'

'Oh, I do just about hope that was right an' all!' replied Maia. 'Only strikes me as he may go an' take against me now, see?'

'Not he!' said Occula. 'Not he! You couldn' have done better! He can' possibly hold it against you; and I shouldn' think any girl's ever treated him like that before in his whole life. He'll be even crazier about you now—you jus' wait and see! He'll think you're the most marvellous thing since Lespa flew away with the goat. He'll probably come round here and ask for you, I expect.'

'But—' Maia spoke hesitantly, frowning and stabbing slowly at the floor with a splinter of firewood—'Meris was saying at the banquet that we're never allowed out, and nobody ever gets to see us.'

'Ah; but that's just as *I* may decide, you see,' said Terebinthia, holding up Maia's Yeldashay skirt to the light and examining it one side and then the other. 'What it comes to is that I certainly don't allow any girl to go out by herself if I feel I can't trust her to do me and the High Counsellor credit. It's most unwise to forfeit *my* confidence.' She patted Maia's shoulder. 'You've made a very good start, Maia. Mind you take care not to get conceited. What is it, Ogma? Has the High Counsellor finished talking to those messengers from Tonilda now? Then I'd better go and ask him whether he wants to see Meris whipped before supper or after.'

'Don't like Meris, do she?' said Maia when Terebinthia had gone. She got up from the couch. 'Meris must have rubbed her up the wrong way good and proper.'

'Absolutely fatal,' replied Occula. 'Anyone could see all along that she had it in for her. Even without last night she'd have got Meris sooner or later. It only goes to show, banzi: one thing you *must* avoid in this game is makin' enemies, and particularly of people who have power over you.'

Maia was rummaging in the alcove for her comb. 'I say, Occula, what's happened to your Cat Colonna as the pedlar gave you? I thought you left it up here on the shelf?'

'Oh—er—I dropped it,' replied Occula after a moment. 'It was only thin pottery, so that was that. No great loss, really, was it? Come on now, banzi, come and gild my eyelids, will you? And then you can do my nipples as well. We've got to get all polished up to attend that wretched girl's whippin'. And we know what Piggy's goin' to want after *that*, doan' we?'

'Blackberries I reckon those are, not strawberries,' giggled Maia, searching along the shelf for the little jar of cosmetic gilt. 'You got a knife or a coin or something? Only this lid's jammed on that tight.'

The punishment referred to by Terebinthia and Occula as 'whipping' was in actuality seldom or never inflicted with a whip, for the bodies of slave-girls of the quality owned by the High Counsellor were far too valuable to be scarred or lacerated. Terebinthia's normal practice—of which he, as a connoisseur, approved, finding it fully as enjoyable as whipping—was to administer a sound smacking on the rump with a broad strip of leather about twenty inches long and perhaps an eighth of an inch thick. As an amusing adjunct to this spectacle Sencho, whose natural pruriency delighted above all in seeing women indecently degraded, had himself designed and had made a special block for the culprit. This consisted of a life-sized figure, carved in black wood, of a naked, grinning savage reclining on its back, the two hands cupped in front of the face to form a kind of perch or saddle. The girl to be punished, having been stripped, was compelled to crouch astride this figure, facing its feet, her buttocks elevated and her groin supported on its hands. In this position, and effectively gagged—for the figure was realistically complete in its semblance of carnal arousal—she presented a charming and elegant spectacle of humiliation which never failed to afford Sencho the keenest enjoyment.

During the smacking of Meris, which Terebinthia, herself stripped to the waist for greater freedom, carried out with brisk and pleasing vigour, the High Counsellor, his couch placed close beside the girl, lay watching in blissful silence. From time to time, signing to Terebinthia to pause, he would stretch out a fat arm to caress Meris's thighs, himself trembling with *frissons* of delicate, cultured pleasure. Indeed, so intense was his delight that he could scarcely bring himself to tell Terebinthia to desist, consenting at length only when the säiyett had respectfully pointed out that the girl was, after all, very valuable. For some time after Meris had been carried out he lay, with closed eyes, in a kind of transport, emitting sighs of satisfaction or sudden, quick groans of reminiscent delight. At length, coming to himself and growing once more aware of the four women waiting to learn his further wishes, he instructed Terebinthia first to undress Maia, whom he wished to remain with him, and then herself retire with Occula and Dyphna.

In the event Maia did not leave the High Counsellor until the following morning.

Her own reactions to the whipping had been startlingly unexpected, and might have puzzled her if she had been in the habit of dwelling upon her own feelings: but such was not her nature. At first she had been filled only with revulsion at the sight of the grotesque, carved face leering up between Meris's legs, at her haunches quivering as Terebinthia struck her, and at the yet more grotesque figure of the High Counsellor quivering ecstatically in harmony. Then, suddenly and entirely without volition, she felt in herself, with a rush of spontaneous excitement, that same pleasure which she knew to be Sencho's. Like a swimmer ceasing to struggle against a current; like a desert traveller gulping down the water that was supposed to last two days; like an enraged soldier who cannot restrain in himself the impulse to strike a superior—so Maia, whether she would or no, was swept away by a surging, headlong exhilaration. Ah! Ah! Meris shuddering, Meris writhing, Sencho panting, Meris uncontrollably pissing in the black man's face ha ha, Terebinthia's big deldas swinging as she wielded the thick, pliant leather smack, oh no it wasn't Meris smack it was that sneering nobleman who had dared to shout at Lady Maia from his boat smack, it was filthy Genshed with his knife smack, oh yes, it was Zuno lolling under his awning harder, harder! while she and Occula trudged in the hot smack sun it was Perdan who had thrown her against the cart on the road oo yes it was smack grubby little Nala threatening to sneak on her and Tharrin oh *smack*! it was Morca Morca Morca *more*!

As the kitchen-maids finally carried Meris away, Maia realized that she herself was panting, hot and viscid. Biting her lip, eyes downcast, she picked up one of Sencho's towels, covertly thrust it between her legs and cast it aside, hoping no one had noticed. Thereupon, turning her head for an instant towards the couch, she realized that her master, at all events, was entirely aware of what she had done; yes and of all—of every last thing—that she had felt. Her own feelings, she knew beyond a doubt, were even now forming a part of that sighing pleasure in which he lay, weak with excitement yet raised—with herself caught up and swirling in the same spiral—to an elation far beyond anything so absurd as pity for a fool like Meris. It came as no least surprise when Terebinthia was ordered to strip her. She would have been astonished—oh, bitterly disappointed!—if it had been otherwise. While Terebinthia obeyed, she sat still and exalted

221

as a princess; and as soon as the others had gone out, herself got up unbidden and quenched two or three of the lamps until the light remaining in the room was to her own satisfaction. Then, climbing on to the couch without a word and needing no instructions from Sencho thank you very much, she began her work without haste, with no vestige of diffidence and without—oh, certainly without—any anxiety that she might show herself clumsy or inexperienced. *She* would be the one to decide what they would do together, and to this the High Counsellor would raise not the least objection.

: 24 :

MATTERS OF STATE

Durakkon sat moodily at the window, watching the rain drifting over the Bramba Tower outside.

'But do you *want* a campaign against Karnat?' he asked Kembri. 'I should prefer to avoid it.'

'What I want to do, sir,' replied Kembri, 'is to reconquer Suba for the empire.'

'But—er—it was ceded to Karnat less than seven years ago, at the time when you and Fornis came up from Paltesh. You deliberately let him take it in return for leaving us undisturbed to depose Senda-na-Say.'

'Yes, and at the time that bargain served its purpose. But nothing's going to alter the fact that the proper place for Terekenalters and Katrians is the far side of the Zhairgen. That's the only logical western boundary for the empire. Otherwise we can't call ourselves secure. If we could only recapture Suba, it would do the Leopard cause a whole power of good; gain us a lot of popular approval and help to put an end to all the trouble we're having in Urtah and Tonilda. Don't you agree, Sencho?'

The High Counsellor replied that he had no doubt of it.

'At the moment we've got Sendekar on the Valderra, with a fairly strong force,' went on Kembri. 'They're spending Melekril in garrison at Rallur. I mean to join them as soon as the rains are over, with enough men to cross the Valderra and recapture Suba.'

'And if you succeed we'll return it to Urtah, presumably,' said Durakkon. 'As you know, Suba was a dependency of Urtah before it was given to Karnat. Does the old High Baron know you're planning to recapture it?'

'No, sir, certainly not. We don't want schemes of that sort leaking out in a place like Kendron-Urtah. They'd never be kept secret: Karnat would get to hear in no time. Besides,' he added after a few moments, 'if we do

222

succeed in getting Suba back, we may not return it to Urtah at all. Queen Fornis, for one, would like to see it become part of Paltesh, and I've been thinking that that might very well be best from our point of view.'

'But that would be totally wrong,' said Durakkon, 'and unjust to Urtah.'

'But it would be most expedient, and a better thing altogether for the Leopards,' said Kembri. 'If we were to make Fornis a present of Suba, she'd be much less likely to start any trouble when her reign as Sacred Queen comes to an end. Have you thought of that, sir?'

Durakkon had indeed been reflecting most uneasily about what was likely to ensue when the time came to insist to Fornis that at the age of thirty-four she could not expect to be reinstated as Sacred Queen of Airtha for a third term of four years. The people as a whole would undoubtedly regard such a step as an affront to the god and therefore very unlucky: but Fornis was resourceful and domineering, a very alarming adversary indeed and a woman not lightly to be antagonized.

'But my immediate worry,' went on Kembri, without waiting for Durakkon to answer him, 'is the prospect of campaigning on the Valderra and in Suba while we still know so little about what may be being brewed up in Urtah without the old High Baron's knowledge. He himself only wants peace and quiet, of course. As long as he's alive, he'll go on preventing the Urtans from flying at our throats for being the villains who gave away Suba. But if he dies—and I'm told now that he may die at any time—what's going to happen then? The heir's Eud-Ecachlon—a slow fellow; not many ideas of his own—but he hates Fornis like poison and who's to blame him, seeing she made him look a complete fool over that betrothal? He could easily be influenced into coming out against us. I don't want to start crossing the Valderra into Suba with Karnat in front of me and then find Urtah up in arms at my back.'

He looked at Sencho, but the High Counsellor said nothing.

'Then there's the bastard,' continued Kembri. 'I mean Bayub-Otal, the High Baron's son by the Suban dancing-girl. He'd been promised the rule of Suba on his father's death, so he's the most embittered Urtan of the lot. I've often wondered about having him killed off, but that certainly *would* lose us the old High Baron's support for good and all. Even if it could be made to look like an accident—and I doubt it could—he'd never believe it: we can't risk it. But Bayub-Otal's up to something on his own account, or else I'm much mistaken. I'd like to know what it is. Sencho, you'd better hit on some way of finding out for us. After all, he's spending Melekril here in the city.'

Sencho, however, did not respond to this as positively as the Lord General had been hoping. The High Counsellor resented being told by Kembri or anyone else how to run his secret intelligence network or where he should put his spies, and had always been firm that he did not act on the orders of the Lord General or of any other Leopard leader. This obstinacy and independence, he was shrewd enough to realize, was ultimately his only safety in dealing with his fellow-conspirators—Fornis, Han-Glat and Kembri. As long as reliable information about threats of sedition could reach them only through him and as long as they did not know how much he knew or where his agents were working, they could not afford to get rid of him.

He began speaking in general terms about Kembri's contention that to reconquer Suba would be good for the Leopards' standing throughout the empire. Ending disaffection, he pointed out, was more than a matter of recapturing an unproductive area of marshland and water-ways and making a present of it to Fornis: while as for Urtah, it was not really this relatively stable, prosperous and civilized province which gave the deepest cause for anxiety, but rather the more inaccessible fringes of the empire: remote, tribal areas, where his spies and agents were unavoidably fewer and whence information took longer to reach him.

'You mean Chalcon, don't you?' said Durakkon.

Sencho nodded, and went on to speak of his uneasiness about that isolated area of foothills and forest where the marches of northern Yelda joined those of southern Tonilda. This was the outlying region—wild country a good three days' journey or more from Thettit—in which, after the Leopards' seizure of power, Senda-na-Say's nephew Enka-Mordet had been suffered to settle on the last remaining family estate. The High Counsellor, whose cunning included an instinctive and often startlingly penetrating ability to sniff out concealed enemies (the strongest reason for the fear in which he was held), felt an intuitive certainty that something dangerously against the Leopard interest was hatching there.

'What, then?' asked Durakkon, forgetting for a moment to conceal his contempt. 'Are you sure you're not just assuming that Enka-Mordet's the sort of man you were yourself eight years ago?'

Sencho ignored this. It was well understood between him and Kembri that provided they refrained from openly quarrelling with Durakkon or sneering at his intermittent, futile attempts to assert his nominal authority, they could always, ultimately, dominate or prevail upon him, since he lacked self-confidence and was dependent upon them to maintain his position.

Chalcon, continued the High Counsellor, might not at this moment seem so great a cause for anxiety as Urtah. Yet as far as Santil-kè-Erketlis, its most influential baron, was concerned, he himself felt more-or-less certain, despite the lack of any specific evidence, that something was being secretly cooked up against Bekla. There had been furtive comings and goings of messengers—too many to be attributable to mere farming and husbandry—between Erketlis and Enka-Mordet; while both were retaining in their households more young, able-bodied men than any normal estate-owner required during Melekril.

'Well, if we're going to take punitive action in Chalcon,' said Kembri, 'it ought to be now, immediately, in spite of the rains; awkward as that'll be. In the first place no one will be expecting it, and secondly it can be done and over before my Suba campaign begins next spring. The last thing we want is trouble on the Valderra *and* in Chalcon at one and the same time.'

'But this jumping to conclusions is unjust,' said Durakkon. 'Santil-kè-Erketlis—you've got nothing definite against the man, and if you kill him you'll only stir up the whole of Chalcon against us, just when there are no men to spare from the Valderra front. Young Santil's father and mine were close friends,' he added inconsequently.

To be sure, replied the High Counsellor: he had never suggested killing Erketlis. He was entirely in agreement that the objections were too strong. Nevertheless, he and the Lord General were both convinced that something—a lesser stroke—ought to be executed in Chalcon, with the object of frightening those heldril who were coming together round Erketlis and of showing them that Bekla, distant though it might be, was well-informed about disaffection and not prepared to let it go unpunished. To take such action during the rains would make the effect more telling.

'Action?' queried Durakkon. 'You *do* mean killing, then?'

Sencho shrugged. What else? On every count, the most suitable man of whom to make an example was Enka-Mordet.

'Enka-Mordet,' said Kembri. 'Yes, he's the right man to put out of the way. We should probably have done it before, but this is a good occasion none the less. He's the only remaining close relative of Senda-na-Say, and that means there's always a danger of some heldro bunch making use of him as a figurehead to mount a revolt. We know he's talked rebellion on and off, but never quite enough for us to arrest him: enough to show the way he feels, though. And now Sencho's found out that he's hatching something or other with Erketlis.'

'Which may be nothing at all,' said Durakkon. 'Mere suspicion. If—'

'The real thing,' went on Kembri, cutting him short, 'is this: when we kill Enka-Mordet, it'll have a salutary effect on every heldro in the province who has a hand in whatever he and Erketlis are up to. Chalcon won't rise on account of Enka-Mordet, though it probably would on account of Erketlis. He's never been a man of that sort of weight. We shall hit them just hard enough to make them think, and no harder.'

The discussion continued for almost an hour, at the end of which, predictably, Durakkon had been prevailed upon reluctantly to agree. As to means, Sencho was reassuring about the practicability of a swift blow. Two hundred reliable men from, say, the Belishban force at present quartered in Bekla should be sufficient for the task. None but the baron and his wife, his two grown sons and a daughter of sixteen need actually be put to death. There were, however, one or two relatively minor matters connected with obtaining further information. If Kembri had no objection, he would himself have a private word with one of the tryzatts before the Belishbans left.

'All right, so we make an example of this man and his family,' said Kembri at length. 'But that still doesn't mean we don't need to find out a lot more about Erketlis and whatever it is he has in mind. As long as we don't know what it is, we can't forestall it; and all we know at the moment is that messengers keep coming and going to his place from Enka-Mordet and one or two more. Aren't there any of his servants in your pay, Sencho?'

The High Counsellor replied that he had always been wary of trying to bribe servants native to a remote area; nothing was easier for such people than to tell their master what was afoot and then go on giving the briber false intelligence. In the case of a man like Santil-kè-Erketlis, trying to bribe his house-servants, most of whom felt themselves virtually members of the family, would simply be asking for trouble, while to plant a stranger in the place would be next to impossible. Even supposing that they were to make use of bribed servants, there was little chance of such people learning anything of a matter which at this stage was probably known only to a few men of rank. Ideally, they needed to get at the messengers; yet to waylay them would be useless, for this would only give the game away.

'Then—?' Kembri put more fuel on the brazier with his own hands and refilled Sencho's goblet.

There was one device, said Sencho, which he himself thought worth trying. He reminded Kembri of the gang of young robbers on the Herl-Dari highway who had been dealt with by the army some four years before. He might remember that they had made use of a girl as a decoy.

Kembri frowned. 'But you can't put just any girl on a job like seducing messengers. She'd have to have a lot more than looks. Looks would be essential, of course, but on top of that she'd need to have all her wits about her; to be sharp enough to ask the right questions without being suspected and understand the gist of anything she managed to get hold of. I doubt we could find anyone capable of it.'

Sencho smiled. It so happened that he had in his household the very girl who had acted as decoy for the Belishban gang. She was an unusually attractive and wanton young woman—both Han-Glat and himself had had a good deal of pleasure from her—and she was not only quick-witted, but also very much on the make. His notion was to promise her her freedom, together with enough money to set herself up as a shearna, in return for finding out what they needed to know.

'All very fine,' objected Kembri, 'but you say the girl's a Belishban, and you want to plant her in Chalcon to seduce local messengers. She'd be far too obviously a stranger. Besides, she couldn't live in the province on her own, indoors or out. Who'd look after her?'

Sencho explained his scheme. The girl had recently neglected her duty and been well whipped for it. Nothing would seem more natural to his own household than a decision on his part to sell her. Lalloc could sell her, by arrangement, to the woman Domris, who owned the Lily Pool in Thettit-Tonilda. At this moment he was making use as an agent of a Tonildan pedlar, a man thoroughly familiar with the whole province. Under cover of selling his wares, he reported regularly to the High Counsellor in the course of periodic visits to Bekla. This man, acting on instructions, would, as soon as the rains ended, unobtrusively convey the girl from Domris's house, after which she would simply appear as his own doxy, travelling with him. In this rôle she could, of course, be as Belishban as she liked. Once they reached Chalcon the two would act on their own initiative, by the kind of methods he had described, to find out what messages were passing to and from Erketlis. In point of fact the pedlar had already told him the names of two men who were acting as messengers; one a man called Tharrin, and the other—

To Durakkon's disgust Kembri, bellowing with delighted laughter, pushed aside the deaf-mute slave and himself took over the task of rubbing the High Counsellor's belly while complimenting him on the ingenuity of the plan. Provided Sencho's assessment of the girl was as shrewd as most of his judgements, it seemed to offer an excellent chance of success. He would like to see this remarkable girl for himself.

He had recently done so, replied Sencho, at his own Rains banquet two nights before.

Kembri was surprised. What, the very pretty child with golden hair? No, not her, said the High Counsellor; the other.

Ah, yes: Kembri remembered her now: a handsome girl. If only she could avoid arousing suspicion, she should prove virtually irresistible in a back-of-beyond spot like Chalcon. And as long as she was apparently chance-met on a road, or at some wayside inn, the fact that she was a Belishban would add to her attraction rather than make her suspect, as it would if she were a servant in some baron's house.

'But it occurs to me,' went on Kembri, 'that whatever you may think, Sencho, of the drawbacks to family servants as spies, it couldn't do us any harm to plant a local girl in Erketlis's house as well. Haven't you got any Tonildan girls?'

Sencho replied that he had indeed, but it was certainly not his intention to send back to Tonilda a young woman who had just cost him fifteen thousand meld and worth every *trug*. He could not resist enlarging a little on the subject. The girl had already shown every sign of a pleasingly carnal disposition. She was a sharp little thing, too—had a good head on her shoulders. As a concubine she was, of course, immature but already capable of a good deal, with a certain capacity for invention to compensate for her rough edges.

'Rough edges?' Kembri, recalling the girl he had seen at the banquet, chuckled. 'That's what you call them, is it? Well, you must let me borrow her some time.' (In point of fact the Lord General, irritated at Sencho's having brushed aside his suspicions and anxieties about the Urtans, had just been visited by an idea for pursuing the matter on his own account, but this he did not disclose to the High Counsellor.)

'On the usual terms.' Sencho began helping himself to buttered crayfish and plovers' eggs, which the slave had just carried in.

'Of course. Yes, I'd fancy her: I'll send someone to see your säiyett—Terebinthia, isn't it?—about an arrangement. But now we'll eat.'

Getting up from beside the High Counsellor, he made his way across to the table.

'Let me pour you some wine, sir,' he said to Durakkon. 'It's no good troubling yourself with doubts and regrets about Enka-Mordet: it's an essential part of the High Baron's job to be ruthless when necessary, you know.'

He poured the wine, but Durakkon, after raising the goblet absently to his lips, had still not emptied it by the time the Lord General and the High Counsellor took their leave.

: 25 :

TEREBINTHIA BRINGS NEWS

'Oh, we used to just about dread Melekril, and that's a fact,' said Maia, stretching a bare arm out of bed for another handful of grapes. 'I can remember waking up and, you know, hearing the rain and that and thinking "Isn't it *ever* going to stop?" '

'We used to take it fairly easy at old Domris's,' said Occula. 'Same as they do here. You couldn't, I suppose?'

'Well, you can't, can you?—not when there's beasts to be seen to, and then sometimes we'd have to take the boat out; and then there'd be firewood to get in—oh, I can remember being almost up to the knees in mud, just going down the lane to borrow a bucket.'

'So you reckon this is a better life?'

'Well, isn't it?' Maia giggled. '*We're* the cows now—someone else has to look after *us*, don't they?'

'Come on, then, pretty cow, let's get up. Stove'll be goin' nicely by now. I'm hungry, aren' you?'

'Oh, the dancing, Occula! That dance you said you'd teach me—the—'

'So I will: soon as we've had somethin' to eat.' She raised her voice. 'Ogma! Can we have some breakfast, dear, please? Dare say I can play a hinnari well enough for all you'll need to begin with.'

An hour later Occula, having laid the hinnari aside on a bench, was standing opposite Maia on the open floor near the pool, her hands moving this way and that in smooth, fluid gestures.

'First thing you've got to realize, banzi, is that this isn' village dancin'. Your hands aren' just somethin' at the ends of your arms. You've got to *use* them, *and* your fingers too. Each finger's got to be able to move separately—like this, see?'

'Oh, I'll never be able to do it, Occula!'

'Yes, you will. If I could, you can. You're made for it, actually; but it takes skill and practice. Wouldn' be any point otherwise, would there?'

'What did you say the two parts are called?'

'The *selpé* and the *reppa*. The whole point of the senguela, banzi, is that although you're only one dancer, you've got to play three parts. First of all you're Lespa, then you're Shakkarn and then you're the old woman. And you've got to *act* each of those parts; *be* them, not just dance them. You've got to act them so well that your audience see what isn' there. In the sort of dancin' you've been used to, there are a lot of other people and every-body more or less has to keep together. But then *they're* only concerned with amusin' themselves and each other. *This* you do alone, and you're doin' it for people to enjoy watchin' you. So once you've mastered the skills and the actin', you can dance more or less as you like; you can pretty well make it up, as long as you're graceful and as long as you act the different parts so well that everybody can follow you. Anyway, let's leave the finger-movements for now: you can practise them half an hour a day. Look, I'm just goin' to keep a rhythm goin' for you—I can' play this thing much better than that, anyway. You're Lespa bathin' in the pool, right? And you've got to *feel* you're Lespa, banzi; you've got to *become* Lespa! Lie down to start with; shut your eyes and *think*: pray if you like. And then you're goin' to *turn into* Lespa, simply burnin' for it, but half-frightened as well. If *you* doan' believe it, nobody else is goin' to. Now then—these are what they call the water-chords. Lie down and concentrate—'

Towards the end of the morning they were still at it when Maia, as deeply absorbed and self-forgotten as even Occula could wish, took a few whisking steps backward among the imagined trees and found the silent Terebinthia at her elbow. She started, stumbled and broke off. Occula stopped playing.

'Well, I dare say you may become quite good in time, Maia,' said Terebinthia, taking her arm to help her regain her balance. 'But take care to develop your own style: don't copy some other girl's. Dyphna's slimmer than you, and that makes a difference. Work *with* your body and not against it.'

'Do you know the senguela, then, säiyett?' asked Occula.

'Very well: I've seen many girls work out their own ideas of it. But now I have to interrupt you on one or two matters. First of all, the pedlar's here again. He's been taking orders for various things the High Counsellor wants from Thettit, and he's setting off again this afternoon.'

'What, in the rain, säiyett?' asked Occula.

'So it seems,' said Terebinthia. 'It's a matter of profit, I dare say. No doubt pedlars ready to travel in the rain make more money, or he may simply have been ordered by the High Counsellor to go at once. He says if you have any messages for anyone in Thettit-Tonilda, he can take them.'

'That's nice of him, säiyett,' said Occula, slackening off the strings of the hinnari and hanging it up on the wall. 'Could he come in for a moment, do you think, if we're not puttin' you to too much trouble? I've a friend in Thettit—one I think he may already know.'

The pedlar, clumsy in great boots reaching to his knees, was carrying a cape shaped, as though for a hunchback, with a recess to contain his pack. Laying this down and opening his tunic at the neck, he leant against one of the columns by the door-curtains and took a long pull at the goblet which Terebinthia offered him.

'Why, you girls live in a bed of roses,' said he, wiping his mouth. 'I don't know where there's a better drop than that—no, not from Bekla to Thettit.'

'I doan' envy you your journey, Zirek,' said Occula. 'You'll be walkin' straight into the rain, too. How far will you get tonight?'

'Oh, I'll get as far as Naksh easily enough,' he answered. 'I'm used to it, you know. I always say if the boots can do it, I can. Still got your Cat Colonna? It *was* you I gave it to, wasn't it?'

'Oh, d'you know, I dropped it?' said Occula. 'It broke, of course: I'm sorry, after you gave it me for nothin'.'

'Well, some cats fall off a roof and land right way up,' said the pedlar, 'but pottery cats you'd hardly expect it, would you? Never mind: I can let you have another, seeing as your master's been kind enough to give me a good bit of profitable business. I think I've got a nice, striped one somewhere.' He opened his pack. 'Yes, here she is: with my compliments. But now I can't stop about—not with seven or eight mile to do before dark.'

'Could you give a message to a friend of mine at the Lily Pool?' asked Occula. 'A shearna called Bakris?'

'Bakris?'

'That's right. Before I left there was some talk of her comin' up to Bekla this spring on business.'

'What d'you want me to tell her, then?'

'Well, I thought if Bakris happened to be here for the spring festival, there might just possibly be a chance for us to meet—at the feast by the Barb in the evenin' perhaps—that's if she can get someone to take her and if I happen to be one of the girls the High Counsellor takes with him. I'd be workin', of course, but there might be a minute or two to spare all the same.'

She glanced a moment at Terebinthia, but the säiyett made no comment.

'Well, that's easy enough,' said the pedlar. 'I'll drop in and give her your message.' He drained his goblet. 'And now I'll be off. See you again after Melekril, for I don't mean to tramp that road twice in the rain, I'll tell you that.'

Bowing to Terebinthia, he went out. Occula was about to take the hinnari down again when she and Maia became aware that the säiyett evidently had more to say.

'One *or two* matters, I said, Occula,' remarked Terebinthia coldly.

'I'm sorry, säiyett: forgive me.'

'I will forgive you. In fact, I have your comfort so much at heart, both of you, that I'm going to make you an offer. Would either of you like Meris's room?'

'Meris's room, säiyett? You mean, change over, and her to have ours?'

'No, that isn't what I said. I asked whether either of you would like Meris's room. If one of you would, then the other can stay in the room where you are now and have it to herself—for the time being, at all events.'

'What about Meris, then, säiyett?'

'Meris is to be sold. In fact, she has already been sold.'

'Cran and Airtha!' said Occula, startled out of her usual deferential manner. 'Bit sudden, wasn' it?'

Terebinthia made no reply.

'Who to, säiyett?' asked Maia.

'That doesn't concern you,' replied Terebinthia. 'Well, am I to have an answer or not?'

Occula and Maia looked at each other.

'I'd really prefer to stay with Maia, säiyett,' said Occula. 'We—well, we're quite happy as we are, you know.'

'Very well: as long as you realize that that means when another girl's been bought, she'll have Meris's room to herself. I don't want to hear any complaints from either of you. And now, something else: suppose I were to agree, Maia, to your going out, do you think you could behave properly and do us credit?'

'Going out, säiyett?' Maia looked up nervously.

Terebinthia, with the complacent air of one who has something unexpected and pleasant to disclose, sat down and called to Ogma to bring some wine, evidently waiting for Maia to question her further. Since Maia said nothing, however, but only continued to look at her with apprehension, she finally turned towards Occula and remarked, 'Apparently Maia doesn't want to go: perhaps you'd better go instead, Occula. What do you think?'

'I've no idea, säiyett, until you tell me,' replied Occula rather pertly.

Maia drew in her breath, but as usual Occula had judged Terebinthia's mood correctly and was sailing with the wind.

'Somethin's pleased you, säiyett, hasn' it?' went on the black girl. 'Woan' you be kind enough to tell us what it is, instead of teasin' my poor little Maia, who really doesn' deserve it after all she's done for the High Counsellor?'

She put one arm round Maia's neck and kissed her. 'Ask her, banzi,' she breathed in her ear. 'She wants it.'

'Well, always do the best I could, säiyett,' said Maia. 'Where'm I s'posed to go, then?'

'Somewhere—very exalted,' replied Terebinthia deliberately. 'That is, if I choose. You may think, Maia, that just because some important personage has taken a fancy to you, I have no say in the matter. But I could quite easily advise that I don't think you're ready yet for an honour of this kind, and that would be the end of it.'

'But wouldn' that rather depend, säiyett,' asked Occula, 'on how badly the—er—personage wanted her?'

'Not at all,' replied Terebinthia. 'It would depend on what the High Counsellor, whose property she is, thought of my advice.'

'Säiyett,' said Occula, 'I doan' think Maia's quite grasped yet what this is all about: but I have. The plain truth is, isn' it, that someone who saw her at the banquet has asked the High Counsellor whether she's—well, available; and you're pleased about it, aren' you?'

Terebinthia nodded. 'Yes. Yes, on the whole, I am. And Maia certainly ought to be.' She paused. 'Now listen, Maia. First of all, if you've got any idea of trying to run away when you get outside, don't. It would be a shame to see a girl like you hanging upside-down, which is what happens to runaway slaves.'

232

'Run away, säiyett?' replied Maia incredulously. 'But I'm better off here than I've ever been in my life!'

This was uttered with such obvious conviction that Terebinthia dropped the matter.

'Now the next thing. Do you know the rules?' she asked.

'The rules, säiyett?'

'No, of course she doesn'!' cried Occula. 'She doesn' even know what you're talkin' about. Oh, säiyett, do tell us who it is! I'm like a goat in heat to know!'

'All in good time. Maia, do you know what a *lygol* is?'

'No, säiyett. Well, that is, I've sort of heard the word, but—'

'A girl like you can expect to receive not less than a hundred meld as a—well—a token of esteem, after a visit of this kind. That's called a lygol. But you are *not* a girl in a pleasure-house, do you see? You're the property of the High Counsellor, lent as a favour to another personage of importance. You don't *ask* for a lygol, either in advance or afterwards. You accept whatever you're given with graceful thanks.' She took a step forward and, putting a hand under Maia's chin, lifted her face to her own. 'And the rule in this household is unusually generous. You're allowed to keep two-fifths of it. The rest is a matter between the High Counsellor and myself; do you see? So don't try to be clever. You'll only wish you hadn't, and I'd hate to see you finish up like Meris.'

As Terebinthia said this, staring into Maia's eyes, she looked, for a moment, so appallingly omniscient and malevolent that Maia, with a little cry, drew back, trembling.

'Of *course* I won't, säiyett!'

'Then we understand each other,' said Terebinthia, patting her cheek. 'Now, as you know, the High Counsellor doesn't keep litter-slaves. In the normal way you'd walk, accompanied by Jarvil or one of the house-servants. However, you can't do that in the rain; you wouldn't arrive fit to be seen. A covered jekzha will be best. When you arrive there'll be someone like me, and *she* will pay the jekzha-man, do you understand? Be ready about two hours after noon tomorrow. In fact, I'll come and dress you myself.'

She drained off her wine and turned towards the door.

'But who *is* it, säiyett?' cried Occula, running after her and seizing her arm. 'Who is it? Who is it?'

'Oh, yes, to be sure; I'd quite forgotten,' said Terebinthia, pausing in the doorway. 'I'm glad you reminded me. It's—the Lord General Kembri-B'sai.'

With a light clashing of the bead curtains she was gone, leaving Occula and Maia staring at each other across the cushioned bench.

'Lespa's stars, banzi!' said Occula. 'Do you realize, my girl, what you've been and gone and done?' She caught Maia's two hands, swung her round and bowed to her like a dancing-partner. Then, imitating Terebinthia's voice, 'The Lord General Kembri-B'sai!'

'Oh, *don't!*' cried Maia desperately. 'Oh, I only just wish it had been you, Occula! Whatever am I going to do?'

'How about lying down on your back, with your legs apart?' said Occula. 'For a start, anyway.' She ran a hand through her wiry curls. 'After that your guess is as good as mine. But do try not to make a mess of it, sweetheart, woan' you? It's one hell of an opportunity.'

: 26 :

KEMBRI'S PLEASURE

Maia, a green silk cloak thrown over her pale-blue metlan, silver necklace and bracelets, was met in the covered forecourt of the Lord General's house by the same gracious, fair-haired woman who had opened her litter on the night of the Rains banquet. Her easy, professional affability was so welcome and reassuring that Maia forgot to ask her to pay the jekzha-man, who stood about stamping his feet and coughing until told sharply to go and see the porter.

Thereupon the säiyett led Maia through the courtyard and up a different staircase, which led into a long gallery. Brilliantly-coloured, woven hangings covered the whole length of the wall opposite the windows, and in front of these, at regular intervals, stood seven jewelled and painted statues representing the gods and goddesses worshipped throughout the empire: Cran, his hair cloven with lightning, his arms lifted in the act of parting the sky from the earth; Airtha of the Diadem, big-bellied and smiling, suckling a crowned infant at each golden breast; Shakkarn, horned and hoofed with topaz, his bearded mouth frothing sulphur as he thrust forward like a spear his ruby-headed zard; white Lespa, a rippling, floating vision of mercy, crowned with stars and bending forward in the act of scattering dreams from her opal-studded basket upon the sleeping earth; Shardik the bear, his eyes two smouldering garnets, one huge, clawed paw raised to smite as he ramped upon his terraced Ledges; Canathron, glaring from a thicket of copper flames and raising aloft his serpent's head and condor's wings; and lastly Frella-Tiltheh the Inscrutable, cowled, her face invisible, poised on Crandor's summit as she pointed with one lean finger to the tamarrik seed sprouting at her feet.

Maia, following her guide and stealing past these tremendous presences

234

in so much awe that she scarcely dared to glance at them—for if asked, she would not have been at all sure that they did not embody the actual deities themselves—came to a dark-and-light, zig-zag-panelled door which recalled to her the decorated walls of the dining-hall above. Here the säiyett stopped and, turning to Maia with a smile, made her a little, ironical bow as she held open the door with one bare, white arm.

'Is—is the Lord General there?' whispered Maia.

'No,' answered the woman. 'You go in and wait, and he'll come.' And then, looking her up and down and speaking in a tone which made it clear that she was paying a playful compliment, 'I shouldn't think he'll keep you waiting very long.'

Maia felt her self-possession swaying like a tree in a gale. For a moment she clasped the other's hand.

'Säiyett—oh, I'm all of a shake—only it's the first time, see, and I don't rightly know—'

The woman's laugh, though condescending, was nevertheless kindly.

'You're lucky, then, Maia, in your first time, for I can tell you, you won't find any difficulty with the Lord General.' And then, as Maia stared back, uncertain what she might mean, she nodded and gave her hand a little pat. 'In you go. You'll soon see!'

She had not been altogether correct, however, in saying that Kembri would not be in the room, for just as Maia went in at the panelled door the Lord General entered through another on the further side. She had no opportunity to take in her surroundings or to become aware of more than a sense of spaciousness, luxury and warmth in the carpeted room. Indeed, she had no time even to utter a word (which was perhaps as well, for she had not the least idea what to say) before Kembri, taking four strides across the room, lifted her bodily in his arms and laid her down on the great, soft bed.

After that it took her no time at all to grasp what the säiyett had meant. As the Lord General's partner she was required to do nothing whatever but submit. He simply did as he wished, with an unhurried yet urgent and almost impersonal power like that of a river in spate, for he—or so it seemed—had little more control over their course than she had. Having seen him before only from a little distance, she had not fully realized what a huge man he was, or how overwhelming was his mere presence. Grim, black-browed and black-bearded, even when naked he somehow seemed invisibly armoured and girt with weapons. They had hardly begun before Maia intuitively grasped a paradox which unexpectedly warmed her heart and restored her confidence. In this voracious, intent silence, this total absence of any courtly attempt to show the least regard for either her inexperience or her pleasure, lay a greater intensity of sheer desire than she had yet encountered. Caught up in this driving storm, it did not consciously occur to her that he had not spoken. She knew only that she liked what was happening. Tharrin had been accustomed to laugh and pay little compliments as he went about his pleasure. Sencho was full of snorting demands for one lewdness after another. This, though not brutal, was raw appetite, unashamed and unreflecting. She was being devoured. She writhed, half-crushed beneath the panting weight, and one of Occula's sayings flashed across what remained of her mind. 'The man wants the girl. But the girl usually wants the man to want her.' 'Dear Lespa, I'm doing this lot to him!' she thought, even as the mountain split and the rocks toppled about her. 'There were hundreds of girls at that banquet, but I'm the one as he sent for.'

She lay in silence, wondering what might now be expected of her: but she did not have to wonder long. Plainly, nothing was expected of her but to be the recipient of the Lord General's apparently insatiable ardour. He had done nothing deliberately to hurt her, yet already she felt bruised from head to heel. When she had cried out with delicious agony, he had paid less heed than if she had been an enemy in battle. And soon after, as she sprawled exhausted, sweating and tousled as a kitchen maid at the spit, another onslaught fell upon her gasping, breathless body.

At length he lay like a felled tree. Asleep? There was no telling—but at all events oblivious of her beside him among the soft, thick rugs. She herself slept for a little, but woke with a quick start, wondering what she ought to do now. Would the proper thing, perhaps, be to get dressed and go? Yes, she thought; for she was a slave-girl, and plainly there was no more for her body to do here. Sliding quietly out of the bed, she slipped on her shift and then her metlan, picked up her cloak and tip-toed towards the door. At this moment the Lord General, behind her, spoke for the first time.

'Come back.'

She jumped like a child caught stealing.

'What's the matter?' he asked, frowning as though she had done something unexpected.

'Oh, my lord, you startled me, that's all!'

He said nothing more and she did as she had been told. Undressing and getting back into the bed, she became aware at once—and incredulously— why he had called her to return. Thereupon, suddenly, the country girl supplanted the timid slave. Putting her two hands on his shoulders, she looked unafraid into the scarred, swarthy face.

'My lord, did you ever hear the story they tell where I come from, about the inn on Lake Serrelind called "The Safe Moorings"?'

He shook his head, but behind the black beard the trace of a smile answered hers; the smile of a man who spares an idle moment to watch a puppy playing with a stick.

'Well, that inn's got a bit of a front on the lake, see, and one day there's this fellow—stranger, like—comes sailing up in his boat. Landlady comes out; "Oh," says he, "I've heard you have good wine here. Bring me out a pot of your ordinary." So she brings it out and he drinks it sitting in the boat. "Ah!" he says. "Well," he says, "I'll try another, the same." So off she goes and gets him another, and he drinks that too. "I'm not sure about this yet," he says. "Bring me another one"; and so she does. So he finishes that and then he says "Yes," he says, "it *is* good wine. Reckon I'll come in and have some."'

The Lord General threw back his head and laughed; then laid hold of her once more, much like a man in haste to quench a thirst. It was as though nothing had yet taken place between them. At one moment Maia found herself actually struggling to breathe. He was, she now realized, not only big but immensely strong. He could easily have crushed her ribs between his hands. And this sense of helplessness—of danger even, for he seemed beside himself as he clasped and strove—filled her with exhilaration, so that for the first time she joined him, spinning in the vortex, and came to herself to find blood trickling down his shoulder.

Dismayed and a little frightened, she picked up her shift—the only thing to hand—and was about to staunch the wound when he took it from her and tossed it aside, laughing down at her as he might have laughed at a nervous and over-conscientious child who in playing has accidentally broken something of no particular value.

She was expecting him to fall asleep again, but now he did not seem so inclined. She herself, dazed and aching, knew without being told that he was pleased. Warm and relaxed, she lay listening to the rain and wondering what would happen next.

At length he asked, 'Have you had enough?'

She giggled. 'S'pose I say no, my lord?'

'Then we shall have to get you another man.'

'Mouse after a bull, that'd be.'

He made no reply, and she wondered whether he might be annoyed. She was surprised when, after a pause, he asked, almost like someone making conversation,

'How do you like belonging to the High Counsellor?'

She knew the answer to this, for Occula had stressed it to her again and again. 'Never gossip to them about one another, banzi—not even if they offer you gold. Long zards are all in a night's work, but long tongues never.'

'Very much, thank you, my lord.'

237

'What sort of things d'you do with him—a man too fat to walk?'

'We do as he wishes, my lord.'

'A great many people come to see him, don't they? From all over the empire. Are you ever there when he talks to them?'

'No, my lord.'

'You know who these people are? You know why he sees them?'

Putting out one hand, as easily as he might have lifted a cushion he pulled her bodily round to face him.

'You do, don't you?'

'Yes, my lord: but we don't get to hear nothing about—about that side of things.'

'What about your säiyett? He's almost helpless without her, isn't he? Is she there when he sees them?'

'If she is, my lord, she never talks to us.'

He said no more for a time, and she hoped they had exhausted the subject.

'Did you see Otavis at the banquet?' he asked suddenly.

'Oh, ah, my lord; that I did! I reckon she's *really* beautiful.'

'Did you know she belonged to me?'

'No, my lord. But—surely I saw her comin' up the staircase from the courtyard that evening, along o' the rest of the girls?'

'Yes. She'd been—elsewhere, working for me. But now she's able to buy herself free, I've no wish to stop her. A shearna can get to talk—and listen—to even more people than a slave-girl.' After a few moments he added, 'You needn't bother to tell the High Counsellor. He'd probably only have her murdered, and I'm sure you wouldn't want that.'

'I don't understand you, my lord; I'm sorry, but I don't know what you're on about at all.'

Kembri took her in his arms. For one incredulous instant she thought he was about to gratify himself yet again. Then he said, 'I didn't send for you this afternoon because I wanted to bed with you.'

At this she burst out laughing. 'Then all I can say, my lord, is you could 'a fooled me.'

His next words cut short her merriment.

'Would you like to make your fortune by taking Otavis's place?'

She stared at him, but could infer nothing from his impassive gaze.

'Well, my lord, I don't reckon the High Counsellor would sell me—not just at present, anyway.'

'I didn't mean that: I don't want to buy you.'

He got up, flung a quilted robe round his great, shaggy body and sat down on a carved chest beside the bed.

'What people tell their rulers is nearly always what they think they want to hear. But the rulers need to know more. I need to know things—things I wouldn't be told if I asked. Do you understand?'

'But my lord, the High Counsellor—isn't that *his* work—all those people who come and talk to him—'

'This is nothing to do with the High Counsellor: I need my own sources of information. There are things I can't leave in the hands of a man who lives as he does. And don't go telling him what I've said, or tell your säiyett, or anyone else, do you see? If I learn that you have, I shall simply say that you're a mischievous little liar and have you put to death.'

Frightened, she said no more. The Lord General, standing up, opened the chest and took out a purse stitched over with white beads. Tossing this up and down in his hand, he sat down on the bed beside her.

'In a city like this—a country like this—men trust only their closest friends; and sometimes not even them. Everyone's on his guard, and the higher up he is the fewer he trusts. Everyone has secrets—secrets about which he means never to talk. But in practice, sooner or later, everyone *does* talk. That's strange, but true: for some curious reason, a secret always gets told—to somebody—'

She stared at him silently.

'But it's very seldom told where *I* can hear it; so someone has to hear it for me.'

He paused, still tossing the purse up and down. The coins clicked rhythmically, like a tiny mill-wheel, and the rain sighed on outside.

'No, naturally they're not indiscreet to me; or to Sencho, or to the Lord Durakkon either. But in bed—or even just in company—with a pretty little slave-girl who looks no more than a child—that's another matter. Otavis—she's very well-known now; yet even so, she still gets to hear a lot.' He smiled briefly. '*You* might hear still more. For one thing, you don't belong to me, you see.'

'But my lord, if I don't belong to you—'

He raised a hand. 'Some things a girl simply *happens* to hear, but that's only a small part of the work. Any girl can do that. But a very pretty, much-sought-after girl—she can often learn what she seeks to learn. However much a man may mean to be on his guard, he may easily find himself talking freely to a girl like that, especially if she's shrewd and knows how to loosen his tongue. I dare say you know the old tale of the girl who refused to bed with the magician unless he agreed to give her the egg that contained his heart? He gave it to her, and she broke it.'

'But if I don't belong to you, my lord, how can I do the work?'

'That you'll be told in my good time. You and I may never actually meet again. It's possible that it could turn out to be dangerous. You'd better think it over. But I'll deal fairly with you, Maia. If you do well—and

239

survive—you'll be set free; with plenty of money, too. Enough to make a good marriage—set yourself up as a shearna—whatever you want.'

As Maia remained silent, trying to take this in, he went on, 'The men you'll have to deal with will be Urtans—touchy, proud, humourless people. You'll need to be resourceful and sharp, so for a start—and as a test—you can find a way of your own to let me know your answer within the next three days.'

Before she could reply he picked up a bell from the table by the bed and rang it two or three times. The fair-haired woman came in and stood by the door, palm to forehead. Kembri tossed the beaded purse to her.

'I like to be generous to a girl who's pleased me. Is my bath ready?'

'Yes, my lord.'

Without another word the Lord General left the room.

: 27 :

WAITING

Maia, upon her return, found Terebinthia, Occula and Dyphna sitting round the stove. This surprised her, for at this time of day either the säiyett herself or at least one girl would usually be in attendance upon the High Counsellor. Before she had a chance to ask questions, however, Occula, jumping up and helping her off with her wet cloak, enquired cheerfully, 'Hullo, banzi; back in one piece? Well basted?'

'Basted? You mean split and sun-dried,' answered Maia, sliding off the heavy silver bracelets, which she found cumbersome. She was in a mood to reply to Occula's ribaldry in kind, for to herself she no longer seemed the girl who had been given her instructions by Terebinthia earlier that afternoon.

'Got the speedin' trick, had he?' said Occula. 'Took you up and took you down; is that the tale? His tail or yours?'

'Here, I'll tell you—' Maia, laughing, stopped suddenly as she saw Terebinthia staring at her in the manner of one waiting for another to remember what she ought not to have to be reminded of. She took out the Lord General's purse and handed it over.

'It's still sealed, säiyett.'

'So I see,' replied Terebinthia. 'If it hadn't been, I should have felt—unpleasantly surprised. The seal is customary, but I deliberately didn't tell you. I suppose Occula did?'

'No, I didn', säiyett,' said Occula. 'To tell you the truth, I clean forgot. Maia deserves all the credit. Can we see what he's given her?'

'We can,' answered Terebinthia, breaking the little red seal and spilling the contents of the purse on her palm. 'Well, well!' Maia had the impression that for a moment she was quite taken aback.

'Whew!' said Occula. 'Two hundred and forty meld! That's about as big a lygol as ever I've heard of, säiyett, but of course I doan' know how they go on in Bekla.'

'It's very good indeed,' said Terebinthia. 'Well done, Maia! Here you are, and mind you look after it.' She counted the coins again. 'In fact, you may have a full hundred. It ought to be ninety-six, but I confess I wasn't expecting the Lord General to be quite so generous, and I can't be bothered to go and find the change just now.'

'Thank you very much, säiyett.'

'Just think, banzi,' said Occula. 'Do that a hundred and fifty times an' you'll be a free girl—long as your back's not broken.'

The night: the close, secret, rain-whispering night. Heads close together under the bedclothes, barely a sound even from lips close to ears. Maia lay trembling in Occula's arms, the black girl listening intently as she clasped her close.

'. . . so then he said . . . put you to death . . . secrets . . . dangerous . . . if you survive . . . a fortune! . . . answer in three days.'

For a while Occula made no reply, merely calming Maia as she might have calmed an animal or a baby, with quiet endearments and soft, meaningless sounds. At last, putting her own lips as close to her ear as Maia's had been to hers, she breathed, 'You'll *have* to do it, banzi: you've no choice. If you tell him you woan', he'll decide you're a risk, however much he enjoyed bastin' you. He'll reckon he's told you too much already; an' that could be fatal.'

'But why ever should he choose *me?*' asked Maia desperately. 'I don't know anything—hardly been in Bekla any time at all—'

'Ssh!' For Maia's voice had risen well above a whisper. 'He told you why himself—or most of it. You look too young—you act too young—to be suspected: that's one thing. But he reckons you're a girl who can turn people's heads—you seem to have turned his all right for a couple of hours, by all you've told me. You doan' realize yet—lots of girls never do realize—what sort of effect a girl can have on men. They're not made like us. They get obsessed, you know—crazed, distracted—like a dog hangin' round after a bitch. They doan' think about warmth or kindness or friendship, like we do. They just go out of their minds to baste you. Sometimes it sends them as near mad as makes no difference, and they'll do anythin', tell you anythin', just to get it. Far as I can make out, Kembri as good as told you that himself, but you doan' seem to have taken it in. And on top of all that, he must have decided that you're no fool.'

'But how could he? He never said a word until—'

'*You* never said a word either, did you? Probably that had a lot to do with it.'

'He said it might be dangerous—'

'There's *always* danger for the likes of us. But cheer up, banzi. It could all turn out to have been worth it, you know. Anyhow, I should try to look at it that way, for you'll have to do it.'

'But he said I was to tell him in three days. How can I?'

'I've thought of that, darling: *I'll* do it for you.'

'*You* will? How?'

'Like this. You tell Miss Pussy-cat tomorrow that while you were with Kembri you told him about your friend the black girl, and he said I sounded unusual and he'd like to have a go at me. That'll sound much more convincin' than if you said he wanted *you* back. You've nothin' to gain out of me goin', you see.'

'But she won't take my word for a thing like that—'

'No, 'course she woan'. But she'll hope to Cran it's true, because she'd like another hundred and forty meld. I bet she'll never give Piggy a trug of what she took off you today. By the way, he's out of order, you know. Gorged himself sick at dinner an' they put him to bed. That's why we were all off-duty when you got back. So she's on her own. She'll send round to Kembri's säiyett, who'll ask Kembri. And he's expectin' to hear somethin' from you, so he'll realize what it's all about and say I'm to come.'

'But he said I wasn't to tell a soul—'

'Ah, but for the matter of that I could perfectly well be bringin' him a message I didn' understand myself, couldn' I? "My friend thanks you for being so kind, my lord, and she'll be happy to do anythin' she can for you." Somethin' like that. Great Cran, there are hundreds of ways I can tell him, sweetheart! Just leave it to me.'

'Oh, Occula, I love you so much! Why, now *you're* trembling! What is it?'

For some time the black girl made no reply. At last she whispered 'Oh, what an evil, terrible city this is! I came to it in bloodshed nearly seven years ago an' it hasn' changed an atom! Pray, banzi—only pray that we both survive!'

The following morning, however, she was her usual self, passing the time by inventing ridiculous games in which she and Dyphna competed first, to tell a story containing the most and biggest lies, and then to dress up as different kinds of men paying court to Maia, whom they hit over the head with a bladder every time she failed to stop herself laughing.

Sencho was still sick; and likely to remain in bed for two or three days, so Terebinthia told them. A doctor had prescribed a purge, rest and quiet. Three or four nondescript people who had come for instructions had been sent away and told to return in three days' time.

Maia, having been made to act out her false message until Occula was satisfied that she could deliver it convincingly, asked to see Terebinthia alone. The säiyett, having heard her, enquired whether the Lord General had given any indication of when he wanted the black girl to come; but here Maia, as instructed by Occula, pretended to be unable to remember. Terebinthia thereupon reproved her for not taking more trouble to commit to memory the details of a message from so exalted a personage as the Lord General, but went so far as to smile when Maia replied that she had really been in no condition to memorize anything accurately when she was feeling less like a girl than a bucket of soapsuds.

The porter's underling having been despatched to make enquiries at the Lord General's house, both girls could not help feeling some anxiety. Occula, however, turned out to have been right in supposing that Kembri would put two and two together. The reply was that the Lord General wished to see the black girl that very afternoon; and after a scented bath Occula, having silvered her eyelids, put on her golden nose-stud and necklace of teeth and obtained Terebinthia's approval of her orange metlan and hunting-jacket, set off in the same jekzha that had carried Maia the day before.

She returned quite late, explaining that as she was about to leave the Lord General's house his säiyett had brought her a message that the young lord Elvair-ka-Virrion wished her to come and drink wine with himself and a few friends in his rooms. Naturally, she had done as required. There had been one or two other girls there, including Otavis and a celebrated shearna named Nennaunir, who was very popular among the younger Leopards.

'But I didn' do any more on my back,' she added, handing over Kembri's lygol of two hundred meld and pocketing the eighty which Terebinthia returned to her, 'I just met several rich young men and did my best to make them remember me. I think something might come of it later, säiyett.'

After supper she complained of a headache and said she was going to bed. Maia remained for some time with Terebinthia, helping her to look through and take stock of the wardrobe of beautiful and expensive clothes maintained for the High Counsellor's girls. The säiyett, having ascertained that Maia could ply a needle at least passably, set her to stitching two or three torn linings and frayed hems, dismissing her only when she was ready to go to bed herself.

Maia, expecting Occula to be already asleep, came into their room to find her sitting by the lamp, bent over the pedlar's pottery cat, which she was holding upside-down on her lap and apparently scratching open with the point of her knife.

'What you on with, then?' asked Maia, sitting down on the bed and reaching for the hairbrush. (Since seeing the girls at the Rains banquet, she had taken to a regular use of brush and comb every night before going to bed.)

Occula put the cat back on the shelf.

'Oh, nothin'. Passin' time—wastin' time. A cat ought to have a venda, banzi, doan' you think? Imagine how miserable you'd be without one.'

Maia shook her head in perplexity. 'Thought you was supposed to have a headache?'

'I have. Come on, let's go to bed and put the lamp out. I'll tell you a story—two stories. I want someone's arms round me who loves me, jus' for a change. You'll do for now.'

Under the bedclothes she whispered, 'Well, it worked, banzi. He basted me for a start, but I think he must really have spent almost the lot on you yesterday. He as good as said so, actually, a bit later on. Didn' stop him gettin' down to work for a quarter of an hour, though, before he thought to ask why I was there.'

'What did you say?'

'I gave him your message; that you were ready to oblige him at any time; nothin' more than that. And then I told him—well, you know—that I was your friend and a bit about how we met and how I'd always done my best to look after you. I told him about that little tick Genshed, too—might do him a bit of harm, you never know. Anyway, after a time he asked whether you'd told me what he'd said to you yesterday, and of course I didn' know a damned thing. So then he said what did I think of you, and I said—oh, banzi, I'm so clever—I said I thought you'd do wonders in time, but I couldn' help bein' a bit worried because you were so inexperienced. And then, as if it was a huge joke, I told him about what happened at Khasik—all about Zuno and the Ortelgan rope-merchant and his golden bear. "See what I mean?" I said. "She turns people upside-down, but she's much better when she's got me to look after her. Still, my lord, I mustn' go borin' you with a lot of silly chatter."

'So then he had some food and wine brought in and we talked about nothin' for a bit, and then he basted me again, and after that he told me to get dressed and go home. I'm certain he was waitin' to see whether I'd bring the subject up again. If I had, of course, he'd have guessed you'd been talkin' to me. I just acted as though I'd completely forgotten the whole thing. He gave me my lygol and I was actually goin' out of the room when he called me back and told me to shut the door and sit down.

'And then, banzi, he told me more or less what he told you; that he needs eyes and ears, and in particular that he wants to know more about the Urtans. What it comes to—or so I believe, though of course he didn' say it—is that for some reason he can' persuade Sencho—or doesn' trust him—to find out whatever it is that he wants to know about these Urtans. Neither of them really trusts the other; crooks never do. But my guess is that Sencho's becomin' less and less useful.' Occula suppressed a chuckle. 'Not pullin' his weight, as you might say. But all the same, you see, he knows so much that nobody else knows, that Kembri and Durakkon daren' get rid of him.'

Maia threw back the covers as far as her waist and lay silently on her back, thinking. A lull had fallen in the rain. She could hear the wind stirring the leaves, and the minute pattering of some small animal—mouse, jerboa or long-tailed *chidron*—along the foot of the wall outside. At last, covering their heads once more, she whispered, 'But what's all this to us? We're just slaves. Whose side are we on?'

'The side that suits us best, of course,' answered the black girl. 'Kembri's said he'll pay you and free you, and I trust Kembri as much as I trust any bastard in this damn' city. Besides, it'll get us out into company, and that's what we need, to get on.'

'Us?'

'Oh, yes; I forgot to tell you, banzi. I convinced the Lord General that you need me to help you. Experienced girl, you know. Whatever this work is—and I doan' know any more than you do—I'm goin' to be in it with you. One or other of us ought to be able to make an Urtan talk, doan' you think?'

But nothing happened. The next day passed, and the next, and another. Sencho, at length recovering from his indisposition, had one of the cooks whipped and sold; and later the same day sent for Lalloc to discuss buying another.

Maia's feelings towards the High Counsellor remained strangely ambivalent, fear and fascination succeeding each other like sunlight and cloud-shadow on a hillside. She came to perceive that for him, as Occula had said, the humiliation of others was an important ingredient of sexual pleasure. One evening, when Maia and Occula were with him in the bath, Terebinthia entered to tell him that a shepherd lad from Urtah, secretly in his pay, had come twenty miles through the rain to report to him, and was waiting wet through in the courtyard. The High Counsellor, having replied that the boy deserved to be treated hospitably, thereupon had him brought in, stripped of his wet clothes and rubbed down; after which he made him sit beside the bath while he himself continued what he had been doing with the girls. At length, telling Maia to remain, naked as she was, and serve the youngster with food and drink, he listened to his report and questioned him, while at the same time plainly enjoying his shamefaced and futile attempts to conceal his natural reaction to the sight of the pretty slave-girl.

On another occasion, while talking to a young soldier who had come on some errand from Durakkon, Sencho asked him whether he thought Dyphna was beautiful: and upon the youth naturally replying yes, told him that he might do whatever he pleased with her, provided he did not deprive him of his very natural desire to watch. And despite his reluctance the young man, before being permitted to leave, was compelled to do as the High Counsellor required.

An habitual amusement with him was to inflict pain under the pretence of play or of a caress, and the girls, while waiting upon him, were often squeezed, slapped, or tormented in some more prurient manner, such as tweaking their nipples or plucking the hair at their groins.

And yet, even in the act of performing some disgusting duty, such as helping the High Counsellor to vomit up his gorge, Maia found herself often overcome by that spontaneous sense of excitement and admiration not uncommon in young people towards someone who has absolute power over them. She had no say at all in what took place between them. Sencho might discuss certain matters with his cooks, but never with his girls; for while what he wanted from the former varied and often required careful thought on their part, what he wanted from the latter did not. In his household only one person's convenience was ever considered; and since Maia had no rights and he could order her to do anything he wanted, she simply accepted the situation, which by the standards of a Tonildan peasant-girl was far from intolerable. Maia, indeed (in contrast to Occula), was not unlike a beautiful hawk or hound. She did not go in for reflection. Sencho was her master and after all her abundant, youthful energy had to have some outlet. To wait on him and to gratify him was easy work, while even to minister to him while he excreted great quantities of ordure was not all that different from mucking out the cows—in fact, more cleanly and much less arduous, for every part of the High Counsellor's house-hold was well-conducted and -equipped, Terebinthia being perhaps the most expert säiyett in the empire in accommodating the needs of a libertine.

Sencho did exactly as he felt inclined from morning till night, gratifying each appetite and impulse in the moment that he felt it and without the slightest constraint or shame either in the act or after. From this self-indulgence he clearly derived that peculiar satisfaction often felt by those who have formerly been, but are now no longer, poor and continually straining every energy to their own advancement. Indolence in itself, for example, plainly constituted one of his greatest sources of enjoyment.

When his greed and lust had for a time been satisfied, he would remain lying upon the couch or in the bath, not sleeping but torpid, like some huge insect, doing nothing whatever, yet plainly with enjoyment. During all the months that she spent in his household, Maia never knew whether or not he could read and write; for though it seemed incredible that he could not, she never once saw him do so, it being his invariable practice to require Terebinthia to undertake such irksome matters on his behalf.

Occula and Dyphna, each in her own way, contrived to exercise a kind of veiled, partial control over Sencho's lewdness and cruelty by means of half-hearted response and an air of detached acquiescence, rather as though humouring a child. Maia, however, could never catch the trick, for—as she had discovered on the night when Meris was whipped—there was some part of her which felt a sort of enigmatic affinity with the High Counsellor. As she stooped over him to pour his wine, dressed in a necklace and jewelled sandals, and felt him pinching or biting at her body, she would often become so much enflamed that she would fling herself into the cushions, then and there to initiate what she should, as a compliant slave-girl, have waited to be told to perform. Of such behaviour, however, the High Counsellor seldom complained. The dangerous unpredictability of his moods formed part of the curious glee which she often felt in his presence, and indeed it once occurred to her that if she had known herself to be entirely safe with him she would have felt no excitement. Underlying everything else was the knowledge that the High Counsellor found her greatly to his taste. She felt certain that he would not have sold her for twice what she had cost him.

The truth was that Maia was uncritically proud of her aptitude for pleasing a wealthy, powerful man like Sencho and even of what she suffered at his hands; just as a young, simple-minded soldier is proud of pleasing his superiors, whoever they may be, and of undergoing fatigue and hardship at their behest, feeling that these prove his manly worth. If she had somehow or other found herself back home beside Lake Serrelind, she would probably have boasted of what Sencho had inflicted on her, knowing that it was on account of her attractiveness to him.

She might well have boasted of more than that, for the girls lived in a luxury almost as great as the High Counsellor's own. Their quarters were comfortable and elegantly decorated, and it was no part of their duties to clean them. Soon Occula, after the manner of her kind, began to need to take care not to grow fleshy, for when attending upon Sencho they were not only allowed but encouraged—since it tended to increase their carnality—to eat as much as they wished. Maia, on the other hand, discovered something that she had never had the opportunity to find out before; namely, that eating to her fullest satisfaction seemed to have no effect whatever on her weight or appearance. To sleep, too, was easy and pleasant, for here were no buzzing night-flies, no crying baby; only Occula in a big, soft bed instead of Nala in a small, hard one; and no early rising, either; for plenty of sleep was important to their looks.

In short, the girls were cared for and tended like the valuable property they were. Terebinthia often examined and massaged them herself, and on the slightest cause, such as a sore throat or a stomach pain, would summon the doctor. When Dyphna was troubled by a corn in the foot, a skilled man was brought from the lower city to remove it. Often they were warned of the severe punishment awaiting any girl who might pick a quarrel or lose her temper. Maia learned that the säiyett's very valid objection to Meris, beauty or no, had been that in her former life she had got into a habit of mischief and violence; and a scratched face or a torn dress was a serious matter, since it lessened the High Counsellor's pleasure and wasted his money.

Indeed, almost as much was spent on the girls' wardrobe as on Sencho's gluttony. When he entertained, he would order Terebinthia to dress them magnificently; and this, as Occula and Maia soon discovered, meant as richly as the finest lady in Bekla. Not only their dresses and jewels, but their undergarments and every least part of their attire were of a quality that Maia had never even imagined; so that now, when she recalled the dress with which the slave-traders had tricked her, she felt ashamed to think she could ever have been taken in by such rubbish.

One evening the girls were called upon to help to regale one Randronoth, the governor of Lapan, who was visiting Bekla on state business and spending the night at the High Counsellor's. Randronoth had a reputation in the empire for gross extravagance and for preferring very young girls. Nevertheless, he was a man of forceful ability and personal magnetism, possessed standing in Lapan as a soldier and leader and was popular and influential among his own people. On this account he had retained his position as governor throughout the Leopards' rule, despite their strong suspicions that he often made little distinction between public money and his own.

It came as no surprise to Sencho when Randronoth showed a marked interest in Maia, and the High Counsellor (who not only had his own reasons for wanting to oblige him, but also felt it flattering that a Lapanese aristocrat should not attempt to conceal that he envied him a valuable possession) hospitably told him that he was welcome to spend the night with her.

Undressing with the care for her clothes which Terebinthia ceaselessly enjoined on them all, Maia realized that her companion seemed almost as much excited by what she was taking off as by what was being revealed.

Handling and examining them, he asked her whether she had any idea what her gown and jewels might be worth in all; and upon her replying that she really could not tell, said that in his estimation she must have had at least seven thousand meld on her back, her fingers and round her neck.

'Don't signify, my lord; what you got in your arms now cost more 'n twice that,' she replied; jestingly, yet letting him see that at all events she knew that much. And this answer plainly stimulated him even further.

The apparently insatiable desire roused in him again and again during the night, not so much by anything she said or did as by her mere bodily presence—the sheer look and feel of her, which seemed to put him almost beside himself—would have struck a more experienced girl as altogether out of the ordinary; even as somewhat unbalanced. It was as though she must correspond to, must be for him the physical manifestation of, some personal, inward obsession. Those who have travelled widely can recognize a prodigy when they encounter it, while by the same token an ingénue may easily take it for granted without discernment or special wonder. Maia, who was still deriving pleasure from the realization that she was exceptionally desirable to men, did not find her night with Randronoth disagreeable—in fact she quite enjoyed it—but by the same token attached little or no consequence to the fervour of his passion. When, next morning, he told her that he must at all costs see her again—that he was utterly set on it—she accepted this as being, for all she knew, the sort of thing men not infrequently said to girls; and when he begged her for assurances that she felt for him as he for her, she gave them as a matter of politeness and of what she thought was only to be expected of a good concubine.

And inwardly? Yes, well, she supposed she'd turned his head all right; that was what she was for, wasn't it? It was quite beyond Maia, even on the evidence, to perceive or have any inkling how completely; let alone to foresee or feel apprehensive about the possible consequences. This, however, was perhaps as well for her, since his infatuation, brought about entirely without her intention, was now irreversible, and no amount of anxiety on her part could have dispelled it.

Her impudent retort about her own value, coming from a child of fifteen, amused Randronoth enough to make him repeat it to the High Counsellor, who nodded approvingly, feeling that she had done him credit. His lygol was exceptionally generous, and the tone of his farewell to her (though she soon forgot it) was more like that of a man parting from some incomparable paramour than from a slave-girl lent to him for a night. Later Terebinthia, in her customarily cool, half-grudging manner, remarked that she appeared to have given satisfaction.

With compensations of this kind such a life, despite its abasements and indignities, could not—to a girl like Maia—help but tend to self-satisfaction, even while Terebinthia held her across the couch for the High Counsellor to slap her plump young buttocks. And this gratifying state of mind, together with the sincere affection of Occula, was more than enough to overcome any boredom she might have felt at passing all her time either in the women's quarters or in attendance upon the High Counsellor. In fact she found plenty to do, for Maia had never been inactive by nature. Encouraged by Occula, who believed strongly in the value of accomplishments, she wheedled Dyphna into giving her lessons in reading and, catching Terebinthia one day in a good mood, persuaded her to hire a skilled sempstress to improve her needlework. She also learned a little of the hinnari—'just enough to be able to accompany yourself, anyway,' said Occula; but the truth was, as Maia knew, that she possessed no more than an ordinarily pleasant voice.

The dance, however, was another matter. In this, more than in anything else, she took pleasure and progressed, and under Occula's tuition would practise for hours not only the flowing, seductive sequences of the senguela but also other dances—Yeldashay, Belishban and the stamping, whirling rhythms of the Deelguy; for at the Lily Pool Occula had watched and talked to many visiting dancing-girls and picked up a great deal.

On certain evenings, when the other girls were on duty in the bath or the dining-hall and she was alone, Maia would sit pensive at a window, her hands in her lap, looking out at the falling rain; neither fretting nor melancholy but, country-fashion, letting her thoughts stray where they would. Sometimes she would choose the long, northern window looking down towards the wall bounding the upper city, the Peacock Gate and the vista of descending streets beyond, from among which soared the lower city's tall, slender towers. These she could now recognize and name at a glance. Or again, she would sit at the west window, with its prospect across the green, dripping garden and bordering grove of birches to the shore of the Barb. A mile away, on the further side of the water, rose the Leopard Hill, crowned by the Palace of the Barons with its twenty symmetrical towers. Once, when the rain chanced to cease for a short while at sunset, the western clouds parted briefly to reveal a huge, crimson sun; a heavy, glowing sphere floating as though half-submerged, borne up, dipping and rolling in a fluid sky—swimming down, she thought, among far-away lands; Katria, Terekenalt and further yet—perhaps over that city of Silver Tedzhek which Occula had spoken of, out beyond the Govig. 'Happen it's shining on that Long Spit up the river, where they hold the fair,' she thought. 'It must just about look pretty, with that red sun setting.' For of course it did not occur to Maia that the time of day would be different in a far-off land—that in Tedzhek it would still be afternoon.

She would recall that drudging childhood she was glad to think she had left behind; of no further interest, remnant as a discarded dress or a faded bunch of flowers. Only for the rippling solitude of Lake Serrelind, and for her happy waterfall, did she still feel a pang of regret, and—yes! for Tharrin, that strolling, smiling, rather seedy adventurer. He was shallow, a rascal, of no account—this she could now see plainly. While she was daily before his eyes he had not been able to resist her; indeed, it had never occurred to him even to try—no, indeed, rather the reverse. Yet once she was gone, he had let that be the end of it. Too bad, but these things happened, didn't they? At least, they always had—to him. Easy come, easy go. 'Wonder what mother said when he came back?' she thought. 'Ah, and what *he* said an' all. Just about nothing, I dare say. All the same, he was kind and good-natured; he liked a good time; he made you laugh; we had a bit of fun. I wouldn't say no to him, not even now. Leastways *he* wasn't one to bite and pinch and set you crawling over the floor. Oh—' and here she gazed down pleasurably at her clothes and the jewels on her fingers and arms—'wouldn't I just about like to rub his face in this lot? "See?" I'd say. "This is what I've got out of you not being man enough even to *try* to get me back. 'Fraid I can't stop now—I've got to go and be basted by the Lord General of Bekla, for more than two hundred meld. Ta-ta!" '

Ah! The Lord General of Bekla. And thus her thoughts came sharply back to the present. Mostly, during the day, she was successful in keeping her anxiety at arm's length. Sometimes she was able to persuade herself that nothing at all would follow from what the Lord General had offered (or demanded of) her. Yet alone, in the rain-scented evening, with the thrushes singing in the green silence, the recollection of what he had said about danger would come trickling back into her mind like water under a door—indisputable evidence of worse outside. What sort of danger? When? Where? From whom? 'If you survive.' This, for all she knew, was probably the sort of thing generals commonly said to their soldiers. She wished Kembri had not said it to her.

Yet here, if the Lord General was to be trusted, lay the hope of greater and quicker gain than she could expect from any other quarter. To be free, and set up as a Beklan shearna, and that before she was much older! This was the thing to dwell upon, this was the thing to hope for. 'When I'm a shearna, I'll—' and as the clouds closed once more across the red sun and the rain returned, Maia's thoughts ran buoyantly on towards an indistinct but glorious future; for she was young and healthy and, like most people until they have met catastrophe face-to-face, had a vague idea that it could never really happen to her. She was lucky! Lucky Maia! Had not her very enslavement turned out, all in all, a big change for the better? As Tere-binthia came in to summon her to the dining-hall she would dismiss her fears, turning from the window and unfastening her bodice to lie half-open in the way she knew the High Counsellor liked.

Occula, too, though she never spoke of it, seemed by no means without anxiety. She had set up in their room the polished, black image of Kantza-Merada, and more than once Maia, returning unexpectedly, would find her prostrate before it, her face—certainly on one occasion—wet with tears. Maia became familiar with the words of that liturgy which she had first heard by the stream between Hirdo and Khasik:

'Most strangely, Kantza-Merada, are the laws of the dark world effected. O Kantza-Merada, do not question the laws of the nether world.'

This and more Occula would repeat nightly, sometimes clasping the figure of the goddess between her hands as she did so; striving desperately, one might think, to wring comfort from it as juice from a fruit.

One night, as they were preparing for bed, Maia, happening to pick up the pottery Cat Colonna, saw that Occula had roughly scratched a few words—presumably with her knife—across the base. Slowly, she spelt them out. ' "Ready—do—as you wish." What's that, then, Occula?'

'That?' For a moment Occula seemed startled. 'Oh, that's—that's what we used to call an incised prayer. You know, you take the trouble to scratch it on, an' that makes the prayer—well, it sort of makes it work. That's a prayer of submission.'

'Submission? To what?'

'Oh, I dunno—everythin': anythin': to whatever has to be done, that's all.' She stood up, yawning and stretching smooth, black arms above her gown of white satin. 'Come on, help me off with this. Cran, it's heavy! Unhook the back, banzi, and then hold it while I step out. Oh, I could sleep for days, couldn' you?'

: 28 :

A LITTLE AMUSEMENT

Maia, making up the charcoal brazier at the further end of the small dining-hall, returned to the High Counsellor's couch, helped herself to a bowl of egg-yolks frothed in lemon, wine and sugar, and lay down among the cushions at his feet.

Sencho had spent the greater part of the morning in questioning and giving instructions to a succession of outlandish, raffish persons, most of whom were obviously poor and one or two, actual vagrants (or might they, Maia wondered, be merely disguised as vagrants?). The girls had not, of course, been in attendance. Terebinthia had brought the men one by one into the High Counsellor's presence, and as each was dismissed paid him whatever meagre sum Sencho ordered. None, however, had been allowed to leave until all had been heard; after which six or seven had been kept back for further questioning until Sencho had resolved to his satisfaction certain inconsistencies in what they had told him. Three, who arrived masked, had been kept in separate rooms until summoned.

Whatever the result of the morning's work, it was evidently pleasing to Sencho. As noon approached he seemed in excellent spirits, instructing Terebinthia to see that the small hall was prepared and that Maia and Occula were ready to add to his enjoyment of a well-earned dinner.

It was soon clear that his satisfaction with the reports of the spies had stimulated his greed to an even greater degree than usual. When at length, after more than an hour, the time came for an enforced rest, he showed no inclination to drowse, requiring instead that the girls should entertain him until he felt capable of eating again.

One of the High Counsellor's amusements at such times was to misuse or spoil food in one way or another; for it pleased him to feel that he, who had starved and stolen as a child, was now able not only to consume excessive quantities purely for his pleasure, but also to waste them if he wished. Sometimes he would have some emaciated beggar brought in off the streets and, having deliberately fouled a dish of veal or a game pie before his eyes, would graciously permit him to eat it before being sent away: or, ordering two or three girls to be brought up from one of the pleasure-houses of the lower city, he would promise a large sum of money to the one who could eat most in half an hour, watching intently as they gobbled, crammed and choked over the rich food to which their stomachs were quite unaccustomed.

Today he caused Terebinthia to fill a great, silver basin with clotted cream until it was almost brimming. Then, himself undressing Occula, he told her to sit down in it. The black girl did so, lending herself to the game by lolling and wriggling from side to side until the cream had covered her smooth, brown body from belly to thighs. Then, getting up, she stood obediently as the High Counsellor proceeded to decorate her loins with an intricate pattern of cherries, almonds, fragments of angelica, sugared violets and the like.

Maia, excited by the extravagance and waste and by the bizarre sight of her pretty friend literally clothed in food, was as usual unable to confine herself to her proper rôle as a slave-girl, but must needs be joining in the sport, hanging pairs of cherries from Occula's ears and nipples and then, laughing at her own ingenuity, peeling the skin from the long finger of an *itarg*-fruit and thrusting it between her legs. Her fellow-feeling for the game pleased Sencho, who at length resumed his dinner by causing Occula to remain beside the couch so that he could lick the creamy confection from her body; while Maia, crouching, made use of the frothed egg-yolks to indulge him in a somewhat similar manner.

The game having concluded, predictably, in an access of contentment for the High Counsellor, Maia (who before the end had become somewhat disarranged) was putting herself to rights, while Terebinthia wiped Occula down with a towel wrung out in warm water, when the ringing of a small bell was heard outside the door. This indicated that a servant wished to speak to Terebinthia; it being a strict rule that no one but the säiyett herself was ever to enter the hall when Sencho was with his girls. She went out and returned to inform the High Counsellor that an aristocratic visitor had called—none other than the young lord Elvair-ka-Virrion—accompanied by a lady, and begged to be graciously permitted to speak with him for a few minutes.

In the normal way Sencho would not have dreamed of allowing such an intrusion upon his dinner, but his satisfaction in the morning's work and the exalted social position of his visitor, as well as the pleasure which Maia had just so skilfully afforded, disposed him to stretch a point; the more especially as he rather hoped that some opportunity might present itself to affront or disgust the unknown lady.

Elvair-ka-Virrion's companion, when he entered the hall behind Terebinthia, proved to be Nennaunir, the shearna whom Occula had met some days before at the conclusion of her visit to the Lord General.

Elvair-ka-Virrion, who was as usual magnificently and flamboyantly dressed and was carrying over one arm a heavy cloak of leopard-skins, greeted the High Counsellor with as much ease and self-possession as though he had not been lying half-drunk among naked girls. Having accepted wine for himself and his companion, and respectfully complimented the High Counsellor on its excellent quality, he went on to say that he had come in person to ask him a favour. He was giving a party the following night, and wished to spare no pains to ensure that plenty of attractive girls should be present.

'You have here, my lord,' he said, spreading his hands and smiling, 'well—what one would expect of an establishment such as yours—the most striking girls in the city. Occula here is unique: I'm sure she sweeps downstream like a Telthearna flood. As for this Tonildan girl, one has only to look at her to suppose that Lespa has returned from among the stars. In short, my lord, if you'll lend them to me tomorrow I'm in no doubt they'll do you the greatest credit.'

While he was speaking Maia, who had begun by taking in every detail of his fine figure and beautiful clothes, gradually became more fully aware of the young woman standing a little apart as she sipped her wine. Nennaunir, she thought, must be about twenty-one. She had dark-brown hair which curled naturally over her shoulders, very fine skin and exquisitely beautiful, delicate hands, on one of which she was wearing a gold ring set with some tawny, translucent stone carved in the form of a crouching leopard. Her close-fitting robe, very slightly transparent above the waist to reveal—or not quite to reveal—her firm breasts, was of a dull-toned, rather dark red, plain except for an inch-deep gold border which matched her sandals. Its surface was without lustre and slightly rough; Maia guessed that it must be made of raw silk. She looked, in fact, not only wealthy but as respectable as any daughter of a baron or wife of an officer.

Apart from her dress and appearance, however, there was about Nennaunir a certain quality which engaged Maia's interest so strongly that after a time she ceased to pay attention to Elvair-ka-Virrion, watching instead the young shearna and trying to enter into her thoughts and feelings as she stood leaning against a column, looking demurely down and idly examining the decoration of the silver goblet in her hand. A man, Maia realized after a little, would see in Nennaunir whatever she intended him to see. To a woman she was inscrutable, for no sooner did one fancy that one had perceived her frame of mind, than one's thoughts stopped short, checked—baffled, even—by an intimation of what seemed the exact opposite. Her eye wandered knowledgeably and appreciatively over the fountain nymph among her jade reeds, the mosaic floor and other luxurious appointments of the hall. Yet at the same time she evinced—or rather, did not quite evince—a faint air of distaste for the High Counsellor. The next moment—and it seemed as though she herself had not changed but rather that Maia's viewpoint had, as it were, altered slightly, as might that of someone looking at the varying colours reflected from the bevelled edge of a glass—she appeared amused, with a hint of excitement, as though it would not take much to make her undress and join the girls on the couch. From this she was restrained only—so she appeared to suggest—by devotion to Elvair-ka-Virrion. At least, this devotion was implied in her eyes, which were frequently turned towards him with a look of admiration. But then again her glance would catch Terebinthia's with the complicit air of one professional to another. Towards Maia and Occula her manner was slightly distant, not unfriendly but a little aloof, as befitting one who had risen above their level. 'You *may* come to be like me, in time,' her brief smile seemed to say. 'I'm inclined to doubt it, but I wish you well all the same.'

Maia felt daunted by her assurance and poise: her mingling of authority with deference, warmth with detachment, honesty with artifice, candour with reticence. Sufficiently sharp to perceive all this and to realize, too, that this skilful balance, no doubt imperceptible to men entirely taken up with her physical grace and beauty, constituted the essence of an accomplished shearna, Maia could not help wondering whether she herself would ever be able to attain such ability. A shearna, she now saw clearly enough, needed to be an actress; yet it would be of no avail merely to copy Nennaunir. Actress or no, her style was individual—it was all one with her looks, her movement (lighter and quicker than Maia's), the tone of her voice and her cast of countenance. This girl had succeeded in becoming what she—Maia—and Occula were hoping to become. And in the very act of leaning by the fountain, toying with her wine and not in the least appearing to be doing five things at once, she was giving an all-too-clear demonstration of how she had achieved her success. 'It's like she keeps putting on different masks,' thought Maia. 'Only they're see-through masks an' all. It's always herself you think you see underneath.'

Sencho replied to Elvair-ka-Virrion that his girls, like everyone else's, were available on terms, and enquired what kind of lygol the young man thought appropriate for their attendance at his party. At this Elvair-ka-Virrion showed slight surprise. Surely in all the circumstances—

Sencho, with an air implying that it was hardly for one such as himself to be put to the trouble of expounding to youths commonplace matters which someone else should already have taught them, waved a shapeless arm towards Terebinthia. The säiyett, smiling deferentially, begged Elvair-ka-Virrion to permit her to explain something of which he himself would undoubtedly become more keenly aware when, later, he came to possess slave-girls of his own. A girl represented a very considerable capital outlay; especially girls like these, hand-picked and in their prime. Inevitably, little by little, time and use took the bloom off them. They were a wasting asset, with a normal peak life of about seven or eight years. The young lord would not, would he now, expect to borrow hounds for a hunting expedition, or a boat for some journey down-river, without agreeing upon a fair sum for wear and tear? There was always good reason behind every generally-accepted social custom.

Elvair-ka-Virrion, no less courteously, was responding to this with some talk of the value of experience and the exhilarating and polishing effect upon girls of mixing in the highest company and becoming friendly with such outstanding practitioners as the lady Nennaunir, when the High Counsellor broke in once more. Having regard to his friendship with Elvair-ka-Virrion's father, he was ready to oblige him. Obviously—and here Sencho's half-buried eyes flickered sharply up at the young man—this party was not an affair of state policy, or his father would have advanced him public funds for it. But—and here he checked Elvair-ka-Virrion, who was about to protest—no matter. The girls might go, and he would expect them to receive whatever generous lygol Elvair-ka-Virrion thought appropriate: less, no doubt, than the four hundred meld apiece which would normally be required for loaning such girls for an entire night; but let that pass. In return, Nennaunir should remain with him for the next hour.

At this the shearna started for a moment, but instantly recovered her self-possession. Occula, catching Maia's eye, quickly glanced away. Elvair-ka-Virrion, plainly disconcerted, replied that he greatly appreciated the High Counsellor's generosity. Nennaunir, however, was a free woman and, like any other shearna, was accustomed to be well paid for her time and accomplishments. He really could not say—embarrassed, he glanced hesitantly towards her.

Sencho said no more, but Terebinthia (and here Maia began to perceive that one of the skills of a competent säiyett was to preserve the dignity of her master, carried away by a compulsion to gratify some depraved impulse, and to intervene on his behalf) suggested that since Nennaunir was today spending time in Elvair-ka-Virrion's company, no doubt it was in his power to compensate the High Counsellor for his generosity by letting her bestow a little of that time on him. Otherwise—she shrugged—perhaps it would be better to forget the whole business—after all, it was not important—the young lord might prefer to look for girls elsewhere—

Nennaunir, having now had time, as it seemed, to deliberate with herself, put down her goblet and walked over to the couch. As she sat down her perfume, a light, fresh drift of planella, reached Maia's nostrils. She would be delighted, she said, provided her friend was agreeable, to render the High Counsellor any service in her power. Indeed, she was only sorry that the opportunity should not have come her way before.

Terebinthia, turning to Elvair-ka-Virrion, said that she would be happy to discuss with him, in the garden-room, the necessary arrangements for the girls' attendance at his party. If he wished, she would show him the clothes which she had in mind for them to wear; of course, if he should have other ideas, she would be only too happy—

Still talking quietly, she conducted the young nobleman from the hall.

An hour later, in the women's quarters, Occula stood oiling and soaping Nennaunir in the bath, while Maia, having carefully selected some matching thread, was mending the hem of her robe where the gold border had been torn. Elvair-ka-Virrion had already left. The shearna, shuddering, buried her face in her wet hands, then bit on one finger, shaking her head from side to side.

'Steady!' said Occula, putting one arm round her shoulders. 'Time to go home now. All finished!'

'Oh, the filthy brute!' burst out the girl. 'How *disgusting!* Oh, I never imagined—'

'Oh, this is the real world here,' replied Occula. 'We handle anythin', you know—'

'You think it's *funny*?' cried Nennaunir, with blazing anger. 'You think—'

'Well, I'll be frank,' answered the black girl, putting down the oil-flask and looking her soberly in the eye. 'I *do* find it a bit surprisin' to see an experienced girl like you thrown off her balance by such things. After all, you must have—'

'*Me*?' cried Nennaunir, stamping her foot in the water. 'To do—*that*, to *me*? Do you know that when U-Falderon took me to Ikat Yeldashay last year I was mistaken for the Lord Durakkon's own daughter? D'you know who gave me that robe there, and what it cost? Do you—'

'That's just why he *did* it, dear,' said Occula patiently. 'Much more fun to do it to someone like you than to trollops like us.'

'But—but what possible pleasure can there be in—in *that*?'

'Why, simply to see you revolted and trying not to be sick,' said Occula. 'You must have come across this sort of thing before, surely?'

'We evidently live in different worlds,' said Nennaunir, with a wretched attempt at superiority.

'Oh, by all means, if it makes you feel better—' answered Occula, shrugging her shoulders.

Nennaunir, stepping out of the water, was silent while Occula rubbed her down. At length she said, 'I'm sorry! I didn't really mean to be spiteful.' She turned to Maia. 'Is he always like that, or only sometimes?'

Maia felt embarrassed. 'Dunno, really.'

'Oh, can' you see,' said Occula, with a kindly touch of impatience, 'that it's just you being an expensive girl and hatin' every minute of it that brings him on? It's much easier for us guttersnipes. He'd do it to the Sacred Queen if he could.'

'The Sacred Queen?' Nennaunir stared. 'The Sacred *Queen*? She'd love every minute of it! Have you ever had anything to do with her?' Occula shook her head. 'Oh, well. It doesn't do to pass on everything you happen to learn, does it? I'd heard stories about the High Counsellor, if it comes to that, but I never really believed them until now.' Overcome once more by her revulsion, she sat down beside Maia and dropped her head between her knees. 'Oh, I'd rather have been whipped! I really would.'

'You wouldn't,' said Terebinthia, who had come into the room as silently as usual. 'But you needn't have put yourself forward so readily this afternoon. I could have got you out of it if you'd given me the time—and the money, of course. It's merely a matter of exercising influence.'

'Influence with the High Counsellor, perhaps,' said Nennaunir, slipping on her sandals and stooping to fasten them, 'but not with Elvair-ka-

Virrion. That was really why I had to agree. His father owns my house, you see, and I live in it for nothing—as long as I'm one of his friends. Even so, I wouldn't have agreed if I'd known—'

'But could you really have got her out of it, säiyett?' asked Maia. She snapped off her thread and spread out Nennaunir's robe on her knee. 'How?'

'Why, he accepts my advice, of course,' replied Terebinthia. 'I can generally change the High Counsellor's mind if I want to. Without me he'd be dead in a month, and he knows it as well as I do. Why do you suppose Meris was sold? If anyone thought I was going to keep a girl like that—couldn't keep her temper, always using her sexuality to make trouble, lucky not to have been hanged upside-down in Belishba—' She looked with approval at the mended rent. 'He wouldn't find another säiyett like me.'

'Well, you live by looking after the High Counsellor,' said Nennaunir. 'You're welcome, I'm sure. Personally, I can't leave too soon.'

'There is a jekzha waiting for you in the courtyard,' replied Terebinthia coldly.

: 29 :

THE URTANS

Maia lay easy and relaxed beside Elvair-ka-Virrion. She was feeling, at this moment, as fully content as at any previous time in her life; and not only in respect of physical satisfaction, or even of pride in the power of her beauty—of which she had just received the amplest proof. Even more than with these, she was filled with a sense of success and of having attained to a new level in her fortunes. It was as though until today, with Occula to guide her, she had been climbing arduously towards a ridge rising above her. Now she was standing on the ridge. Whatever lay in the future, she was no longer—would never again be—that plodding girl. Dangers there might be, but no more clambering. Serene in her beauty, energy and health, she felt equal to any future uncertainty; capable, even, of turning it to account. Stretching lazily, she rubbed her cheek against Elvair-ka-Virrion's shoulder.

Upon her arrival with Occula—and before she had even seen any of the other guests—she had at once been taken upstairs to Elvair-ka-Virrion's room, where he joined her after a few minutes. Taking her in his arms, he kissed her passionately and at once set about giving expression to the feelings he had declared so ardently at the Rains banquet. He had certainly proved himself no liar, she thought.

259

And something else he had shown her, too—the difference between a nobleman and a tavern-stroller. Sencho, of course, did not enter into this. All that she had ever done with Sencho had been the work of a slave-girl, and her only satisfaction had come from doing a thorough job and climbing into her master's good graces. Neither did she count Kembri, for plainly almost any girl would do for him. She now believed only too well that when he had told her that he had not sent for her primarily because he wanted to bed with her, he had been speaking no more than the truth. Throw almost anything you like in the water, she thought, and a pike'll take it if he's on the feed. No, it was Tharrin whom Elvair-ka-Virrion had put in the shade, and not merely by wealth, or even by youthful virility. Tharrin's playfulness, she now realized, though it had amused and pleased her at the time—oh, he wasn't a bad sort—was all of a piece with his weakness. He wasn't—he never had been—a man who picked life up and shook it. He was footloose, fugitive, a stray cat round a back door. He had no real dignity—no, not even in a girl's arms. He was a born scrumper of apples, a pinch-and-run exponent—'What, me, sir?'—one who had always preferred to nibble and move on rather than stay to make a job of anything. And this had shown—oh, yes, very much—in his love-making— light-hearted, trivial, what's a bit of fun between friends? As she lay here now, with Elvair-ka-Virrion's arm under her head, she was not even think- ing of Tharrin's responsibility for what had happened to her, but simply of how much more satisfaction she had just received than ever she had from him. From all she had heard, Tharrin's whole life had been precarious. He was precarious by nature, and unconsciously she had felt precarious as his lover. Events had proved her right. By contrast, Elvair-ka-Virrion had taken her with a kind of smooth, natural mastery in which there seemed no hint of weakness: and (unlike his father) he had shown consideration for her as well as himself. She felt respect for him. Although she knew that he must have had many girls, she believed what he had said to her—that since he had first seen her he had felt more desire for her than for any other girl in the city. She had had no choice in the business, of course, but that did not matter, for the truth was that she had gone along with it altogether. In fact, she had never enjoyed anything so much. To be with a handsome, warm-hearted, well-mannered man not many years older than herself, who behaved unselfishly, yet took what he wanted with an ardour which she knew to be the effect of her own beauty—this, for Maia, was a new and wholly delightful experience.

As a Beklan slave-girl, with a long road still ahead of her to freedom and fortune, she should no doubt have been thinking less of pleasure than of how she could best turn this highly-placed young man's favours to advan- tage. But Maia still lacked professional detachment; and it was, of course, this very deficiency which made her so attractive to Elvair-ka-Virrion. She was still brim-full of unfeigned spontaneity, and he, perceiving this, had been seized with a very natural desire to make the most of it.

Lying beside him now, Maia had no least thought of how much money he was going to give her, or even of what advancement she could hope for. In point of fact she was simply hoping that next time they might be able to spend rather longer together. Nice as it was, it had been over too quickly. But then what else could you expect, just before a party of which Elvair-ka-Virrion was the host? He had simply taken his opportunity. She would have been disappointed if he had not; but at any moment he was likely to be missed. Outside, not far away, she could hear his merry-making guests; voices raised in song, and then a burst of laughter which broke off in shouts and cheering.

'Ought you to go back, my lord?'

He had been so charmingly self-forgotten that she felt obliged to ask. It did not, of course, occur to her that from his point of view, good manners might all be part of the game: a subtle way of gratifying himself still further, to treat a little Tonildan slave-girl like a princess; just as it excited Sencho to degrade a celebrated shearna.

'Why, you don't want to leave me, do you?'

'Oh, no, my lord. I was only afraid they may be missing you.'

'Never mind: we have to talk, you and I.'

'About Nennaunir?' This was impertinence, but if Maia had been a mere professional she would never have troubled to taunt him at all.

He felt enough respect for her, it seemed, to give her a serious reply.

'I've never made love with Nennaunir. If you don't believe me, you can ask her yourself.'

Still she teased him. 'Wonder why not?'

'I just don't fancy her: I told you, I've not fancied anyone else since that day when I first saw you in the Khalkoornil.'

'But Nennaunir was with you yesterday when you came to the High Counsellor's?'

'I'd taken her with me to see Eud-Ecachlon, the heir of Urtah, and ask him to come tonight with his friends. But that was only to help him make up his mind. *He* fancies her very much, you see; only he's never been able to persuade her. She's a self-willed girl, Nennaunir—she picks and chooses. She's so much sought after that she can afford to, and of course that adds to her attraction in a lot of people's eyes. I asked her to promise Eud-Ecachlon that she'd be nice to him if he came to this party. That decided him all right: otherwise he might not have come. The Urtans only pretend to like us, you see; and can you wonder? My father sold Suba to Karnat— he and Fornis.'

'Why d'you reckon Nennaunir agreed, then? I mean, if she doesn't really fancy him?'

'Why, because she—knows.'

'What does she know, my lord?'

'She knows how much Bekla needs her help. And Bekla needs *your* help, too, Maia.'

'*My* help?'

'Well, you told my father you were ready to help us, didn't you?'

She drew in her breath sharply, and for an instant shrank down where she lay in his arms. In her simplicity, it had not for one moment occurred to her that her undertaking to the Lord General would be required of her tonight.

He smiled. 'You weren't expecting me to say anything like this?'

'No, my lord!' She was close to tears. 'I thought—I thought you'd asked me here because—because you wanted me—because of what you said to me at the banquet—'

'Oh, Maia, I meant every word I said at the banquet! I still mean it. You're wonderful! You're not like—well, you're not like that hard-faced Belishban girl you were with that night, for one. Don't ever stop being yourself. Don't *ever* stop talking like a Tonildan girl; promise me!'

She laughed. 'That's easy promise, I reckon.'

But now he was grave again. 'What do you want most in all the world, Maia? To be free? To be rich—as fine a shearna as any in Bekla? Or would you rather go back to Tonilda—live in your own house, with servants to wait on you and tenants to work on your land? All those things are possible.'

'Oh, now you're just making fun of me, my lord.'

'By Cran and Airtha, I'm not! You don't understand, do you? If only you can succeed in doing what we want, no reward will be too great.'

Maia was silent. At length she said, 'I must believe you, my lord. Only 'tain't easy for me to take it all in, see? Seems only just the other day as I was back home, wearin' sacking and glad of a bit of black bread.'

'But my father told you, didn't he? A girl who really *is* a banzi straight from the back of beyond, that's a thing that can't be faked; not day in day out. We've got to have someone who really *is* what she seems to be.'

She slipped out of his embrace, sitting up in the bed and tossing back her hair. He reached up and gently fondled one breast.

'What is it, then, my lord, that you want me to do?'

'All we want you to do tonight is to turn someone else's head as thoroughly as you've turned mine. No more than that. Don't, whatever you do, give him what you've just given me. Just make him very much want to see you again. Can you do that?'

'All depends, my lord, doesn't it, whether *he's* goin' t' fancy *me*?'

'He'll fancy you all right. Just pretend you're back home in your own village and be yourself. Listen: I'll tell you a story. When Durakkon's wife went into labour a year or two ago, the doctor was very nervous to think he was attending the wife of the High Baron. Durakkon told him to imagine he was delivering a girl in the lower city. It worked like a charm. I bet you had one or two lads on their toes in Tonilda, didn't you, before you came here?'

'But this man, my lord—he'll know I've been with you.'

'He won't: I took the greatest care. They'll just be starting supper now. Come with me and I'll show you your man without him seeing you. Then we'll go down to the hall separately.'

Obediently, Maia got out of bed and dressed. Picking up a lamp, Elvair-ka-Virrion guided her along an empty corridor and up a steep flight of steps. At the top he blew out the lamp and opened the door of a small, unlit room. She could hear the rain drumming on the roof overhead.

The opposite wall consisted of nothing more solid than decorative wooden tracery, through which lamplight was shining. From below rose sounds of talk and laughter and the clatter of plates and goblets. Elvair-ka-Virrion, turning to her with a finger on his lips, led her across to the tracery wall.

Through this Maia, from a height of perhaps thirty feet, found herself looking down into the Lord General's dining-hall. It was less crowded than on the night of the Rains banquet, for Elvair-ka-Virrion had invited no more than sixty or seventy people altogether, men and girls. The serving-tables were spread with food—the mere sight of them, together with the smells of roast meat, vegetables, herbs and sauces, aroused Maia's appetite—and the flower-crowned guests were moving among them for slaves to fill their plates and goblets. Several men had already seated themselves at tables on the dais itself, while others, accompanied by their girls, had strolled further down the hall, forming casual groups. Maia could see Nennaunir, in a saffron robe and a necklace of what looked like real rubies, talking with two young men who were obviously competing for her favours. As she watched, one of them suddenly turned towards the other with a quick look of anger, whereupon Nennaunir burst out laughing, slapped his hand and held out her goblet for him to go and refill.

Elvair-ka-Virrion pointed towards the right-hand side of the dais. Here a little knot of five men were talking among themselves as they sat together round the end of one of the tables. All had long hair gathered behind their necks in the Urtan style, and wore daggers at their belts. In guests from any other part of the empire this last would have been regarded as an insult to their host, but among the Urtans wearing daggers at all times was a custom so obstinately retained that it had become tolerated, so that shearnas were sometimes asked jestingly whether they wore them in bed.

Although the group included no girls, they were plainly enjoying themselves, laughing and talking animatedly and sometimes turning their heads to call out to passers-by or guests at other tables. Suddenly Maia saw Occula (to whom Terebinthia had given a tunic made entirely of overlapping, scarlet feathers, which left her oiled limbs bare except for a pair of belled anklets and a serpentine brass torque on one arm) saunter across to where they were sitting and offer one of them—an older man who looked to be in his mid-thirties—a dripping rib of beef. As she bent and whispered something in his ear he laughed, whereupon she sat down on his knee and, with one arm round his neck, shared the meat with him, from time to time putting her hand on his to turn the bone for the next bite of her gleaming teeth.

Maia, eyebrows raised, turned enquiringly toward Elvair-ka-Virrion, but he shook his head, whispering, 'No, that's Eud-Ecachlon, the heir of Urtah.'

'Then which?'

'The man on his right; his half-brother.'

Maia looked down once more. Beyond Occula's be-feathered, red shoulder she now observed a thin, dark man; rather tall, it seemed. Half a fowl was lying on the dish before him, and as she watched he put down the drumstick he had been gnawing and turned for a moment to speak to Occula. Maia, quick as always to form a first impression, thought she perceived in his manner a kind of detachment, almost distaste. As he looked at the black girl where she sat on Eud-Ecachlon's knee, his rather narrow, unsmiling face had an expression she could only describe to herself as haughty. A clever but humourless man, she thought: tense, highly-strung yet tenacious, not altogether at ease among his companions; for that matter not at ease, perhaps, in the world itself, yet determined to hold his own. He might be twenty-four or twenty-five, but the lamplight and the distance made it hard to judge.

As she watched him talking to Occula—the black girl leaning across to answer him, so that her necklace of teeth hung forward like a row of tiny, curved knives—she noticed something odd. The Urtan sitting on his further side—a big, good-natured-looking fellow with a fair beard and gold earrings—leant across, took the fowl in one hand and proceeded to slice it with his knife. The dark man glanced towards him with a nod of thanks, then stuck the point of his own knife into a piece of the cut-up meat, dipped it in the sauce beside his dish and ate it.

Elvair-ka-Virrion, his face dappled by the light shining through the tracery, again caught her eye, nodded and led her back into the corridor, closing the door silently behind them.

'You'll know him again?'

'Yes, my lord; who is he?'

'His name is Bayub-Otal: he's a natural son of the High Baron of Urtah.'

'A *natural* son?'

'He might very well have had no standing in Urtah at all. He might have been sent away—brought up as a peasant—and no wrong would have been done either to his mother or himself. But she was a great beauty and a much-admired and very charming woman—to say the least. The High Baron loved her passionately—more than he loved his wife, for that was nothing but a political marriage between baronial families. Bayub-Otal's mother was a Suban dancing-girl. When she died—well, never mind how she died—the High Baron was heart-broken. That's why Bayub-Otal's always been treated as though he were a legitimate son. And if it had remained under Urtan dominion, he'd have stood to inherit Suba. He'd been promised Suba: that was what his father intended for him.'

This last was of little interest to Maia: but what she had actually seen was.

'That other man—he was cutting up his meat for him?'

'Bayub-Otal has a withered hand. It was—injured, when he was a boy.'

As they walked back down the corridor Maia was silent. At length she asked, 'What—what sort of a man is he?'

'That I can't tell you, Maia: I've had very little to do with him. They say, though, that he's full of resentment and that he's no fool.'

'And *I'm* to deceive him?'

Elvair-ka-Virrion stopped short and turned to face her.

'Who said that? Not I!'

Half-child as she was, she gave way to a touch of impatience.

'Reckon you did!'

'I did not. Maia, understand, you're simply to make him like you, talk to you, want to see you again—nothing more than that.'

'But why, my lord? I mean, what for?'

'Never mind. Trust me, it'll all turn out very much to your advantage. Now I'm going to leave you. Wait here a minute or two, then go down this staircase and Sessendris—you know, my father's säiyett—will be waiting for you. Go in and have supper with the Urtans. Remember, I hardly know you—I've only seen you at Sencho's. Sail your boat well, pretty Maia! I'm sure you can. Thank you for my pleasure. It was much the best I've ever had in my life! I'm not going to spoil it by giving you a lygol, but believe me I'll do far more for you than that one day.'

He kissed her unhurriedly, tilting her face between his hands, smiled and was gone.

Sessendris, seated in a cushioned recess opposite the foot of the staircase, looked up at her as she came down the stairs.

'You're becoming quite a regular visitor, Maia.'

'Thank you, säiyett. Come to that, I'm beginning to feel quite at home.'

She'd best start acting her part directly, she thought. For all that this woman was supposed to know, she had no reason to feel nervous. Rather, indeed, the reverse, for had she not just received a favour with which any slave-girl in Bekla would have been overjoyed?

Sessendris evidently felt this too, for she showed every intention of keeping on the right side of a girl who was so clearly on the way up.

'Is there anything you need before you go in? There's a nice, big mirror in that room over there; and you're welcome to use this comb, if you like—it's my own.'

As they walked across the lobby together she went on rather archly, 'Well, and which do you like best—the son or the father?'

Maia, turning her head for a moment to look her in the eye, gave her a smile which meant 'You surely don't expect me to answer that?'

'No preference?' persisted Sessendris teasingly.

Maia tossed her head. 'Spring's nice. So's summer, isn't it?'

The polished silver wall-plaque was, if anything, bigger than the one at the High Counsellor's. She surveyed herself in it with no little satisfaction. She was wearing a dress of soft, fine wool—blue flecked green, with an open weave. The effect of the pale-green satin under-skirt was to make the wool above it appear of a different shade, lighter and greener than the bodice. Her only jewellery was a necklace of the creamy, dusky-streaked beads of semi-precious stone called *eshcarz*, which the Ortelgans dived for in the Telthearna and traded in Bekla, together with their rope and feathers.

Sessendris obligingly held a towel for Maia to dry her hands.

'I expect you're feeling pleased, aren't you? I wouldn't be surprised if you received some more favours tonight.'

'I'll need to eat something first, säiyett,' answered Maia. 'I'm that sharp-set, I'd say no to Shakkarn himself until I've had some supper.'

'Of course: you're used to plenty of that at the High Counsellor's, I dare say.' Sessendris spoke as pleasantly as ever. 'I notice your black friend's putting on a little weight, isn't she?'

'Urtans seem to like her, anyway,' replied Maia.

'Really?' Sessendris seemed surprised. 'How do you know?'

Maia bit her lip. Here was a fine start to a career of adroit deception!

And Sessendris must, of course, know of the existence of the upstairs room overlooking the hall.

'Well, Lord Elvair-ka-Virrion said to me as the Urtans had told him they'd heard of her from someone in Thettit, that's all. That's why he asked the High Counsellor to let her come tonight.'

To this the säiyett replied with a nod, and Maia could only hope that it had sounded convincing.

Strolling unhurriedly through the colonnade and down the steps, she helped herself to a crown of jasmine from a tray held by a slave. Several young men turned to stare at her, but Elvair-ka-Virrion, who was talking with Nennaunir and another girl, did not give her a glance. Going across to the supper tables, she stood demurely on the carpeted dais, letting another slave make her up a plate as he thought fit. Holding this in one hand and a full goblet in the other, she glanced around her, pretended to notice Occula for the first time and went towards the table where the Urtans were sitting.

She walked slowly, for she was feeling rather nervous and wanted to begin by observing the Urtans at closer quarters and if possible weighing them up a little. She noticed at once that of the five, the two older men— Eud-Ecachlon and the dark, detached Bayub-Otal—were obviously of higher rank. Not only were their clothes finer, but there was about them an unmistakable air of accustomed authority, of which the three others were clearly sensible even in the midst of their merriment and high spirits.

Eud-Ecachlon, a man already, to Maia's eyes, middle-aged, was of medium height, rather thick-set, with touches of grey in his hair and beard. Something in his rather slow movements and the steady gaze with which he sat listening to one of the younger men suggested to her someone of stolid dependability—even, it might be, a shade slow; not a quick mind or a natural leader. Without giving the impression of being a fool or not up to his position, he nevertheless had the air of a conventional, perhaps rather uninteresting person, content with and even preferring things as he had always been used to them.

Still, never mind 'bout him, she thought as she drew nearer to the table. It's t'other as matters to me.

Bayub-Otal had also turned towards the young man who was speaking. The sight of him at closer quarters confirmed the notion she had already formed. This was a keener, tenser, more restless character altogether; and also, in some way or other, a man apart. There was, or so she vaguely sensed, something in him awry; a kind of estrangement from natural, spontaneous life, as though if he were to laugh it might be because he thought it appropriate to do so rather than because he could not help it. A kind of invisible veil or screen seemed to lie between himself and his companions. Energetic and clever he certainly looked, yet somehow clouded with—with what? She could not tell, yet her spirits faltered. She knew nothing, she felt, about such men as this. Was he really at all likely to fancy her? She rather doubted it. If he did not, she had no idea of how to go about inclining him to do so.

At this instant Bayub-Otal looked up and saw her. His immediate reaction was so extraordinary and unexpected that she felt actually alarmed. He started violently—though this, as the young fellow opposite reached the riotous climax of his anecdote, went unnoticed by his companions—and then, with one hand gripping the edge of the table, stared at her open-mouthed, with a look not unlike fear—almost as though he were about to leap up and run away. She, for her part, came to a dead stop, quite disconcerted and not knowing what in the least to do. Gradually, though he continued to stare at her, his features became composed. He looked away for a moment, then once more looked back, slightly shaking his head. Whatever had dismayed him, he evidently now had it under control. She was the one who remained dismayed. Could there be something wrong with her dress or her hair? Had she unknowingly done something indecorous? She couldn't think of anything. Could he be some kind of nervous eccentric—perhaps even afflicted with fits? If so, why hadn't Elvair-ka-Virrion warned her?

Well, there was no time to wonder. She could only pretend to have noticed nothing and go on. To cover her confusion she greeted Occula first, smiling and embracing her where she sat on Eud-Ecachlon's knee.

'And who's this?' asked Eud-Ecachlon, clearly pleased.

'Maia, from Serrelind. She puts me in the shade,' answered Occula. 'Doan' you see how dark I've gone? That's with blushin'.'

Eud-Ecachlon rubbed his hand along her bare arm. 'You must be right. Nothing's come off on me.'

'How do you know?' asked Occula, stroking his cheek. She held out her pink palm. 'See? It's on you now.'

There was a general laugh. 'Well, why don't you let Maia from Serrelind sit down?' said Eud-Ecachlon to the rest. 'Come on, Haubas,' he added, to the big young man sitting on the further side of Bayub-Otal, 'move up and make room for her.'

Haubas obediently moved along the bench, whereupon Bayub-Otal—perhaps, thought Maia, because he wanted to remain next to the man who cut up his food—did the same. She sat down between him and Eud-Ecachlon and without more ado fell to work on her supper. She was so hungry that the first gulped mouthful stuck rather uncomfortably in her throat.

'You seem to be ready for that,' said another of the young Urtans sitting opposite her. She smiled and nodded, swallowing another large piece of partridge.

'You've only just arrived, haven't you?' asked the man on his left, hardly raising his eyes from her breasts even as he spoke. 'I saw you come in.'

Soon they were both talking to her with so much animation that she had nothing to do but listen, smile and answer an occasional word. The effect of her beauty was not only to excite them but to make them rather self-conscious and coltish. They laughed a great deal, paid her compliments, teased and contradicted each other, often asked her to corroborate them and continually called the slaves over to serve her with food and wine for which she had not asked. Meanwhile Bayub-Otal, seated on her right, remained silent. Yet it struck Maia that although he was not by nature the sort of man to let himself go, he was nevertheless taking good care not to appear entirely out of accord with the younger men's brash high spirits. It was clear that they respected him and accepted his watchful, attentive manner as his own way of being in their company. Whenever someone addressed a remark to him, he replied readily and pleasantly enough, once turning a sally against the man who had made it. Maia noticed, however, that he said almost nothing except in answer to somebody else; nor did he speak directly to either Occula or herself.

'He's sharp enough to hold his own,' she thought, 'but far as I can see he's kind of got something on his mind. Reckon Kembri's picked the wrong girl. Don't seem like he's one to have his head turned in a hurry. All same, I'll have to have a go.'

At this moment, however, Bayub-Otal asked her quietly, 'How old are you? Young enough not to mind being asked—I can see that.'

In point of fact Maia was, of course, so young as to resent being asked. Just in time she choked back the kind of retort she would have made in Meerzat. Leaning towards him and speaking as though she were telling him something confidential, she replied in an equally low voice, 'I'm fifteen, my lord.'

'Fifteen?' He paused. 'You're sure of that?'

She laughed. 'Well, of course. I'll be sixteen in a few days, actually.'

'And how long have you been in Bekla? You come from Tonilda, your friend said?'

'Not very long. Yes, I come from Lake Serrelind.'

'I was there once: I went sailing on the lake with a friend.'

'Then I may have seen you, my lord. I used to swim in the lake a fair old bit.'

'I should *certainly* remember if I'd seen *you*.'

Yet it was said without a smile or any particular warmth, and Maia felt

269

puzzled. A moment later he had turned to Haubas on his other side and the two men opposite were at her again. Occula had slid off Eud-Ecachlon's knee and was now sitting beside him, eating grapes and wiping the pips with the back of her hand from between her soft, thick lips.

It was plain that one of the young men was growing tipsy and not altogether pleasant with it.

'Where do *you* come from?' he asked suddenly, grinning at Occula in a provocative, taunting manner. 'Nowhere in the empire, I'll bet: unless it's Zeray.'

'No, a bit further than Zeray,' replied Occula. 'I shan't be endin' up there, either. Will you?'

'Taken in war, then, were you?' asked the young man. 'Your lot ran away, did they, and left you for the Beklans? Any regrets?'

Eud-Ecachlon, shaking his head, seemed about to remonstrate, but as he hesitated Occula spoke first. Her voice was conciliatory; low and pleasant, but Maia, knowing her so well, could sense her controlled anger, like the twitching of a cat's tail.

'People always regret leavin' me. Sometimes they regret teasin' me, too; but only when I decide I've had enough.'

'Hoo, what a lot of words!' answered the young man, with a kind of sneering laugh. 'That supposed to be clever?'

'Ka-Roton,' interjected Bayub-Otal quickly, 'don't be stupid!' His tone contained no surprise, and Maia wondered whether Ka-Roton commonly gave this kind of trouble after a few cups of wine.

'Well, hardly, I should say,' replied Occula, smiling. 'Why doan' we—'

'*You* should say!' interrupted Ka-Roton. 'A *black* girl! Cran preserve us!'

As he spoke he swirled the wine in his goblet, and by mischance a few drops spattered over Occula's bare arm. Eud-Ecachlon, bending forward, grasped him by the wrist, but Ka-Roton jerked it away.

'How d'you keep her in order, this black leopard?' he asked Maia. He had, she now noticed, a gap between his top front teeth, in which a shred of meat had remained stuck.

'I don't,' answered Maia. 'She keeps me in order.'

'You look much less of a savage. You're the one I fancy.' He picked his teeth for a moment, then leant forward and squeezed one of her breasts.

'You're right: I'm the savage one,' said Occula suddenly and sharply. 'If I wanted to I could make you stab yourself to the heart!'

Ka-Roton slapped his thigh and roared with laughter. 'I'd like to see you try!'

'Would you really?' replied Occula. 'Like to bet two hundred meld on it?'

'Have you *got* two hundred meld?' asked the young man contemptuously.

Both Eud-Ecachlon and Bayub-Otal seemed to have abandoned any further notion of controlling the conversation, though they were listening intently. Occula's manner had compelled everyone's attention.

'Yes, I have,' answered Occula. 'You accept, then, do you?'

'Certainly, if you're such a fool as to want to throw your money away,' said the young man. 'I don't know what you've got in mind, but I warn you—'

Occula laid a hand on his shoulder. 'Well, doan' run away, then, will you?'

Thereupon she stood up and made her way across the hall to where Elvair-ka-Virrion was sitting. Maia could see them in conversation, Occula smiling and gesturing, Elvair-ka-Virrion evidently asking several questions and nodding at her replies. At length he beckoned to a slave, gave some instructions and then, as the latter accompanied Occula out of the hall, resumed his conversation with the man beside him.

A minute or two later the slave returned and, helped by two others, began putting out several of the lamps.

Throughout supper the hall had been bright with lamplight—brighter, indeed, than was customary at the High Counsellor's. Now, as the lamps went out by ones and twos until only about a quarter of those in the hall were left burning, Maia felt a tremor of apprehension; half exciting, as though someone were about to begin a tale of ghosts or demons; but half disturbingly real—an onset of anxiety and foreboding. What had Occula arranged with Elvair-ka-Virrion? The young Urtan had angered her; and Maia knew her well enough to feel trepidation. She remembered the previous occasions when she had seen Occula angry—at Puhra, and in Lalloc's depôt on the night when they had arrived in Bekla. Yet what possible scope for violence could she have here, a slave-girl among the aristocracy of the upper city? That Occula could be both impulsive and tempestuous she had seen: so far she had always got away with it; had always just skirted the brink of self-destructive rashness. Part of the admiration and affection which Maia felt for her stemmed from the knowledge that she had always been ready to run real risks whenever she felt herself to have been slighted; and from the fear that one day, doing it once too often, she might herself be swept away in the fury welling up like blood from the wound still unhealed in the daughter of Silver Tedzhek enslaved among barbarians.

She felt herself on the point of getting up to go and beg Elvair-ka-Virrion to call Occula back, to tell her not to go on with it—whatever it might be. Yet she did not. Even now, in her absence, Occula's ascendancy

271

prevailed. It wasn't for the likes of her to interfere with Occula. If Occula was about to destroy them both—for what would become of herself without her?—then it must be so. She remained seated among the Urtans, saying nothing, yet full of uneasy misgiving.

She looked up quickly as Nennaunir appeared beside them; Nennaunir come, as it seemed, to take Occula's place. Probably Elvair-ka-Virrion had sent her. 'I asked her to promise Eud-Ecachlon she'd be nice to him.' Eud-Ecachlon, hands spread wide and mouth open with delight, made as though to draw her, too, down upon his knee; but Nennaunir, smiling graciously, seated herself on his left, opposite Maia, the two younger men sliding down the bench to make room for her. She seemed about to speak, but before she could do so the knock and boom of drums began to sound from the corridor on the other side of the colonnade.

Conversation ceased. Everyone became attentive, waiting. From the dimmed light and the mounting throb of the drums it was plain that some kind of show was about to begin. Most of the central floor was now in shadow, tracts of near-darkness or dappled gloom separating small islands of brighter light. The pool, too, lay dark, for the lamps below its floor were all out.

From the colonnade, however, light still showed, and here the drummer now appeared, a black silhouette between two pillars, his hands, the fingers tipped with bronze thimbles, rising and falling as they beat here and there upon the long, curved drums hung at his waist.

At this time in Bekla's history, five or six different styles of drumming were practised in various parts of the empire, as accompaniments to as many kinds of dance. The drummer was using *lembas*—a pair of drums usually played by a single musician; one, the *zhua*, made of skin stretched over a deep bronze bowl; the other, the *lek*, a hollow cylinder of *bola* wood, thin in some parts, thicker in others, capable, in skilled hands, of producing many different tones—hollow knockings, rattlings, sharp tappings, quick, pattering sounds, wooden susurrations and light scrapings like those of branches in the wind. A skilled player could lull his hearers like a stream in summer, or fill them with the frenzy of men eager to storm and loot a burning town.

The drummer, his lembas swinging slightly on his heavy belt as the upper part of his body swayed between one and the other, was beating out a deep, unvarying rhythm on the zhua, while from the lek came abrupt, intermittent sounds, like pecking or the snapping of sticks. The effect, in the darkened hall, was as though the quiet of some shadowy place—a ravine or forest—was being broken, at irregular intervals, by creatures moving unseen; concealed perhaps, yet not far away.

Slowly the drummer descended the steps and, keeping among the shadows, moved away into a recess of the hall, where he remained invisible, the sound of his lembas continuing to act like a spell upon his audience. Nennaunir leant across the table towards Maia.

'What is it—a kura? No one said anything to me about a kura.'

'I don't know,' answered Maia. The wine, the half-darkness and the unrelenting, rhythmic drumming were combining to intensify her disquiet. She found that unconsciously she had taken hold of something unnaturally cold and limp, and then realized that it was Bayub-Otal's withered hand. However, he did not remove it, and to spare him possible embarrassment she let it remain lightly in her own for some moments before gently relinquishing it and resting her chin on her fingers.

And now Occula was among them: Occula, a dark, lithe shape against the light at the top of the steps, the feathery tunic devoid of colour, its outline like a shaggy cape, like a pelt stripped from a beast. As Maia stared up at her she turned quickly to one side, glanced down and gave it a little twist and tug, as though releasing it from invisible briars. Surrounded by the all-enveloping shadows and the throbbing beat of the zhua she came limping slowly, wearily down into the forest glade of the hall, picking her way between clumps of tall weeds, ducking under low branches, momentarily shading her eyes from a quick dazzle of last light falling between the trees. She was tired out—exhausted: they could all see that. She must have come miles: and the spear she seemed to be carrying, though only a light, throwing javelin, would weigh heavy after so many hours afoot.

The light was fading. The drums said so. Yet as the day-time forest sank to sleep, another forest began to stir, rousing itself to people the falling night. The girl, it was clear, was unsure of her way. She hesitated, listening and gazing, once or twice retracing her steps to seek another track. The rustlings and whisperings about her were growing more numerous; yes, and more purposeful—sounds of night and active movement, no longer sounds of evening. Yet she herself stole among the trees without a sound, in and out of the last light; pausing to rest, raising one forearm to lean upon a tree-trunk, round which she peered fearfully into the dark, empty stillness beyond.

The rhythm of the zhua was changing—slower, more ponderous as the light ebbed. In the darkness, some larger creature was moving. The girl could hear it. Noiselessly she vanished between the hanging creepers, laying down her spear to part them with both hands and drawing it after her into the recesses of the undergrowth. Not a soul present but could feel, now, her dread as the unknown beast came nearer. Was it only by chance that it approached, or had it scented what it was seeking?

When the girl reappeared it was unexpectedly; from a different place, to which she must have crept, smooth as a serpent, through the close cover.

She had shed her cloak now and stood naked, a black shadow in the forest, agile and wary as a hunting cat. Her spear was raised, balanced in one hand. This was kill or be killed; and she, perforce, must become savage as her pursuer. She sniffed at the dark air, teeth bared, sweat gleaming on her bare shoulders. As she stole on through the gloom, the onlookers felt themselves brushed by the wing of fear—that fear which springs from the knowledge that sight and hearing are bewitched and playing false. Eud-Ecachlon, staring fascinated at the padding, prowling girl, suddenly started and turned, clapping one hand to his shoulder as though he felt the prick of thorns or the bite of an insect. A warm air seemed moving, foetid with the odour of swamp-mud and decaying leaves. The rapid, tremolo chattering of the lek had become the croaking of frogs.

But was this the huntress or the beast that came forth at length from the blackness at the foot of the steps? Its savage eyes, in a brief glimmer of lamplight, were bloodshot, its wide nostrils dilated, lips parted and speckled with beads of foam. It slunk on and disappeared. Then, not ten seconds after, out of the same shadow emerged a different being—the huntress, wild with terror, tripping and falling, clambering up again, dropping her spear as she staggered and rocked on the brink of the dark pool. The drums closed in upon her as in desperation she slid into the water, slipping under without a sound, reappearing on the further side as a glistening shape which dragged itself through the reeds and was gone once more between the trees.

Now there were only the drums in the dark—the ripple of the water, the heavy, squelching tread of the pursuing beast in the swamp-shallows. Maia felt ready to scream with terror. If only this dread had been disclosed in a picture, or at a distance—if only it had not been spread like a net round one's feet, if the very walls had not been dissolved, in the gloom, by the ceaseless booming and knocking of the drums—if only the drums would stop! From behind her came the quick, frightened sob of some other girl. Nennaunir was sitting still as stone, her knuckles white against the table.

Yet it was no beast or huntress who finally reappeared, but a third being, neither brute nor human; one the very sight of whom was enough to wither the hearts of any encountering her in that solitude. Like a snake she rose up from the forest floor, swaying and ghastly. Blood dribbled from her mouth. Her unblinking eyes, fixed and staring like those of a corpse, yet held in them a malevolent intelligence more dreadful than any human hatred. The rolling of the drums poured from her outstretched hands, from her shuddering loins and thighs. She quivered, exultant with the power of evil. As she slowly raised one black arm they saw—they all saw—in her hand the gleam of a knife, reflective yet transparent; a horrible, spectral knife, which she tossed and caught, plunged into her arm and left hanging there as she bobbed and nodded grotesquely, bent-kneed and grinning. She drew it out bloodless and it disappeared in her hand; yet an instant later, as she stretched out her arm, it seemed to leap towards her out of the dark, out of the stench and blackness of the swamp.

And now she was advancing, step by silent step across the floor, and as she did so the young Urtan Ka-Roton, powerless to resist, stood up to meet her; the bridegroom of death, his lips smiling, his arms outstretched towards her arms. Onward he moved in a trance, pace by pace, never taking his eyes from hers. Coming to the edge of the pool, he received the knife from her hand. Yet in the very moment that he plunged it into his breast, it once more vanished and he fell forward, prone on the ground as the drums at last faded and ceased.

Eud-Ecachlon, leaping to his feet, ran forward, knelt and lifted Ka-Roton's head on one arm. All across the hall men and girls were crying out and starting from their places. The slayer had disappeared in the tumult, by the very act of her departure dissolving her own spell. The drums were a quenched fire. By the pool there was no one to be seen but Eud-Ecachlon, dashing water into his friend's face as he repeated his name again and again.

Elvair-ka-Virrion called for lights and little by little the secure, familiar hall was disclosed. Supported by Eud-Ecachlon, Ka-Roton stood up, wiping the sweat from his face and gazing about him dazedly. It was obvious that he could recall little or nothing of what had happened. Slowly he walked back to his place and sat down, but seemed either not to hear or not to comprehend the questions of his friends. After a few minutes Elvair-ka-Virrion came over to enquire after him and, seeing how matters stood, suggested to Eud-Ecachlon that someone had better take him home. Then, turning to Maia and speaking as though he were angry, he said, 'Where's your friend?'

'I don't know, my lord.'

'Did you know she meant to do this?'

'No, my lord: I thought as she'd spoken to you about it. Didn't she say—'

But as Maia uttered these last words, Elvair-ka-Virrion simultaneously began, 'Didn't she say—': whereupon neither of them was able to suppress a smile. He, turning quickly back to Eud-Ecachlon, said, 'I'm sorry: I hope your friend'll soon be feeling himself again. I assure you I had no idea beforehand how this was going to turn out.'

Eud-Ecachlon nodded, murmuring a few polite words, and Elvair-ka-Virrion returned to his own table.

Maia was feeling sick, as much with nervousness on Occula's account as with the fear and excitement which she herself had undergone. Wiping her sweating forehead, she leaned forward and closed her eyes. As she remained thus, trying to breathe slowly and deeply, Bayub-Otal's voice beside her said, 'Perhaps you'd be the better for some fresh air. Shall we stroll outside for a minute or two?'

She stood up, and they walked side by side through the colonnade and out into the empty corridor. At the far end, near the foot of that same staircase which she had descended earlier in the evening, they came upon a doorway leading outside, into a covered gallery overlooking the courtyard, where two or three lamps were burning. The outer rails, no more than waist-high, supported an arcade open upon the night, and here, in the cool, rain-scented air, they took a few turns. The light wind was blowing westward, away from them. Maia, stretching out one arm, could not feel the rain under the lee of the wall.

'Better?' asked Bayub-Otal.

'Oh, 'twas nothing, really, my lord. Just give me a turn, that's all. Reckon I wasn't the only one, either.'

'I thought that girl was a friend of yours?'

'She's my closest friend.'

'But you've never seen her do that before?'

'No, I never. Nor I never knew she was going to, neither.'

'Was that why it frightened you?'

'Well, didn't it you?'

'Not particularly.'

'Oh, go on with you!' said Maia, unthinkingly. 'Can't have been no one in the hall as wasn't frightened! Not when she—you know, the knife?'

'What knife?'

'The knife she give your friend—at the finish—and her mouth all over blood—'

'I saw the blood. That's an old stage trick—they keep it in a little bladder in their mouths. But I didn't see a knife.'

'Well, I did. And your friend must have, 'cos he took it from her and stabbed himself.'

After a few moments' reflection Bayub-Otal replied, 'Well, as to that, we can ask him, I suppose.'

'That wouldn't signify. Like enough he won't remember. He looked that way to me.'

Again Bayub-Otal was silent. At length he said, 'Well, Maia—it is Maia, isn't it?—I'll tell you what *I* say, and you can believe me or not as you please. Your friend performed a very original act, which led up to her being able to hypnotize Ka-Roton. He's young, of course, and not terribly clever; it's always easier with that sort of person. The darkness and the drums, and that trick of being able not to blink—it's very effective. Quite possibly he *did* think he saw a knife. But I'm surprised to hear *you* did.'

Maia was nettled. 'There was plenty more than me saw it, my lord.'

He half-turned towards her where he sat on the stone parapet. Below them, the surface of the wet courtyard glistened for a few moments as a door was opened and shut. 'So your friend's a sorceress?'

'Occula? Never!'

'Well, what I'm really asking is whether she often makes people—people like Ka-Roton, I mean—think they see what isn't there?'

'I told you; I've never seen her do anything like that before.'

'Other things?'

'Why don't you ask *her*, my lord?'

She half-expected a sharp rebuke, but to her surprise he only replied,

'Well, perhaps I will. Shall we go back now? Someone ought to pay the girl her two hundred meld. In fact, I will. She certainly won them.'

: 30 :

BAYUB-OTAL

Occula was neither at the Urtans' table nor elsewhere that Maia could see. She sought out Sessendris, who told her that the black girl had come over faint on leaving the hall.

'And can you wonder?' added the säiyett, who was plainly, despite herself, full of compelled if uneasy admiration. 'It must have taken everything out of her. Were you frightened, Maia?'

'Yes, I was. Tell me, säiyett—at the end—did you see a knife?'

'That's what everyone's asking one another. I think I did, yes. But one thing's sure—the Urtan boy did, didn't he? No doubt about that.'

Maia asked whether she might be taken to see Occula. Sessendris led her along two corridors to a small room where the black girl was lying on a couch wrapped in a fur rug. She looked haggard and consumed. Sessendris—who was plainly nervous of her—having made the briefest of polite enquiries, left them together.

'Thank Cran it's you, banzi!' said Occula. 'None of these bastards has offered me a drink. Go an' get me a good, big one, there's a pet.'

When Maia returned, she drank off the whole goblet at a draught.

'That's better.' She sat up. 'I'm fine.'

'Bayub-Otal wants to pay you your two hundred meld,' said Maia.

'Two hundred meld my venda! I didn' do it for two hundred meld!'

'What for, then, dearest?'

'Why, because that little tairth made me angry, that's why, sittin' there, pawin' your deldas as if he'd bought you. Well, he woan' be tryin' it again for a bit, I dare say.'

'And that's really why you did it?' said Maia. 'All that—just for me?'

'Well, it's like this, banzi,' replied Occula. 'You and I, we want to go up, doan' we, not down? I doan' mind you bein' basted by someone who's goin' to do you a bit of good and get you further. We were brought here for the Urtans, right? But when we actually come down to it, it's obvious that only two of them count for anythin'. And of those two, one's not interested. Ever seen a dead ox? Am I right?'

Maia could not help smiling at Occula's down-to-earth assessment. 'Just about.'

'Whatever Bayub-Otal wants, it's not either of us. So then as soon as I've gone Nennaunir turns up—oh, yes, I saw—and it's obvious that Elvair-ka-Virrion's sent her for that Eud-Ecachlon—*and* paid her, you can bet on that. So where does that leave you an' me? To go to bed with the rubbish? Not *this* girl, banzi, slave or no slave! Start as you mean to go on. I wasn' goin' to do it and I wasn' goin' to see you left to do it.'

'But Elvair-ka-Virrion—he come over afterwards—he seemed real mad—'

Occula slewed round where she sat and put her hands on Maia's shoulders. 'That Urtan fellow made *me* mad; that's what started me off! I knew if it worked it'd be somethin' they wouldn' forget in a hurry. Never mind about Elvair-ka-Virrion. He's not a danger to us. You jus' wait a few days, till everyone's heard about it—'

'But Occula, I was real scared—so was everyone else. I mean, can you do that any time you want?'

The black girl shook her head. 'Somethin' has to happen to make you *want* to do it—sort of get you up to it; because a thing like that, when you start you never know how it's goin' to turn out. I doan' know now, come to that. I mean, *did* they all see the knife?'

'Far as I can make out just about everyone saw it. *I* saw it, anyway. It was horrible!'

'Yes, well, you can' do that, you see, unless somethin' happens to make you able to. It's got to come from the goddess; come boilin' out of you and all over them. The act—anyone can learn that. I learnt it from a Deelguy girl in Thettit. But whether you succeed in makin' them actually see what isn' there—that's another matter. Is the boy all right, by the way?'

'They've sent him home.'

'Good! I was takin' a chance, banzi, really. Well, I mean, the drummer, for a start: I only had a few minutes with him, just long enough to tell him more or less what I wanted. He had to follow me best he could. Actually he turned out very good—better than anyone in Thettit. Well, this *is* Bekla, after all, an' the upper city at that. He ought to have fifty meld. Doan' let me forget; we might need him again some time. Oh, and banzi, can you go and make sure of my feather tunic? I forgot all about it, and Terebinthia'll play hell if it's lost. Besides, I've got nothin' else to put on.'

Maia jumped up. 'I'll go and get it now.' She picked up the goblet. 'D'you want another drink, while I'm there?'

Just at that moment, however, Sessendris returned.

'How are you feeling now, Occula?'

'Tired, säiyett.'

'How's the headache?'

'Jus' about gone.'

'Do you feel well enough to give a little pleasure, or shall I make your excuses?'

'Who to, säiyett?'

Sessendris laughed. 'Well, the short answer to that, Occula, is "Almost anyone you like." And I'd imagine you could expect very generous lygols. Something like fifteen young men have approached me and asked whether you're feeling better. One of them, you may not be entirely surprised to hear, is Lord Eud-Ecachlon, who seems most anxious to see you again.'

'I suppose he's angry, säiyett, isn' he?'

'I think not. I haven't been a shearna and then a säiyett for quite some time without being able to tell when a man's strongly attracted. It's annoyed Nennaunir very much. She's gone home in a rage.'

'Sorry to hear that, säiyett,' replied Occula, keeping an admirably straight face. 'And after all Lord Elvair-ka-Virrion's trouble, too! Well, I'd better not disappoint Lord Eud-Ecachlon, then, had I?'

'Am I to go back to the Urtans, too, säiyett?' asked Maia.

'I don't think you need,' answered Sessendris. 'The three younger men were asking for you, but they were all so impatient that by now they've suited themselves elsewhere. That just leaves Lord Bayub-Otal. I was going to ask him whether he'd like to see you again, but before I could, Lord Eud-Ecachlon took me aside and told me that he never goes with girls at parties. Apparently he's—' she paused and shrugged—'fastidious in some way or other.'

Maia could see that Sessendris felt she had failed and was glad to see her taken down a peg. Her polite smile meant, 'You thought you were irresistible, didn't you?'

She felt mortified. Not that she had herself been attracted to Bayub-Otal, but she had been instructed to attract him and assured that she had the power to do so. What would Kembri and Elvair-ka-Virrion think of her now?

'At that rate, banzi,' said Occula, 'if he's too stupid to want a girl like you, you'd better come along and lend me a hand with Eud-Ecachlon, and we'll split his lygol between us. By the way, säiyett,' she went on, before Sessendris could express a view on this proposal, 'd'you happen to have seen my feather tunic? I suppose someone picked it up?'

'I brought it round for you,' answered Sessendris. 'It's hanging up outside.'

'Thank you very much, säiyett. I came down here in a blanket,' she explained to Maia, 'but I'd rather not go back in one.'

Eud-Ecachlon, whom they found walking impatiently in the colonnade, spoke pleasantly to Maia but, in spite of the broadest hints that Occula could let fall, showed no inclination for her company in addition to the black girl's. After a short conversation he excused himself and led Occula away. Evidently he had already made his arrangements with Sessendris, for he clearly knew where they were going.

Maia, left alone, felt depressed. In spite of what Sessendris had said, she was not sure whether one or other of the younger Urtans might not still be looking for her, and she had no heart for such an encounter. However, she was still supposed to be working and she had no wish to turn her failure into a disaster by letting Sessendris or even, perhaps, Elvair-ka-Virrion himself come upon her wandering about at a loose end.

She went back into the hall. There were not more than fifteen or twenty people there altogether, most of Elvair-ka-Virrion's guests having, as it seemed, dispersed about the big house for the same purpose as Eud-Ecachlon. A little group of four or five young men, all wearing Leopard cognizances, were talking with some girls under a cluster of lamps at one end of the dais. From their unhurried, easy gestures and general air of relaxation, Maia could perceive that they had already satisfied their desire and were now probably having a friendly drink before going home. That would be the right sort of company for her, she thought, to keep out of harm's way until Occula returned.

While she stood hesitating one of the young men, glancing round and catching sight of her at the foot of the steps, came over and began talking to her. Answering rather abstractedly, she allowed him to bring her some wine and then lead her across to join his companions.

'You're a friend of that black girl, aren't you?' asked a second young man, whom she remembered having seen with Elvair-ka-Virrion earlier in the evening. 'Weren't you both with the Urtans during supper?'

She nodded, and at once all the young men showed interest.

'Are you together, then? Whose household are you in?'

'I saw you at the Rains banquet, but I don't remember seeing her. She's really amazing!'

280

'How long has she been in Bekla? What's her name?'

'Perhaps *you* can tell us, then: was there really a knife?'

They continued for some time, the girls almost as inquisitive as the men. Maia did her best to create an impression of Occula as a smouldering, passionate girl from a far country, possessed of virtually supernatural powers. She must have been fairly successful, for two or three of the young men, apparently too much intrigued to feel restrained even by the presence of their partners, asked whether Occula was allowed to accept invitations and what kind of lygol she usually received. It was clear that they were afraid of the High Counsellor and daunted to learn that whatever her price, Occula's favours could be obtained only through a request to him or to Terebinthia. Maia felt that none of them was interested in herself. Determined to improve Occula's chances all she could, she was just suggesting that one possible approach might be through Jarvil, the porter, when she felt a touch on her arm. Looking round, she was surprised to see Bayub-Otal. Without speaking to any of the others he murmured, 'Can you spare me a few more moments, please?'

Before she had even time to excuse herself to the young men, he had turned away. Following him across the hall, she overtook him at the foot of the steps and for the second time they went out together through the colonnade.

For a while he said nothing, walking slowly along the corridor as though abstracted, his eyes upon the ground. Just as she was plucking up courage to ask what was on his mind, he asked, 'Have you enjoyed this evening?'

Disappointed as she was—and particularly with him—the enquiry vexed her. 'A slave-girl doesn't answer a question like that, my lord. If you have, then I have.'

'So you never allow yourself to express any sincere feelings? My mother did, in your position.' He smiled slightly. 'That's why I'm here.'

Now she felt afraid to have spoken out sharply. His bad opinion might well do her harm. 'I'm sorry, my lord: I didn't mean to speak out of turn. Yes, I've very much enjoyed meeting you and Lord Eud-Ecachlon, and so has my friend, I'm sure.'

'Your friend? Oh, the black girl—where is she?'

'With Lord Eud-Ecachlon.'

He threw back his head for a moment, expelling his breath with a sound suggestive of contempt.

'For *money*, I suppose.'

'Well, yes, he'll give her a lygol, my lord, I expect, don't you? It's the custom, after all.'

'Oh, naturally! Everything in Bekla's to be bought and sold, isn't it? After all, they paid Durakkon to murder Senda-na-Say, didn't they? And Karnat's price was Suba.'

Maia looked quickly over her shoulder. ''T'ain't rightly for me to say it, my lord, but p'raps you ought to be more careful, just. I wouldn't want you to speak out of turn and end up in trouble.'

'You're right, of course, Maia. Foolish to let one's tongue run away to no purpose except the relief of feelings better suppressed. Well, and so they brought you up from Serrelind to Bekla to learn a trade. Are you learning it?'

His sarcasm was plain. She bit her lip.

'What else can I do, my lord? What's the good o' talking to me like that?'

'None, I dare say. But I'm one person who's *not* going to advance your education. You'll get no lygol out of *me*.'

She blushed with anger, wondering how far a slave-girl could safely go in retorting to such an insult.

Suddenly he stopped in his pacing and turned to face her. 'Would you like to see me again?'

He seemed to be expecting a serious answer. She could not tell what to make of it and, confused, could find no reply. After a few moments she sat down on a bench against the wall. He made no move to join her, merely leaning against a pillar and looking unsmilingly down at her as he waited for his answer.

This extraordinary man, she thought, had just spoken to her with contempt and decisively rejected her. And now, in the next breath, he was apparently asking to see her again.

Inexplicable—and infuriating—he might be; but one thing she realized immediately. However badly the evening had gone for her and however galling his behaviour, he had now—whatever the reason—made it possible for her after all to tell Elvair-ka-Virrion that she had not altogether failed. In the light of this, her feelings of personal dislike for him mattered nothing.

She stood up, smiling. 'Yes, very much, my lord: I'll look forward to it.'

'Where shall I find you, then?'

'At the High Counsellor's.'

He stared at her as though taken by surprise and utterly disgusted. 'You belong to *him*?'

'Yes, my lord: I thought you knew.'

He shook his head without a word.

'The truth is, my lord, the High Counsellor often leaves such matters to our säiyett. I think perhaps you might be able to come to an arrangement with her without troubling him.'

'I dare say,' replied Bayub-Otal. 'But he knows too much. He's a man everyone fears. Anyway, here's your friend's two hundred meld.'

'Why, you can give it to her yourself, my lord,' said Maia. 'Here she comes, look, and Lord Eud-Ecachlon with her.'

Occula, scarlet-plumed, and Eud-Ecachlon—plucked, one might say—came down the corridor together, arms round each other's waists. It was clear that Eud-Ecachlon was feeling contented. He greeted Bayub-Otal with a smile and at once fell to praising Occula in a manner implying that he too had acquitted himself in no mean fashion. Occula, having allowed him to run on for a time and corroborated him whenever he seemed to be expecting it, at length put her lips to his cheek and asked whether he would now be so good as to escort her friend and herself to the lower courtyard, where a jekzha—so she believed—was awaiting them; and then return to convey thanks and farewells on their behalf to Lord Elvair-ka-Virrion.

'For the truth is, my lord,' she explained, 'that after what you've given me I shan't want any more for a week, and I'd rather not be put to the embarrassment of refusing anyone else.'

Eud-Ecachlon, smirking with satisfaction, gave her a purse containing her lygol and readily undertook to do as she asked; and forthwith Occula, having sought out and paid the drummer and relieved Bayub-Otal of both her two hundred meld and Maia, made their departure.

Once in the jekzha, however, she drew down the rain-curtain and leant back, fanning the humid air and gripping Maia's hand like a child seeking comfort in the dark.

'I'm nackered, banzi! Tell you the truth, it was as much as I could do to give that Urtan dolt what he wanted. Never mind: we've got his lygol and two hundred meld on top. I shan' say anythin' to Terebinthia about that: she'll never find out. You didn' tell anyone, did you?'

'No, darling; there's no one but us and the Urtans knows anything about it.'

'I saw you talkin' to Bayub-Otal, but I couldn' for the life of me make out whether you'd done anythin' or not. How did you get on?'

'Well, tell you the truth, Occula, I'm blest if I know.'

And therewith Maia proceeded to tell of Bayub-Otal's odd behaviour.

'Well, that *is* a rum go!' said the black girl. 'Didn' want to do anythin' an' then asks whether you'd like to see him again? They certainly do come all sorts, doan' they, banzi? Only thing I can think of, he didn' feel like it tonight but reckoned he might some other time.'

'Oh, I do just about hope so! Only you see, Occula, Elvair-ka-Virrion told me tonight—I was sent upstairs to him as soon as we arrived, you know—'

'*Were* you, banzi? Cran's zard, I wondered where you'd got to! Was it a success?'

'Oh, yes! He enjoyed it, and so did I. I reckon he's nice! But then he told me—you know, afterwards—that I was to go and join the Urtans and make Bayub-Otal like me and want to see me again.'

Occula whistled. 'So *that's* what it's all about! They've got their suspicions about Bayub-Otal, have they? And they're hopin' he may let some cat out of the bag to *you*?'

'But if they want information so badly, why can't they get it from Sencho? I thought he was supposed to know about everyone all over the empire?'

'I doan' know, banzi, but if you ask me, it's like I told you—Kembri doesn' trust him any more. So Elvair-ka-Virrion gave you a good bastin' and then went on straight away to tell you to get Bayub-Otal into bed? I reckon that was a dirty trick, even if we *are* slave-girls. He might have wrapped it up a bit nicer than that.'

'No, Occula, that's just it. He told me I *wasn't* to let Bayub-Otal have anything, not on any account. I was to refuse him, but try to make him want to see me again.'

'And you say he means to?'

'Well, I don't rightly know. When I told him we belonged to Sencho, you could see he didn't like that at all. It seemed to sort of change his mind, like.'

'Well, at that rate we can only wait and see,' said Occula. 'But I shouldn' break your heart if nothin' comes of it. You'd be best out of this Urtan lark, I reckon. Plenty of people'll soon be interested in you without the risk of that—whatever it may be.'

'But Occula, listen! Those young Leopards I was talking to while you were with Eud-Ecachlon—there wasn't one of them particularly interested in *me*. It was *you* they were all asking about.'

'Ah, but then they'd all just had a bit of yum-yum, hadn' they? If we were still there now, you wouldn' have to wait long.' Occula paused. 'Yes, well, I dare say my act may have got them interested. It was meant to. We must think up somethin' for you, too, banzi. You see, however pretty a girl is, for the upper city she really needs more than just looks: she needs somethin' to make them think she's out of the ordinary. These Leopards help themselves to the cream and leave the milk for the lower city. Up here, just pretty girls are ten meld a dozen. Look at Meris—she was pretty enough. But you just compare her with Nennaunir. D'you know what Nennaunir's like? She's like a story people want to hear again and again—because they keep findin' new things in it. She's a clever girl, too: Terebinthia told me about some big Leopard she was with who asked her to advise him about his money, and apparently she did it so well that he made a fortune and gave her a bastin' great lump of it to keep for herself.'

'Can't see me ever doing anything like that,' said Maia.

'Nor me neither. But I *can* make people see knives that aren' there: well, sometimes, anyway—you know, when they've all had a few drinks. But we've *got* to find somethin' distinctive for *you*. Well, of course! We'll make you a dancer!'

The jekzha stopped and she peeped out through the rain-curtain. 'But jus' now what we seem to have found is old Piggy's house, so we'd better go in, I suppose.'

: 31 :

MILVUSHINA

Nevertheless, Occula refused to get down in the rain, insisting that the jekzha-man, before being paid and dismissed, should call the porter to open the gate and then pull them into the covered courtyard. To the sleepy Jarvil, however, she was all civility, thanking him for his trouble and even, with a detachment worthy of a baron's wife, sliding two meld of her own into his palm before taking the lamp he proffered and disappearing down the corridor to the women's quarters.

'D'you think there'll be any hot water?' said Maia, pausing at the door and taking the lamp from Occula to light another on a ledge near-by. 'I wouldn't half like some, but I'm not going to knock poor old Ogma up at this time of night—'

'What in Cran's name's that?' said Occula suddenly, grasping her wrist. 'Did you hear it?'

They both stood still, listening. For some moments there was no sound. Then, from somewhere beyond the door, they both heard muffled weeping—sobs, a shuddering, indrawn breath and then silence once more.

The two girls stared at each other.

'Dyphna?' whispered Maia at length.

'No, nor yet Ogma,' answered Occula. 'Someone else.'

'Ought we to get Terebinthia; or Jarvil?'

'No, to hell with that!' said Occula. 'If it were a man—but it's not. We'll find out for ourselves. Come on!'

Opening the door quietly, they went on through the bead curtains and across the main room, where the still pool lay glimmering in the reflection of their lamps. Their own room was empty.

'Dyphna can't be in her room or she'd have heard it too,' said Maia.

'No, she's probably with Piggy,' replied Occula. 'Meris's room—we'd better go and look.'

Picking up the lamp, she led the way. Maia, following and peering over her shoulder in the doorway, saw that there was indeed someone in the room—a girl sitting up in the bed, clutching the coverlet about her and cowering from the strange, black face of the intruder.

Slipping past Occula, Maia sat down on the bed and took the girl's hand in her own.

'You don't have to be afraid of us,' she said. 'Tell us who you are.'

The girl, without replying, tugged to release her hand. Maia let it go and put an arm round her shoulders.

'Don't know whether anyone's hurt you since you come here,' she said, 'but *we* shan't, tell you that.'

The girl, she now saw, was not much more than her own age, though slimmer and lighter. She had unusually large eyes, dark-brown hair and beautifully-shaped lips. What with the lamplight and her face smeared and contorted with weeping, it was difficult to make out more.

'You know who this'll be, doan' you?' said Occula to Maia, sitting down at the other end of the bed. 'The girl to replace Meris. Well, I knew Terebinthia was a bastin' cow, but I wouldn' have believed that even she'd have shut a banzi like this in here on her own and then gone off to bed.'

'Careful, Occula,' whispered Maia. 'She might be just outside the door.'

'I doan' give two farts if she is,' said Occula loudly. 'Let her come in, and I'll give her a piece of my bastin' mind! Everybody knows if a girl who's pitchforked into this game's to get over the shock and turn out any good at all, she's got to be looked after and let down light to begin with. Even old Domris knew that. Terebinthia's not fit to be a säiyett: goin' the right way to ruin her master's property, and I've a damn good mind to tell him so.'

'Might do more good just now to get this girl straightened out a bit,' said Maia. 'Suppose we—'

'—do the säiyett's damn' job for her,' said Occula, 'just to top off a jolly evenin' with the Urtans! Yes, all right, banzi. I know there's some wine left in that cupboard by the pool, and I dare say there may be somethin' to eat somewhere. Keep her happy: I'll be back before a dog can piss on a wall.'

'You needn't be afraid of her,' said Maia, as Occula disappeared into the passage. 'Dare say you've never seen anyone like her before, but that's just her natural colour. She talks rough, but she's got a very kind heart. Come on, now, try and tell me about yourself. What's your name?'

'Milvushina,' answered the girl quietly. Her voice was unexpectedly low and smooth. She had stopped crying and was now leaning back against the wall, breathing slowly and deeply.

'Where you from?'

'Chalcon.'

Maia, filled with curiosity, was about to go on to ask her how she had come to Bekla and whether it was Lalloc who had sold her to Sencho, when it occurred to her that probably this would only add to the girl's misery and upset her further.

'Have you had any supper?' she asked.

'Yes, thank you,' answered the girl. She leaned across, picked up a towel and wiped her face. 'It's good of you to have come in. I was—I—' She seemed about to break down again, but then, controlling herself, said, 'I'm sorry to have given you the trouble. You can go now, if you like.'

Maia was startled to realize, from her manner and tone of voice, that this must be a girl from a well-to-do family. Despite her earlier tears, she was now trying to put on a show of self-control and even detachment. Her air bore some faint resemblance to that of a lady addressing a servant. In other circumstances this would have angered Maia. As it was, it merely made the girl seem more pathetic. She decided to refrain altogether from further questions and merely to talk in a friendly, reassuring way until Occula returned.

'There's three of us here just now,' she said. 'Not counting you, I mean. It's not so bad, really, once you get used to it. The important thing's to keep on the right side of the säiyett, 'cos she's the one as really says what's to be done, see? The High Counsellor can't hardly do without her.'

Milvushina shuddered, biting her lip. Maia guessed that she might already have been inspected and approved by Sencho in much the same way as she herself had been.

'You can work for your freedom, you know,' she went on. 'If a girl can get the price together they've got to accept it and write her free; that's the law. That's why you want to keep in with Terebinthia; only she can either help or hinder you, see—makes all the difference. Dyphna'll be buying herself free any time now, and she's not much older than Occula. She'll probably be a shearna by the spring.'

'I don't want to be a shearna,' replied the girl coldly. She buried her face in her hands; not, as it seemed, to conceal more tears, but rather to shut out what lay around her.

Maia got up, went across to the window and stood looking out into the rainy darkness. A few moments later Occula returned, carrying a plate and wine-flask. Milvushina started and drew in her breath sharply.

'Oh,' she said. 'You startled me!'

'Oh, I scare the bugs out of the woodwork,' replied Occula. 'Now you listen to me, my lass. It's late at night, you're half out of your mind and I doan' blame you. We're not goin' to talk and you're not goin' to argue. You're just goin' to let us look after you.'

Before Milvushina could reply she went on, 'It'll be easier if you do what I say. Eat this—it's bread and cheese—best I can do at this time of night—and drink this wine; I've warmed it over the lamp. After that you're goin' to sleep with Maia here, in the other room, so that there'll be someone with you. I'll sleep in here.'

The girl hesitated and seemed about to reply.

'I doan' want to hear anythin' more tonight,' said Occula. 'I just want to get to bed myself.' She stood up, leaning against the wall with folded arms. 'There *is* some warm water, banzi. I've put it in the basin in the other room, so get on and doan' let it get cold.'

Maia, giving her a quick kiss, slipped out. She had just finished washing when Occula came in, her arm round Milvushina's shoulders. Having helped the girl into bed she drew up the coverlet and sat down beside her. In a matter of minutes Milvushina was asleep.

'I doan' think she'll give you any trouble, banzi,' whispered Occula, hanging up Maia's towel and helping her on with the supportive bodice which Terebinthia had told her to wear in bed. 'If I know anything about it, she'll sleep for about ten hours.'

Maia frowned, puzzled. 'Why? How's she gone off so quick, anyway?'

''Cos I've bastin' well drugged her, that's why,' answered the black girl shortly.

'*Drugged* her, Occula? What with?'

'With tessik, that's what.'

Maia shook her head.

'Tessik's a drug the Ortelgan priestesses make on Quiso—their Tel-thearna island, you know. I got some a year or so back, from a fellow in Thettit—the same one as gave me the smoke, remember? I never thought I'd have any use for it, but at least I took the trouble to find out what the dose is. Doan' let anyone else know we've got it, banzi; certainly not Pussy-cat. Now get off to sleep yourself. If you're as tired as I am, neither of us'll be missin' the other much tonight.'

An hour or so after dawn the following morning Maia, having woken to the familiar sound and scent of the rain, slipped out of bed, leaving Milvushina still in a heavy sleep, and went along the passage to the main room, where she found Ogma scrubbing the drained pool. Sending her off to the kitchen to fetch some breakfast, she sat down beside the newly-lighted stove and was reflecting on Bayub-Otal's curious behaviour of the night before when Occula came in, washed and dressed, with gilded eyelids and scarlet finger-nails.

Maia stared at her. 'It's not that late, surely? He won't want us before mid-day.'

'Well, apparently he woke early,' replied Occula, 'and told Terebinthia one of us was to come as soon as he said. That's me, banzi—always live and ready. But now it seems he's gone back to sleep again.'

She sat down, staring at the flames and drumming her fingers on the bench.

'Something on your mind?' asked Maia.

Occula, without turning her head, nodded, but still said nothing. At length she asked, 'Would you say I was tough?'

'Very.'

'That's what *I* thought, too. Well, now I just want to be sick—all over everyone in this bastin' house. I wish I'd stayed down in Thettit; I really do.'

'Why, for Cran's sake? What's up?'

At this moment Ogma came back with Maia's breakfast—eggs, milk, butter, fruit and warm bread. Maia, jumping up, went across to the table and set to.

'Shall I bring you the same, Miss Occula?' asked Ogma. 'Very likely you'll have time before the High Counsellor wakes up again.'

'I'll call you,' replied Occula absently. 'Just leave us for now, Ogma, there's a dear.'

When the girl had gone she came over and sat down opposite Maia, elbows on the table and chin in her hands.

'I've been talking to Dyphna.'

Maia scraped her egg. 'How nice for you!'

'Doan' give me that shit, banzi!' stormed the black girl, banging her fist on the boards, 'or I'll knock your blasted deldas off! I'm just in no damn' mood to—'

'I'm *sorry*, dear!' replied Maia, surprised. 'Whatever's upset you so much?'

'Dyphna's been tellin' me who that Chalcon girl is and why she's here.'

Maia waited.

'D'you *know* who she is?' asked Occula.

'No, 'course I don't.'

'She's the daughter of a baron called Enka-Mordet, in Chalcon; a friend of Santil-kè-Erketlis, Dyphna said. That's to say, he was.'

Maia put down her bread and stared. The black girl continued in a low but steady voice.

'You know who the *heldril* are, doan' you? It means "old-fashioned people"—landowners out in the provinces who go as far as they dare to show they doan' like the Leopards. There's always been a lot of heldro feelin' in Tonilda—'specially in Chalcon. They're all heldril there, and the Leopards know it. Probably the most disaffected province in the whole empire. Everyone knows Sencho's been watchin' them for a long time now. Erketlis is still quite young, you know, but he's the biggest baron in those parts, and if he came out openly against the Leopards there'd be plenty who'd follow him. Those men who were here the other day—you can be certain some of them were agents from down that way.'

She crossed the room, went through the bead curtains to the outer door and listened carefully before coming back to the bench.

'It was Dyphna who told me about Enka-Mordet of Chalcon, this mornin'. Apparently Sencho was talkin' to her last night, in between enjoyin' himself. He was so pleased with his own cleverness he couldn' resist tellin' her. Enka-Mordet was Senda-na-Say's nephew, and he had a wife and two grown sons.'

'You mean the Leopards have killed them all?' asked Maia.

Occula nodded. 'Dyphna says Kembri sent about two hundred men, an' they reached Chalcon from Bekla in less than three days.'

'Through the rains?' asked Maia. 'Surely not?'

'Yes, they did. Apparently half of them are down with fever now; but they finished what they went for, so Kembri woan' be mindin' about that. They killed Enka-Mordet and his wife and sons. But now hear this. On Sencho's personal orders the daughter, Milvushina, was brought back here, for him. "So she hasn't cost me a meld," he said to Dyphna.'

Maia was silent for some little time. At length she said, 'Well, s'pose it's no worse for her than it was for you.'

'P'raps not,' answered Occula, 'but I doan' care to hear you talkin' like that, banzi. Believe me, it's a great mistake to let yourself get so tough that you never feel sorry for anyone. It shows in your face after a time, and that's when you're on the way out—hard as nails and look it. Meris was beginnin' to look that way. I feel sorry for this wretched girl. *You* ought to feel sorry for her. But you doan' like her, do you?'

'I never said so.'

'No, but I can tell what you're thinkin'. "She's a baron's daughter, ha, ha, and now she's come down to no better than us." Yes?'

'I never—'

'Yes, you did,' said Occula sharply. '*Of course* it's bad for slaves, banzi— it's a rotten world—but it's even worse for that poor girl. It's not her fault who she is or where she was born. She's been through enough to drive any girl stark, ravin' mad and if we doan' look after her, she probably *will* be.'

'Cran, I've just thought!' said Maia, jumping to her feet. 'Where's your knife, Occula? Is it in your box? She might wake up and find it.'

'Yes, I'd thought of that, too,' replied Occula. 'It's hidden, along with the tessik. But somehow I doan' think Milvushina's the sort to do herself in. I'm not really worried about that. I'm much more bothered about Piggy and his jolly fun.'

'You don't think he might drive her to it?'

'No—because we're goin' to help her to turn herself from a baron's daughter into a crafty, hard-headed slave-girl. Oh, *you* were no trouble, banzi; you're a tough little thing, aren't you? You quite enjoy ruttin' about with Piggy, doan' you? Uh-huh, I've seen you: *and* he knows it. But d'you realize what it's goin' to be like for *her*? That's why he had her brought here, the bastard—partly that and partly so's he could feel he'd got twelve thousand meld's worth for nothin'.'

Maia looked up quickly, finger to lips, as the door beyond the bead curtains opened softly. A moment later they stood up as Terebinthia came in.

'Ah, there you are, Occula,' said Terebinthia. 'You may go to the High Counsellor now. I don't think he's very well this morning, but no doubt you'll be able to make him feel better.' Then, turning to Maia, 'Where's the Chalcon girl? You've seen her, I suppose?'

'Yes, säiyett. We put her to sleep with me in the big bed—jus' so's I could keep an eye on her, like: only she was a bit upset last night, see. Thought I'd sit in there and do a bit of mending till she wakes, and then Ogma can get her something to eat.'

'Yes, that will do,' replied Terebinthia, 'and you'd better tell her that the High Counsellor will want to see her later on, at supper-time.' She stooped, holding her hands to the stove, and then added quietly, 'He's greatly looking forward to it.'

: 32 :

MAIA AS COMFORTER

Nevertheless, the High Counsellor did not send for Milvushina that evening. At dinner next day, when he was attended by Occula and Maia, he was listless and petulant, cutting short his gluttony and showing no inclination for other pleasures. Although replying to Terebinthia, with testy annoyance, that he did not feel ill, he plainly lacked the energy and zest to enjoy the humiliation of a baron's daughter turned concubine. Early in the afternoon he dismissed the girls, but later recalled Occula to bath and massage him, after which he fell asleep without even attempting to gratify himself.

The next two days brought no change and Maia, to her own surprise, realized that she was beginning to feel frustrated. It had never occurred to her that what she had become accustomed to doing for the High Counsellor gave her any satisfaction; indeed, she had now and then, in the secrecy of their bed, expressed to Occula her disgust. Now she began to understand that her feelings were not as simple as she had supposed.

She had never forgotten the day when Lalloc had first displayed her—the day when Sencho, beside himself at the mere sight of her, had vainly tried to raise himself from the cushions. Nor did she forget the night of the Rains banquet, when Meris had failed him and she herself had not. She was also well aware, of course, that he felt not the least affection for her and that if for any reason, such as illness or injury, she were to become less attractive he would simply sell her off for the best price he could get. Yet in a strange way this state of affairs suited her. She enjoyed the fact that her beauty and wantonness were sufficient in themselves and needed no supplement of emotion. Her own nature was down-to-earth. So was Sencho's. Despite his delight in humiliating his girls, he was in this respect an easy master, since he wanted and expected nothing but pleasurable sensations, which Maia could provide without difficulty. If questioned about her work, she would probably have answered much the same as a farm-hand—that she could do it all right, but would have been happier if there was less of it. Dyphna, she knew, would have liked a more cultured, aristocratic master, and Occula one in whose house there was more social life and opportunity for her ambition and quick wits. She herself had no such feelings—the reason, she had hitherto thought, being simply that she was not required to do anything beyond her.

She now discovered that there was more to it than this. Occula and Dyphna despised Sencho and found him tedious. To her his vulgarity, cruelty and salacity were off-set by another quality—his enormous capacity for enjoyment—together with the knowledge that she herself was what he particularly liked. The transient indolence of his intermittent satiety—that too had been acceptable to her, as a night is acceptable between two days; but this new listlessness, unrelieved as one day succeeded another, began to seem like a long spell of rainy weather. Hunching her shoulders, as it were, she looked about her at a household become more wearisome than she had hitherto found it. If Sencho could not gormandize or rut, she was as much at a loose end as a farm-lad kept idle by snow.

'He keeps telling Terebinthia there's nothing the matter,' she said one afternoon, after she had finished practising the senguela—at which she had greatly improved—and she and Occula were lying together in the pool. 'And if I ask her whether he's really ill, she gets cross. But if there's really nothing the matter, why doesn't he want anything? Don't want any girls, don't want any dinner: I just about wish he did, and that's the plain truth.'

'It often takes them like that, so I've heard,' replied Occula. 'Gluttons, I mean, and lechers: people who've lived a long time the way he has. They get so their bodies jus' can't respond any more. Well, when there's nothing left in a barrel it runs dry, doesn' it? And take it from me, that's what's frightenin' old Pussy. She's afraid he's going to die.'

'D'you reckon he is, then?'

'I doan' know, banzi. Always been in steady employment, myself. I jus' doan' know enough about people like Sencho. But I'll tell you one thing—we ought to take damn' good care he doesn't have a fit or somethin' while we're stuffin' him or workin' him up to a bit of fun. We could easily get the blame, you see.'

Nevertheless, it was remarkable to Maia that during these days Occula spent more time with Sencho than did any other member of the household—more even than Terebinthia. He would send for her in the course of the morning, and she would remain with him for several hours. Once or twice Maia, entering the room on some errand from Terebinthia, had the notion that she had interrupted a conversation. Also, she received a vague impression that in some way Occula was influencing the High Counsellor. One evening, for example, having been called unexpectedly to the small hall and finding, to her surprise, that he wanted her to gratify him, she sensed that in fact this had been instigated by Occula, who remained to encourage him and urge him on to satisfaction. Another day Occula was successful to some slight extent in re-awakening his greed, yet to Maia it seemed to come from the strength of her will rather than from his own appetite.

Formerly, the High Counsellor had not been in the regular habit of requiring a girl to spend the whole night with him; but now, more often than not Occula would remain with him all night and herself perform those menial tasks, such as bringing water, cushions or fresh towels, which would normally have been the duty of Ogma. Maia, herself puzzled, was secretly amused by the greater bewilderment of Terebinthia. Plainly, the säiyett did not know whether to feel vexed or relieved, for on the one hand Occula had to a considerable extent assumed her functions, while on the other the black girl seemed the only person able to soothe and relieve the malaise of the High Counsellor. Under her ministrations he would pass each day in a kind of lethargy, occasionally rousing himself to eat, but for the most part drowsing in the bath, sleeping, or simply listening to Occula, whose whisperings and occasional chuckling laughter—about what? Maia wondered—clearly possessed some odd power. She herself had never had much occasion to converse when she was with the High Counsellor.

These long absences of Occula from the women's quarters left Maia a good deal together with Milvushina, about whom Sencho seemed for the moment to have forgotten. She herself was, she now knew, jealous of Occula's pity for the wretched girl, but of this she did not feel particularly ashamed. Family disaster, violent death and enslavement, though certainly out of the ordinary, were nevertheless recognized hazards throughout the half-barbaric empire, and Milvushina's luck was no different from that of the daughters of many a ruined man. The last people from whom those who have come down in the world can expect pity are those who have never been up in it. Milvushina had scarcely anything in common with Maia. Paradoxically, however, this proved a source of strength to her. A more sympathetic and understanding girl might well have increased Milvushina's grief beyond endurance, simply by feeling and reciprocating it more fully. Maia, by her ability to feel only a limited sympathy, blunted—a little, at least—the fearful edge of Milvushina's misery.

Yet, peasant lass as she was, she was not lacking in a peasant's homely kindness to someone in trouble. If nice cups of tea had been known in Bekla, Maia would have made a nice cup of tea. The unspeakable horror which had been inflicted on Milvushina might be as much beyond her powers of empathy as was the Chalcon girl's aristocratic sense of her degradation and shame. (Maia had never felt in the least *ashamed* of becoming a concubine.) Yet it was not beyond her to persuade Milvushina to eat, to send Ogma out to buy her a brush and comb, or to hold her in her arms and soothe her when she woke screaming in the night. If the girl had not been plainly on the verge of collapse—even of madness—Maia might very well have given way to her natural feelings of resentment, for there were times when Milvushina unconsciously revealed that she regarded her in much the same way as she had once regarded her dead mother's servants; not, indeed, by ordering her about or saying anything contemptuous (her careful good manners, in fact, rather added to Maia's annoyance, since to her they seemed affected beyond anything she had ever been used to), but by her maintenance of a kind of reserve and distance, even when she was doing her best to be friendly, and by her inadvertent way of showing that she saw the world from a higher standpoint. 'But that was long ago,' she said once, recalling some memory of childhood, 'before we had even fifty men on the place.' And again, 'My mother didn't possess a great many jewels, really.' Maia made no rejoinder, for the tears were standing in Milvushina's eyes as she spoke, and after all it was she herself who had led her on to ease her mind by talking.

To Milvushina the company of Maia, as pretty and about as cultivated as a gazelle, often seemed rather like that of the fire on the hearth. Creatures and elements have their fixed properties, which cannot alter, and in deep misery it is often easier to whistle to a bird or tend a fire than to make the effort to talk to an educated person. All the priests of Cran could not have influenced Milvushina to try to preserve her self-respect so effectively as did Maia by her mere presence. The educated person will indulge, excuse and make allowances for you; but you have to feed the bird and you have to tend the fire—or else do without them. Milvushina could hardly do without Maia, for Dyphna, polite but withdrawn, was bound up in her own professionalism and imminent prospect of freedom, while Terebinthia, relishing cruelty cat-like and sensing that Milvushina found it well-nigh intolerable to be at the orders of a woman like herself, seldom spoke to her without exercising her authority or going about to abase her in one way or another.

Maia, however, with her ingenuous, bouncing warmth, often felt herself snubbed by Milvushina, and more than once expressed to Occula her annoyance on this account. Yet how could anyone—let alone Maia—long remain resentful of a girl whose father and brothers were just dead, who had actually seen her mother murdered and then been dragged to Bekla to become the slave of a man like Sencho?

Sometimes Milvushina would speak of her former life in Chalcon, but this was always of her own accord and not in reply to any questions from Maia. One day, to Maia's astonishment, she told her that she was still a virgin. To those who had attacked her home, looting and raping without restraint, orders had evidently been given that she was not to be touched; and she had been brought to Bekla under guard of a tryzatt especially told off for the purpose. She asked Maia whether she had heard tell beforehand of any plans on Sencho's part; to which Maia replied that although she had heard nothing whatever, she could guess that at the time when he had agreed with Kembri to kill her parents and family, the High Counsellor must also have decided to take her for himself. At this Milvushina wept bitterly, fearing that her very existence, known to Sencho through his spies, might have been a motive for her parents' murder. Maia felt this unlikely and said so; yet, as so often, had the impression that Milvushina attached little weight to her opinion.

Often enough she felt that the Chalcon girl was keeping her at arm's length. More than once, when Maia had been telling her about Morca and Tharrin, or about swimming in Lake Serrelind, and then awaited some reciprocal narration, she met only with polite but mortifying evasion. All too plainly, Milvushina had no wish to become unduly intimate with a little Tonildan tart who could not write her own name.

'Wants it all ways, she does,' Maia said to Occula one night, when Milvushina was out of hearing. 'Ten meld to talk to her, Lady Heldro, that's about it.'

'Oh, give her time, banzi!' answered Occula. 'For Cran's sake, only give her time! In a life like ours, your friends are the people you find beside you. She might come in very handy one day, you never know. Meanwhile jus' *try* to remember what it's all been like for her. *And* she doesn' know when Piggy might not start feelin' inclined for a bit of fun. Neither do I, come to that—though I'm doin' all I can.'

So, little by little, despite a good deal of mutual incomprehension, the two girls came after a fashion to accept and respect each other. One day Maia, to her own surprise, found herself defending Milvushina against an unjust rebuke from Terebinthia for putting Ogma to unnecessary trouble. After all, it had taken her some time to get Milvushina to feel it worthwhile to give Ogma any orders at all.

: 33 :
AN ODD BUSINESS

Despite her anxiety on behalf of the High Counsellor, Terebinthia, during these days as the rainy season began to draw to its end, was not without cause for satisfaction. In the licentious society of the upper city, every säiyett hoped for profit from the girls in her charge and, insofar as their master would permit, encouraged them to become popular with rich men. Occula, returning from Elvair-ka-Virrion's party, had told Maia that she thought she had succeeded in interesting some of the young Leopards and their friends. The next few days proved her abundantly right. Despite the universal fear of Sencho, lying like some bloated spider in the midst of his web of spies and secrets (a spider which might at any moment turn dread to terror by suddenly moving very fast to seize and clutch), a number of wealthy young men—respectful and open-handed—having heard, perhaps, through the network of rumour, that the High Counsellor was indisposed and in no condition to be told of their interest or to give it his personal attention, called at the gate, asking to speak to Terebinthia, and if they got as far as an audience invariably asked whether it might be possible—for an appropriate consideration, of course—to make the closer acquaintance of the black girl who had literally ensorcelled more than sixty people together in the Lord General's hall. Occula's performance, it now appeared, had not only frightened and fascinated her spectators but had also—after the manner of shocking experiences, from whippings to earthquakes—had an aphrodisiac effect, leading to a general, orgiastic release of tension, highly exciting and pleasurable, which some supposed she might be able to repeat on demand. Terebinthia, who had been told nothing about the affair either by Occula or Maia, was puzzled but pleased enough. Occula, she replied to the young men, was no ordinary girl. She was particular about her admirers—she could afford to be—and accustomed to receive a generous lygol. Furthermore, she was not often available, being, as one might suppose, in great demand with her master. However, she would see what she could do—that was to say—er—if the young gentleman really felt it—er—worth his while. Most of the young gentlemen did, and showed it, but Terebinthia, though she had never had such a pearl in her hands before, was too clever and experienced to make Occula freely available, even to the wealthy. For one thing, she wished if possible to keep the matter (and the money) from Sencho. This, of course, was perilous, but his present condition made it a chance worth taking. Again, she had assessed Occula as a girl of exceptional style, with far more than the kind of short-term basting appeal of a beauty like Meris, and she did not mean to let her attraction burn up and blaze out like a fire-festival bonfire. It had already occurred to her that if the High Counsellor were to die, as now seemed a possibility, she might be able to arrange Occula's sale, or even marriage, to her own profit.

Finally, there was the hard fact that in practice she had less control over the black girl than she allowed people to think. For one thing, Occula was not only spending many hours each day with the High Counsellor: she was clearly—and this was mysterious—content to do so. On certain days she was with him from morning till night, and did not even show any particular haste to be done. If she found her task burdensome she never said so. In the second place, she clearly had her own ideas on how best to pursue her career in the upper city. Terebinthia felt herself to be acting as bawd to an old head on young shoulders—a head which it would probably be more profitable to take into partnership than try to order about. Occula, in short, wielded the same kind of power as a highly talented dancer or singer. Self-willed and wayward though she might appear, she yet possessed an authority firmly grounded upon her ability to land the prizes if left to do it in her own way.

It soon became plain that she was more interested in the powerful than the merely wealthy. Despite every opportunity which Terebinthia could make for her, the hours she apparently felt able to spend away from Sencho were few and these—since she was in a position to exercise her own choice—she used almost entirely in meeting men of consequence. When one of the wealthier cloth-traders in Herl-Belishba, having heard of her fame while on business in Bekla, asked her to dine with him, she suggested to Terebinthia that perhaps they might pass the invitation on to Dyphna, since she herself felt she could not leave the High Counsellor. Yet the following afternoon she spent with a close friend of Elvair-ka-Virrion and the next with Kerith-a-Thrain, the commander of the Beklan regiment, an officer of no great wealth but much standing as one of the staunchest supporters of the Leopards throughout the army. Sometimes she would accept an invitation to a party, but on these occasions, though always pressed, she never consented to repeat her act as the jungle huntress. Although the refusal disappointed her hosts—one or two of whom complained to Terebinthia that this slave-girl ought to do as she was told and stop telling her betters what she might or might not have a fancy to perform—she possessed other erotic accomplishments so remarkable that requests for her company continued to pour in unabated.

Maia felt no jealousy, Occula being the only person in the world whom she sincerely loved. Besides, she well remembered the black girl's genuine pleasure when she herself had been preferred to go to the Rains banquet and subsequently summoned to gratify the Lord General. No; any difference in success between her and Occula, she felt, could only be for herself to adjust. As Occula had said, in the upper city mere beauty was not enough; she had to develop a distinctive style of her own. Stories began to filter back to her, through Terebinthia, through Ogma and the other servants, of Occula's prowess—how she sometimes terrified her lovers in bed, snarling like a beast in transports of savage pleasure and sinking her teeth and nails in their naked flesh; of an extraordinary kura that she had performed with three young men simultaneously; of a wager she had won that she would drink half a gallon of wine on a tight-rope; of how, to make up for the night when she had won his two hundred meld, she had led half a dozen girls in stripping naked and playing a game of blind-man's buff with Ka-Roton and two other Urtans, the understanding being that they should then and there enjoy anyone whom they might succeed in catching. Occula, relaxing for an hour in the pool, or returning after midnight to find Maia waiting up for her, never recounted these exploits herself, and if Maia asked for corroboration of what she had heard, would merely make some such reply as 'Randy bastards pay best' or 'Which blind man told you that?' Often she would bring back forty or fifty meld over and above her sealed lygol, and this she invariably split with Maia, the two girls hiding the money, wrapped in old rags, under the floor-boards. Maia felt that she would do anything in the world for Occula.

Quite early one morning, towards the end of the month Thakkol, Eud-Ecachlon's servant, appeared at the gate with a letter for Occula. This was brought to her personally in the women's quarters, since Terebinthia was not yet up and would have bitten the head off any household slave who had ventured to disturb her. Occula, however, uncertain of the Urtan hand-writing, made no bones about waking Dyphna to read it. Eud-Ecachlon wrote that owing to the illness of his father, the old High Baron, he had been called back to Urtah urgently, would be leaving Bekla next morning and earnestly begged Occula to spend a last afternoon or evening with him.

'That one-balled Urtan goat!' said Occula, rubbing the sleep out of her eyes and pulling up her night-shift to scratch her ribs. 'Thanks, Dyphna. He can't even do it—he jus' enjoys tryin'.'

'I expect you can get him up to it, can't you?' asked Maia.

'Cran and Airtha, banzi!' answered the black girl. 'You talk as if he'd been on and off me like a crow on a roof! I doan' spend any more time with the Urtans than I've got to, you know. All the same,' she continued, as they left Dyphna and strolled back to the pool room, where Ogma was waiting for the reply, 'I'll have to go, little as I fancy it.'

'Why, dearest?' asked Maia.

'Because,' replied Occula, whispering, 'Elvair-ka-Virrion told me at a party the other night that if we got the chance, one of us—you or me—must do all we could to spend more time with Eud-Ecachlon before he left Bekla and report anythin' he might say about Suba: that's why. Ogma, will you tell Lord Eud-Ecachlon's man that I'll have to speak to the säiyett as soon as she's up, but I'll probably be able to come this afternoon?'

An hour after mid-day, however, she slipped down from the garden room, where Sencho was dining—after a fashion—with the help of Terebinthia and herself, and interrupted Maia's dancing-practice.

'I'm not goin', banzi,' she said. 'Doan' ask me why; I'll tell you another time. I've told Pussy and she's agreed that you're to go instead.'

'Me?' said Maia, astonished.

'Yes, you!' replied Occula impatiently. 'Doan' look so damn' surprised, as if you didn' know a zard from a parsnip. Get your deldas pulled up and your dress on. And look sharp too—the jekzha's here.'

The next moment Terebinthia appeared to corroborate Occula. 'The High Counsellor says he can't spare her this afternoon,' she said. 'He's still not himself, I'm afraid. Your powder-blue dress will do very well, and as it's an Urtan you'd better wear plenty of jewels—that always impresses them.'

'Now listen, Maia,' she added later, when she had given her her cloak and was walking with her to the courtyard, 'Eud-Ecachlon's lodgings are in the lower city—somewhere near the Tower of the Orphans, I believe. You're to go straight there and come straight back, and you're not to get out of the jekzha on any account, do you understand? A slave-girl of the High Counsellor has a position to maintain, and if I hear that you've been racketing round any shops or bazaars by yourself there'll be serious trouble. If Eud-Ecachlon chooses to take you, of course, that's another matter. You shouldn't be away more than four hours at most—the High Counsellor may want you at supper-time. I'm sure we all hope he will.'

It so happened that, as sometimes occurred during Melekril, the rain had let up for a few hours. Maia set off in high spirits. This would be the first time she had been out of the upper city since Lalloc had sold her to

Sencho. In her restricted life to go out at all was an excitement, but to be bound for the lower city—smoky, pungent, clamorous, spread out before her like a sunset sky full of rooks—was exhilaration itself. As soon as they were well outside Sencho's gate she began chaffing the jekzha-man, giving as good as she got all the way down the walled road to the Peacock Gate. Going through the Moon Room by herself—for the jekzha-man, of course, was known and required no scrutiny from the guards—was somewhat daunting, but once back in the jekzha and trundling comfortably down the steep Street of the Armourers towards the Caravan Market, she quickly recovered her vivacity, gazing about her with delight. At the entrance to the paved market they had to stop while a string of pack-oxen plodded by, their bales covered in rain-soaked sacking. An apothecary's 'prentice, standing at the door of his master's shop, gazed at Maia admiringly.

'Where are you off to, sweetheart?'

Maia, leaning round the side of the jekzha, let her cloak fall open for his benefit and gave him a warm smile.

'To see a friend from Urtah.'

'Urtah?' said he, tossing his head. 'You'd much better come in here. I'll teach you all about pestles and mortars, if you like.'

'My friend's a champion javelin-thrower!' retorted Maia as the jekzha moved on: at which the young fellow roared with laughter and stood watching her out of sight.

They found the house without difficulty and Maia paid the man while the porter's boy went up to Eud-Ecachlon's rooms. The Urtan came down at once: his face, when he saw Maia standing at the foot of the stairs, fell all too plainly.

'Maia?' he said, stopping short on the lowest step. 'But I thought— Occula—'

Maia had already anticipated this. At least he remembered her name, which was better than she had expected. Taking three quick steps forward, she put a hand on his arm, looking up at him and smiling as she unfastened her cloak.

'Occula's so sorry, my lord. Sometimes things happen when girls aren't quite expecting them—you know? But I'll tell you something else if you like.' She looked round, then stood on tiptoe and whispered, 'I wouldn't let anyone else come instead; only me. At the party—that night—when I first saw you, I felt—oh, can't we go somewhere where I can say what I really *mean*? It's not just by accident I'm here, tell you that.' And with this she half-closed her eyes and took another step upward, so that she was standing beside him. Eud-Ecachlon, without a word, led her up the staircase.

Thereafter there was not much that he or any other normal man could have done to resist her, for Maia entered upon their business with a fervent, happy confidence that carried all before it.

The occasion proved more successful than she had dared to hope. She surprised even herself. Indeed, it was during this same afternoon that Maia came to realize that she had the luck to possess not only exceptional beauty but also an exceptional erotic aptitude. Occula, she knew, despised Eud-Ecachlon and had formed a poor opinion of his virility. Very well: it took all sorts to make a world; if Occula couldn't get the bull through the gate, she'd just have to do it for her, wouldn't she? Sharp-set after her recent, frustrating days, she was eager for pleasure and by no means disposed to be critical. Her forthright ardour was something for which Eud-Ecachlon, rather impassive and a little slow off the mark by nature, was quite unprepared. Despite being the heir of Urtah, he was not really very self-confident, and in his dealings with girls had become all-too-used to tepid acquiescence. This tended to make him nervous and often barely successful—as with Occula; but no one could have felt nervous of a happy-go-lucky, frisking child like Maia. With a kind of rapturous astonishment, Eud-Ecachlon suddenly found himself giving as good as he got. The afternoon took on an unreal, extravagant quality, with after-play imperceptibly turning into fore-play and pleasure becoming unco-ordinated, to everyone's enjoyment and no one's frustration. Kembri had been accurate in judging Maia's artless charm capable of exercising a strong appeal. The essence, of course, lay in her being as yet a stranger to dissimulation.

At length, roused out of sleepy contentment by the gongs of the clock towers sounding for the sixth hour after noon, she sat up in panic.

'O Lespa! That's never the time? Oh, I'll just about have to fly! No, don't try to stop me, my lord' (as he put his arm round her), 'you'll only get me into trouble. But next time you're in Bekla—oh, soon soon soon!'

'It can't be too soon for me,' he answered. 'I'll let you know in good time, Maia, when I'm coming back. To tell you the truth, I like you better than Occula.'

Occula's sophisticated expertise might perhaps have been a little too much for him, she thought. Indeed, now that she had got to know him for herself, she could sense as much. So she, Maia, could actually manage something Occula couldn't! Eud-Ecachlon was the better for her, and she was the better for knowing it. He wouldn't forget her: that she was sure of. (Nor, as will be seen, did he.)

Dressed—more or less—and climbing into the jekzha for which the porter's boy had run out into the rain, she leaned back in a state of delightful self-satisfaction, fingering the lygol in her pocket (which felt heavy) and with her other hand fanning the humid air before her face.

It was not Maia's way—as it is many people's—to cool down excitement or gratification by searching for snags. (If only it had been, of course, she would probably never have become a slave-girl at all.) On the contrary, she normally gave full rein to every mood, one way or the other, until the fit was out. Now, triumphant in the waning light, she pulled aside the rain curtain and rode down the street like a princess, gazing from side to side and even, once or twice, happily waving to those passers-by (and there were more than a few) who chanced to look at her.

Thus gazing about her, she noticed a sweet-shop a little way up the road. Its lamps, which had already been lit, glistened invitingly on ju-jubes, crystallized fruits, slabs of toffee and honey-nut thrilsa like that which Tharrin had given her in the fishing-net. After all her romping activity, Maia was hungry (and to do him justice, Eud-Ecachlon would probably have done something about this, if only she had given him time). At the mere sight of the confectionery her mouth began to water, and a moment later, as the jekzha moved nearer, she caught the spicy, nutty smell of the shop, warm from the lamps.

Oh, bugger Terebinthia! she thought. Who did she think she was, anyway? When Terebinthia was an old hag with rotten teeth, she, Maia, would be a golden shearna and the friend of princes. And talking of teeth—

'Stop a moment!' she said to the jekzha-man. 'I'm going into that sweet-shop; I shan't be a minute!'

Taking his hand to help herself down, she crossed the paved, well-drained footway—it still delighted her that in Bekla the rains were mud-less—and went in under the propped-up, pent-house shutter of the shop.

Beside the scales, with their pile of little, brass weights, an old woman, black-clad, was sitting on a stool, while near-by a sturdy young fellow, holding a stick, leant against the wall. Maia could guess well enough what his job was, for in cities of the Beklan Empire sweet-shops had an effect no different from that which they have always had on penniless urchins.

'Good evening, mother!' she smiled, throwing back the hood of her cloak and giving the old woman the full benefit of her happy elation. 'Would you like to sell me some thrilsa?'

The old woman, who knew all the local shearnas by sight, stared to see such a young, pretty girl out by herself. At all events, she thought, the customer looked well-dressed and prosperous.

'Is it the best you'd like, my dear?' she said. 'There's two or three kinds, but this one's made with serrardoes, look—very nice.'

She held up a piece between a none-too-clean finger and thumb.

'Oh, yes, that does seem nice,' said Maia, bending forward and sniffing. The smell vividly recalled Tharrin and the net. 'It looks even nicer than the kind the High Counsellor usually has. D'you reckon p'raps I ought to take him some back for a treat?'

In her high spirits, the idea of standing treat to the High Counsellor struck her as exquisitely funny, and she roared with laughter.

The old woman stopped hitting the slab of thrilsa with her little hammer and looked round at her sharply.

'Are you the girl from the High Counsellor's?' she asked.

'Yes, I am,' answered Maia, in a tone that meant 'and proud of it, too!'

The old woman put her face close to Maia's.

'Why have you come here yourself?' she whispered. 'D'you want to get us all killed?'

'What—whatever do you mean?' gasped Maia, stepping back in astonishment and alarm. Presumably the poor old thing must be a little touched.

The old woman paused, uncertainly it seemed, as though in her turn wondering what to make of her visitor. Then, turning back to the tray of thrilsa, she said, 'Oh, just my little joke, my dear: you mustn't mind me. Oh, look over there, now! There's my old cat coming in, see? Need a sharp cat in a sweet-shop, you know: Colonna, we call her.'

This brought to Maia's mind the recollection of Zirek and Occula chaffing each other about the pottery ornament. She had never understood the joke, whatever it might be. All the same, perhaps she could make use of it for a bit of light conversation to turn what had seemed to be going to be an awkward corner. For all she knew the point might be something quite clever and amusing.

'Well, you call her Colonna, mother, and I'll call her Bakris, and let's see which one she answers to, shall we?'

In an instant the old woman had grabbed her by the wrist and half-dragged her into the back of the shop. Maia, really frightened now as she remembered the jewels she was wearing, was beginning 'Let me go! The High Counsellor—' when the old woman, speaking low and quickly, said 'You little fool! Why did you come yourself? Thought you had more sense! We'd have found a way to let you know. But since you're here, listen! The night of the New Year festival, in the *zoan* grove at the far end of the Barb gardens. Repeat it!'

Maia, stammering, did so, and the old woman released her.

'Now get out quick! And put your hood up, too.'

Now that she knew she was not going to be robbed or hurt, Maia began to feel angry. 'My thrilsa—'

'Oh, take it! Take it!' cried the old woman, grabbing up a slab and thrusting it, unweighed, into her hand. 'And don't you never come back here no more, d'you see? O Cran have mercy!—' and with this she disappeared through some dark recess between the store cupboards.

Maia, utterly bewildered, dropped a two-meld piece into the scales and returned to her jekzha.

Arrived back, she found Occula alone by the pool, gently plucking the hinnari and running through the ballad—a favourite with shearnas called upon to sing—of U-Deparioth and the Silver Flower. Seeing Maia come in, she broke off.

'Cran's teeth, banzi, we've had quite a time since you left! How'd it go? Could he do it?'

'Oh—yes, fine, thanks,' replied Maia rather absently. 'What's up, then?'

'Oh, Piggy finally remembered about Milvushina,' said Occula. 'We had to take her up to him.'

'What happened?'

'Well, he made her do one or two things—nothin' to hard cases like you and me, but no fun for her, of course. She took it very well, really: I'd had a word with her outside, you see. "More fuss you make," I said, "more he'll enjoy it. Just pretend you're milkin' a cow or somethin'." And d'you know what she said? "I've never milked a *cow* in my *life*!" So I said—'

'Occula, there's something I want to tell you about; something queer as happened when I was coming back—'

At this moment, however, Terebinthia appeared and, being in a good mood on account of the improvement in the High Counsellor's spirits—a mood which improved still further when she had opened Maia's lygol—remained chatting for some little while. Later, at bed-time, Maia slipped into Occula's room and told her what had happened at the confectioner's.

'*What* d'you say she said?' asked Occula, her mouth full of thrilsa. '"The zoan grove at the far end of the Barb gardens?" Sounds crazy to me: but then a lot of those old dears get a bit that way, you know.'

Maia told her how the old woman had bolted out of sight without waiting to be paid.

'Nutty as the thrilsa,' said Occula. 'Can only be! Well, *that's* all right, anyway: give us another bit, banzi: thanks. I shouldn' tell anyone else about this if I were you,' she went on, munching. 'Not Dyphna or Milvushina, I mean. They'll only let it out, and if Pussy gets to hear, you'll be in the shit for goin' into a sweet-shop at all, woan' you? Anyway, tell me about Eud-Ecachlon. You say he was hot stuff? I'd never have believed it! You doan' know your own strength, banzi, that's what.'

: 34 :
AN UNEXPECTED RE-ENCOUNTER

About noon next day Maia, under Occula's tuition, was practising the
reppa—the spectacular though enormously demanding closing sequence of
the senguela—when Terebinthia came in. She broke off at once, but to her
surprise the säiyett told her to continue and stood watching for some time.

'You have quite a gift, Maia,' she said at length. 'At this rate you'll soon
be ready to show it off a little. We must find you an opportunity.'

'Oh, I don't just rightly know about that, säiyett,' answered Maia,
panting and leaning against the wall. 'It's only just passing time on, really.
But I do enjoy it.'

'Well, we shall see,' said Terebinthia. 'If you keep up this sort of progress
there may be prospects.' She sat down. 'However—'

'Can we help you, säiyett?' asked Occula, smoothly anticipating whatever she had been about to say.

'Yes,' replied Terebinthia, 'as a matter of fact you can. You can get
Maia ready to be at the Barons' Palace in about two hours' time.'

'The Barons' Palace, säiyett?' said Maia.

'The governor of Lapan has asked for you,' answered Terebinthia. 'It
seems he's in Bekla again. If it hadn't been for the High Counsellor not
being himself, he'd have been here in person. That's a disappointment he
can bear, apparently, but the idea of not seeing *you* again, Maia, he found
quite unendurable.'

Maia felt elated. She remembered the governor of Lapan, and the saucy
answer she had given him when he had remarked upon the value of her
clothes and jewels. Evidently he had not forgotten it, either. She would
enjoy showing him how much she had improved her sexual accomplishments since last she had been in his company. Recalling how much her
sumptuous clothes had seemed to excite him, she persuaded Terebinthia to
let her put on a full-skirted, cream-coloured gown, ornately brocaded with
vine-leaves and leopards, bought only recently and never as yet worn. To
this the säiyett added a diamond pendant on a fine gold chain.

Having arrived, somewhat overawed, at the Barons' Palace, she was
received with few words by a grave, elderly säiyett and conducted to a
room high up on the south wall, below the Lily Tower. A fair-haired
Yeldashay lad, who had just finished making up the stove, bowed to her
and slipped out, leaving her alone.

She wondered whether she should undress at once or wait until Randronoth came to join her. In view of his pleasure in clothes, she decided to
wait. Anyhow, she reflected, it would be next to impossible to get out of

this dress without someone else's help; and he would no doubt enjoy being the helper.

The rain billowed on outside. Through the window she could see the sodden slopes of Crandor rising to the stone quarries and the citadel—a bleak, hazy solitude, indistinct behind the drifting curtain of rain. How nice, she thought, to be paid for doing what you like! The prospect of an afternoon spent with a warm, good-humoured admirer, a sound basting or two and a nice, fat lygol to take home afterwards, was by no means unpleasant. Turning away from the window, she sat down on a bench in front of the stove and held out her hands to the blaze.

The door opened, a deep voice outside spoke a word of dismissal to someone in the corridor, and a moment later not Randronoth, but Kembri entered the room. Taken by surprise, Maia stood up in confusion, raising her palm to her forehead.

'My lord, I—I wasn't—'

'Sit down,' said the Lord General unsmilingly. Maia obeyed, the heavy folds of her skirt spreading about her.

'You weren't expecting me?' he asked.

'No, my lord; that I wasn't. Only they told me, see, as the governor of Lapan—'

'It was I, not Randronoth, who had you brought to the Palace. Now understand this, Maia. No one's to know that you've seen me—no one at all, do you understand? The purpose of that message was simply to mislead the High Counsellor's household. Your säiyett's not to know that you've seen me. You'll be given a lygol and you'll say that the governor of Lapan gave it to you.'

After a moment he added, with a grim smile, 'You won't even have to work for it: I merely want to talk to you.'

Her pride aroused, the Tonildan urchin peeped out. ' 'Twouldn't be no trouble to me, my lord—' but clearly he was in no mood for such sallies. Silencing her with a gesture, he sat down on the opposite side of the stove, leaned forward and rested his elbows on his knees. She waited silently.

After a time he asked, 'The High Counsellor—is he seriously ill?'

'He's—well, he's not been at all himself just lately, my lord, and that's a fact.'

'I know *that*.' His tone was brusque. 'Anyone else could say as much. It'll be best for you to speak frankly and straight to me, Maia. Forget you're a slave-girl and forget who you belong to. You're an informant, now, telling me as much as you can in reply to my questions, d'you see? The more you can tell me, the better I shall be pleased; as long as it's the truth. When I send messengers to enquire after the High Counsellor's health, they're told what he wants me to hear—or perhaps what that säiyett of yours wants me to hear—that he's suffering from a temporary indisposition. She wants me to think there's nothing wrong. I need to know the truth. What *is* the truth?'

'Well, 'tis hard to tell, just, my lord, with a man like that. Way he goes on, you see, he's bound to be taken bad every now and then. He gets bilious, like, in his stomach, or else he wakes up with headache an' that. I've seen him bad of a morning and then come the evening he'll be right again and stuffing himself.'

'And you admire that, don't you?'

'Well, want to know, my lord, I reckon he knows how to enjoy himself; leastways that's to say he did, till a little while back.'

'But this—now. Is this different—serious? Is there any more to it than after-effects?'

Maia considered. 'Yes, my lord, happen there is; only it's hard to say 'zackly what. It's bin going on that long now, you see, and it comes and goes, like.'

'Is he going to die, Maia?'

'I don't reckon so, my lord: but then of course I don't know a great lot about such things. It's more as though he was kind of—well, bemused—fuddled, like. Occula could probably tell you more. Only he seems to rely on Occula a great deal these days.'

'If ever you have reason to think he's going to die, Maia, you're to let me know at once—before anyone else. Either you or Occula must find a way to tell me—quickly: do you understand?'

Maia looked up into the scowling, bearded face, tawny in the firelight.

'You told me as I was to speak freely, my lord, so I'll ask you. Do you *want* him to die?'

'No, I didn't say that. And it's not going to be any part of your work to kill him, either, if that's what you mean.'

Maia was genuinely shocked. 'Well, of course I didn't mean that, my lord! I'd never do such a thing!'

'If I require it, you may find yourself doing just that, though not to the High Counsellor. But killing's no part of what I want to talk to you about now. I was merely enquiring after your master's health, which is a serious matter to me.'

He went to the door and called. After a short delay the elderly säiyett entered, carrying a tray with fruit, a flagon and wine-cups. Kembri, having filled a cup for himself, motioned to her to set down the tray and go. As the door closed he turned back to Maia.

'You remember an Urtan—a man called Bayub-Otal?'

'Yes, of course, my lord; at your son's party.'

307

'You were told—my son told you, didn't he?—to do your best to attract him.'

She nodded.

'What came of that, Maia? How successful were you?'

'Well, tell you the truth, my lord, I couldn't just make him out at all: and as to being what you call successful—'

'Why couldn't you make him out?'

'Well, first he was on talking very scornful-like about—well, about girls like me going with men and being given lygols and all such things as that. "You'll get no lygol out of *me*!" he says—kind of sneering, like. So naturally I reckoned he must just about hate me. But then next minute he was on asking whether I wanted to see him again. It just didn't make no sort of sense.'

'What did *you* say?'

'I said I'd be glad to meet him again if that was what he wanted.'

'Was that all that happened?'

'Yes, my lord. Well, only other thing was that when he asked where he could find me and I said at the High Counsellor's, you could see he didn't fancy that at all.'

'What did he say about the High Counsellor?'

'He said "He knows too much. He's a man everyone fears." I reckon that's why he hasn't tried to see me again. But then, why did he ask me in the first place whether I wanted to—I mean, if he didn't fancy me?'

Kembri, standing up, laid a hand on her shoulder. She realized with surprise that he was pleased.

'You've done well, Maia. You see now, do you, how easy it is to do well, just by doing what you're told?'

He filled the other wine-cup and handed it to her.

'*I* can tell you why Bayub-Otal hasn't tried to get in touch with you again. He left Bekla suddenly, the day after that party. He went back to Kendron-Urtah, but from there he disappeared altogether; for some considerable time. Those whose job it is to watch him lost track of him entirely.'

Maia sipped her wine and said nothing.

'Travelling in the rains,' went on Kembri. 'That's suspicious, for a start. But from Urtah, there's only one place to which Bayub-Otal would be likely to vanish altogether—where he couldn't be traced—and that's Suba. Marshland—water-ways—grass half as tall as the trees. Some secret meeting-place. Do you understand what I'm saying?'

'No, my lord. Fact is, I don't know what you're on about at all.'

He nodded. 'That's all to the good: you'll be all the more convincing if you're really what you seem to be.'

He threw two or three logs into the stove. They caught the blaze at once, with a resinous scent, and the gum began to ooze, hissing, from the wood.

'Bayub-Otal's returning to Bekla at this moment. In fact, he may already be here. I happen to know that he spoke to someone about you and said he meant to see you again.'

Maia, shaking her head, held her hands apart in a gesture of incomprehension.

'You're to do your best to find out where he's been; and what he went for, too, if you can,' said Kembri.

'But how, my lord? I told you, he didn't fancy me—'

Kembri held up a hand.

'You're young and inexperienced, Maia, and what little experience of men you *have* had has been concerned with only one thing. I don't understand Bayub-Otal any more than you do, but I know a great deal about him. Either he doesn't care for girls or else he pretends he doesn't, out of some sort of pride. It's not boys, either—we know that. But for your purpose and mine it doesn't matter what's at the back of it. He may not want to go to bed with you, but he wants to see you again—that's good enough for us.'

'Where he went to and why—is it just that you want me to find out, my lord?'

'As much as you can: anything he'll tell you; his hopes, his plans. He may be innocent; but we think not.'

'I wonder you don't have him killed, then, my lord. You easy could if you wanted, I suppose.' This was insolence and meant to be. She was speaking sardonically, out of a peasant's well-founded resentment against all callous rulers and oppressors. He answered her seriously, however.

'Kill the love-child of the High Baron of Urtah? They hate us enough as it is. That would bring the whole place round our ears.' Again came the grim smile. 'His father loves him, Maia, even if you don't.'

'Can you tell me any more about him, my lord?'

'I'm deliberately not going to tell you anything at all: then you can't reveal, can you, that you know more than if you were completely innocent? He didn't want to bed with you at the party. He may change his mind later, or he may not. For our purposes it doesn't matter. You may not know this, Maia, but a few men, here and there, prefer a girl who doesn't fall on her back straight away—even a slave. Perhaps he wants to believe you're pure at heart. If you decide, when you've got to know him better, that that's what he wants, you must do all you can to go along with it. *I* can't tell you how to win his confidence. You're the woman, not I.' He paused. 'Well, now you know that he means to see you again, and you've heard what I want you to do. How do you feel about it?'

Maia had in fact been recalling the contempt with which Bayub-Otal had spoken to her. 'Are you learning your trade?' 'You'll get no lygol out of *me*.' Remembering her mortification, she felt herself once more full of annoyance. Why ever should Bayub-Otal want to see her again? She neither knew nor cared. She could not choose but do this work for the Lord General, but she would much prefer to find herself in a straightforward sexual situation, with a normal man whom she could understand. If only, she thought, it had been Eud-Eachlon they had wanted her to find out about.

She raised her eyes. 'All I was thinking, my lord, is that if you're looking for a girl as'll make him forget himself—I mean, strike him as young and innocent, the way you said—then I know one as'd likely do much better for the job than me.'

'I'm the one to decide that, Maia, not you,' replied Kembri.

Now she'd angered him, she thought. She looked down into her cup, swirling the wine in the bowl and wondering whether or not to go on. In the silence she could hear the rain beating in gusts against the stones of the tower outside.

'Who is this girl?' asked the Lord General at length.

'Her name's Milvushina, my lord. She's with me in the High Counsellor's household.'

'And what makes you think she'd do better than you for Bayub-Otal?'

'Because she's a baron's daughter, my lord.'

'A *baron's* daughter? A bed-girl in Sencho's household? What do you mean? How did he come by her?'

'You mean you don't *know*, my lord?'

There was no question of him thinking her impudent now. The startled sincerity of her question carried its own conviction.

'You'd better tell me, Maia. Whose daughter is she?'

'Enka-Mordet's, my lord; the baron you killed in Chalcon.'

At this he stared. It was obvious that he knew nothing of Milvushina. She told him all that she had learned, together with an account of how she and Occula had found Milvushina at Sencho's upon their return from Elvair-ka-Virrion's party, and of the way in which Milvushina had borne her affliction since then.

'We heard, my lord, as you'd told your men to bring her back for the High Counsellor.'

'Did you indeed?' replied Kembri. 'Well, one day I may decide to see this girl for myself. Meanwhile, you can take it from me that she wouldn't do for this work with Bayub-Otal. There's a particular reason why you've been selected. When you succeed in finding out what it is, you'll know you're well on the way to success.'

This was baffling; but the Lord General said no more by way of explanation. For some little time he remained standing with his back to her, looking out at the rain. Maia, having drained her cup, tilted it in her hand and sat tracing the serpent pattern with one finger. Twilight was falling, but despite her disappointment over the way the afternoon had turned out, she felt in no hurry to return to Sencho's. The red glow of the stove seemed inviting her to linger before its warmth and let the wine finish its work.

'I'll give you a piece of advice, Maia,' said Kembri suddenly, turning back into the room. 'I'm speaking to you now simply as a man to a woman. Only a few slave-girls get as far as the upper city. That means they leave behind them far more who don't: and often that's the ruin of them, because they start forgetting where they came from and deceiving themselves into thinking they're exceptionally gifted—' he shrugged—'too clever to lose. The vital thing for adventurers—whether they're men or women—is never to forget that they're insecure. Self-deceit's fatal; it only leads to a dangerous sense of over-confidence. A girl in your position's entirely dependent on her wits. If they fail you've nothing to fall back on at all.'

Suddenly Maia felt that they were indeed talking on equal terms.

'*You're* an adventurer, aren't you, my lord?'

A brief, surly nod. 'You're young, Maia, but as far as I can see you're no fool. Just don't start thinking you're beyond the reach of disaster, and you might go a long way. I've already told you something about Otavis. I remember her when she was a young, inexperienced girl like you. She gave us a lot of help, so *we* helped *her*. That's why she's free now, with enough money to set herself up in the style a high-class shearna ought to have.'

As though about to go, he walked round the end of the bench towards the door. But his sudden, gratuitous advice, not unkindly spoken, had induced in Maia a typically spontaneous impulse towards the only kind of reciprocation at her command. Getting up, she stood with one bare arm outstretched along the back of the settle.

'You wouldn't care for something before you go, my lord?'

He turned, and from the shadows by the door looked back at her where she stood in the orange glow from the stove.

'You little trollop! Are you importuning the Lord General?'

She giggled. 'Well, without you help me, my lord, I can't get out of this dress, see?'

He hesitated a moment; then bolted the door.

Before she left he said, 'Well, audacity can be an advantage—some-times—to a girl like you. You've still got a light heart, Maia, and a trick of making men go along with it. It's a natural gift; if I were you I should hold on to it as long as you can.'

BAYUB-OTAL'S STORY

Stirring uneasily, Sencho woke little by little from a confused sleep to meet the dark-brown, slightly bloodshot eyes of the black girl gazing down at him. The sight of her, sedulous and compliant, was reassuring, recalling to him that he was now High Counsellor of Bekla, wealthy and powerful, master of spies throughout the empire, possessor of information indispensable to Durakkon, Kembri and the Leopard régime. For a few moments, still half-asleep, the stupor of his fancy identified her with his own dark, hidden knowledge of plots and conspiracies running underground—plots which he would reveal and bring to ruin as soon as he was ready. This girl was his to do with as he might wish. But she, like his secret knowledge, was too valuable to him to part with or expend lightly. He was reliant on her: she was his security.

Laying her hands on his swollen body, the girl began to knead and caress him, murmuring gently the while in her own tongue, to the sound of which, though he understood not a word of it, he had become more and more used during these past days while she had attended him, easing the strange infirmity clouding both his mind and his luxury. Her soft speech was like a spell to assuage sickness and anxiety. Relaxing, he gave himself up to the soothing sense of being enfolded, body and mind, in her skilled attentions.

He could not remember exactly how or when the illness—if illness it was—had come upon him. Indeed, he did not believe himself truly ill, for he had suffered no pain or fever; and of poison he had no fear. Not only were his cooks reliable but Terebinthia, he knew, was continually vigilant.

His lassitude and loss of appetite and lubricity, so it seemed, had stolen upon him by slow degrees, as gradually as winter. At first with impatience, he had felt in himself a disinclination for those pleasures which he had formerly found so enjoyable. His sleep, too—once a smooth refreshment after gratification—had become broken, and troubled by disturbing dreams—fantasies which tended to linger after awakening and from which he could find relief only in the black girl's ministrations.

In lucid moments he felt her presence as a danger. He must make himself do without her—sell her; have her killed, perhaps. She was a sorceress (for Sencho, like many of the cunning and cruel with no belief in religion, was full of superstition and vague notions of necromancy). He had become addicted to her; less to her body—for the intermittent pleasure he could still derive from that was not exclusive of others—than to her mysterious, sustaining power, like a thick, dark fluid which seemed continually passing from her into himself. Sometimes this seemed to him an actual reality; she represented a kind of drug, at one and the same time euphoric and harmful, which he knew to be nocuous yet could not do without. When she was absent he became peevish, full of vague dread and at the mercy of all manner of nebulous fears. Yet when she returned, he felt her spirit scattering those fears only the better to dominate him itself. When he dined, solacing himself with no more than a shadow of his former gluttony, it was by her will; and when he gratified himself, whether by means of her body or another's, it was as though she led him out into a paddock and stood by while he carried out what her husbandry had appointed. Her pig to be fattened; her goat to perform its task.

There were days when he could recall clearly the instructions he had given to his various agents; and the suspects—each one of them—for whom he had laid snares. Chalcon was a dangerous centre of disaffection. Tonilda, he had long been aware, was full of spies and counter-spies, many already known to him. He had a list of names—more than fifty, ranging from servants, shopkeepers and secret messengers to disaffected barons—against whom treason could be proved. At the right time, when it suited him, he would have them arrested. The right time would be when he had enough evidence against Santil-kè-Erketlis, whom he knew to be the Leopards' most influential enemy. The killing of Enka-Mordet had possibly been premature, he reflected. Perhaps, on the other hand, it had put a stop at the outset to what might otherwise have become a full-scale revolt. Other heldril, minded like Enka-Mordet, would not have failed, now, to realize that there was little which remained unknown to the High Counsellor. Ah! but to have acquired his haughty, delicate young daughter for nothing—and without even Kembri's knowledge, too—that had been extremely clever. As soon as he felt better, he would apply himself properly to breaking her in. Some reason might be found for Terebinthia to whip her; yet there were subtler and more enjoyable forms of degradation; delightful inventions of his own, for which at the moment, however, he lacked true inclination or energy. For the time being he must confine himself to milder humiliations.

Once or twice, during these last few days, he had felt about to rouse himself sufficiently to hear and give instructions to some of the spies who had come to report to him. More often, however, he had let matters slide, simply telling Occula to see that they were paid and dismiss them until they were due to return.

He fell asleep again, and in this sleep dreamed of an unknown, black goddess with white slits for eyes; thick-lipped, her breasts sharp and pointed as weapons, who revealed to him the likeness of Fravak, his long-dead master; then of the Katrian boy executed for his murder; of the servant-girl raped in Kabin—these and more. 'How is it that you know these people?' he challenged her; and to this she replied, in some strange tongue which in his dream he nevertheless understood, 'Most strangely are the laws of the nether world effected. Do not question the laws of the nether world.'

Waking in discomfort, he called once more for Occula, and when she came told her to ease the itching and prickly heat tormenting him. The black girl, gazing at him gravely, assured him that all would be well if only he would do as she said. He should order the slaves to carry him into the small hall: he would find himself more comfortable there. Indeed, she assured him, for his own ease and well-being he would in general find it best always to go wherever she suggested. Complying, he felt the power of his own cunning compromised and diminished, yet felt, too, immediate relief and reassurance as she caressed and whispered to him, changed the sweat-soaked cushions and fanned him while he drank the wine she had brought.

Sometimes Dyphna or the Tonildan girl would take Occula's place, but at such times he was disturbed and fretful, for he felt at the mercy of shadows—had she conjured them?—and dared not let her be absent for long, his enigmatic comforter. All was paradox. 'I am bewitched: I am not my own master,' he once broke out suddenly to Terebinthia. Yet when she asked him what he meant, he was not aware that he had spoken but, queasy and restless, merely told her that he felt disinclined for supper tonight, and once more fell asleep, to dream of Occula, transformed to Frella-Tiltheh the Inscrutable, preserver and destroyer, floating with him upon dark water towards some undisclosed destination of voluptuous enjoyment and impending menace.

Bayub-Otal drained his goblet, gestured for it to be refilled and leaned back in his chair, smiling at Maia across the table. His face, in the candle-light, was flushed and a few drops of sweat glistened at his temples. During dinner the room, which was not large, had become too warm. Now that the shutters had been opened to cool it, they could hear that the rain had slackened. Light gusts of wind were blowing and the air smelt fresh. In the colonnade below, a girl's voice, soliciting, spoke to some passer-by, who replied sharply and presumably walked on. The exchange gave Maia a pleasant sense of satisfaction. Even if she did not care for Bayub-Otal's company, at all events she was not plying for hire on the streets of the lower city.

They had dined well, in a private room at 'The Green Grove', a well-known tavern situated on the north side of the Caravan Market. 'The Green Grove' catered not only for prosperous traders and merchants but also, on demand, for aristocratic customers prepared to pay for the best food and wine. During Melekril there was little in the way of custom from provincial traders and the like, and Bayub-Otal's small party—himself, Haubas, Ka-Roton and three girls—had had the benefit of the best cooking and service the house could provide. Maia, who still could not take for granted the marvel of unlimited, delicious food, had not allowed her task of cutting up Bayub-Otal's meat to interfere with doing the fullest justice to the hare soup, baked carp, stuffed lamb and succeeding dishes, and was now sitting alone with Bayub-Otal over mulled wine, figs and thrilsa. She was glad the other Urtans had taken their girls upstairs for a time, since both—strangers to her—were prosperous shearnas a good six or seven years older than she, and neither had shown herself particularly friendly to the sixteen-year-old slave-girl. 'Why couldn't he have let us bring Actynnis?', she had heard one of them whisper. 'She was dying to come.' 'Little slave-girls are cheaper,' giggled the other, but broke off as Maia leant across to ask her for the salt.

'Did you enjoy the dinner?' asked Bayub-Otal, fanning himself with a fig leaf pulled from the basket.

'Very much, my lord,' replied Maia. Then, making no attempt to suppress a belch, she laughed and added, 'That's how much!'

'You'll never grow up to be a shearna at that rate.'

Her task, she reminded herself, was to appear as simple and innocent as possible.

'P'raps I don't want to be a shearna.'

'What would you like to be?'

Maia paused, smiling at him between the candle-flames. 'There were four of us girls back home: I was the eldest, but dare say Kelsi'll be married now 'fore ever I am.'

Bayub-Otal made no answer and she went on, 'I told you how I used to swim in the lake—oh, sometimes for hours. It was lovely.'

He pushed the candlesticks to one side, so that the light no longer lay directly between them.

'When you told me you belonged to the High Counsellor, I was in two minds whether to see you again.'

'It's not my fault, my lord, if I belong to the High Counsellor. I'm still the same girl.'

'The same girl as whom?'

'As swum in the lake.'

'You won't be for long if you stay in *his* household. You tell him all you get to hear, I suppose—you and your black friend. That's the other use he has for you. Very serviceable, I'm sure.'

A more experienced girl would have passed over the taunt. Maia felt nettled and showed it, for he had, of course, come close to the truth.

'We're not spies, my lord; we're his household girls. I shan't go telling him anything you say. If you don't believe me, why do you want my company?'

He walked across the room and closed the shutters on the dripping darkness outside. Then, turning to the slave who had waited on them and pressing a couple of coins into his hand, he said, 'Bring us in some more mulled wine. After that you may go.'

'You're angry,' he said, when the door had closed.

'Don't make much difference, my lord, does it, whether I am or not? I'm here to do as you like.'

He cracked and peeled a nut with his left hand.

'What I'd like? Then what I'd like is simply for you to listen to me for a little while: I'll tell you a story which I dare say you may not have heard, though it's certainly known to the High Counsellor. Do you want to hear it?'

'Seeing as you want to tell it to me, my lord.'

'When I was born, my mother was a girl little older than you are now. She came from southern Suba—the marshland delta where the Valderra runs into the Zhairgen. There are more channels there than a cat has whiskers.'

Maia, forgetting her annoyance, laughed. 'How many's that, then?'

He smiled back. 'I don't know, but that's what they used to say when I was a child. Ah! "When I was a child": we all love the place we come from, don't we? You loved your lake. In Suba the grass grows very tall—as tall as a man—in great swamps, with *sheldin* trees lining the banks of the channels. Evenings, the sun sets—oh, far away, out beyond Katria—and there are shoals of little silver fish—*margets*, they're called—that leap out of the water, here and gone, like rain pattering. It's all water-ways there—water-ways and reeds—and the children can paddle a raft almost as soon as they can walk. The Urtans call us marsh frogs: they say that when our enemies come we dive into the water.' He laughed. 'So we do. People who want to be lost take a lot of finding in that country.'

'Lespa of the Stars—didn't she come from there, my lord?'

'So they say. But if she did, she couldn't have been more beautiful than my mother.'

He pushed the wine-flagon across to her and waited while she refilled her goblet.

'My mother was a dancer—the most famous and beautiful in all Suba; in all the empire, really. At festival-time men used to travel three, four days' journey just to see her dance. I hardly ever saw her dance, myself;

but I've talked to men who did, before she was—before she was *married*,' said Bayub-Otal with emphasis. 'That's to say, before I was born, when she was at her greatest as a dancer.

'The baron of southern Suba at that time—Nor-Zavin; he's dead now— he was suspected by the Urtans—I don't know how justly—of secret dealings with Terekenalt, and he badly needed to convince the High Baron of Urtah that he was loyal to him. He sent him all sorts of gifts—unusual, singular things that they'd never seen in Urtah. He knew of my mother, of course. All Suba knew of her. So he bought her from her parents. It was a forced sale: he was a baron, and even though she wasn't a slave they had no real choice, though I suppose you could say it was a fair deal in its way. He paid them far more than she'd have fetched in the hands of men like Lalloc. It kept them in comfort for the rest of their lives.' He paused. 'Break up this thrilsa for me, Maia, and have some yourself.'

Maia did as he asked. The slave returned with the mulled wine, put it down and went out.

'Well,' went on Bayub-Otal slowly, 'so she was taken away—crying, I dare say—to Kendron-Urtah. And there she danced for the High Baron and his court. Do you know his name?'

'No, my lord, can't say as I do. Is he still alive?'

'Yes, he is. He's sixty-two. His name is Het-Otal-Ecachlon. At the time I'm speaking of, he was about thirty-four or thirty-five. It's—well, it's always been widely known—that things weren't smooth or happy between him and his wife. She was a Palteshi, very well-born; it was a political marriage. Many a ruler, many a great man in that situation's found himself as badly off, I dare say.

'The High Baron fell deeply in love with my mother. Possibly that may have been Nor-Zavin's idea from the start. But then everyone in Kendron-Urtah was in love with her, really. They still speak of her: she's become a legend.'

'What was her name, my lord?' asked Maia.

'Her real name was Astara. But everyone called her "Nokomis": that means "The Dragonfly", you know.'

'What tongue's that, then? Never Beklan.'

'Old Urtan—hardly anyone speaks it now—only a few peasants up in the north. The High Baron became my mother's lover. He told her,' said Bayub-Otal, 'and she told me—that he'd never truly loved any other woman in his life. I suppose a lot of people would laugh at that—it's what any philanderer says, isn't it?—but my father always had the reputation of a chaste and upright man. I doubt he'd ever had any other woman apart from his wife.

'My mother loved him as deeply as he loved her; and not just because he

317

was the High Baron, rich and powerful. She understood him. They made each other happy, that was what it came to.

'You can guess how much his wife liked the dancing-girl from Suba. If only she hadn't been a dancer, perhaps she might have been able to conceal it when she became pregnant. But of course it became plain soon enough. And one day there was an attempt on her life which nearly succeeded. My father grew afraid for her and sent her back, secretly, to Suba: not to her own village—that would have been too dangerous; but to another place, more remote. He used to come and visit her there as often as he could. He came alone, or else with just one trusted servant. It was known, of course, in Kendron-Urtah—or suspected, anyway—that he went to Suba. But once across the Valderra, even a High Baron can disappear and no one could tell for sure where he might be. There's another saying, you know, in Suba: "Plenty of long grass."

'When I was born—a boy—my father was so happy that he couldn't keep the secret, though I dare say it would have been bound to leak out anyway. He made sure I was taken every care of. There's a lot of damp and fever in Suba, of course—not good for babies, very often. I can remember him—I must have been—oh, three, I suppose—I can smell the river-mist now—striding through the door one night after dark, covered with mud to the knees, and my mother jumping up, crying for joy. Sometimes he'd stay as long as five or six days.' Bayub-Otal paused. 'I've never seen two people happier together than my father and mother.

'But it was always dangerous. We used to move continually from one village to another. I'd realized that we were in danger long before I was old enough to be told in so many words. My father was always afraid, you see, that his wife would find out where my mother was living. He didn't dare have it out with her openly, because he had to do his best to stay friends with Paltesh. I suppose that makes him sound like an underhand, crafty sort of man, but he wasn't. It was simply that he had a responsibility as a ruler: he had to put the good of Urtah before anything else. A High Baron can't be like ordinary people, you know.

'As I grew older, I came to love him dearly. He kept me company every hour he could. He taught me to read—my mother couldn't read—and how to use a bow, and to fish and hunt. Often we'd be out together all day. That was the happiest time I can ever remember.'

Bayub-Otal bit his lip. 'Well, I'll get on a bit. I was ten years old. It was the end of summer—burning hot and everything dry as tinder. We woke one night to find the house burning. My mother—my mother died. The servant died. People dragged me out. My hand had been trapped under a burning beam. No one ever knew whether or not the fire was an accident.

'I lived for the next few weeks with an old couple near-by. They were kind enough, but it was a very bad time. Then news came that my father's wife had died. It can only have been a coincidence: he'd never have harmed her. She'd been ailing for some while. I've often wondered—suppose she'd died three months earlier? Well, no good thinking about that. And a few weeks later, when the decencies had been observed, and I'd recovered—or as much as I ever will—my father brought me to Kendron-Urtah and acknowledged me as his son. He said he wasn't ashamed of having loved a woman whom he knew all his people had loved too. And I've never heard anyone in Urtah say a word against either of them from that day to this.

'My father's always been fair and just to both his sons—my half-brother Eud-Ecachlon and me. He's never favoured either of us. When Eud-Ecachlon came to be twenty-one—that was three years after his betrothal to Fornis of Paltesh had come to nothing—I was fourteen—nearly fifteen. My father called the two of us together and made us swear by the Streels of Urtah that we'd never—'

Bayub-Otal stopped and glanced quickly at Maia, at the same time making a swift, criss-cross gesture in the air with his fore-finger.

'Do you know what the Streels are?'

'No, my lord. Leastways, that's to say—'

'Yes?' His voice was sharp.

'I just know what an Urtan girl at Lalloc's said when me and Occula was there. She said something about the curse of the Streels; and then she said it was a very dreadful thing and she shouldn't have let it out. That's all I know, my lord.'

'I see. Well, you can take it from me that it's a strong oath for an Urtan, to say the very least. We swore to him that we'd never be rivals for power or try to harm each other. And then he told us that Eud-Ecachlon was to inherit Urtah; everything east of the Valderra. "That's just and right," he said, "for he's my elder son and the lawful heir. And you," he said to me, "for your dear mother's sake, you're to inherit Suba; all that lies between the Valderra and the Zhairgen. Swear to me now, both of you, that you'll never go against this or try to harm each other."

'We were both glad to agree to the wishes of so good a father. Eud-Ecachlon and I, we haven't much in common; but he's never grudged me the inheritance my father promised me. And the Subans—well, they were delighted. To them I've always been "Anda-Nokomis"—the Dragonfly's boy. The year I was sixteen I travelled over almost every mile of the province—by boat, mostly—meeting the people, getting to understand their problems and dissensions and so on, as well as a youth of that age can. I was starting as I meant to go on.'

Bayub-Otal drank deeply; then got up and began pacing the room, his light, cream-coloured robe swishing softly each time he turned about.

'Well, you know what happened, I dare say?'

'No, my lord. You forget, I'm only sixteen and not been long in Bekla at that. You're talking to a girl from the Tonildan Waste.'

'Well, Shakkarn be thanked for that!' answered he. 'Nearly seven years ago—oh, I must be careful what I say, mustn't I?'

'Why, my lord?'

'You know why. And yet,' said Bayub-Otal, stopping in his walk and looking directly at Maia where she sat at the table, her cloud of golden hair framing her face and shoulders, 'and yet, why should I? My feelings— the High Counsellor, the Sacred Queen—they'd be stupider than oxen, wouldn't they, if they hadn't known from the start what I felt when the King of Terekenalt took Suba with their connivance?'

'When was that, then, my lord?'

'When you were about eight or nine years old. That's to say, when the Leopards came to power.'

Maia recalled what Occula had told her. 'When the Sacred Queen first came to Bekla, my lord?'

'Ah, yes, the *Sacred* Queen! Fornis of Paltesh! Have you ever seen her?'

'No, my lord, that I never.'

'Well, I dare say you will before long. She was the only daughter of the High Baron of Paltesh, and when she became Sacred Queen—when Sendana-Say was murdered and the Leopards made Durakkon High Baron of Bekla—King Karnat crossed the Zhairgen and took Suba for Terekenalt. Fornis had told him that Paltesh would offer no resistance. In return, he was to take no further advantage of the civil disturbances caused by the Leopard revolt. It was a very good bargain—for him. He knew Urtah couldn't resist him unsupported.'

Stopping beside Maia, Bayub-Otal half-sat on the edge of the table and stared down at her bleakly, covering his mutilated hand with his other sleeve.

'But if you were the rightful heir of Suba, my lord,' said Maia, 'then why—' She stopped, overcome with embarrassment. Would he give her the same answer as Kembri? How did he see it? she could not help wondering.

'Why haven't they killed me? That's what you mean, isn't it?'

She nodded dumbly.

'Oh, no, Maia; why bother to make a martyr, when you've already got something much better—an ineffective, contemptible loser on public display? The High Baron's bastard son, who can't even draw a bow or cut up a chicken?—a fellow not worth the killing; unless he starts making a nuisance of himself, of course. Perhaps if I were to cross the Valderra into Suba—oh, yes, if I were just to go home, as any ordinary man's free to go—*that* might be grounds for putting me to death, I dare say. But the dancing-girl's dispossessed son, a man who can't even see any way to avenge his own honour, left free to kick his heels—to take to drink, perhaps, or chasing worthless girls; to be a laughing-stock behind his back—'

Maia was genuinely moved to see tears in his eyes. She put a hand on his arm.

'What's the good, my lord? Trouble—the whole world's full of trouble; worse nor yours, and mine too. But we're here in a clean, warm room. We're not hungry or cold or ill. You've money, and wine—yes, and me, too, if you want. Far as we know, neither of us is goin' to die just yet. There's thousands as that'd be more than enough for.'

He touched her forehead with his lips. 'Yes, of course.'

'Listen, my lord. There's a girl with me now in the High Counsellor's house. You talk about loss and trouble—'

She began to tell him about Milvushina, but after a time he stopped her, resuming his restless pacing.

'Strange things happen, don't they? An enslaved girl's loved honourably for years, by a High Baron; and a baron's daughter's enslaved and becomes the victim of a filthy libertine.'

' 'Tis all a dream, my lord. That's what old Drigga used to say—her as told the stories back home. When Lespa wakes us—'

'*Now* do you understand why I don't feel inclined to go to bed with you—or with any girl? Do you think I'd buy a girl's body, or compel a girl to bed with me, after what I've told you; yes, and after what you've just told me? This whole city's full of wretched girls yielding to men because they've no choice. And wouldn't those men love to see me become as dissolute as themselves?'

'You take it too hard, my lord, that you do. It's pleasure and comfort, after all. Where's the harm, long as the girl's willing—?'

'Yes, for a lygol!' He spat the word. 'Where's the dignity, the sincerity, in what *they're* doing?' He pointed upward. 'Where my father bedded, there he loved. And where he loved, there he honoured and cherished.' His voice rose. 'I'm speaking of the sense of responsibility that ought to go with desire for a woman.'

'And d'you know what I reckon, my lord? I reckon you're just cutting off your nose to spite your face. There's thousands have lost everything and had to make the best of what's left. You should, too.'

'I will: when Suba's free. I have a sacred duty to my people, you see. But that's enough of such talk.' He smiled into her eyes, his pale, rather fine features (did he take something after his mother? she wondered) seeming to express amusement at the futility of his own outburst. 'You told me *you* dance, sometimes. Will you dance for me now?'

'Oh, I'd not have the face, my lord; not after what you told me—about your mother, I mean.'

'If I were to tell you to take off your clothes and go to bed with me, I suppose you'd raise no objection at all. Yet you're reluctant just to dance. I find that rather depressing.'

'One's difficult and I'd do it badly. T'other's easy and I'd do it well.'

'All in a day's work, eh?'

'I know how to give pleasure, my lord. Ask anyone you like! You can start with Lord Eud-Ecachlon, and—'

'I don't think I'll bother,' interrupted Bayub-Otal bleakly. 'But I *will* trouble you to dance for me: I've a particular reason. Please go and ask them to send in a hinnarist.'

Maia could only obey. When she returned Haubas, Ka-Roton and the two shearnas had come back downstairs. As they lolled half-dressed in one corner of the room, yawning and barely attentive, Maia did her best to tell the accompanist what she wanted and then, sadly devoid of any real confidence, entered upon the reppa of the senguela, which depicted Lespa's apotheosis to become the consort of Shakkarn and divine mistress of stars and dreams.

As she danced, unable for a moment to discard her awareness of the inadequate space, of the spent, drowsy Urtans and the indifferent hinnarist with whom she had not rehearsed, Maia had never felt so clumsy, so incapable of forgetting herself or of becoming in her heart the goddess whom she was supposed to be representing. She had forgotten to ask for the floor to be swept, and once, treading unexpectedly on a broken nut-shell, she stumbled and could barely control a cry of pain. Yet Bayub-Otal, watching gravely, gave no sign of disappointment. As she came to the close—the beautiful, beneficent young goddess gazing down upon her sleeping earth-people between the clouds invisibly spread below her—dismally aware that she was two beats ahead of the hinnari, she felt full of chagrin. It was the first time she had danced for anyone but Occula, and a sorry go she had made of it.

'Maia,' said Bayub-Otal after a few moments, 'I can tell what you're feeling. Will you believe me if I tell you that you're a great deal better than you suppose? Given the opportunity, I'll prove it to you before much longer.'

She made no reply, but he seemed to expect none and, having paid and dismissed the hinnarist, opened a shutter upon the Caravan Market.

'It's late,' he said, as the clock-lanterns opened and shone for midnight, 'but there's still no rain for the moment. You have to go back to the upper city, don't you? I'll go with you as far as the Peacock Gate. Then you can take the jekzha on and I'll walk back.'

322

Out of the tail of her eye, Maia saw Haubas glance at Ka-Roton and Ka-Roton shrug.

'Just as you wish, my lord.'

They went out into the colonnade while the landlord's boy ran for a jekzha. As they were getting into it Maia caught a glimpse, in the shadows, of a solitary girl—no doubt the same one whose importuning voice she had heard earlier in the evening. She looked haggard, dingy and considerably older than Maia.

'Is that your lygol?' asked Terebinthia grimly. 'Are you sure you haven't been tampering with it?'

'When did I ever tamper with a lygol, säiyett?' said Maia. 'They're Urtans. Why do I have to go with them?'

'You needn't again,' replied Terebinthia, 'if they can't do better than that.'

: 36 :

A SIGN FOR OCCULA

'When are you going to take the field, then?' asked Durakkon. With any luck, he thought, and if Melekril were really ending (for sometimes the rainy season would appear to be over, only to resume for as long as two weeks), Kembri might leave Bekla within the next few days and remain several months with the army.

He wondered, not for the first time, what good he had ever done anyone throughout the empire by seizing the lordship of Bekla. As for himself, fear and anxiety never left him. He was surrounded by and dependent upon men whom he disliked and despised—men who had corrupted the city and alienated many parts of the provinces. Day in and day out, simply to maintain power, he lent his name to a régime of intrigue, double-dealing and subterfuge. He had accomplished nothing of what he had first intended: this bore no resemblance—none—to the benevolent rule with which he had planned to replace Senda-na-Say's.

'Give the roads a few days to dry,' answered Kembri, 'and I'll take the Tonildan and Beklan regiments to the Valderra to join Sendekar.'

'Has Sencho found out anything yet about Karnat's whereabouts and plans?'

'The truth is,' said Kembri, 'that Sencho's becoming less and less useful. It was only to be expected, I suppose. Lately, apparently, he hasn't even been capable of seeing his own men or hearing their reports. Anything could be brewing and we might not hear about it until too late, simply because he's sick or dying.'

'*Is* he dying?' asked Durakkon.

'His säiyett won't say a word one way or the other. One of his girls—a Tonildan—is reporting to me, and she thinks not; but she's only a child and she could be wrong—she admits it herself. As far as I can make out, he seems to have become completely dependent on the black girl—you know, the one all the younger men are talking about.'

'The sorceress?' asked Durakkon. 'Didn't she do some extraordinary sort of act with a knife—someone told me—'

'I don't know,' replied Kembri shortly. 'I wasn't there. She certainly seems to have acquired some extraordinary sort of influence over Sencho. The Tonildan's been with Bayub-Otal a couple of times. He seems to fancy her in some way of his own. I've told her to do everything she can to win his confidence. If only he'll talk freely to her, we might learn a great deal about Urtah—and Suba too; more than Sencho's likely to find out for us in his present condition. She's here now, without Sencho's knowledge. That's one advantage of him being sick, at least.'

'Well, we'd better have her in then, I suppose,' said Durakkon, with an air of distaste.

'I think not,' replied Kembri. 'If we do, at least one person—my säiyett— is going to know that you and I talked to her together, and possibly draw conclusions. No, I'll have her taken into a bedroom: nobody's going to wonder about *that*. There's one with a concealed screen, so you can easily come and hear what she's got to say.'

A few minutes later Durakkon, seated in darkness behind the screen and looking into the lamp-lit room, saw the girl come in. He remembered, now, having noticed her at the Rains banquet—a golden-haired lass, strikingly beautiful. Raising her palm to her forehead, she stood before the Lord General in an attitude of expectant submission.

'You won't be here long today,' said Kembri, 'and don't try to do what you did last time, or I shall be angry; do you understand?'

'Yes, my lord.'

'You've been with Bayub-Otal again?'

'Yes, my lord.'

'Were you alone with him?'

'Well, quite a while I was, my lord, yes.'

'Did he say anything about Suba?'

'He said he'd not be able to take life easy, my lord, till Suba was free; on account of he had a sacred duty to his people.'

'Nothing more?'

'No, my lord.'

'You didn't think of asking him what he meant by that, or how he intended to go about it?'

'Well, I would have, my lord; only then he broke off the talk himself, see, and made me dance; and after that he said we'd go home, so I never had the chance to ask him any more, like.'

'Well, that's useful information as far as it goes,' said Kembri. 'How is the High Counsellor today?'

'About the same, my lord, I reckon: kind of sleepy, like. Not himself at all. It's like as if he was bewitched, sort of.'

'What else did you talk about with Bayub-Otal?'

'He was on telling me about his father and mother.'

'That old tale again,' said Kembri.

'Well, I thought 'twas very sad, my lord, the way he told it to me.'

'I'm sure it was,' said Kembri drily. 'You enjoyed listening to him, then?'

'Well, reckon I did, my lord, yes. He told me how he'd grown up in Suba and how he'd been promised the rule of it by his father; and then how it had been given to this King Karnat.'

'It's time you understood a little more about this matter now, Maia,' said Kembri. 'If Bayub-Otal wanted Suba badly enough, he might—mightn't he—offer to rule it as some sort of vassal of King Karnat? Offer to pay him tribute and so on, if only he'd let him rule the country his father promised him?'

'I s'pose he might, my lord.' She frowned, plainly perplexed and out of her depth: then suddenly laughed, showing her white, even teeth in the lamplight. 'More 'n I'd want, I know that! Strikes me 's nothin' but a peck of trouble—'

'Never mind,' said Kembri brusquely. 'King Karnat, if he were to give Bayub-Otal the rule of Suba, would want him to give something in return. And it might be something we wouldn't want Karnat to have, mightn't it?'

The girl frowned again. 'Don't see what he's got to give him, my lord.'

'He could order his Subans to fight for Karnat,' said Kembri. 'He could persuade them that it would be in their own best interests to help Karnat to conquer Paltesh or even Bekla itself, in return for giving them back their freedom. Now tell me, did Bayub-Otal tell you where he'd been since he was last in Bekla?'

'No, my lord. Nor I didn't see how I could ask him without him getting suspicious of me, like.'

'He didn't tell you he'd been across the Valderra, or gone into Suba, or anything like that?'

'No, my lord.'

'Now that you know what I've explained to you, can you remember him saying anything that makes you think he might be in touch with King Karnat?'

'No, my lord. But you see, he kept on saying he expected I was going to tell everything to the High Counsellor, so he wasn't going to say anything as everyone didn't know already. He was very much on his guard, as you might say.'

'Did he bed you?' asked Kembri.

'No, my lord. He told me—well, he kind of said as he didn't go in for such things, like, on account of his father and mother an' that—'

Kembri waved a hand. 'All right. Now listen, Maia. I want you to get to know him still better. Tell him you go along with these ideas of his and that you think he's a sadly-wronged man. You must get still further into his confidence. Tell him you hate the Leopards, hate being a slave and so on. But don't overdo it, or he'll get suspicious. You're to go on being a simple, country girl. But above all, get him to talk about Suba. Tell him it sounds a wonderful place—that you'd love to go there—anything you like. He's up to something or other; of that we're certain. Find out what it is, Maia, and from that day you shall be a free woman. Do you understand?'

The girl's face lit up. 'So soon, my lord?'

'So soon. But don't try making anything up for my benefit, or saying what you think I might want to hear: I should only find out in the end. Now there's your lygol. What are you going to say to your säiyett?'

'Why, as the governor of Lapan basted me, my lord.'

She gave him a mischievous smile, but Kembri only nodded and turned away. The girl raised her palm and went out.

When the door had closed behind her Durakkon came forward into the room.

'I can't see that that poor girl's found out anything of importance to us about Bayub-Otal.'

'What I suspect is this,' said Kembri. 'He's been secretly in touch with Karnat, who's promised him the rule of Suba in return for getting the Subans to fight on his side; helping him to cross the Valderra and attack us. From his point of view it's a case of half a loaf being better than no bread. But there could be more to it than that. For instance, suppose Sencho knows about it too, and Bayub-Otal's the go-between? Sencho agrees with Karnat to give us misleading information and so on. Karnat crosses the Valderra with Suban help, conquers Bekla, puts us out of the way and then gives Sencho all he wants to gorge and baste himself to death—pensions him off. Meanwhile Bayub-Otal retains the rule of Suba as a vassal of Karnat and everyone's happy.'

'Oh, this vile business of playing games with people's lives!' burst out Durakkon. 'To think there was a time when I believed the Leopards were going to bring prosperity and happiness to the common people!'

To this Kembri did not trouble to answer. 'Well, let's hope this girl *can* find out something more. We've nothing whatever to lose by letting her try.'

'She seemed a nice little thing,' said Durakkon. 'You mean to free her, then, when she's done her job, and send her back to Tonilda?'

'Well, if she finds out anything of real importance, of course, she'll probably have to be done away with,' answered Kembri. 'These people outlive their usefulness, you know, once they're known to have been agents; and once they know more than we want to risk them talking about elsewhere.' He shrugged. 'There are always plenty more where she came from, after all. But now, another thing, sir. I beg you, please, while I'm absent from Bekla, and as long as the High Counsellor's still not himself, to make sure of obtaining frequent reports about the state of affairs in Chalcon: and particularly as regards Santil-kè-Erketlis. There's not a doubt that in spite of our killing Enka-Mordet, he's still a very real danger. Here's a report I received only this morning, for instance, about a man named Tharrin—'

Upon her return Maia, pushing open the door that led to the women's quarters, was startled to see Milvushina standing in the passage immediately behind it. Before she could speak the Chalcon girl took her by the wrist.

'Maia, listen—'

'What's up, then?' Maia, alarmed, replied sharply.

'It's Occula. I've been waiting for you—'

'What about Occula?' Then, in sudden panic, 'He hasn't *sold* her?' Her voice rose, and Milvushina hastily motioned her to silence.

'No, no! We'd better whisper—'

'Where's Terebinthia?' asked Maia.

'With—' Milvushina, who never referred directly to the High Counsellor unless it was quite unavoidable, made a movement with her head. 'Is that door quite shut?'

'Yes, yes! Come on, what about Occula, then?'

'She's—well, she seems frightened and upset—not like herself. She's in her room—'

'Occula frightened? I don't believe it! What on earth of?'

'I don't know, Maia. But either that or else she's ill. She came back from—' again the movement—'about an hour ago and she seemed—well, as I say—upset. I've never seen her like that before. I asked her whether I could help, but I'm not sure whether she even took in what I was saying.'

Maia, entirely forgetting that her first duty was to send Ogma to tell the säiyett that she herself had returned, hurried through the pool room and down the short corridor beyond.

Occula, dressed only in her shift, was lying face down on the bed, her arms stretched in front of her. Between her hands was the black image of Kantza-Merada. She was breathing heavily and slowly, as though struggling to endure some inward pain. Each time her shoulders rose, the muscles contracted as she clutched the goddess more tightly.

Maia, who had never once seen her friend unnerved since the night at Khasik when she herself had stolen the Ortelgan merchant's golden bear, stood perplexed, anxious to help but at a loss to know how. After some moments she sat down on the bed and laid a hand on Occula's arm. At once the black girl looked up quickly, revealing tear-stained eyes and a face covered with sweat.

'What day is it? Have I been asleep?'

Maia stared in fear, for Occula seemed scarcely to recognize her. She had heard tell of people being driven out of their minds by sorcery and curses. The dreadful thought occurred to her that her friend might perhaps have been bewitched or poisoned.

'Asleep?' she faltered. 'I—I don't know. I only just got back, Occula. Are you sick? What's the matter?'

'Ah, nothin', my pretty banzi,' said Occula. 'Nothin', nothin' in the world! Oh, if only I could get out of here somehow! Out of Bekla! Out of this whole bastin' empire! Get me out, banzi—if you love me, only get me out! I can' go on with it! I've lost my nerve!'

Drawing Maia to her, she kissed her passionately. Maia felt her tears against her cheek.

'I don't understand! What is it? You're frightening me, Occula!'

'*I'm* not frightenin' you, banzi,' whispered Occula, releasing her and stroking her shoulder. 'I'm more frightened myself than ever I've been since the Govig.'

'But what of?'

'But how can I stop now? It's what I *came* here for—'

Quickly, roughly, she wiped her face with a corner of the coverlet. 'Pray for me, banzi! Pray for me if you never prayed for anyone in your life.'

''Course I will, dear.' Maia, bewildered, spoke as to a child. 'But—well, it's not like you—can't you tell me the trouble?'

'No, you keep out of it!' retorted Occula immediately. She looked quickly round. 'Where is she?'

'Terebinthia? With Sencho, Milvushina said. Shall I shut the door?'

'No; that'd be worse. She might come and listen outside and we'd never know she was there at all.'

Sitting up on the edge of the bed, she buried her face in her hands. Maia .

sat beside her in silence. After what seemed a long time, Occula whispered, 'Where have you been?'

'With Kembri. He was asking me—'

'With *Kembri*? *Not* with the governor of Lapan?'

'That's right. He—'

'Did he say when the spring festival would be held?'

'No; he was on about Bayub-Otal. He—'

'But he must *know*, banzi! He *must* know! Melekril's as good as over. They *must* have fixed a day by now!'

She gazed at Maia with a look of entreaty.

'Well, but he didn't say anything about the festival,' answered Maia. 'What's so important about the festival, anyway? Will it be soon?'

'Yes, of course it'll be soon, banzi! It's always held within a few days of the end of the rains. They must be goin' to announce the day—'

'Hush, dear! Try and take it easy, do! She may come along any minute. Why's it so important?'

'Because—oh, banzi, I can' keep it up any longer! It's like tryin' to keep holdin' somethin' heavy above your head. I'm exhausted! I'm finished!'

'No, *that* you're not!' cried Maia with all the confidence at her command; for though she had no notion what could so much have dismayed her friend, her whole spirit rejected the idea of her Occula being unequal to any turn of fate whatever. 'You're not to talk like that! If it's someone that's trying to hurt you, tell me who it is. I'll go to Kembri—I'll do anything—'

'He was better today,' whispered Occula. 'He ate—like he used to; and then he had Milvushina in by herself.'

'Sencho?'

'When I saw the rain had stopped, I tried whether I could get him to tell them to carry him out on to the terrace; but I couldn' do it—it didn' work. I could feel it all tearin' up and breakin' to pieces inside me, like an old bit of cloth you can' patch any more; like a blunt knife that woan' cut. I've lost the trick, banzi. Whatever am I goin' to do? If I can' get him to the right place when the time comes—'

Maia shook her head. 'You're tired out, dear. Why don't you go to sleep? Come and sleep with me tonight, like we used to. I'll tell Milvushina.'

'No: Terebinthia'd only wonder why. If only they'd announce the festival—'

'Old Drigga used to say "Everything looks worse to tired eyes." I'll make you some hot wine with honey. The fire's still in.' Maia stood up.

'It mustn' go wrong now,' whispered Occula, rocking backwards and forwards where she sat. 'O Kantza-Merada, remember thy faithful servants robbed and murdered! Give me thy power only a little longer! Kantza-Merada, give me thy power!'

She slipped to the floor and knelt there with bent head; then spread out her arms, palms downward on the floor on either side of her body; and so remained, as though waiting for some answer from the grim, black image above her on the bed. Maia, not knowing what more to say, folded her hands in her lap and waited.

At length Occula rose to her feet, blew out the lamp and stood motionless, facing the barred window. As Maia's eyes grew accustomed to the darkness, she could see clearly the square of night sky, twinkling here and there with the faint points of stars. There was silence except for a gentle patting of wind.

Suddenly a wild shriek, savage and fierce, tore through the stillness. Hard upon it came the short, cut-off squeal of some small creature stricken and seized. Maia started back against the wall, but Occula made no least move. A few moments later the dark shape of the owl, clutching its prey, flew silently across the window-space and vanished.

Occula spoke in her normal voice. 'Get me the wine, then, banzi: and after that I'll go to bed.' Then, as Maia hesitated, 'Go on, before the fire's out. Bread, too! I'm damn' hungry!'

When Maia came back, carrying the bread and wine in one hand and a newly-lighted lamp in the other, Occula had put the image away, but was still standing at the window. Turning, she smiled and took the wine-cup from Maia's hand.

'That's good enough for me, banzi! I would be a fool, wouldn' I, not to trust in—' She broke off.

'Not to trust?' asked Maia hesitantly. She was feeling somewhat shaken.

'A sign—an omen—as plain as that.'

Maia shook her head in bewilderment. Occula laughed and kissed her.

'You doan' understand? So much the better for you!' Then, with a complete return to her normal manner, 'Never mind! Just forget every bit of it! Listen; I'll tell you somethin' else—nothin' to do with owls. D'you remember Zuno and his white pussy-cat?'

'Yes, 'course.'

'And how I said I'd do him a bit of good if ever I got the chance, all along of those robbers on the road between Hirdo and Khasik? Well, I reckon I've done it, like as not.'

'Get away?' replied Maia, surprised. 'I never thought you really meant it.'

Occula, munching, sipped the hot wine.

'Elvair-ka-Virrion—t'other night—I never told you. He was sayin' that apparently the Sacred Queen's lookin' for a new household steward. The last man—she was angry with him. Lucky to get off with his life, Elvair-ka-Virrion said.'

'What had he done, then?'

'Playin' around with one of her girls. So I upped and said that Lalloc had this very superior young man in his employ, natural gift of authority, well-spoken and all that, who'd *never* want to touch the girls. And Elvair-ka-Virrion said that as it happened he was goin' down to see Lalloc about buyin' a lad to look after his hounds, so while he was there he'd just have a look at Master Zuno and possibly recommend him to Fornis.'

'I wonder you was at the trouble,' said Maia, recalling how they had trudged beside the jekzha in the burning sun.

'Oh, banzi,' answered Occula, gulping down the last of the wine and climbing into bed, 'it's not a question of *likin'* him; though I must admit I doan' altogether dislike him. But that's the sort of fellow who'll be able to keep his head, even in a household like the Sacred Queen's. And if he's pleased and she's pleased, you never know when he might not be able to do us a bit of good.' She paused. 'That's if *anythin's* goin' to be able to do me good. But I doan' mind now. Where Kantza-Merada went, I can go.' She laughed. 'Huntin' in the dark, I mean. "Do not question the laws of the nether world." Did old Kembri baste you again, then?'

Maia smiled. 'No, but I got a lygol all the same. O great Cran, and I've just remembered—I never told Terebinthia I'd got back. I must go and find Ogma—'

'How long have you been back, Maia?' Terebinthia was standing in the doorway.

Maia raised her palm to her forehead. 'A little while, I'm afraid, säiyett: I'm ever s' sorry! Only I found Occula taken bad, see, and that put it out of my head. But here's the governor's lygol.'

Terebinthia, taking it from her, put it into her sleeve unopened. 'What's the matter with you, then, Occula?'

'Nothin', säiyett. I've just been sick, that's all. Somethin' at dinner, I s'pose. I was just goin' to bed—unless there's anythin' you want.'

'No,' replied Terebinthia rather absently. 'Maia, have you ever mentioned Milvushina to Lord Elvair-ka-Virrion?'

'No, säiyett: I haven't seen Lord Elvair-ka-Virrion at all since the night Milvushina was brought here.'

'Well,' said Terebinthia, 'you'd better understand this, Maia. The High Counsellor doesn't wish anything to be said outside about how Milvushina came to be here. If I learn that you've been gossiping, I shall be extremely angry, do you see?'

'Yes, säiyett. I won't say nothing.'

331

'I've just been telling Milvushina herself the same thing. She's to say nothing to anyone of how she came here, on pain of the most severe punishment. Now listen to me. Lord Elvair-ka-Virrion has asked for you to go to a party at the Barons' Palace tomorrow night, and he wants Milvushina to go with you. I wasn't aware that he even knew of her existence. In the normal way I certainly wouldn't permit it, but the fact is that Lord Elvair-ka-Virrion was—er—well, very generous and very pressing. So I've decided to let you both go. No doubt there'll be generous lygols if you do well.'

'Thank you, säiyett.'

'Now it's time both of you were asleep. Milvushina's in bed already.'

'Is Dyphna back yet, säiyett?' asked Occula innocently.

'Dyphna? Tomorrow,' replied Terebinthia; and was gone.

'Cran and Airtha! She's goin' to slip up one of these days, banzi; she's bound to,' whispered Occula. 'Piggy'll find out she's featherin' her nest on the quiet and have her hangin' upside-down as sure as a cow can fart.'

'Either that or she'll make her fortune,' said Maia. 'Elvair-ka-Virrion must have slipped her a hell of a lot to let Milvushina go out. Old Sencho'd never dream of allowing that if he knew.'

'She must be better off than ever Domris was, right now this minute. Just think, every time one of us gets basted—oh, well. Why doan' I stop talkin' and go to sleep?'

'Think you will now?'

'Sounder than a tree in winter. Good-night, pretty banzi.'

: 37 :
THE SENGUELA

The early afternoon sun, slanting through the trees, shone on the bushes, the long, wet grass and patches of red-brown soil, drawing up a fresh-smelling warmth from the floor of the Tonildan glade. Close by, in a thicket, a greenbreast, with many pauses, was letting fall one slow, clear phrase after another; its song, in the silence, as joyous and untroubled as though there were no harm or danger in all the world. Winged flies, survivors of the previous summer, roused from the bark crevices or subterranean cells where they had sheltered through the rains, glittered in the soft air; many, in their first, unwary flutterings, snapped up by the pouncing sparrows. High above, in the newly-revealed, blue sky, a buzzard hovered, waiting to drop upon any small creature decrepit or injured, slow-witted, or simply deceived into momentary inattention by the benediction of returning spring.

Brown and spare, the young pedlar Zirek, stripped to the waist in the sunshine, stood leaning against a tree-trunk, one knee bent and foot raised as he scraped with a pointed stick at the mud caked on his boot. His pack lay in the grass near-by and across it he had thrown his white-striped jacket and scarlet leather hat.

'So now you know—well, all there is to know,' said he, looking smilingly down at his companion.

Meris, sprawled on his cloak, did not return the smile.

'But you *did* work for Sencho, all the same? As well as for Santil?'

'Well, I had to,' answered the pedlar. 'Else it wouldn't have been convincing. Some of the information was useful to him, too, I'm afraid—it had to be. Some of it was misleading, but some of it wasn't. It was a question of how little I could get away with. I've managed to avoid suspicion, anyway.'

'And are there many, then, like you? Playing it double, I mean?'

'I don't know,' said he. 'I don't know anything except what I'm told. Those who don't know can't tell, can they?'

'Is that why you became a pedlar—to do this work for Erketlis?'

'No; I was a pedlar first; it was the Leopards—well, one of Sencho's agents—who first got hold of me, at Khasik, and said Sencho would pay me to work for him. A pedlar, going all over two or three provinces—I'm licensed from Kabin down to Ikat, you see—there's plenty of opportunities to pick up information. I accepted; but then I managed to let Erketlis know what had happened. He's made good use of it since.' He broke off suddenly. 'Listen! What's that?'

The glade was only a bowshot from the road by which they had come from Thettit-Tonilda. Zirek, following Sencho's instructions of a few weeks before, had called at the Lily Pool early that morning and taken charge of Meris, whom Domris had woken and handed over to him before anyone else was about. Since then they had walked some eight miles, first among fields and hamlets surrounding the city and then through the open forest-land east of Hirdo. Meris had at first supposed that they must be on the Ikat road and going south, for she had been told that the pedlar would be taking her to Chalcon. It was only gradually that she realized by the sun that this could not be their direction.

At last she had asked him directly what his plans were; and at this he suggested that they should turn aside into the trees for a bite and a rest. Meris had supposed that his reason would prove to be the one she was accustomed to; nor did she feel unwilling. She had not in the least been expecting what he had just disclosed to her and it had come as a considerable shock.

They both listened intently. From the direction of the road sounded voices and laughter, followed by crackling sticks and a rustling of the bushes.

'It doesn't matter, does it?' said Meris. 'After all—you and me here—why not?'

The pedlar, without answering, stole away through the trees. He returned a minute later.

'Four or five young fellows with a couple of bullock-carts—no one I've ever seen before on this road. They've gone now, anyway.'

'What were you afraid of?'

He sat down on the cloak beside her. 'Well, in this game, you see, you never know who might have been put on to watch you; or who by. Sencho doesn't really trust anybody. But I believe Erketlis trusts me, even though I've never seen him in my life.'

Meris frowned. 'You've never *seen* him?'

'Oh, great Cran, no; that'd be much too risky! If you're—well, what I am—you don't meet heldro leaders in person. You meet carters along the roads—old women in sweet-shops in the lower city—wood-cutters—whoever you're told to meet. You don't know them; you exchange a password. "Colonna"—"Bakris"; that sort of thing. You may never see them again. No, I've never met Erketlis, but I get his orders all the same.'

'D'you think there may be people like you the other way round—working for Sencho?'

'I'm certain of it.'

'Enka-Mordet—who gave him away?'

'I don't know,' said Zirek, 'but it only goes to show you can't trust anyone. Sencho had someone among Enka-Mordet's people; he must have. Or more likely Sencho just had some personal reason to want him dead.'

Meris stretched lazily in the sunshine.

'You know what I was told I was going to have to do?'

He laughed. 'What you're good at, by all I've heard. Had some practice, haven't you?'

'Plenty: I was looking forward to it. Be like old times, taking men into the long grass again. They said they'd free me if only I could find out what Erketlis is up to.'

The pedlar put one arm round her and kissed her bare shoulder.

'Well, you won't be able to do that now, will you? What it comes to is this: you've got a choice. I can leave you with a friend of mine at Hirdo: but of course you realize, don't you, that whether I succeed or fail, they're bound to look for you? All the same, you may think it's your best chance. Kalton—my friend—he'd do all he could for you, I know that.'

'And the other?' asked Meris.

'The other's to come along with me and help me. If it fails, I promise I'll kill you quick—this dagger here, see? But I believe myself that if only Occula can pull it off, we'll succeed. It's afterwards is going to be the hardest part.' He paused. 'Well, how d'you feel? Do you hate them enough to try it?'

'Hate them?' answered Meris. '*Hate* the Leopards? O Shakkarn, if only you'd seen Latto hanging upside-down by the road! You couldn't even see his wounds for the flies!' She clenched her fists. 'And Yunsaymis—she was in Sencho's household, you know. He had her whipped, like me—he sold her—he—'

'All right, I've got it: you don't like them,' said Zirek. 'Well, now's your chance; and a better one than working for Sencho in Chalcon, I'd say. Him? When you weren't useful any more, he'd simply get rid of you. He certainly wouldn't free you, whatever he may have promised.'

'But how's it to be done?' asked Meris. 'If only I thought there *was* a chance—'

'Why, there's a fair enough chance,' answered he. 'In a day or two it'll be the New Year festival. There'll be crowds coming into Bekla from all over the provinces, and if only you can walk the distance in two days, we can be in the thick of them. I've got my pedlar's pass into the upper city. Durakkon'll be giving a feast by the Barb that night.'

'Well?' said Meris tensely.

'I'm not saying any more,' replied the pedlar. 'Those who don't know can't tell. But I work to Santil's orders and I trust him. He wouldn't send me there without we had a fair chance.'

'But how can we expect to get out of the upper city? There isn't any way out, except through the Peacock Gate.'

'And *that* I'm not telling, either. But you can believe me when I say I believe we *shall* get out. Else I wouldn't be going.' Putting his hands on her shoulders, he turned her to face him. 'If you don't fancy it—and I shan't blame you if you don't—say so now. It'll certainly be safer for you at Hirdo, with my friend.'

Rising to her feet, Meris stood looking down at him. At length she said, 'You mean I could really *help* to kill him, myself? I could actually *see* the bastard die—see the shit pouring out all over his filthy belly? Hear him choking in his blood—'

She stopped, panting and biting on her fingers.

'Steady, now, steady!' said Zirek, grinning. 'Well, perhaps there might not be quite enough time for all that. Once it's done we'll have to be off sharp, you know—no fond farewells like you seem to have in mind. But since you're feeling so enthusiastic—'

'Do you remember,' cried Meris, 'do you remember what I offered you in Sencho's house, the day you gave that pottery cat to the black girl?'

335

'I wouldn't be likely to forget it,' answered Zirek.

'Well, you *needn't* give me a flask of kepris today,' said Meris. 'And we don't have to be all that quick about it, either.'

As he took her in his arms, she felt for the fastening at the neck of her robe, but his hand had reached it before hers.

'I'll come with you,' she whispered, as they sank down together on the cloak. 'Oh, yes, I'll come with you! Ah! Ah! Ready, weren't you?'

Afterwards, stretched at ease, she asked, 'D'you remember how Occula prevented us, that day? I could have killed her. I wanted you then; much as I've ever wanted a man; more.'

'I remember,' said Zirek. 'Well, whatever you may think of her, everything depends on Occula now, I'll tell you that.'

'I was afraid of her,' said Meris. 'She was—well, like a witch, sort of.'

'Just so,' said the pedlar. 'That's what she is. There's some sort of strange power in Occula: that's why she's there. But now; it's a shame to put clothes back on a body like yours, but we have to get to Hirdo tonight, my lass, and if we want a comfortable bed we'd better be off, for there'll be travellers enough now the rains are over.'

'One thing more,' he added, as she helped him on with his pack and eased the straps over his shoulders. 'What's mine's yours now. I won't come out of Bekla without you—that I promise. You be straight with me and you'll find me straight enough with you.'

The party, when Maia and Milvushina arrived at the Barons' Palace on the evening after Occula's strange turn, proved in fact to be given not by Elvair-ka-Virrion—though he and several of his friends were present—but by U-Sarget, a wealthy wine-merchant who stood well with the younger Leopards and was said to have lent money to several of them. Whatever the truth of such rumours, he evidently intended on this occasion to leave no one in doubt that he was a man of means. One of the smaller halls of the palace had been entirely re-hung with new, woven fabrics dyed in contrasting shades of green. At this early time of year few flowers were yet in bloom, but Sarget had procured banks of ferns, overhung with trailing creepers, and these—continually sprinkled with water by pretty little girls dressed as different kinds of bird—gave off a scent of herbage and moisture among the tables. Each guest, upon greeting Sarget, was presented with a bronze wine-cup of Gelt workmanship, which was filled then and there from a cask of Yeldashay, so that he or she might drink the host's health. When all the guests had arrived, a choir of boys and girls sang a song of welcome to the returning spring, composed for the occasion by Sarget himself. This anthem having been warmly applauded (it proved, in fact, a lasting favourite, often performed in after-years) the choir left the hall.

The musicians, however, remained, and continued to play throughout supper. These were the best in Bekla, for Sarget, money-lender and place-seeker though he might be, was a wholehearted lover of music and himself a good hinnari player—an accomplishment for which he was sometimes sneered at, behind his back, by people who considered such skills appropriate only to slaves or hired professionals.

If Sarget had spent heavily, he had certainly achieved his object—a striking display of taste and style—and in addition had proved lucky in his choice of the day. It was now virtually certain that the rains were over. At noon Durakkon himself, speaking, in accordance with custom, from the Bronze Scales in the Caravan Market, had proclaimed that the Sacred Queen's ritual congress with the god would take place in two days' time, and be celebrated with the customary festivities throughout the upper and lower cities. Already a spirit of approaching carnival was abroad, even among slaves and beggars, and the guests, as they assembled, were in good humour and wholeheartedly disposed to enjoy themselves. At the outset Sarget, a shrewd judge of what was likely to go down well, improved upon the occasion by personally reconciling, in front of the company, two young men who were known to have been at daggers drawn over a girl, and whom he now begged to honour him by drinking a health to each other before everyone sat down to supper. Amid cheers and acclamation they complied, after which both, having been crowned with flowers, held tapers to either end of a flat, dry reed, on which had been painted the words 'Rains' and 'Discord'.

Maia, laughing and applauding with the rest, looked round to find Nennaunir standing beside her. Smiling rather timidly, she was surprised to be clasped by the shearna in a warm embrace.

'You here as well, you pretty little thing?' whispered Nennaunir in her ear. Then, releasing her and holding her at arm's length by the shoulders, 'Not so darned little, either! And you're glad enough to get away from that filthy brute for once, I dare say?'

For a few minutes they chatted, strolling across the room. Maia felt that Nennaunir, like Sessendris, had decided that, slave-girl or no, she had evidently acquired some kind of standing among the Leopards, and that accordingly nothing was to be lost by being pleasant to her. She took the opportunity to introduce Milvushina and was amused to see that the shearna, with professional shrewdness, at once grasped—and was puzzled to grasp—that this was a young lady of birth. Looking round, she recognized by sight several other shearnas and guessed that in all probability she and Milvushina were the only slave-girls in the company.

Elvair-ka-Virrion had been standing with Sarget at the further end of the hall, but now both he and the wine-merchant—who was wearing a crimson robe magnificently embroidered with a hunting scene in silver—deliberately made their way to where the three girls were talking together. Nennaunir, of course, was already acquainted with Sarget, and at once began congratulating him on his generosity and on the decoration of the hall. Sarget, having replied appropriately, drew Maia into the conversation by admiring her dress. It was one of three or four which Terebinthia had bought in anticipation of the spring festival: close-clinging silk, of a soft, cherry colour, the bodice glittering with minute crystals. As soon as he learned that she came from Lake Serrelind, Sarget began telling her about a hunting expedition he had once made to the Tonildan Forest. Maia, who had never in her life been even as far east as the Thettit–Kabin road, and knew no more of the Tonildan Forest than she did of the Deelguy Desert, nodded and smiled and opened her eyes wide; and soon felt in no doubt that Sarget thought her as charming a girl as Elvair-ka-Virrion had no doubt told him she was.

She had some little difficulty, however, in concentrating on this conversation, being distracted by her realization that Elvair-ka-Virrion was deep in talk with Milvushina. Milvushina's voice was always low, and Maia could hear nothing of whatever she might be saying. From time to time, however, she caught a phrase or a few words from Elvair-ka-Virrion. 'In Chalcon?' 'I'd never have believed . . .' and at length, with emphasis, '. . . assure you my father knew nothing whatever about it.'

If Terebinthia, thought Maia, had in truth cautioned Milvushina as she herself had been cautioned, it was evidently having very little effect. She could not help feeling some anxiety on her behalf.

After some minutes the guests began moving towards the tables, and at this moment Maia, in the middle of telling Sarget about the fish-charming songs of fishermen in Meerzat, suddenly stopped in amazement, hearing a sound she instantly recognized for what it could only be, even though she had never heard it before. She looked round. Milvushina, walking across the hall beside Elvair-ka-Virrion, had burst into laughter.

'And do they really believe in the magical power of these songs?' asked Sarget with interest.

'What? Oh, ah; yes, they reckon a whole lot to them,' answered Maia. She glanced round again, but this time could catch no more than a glimpse of Elvair-ka-Virrion's silver-tasselled shoulders disappearing beyond a tall, fair-haired shearna who rather reminded her of Sessendris.

'I wish you'd sing one of them for us later on,' said Sarget, taking her arm to lead her to her place. 'We seldom hear country music in Bekla, you know, and when we do it never really sounds genuine—not as it would on Lake Serrelind, I'm sure.'

'Oh, but I've no voice, U-Sarget,' answered Maia smilingly. ''Sides, I don't know as I could just remember any of those old songs now; though I dare say if I was swimming in the lake they'd come back easy enough.'

'Then we must get you swimming in the lake—or *a* lake,' said Sarget. 'The Barb, perhaps—'

'Good evening, Maia,' said a voice behind them.

It was Bayub-Otal. Maia had not noticed him among the guests, and it had certainly not occurred to her that he might be a friend of Sarget. However, from the obvious pleasure with which Sarget now greeted him, this was evidently the case. He was wearing a plain, grey robe, without ornament, and round his neck a heavy, silver chain of striking work-manship, the individual links fashioned to resemble reed-clusters, rippling pools, willows, fish, water-fowl and the like. Sarget, smiling, raised a finger to touch it.

'I'm one person who's glad to see you're not afraid to wear a chain like that in Bekla.'

'There *is* no chain like that,' replied Bayub-Otal, returning his smile.

'I don't doubt it,' said Sarget. 'It's an heirloom, I suppose?'

'My father had it made for my mother.'

'I never had the luck to see her, but I've often heard tell of her. Well,' went on Sarget, 'here's the young lady you asked us to make sure of. Elvair-ka-Virrion can usually get what he wants if he puts his mind to it.'

'I'm indebted to him—and to you. By the way, your spring hymn was really excellent—too good for the audience, perhaps. You should keep work like that for your friends in private. But we're delaying the others, aren't we?' And indeed those round them were clearly waiting only for their host to take his place. Sarget, bowing to Maia as though she had been a baron's wife, turned and went to his seat, leaving her with Bayub-Otal.

Here was a nice damned state of basting affairs! she thought angrily. Terebinthia had told her that Elvair-ka-Virrion had asked for her and Milvushina to go to a party. She had said nothing about Bayub-Otal. But then, she thought, in all probability Terebinthia had not known herself. Elvair-ka-Virrion would not have said anything. In the ordinary way Occula might have guessed at the likely truth of the situation and pointed it out, but then she, of course, had not been herself last night.

Maia strove to control her disappointment. She had been simple enough to suppose that Elvair-ka-Virrion must want her again for himself. She might have realized that what was in fact going to be required of her was to continue her work on Bayub-Otal. And Nennaunir had remarked that she must be glad to get away from the High Counsellor for a while! If only Nennaunir knew! she thought. She would actually have preferred Sencho, restored to his normal appetites and ready for the attentions of his favourite, than an evening with this cold, embittered Urtan who seemed—perhaps because no Beklan ladies of birth would consort with him—only to want to treat her as something she was not. Still, if she wanted to go on making progress in Kembri's good graces she had better get down to her job.

'You *asked* for me to come here tonight, my lord?' she said, leaning back on her arm and smiling up into his face.

'I hope you're not sorry,' he answered. 'Between ourselves, it's not the kind of occasion I care for much, but Sarget's one of the few people in Bekla whom I regard as a friend. I didn't want to refuse, and I thought if anyone could help me to enjoy it, it would be you.'

'I'm going to see to it as you do, my lord.'

It did not, in fact, prove such very hard work. The excellent dinner and wine, the luxurious surroundings, the friendly amiability of Nennaunir and others, Maia's confidence in her own beauty and the desire she obviously excited in everyone, it would seem, except Bayub-Otal: these were more than enough to enable her to feel not unkindly towards him. She'd got the measure of him now, she thought, well enough. He didn't know what to do with a girl, but none the less—poor, disappointed loser—like anyone else he wanted to be able to show one to the world: and even apart from her own interests with Kembri, her easiest course was to try to get on with him as well as she could. Irritation might come easily to Maia, but her natural good nature did not readily admit of sustained dislike.

From time to time her eyes wandered to the next table, where Elvair-ka-Virrion was sitting near Sarget. Milvushina was beside him, and it was clear enough that he was enjoying her company. The Chalcon girl had resumed her habitual, grave demeanour and appeared to be doing little more than reply courteously to his remarks and questions. Maia could not help thinking that her sombre self-possession became her very well; Elvair-ka-Virrion obviously thought so too, for he continued talking to her almost exclusively, apparently making every effort to suit his manner to her own. Once or twice—half-reluctantly, as it seemed—she smiled in response.

S'pose she reckons she's back among her own sort, thought Maia; and for a time, jealousy and resentment overcame her. Yet soon these, like her earlier annoyance, were at least to some extent dispelled by simple enjoyment and absorption in her surroundings.

The truth was that this evening Maia was beginning for the first time to grasp something of the difference between style and the mere show of opulence. This, not surprisingly, was a matter to which she had never previously given thought, since neither one nor the other had been exactly plentiful along the shores of Lake Serrelind. Now, she unexpectedly found herself contrasting the hall about her with the rooms in Sencho's house.

Upon her arrival she had been surprised to see so few obviously precious things displayed. Sencho's two halls, as well as the garden-room, were full of hangings, furniture, statues and ornaments—many from the houses of enemies and victims—the costliness of which was plain enough. It suddenly occurred to Maia to wonder whether he would notice if some of them were stolen; and whether Terebinthia might in fact have sold a few without his knowledge. Be that as it might, it crossed her mind (in the act of gnawing a roast duck leg) that clearly someone—presumably Sarget himself—must have given careful thought to the appearance of this hall as a whole, and that his aim had been a display less of wealth than of restrained and congruent beauty and harmony. Restraint, she now realized, was not necessarily a sign of indigence. The purpose and effect of the moist ferns and varied green wall-hangings—however much or little they might have cost—were simply to provide a relatively unobtrusive yet appropriate setting for the guests' own magnificence—for Elvair-ka-Virrion's black-and-crimson, silver-tasselled abshay, Nennaunir's night-blue robe and Bayub-Otal's unique silver chain.

Even more strongly than the decoration of the hall, however, the music made Maia aware of a difference in quality between Sencho's pleasures and those of Sarget and his friends. The very notion of music was so alien to the atmosphere of the High Counsellor's household that it had never before even entered Maia's head to think of it as a deficiency. She would as readily have thought of missing the stars from a cellar. Yet it now struck her that obviously Sencho, if he wished, could well afford musicians as good as these; and thereupon she realized also, not only that he did not want them—that music meant nothing to him—but also that this insensitivity could not really be attributed solely to the poverty and hardship of his origins; for Tharrin, if he were somehow or other to become rich, would certainly take pleasure in having his own musicians: so, probably, would Zuno. She began to perceive more clearly why so many of these people despised Sencho even while they feared him and perforce afforded him the show of respect.

Smiling and conversing with Bayub-Otal, teasingly or otherwise as the mood took her (for Maia's conversational style knew little of reserve or convention), she was nevertheless almost continuously aware of the softly plangent, bitter-sweet tone of the hinnaris interweaving, darting here and there like swallows, back and forth in a patterned harmony above the dark water of the drums. In her fancy the intermittent flutes became gleams of light, the soft crescendos of the zerda and derlanzel a distant rustling of leaves. The minor, repeated phrases of the Palteshi *rogan* which they were playing seemed infinitely vivid and compelling, moving her almost to tears. Bayub-Otal, she sensed, felt this also, and was aware that she felt it too; for gradually his conversation ceased and he sat unspeaking, gazing into his wine-cup and silently—almost imperceptibly—following the rhythm of the drums with his finger-tips. Once, turning his head, he caught Maia's eye with a half-smile and she, her task of pleasing him become that much easier, smiled back and for an instant rubbed her shoulder against his.

At this moment, once more catching sight of Milvushina, she was surprised to find herself thinking how beautiful she looked. Her great, dark eyes and delicate, olive-skinned features, which to Maia had always seemed so lacking in vitality and warmth, were now turned towards Elvair-ka-Virrion, if not with animation, at least with alert attention. After a few moments, as he ceased speaking, she smiled and replied a few words, upon which he at once resumed, nodding in corroboration of what she had said. Maia had always thought Milvushina naturally aloof. Now she began to wonder whether the truth might not be that in the women's quarters at Sencho's she had merely been unable to feel interest in anyone or anything around her: whether, even setting aside the natural effect of her misery, she had found no one capable of making her feel inclined to say much more than she had to. Tonight it seemed as though some hitherto-withheld part of her was hesitantly re-emerging. Either Elvair-ka-Virrion had been able to make her—at least to some extent—genuinely forget her grief, or else self-respect was impelling her to assume, for his benefit, some semblance of the one-time baron's daughter of Chalcon.

Without going so far as actually to feel selflessly happy on Milvushina's account (bearing in mind her disappointment over Elvair-ka-Virrion, this would scarcely have been natural), Maia, to her credit, was genuinely pleased to see that her frozen grief was apparently capable of being melted, and hoped that more might come of it. To see Milvushina at last showing a little—however little—warmth made her feel that after all they might yet find that they had something in common.

Once more drawn by the music into a delicious oblivion of her surroundings, she closed her eyes, listening with parted lips and even holding her breath in the intensity of her pleasure. With Maia, delight in music had always involved a physical response, at least with her body if not with her voice as well. Now, without reflection or self-consciousness, she began to sway gently where she sat. Once or twice she nodded her head, as though with inward corroboration that the music had indeed taken that delightful turn which she had expected; and once she spread her hands, as though to represent the gesture of the goddess by whose liberality such beauty was vouchsafed to humankind. Two or three men sitting near-by caught each other's eyes, smiling at the naïveté of the pretty child, while one made a facetious pantomime of craning his neck and shaking his head as he looked into her wine-cup.

342

Supper was nearly at an end. In accordance with Beklan custom some of the guests, in twos and threes, were beginning to get up and stroll out of the hall, either into the corridors or as far as the westward-facing portico of the palace, whence they could look out across the city walls towards the afterglow beyond the far-off Palteshi hills. The rest, either still inclined for eating, or simply for remaining where they were to converse or to listen to the music, relaxed luxuriously, while their shearnas fanned them and the slaves carried round trays of sweetmeats.

Throughout the whole of this gentle disturbance, Elvair-ka-Virrion still sat absorbed in talk with Milvushina. One or two of his friends, having failed to distract him, gathered about Sarget on their own account, enquiring banteringly—for they knew his somewhat staid reputation—what he had in mind for their entertainment and whether he had ever composed any music for a kura. The fastidious Sarget, though on the one hand wishing to continue to stand well with these young men, on the other hoped to avoid seeing his supper-party take on the tone of the Rains banquet and such-like functions governed by the tastes of men like Kembri or Sencho. As he sat smilingly temporizing and assuring a young man named Shend-Lador, the son of the citadel castellan, that he knew Nennaunir was anxious to get to know him better, Bayub-Otal, appearing quietly at his shoulder, stooped and whispered a few words in his ear.

Sarget, rising, at once took the Urtan's arm and led him out into the corridor, leaving the young Leopards to mutter and shrug their shoulders over what they regarded as an intrusion. A minute or two later, however, the two returned and walked over to where the musicians were squatting together near the centre of the hall. The music died away, and as it did so Maia looked up, opening her eyes and giving a little shake to her head, as though awakening.

Fordil, the elder of the two hinnarists, a musician whose name and skill were known from Kabin to Ikat, nodded as he listened to U-Sarget, from time to time looking round at his drummers to make sure that they too had understood the patron. Maia, watching them and wondering what was in preparation—some kind of Urtan music, presumably (why should that wretched Bayub-Otal have gone and interrupted her enjoyment?)— was suddenly puzzled and confused to see them all looking round in her direction. She dropped her eyes and reddened, wondering what might have been said. The next moment Bayub-Otal was standing beside her.

'Maia,' said Bayub-Otal—and now, or so it seemed to the disconcerted Maia, everyone was listening—'U-Sarget wishes you to dance for us.'

Maia, a clutch in her stomach, stared at him speechlessly.

'I've told Fordil,' added Bayub-Otal, smiling; in earnest or in mockery? she wondered, 'that you'd probably like to dance the senguela. I assure

343

you that you'll find him an accompanist of very different quality from that man at "The Green Grove"; and the floor's all that even my mother could have wished. They're sweeping it now, as you can see.'

Maia, looking round her in a daze, saw that Sarget himself was personally directing two slaves with brooms.

'My lord, I can't, really I can't—oh, my lord, you must tell him—you must tell U-Sarget, please—'

'Maia,' replied Bayub-Otal, scarcely moving his lips, 'Elvair-ka-Virrion brought you here at my request. U-Sarget and I wish you to dance.'

His manner, following upon his courteous, friendly behaviour during dinner, filled Maia with sudden rage. If ever Occula's dreams were to come true, and the two of them became shearnas with all Bekla at their feet, then first and foremost she would settle accounts with this bloodless, high-handed bastard of an Urtan baron. Meanwhile she could only set her teeth and do her best to show him he couldn't put *her* out of countenance— for that could only be what he was trying to do. Without another word she stood up, raised her palm to her forehead with a gesture as ironic as she could make it; then turned and walked—steadily, she hoped—across to the musicians.

'I have no money, U-Fordil,' she said, pulling up the hem of the cherry-coloured skirt and dropping to her knees beside him on the floor. 'I'm only a slave-girl as yet. But do your best for me and I promise I won't forget you.'

Old Fordil, smiling, inclined his grey head towards her with a fatherly look.

'We don't need to be asked for our best, my lass. We *are* the best. Lean on us as hard as you like—the rope won't break. You're going to dance the senguela?'

'Yes.'

'Selpé and reppa? The whole thing?'

She nodded.

Fordil smiled again. 'Sure you can manage it? If it's just on account of orders and you feel it's too much, I can probably get you out of it. Only it's generally better, you know, to stick to something you're sure of.'

'I'm going to dance the whole thing,' answered Maia firmly.

'Then Lespa be with you, little säiyett,' replied Fordil. 'I shall be, anyway.'

Maia, leaning over, gave his bristly cheek a kiss. 'Thank you, U-Fordil. No one's ever called me "säiyett" before. I'll remember that.'

One of the drummers looked up from tightening the cords round his zhua. 'That dress—think it'll fall quick enough?'

Maia nodded again. 'It'll fall.' Thereupon she rose to her feet, walked a few steps into the middle of the empty floor, turned towards Sarget and stood waiting for the *frissoor*.

It was customary in Bekla for a dancer or singer to await from her host, initially, a signal of invitation, known as the frissoor. Once this had been received the performer, even if a slave, had the complete right to order everything as she wished—the space about her, the lamps, the music— even, if she insisted, the dismissal of anyone unwelcome to her. Thus, the leader of the Thlela had sought the frissoor from Durakkon at the Rains banquet, and Occula from Elvair-ka-Virrion before her now almost legendary act as the doomed huntress. As soon as Sarget, smiling reassuringly, had extended his left hand and then lowered it to his side, Maia, with the best air of authority she could muster, beckoned to two slaves and, having told them what she wanted, stood impassively while they moved or extinguished sufficient lamps to make one side of the central floor bright and the other shadowy and dim.

The hall seemed to have filled again. Word, it appeared, had got round that she was about to dance, and men and girls had come back, some to their former places, others merely to stand wherever it might suit them—a few near the doors, ready to slip out again if she should prove a disappointment. With a quick smile she gestured to Shend-Lador and a girl with him to move back from the edge of the floor, and felt delighted surprise when they did so at once. Whoever would have thought it? It worked for her, just as for anyone else who had received the frissoor.

Suddenly she knew that Lespa was with her. Kind, merciful Lespa was looking down from the stars at her servant about to honour her—Lespa of the heart's secrets, Lespa, sender of dreams! A few moments more she stood in silence, offering herself to the goddess. Then she spread her hands; and at once the zhuas began the low, throbbing opening of the selpé.

She was Lespa—mortal Lespa, the prettiest village lass that ever walked the earth—Lespa on her way to the greenwood, tripping through the meadows of spring. The grass was cool at her feet, the flowers were springing—ah! and here was a patch of muddy ground she had to cross. Pouting, she stopped and wiped her feet, one and then the other; then stooped to pick a yellow spear-bud and put it in her hair. Her body was burning with frustrated longing, with desire for her lover, for poor young Baltis gone to the wars.

During this first, opening minute she realized what Bayub-Otal had meant in speaking of Fordil. She had never conceived of any accompaniment of this quality. She would not have thought it possible. The quick, pattering notes of the hinnari seemed actually created by her own movements. They did not follow her; they led her on and bore her forward. It was Fordil who was really dancing, except that she, happening to be young and a girl, was acting on his behalf. She was his reflection, and therefore they could not be out of accord.

A kynat, migrant of spring, purple and gold in the sunshine, flashed suddenly out of the distant trees and she stood entranced, shading her eyes to gaze after it as it flew. Then, recalling her errand, she went on up the course of the little brook towards the watercress-edged cattle-wade on the outskirts of the wood.

When dancing for Occula Maia, throughout this first episode of the selpé, had always felt, above all, the pathos of a girl left forlorn in spring; intensely aware of the multifoliate burgeoning of the new year all about her, yet separated from it by her loneliness. To stress this sense of loneliness, she knew, was important as a contrast to the excitement to follow. She was a girl sad in springtime: this was what she had to express; and now the hinnari, with a soft sobbing of zhuas beneath, was saying it for her as, in Occula's hands, it had never been able to.

How long should she give it? Not very long, for this was only the prelude to her story. Bending down, she pulled some strands of watercress and nibbled them; then sprawled on the short grass in the sunshine, first picking her teeth with a twig, then rolling quickly over to catch a tiny frog and let it jump off her hand into the water. So clearly did she mime these things and so closely did the drummer follow her, that the frog's leap was represented by a quick, sharp stroke of his thimbled finger on the side of the hollow lek, at which Maia herself, watching the frog, spontaneously gave a little jump. The watchers laughed, not only at the joke but with pleasure in the skill which had enabled them to recognize it. A moment later she got up and, disentangling her skirt from a spray of bramble as she climbed the fence, entered the wood, disappearing into the darkness on the lampless side of the hall.

Almost at once—more quickly than she would have wished, but she guessed that Fordil wanted to forestall any possible outbreak of chatter or restlessness among the audience—the music changed to the quick, light knocking of the two leks, playing alone. Yet she herself must wait a moment; she could not change her rôle so quickly. This was Shakkarn coming— Shakkarn stolen away in spring from the palace of the gods to wander footloose among the fields and woods of earth. Far off he was as yet, his footsteps faint but coming closer, sending before them the disquiet and apprehension latent in all sounds of approach by someone or something unknown to the hearer. And at this moment, as luck would have it, two of the lamps, their oil exhausted, simultaneously flickered and died. A total silence fell throughout the hall, save for the tapping of the leks answering each other, hoofed footstep and echo, among the rocks high up in the wood.

Occula had told her that sometimes a girl would elect to play Shakkarn masked and horned, and thus disguised as the god would appear in full light as plainly as in the part of Lespa. Yet this was not the true style of the senguela, the *tonda* and the other great traditional dances. 'So often, banzi, a pretty girl wants to show off as Lespa, but she only wants to dress up as Shakkarn. That's not real senguela! You've got to *be* Shakkarn— make them believe you're another person—well, almost.' And had not Maia seen Occula herself perform just such a feat on the night when Ka-Roton had taken the phantom knife and stabbed himself?

Here came Shakkarn; barely to be seen, a shadow among dark trees; half-brute, peering from side to side, pausing to sniff the air, plunging into the stream and shaking the water from his back as he lurched himself up and out; Shakkarn grinning and licking his lips like a hound, pausing to rub himself against the stump of a tree. Then, almost as soon as glimpsed, he had vanished again into the blackness; but it was enough. A noise of running, and on the flutes startled birds flew up in the distance. Something umbral was slinking away, disappearing between the tree-trunks; re-emerging for a moment to peer out, round-eyed, slobbering with excitement, kindled by what he had caught sight of in the glade below. Then once again, swift as a lizard, he was gone.

Maia, racing silently round the darkened edge of the hall, reached the opposite side quickly enough to create the effect of surprise she wanted. Hardly, it seemed, had the wanton god been lost to sight in the forest than here came pretty Lespa, gathering sticks, getting together a good, stout faggot to carry home; pausing to listen to the song of a greenbreast from the outskirts of the wood. Still going about her work, she came upon the pool; brown and clear, not too deep and not too cold, for she dabbled one foot in it to try.

As the hinnaris rippled about her in liquid cascades of descending quarter-tones Maia, with a single, swift movement, loosed the halter of the cherry-coloured robe, let it fall to her ankles and stepped naked into the pool, giving a quick shudder and clutching her arms about her as she felt the first chill. She was still standing on the floor of the hall, yet now the water was nearly up to her shoulders and her feet were groping on the stones as she waded slowly forward. Cupping her hands, she splashed water into her face, laughed and tossed back her wet hair. She, at all events, knew where she was now; under the falls on the edge of Lake Serrelind.

For a little she made all she could of this most beguiling of scenes, bringing to it every scrap of invention at her command. She had been naked often enough for Sencho. She had been naked for Kembri, for Elvair-ka-Virrion, for Eud-Ecachlon, for Randronoth of Lapan; but never before for the delectation of eighty men and women at once. Under the bravado which she had assumed to Fordil and his drummers she had been very nervous, but had thrust the fear away by telling herself (as might a soldier) that it had simply got to be done and that was all there was to it. Now that it was here, however, she was delighting in it. Intermittently, glancing up through the splashed water and her own wet hair, she glimpsed, on the edge of the surrounding lamplight, the fascinated eyes of the watchers, and felt her power over them. 'I am Lespa,' she thought. 'I am Lespa of the inmost heart.' Her nakedness was no mere matter of tantalizing young men like Shend-Lador. It was the revelation of womanhood by the goddess. Not to be naked now would have been irreverent and impious.

Ah, but it was heady stuff, this! And here she might have remained, displaying herself in the pool, and well content would they have been to watch on, even until she had dishonoured the goddess with her selfish vanity. Some girls did, and so she had been warned. But against this the good Fordil stood her friend. Oh, but one moment, Fordil! Just one more plunge, turning on my back and sliding upward to the bank! I do it so well! But no—she must obey him, must obey the goddess, obey the story and the music. For here, broken loose, straying aimlessly one might suppose, never a care, no harm in the world, down through the wood and grazing as he wandered, came the goat Shakkarn. Oh, but such a goat, the music said, such a goat as no lout of a farmer ever held on a chain; milk-white, silky-coated, his great, curving horns like the frame of a lyre, his hooves shining smooth as bronze. From the pool Lespa stared in wonder, her eyes following the goat rambling here and there as he cropped the green leaves. Then, as he hesitantly, almost timidly, approached to drink, she rested her two hands on the bank, drew herself out of the water and sat close by him in the sunshine.

Everyone in the hall could see the magnificent creature—not merely because his likeness was carved on the walls of temples all over the empire, not only because he lay in their minds and their dreams as surely as doomsday or the flood, but above all because he was real to the girl sitting beside him, her body seeming to glisten with water-drops as she gently stretched out one hand to touch him, to stroke his back as he stood docile on the margin of the pool. She put her arms round his neck and rubbed her cheek against his ear.

Then followed the slow dawning in Lespa's mind that this paragon of beasts was indeed male: and that she herself—ah! Round-eyed, open-mouthed, she sprang up, fleeing a little way in hot shame: yet still her companion made no move and showed no impatience as the inmost secret stirred in her, revealing to her that she herself, she too—And here Maia stood for long moments down-glancing, trembling, bewildered. At last a little smile came to her lips and she took one single, tentative step to return to him whom she herself had summoned unaware.

The mounting excitement as Lespa, of her own accord, began their love-play was conveyed by Maia, as Occula had taught her, shamelessly, in the sense that shame had been discarded, a thing of no meaning to the consort of a god (''cos you can be sure of one thing, banzi—whatever goddesses have, it's not shame: else they'd be liars'). As at length he seemed to draw back, tantalized beyond endurance by the touch of her hands, only next moment to press himself yet more eagerly upon her; and as she rose, laughing, inviting him to go with her into the recesses of the wood, more than one couple followed her example and slipped away out of the hall on their own business.

And now Maia, once again out of sight in the darkness, found herself faced with a dilemma, unforeseen in her agitation at being so suddenly called upon to dance. Now she had to become the prying old woman—and here she was, naked and costumeless, without even a dresser to help her. Fordil himself had not anticipated or remembered this. Whatever was she to do? At all costs things must not go wrong now! In desperation she beat her fist on the wall; and as she did so felt the smooth texture of one of Sarget's panels of green cloth.

The panels, side by side and slightly overlapping, had been hung one above another in two rows. Each woven piece measured about seven or eight feet square, with loops at the upper corners by which it was hung on nails driven between the stones. Standing on tiptoe, she lifted down a square of fabric, wrapped herself in it from head to foot and drew up one corner as a hood. Then, as the zhuas began the comic, shuffling rhythm of the old woman's gait—*boom* da-da-da, *boom* da-da-da—she came hobbling once more into the light.

The peering, prurient curiosity of the old woman, her outrage at what she saw, her envious disgust, her hurry-scurry back to the village, her jabbering to her cronies and their setting forth in a body to put paid to the shameless hussy up in the wood—these things Maia rattled through, playing them very broadly, Meerzat festival-fashion, a peasant making fun of peasants. Perhaps, indeed, she overdid it a little, for the old woman in her haste need not really have trodden in a cow-pat and gone hopping about; but it got a laugh. Off they all hurried to the forest, and in the emptiness left behind, the two hinnaris began the reppa—the universally-known song of Shakkarn, hymn of Lespa's humility and acceptance of the inmost longing revealed. The audience began a low clapping to the rocking, thrusting rhythm—for it was impossible not to reciprocate—and all eyes were turned once more towards the dim glade whither Lespa had stolen away with her divine companion.

But Maia was not where they had expected. Exercising the privilege of the frissoor, she had taken possession of the dais behind their backs; and here she was lying on the great table, all among the scattered flower-garlands, her parted legs, bent at the knees, clasped about her invisible lover as Lespa writhed in her joy. No one saw her until, as she gave a swift, inarticulate cry of pleasure—the only sound she had uttered all through the story—they turned in surprise, pressing forward, all of them consumed to look at her once again as she lay striving in the half-light, head flung back and hair streaming.

So now they themselves had involuntarily assumed the part of the villagers—the mean-minded louts and harridans come to besmirch her bliss, to rub the butterfly's wings between their dirty fingers and thumbs. Lespa, suddenly aware of them, buried her face in her hands, rolled quickly over and dropped off the table into the shadow beneath.

Following the tradition of the senguela, the climax of the reppa—the apotheosis of Lespa through the celestial love of Shakkarn—could be represented in various ways, according to the resources of the occasion and the temperament of the dancer. Sometimes, when her surroundings made this practicable, the girl would pace, divine and unheeding, straight through the audience, ascend a staircase and so be gone; or again, she might be escorted by children dressed as cherubs to a goat-horned throne set among clouds and stars. But no such help was available to Maia. Neither could Fordil help her. Yet on the music went, an audible expression of that ineffable harmony for ever sounding in the ears of the gods, and on she must go with it. Slowly she stood up, her face radiant (and goodness knows I got something to be happy about, she thought, else I'm very much mistook), and began, on the level floor of the dais, to climb easily upward, her limbs unhindered by the least weight from her body—for had she not become a goddess?—first through the trees (she parted their branches before her), then through the clouds and at last among the glittering aisles of the stars. Once or twice she stretched out a hand—the graceful, sturdy girl—to that of her divine lover, manifest now as the god Shakkarn, he whose animal nature she had accepted in herself and embraced in her erstwhile humanity. He ascended with her until, among the last whisperings of the hinnaris and the lightest breathings of the flutes, she stood motionless, arms outspread, head down-bent in blessing, to take up her eternal, nightly task of scattering truth in dreams to all the dwellers upon earth. And thus she remained, aloft upon the table and gazing gravely downward as the music at last died away and ceased.

For long seconds there was silence throughout the hall. Then a murmur like a sigh rose from her audience. As it died away a man in a blue robe, standing a few feet from Sarget, asked him, 'Who is the girl?' Before

Sarget could reply, however, Elvair-ka-Virrion, looking quickly round, answered 'She's Maia—from Serrelind!' At this others, laughing, began teasing the blue-robed man, turning towards him and echoing, 'Maia! She's Maia!'

Gradually this took on the nature of an ovation. 'Maia!' called Elvair-ka-Virrion again, raising his hand in the traditional sign of salute to the winner of a contest. Shend-Lador and several other young men took it up. One, pushing his way forward, climbed the steps of the dais and fell on his knees before the table. From all sides came cries of 'Maia! Maia!' as the company, both men and women, raised their hands, fingers outspread, in the gesture of acclaim.

Maia, bewildered now and uncertain what it would be best for her to do, still made no response, even with a glance or a smile. During the close of the reppa she had become virtually oblivious of being watched. Self-forgotten as a child in play, to herself she had been Lespa, and had even seen the dreams drifting like snowflakes from her down-turned fingers upon the sleeping earth below. She had not forsaken her audience; she had transcended them. She had, in fact, been not far from the presence of the goddess; and was seldom to feel herself so close again (such moments, not to be commanded even through the greatest skill or experience, being a matter of grace and coming when they will). At no time, of course, had she ceased being to some extent aware of her real surroundings, but during the dance their aspect and her relation to them had become transformed. Now they slowly resumed once more their normal, mundane properties. The effect was a kind of shock. As everyone round her was noisily affirming, she was Maia, standing naked on a table before the eyes of some eighty men and women whom she had just excited to fever-pitch. What should she do now? Climb down from the table, scramble back into her dress and accept a drink? This struck her as less than seemly. Yet for the life of her she could not think of any truly fitting way to conclude what she had accomplished.

So there she stood, unmoving. It was Sarget himself—probably the most sensitive man in the room—who, discerning her predicament, came to her rescue. A slave had already retrieved her dress from where she had shed it and was now standing near the doors, holding it over his arm. Sarget, however, ignored him, went quickly out into the corridor and, before the ovation had subsided, returned carrying a fur cloak. Climbing on to the table, he stood for a few moments beside the still-rapt Maia, smiling and waving acknowledgement on her behalf. Then, wrapping the cloak round her shoulders, he helped her down and gave her his arm out of the hall.

Sarget, having led her to a room along the corridor, remained only to speak a few words of praise—Maia could do no more than smile in reply—before leaving her alone. What he might be going to arrange she had no idea and felt too much exhausted even to wonder.

A minute later Nennaunir came in, carrying the cherry-coloured dress.

'Do you know what you've done, my dear?' she asked. 'They've all gone mad for you! There are forty goats out there, not just one—and if they're not gods, at least they're real. Gods don't give lygols, either. If you want your pick I shouldn't leave it too long, 'cos you've put all the girls in heat as well.'

'The girls?' answered Maia vaguely. 'How's that, then?'

'Oh, really, my dear, surely you know—women get almost more excited than men when they watch that sort of thing. Every woman fancies it's herself up there, driving all the men out of their minds. But you were splendid, you know. Wherever did you learn?'

'Occula taught me—just to pass the time, kind of style.'

'Really? Then, Maia dear, all I can say is you've got great talent: you certainly mustn't waste it. I'll gladly help you. I'll—' She broke off. 'But how can I, while you belong to that pig? Does *he* know you can do that?'

Maia laughed. 'Didn't know it myself. No, he don't; nor he wouldn't care if he did.'

Suddenly there rose before her mind's eye the face of Chia, the cast-eyed girl whom she and Occula had met at Lalloc's. What sort of luck might Chia have had since then? Little enough, most likely. How strange, she thought, to find myself sorry to belong to the High Counsellor of Bekla! Don't know when I'm well off, do I?

'Whose is this cloak, d'you suppose?' she asked, to change the subject; for Nennaunir would not want to continue talking about Sencho. 'What a beauty, isn't it?' She slipped it off and began getting dressed.

'It's mine,' said the shearna. 'I told Sarget to take it for you. The governor of Kabin gave it me last time he was here. It cost eight thousand meld.'

'Eight thousand meld?' Maia stared.

'Governors collect taxes; didn't you know? Otherwise why be a governor? Don't worry, pet—you go on as you've started and you'll be getting as good before long, take my word for it. Anyway, I'll give you a hand with your dress if you like: and here's a comb. You ought to go back while they're still asking for you, you know. Who's the girl who came with you, by the way? Pretty, isn't she? Does *she* belong to filthy Sencho, too?'

'Yes; he got her after Meris was sold.'

Nennaunir waited, clearly expecting more. After a few moments, as Maia added nothing, she said, '*She's* no peasant: anyone can see that. Father ruined, or something?'

'I'm not just too sure about the rights of it, tell you the truth.' Maia had no intention of risking the punishment which Terebinthia had threatened.

'*Aren't* you?' replied Nennaunir rather curtly. 'Oh, well, if you don't— Anyway, she's evidently made a great impression on Elvair. They've been together all the evening. Sarget brought a girl for Elvair but in fact he's hardly spoken to her. Never mind—I hope it does your friend some good, the poor banzi. She's lost more than most, if I'm any judge.'

There was a tap at the door. Maia, a slave with no claim to privacy and in any case unaccustomed to such niceties, made no response, but Nennaunir called 'Come in!'

Bayub-Otal entered, followed by a servant with wine, fruit and biscuits. Maia, rather taken aback, was slower than she should have been to look delighted, but her lapse was expertly covered by the more experienced Nennaunir, who was on her feet in a moment, all smiles.

'Come to congratulate her, my lord, or to get ahead of the others—or both? U-Sarget told me it was your idea for her to dance. You knew then, did you, how good she was?'

'She may *become* very good, I think,' replied Bayub-Otal composedly, 'in time.' He crossed over to the table, poured some of the wine and handed a goblet to each girl. 'And with more practice.'

Nennaunir was far too adept to be provoked or to take up cudgels. 'Well, if *you* think that, my lord, I'm sure she can feel really proud. There's plenty of girls who'd like to have been standing on that table tonight, but none I know who'd have got the acclaim she did.'

Bayub-Otal made no reply and after a moment Nennaunir, murmuring something about needing to have a word with U-Sarget, slipped out of the room.

Maia went on combing her hair, which crackled and floated above her bare shoulders. She wondered in what manner this strange man would embark on the business of expressing his desire—for this was obviously what he must have come for. In a way, she reflected, he had already begun to do so, by compelling her to perform the senguela. He had clearly been determined to see her dance again. He had placed confidence in her. However slight her natural inclination towards him, she could only feel deeply grateful for that. It was entirely to him that she owed this outstanding success, which might very possibly lead on to—who could tell what? Well, she would certainly pay her debt to him, and warmly and bountifully at that, even though he might not be exactly her idea of Shakkarn incarnate. Her beauty, her body, was all she had to give him, and her gratitude was as sincere as it could be. Indeed, at this moment Maia had quite forgotten her ulterior, secret purpose—Kembri's purpose. Why, now she came to think about it, she would positively enjoy giving herself to him—yes, really! She'd no doubt be able to help him—teach him a thing or two. Oh, yes, he had a funny way with him, but then he'd had a funny life—and his poor hand and all. After this evening she really couldn't find it in her heart to deny him. He deserved a nice time, he really did.

He had still done nothing to break the silence. Why not a hand on her shoulder? Or better still, his lips to her shoulder; then her cheek could turn just a little and touch his. What a pity he seemed never to have learned any such ways! Well, but even so, he could at least speak, surely? He'd had time enough now, in all conscience, to think of something to say.

She turned round on her stool. Bayub-Otal was sitting on a bench, his back against the table, gazing absently down into his wine-cup with the air of one waiting without impatience. He certainly didn't look nervous or tense; not in the least like a man wondering what best to say or how to say it. Glancing up, his eye met hers, whereupon he smiled slightly, nodded and sipped his wine.

'Nearly ready?'

Perplexed, she frowned a moment. 'Oh, yes, I'm quite done, my lord.'

She stood up, turning one way and the other to make sure her skirt swung freely. 'Were you waiting for me? I'm ready all right!'

She crossed over and sat beside him on the bench. 'My lord—I can't thank you enough for making me dance tonight. I was nervous—I was real scared—when you first told me; but you knew better than I did, didn't you?'

'I thought you ought to have the opportunity. One can't always expect to have Fordil, you see.'

'Oh, he was wonderful! I never knew—I couldn't have imagined—and the drummers, too—I mean, I couldn't have gone wrong if I'd tried.'

'I've paid him for you, by the way. I gave him what he'd have got from a shearna.'

This was her cue—all the cue she seemed likely to get, anyway. She flung her arms round his neck, and would have kissed him; but he turned his face aside.

'Oh, thank you, thank you, my lord! And did *you* like it? Did I do as well as you'd hoped?'

'You weren't bad as Shakkarn.' He paused, considering. 'And you were most resourceful, I admit. It hadn't occurred to me—it should have, of course—that without a costume or a dresser you'd be in difficulties over the old woman. I blame myself for that. But you certainly got over it very neatly.'

'You've been marvellously good to me, my lord, really you have. I'm so grateful! What can I do to show it to you?'

He shrugged. 'Practise, I suppose.'

354

She waited for him to go on, but he was silent. Elated and full of her triumph, she was now consumed with sheer, raw desire. For him? she wondered. For a man, anyway. Then, Yes! yes! certainly for him! Yes, of course, for him! Come on, then!

She rose, put her wine-cup on the table and sat down on his knee. After a moment, since he made no move to support or embrace her, she once more put her arm round his neck. Her other hand, finding his, drew it up to her bosom and fondled it back and forth.

'You're the kindest man I've ever known. I mean it, truly. Oh—' She looked impatiently about the room—'isn't there somewhere we can go—?'

Rather absently, he drew his hand away. 'Well, I came to take you—I can't call it "home", unfortunately for you—but to where you live, anyway.'

'To take me *home*, my lord?'

'Well, you see, there are a great many people in the hall who want to—well, give you money and so on. Here's Sarget's lygol, by the way. I asked him to give it to me, so that you wouldn't have to go back. That'll keep your säiyett happy, I suppose. And Elvair-ka-Virrion will be seeing to your friend, I'm told.'

Maia stood up, and at once he did so too.

'What do you mean, my lord, "I won't have to go back"?'

'There's a jekzha waiting for you in the courtyard,' replied Bayub-Otal, 'just along the corridor.'

Before she could control herself, Maia had hurled her bronze wine-cup across the room. Dented on one side, it leapt, rolled a few feet and came to rest in a corner.

'And suppose I happen to want to stay here, my lord?'

Bayub-Otal picked up the goblet and put it back on the table.

'There seems little point in staying in this room.'

'I mean, suppose I happen to want to go back into the hall?'

'I'm afraid you can't: I don't wish it.'

'And I *do*!'

'As I've already told you once before this evening, Maia, you were brought here at my request. It would be a pity if Elvair-ka-Virrion had to tell your säiyett that you wouldn't do what you were told.'

Maia walked over to the window and stood staring out into the moon-light. Tears of mortification filled her eyes. Yet there was no point in saying more: Bayub-Otal, she knew, would be immutable. But what could he want? What did he mean by subjecting her to this motiveless, pointless humiliation, involving no gain to himself?

'Just as you wish, my lord. But perhaps you'd kindly allow me to go back alone to the High Counsellor's. It's only a mile through the upper city, so there's no danger.'

'I'll fetch your cloak,' replied Bayub-Otal.

Maia, left alone, stood with closed eyes, gripping the edge of the table. Gradually she sank down until she was kneeling, her forehead resting on the wood.

'O Cran and Airtha, curse him! Lespa, darken his heart! Shakkarn, send down on him the Last Evil!'

Realizing that she was kneeling in the spilt wine, she got up. Anyway, where was the sense? She was no priestess; she hadn't the power of cursing. She had no power at all—yet. Ah! but she'd a fair taste of it tonight, before he'd gone and spoilt everything.

'To be desired,' she said aloud—and now she spoke calmly—'to be desired by everyone—that's power! To be desired, that's—an army of soldiers. If ever I can harm him—oh, if ever I can harm him, I will!'

: 38 :

THE TEMPLE OF CRAN

It was two hours after dawn. Durakkon, clad in the golden, black-dappled robes of the High Baron, was standing with a small entourage on the rostrum outside the Blue Gate. On either side of him rose the backward-sloping walls of the outer precinct, forming a kind of funnel down which the paved roadway led eastward from the gate itself to the junction, outside the city, of the highways from Thettit-Tonilda and Ikat Yeldashay.

In spite of the water sprinkled on the stones below, dust covered Durakkon's robes and had filled his mouth and nose. For half an hour he had been standing on the platform, while below him the Tonildan and Beklan regiments, some three thousand men in all, marched out of the city for the Valderra front. The two contingents, having mustered in Bekla upon the first slackening of the rains and spent several days in equipping and refitting, had been assembled by Kembri at dawn that morning in the Caravan Market. Apart from his anxiety to reach the Valderra as soon as possible, the Lord General wanted no delay in getting the men out of the city, where soldiers in the mass were always liable to cause trouble through fighting, theft, rape and the like. Watched by the usual crowd of grieving girls, proud but sorrowful parents, envious younger brothers and angry tavern-keepers, trulls and similar creditors making last, vain efforts to collect what was due to them, the regiments had been inspected and addressed by Kembri and then marched out of the city by the nearest gate.

Durakkon, thinking it only fitting that the High Baron as well as the Lord General should be present at their departure, had decided against coming to the Caravan Market (where he could only appear second in importance) and taken up his position outside the Blue Gate. Notwithstanding the dust and discomfort, it had proved worthwhile. Several of the companies had cheered him as they passed and he had spoken personally with eight or nine senior officers.

Although it was common knowledge that as High Baron he lacked force and domination, Durakkon had a fine presence and a name for honesty and benevolence at least. The feeling of most of the men, as they recognized him standing on the platform, had been that although it was not going to make any difference either to their comfort or their success, he had nevertheless done the decent thing in turning out to see them off, and accordingly they cheered him sincerely.

There was another good reason for the regiments' early departure. This was the day fixed for the spring festival. Kembri had originally intended to get them out the morning before, but had been unable, owing to the late delivery of certain supplies. It was now vital that they should be gone before the festival began, for otherwise they—or even the city itself—might very well get out of control. During the past three days crowds from all over the provinces had been pouring into Bekla. The lower city, even without the soldiers, was already thronged to overflowing, and the householders on whom they had been billeted were impatient to see the back of them and attract paying lodgers instead. From the point of view of law and order they were probably leaving in the nick of time.

During their departure all incoming traffic through the Blue Gate had been stopped. As the last company of the Tonildan regiment came out from between the walls, turning north and then west in the rear of the column, hundreds of wayfarers, who had been waiting beside the road as the soldiers went by, came surging down the outer precinct towards the Blue Gate.

Durakkon, not having foreseen this, found himself cut off on the rostrum and unable to take his departure, for clearly the High Baron could not jostle his way back into the city among pilgrims and drovers. His entourage was insufficient for an escort and in any case the crowd was too dense. So on the platform Durakkon remained, coughing in the dust raised by the sweating, shoving tide below. He had despatched one of his aides for an officer and thirty men to accompany him back to the upper city. He could do no more.

Durakkon had always had a sincere feeling for the common people. That, indeed, was what had seduced him into the seizure of power and the predicament of rule. Now, not ill-humouredly despite his discomfort, he

357

stood looking here and there about the precinct below, observing this person and that among the multitude pushing on towards the gate. Here, if anywhere, he could see, almost as though depicted on a great scroll, the range of his subjects—men and women from every part of the empire, as well as some from beyond its borders.

A gang of thirty or forty market women, typical of those who regularly tramped the twenty-odd miles to the big commercial gardens along the banks of the upper Zhairgen to buy fruit and vegetables for sale in Bekla, went past together, each carrying on her head a full pannier. Close behind came a Kabin bird-catcher, capped and belted with bright feathers and hung about with wicker cages containing his prisoners for sale. Two, Durakkon noticed, were already dead. Three solemn-looking, grey-bearded men, each wearing the corn-sheaves emblem of Sarkid—by their bearing, persons of standing back home—looked up as they passed and saluted him by raising their staves. Following them, singing raucously and waving leather bottles as they rallied those around them in the crowd, came a troop of long-whiskered Deelguy with silver rings in their ears and at least four knives to each man's belt. Among these, and apparently accepted by them as companions, were a lank, tough-looking young man in the uniform of a licensed pedlar, and a pretty, dark-haired girl—Belishban, by her appearance—who was limping and plainly very tired. Probably, thought Durakkon, she had been walking all night. For a moment he had a vague notion that he had seen her somewhere before. However, he could not remember where, and next moment she was gone, leaning heavily on her pedlar-lad's arm.

But now the High Baron recognized a wealthy Gelt iron-master, one Bodrin, carried in a chair on the shoulders of four slaves. Calling down to him by name, he invited him to join him on the rostrum. The man climbed up, and after the usual courtesies Durakkon began questioning him about the supplies of iron to be expected from Gelt now that the rains were over. (Although a paved road ran sixty miles from Bekla to the Gelt foothills, consignments of iron were suspended during Melekril.) Below, the festival crowds surged on—pilgrims from as far as Ortelga and Chalcon, craftsmen and merchants up from Ikat, from Thettit, from the upper Zhairgen valley, from Cran alone knew where; some with their women and some without; and all manner of strange earners of livings—piemen and itinerant confectioners, quack-doctors, travelling actors and their wenches, professional letter-writers, hinnarists, cloth-sellers, vendors of knives, of glass, of bone needles and cheap jewellery; and along with these, plain sight-seers and folk up for a frolic; people who had come to see the Tamarrik Gate and people who already knew it well. Many of these, unable to obtain lodgings, would sleep on the streets.

At length Bodrin, palm to forehead, took his leave, descended from the rostrum and continued on his way. Durakkon, still aloft above the crowd, felt suddenly old and tired, a prisoner cut off from all the energy and vibrant life below. Wearier than the poor lass with the pedlar, he thought, for he had been tramping for seven years to stay in the same place. Once he had been full of confidence and determination to be a just ruler, to put down oppression and champion ordinary folk against those who cheated and exploited them. He had even had some idea of an end to slavery. But his vision, like the charitable bequest of some stupid, kindly old lady, had never reached its intended recipients. Somewhere along the way it had been intercepted, pilfered, nullified; by Kembri, by Sencho, by Fornis, by men like Lalloc. Was there, he wondered, one single peasant— man, woman or child—whose life was any the easier for his rule?

He thought of his wife, the daughter of a baron of Sarkid, whom he had married twenty-eight years ago, loyally fulfilling her rôle as High Baron's consort in a society where many now regarded the very concept of marriage as obsolete foolishness; of his sons, one on the Valderra, the other an officer in the new fortress at Dari-Paltesh. He called to mind, too, the pretty, golden-haired girl, with her soft Tonildan burr, whom he had watched Kembri question and browbeat the other night; a child enslaved, snatched from her home, eager to make her fortune by whoring, spying and delation. Whatever good she might contrive to dredge up for herself from the mud into which she had been pitched, he had conferred none on her.

He wondered how much longer he would have to go on living. At his age he could not realistically seek service—and death—in the field. Already he was showing signs of infirmity and it would look merely foolish. The prospect of something like another twenty years of increasing inability to hold his own against Kembri and Sencho seemed to him like slow death in a dungeon. Yet at all costs he must try to keep his dignity for the remainder of his life—whatever that might be.

From somewhere away to his right he heard shouted commands and men marching. The soldiers were coming through the gate to escort him back to the upper city, opening a lane through the crowds, pushing people back with the shafts of their spears. Their officer, reaching the foot of the rostrum, looked up and saluted, right forearm across his chest.

'If you'll allow me to say so, my lord, I wouldn't delay. My men can't hold back a crowd like this for long.'

'Thank you,' replied Durakkon. 'I'm coming.'

In the High Counsellor's house also, preparations for the spring festival were proceeding. Sencho, irritated by the prospect of the three-quarter-mile journey down through the lower city to the Temple of Cran, the long, tedious rites and the unavoidable forgoing of dinner and other customary pleasures, lay morosely in the bath while Terebinthia laid out his robes and regalia.

Slave-girls, of course—even the High Counsellor's—could not be present at the temple ceremony, but since Sencho was virtually helpless without attendants, Occula and Maia were to walk beside his litter as far as the temple precinct, wait until the ceremony was concluded and then accompany him back.

For the Sacred Queen's spring festival the aristocracy of Bekla, as well as the numerous provincial barons who made the journey to attend, were usually dressed, in accordance with ancient custom, as though for a wedding, while those of rank wore or carried their privileged insignia. By the same token propriety required that slaves, insofar as their presence might be unavoidable, should be dressed plainly and inconspicuously: or rather, this was what would once have been expected, in the days of Senda-na-Say and his predecessors. Of late years, however, fewer and fewer inhabitants of the upper city had continued to regard the ceremony with the fervour felt by their forefathers. The rites were not, indeed, cut short or treated lightly, but they were observed rather than celebrated—a tradition of the empire rather than an invocation of the god from the hearts of his worshippers. The dignitaries attending did so because it was expected of them, and because to have been absent would have given rise to criticism.

Accordingly, in the matter of dress, no one was particularly concerned to find fault with departures from the sober ways of the past, those who might privately feel troubled preferring not to risk being thought hidebound or puritanically out of date. Least of all was anyone likely to suggest that so powerful and vindictive a public figure as the High Counsellor might be acting tastelessly or irreverently by attiring his slave-girls in travesties of traditional styles. Occula was dressed in a plain white frock of fine wool, its long sleeves slashed and the weave, from shoulders to knees, so open as to reveal her body beneath. Maia's dress, which in cut followed exactly the homely garment of a household servant of a hundred years before, was made of very thin blue silk which clung so closely that the effect was, and was meant to be, immodestly provocative.

'Great hoppin' Shakkarn, banzi!' muttered Occula, as on Terebinthia's instructions they went together to fetch hot towels from the steam-room, 'you hang around the Tamarrik Gate like that for a bit and half the jig-a-jigs in town'll be rubbin' themselves up against you.'

'Reckon *you'll* be safe, then, do you?' answered Maia, trying the heat of a towel on her bare forearm, clapping the steam out of it and dropping it into the basket.

'Oh, they'll all have come off jus' lookin' at you before they get anywhere near me,' replied the black girl. 'Anyway,' she went on, with a certain change of tone, 'Kantza-Merada's protectin' me today. And you'll remember I said that, woan' you?' she added, turning to look directly into Maia's eyes. 'Do you love me, banzi? Really?'

'You ought to know.'

'Then remember this. Tonight, at the Barb, whatever I tell you to do, *do* it, and doan' ask any questions. No' (holding up a pale palm), 'that's enough! But remember we were lovers, banzi, and that I was always straight with you.'

Before Maia could reply she had taken the basket and was leading the way back up the passage.

When the girls had finished dressing the High Counsellor and helped him into the small dining-hall to await the arrival of his litter, Terebinthia, kneeling, begged him, in the customary terms, graciously to hear the petition of his faithful and devoted slave Dyphna, who had completed five years in his service. This was the signal for Dyphna to come forward, prostrate herself, offer the payment for her freedom and formally request Sencho to grant it to her. Usually, in Bekla, the freeing of a girl who had earned her price and given her master pleasure and satisfaction was the occasion for mutual compliments and some little informal ceremony. The girl would be asked to rise and drink with her master and would receive his thanks, good wishes for her future and so on, before receiving a present and taking formal leave of the household; sometimes being escorted by an admirer (invited beforehand) to begin her new life as a shearna or sometimes even as a wife.

Such wearisome niceties, however, were not for Sencho. Having told Terebinthia to count the money, he lay silently, with closed eyes, from time to time scratching himself under the oppressive robes; and as soon as the säiyett had assured him that the sum was correct, waved the girl away, at the same time calling for Milvushina to hold a pot for him to pass water before setting out for the lower city.

At one time Maia would have been overcome at the idea of being seen publicly in such a dress. Feelings of shame, however, usually stem not directly from ourselves but rather from anticipation of what we know or suppose others are going to think of us. Also, such feelings tend to vary according to one's self-confidence or social position. It was only a few months since Maia, in her one good dress, had sat with Tharrin in the tavern at Meerzat, nervous of the unaccustomed wine and embarrassed by the hot glances of the fishermen. Ah! but things had changed, she reflected. She'd learned now all right, no danger, what people in Bekla reckoned to a girl whose looks and accomplishments could attract the favour of the rich

361

and powerful. As long as she could maintain that favour, even poor people, acquiescent in the ways of their rulers, would accept her at those rulers' valuation and never think of her origins—except perhaps to admire her for rising above them. Nor would they stop to consider that it was their taxes which had put gowns on her body and jewels round her neck. Only if she fell from favour would their envy and malice come to the top. Meanwhile she and Occula represented that very best which some could afford while others couldn't.

The only modesty she felt now was that appropriate to a junior; a prudent sense of the unwisdom of making enemies through showing conceit or presumption. The cobblers, weavers and potters along the streets were welcome to stare out of their doors at her and imagine, poor fellows, what they would like to do to her. That did not matter. The important thing was, in the event of meeting such as Sessendris or Nennaunir, to be careful to assume an air of demure gratitude for favours received; and on no account publicly to claim acquaintance, act familiarly or even smile at any aristocrat who might have bedded her or watched her dance naked in the Barons' Palace.

This morning the Peacock Gate stood open and the guards were concerned only to watch for unauthorized ingress from the lower city; not that anyone wished to go that way, for as the hour of noon approached almost the whole populace wanted only to get as near as possible to the Tamarrik Gate, or at least to line the streets leading to it and watch the nobility assembling for the ceremony. Many of the country people who had earlier flocked past Durakkon at the gate were standing on each side of the steep Street of the Armourers, or thronging the Caravan Market and Storks Hill, down which the dignitaries from the upper city would be coming.

Soldiers lined this route. Those between the Peacock Gate and Caravan Market were from the Yeldashay regiment, but lower down, Durakkon's Green Guard had been posted along Storks Hill as far as the Temple of Cran itself. These men, all above normal height, made a fine spectacle with their open-link mail over jerkins of green-dyed leather, and polished helmets flashing above the crowd whenever one or another of them turned his head.

The flat-roofed, stone buildings shone white in the noonday sun. The rainless air itself seemed fulgent and there was an unbroken murmur of expectant talk among the crowds, every now and then rising in excitement as they recognized some well-known figure passing. Old men nodded and mumbled to one another about festivals of years gone by. Women chattered, children squealed and pointed, lasses rolled their eyes and flaunted their finery, sweet-meat vendors pushed about, crying their wares.

Municipal slaves went continually to and fro, sprinkling water to lay the dust.

It was along the paved route kept open by the soldiers through this staring, babbling throng that the two girls were required to walk, gazing nowhere but straight ahead as they followed the litter in which sprawled the monstrous, bloated figure of the High Counsellor. Continuously, from about a hundred yards in front, a sound of cheering preceded them as Elvair-ka-Virrion, accompanied by Shend-Lador and three or four more of his closer friends, made their way down together on foot. The cheers, dying away as the young Leopards passed on, were not renewed for Sencho.

Maia, shortening her pace to accord with that of the litter-bearers as they began the final, steep descent of the Street of the Armourers into the Caravan Market—the spot where she had exchanged ribaldry with the apothecary's 'prentice on her way to Eud-Ecachlon's lodgings—constantly heard murmurs rising on either side. The countless pairs of eyes round her, which she could sense but not return, seemed stripping her naked. Well, but they're only people, she said to herself. Ah, yet if only she'd been free just to gaze back at them! This enforced detachment and indifference, she thought, didn't suit her style; she felt as though she were pretending to be a creature of some other species, kept for its beauty yet not consciously aware or concerned that these were men around her—a peacock on a lawn, perhaps, or Zuno's white cat among the guests at the inn.

The litter swayed on across the Caravan Market, past Fleitil's brazen scales towards the colonnade in which stood 'The Green Grove'. Once a child's clear voice reached Maia, 'Oh, look, mum, the pretty ladies!' and a minute or two later, lower but still plain, a man's, 'No, the fair one in the blue.' She felt a quick spurt of superstitious reassurance, for the accent had been unmistakably Tonildan.

At the entrance to Storks Hill the litter stopped, evidently in response to an order given by Sencho, for they could see the tryzatt bend down as though listening to him. The girls, standing still in full view of the crowd, resembled, in their exposed yet inaccessible youth and beauty, ripe fruit on the trees of an enclosed orchard; a provocation the more alluring for being forbidden; enough to make a man forget all normal promptings of safety and common sense. Suddenly, Maia heard from only a few yards away a sharp cry, 'Back! Get back there!' and, turning her head in alarm, saw a soldier ramming the butt of his spear into the stomach of a big, shambling fellow, whose eyes remained fixed on her even as he went down among the crowd.

'Piggy gone mad, or what?' muttered Occula out of the side of her mouth. 'We'll all be basted to buggery in a minute, standing here.'

The tryzatt, straightening up, now turned and beckoned Maia to the side of the litter. Sencho, clutching her by the arm, told her to go into 'The Green Grove' and fetch him some cooled wine. The kindly tryzatt, however, overhearing, anticipated her and brought it himself. Sencho, having gulped at leisure until he had finished the entire beaker—Maia standing by him the while—then required her to take a towel and wipe the sweat from his face and shoulders. She returned to her place beside Occula flushed with embarrassment.

'What was all that about?' asked the black girl.

'Drink,' replied Maia in a whisper.

'That all?' said Occula. 'Thought you must be havin' a quick thrash.'

At the foot of Storks Hill an even thicker crowd surrounded the Temple of Cran. In the tile-paved precinct below the portico, close by the new statue of Airtha, the tall figure of Durakkon was standing among his barons and such of the army's senior officers as were not on the Valderra or at Dari-Paltesh. Their wives, together with the company of the Thlela, were assembled a little apart. Each new arrival, as he reached the precinct, formally greeted Durakkon, whereupon he was either, if of sufficient importance, invited to join those round the High Baron or else courteously conducted to some other group, among his equals. There was a blaze of colour from cloaks, robes and plumed hats, and a mingling of scents on the air, not only from perfumes but also from the spring flowers bedded round the edge of the precinct. Viewed from a little above, as one descended Storks Hill, the scene conveyed a breath-taking impression of wealth and power, so that even Occula momentarily lost her *sang-froid*, murmuring 'Kantza-Merada!' in a tone of startled admiration which Maia had never heard from her before.

Yet now before the girls' eyes was disclosed a sight even more astonishing than that of the Leopard gathering. Beyond the precinct, on the right bank of the Monju brook where it ran out of the city beneath the walls, stood the fabled Tamarrik Gate, designed and constructed eighty years before by the great Fleitil, grandfather of Fleitil the sculptor. This, a wonder of the empire rivalled only by the Barons' Palace and the Ledges of Quiso, was (until its destruction by the Ortelgans several years later) an integral part of the cult of Cran, conferring upon it a numinous splendour virtually irresistible alike to the dullest heart and the most sceptical mind. In function it was a water-clock, driven like a mill by the brook; but this is like saying that Alexander the Great was a soldier.

A swift-flowing carrier from the Monju encircled the whole area of the Tamarrik, its shelving inner bank planted with tall, plumed ferns. At intervals, ducts admitted water into one or another internal part of the complex. Along the lower courses of the walls of these ducts grew expanses of green liverwort, while the parapets, where the stones remained dry, were covered with blue-tongued lichens, their scarlet apothecia upstanding like myriads of minuscule warriors on guard above the sacred water below.

Immediately within the ring of the carrier stood a double half-circle of sycamores, between the leaves of which (the water driving their concealed mechanism) appeared from time to time, half-visible, the likenesses of the seven deities of the empire—Cran, Airtha, Shakkarn, Lespa, Shardik, Canathron and Frella-Tiltheh the Inscrutable.

The Tamarrik Court itself faced due south towards the temple precinct and Storks Hill. In the centre, on a circular bronze platform ten yards in diameter, stood the sundial of Cran. The life-sized, naked figure of the god, cast in bronze covered with silver leaf, reclined on a bed of malachite grass, speckled with red and blue flowers of carnelian and aquamarine. Its great, erect zard, stylized and engraved with fruit, flowers and ears of corn, formed the gnomon of the dial, and round it, in a shallow spiral precisely designed and placed for the indication of time throughout the day, stood, in various postures of an arrested, ecstatic dance, twelve silver girls, each the guardian of an hour-point on the dial at her feet and herself representing one of the empire's twelve provinces or independent domains—Bekla, Belishba, Chalcon, Gelt, Lapan and Kabin of the Waters: Ortelga, Paltesh, Tonilda, Urtah, Yelda and Sarkid of the Sheaves. The spiral dial above which they danced was a concave groove, about a foot broad. At its summit sat a golden, purple-lacquered kynat-bird, which every hour, by the operation of the water, released, as though laying an egg, a silver ball to roll down the spiral and be caught at its foot in a cup held by the figure of a kneeling child. (To keep the sundial and water-clock in synchronicity, a skilled task, required continual vigilance and adjustment and was carried out by six of the priesthood, their sole duty being to attend to this business from dawn till sunset.)

Behind and above the dial, but in front of the square gateway at the back of the Tamarrik Court, stood the famous concentric spheres of silver filigree—threads criss-crossing between slender, silver ribs—which represented the city and the sky above it. Bekla, standing in the midst of an open plain, commanded a virtually hemi-spherical view of the stars and accordingly, accurate observation of their places and movement had been a function of the priesthood from earliest times. The inner sphere, over five feet in diameter, was fixed, and reproduced on its upper hemisphere all the principal features of Bekla—Mount Crandor and the citadel, the Barons' Palace, the Barb lake and the various towers and gates of the lower city. Its under-side represented in relief Cran and Airtha in majesty, their arms extended to uphold the city above them. Enclosing this, yet sufficiently open in workmanship to leave all these details plainly visible, the outer sphere bore, upon its thin, curved ribs of silver, great jewels set in the forms of the various constellations. This had been constructed to be manually rotated in conformity with the movement of the heavens themselves and, like the dial, required constant attention to ensure its precision.

A stone canopy protected the spheres from wind and weather, and this bore on its pediment four dials which showed the month of the year, the phase of the moon, the day and the hour. From its roof one end of a narrow bronze bar, trough-shaped, projected over the courtyard below. This was balanced on a fulcrum mounted on the parapet, and its padded inner end rested on the surface of a deep silver drum. At sunset a priest, climbing to the roof, would scatter corn into the trough. The sacred white doves, alighting to eat, as they came and went would cause the finely-balanced bar to tilt and fall back, so that the drum seemed to beat of itself, to signal to the city the end of work for the day. Aloft, crowning the edifice, rose on its pedestal the wind-harp known as the Voice of Airtha, from whose music omens were divined.

Beyond the gate, just outside the city walls, stood the grove of tamarrik trees universally believed to be sprung from the seed cast down from Crandor's summit, ages before, by Frella-Tiltheh the Inscrutable. That the whole marvel stood in a deliberately-made breach in the walls symbolized the impossibility of an enemy ever taking the city by storm.

Occula and Maia, halting on the edge of the precinct while the High Counsellor's litter was carried on into the temple, stood gazing in awe and astonishment at one and another part of the wonder before them. Maia, unable to imagine the purpose or meaning of the dials (except that they were obviously magical and on that account disturbing), was nevertheless delighted by the nympholeptic spiral of hours, the reclining god and the purple-and-gold kynat above. Gazing, she remembered with amusement how, on the night of the Rains banquet, she had been disconcerted by the sight of the erotic fountain in the Lord General's lower hall.

'What the hell are you gigglin' about?' asked Occula rather tensely.

'Just thinking I know now why you're always swearing by Cran's zard,' answered Maia.

'He did even better than that, though, did Fleitil,' said Occula, with more composure. 'D'you know what happens at the ceremony?'

'Well, yes, kind of—that's to say, Tharrin told me a bit about it, once.'

Suddenly she caught her breath, all her ribaldry gone as for an instant the face of Lespa looked out at her from among the leaves.

'Oh, Occula! Did you see?' She turned and, despite the crowd and the blaze of noon, seemed almost ready to run.

'Steady!' said the black girl. 'It's only a trick, banzi. Cran and Airtha!

you were Lespa yourself the other night—and very good, too, by all I hear.'

'Why, whatever can valuable property like you two be doing standing out here in the boiling sun?' said a voice behind them.

They both looked round. It was Nennaunir, strikingly beautiful in a purple robe cross-stitched with gold thread, her high-piled hair fixed with jewelled, ebony combs. Maia, hoping she had not noticed her naïve alarm at the face in the leaves, smiled back at her.

'Oh, we're just gettin' toasted, ready for the supper-party by the Barb tonight,' said Occula. 'It'll go easier with sunstroke, I dare say.'

'But have you really been told that you've got to stand out here all through the ceremony?' persisted Nennaunir.

'Well, tell you the truth, I'm not sure,' answered Maia. 'Reckon as long as we're back here 'fore the end—'

'You can't go in?'

'We're slaves, aren't we?' said Occula.

Nennaunir looked quickly and covertly round the crowded precinct, rather like a child contemplating mischief. Then, dropping her voice, she whispered, 'I'll get you in, if you like—both of you,' and at once began leading Maia towards the temple. Occula hesitated a moment and then, shrugging her shoulders, followed.

The temple steps and portico, built of stone blocks, faced east across the precinct, presenting a solemn and majestic front. The rear of the building, however, rather like that of a theatre (which to some extent it was), comprised all manner of storage and robing rooms, administrative quarters and other odd corners—the priests' refectory and kitchen, offices for conducting temple business, tally-rooms, cellars, a yard and shed where parts of the mechanism of the Tamarrik Gate were overhauled and maintained—and so on. Nennaunir, slipping quickly along a sunk path running beside the temple's south wall, turned, between two out-buildings, into a paved yard piled with firewood on one side and empty wine-casks on the other. Here a dark, scowling young man, dressed in the grey-green smock of a temple slave, was sitting on a stool, peeling brillions into a pail with a broken-bladed knife. He had dirty finger-nails and a stubble of beard, which he scratched with the knife as he paused, looking up at the newcomers.

'Hullo, Sednil,' said Nennaunir, halting beside him in a cloud of perfume and trailing gauzes. 'Found you easily, didn't I? How are you, my darling?'

The young man looked up at her with a grin which, while probably meant to express bravado, only succeeded in making him look mortified and rather pathetic.

'I was all right until just now. What d'you want to come round here for, looking like that?'

'I didn't come here to torment you,' said Nennaunir. 'Really I didn't, Sednil. Cheer up! Honestly, I believe it won't be much longer—'

'Three years,' said he. 'D'you call that long or short?'

'It might be much less,' answered Nennaunir. 'It might, Sednil, truly. I'm doing my best, but it's a matter of finding the right person and the right moment.'

'Like when you're on your back with someone else, you mean?' said Sednil, spitting into the peel-bucket.

'Well, that might turn out to be a good time, yes. You must be realistic, darling. I shan't miss any opportunity I get, I promise you.'

Sednil made no reply, only continuing to gaze at her like a man looking through the barred window of a cell.

'Sednil, it *will* be all right—you wait and see! And look, I've brought two charming friends of mine to meet you—Maia and Occula. They both belong to Sencho, poor girls.'

'Cran help them!' said Sednil. 'Why aren't they squashed flat?'

'Well, there you are, you see; there's always someone worse off. They want to go in and watch the ceremony. You'll help them, won't you?'

Sednil said nothing.

'Won't you?'

'It's risky,' said Sednil.

'I'm sure they'd really appreciate it. They'd show themselves very very grateful, I expect.'

At this moment there rang across the city the clangour of the gongs striking noon, and from the steps of the temple a trumpet sounded.

'Yes or no?' said Nennaunir. 'I'll have to be quick: I've got a friend waiting.'

'Oh, twenty, I dare say,' answered Sednil bitterly. 'All in line.' He turned to the girls. 'Well, come on, then!'

By this time Maia, who had not been paying much attention to the talk, was as much agog as a child being taken to a treat. Smiling at the young man and taking his arm, she thanked Nennaunir warmly and then set off with him through the door, across an untidy, deserted kitchen and along a stone-floored passage.

'You're a friend of Nennaunir?' she asked conversationally.

'I used to be,' said he.

'Before you came to the temple, you mean?' Maia was puzzled.

'How long did you get?' asked Occula from behind them.

'Five years. Oh, she's not a bad sort, I suppose. All the same, she knew the truth of it and never said a word. Oh, never mind! What's the use?'

Maia still felt none the wiser.

'You mean you're here against your will? Couldn't you—well, run away or something? I mean, all these crowds of people from all over the empire—'

'Run away? Where d'you come from, lass? Look!' Sednil, pausing by a window on the staircase they were now climbing, stretched out one hand. Across the back extended a white scar, fully three inches broad, in the shape of a pair of crossed spears. In parts the flesh was proud, and in one place the wound had not entirely healed.

'M'm—so that's the forced service brand, is it?' said Occula, craning over Maia's shoulder. 'I've never seen one before. Did it hurt?'

''Course it basting well hurt!' replied Sednil irritably. 'What d'you think?'

'I don't understand,' said Maia. 'You mean it's—'

'If a man who's been branded like that can't show a token—either from whoever he's workin' for or else a "released" token once his time's up— it's death straight away,' said Occula. 'That's why he doesn' run, banzi. He'd have to run to Zeray.' She turned back to Sednil. 'I didn' know they sent people like you to the temple. It's usually the Gelt mines, isn' it, or somewhere like that?'

'Yes, but Nennaunir persuaded one of the priests to ask for me, on a promise of good conduct. She's got friends everywhere, that girl—priests and all. I've seen one or two things while I've been here, I can tell you.'

They had reached the top of the staircase and now Sednil, turning to the left, led them into a gallery which ran the length of the back of the temple. About thirty yards along this was a door set in the inner wall. As he opened it the girls could hear from below the murmur and movement of a crowd.

'Now, we've got to keep quiet,' whispered Sednil, 'and mind you do.'

Maia followed him into what seemed for a moment to be darkness, the more so as he immediately closed the door behind them. Then, as she stood still in uncertainty, she became aware of light, its source, however, somewhere below them. Sednil, taking her hand, led her forward until she found herself looking down, from the rather alarming height of a roof-level balcony, into the interior of the Temple of Cran.

Fifty feet below lay a circular, tessellated pavement, some nine or ten yards across, slightly sunk below a surround of veined, grey marble. Immediately within this surround the tiles formed a border depicting a crested serpent with red, green and blue scales, which stretched entirely round the edge of the pavement until, at the eastern point, it grasped its own tail between its jaws. Round its body was twined an intricate design of vines, fruit and corn, the various motifs being repeated at regular intervals throughout the circle. Within this again was a variant of the divine group represented on the inner sphere of the Tamarrik Gate. Upon a ground of green malachite inlaid with coloured blooms and with animals, birds and fishes, the golden-bearded figure of Cran stretched out his arms, whilst opposite, Airtha of the Diadem extended hers towards him. Each of their hands rested upon the base of one corner of a rectangular marble slab, about two feet high, standing in the centre of the pavement.

Maia was so much fascinated by the design and by the brilliant colours in the pavement—of which, of course, looking directly down from above, she had the best possible view—that it was some little time before she began to notice the less ornate central altar-slab and the figure lying upon it. When she did so, however, her first reaction was one of bewilderment and disappointment. Somnolence and passivity was not what she would have expected at the very core of the empire's worship. She had always imagined the god in his temple armed with lightning, majestic, vigilant and mighty to protect the empire. The reality was much unlike.

The low, marble slab was carved in the form of a couch resting upon scrolled clouds. Upon this lay a life-sized, bronze figure of Cran; but very different from that of the Tamarrik dial with its attendant circle of ecstatic nymphs. The god, his head and shoulders raised on marble pillows, was supine, in the posture of one asleep. Indeed, he plainly *was* asleep, for his eyelids were closed, giving him—since his body was unmoved by breathing—the appearance almost of one dead. He was naked, and his flaccid zard, like any mortal man's, lay across the hollow of his thigh. Something about its appearance puzzled Maia, though from this height she could not quite make out what it might be: it was flexed, and seemed to be fashioned out of narrow, overlapping, cylindrical scales. But apart from this, she had never before seen the god represented without his attributes—crown, lightning and serpent torques. She would hardly have recognized him. The figure, in fact, displeased her. It seemed an unworthy, almost impious, representation, not at all god-like, inappropriate in its resemblance to mere humanity.

The three of them were standing, she now realized, near the top of an octagonal lantern tower, the whole of the interior of which was open to and visible from the floor of the temple. This was supported upon the lintels and square columns of a circular arcade surrounding the pavement below. At a height of about thirty feet, a narrow gallery ran round the lantern (their own standpoint was a mere box just below the roof), and below it were narrow windows admitting daylight to the floor of the temple below. This was augmented by eight branched candlesticks, each carrying some twenty or thirty candles, which had been placed round the edge of the pavement, one in front of each column.

Looking between the columns to the further side of the arcading, Maia could glimpse tiers of stone seats rising one above the other. It seemed strange to her that the temple should apparently not be lit by windows at ground-floor level. She was not to know that these had all been shuttered, to intensify the effect of the lit central pavement and the sleeping figure of Cran.

The temple was filling. As the girls continued looking down, a scarlet-robed priest, carrying a staff, entered beneath one of the lintels, followed by Durakkon and a train of barons and other nobles. These, conducted round the edge of the pavement to the west side of the arcade, passed between the columns and seated themselves within. On Durakkon's right, Maia noticed, was her admirer Randronoth, the governor of Lapan. Sencho himself she could not see anywhere, and could only suppose that special arrangements must have been made to spare him the unendurable discomfort of having to sit upright.

The placing of the various notables, their wives (who occupied a separate bay of the arcade) and the remainder of those eligible for admission, took a considerable time, the priests continually disappearing between the columns, re-emerging, conferring under the candelabra, and once or twice leading out some important personage to seat him more befittingly. The assembly, however, showed no impatience and there was no noise above a low murmur of talk as they waited for the ceremony to begin.

At length the priests retired, the central circle stood empty; and complete silence fell. It was hard to believe that nearly a thousand people were seated in the twilight beyond the columns. Maia, allowing herself a tiny, nervous cough, was overcome as the sound seemed to fill the roof and echo round the walls. Frightened, she crouched quickly down behind the balustrade. After a moment Sednil's hand, trembling slightly, and rough compared with those she had become accustomed to, caressed her shoulders and drew her back up beside him. Glancing sideways, he put a finger to his lips and then returned to watching the floor below.

Side by side two files of priests were entering in procession. Parting, they paced slowly round either edge of the pavement until the leaders met once more, whereupon all halted, turning inward to face the central stone before which their leader, advancing, had taken up his station.

Maia, though familiar from infancy with the myths and legends of the gods told her by old Drigga, had heard relatively little about the actual worship of Cran as performed in Bekla. To her, therefore, as perhaps to no other person in the entire temple, everything seemed fresh, direct and heartfelt. The chief priest, in an invocation to the god interspersed with chanted responses from his followers, told of the harsh quenching of the land and the hardships suffered by the people during Melekril. While he still slept, Cran's sacred empire had been threatened by the chaotic powers of winter—storm, rain and darkness. Of themselves his people had no resource or defence, weakened as they were by hunger and by their sins. They implored him to waken and renew the fertile year.

This opening part of the spring liturgy, which was very ancient and couched in ornate, archaic language, expressed a dignified yet heart-broken sorrow which overpowered Maia entirely, leaving her beyond even tears. The priests' hymns, supporting their leader's pleas with lyric descriptions of the failing land and of mountains, plains and forests languishing under the long weeks of cloud and rain, found a ready response both in her imagination and her memory. She even found herself feeling sorry for Morca, huddled in the draughty hut with the mud outside stretching down to the bleak shore.

Symbolic fire was carried in—a brazier borne between two priests on an iron pole—for the burning of the past and the winter season. And now the chief priest, kneeling, again implored Cran to waken and return to his people. Yet still the god lay sleeping on his marble bed.

At this point Maia, who as an audience was never insensitive or slow in response to a story or a dance, began to feel a mounting tension and superstitious dread. This, she realized, stemmed not from the priests' expressed fear that the god would not waken, but on the contrary from her own inward realization that inevitably he would. All her life she had been listening to tales by the fire, playing singing-games and at village festivals taking part in old dance-rituals and the like. Without reflection she knew that in stories and dramas the thing that seems impossible is always the thing that finally happens. The haughty maiden, rejecting gift after gift from her suitor, finally relents; the forgotten, friendless prisoner is released, the invincible giant falls to a trick, the magically trance-bound sleeper wakes. As the next part of the ritual began, with the bringing to the god of gold and jewels—the temple treasures—as a further inducement to return, she felt the hair rising at the back of her neck. Against all course of nature and possibility, ultimately the bronze figure below was going to waken. But how? And what would come to pass when it did? Craning forward, she looked down more intently still. No—she was certain that no human being could be concealed within that case of jointed metal.

Each episode of the service lasted for some time, for as one offering after another was vainly made to the god, the priests extolled its particular properties and merits in a succession of anthems—some solemn, some lively, but all appropriate. Their rhythmic power and melodic beauty made Maia want to dance. Swaying silently in harmony with the lilt of a song in praise of wine (while flagons were poured into crystal jars placed before the god's couch) she felt her hips gently pummelling against Sednil's and turned to smile at him, feeling a natural pleasure in being close to a young fellow before whom she did not have to act the part of the compliant slave-girl. Sednil, looking round at her and licking dry lips, put an arm round her shoulder and pressed her against his side; but to this Maia, who in imagination was back among her younger sisters, dancing in the dust outside the door, attached for the moment little importance.

After the gold, jewels and wine, fine robes and then weapons and food were offered to the god; ornamental spears of silver; tasselled, polished bows and an inlaid, damascene sword and shield; roasted haunches from a goat, a sheep and a bull-calf, while the priests sang in praise of food and feasting. The smell of the roast meat, wafted up to the roof, made Maia's mouth water, for she and Occula, both become accustomed to good living, had today eaten nothing since an hour or so before setting out from the upper city.

At last the worshippers seemed driven to despair. The priestly chorus, prostrating themselves round the edge of the pavement, proclaimed, in a sobbing lament, that the god must himself have become the victim of winter and accordingly would never return. The chief priest, casting off his robes to reveal, beneath, the leather jerkin of a slave, called aloud upon any man or woman whatsoever who would come forward to save the empire in its peril. At the same time the candles round the arcade were extinguished and from outside the wailing of mourners was heard. As they ceased and all became silent, the god, in the dim daylight slanting down from above, lay alone among his unavailing gifts.

After a pause, during which the frightened weeping of a young girl—too young to be present, perhaps—could be plainly heard from among the women's seats, the silence was broken by a sudden, heavy knocking on the great door of the temple. The chief priest, rising to his feet, looked about him in apparent surprise. Taking up his staff, he made his way out and could be heard ordering the door to be opened. A few moments later rose the sound of girls' voices singing as they approached. Then a beautiful little child, about eight years old, crowned with spring flowers, ran into the middle of the pavement, flung out her arms and cried, 'The Sacred Queen! The Sacred Queen!'

The girls, dressed alternately in green and in white, their arms laden with blossom (the scent of which rose up to Maia), entered, as had the priests, in two files, singing, as they came, that the empire was about to be delivered, since they were now bringing to the god the most precious gift in heaven and earth. When at length they too halted, each was standing beside one of the prostrate priests, whom she raised to his feet, smiling at him in comfort and reassurance.

The girls, all young and beautiful, mimed this part of the ceremony with

373

an air of happy gaiety, to which the priests responded by showing first astonishment, then disbelief and finally, puzzled expectation as their new companions turned towards the eastern entry, each raising one arm, both in indication and in greeting. The chief priest resumed his robes. Then, as he knelt to receive her, trumpets sounded and Queen Fornis herself entered alone.

Since becoming Sacred Queen of Airtha, Fornis had had the shrewdness to modify considerably the ways of her youth and to appear in public only to planned effect. (Maia, for example, had never yet set eyes on her.) She took the greatest care of her appearance and now, although in her thirty-fourth year, still possessed the flawless skin and almost luminous auburn hair which had made so deep an impression on the eleven-year-old Occula in the palace of Senda-na-Say. Together with these she had retained an extraordinary, energetic vitality, which was manifest in her manner, her movements and everything she did. A kind of swift, confident power and domination emanated from her, exhilarating in their effect and to most of the people evidence enough, together with her beauty, that she must be god-favoured, the veritable talisman and luck of the empire.

As she now appeared, pausing for a few moments under the eastern arch, Maia heard Occula, beside her, utter a kind of stifled moan. She turned quickly towards her, but the black girl had already controlled herself and was once more looking down in silence, biting her lip.

Queen Fornis was dressed in the white, full-skirted robe of a Beklan bride and carried a long, trailing bouquet of green-and-white *golian* lilies, the first flowers of spring. In this she conformed to tradition. Like Sencho, however, she did not hesitate to modify old forms of dress to her taste. Her present robe, like the one in which Occula had first seen her, was half-transparent, ornamented with green ribbons at the sleeves and shoulders and gathered at the waist with a broad, green sash. Upon her head was the crown of Airtha, most sacred and costly of the temple treasures, its aqua-marines and huge, irregular emeralds catching the light of the re-lit candles as she stepped forward onto the central pavement. Maia, staring, caught her breath.

'Never seen her before?' murmured Sednil in her ear.

Shaking her head, Maia became aware of Occula leaning towards her on the other side.

'Those emeralds are Zai's,' whispered the black girl through clenched teeth.

'But the crown's old, surely?' answered Maia.

'I doan' care,' said Occula. 'That big one in the middle—I've held it in my hand—I'd know it anywhere.'

Now began a ritual of question and answer between the chief priest and the beautiful lady. Who was she, he asked, and whence had she come, professing power to save the empire and revive the year? In a clear, musical voice, with no more than a trace of Paltesh in the accent, she replied that Airtha of the Diadem had spoken to her, bidding her have no fear to put herself forward, for the goddess had appointed her as her chosen vessel.

Yet why did she think she could succeed where all other attempts had failed? Because, she answered, Airtha possessed her. This was even now Airtha of the Diadem speaking through her lips; she who had power to succour all things living, yes and even to raise the dead in the world beyond. She had come to awaken the god by bringing him the most precious gift in the world.

At this the chief priest prostrated himself; yet, giving as justification his sacred responsibility, he still wished to learn what warrant she might have for saying that she was the chosen incarnation of the goddess. To this she made no spoken reply at all, merely standing motionless while two of her maidens came forward, took her flowers and then divested her of her robe. It was fastened down the front with gold clasps, and as it fell open and was smoothly drawn away from her shoulders and arms, leaving her completely naked, neither her easy posture nor the calm, joyous expression of her face altered in the slightest degree. 'Here is my warrant,' she seemed to say. 'Judge for yourself, since you have sought to know. Before, in using mere words, I was making a concession to your human nescience.'

The chief priest, veiling his gaze, as though dazzled, with a forearm before his brow, begged her to deign to tell them what gift it might be—this greatest gift—which she had brought to waken the god and rejuvenate his power. And to this she answered 'Love.'

Thereupon began, somewhere beyond, a low, barely-audible throbbing of zhuas. The chief priest and his followers withdrew, while the queen's attendants re-grouped themselves under the eastern arch, singing as they did so the wedding hymn with which all brides in Bekla were customarily escorted to the marriage-chamber. Meanwhile the little girl, unaided, extinguished the candles for the second time and then, once more raising her arms to the assembly, preceded the women out of the temple.

The queen, left alone with the sleeping god, turned, walked slowly to the side of the marble couch and, kneeling down, took his bronze fingers in her own. Maia, watching spellbound and recalling what it felt like to act before an audience a part of this nature, could detect in her manner no hint of artificiality or of anything that did not appear spontaneous and natural. Bending forward, Fornis kissed the god's lips and then, lying down lightly and easily beside him, put one arm round his shoulders and pressed her body against his.

And now it was all that simple Maia could do not to cry out in fear, for as she watched, the god's bronze eyelids slowly opened, disclosing blue-irised, black-pupilled eyes which, though unmoving and lacking speculation, appeared nevertheless most startlingly alert. The figure, too, seemed to be raising itself from the hips, and as it did so the queen, stretching one arm behind the head of the couch, picked up a cushion to support its shoulders.

Who will take it upon themselves to condemn what followed as lewd or unnatural? The Shilluk of the White Nile, perhaps, whose custom it once was to wall up their king, together with a nubile virgin, to die in the dark of hunger and thirst? The ancient Carthaginians, who sacrificed children by fire to a calf-headed image, playing music the while to drown their screams? The inhabitants of Quilacare in southern India, where every twelve years the king, standing on a high scaffolding, would cut off his nose, ears, lips and genitals, scattering them among the people before cutting his own throat? Or the Christian peasants who on St Stephen's Day hunted down wrens along the hedges? The celebrant who to one is clearly nothing but a capering, mud-smeared charlatan of a witch-doctor, to another is a dread figure of power, expert by long study in dangerous communion with ghosts and gods. What to an alien is indecency, to the devout and instructed is a symbolic enactment of the magnanimity of the immortals, by whose mercy men live and in whose grace they hope to die.

Before the eyes of the rulers and dignitaries of Bekla, Fornis lay beside the god, kissing and stroking him like any lass with her mortal lover. She fondled his shoulders, his smooth-plated belly and gleaming thighs. Then, laughing with mischief and half-pretending shame, as girls will in play, she performed for him such other things as are done by lovers in the mounting excitement of desire. So realistically did she enact her part that Maia, utterly absorbed, felt her own loins moisten and her breath come short.

As she gently caressed and drew apart the overlapping bronze scales so cunningly fashioned by Fleitil, the god's zard lengthened and grew rigid in his lady's hand, at its full extent locking with a minute click, inaudible to the watchers but to the queen the signal that she needed to hear. Thereupon, mounting her lover and drawing his jointed arms about her shoulders, she sank down astride him, crying out ecstatically and displaying to her worshippers, in the plunging of her thighs, all that they needed, for their spiritual renewal and fulfilment, to behold: and in what ensued she displayed the most skilful artistry, for not only did the great crown remain in place round her glowing hair, but never once did she lose the sacred thing which she had received.

Maia, hardly aware of what she did, turned and pressed herself against Sednil, thrusting her tongue into his mouth and at the same time pushing him back into the shadows. An hour ago it had briefly occurred to her to wonder why Nennaunir should have been at the trouble of seeking out this lad and asking him to run the risk of taking them into the temple. She knew now all right, no danger. Whatever it was that he might have done, Nennaunir evidently felt she owed him a good turn; and at this moment Maia felt no least objection to performing it for her.

'Sednil! Oh, Sednil—'

'Well, that makes things a lot easier, banzi,' remarked Occula composedly. 'I knew it was goin' to be one of us, but I'm not really in the mood, myself. You could charge him double if you like—he's got nothin'.'

'Not here, not here,' muttered Sednil. 'Your clothes'd get dirty and it'd show. There's a room along the gallery. But we'll have to be quick! We haven't got long.'

Coming out into the yard, Occula and Maia made their own way back to the precinct, where Durakkon and some of the other nobles, in accordance with custom, were tossing handfuls of small coins among the crowd. After the girls had stood waiting for a considerable time in the blazing sun, the tryzatt of the litter-bearers came out to summon them back to the rear of the temple. Sencho, who had decided that it was not necessary for him to appear a second time in the hot, crowded precinct, had been lying down in the chief priest's private apartments. Here, having deigned to spend three-quarters of an hour over a light meal, he was ready for the girls to help him to his litter.

The return to the Peacock Gate was arduous for the soldiers who, partly through heat and the weight of their burden and partly on account of the crowds, were several times forced to put the litter down. While the High Counsellor had been taking his ease in the temple, the sentinels lining the roads had been dismissed, and again and again it was necessary for the tryzatt to go ahead to clear the way. Sencho, however, drowsing in the cushions, showed no particular impatience, merely telling Occula to close the curtains and leave him undisturbed; and the good-natured tryzatt, emboldened by the High Counsellor's lethargy to act on his own initiative, lent Maia his cloak, remarking tactfully that it would keep off the dust. Maia was glad to cover herself, having already attracted more than enough unwanted attention while crossing the Caravan Market.

'Nice bastin', banzi?' asked Occula as they plodded uphill in the wake of the litter. Her sarcasm was no more than teasing, but Maia, sweating and uncomfortable, was quick to resent it.

'Yes, it *was*!' she replied sharply. 'And you needn't be so damned spiteful, either. I was sorry for the poor boy, that's what. He's a prisoner in that place, isn't he? He was desperate for it.'

'He wasn' the only one,' said Occula. 'Cran! *you* were like a damn' cat on a roof—just with watchin' that cruel, wicked woman, that's what.'

Maia was about to retort when something in Occula's voice checked her. Turning her head, she saw that the black girl was on the verge of weeping. She took her hand and kissed it.

'I'm sorry, dear. I don't wonder it upset you. You hate her, don't you?'

'Of course I hate her!' cried Occula. 'Didn' she murder my father—'

'Hush, love, hush! Someone'll hear—'

'And you mark my words, banzi, one day I'll—'

As the black girl bit on her fingers, Maia could see the tears falling on the back of her hand.

'Seven years! Seven years, and Zai's spirit—'

'Try not to take on, dear! You're not yourself—it's the sun and all the standing about. Anyhow, thank goodness here's the gate, and about time, too. Oh, I *shall* be glad to go in the pool when we get back, won't you? I hope he'll let us have a bit of a rest, seeing as we've got to go to that Barb party tonight. I wonder whether—O great Cran! Occula! Look! That's Meris over there! Meris! And the pedlar man—what's he called? Zirek. Look! going through the gate now!'

'Strikes me you're the one's been in the sun, banzi. How the hell can it be Meris when you know perfectly well she's been sold into the back of beyond?'

'But I tell you it *was* Meris, Occula! They've gone now, but—'

'Banzi,' said Occula, gripping her wrist and turning upon her with a look of desperation, 'shut up! Doan' ask me why—just shut up! Tell me about your lake in Tonilda, go on! Tell me about Tharrin—tell me about any damn' thing you like!'

Maia, frowning with vexation, made no reply, and together with two or three other groups of nobles and attendant slaves they passed on under the arch into the upper city.

'Banzi,' said Occula presently.

Maia went on humming the wine anthem without replying.

'Banzi.'

'Well?' Maia felt tired and sulky. 'Got yourself into a better temper?'

'There's somethin' else I've just thought of, and it's very, very important. Piggy may sleep this afternoon—probably will, I dare say. But *if* he sends for you, doan' let him have anythin', d'you see? Tell him it's the wrong time of the month, tell him you've broken your wrist, hurt your mouth— tell him anythin' you like. But whatever you do, *doan'* let him have any-thin'! *You* can get away with it. He'll take it from you.'

'But why, Occula?'

'Never mind. Just do as I say. Anyway, p'raps you woan' have to.'

In the event this last proved correct. Sencho, carried to the small hall, told Terebinthia that he would sleep until sunset, when he was to be

378

awakened for the supper party. He confirmed that Maia and Occula were to accompany him. The following day he wished to see Lalloc about buying a girl to replace Dyphna.

: 39 :

BY THE BARB

By sunset Maia was feeling refreshed and ready for the evening. Despite Occula's reproach, she felt neither shame nor regret about what she had done with Sednil. His famished necessity and corresponding ardour, his being a person of much the same station in life as herself (which had made her feel delightfully relaxed) and (perhaps most pleasant) the knowledge that she had enjoyed something illicit which could not now be taken away—all these, adding up to a real sense of satisfaction, had left her in a happy, confident mood, so that Terebinthia, while looking through the wardrobe with her, thought fit to remark that she had better take care not to let her high spirits run away with her at the Barb party; to which Maia replied pertly that she felt sure Terebinthia would like her to do all she could to bring back a good, big lygol.

'I doubt there'll be any lygols tonight,' answered Terebinthia. 'I rather think the High Counsellor will want to keep you both to himself. And you'd be well-advised to remain content with that. Remember Meris.'

'Why isn't he taking Milvushina, though, säiyett?' asked Maia. 'I mean, I thought he liked to show what a lot of everything he's got, and we've been out in public once today already.'

'I rather imagine—' Terebinthia hesitated. 'A lot of provincial barons will be there tonight and I think that possibly he may not want to run the risk of anyone recognizing her. But you're not to repeat that.'

'No, säiyett, 'course I won't. Oh, look! Can I wear that?'

It was a yellow-and-white tunic, broad-lapelled and buttoning down the front, with flared, embroidered lappets doing duty for a skirt. The buttons were topaz, as were the eyes of the leopards embroidered on the flapped pockets. Maia tried it on. It fitted well, and Terebinthia nodded approval.

'You'll need to wear a low-cut shift underneath, and short enough in the hem not to show beneath the lappets, too. With legs like yours that will do very well.'

Neither Terebinthia nor Maia could have had the least inkling of how well it would have to do—or for how long.

At this moment Occula appeared. She seemed edgy and preoccupied. She was wearing her orange metlan and leather hunting-jacket, her gold nose-stud and necklace of teeth—the costume which Maia had first seen in the slavers' depôt at Puhra. It certainly *did* suit her, she thought; and it was nice that as a result of her own widened experience of clothes during these last months she had come to think more and not less highly of Occula's taste.

'Do you think that's quite suitable for the High Baron's party, Occula?' asked Terebinthia. Once, thought Maia, she would simply have told her to go and take it off.

'I'd like to wear it, säiyett, if I may,' answered Occula. 'Yes, I think it suits me and I always feel confident in it.'

'Well, I don't know whether the High Counsellor's going to agree with you,' said Terebinthia. 'But if that's how you—What is it, Ogma?'—as the club-footed girl came hurrying in.

'The High Counsellor's awake, säiyett, and wants you to go and see him at once,' said Ogma.

'Banzi,' said Occula, as Terebinthia went out, 'just come back to my room for a minute.'

Once there she closed the door and then, taking out of her box the squat, black image of Kantza-Merada, placed it in Maia's hands.

'Keep her safe, banzi,' she said. 'Either keep her yourself or if you have to, destroy her—burn her—d'you see? Doan' lose her, and doan' ever let anyone else have her.'

'Why, Occula, whatever's the matter? You've been so strange—well, all day, really. Is it an omen you've had, or what? Anyone'd think you reckoned you weren't coming back here.'

Very deliberately, Occula put her two hands on Maia's shoulders and kissed her.

'I loved you, banzi. I was always straight with *you*. Doan' ever forget that, will you? Look, I'm goin' to hide Kantza-Merada under the floor-board here, along with the money.' Then before Maia could answer, 'Now let's get you dressed in that tunic thing. Are you goin' to put your hair up? I think you should—but at that rate you'll need combs. Where are they? Then we can all go and have a jolly romp with Piggy, can' we?'

Sencho was also in good spirits, and with reason. Four years before, in return for his part in the appointment of the present chief priest of Cran, he had succeeded in bringing it about that the High Counsellor should in future receive one-twelfth of the annual temple revenues, payable after each spring festival. While eating the chief priest's roast quails that afternoon, he had learned that the twelfth due to him for this year was a larger sum than he had expected, partly on account of the temple's recent recovery, with substantial interest, of a loan made to Lalloc, and partly on account of its share of the confiscated estate of Enka-Mordet. He was also twelve thousand meld to the good over Dyphna, and expected to get a new girl for not much more.

The Barb party was an occasion which he usually enjoyed. Flattery, sycophantic servility from men higher born than himself, the exercise of power and the granting of favours on profitable terms as and when it suited him—these things he relished. The food would be excellent; and there would, of course, be other pleasures. He felt fully recovered from his recent indisposition (which must, he now felt, have been due to nothing more than the depressing effect of the rainy season) and delightfully full of his customary appetites. During the time when he had not been himself the black girl had done well. She had turned out most skilful and reliable. Expensive as they had been, he had shown himself sharp in buying her and the Tonildan. Lying in the bath and enjoying Milvushina's ill-concealed aversion to washing him, he had the two girls brought in, approved their clothes and then told Terebinthia to make sure that they were equipped with towels, extra cushions and everything else necessary to his comfort. Milvushina had just finished drying him when Ogma appeared to announce the arrival of the litter-bearers.

The distance to the lake known as the Barb, beside which Durakkon's guests were to meet, was not much over half a mile—about twenty minutes' journey for the heavy litter. Near the foot of the Leopard Hill the curving, northern shore was laid out as an arboreal garden, its lawns extending down to the water. There were groves of willows and cypresses, and two great zoan trees standing on either side of the inlet known as the Pool of Light. Planted about the lawns were scented shrubs—flendro, witch-hazel, jain-gum, capercaraira and many more—and arbours of evergreens to give shelter, when necessary, from the wind.

Tonight, however, was almost as mild and balmy as midsummer, with a half moon already high in a cloudless sky. The scent of spring flowers filled the air and not the least breeze ruffled the surface of the water or stirred the foliage. Nevertheless, in case anyone should feel cold, charcoal braziers had been placed here and there, and from a distance these glowed and twinkled between the trunks of the trees. A chain of coloured lamps—pink, blue and green—surrounded the widest of the lawns, ending (or beginning) at the entrance in a serpent's head and tail, in imitation of that encircling the pavement of the temple. Here a gold-clad equerry was receiving the guests and presenting them to Durakkon and his wife, beside whom Elvair-ka-Virrion was standing as proxy for his father. Fordil and his musicians were already playing—some gentle, plaintive Yeldashay melody which carried softly on the shadowy air; while some way off, beside a grove of birches, the cooks had set up their kitchen, with fires burning in trenches under grills and spits. At a little distance beyond, the southern end of the gardens was closed by a thicket of zoan trees, mixed with evergreens—juniper and ilex.

A considerable number of guests had already arrived and were strolling on the grass or sitting on benches near the water. Maia caught sight of Sarget and two or three of his friends, and as she and Occula followed Sencho's litter several young men, including Shend-Lador, smiled or waved to them, but clearly felt it more prudent, in the High Counsellor's presence, not to go the length of approaching or speaking to his girls.

It did not take Maia long to realize that they might have another reason. This was, she sensed, a rather more staid occasion than any upper city party which she had hitherto attended. It was true that a few shearnas were present in company with younger men, but most of the women looked like the wives or grown daughters of barons and similar notabilities. Also, she soon perceived that a large proportion of the guests were visitors from the provinces, and important ones at that. Many were wearing jewelled cognizances—the fountains of Kabin, the Paltesh fortress, the corn-sheaves of Sarkid and the like. Once, as they passed by, she heard Yeldashay spoken, and a few minutes later quickly averted her gaze from a dark man of about twenty-eight or nine, his face sickeningly disfigured and seamed with scars, whose fur-cloaked shoulder was adorned with a golden bear emblem.

'That's Bel-ka-Trazet, the High Baron of Ortelga,' whispered Occula. 'Give me a regular turn, he did! 'Nough to give anyone the creeps!'

'He's famous as a hunter. Durakkon invites him to hunt.'

While many of the guests—especially the Beklans—were dressed in the fine, well-cut materials and glowing colours to which Maia had grown accustomed in the upper city, the clothes of several of the older provincial visitors suggested clearly enough that they were not—to say the least—over-particular about niceties of style and fashion. Her eye fell upon a shock-haired, stubbly-bearded man leaning on a thumb-stick and looking like nothing so much as an old drover, who was surrounded by five or six people plainly full of respect and gratified to be in his company.

'Whoever's that?' she asked Occula.

'No idea, banzi, but he could easily be a baron from somewhere quite important. A lot of the provincial barons make a point of comin' up to Bekla for the spring festival. Their wives enjoy it, and I dare say they often feel like a bit of an outin' themselves after being shut up all through Melekril; and then, of course, some of them have to pay their tribute, renew their vows to their overlord—all that sort of thing. Or they may want to have a word with Durakkon, or just let him see they're still about. Barons who sulk in their own dumps all the year round are apt to be regarded with suspish, you know. You can bet Piggy's goin' to be noticin' all right—who's here and who isn', I mean. A lot of them almost make a point of *not* dressin' up for it—you know, they're not all that wealthy, some of them, and they're proud. They reckon what's good enough for Kowshittika's good enough for Bekla, and they doan' care who sees it.'

'Well, I reckon, all this lot, 's a pity Milvushina isn't here 'stead o' me,' said Maia. 'Be more in her line than mine. Might have done her a bit of good, too.'

'That's why she's not been brought, of course,' said Occula. 'Truth is, I think Piggy's begun to realize he may have bitten off a bit more than he could chew when he helped himself to Milvushina like that. I only hope to Cran he doesn' decide the safest thing's to put her out of the way.'

'You really think he'd do that?'

'I'm bastin' well sure of it, banzi. You've never really got it through your head, have you, what a cruel brute he is? Still, never mind that now. Here we are, I think.'

They had come to a stretch of turf close by the water-side and not far from the kitchens and supper tables. The soldiers put the litter down and Sencho was helped by the girls to rise and take a few steps as far as a low bank, bordered by flowerbeds, where a kind of divan had been prepared with cushions and brightly-coloured rugs. Maia busied herself in making him comfortable, while Occula gave instructions to Durakkon's butler—who had been waiting for the High Counsellor—about what he wished to drink.

Maia herself was exhilarated by the atmosphere and arrangement of the party, which was rather like an aristocratic version of a village festival. For those who wanted to eat formally there were tables under the trees, and here slaves waited upon any guest who came and sat down. Many, however, preferred simply to go to the cooks' tables, get their plates filled and then join groups of friends beside the water or in the arbours. She caught sight of the drover-baron walking about, gnawing a drumstick as he made himself agreeable to old friends: no one appeared to think him in the least odd.

Sencho displayed all his habitual gluttony, more than once requiring Maia to bring three or four different dishes together, in order that he might taste each before deciding what to enjoy next. His greed, however, was leisurely and interspersed with much talk and business. The two girls, carrying out their duties as unobtrusively as possible, were frequently required to stand aside as people approached, ostensibly to greet him and pay their respects, but in reality to beg favours, offer some promise, bribe or bargain, or circumspectly try to influence him against an enemy or rival. Sencho, often seeming, disconcertingly, to know as much about their affairs as they did themselves, said for the most part much less than the suppliants, while they for their part became more and more loquacious and self-revealing in their efforts to move him. Now and then he was deliberately and insultingly inattentive; yet once, when a baron from Paltesh mentioned something relating to the affairs of an Urtan dowager who had begged a favour of him an hour earlier, he instantly connected the two and told Maia to go and find the woman and tell her to return. It was clear to both girls—the only witnesses of the earlier interview—that he meant to make use of the young baron to prove her a liar and put her out of countenance.

Going up through the gardens on this errand, she happened upon Elvair-ka-Virrion. He was leaning against a tree, sharing raisins from a silver bowl with a tall, dark-haired young woman and her brother (or at all events, thought Maia, the two of them looked very much alike). Seeing her, he at once called her over.

'Maia!' said Elvair-ka-Virrion, smiling and taking her arm for a moment as though they had been equals. 'You grow more beautiful every day.'

She felt embarrassed, knowing that if he persisted in conversing with her it must sooner or later transpire that she was a slave. Might as well get it over with, she thought. She murmured something, raised a palm to her forehead and stood waiting with bent head.

'This is what our slave-girls look like in Bekla nowadays,' said Elvair-ka-Virrion to his companions. 'You ought to come and live here, T'maa.'

The young man laughed and said something complimentary.

'Are you attending on the High Counsellor?' asked Elvair-ka-Virrion.

'Yes, my lord. I must go now, an' all—he's sent me to find someone, you see.'

She was off before he could say more, but after a few yards found him at her elbow.

'Maia, is Milvushina here tonight?'

'No, my lord. He left her at home.'

'That's the son and daughter of a Yeldashay baron with me. They've been asking about her. They knew she was alive: they say everyone in Chalcon knows what's happened to her.'

Maia made no reply.

'If the three of us were to go to Sencho's house now, do you think your Terebinthia woman would let us see Milvushina?'

'For money, my lord, yes, I'm pretty sure she would. But you really must let me go now, please: I'll be in trouble else.' And once more she left him.

However, her errand was still not to be free from interruptions. Searching along the water-side, she could not resist stopping for a moment to

384

admire the swans. Three or four of them, attracted like moths to the light, had swum up to the edge of the lake and, their white plumage tinged now rosy, now blue or green as they oared back and forth between the lamps, were taking food thrown to them by the guests. One of these, turning suddenly, revealed himself as Bayub-Otal. Before she could hurry away he had caught up with her.

'I suppose you're with the High Counsellor, Maia,' he said, falling into step beside her on the path.

'Yes, my lord.'

'And is that pleasant?'

'I've told you before, my lord; I'm a slave.'

For a few moments he made no reply, only watching her as she darted glances among the people they passed.

'Whom are you looking for?'

'A lady as the High Counsellor's sent me to find.'

Suddenly he stopped dead, gripping her by the wrist so hard and un-expectedly that she was brought up standing with a jolt. She gave a quick cry of vexation, but then, restraining herself, stood looking up at him silently.

'You—you don't have to go on being a slave, you know,' he said abruptly.

'What, my lord?'

'I said, you needn't go on being a slave. You can leave that brute before he does you any more harm. If you want, you can leave Bekla and become— well, become a real woman.'

'I don't understand, my lord. What do you mean?'

'Not what I believe you suppose. I won't say more now, but if ever you come to think better of yourself, Maia—if you want to leave Bekla— you've only to tell me—that's if I'm still here to be told.'

'If you mean as you want to buy me, my lord, then I think you'd better speak to the High Counsellor yourself. Then you—'

But he was gone, turning on his heel and striding away between the bushes and the coloured lamps. She stared after him a moment, then shrugged her shoulders and was going on her way when suddenly she caught sight of the Urtan dowager talking to Durakkon himself.

The lady, plainly flustered by Maia's message, immediately excused herself to Durakkon (shows which one she's more afraid of, thought Maia) and hurried away over the lawn. Maia followed more slowly, won-dering exactly what Bayub-Otal might have meant. She had better consult Occula, she thought, once they could be alone together.

At this moment she was surprised to see Occula herself approaching along a path through the trees. She was plainly in a hurry, peering here

385

and there and looking, thought Maia, really upset—almost beside herself. Several people turned to stare as she passed them.

Maia ran up to her. 'Occula, I couldn't help it! I only just found the old lady—she was talking to the High Baron. She's gone to see Sencho just this minute—'

Occula appeared scarcely to have heard her.

'Banzi! Thank Cran I found you! Look, keep away, d'you see? Doan' go back to him—not on *any* account! Leave him to me, d'you understand?'

'Oh, Occula, is he angry? Honestly, I couldn't have been any quicker—'

'No, no, he's not angry: I can' explain. But keep away! Doan' go back, that's all! Leave me to see to him.'

'But whatever—I mean, how long for?'

'Well—until—oh, banzi, doan' ask!'

Occula paused. Her breath was coming fast and she was trembling. 'Hell, I ought to have sent you back home to fetch somethin', oughtn' I? You'd have swallowed *that*. Look, banzi, just keep out of the way for—well, say, for half an hour.'

'All right, dear; if you say so. But are you sure you can manage him by yourself?'

'Yes! Yes! Give me a kiss, banzi; my dear, dearest banzi! Good-bye!'

Maia kissed her and Occula, with what sounded like a quick sob, instantly suppressed, hastened away across the grass.

Maia, once more alone, tried to imagine what could possibly have put her into such a state. It was bewildering. At least, however, she had said that Sencho wasn't angry; that was reassuring.

Suddenly she knew what it must be. That crass, clumsy fool Bayub-Otal had then and there gone and asked Sencho to sell her to him. Yes, of course, that must be it! And Occula had been afraid that if she, Maia, came back in the middle, while Bayub-Otal was still talking to Sencho, he might make a scene, or she might lose her head and start begging Sencho to let her go. Whereas Occula reckoned that if she herself could only spend half an hour alone with Sencho when he'd got rid of Bayub-Otal, she could probably cool him down.

But then, how ought she to act when she did return? Oh, simply wait and see; it would all depend. He might be drunk by that time, or Occula might have gratified him and got him off to sleep. Or better still, he might want her, Maia, to gratify him: that would put her beyond any risk of his displeasure.

The mood of the party, she noticed, was beginning to change. Most of the older people seemed to be leaving. Not far away, a little group of obvious heldril were making their farewells to Durakkon, while near-by she could hear a grizzled baron saying something to his wife about the evening having lasted long enough. She turned back towards the lake, and as she did so two young men ran past her, one waving a flagon and calling out the name of Shend-Lador. Evidently the younger Leopards were now intending to make a night of it. Would Sencho be more likely to stay or go? she wondered. On the one hand his greed, now indulged, might dispose him to sleep, but on the other his lust might cause him to remain awake for a while yet.

A little distance away she could hear shouts and laughter. There were cries of 'Go on!' 'Go on, Sychar!' Then a splash was followed by ironical cheering. Looking in the direction of the noise, she could make out dark figures dodging about, obscuring and again revealing the coloured lamps among the trees.

The swans were no longer to be seen. How nice it would be, she thought, simply to take off her clothes and plunge into the water—just to strike out into the moonlit emptiness for a good, long swim. Of course, this silly old Barb was nothing to Lake Serrelind. How long was it, she wondered—half a mile? Not much more. The further end was only two or three hundred yards away from Sencho's house. What fun it would be to swim down there—she could do it in half an hour, easy—oh, yes, less— and then just climb out, like one of those water-nymphs in old Drigga's stories, and walk in. Ah, and she could just see Terebinthia's face an' all—

'Maia! All alone? What are you doing now—just going to bathe, were you?'

It was Elvair-ka-Virrion, sauntering alone, apparently at a loose end. As she turned and smiled at him he took her in his arms and kissed her warmly, fondling her body up and down through the smooth, supple material of the tunic.

'Why, my lord, I thought you said as you were going off to see Milvu-shina?'

'T'maa and his sister have gone. I'm joining them there later. But never mind about that. A moment ago, before you saw me, you were looking as if you'd love to dive in.'

'So I would, my lord. Nothing I'd like better!'

'It's deep, you know—deeper than you think. The Pool of Light's more than three times as deep as a man.'

'Wouldn't worry me, my lord. Deeper the better!'

'You really *can* swim, then?'

'In the lake, back home, I used to swim—oh, ever so far.'

'*Did* you?' He stooped quickly, drew one of her arms round his neck and then, with the other under the crook of her knees, lifted her bodily.

'Oh, please don't throw me in, my lord! Not in these clothes—that'd make a right old lot of trouble for me, that would!'

'I'm not going to.'

He was carrying her easily along the shore in his arms. Although she had no idea what he had in mind, she could not help enjoying it. Within a minute they had reached the outskirts of the frolic going on round the Pool of Light. About twenty or thirty young Leopards, together with perhaps half as many girls, were gathered along the shore, shouting with laughter as they pelted and cheered on a young man who had plunged in fully clothed and was laboriously splashing his way across the pool, supporting himself on a floating wine-cask. Looking at him, Maia could feel only contempt for his stupid clowning. He was, she felt, merely spoiling and uglifying the whole notion of swimming. It was like as if he'd started hopping about while Fordil was playing the music for the senguela.

Elvair-ka-Virrion put her down.

'Can you swim better than that?'

'Than *that*, my lord? Dear oh law, that's not swimming! Why, I could dive out of that zoan tree there and be half-way 'cross the pool 'fore anyone'd seen me go!'

'Could you indeed?' said Elvair-ka-Virrion. 'Well, if you really can, I'll—'

He stood laughing down at her, his teeth very white in his shadowed face. A girl ran past, calling 'Elvair, come on! We're going to pull him out!' Elvair-ka-Virrion ignored her and she disappeared among the bushes.

'Can you?'

'Whatever you say, my lord. But's anyone going to mind if I'm naked? Only—well—all these old heldril, and the High Baron's not far off, either. I don't want no trouble—'

'Trouble—*you*—naked?' said Elvair-ka-Virrion. 'Ha! Don't worry; I'll see to that.'

Maia, drawing the combs out of her hair and pocketing them, unbuttoned the embroidered tunic and took it off, together with her shift. Elvair-ka-Virrion stretched out his arms to her, but she smiled and shook her head.

'One thing at a time, my lord. On'y this is serious stuff, see?'

With this she ran across the grass to the foot of the zoan not thirty yards away. No one seemed to notice her, for they were all watching the young man struggling out on the further bank. In a moment she had seized a low branch and pulled herself up into the fork. Having taken stock of the tree, the pool and her potential audience, she began edging up a long, sloping bough which extended over the water.

From one branchy hand-hold to another she inched her way outward, until the thinning bough began to sag under her weight. Go out any further, she thought, and I won't have enough support for a dive. Ah, here was a good place, though—nice and open, no other branches to get in the way and the water—oh, eleven or twelve feet down, perhaps; hard to tell in this light, but it looked deep enough.

At this moment two young men walking along the bank looked up, saw her and stopped in amazement. Pointing, they called out to others further off. People began running towards the zoan, staring and exclaiming.

'Careful—you'll fall!' 'No, she won't!' 'What a pretty girl!' 'Why not come down and go to bed with me?' 'Who is she?' 'Look out!'

'It's the senguela dancer!' cried a voice.

'She's going to dive!' shouted Elvair-ka-Virrion at the top of his voice.

At this there was some derisory laughter and someone shouted 'When? Next year?'

Maia, facing the full moon, her toes flexed on the rough, fissured bark, was on the very point of diving when suddenly she saw through the foliage a woman gazing directly up at her. The glimpse, between the faintly-moving, silvery leaves, was like a face seen in a dream—indistinct yet disturbing; arrestingly beautiful, yet in some way menacing too. The wide, commanding eyes, framed in an aureole of hair gleaming in the moonlight, were staring—with approbation, certainly—but also with a kind of intent rapacity which frightened her even as she sensed it.

Startled and thrown off balance, she swayed and for an instant tried to stop short. But this was no longer possible. Thereupon the naturally-acquired skill of years came to her rescue. Her body knew instinctively that it must dive.

To the watchers below there seemed no trace of hesitation. One moment she was standing in the moonlight, high among the zoan boughs. The next she had dived outward, straight and taut, hair streaming and the leafy branch thrashing behind her, to plunge through the surface of the lake with a single, quickly-gone splash and a symmetry of outward-flowing ripples.

In the instant of diving Maia had recognized the watcher below her. It was the Sacred Queen.

These Beklans were no swimmers: that she had known all along. To them, a girl who made nothing of plunging twelve feet into deep water seemed almost miraculous. All round her, from both banks, arose cries of wonder and acclamation. Waving, she turned on her back, arching her breasts clear of the surface and then, with hands gently fanning beneath her, eased herself smoothly towards the centre of the pool.

The water was warmer than she had expected. It really was a lovely night for a swim. Should she, after all, simply swim away down the length of the Barb? Ah, but the High Counsellor? And then again, she'd better not lose touch with Elvair-ka-Virrion, who'd promised to keep her out of trouble. Still, all these rich people—she might as well show them a thing or two now she'd started. One thing might lead to another, as Occula was always saying.

Swimming towards the shore, she stopped some yards out and lowered her feet, but found no bottom. A small crowd had gathered on the bank, as near to her as they could get. One young man knelt, miming anguished longing and holding out his hands in mock entreaty, while another took off his gold chain and held it up, offering to give it to her if only she would come ashore and let him put it round her neck for himself.

Exhilarated, she began to tantalize them, jumping herself up and down in the water and opening her arms in invitation.

'Who's going to join me?' she cried, laughing up at them. 'Isn't there a single one of you man enough to come in and catch me?'

'It's too deep, Maia,' called Shend-Lador. 'Come a bit further in, where we can wade!'

He pointed along the curve of the shore. After one quick look to make sure of her direction and the distance, she dived under, swam a dozen strokes and came up to find herself just in her depth and about twenty yards out from the bank.

'You're afraid, aren't you?' she called to Shend-Lador. 'You're afraid to come in and catch me!'

For answer he began taking off his clothes, tossing them here and there and then sitting down while two of the girls, shouting with laughter, pulled off his shoes and breeches. Four or five other young men followed his example.

'What's the reward, Maia?' shouted a young gallant with a wreath of scarlet trepsis round his shoulders.

Before she could speak, Elvair-ka-Virrion's voice answered.

'Anyone who catches her can have her—that's the reward!'

Already Shend-Lador and three more had leapt into the water and were wading out towards her. One of these, an older man, tried to clutch Shend-Lador and pull him back, but himself overbalanced and fell his length amid roars of delight from the spectators. Maia, waiting until the last possible moment, swam a few lazy strokes further out. Shend-Lador plunged after her up to his neck, whereupon she turned and slipped shorewards past him, stroking his cheek with her fingers and gliding away as he made a clumsy grab which missed her by a foot.

Now she was swimming back and forth between them as they floundered and clutched this way and that; pretending to offer herself and vanishing under water just when they all felt sure she must be caught; coming up behind Shend-Lador and nibbling his shoulder before he had even realized she was there. Then, swimming inshore again, she stood up no more than knee-deep, displaying herself in the moonlight, imploring them to make haste, for she felt so lonely and feared she would never be caught at all. At this a big, bearded man, still in the act of undressing, leapt off the bank in his breeches and came splashing towards her. Maia, diving quickly, pulled them round his knees as he lunged forward, groping. Shouts of laughter and derision rose from the bank as her prank revealed that he had plainly been very eager to catch her indeed.

Although their admiration and her own sense of supremacy were delightful, nevertheless she could not help beginning, now, to feel a trifle weary of the game. She had hoped that there might have been one swimmer among them at least. As it was, the whole lot of them together couldn't have caught her if they'd tried all night, and her common sense told her that however desirable she might be, they would soon get tired of being made to look fools. Yet how best to bring it to an end? She had not foreseen that Elvair-ka-Virrion, in his high spirits, would take it upon himself to offer her as a prize. All the same, she thought, she'd have had no real objection. They were all rich and high-born, else they wouldn't be here. The story would have got around and likely increased her popularity; and besides, there'd almost certainly have been a generous lygol into the bargain. She could simply have picked out a man she fancied, let herself be caught in some amusing way and then done what was expected of her. But what put all this out of the question was the High Counsellor. Ah, and it must be about time she was getting back to him an' all. Perhaps he was already asking where she'd got to? If he were to miss her and then learn that she'd been—She thought of Meris. Oh, Cran, there was no time to be lost; no, not a minute! She'd better just swim straight back along the lake—they'd never let her go else—never mind her clothes—she could always ask a slave to go and fetch them back from Elvair-ka-Virrion.

Suddenly, cutting through the hubbub, there came a different kind of cry—quick and desperate, a yell of fear cut short in a choking gasp. Shend-Lador, in his eagerness to reach her, had missed his footing and was struggling in deep water. As she looked, his head went under, reappeared for a moment and vanished.

Most of those on the bank were still running about laughing. Only a few had seen what had happened, and these were shouting helplessly and pointing to where Shend-Lador had disappeared.

Maia, reaching the place in six or seven strokes and diving instantly, came upon him a few feet below the surface. He was still struggling, but feebly. As she seized him he grabbed her in panic and she bit his hand as hard as she could. He let go and she kicked upward, got his head above water, turned on her back and dragged him some five or six yards towards the bank. Splashing and jerking, he clutched her again and almost pulled her under; this time she could scarcely break his hold and, having done so with difficulty, was forced to let him go while she recovered herself. They were both in their depth now, but he could not stand unaided. She put one arm round him, trying to reassure him as he leant upon her, vomiting water over her shoulder.

'All right, Maia, leave him now. You've done enough!'

It was Elvair-ka-Virrion, together with some other young man whom she did not know. Together they took Shend-Lador between them and began wading back towards the bank. Maia, swimming, reached it before them, put her hands on the stone coping, vaulted out and turned, sitting with her legs in the water. She felt exhausted, and now noticed for the first time a deep scratch along her arm. It was bleeding and it hurt. No one was paying any attention to her. They were all gathered round Shend-Lador as Elvair-ka-Virrion heaved him up onto the grass.

'What's your name, child?'

She looked up. Standing over her was the Sacred Queen, gazing down with the same intent, unsmiling expression that had startled her in diving from the zoan tree.

Maia, having no idea what it was correct for her to do, and all-too-conscious of her wet, bleeding, dishevelled nakedness, scrambled up and knelt at the queen's feet.

'I said, what's your name?'

'Maia, säiyett. Maia of Serrelind.'

'Stand up.'

Maia did as she was told. The queen was only slightly taller than herself. She was wearing a white cloak over a pale-green robe gathered at the waist with an enamelled belt, in which was sheathed a pair of silver knives. A little way behind her stood a dark, middle-aged woman in a plain but very fine dress of grey silk who must, Maia realized, be in attendance.

'What are you doing in Bekla, Maia? Have you come up for the festival?'

'No, säiyett. I'm in the household of the High Counsellor.'

'In the household of the High Counsellor. *Are* you? Do you know who I am?'

'Yes, säiyett.'

'You call me "esta-säiyett". You're a slave, you mean? A bed-slave?'

Maia nodded.

'How old are you?'

'Sixteen, esta-säiyett.'

The queen unexpectedly stretched out one hand, rubbed her fingers along Maia's bleeding arm and licked them.

392

'Then why aren't you with the High Counsellor now?'

'I ought to be, esta-säiyett. I was just going to—'

She stopped, confused, for the queen, without the slightest alteration of manner, had begun to stroke and pinch her wet, naked buttocks.

'Plump, aren't you? You eat well, I suppose?'

Before Maia could answer, a sudden, bellowing cry—unmistakably the cry of a man in mortal agony—carried across the entire length of the gardens, instantly silencing every vestige of talk and murmur between. Hard upon it came the screaming of a girl and terrified calls for help. The voice came from among the trees more than four hundred yards away, but Maia would have known it at any distance, for it was Occula's.

Sencho, gulping the last of a bowl of thrilsa mixed with mulled wine and honey, lay back in the cushions and signed to the black girl to rub his belly. He was enjoying a happy sense of full satisfaction. The petty deception attempted by the Urtan dowager, who had returned in alarm and self-abasement, had been exposed, and her mortification had been most enjoyable. Although he knew that several other provincial dignitaries were hoping to speak to him, he did not intend to talk to anyone else tonight. Replete with the excellent and copious dinner, he now felt disposed towards pleasures less mentally strenuous than those of withholding sought favours or playing off one petitioner against another. Besides, his cunning mind knew very well when it had exerted itself sufficiently for the time being. Though by no means incapable, he nevertheless knew that he would now do better to desist from further business.

He felt inclined for the Tonildan girl, but she had not as yet returned from her errand to fetch the dowager. Still, there was no immediate hurry. He would rest for a time and allow his dinner to settle, for the girl, being young and enthusiastic, often tended to be somewhat over-energetic as well. Half-dozing, he began to indulge one of his favourite fantasies—that of devouring the world and everything in it. In his imagination he gorged like an ogre on great flocks of cattle, acres of crops and teeming cities; gulped down pools, lakes and rivers; stuffed himself with basketsful of fat babies and barrow-loads of succulent, chubby little boys and girls. Then, when nothing remained of his feast, he would sleep it off while the gods, at his command, created a fresh world, ready to be consumed when he awoke.

Soon his meditation turned to imaginings of delicious cruelty. He thought, one by one, of the personal enemies whose ruin he had contrived, and of all those by whose deaths he had profited. He had watched them die, some of them, and been present, too, when they were condemned. Some had begged for mercy, offered all their wealth in exchange for their

393

lives—wealth which the Leopards had acquired anyway, through the forfeiture of their estates. Half of Enka-Mordet's estate would come to him shortly. Ah, but the singular, subtle pleasure of enslaving his daughter—he had had to take special, discreet steps to make sure of that! It had been expensive, of course—the secret instruction and bribery of the soldiers—but it had been worth it.

The infliction of humiliation and anguish on a well-bred girl was a pleasure for which, unfortunately, opportunity all too seldom arose. The sort of women who fell into his power rarely had enough pride or social standing to make their humiliation really amusing. Indeed, many of the coarser kind of young women often seemed positively to enjoy being ill-treated by a man as exalted as himself. It had certainly been pleasant to debase and nauseate that expensive shearna who had come to his house with Kembri's son a few weeks ago. She had thought herself become too exalted for such pastimes: she had found out that she was wrong. Nevertheless, where popular, well-connected shearnas were concerned, one had to be careful about giving way to impulses of that kind. Yet where was the pleasure in degrading slave-girls who had no dignity of which to be deprived?

As the sensations of satiety in his distended belly began to subside under the skilful ministrations of the black girl, his lust became more urgent and he looked about in growing annoyance for the Tonildan, who should certainly have come back by now. She was beginning to fancy herself too much, was that child. She probably even supposed that he entertained some sort of feeling for her. He knew very well that she thought herself his favourite. Her disillusionment in this respect might, perhaps, be coupled in some way with tormenting Milvushina. Perhaps Terebinthia would be able to devise something really original. Meanwhile his immediate craving was simpler.

The black girl was bending over him, whispering solicitously and sliding her warm, pink tongue between his lips. She was good at her work. He had grown to trust her; she had shown herself one of his best purchases ever. During his recent indisposition she had proved better than Terebinthia, seeming to know exactly what he needed and how to help him to recover his spirits. The true reason for this, he knew, was the existence of some strange affinity between them. She possessed, he had come to realize, a ruthlessness, a well-masked savagery in certain ways akin to his own. At his heart lay a murderous hatred of the rich world that had spurned a starving ragamuffin from its doors—until that ragamuffin had learned to pander to its filthy desires. He longed for that world's destruction. So did she. At least, she longed for some sort of destruction. He was no fool; he could perceive that. She was like him to the extent that hatred was what

394

made her live; though hatred of precisely what he had not as yet been able to discern, for she was inscrutable. Now that he came to think of it, she might make a useful secret agent.

Now she was looking into his eyes, murmuring very close and low in a language unknown; sibilant and eager, an invitation, a promise of something lewdly delectable. In response to this cryptic incitement he began to have second thoughts. To have her to gratify him now would be more enjoyable, all things considered, than the Tonildan. How pleasant his life was! His great wealth, his enemies destroyed, every luxury and indulgence at his command! Her strange, unknown words sounded in his ears like an affirmation of security, an invincible charm. Yes, she understood him very well, this fellow-pirate. He was in haste for her.

Even the High Counsellor could not gratify his lust openly, in the gardens of the Barb and the presence of provincial barons and their wives. Impatient, he raised himself in the cushions and looked about for the soldiers.

'The boat, my lord,' whispered the black girl. 'There's a boat, do you see? Just down there, look. We'll go a little way off, in the boat. That'll be the easiest way.'

Two of the attendant soldiers came forward to help him to his feet, but he waved them away, content to clutch her arm. Ah, but he hardly needed help! He felt young again, on his way to the iron-hills of Gelt, on his way to make money once more in Kabin of the Waters: a sharp fellow, one who knew very well how to sail with the stream; one who had grown fat on the blood of his enemies. Only a few steps, yes, just a few gasping steps to the water-side. Slaves had filled the narrow flat-bottomed boat with cushions and into these he sank, while the black girl, seated at his feet, loosed the cord, took up a paddle and pushed gently away from the bank.

'We needn't go far, my lord,' she said, smiling down at him. 'Just up among those trees. No one'll see us there.'

Now the boat was gliding smoothly, only a few feet from the bank, slipping quietly up the margin of the lake, past the scullions dowsing their fires and the cooks packing up their utensils after the evening's work. There was a pleasant smell of smouldering logs. The black girl had slipped out of her clothes and now sat naked on the thwart, her body gleaming in the moonlight as she bent, dipped her paddle and rose again, this side and that, gently guiding the boat towards the zoan grove bordering the far end of the gardens. The moon had dropped behind the trees and the inshore water was lying in deep shadow. Into this warm seclusion the boat slid with scarcely a ripple—merely a light chuckling under the bow and then a gentle scraping as it touched the bank and came to a stop. Laying down her paddle, the black girl knelt and secured the cords fore and aft to two projecting roots.

395

Now she was stretched beside him, fondling him, her fingers deft and busy under his thin robe. In growing excitement he began caressing her thighs, clutching her, fondling her breasts.

'You're the god Cran, my lord,' she whispered, 'and I'm your Sacred Queen.'

Laughing, she mounted astride him, sinking down upon him, panting. Her rapid plungings began to shake and agitate the boat, sending a succession of ripples out across the water.

'Ah, *now*, my lord!' she cried. 'Now! Now!' Yet thereupon, unexpectedly, she rolled quickly over and away from him, slipping out of his embrace.

As she did so, two figures rose silently out of the undergrowth of the zoan thicket. The taller, holding a wooden stake sharpened to a point at one end, plunged it downward into the huge belly, leant on it and then, jabbing, levered it back and forth. His companion, a woman carrying a knife, crouched down and drove it again and again into the folds of fat at the High Counsellor's throat. Once only he cried out—a roaring bellow which died away as the blood filled his mouth and spurted over his neck and shoulders.

The black girl, snatching the knife, drove it twice into her own thigh and once into her arm. Then, while the attackers made off, one dragging the other by the wrist, she began to scream. As her blood ran down, mingling with her master's, he clutched in agony at the stake jutting from his paunch, shuddered and lay still.

When the first of the soldiers and kitchen-slaves came bursting through the undergrowth from the gardens, they found only the High Counsellor's concubine beside the body, sobbing hysterically, calling on her gods and beating blindly, with bloody hands, at assailants who were nowhere to be seen.

: 40 :

INVESTIGATION

The murder of Sencho-bè-L'vandor, High Counsellor of Bekla, at a state festivity, within earshot and almost within sight of the High Baron, the Sacred Queen and some two or three hundred assembled dignitaries of the empire, spread not only shock but something close to panic, first through the upper and then the lower city. The deed was bewildering and minatory as an earthquake tremor. None could tell what might be going to follow; whether this was simply an isolated act of vengeance carried out by two of the great number with good reason to hate the High Counsellor, or the prelude to an organized, armed insurrection against the Leopard régime. How many murderous agents might there be in the city? How many in other cities—in Thettit, Ikat, Dari-Paltesh? Who might be those marked down as their victims?

Fear and suspicion ran everywhere: among the guests, making haste to be gone from the gardens; many, as they went, arranging to remain together for the rest of the night and set out for home no later than dawn; among slaves and servants, warned by their masters to go armed, to keep strict watch and trust no one: among soldiers, an hour ago glad not to have been sent to the Valderra, now ordered to search cellars and attics in the dark; among tradesmen and merchants, fearful for their stock; among shearnas and their admirers, both, as they learned the tidings, reflecting how little they really knew of this other who lay staring and wondering beside them in the lamplight; among the priests of Cran, hiding the temple treasures and sending young Sednil hotfoot to the upper city with an urgent request for the guard to be doubled. Fear was in the creak of a door, the howling of a dog, the sound of footsteps outside.

The sheer audacity of the killing intensified the dread it evoked. If the High Counsellor, in the very midst of his luxury, could fall a victim, with slaves and soldiers on every hand, then who could count himself safe? And the unknown killers had vanished like ghosts at cock-crow. From the upper city, completely walled round and sentinelled, out of which was no egress save by the Peacock Gate, they had simply disappeared. Search, next day, of every slope and cleft on Mount Crandor revealed no least trace of them. So incredible was this that many wondered whether in fact there had ever been any assailants at all. The High Counsellor's black concubine, who had been with him when he met his death, had, of course, been held for questioning, as had the other, the Tonildan girl who had accompanied him to the gardens that night. To some, despite the gruesome and brutal nature of the High Counsellor's wounds, it seemed more likely that the black girl herself had killed him than that two intruders, for whose existence there was only her word, should have contrived to escape from the upper city unseen. But no, said others: she might, to be sure, have taken a knife with her in the boat unnoticed by her tipsy, lecherous master; but the stake had been cut from the zoan thicket and sharpened there (shavings had been found; and the stump). And this the girl would not have had time to do, even supposing that her master had been too gorged and heedless to stop her. Ah, but might it not have been left there, ready for her use, by an accomplice? Well, possibly. Anyway, they all concluded, she was unlikely to come out of the business with her life. Whatever part she might or might not have played, the authorities, if only to be on the safe side, would no doubt put her out of the way.

397

Such was the general opinion, which did not fail to reach the ears of Maia in her cell in the temple of Cran.

By noon of the third day after the murder the Lord General was back in the city, having been overtaken by the news when no more than two days' march away. He, after no more than the barest of consultations with Durakkon, at once set about seeking the truth. So far as was known, Sencho had never made any written lists of suspects or known dissidents, preferring to keep what he knew in his own head. A few names, however, were already known to the Lord General, while others were now given to him by certain of Sencho's agents who, scenting blood-money, came forward of their own accord. Kembri at once sent lists to the various provincial governors, ordering the arrest of all known suspects of secondary importance—servants, drabs, watermen and the like. Those of higher rank, he judged, would be best left alone for the time being. Apart from anything else, most would not be easy to apprehend without using soldiers—soldiers whom at the moment he could ill spare. Meanwhile the lesser fry—perhaps fifty or sixty in all—were to be sent under guard to Bekla.

Kembri, flanked on one side by the chief priest of Cran and on the other by the governor of Tonilda, looked up at the black girl standing before him on the other side of the table. Her eyes, bloodshot and heavy-lidded with sleeplessness, nevertheless returned his gaze steadily.

'You say,' said Kembri, 'that the High Counsellor wanted you to go with him to some secluded part of the gardens?'

'Yes, my lord.'

'Who actually suggested that—he or you?'

'He wished it, my lord. He wanted me to do what he usually required one or other of us to do after he'd had supper: but since we were in the gardens and not in his house, we had to go somewhere out of the way.'

'Very well: but the soldiers are clear that they heard you suggesting the boat.'

'Yes, my lord. Seein' what he wanted, to take the boat was the most discreet and convenient thing. I simply told the slaves to put cushions in the boat and then I helped the High Counsellor into it.'

There was a pause.

'Well, go on,' said Kembri.

'I took the boat up under the trees, my lord, where we couldn' be seen, and began doin' what the High Counsellor wanted.'

'And then, according to you, two people came out from among the trees and attacked him?'

'Yes, my lord.'

398

'You were actually lying above him at that moment? Isn't that so?'

'Yes, my lord. One of them pulled me away and stabbed me while the other set on the High Counsellor.'

'Why didn't they kill *you*, do you suppose?'

'They tried to, my lord, but I fought and struggled and I suppose they must have been in a hurry to get away.'

There was a longer pause, while the Lord General continued to stare up at the girl. At length he said, 'If you want to avoid torture, I suggest you tell me now what more you know about this business.'

'I know nothin' more, my lord.'

'Then I'll tell you what *we* know. You came up to Bekla several months ago from a house in Thettit called the Lily Pool: you came at your own request. Among the men who sometimes came to that house there was a licensed pedlar, who also used to go from time to time to the High Counsellor's house here, in the upper city.'

'Yes, Zirek: I know him, my lord.'

'Some little while ago the High Counsellor sold one of his girls, named Meris, to the Lily Pool. You know that?'

'I knew she'd been sold, my lord, but not where she'd gone. We weren' told.'

'That girl and the pedlar left the Lily Pool together a few days ago, before the spring festival. Since then they've not been seen. But you were the last person to see them, weren't you?'

'If you're askin' me whether they were the ones who did the killin', my lord, I can' say one way or the other. It was dark and the attack was very swift and violent. I couldn' have recognized anyone, whether I knew them or not.'

'No, you didn't need to, because you knew they'd be waiting there, didn't you? That was why you took the High Counsellor there.'

'No, my lord: I was well off in that household, as the säiyett Terebinthia will tell you. The High Counsellor liked me: I had no reason to kill him. May I also respectfully point out that if I'd been an accomplice I might have been expected to have escaped with the killers?'

'Take her away!' said Kembri. 'And bring in the Tonildan!'

The black girl, clearly still in pain from her wounds, limped out between the two soldiers in attendance.

'What do you make of that?' asked Kembri, turning to the governor as the door closed.

The governor, an elderly, shrewd man, hesitated.

'You're asking, of course, whether I think she knows more than she's telling us. It's tempting to conclude that she might, but it seems to me just as likely that she mightn't. After all, when she persuaded this woman in

Thettit to send her up to Bekla, neither she nor anyone else could possibly have known that Sencho was going to buy her.'

'No; but Lalloc may have thought that Sencho was likely to fancy her.'

'Lalloc, Lord General? He'd be the last man to join in a plot. All the slave-traders are Leopards to a man: they know which side their bread's buttered.'

'That's true,' replied Kembri. 'We can leave Lalloc out of it. But in fact I'm less interested in this girl's personal guilt or innocence than in how much she may know. Do you suppose she knows who was behind the killing and what they mean to do next?'

'She may very well have had some sort of hand in it and yet still know next to nothing,' cut in the chief priest. 'She could have been given instructions without knowing where they came from, let alone anything about the people at the top. She'd better be tortured: that's the only way to make sure.'

The door opened and the soldiers brought in the Tonildan girl. She was plainly terrified; staring wildly about her and scarcely able to put one foot before the other. Her long, fair hair hung in a dishevelled mass about her shoulders. Her face and hands were grimy and her eyes circled with dark rings. Appearing thus, she looked even younger than her years—a mere child, devoid of all self-possession or power to dissemble. Kembri found himself thinking that if she was innocent he felt sorry for her.

'Bring up that bench,' he said to one of the soldiers. 'Let her sit down.'

The girl half-fell on to the bench, breathing hard and staring out of her blue eyes like a trapped animal.

'You come from Tonilda, don't you?' said Kembri.

The girl nodded speechlessly.

'Did you know Occula before you came to Bekla?'

'No, my lord: we met on the way here. At Puhra, 'twas.'

'I see,' said Kembri. He leaned across the table. 'Now, if you don't want to die, tell me who told you that the two of you were to take part in murdering the High Counsellor.'

At this the girl broke into a torrent of weeping.

'I never knew nothing about it, my lord! I wasn't nowhere near when it happened, even! I—'

The soldiers shook her and she became silent.

'We know that,' said Kembri. 'The truth is, you weren't where you should have been, were you? You were supposed to be attending on the High Counsellor. You had no business to leave him—'

'But he'd *sent* me, my lord! He'd sent me, himself, to find an Urtan lady and tell her as he wanted to see her—'

'Yes, we know that, too. But after you'd found her and delivered your message you didn't go back to him, did you? Your job was to distract attention; to entice everyone you could to watch you in the water down at the other end of the garden. What happened when you went to look for the Urtan lady, and why didn't you go back to the High Counsellor as soon as you'd found her?'

'First I happened to meet Lord Elvair-ka-Virrion, my lord, and he began talking to me, but I told him as I had this errand to do. And then, while I was on looking for the lady, I met Lord Bayub-Otal.'

'Bayub-Otal?' said Kembri sharply. In all the turmoil of the last few days he had forgotten this girl's connection with Bayub-Otal—a suspect if ever there was one. Now it returned to him forcefully. 'Well, and what did *he* say to you?'

'He said, my lord, as I needn't go on being a slave-girl if I didn't want. And then—'

'He said *what*?' asked Kembri. The chief priest, who had been conferring with the governor of Tonilda, looked up sharply.

'My lord, he said if ever I wanted to leave Bekla I'd only to tell him.'

Kembri and the governor looked at each other.

'And what did you reply to that?' asked the governor.

'I said, my lord, that if he meant as he wanted to buy me, he'd better speak to the High Counsellor, not to me: and then he was off; he just went away very sharp, like.'

'To speak to the High Counsellor, you mean?'

'I can't say, my lord. At the time I reckoned he must have, and I thought as that was likely to make the High Counsellor mad at me. I mean, he might think I'd suggested the idea myself, like. So I reckoned I'd wait a little while 'fore I went back; only he was always in a better frame of mind after he'd been with a girl, you see.'

'You mean, you thought you'd leave him to Occula?'

'Yes, my lord, I did think that.'

'Well, and what then?' said the governor.

'So while I was waiting, Lord Elvair-ka-Virrion, he come up to me again, and asked was I a good swimmer?'

'Why did he ask you that?'

'Well, his friends was all playing round the water, see? So I says yes, I was good, and then he said if I could swim so well I'd better show everyone. So I just done what he said.' She paused; then burst out passionately, 'It's true, my lord! He'll tell you himself!'

'You can leave that to us,' said Kembri. 'All right; take her away!'

When the soldiers had gone he said, 'My son's already told me that it was he who put her up to the swimming game: but I wanted to hear what she had to say herself. Actually, I doubt she was deliberately trying to distract attention from the killing.'

'Still, both girls had better be tortured,' said the chief priest. 'Don't you agree?'

Kembri made no immediate reply. The truth was that for various reasons he felt disinclined to consent. Judicial torture in Bekla (which by law could be used only upon slaves) was a function of the priesthood of Cran. Kembri had never liked the chief priest, whom he had always suspected of being in some sort of secret understanding with Sencho. It now appeared to him that the chief priest—a celibate but not a eunuch—seemed distastefully eager for a little torture—more so than he would have been if the suspects had been labourers rather than pretty girls. As concubines these two were above average and likely to become excellent shearnas. They were popular. One or two of the young Leopards, in fact, had already mentioned to him privately that they hoped he might be able to avoid torturing them. Besides, they were valuable property, no less than jewels or silver. Sencho had left no heir and everything he had possessed now belonged to the state—strictly speaking, to the temple: but Kembri himself and other Leopard leaders would come in for a cut. The idea of torturing, and thereby ruining, or at least gravely damaging, a couple of girls worth fourteen or fifteen thousand meld apiece, simply on the chance that they might know a little—not much—more than they had already told, struck him, on balance, as more loss than gain. What he was really seeking at this juncture was clear evidence against Santil-kè-Erketlis, which was more likely to be obtainable from arrested Tonildans than from secluded Beklan dwellers like these girls. Lastly and most important, what the Tonildan child had said about Bayub-Otal had just suggested to Kembri an entirely new means of gaining information, which he felt strongly ought to be made all possible use of.

The governor and the chief priest were awaiting his answer. He thought quickly. It would hardly do simply to set aside the chief priest altogether and order the release of both girls: better to settle for releasing the Tonildan, who in any case was almost certainly innocent and for whom he now had a special use. The black girl, against whom suspicion was stronger, would have to be relinquished to the priests. A pity, but there it was.

'The black girl, yes,' he replied. 'As for the Tonildan, though, I'd like to tell you something that's just occurred to me with regard to Bayub-Otal. If I'm not mistaken, it could turn out very valuable indeed.'

Once more Maia, this time with unchained hands and no soldiers behind her, sat on the bench facing the Lord General. Until this moment, she had been close to hysteria and collapse. Only her fear of her questioners had enabled her to control herself sufficiently to answer them. During the past few days, since the killing, she had suffered unspeakable agonies of terror and anxiety, unable to eat and scarcely to sleep, anticipating every dreadful conclusion to what had become a continuous, waking nightmare. Often she called to mind the ghastly corpses which she and Occula, on their way to Bekla, had seen hanging by the road; and at such times, crouching in the cell where they had locked her, she would cover her face and rock to and fro, sobbing and calling on Lespa and Shakkarn to put an end to her life. The knowledge that she was innocent comforted her no more than it has ever comforted any helpless person in arrest under a despotism. What she knew was that she was in dire trouble, that the authorities were looking for culprits and that she had no influential friend to speak for her. She had given herself up for dead and hoped only that the horrible business might somehow be over quickly.

Throughout all this time her one coherent thought had been for Occula, whom she had not seen since they had parted in the moonlit gardens by the Barb. Occula, she now realized, must of course have played a vital part in the killing of Sencho, the killing itself having been carried out by the pedlar Zirek, no doubt helped by Meris. Yet this—or so it seemed to her—could be proved only if she herself were to tell all she now knew—of the messages passed by means of the pottery cats, of the old woman in the sweet-shop, the omen of the hunting owl and her own brief glimpse of Zirek and Meris in the crowd near the Peacock Gate. Only these could condemn Occula, for to all appearances it was plausible enough that she and Sencho should have taken the boat up the lake to a secluded place. Maia, of course, was ignorant that Kembri and Sencho themselves had sent Meris to the Lily Pool in Thettit or that Zirek, as an agent of Sencho, had been ordered to collect her from there and take her to Chalcon. She supposed that if only she herself could succeed in maintaining the appearance of one who knew nothing, there could be no case against Occula, since Sencho had enemies enough for forty men.

She had come back into the room full of dread. Yet now, facing Kembri for the second time, she almost at once perceived intuitively—as does any accused or suspect, if it occurs—a certain easing of the atmosphere. At first with incredulity, for she was superstitiously afraid even to entertain the idea, she sensed that apparently it was no longer their intention to fasten guilt upon her: their questions were no longer directed to suggesting that she might have devised the swimming game as a distraction to cover the murder. Then it occurred to her that Elvair-ka-Virrion must have corroborated what she had already told them about his part in it.

'We know, because the soldiers and the black girl have told us,' said the Tonildan governor, 'that in fact Bayub-Otal *didn't* speak to the High Counsellor about buying you.'

This came as a surprise to Maia who, ever since Occula had warned her, in the gardens, not to return to Sencho, had continued to suppose that Bayub-Otal must have asked him to sell her. Yet if he had not, this only made it all the more vital that no one should learn that Occula had sought her out and told her to keep away. She said nothing.

'However, we'll leave that for the moment,' interposed Kembri, in a tone which brought to Maia an immediate sense of relief. 'I want to talk to you again, Maia, about this conversation you say you had with Lord Bayub-Otal in the gardens that night. Are you sure that he said that if you wanted to leave Bekla you had only to tell him?'

'Yes, my lord; I'm absolutely certain about that.'

'And do you like Bayub-Otal?'

'No, that I don't, my lord. One time I thought I did; but now I *hate* him!'

'Why?'

Maia hesitated. She could hardly reply, 'Because I offered myself to him and he rejected me.'

'Well, never mind,' said Kembri briskly. 'If you hate him that'll be all to the good, as long as you never let him see it. He's almost certainly a secret enemy of Bekla. We believe he may very well have entered into some sort of agreement with King Karnat, and that's what we need to learn more about, do you see?'

'Yes, my lord.'

'We're going to let it be known publicly that both you and the black girl are being held here for further questioning, and in fact it will be made to look as though you've been questioned in the usual way. Then, late tomorrow night, you'll make your way to Bayub-Otal's lodgings. Do you know where they are?'

'No, my lord: I've never been much in the lower city at all.'

'No matter. It'll be very late—after midnight. Someone will guide you there and leave you outside. Then you'll wake Bayub-Otal, tell him that you've escaped from the temple and beg him to help you to get away from Bekla. After that you'll have to rely on your own wits.'

'You mean, he'll take me away with him?'

'That's what we hope.'

'But, my lord—' She was perplexed. 'Suppose I do find out something—say he gets a message from this king or something o' that—how'm I to pass it on to you?'

'That'll depend entirely on yourself. You'll have to find the best way you can. It's a matter of keeping your head. You may have to get back here alone. You may even have to kill him first. I repeat, this is risky work, Maia. But it's of great importance; and if you succeed—whatever success may turn out to be—the reward will surprise you—your freedom and more besides, I assure you. But don't try to run away or betray us, do you see? because that would turn out very badly for you in the long run: very badly indeed.'

'No fear of that, my lord: I'll do all I can. Only could I—?' She stopped uncertainly.

'What?' asked Kembri.

'Could I sleep now, my lord? Only I'm that tired, I can't hardly think.'

'Very well,' said Kembri. 'I'll tell you more tomorrow.'

The girl, about to get up, suddenly hesitated.

'Occula, my lord! Occula never done anything! You'll let her go?'

'We ask the questions, not you,' interposed the chief priest. 'She's being held here for questioning. That's enough!'

The girl half-rose, gripping the edge of the table. Kembri was about to call in the guards to remove her when the door was opened from outside by a soldier who, raising his palm to his forehead, announced 'My lord, the Sacred Queen!'

Next moment Queen Fornis, attended by the same dark-haired woman whom Maia had seen with her by the Barb, entered the room. The three examiners rose to their feet, Kembri motioning to Maia to go and stand against the further wall.

The Sacred Queen was dressed in a clinging robe of vivid purple, the crimson hem of which fell almost to her silver, bead-embroidered sandals. Her amazing hair, now piled on her head, was held in place by two jewelled combs and by a gold chain wound in and out of the tresses. Round her neck, on a second, finer chain, hung a silver leopard as big as her thumb. Her finger-nails were lacquered crimson and on her left fore-finger was a spiral ring in the form of a gold serpent with ruby eyes.

Unhurriedly, she crossed the room and then motioned to her woman to drag Kembri's heavy, carved chair into the sunlight by the window. Having seated herself, she remained gazing towards the Lord General with a slight smile and an air of complete composure. Looking at her, Maia received an overwhelming impression of assured, self-seeking potency. It was as though she were possessed by an intense, ruthless force, at this present moment less evil than simply inhuman; a force which, like an animal, would unthinkingly and of its very nature pursue its object with no thought of anything beyond self-interest. The mere sight of her was disturbing, conveying as it did a sense of one possessing both more and less than normal human nature.

Maia realized furthermore that the three men, now seating themselves once more in response to her gesture, also felt—to some extent, at any rate—the same disquiet as herself.

'Well, Kembri,' said the Sacred Queen at length, with a certain air of having waited long enough to be sure that no one was going to have the temerity to speak first, 'have you found out the truth about the High Counsellor's death?'

'Partly, esta-säiyett. But before we can be sure we shall need to examine several of those about to be arrested in the eastern provinces.'

She spread her hands. 'You have to do all this in order to work yourselves up to kill Santil-kè-Erketlis? Why not simply go and kill him?'

'I've already considered that, esta-säiyett, but Chalcon is remote, difficult country. We shall need to raise a special force for the purpose. In my view the real question is, once we openly declare Erketlis to be an enemy, how much support will he be able to attract to himself? We don't want to turn him into a heroic victim of Leopard tyranny throughout the eastern provinces. If only we can get positive proof that it was he who planned Sencho's death, then we've got law on our side: we can declare him a traitor and call him to account. Many more people will think twice about supporting him then.'

She nodded absently, as though bored with all this reasoning, and merely waiting for him to be done. While he was still speaking she made a gesture of dismissal to her woman, who raised her palm to her forehead and went out.

'The High Counsellor's house—his property—that's being guarded, I suppose?'

'Naturally, esta-säiyett: there are soldiers there, and the domestic slaves have been left in the house for the time being.'

'Including the woman Terebinthia?' asked the Sacred Queen.

Kembri looked embarrassed. 'She—er—she left the city very suddenly the day after the murder, esta-säiyett. We don't know where she's gone. However, she's not under suspicion, for we know she never left the High Counsellor's house at all that day.'

'Perhaps not,' replied the Sacred Queen, 'but I think you know very well why she left the city so quickly, don't you?'

Before the Lord General could reply she went on, 'And the High Counsellor's girls?'

'Two of them were with him in the gardens that night, esta-säiyett—'

'I know that.'

'Naturally, we're holding them for questioning.'

'Naturally. But there was a third girl: I don't mean Dyphna, the one who bought her freedom that morning. Whom do I mean?'

Kembri hesitated. Maia could see that he was uneasy. The extent and accuracy of the queen's knowledge had evidently taken him by surprise. Fornis, now looking directly at him, spoke a little more sharply.

'I mean a girl named Milvushina. Where is she now?'

'She is—just at the moment—that is, while the household is being fully inventoried, you understand, esta-säiyett—she is being looked after by my son.'

'Yes. What you mean is that Elvair-ka-Virrion bribed Terebinthia and helped himself to the girl before any inventory of the High Counsellor's property had been submitted to the temple or to the High Baron?'

'Well—er—I dare say you know, esta-säiyett, that the girl is well-born— she came from the baron Enka-Mordet's family in Chalcon; a family we unfortunately had to destroy for sedition. I was quite unaware that the High Counsellor had issued private instructions to the soldiers and enslaved her. Had I known, I would never have agreed. I think it's very doubtful in law whether she can be held to be a slave at all. In all the circumstances my son took pity on her. He thought that she—well, that she ought to be properly cared for.'

'How very considerate of him! He probably also thought that I wouldn't come to learn of it. You know, of course, that by law all slaves in the household of a man who dies intestate without heirs belong to the temple?'

'Well, strictly speaking, esta-säiyett—'

'Yes, I am speaking strictly,' replied she. 'But perhaps Elvair-ka-Virrion consulted the chief priest before he helped himself to this girl, did he?'

The chief priest said nothing. The queen stood up.

'What a strange empire this is! Santil-kè-Erketlis must have every benefit of the law, but for the god Cran it's apparently otherwise. Let's hope he's not angered. Luckily he has at least got me to defend his interests.'

She turned and looked at Maia, still standing against the wall in the posture of a waiting slave, head bent and hands clasped below her waist.

'This child was one of Sencho's girls too, wasn't she? What are you going to do with *her*? Help *your*self? Or perhaps she's already earmarked for the governor here, is she?'

Kembri seemed to be controlling himself with an effort. 'Esta-säiyett, if I may say so, you are a shade too exacting. The city has been turned upside-down by this murder. Everything has been in confusion—'

'Oh, very much,' said she. 'I'm confused myself; and not least by your son's blasphemous temerity.'

'Esta-säiyett—'

Fornis turned her back on him. 'Come here, child.'

Maia, startled and blushing, obeyed. Fornis looked her slowly up and down.

'She looked much better when she was swimming in the Barb the other night. I'm afraid you can't have been looking after her very well, poor girl. She ought to have been treated in accordance with the law, of course. Never mind; I'll see to it for you. That will save any risk of further irregularity, such as household säiyetts accepting bribes to hand over girls who are temple property and then leaving the city before they can be called to account for it.'

'Esta-säiyett,' said Kembri, 'for the sake of public safety and our own safety too, let us both be plain. I confess my son helped himself to the Chalcon girl and that he had no legal right to do so. But at least that causes no real harm. The Tonildan girl I need. She is vital to a secret and important scheme which could very well turn out to be of great advantage to us all.'

The queen raised her eyebrows. 'This child?'

'This child, esta-säiyett. As things stand, no other girl will do. I beg you not to make too much of my son's—lapse. This girl here may quite possibly be able to effect something of critical value to us all. Let me explain to you what I have in mind.'

'No, you needn't,' she said, raising her hand, on which the snake ring, catching the light, flashed an instant in Maia's eyes. 'I can guess well enough. Some man is to be decoyed—enticed—betrayed. How else do you work, and what else could such a child be good for? As for your son, I was on my way to speak to the High Baron about this profane act on his part—'

'I'm convinced, esta-säiyett, that all he wanted was to show some kindness to a young woman of good family who should never have been enslaved to a man like Sencho—'

'And do you expect either me or the High Baron to believe that? For one thing, your son's ways are notorious.' She paused reflectively. 'But also I rather suspect, Lord General, that you may be entertaining certain notions on your own behalf regarding the future of the girl Milvushina. However, I'll say no more of that. In fact I'll oblige you: I'll oblige you in two respects. I'll disregard your son's sacrilegious behaviour—for the moment—and I myself will look after this girl—this piece of temple property—until further notice.'

'But I need her tomorrow, esta-säiyett.'

'Then you may send to me and ask for her!' flashed the queen in a tone of conclusive finality. 'The girl is temple property—not yours. Maia!' (Maia jumped.) 'My säiyett is waiting for you in the corridor.'

Thereupon she swept out of the room. Maia, bewildered, afraid to obey her and afraid not to, remained where she was beside the chair. After some moments, however, her eyes brimming with tears of nervous anxiety, she fell on her knees before the Lord General.

'My lord, Occula! If you'd only let me see Occula—just for a few moments—'

'You'd better hurry up and obey the Sacred Queen,' replied Kembri coldly. 'Whatever else you do, I don't advise you to displease *her*.'

Maia, raising her palm, stumbled from the room. Outside, the Palteshi woman, giving her a half-smile, wrapped a cloak round her shoulders, took her arm and led her along the corridor and down the temple staircase.

QUEEN FORNIS

For a good nine hours and more Maia lay sleeping in a great, soft bed, while the sunlight moved slowly across the floor until at length evening fell with a gradual melting and vanishing of the hard, black shadows of the afternoon. The unexpected lifting of the horrible fear in which she had lived since the killing of Sencho; Kembri's plan to make use of her against Bayub-Otal; the unexpected appearance of the Sacred Queen and her own sudden removal—whither and for what purpose she had no idea: these had left her as much confused and bewildered as a bird flown by chance into a lighted room.

She had not even had the self-possession to ask Queen Fornis's säiyett where they were going, but only hobbled on, leaning on the woman's arm and taking in little or nothing of their surroundings. They stopped. She found herself in a jekzha. A quarter of an hour later she could not even have said whether or not they had passed through the Peacock Gate. Two things she knew—that she was no longer a prisoner and that she longed above all for sleep.

When at length they reached their destination, she was aware—vaguely—only of a great, stone-fronted house, a flight of steps and a heavy, panelled door which was opened to the woman's knock—by whom she did not notice. Inside was coolness and two rows of green columns between which hung suspended some huge, dully-gleaming, winged effigy. She was led up one staircase, then another, and finally into a sunny, clean-smelling room with a bed. The woman undressed her, tut-tutting at the state of her tunic, which she simply threw outside the door as though to be rid of it; and thereupon Maia, all dirty as she was, climbed into the bed and was unconscious almost before the woman had left her.

When she woke, the room was in twilight. Through the windows opposite shone an afterglow sky of ochre and pale-green, and from somewhere just outside came the low cackle of birds settling to roost along a cornice—mynahs or starlings. The air smelt of evening—wood-smoke and moist herbage. She must be high up, for from where she lay she could see neither roofs nor trees. It was quiet—too quiet, she thought, for the lower city.

For some time she lay still, listening to the gentle commotion of the birds as the last light ebbed out of the sky. In spite of her complete ignorance, both about her situation and the future, she felt full of relief and even a curious kind of confidence. Whatever lay ahead, it could only be better than the horror behind. Evidently Queen Fornis had a use for her, though Maia could not remember what, if anything, she had said about it.

Well, and come to that Sencho had had plenty of use for her, too. Strange to think that she would never again feel him panting and shuddering as she did what he liked on the big couch in the fountain-room. What would become of his household now, she wondered—the cooks, Jarvil the porter, Ogma and the others? No doubt the skilled ones would be able to take their skills elsewhere. Lucky Dyphna, getting out just in time! And apparently Elvair-ka-Virrion had taken Milvushina: to keep or to set free?

Suddenly, with a quick darkening of the spirit, she remembered Occula. Occula was still held in the temple for questioning. Whether she told them anything or not, a slave had no rights at law: for a slave to be condemned, only suspicion was necessary. Occula's only hope was that some influential person might speak for her.

Who might be ready to do it? Shend-Lador or some of his Leopard friends? Yet they were only young blades—not men of influence. Even Elvair-ka-Virrion did not strike her as likely to be of much help here. Suddenly she thought of Sarget. Sarget—a middle-aged, wealthy man, not profligate, widely respected for his culture and good sense. Not a nobleman, true, but at least a man who had lent money to noblemen. After she had danced the senguela, Sarget had given her his arm out of the hall and praised her warmly. Could she possibly get a message to him now, begging him to intercede for Occula?

At this moment she became aware, beyond the far end of the big, shadowy chamber, of lamplight behind a curtained archway. Someone was moving quietly about in the adjoining room.

She coughed two or three times. The lamplight grew brighter, the curtain was drawn aside and the Palteshi woman came in, carrying lighted lamps on a tray. Three of these she placed on stands about the room, then came across and sat down on the edge of the bed, smiling at Maia as she put down the fourth lamp on the table close by.

'Good sleep? Feeling better?'

Maia nodded. 'Where am I?'

The other looked surprised. 'Why, in Queen Fornis's house, naturally! Great Cran, girl, you look frightened to death! You've nothing to be afraid of, you know. You ought to be thanking the gods for your good luck!'

Maia managed to smile. 'Well, only it's all a bit sudden, like; and I've had a real bad time.'

'But it's over now.'

'Will you tell me,' asked Maia hesitantly; 'well, who you are, säiyett; why I'm here and what I've got to expect, like?'

The woman laughed. 'Well, for a start, I'm Ashaktis, and you can call me that; you needn't call me säiyett. But before I tell you any more—Maia, isn't it?—you'd better come along to the bath. The queen will want to see you as soon as you're fit to be seen—'

'What for?' Maia's fingers tightened on the coverlet.

'What for? Don't be silly! Are you afraid of her?' asked Ashaktis.

'Yes, I am. Reckon I'm not the only one, either.'

'But you used to be with Sencho, didn't you? Anyway, the bath now!' said Ashaktis peremptorily. 'Put this wrap round you and come with me.'

Evidently the bath had already been prepared, for as they walked together along the open gallery outside, Maia could smell the perfumed steam. The bathroom, when they reached it, fairly took her breath away. It was even more luxurious than Sencho's. Half of one wall consisted of a broad stone hearth spread with glowing charcoal, and here two great cauldrons of water, each with a long-handled iron dipper, stood gently bubbling. The circular bath, a good seven feet across and made of green malachite, was sunk in the floor and surrounded with glazed, crimson tiles, each bearing a different design of a bird, flower or animal. On shelves along the opposite wall were laid out any number of flasks of scent and perfumed oils, smooth and rough pumice-stones, scented soaps, small files and pointed wooden spills. To one side stood the cold-water cistern, from which a copper pipe, stopped with a wooden plug, led down into the bath. There were two carved, wooden couches covered with thick towels and rugs, and a deep, open-fronted recess stacked with wraps, slippers, brushes and at least three silver hand-mirrors.

A Deelguy slave-girl, dark-eyed and broad-nosed, her black hair in a plaited rope down her back, was kneeling to fan the charcoal. Ashaktis, dismissing her, took off Maia's wrap and hung it on a peg, gave her her hand to step down into the bath and then seated herself near-by.

Maia, used as she had become to luxury, had never experienced opulence like this. Always capable of setting aside her worries in any pleasure which the immediate moment might offer, she spent plenty of time in the water, feeling the tension and grime of days disappearing like smoke on the wind. When she had finished washing her hair, she asked Ashaktis whether she might let some of the water out and add more from the cauldrons on the fire.

'Oh, I'll see to that,' said Ashaktis, getting up and plunging a bared arm into the bath to grope for the plug. 'Just stand out of the way while I pour this boiling water in.'

'Can you tell me what this is all about?' asked Maia, slipping back into the hot water with a wriggle of pleasure and splashing it over herself.

Ashaktis, laying aside the dipper, sat down again.

'How much do you know about the Sacred Queen?' she asked.

411

Maia recalled all that Occula had told her of Fornis of Paltesh; of her unscrupulous rapacity, her cruelty, her relentless and cunning tenure of power; of the admiration she inspired and the fear she was capable of inspiring when she wished; of the many men, dazzled, who had tried to gain her, and how none had been even so much as rumoured to have succeeded.

'Reckon just about nothing,' she answered.

'I've been with her for twenty years,' said Ashaktis, 'ever since she was a girl in her father's house in Dari. I was with her when she took the boat and sailed it to Quiso. You'll have heard *that* tale, I suppose?' (Maia nodded.) 'Cran only knows what I've done for her since, and Cran'll destroy me for it one day, I dare say, for she's thumbed her nose at him and every one of the gods for years. But it'll have been worth it. Perhaps you've learnt something yourself already, have you, about the difference between scrubbing floors for the bare living and doing what rich people want done by girls who know how to stay on the right side of them and keep their mouths shut?'

'Ah, that I have,' replied Maia decisively.

'Life's not easy with the queen,' went on Ashaktis, 'but at least it's never dull. There's times she makes your hair stand on end. You've got to look alive with her. For a long time now I've had more than enough money to buy myself free, but I never do. She's like one of those drugs the Deelguy sell: people keep saying they'll give it up, but they don't. I've become addicted to Miss Fornis. One day she'll be the death of me and that'll be that.'

Maia felt emboldened by the woman's friendly loquacity. 'Go on, then; tell me something you've seen her do. Something out of the ordinary, like you were saying.'

Ashaktis was silent for a time, reflecting. Maia, looking this way and that to admire the serpents, porcupines, gazelles and panthers depicted on the bath-tiles, waited expectantly.

'Well, one time, several years ago now,' said Ashaktis at length, 'we went up into Suba. It was only about three months after we'd got back from Quiso; that's to say, before those uncles of hers had really got it into their heads that she didn't mean to marry. She'd told them she wanted to go to Suba to hunt duck and water-fowl. There weren't many of us; one of the uncles and his daughter, a girl of about twenty; a couple of huntsmen, Miss Fornis and me. The cooks and guides and the rest we hired once we'd crossed the Valderra. You've never been in Suba, have you?'

'Never,' said Maia.

'It's a strange place, and the people are strange, too. It's like nowhere else in the empire—half land and half water. You travel everywhere by boat, down the water-channels; like corridors of water they are, between one village and the next, and the reeds and trees standing high all round you. You hear bitterns booming in the swamps and I've seen black turtles—oh, big as a soldier's shield—lying out on branches above the water.

'After about ten days poor old uncle was tired out, so Miss Fornis went out alone with me and four men—two Subans and our own two Dari huntsmen. We came to an island in the swamps and in the middle was a heronry. We could see the big, ramshackle nests, high up in the tops of the trees. You know the way they build?'

Maia nodded.

'Well, we'd no sooner got to this island than Miss Fornis looks up at the trees and says "Ah, herons! I've always fancied young herons would be good in a pie; better than pigeons. Phorbas," she says to one of the Suban lads, "just climb up and bring me down half a dozen, will you?" "No, säiyett," says the boy, "that I won't! I value my life and that's the truth. There's no living man could reach those nests, and even if he did the herons would be at him like dragons." "Why, you damned, cowardly, Suban marsh-frog!" she said to him. "I don't know why ever I hired the likes of you! Go on, then, Khumba," she said to one of our huntsmen, "you'd better just show him how to do it, hadn't you?" "I'm very sorry, säiyett," says Khumba, "but I reckon yon Suban fellow's in the right of it. I'm no more going up there than he is. My wife wouldn't fancy me with a broken neck, that's about the size of it."

' "Cran and Airtha! Well, here goes then!" says Miss Fornis, as if she was stepping out of doors into the rain. "And since you're not a man," she said to the Suban, "you can just give me those breeches of yours to keep my legs from getting scratched. Come on, hurry up!" And she made him take them off. They still thought it must be some joke she was up to. She was only just seventeen then, you see, and in those days her ways weren't so well-known.

'She put on the breeches and stuck a short spear in her belt and then she was up the tree like a squirrel. She'd gone something like thirty feet before any of them really understood she meant to do it. After that they just stood and watched like folk round a burning house. Khumba kept saying "O Lespa, make her come down! O Shakkarn, what am I going to say to her uncles when she's dead? They'll hang me upside-down!" I admit I was praying myself. It would have frightened anyone to see her.

'She got up to the nest she'd had her eye on—must have been all of eighty feet, and the upper branches swaying under her like grass in the wind. Both the herons went for her. She killed them with her spear, and after that she wrung the necks of five young ones and carried them down—she couldn't throw them down, you see, what with all the twigs and brush below her. "There!" she says to the Suban boy. "And I've a good mind to

413

make you eat one raw. The next time I tell you to do something, you damned well do it, d'you see?" He never answered a word; and he never came out with us again. But there were plenty more who were only too glad to, for the story got around, you see; and she always paid well. I don't believe there was anyone else in the empire, man or woman, who'd have climbed that tree. But that was nothing at all, if only we'd known what was to come.'

'And you say she's got a use for *me*?' asked Maia, with considerable apprehension. 'Only if it's along of the swimming—'

Ashaktis burst out laughing. 'The swimming? Are you ready to come out now? I'll rub you down.'

Maia did so, dried her face and stretched out on the couch while Ashaktis towelled her.

'What's the Sacred Queen's vocation?' asked Ashaktis after a little. 'Do you know?'

'Why, she's the bride of Cran,' said Maia. 'She's Airtha in human form, isn't she, as makes the crops grow and the babies come?'

'Yes, that's quite right. The Sacred Queen doesn't have to be a virgin— there's never been any fixed law about that. Occasionally in the past she's been a married woman or even a shearna. It's entirely a matter of popular acclaim—or it's supposed to be. But all the same, Miss Fornis has always taken good care that in spite of all her wild ways, no one's even been able to link any man's name with hers. That adds very much to her real power, of course.'

'I see,' said Maia, shuddering deliciously as Ashaktis's strong fingers massaged the muscles along her shoulders.

'But she's still flesh and blood, for all that, isn't she?'

'Flesh and blood? Well, yes, I s'pose so, kind of.'

'She gets to learn a lot about almost everyone in the upper city,' went on Ashaktis. 'She knew a lot about Sencho, for instance. You were quite a favourite with him, weren't you? You were very good at doing what he liked—you used to put your heart into it?'

Maia felt flattered. She did not know that she had acquired so wide a reputation.

'Well, 'twasn't all that difficult; not really.'

'You mean because you enjoyed it yourself?'

'Well, yes, I s'pose so. Only he'd send for me and no one else, see? And then he used to get that worked up sometimes, it made me feel—well, made me feel I was good at it.'

'Well, the Sacred Queen feels you probably are, too.'

Maia, rolling over on the couch, stared up at her.

'She really takes an interest in nice, spirited girls,' went on Ashaktis. 'Of course, some of us aren't as young as we were—that can't be helped. But I don't bear you any grudge, I assure you. All you've got to do is show her your talents—just as you did with Sencho.'

Maia was about to reply when suddenly her earlier thoughts returned to her mind with force.

'Oh, säiyett—Ashaktis—there's something you've *got* to do for me! Please! Only it's terribly important. Do you know U-Sarget? He's a rich man in the upper city. You *must* know him! I've got to get a message to him—about my friend Occula!'

'Now just calm yourself, child,' said Ashaktis, putting her hands on Maia's shoulders. 'You obviously haven't grasped what I've been telling you. Do you realize that by tomorrow morning you'll probably be able to ask favours of the queen herself?'

Before Maia could answer, the Deelguy bath-slave drew aside the door-curtains and, palm to forehead, announced 'Säiyett, the Sacred Queen!'

Maia, looking frantically round for something to put on, could find only the towels on which she was lying; and with these she was still fumbling as Fornis entered the bathroom. It did not occur to her that some few days before she had stood naked beside the queen on the shore of the Barb.

On this occasion, however, Queen Fornis was less alarming. Indeed, not only her appearance but her whole manner was altogether different. There was nothing in the least imperious or daunting in the way she came up to Maia, took her by the hand and, smiling, drew her down to sit beside her on the couch.

Her hair, now gathered behind her head, like any village girl's, with a plain green ribbon, fell nearly to her waist, flaring out on either side almost like a cloak. She wore no jewels, the lacquer was gone from her nails and she was bare-footed. Her thin, white surcoat, belted with a green cord and buttoning down the front, was stitched from neck to hem with a pattern of flying dragons in minute, brilliantly-coloured beads. Neither the material itself nor the beads were of any great value. All lay in the workmanship, which must have taken months to complete.

'Well, Maia,' she said, smiling and speaking as to a guest, 'you're looking much better now; and feeling better, too, I hope. Has Ashaktis been looking after you properly? I always seem to meet you when you've been in the water, don't I? I didn't think that tunic thing you've been wearing was going to be much more use, so I've brought you a new robe. Are you ready to put it on?' Pulling aside the towel, she rubbed her hand up and down Maia's back from neck to thighs. 'Oh, yes, you're quite dry enough. And you must be starving for some supper. As soon as you're ready we'll go and eat.'

Thereupon she clapped her hands and two chubby little boys, about nine or ten years old, came in through the curtains, carrying between them a plain but very soft and finely-woven woollen robe of pale blue. Both children were exceptionally beautiful, with long hair falling over their bare shoulders, white, even teeth and the fair skin and blue eyes of Yeldashay. On their heads were crowns of scented, white tiare blossom, but otherwise they were naked.

'Aren't they lovely?' said the queen, as the two children, without a trace of self-consciousness, stood beside Maia and held up the robe for her to put on. 'I only bought them a few weeks ago, but they're learning well. What is it you need—' seeing Maia glancing round the room—'a comb?'

'Well, yes, esta-säiyett—er—that's to say, if it's no trouble,' faltered Maia.

'I'll do it for you, if you like,' said the Queen, taking a heavy, carved comb which one of the little boys, without being told, at once brought to her from the shelved recess. 'What beautiful hair! Is it your father's or your mother's?'

Maia, who was beginning to feel more relaxed, laughed. 'Don't know, really, esta-säiyett. Reckon it's mine!'

'You needn't call me "esta-säiyett" now,' said Fornis, stroking her hair as she combed it. 'What am I called, Shakti?'

Ashaktis smiled. 'Folda. But Maia won't know what that means.'

'What does it mean, Maia; do you know?'

'No, I don't, esta-säi—I mean, Folda.'

'It's old Urtan for a hunting-knife. But your hair,' she went on, working out a wet tangle with the comb. 'You mean you've never had to curl it; not even with all that swimming in Lake Serrelind?'

'But did I ever tell you about swimming in the lake?' said Maia, confused. She looked up into the green eyes and, as the queen's lips, prompting her, pouted to shape the word, added 'Folda.'

'No, you didn't,' replied the queen, 'but you told me you came from Serrelind, and where else would you have learnt to dive and swim like that? Tikki, my sweetheart,' she called to one of the little boys, 'where are the nuts?' In an instant the child was beside them, offering a silver basin of serrardoes mixed with flakes of a gingery spice.

Fornis, putting one arm round him, nibbled his bare neck and shoulders. 'M'mm! Keep still!' Then again to Maia, 'Tell me about Lake Serrelind! I've never been in Tonilda, you know.'

Diffidently at first, but then with increasing confidence and freedom, Maia found herself talking about her childhood in the hovel; of the increasing burden, as she grew older, of being the eldest of four, and of how she used to escape, in summer, to the falls and the solitude of the deep water.

'Never had a stitch on, sometimes, half the day. It was the only place, you see, where I could be sure of being left alone.'

'A naiad! And how did you come from that to Bekla?' asked Fornis, laying aside the comb and again fondling the little boy as he came up to take it away.

Maia, who had been chattering happily enough, hesitated and fell silent. The queen must know very well that she had come into the possession of Lalloc, who had sold her to Sencho. About this, and of her journey from Puhra to Bekla, she was perfectly ready to talk. What she did not want to speak about was her seduction by Tharrin and how her own mother had sold her to the slavers. For the first time she found herself wondering whether Morca might later have come to feel sorry for what she had done.

Fornis perceived her reluctance. 'Sad story? They always are. I shouldn't have asked. Never mind; wouldn't want to go back, would you?' She stood up. 'I've kept you talking too long, but I was so fascinated by what you were telling me. You can go on over supper. There'll be no one except you and me and Shakti here, so you can feel quite free.'

The gallery, Maia now realized, as they strolled along it, with Ashaktis and the little boys following, ran entirely round the interior wall of the building, which was a hollow square. They were two floors up. Although darkness had now fallen, she could make out below, through the trellised arcading, a garden courtyard with a carved, central fountain-basin. There was a smell of jasmine, and great moths were flitting here and there. The roosting mynahs had settled down: she could see them in the dark—little groups of darker black—crowded together under the opposite cornice.

'The whole of this upper storey's private, you see,' said Fornis, as they turned a corner of the gallery. 'No one ever comes up here except my personal people.' She turned into a doorway. 'This is my supper-room. I designed the decoration myself; it's in traditional Palteshi style—to remind me of home, you know.'

Maia, however, although she had been virtually asked to do so, was too much startled to admire the room, for standing just inside the doorway, in the attitude of a dignified, respectful upper servant, was none other than Zuno, dressed in a gold livery embroidered across the breast with a leopard in silver thread. His hair was trimmed and curled in imitation of the style in vogue among Elvair-ka-Virrion and his friends, and in one hand he was holding a white wand almost as tall as himself. Upon the queen's entry he bowed, so that Maia recognized him a moment before he, returning to the upright, recognized her. With this advantage, she had just time to compose her features, meet his eye gravely and enjoy his startled though instantly-controlled reaction.

'Everything in order, Zuno?' asked the queen, looking round the tranquil, candle-lit room.

Zuno bowed again.

It plainly was. The honey-coloured panelling of the little hall, which measured about twenty-five feet by fifteen, had been polished with pine-scented beeswax, so that the walls and floor, gleaming gently in the candlelight, gave off a light, resinous aroma. A single step of smooth slate, banded cream and grey, surrounded the sunk rectangle of the central floor, in the middle of which stood the flower-strewn supper-table. Beside this were two couches, spread with as many cushions as even Sencho could have wished. A charcoal brazier glowed in one corner of the room and near it stood a third, slightly older boy, as handsome as the queen's two pages now taking up their places to wait at table. Several copper vessels were standing on the charcoal, and from these came a mixture of delightful odours which made Maia realize how hungry she was.

'Come here, Vorri,' said the queen, calling the lad over from beside the brazier. 'M'm, getting a nice, big boy now, aren't you? Almost too big to be hanging round the Sacred Queen. I shall have to start thinking what I'm going to do with you; but just now you can pour me some wine.'

'Oh, esta-säiyett,' he answered, with a charming, rather coltish manner, somewhere between the studied deference of Zuno and the artless grace of the little boys, 'I daren't leave the cooking, or your savoury pancakes will be spoiled.'

'Why, are *you* cooking the supper, then?' asked Fornis, surprised.

'No, esta-säiyett,' interposed Zuno, again inclining gracefully from the waist ('He don't miss any chance o' doin' that,' thought Maia), 'the dinner itself—the trout and the boar—are being prepared in the kitchens, as usual, and the children will go down for them. But I thought the soup and the crayfish pancakes would be better if they were prepared here.'

'Excellent!' said the queen, motioning Maia to one of the couches and settling herself on the other. 'Then pour the wine yourself, Zuno. And you'd better get back to your pancakes, Vorri. Oh, you're like a little pancake yourself, aren't you? M'm, take care I don't eat you by mistake!'

To Maia the dinner was exquisitely enjoyable, as much for the comfort and surroundings as for the food. Nor was conversation any problem, for she had nothing to do but lie basking in the queen's favour. Fascinated by the charm of this extraordinary woman, who only a few hours before had struck the fear of Cran into her, she no longer felt in the least out of her depth or nervous of her ability to reciprocate. Fornis, with no trace of condescension, put her entirely at her ease. They might almost, she thought, have been two young women back in Meerzat, having a bit of a gossip. In her pleasure and excitement, one detail escaped her notice. Ashaktis, sitting on a stool beside Fornis's couch and from time to time joining smoothly in the talk, tasted everything the queen ate before serving her.

Although Maia stuffed herself heartily (which clearly pleased the queen), she was careful not to drink more than a little of the excellent wine. 'Never do 'f I was to get tipsy,' she thought. 'That'd be a right old mess, that would, on top of a bit of luck like this.'

As the courses, carried up from below, succeeded one another and sheer appetite began to slacken, she became, as she had at Sarget's party, more aware of the elegance and style of her surroundings. Although nothing could have been called ostentatious, no one suddenly set down in it by magic (which was just about what had happened to her, she reflected) would have had the least difficulty in at once perceiving this to be the dining-hall of a wealthy aristocrat. It resembled, she thought, one of Sencho's rooms to about the same extent as her pleasure with Elvair-ka-Virrion had resembled the kind of thing Sencho used to require of her. The truth, she now realized, was that whatever the future might hold in store, she was glad to think she had done with Sencho.

'Barla, little sweetheart,' said Fornis at length, 'do you think you could go down all by yourself to the kitchens and bring up the syllabubs? Tell them to give you another bowl of serrardoes, too, and some *lipsica*. Have you ever tasted lipsica?' she added to Maia, as the little boy, naked as he was, took up a silver tray and went out of the room. 'It's made of fermented peaches. Ikat's the only place where they know how to make it.'

'No, I haven't,' said Maia. 'That's something I don't think even the High Counsellor went in for—not while I was with him, any road.'

'What sort of things *did* he go in for?' As she spoke, Fornis got up, walked round the table and seated herself beside Maia.

'Well, there was one drink he particularly liked as was made of a mixture of pears and white grapes,' answered Maia. She giggled. 'Sometimes I had to give it to him in a spoon; that's when he'd got too full up to move, you know—'

'I didn't mean his drinks,' said Fornis. Maia, leaning back on the cushions and looking up at her, now saw again the sorceress who had gazed up through the moonlit leaves of the zoan tree. 'You did *other* things for him as well, didn't you?'

Maia's answering smile was complicit. 'Oh, ah! All sorts of funny things.'

'Tell me. Come on, tell me!'

Maia, disconcerted now, looked down, picking at the gold tassel of one of the cushions.

'The candles make it rather hot in here, don't they?' said Fornis. 'Let's go outside and get some fresh air.'

The moon had risen, throwing, through the trellised arcading, criss-cross patterns of light over the tiled floor of the gallery. Scents of tiare and lenkista filled the cool, shadowy air. Without the least hesitation or uncertainty Maia took the Sacred Queen of Airtha in her arms and kissed her again and again. Together with gratitude for her release, she felt full of a passionate delight both in her surroundings and her good fortune. To her surprise, she realized that she genuinely desired the queen, who was responding to her with a kind of obeisant but passionate self-surrender, leaning backwards with closed eyes.

'Bite me, Maia! Harder! Harder!'

Beyond the roof-tops an owl called somewhere in the trees, and the sound, agonizingly, brought back Occula to Maia's mind. At all costs she must find a way to intercede for Occula. Yet if she were to confide in the queen, might not the queen become jealous? How soon could she safely introduce the subject? She considered, even in the act of complying with the lithe, panting woman in her arms; and answered herself, sensibly enough, 'After she's had what she wants.'

'What sort of things *did* you do for Sencho, then?' whispered Fornis, releasing her. 'Did you ever have to punish him?'

'*Punish* him, Folda?' Maia was puzzled. 'How d'you mean?'

At this moment there broke out from below a sudden clamour; a crash and clatter of something falling was followed by the terrified screaming of a child, the growling and snarling of some fierce animal, stumbling feet and cries of alarm. Zuno came darting out of the supper-room, leaving the door open behind him, ran to the stair-head and vanished down the stairs.

Without the least appearance of haste or discomposure Fornis nevertheless moved very swiftly. She seemed not to run, yet Maia found herself running to keep up with her. When the noise broke out they had been some little way along the gallery, the supper-room lying between them and the stair-head. Pausing an instant at the open door to call to Ashaktis and the two boys, 'Stay where you are!', Fornis shut it and then, with a kind of rapid gliding, descended the stairs two at a time.

The staircase consisted of two short flights running one way and the other, with a small landing half-way down. As Fornis and Maia reached this and turned, they saw below them, at the foot of the stairs, a group of four or five house-slaves pointing and gabbling as they stared at something out of sight. Becoming aware of the queen, they fell silent.

'Get out of the way!' said Fornis. Passing through them, she turned into the corridor, followed by Maia.

The little boy Barla was lying on his back on the floor. Beside him was his silver tray and the wreckage of the syllabubs and other delicacies which he had been carrying. He had stopped screaming, but was beating feebly with his hands at an enormous hound, which had him by the throat. Two youths were shouting at the hound and trying, quite ineffectively, to make it let go. One was holding a chain from which dangled a broken leather collar. The other kept repeating hysterically 'It'll *kill* the boy! It'll *kill* him, for Cran's sake!'

Fornis, having paused a moment to take in the situation, went unhesitatingly up to the hound and seized it by the back of the neck. After a few moments, however, since it had no collar and she could not get a purchase, she let go and took up a stance astride it, facing its head. Then she bent forward, gripped its front legs and pulled it bodily upwards, her bare hands on either side of its jaws. Since the hound, however, did not release the child's throat, the upper part of his body was also lifted, his head hanging backwards and his long hair brushing the floor. Fornis, still holding the beast's legs and speaking to it in a low, firm voice, struck the side of its head two or three times with her elbow, whereupon it loosed its hold and the little boy fell back, to be instantly dragged clear by one of the youths.

'Chain!' said Fornis, holding out one hand and snapping her fingers without looking round. The other youth put the chain into her hand. Having secured one end round the dog's neck, she mutely held out the other to be taken from her. Then she straightened up and looked about her.

'Is the child much hurt?'

'No, Cran be praised, esta-säiyett,' replied the first youth, who was holding the little boy in his arms. 'Nothing serious, as far as I can see. But it—'

'Then put him to bed. And as for you,' she said, turning to the other youth, 'what the hell do you suppose you were doing? You're in charge of the dog, aren't you?'

'Esta-säiyett, I was patrolling the house as usual with the dog on its chain. When it saw the little boy it turned savage. Those children very seldom leave the top floor, you see, so it doesn't know them. I did my best to hold it, but it broke its collar and got the child down.'

'And why did it break its collar? Isn't that part of your business, to see that the collar's sound?' The youth made no reply and she slapped him hard across the face. 'Why should I have to drag your damned dog off my page with my own hands? You'll get a good whipping for this. Well,' she said, turning sharply round upon the watching house-slaves, 'why are you all standing there like a pack of fools? Clear this mess up, and then get back where you belong! And where have *you* been?' she added, as Zuno appeared at the far end of the corridor, followed by a man wearing a leather coat and knee-boots.

'Esta-säiyett, I went to fetch the kennel-man.'

'And a damned lot of use that would have been by this time!' said Fornis. With this she took Maia's arm and led her back up the staircase.

'You can come with me tomorrow and watch him whipped, if you like. This man I've got now does it really splendidly.'

Maia, who was feeling a good deal shaken, made no reply. The queen turned towards her with shining eyes.

'Would you like to whip *me*? You would, wouldn't you?'

Without waiting for an answer she called through the door of the supper-room, 'Shakti! Send the boys! We're going to bed!'

'You need them, do you, to see to the lamps and that?' asked Maia. 'Only I can easy do that, and we can be alone.'

'Oh, no, Maia,' replied Fornis, putting her arm round her as they walked together down the moonlit gallery, 'I don't need them for the lamps! They're going to stay with us all night.'

The mynahs were moving and rustling outside the windows, uttering their liquid whistles in response to the first light. On cushions strewn upon the floor the little boys lay sleeping as only children sleep—with the appearance of having been absorbed into a higher state of existence, a better world where they abide perfect as summer leaves or pebbles in a clear brook. And a right old job it'd be to wake them and all, thought Maia enviously, recalling how often she had had to shake and pummel Kelsi and Nala out of bed in the mornings.

Fornis, sprawled beside her, stirred and muttered a few words in her sleep. 'They'll never taste it, Shakti.' She was no sort of sleeper, thought Maia; a kind of intruder or fugitive in that country which the little boys entered as of right. She had been in and out of sleep all night, dragging Maia behind her like a beast on a rope.

Ah, and some right old tricks they'd been up to an' all, thought Maia glumly; and none of them had really worked. To her it had been as though Fornis were seeking to satisfy hunger with hay, flowers, reeds—anything but food. Short though her amatory career had been, Maia could tell when mutual accord was present and when it was not. Some people, like Sencho, were incapable of it anyway and one therefore left it out of account when dealing with them. But Fornis, lacking it, was like a bird with an injured wing; flying lop-sided for a spell; alighting perforce, yet almost at once impelled to try to fly once more. All this Maia knew well enough because she had felt it no less in herself. They just hadn't hit it off. Her racking anxiety for Occula might have had something to do with it, but apart from that she knew that what Fornis wanted she, Maia, didn't like—to say the least—and was unable to give. It was a more than disappointing outlook for a girl in her situation.

422

Fornis rolled over, clutching at Maia in her sleep, but then started, as though frightened at finding another's body in her arms. She struggled a second and opened her eyes, staring into Maia's for some moments before recognizing her. Maia kissed her and stroked her shoulders.

'Is it morning?' asked Fornis.

'Just about.'

'O Cran and Airtha! Did you sleep?'

Maia, shaking her head, could not suppress her chagrin. 'You always that restless?'

Fornis smiled. 'Some people I've slept with have said I chased them up and down the bed. I hate sleep, anyway: it's a waste of time.'

She got up, naked as she was ('and she's all they say, no danger,' thought Maia), walked across to the window, stepping over the sleeping children, and opened one of the shutters. The first light glinted on her hair and the creamy skin of her shoulders.

'You're right, it's dawn.' She shivered a moment. 'Chilly, too.'

Once again Maia set herself, as convincingly as she could, to simulate eagerness and renewed appetite. 'Come back to bed, Folda.' She opened her arms. 'Come here and kiss me.'

The queen blew out the lamp, lay down beside Maia and gazed into her face, cupping it between her hands.

'I took a fancy to you that night by the Barb because you're so pretty and beautifully made. I dare say there's not a prettier girl in the empire.'

Maia, sensing more to come, made no reply.

'But now I'll tell you something, my child,' said Fornis, 'seeing that I've been at it for years. If two people like us fancy each other for their looks but aren't actually in love, it only works if they like the same things. You're as pretty as a lily in a pool, but you don't come with me, do you, to where I want to go?'

Still Maia said nothing.

'Tickle, tickle,' went on Fornis, 'anyone can do that. The little boys can do it: but that's not what I wanted from you. The truth is, my nasty tastes simply aren't yours, are they, however hard you try? In fact, they disgust you—No!' (holding up a hand) 'you needn't try to tell me they don't.'

She flicked one of Maia's nipples with her finger-nail, hard enough to hurt.

'I thought Sencho would have turned you into a real, depraved little beast. From what you said to me, I believe you yourself even thought he had. So let me tell you, dear, that whatever you may have thought, he hasn't. I *am* depraved and I know. You're not even cruel, are you? Cran only knows how or why, but you've remained naturally *decent*.' (She uttered the word contemptuously.) 'One day it'll catch up with you, I expect—if you live that long. You'll end up dull as a cow in a field.'

Maia spoke at last. 'I done my best, Folda.'

'Oh, I know: but I'm talking about natural inclination—and you haven't got it.'

'Well, not for—' Maia hesitated. 'No.'

There was a pause. 'As a rule,' said Fornis at length, 'when anyone's been with me like this, and I find they don't suit me, I get rid of them for good.'

Maia turned cold: she felt her bowels loosen. 'You've—you've done that?'

'Oh, yes!' replied Fornis lightly. 'It would never do, you see, to have people around who could repeat scandal about the Sacred Queen. So one way or another they have to disappear. That's part of the fun, actually. Now and then it might be Zeray, but sometimes even Zeray isn't far enough.'

Maia clutched at her, sobbing. 'Oh, esta-säiyett, please! I didn't mean—'

'Quiet!' said Fornis quickly. 'You'll wake the boys. But I've decided not to put *you* out of the way, Maia, because of this plan that Kembri's got for you: and if you and he think I don't know what it's all about, you must be even bigger fools than I took you for. I agree with him that if only you can bring it off, it could be very valuable. In my opinion Bayub-Otal's a most dangerous man; and since he's taken this fancy to you—which is perfectly understandable—you're probably the only person who *can* bring it off. I hope you do.'

'Oh, Folda—thank you—thank you! I'm sorry—I'm ever so sorry I couldn't—'

'You think it's blasphemy, don't you?' flashed the queen suddenly, gripping her upper arms and digging her nails in so hard that Maia cried out.

'I never said so!'

'No, but you were thinking it. "What am I doing, polluting the Sacred Queen?" That's what you were thinking.'

Since the truth was that Maia had begun thinking exactly this from the moment when she realized that she and the queen were not sensually at one, she could find no reply. As she hesitated, the child Tikki stirred in his sleep, and this distracted Fornis, who turned her head to look at him.

It was at this instant that Maia was seized with a sudden, desperate inspiration. There was no time to consider it, the idea that had leapt into her mind. She knew only that it offered a chance to save Occula from torture.

'Folda, please don't be angry. You see, I can still do you a very good turn—better 'n what you can imagine. Now that I've been with you and

424

realized what you like, I know someone who'd suit you right down to the ground—someone as might 'a been made for you.'

Fornis laughed. 'Maia, you're simple, aren't you? I know you mean well, but even *I* can't reach out and help myself to other people's property just as I've a mind to. Some other girl you know in someone's house, is it? I can't go taking any slave-girl in the city. Apart from anything else, I have to be very discreet about my pleasures. That's why I have the little boys.'

'I know all that, Folda: but as it happens, this girl's your own property. She's down in the temple of Cran at this minute. It's my friend, Occula. She never killed Sencho, I can promise you that. She didn't know anything about it. Did, she'd 'a told me.'

'You mean the black girl who was with Sencho that night?'

'Yes, esta-säiyett. Occula—she's exactly what you want, believe me.'

'How very interesting!' said Fornis. 'What makes you so sure?'

'Because we was months together at Sencho's and I know what she likes: her tastes an' that.'

'I see.' Fornis paused. 'Well—and yet you say she didn't kill him?'

'I know it, esta-säiyett.'

'What a pity!' said Fornis unexpectedly. 'Sencho'd lived too long. He wasn't useful to us any more. Perhaps *I* killed him, did I?' She laughed again. 'No, I didn't, as it happens; but I rather wish I had. Well, we'd better start thinking what we're going to do, hadn't we? I'll write to the chief priest under my personal seal, saying that I've decided after all that you're available to be used as Kembri wishes, but he's to send me Occula instead. Then Shakti can take you down to the temple this morning and bring Occula back with her.' She paused. 'But mind this, Maia, and make very sure you don't forget it! One word about last night to anyone at all, and that gorgeous body of yours will be hanging upside-down by the road for the flies to blow. Have you got that? Now let's go and bath, and if that Deelguy girl hasn't got the water hot I'll have her whipped as well as the dog-boy.'

: 42 :

A NIGHT JOURNEY

It was after midnight. Maia, who had been awake—how long? she wondered; well over an hour—was looking out from the temple of Cran over the still, moonlit city. The room where they had told her to sleep until it was time to set out was high up, under the cornice, and from its window she could see, across the roofs of the lower city and the great

425

square of the Caravan Market, the dark shape of the Peacock Gate and the walls extending on either side of it.

To the right and beyond, a mile away on the Leopard Hill, rose the Barons' Palace, its slender towers soaring, in the moonlight, above the deep-shadowed outline of its north front. Remote and far-off it looked now; nothing to do with her any more, the girl who had danced the senguela to the acclamation of Sarget's guests.

There was not a breath of wind. She looked down on the flat roofs tilting this way and that below her. The shadows of their parapets cast hard, slanting lines and the moonlight picked out, here and there, a medley of objects; brick cisterns, pear-shaped water-jars, shrubs growing in pots, here a coil of rope, there a pallet-bed for use in the heat of summer. The moon, now risen high over Crandor, had dimmed Lespa's stars with a light almost as bright as day.

Somewhere a dog was howling and from another direction, so far off that her ear caught it only intermittently, came a sound of music. Here and there a few lamps still burned in windows, but since she had begun her pensive, melancholy watch they had grown fewer and fewer, until now only two or three remained: watchers by the sick, perhaps, she thought; or lovers abed who preferred a dim light to darkness. It seemed much longer than an hour since the lamp-shutters of the clock towers, both of which she could see, had swung open to signal midnight. Surely they must be due to open again any moment now. There was not a soul in the streets below; the Kharjiz, Storks Hill and Masons Street all empty. Only in the distant Caravan Market a few figures—porters or sweepers, perhaps—were moving slowly here and there; like autumn flies on a window-sill, she thought. How long now till someone came for her?

Her shoulder was hurting, as it had for hours past, and she could not bear to think what she must look like. Kembri and the chief priest, who had seen her again that morning to give her her detailed instructions, had assured her that she would not have to suffer a great deal to make it look as though she had been questioned. The temple guards, however, told off to see to the actual business, had taken a rather different view. They had not been as brutal as if she were a real prisoner, but Maia in all her life before had never been really knocked about or ill-used, and the fear and shock had been almost worse than the pain. She had a black eye and a badly swollen lip, a four-inch burn across her right shoulder and livid bruises across her thighs and buttocks. The soiled white tunic—which Bayub-Otal might remember her to have been wearing in the gardens—had been brought down from the queen's house and she had had to put it on again. Hair, finger-nails, knees, feet—all were filthy. Probably, she thought, the tracks of her tears showed plain down her grimy face.

426

The chief priest, cold and reserved (disappointed, perhaps, in his hopes), had refused to let her see Occula. Maia had half-expected as much, and on the way from the queen's house to the temple had begged Ashaktis to look after her friend and give her all the help she could. This Ashaktis had promised, though rather casually.

'That's if the queen likes her, of course,' she had added; and Maia had judged it best to say no more.

What she now felt above all, leaning on the sill and looking out over the chequered, sleeping city—more than her injuries and dirt, more even than the danger into which she was going—was her loneliness. For the first time since the day when she had been carted by the slave-traders to Puhra, she had no friend to whom she could turn, no one to comfort or help her. The exploit on which they were sending her, she knew, was a pure gamble on Kembri's part. She was being thrown down like a die on a gaming-table. If the throw proved a loser, they would merely shrug their shoulders: she would be no great loss. If she won for them they would pocket the winnings, and for what they might award her in return she had nothing but Kembri's word, given as an inducement. Yet what else could she do but try to succeed? She could not hope to escape. Where to, anyway? She had no money and knew next to nothing of the empire, its various provinces and towns; while as for trying to get out of it on her own, she would not know how to begin. She could only go through with the adventure. If she succeeded she must, surely, end up better off. Yet if only there had been a mate, a friend, someone to share the frightening, hazardous future!

There were fewer lights now. The dog howled on. In the nearer clock tower, a few hundred yards to her left, the shutters opened and the lamps beamed out for the hour, followed at once by those of the further tower half a mile away to the west. At this moment she heard footsteps outside the door and the latch was lifted.

'Maia? Ah! Waiting, were you?'

It was Sednil, carrying a candle. It had not occurred to her that it might be he who would come. She flung her arms round his neck and clung to him, weeping.

'Oh, Sednil, I'm so frightened! I just wish to all the gods as I was back at home! I'd never—'

'Easy, girl, easy now! It'll only be worse if you let yourself go to pieces. As for the gods, you can forget about them: they won't help you.'

'It's the being alone, like; the having to go alone. I need—oh, someone to help me—'

He held her away from him, looking at her intently, a young man, yet already with every mark of scepticism and disillusion on his drawn, hard face.

'People's no different from animals—clawing each other; who's strongest, which can make t'other most afraid. Just set yourself to do what the animals do, girl: survive! Once you stop taking *that* much trouble, no one's going to do it for you, no more 'n if you were a rat in a ditch.'

She nodded, paradoxically comforted a little by his bleak words, as people sometimes find themselves when unrealistic longings are cut away like broken tackle in a storm and at least they can see clearly what they have no alternative but to make the best of.

'People like you and me,' whispered Sednil, fondling her, 'we can't afford to be fools. Crying and carrying on—that's a luxury; that's only for rich people. Listen, d'you know what that Tamarrik Gate's made of? I'll tell you: tears! The tears of thousands of ordinary people who were taxed and starved to pay for it, that's what. So it come expensive, didn't it?' He spat on the floor. 'Wasn't me made that up, either.'

'Who, then?'

'Oh, some drunken poet used to be a friend of Nennaunir. He's dead now, anyway. You better come on now, Maia, else there'll only be trouble. They've told me to go with you as far as What's-his-name—Bayub-Otal—where he lives.'

'Oh, I'm glad it's you that's with me, Sednil. That makes it a bit better, sort of.'

He nodded without replying and she followed him out of the door. There was no moonlight in the gallery or the staircase, and the candle, as they went on, threw a dreary succession of shadows which rose up before them and wavered either side before merging into the blackness behind. Once she heard a squeak and scamper in the wall and once drew back her bare feet from a cockroach scuttling out of the light.

At the foot of the stairs a priest was seated by the door. Raising his lamp, he looked Maia up and down in silence. Having apparently satisfied himself that her appearance was sufficiently bedraggled and wretched he nodded, slid back the bolts and held the door just wide enough for them to slip out one behind the other, into the moon-blanched courtyard.

Neither spoke until they had left the temple behind and were walking side by side down the Kharjiz, empty as a forest track.

'Not even a beggar. No one—nothing,' murmured Maia.

'They don't let beggars sleep along the Kharjiz,' replied Sednil. 'There's rich merchants live round here, and they wouldn't want beggars dying outside their homes, would they? When the prisoners are marched to work in the morning, they have to pick up their chains and carry them, not to wake the rich people up.'

They passed through the Slave Market, with its carved reliefs along the bases of the rostra, and Maia remembered as though it were long ago her shocked embarrassment when she and Occula had first seen the platform for the girls.

'What you said back there,' said Sednil after a little, as they turned out of the Khalkoornil and entered the tangle of narrower streets near the western clock tower. 'Said you didn't like being alone. But that's when you're safest, when you're alone: there's no one to twist you or let you down then, is there? Just remember that, and you might come back safe.'

She nodded, blinking back her tears. Sednil stopped and looked about them for a moment. 'It's only just round the corner now.' Suddenly he gripped her arm. 'Here's a night-patrol coming, see? I've been wondering when we'd meet one.'

Two soldiers in light armour, swords at their belts but without shields, were approaching at the unhurried pace of sentinels or watchmen. One carried a lantern, its flame barely visible in the moonlight. Sednil stood still as they crossed the street and came up to Maia and himself.

'What are you doing out at this time of night? Where are you going?'

'I'm a temple servant on business for the chief priest,' replied Sednil. 'Here's my token.'

He drew out of his pocket a flat piece of wood about two inches square, which bore lettering and a painted Leopard cognizance. The soldier, taking it from him, examined it.

'Never seen one of these before.'

'Keep it; I'm carrying several. That's what they're for. Take it to the temple if you want. They'll tell you I'm authorized.'

The man paused and shook his head, clearly in two minds.

'This young woman—is she a temple servant too?'

'I'm escorting her to where she has to go.'

The two soldiers looked at each other. 'The fun sometimes gets a bit rough in the temple, does it?' asked the second soldier sardonically. 'How did her face and clothes get in that state?'

'I've no idea,' answered Sednil, 'but I know what my orders are, and if you hinder me you'll have to answer to the temple for it.'

There was another pause. Then the first soldier, pocketing the token, said curtly, 'All right, not so much of your damned lip. 'Way you go.'

Round the next corner, standing in the shadow of the western clock tower, Sednil pointed to one of a row of small, stone-built houses opposite.

'That's it; the third one, see? But how you're going to wake him—' Suddenly he gave a low whistle. 'Why, there's a light, look, shining through the ground-floor shutters—see it? Either someone's up or else they've forgotten the lamp. Were you told he'd be up?'

'No,' said Maia.

'We'd better have a look, then,' said Sednil. 'Quiet, now.'

Maia followed him across to the front of the house. In the room behind the shutters she could hear someone moving quietly about. After a few moments Sednil plucked her sleeve and pointed silently to a chink. Shutting one eye and peering through, Maia saw Bayub-Otal pass across her line of vision carrying a folded garment. A moment later he came back the other way, empty-handed.

Sednil, leading her back to the opposite side of the street, took her in his arms and gently kissed her swollen mouth.

'Good luck! And don't forget what I told you. Keep a jump ahead of the bastards—whoever they are—and maybe we'll meet again yet.'

Maia was filled with sudden panic.

'Oh, Sednil!' She looked at him piteously. 'Come with me! Come on! You could be free! You could escape! I'll tell him—'

'Don't be daft! The guards on the gate have been told who they're to let through. You know they have.'

With this he turned and walked away, leaving her alone.

Now that there was nothing to do but go on, Maia felt a sudden access of resolution. Pausing only a few seconds, she ran across the road and knocked rapidly three or four times on the shutters.

There was a sudden, startled movement in the room, but no one spoke. She knocked again.

'Who's there?' said Bayub-Otal's voice sharply.

'My lord, it's Maia! Maia! Let me in, for pity's sake!'

'Maia!' A panel of the shutter opened and she saw him standing before her. 'What are you doing here?'

'Oh, let me in, my lord! Please let me in quickly!'

Swinging back a second panel to widen the opening, he helped her into the lamp-lit room. As he closed and barred the shutters behind her, Maia sank down on the floor as though exhausted. Bayub-Otal supported her to a bench by the table.

'I heard you'd been taken to the temple for questioning.' Then, for the first time catching a clear sight of her face, 'Gods! What's happened? What have they done to you?'

'Oh, my lord, there's no time to explain! Won't you help me? You promised—you promised you'd help me to get out of Bekla if ever I asked you.'

'But I don't understand,' replied Bayub-Otal. 'How do you come to be here?'

'I escaped, my lord; from the temple; not an hour ago.'

'From the temple? How?'

'One of the guards—I gave him—I gave him what he wanted, to let me go.'

'I see. And do you think they've found out yet that you've escaped?'

'I don't know. Not yet, perhaps, but they're bound to soon. Oh, please help me, my lord!'

'But how did you know where I was?'

'I knew where your lodgings were, my lord. Sencho knew—he knew everything like that. You *will* help me, my lord, won't you? If they catch me now—'

'Yes, I'll help you,' said Bayub-Otal, 'but we'll have to be quick. You're lucky to have found me here. I was warned, not an hour ago, to leave the city at once. I was intending to leave tomorrow anyway, but apparently they mean to arrest me on suspicion of having to do with the murder.'

Kembri must have arranged this, thought Maia, to make sure that Bayub-Otal would be up and setting about his own flight when she arrived. That would make him less likely to question her too closely.

'I was just putting some things together.' He pointed to a half-filled pack lying on the floor. 'We must be off at once, before they know you're gone.'

'Can I wash, my lord? Is there time? I'd feel so much better—'

'Yes, of course. Are you injured—wounded?'

'My shoulder hurts.'

'Let me see.'

She pulled the tunic to one side so that he could see the burn.

'O Shakkarn!' he said. 'The brutes! This damned city! One day—Did you tell them anything?'

'I couldn't, my lord, 'cos I don't know anything; not about the High Counsellor's murder.'

'Neither do I, but I wish I did. I'd gladly have played a part in it. That's why I'm suspected, I suppose.'

Crossing to a door on the further side of the room, he called in a low voice, 'Pillan!'

There was no response and after calling once more he went out into the passage, returning a minute later with a grizzled, stooping man carrying a towel and a pail of water.

'This water's not very hot—the fire's been out an hour or two—but at least it's not cold. You can wash in here—we'll leave you—but be as quick as you can. And here's something to tie round your shoulder. At any rate it's clean—better than nothing.'

Maia, in the act of taking the cloth from him, suddenly saw that the servant was staring at her with an expression of fear and amazement, making the sign against evil with a hand held before his face. She had not imagined that her appearance could be so grievous as to give rise to feelings of this kind, and herself felt frightened to see him muttering and gesticulating.

'Anda-Nokomis,' stammered the man, turning to Bayub-Otal and speaking in an Urtan argot that Maia could barely understand, 'what does—what does this mean? Who is this girl?'

He seemed almost about to run from the room. Bayub-Otal replied sharply.

'Control yourself, Pillan! Stop this superstitious nonsense at once! I'm quite aware of what's troubling you; but there's nothing to be afraid of, do you understand? Just pick up that pack and bring it into the kitchen with you. Be quick, Maia! As soon as you're ready, just leave the water and come through: we'll be waiting for you. I've got a cloak you can wear, but no sandals, I'm afraid.'

'I'll be quick, my lord.'

They went out. She stripped and washed, wincing as she touched her bruises and in her haste splashing a good deal of the tepid water over the floor. Then, clenching her teeth with disgust, she got back into her grimy shift and the once-white tunic, now stiff with sweat and dirt, and fastened its four remaining topaz buttons.

If only I could get some clean clothes, she thought, wouldn't matter how rough. Oh, I could cry with it!

The short passage let her into a brick-floored kitchen where—or so it seemed—Bayub-Otal was vehemently warning or admonishing his servant in some way. He broke off as she came in. The man, with a surly air of acquiescing rather than accepting whatever his master had said, went across the room to where his cloak was hanging on a peg. Bayub-Otal handed her a dark, smoothly-lined cloak—no doubt his own—and wrapped himself in a rougher one of coarse, grey cloth. Pillan blew out the lamps and they went into the courtyard. At the gate Bayub-Otal motioned to Maia to wait while Pillan, silently lifting the latch, stepped out into the street and stood looking this way and that. After a few moments he turned his head, nodding, and they followed him out.

It was barely three hundred yards back into the Khalkoornil and in less than five minutes, without encountering anyone at all, they were descending its final length towards the Gate of Lilies. A dim light was shining from the half-open guard-room door, but the only soldier to be seen was the sentry on duty who, having taken off his helmet and leant his spear against the near-by wall, was sitting on a bench in the shadow of the arch. Becoming suddenly aware of their approach he hurriedly sprang to his feet, snatched up his spear and challenged them.

Bayub-Otal, throwing open his cloak and spreading his arms wide to show that his sword and dagger were both sheathed at his belt and that he carried no other weapons, walked up to the sentry and stopped in front of his extended spear-point.

'I'm travelling to Urtah: I need to make a very early start. These are my servants, who are going with me. Will you please let us out?'

'No one's allowed out, sir,' replied the boy. 'Not until the gate's opened at dawn, and that's another three hours and more.'

Maia had already been told by Kembri that the sentry would refuse to let them out; and that she was thereupon to say, as a pre-arranged password, that she was as thirsty as an ox and to ask him whether he could give her something to drink. She said this now and at once the soldier, replying that he would see what he could do, went into the guard-house and returned with the yawning tryzatt. While Maia drank some of the sharp wine which the boy brought her, the tryzatt conferred with Bayub-Otal over a bribe. Maia, well aware that the man must have received secret instructions to let them go, felt impatient of this play-acting. Whatever sum was finally agreed, Bayub-Otal was plainly not concerned to drive a bargain. A quick clinking of coins was followed by the unbolting and opening of the postern to one side of the main gates.

They passed through. Before them, in the light of the now-setting moon, lay the empty length of the highway to Dari-Paltesh. Maia's bare feet, used as they had once been to stones and miry lanes, had grown soft during her months in the High Counsellor's household. Seeing her shrink, Bayub-Otal gave her his arm. Pillan fell in behind them, and as the postern shut to at their backs they set out towards the wooded country west of the Beklan plain.

: 43 :
NORTHWARD

After following the paved highway for some time they reached its junction with the road running north into Urtah. This was not much more than a broad track, its ruts and marshier places mended with stones or felled saplings laid side by side. After some three miles it entered woodland, where trees stood thick about the verge and in places overhung it. The moon had set and in near-darkness Bayub-Otal and Pillan went forward warily, with drawn swords. They met no one, however, and within the hour, from an open place, saw first light creeping into the sky on their right.

Soon the track forked and here Bayub-Otal slid off his pack, sat down and turned to Maia with a smile.

'Tired?'

She laughed. 'Never in the world, my lord. I can go 's far as you like.'

'There wasn't time to offer you food when you came. Would you like some now?'

'Oh, that's kind of you, my lord, but not yet.' (The priests had in fact given her a good meal late the previous night.)

'You're probably right.' He evidently interpreted her refusal as a prudent wish to put first things first and push on. 'We'll both have been missed by now. We'd better not stay on the direct road to Urtah: we'll play safe and lose ourselves.'

'What's your plan, then, my lord? Where are we making for?'

'That all depends on the news I get; if I get any. I may or may not go to Kendron-Urtah: but if I do, I shan't take *you* there.'

'Why not, my lord?'

'I'm afraid you must leave the decisions to me.' The cold, almost contemptuous note she knew so well had crept back into his voice.

'But what we have to think about now,' he resumed after a few minutes, as they went on down the narrower, divergent track, 'is getting into Urtah by back-ways. Once we're actually there—across the Olmen, I mean—we'll be able to take things more easily. We'll be safe then. My father would never give me up to Bekla, and the Leopards couldn't make him.'

'How far's that, then, my lord, d'you reckon?'

'Forty miles at least; it could be fifty. But with luck we ought to reach the Olmen the day after tomorrow. Can you do fifteen miles a day for three days?'

'I reckon so, my lord; but I'd go a lot easier if only I had some sandals and if I could get rid of these filthy dirty clothes.'

'I think you may be able to, tonight.'

Once again she felt what a strange, incomprehensible man he was. He had shown himself ready to risk his life to save—as he supposed—that of one of the most desirable slave-girls in Bekla. Now he was speaking matter-of-factly of not taking her with him to his destination. What was she to make of it? And at this rate how could she hope to obtain any information of value to the Lord General?

Dawn was now breaking along the eastern skyline in a long, smooth band of ochre, and the woodland round them was full of bird-song. The dark-red east turned first to crimson and then, as the sun itself appeared, to a dazzling gold too bright to look at. The zenith became clear blue, while before them the northern horizon lay in a purple haze, foretelling a hot, cloudless day.

Some way ahead, at the foot of an open slope, stood a grove of empress trees, covered with their mauve, trumpet-shaped blooms, and suddenly, as she looked down at them, a kynat, the purple-and-gold harbinger of summer, flew out from among the branches, uttering its fluting call. In the

434

distance shone a soft, yellow mist of wattles in bloom, and beside the track were growing clusters of three-petalled trillium lilies. Stooping, she picked one and tucked it behind her ear. The return of summer had been a familiar blessing all her life, and now she responded to it almost unthinkingly, one of thousands of living creatures to whom it meant the restoration of energy and confidence. She was lucky Maia, secure in her youth and beauty. The dread of torture was gone: the filthy prison was gone. Why look for more just now? Something would happen: things would turn out all right, as they had before.

One thing, however, remained mysterious and disconcerting—the bearing of Pillan. Plainly, he still regarded her with disquiet, though why she could not imagine. From time to time, she noticed him staring at her uneasily but then at once glancing away, as though afraid to look and yet unable not to. Since their setting out, he had not once addressed her directly, and seemed to be taking care to remain at a little distance from her. Once—it was shortly after they had turned westward off the Urtah road—when she had asked him for water, he had taken the bottle off his belt without speaking and passed it to Bayub-Otal to give to her.

At the bottom of it, she felt, there could only be some sort of superstition. Did he perhaps suppose that she had bewitched his master? She only wished she had. Or might it, after all (he being obviously a devoted servant), be nothing but jealousy? Yet he looked too old and steady a man to give way to such feelings. She hoped he was not going to make himself her enemy. His manner, however, suggested not so much hostility as a kind of perturbation and bewilderment. Well, she wasn't going to do anything about it. He'd just have to come round in his own time.

Bayub-Otal's withered hand, she came to perceive during the next hour or so, was more of a handicap to him than she had hitherto realized. During the time when she had been with him in Bekla he had seldom or never had to compass anything more awkward than eating and drinking. Now, as she saw him fumbling, however dexterously, with his sword-belt, his pack or the ties of a sandal, or merely moving in a slightly unnatural way on account of the wrist that did not co-ordinate like another man's; and observed how unobtrusively he contrived to minimize the disability, she began, against her natural inclination, to feel both sympathy and respect. She had not been wrong, either, in judging that Pillan, though dour by nature, both liked and esteemed his master.

If Pillan was indeed a free man, she thought, as his manner suggested, he seemed hardly the sort to remain, however well-paid, in the personal service—dangerous, too—of someone he did not hold in regard. Besides, in a cryptic way the two of them were on familiar terms. They had a kind of game, played now and then to their evidently mutual though

435

unexpressed amusement, which consisted of Bayub-Otal exaggerating the rôle of the gilded gentleman, while Pillan responded in the part of the gruff, earthy retainer.

'That purple blossom on the trees is remarkably beautiful, Pillan, don't you think?'

'Don't last long.'

'Yet it's quite exquisite while it's here.'

'All right for them as likes that sort of thing.'

Bayub-Otal sighed deeply; Pillan spat on the ground; and both walked on in silence.

She began to understand also why, since Bayub-Otal was regarded as a danger to Bekla, Kembri had jumped at the chance to put a spy actually in his company. In this lonely country he could never have been followed without becoming aware of it. And not only did his destination remain unknown—apparently even to himself—but as the morning wore on their very route became more and more involved and unpredictable. He was at particular pains to avoid meeting such few wayfarers as they saw, now and then, approaching from the opposite direction, and would lead herself and Pillan off the track into cover. Once, seeing two pedlars coming across an open stretch where there was no chance of concealment, he simply sat down, wrapped himself in his cloak and assumed the part of a solitary traveller resting, while Pillan and Maia walked on as though they had nothing to do with him.

Maia, still young enough to feel pride in showing two older men that she could accomplish more than they might have expected, was by this time rather enjoying herself. Nennaunir could not have walked fifteen miles; neither could Dyphna. The going was easy enough and her feet, like oxen back in the shafts after winter, were beginning to remember their manage. The men were not walking fast—indeed, she could have walked faster—but then she was not carrying a pack, and Bayub-Otal firmly refused her every attempt to take a turn with his.

By about two hours before noon the sun had become too hot for comfort. The sweat was running down Maia's back and between her breasts, and she felt altogether imprisoned in the heavy material of the tunic. When they approached a stream and Bayub-Otal turned off the track towards it, she ran ahead and, kneeling down, first drank and then bathed her arms, feet and face. The others came up as she was shaking the water from her dripping head.

'We'll stop here,' said Bayub-Otal, pointing to a yew thicket a little downstream of where they were standing. 'Suitably secluded, Pillan, would you not conjecture?'

'No good at all.'

'You needn't stop on my account, my lord,' said Maia. 'I'm not done up yet, not by a long ways.'

'I dare say,' said Bayub-Otal, 'but if we try to go on in this heat you will be, and so shall we. Why isn't it any good, Pillan?'

'Scent. Might be usin' dogs.'

'So they might. Well?'

'Best go upstream, my lord. Going down's easier, so they'd likely reckon we'd done that.'

Without another word Bayub-Otal stepped into the water and began wading upstream. For a good hour they made their way through shallows and small pools, ducking under branches and clambering up the few small falls they encountered. This last, as Maia could see, was by no means easy for Bayub-Otal. Pillan, however, seemed to know from experience when his master required help and when he was better left to himself.

At length, in the full heat of the day, they came to what looked like the outskirts of an extensive forest. Once among the first trees, Bayub-Otal climbed out of the stream and sat down.

'We'll leave it at that, Pillan. Food and rest now, until it's cooler.'

They ate bread and cheese, dried figs and last year's apples, soft and wrinkled. Maia, having wandered a little way along the bank, stripped off the horrible tunic, wrapped herself in her cloak and fell asleep almost at once, without even a thought of possible wild beasts. It had, however, occurred to her that she could rely on not being molested by her companions, and this was pleasantly reassuring.

When she woke, the sun was sinking behind the forest. Long shadows were falling across the rough ground beyond the edge of the trees, and from somewhere not far off came the evening sound of a *semda* singing its falls and trills. Buttoning on the tunic (which by now felt almost like leather, particularly under the armpits) she returned to the others. Bayub-Otal was keeping watch from a tree while Pillan, seated on a log, was mending a sandal-strap with twine. She picked up one of the packs and slipped the straps over her shoulders.

'Don't do that,' said Bayub-Otal. 'Until we can get hold of some sandals for you, you've got to go easy on your feet. If they give out we're all in trouble.'

She was compelled to give him the pack.

For a time they went north along the irregular edge of the forest, until what little they could see of the sunset had begun to fade behind the trees. Maia, anxious at the prospect of spending the night in such a wild, lonely place, was on the point of asking Bayub-Otal what he meant to do, when in the distance they caught sight of a man rounding up a flock of sheep with two dogs.

'We'll try him for a night's lodging,' said Bayub-Otal. 'He might give us away, I suppose, but I think the odds are against it. After all, he's not to know who we are.'

The shepherd, who seemed good-natured enough, showed no particular surprise at their request, merely replying that they had better come back with him to the farm and have a word with his master. Someone further off, however, had evidently seen them approaching, for when they reached the gate of the stockade surrounding the big farmhouse and its barns, they found a group of ten or twelve men and girls already gathered to have a look at the strangers. Bayub-Otal, greeting them courteously, left Maia and Pillan to wait while he went to see the farmer.

Pillan was not one to take the lead in talking with strangers and Maia, for her part, thought it best to assume the rôle of the modest wench, diffident of speaking up before her betters had settled what was to happen. One or two of the girls smiled at her and she smiled back, but nevertheless remained demurely seated beside Pillan on a pile of planks in one corner of the yard.

After a short time the farmer, a burly man of perhaps forty or forty-five, came strolling across the yard, chatting with Bayub-Otal as he came. Evidently the two of them had hit it off well enough and reached an understanding. Pillan and Maia stood up respectfully, but the farmer did not trouble himself to speak to them, merely calling forward another man—the stockman perhaps, thought Maia, or the head forester (for timber was plainly a substantial part of the business)—to see to the gentleman's servants. A minute or two later she found herself among six or seven lasses, all somewhere around her own age, who had been told to take her with them to supper. Just as she was going, however, Bayub-Otal called her back and, slipping a hundred meld into her hand, suggested that she should try to use it to get some sandals and fresh clothes.

Maia soon gathered that the farm, though no more than sixteen or seventeen miles from Bekla, was regarded by the girls as an isolated place, off the beaten track. The chance arrival of a stranger, and one who had actually lived in the great city at that, was a godsend—a most welcome break in the routine of their lives. Only two or three of them had ever been to Bekla. During supper—strong broth, weak beer, bread and cheese but plenty of it, dispensed by a good-natured, rather deaf old woman whom they called 'säiyett' when they remembered—she was fairly pelted with questions, but had little or no trouble in answering them or in giving a convincing account of herself; for though perky and inquisitive as blue-tits, they were not in the least sceptical and ready enough to accept whatever she told them. How had she hurt her face so badly? Oh, she'd been tripped up in the market by some lout who thought it was funny. One of her boy-friends had thrashed him for it. They must have had a rough day's journey: her clothes were in such a state? Oh, this had once been a party tunic belonging to a rich Beklan lady—a friend of her master—who'd given it to her as a cast-off. That's why there was leopards on the pockets. It had been nice once, but since it was as good as finished she'd thought she might as well wear it out on the journey. It hadn't been a good idea, though; it was too thick and held the sweat. She was hoping to pick up something else. They were a long way off the direct road to Urtah, surely? Oh, her master had some relatives he wanted to visit further west—no, she couldn't say exactly where, never having been there as yet—but that was what had taken them out of their way.

Then, after a pause in the talk, 'Are you a slave?' asked one of the girls suddenly, in a kind of quick little spurt of utterance, as though she had finally screwed herself up to the point of asking. One or two of the other girls giggled with nervous embarrassment, but nevertheless it was clear that they were all waiting for her reply.

'Not any more,' answered Maia, smiling. 'I've been freed.'

This let loose a flood of exclamations and further questions. 'But you're no age!' 'Were you born on a slave-farm?' 'How long have you been free?' 'Did you have to pay?' 'You don't look a bit like a slave!'

Maia, catching on to the last of these as the easiest to answer, asked teasingly, 'What d'you reckon a slave looks like, then?'

To her surprise this did not seem to go down very well. Most of the girls looked grave and there was a little pause. Then one said, 'Well, o' course we didn' mean nothin' personal, not if you've *been* a slave, like, but so happens there's one of these new slave-farms not so very far off from here, where the poor children's actually bred for slavery, to be taken away when they're old enough. We all feel sorry for them. My dad told me it belongs to some of those rich Leopards up in Bekla.'

'Ah, that's right,' said an older lass, 'and 'twas the Leopards as brought the farms in, too, 'cause they wanted even more slaves—more than they dared take from the villages and from ordinary folk like us. There weren't any slave-farms, my mum said, not when she was a girl.'

'I didn't come from a slave-farm,' said Maia.

'Then were you—' began the girl; but another, interrupting her, cut in, 'We heard about that big Leopard baron, or whatever he was; him as was murdered at the festival—terrible bloody murder, they say—and they've never found the ones as did it, neither.'

'Oh, I can tell you all about that,' said Maia, glad of an opportunity to distract them from any further enquiries about herself. 'I was actually in the gardens by the lake that night, when it happened.'

This, of course, had all the effect she was hoping for, and the whole group listened agog to her description of the party by the Barb, the murder of Sencho and the mysterious disappearance of his assailants. Of her own relationship to the High Counsellor she naturally said nothing.

'Must 'a bin someone important behind it, though, mustn't there?' said the older girl, when Maia had finished.

'Well, 'twasn't *you*, Gehta, anyway,' cried a little, merry girl, with black eyes and a snub nose. 'That's for sure!' Then, turning to Maia, she added rather unnecessarily, 'I'm only teasing, you know. But Gehta's a real Leopard—we all tell her so. If she'd 'a bin there she'd have gone and saved that fat old Counsellor, sure enough.'

'Now then!' cried the deaf old woman, shaking her ladle at them with mock minacity. 'How much longer you lazy wenches goin' to sit there on your bums? Anyone for any more, 'fore it's cleared away?'

Everyone, however, seemed as replete and contented as Maia felt herself. Indeed, they struck her as such a cheerful, good-natured little society and the whole atmosphere seemed so pleasant, that she couldn't help feeling, rather wistfully, that she'd have liked to stay with them. Well, but it was only a fancy, she thought, as she began helping to clear away. Like enough she'd soon be tired of getting up early to milking and dirty hands from morning till night.

She watched her opportunity to take the older girl on one side and ask her about clothes. As she had hoped, Gehta proved helpful. Between them, she and the deaf old woman fitted her out with a tidy, serviceable smock, as well as a clean shift, neither much the worse for wear, and a pair of sandals. They firmly refused to accept so much as a meld.

'Never in the world!' cried Gehta, closing Maia's fingers over her money and pushing her fist back into her pocket. 'Think we're going to take money for helping out a guest? You'll be helping *us* one of these days. Fact, you can,' she added in a lower voice (though the old woman was their only company). 'Let's you and me just have a little stroll outside, shall we?'

She led the way across the yard to the gate of the stockade, where a fire was burning in an iron basket and the night-watchman was already pottering about near his hut beside the sheep-pens.

'We're just going for a bit of a turn before bed-time, Brindo,' said Gehta. 'We'll be back directly—don't worry.'

The old fellow, smiling as he pretended to grumble, unbarred the gate and the two girls went out into the big, smooth-grazed meadow beyond.

'They let you go out alone after the gate's been shut?' asked Maia in some surprise.

'Well, we're not really supposed to,' replied Gehta, 'but Brindo's never one to make trouble, and everyone here takes the rules pretty easy. The land's open as far as the forest, you see, and there's not really much harm you could come to.'

The moon, directly ahead of them, had already risen clear of the distant trees. Bats flitted noiselessly here and there and the breeze carried a resinous scent from the pines.

'Peaceful, isn't it?' said Gehta after a minute or two. 'You wouldn't think there was any danger in all the world, would you?'

Something in her tone made Maia turn her head and look at her.

'What's up, then? You mean, there is?'

'Well, that's what I wanted to ask *you*, really,' replied Gehta, 'but I didn't want the others to hear. You've been living in Bekla, haven't you—working in that gentleman's house as you're with? I don't want to ask a lot of inquisitive questions, only I thought p'raps you might sometimes have heard one or two of these big barons and such-like talking—you know, at their parties and dinners and that.'

'What about?' asked Maia.

Gehta stopped and faced her squarely. 'I'll tell you straight out. My dad's got a farm—not so big as this—about twenty miles west of here. One day it'll be mine and my husband's; when I've got a husband, that's to say; only I've no brothers, you see. I'm here for a bit to learn one or two things—well, like buying and selling the timber—that I couldn't pick up so well at home. But never mind that—what I want to find out is whether there's going to be trouble—you know, real bad trouble.'

'D'you mean the war?'

'S'ssh!' said Gehta; though there was no one in sight. 'Everything we hear—you know, from pedlars and visiting timber-dealers; oh, yes, and from our own men when they take stuff up to Bekla: they believe there are barons—you know, heldril—in some of the outlying parts that are getting ready to make trouble for the Leopards. They're the ones that really killed that fat old Counsellor or whatever he was, because he was the one as knew most about what they're up to; he had his spies everywhere, or so we heard. They say some of the barons living right the way over there'—she pointed eastward—'they'd even be ready to see King Karnat take Bekla, because they reckon they'd be better off than they are under the Leopards.'

'The Leopards tax the farmers and peasants and favour the merchants and city people,' said Maia. 'I've heard that said again and again.'

Gehta looked at her with tears in her eyes. 'If King Karnat crosses the Valderra river and makes for Bekla, dad's farm's slap in the way, near enough. *That's* why the other girls say I'm a Leopard—because I'm afraid of what might be going to happen. If there's going to be fighting, I want to go back home now, before it starts. That's my proper place—with dad

441

and mum. Only you can't get any reliable news, living here. I thought if you've been—well—in service in the upper city, p'raps you might have heard—you know, something or other—'

'Well, truth is I reckon *you* know more'n what I do,' said Maia. 'About the Leopards, I mean. All I know is they're all in a great taking about the killing.'

'I know the Leopards are hard on farming folk,' said Gehta, 'but even that's better than war. I was only nine when Queen Fornis and her lot came up from Paltesh to Bekla. They took everything we had; and the soldiers, they—you know.' She began to cry. 'If there was to be all that over again—oh, what's going to happen, Maia? What ought I to do?'

Maia, liking her and grateful for her help over the clothes, longed to be of some comfort. 'I reckon you're troubling yourself too much. I've heard General Kembri talking; I've—well, I've waited on him at dinner, you know, and that kind of thing. And I've never heard him speak as if he thought they couldn't stop King Karnat crossing the river. As for the heldril, well, it's true you hear a lot of talk about trouble and rebellion and so on, but it never seems to come to anything.'

'Oh, I do just about hope you're right,' said Gehta. 'It's such a worry. 'Course, I know there's nothing I could really do to make Dad any safer if I did go home, but all the same, if there's going to be trouble I'd rather be there than here; it's only natural.' She paused. 'Anyway, thanks, Maia. At least it's some relief that *you* don't seem worried. We'd best go back now, 'fore old Brindo starts shouting after us.'

Before the night was over Maia experienced another instance of the easy-going ways of the farm. Given a very comfortable spare bed at one end of the girls' big sleeping-shed, she quickly fell asleep. Waking some time during the night she sensed, drowsily but surely enough, a kind of muted disturbance near-by. After a few moments she realized what it was. One of the girls was not alone in bed, and unless she was much mistaken her companion was not another girl. Turning over, she saw in the moonlight that Gehta, next to her, was also awake. Putting a finger to her lips, Gehta beckoned to her and, leaning a little way out of bed, put her mouth to her ear.

'We never tell: you won't?'

Maia shook her head and fell asleep again.

As she had expected, the girls were up soon after dawn to milking, fowl-feeding and the other tasks of the farm. After breakfast they said good-bye to Maia with warmth and regret on both sides.

'We don't often get someone like ourselves stopping by,' said the little, black-eyed girl. 'Makes a nice change.' She kissed Maia. 'What a pity you couldn't have stayed a bit longer.' Maia was soon to find herself in full agreement with this.

44

LENKRIT

'You got your clothes and sandals all right, then?' asked Bayub-Otal, as they set out across the big meadow.

'Yes, thank you, my lord; no trouble.'

'Did you have to pay much for them?'

'Nothing at all, my lord. Only they wouldn't take anything, see? Here's the money.'

'You'd better keep it. You may need it. That was very kind and hospitable, don't you think, Pillan? Very kind indeed.'

'No such thing.'

'Dear me, why ever not?'

'That coat what she had on yesterday: them yellow buttons must 'a bin worth a sight more 'n anything they've give her.'

There could be no answer to this, even though Maia did not believe that either Gehta or the old woman had thought twice about the topaz buttons. Still, neither had she, and she felt annoyed to have been so careless. She ought to have pulled the buttons off and kept them.

'Did you enjoy your company last night, Pillan?' asked Bayub-Otal.

Pillan became unwontedly fluent. 'One of 'em I'd have given something to remember, only for you bein' up at the house and we didn't want no trouble.'

'Oh dear! I suppose he called you a Suban marsh-frog, did he?'

Pillan grunted.

'One gets used to it. You never know, you might have the opportunity to do something quite drastic about it before much longer. Did you manage to buy any food?'

Pillan jerked his thumb at his pack. 'Bit in here.'

'And you, Maia?'

' 'Fraid not, my lord.' She had never given it a thought.

'It doesn't matter,' said Bayub-Otal. 'I got some, too, so we'll have enough between us for today.'

They came to a rough track running north and followed it. It led to no farm or dwelling, let alone a village. All that day, as they went steadily uphill and northward, the country became more lonely, barren and wild. It was, indeed, the most desolate Maia had ever seen; part sandy waste covered with rough grass and scrub, part rocky, with a few stunted trees and tracts of some mauve-flowering, sage-like shrub which harboured clouds of flies. During the late afternoon, as she was plodding onward with eyes half-closed against the glare and sucking a pebble to ease her thirst—for they had no water left, having come upon none since mid-morning—she suddenly realized that at last they were on level ground: in fact they had begun, though almost imperceptibly, to descend. Shading her eyes, she saw ahead and below a smooth, green plain, speckled with brown and grey patches which were mud-built villages. Far ahead, perhaps ten miles off in the heat haze, she could just make out what looked like the irregular line of a river.

Bayub-Otal, wiping the sweat from his face, pointed towards it.

'That's the Olmen. With luck we'll cross it tomorrow; then we'll be in Urtah.'

'We got to go much further today, then, my lord?'

'No; we'll get down off this crest and find somewhere to lie up for the night. We daren't risk a village—not in a place as frequented as the plain. We're still in Bekla province, you see, and likely enough there's a price on our heads by now. We'll make for those trees: ought to be some shelter there.'

The woodland which they were approaching covered most of the rocky slope below. Soon they found themselves among outskirts of scrub oak, long-leaved *nakai* and evergreen sweetspires, several growing almost horizontally out from the faces of steep little bluffs. A few of these were precipitous, and more than once they were forced to go some distance along a sheer edge before they could find a way down.

Maia, at the end of this second long day, was feeling weary, due partly to the rough going, but mainly to her increasing anxiety and uncertainty. Normally, her instinct in such a situation would have been to do what she was told and leave everything else to her older and more experienced companions. But these Subans—she was their secret enemy. If in some way or other they were to find out the truth, they would probably kill her. Not for the first time that day, the idea occurred to her, 'Why not *tell* them? Tell them I was forced into it—that I'd got no choice?' But what would they do then? They might not kill her, but obviously they would unburden themselves of her in one way or another; and what had she to hope for, left alone in unknown country?

Rapt in these dismal meditations and in the listlessness of fatigue, she did not notice, until Bayub-Otal called out to her, that he and Pillan had stopped at the foot of the last bluff they had descended, and were sitting among the rocks. She went back to them. Bayub-Otal nodded over his shoulder. 'That cleft—there's quite a fair-sized cave inside. If you don't mind sharing it, I think it'll do us very well. There must be water somewhere fairly near, and we can cut branches and scrub to sleep on. Have a look and tell me what you think.'

She smiled. 'I'm not used to being asked what I think, my lord.'

444

'Then you can get some practice now,' replied Bayub-Otal.

She felt irritated. Whether or not he really supposed he was giving her any power of choice she had no idea. As far as she was concerned he had as good as told her what they were going to do. Why couldn't he have said so and left it at that?

Except for the narrow opening, which made it gloomy and dark, there was nothing wrong with the cave. It was all of thirty feet long, with plenty of room for her to sleep apart. Bayub-Otal set off with the water bottles while she and Pillan began cutting scrub-willow and oleander branches for pallets.

Later, when they had eaten and drunk, she made her own way down to the brook, washed and bathed her feet.

'I don't think we should make a fire, do you?' Bayub-Otal was saying to Pillan as she returned. 'We don't want to risk anyone knowing we're here.'

'Wood burns that quick, my lord, we'd never be done gett'n enough.'

'I'm afraid we'll have to take it in turns to keep watch, though,' went on Bayub-Otal. 'You can start, Pillan, and then wake me; and I'll wake you, Maia, an hour or two before dawn. You needn't be afraid: animals are easily scared off even without a fire, and you can always wake us if you think anyone's coming.'

Once she had lain down she found herself more comfortable—or else more tired—than she had expected, and slept without stirring until Bayub-Otal woke her.

The moon was almost set. She felt stiff and cramped from the hard floor. He'd left her late, she thought. He'd given himself the most inconvenient watch, too; the one that broke a night's sleep in half. She wished he wouldn't always be so scrupulously courteous and considerate. From a man who had rejected her it came cold, and only made her feel inferior and ill-at-ease.

For a while she sat just outside the cave, wrapped in her cloak and listening, in the yellow moonlight, to the innumerable small noises all around her—patterings, rustlings and the quiet movement of leaves and branches. With moonset, however, it grew very dark and a chilly wind got up from the east. She began to feel shrammed. After a time it occurred to her that since she could see nothing and her watch now consisted only of listening, she could do it as well inside the cave and out of the wind. She went back to her pallet near the cave-mouth and lay prone, her chin propped on her hands: but still she felt cold. She shivered, hunching her shoulders.

Further back in the cave, Pillan lay stretched asleep on the stones. She could just hear his breathing in the darkness. Moving slightly, he muttered an unintelligible word or two and was quiet again. She made a little joke in her thoughts: 'Does he say more awake or asleep?'

His strange, alarmed reaction when he had first seen her at Bayub-Otal's lodgings—after two days in his company it struck her as oddly out of character. This rather grim, unexcitable man, who seldom wasted a word—for some reason the mere sight of her had put him in fear, and that to such an extent that Bayub-Otal had had to check him. Try as she would, she could think of no plausible reason. First time anyone's ever been afraid of me, she thought, without it was Nala.

She was feeling warmer now. Resting her forehead on her forearms, she relaxed, breathing slowly and deeply. Her thoughts began to wander into fantasy. She imagined herself back in Bekla, a famous shearna, her fortune made; living with Occula in their own house; sought after, receiving and refusing whom she would; lying late, rising in the afternoon, calling their maid to help her bath and dress for the evening. Five hundred meld a night. A thousand meld a night! A great, soft bed all covered with silk— ah!—soft as—soft as—the lake—floating—under the waterfall—scent of water-mint—wavering down, deep water. Deep.

Her body was jarred by a thudding blow. For an instant it formed part of her dream as a kind of explosion, shattering from about her the lake, the sun and the sky above. She struggled against it, trying to hold on to the lake, trying to stop the fragments dispersing. Then came the inrush of shock and she leapt wide awake as a second thud jolted her against the stony floor of the cave.

It was grey daylight; not yet sunrise, but fully light enough to see. A man was standing over her. For a moment she thought it was Pillan; then realized with terror that it was a stranger, a man she had never seen in her life. As she sprang to her feet, stumbling over the hem of her cloak, he grabbed her by the arm, jerking her up and forcing her round to face him.

He was bearded, dark and stocky; broad-featured, perhaps forty years old, with the weathered appearance of a soldier or a hunter. There was about him also the air of a man accustomed to command. Ruthless and hard he certainly looked, yet no ruffian. His eyes, as they stared into hers, had a look of assurance and authority, as though he were one who seldom needed to use violence except in the last resort.

He was wearing a padded leather surcoat, a sword at his belt and a helmet of smooth, hardened leather. His left hand gripped Maia's arm: his right was holding a dagger, its point towards her.

Speechless with fear and the shock of her awakening, she now saw that this stranger was not alone. With him were two younger men, similarly

446

armed. One of these, also holding a dagger, was kneeling beside Pillan, whom he was shaking awake. The other, black against the light, stood at the mouth of the cave, his sword drawn in his hand.

The dark man spoke in an accent strange to Maia, but perfectly intelligible. 'What are you doing here? Who are you?'

The unfamiliar cadence, which seemed all of a piece with his bellicose appearance, frightened her still more. For an instant the thought whirled across her confused mind that perhaps he was not human. Old Drigga had told her of forest demons who had power to take the semblance of men, yet always with some revealing imperfection—ears, hands, voice or the like.

Cowering from him, she would have fallen, but his grip literally held her upright: as her eyes once more met his, he shook her so that she lurched against him.

'Come on, answer me! Who are you?'

Pillan was awake now. The man kneeling on the floor had his knife at his throat.

'I think this is a Suban, sir.'

The dark man, without relinquishing his agonizing grip of Maia's arm, was about to answer when Bayub-Otal's voice spoke from the back of the cave.

'Lenkrit! What on earth are you doing here?'

The dark man, startled, let go of Maia, who fell against the cave-wall as Bayub-Otal, still wrapped in his cloak, came forward, stepped over Pillan and stood smiling in the light from the cave-mouth.

'You'd better sit down, Lenkrit. And for Cran's sake put your knife away. You're terrifying the poor girl.'

'Anda-Nokomis!' replied the dark man, staring. Then, so suddenly that, far from reassuring her, it only added to Maia's dream-like bewilderment, he burst into a great shout of laughter. 'Anda-Nokomis! O Shakkarn, and we nearly cut all your throats! That'd have been a right start to the war, that would! Here, Thel, get up, man! Get up and let that fellow alone! What's his name, Anda-Nokomis—I remember him—Billan—Tillan—something or other?'

He sheathed his knife and, stepping forward, flung his arms round Bayub-Otal's neck and embraced him.

'Pillan. Who's with you; just these two lads, or are there any more?'

'No, just the three of us. This is Thel, and that's Tescon. Their fathers are both tenants of mine. You'd better come back here now, Tescon. If you never saw him before, this is Anda-Nokomis.'

Both the young men, smiling, stood in front of Bayub-Otal, raised their palms to their foreheads and then offered him their daggers, holding them

447

by the blades. Bayub-Otal, also smiling, took each in turn for a moment and then returned it to its owner. Pillan, who had uttered no word since he was woken, was now standing behind Bayub-Otal with folded arms.

'And the wench?' asked the dark man.

Bayub-Otal, as though recollecting himself, went quickly across to Maia, put his arm round her and supported her to a low rock near the cave-mouth.

'You've frightened the life out of her, Lenkrit. She's still trembling and can you blame her? What happened, Maia? Did they rush you or didn't you hear them coming?'

'I—I was asleep, my lord: I'm very sorry.'

'That's right!' cried Lenkrit, with another great laugh. 'All the damned lot of you, sound as toads in a winter ditch! Lespa's stars, Anda-Nokomis, it's lucky for you she *is* a wench: else we'd likely have knifed the lot of you in your sleep and that would have been that. What's she doing here, anyway?'

'Either you're rather forgetful, Lenkrit, or else you're rather unobservant,' replied Bayub-Otal. 'Your lads here are too young, but you're not. Take another good look at her now.'

Lenkrit turned and regarded Maia steadily in the now-clear light. When he next spoke it was in a quieter, rather hesitant tone of voice.

'I—see, Anda-Nokomis. I wonder I didn't before. But the light was bad, of course, and we were all a bit flustered. And then, poor girl, someone's been knocking her about, haven't they? But—well, it's incredible—amazing! Your sister, is she? I never knew you had one.'

Bayub-Otal shook his head. 'As far as I know, she's no relation at all. Her name's Maia and she comes from Tonilda. Strange, isn't it? In Berkla she belonged to that brute Sencho: she was—well, in his household.'

Lenkrit drew in his breath sharply. 'Was it her that killed him, then? And you got her out? Is that it?'

'No, she didn't kill him, but she was being questioned by the priests. She managed to escape from the temple and we got her out of Bekla with us the night before last.'

Lenkrit took Maia's two hands in his own and kissed them.

'Well, Shakkarn be praised I didn't kill you, Maia.' Then, seeing her puzzled expression, he turned back once more to Bayub-Otal. 'Hasn't she been told?'

Again Bayub-Otal shook his head. 'Not yet. And not until I say.' Then, abruptly, 'Have you got food? Let's talk while we eat. Maia, I must explain to you. This is Lord Lenkrit-Duhl, the Ban of northern Suba. He and I are old friends, but what he's doing here I don't know any more than you do. No doubt he's going to tell us.'

They sat down and the two young men, opening their packs, took out

448

hard bread, cheese and dried tendrionas. Maia, who was still feeling badly shaken, did her best to swallow a few mouthfuls. She had grasped little of the conversation, but at least she knew that she was no longer in danger of her life.

'You were in Bekla when Sencho was killed, then, Anda-Nokomis?' asked Lenkrit.

Bayub-Otal nodded. 'I was in the gardens that night. So was she—she was actually one of the girls attending on him.'

'So of course they arrested her: I see. And they've been setting about her, by the looks of it. They didn't arrest *you*, though?'

'They would have, but two nights ago I got a warning to clear out. I bribed the tryzatt at one of the gates and we were away before dawn. But what can *you* tell *me*, Lenkrit?'

Lenkrit wiped his mouth with the back of his hand and tossed what was left of his bread to Thel to put back in the pack.

'Karnat himself's in Suba now. He must have got about six thousand men there: and Suba itself's been preparing since the end of Melekril.'

Bayub-Otal nodded. 'That was why I stayed on in Bekla—to do my best to mislead them and disarm suspicion.' He held up his right hand in his left and let it drop again. 'More useful in my case than reporting to Karnat for sword-practice, wouldn't you agree?'

'Not at all, Anda-Nokomis. Karnat's publicly declared you the rightful Ban of Suba. We're all waiting for you.'

'Was it Karnat who sent you here, then?' asked Bayub-Otal.

'Karnat wanted someone to cross the Valderra and find out as much as possible, so I took it on, with these lads here. There were two things he wanted us to do and we've done them—or as good as. One was to reconnoitre a route for the army from the Valderra to Bekla, and the other was to find out what was going on in Chalcon. We've been the very devil of a way east, Anda-Nokomis—well to the other side of the highway from Bekla to Gelt. And if he takes my advice, that's the way Karnat'll be coming; east as far as the Gelt road and then straight down it to Bekla— keep north of all that rough country you must just have come through. The Leopards won't be expecting that.'

Bayub-Otal nodded and after a moment Lenkrit went on, 'We're on our way back now. We must have done something like twenty miles since yesterday evening. We've been going by night, you see, ever since we crossed the Valderra. We happened on this cave on our way east five nights ago, and lay up here for a day. We were reckoning to get back to it this morning and what do we find but you? You were lucky, because it's been daggers first and questions afterwards—not in Urtah, but all the time we've been in Bekla province. It's much too obvious that we're Subans, you see.'

'Well, but the Chalcon news?' said Bayub-Otal.

Lenkrit paused a moment; then drew from beneath his cloak a wooden, tubular object, pierced with holes and roughly stained red and blue. Maia, taken unawares, could not suppress a quick 'Oh!' of recognition and surprise. It was a Tonildan shepherd-boy's home-made pipe—an object familiar to almost any Tonildan. She had once made one herself; and played it, too, after a fashion.

'You've seen one of these before, then?' asked Lenkrit, looking round at her.

She nodded, but said nothing. 'Daggers first and questions afterwards.' Had they, then, killed the Tonildan boy the pipe had belonged to?

'Don't worry, Maia,' said he, reading her thoughts. 'It was fairly come by. I was given it two days ago by a little lad herding goats on the edge of the Tonildan Waste. Shepherd-boys were about the only people we dared question, you see. Grown men and women would have been much too risky. We told these boys we were travelling merchants and asked them what news they'd heard lately. This particular lad was very sharp and sensible. He told us his father was just back from Puhra, where all the market-talk was about Chalcon and Santil-kè-Erketlis. I was so pleased with him that I gave him five meld—more than he'd ever had in his life, I dare say—and *he* was so pleased with *me* that he gave me his pipe.

'Well, the news, Anda-Nokomis—and I think it's probably reliable—is that Santil's near enough openly in arms against Bekla. He wasn't going to wait to be treated like that other poor fellow—what was his name?— Enka-Mordet. He's left his estate and gone into the Chalcon hills—taken his servants, tenants—the lot. And men are joining him from all over, apparently.'

'Have the Leopards sent anyone against him, then?' asked Bayub-Otal.

'The lad couldn't say. But he did tell us one other thing which made me prick up my ears. He said his father had heard rumours of some sort of trouble further south, too. Who would that be, do you suppose?'

'Elleroth of Sarkid; the Ban's son? He's the most likely.'

'Just what I thought myself. Listen, Anda-Nokomis: suppose—just sup-pose—that Karnat, with his army half as big again with Suban auxiliaries, crosses the Valderra and succeeds in going straight on to Bekla.'

'Well?'

'Then Suba's rewarded for its indispensable help by being made an independent province in its own right—which it always should have been. You rule it, Anda-Nokomis—which everyone wants, seeing you're the rightful, legal heir, and son of the finest Suban girl that ever—'

'And Karnat?'

'Once there was peace, I doubt Karnat would require a great deal more from Suba. Well, come to that, we haven't got much to give him, have we? Frogs, ducks, reeds—Suba's always been a place on its own. Karnat himself's only valued it because it put him east of the Zhairgen. But you must come and talk to him yourself, Anda-Nokomis.'

'I fully intend to,' replied Bayub-Otal, 'as soon as I can get there. He's at Melvda-Rain, I suppose?'

Lenkrit nodded. 'He's an honest man: we all think so. As for the Subans, it's you they're ready to fight for—Nokomis's boy, that that damned Fornis cheated out of his inheritance.'

'Well,' said Bayub-Otal, standing up somewhat abruptly, 'when do we start? You'll be wanting to sleep now, I dare say, if you've come twenty miles during the night.'

'Yes, we'll lie up here today, Anda-Nokomis, and get across into Urtah tonight. After that it'll be easy enough until we come to the Valderra. You see, the Beklans have got outposts—standing patrols—all along the east bank, from Rallur right up to the hills in the north.'

'Where's the main Beklan army itself, then?' asked Bayub-Otal.

'At Rallur. They've built a light bridge across the Olmen—just above where it runs into the Valderra—so that they can move south quickly if they have to. But all the signs are that they think they *won't* have to; anyway, they've got hardly any outposts downstream. They must feel sure that we can only get across upstream.'

He smiled and Bayub-Otal, nodding, smiled too. To Maia, though she had not really been following all that Lenkrit had said, it was clear enough that they had some unspoken knowledge in common.

'When the three of us came across,' resumed Lenkrit after a few moments, 'my people put on a little act about half a mile away—you know, shouting and pretending they were coming over—to distract the Beklan patrol: so we got across the ford without being spotted. But there'll be nothing like that coming back. It's true there are several fords to choose from, but every single one of them's watched. I think,' said Lenkrit with a certain relish, 'I think we'll hardly avoid a little scuffle.'

Bayub-Otal nodded again. 'Well, you'd better sleep now. That boy there's half asleep already.'

45

ACROSS THE VALDERRA

To Maia there was no tedium in idling away the hours. After the past two days, merely to lie in the sun and do nothing was pleasant. Besides, she had been used enough, in years gone by, to minding sheep and goats on the waste, and this was not much different. The sun moved. The leaves rustled. One lay on one's back and looked up at the marching clouds. After a time evening came.

They set off about two hours after sunset. According to Lenkrit it was no more than six or seven miles to the Olmen, but after some time Maia reckoned that they must already have gone further. At first they went straight down through the woods, but once out on the open plain Lenkrit proceeded cautiously, keeping wide of the two or three villages they encountered. Once, when dogs began to bark, he went back a good half-mile before taking them off the track and round by way of the village fields.

Despite this caution she became keenly aware—for it frightened her—of a potential ruthlessness in her new companions. 'Tain't so much what they're doing now, she thought, it's what they'd be ready to do if they was put to it. It was true that the Subans were not looking for trouble; but they were clearly prepared to shed blood if they had to. Once, when two drovers, who from their overheard talk seemed to be out late in search of a strayed beast, passed close by without seeing them, it was plain enough that at a word from Lenkrit the young men would have knifed them. Maia wondered how many people they had in fact killed since first leaving Suba.

The river, when at length they reached it some two or three hours after midnight, was much as Lenkrit had already described it to her—slow-flowing and about sixty feet wide, meandering across the plain between treeless banks. One of the young men took a cord from his pack, tied one end to the hilt of his knife and plumbed the depth. It was about five feet under the bank.

'We did better coming,' said Lenkrit. 'It was only waist-deep. Still, we can't spend time looking for a better place. We'll just have to flounder across as best we can.'

'It's flowing so slowly, it'll be very little deeper in the middle,' said Bayub-Otal. 'We ought to be able to wade it, just.'

'But do you think the bottom will be firm enough, Anda-Nokomis?' asked Tescon.

As they stood debating the matter among themselves, Maia began to feel a mixture of impatience and mischief. No one had consulted her: it had not even occurred to them that she, a girl, might be of any use.

In the near-darkness, she wandered quietly a little distance upstream. Then, sitting down on the bank, she slipped off her clothes, rolled them round her sandals and, holding the light bundle over her head, slid down into the water and turned on her back.

To get across took her less than half a minute. She had drifted scarcely any distance with the current. Pulling herself out, she walked back until she was opposite the Subans.

'My lord!'

They spun round, clutching their weapons as though Kembri himself were upon them. All but Pillan looked startled out of their wits. For a few moments none said a word. Then Bayub-Otal, taking care not to raise his voice, said, 'Maia! How did you get over?'

'Swam, my lord. Would you like me to take the packs and that over for you?'

And without waiting for an answer she once more lowered herself into the water and swam across.

They were embarrassed out of countenance, these neck-or-nothing desperadoes. They would not look directly at her. After some moments Bayub-Otal said, 'Come on, Lenkrit, give her your pack. We're lucky to have her to help us.'

Without replying, Lenkrit stooped and lowered his pack down to her. She took it over dry and then came back for Thel's. When all the packs and weapons were across she offered to take their clothes, but the men would not undress, choosing to splash and flounder as best they could through the bed of the river, emerging wet from head to foot.

They sat on the bank slapping themselves and squeezing the water out of their sleeves. Maia, having dressed again, remained carefully silent. At length, with an air of mingled curiosity and resentment, Lenkrit said to her 'You don't *mind*—men—seeing you naked?'

'All depends, my lord.'

'On what?'

'Well, just struck me as I could help you, that's all.' For the life of her she could not keep a note of irritation out of her voice. They might at least have thanked her, she thought; on impulse she added, 'In Bekla no one'd think twice.'

'Oh, wouldn't they?' replied Lenkrit contemptuously. 'I see.'

'Might be one or two things changed in Bekla 'fore long,' muttered Thel.

'Let her alone!' said Bayub-Otal sharply. 'She helped you, didn't she?'

'Dare say she did,' persisted the boy, with sullen obstinacy. 'All the same, there's some things—'

'Stand up!' cried Bayub-Otal, himself springing to his feet. 'Who am I? Answer me!'

'A—Anda-Nokomis,' stammered Thel, facing him in the moonset. 'I'm sorry—my lord—'

'Right, let's get on!' snapped Bayub-Otal, turning away and picking up his pack. 'Now we're in Urtah we can stop as soon as it's light and get dry by somebody's fire.' He touched Maia's hand. 'Thank you, Maia. They're grateful, really. It's just that people in Suba see one or two things a little differently, you know.'

It was on the tip of her tongue to reply 'And silly they look with it,' but she swallowed it down and set off behind him.

Two nights later Maia, wet through, was lying prone in a marshy thicket beside her five companions. Seventy or eighty yards away, on the nearer bank of the Valderra, firelight flickered between the trees, and from time to time could be heard voices, the snapping of sticks and the clink of a cooking-pot or a weapon.

'There's no telling how many of them there are,' whispered Bayub-Otal. 'Do you want to try somewhere else?'

'Again?' replied Lenkrit. 'It'd be the same at any other ford: they're *all* watched. We've got to chance it, Anda-Nokomis. I doubt there are more than nine or ten men there at the most. What do you think, Tescon?'

'Ay, get in among the bastards, sir, 'fore they know what's happening.' After a moment he added, 'They're only damned Tonildans; they won't fight.'

'They'll not be expecting anything from this direction, sir,' said Thel. 'Their job's to watch the ford.' He fingered his dagger.

'Waste of time going anywhere else, Anda-Nokomis,' pursued Lenkrit. 'It's getting on for first light now. It'd mean another night gone, and time's very short already. You ought to be down in Melvda as soon as you can. It'd look bad if Karnat decided to make a start without us, wouldn't it? Anyway, I've got to get back to my men. I've had enough of this.'

And so had she, thought Maia. Physically she had never felt so worn out in her life. Since crossing the Olmen they had gone no more than twenty miles in two days, but although Bayub-Otal, as usual, had shown her every consideration, the distance had proved more than enough. Her feet were blistered and she had an upset stomach. Although they had spent the previous night under a roof, she would honestly have felt better if they had not. The place called itself an inn. The kitchen, which was also their sleeping quarters, had a boarded partition down the middle, on the other side of which were stalled cattle. The supper had been cooked in rancid fat and the privy was so vile that she could not bring herself to use it. After an hour or two's sleep she had woken to find herself bitten from head to foot. Weeping from the sheer accumulation of discomfort, she had let herself out into the clean darkness, where Lespa's stars were paling in the first light, and lain on the grass for an hour. She had felt done up even before they set out.

Soon after nightfall they had approached the wooded eastern bank of the Valderra, making for the ford by which Lenkrit had crossed from Suba. As they made their way through the trees, however, it became clear from the noise and the number of fires that the Beklan outpost must have been strengthened. There seemed to be two or three dozen soldiers at least. Stealing away, they had gone about three miles north in the dark, through woodland, water-meadows and brooks, only to find at the next ford another strong outpost, where they had narrowly avoided blundering into a sentry.

It was now long after midnight; they had reached a third ford and Maia, chilled, aching and exhausted, felt past caring what happened.

All day she had been wondering whether she could not manage to get away from them: yet how, without help? Kembri had told her that certain Leopard agents in Urtah might be able to get in touch with her, but none had made any approach. Last night she had had some idea of throwing herself on the mercy of the innkeeper and his wife, but (as the state of their house showed) even by rustic Urtan standards they were blockheads: there was no telling how they might have responded.

So, with ever-falling spirits, she had trudged on with the Subans. Yet until nightfall she had not really believed—had not really faced the fact— that she was going to be taken across the Valderra. Something would surely happen to prevent that. Lespa would not let it happen. Yet here she was. And once across the Valderra, how could she ever hope to get back?

And then, suddenly—or so it seemed—opportunity was staring her in the face. If they were going to attack this outpost, could she not run away in the confusion? There must be some place—some house, some village— she could hope to reach. They would be wanting to get on across the river; they wouldn't want to waste time searching for her. What might happen after that was another matter; but anything—anything offered more hope than being taken across the Valderra.

Some sort of argument had begun.

'But why has someone got to stay with the girl, Anda-Nokomis?' said Lenkrit. 'We're few enough as it is.'

'Because if it turns out badly, there's got to be someone to get her away and look after her,' answered Bayub-Otal. 'She's not going to be taken prisoner and dragged back to Bekla, and that's all there is to it.'

'Then you'd better stay yourself,' said Lenkrit brusquely. 'It comes down to a question of who's going to be most use—'

'*Don't* speak to me like that!' replied Bayub-Otal, still whispering but with fierce authority. 'I have my servant here, and he's under my orders, not yours. Pillan, you're to wait here with this girl until we've finished: is that clear?'

'Very good, my lord.'

For a moment it looked as though Lenkrit was going to take it badly. His two followers, muttering to each other, were clearly expecting him to protest. Then, shaking his head with the air of one acquiescing in a bad business, he drew his sword. 'Very well, Anda-Nokomis. Let's get on, then.'

Immediately they were gone, the four of them, creeping noiselessly away through the bushes. Even with Pillan beside her she would have taken her chance and run, but he was gripping her wrist, presumably by way of reassurance. Suppose she were to scream and warn the outpost? But that would only mean her own death at Pillan's hands. No, there was nothing she could do. She began to tremble, and he put his arm round her shoulders.

'Easy, girl. Won't be long.'

She shut her eyes and bit her lip, tense as a runaway thief hiding in a ditch. All around seemed complete silence, but this, no doubt, was because she could hear nothing but the blood beating in her own head. O Lespa! she prayed. Lespa, only help me!

Suddenly uproar broke out on the bank ahead; curses, shouting, the clash of metal, cries of aggression and alarm; she heard Lenkrit's voice above the hubbub and, looking up, could see black shapes running and stumbling, here and gone against the firelight. There was a heavy splash and then, horrible in its shrill agony, a scream, cut suddenly short. Lenkrit's voice shouted, 'Let them go, Anda-Nokomis!' and then 'Pillan! Come on! Quick, man!'

Dragging her to her feet, Pillan began thrusting through the undergrowth, pulling her after him. Twice she tripped, the second time striking her shin so painfully that she cried out and fell to her knees, gasping and dizzy. Pillan, stooping, put an arm under her shoulders, hoisted her bodily to her feet and held her up as she tottered forward, sobbing and breathless.

Lenkrit's voice, closer now, shouted again. 'Pillan! Don't stop! Straight into the water!' This was followed by further sounds of fighting and commotion. A few moments later, struggling through a tangle of creepers and bushes, the pair of them came out on the bank.

Two fires were burning on either side of a ramshackle, open-fronted shed made of poles and branches. Beyond lay the river, a good fifty yards wide, turbid and running strongly, its main current closer to the nearer bank. This ford, which had never been one favoured by regular travellers, was in fact little more than a spot where it was more-or-less practicable to wade across in summer. Once it had been marked by posts driven into the bed, but some of these had carried away in the winter floods and most of the rest had been broken or pulled out by the Beklans to hinder any possible crossing. The nearer bank was open, running rather steeply down to the water, but the far side had no definable margin, the river losing itself in a wilderness of marsh, tall grass, pools and clumps of trees.

Maia, of course, took in virtually nothing of all this, being prevented not only by the darkness, haste and confusion, but also by her own pain and terror. Before she had taken ten steps into the clearing, however, another and even more dreadful distraction lay before her eyes.

On the ground, drenched with blood, were sprawled the bodies of three men. One, with the crescent badges of a tryzatt, wore a leather helmet and iron-ringed corselet. The other two, no more than youths, lay in their shirts and breeches, having evidently been caught unawares—asleep, perhaps, in the hut. One of these, on his back close beside the fire, glared up into her face with fixed and terrible eyes. His hands were clutched over a gash in his chest, and blood was still oozing between his fingers.

The Subans had already plunged into the ford. From beyond the firelight she could hear splashes and shouting, and glimpse here and there the glint of broken water. Pillan had let go of her wrist and was striding ahead of her, but as she faltered, recoiling from the bodies, he turned quickly.

'Don't stop there! Them as run won't be gone far.'

Suddenly another, faint but appalling voice spoke from close by.

'Oh, mother! Mother!'

Maia stopped dead, looking about her. Close by, just beyond the light of the fire, lay a boy little older than herself. He was stretched on his stomach, his hands beneath him, and as he moaned his head twisted from side to side.

'Mother! Mother!'

The accent was unmistakably Tonildan. Maia dropped to her knees beside him. Putting her hands under his shoulders, she tried to turn him on his back, but at this he gave a cry, wrenched himself from her grasp and fell back on his face. The sand beneath him was sodden and there was a smell like that of a slaughtered beast. Bending down, she put her mouth against his ear.

'I'm from Tonilda. What's your name?'

His lips were moving. Stooping still lower, she could just catch his answer. 'Sph—Sphelthon. Sphelthon.'

'Sphelthon. Where's your home?'

But now it seemed as though he could no longer open his lips. For a moment only a low, humming sound came through them.

457

'M'mmm—M'mmm—Meerzaaa—'

She was jerked to her feet. Someone had her by the arm, someone was speaking in a curious, distorted voice.

'Maia, come on, before we're all killed!'

It was Bayub-Otal, dripping wet, his dagger clenched between his teeth.

Out of the firelight: stumbling down the steepness of the bank. Water over her feet, ankles, knees. Now she was struggling in the river for a foothold, clutching at Bayub-Otal as she tried to keep her balance in the current, ankles turning, stones moving under her sandals, firelight receding behind them as they pushed their legs forward into the deeper water. Here's a broken post—clinging to it—stones grinding in the river-bed beneath—giving way—tilting—toppling over—gone; another; now none; only the chattering, swirling pressure round thighs and waist, a cold demon trying to sweep her legs from under her. Somewhere in the darkness Lenkrit was shouting.

'Thel's gone! Don't stop—fatal!'

Another step. Another. Which way—which way were the others? Nothing to be seen, no one, no mark to make towards. Only the swirling water in the dark. Don't stop! One foot sliding forward, groping along the uneven stones. Leaning into the current, her body at an angle, the flowing water nearly up to her shoulders.

Bayub-Otal's voice shouted 'Maia!'

'Help!' she answered. 'Help me!'

He was beside her. He had her by the hand. Again she was lurching forward, forcing one leg and then the other through the heavy, wavering pressure of the water.

'Another yard!' he shouted.

With a cry she lost her footing; but he had stayed beside her, down-stream; the current swept her against him. He steadied her, leaning against her, keeping his balance, straddle-legged, until she could stand again. Another step and the water—surely—was shallower—slacker? Yes, it was slacker. She could walk. She took three slow yet steady steps. Bayub-Otal, stepping past her, took her hand and thrust it into his belt.

'Keep hold!'

He himself was holding Lenkrit's belt, but there were no others.

A minute later they stopped, knee-deep in stiller water, swamp-grass high all round them, trees overhead forming a cave from which they looked back at the turbulent river and the watch-fires burning on the other bank. Men were bending over the dead and a voice was shouting angrily.

Pillan appeared out of the swamp behind them. Lenkrit turned to him. 'Tescon?'

Pillan jerked a thumb over his shoulder. 'Leg's hurt, though.'

'Badly?'

'Can't say.'

His own forearm was gashed and bleeding. His head hung forward, gaping, grinning for air: a froth of saliva covered his chin. And now before Maia's eyes his bearded face, in the gloom, seemed floating bodiless. Ah! and she was floating too—surrounded—dear Cran!—by men tall as trees, their lips moving, speaking without sound, all swirling, spiralling together in a slow vortex.

The next moment she had pitched forward in a faint. Pillan and Lenkrit, grabbing, were just in time to catch her.

Followed by Bayub-Otal and the limping Tescon, they carried her along the muddy track through the swamp, laying her down on the first dry ground they came to. It was almost morning, and in the grey light they could make out, not far off, a group of Suban huts raised on stilts above the mud. Two or three of the villagers had already seen them and were approaching.

: 46 :
SUBA

Coming to herself, Maia's first sensation was of a humid, fenny odour of mud and old leaves, and a damp air so heavy as to seem hard to breathe. She could feel soft ground beneath her, warm and moulded by the pressure of her body; and then the throbbing of her wounded shin. It must be daylight now, for there was red behind her closed eyelids. Recalling the crossing, she realized that they must have carried her out of the river: so now she was on the other side of the Valderra—in Suba. This knowledge came flooding into her like icy water, bringing with it a sense less of danger than of being utterly adrift, beyond all possible benefit of past experience or common sense. Had Kembri envisaged that she might be taken into Suba? Probably he had supposed that if Bayub-Otal had any intention of crossing the Valderra, he would find it impossible because of the watch on the fords.

Not even at Puhra, when Occula had revealed to her that she had been sold into slavery, had she felt so helpless to envisage how she stood or what was likely to befall her. What sort of a place was this? Would the Subans be friendly, or would she be entirely dependent on the protection of Bayub-Otal? This King Karnat—the arch-enemy of Bekla—was she likely to cross his path?

She knew the answers to none of these questions. The prospect of opening her eyes—of showing that she had regained consciousness and thereby returning once more to all the stress and anxiety of the past few days—frightened her. As long as she remained unmoving, with closed eyes, she had a respite. She lay still; but listened intently.

Some sort of movement was going on near-by. A shadow fell across her eyelids. Then it seemed that two people were kneeling—or sitting, or crouching—beside her. Someone felt her pulse; she was careful to keep her wrist limp and let it drop when it was released. A voice she did not know, but could now recognize as Suban, said, 'And how did she come by that burn on her shoulder, Anda-Nokomis?'

Bayub-Otal's voice replied, 'Oh, in Bekla, too. That's what their priests call questioning.'

'I don't think she's in any danger,' said the first voice. 'Pulse is steady—breathing's easy—no recent injuries except the shin there. Fine-looking girl, isn't she? And the resemblance—as you say, it's amazing. How was she on the journey?'

'Like a falcon,' replied Bayub-Otal. 'She never complained, either.'

'You say you lost poor young Thel in the river?'

'I'm afraid so.'

There was a pause.

'Well, you'd better put her to bed, Anda-Nokomis: I think she's nothing more than tired out; certain amount of fear and strain, too, I suppose.'

'She can't have been free from fear for days,' said Bayub-Otal.

'But she didn't say so?'

'No.'

The voice uttered a sympathetic murmur. 'Don't worry, Anda-Nokomis; I'd expect her to recover by tomorrow.'

This exchange made Maia feel a good deal less apprehensive. The voice, which was slow, deliberate and rather deep, sounded like that of quite an old man. Obviously he was friendly towards both herself and Bayub-Otal: and she was not going to be made to get up and go on; or not just yet, anyway. To go to bed and stay there—that was more than enough for the moment. Sooner or later she would have to let them see she was conscious, so it might as well be now.

She moaned slightly, drew a couple of deep, sighing breaths, opened her eyes and looked round her. She was lying near the edge of a long, more-or-less triangular patch of rough grass, bordered on either side by dense trees. The point of the triangle was behind her, to her right, and here a track came out from among the trees, leading on past her to a cluster of stilted huts about a hundred yards off. Near these stood a little crowd of dirty, rough-looking people—men, women and children—all staring in her direction. They did not seem to be talking much and were showing no

460

particular excitement. In fact, she thought, they rather resembled cattle in a field gazing at a stranger.

Lenkrit and Pillan were standing a few yards away, together with two or three other men—obvious Subans; short, swarthy and broad-featured—all bare-footed and dressed in the same sort of garment; rough, shapeless smocks made out of some kind of smooth, greyish skin unknown to her.

Bayub-Otal was kneeling beside her, together with an old man with a lined, brown face, deep-sunk eyes and a shock of grey hair. Round his neck, on a leather cord, was a bone amulet in the shape of a fish with gaping, toothed jaws. This, in fact, was the first thing Maia saw as she opened her eyes, for since its owner was bending over her it was hanging forward almost into her face. A good deal of the foetid, muddy odour, she now realized, came from him: at least, it was all around, but it would have been less strong if he had not been there. His look, however, was kind enough. Meeting it, she felt still less afraid, and for one strange, here-and-gone moment even had the notion that she had seen it somewhere before. It expressed not only concern but also a kind of firm, undemanding patience, suggesting that by and large he expected to find people suffering and that even if he could not do a great deal about it he was in no particular hurry to leave them and be off about his own affairs. Nevertheless, he was a somewhat startling figure with whom to be confronted at close quarters, and Maia involuntarily drew back a little, turning her gaze towards Bayub-Otal.

He, though looking as tired as she felt, smiled down at her reassuringly.

'You've nothing to be afraid of, Maia. We're in Suba. No one can take you back to Bekla from here.'

Uncontrollably, the tears sprang to her eyes. She sat sobbing on the spongy, warm ground, her wet hair hanging round her shoulders, her mouth and nose running down her chin. Bayub-Otal put his arm round her, then rolled up his cloak and, placing it behind her head, pressed her gently back until she was once more lying down.

'Let her cry if she wants to, Anda-Nokomis,' said the shaggy man. 'It'll do her good. She couldn't very well cry before, could she?'

'Well, she didn't, anyway,' replied Bayub-Otal.

Tescon came up the track from the direction of the village and spoke to Lenkrit.

'They've got a hut ready for us now, sir, and some food.'

'What about Maia?' asked Lenkrit.

'One of the women's going to look after her, sir.'

'Do you think she can walk, Anda-Nokomis, or shall we carry her again?' asked Lenkrit.

The shaggy man, stretching out a hand, helped Maia to her feet. Her sense of not wanting to go on, of not being able to face anything new, had returned. She felt all reluctance; yet she let him give her his arm and went with him across the grass, past the staring, muttering group and on between the huts. Hard-trodden earth; wood-smoke; a peering face at a window; scraggy fowls pecking here and there, a fishing-net spread to dry, the crying of a baby, tattered garments hanging on a line. He helped her up a short, rough ladder into a murky hut where her feet sounded hollow on the boards, and here an old woman spoke to her—something about food— she could hardly understand a word. She heard Bayub-Otal replying that she was exhausted and needed sleep. The old woman, clucking and nodding sympathetically, knelt beside a pallet on the floor, drew back the coverlet and pummelled a couple of dirty cushions. Maia, smiling as best she could and wiping her running nose on her arm, lay down and shut her eyes. After a minute she asked for water, and as soon as she had drunk it—it tasted muddy—she fell asleep. Not even the excitement of the villagers below disturbed her, as Lenkrit, their baron, told them that the stranger who had forced the ford with him by night was none other than Anda-Nokomis, the defrauded and rightful Ban of Suba.

Not long afterwards all four of the Subans—even Pillan could hardly stay on his feet—having eaten, went to bed and slept as soundly as Maia.

Maia herself woke about the middle of the afternoon. She no longer felt exhausted, but her shin was painful and she had a headache. The room was close and stuffy and the muddy smell seemed everywhere—in the air, in her mouth, on her very skin. For some time she lay unmoving, conscious only of her discomfort. At length, when some creature stirred in the thatch above—a dry, stealthy rustle followed by a brief scuttling—she turned her head quickly in the direction of the noise. Sometimes, as she well knew, things fell out of thatch and landed on you. As she did so she saw Bayub-Otal standing with his back to her, gazing out of the window-opening. Hearing her move, he looked round and smiled.

'Feeling better?'

She nodded and tried to smile back, but her heart was like lead. She sat up, pressing fingers over her aching eyes.

'Are you feverish?' he asked. 'Tell me—really—how you feel.'

'I'm all right, my lord: only I've got a headache and my shin feels that bad.'

'Try to eat something: you'll feel better. People often get headaches when they first come to Suba—it's the marsh air—but it soon passes off.'

'I'd like to wash, my lord. Reckon that'd make me feel better than anything.'

He sat down on a rickety stool under the window.

'Suban people mostly wash out of doors: I'll call a girl, shall I, to show you wherever it is they go here?'

'Oh. Well—well, at that rate, my lord, I think I'd rather eat first.'

'Just as you like.' He smiled again. 'Just as *you* like, Maia. You're not a slave any more, now.'

He called from the window and after a little the old woman clambered up into the room, carrying a flask and a clay bowl. These she put down, smiled toothlessly at Maia, mumbled a few words to Bayub-Otal and disappeared again.

'She's gone to get you some bread and fish. People eat a lot of fish here; there's not much else, you see. This will be fish soup, I expect—*akrow*, they call it.' He filled the bowl from the flask. 'Yes, it is. It's good, too. I had some myself earlier on.'

She took the bowl from him. The liquid was pale yellow, not much thicker than water and surfaced with tiny, iridescent circles like a clear gravy. White fragments of fish were floating in it. Seeing her hesitate, he shook his head.

'You just gulp it down. No spoons here. Pick out the big bits with your fingers, but watch for bones.'

She tilted the bowl to her lips. The soup was hot enough, and its taste not unpleasant. It left a coating of grease on her lips and the roof of her mouth.

The old woman returned with wine, black bread and two crisp-skinned, baked fish on a plate.

'Would you like me to break these up for you?' he asked. 'It can be awkward till you've got the knack.' He laughed. 'I'm rather good at it; or I used to be.'

He was plainly in good spirits. She watched as he slit each fish along one side with his knife, took out tail, backbone and head in one piece and threw it out of the window.

'And *that*, too, you eat with your fingers,' he said, handing the fish to her. 'Makes it taste much better, I assure you.'

For the life of her she could not bring herself to take it in good part. The room seemed stifling and her headache, if anything, worse.

'Are the people all so poor?'

'Oh, no, these people aren't poor: they just haven't got any money.'

She ate the bread and fish, sucked her fingers and wiped them on the coverlet, which from the look of it was not going to take any harm from a little thing like that. When she had eaten a few figs and swallowed down some of the rough wine, her headache grew duller and she began to feel drowsy again.

He watched her, sitting on his stool.

'Poor Maia! How many days is it now since we left Bekla?'

She knew that. 'This is the sixth day, my lord.'

463

'Don't call me that any more. Call me Anda-Nokomis, like everybody else. Six days—so it is. I don't wonder you're tired out. I'm sure there are very few girls who could have done it at all. You'll need at least another day's rest: but don't worry, Maia—I'll leave you in good hands, I promise.'

She stared at him, frightened. '*Leave* me?'

He got up and once more stood looking out of the window. After a few moments he replied rather hesitantly, 'Well, as far as I'm concerned, you see, it's become very urgent. I've got to get down to Melvda-Rain as soon as I possibly can, and so has Lenkrit. He tells me his son will be there already, with the men from upper Suba. I've no idea what Karnat's planning to do. If he was one of our own people it would be different, but with allies there's always the risk of misunderstanding and ill-feeling. He's got to be able to trust us; he's got to believe that we mean what we say.'

Maia could make little of this, except that he meant to go away and leave her behind. Her silent incomprehension seemed to recall to him that he was speaking to her in particular. He came back across the room and sat beside her on the floor.

'I'll explain,' he said. 'King Karnat of Terekenalt has his army in camp about thirty or forty miles south of here, at a place called Melvda-Rain. We—that's to say the Subans—are joining him as allies, which means that Lenkrit and I, as Suban leaders, need to get down there at once. We're leaving now—before dark. We're going by water—all travelling's by water in Suba. We'll get there about mid-day tomorrow. Once we get clear of these eastern marshes it's more or less straight all the way, down the Nordesh. You'll be following as soon as possible—'

'Me, my lord—I mean Anda-Nokomis: why me?'

'Oh—well—' He hesitated. 'I won't explain now: but I'll see to it that you're told before you get to Melvda.'

'If I've got to go, Anda-Nokomis, can't I go with you?'

'You're not fit to travel tonight, Maia, that's certain. You need more rest and sleep. I've suggested you start tomorrow, in the afternoon. Lenkrit's leaving Tescon, so that you'll be able to travel with someone who's not entirely a stranger; and I've found a sensible, steady girl to go with you.'

'No one else? Just those two?'

He was silent, thinking. 'Yes, of course there ought to be an older man as well. I don't know who'd—' Suddenly he looked up, smiling. 'Well, of course! U-Nasada's going to Melvda—he can easily wait and go with you! There couldn't be anyone better.'

'U-Nasada?'

'The old man you saw this morning—the doctor. You'll be safer with

464

him than you would be with forty soldiers. Everyone in Suba knows and respects Nasada, you see. He goes everywhere—all over the place.'

'Is he a priest?' To Maia, as to everyone in the empire, healing was associated with religion, or at least with magic.

'I believe he was once: I remember hearing that he started as a priest, so I suppose strictly speaking he still is. But ever since I can remember, he's been known simply as a doctor. Everyone looks up to him because he gives his skill for nothing; or for very little, anyway. It's not every doctor who understands our illnesses in Suba, you see—the marsh-fevers, the agues and all the rest of it. Very few doctors want to come here. It's not like any other province, and there's nothing to be made out of people who've got no money. Nasada knows more about Suba than anyone else; and no one's going to make trouble for *him*. They're only too glad to see him coming.'

'Does he live here: in this village, I mean?'

'He doesn't really live anywhere: he's nearly always on the move. It was a piece of good luck for us that he happened to be here last night.'

She could not find it in herself to respond to his cheerfulness. Her own feelings were not far removed from despair. She might as well, she thought, have been swept away with Thel in the Valderra. Used though she had always been to making the best of things, what was there now to make the best of? She recalled something Occula had once said: 'Wherever else you go, banzi, keep out of Suba. You want the blood running out of your tairth, not your venda.' Suba was a by-word for every sickness of the stomach and bowels. This headache and malaise—might it be the bloody flux that was coming on her now? She had heard tell, too, of the marsh-fever, that could knock down a strong, healthy girl like a blow from a fist and kill her in a few hours. Her body—her beautiful body! She thought of Sencho fondling and grunting with pleasure in the cool, scented, fly-screened cleanliness of the garden-room. 'The marsh for frogs,' ran the saying, 'and Suba for the Subans.' Kembri would learn soon enough, after last night, that she had been taken across the Valderra. She would be written off as dead.

Bayub-Otal stood up with the air of a busy man unable for the moment to spare her more time. 'Well, I may see you again, Maia, before I go: but anyhow we won't be apart for long. I'll ask the girl to come and see you. Her name's Luma, by the way.' Stooping, he touched her hand for a moment and was gone down the ladder.

The girl did not come at once, however, and Maia, dropping off into a half-dream, seemed to herself to be walking round the pain in her shin, which had become a kind of heavy, carved block, like those in the Slave

Market at Bekla. Somewhere Nennaunir, cool and inaccessible, was standing at the top of a staircase among sycamore trees.

She woke slowly, and lay sweating as the dream gradually dispersed.
The flies buzzed in the dusky roof and a gleam of red sunlight, slanting
through a crack, dazzled a moment in her eyes. After a time she became
aware of a curious, droning sound, something like the wind against the
edge of a shutter, but varying in tone, rather as though some large flying
insect were in the room. Raising herself and looking round her, she saw a
girl sitting cross-legged on the floor near the ladder-entrance. Her back
was half-turned towards Maia and she was gazing idly downward. The
droning—a kind of humming murmur—came from her. It was repetitive,
a succession of five or six sustained notes, predictable as the song of a bird.
There was no clear beginning or end to the cadence and the singer, indeed,
appeared no more conscious of making it than she might be of breathing
or blinking. With one fore-finger she was slowly tracing an invisible pattern
on the boards, but this movement, too, seemed recurrent, a kind of counter-
part of her drone. On the one wrist which Maia could see was a
notched, rather ugly wooden bracelet, stained unevenly in blue and green.
Her dirty feet were bare and her hair was gathered in a plait tied with a
ragged strip of leather.

This, surely, must be the girl of whom Bayub-Otal had spoken. Watching
her, Maia began thinking how best to go about making use of her for her
own comfort and relief in this dismal place. Yes, and for her instruction,
too, for there must be plenty she would need to learn. It was a pity she had
nothing to give her, for it was important that the girl should not think her
stuck-up or feel impatient with her for not knowing Suban ways.

The thought of pestilence came scuttling and creeping back into her
mind: her very life might well depend on the girl. There must be ways of
protecting oneself—things to do and things to avoid. If only she could
contrive to avoid getting ill, then one day, somehow or other, the opportunity might arise to escape: though how—and here her despair
returned, so that she shivered in the stuffy room—she could form no least
idea. Better to think no more about that, but get on with what was
immediately to hand.

She tried to impart a friendly tone to her voice. 'Are you Luma?'
She had expected the girl to start or jump up, but on the contrary she
gave no immediate sign of having heard her. Then, rather as though
reluctantly turning aside from something else which had been absorbing
her attention, she lifted her finger from the floor, raised her head, blinked,
smiled and nodded. She had dark, heavy-lidded eyes, a broad nose and full
lips; and might, thought Maia, have been quite a pretty girl—something
after the style of the Deelguy—if it had not been for her sallow, mottled

skin and a weeping sore at one corner of her mouth, which she licked nervously before replying.

'Luma.' She nodded and smiled again. Maia guessed her to be about seventeen.

'I hope you're going to be able to teach me how you do things here,' she said. 'Only I've never been in Suba in my life, see, and where I've come from it's all different.'

The girl spread her hands, smiled again and said something that sounded like 'Shagreh.'

'Anda-Nokomis said you're going to come with me to Melvda-Rain,' said Maia. 'Do you know it? Have you been there before?'

The girl nodded. This was better than Maia had hoped for.

'You have? What's it like?'

'Shagreh,' said the girl, smiling. Then, as Maia paused, puzzled, she said, in a thick Suban accent, 'You'd like some food?'

'What? Oh—no; no, thank you,' answered Maia. 'I had something not long ago.'

The girl, however, appeared to take this for an assent, for she got up and was plainly about to go down the ladder. Maia called her back.

'What I really want,' she said, standing up and smiling, 'is to *wash*.' The girl looked at her nervously, scratching at one armpit and apparently wondering what she had done wrong. 'I want to wash,' repeated Maia. Still getting no response, she began to mime the act of stooping and splashing water over her neck and face.

At all events there was nothing wrong with her mimicry. The girl's face lit up with comprehension.

'Oh, *wash*?' she said, laughing with pleasure at having grasped Maia's meaning. She paused, still smiling. At length she added, 'You want— *now*?'

'Yes, please,' said Maia. 'You wash out of doors here, don't you?' She pointed through the door opening. 'Will you show me where it is?'

Luma nodded, raised her palm to her forehead and stood aside for Maia to go first down the ladder. Outside, a light breeze was blowing, stirring loose wisps of thatch under the eaves and rippling the tall, yellow-brown grass beyond the huts. As they set off together, a little group of staring, pot-bellied children, some naked, others in rags, fell in at their heels and followed until Luma, turning and clapping her hands as though they had been chickens, sent them scattering.

It was early evening; an hour, certainly, when any village might be expected to be ceasing from labour, changing the rhythm of the sun for the gentler rhythms of nightfall, supper and firelight. Even so, Maia was struck by the listlessness which seemed to fill the whole little settlement, as though (she thought) they were all under water, or in one of those dreams in which people can move only like beetles crawling over each other on a branch. Everyone she saw appeared languid and apathetic—nowhere a song or a burst of laughter. The very birds, it seemed, were not given to singing, though now and then, as they approached the further end of the village, the harsh cry of some water-fowl—coot, perhaps, or *jabiru*—echoed from the surrounding swamp.

Luma appeared to feel no particular obligation to talk and Maia, after a few attempts to do so herself, walked on beside her in silence. At length she asked 'How many people are there in the village? About how many, I mean?'

Luma smiled and nodded.

'How many?' persisted Maia, pointing to the huts.

'How many *you* think?' replied Luma, with an air of deferring to higher wisdom.

'I don't know. Three hundred?'

'Shagreh, shagreh.' Luma nodded corroboratively.

'Or five hundred, perhaps?'

'Shagreh.'

They had now left the huts and were walking between clumps of grass and rushes, on a path that wound between shallow pools and mud that was half water. Here the marshy smell was mingled with the scent of some kind of wild herb, peppery and sharp, and now and then with a sweeter fragrance, as though somewhere near there must be a bed of marsh lily or roseweed. In places, split logs had been laid together, flat side up, to pave the path, and over these Luma led the way, her bare feet pressing down the wood so that now and then the warm, stagnant water rose nearly to her ankles. The light was fading and as they went on the croaking of frogs, which at first had been intermittent, became continuous, spreading round them on every side.

Passing through a thicket of plumed reeds and club-rushes taller than themselves, the two girls came to a still, open pool about thirty yards broad—some backwater of the Valderra, Maia supposed, for it did not seem to be flowing. In several places here the short-turfed, level bank had been cut into, to form a succession of regular inlets, each a few yards long and about three feet deep. In four or five of these, girls, either naked or stripped to the waist, were splashing and washing themselves. One, looking up, called a greeting to Luma.

Even on the Tonildan Waste Maia had possessed a towel of sorts and (as will be remembered) Morca used to make soap from tallow and ashes. Such refinements, however, seemed unknown here. Luma, pointing and smiling, became unexpectedly articulate.

'This is a good place. Not many others—' (Here Maia lost her drift.) 'You needn't worry; none of the men come here. Have their own place.'

Stooping, she pulled off her dull-grey, curiously supple smock (Maia could still form no idea from what it could be made), stepped into one of the inlets and began sluicing her head and shoulders with her hands. Maia, strolling a little way along the bank, looked down into the dark, smooth water. She could not see the bottom: it must be all of eight or ten feet deep and it was weedless. She dipped one hand in. It felt pleasant—somewhere between cool and lukewarm; if anything, a shade warmer than Serrelind at this time of year. In fact, it was just what she needed. She undressed and, kneeling above the water, became conscious once again of the beauty of her own body. She bent over the calm surface. It was not a perfect reflection— since leaving Fornis's house she had had no sight of a mirror—but as near as she could tell, neither her black eye nor her bruised lip were still noticeable. Looking at her breasts, she smiled to remember how Meris, on the night of the Rains banquet, had shown her jealousy of their firm prominence.

'Ah!' she whispered. 'I've still got myself: that ought to be good for something, even in Suba.'

Rising quickly to her feet, she plunged into the water and struck out, delighted to be swimming once again. Any road, she thought, this is something that hasn't changed. Water's where I'm at home. Water loves me.

She duck-dived a foot or two into the green gloom, swam on until she was breathless and came up through a surface glowing and reddened by the setting sun.

The splash and smack of the water filled her ears: there was no other sound. It was close, protective, a helmet of sound—only herself and the water—like old days on Serrelind, with the evening light fading before supper-time. She swam a dozen strokes, then turned on her back and floated, looking up at the pink-tinged clouds.

Suddenly she became aware of a turmoil of high-pitched screeching coming from the bank. Luma and the other girls were gathered in a cluster, some clothed, some still undressed, but all waving at her, gesturing and calling shrilly. Since they were all shouting together—and in their Suban dialect, at that—she could make out very little, but what was clear enough was that they wanted her to come back at once. Whatever it was all about, it was evidently urgent and important to them. What a pity, she thought, just as she was enjoying herself. Still, she was in their hands: it wouldn't do to upset them.

She struck out for the bank and as she did so felt a sharp little stab at the back of one knee, like a needle or the bite of a horsefly. This was followed, a moment later, by a similar pain in her ankle. Each, if there had not been two at once, might almost have been—ow! there was another, in her thigh—one of those little pangs that everybody feels at times, but which seem to have no perceptible cause. Reaching the bank, she stretched up her arms to pull herself out, but before she could do so two of the girls had caught her hands and hauled her bodily on to the grass. They were all chattering together.

'Why didn't you tell her?'

'How could I have known?'

'She's a foreigner, she wasn't to know—'

'Stupid thing to do—'

'Take her back quickly, Luma!'

Maia, sitting up on the grass and looking down at her ankle, saw, just above the heel, a glistening, liver-coloured strip some three or four inches long and not quite as thick as a rat's tail. As it compressed and then extended itself with an oozing, undulant motion, she realized with horrified disgust that it was alive. And now that she could see it, she could also feel that it had pierced her skin and was sucking. Overcome with nausea, she was about to pluck at it when Luma caught her wrist.

'No, säiyett, no!'

'Let me go!' She struggled, retching and crying. She could now feel at least two more of the loathsome creatures on her legs and body. Why were the girls preventing her from pulling them off? It must be some horrible, crazy superstition: they were sacred; or else she, as a stranger, had to give them blood—something like that. She screamed, struggling in hysterical frenzy. Four girls were holding her down now, one to each arm and leg.

An older woman, swarthy, with discoloured teeth, was bending over her, trying to speak. From sheer breathlessness Maia became silent and listened.

'*Akrebah*, säiyett: akrebah only come in the deep water. You should have stayed in one of the pools by the bank. If you try to pull them off they break; the head stays fastened on, then it has to be cut out. You have to touch them with a smouldering twig, then they let go.'

The woman's look was direct and down-to-earth, but at least there was nothing contemptuous or unkind in it. She did not think her a fool for not knowing. Blinking back her tears, Maia did her best to pull herself together.

'You mean I got to go back to the village 'fore they can be took off?'

The woman nodded. 'It's not much, really, long's you let them alone. But if you'd stayed out in that deep water, you'd have had thirty or forty—they're like flies. Then you'd have been real bad.'

'How was I to know she didn't know?' Luma was indignant. 'Even the children know about akrebah!'

Maia, determined to do what she could to recover the respect of these girls—one or two of whom clearly thought her either a born fool or else a spoilt lady too fine to blow her own nose—walked back to the huts uncomplaining and trying her best not to hurry. Clearly, she was just beginning to scratch the surface of Suba, a country where one had to beware of water, the natural blessing and plaything of mankind. No doubt she had more to discover. The air, of course (which she was drawing into her lungs), was tainted: that was common knowledge. How about the earth? It was difficult to see how fire could be, but perhaps burns turned putrid here.

As the woman had said, the removal of the leeches turned out to be a matter of no great difficulty. At the first hut they came to, behind which a fire was burning in an iron basket, matters were explained to the woman and her husband (who was eating his supper). The man, with a few perfunctory words of sympathy, broke off his meal and disappeared, Maia stripped yet again and the goodwife, taking a glowing twig, went to work so quickly and deftly that she felt almost nothing. About to dress again, she became aware that her hostess, who had slipped indoors, had brought something in a clay bowl which she was now offering to her.

'What is it?' she asked rather shrinkingly.

They all laughed. 'Where's she from, then?' asked the woman. But on being told 'Bekla', she said 'Well, if they're all as pretty as she is, p'raps Bekla may be good for something after all. You haven't got no akrebah then, in Bekla?' she asked Maia.

'Dunno as we have,' replied Maia, smiling. 'Maybe you could spare us a few, could you?'

They laughed again, more kindly this time. Maia felt bold to ask once more what was in the jar.

'It's what we put on bites and that,' said Luma. 'To clean the place, like.'

The woman dipped two fingers into the sharp-scented unguent, but then seemed restrained by a kind of doubt about actually touching Maia's naked body.

'Shagreh?' she asked rather hesitantly.

Maia nodded. 'Shagreh.'

A minute later she was dressed, the husband had come back and she was thanking them both, again silently regretting that she had nothing to give. However, they did not seem to expect anything. Everyone appeared pleased and clearly felt that the business of helping the poor, ignorant stranger had been adroitly handled.

Returning to her hut in the dusk, she and Luma were met by the old woman who, having greeted Maia palm to forehead, told her that Anda-Nokomis and Lenkrit had already left for Melvda-Rain.

'He couldn't wait, but said to give you his blessing, säiyett, and U-Nasada will go with you tomorrow.'

'Thank you,' replied Maia rather distantly. She was not sorry to have missed the departure of Bayub-Otal. Other things were on her mind; chiefly the business of self-preservation. She was as good as a prisoner: nor was there here a single man of wealth or standing whom she might set out to attract with a view to acquiring a protector. No, all she could do for the time being was devote her wits to the business of not getting struck down by any of the hundred and one plagues that stalked this swamp.

Turning to Luma, she took her by the shoulders.

'Listen,' she said, speaking firmly and unsmiling, 'make a fire, bring the biggest pot you have, fill it with water and boil it. Do you understand?'

It took her some time to convince the girl that she meant what she said. Apparently everything here was governed by the time of day, and this was neither the time for lighting fires nor for boiling water. Luma had not expected to be set to work at this time. What did the young säiyett want water for? Hadn't she just bathed? Finally Maia had to threaten to take the matter to U-Nasada and also to report it to Anda-Nokomis as soon as they reached Melvda. At this Luma sulkily fetched the old woman and together, grumbling, they lit a fire and boiled three or four gallons of water. This Maia made them carry up the ladder into the hut. Although a good deal of it was spilled on the way, enough was left for her purposes.

As best she could, she washed herself (including her hair) from head to foot, and then her clothes and sandals. After this she put her wet clothes back on her wet body and felt a good deal better. She had already thought about the next problem—supper. She called Luma in from beside the fire, where she was sitting with the old woman. It was clear enough that she had forfeited any liking the girl might originally have felt for her, but she was past caring.

'Luma,' she said, 'will you bring me some supper now, please?'

'Shagreh.' Abruptly, the girl turned to go. Maia called her back.

'I want three hard-boiled eggs' (holding up three fingers) 'and five tendrionas with the skins left on. Nothing else. Do you understand?'

'No eggs, säiyett.' Explanations were clearly about to follow, but Maia checked them.

'If there are hens there are eggs. That man was eating eggs for his supper. You boil me three eggs. Shagreh?'

'Shagreh, säiyett.'

Even in Suba, thought Maia, it would surely be difficult to contaminate shelled eggs and rinded fruit. It was a poor enough supper, but better than getting infection of the bowels.

She was finishing her meal by the dimmest and smokiest of lamplight when she heard someone on the ladder. 'Luma?' she called. There was no immediate reply, but after a short pause a man's voice asked, 'Can I come in?'

Maia, carrying the lamp over to the entrance, recognized Nasada. Putting out a hand, she helped him up into the room. As she did so she noticed, to her surprise, that he was now dressed like any Beklan, in a clean, if much mended, robe, and that the muddy smell which she had noticed that morning was no longer perceptible. The hand clasping hers, too, though rough and hard, was clean.

She looked at him rather timidly in the flickering light, not sure how she should address him, for in spite of his short stature and squat build he possessed a peculiar dignity which made her feel—as she certainly had not for many months past—younger than her sixteen years. She wondered why he had come; not, she felt intuitively, for the reason which would have brought many men. As this thought crossed her mind it was followed by another and stranger one, namely that although the one thing she would have thought she would have leapt at was for some influential man to show himself attracted to her, for some reason she would have felt disappointed if this man had done so.

'Why, your dress is wet—wet through,' he said, looking her up and down from under his bushy eyebrows. 'Did you go in the water in it, or what?'

She laughed. 'Oh, no, U-Nasada. I've just washed everything and I've nothing else to put on, see?'

'Well, then, we must get you something,' said he decidedly. 'It's not healthy to have wet clothes here, even though you mayn't feel uncomfortable. The girl should have lent you something.'

He called to Luma, but neither she nor the old woman appeared to be within earshot.

'It doesn't matter, U-Nasada,' said Maia. 'I only washed them for fear of infection. They'll dry off soon enough.'

'You're afraid of infection here?'

With anyone else, she would have been worried that he would think she was slighting his country or his people. But there was something reassuring in his plain directness. He had asked the question because he wanted a truthful answer.

'Very much, yes.'

'I heard you'd been in the water. Well, you weren't to know: it must have been upsetting for you. Is that what's made you worry about infection?'

She nodded. 'Well, yes—partly.'

'I don't wonder. You'd better let me have a look at those leech-bites. It's not likely you've taken any harm, but it's best to be sure.' He smiled. 'I'm a sort of doctor, you see; the only sort there is here, anyway.'

'I know. Bayub-Otal—Anda-Nokomis—told me.'

'I'll get the girl to come in.'

'What for, U-Nasada? I don't mind if you don't.'

Suddenly she felt absurdly light-hearted. It was all so unexpected. With this man she could be her natural self. Not only was he not seeking anything from her; he would not, she felt sure, criticize or judge her—not even in his own mind—whatever she might say. In a word, she trusted him. She felt more at ease than at any time for days past—than at any time, indeed, since she had last been with Occula. It was a reassuring feeling, a feeling of release; and being Maia, she acted on it with characteristic, impulsive gaiety.

'It's kind—it's very kind of you to have come,' she went on. 'Oh, this is so wet, I can't pull it off. D'you mind helping me?' She laughed. She couldn't help thinking it was funny that he should have supposed that she might want another girl to be present. It did not occur to her that perhaps he himself might have preferred it.

If so, he made no more of it, but helped her off with the damp, clinging dress and shift as smoothly as even Terebinthia could have done.

'You feel quite easy and natural with nothing on, do you?'

'Oh, that's what U-Lenkrit asked me on the river bank.' She found herself pouring out to him the story of the Olmen crossing, for it still rankled.

'So that was all the thanks I got,' she ended.

'Well,' he said, 'they were the ones who lost dignity there; not you.'

'Lost dignity, U-Nasada? That seems a funny old way of looking at it.'

'Well, maybe,' he answered, smiling at her in the most relaxed way as she sat naked before him. 'Anyway, I'd better have a look at the bites. How many were there, do you know?'

'Well, three for certain—the ankle here, and the back of the knee, and this thigh. But might be one or two more for all I know.'

'None between your legs—I mean, in the private parts? Only that can be serious, especially if it goes unnoticed: we'd better make sure. You don't mind that, either? My hands, I mean?'

Lying down on the bed, she answered, 'I shan't bite, U-Nasada.'

'Bite? Like the akrebah, you mean?'

'No; like the Sacred Queen's dog.' And while he examined her she told him the story of Fornis's unhesitant handling of the guard-hound which could have bitten either of her hands through.

'Well,' he said at length, 'I'm as good as certain you've got nothing to worry about, though it might be as well to make sure tomorrow. My eyes are every bit as old as I am, you see, and though doctors often have to work by lamplight, it's not ideal. You're not to go putting those wet clothes back on: you're to get into bed now, Maia of Serrelind. That was my other reason for coming—to make sure you get a good night's sleep. Will you take a sleeping-draught if I make one? It's not very strong.'

'Yes, I'll do whatever you say, U-Nasada.' She drew up the ragged coverlet and put a cushion under her head.

'Comfortable?'

'I never noticed this morning—I was that tired—but it's a deal more comfortable than I reckoned. What's in this mattress, then?'

'Dried sedge and rushes are what they mostly use here. A few feathers, perhaps. Better than straw, I've always found.'

He pulled up his sleeve, disclosing round his forearm a broad leather strap with six or seven small pockets, each of which contained a stoppered, bronze phial. Seeing Maia stare, he unbuckled it and handed it to her.

'Never seen anything like that before?'

'No, I never.' Maia was fascinated by the novelty of the contrivance and the neatness of its workmanship.

'I made it myself. It comes in useful.'

'You ought to make some more. You could sell them in Bekla: get rich.'

He laughed. 'Perhaps I will one day. Tell me about Bekla. Is that where you learnt not to be ashamed of showing people that you're beautiful?'

She told him how she had been enslaved; about Occula, Lalloc, Terebinthia and the High Counsellor. She found herself longing to tell him the truth about Kembri and her flight from Bekla, and with a little encouragement might even have done so. He listened silently, however, sitting hunched on the three-legged stool and scarcely moving except now and then to trim the smoking lamp.

'And are you tired of all your adventures?' he asked at length. 'You're young to have had so many.'

'Oh, U-Nasada, it's the *danger* I'm so tired of,' she answered. 'You can't imagine how tired! Danger—it scares you—it wears you out.'

'You're not in danger now.'

'No: but I wish I knew what was going to happen.'

'I think I can help you there: we'll talk tomorrow evening. It's too late now—time to sleep.'

Searching, he found a clay cup, into which he poured the contents of one of the phials, mixing it with water from the covered jar by the bed.

'This is just dried *okra* leaves, really. There's some tessik mixed in, but only a touch.' He smiled. 'You'll wake up in the morning, I promise.'

She drank it down. It was bitter and sabulous, leaving grains on her tongue.

475

'Did you like being at the High Counsellor's?' he asked.

Maia realized that if Bayub-Otal or Lenkrit had asked this question, she would unthinkingly have replied 'I was a slave-girl.' But for some reason that was not good enough for this man. He deserved a better answer—chiefly because he had not asked the question contemptuously, as they would have done. He knew very well, she thought, that there were some things about the High Counsellor's which she *had* enjoyed; and he wasn't blaming her for it, either.

'I didn't like being shut up indoors so much.' He waited. 'Oh, but the clothes, U-Nasada, and the food! A girl like me, see, couldn't ever have expected to live like that. The upper city—you've no idea—oh, I'm sorry, I didn't mean—'

He was not in the least offended. 'And did you enjoy giving him pleasure?'

'Well, I did after Occula'd taught me the right way to look at it. It was work, see? I didn't get much real, bodily pleasure myself—well, you couldn't, could you?—but I did enjoy feeling he was rich and powerful and could have anything he liked, and that what he liked was me. He was a brute, really—a filthy beast, everyone knew that. If I hadn't suited him, he'd just have got rid of me. But he didn't; that's the truth of it, U-Nasada. I mean, that was what I liked.'

'Did you always live by Lake Serrelind—before Bekla, I mean?'

'Yes, all my life.'

'You're quite sure?'

She frowned, puzzled. 'Yes, of course. Why?' Then she laughed. 'Dare say that's why I took to Bekla, d'you reckon? Country girl never been anywhere before?'

'And your father—he died when you were still quite a little girl?'

'No, I was nine when he died: I remember him well. I liked Dad: he was always good to me. It was only after he died, really, that Mother got so bad-tempered and sour.'

'I suppose there's never been any doubt that he *was* your father? Has anyone ever told you anything else?'

If she had not taken such a liking to him—and if she hadn't been beginning to feel so drowsy—she would have resented this.

'Never.' She giggled. ''Course, I wasn't just exactly there at the time, was I?'

He laughed too; then shrugged, evidently dismissing the subject. 'Feeling sleepy?'

'M'm, very. Thank you, U-Nasada. I don't feel half so bad about everything now. *You'll* see I don't get ill, won't you?'

'Well, that's what I promised Anda-Nokomis. If only you do what I tell you, there's no reason at all why a healthy girl like you should get ill here. Suba's not half as bad as it's painted, you know, to people who understand it. Shall I tell Luma to bring her bed in? You won't wake, but you may as well have her here. Looking after you's what she's been told to do.'

'Yes, ask her.' But before the Suban girl had dragged her mattress and blankets up the ladder, Maia was sleeping so soundly that she did not stir even when Luma stumbled over her sandals in the dark.

: 47 :

AT LUKRAIT

It was an hour after noon, still and humid among the overhanging trees and beds of reeds. There was not the least breeze. The only sound near at hand was the hollow *slop-slop* under the rectangular, flat-bottomed boat as it made its way over tangles of weed, muddy shallows and deeper places. One could more or less tell the depth of the water, thought Maia, by the sound it made under the planking. It was like one of Fordil's zhuas, rim and centre—above deep water the boat made a more cavernous sound. One might make a dance out of it. She and Fordil might devise a dance about the swamps and their miles of shady, watery waste. What would the story be? What stories did these people tell among themselves? Anyway, when would she ever see Fordil again?

She was sweating all over, and although she kept trying to cool her face with a cloth dipped in the water, the water itself was lukewarm. She felt dirty and untidy. What on earth would they say in Bekla to see her now, the High Counsellor's fifteen-thousand-meld bed-girl, with black finger-nails, her golden hair full of dust of ashes, a torn smock and hairy armpits? O Cran! she thought, and what are they going to think when we arrive at this Melvda place and maybe that king's going to be there an' all? Likely they'll put me on scrubbing floors—that's if there are any to scrub.

They had left the village in the boat—a *kilyett*, as they called it—a little before noon—U-Nasada, Tescon, herself and Luma. All three of the others appeared equally at home when it came to paddling and steering what seemed to her a heavy, clumsy craft, not even quite regular in shape. Tescon had explained to her that Subans, as marsh-dwellers, used two or three different kinds of boat, according to the particular need. For fishing and for short trips—which might be no more than a couple of hundred yards—they used either rafts or else what they called *dords*—light, oval coracles with a kind of well or hollow keel for carrying gear. For longer journeys, however—especially such as might involve moving through tracts of swamp between villages—the proper craft was the flat-bottomed kilyett, fourteen or fifteen feet long, which drew no more than a few inches and in which one could sleep at a pinch. Unless it was actually stuck on mud, a kilyett could be forced through almost anything in the way of reeds or undergrowth, while if everyone got out it could even be dragged for short distances overland.

The village, she had discovered when they came to leave it, lay on a kind of spit or neck of firm ground between the Valderra to the east and a wide expanse of marsh on the west. It was through this marsh that their journey had at first lain; though how anyone could tell the way was past her comprehension. In and out of the mournful swamps they had wandered, under and between trees festooned with pendent moss and shaggy creepers; over shallow mud beds where the boat had skirred, slowed and grated, until she felt sure they were going to stick fast: across pools and small lakes, heading straight for what looked like impenetrable banks of reeds on the further side, through which, at the last moment, they pushed and crushed their way into the next pool; down corridors of water flanked by boggy thickets, out of which, at their approach, flew great flocks of long-billed waders. Once or twice Maia ventured questions or offered help, but although the Subans always answered her courteously, she soon grasped that she was more hindrance than use and might as well accept that she was about as valuable as a tailor in a smithy.

Together with her anxiety about the future, she was now beginning to feel, more acutely than at any time since leaving Bekla, two further deprivations. One was of the luxury and comfort of the High Counsellor's household, which had softened her and to which, she now realized, she had become more accustomed than she had supposed. During the first two or three days she had enjoyed standing up to the journey, never envisaging that anything could go wrong with Kembri's plan. Now, however, it was no longer a matter of bearing hardship with the prospect of reward. Gone for ever were the delicious meals, the soft bed, the clothes and jewels, the ready availability of Ogma to do whatever was wanted, the admiration of the Leopards and her own future as a dancer. Oh, and above all, she had lost Occula! 'Kantza-Merada blast this damned, dirty sink of web-footed bastards!' she whispered under her breath.

Her other need was simpler and deeper. She wanted a man. Ever since Tharrin, she had hardly been without one for more than a few days. She remembered how once she had been cross with Occula for taking her up short when she had talked about randy goats in the upper city who couldn't go without. 'Banzi, you think men are randy and you're not? Doan' you know it goes far deeper with girls? Men—they talk and boast about it and we doan': and you take all that at face value. But men have a sort of silly

478

notion there's somethin' clever about doin' without. Food, drink, sleep, women—oh, doan' they just love to boast that they're brave, brave soldiers who can go without if they're put to it? So can we. But when did you ever hear a girl *boastin'* about goin' without? Girls who have to go without bastin' just feel sorry, not proud. One day you'll find out that I'm right.'

She'd found out now, she thought. On and off for hours she'd been tormented, not by any longing for this man or that—not for the devouring potency of Kembri, the elegant style of Elvair-ka-Virrion, the lewdness of Sencho—but simply for the thing itself. Her mind kept dwelling on the actual physical sensations, like that of a near-starving person obsessed with food; and the recollection of her sufferings—the river crossing, her wounded shin, the leeches—only seemed to sharpen it, as Sencho had once told her that girls were often sharpened by a good whipping. Oh, I'd take just about any man! she thought; that I would!

Lying prone on the raised, flat stern and trying to turn her mind to something else, she began considering the strangeness of coming, in this wilderness, upon so unexpected a person as Nasada. He puzzled her. It was nothing to do with his having no sexual interest in her. After all, neither had Zuno; nor had Sarget on the night of the senguela, whatever might have been his private feelings. Maia had no general objection to men not showing desire for her. Her dislike of Bayub-Otal stemmed not from this, but from his actual rejection of her advances—that and the contemptuous way in which he had spoken of what he regarded as her degradation in the High Counsellor's household. Nasada, on the other hand, she not only liked—and wanted him to like her—but also intuitively trusted as she had never trusted anyone else. This was not simply a matter of his being a doctor and having taken the trouble to come to see her last night. No, it was an attraction the nature of which she could not really explain to herself. He was wise, yet he didn't talk down to her. He made her feel secure. She wanted to get to know him better, to talk to him, to tell him more about herself, ask him all manner of questions and hear what he had to say in reply; to be—well, to be his friend. He made her feel she was valuable as a person, not just as an expensive and beautiful concubine. She didn't desire him—oh, no, the very idea was out of the question; that would spoil it all; nor did she entertain any hope that he would help her to escape from Suba. Yet he had put new heart into her, and a feeling that she could face the future. If he had not been with her now—if there had been no one but Luma and Tescon—she was not sure but what she mightn't have been driven to some desperate turn.

She came out of these reflections as Tescon spoke.

'Well, Shakkarn be thanked, that's the worst of it, U-Nasada. Here's Dark Entry at last.'

For some time they had been paddling cautiously through a watery grove of huge trees stretching out invasive roots under the shallow water, many of which extended for yards and were like submerged rocks on which a boat could ground or even hole itself. As Tescon spoke he made two quick strokes on each side and the kilyett, immediately gaining speed and thrusting its bow into a kind of deep cavern of overhanging branches, came out beyond into slow-moving, open water—the first flowing water Maia had seen since they started. The breadth across to the opposite side—another line of trees and reeds—was about thirty yards. Looking one way and the other as Tescon, back-paddling, turned the boat through a right-angle and headed it into the current, she saw the vista of a long channel, for all the world like a track through a forest, extending away in each direction.

Tescon glanced at her. 'This is the Nordesh. Runs clear all the way to Melvda.'

She smiled and nodded. He settled back silently, letting the boat drift with the current and using his paddle merely to keep it on course. Luma, further forward, fell once again into the same monotonous drone which Maia had heard the day before. Proper high-spirited bunch, aren't they? she thought. Wonder where we're going to stop for the night? As she looked up into the green gloom, they approached and passed beneath a great, black turtle, motionless on a branch overhanging the stream. She fell to wondering how they mated and whether they enjoyed it.

All that afternoon, at the speed of a man strolling, they travelled on down the Nordesh. What with the humidity, the unvarying sameness of the stream and the tunnel of trees above, the journey became almost like a trance. Subans, Maia felt, seemed no more conscious of tedium than the water-fowl among which they lived; nor, for the moment, was she disposed to blame them. To her, one part of Suba seemed as monotonous as another and she was in no particular haste to arrive at any destination. Luma, for her part, showed less interest than an animal in what lay around them, sitting with bowed head for half an hour at a stretch, and merely nodding, or murmuring 'Shagreh', when anyone spoke to her. Maia wondered why she couldn't go to sleep and be done with it.

The light—such as it was—was at last beginning to fade when, as they drifted round the curve of a long, regular bend, they saw ahead of them another kilyett, smaller than their own, moored against the right bank. At first it seemed to be empty, but on coming closer they saw two youths stretched out in the bottom, either asleep or dozing. Tescon hailed them and they both sat up quickly, one calling out 'U-Nasada?'

Nasada answered, whereupon they untied their boat and took up their paddles.

'We're from Lukrait,' said one, palm to forehead, as Tescon, who could steer the heavy *kilyett* to an inch, slid alongside. 'Our elder sent us to wait here and guide you in when you came.'

'That's still U-Makron, I hope?' asked Nasada and, as the lad nodded, 'It must be—oh, two years, I suppose, since I was last at Lukrait.'

'And two months and three days,' replied the lad, smiling. 'You don't remember me, then, U-Nasada?'

The old man frowned, thrust forward his head and stared piercingly at him, making a comical act of it. Then he smiled and put a hand on the lad's shoulder.

'Yes, I do—you're Bread or Crumb or something, aren't you?'

'Kram.' He looked delighted.

'That's it; Kram. I scratched your arm for you, didn't I? But I had to leave before I knew what came of it. Did it work?'

'Yes, it did. For about three days after you'd gone I felt terrible. Everyone said you'd poisoned me—'

'I had.'

'My mother was ready to kill you. Then I got well and I've never had a day's fever since.'

Nasada nodded. 'I thought it would probably suit you. It doesn't suit everybody.'

'You mean I'll never have the fever again?'

'Well, that I can't promise,' said Nasada. 'But if I scratch you again in about another three years, you ought to be safe for a good long time.'

Following Kram's boat in the failing light, they now began another bumping, winding course through the swampland.

'Have you seen Anda-Nokomis, then?' asked Tescon. 'Was it he who told you we were coming?'

'He and U-Lenkrit arrived late last night,' replied Kram. 'Too late to try to get through here, I'd have thought, but they managed it. U-Makron saw them, but they left again soon after dawn this morning.' After a pause while they negotiated a wide, reedy mud-bank, he added, '*We're* coming down to Melvda with you tomorrow; and one or two more as well.'

'Aren't you too young?' asked Nasada.

'No one's too young to strike a blow for Suba, U-Nasada,' said the second youth. 'Besides, Anda-Nokomis told U-Makron that everyone— every single man—who goes will get his reward.' He laughed. 'So we're not going to miss ours!'

Emerging at length from among the trees, they saw ahead of them the outskirts of a village which to Maia looked much like the one they had left that morning. By the waterside were moored boats, nets spread to dry, a rickety-looking watch-tower and two fish-breeding ponds closed off by

481

means of wicker hatches. A path led up through trees to the village itself, about two hundred yards away on slightly higher ground.

Nasada told Kram to take the girls straight to their sleeping-quarters while he went to pay his respects to Makron. The lad led them up the path to the village, which Maia could now see was not only larger than the other but also somewhat more prosperous-looking—though that wasn't saying much, she thought. Still, at least there seemed to be fewer sores and rags and more cheerful children. One little girl, aged about nine, ran up to them of her own accord and asked smilingly, 'Who are you?' Maia smiled back, but thought it best to leave Luma to answer her in their own dialect.

Their hut, too, was a pleasant change for the better. It was quite spacious, and had been fumigated by burning some sort of herb which had left a clean, sharp smell. The ladder was new and firm, and the floor had been covered with fresh rushes. As they entered, an elderly woman sitting by the window stood up, put a quick question to Kram and, having learned that they were whom she had thought, came forward to greet them. She seemed to have put on her best clothes for the occasion, being dressed not in the usual sheath-like smock, but in a faded, blue, woollen dress a little too large, which could only have come from somewhere beyond Suba. Her gracious, unhurried manner suggested that she was—or felt herself to be—a lady of some standing. Maia hoped she would not converse for long, since all she herself wanted was to wash, eat and sleep.

'My dear,' said the old lady, taking her hands, 'Anda-Nokomis told us—we were most pleased—that you—' Suddenly she stopped, catching her breath. 'Oh!' Still holding Maia's hands, she stared at her intently, with an air of amazement. 'Anda-Nokomis told us, but I never imagined— of course, it's more than sixteen years now—'

'Excuse me, säiyett,' said Tescon, who had followed them into the hut, 'but U-Nasada asked me to explain to you that Maia hasn't been told anything about this yet. He's going to have a talk with her later this evening.'

'Oh, I see.' The lady, who in any case had recovered herself almost at once, took this smoothly in her stride. Still gazing at Maia, however, with a kind of mannerly-controlled wonder, she went on, 'We're very glad you'll be staying with us tonight. You too, my dear,' she added politely to Luma, who put her palm to her forehead but made no reply. 'One of my girls will bring you some hot water' (I can't believe it! thought Maia), 'and then she'll get your supper. Please don't hesitate to ask for anything else you want. My name's Penyanis, by the way,' she added smilingly. 'I'm U-Makron's wife. I hope you're not too tired after your journey?'

Although her Suban accent would have marked her out instantly in Bekla, Maia could nevertheless understand her well enough—better than

482

she could understand Luma—and guessed that in years gone by she must have spent some time in one of the cities of the empire. She herself, of course, had virtually no experience of talking to ladies of consequence, but for the few minutes until the hot water arrived she did her best and felt she had come out of it at least passably; perhaps because the old lady seemed almost bemused merely by looking at her, and on that account hardly concerned to pay any very close attention to anything she actually said. Soon she took her leave, hoping they would be comfortable and once more begging Maia to ask for anything she lacked.

An hour later Maia was feeling, if not altogether at ease, at least less uncomfortable than at any time since leaving Bekla. Her shin seemed almost to have stopped hurting. She had washed from head to foot with soap, combed her hair and cleaned her teeth with a frayed stick. The supper, though nothing more than fish, eggs and fruit, had been good and Penyanis's maid had served it well. The wine, too, had been a delightful surprise, for it was Yeldashay—even Sencho might have appreciated it— and there was plenty of it. Having thanked and dismissed the maid, she refilled her cup and stood at the window looking out into the twilight, where supper fires were burning behind the huts and lamps shone from windows. In the cool, mud-smelling mist beyond, the frogs were rarking far and near, and a belated heron flew slowly over, with back-bent neck and trailing legs. 'Go on—fly to Serrelind,' she said aloud. 'Tell Kelsi her sister's in a mess and needs her.' And oh! wouldn't she just about be glad, she thought, to see Kelsi come walking up through the village now, in her sacking smock and bare feet?

Whom she actually saw a moment later was Nasada, deep in conversation with an even older man who was walking beside him, leaning on a stick. At once she waved, called out 'U-Nasada!' and then, mischievously, 'Shagreh?'

He looked up and raised his hand. 'We're coming to see you.'

'Luma, help U-Nasada and the other gentleman up the ladder.'

'Shagreh.'

A minute later they were in the room and Luma, at a few murmured words from Nasada, had left it. Nasada smiled at Maia, nodding approvingly.

'Well, you don't look as if you'd come twenty miles down the Nordesh. You look as if you'd just come from your upper city in a litter.'

She curtseyed, tossing back her combed hair.

''Tisn't true, U-Nasada, and I reckon you know that; but it's nice to have anyone say it, specially you.'

Nasada turned to his companion. 'Were you ever in the upper city, Makron? It must be a dangerous place, don't you think, with girls like this about?'

483

'I've never been to Bekla, Nasada,' answered the old man. 'But now I've seen *her* I don't think I need to.'

'Well, I suppose we shouldn't go on talking about her like this, us two old storks,' said Nasada. 'I'd better introduce you. This is U-Makron, elder of Lukrait—Maia of Serrelind.'

Maia curtseyed again and raised a palm to her forehead. 'Thank you very much for the beautiful wine, U-Makron.'

'Oh, you liked it?' he said. 'That's good. King Karnat sent it to me a year or two back, but we're not really expert in such things here, you know. I'm glad to have been able to give it to someone who appreciates it. Still, I dare say you've been used to better in Bekla?'

She shook her head and smiled. 'None better, sir.'

There were several stools in the room. She motioned to them to sit down, rinsed two cups and poured more of the wine. The elder enquired about her escape from Bekla and the dangerous Valderra crossing, and went on to deplore the discomfort of Suba to anyone not used to its mists and marshes. To all of this she replied as she hoped he would wish.

'And—er—you grew up in Tonilda?' he asked at length. 'On Lake Serrelind? That's near Thettit, isn't it? You've really lived there all your life?'

'Almost all sixteen years of it, U-Makron!' she smiled.

'Something over sixteen years since you were born?' said he, sipping his wine with a thoughtful air. 'Well, I myself never saw Nokomis, you see, though my wife did.' He paused. 'She tells me it's more than strange. I'm glad to have had this chance of seeing *you*. I wish you luck: but I must leave you now. I've got to talk to the young men before they go to Melvda tomorrow.' She stood up, and he took her hands. 'We shall meet again before you go. I feel honoured to have met you, Maia of Serrelind, bringer of good fortune—as I'm sure you are.'

'Good-night, U-Makron.' (And I wonder what he'd call me if he knew how I lived in Bekla?)

As Makron went down the ladder Nasada picked up one of the lamps and put it down by Maia's bed.

'You've had a long day: why don't you lie down? You'll be more comfortable.'

She did so. He remained standing, sipping his Yeldashay and looking down at her.

'You'd like a man in that bed, wouldn't you?'

She looked up quickly, angry for a moment; but his tone was entirely matter-of-fact and there was no mockery in his eyes.

'Yes, I would.'

'Natural enough, wouldn't you say, for someone who's lonely and anxious in a strange place? Who likes being alone in the dark?'

'I never thought of it that way, U-Nasada: I just like—oh, well, I just enjoy basting, I suppose.'

'Great Shakkarn!' he said. 'Any reason why you shouldn't? People do, or none of us would be here, if you come to think of it.'

'Well, that's one thing, U-Nasada, but—' She stopped.

'Well, what's another thing?' He sat down beside the bed. She pondered, and as she did so realized with delight that he was in no hurry and glad for her, too, to take her time.

'Well,' she said at length, 'I suppose I meant that in Bekla men just used me, really, same as they might use a hawk or a dog, for sport; and I enjoyed it—or a lot of it I did—'cos it meant they admired me and wanted me. It was a sight better 'n working in a kitchen, too, wasn't it? But some of them despise you as well—for what you are, I mean—even though it's none of your own choosing; and that just about makes me mad. It's crazy, really, U-Nasada. You're supposed to like it, because that's what they want—to think they've made the girl enjoy it: but then there's some people, if you act natural they just despise you, like Lenkrit and the others that night when I took my clothes off to cross the river.'

'Well, I don't despise you,' he said. 'In fact, if you want to know, I very much admire the way you seem to be able to stand up to anything still keep your spirits up. But Lenkrit, yes; I'm glad you reminded me of him. Can you remember what Lenkrit said when he first saw you? I'd be interested to know.'

'Let me think. Only I was that frightened that morning—Far as I can remember, Bayub-Otal said to Lenkrit as he must be forgetful—something like that—and to look at me again. And then Lenkrit said something about he wondered he hadn't seen it before, only the light was that bad.'

'And that's all?'

'Far's I can recollect. No, wait! I remember now, he asked Bayub-Otal whether I was his sister; that's right.'

'But you don't look much like him, do you?'

She laughed. 'I don't reckon old Sencho'd have given fifteen thousand meld for me at that rate, do you?'

'You're proud of that, aren't you?'

She nodded.

'I'm not surprised. Why shouldn't you be? And Bayub-Otal?'

'Well, then he kind of cut Lenkrit off short. But I was that upset and moithered with everything—you ever had a knife held at *your* throat, Nasada, have you?—tell you the truth I wasn't really taking in all that much of it.'

'What do you know about Bayub-Otal? Do you know about his father and mother, and how he grew up?'

485

'Oh, he told me all about that, yes: how his mother was sent to Urtah as a dancing-girl, and how the King—High Baron—whatever 'twas—fell in love with her and hid her away in Suba to save her from his wife. And about the fire—why, whatever's the matter, U-Nasada?'

To her horror, she saw tears running down his rough, wrinkled cheeks. For an instant he actually sobbed.

'You're very young, Maia: young people are often unfeeling—until they've learned through suffering themselves. It wasn't really so very long ago. Nokomis—she was like moonlight on a lake! No one who saw her dance ever forgot her for the rest of his life. All Suba worshipped her, even those who never actually saw her. When she died, the luck ran out of Suba like sand out of a broken hour-glass. You never saw Nokomis—'

'Well, how could I?' she answered petulantly. 'I wasn't even born when she died.'

'As far as any of us here can make out, you were born more or less *exactly* when she died. The night of the tenth Sallek?'

Maia stared. 'What do you mean, my lord? Why do you say it like that?'

He drank off his wine and put the cup down on the table. 'And then,' he said, as if continuing, 'last night I asked you whether you were sure about your father. You were.' He paused. 'So that just leaves us with the will and power of the gods, doesn't it?'

'The gods? I don't know what you're on about, U-Nasada, honest I don't.'

'And you say Sencho paid fifteen thousand meld?' he went on. 'Well, for what it's worth, that's what Nor-Zavin, the Baron of southern Suba, paid her parents for the daughter they'd called Astara. I happen to know that. I'm not sure who first nicknamed her Nokomis, but I suppose that doesn't really matter.'

It may seem incredible that no inkling had dawned earlier in Maia's mind. Yet just so will a person often fail to perceive—resist, even, and set aside—the personal implications of a dream plain enough to friends to whom it is told.

'U-Nasada, are you saying that I look like Nokomis?'

He paused, choosing his words. At length he answered, 'To someone like myself, who remembers her well, it would be quite unbelievable—' he smiled—'if it weren't here before my eyes.'

She reflected. 'Then why doesn't everybody see it? Tescon, say, or Luma?'

'Because they're too young. It's more than sixteen years, you see, since Nokomis died. But as well as that, you have to realize that Suba isn't Bekla. This is a wild, marshy country and most people seldom travel far. Everyone in Suba knew the fame of Nokomis—she was a legend—but

486

thousands never actually saw her. No one in that little village we left this morning, for instance, had ever seen Nokomis. But Penyanis, Makron's wife—she saw her more than once. How did she take it when she met you this evening?'

'She seemed—well, kind of mazed, like.'

'And Makron—well, did you think it strange that they didn't ask you to have supper with them?'

'I never really thought.'

'Anda-Nokomis had already told them what to expect, you see. They have some old servants, some of whom would also remember Nokomis, and they thought it better not to set the whole place buzzing with tales of witchcraft and magic and so on. I suppose—'

She blazed out, interrupting him. 'But why didn't Bayub-Otal himself tell me all this in Bekla? Why? Or Eud-Ecachlon, come to that? Cran and Airtha! I went to *bed* with Eud-Ecachlon! I—'

'I doubt whether Eud-Ecachlon ever saw a great deal of Nokomis. In fact he may quite possibly never have seen her at all. Younger boys are brought up rather secluded in Urtah, you know. He'd have been—let me see—scarcely nine when Nokomis left Kendron-Urtah in fear of her life, so in any case he wouldn't have a very clear memory of what she looked like. As for Bayub-Otal, this is really what I came to talk to you about.' He paused. 'What do you think of Bayub-Otal?'

She said nothing.

'You can trust me, Maia.'

'Well, tell you the truth, not a great lot.'

He took her hand. 'I think I know why, but I'd like you to tell me.'

'Well, I can't make him out, U-Nasada, and that's the truth. He's not like any ordinary man. In Bekla he didn't want to make love to me and yet he wouldn't let me alone. And then he kept on saying sort of spiteful things—nasty, contemptuous things—about—well, about me being a bed-girl', (she was crying now) 'as if I could help that! And about me being with Sencho and taking lygols and all such things as that. As if all the girls didn't take lygols! *That's* the real reason why I was what you called—what was it?—defensive just now, when we were talking about basting. He was always so sort of scornful and sneering in his talk, like. And then, when he'd as good as ordered me to dance the senguela in the Barons' Palace—I couldn't never have done it if he hadn't made me, but afterwards everyone thought the world of me—and I wanted to show him how grateful I was and I as good as told him I'd like him to make love to me, he—he just said—' And here poor Maia rolled over on the bed, sobbing with the recollection of that humiliating mortification and beating her fists on the pillow.

487

'How very disappointing,' said Nasada, 'for an ardent, warm-hearted girl like you! Anda-Nokomis really is a fool sometimes. Obviously you must have felt very upset. But he had his reasons, hadn't he? as you can no doubt see now.'

Maia was half-expecting him to go on to say something like 'I wonder, at that rate, that you went straight to him when you'd escaped from the temple.' But he did not.

'Bayub-Otal,' he continued at length, 'he's had enough to make him feel bitter, if ever a man had. His mother a renowned beauty, the most famous and idolized dancer in the empire, his father the High Baron of Urtah. When he's ten his mother dies—murdered, so most people believe—and he himself's maimed so that he can never hope to be a warrior or try to compete normally with other lads. But his beloved father doesn't disown him: no, just the reverse. He gives him everything to live for. He promises him the rule of Suba—something at which he *can* hope to succeed, for he's got a gift of authority and a good head on his shoulders. The boy starts as he means to go on. He puts everything into learning about the province he's going to rule. And then Fornis—with no legal right in the world— trades it off to Karnat while she seizes Bekla.'

'But what's all this got to do with me, U-Nasada?'

'He's not even worth murdering,' went on Nasada, ignoring her. 'That wouldn't be politic, would it?—it'd only antagonize his ageing father, and the Leopards aren't too sure of Urtah anyway. So he's left to moon about between Urtah and Bekla. With any luck he'll go to the bad with drink or women or something, and then the Leopards'll be able to say "Look at the former heir of Suba lying there in the gutter!" '

'What's that to me, U-Nasada?'

'However, he doesn't go to the bad. He puts on an act of being at a loose end, under cover of which he manages to enter into secret negotiations with King Karnat. And then one day the gods send him a sign. Quite unexpectedly—and it's an enormous shock, of course—he comes upon a girl who looks almost exactly like his fabled mother as he remembers her. Only as it happens she's enslaved—to the most disgusting libertine in Bekla. She's loaned out to be basted for money, too. He finds this—well, a trifle distasteful, shall we say? But when, in his rather diffident, prickly way—for naturally, after all he's been through, he's become distinctly stand-offish and sensitive—he does his best to get to know her better, this is—oh, very naturally: no one's to blame—misunderstood and taken the wrong way. The poor girl's looking for money to buy her freedom, but of course this isn't at all what Bayub-Otal has in mind. How can he explain? March up to her and say "It's most peculiar, but do you know, you look exactly like my mother?" Would that go down well, I wonder?'

488

For the first time since they had begun talking, Maia laughed.

'But that's not his only problem,' went on Nasada. 'The resemblance is so uncanny that doubts and questions begin to arise in his mind. Surely the only possible explanation is that he and she must be related in some way? This is something he obviously can't set aside, but of course it doesn't alter—oh, no, it only strengthens—his determination to get her out of Bekla if he can, and make her a free and honoured woman.'

There was a long silence. Nasada got up, filled Maia's cup and his own with the last of the wine, sat down again and drank deeply. 'Well, it's made me quite dry—saying all that.'

'U-Nasada,' said Maia at length, 'are you telling me that Bayub-Otal loves me?'

'Certainly not. *He's* the only person who could say anything like that.'

'Well, then, do you know whether that's what he feels? Has he said anything to you?'

'No, he hasn't—nothing of that kind at all. But as I keep on telling you, Maia, he's a very reticent, diffident sort of man; reserved and constrained—with good reason.'

'Then how do you know all this as you've been telling me?'

'Well, partly because he's told me a certain amount himself, and partly because I know him and I know Suba. And then again, you see, I'm old, and when you're old, if you'll believe me, you often find that you see quite a lot of things without actually being told, because of all you've learned and experienced yourself.'

As she remained silent, perplexed, he added, 'I'm not talking about love. That's nothing to do with me and I'm not trying to give you any advice one way or the other. I can't say whether or not it comes into the business at all. All I've tried to do is explain to you how you're situated here in Suba and the reason for what you've very naturally seen as Anda-Nokomis's strange behaviour towards you.'

'I can't hardly take it in at all.'

'I'm not surprised. I can't myself; yet here you are, before my eyes.'

After a little she asked, 'Where are we going?'

'To Melvda-Rain. "Rain" means a meeting-place, you know.'

'What for?'

'You may well ask. Karnat's there, with his army from Terekenalt. And Anda-Nokomis has promised him the help of three thousand Subans, to be commanded by himself and Lenkrit. They're assembling now.'

'What *for*?'

'I don't know,' he answered. 'But I should imagine to cross the Valderra and defeat the Beklan army, wouldn't you? What else?'

'But why are *we* going to Melvda-Rain, then, you and me?'

'I, because I'm a doctor. You, because of what I've just told you. Anda-Nokomis thinks that the mere sight of you at Melvda is bound to have a tremendous effect.'

'You mean they'll think I'm Nokomis come back?'

'Some of them may really think that. They're simple folk, most of them. But they'll think you're magic, anyway. Perhaps you are—how would I know?'

'You mean I'll be made to go where there's fighting?'

'Oh, Lespa, no! They wouldn't take you across the Valderra: not at first, anyway; you're far too precious. It'll be quite enough for them to see you at Melvda. You'll be their magic luck.'

Maia said no more. Her heart was surging with excitement and fear, dismay and wonder. After some time Nasada said, 'The agreement between Karnat and Anda-Nokomis is that if Karnat takes Bekla with the help of the Subans—and he can hardly hope to do it without—he'll give back the rule of Suba to Anda-Nokomis. Such things don't really concern me, but I do know that much.'

'Then what *does* concern you in all this, U-Nasada?'

He looked surprised. 'Why, there's going to be a lot of work for me, of course. People are going to get hurt.'

'Oh, U-Nasada! Like—like on the river bank? Oh, *no*! No!'

'On the river bank? When you came over the Valderra, you mean, the night before last?'

'Yes; then. There was a boy—one of the soldiers—he came from near my home in Tonilda. Lenkrit killed him—he was crying for his mother on the bank! The blood—the smell—oh, I can't tell you how dreadful it was!'

She began to weep again. He stroked her cheek gently.

'I hate war as much as you do: but there's no stopping this, I'm afraid. Go to sleep now, Serrelinda. A good night's sleep makes everything look better. Would you like another of my night-drinks?'

'Yes, please.'

As he was preparing it she asked, 'U-Nasada, what are their clothes made of here? I've never seen anything like them anywhere else.'

'They're the cured, treated skins of a fish called *ephrit*—stitched together, you know. Same idea as leather, really, except that it's fish-skin; comfortable enough once you're used to it.'

'Is that why they all smell?'

He laughed. 'Yes. So do I, when I'm travelling and working among them. After all, I'm Suban and it helps ordinary people to trust me and feel I'm one of them—which I am. But I changed into a robe for you—I even washed!—for the same reason, I suppose. Here you are, now. Drink it up, and I'll call Luma. Do you think you'll be all right?'

'As long as I can count on you, U-Nasada, I'm sure I will.'

: 48 :
THE GOLDEN LILIES

The kilyett was drifting on down the Nordesh. The warmth of the early sun had not yet pierced the foliage or drawn out the humid vapours from the swamps. It was cool, even chilly, along the water under the green tunnel, through which could be glimpsed, here and there, patches of lightly cloudy sky. Off to the left, at the edge of a shallow among the bordering trees, a flock of ibis were stalking and stabbing in the plashy mud with their curved, dark-red bills.

Behind came two smaller kilyetts carrying Kram, his friend and four or five other young men from Lukrait. All were armed with fish-spears and light, fire-hardened wooden shields. Unlike Beklan soldiers, none had any body-armour. They could not afford it, Maia supposed, for Gelt iron was there for the buying and she remembered having heard tell that Kembri himself had once made unavailing attempts to stop Gelt selling to Terekenalt.

Green and blue dragonflies were hovering and darting across the water, and several times, from one side or another, came a sudden, light pattering, rather like hail. Maia, turning towards the sound, was never quick enough to spot what had made it; nor could she anticipate where it was likely to come from next. After watching her for a while with some amusement, Nasada laid a hand on her arm and silently pointed ahead of them towards the mouth of a side-channel leading away between tall reeds. Looking along its length as they drew level she saw, all in a moment, the still surface come alive as a shoal of little silver fish leapt a foot or two clear of the water, falling back again with the pattering noise she had heard.

'*Margets*, we call them. You don't have them on Serrelind?'

'No, Nasada, not as I ever saw. They're pretty.'

'They always jump like that at sunset and often in the early part of the morning, too: never in the heat of the day. They like still, narrow water.'

'Oh, I remember now; Bayub-Otal was on about them once.'

'A few years ago, when I was living away from Suba, I found I missed that noise. To me, it's the sound of travelling alone down these water-ways. The sound of solitude—the sound of arriving in time for supper, too.'

'You lived away from Suba? Where; in Bekla?'

'No; on an island called Quiso, in the Telthearna. That's up in the north, you know, beyond the Gelt mountains.'

'What took you up there, then, Nasada?'

'Oh, I wanted to learn more about doctoring from a certain wise woman. There's a female priesthood on Quiso—it's part of the cult of Shardik, you know. I learnt a lot from them—well, from the Tuginda, anyway.'

They talked on for a time; about his wanderings up and down the marsh country, and of her life on the shores of Lake Serrelind. She found herself avoiding any mention of what he had told her the previous evening, and he for his part spoke no more of it. After a while, feeling drowsy, she went back to the stern and lay down on the smooth wood, listening to the lapping of the water, the splash of the paddles and the intermittent, raucous cries of the birds in the swamps.

The night before, she had soon fallen asleep, tired out with the day's journey and feeling quickly the effect of the drug. Their departure that morning had been hurried—breakfast, followed by thanks and farewells to Makron and Penyanis, with little or no time to ponder on what she had learned. She could not get the strange business sorted out in her mind; could not decide what she really thought about it. Was she glad or sorry that she bore this extraordinary resemblance to the legendary Nokomis? Did she now feel any more sympathy for Bayub-Otal? And her freedom— she was supposed to be free: she was no longer a slave. Yet how free was she? As far as she could understand, they meant to make a sort of princess out of her—for their own purposes. She imagined herself telling Occula; and that young lady's reactions. 'Princess of frogs, banzi? Hope you enjoy it. Personally, I'd rather take over from Nennaunir at six hundred meld a night.' Free? Well, there's some might call it that, she thought. But if ever I had any least chance of getting out of Suba, I reckon this lot's going to make it next to impossible.

The truth was that Maia, inexperienced and living largely without re- flection, through her senses and emotions, was not really capable of weigh- ing one thing with another and reaching a considered view. Such was her respect for Nasada that if only he had told her what she ought to think, she would most probably have found herself thinking it. But he had deliber- ately not done so. Life had so far afforded her virtually no practice in exercising the power of choice: nor was it doing so now. With her, things simply happened; and by a mixture of patience, cunning and pluck one made the best of them. Unconsciously (and quite unlike Occula) she had come to think of life in this way.

Yet also strong in her—and of a piece with her habit of responding impulsively and living in the immediate moment—was the peasant's quickly-injured pride and resentment of anything felt as condescension;

'Who the hell do they think they are?' Poor Milvushina, for all her help-lessness and misery, had been enough to spark it off, let alone Bayub-Otal. One thing Maia certainly felt now, more than all her confusion and per-plexity, was tart annoyance that apparently she was not wanted for herself, but only on account of her random resemblance to this Nokomis, whom she had never seen and who had died more than sixteen years before. I don't care if she *was* the most wonderful dancer in the world, she thought. I'm not her, I'm me!

As they glided on downstream and the sun moved towards noon, the channel of the Nordesh gradually widened, entering at last a broad lake, smooth and dark-surfaced under an open sky. Out of its further side ran three or four different water-ways, one disappearing into woodland, the others leading away through low-lying, spacious country; part fen, part tall-grassed meadowland where in the distance cattle could be seen graz-ing.

'Not far to Melvda now,' said Nasada over his shoulder.

Maia, eager to learn more, scrambled down from the stern and went forward to sit beside him again. He pointed ahead. She could make out fences, barns, stockades and folds, with broad, green paths leading between them.

'Do you like the look of it?' he asked.

'Better 'n what we've left behind I do.'

'We're quite a way down into lower Suba here. A lot of it's very open compared with the swamps further north, and there's more firm ground. Melvda's not really what *you*'d think of as a city: there's nothing built of stone or brick at all. Still, insofar as Suba has any towns, Melvda's the principal one. They mostly breed sheep and cattle. There are two big fairs every year: that's why it's called Melvda-Rain. The town's really just a lot of farms—those and the houses of people who live by the farmers—you know, wheelwrights, drovers, woodmen—people like that.'

'You say King Karnat's here?'

'Oh, yes, he'll have been here for some days now. There must be thou-sands of soldiers camping and bivouacking: Katrians, Terekenalters; and a lot of our own people as well, coming in from all over. Anda-Nokomis told me he thought there'd be something like nine thousand altogether.'

'Why, however do they all find enough to eat?' asked Maia.

'Well, that's it. They can't stay here for very long, you see. Once an army's been got together it has to be used or it starts melting away. There's a saying, "Sun on the snow and hunger on an army." Or sometimes it's "Sickness on an army." That's where I come in.'

'Where are they going, then, Nasada?'

'I don't know,' he replied. 'That's not my business. I doubt anyone

493

knows but Karnat and Anda-Nokomis. But if Subans are going to be wounded, that *is* my business; and I'll stick to it.'

Soon they were among the grazing-meadows; watercress flowering white in the shallows, yellow water-lilies and patches of pink bogbean. Herd-boys called and waved to them and Kram and his friends called back, asking why they didn't leave their cattle and come and fight for Suba. Not far off, above the tall grass, Maia could now see acres of long, single-storeyed buildings like great sheds, roofed with shingles stained or painted in bright, contrasting colours. These formed patterns and in a few cases even pictures. One roof that she saw depicted a green field with brown, black and white cows, all picked out in coloured shingles. And then—oh, how unexpected and delightful!—there on another roof was Lespa—Lespa herself, golden-haired, clouds drifting across her white nakedness, standing among her stars against a dark-blue sky.

The roofs stretched away into the distance. Among them were groves of trees, mostly willows and trailing zoans, and here and there gardens and pools with water-flowers. They passed a smithy fronting the water, where men were at work round a blazing forge, tapping and clanging so intently that none looked up as the kilyett slid past. At their feet lay a pile of sword-blades, some with the hilts already fixed.

There seemed to be no shops, but Maia saw a timber-yard, sawn planks piled one side, trimmed tree-trunks the other, all stamped in red with characters and brands which meant nothing to her—signs denoting their vendors or purchasers, perhaps, or their destinations. A little further on they came to a temple of Shakkarn, upon whose crimson roof was depicted the goat-god himself, with shaggy hide and golden horns. She raised her hand in salutation. Ah! great-hoofed thruster, remember me, for I'm in sore need of good luck!

The buildings gave place to another stretch of fields. Yet these held no cattle, but an untidy camp of ramshackle huts, low tents and rough shelters of goatskin and cow-hide. Fires were smoking, men were cooking, lazing in the sun, rolling dice, fettling weapons. There were smells of trampled grass, ashes, excrement and the rotten-sweet odour of old vegetables and other such garbage. Not far ahead, a little crowd of young fellows were splashing naked in the water. Although it meant nothing to Maia, she thought it best to follow Luma first in averting her eyes and then in lying down on the floor of the boat as they passed.

'We'll be there directly,' said Nasada, putting out a hand to help her up again. 'Are you ready to meet Anda-Nokomis and the king?'

'The king?' cried Maia in panic. 'But you never *told* me!'

'Well, I can't say for certain that he'll be at the landing-stage, but I wouldn't be at all surprised. Anda-Nokomis is bound to have told him.

Stop a moment, Tescon, there's a good lad. We must give Maia a chance to get ready.'

'But U-Nasada, how *can* I get ready?' cried poor Maia, nearly weeping as Tescon turned the kilyett and drove its bow six feet into a deep clump of rushes bordered by a bed of yellow water-lilies. 'I've got no shoes, no jewels, not even a necklace—and now you say meet the King! It's like a bad dream! I haven't even got a decent dress! Look at this thing!'

'You could take it off, I suppose.'

That was an idea! Maia looked quickly round to see whether he was serious; but he only smiled wryly, shaking his head.

'In Bekla, perhaps, Serrelinda: not in Suba, I'm afraid. We'll just have to do the best we can. Luma, will you help Maia, please?'

'Shagreh.'

It was all Maia could do not to slap the girl, who was plainly completely insensitive to her predicament, let alone possessed of any suggestions for helping her. Miserably she washed her face, neck and arms in the water, combed her hair with her fingers and tidied it as best she could. Sitting on the bow, trying to pull to some sort of rights the smock which Gehta had given her, she was struck by a sudden thought. That morning Penyanis's maid, sent to wake herself and Luma, had brought presents—a new shift for each of them. They were Palteshi work, of fine linen, beautifully embroidered. The kind-hearted Penyanis had ventured to hope that they would prove acceptable. Luma had become almost loquacious with pleasure. At breakfast Maia had thanked and kissed Penyanis, but inwardly had not really felt as much pleased to receive the gift as the old lady had evidently been to make it.

However, its possibilities now seemed rather greater. Pulling off her smock, she examined the shift carefully. It was brand-new and looked it: and it was still fresh and clean, for as yet she had scarcely begun to sweat. The embroidery was really much finer and prettier than she had noticed that morning, with a border of flying cranes in red and blue round the yoke and another, flying the other way, round the hem. It fitted her a shade closely, having probably been intended for a less buxom girl; but that might perhaps prove, if anything, a fault on the right side. It left her arms bare and fell to just above her knees. Her arms weren't scratched or marked at all. Her shin was still rather badly bruised, of course, but that would have shown anyway.

'Luma,' she said, 'please pull me a whole lot of those yellow water-lilies. Just go on pulling them till I tell you to stop.'

The long stems were hollow, pliant and fibrous, easy enough to pierce and thread through one another. She took her time, carefully making a broad crown of bloom for her head, a double garland for her neck and a

495

bracelet for each wrist. When she had finished and put them on she stood up, swayed back and forth a little to make sure they were firm and would not break or fall to pieces; then stepped carefully down the length of the boat to where Nasada and Tescon were waiting with their backs turned.

'This is the best I can manage, U-Nasada. D'you reckon it might do?'

He turned, and for several moments sat looking up at her without replying. At length he said, 'To be young—as young as you are—as well as very beautiful—that's rather like being able to fly or disappear, you know. There aren't any rules for someone like you.'

She was too flustered to grasp what he meant. 'Is it all right, Tescon?' she asked with anxious impatience.

He answered simply 'Yes,' never taking his eyes off her as he backed the kilyett out of the rushes and turned the bow into open water. Then, with the other two boats following, he began paddling slowly downstream towards the buildings in the distance, beyond the camp.

As they drew closer, a sharp bend and a grove on either bank cut off their view ahead, but when at length they came floating out from among the trees Maia saw, about two hundred yards away, a wooden landing-stage which extended along the riparian side of a courtyard strewn with rushes. Round the other three sides stood the same kind of long, shed-like buildings that she had seen earlier; yet these were still more ornate, their walls decorated with stylized, brightly-coloured likenesses of beasts and birds, their roofs painted blue, with yellow stars. Everything was constructed of unpolished wood; yet such was the trimness and quality of the workmanship that the place certainly did not lack dignity and even a certain grandeur. Whatever else they might or might not be, thought Maia, the Subans were clearly carpenters.

A number of boats were moored against the landing-stage, but apart from two or three sharp-featured, foreign-looking soldiers with spears and helmets, and a little group of Subans gathered about an upturned boat which they seemed to be repairing, there was no one in the courtyard. Suddenly a boy, happening to look up in the direction of the approaching kilyett, called out and pointed, whereupon they all turned, staring. Someone spoke to the boy, whereupon he ran across the courtyard and disappeared through an open doorway.

'Maia,' said Nasada, 'I think you ought to go and stand well forward on the bow. And Luma, you come back here, near me, will you?' He picked up a paddle and moved aft to sit beside Tescon. 'Right up on the front, Maia: we'll keep it steady—we won't let you overbalance.'

As she hesitated, she saw Bayub-Otal come out into the courtyard, followed by several soldiers. He was dressed in light armour, over which he was wearing a short, blue cloak, with a sword on his right hip. As he raised his hand to her in greeting the soldiers broke into cheers. A few moments later a pair of double doors on the far side of the courtyard opened and through them, stooping under the lintel, appeared an immensely tall, broad-shouldered man, accompanied by a group of officers and a few women. All were dressed in uniforms and robes as fine as any to be seen in the upper city, though there were certain differences of style which Maia, though she vaguely noticed them, felt too much agitated to take in in detail. The big man spoke to one of his followers, shading his eyes to look at the boat. Then he, too, with an unhurried, easy gesture, raised his hand, though whether to Nasada or herself she could not tell, and thereupon strode across the courtyard to the edge of the landing-stage. Out of the doors behind, more men and women came pouring, so that soon the courtyard behind King Karnat—for it could be none other than he—was full of people, all plainly excited and eager to join in welcoming the newcomers.

As the warmth of spring draws a butterfly from its crevice—that is to say, without will or decision on its part—so Maia was affected by the spontaneous excitement of those gathering along the shore. To act on the inspiration of the moment—whether it was a matter of putting on the slave-traders' decoy gown, of gratifying the High Counsellor at the Rains banquet or of responding to the inner certainty that Lespa was with her as she began the senguela—this was her nature. Even when, as now, she felt full of uncertainty and was far from clear what was required of her, still her instinct was to respond rather than to hang back.

She went forward to the raised, square bow—one corner was daubed with soft earth from the bank into which Tescon had driven it, but there was no time to bother with that now—and took up what she hoped was a gracious, courtly stance, her bare feet several inches above the gently rippling water, the flying cranes round the hem of her new, linen shift twirling slightly in the breeze of the boat's movement, the stems of the water-lilies cool and smooth round her wrists, her brow and neck.

In after years the tale of her arrival at Melvda was often told, both in Suba and in Terekenalt; how King Karnat, at the Star Court, upon hearing news of her approach, came down with his captains to the waterside to greet the miraculous girl who had crossed the Valderra by night with Lenkrit and Anda-Nokomis. True, not many people were actually in the courtyard at the time—perhaps fifty—though later, many more claimed that they had been. The tale grew in the telling, and some, as they grew older, would weave into it all manner of fancies born of later musings.

'What was she like?' younger men would ask some greybeard, when enough sour Suban wine had loosened tongues. 'Tell us what you saw that day.'

'Why, she was—well, d'ye see, she wasn't just like any lass that you'd catch sight of in the market, nor yet at a festival, and think "That's a pretty one: I wouldn't mind her." Oh, no! She looked—well, I'll tell you now, she looked as though she'd come from some other world to put this one to rights for good and all. She looked like someone who could never grow old or die.'

'But was she really as beautiful as they say?'

'She was more beautiful than I care to remember now, for when you're old it hurts, and that's the truth. But what I most recollect—there was a kind of a brightness about her, like. It was as though light was actually shining from her—or at least, that's just how it struck my fancy at the time, you know. It was mid-day, to be sure, but all the same she seemed brighter than anything round about her.'

'But what was she wearing, grandad—how did she look?'

'Well, that's just it. She'd got no jewels nor nothing of that, but you felt you'd as soon go putting jewels on a rose or a goldfish. Her arms and legs were bare—I remember that—and her hair over her shoulders was all gold—shining in the sun, it was. She was wearing a kind of a short, white dress all embroidered with birds, and those golden lilies—real lilies, they were—round her neck and her head. They'd left drops of water on her arms and I remember as the boat tipped a bit, one of them twinkled a moment, you know, in my eyes.'

'But wasn't there any show to it, then—no music or flags—nothing of that?'

'Well, I suppose it seems strange—yes, it would—if you weren't there—but no, there was nothing of that at all. It was really more the kind of startling of it, you see; unexpected, like waking up to snow. It was like you'd be out in the woods and then suddenly, before you've had time to think, there's some bird or creature you've never seen in your life—never knew there was such a thing. That's the part that's hardest to describe. In one way she was just like that—a flesh-and-blood creature, what you'd call arresting, like it might be a leopard or a humming-bird. But in another way there was something about her you couldn't pin down—as though we'd all been blest; and as though she could never be harmed or hurt. But the exact look of it all—in my mind's eye, you know—that's gone: that's like a tune that's vanished away out of my head. I wish it hadn't. All I know now is, it was the best one I've ever heard. I'd like to hear it just once again—ay, that I would.'

'What did the king do?'

'Well, he was stood there waiting, d'ye see, as the boat came up to the landing-stage, and he was just about staring at her, too. Of course, everyone was staring at her, but then King Karnat was that tall—he was a big, fine

498

man to look at, you know—he was head and shoulders above the rest, so they couldn't help but see how he never took his eyes off her. And then Anda-Nokomis stepped up beside him and U-Lenkrit and one or two of the other captains, they came crowding round so it was a wonder, really, as no one got pushed into the water. And then the king came forward and offered her his own hand out of the boat, and she smiled at him and bent her head and put her hand to her forehead. But then the king, if you'll believe me, he put *his* hand to his forehead! Well, so she blushed at that, right down to her shoulders, and he spoke to her—something or other—I don't know—in Beklan. Only King Karnat, he couldn't speak a great lot of Beklan, you see—no more than just a few words as he'd picked up. So then Anda-Nokomis spoke to her and said the king had said he was honoured to meet her—I was quite near, y'know, I heard that much—and then they all got to laughing, because Anda-Nokomis could only speak a few words of Chistol, you see. So the king, he tells someone to go and fetch his young captain-fellow—very fine-looking, handsome young chap he was, too. What was his name, now? One of those Katrian names—ah, Zen-Kurel, that's it—only he was the king's interpreter, you see, as used to question the prisoners and so on. So while he was coming, the old doctor, U-Nasada, he followed the girl out of the boat on to the landing-stage and Anda-Nokomis presented him to the king. And the king said— in a kind of halting way, making a joke of his bad Beklan, you know—he said "Oh, I've heard of you. You're the man who can keep my soldiers alive, aren't you?" And then the girl—it was the only thing I heard her say—I'd been wondering what her voice would be like. It was soft and kind of slow, like pouring cream—she came from somewhere over in the east, you know—she says, "Oh," she says, "but *I* shall need him, your majesty, to keep *me* alive, too." And the king answered—well, you know, some joking sort of thing—and then this young Captain Zen-Kurel came out and the king and all of them walked back up into the big hall, talking together.'

'She began talking with the king then, did she?'

'I was surprised she seemed so much at ease with the king and the rest, but I reckon the way of it was, you see, it was almost same as though she'd been a first-rate huntsman, say, or a river pilot—something of that. You know how it is—those kind of people have their skills and their knowledge that the quality need and respect. I mean, when it comes to hunting, the huntsman knows more than the king, doesn't he? So sometimes the king acts like he's an equal—jokes with him, lets him take liberties and that. It was the same, really, with this golden lily girl. It wasn't so much that they'd have liked to have her, every one of them, but—well, there was kind of a sense in which they felt she really was above them by nature. They felt

499

a kind of respect was due, like, to anyone as beautiful as she was. They wanted to keep her in their company—made them feel lucky, I reckon. It did *me*, any road, just to see her that day.'

'But then there was a lot more than that to the business, grandpa, wasn't there? Later on?'

'Oh, ah, there was a whole lot more to it than that. Ay, that there was—'

: 49 :
A CHOICE OF DAGGERS

Seated at supper between Zen-Kurel and Bayub-Otal, Maia was doing her best to appear relaxed and easy. From time to time the king, sitting beyond Zen-Kurel on her left, would lean forward and speak to her through him, and she would answer, not sure how warm or open a response it was fitting for her to make. That he admired her he had made plain enough, but she was used to that and it had already occurred to her that if he thought of her—as no doubt he did—as in some degree belonging to Bayub-Otal—the girl he had helped to escape from Bekla—he would want to steer clear of any possible ill-feeling. Karnat's reputation was that of a warrior and general, with enormous personal hold over his followers, who were said to regard him almost as a god. At this very moment, indeed, there was about him an air which suggested to her that he never entirely cast aside the burden of this leadership. Mixed with his friendliness and warmth was a certain restraint—the self-restraint of a commander. He was not acting a part, but he was nevertheless conscious of his position and of the presence of his captains and his Suban allies. Whatever his inward inclinations, he would take care that no remarks were passed behind his back about the general being struck on the Tonildan girl. Besides, he was a king. If he did want her, no doubt he would send for her privately, as Kembri had done. So she gave smiling, neutral answers, complimenting him on the bearing of his soldiers and on all she had heard (which in fact was little enough) of Terekenalt. When he spoke to her of Bekla, she said she had been unhappy there, was delighted to have escaped and very glad to find herself in Suba.

Yet despite the honour being shown to her, this last was no more true now than when she had first crossed the Valderra. After her triumphant arrival at the Star Court that morning, three or four Suban ladies, the wives of notables, had taken her into their care, summoned their maids to bring her food and attend her in the bath, and then put their own wardrobes at her disposal. Two of these ladies had known Nokomis, and Maia once again responded as well as she could to their expressions of incredulous astonishment, assuring them that she was in no way related to the legendary Dragonfly of Suba.

By Beklan standards the dresses were disappointing—their style dowdy and dull for a girl like her—but she had chosen the best of them, a pale-grey robe with a shower of yellow stars spreading outward from bodice to hem; and in this, with her hair freshly washed and set with combs, and a translucent necklace of Telthearna aquamarines, she felt as confident as was possible without actually seeing herself (for, looking at the Suban ladies, she could place little reliance on their assurances and praises).

The thought of passing the rest of her life in such a society depressed her unutterably. In some respects, so it seemed to her, Melvda—the whole place—was not all that far above her mother's hovel. Most of the servants were dirty (dirtier than ever me or Kelsi was, she thought), but no one seemed to notice this or think it unusual. The bath-water, though hot enough, was brown and smelt muddy. Her thin towel was soaked through before she had nearly finished drying. When one of her hostesses opened a wardrobe door to show her her dresses, there was a scurrying of roaches or beetles, but at this the lady showed no particular surprise or discomposure. Since no one had offered her a mirror, she concluded that there was none in Melvda.

However, she had felt a little comforted when they took her to her own quarters. This time there was no ladder. The small, neat house stood apart from any others, at the top of a short slope of grass and flowering bushes. Beyond, a medley of fields stretched away towards distant woodland. The table, cupboards, stools and benches were well-made and looked almost new. The bed was more than four feet wide—they had given her their best guest-house, they explained, usually allotted to a couple—while the sedge-filled mattress was softer than the one she had praised to Nasada two nights before.

'Would you like the girl who came with you to sleep here?' asked her hostess.

Maia declined, asking only that Luma should bring hot water and breakfast in the morning. She would, she assured the Suban lady, be perfectly happy to sleep alone in the guest-house. After all, there was none but friends all round her.

She was hoping that Nasada might drop in that night for another talk. There was much more she wanted to ask him; and not only that, but she had almost made up her mind to tell him the truth and beg him to advise her. Like most girls, Maia found it next to impossible to keep a secret if she could not disclose it to anyone at all.

That afternoon she had accompanied the king, Bayub-Otal, Lenkrit and Nasada as they walked through the camps speaking to officers, tryzatts and soldiers. Karnat's army, both Katrians and Terekenalters, were encamped along the eastern edge of Melvda-Rain, in meadows divided every sixty or seventy yards by irrigation channels and ditches. Over these the soldiers had thrown narrow, makeshift bridges of planks or tree-trunks, across which Karnat led the way, always turning to offer Maia his hand. Although she had not the least knowledge of soldiering, she was struck by the obvious professionalism of Karnat's men. The camps were clean and tidy. There were trenches for burning or burying rubbish and these, as well as the cooking-fires, always seemed to be down-wind of the nearest huts and shelters. The latter were plainly the work of experienced hands; sound and firm, spaced equally and at this time of day opened up, by the removal of some of their timbers or branches, to let in the breeze.

Karnat seemed to know the faces and names of hundreds of men, and from the way in which they answered him, gathering eagerly round, each man hoping to be noticed, it was plain that they not only respected but liked him. Almost every soldier Karnat spoke to possessed a confidence and alertness which impressed Maia. These, she felt, were real men. Beklan, of course, was not their tongue and in any case it would scarcely have been appropriate for her to converse directly with them, but here and there she made use of Zen-Kurel to ask a question or utter a few words of praise. These Terekenalters, she reflected pleasurably, saw her as herself and not as the ghost of Nokomis, of whom they knew little or nothing.

By contrast the Suban camp, along the edge of which their boat had passed that morning, was a somewhat unattractive spot. To be sure, the men were in good heart—as lively and ardent as any captain could wish—and Lenkrit and Bayub-Otal met with nothing but eager enthusiasm. There were cries of 'How far to Bekla, sir?' 'Tell them Terekenalters we'll show 'em the way!' and so on. Yet the whole place was so befouled and the men themselves so dirty and undisciplined that it was hard to think of them as an army. Karnat, for the most part, had received straight, soldierly answers to straight questions, but here, by and large, the men seemed much less clear about where they belonged or what their jobs were. The diversity of weapons, too—many of them nothing but farming or forestry implements, more-or-less adapted for service—made them seem not so much like soldiers as a mob of rough, hardy men, willing enough but lacking any real training or cohesion. Several times Nasada shook his head over the filth and stench. At length, while Bayub-Otal and Lenkrit were at a little distance, talking to five or six men gathered round a grindstone, Maia saw him draw Karnat aside and begin speaking to him earnestly and emphatically. The king listened and nodded with an air of agreement.

'They'll fight well enough, you know, your majesty,' said Bayub-Otal, returning. 'Of course, they haven't the experience of your soldiers, but they're as keen as rats in a granary. They'll chew up the enemy all right, you'll see.'

'Have you met all your officers and talked to them?' asked Karnat courteously but rather gravely.

'Those I'm leading myself I talked to this morning,' replied Bayub-Otal. 'I haven't met Lenkrit's officers yet—I've arranged that for tomorrow.'

'Well, I'm very glad you're here, Anda-Nokomis,' said the king, 'and I'll be still more glad when we've won back your inheritance. I only hope you're not going to find that hand of yours a personal disadvantage, but whether or not, I know the Subans will follow you and Lenkrit: I've never had the least doubt of that.'

'Don't worry, sir,' answered Bayub-Otal. 'If I can rule Suba left-handed, I can fight for it left-handed.'

Karnat laughed, clapped him on the shoulder and began speaking about the arrangements for striking camp. Maia, startled by what she had heard, fell back a step or two and plucked Nasada's sleeve.

'Is he really going to join in the fighting?'

'So he says.'

'But, Nasada, how can he, with that hand?'

'He can't be stopped. He's Ban of all Suba, you see. The men know that, and they admire him for not crying off. If he didn't at least try to lead them in battle he'd have no real chance of ruling Suba after Karnat's won.'

About the effect of her own appearance in the Suban camp there was no doubt. Before they had been there three minutes a grizzled, gap-toothed man in a torn jerkin and goatskin breeches, who looked well over forty, stopped dead in his tracks, stared at her a moment and then cried out 'Lespa's stars!' Behind her, Maia could hear him jabbering excitedly to four or five others, and soon (as there would not have been, she felt, in Karnat's camp, even had her likeness been known there) a rag-tag crowd was following at their heels and men were converging from every side. Again and again came murmurs of 'Nokomis!' 'Nokomis!' They seemed less excited than wonder-struck—almost afraid. No one spoke directly to her or tried to question her. Becoming nervous herself of the unceasing staring, whispering and pointing, she took first Nasada's arm and then, as he turned back to her and offered it, Bayub-Otal's.

'Do they really think I'm Nokomis?' she whispered.

'They're puzzled,' replied Bayub-Otal. 'They don't know what to think. They can't make it out as yet, but they know you must be a sign from the gods, and that's all that matters. Tomorrow I want to present you a little more formally to the officers.'

'How will they take it, d'you reckon?'

'Why, as we all do, of course,' he answered. 'For the best omen we could possibly have had. And when Suba's free, we'll—'

But now more soldiers were crowding round, and he broke off to speak to them. The continual, muttering excitement, together with the acrid smoke and muddy squalor of the camp, had begun to exhaust and repel her. She did not resume their conversation, and was glad when, soon after, the king called for a boat to take them back to the Star Court.

Here several people, some officers, others older men—contractors and petitioners—were waiting to speak to Karnat; but after listening to the first for no more than a few minutes, he broke off to ask Bayub-Otal to arrange for supper to be served within the hour. This seemed to surprise the Subans—as indeed it did Maia, since from what little she had seen of this country, the customary time for supper was either sunset or soon after, and to that it still wanted more than two hours. However, no one was going to disagree with the king, whose fine presence and gracious manners gave him a natural authority accepted by everyone; and Maia had hardly had time to wash the mud from her feet and rinse her eyes and mouth (which felt gritty) before Zen-Kurel was outside the door of the ladies' quarters, presenting his majesty's compliments and hoping that the young säiyett would do the king the honour of sitting near him at supper. It was this that had first made her begin to wonder what his personal feelings might be, but by the time the fruit and rather insipid sweetmeats had been served, she had decided that his warmth stemmed from nothing more than diplomacy. She was the luck of Suba and he was treating her accordingly.

The same, however, could certainly not be said of the young staff officer, Zen-Kurel. He was plainly fascinated by her. Throughout supper he had talked to her warmly and freely in his excellent Beklan, partly about his military service and close connection with the king and partly about her night crossing of the Valderra, which he obviously thought showed great courage on her part. If that was what he chose to think, Maia had no wish to disillusion him. She told him nothing of what had really happened and, as soon as she could, led him on to tell her something of himself. His mother, now dead, had been a Beklan girl (a shearna, she somehow suspected) who had married a Katrian baron, Zen-Bharsh-Kraill. They had apparently met in Dari-Paltesh, though he did not say how. He himself had never lived in Bekla, though as a child he had spent several years in Dari. 'Of course, that was long before the king occupied Suba.' His father was getting on now. One day he would have to go home and take over the running of the family estate in northern Katria. 'But not too soon, I hope,' he said. 'Soldiering—it's a wonderful life, especially now

I'm actually with the king. I don't want to stay at home and breed goats—not yet. Or even get married,' he added, smiling.

'No, that's dull,' said Maia. 'Breeding goats, I mean,' she added.

Zen-Kurel laughed. 'I'm sure you had something better to do in Bekla than breed goats, hadn't you?'

'Yes, I was a dancer. But I've *danced* as a goat—well, that's to say, as Shakkarn. Do you know the senguela—the dance about Shakkarn and Lespa?'

He did not, and listened attentively as she described it and went on to speak of Fordil's extraordinary skill as an accompanist.

'But if you danced in the Palace of the Barons at Bekla, you must be a very good dancer?'

'Well, I don't know. It was just that there was this party, see, and I happened to be there. I was surprised how much they seemed to like it. But then if you're attending on the king, *you* must be a very good officer.'

'Well, not really. It's just that I happen to speak Beklan, you see—'

They both burst out laughing again, thoroughly pleased with themselves and each other. He was an extraordinarily fine-looking young man, possessing both style and charm, and merely to have him seated beside her, hanging on her every word and never taking his eyes off her, was making her feel better and forget the strain and eerie bewilderment of the afternoon. She might not have known how to handle that—who would? she thought—but she knew how to handle this all right. Ah, if only they had been in Bekla!

'I suppose there'll be dancing or juggling and that after supper, will there?' she asked. 'Is that why the king wanted it early—to leave time?'

'Nothing so pleasant, I'm afraid,' answered Zen-Kurel. 'No, the truth is—' dropping his voice and glancing sideways for a moment at Karnat, who was talking to his other neighbour—'the king's called a captains' meeting to be held after supper. I can't imagine what about. I thought we'd finished for today, but with him you never know. He may do anything at all, and he quite often does. Once, for instance, when we were down on the Belishban frontier—'

He was good enough to eat, she thought. He was even better than Elvair-ka-Virrion. His warmth and gallantry, his high spirits, his good manners—Suddenly she knew that if she could possibly help it she wasn't going to waste an opportunity like this.

'I dare say you'll be—er—very busy, then, all the evening?' she said, looking down at the grape she was peeling and slowly laying the strips of skin one by one along the edge of her plate.

'Well, as to that I can't say,' he answered ingenuously. 'A captains' meeting, you see—that could mean anything—'

Maia, still looking at her plate, let her knee touch his for no more than a moment. 'Why?' he went on. 'Is there anything I can do to help you?'

'Well, the thing is, I very much need a new knife—a dagger, really—something with a blade and a point—and I was just wondering whether you could possibly get hold of one for me. Only I lost mine crossing the Valderra, see—it was a good one, too—and these Subans don't seem to have anything that suits me at all.'

'I'll bring you four or five to choose from,' he said, 'and sheaths to go with them. Shall I bring them round to your lodging? I don't know where it is, but if you can give me some idea—'

'Oh, that would be kind of you! I'd be so grateful. Only perhaps we'd better keep it a secret, do you think?—it's only—well, the Subans—they can be so touchy, you know.'

'I won't give them the chance.'

'I'll tell you where to come, then. You go—'

But at this moment they were interrupted, as Bayub-Otal broke off his conversation with the Suban lady on his right and once more turned to Maia at the same moment as the king. Soon Zen-Kurel was smoothly putting into Beklan the king's account of how he had once crossed the Telthearna into the wild land of the far north, where for the only time in his life he had seen the great blue eagles; that was in the Shardra-Main, the Bear Hills. Had Maia ever seen these eagles? Never, she replied, and to please him asked what they were like. Looking into Zen-Kurel's eyes as she listened to his smiling description, she felt she could have melted acres of the snowy wastes which they frequented.

Soon after, with supper ended, Karnat apologized to the ladies for the tedious necessity of holding a meeting of captains, both Terekenalt and Suban: however, he assured them smilingly, he would not be long about it—there were just a few trifles that needed discussion, nothing more.

Left among the ladies who had befriended her that morning Maia, after a decent interval of conversation, had no difficulty in pleading sleepiness and fatigue, and eagerly slipped away to her little house on the knoll. A lamp was burning, placed in a bronze basin as a precaution against fire, and three or four more had been left near-by, ready for lighting. She lit the lot, wishing as she did so that she had some pretty night-robe or dressing-gown, like the one she had put on—and then taken off—for Randronoth of Lapan on the night when he had stayed with Sencho. Well, there was no help for it. She would have to remain in the dress she had worn at dinner, and when Zen-Kurel came, pretend that some preoccupation or other had made her forget about changing. If he delayed too long, it wouldn't seem very convincing. Never mind, she thought. He liked her: she liked him;

and anyway, for all she knew Katrians cared little or nothing for such niceties.

She lay down on the bed to wait. A long time seemed to pass. It grew dark and the half-moon, already risen during the day, stood bright in the sky and shone in through the window. Moths fluttered and dropped about the lamps. She became impatient, then angry, then mortified and at last bitterly disappointed, lonely and depressed. So he hadn't taken her seriously after all! Yet it hadn't seemed like that during supper. No doubt he'd already got a girl somewhere in Melvda. It was only too likely—a young fellow like that. Or else the king had sent him off on some errand or other. But he might at least have let her know—sent a soldier or something. Well, she might as well go to bed. Damn and double-damn Suba, baste the frogs, baste the blasted marshes! Black Kantza-Merada come and rip up Karnat and all his—

At this moment there were footsteps outside, a quiet knock at the door, and Zen-Kurel's voice called 'Maia?'

He had brought a number of daggers for her to choose from, but after a short time they found themselves entirely agreed upon the one to suit her. It answered well in the hand and fitted its sheath perfectly.

She lay in serene joy, her head on Zen-Kurel's shoulder, one arm across his waist, her hair tumbled over his chest. The relief, the ease, the beautiful, smooth tranquillity of her body, was like a transformation. She no longer felt the same girl. Everything—the marshes, the mud, the grimy soldiers, Bayub-Otal, Lenkrit—was changed and become acceptable in a warm haze of delicious, sleepy amazement and satisfaction. She felt equal, now, to all of them—equal to anything. O Shakkarn, he was marvellous! She'd never imagined anyone could be so marvellous! Tharrin, Sednil—how far off, how contemptible! There was no comparison. Whatever could she have been thinking of? She pushed the thought of them impatiently away, like a mistress rebuking some loutish servant—'*Don't* bring those things in here!' There were no words, no thoughts even, to express her joy. It lay all about her, hanging like crystal over the bed, filling the shadows of the room, pouring from her own body. She herself was the source of joy, a still centre, a fountain for the world. This, she now knew, was the man she loved and would never cease to love.

'Are you crying?' he asked suddenly. 'My shoulder's wet!'

'I'm so happy!'

'It really meant so much to you?'

'Not did—does. It does—it always will! If only you knew how much!'

'You needed it, then.'

'Oh, Zenka, it's much, much more than that—really it is. Do believe

507

me! Yes, I did need it, but—oh, I don't want to go saying a lot of stuff as you mayn't want to hear. I dare say you meet a lot of girls—'

He put one hand on her shoulder, gently pushed her over onto her back and silenced her by placing his other hand over her mouth.

'No; no, not like you, Maia. Can't you tell? You ought to be able to. You're far and away the most beautiful girl I've ever known in my life. When you came up to the landing-stage this morning, you looked like a goddess, do you know that? Everyone said so—even the king. Those yellow lilies—to tell you the truth, I've been able to think of nothing else but you all day. I'm utterly in love with you. I love you—sincerely.'

'Do you know—' She hesitated. Then, 'Can I tell you something?'

He waited silently. The tears were standing in her eyes. They glittered but did not fall, and after a moment she brushed them away.

'When I was just a banzi, my step-father basted me because I was beautiful. Then my mother found out and hated me, because I was beautiful. The slave-traders bought me because I was beautiful. They got fifteen thousand meld for me in Bekla because I was beautiful. And after that—oh, never mind. Now you say you love me because I'm beautiful—'

'Well, you are,' he answered composedly, smiling and not in the least disconcerted by her outburst. 'What's all that got to do with us? That's over now. None of those people matter to us. You wouldn't really like it if I said you *weren't* beautiful, would you? You're just imagining trouble where there isn't any, my darling. It's pointless to ask would I love you if you weren't beautiful. That's like saying would I love you if you were someone else.'

She laughed. He made everything so easy. It was like waking up to a new day after a good night's sleep. A little early morning mist on the lake, but the sun was quickly dispersing it.

Later, after they had made love again, she suddenly said, 'Reckon you can have all my authority: I don't need it now.'

'Your *what*?' He was puzzled.

'Oh—I was just sort of making a joke all to myself, really. A great friend of mine—kind of a rather tough girl, like, in Bekla—told me once that when you were with a man you should always be sure to hang on to your authority. But it's much nicer not to.' She sat up, looking down at him through her falling hair. 'My lover! My lord! Tell me what you want me to do and I'll do it. There, so much for my authority!' She made a gesture of throwing something away.

'Maia, I only want you not to forget me; ever. I can hardly believe this has really happened. I love you. I'll always love you. I want to marry you. But for now, I promise I won't forget you. You won't forget me, will you?'

'Forget you? What d'you mean? Why, I'll make love with you again tomorrow and the day after that and the day after that! Whenever you like. There's no question of forgetting you! I'll—'

He only shook his head, staring up at her. Filled with a sudden misgiving, she stopped.

'There is.'

'Why?' He did not answer. 'Why, Zenka, why?'

'Because I shan't be here.'

'You mean—you mean—you mean the king's sending you away somewhere?'

'I ought not to be here as it is: I'm risking trouble for your sake.'

Misunderstanding him—this fine young gentleman—the Tonildan peasant was suddenly angry, resentful. 'Risking trouble? What, by making love to the likes of me, do you mean? Oh, you'd better go, then, hadn't you? Go on! Hurry up!'

'Oh, Maia, don't! Don't spoil it! That wasn't at all what I meant! If only you knew—'

'But I don't, do I? One moment you say you love me—'

He seemed utterly desperate. 'You're entirely mistaken!'

'Am I? I don't reckon so. You said—'

'Oh, how can I *expect* you to understand? You can't have any idea unless I tell you. Listen, then, and I'll tell you everything. I'm not supposed to—it's the closest possible secret—but it can't do any harm now, and anything's better than that you should think—When I say I shan't be here tomorrow, I mean *nobody* will.'

'Nobody?'

'D'you remember at supper I said you never knew what a man like Karnat might be going to do next? Well, what he's going to do now's just a little matter of defeating the entire Leopard army and conquering Bekla, that's all. At the captains' meeting—'

'Tonight—just now, do you mean?'

'Yes; yes! Listen, Maia, and I'll tell you. Then you'll understand what I meant by saying I ought not to be here. The plan's a masterpiece. It's based on two things. One is that Karnat'll have the help of Anda-Nokomis's Subans, which makes his army about one and a half times bigger than the Leopards think it is: and the other is that although the Leopards think the Valderra can't be crossed below Rallur, we know a place where it can be—just. Only just, but that'll be enough.'

'But how can your king be sure the Leopards don't know? P'raps he's not as clever as you think.'

'Oh, yes, he is. Since Sencho was killed their spy network's fallen to pieces. We know that. Sencho used to keep everything in his own head, you see, to make sure that he stayed in power and Durakkon and Kembri couldn't do without him. Since his death, all his agents have been at sixes and sevens. He was the only one who knew who some of them were, even. But as well as that, we've stopped anyone leaving Suba for the last month and more.

'The ford—well, you can't call it a ford, really—the crossing-place—it's about two miles below Rallur. The Beklans have got a bridge across the Olmen at Rallur, but they've got no outposts downstream at all, except for three hundred Tonildans on their own, all of two miles downstream from where we shall be crossing. Above Rallur, of course, they've covered every single ford. That's a good joke—we shan't be there!'

'You're sure of getting across, then?'

Her voice held little warmth, but his ardour and confidence took no account of this. He meant her to feel his own pride in the great victory in which he was about to take part. There would be no more doubt in her heart then.

'We've got Ortelgan ropes, brought here secretly. An advance party under the king himself will reach the ford about midnight. I shall be one of those with him. He's going to wade across with the first rope himself, and even he'll be up to his neck—over his ears in places, probably. Then we'll get two more ropes across. After that, we reckon the best part of a thousand men will be able to cross in an hour. They'll go straight upstream and destroy the Olmen bridge—it's only rough timber, of course. Then they'll stay there to stop the Beklans getting over the Olmen while the rest of the army crosses the Valderra. Even allowing for accidents, everyone should easily be across by mid-day tomorrow. By that time the Tonildan outpost downstream will have been completely destroyed—cut to pieces—and we'll go hell for leather for Bekla. The Leopard army will follow us, of course, but we can deal with that. We won't have to fight our way through them to get to Bekla, that's the point. It's sheer genius!'

Maia was about to reply but Zen-Kurel, his eyes alight with excitement, went on, 'There's a general for you! Every man in the army would follow him anywhere! *Now* you'll understand, my dearest Maia, won't you, that it's not just some fiddling little business that I've got to leave you for? Until the meeting after supper I didn't know it was to be tonight. No one did. We've been waiting, you see, for the last few hundred Subans to arrive. But apparently this afternoon U-Nasada warned the king very seriously that the Suban camp was in such a filthy state that pestilence might break out at any moment. "And if that happens," he said, "you won't have an army at all. If it's the bad-water sickness, they'll just go down in cursing rows in a matter of hours—the Subans and your men as well." That decided the king: he made up his mind for tonight.

'The men are being told at this very minute. We're due to start in an

510

hour. I'm supposed to be with the king now—on instant call, anyway—but I came here to be with you. No one but you, Maia—believe me, no one in the world—could have made me take a risk like that—my place with the king, my reputation, future, everything. *Now* do you realize how much I love you?'

She could find no words.

'But whether or not you believe in my love, my darling, there's no two ways about it, I must go now.'

Hastily, he got out of bed and began dressing. 'Wish me luck! Oh, the daggers! Never mind! Keep the lot!'

Dazedly, hardly knowing what she said, she asked, 'But—but how will you reach the river in the dark? The swamps—'

'The river? Why, it's not far from where we are now—over that way.' He pointed. 'Didn't you know? The woods screen it, else you could almost see it.'

'But you said—downstream—'

'Yes, the crossing-place is about three miles downstream from here. There's a track. We've got guides posted along it already. Now kiss me, Maia; dear, darling Maia! I can't tell you how much I love you! I was going to kill ten Beklans; I'll make it twenty for you.'

'Oh, Zenka, don't go! You'll be killed, I know it!'

He laughed. '"Don't go!" What kind of talk's that, Miss Maia? You know I must.'

'Oh, I love you, Zenka! I can't bear to let you go! I love you!'

'I love you, too. And this isn't the end; it's only the beginning, Maia, as far as we're concerned. Believe me, we'll meet again in Bekla, when Karnat's taken it; and I'll marry you, if only you'll have me. Will you? Will you marry me?'

'Yes—yes! Of course I will! I'll marry you and make you happy for ever! I'd go anywhere, do anything for you!' She clung to him, weeping. 'If only there wasn't to be the fighting—'

At that moment a distant trumpet sounded. Zen-Kurel, starting, thrust her quickly from his embrace. 'O gods, the king! I never dreamt it was so late! The king'll be furious!'

Fumbling at the buckle of his belt, he ran out of the door. The sound of his pelting footsteps receded and vanished, merging into the distant tumult of assembly that now reached her ears across the intervening meadows.

DESPERATION

Dressed once more, she stood in the doorway, gazing across the meadows faintly lit under the setting half-moon. In one or two houses, beyond the foot of the little slope, lamps were burning, but she could hear no voices and there was no one to be seen. The news, she supposed, had by now spread through Melvda, and almost everyone would be down at the camps, whence the first companies must already be on the point of leaving.

Below her she could see the Star Court and the faint, glinting line of the stream up which her boat had come that morning. The courtyard itself was lit by the smoky, orange light of pine torches, and people—black shapes against the flares—were appearing and disappearing, some walking, some running, but all moving purposefully in the same direction. The camp sites beyond were indistinguishable in a hazy distance of moonlit marsh-mist. Their fires, she thought, must all have been quenched. Even as she gazed she caught sight, far off, of a twinkling spray of sparks which vanished all together on the instant—a bucket of embers, no doubt, flung into the stream. Yet there was little noise—only that same far-off, muted commotion into which the sound of Zen-Kurel's footsteps had been swallowed. Probably the men had been ordered to keep silence as they formed up and marched off.

Those black figures moving against a background of leaping fire—they filled her with unease; with dread, indeed. Where had she seen them before? In the gardens by the Barb? No, not that: no, something worse—worse. Suddenly, with a low cry of horror, she recalled crouching beside Pillan in the undergrowth as the Subans crept forward to attack the Tonildan patrol at the ford.

Now she saw again—dreadfully clearly—the staring eyes of the lad lying on his back beside the fire, the blood oozing through his hooked, clutching fingers: and the other—him, Sphelthon—the boy from Meerzat, crying for his mother. The sodden earth, the butcher smell. It would never leave her now; she was tainted with it for ever.

Dizzy and nauseated, she clutched at the doorpost; then, burying her face in her hands, sank down on the step. She thought of the detachment of three hundred Tonildans downstream of Rallur; and of Karnat's troops crossing in the night, cutting them off from the Beklan army. 'The Tonildan outpost downstream—they'll be completely destroyed—cut to pieces—cut to pieces—' Boys from Thettit, from Puhra, from Meerzat—

And Zenka, her beautiful lover, who had begged her to marry him—all warmth and ardour, a very gods' pattern of young manhood—one of the king's personal aides, in the thick of it, carrying the king's messages on the battlefield; what were his chances? She began to sob again, as much with frustration as with grief. She was helpless; a woman. A terrible vision of war—of a world defiled and desolated by separation, fear, wounds, death and bereavement—opened before her inward eye. She beheld an infinity of waste, of mutilation and agony; of sobbing wives, mothers, children, their lives spoiled for ever.

She tried to imagine three hundred men lying on the blood-soaked ground, each one crying like Sphelthon. 'Destroyed—cut to pieces.' How many people—how many women like herself knew what really happened—what it looked like—when men fought and pierced and killed one another?

After a time the intensity of her paroxysm began to subside. She stood up, leaning against the wall inside the doorway. Becoming aware of a voice, she realized that it was her own, emptily repeating aloud, 'How many women? How *many* women?'

There came into her mind the memory of Gehta, the girl at the farm; Gehta walking beside her at dusk in the big, smooth-grazed meadow. The scent of the distant pines.

'If King Karnat makes for Bekla, dad's farm's slap in the way. I'm afraid—afraid—dad's farm's slap in the way—'

Passionately, she stood and prayed, arms extended, palms raised.

'If only I could stop it! O Lespa, I'd give anything, anything in the world to be able to stop it! Only hear me!'

The ribbon of the distant stream glimmered below her. In the Star Court, somebody was quenching the torches one by one. When I swam in the Barb, all the young men went mad for me. O Lespa, I'd give *anything* to stop it, to save the Tonildans, to save my Zenka—

Suddenly the goddess spoke in her heart. 'Very well—'

Maia turned cold and faint with apprehension. She sank down, crouching on her knees.

'Lespa! Dear goddess, no, not that! That would be death! I can't do that! Not that!'

Afraid—afraid—afraid—the beating of her heart seemed jolting her body.

'Very well,' replied the goddess. 'Never ask me for anything again.'

Going back into the bedroom Maia, having selected the dagger with the slimmest and sharpest blade, cut the coverlet into long strips. These she wound round her legs from ankle to knee, tucking the edges under at the top to hold the binding in place. After this she bound her upper arms in the same way from elbow to armpit. There was one strip left: this she threaded through the sheath of the dagger and then knotted it round her waist like a belt.

Two minutes later, having blown out the lamps and shut the door, she was making her way eastward across the outlying fields of Melvda towards the edge of the distant woodland beyond which lay the Valderra.

: 51 :

MAIA ALONE

At first the way, though rough and awkward, was clear enough. Her eyes adapted quickly to the half-darkness and she was able to keep a more-or-less straight course, looking up every minute or so at the black line of the trees against the night sky. As in the camps that afternoon, she continually came upon little streams and ditches, but now there were no bridges across them, makeshift or otherwise. Stubbornly she clambered down and up, down and up, wading and scrambling until she was coated with mud from head to foot. Twice she passed through herds of cattle, the beasts looming suddenly out of the night, gathering about her inquisitively, breathing hard, plodding after her until at the next dyke she left them behind. Lonely sheds, too, she passed, and a ruined hovel, its bare rafters a lattice of blue-black squares against the night sky, with here and there a dim star twinkling through.

Were those the same woods in front of her, or had she unknowingly altered direction? She stood still, trying to hit upon something—anything—which might help her. Which way had the ditches been flowing? They had so little current that she had not noticed. There was no perceptible wind. The moon was almost set: it had been behind her and still was. There was nothing else to rely on. She could only go on towards what she must hope were the right woods.

She could not tell how long she had been walking, or how far, but tension and fear had already tired her when suddenly she realized that she had come to the border of the woods—or of some woods, anyway. There was no fence or ditch, and this surprised her—were the cattle, then, free to wander into the forest?—but the edge of the trees was unexpectedly regular; as far as she could see, a more or less straight line stretching away into the gloom on either hand. Not far to the river, Zenka had said. If that was right, then perhaps she was now quite close to it. She stopped, listening, but could hear no sound like that of the torrent which she had crossed with the Subans. Not knowing what else to do, she pushed her way in among the trees.

At once she realized why there was no need of any ditch or fence to keep back the cattle. The wood itself was the fence. The Subans, when they cleared the ground for their meadows—however long ago that might have been—must have felled as much as they could of the primitive woodland and simply left the rest. What she found herself in was an almost impenetrable thicket. There was no least glimmer of light. The thin, spindly trees stood close, crowded one against another, their branches interlacing; and below the branches lay a mass of thick undergrowth full of creepers, thorns and briars. There was no telling right from left or, if she were to go any distance into this place, forward from back.

Maia began to weep. She did not sob or whimper: these were not tears of lamentation or protest, but the silent weeping of despair. Despite her terror upon setting out, she had at least possessed resolution: she had been determined not to give up. But there could be no finding a way onward through this.

For what seemed a long time she sat hunched on the ground, so still that the minute, nocturnal sounds of the wood resumed about her. As her weeping abated, she became aware of faint rustlings of roosting birds above. Then, with a clutch of fear, she realized that quite close to her some fairly large creature was moving.

She sat motionless, holding her breath. The animal, whatever it was, passed within a few yards of her, crackling its way among the bushes. Then, with unnatural suddenness, the sound vanished. A few moments later it resumed below her, yet somehow altered; in some odd way louder, though more distant than before. After a few moments the explanation came to her. The ground immediately ahead must be sloping downward, and the animal was making its way down some sort of cleft or gully, where such noise as it made would be magnified between the funnelling sides. And surely it could only be towards the river that the wood sloped.

Drawing her dagger, she began to crawl forward on hands and knees, cutting her way foot by foot through the undergrowth. It was desperately slow work, and soon both her hands were bleeding, so that it was all she could do to reach out for another tangle and sever it strand by strand. But she had been right—the ground was indeed falling away in front of her.

She had heard tell of tracts of poisonous growth in forests such as this—ivies and nightshades which inflicted horrible pain and illness upon any creature wandering into them unawares. She could feel and smell leaves and trailing plants all around her as she crawled on, her hands always lower than her knees, her head lower than her body as the descent grew steeper. The whole forest seemed to have fallen silent: her own pain, her own breathing enveloped her. As often as she stopped, she listened with the tension and fear of an animal; and at these moments it seemed as though Shakkarn himself must be following, pit-pat, pit-pat over the fallen leaves.

Now, as though under closed eyelids, she seemed to see, swimming before her, ahead and below, an indistinct, faintly-shining swirl; a glimpse of silvery-grey in ghostly, silent motion, as though the ground itself—or perhaps the air—were actually sliding away. This, she knew, could only be some kind of illusion. Fear must have affected her eyesight. Yet still she went onward and downward, reaching out her arms and clumsily sliding her bruised knees one before the other.

Suddenly she found herself groping in a thick, muddy pool. On each side of her were others. The trees were fewer, bigger, further apart. Above she could make out faint light—a patch of open sky. Cautiously, she stood up. With a kind of slow dissolving of unbelief she grasped—what else could it be?—that she must have reached the swamp bordering the Valderra. The spectral, silvery flow was the river itself, gliding away towards her right.

Sinking at every step into the swampy, rushy ground, she struggled through the trees. As at the ford, there seemed on this side of the river no distinct bank; only the marsh, interspersed, further out, by channels of flowing water. Now it was growing deeper, the water, and there was no longer any firm ground between the pools merging one into another, becoming the river's edge under the faint starlight.

She was up to her knees. If she tried to wade on she would sink in and stick fast: yet if she tried to swim there would be submerged roots and sunken branches to rip an arm or a thigh. Lying down in the water, she thrust warily forward, sometimes braving a few strokes, hands always in front to feel for danger.

At length she reached a little island overgrown with reeds, and crawled across it. On the further side was disclosed the river itself, open to the sky, broader than she could have imagined, revealing itself at last like an enemy ready and waiting. There was no guessing the depth; and peering, she could make out no trace of the opposite bank.

Never a sound it made; very black where the dim light did not strike the surface, and terrifyingly swift, racing down out of darkness and disappearing into darkness again. Suddenly, out of that darkness, like the sneering taunt of a giant—let me just *show* you, dear!—the river displayed, a few yards out on the current, the body of a goat, swollen and distorted; a sodden, bobbing bundle with bared teeth and pecked-out eyes. Swiftly it was gone, remaining no longer than the river needed to make plain to her what it was.

'Lespa, you sent me here. I've obeyed you, mistress of stars and dreams. Guard and save me now!'

Quickly Maia stripped, retaining only her sandals and the knife-belt round her waist. Her clothes she flung into the water: they floated a moment and were swept away. Then, with a last glance upward towards the clouds covering the stars, she plunged into the Valderra.

: 52 :

ORDEAL BY WATER

The moment that Maia had dived into the river she felt certain of her own death. She had never known any water like this. She was powerless in it. This was not water as she had always known and understood it. It was as though she had put a taper to a fire laid on a hearth, to see it instantly leap out and blaze about the room. In panic she tried to struggle back to the bank; but in this current there could be no reaching it. In the moment that she desisted she was spun round, her body vertical in the water, arms flailing as she tried to raise herself sufficiently to breathe, to swim at all, anywhere, in any direction. She was, she now realized, no more than a fragment in a torrent like a vast mill-race. If only she had been able to see it clearly, by day, she would never have attempted to cross it; would have turned tail and made the best of her way back to Melvda. But now there could be no going back. She was fighting for her life—or for a few more minutes of life—in a current malignant as a demon. This was a demon's domain: Lespa herself was powerless here.

Always, before, she had thought of water as her own, kindly element. The tutelary spirits moving in water had known and loved her, their infant splashing about the shallows, their pretty lass half a mile from shore, lazing homeward under a red sky. And yet she had intuitively known— had known three hours ago, when Lespa first spoke in her heart—that to try to swim the lower Valderra would most likely prove her death. If it were not so, Karnat would have found some way to cross it long before this.

The swirling, broken current changed to a strong, steady flow. It seemed now that she was being carried down a great pool in the dark. The river had not yet succeeded in killing her: she had a respite while it prepared for a second attempt. A particle of courage returned to her. She was Maia of Serrelind, not a drowning goat. If Lespa had lost sight of her, if the water had betrayed her, if the demon was going to kill her, at least she would make it as hard for him as she could. In her first panic she had thought of nothing but keeping afloat. Now, in this breathing space, she was able to recall that however dark and wide the river, the opposite bank must lie somewhere to her left. She turned on her belly and as best she could began to swim in that direction.

517

Yet in such a current her strongest efforts were puny and futile. Each stroke with her left hand seemed all-consumingly arduous, like trying to hoist herself up a rope with one arm. Each stroke with her right hand instantly swung her downstream, struggling to turn and commence the whole weary task again.

She felt herself beginning to fail. Already in the forest and the swamp she had been tired, before ever she began this losing fight with the water; and even had she not been tired it would still have been beyond her. As the force of the current strengthened again she abandoned all attempt to swim steadily across it, merely drifting passively and then suddenly snatching a quick stroke or two, for all the world as though hoping that the demon might not catch sight of her in time. She must be in midstream now—of that much she felt sure—but still her half-blinded, water-filled eyes could make out no trace of the opposite bank.

Suddenly pain ripped down the length of her right thigh. Something jagged had pierced her, torn her. Clutching at the place, she was instantly pulled under, mouth and throat full of water, choking; kicking to get her head above the surface. She came up to find herself drifting backwards, and as her eyes cleared saw flash past her in the gloom a glistening, humped, irregular shape, solid amid spatterings of grey foam. An instant later it was followed by another. She was among rocks. It must have been a sharp rock which had gashed her.

Even as she realized her danger the shape of another rock as big as herself came rushing towards her out of the blackness of the river. There was turbulent noise all round her now—a jagged expanse of broken water, roaring and booming. It was like being among a herd of stampeding beasts.

Thrusting out both hands, she clutched at a pointed, uneven projection of rock and clung to it amid the tumult, seeking no more than to hold herself where she was. Now that the demon had driven her into a trap from which all her strength and skill as a swimmer could not save her, now that her death was certain, her only thought was simply to survive the next moment. Soon she would not have the strength even to retain her hold on the smooth, wet stone. There was no pain along her thigh now, but the water, in the gash, felt very cold: she must be losing blood fast.

It was then, as she hung swaying to and fro at the end of her clenched fingers, that she suddenly glimpsed a glow of fire in the dark. Far off— what did 'far off' mean, in this welter where she could move no way but deathward?—yet it was real, it was not her fancy. It was downstream of her and on her right. It was not a lamp or torch, but the redness of a burning fire; and for an instant—or so it seemed to her—she could hear voices. With all her remaining strength she shouted; listened, then shouted again. There was no reply. Yet the fire burned on. And if she could reach it she would live and not die.

She let go of the rock, giving a strong push with her legs, lunging away, thrusting herself as hard as she could across the current in the direction of the fire. Instantly there appeared another rock, low in the stream, almost level with the surface, split and fissured. The water poured over and through it. Trying to cling to it, she could find no hold and was swept onward.

Then began a nightmare of scraping and jarring, of grabbing, of seizing and losing hold, of gasping and choking and an endless succession of heavy, horribly painful blows, as though she were being beaten with stone hammers. Sometimes she clung, sometimes she knelt, sometimes she fell. Once, in struggling, she kicked a rock and screamed with pain, sure that she must have broken her toes. Yet surely the fire was nearer?

As often as her head went under the water resounded far and near with the chattering of stones. She was bemused now, no longer capable of thought, mindless of past or future or of where she had come from. She had never done anything in her life but struggle and writhe in this howling, rock-strewn darkness, the fanged mouth of the water demon, to be bitten small and gulped down into the Valderra.

A voice was shouting: her own voice or another's? In her own mind, or the voice of some bygone victim, some water-ghost wailing in the cataract? Why must she go on suffering, why could she not submit herself to the river and drown? Yet she could not, but still gulped and fought for air, no longer swimming, become nothing but flotsam tossed and battered from rock to rock. Looking up suddenly, she saw the fire quite plainly. It was level with her; and it must be close, for she could actually make out the shape of a blazing log. There were—O Lespa!—there were *men* beside it; men standing secure on dry land, not thirty yards away!

Next moment her head struck heavily against a rock. For a moment she felt a dizzy, sickening pain, and then nothing more.

At first she was aware of nothing but pain. She did not wonder whether she was dead or alive, whether she was on dry land or still in the river, whether she was alone or with others. Pain, lying over her body like thick mist, blotted out all else. She knew only that she was covered in pain from head to foot. She could feel, like a kind of spring from which one particular pain was welling up and flowing out, a great contusion, tender and throbbing, across her right temple. One forearm, too, was horribly painful, as though it had been scraped and torn up and down with a grater. She could feel the wound in her thigh throbbing and as she moved that leg, a sudden agony from her toes shot up it, making her cry out.

There were voices near-by, but it was as though she were hearing them through the thickness of a wall. They were Tonildan voices, but she could not make out what they were saying. How could she be in Tonilda? A voice spoke close to her ear, and as it did so she remembered the river, the rocks, the fire. A moist finger was rubbing her lips with something bitter and strong. She recognized it: it was *djebbah*, the raw spirit the peasants distilled from corn. Tharrin had once given her some, and had laughed when she choked on it.

She opened her eyes. She was beside a fire—that very fire—yes, it could only be—which she had seen from the river. She was wrapped in a cloak and lying on a rough blanket. Her thigh was tightly bound up—rather too tightly. A soldier was kneeling beside her, supporting her head on his arm. Three or four more soldiers were looking down at her.

So she *had* crossed the river! An enormous sense of achievement and satisfaction rose up in her. The pain was still very bad—the worst she had ever known—but now she could endure it. She was among friends: she was not going to die in the river.

'Lespa be praised!' she whispered aloud.

The soldier supporting her, a big, burly fellow, said, 'How you feeling, lass?'

'Bad,' she moaned. 'Reckon I'm bad!'

'Have a drop more of this. It'll kill the pain—deaden it, like.'

Little by little Maia's circle of awareness was growing. The light of the fire made it difficult to see much beyond, but she could hear the river close by, while on her other side stood two or three huts, one with a stack of spears piled against the wall. The man supporting her head was wearing the badges of a tryzatt.

'All right, lass,' said the tryzatt. 'Just try'n take it easy, now.'

'What—what happened?' she asked. 'You pulled me out?'

'Jolan here got you out,' he said. 'We heard you shouting in the river, and he went in after you. It was a miracle you weren't swept away, only you were jammed in between two rocks out there, see?'

'Thank you,' she said, trying to smile at the man towards whom the tryzatt was pointing. 'I can't say n'more. Hope you're not hurt.' The man grinned and shook his head. His forehead was bleeding.

'How did you come to be in the river?' asked the tryzatt. ''Twasn't no accident, was it? You in trouble? Tryin' to make away with yourself, were you?'

Now, and only now, Maia remembered everything—Zenka, the Terekenalt night attack, her own desperate resolve. She tried to stand up, but at once fell back with an appalling spasm of pain up her leg. The tryzatt caught her.

'Easy, now, girl! Nothing's that bad. You're not the first and you won't be the last.' Suddenly he paused, looking at her sharply as a fresh thought struck him. '*Did* you throw yourself in—or did someone push you? Come on, now—what happened? Just tell us the truth of it.'

'Easy, tryze,' said one of the men. 'The poor banzi's all in. Why not leave it till morning?'

'Ay, maybe you're right,' answered the tryzatt. 'Then we can—'

Maia clutched his arm. 'Tryzatt, listen! You must take me to Rallur at once—'

'No, not tonight!' he said. 'You just forget your troubles for a bit, lass, and go to sleep. We'll look after you, don't worry.'

'No! No!' She was frantic. 'They're *your* troubles! Listen—'

'She's off her head,' said the man called Jolan. ''T'ain't surprisin', considerin'—'

'Listen! You *must* listen to me!' But now her head and every part of her was hurting so badly that she could not even collect her thoughts, let alone talk. At last she managed to say, 'I've swum the river from Suba.' And then 'King Karnat—'

'Steady, girl,' said the tryzatt again. 'No use tellin' us a lot of old nonsense, now. That's not goin' to make your troubles any lighter.'

'Oh, *please* listen to me! I tell you, the Beklan army's in terrible danger! Those Tonildans south of Rallur—'

'Why, what do you know about Tonildans south of Rallur?' asked the tryzatt sharply.

Maia was trying to gather strength to reply when suddenly Jolan came forward, stooped and looked closely into her face.

'Hold on, tryze,' he said. 'Wait a minute. *You're* from Tonilda, aren't you?' he asked Maia.

'Yes.'

'Whereabouts?'

'Near Meerzat.'

'Well, if you know Meerzat,' he asked her quietly and in no tone of disbelief, 'what's the name of the inn by the harbour?'

'"The Safe Moorings". It's kept by a woman called Frarnli, with a cast in her eye.'

'I've seen you there,' he said. 'I knew I'd seen you somewhere. Who were you with?'

'Tharrin. He's my step-father.'

He nodded. 'That's right enough, tryze. I *have* seen her in Meerzat and I know Tharrin, too.'

'Well, but if you're from Meerzat, what are you doing here?' asked the tryzatt.

'General Kembri—an agent. I crossed—into Suba—three nights ago.' Then, seeing his look of unbelief, she clutched his wrist. 'It's the truth! I've come from a place called Melvda. I swam the river—'

'Listen,' said the tryzatt, 'we're two miles down from Melvda, d'you know that? Anyway no one could swim across the river here.'

'I tell you Karnat's crossing the river tonight! How far are we from Rallur?'

All the soldiers were gathered round her now. ''Bout a mile, near enough,' answered one of the men.

'Ah, bit less, maybe.'

'You *must* take me to the commander in Rallur. Karnat's crossing *now*, I tell you!'

'What's his name, then, the commander?' asked the tryzatt. 'You say General Kembri sent you—'

'Sendekar of Ikat.'

There was a pause. 'Reckon we'd best take her, tryze,' said Jolan at length. 'Only if what she's saying's the truth, see, and it comes out later as we didn't—'

There were mutters of agreement from the other men.

'Reckon she's hardly in no state to go, though,' said the tryzatt uncertainly. 'Are you?' he asked Maia. 'And as for saying she's swum across the river, that's just plain ridiculous—'

'Carry me!' said Maia. 'You must!' The thought of being jolted a mile to Rallur was almost unbearable, but even worse was the prospect of failing now, at the end; of all she had done and endured going for nothing.

The tryzatt pondered with maddening deliberation. 'Well,' he replied at length, 'dare say we can fix up something to carry you on, but it won't be all that comfortable, mind. And you'll have to watch that leg: that's nasty, that is; you've lost a lot of blood. Jolan, boy, you'd better run on ahead— tell them to wake the general and tell him she's coming.' He turned back to Maia. 'You're sure now? Only you said it, lass, we didn't.'

She nodded. 'I'm sure enough.'

Within the hour General Sendekar, roused from his bed in Rallur, was sitting beside Maia's as she told him of Karnat's crossing and the plan to destroy the Olmen bridge. After about ten minutes she fell back in a faint, but he had already heard enough.

Throughout the early hours of that night—the night of the 15th/16th Azith—King Karnat's army, supported by an auxiliary force of about two thousand Subans, marched in successive companies to the place downstream of Melvda-Rain which, his Suban allies had advised the king, was feasible for a crossing. At this point the river was relatively broad and accordingly somewhat (though not a great deal) less swift and deep. Karnat himself, the strongest and tallest man in his own army, waded into the water with a rope paid out behind him, and carrying a forked pole with which to steady himself against the current. Twice he was swept downstream and pulled back to the western bank. At the third attempt he succeeded in crossing and securing the rope to a tree-trunk on the eastern side. Other ropes were then put across.

The rest of the spearhead force, consisting of about four hundred Terekenalters, two hundred Katrians and as many Subans under the command of Anda-Nokomis, their Ban, crossed in something less than two hours and at once set out upstream to destroy the bridge over the Olmen south of Rallur. Unexpectedly, they found it defended by two hastily-assembled companies of Tonildans, whom they attacked vigorously, the king himself leading the assault. The Tonildans, however, were able to prevent the destruction of the bridge and, as the confused, nocturnal fighting continued, were reinforced by Beklan troops commanded by Sendekar in person. For a matter of some three hours the main Terekenalt army, to the south, continued their crossing of the Valderra in accordance with the king's original plan, he himself trusting that enough men would get over to enable him to drive back the Beklans and destroy the bridge. At length, however, realizing that with the unexpected loss of surprise success had slipped from his grasp, he sent back orders to Lenkrit to halt the crossing and withdraw across the Valderra. He himself, as the Beklans gradually gained the upper hand, defended his contracting bridgehead by a brilliantly-conducted fighting retreat which effectively discouraged the enemy from pressing home their advantage, mauled as they were by one determined counter-attack after another. During one of these Anda-Nokomis, who in leading his Subans had shown throughout the night a total disregard for his own safety, disappeared among the thick of the enemy, and when Karnat, arrived back at the crossing-point, re-formed his depleted force, remained unaccounted for.

The greater part of the Terekenalt army re-crossed to the west bank successfully, and losses among the king's spearhead troops turned out not to have been unduly heavy. Among them, however, was the Katrian staff officer Zen-Kurel who, smarting under a stern rebuke from the king for having absented himself at Melvda until the army was on the very point of setting out, had been continually and recklessly taking part in one foray after another. Next morning a wounded tryzatt told the king of having seen the young man slip and go down on muddy, trampled ground, but in the half-darkness there had been much disorder and he could not tell what the end of it might have been.

Having grasped that the enemy were in full retreat across the river,

Sendekar broke off the fighting, glad to see the back of them so cheaply. About two hours after dawn they cut the ropes, the King himself being the last man to cross.

There could be no doubt—as Sendekar emphasized in reporting to General Kembri—that the failure of the attack had been largely, if not entirely, due to the courage and resourcefulness of the Tonildan slave-girl Maia of Serrelind, who, alone and entirely without help among the enemy at Melvda-Rain, had not only succeeded in discovering their plans but had thereupon escaped, swum the impassable Valderra by night—an all-but-incredible feat, in the course of which she had sustained severe injuries—and brought warning to Rallur in the nick of time. In the circumstances he had thought it only fitting to order the news of her heroism to be proclaimed throughout the army.

PART III

THE SERRELINDA

SELPERRON BUYS SOME FLOWERS

It was not often that Selperron—a merchant of Kabin—came up to Bekla. Indeed, he had done so only twice before in his life; once as a youth, together with his parents, though that, of course, had been many years ago now, and in the time of Senda-na-Say. Selperron was a dealer in ox-hides and other animal skins, though he was also not above such side-lines as river shells and the plumes marketed by the Ortelgan forest hunters. For some time past business had been improving. Apart from the buoyant state of the market, however, his elder son was now of an age to be useful in the business, while his second wife (for Selperron had been widowed some four years before) was a brisk, competent woman, as good as a man when it came to dealing with customers and reckoning profit and loss.

For the first time in years, therefore, he had felt able, this summer, to afford time and money for a trip to Bekla, leaving the business in safe hands. It should not, in fact, prove an unduly expensive jaunt (unless he were to make it so), since he had arranged to stay with an old friend, one N'Kasit, a Kabinese in the same line of business, who had rather unexpectedly uprooted himself and gone to Bekla four years before. N'Kasit had been fortunate enough to obtain from General Kembri a contract (though not a monopoly) to supply leather to the army, and was now doing well. Selperron had sent him consignments of hides at profit, for Bekla's selling prices were higher than Kabin's; and N'Kasit, during a visit home the year before, had suggested that Selperron should himself accompany his next consignment up to Bekla. Selperron had felt attracted by the idea; and now, in short, the trip had really come about.

The journey, in a convoy of ox-cart carriers, slave-gangers and their wares, three or four other travellers like himself and the usual half-company of soldiers for protection (who cost far too much, but it was that or nothing), had been somewhat wearisome. Once, he might rather have enjoyed it, but Selperron had now reached a time of life (and fortune) when he preferred comfort and good food, and somehow the inns along the road had not proved all that he seemed to remember. Among the slaves there had been a girl who wept continually, and this, too—being a kindly and impressionable man—he had found a trial.

Once they reached Bekla, however, he had at once felt all the fascination and excitement of earlier days. At the first, distant sight of the slender, balconied towers, the Peacock Wall extending above the lower city and the Palace of the Barons crowning the Leopard Hill beyond, his spirits had soared. Coming in through the Blue Gate, he had been delighted by the tumult and crowds all about him. Forgoing a jekzha—for he fancied the idea of stopping as he pleased to look around him—he had hired a lad with a barrow for his baggage-roll and strolled beside him along the streets, noting not so much the buildings, or even the Tamarrik Gate and the temple, as the goods displayed for sale and the trafficking at the shops and stalls. Merely to see brisk business going on and things being bought and sold gave pleasure to Selperron, and by the time he reached N'Kasit's house, near the western clock tower, he was in even better humour and more than ready to reciprocate his friend's greetings and polite enquiries after his family and old acquaintances in Kabin. That first evening they had dined at home, after which Selperron had slept long and comfortably, undisturbed by any night-sounds of the city.

And now here they were together, idling on a midsummer day, taking their leisure and seeing the sights, the sun pleasantly warm on their backs and the city babble and savours and throngs all around them as they sauntered up the Kharjiz towards Storks Hill and Masons Street. On the bridge over the Monju Brook N'Kasit stopped and they leaned side by side over the parapet, looking upstream to where the water ran glittering round the curve at the base of the Tower of the Orphans. Further down in their direction was a little garden, and here a weeping willow overhung the stream, its branches forming a kind of watery arbour as they trailed in the slack current.

'Did you do well this last Melekril?' asked Selperron after a time. He spoke with appropriately off-hand diffidence—a blend between the natural interest of a business associate and a friend wishing to seem politely but not unduly inquisitive.

'That's—well—quite a difficult question to answer, even two or three months after,' replied N'Kasit. 'As things have turned out, I'm still over-stocked. It's a damned nuisance having money tied up in stuff that's been on my hands as long as this.'

'Well,' answered Selperron, 'one beauty of our line of business is that at least stock doesn't go bad on you. That market-girl over there's got to sell her fruit quick, but you and I can always hang on to hides and wait for our return.'

'Normally, yes,' said N'Kasit, 'and as a rule, if a proportion of Melekril stock's not been taken off my hands before the spring festival I'm not much troubled; but this time I was fully expecting to be robbed and possibly murdered into the bargain.'

Selperron stared and shook his head, looking suitably concerned. 'We heard all kinds of rumours in Kabin, but thank Cran everything stayed quiet enough down there.'

'You should just have been up here, then,' replied N'Kasit. 'After the

528

murder of the High Counsellor that night, no one knew what to expect. People were burying their valuables and even sending their wives and children away—those who could afford to. A lot of them were expecting another revolution, like the time when Senda-na-Say was killed.'

'But of course it didn't come to that,' replied Selperron.

'No: but there was a fair amount of robbery and looting, you see, and some people were saying it must have been organized. And then not long after the murder Santil-kè-Erketlis came out against Bekla, and young Elleroth joined him from Sarkid. So we didn't know but what there mightn't be some sort of heldro bunch organizing trouble here in the city—just as Fornis's supporters did before she came up from Dari getting on for eight years ago. I don't mind telling you, I was scared. There simply weren't enough soldiers here, you see; most of them had just left for the Valderra. I asked for an armed guard for the warehouse, but I never got a man. Think of it—forty or fifty thousand melds' worth of portable stock and only me and a night-watchman! I slept there myself for three or four nights—me and my man Malendik. We had one sword and a knife between us, that's all. But nothing came of it, thank the gods; and as I was saying, about half the stock's still there now, waiting to be sold. Well, it's no good worrying.'

Wandering on down the Kharjiz, they came to the foot of Storks Hill and then to the edge of the temple precinct and the Tamarrik Gate beyond. Here they stopped to watch Fleitil and his men on their scaffolding, putting the finishing touches to big-bellied Airtha of the Diadem, while below, a painter was beginning his task of colouring the relief panels round the plinth, which depicted the seven beatific acts of the goddess. Selperron wondered what proportion of the taxes he had paid last year might have gone into the gold leaf of the goddess's cloak, her jewelled nipples and the silver wire braiding her hair. He himself was not much in favour of spending public money on this kind of thing, but maybe such civic splendours were indirectly good for business—who could tell?

'They say Santil's got all of two thousand men under arms in the Chalcon hills,' said N'Kasit after a time.

'I suppose he would have, counting Elleroth's lot,' answered Selperron. 'But surely that's nowhere near enough to bother the Leopards, is it? After all, he can't really do more than lurk about in Chalcon, playing tip-and-run. He couldn't even consider trying to take Thettit, for instance.'

'Maybe not,' said N'Kasit. 'But all the same, the Leopards have got to take *some* notice of him, haven't they? Kembri's had to drop his idea of attacking Karnat in Suba, I know that. Thettit's been garrisoned, you know, and that takes men away from the Valderra for a start.'

'Was anyone ever arrested for the murder?' said Selperron.

N'Kasit shook his head. 'That's the extraordinary thing. Of course, there were hundreds of people coming into the upper city all that afternoon and evening—guests and so on—and I suppose the surveillance at the gate can't have been as strict as usual. After the murder, of course, the whole place was searched from end to end, but there wasn't anyone who couldn't account for themselves.'

Selperron chuckled. 'That High Counsellor—he was basting one of his girls in a boat, or something, wasn't he? A black girl, didn't I hear?'

'Yes, that's right. They had her into the temple for questioning, and that's the last I remember hearing about her. But if they've put her to death it certainly wasn't in public, so I suppose they must have decided she wasn't involved. She was rumoured to be some sort of witch or sorceress, I remember hearing. Quite a lot of the young bloods in the upper city were very taken with her at one time; but that was last year. Once the temple got hold of her she just vanished; dead, for all I know. Anyway, no one's any nearer the truth about the murder.'

'There've been arrests in Kabin, you know,' said Selperron. 'Eight or nine since the spring, and more than that in Tonilda and north Yelda, so I heard: people who've been acting as messengers between heldro barons and so on.'

'They're contenting themselves with arresting little people because they can't spare troops to tackle the bigger ones,' said N'Kasit, 'that's about the size of it. They'll bring them up here and execute them and hope that'll damp the heldril down until they can spare more troops from the Valderra and mount an expedition against Erketlis in Chalcon.'

They turned up Storks Hill, N'Kasit heading for the Caravan Market and 'The Green Grove', for he was prosperous enough to be able to afford the best class of tavern, and anxious to show as much to his friend.

'All the same, no great loss, Sencho, was he?' asked Selperron in a cautious undertone, as they came within sight of the colonnade. 'He was a foul brute, by all accounts.'

'That's true enough, but all the same he's a loss to us, as merchants,' said N'Kasit. He grinned sideways at Selperron. 'Why not admit it? He only did what we'd all like to do. Wasn't it only last night you were talking about Beklan shearnas and saying you wouldn't mind meeting a nice one?'

'I wouldn't, either,' replied Selperron. 'Beautiful girls, some of them, a captain of the guard in Kabin was saying only the other day. He told me they—'

'Yes, but the really good ones are impossibly expensive,' broke in N'Kasit. 'Upper city stuff, you know, and inclined to be choosy with it even then. Sencho didn't bother with shearnas, though. Bought his own girls and kept them for himself.'

Selperron fell silent. The truth was that he did indeed take a keen interest in girls, but in a somewhat less carnal way than his friend supposed. To him they were less a means of gratification than one of the most delightful forms of beauty, like jewels or flowers. His head was often turned, but he seldom went further, and in his memory certain girls whom he had never actually possessed tended to stand out as vividly as those he had.

'So a lot of your last year's stock's still in the warehouse?' he asked, to change the subject. 'Do you think the army'll buy it off you soon?'

N'Kasit wrinkled his nose and spat in the dust. 'Well—they've given me an advance to secure it, though not nearly as much as I was hoping for. The trouble is, as I was telling you, that the Lord General was expecting a hard summer's campaign in Suba, with quite a bit of wear and tear. There'd have been reinforcements to equip and so on. But as things turned out, Karnat moved first, and Kembri and Sendekar were lucky not to be taken completely by surprise. Amazing thing, that; all on account of one girl, acting entirely on her own. You heard, of course? She saved Bekla, did that lass, nothing less. Saved us all.'

'Yes, everyone's been talking about it in Kabin,' replied Selperron. 'Tonildan girl, isn't she? I know she swam across the river and brought news of the attack in time for Sendekar to put paid to it, but there's a lot I don't really understand. I mean, what was she doing in Suba in the first place, and how did she come to find out about Karnat's plans at all?'

'Nobody knows,' answered N'Kasit. 'Whatever it was, they've kept that part of it very quiet—the Leopards, I mean. I've got a customer I'm on fairly close terms with, a wine-merchant called Sarget, who's done so well that he actually lives in the upper city now, and he told me that even up there no one really knows. All he could say was that the girl belonged to Sencho at the time he was murdered and she was in the gardens with him the night he was killed—she and the black girl. They were both taken to the temple for questioning, but somehow or other she escaped and actually managed to get as far as Suba—'

'By herself? I don't believe it!'

'Nobody knows whether she had any help or not. All that's known is that she happened to be in Suba.'

'She must have had something to do with the murder, don't you think, and been trying to clear out of the empire altogether; to Katria or somewhere like that?'

'Well, that's what anybody would have thought, I suppose; but what happens then? Somehow or other she finds out that the Terekenalt army's going to cross the Valderra at a place Sendekar hasn't got guarded. In the middle of the night, she finds her way alone to the Suban bank of the

Valderra and proceeds to swim it. Well, that's not just heroism; that's a basting miracle. No one, man or woman, could swim it; it's a raging torrent for miles above and below Rallur. Even the soldiers who pulled her out couldn't believe she'd swum it; they thought she must be an Urtan girl who'd been trying to make away with herself.'

'But *had* she swum it, then?'

'She *must* have, because she knew about Karnat's plan. That's why Sendekar was able to drive him back across the river: otherwise he might very well have reached Bekla in three days. He'd have had complete surprise, you see.'

'Well, perhaps she *did* mean to get out of the empire in the first place, but then, somehow or other, she happened to find out the Terekenalt plan and saw it as a chance to make her fortune.'

'Not if it meant swimming the Valderra, Selpo. Cran, you should just see it! I was up in Rallur myself three years ago, buying from the Urtan graziers. That was just before midsummer—this time of year, more or less—and even then it was like nothing so much as a boiling cauldron full of axe-heads.'

'D'you think perhaps the Terekenalters may have found out she knew, and thrown her in to drown, but somehow or other she just didn't?'

'Well, you can think that by all means, but if I were you I shouldn't be heard saying it. The whole city's crazy about the girl. One of my tanners actually told me he believed she was Lespa come down to save the empire. Made her fortune? Great Cran, *she's* made her fortune all right! They'd give her the stars if they could!'

'Well, what does *she* say happened?'

'Sarget told me she's never said a word about it to anyone in the upper city: so probably no one ever will know precisely what happened.'

'Oh, how I'd love to see her!' said Selperron. 'Just to be able to say I had, back in Kabin, you know.'

'I doubt you'll have the chance,' replied N'Kasit. 'It's not as if it were the spring festival, you see, or the Sacred Queen's birth ceremony. There's not a great deal to bring upper city people down here at this time of year.'

'Is she living with one of the Leopards, or what?'

'No; I'm told she hasn't taken a man since she got back. But everyone's expecting her to make a wealthy marriage as soon as she feels ready. She could have anyone she likes, you see, but for the moment she's probably in no hurry. After all, the Council voted her a house, and money, and Cran knows what besides. I believe the army would have mutinied if they hadn't. Half the officers are said to be wild about her and I don't know that I so very much blame them. After all, *they* wouldn't have lasted long, would they, if Karnat had got to Bekla?'

During the days that followed, the thought of the miraculous Tonildan whose lonely heroism had saved the empire kept recurring to Selperron. She must be a most remarkable girl. What did she look like, he wondered, and what could be the real truth behind her incredible exploit? Had she ever been in love? What sort of a girl was she really, alone or among her friends, behind her radiant guise of a saviour princess so dazzling that simple folk could actually see her as Lespa incarnate?

'Just suppose,' he thought, awake in bed one morning before N'Kasit's servant had come in to call him, 'just suppose I happened to meet her, what would I say to her? And what would she say to me, I wonder? I'm not really all that old: forty's no age.'

He tried to imagine the Tonildan girl breasting the cataract in the roaring darkness, the whole fate of the empire resting on her shoulders as she struggled on. Suppose it had been *he* who had pulled her out on the bank, *he* who had first perceived that she was telling the truth and ordered that she should be taken at once to General Sendekar? Sighing, he heaved himself out of bed and began to dress. Tomorrow he had to start the journey home.

'N'Kasit's a good friend,' he thought. 'I must slip off on my own and buy him a present today—a good 'un, ay. He's really done me very well and I've had a fine time up here. Only I can't help wishing I'd just *seen* the Tonildan girl. People in Kabin are sure to ask, when I get back.'

That afternoon he accompanied N'Kasit to his warehouse. This lay high up in the lower city, south of the Tower of Sel-Dolad and actually abutting on the western ramparts. Like almost every building in Bekla it was of stone, its long rows of recessed bays cool and dusky, the whole place echoing whenever a door slammed or a crate was grounded by the winch. Selperron could not help envying his friend these solid, well-appointed premises which, compared with his own at Kabin, seemed so secure against fire and robbery.

'I only rent the place, of course,' said N'Kasit, in reply to his admiring remarks. 'And quite enough it costs me, too. But you know how important it is to keep up an appearance of prosperity—even more here than in Kabin. Can't make money without spending it, can you?'

'Who's the landlord?' asked Selperron.

'It used to be the High Counsellor. He owned half the city—or so you'd have thought. He left no heir, of course, so all his property's been taken over by the temple. I don't know whether they'll sell me this place—I've made them an offer—but in point of fact it's the Sacred Queen I'm paying rent to now. So I shouldn't think the temple sees much of that, would you?'

Before Selperron could hear more about this interesting state of affairs, however, the quartermasters of the Belishban and Lapanese regiments—whom N'Kasit had been expecting—made their appearance and began discussing such matters as shoe-leather, helmets and shield-facings. As N'Kasit got up to conduct them through the warehouse and show them the various qualities of leather in stock Selperron, taking his opportunity, slipped away as he had planned, merely telling his friend that he would see him back at home for supper.

He had already decided that N'Kasit's hospitality—to say nothing of his own business prospects in the capital—called for nothing less than some kind of gold artifact as a farewell present, and accordingly he made his way downhill towards the Sheldad—the thoroughfare running westward from the Caravan Market—out of which branched the streets of the gold-smiths' and jewellers' quarters. Although he was carrying a considerable sum in coin he was not afraid of robbery, for the streets were well fre-quented in the cooling afternoon, he did not look a particularly wealthy or likely victim and his business was going to be transacted behind the locked door of a reputable dealer to whom he had been recommended in Kabin.

He was still some way short of the side-street leading to his destination when he became aware of some sort of commotion in front of him, appar-ently near the point where the Sheldad ran into the Caravan Market. He stopped, looking ahead rather nervously, for after N'Kasit's account of the troubles in the spring he had no wish to find himself caught up in a riot or a street-fight. He hoped, too, that it would not turn out to be prisoners or criminals being led through the streets (for to his credit Selperron was sensitive and hated the kind of ugly jeering and mob cruelty that commonly took place at such times). In a few moments, however, he realized that whatever else it might be, this occasion was neither brutal nor violent. The clamour ahead was plainly some sort of acclamation. It had a happy quality, as if those shouting were taking part in some kind of shared delight, such as a homecoming or a wedding. People began running past him, some calling out to others in front. Selperron, excited, ran too, jostling along with the rest.

'What is it?' he panted to an old woman whom he found beside him. 'What's all the fuss about, grandmother?'

Beaming, she turned her wrinkled face towards him and toothlessly mumbled something that sounded like 'Share flinders'. Selperron, mys-tified, elbowed his way on, finally coming out into the sanded space of the market. He looked about, but could still see very little over the heads of those around him. Suddenly he realized that he was standing beside the plinth of the brazen scales of Fleitil—one of the wonders of the city, which could weigh an ox, a cart and its contents without unloading—and all in a moment had scrambled up it as nimbly as any street lad. A green-uniformed market official shouted angrily to him to come down, but Selperron ignored him, clambering round the plinth to gaze in the direction of the excitement—whatever it might be.

Across the sanded expanse of the market was approaching a jekzha, drawn by two soldiers of the Beklan regiment, resplendent in their undress uniform of scarlet surcoats with silver lacing and Leopard cognizances. But such a jekzha! Its workmanship was so delicate and fine as to create the illusion of a kind of celestial car, lighter than air, floating on the ground as a bubble on a stream. The doors, as well as the foot-rail and screen, all made of gold filigree, put Selperron in mind of the sparkle of gossamer on a clear autumn morning. The slender spokes of the wheels were painted alternately red and blue, so that in turning they merged to form a flickering, vivid purple. From the top of the canopy rose long, bronze-coloured plumes—whether of eagle, heart-bird or kynat he could not tell. Nor, for the matter of that, did he spend much time glancing at them, for his eyes were drawn elsewhere as a needle to the north.

Seated in the jekzha was a girl so beautiful that, gazing at her, he was overcome by a sort of stupefaction, as though he had not hitherto known (as indeed he had not) that any such being could exist. In this moment he was not unlike a small child seeing for the first time a crimson hummingbird, coloured lamps at a festival or moonlight upon a lake. This was the stilled amazement of revelation. Yet though startled beyond reflection, he was instinctively in no doubt that this could only be the Tonildan, the saviour of Bekla.

Like a flame the sight of her leapt upon him, consuming in an instant all the outworn trivialities about girls littering his memory. He found that he was trembling, and steadied himself with a groping hand upon some random projection of the scales. As the girl drew nearer, it appeared to Selperron as though she shed about her a kind of radiance, airy and fertile, like a sunlit drift of pollen from catkins. All gold she seemed—hair, shoulders, arms; and golden sandals enclosing the feet which rested side by side on the rail in front of her; feet made for dancing, surely. They were like golden butterflies: if they happened at this moment to be still, poised fan-like in the sunshine, nevertheless that very stillness implied a kind of tension, the suggestion that it was their nature at any moment to be up and off about their happy mystery of swift play. But that, indeed, was no more than might be said of the girl herself. Her posture, leaning a little forward, one perfect, bare arm resting on the rail beside her, was instinct with a light, quick energy, as though from sheer vitality she might leap suddenly forward, land weightless as a dragonfly and pirouette on the sand.

Most of all he was astonished by her graceful elegance. In talking to N'Kasit, he had formed in his mind a picture of a big, strong girl, hefty, a sort of warrior lass, a hardy survivor in rough places. Sturdy and well-built she was certainly, but with a kind of softness and the air of a merry child, mischievous and innocently sensual as an urchin with a stolen pie. She was smiling on those around her and gazing down from huge, blue eyes; yet a little disconcerted, too, she seemed, as though by no means sure how to maintain her self-possession in the face of such a welcome; and as she turned her head Selperron was deeply moved to see in those eyes a glint of unshed tears.

And well she might, he thought, be moved to the verge of weeping. Round the jekzha, as it was wafted on across the market-place, people were hastening together from every direction—porters, baggage slaves, hawkers, beggars, guttersnipes, street-traders, nondescript idlers, passers-by like himself and others whose dress—Ortelgan, Belishban or Yelda-shay—denoted them as from the provinces. From all sides came cries of greetings and praise. 'May all the gods bless thee, my little swimmer!' called out a brawny market-woman, flinging up her rough, red hands as the jekzha came abreast of her stall. The lovely girl responded with a wave of her hand before turning to her other side to touch the hilt of the sword which a Beklan tryzatt was holding up to her in an improvised gesture of allegiance and devotion.

'Long live the Serrelinda!' shouted a voice from some rooftop. 'Serre-linda! Serrelinda!' echoed others, and for a few moments a perfect storm of acclaim broke out round the jekzha, which was forced to a gradual halt in the crowd like a boat grounding on the slope of a sand-bar.

'Come along now, missus! Easy there, sir, please! Easy now!' repeated the soldiers in the shafts, wiping the sweat from their foreheads and grinning about them like men not unused to it all. 'Let the young säiyett through, now. We've got to get her home safe, you know!'

'She can have my home!' shouted a young fellow in a leather apron, who was carrying in one hand a newly-turned chair-leg and looked as though he had downed tools and left his work-bench the minute before. 'Ah, and mine, bed and hearth!' bellowed a red-haired man in the livery of Dur-akkon's household.

Helpless to prevail, as it were, against this deluge of benediction, the voices tossing hither and thither about her like gusts of wind, the girl could only smile speechlessly and then, with a charming pantomime of help-lessness and frustration, hold out her arms and shake her head in a mute appeal to her well-wishers to let her pass. She was clad, Selperron now noticed for the first time, very simply, in a short dress of white silk, low-cut and gathered at the waist with a gold belt matching the only jewel she was wearing, a brooch in the likeness of a leopard holding a golden lily. As she half-rose in her seat, grasping the rail and leaning forward to speak to

536

her soldiers, he caught sight, along her lower thigh, of a long, livid scar, plainly the vestige of a wound as grievous as any battle-hardened veteran could boast of. Evidently she was not concerned to hide it. Selperron, as he realized why, was carried away by a surge of adoration and fervour, such as he might have felt in watching some sacred dance performed by the Thlela. If he could have found words, he might perhaps have declared that despite all its folly and vice, there must be something to be said for the human race if it could produce a girl like this.

Such feelings must find expression or else tear him to pieces. Leaping down from the plinth, he ran across the market-place towards the Street of the Armourers where it curved uphill to the Peacock Gate. Here, just at the foot of the hill, a flower-seller was seated, surrounded by her summer wares—tall, maculate lilies in tubs of water; roses and scarlet trepsis, sharp-scented planella, pale gendonnas and ornate, curve-bloomed iris—yellow, blue and white.

'Give me those—and those—and those!' he said, pointing here and there and in his impatience tugging out the bunches with his own hands and piling them into her astonished arms. 'Ay, that'll do!'—for the jekzha was fast approaching.

'Wait, sir! Oh, can't ye just *wait* a minute, now!' cried the old soul, flustered, and torn between annoyance at his haste and gratification at making such a fine sale. 'Let me see, that's twenty meld the lilies, fifteen the roses; and this planella, now—'

'Oh, never mind!' cried Selperron. Dragging out his purse, he thrust five twenty-meld pieces into her hand, gathered up the flowers in one great scented, dripping mass and turned about just as the soldiers reached the foot of the hill. Stumbling forward, he gripped the jekzha's nearside shaft and looked up into the girl's face. At this moment there was nothing in the world but himself and her.

'Säiyett, honour me by accepting these!' he said, lifting up the flowers. 'They're nowhere near so beautiful as you, but take them all the same, so that I may never forget you till the day I die.'

For a long and terrible instant he waited, standing at the shaft, seeing her initial, startled look and the surprise and uncertainty momentarily crossing her face. Then she smiled full in his eyes, bent forward and took the flowers from him in a single embrace of her open arms. Her neck and shoulders were covered with drops of water and the upper part of her dress was soaked; but of this she took not the least notice. For an instant only she looked away from him to lay the huge, tumbling bouquet beside her on the seat. Then, once more stooping, she took his face between her two hands and kissed him.

'Happen I shan't forget you, either,' she said.

Then the wheel went over his foot. But it was not very heavy, and even though he stifled a quick cry and doubled up his leg, he was hardly aware of the pain, for as the jekzha rolled away up the hill, the girl turned her head, looked back at him and waved.

Selperron was as good as his word. He never saw the Serrelinda again; and he never forgot her for the rest of his life. N'Kasit's present, perforce, was not quite so lavish as he had originally intended, but what matter? He could always give him another next year.

: 54 :

HIGH LIFE

The soldiers always began by declining the money which Maia offered them, and always she insisted that they should accept it—a fraction of what she herself could have come by in far less time and without exertion. Among the many privileges conferred upon her together with her beautiful little house beside the northern shore of the Barb, was that of calling upon soldiers to draw her jekzha whenever she had occasion to fare abroad. Otherwise she could certainly never have visited the lower city at all, to go on foot being out of the question, while no jekzha-man or attendant slave could possibly have protected her from the adulation of the common people.

It was seldom that she passed the Peacock Gate, however. The crowds and their devotion half-frightened her, and although she always responded as she knew they wished, yet upon coming home she would find herself exhausted, consumed with a sense of the precarious and unnatural, as though looking vertiginously down from some dizzy pinnacle upon that real world to which she could never descend.

For three weeks and more after the Terekenalt army had been thrown back across the Valderra she had lain gravely ill, scarcely able to tell night from morning, let alone to understand the full import of what she had achieved or of the news which had been proclaimed throughout the army and the city. A frailer girl would have bled to death, they had told her, or else died from shock and exhaustion. As it was, she had often been in worse pain than she had imagined possible, at times being afraid even to stir, for every least movement seemed to bring agony spurting from an injured limb. What had really carried her through—as on the river bank with the soldiers—had been the knowledge that she had succeeded—had not Sendekar himself told her so?—had prevented the bloodshed and saved the lives of the Tonildans stationed down the river. Their commander had come on tiptoe to visit her, a gruff, taciturn man standing almost inarticulate beside her bed, trying as best he could to convey their thanks: but she no less than he had found few words, slipping back into half-oblivion even before he was gone. The clamps with which they had fastened her gashed thigh caused her continual discomfort, and she had had to be scolded for worrying at them like an animal.

Her litter-borne return to the city had been secret and nocturnal, for although she was sufficiently recovered to leave fortified Rallur—no place for a convalescent—Sendekar had been advised that she must at all costs be spared the crowding and ovations inseparable from a daylight entry into Bekla. Also, as he—a Yeldashay professional soldier, not on close personal terms with the foremost members of the Leopard régime—had come to realize, there were those in the upper city who would in any case have sought to prevent it.

Arriving tired out after the trying, five-day journey, Maia had been touched and comforted to find Ogma already installed as her housekeeper, together with old Jarvil, the porter from Sencho's former household, with whom she had always got on well. Ogma—who had, of course, been expecting to be sold on the open market, like the rest of Sencho's slaves— had been even more startled and delighted than Maia by this caprice of fortune (the idea had originated with Elvair-ka-Virrion) and at once set about looking after her devotedly. Thanks largely to her attentions, it was not long before Maia felt well enough to begin the exciting business of ordering her life in Bekla for herself.

She had been surprised—despite her incomparable celebrity, happily and unexpectedly surprised—by the genuine warmth and kindness shown to her by Nennaunir, as also by Sessendris, Kembri's household säiyett. In the days when she had been a slave at Sencho's she had always assumed (as she had, for example, at Sarget's party) that Nennaunir's friendliness was to a large extent no more than politic—a keeping-in with a girl whom she had perceived to stand well with the Leopards. She had certainly felt this about Sessendris on the night of Elvair-ka-Virrion's party—that night when she had first met Bayub-Otal. Not long after her return to Bekla, however, something took place which showed her that (over-influenced, perhaps, by Occula's worldly-wise scepticism) she had in this instance been somewhat too canny.

One beautiful evening, about ten days after her arrival, as she was sitting at the open window of her parlour overlooking the Barb, watching the cranes feeding in the shallows and listening to one of Fordil's hinnarists whom she had hired to play to her (it delighted her to be able, now, to spend money in this way), Ogma came in to tell her that an unaccompanied lady was at the door. It turned out to be Sessendris. Maia, surprised and taken rather unawares, was at first constrained and on her guard. After several minutes, however, she began to feel intuitively that whatever motive the handsome, urbane säiyett might have in coming to see her, she meant her no harm. For a time they conversed of those matters which had all Bekla by the ears—the killing of Sencho, Maia's swimming of the Valderra and Sendekar's capture of the traitor Bayub-Otal in the course of Karnat's retreat. Maia, however, recounted little of her own experiences, and in particular omitted any mention of her journey to Urtah with the Subans or the night crossing at the ford. As the evening light faded from the sky, leaving at last only streaks of pale rose and darkening purple reflected from the windless expanse of the Barb, Ogma brought in serrardoes and a flask of Yeldashay and Maia, sipping and nibbling in the window-seat, fell silent and waited, feeling that someone as experienced as Sessendris should need no further encouragement to bring her to the point of her visit, whatever that might be.

'Well, Maia Serrelinda, saviour of Bekla, princess from Tonilda—' Sessendris, seated on a polished stool with up-curved, scrolled arm-rests, leant back against the table, smiling at Maia over her wine-cup—'what now? How does a girl follow up a conquest like yours?'

'Don't know as I've had all that much time to think about it,' answered Maia. 'It's all like a dream still: I'm just taking things easy. My leg won't be right for a bit yet, they say, though it's nowhere near as bad as 'twas.'

'And who else has been to see you?' asked Sessendris. The question, which might have been typical of idle conversation, was asked in a tone which made Maia look up quickly, sensing something direct and concerned in the säiyett's voice.

'U-Sarget's been,' she replied. 'Matter of fact, he was here very soon after I arrived: and then Shend-Lador and two or three of his friends, along with Nennaunir. Of course I'm not up to all that much yet, you know. Eud-Ecachlon called only yesterday evening, but I was feeling that done up I had to tell my porter I couldn't see him.'

'But the Lord General hasn't been, has he?'

'No.'

'Nor the Sacred Queen?'

'Well, no.'

Sessendris waited, gazing at her with raised eyebrows.

'You mean—well, but I don't see a great lot in that,' said Maia. 'I mean, people like that, if they want to see you, they send for you, don't they? And I dare say they reckon I'm not back to rights yet. Nor I am.'

'Yes, but Durakkon came? And you'd never met *him* before, had you?'

'Oh, I hardly knew what to say!' Maia flushed at the recollection. 'He gave me these diamonds—did you ever see the like?' (she touched her neck) 'and then he said as he'd come to thank me on behalf of the city and the empire, and that neither he nor anyone could ever—' She broke off. 'Well, don't matter all he said, but I'll not forget it, tell you that. He put it—well, what you'd call stately. I reckon he *deserves* to be High Baron. No, I *hadn't* met him before, but I'd say he's what a High Baron ought to be.'

Sessendris shrugged her shoulders and was silent for a little. At length she said, 'I've taken a risk coming here, you know. I always pretend I don't hear anything, but of course any good säiyett knows how to pretend that. Let's go on pretending, shall we? For instance, can you tell me—for I simply can't imagine—whose idea it was that you should join Bayub-Otal and leave the city by night for Urtah?'

Maia started. 'Bayub-Otal?'

Sessendris smiled. 'You thought I didn't know? Who do you suppose took the Lord General's message to let you through that night to the guard commander at the Gate of Lilies? Oh, Maia, you're such a dear, beautiful baby still! You don't really understand anything, do you? Listen: all the common people from here to Paltesh are wild about you. They know you saved us all. They'd give you the moon if they could. And Maia, *I'm* common people! My father was a baker in Sarkid. *I* love you too, and I feel grateful to you from the bottom of my heart. But has it occurred to you that there may be people who don't?'

Uncomprehending, Maia was nettled. 'Don't know as I ever really thought about it all that much.'

Sessendris bit her lip with frustration. 'Look; here's a girl who's sent on an utterly desperate assignment. She succeeds beyond anything that could ever have been expected, she's battered almost to death in doing it and saves an army and probably the empire as well. The Leopards vote her a house, servants, money, privileges, attendance by uniformed soldiers. By Airtha! and they just about knew what was good for them, didn't they? If they hadn't, the army'd likely have torn them to pieces. The High Baron, who's at least got the bluest blood in Bekla if he hasn't got anything else, visits her in person to thank her. But the man who actually sent her, and the woman who consented that he should—*they* don't come. Why not, do you suppose?'

'General Kembri, d'you mean? Well, but he must have everything to do from morning till night, what with the war and that. That rebel baron, Santil What's-his-name in Chalcon, on top of all the rest, and then—'

'Maia, dear, I can't stay much longer: I'll have to go before I'm missed. But I'll ask you something else. How long does the Sacred Queen normally reign, do you know?'

541

Maia pondered. 'Well, I can't just rightly say. Four years, isn't it?'

'And how long has Queen Fornis reigned?'

'Well, I suppose two lots of four years: I never really thought about it.'

'Start now. This next Melekril her second reign's due to end. She's thirty-four or thirty-five—I forget which: older than any Sacred Queen before her, anyway. The other morning, while I was down in the lower city on the Lord General's business, I overheard two porters talking in the colonnade. One of them said, "Why don't they make the Serrelinda Sacred Queen? That'd bring us all the luck in the world, that would, for if ever the gods loved a girl it's her. Must do, else she'd 'a bin dead by this time."'

Maia laughed. 'Why, I couldn't be Sacred Queen: that's crazy! Everyone knows I've been in and out of bed—'

'But Maia, that doesn't matter! The Sacred Queen doesn't have to be a virgin. It certainly wouldn't stop the people acclaiming you; and there are certain Leopards who'd like to get rid of Kembri and put themselves in his place, you know. They'd quite ready to make use of you if they decided it would serve their purpose. When you were a slave-girl you hadn't any enemies. Now you've saved the army and the city, you have. That's how the world works, dear. But *I'm* not your enemy, and that's why I'm here this evening.'

'General Kembri wouldn't harm me,' said Maia. 'I'm sure of that. Why, he promised me my freedom and Cran knows what else if only I could do what he wanted, and I reckon he's been as good as his word and all.'

'He couldn't dare be anything else, after Sendekar'd told the army what you'd done. And you're quite right to think he hasn't got anything against you personally. But what I'm trying to tell you is that you're a public figure now, and whether you like it or not, you're almost certainly seen as a rival by Fornis, whose position's difficult enough anyway at her age, with her second reign due to end in a matter of months. Fornis can be like a raving maniac when she hates someone, you know. She'd be ready to let Karnat in—burn the city—smash the empire—anything at all, before she'd give up her power. She wouldn't care *what* she did!'

Maia stood up and began walking to and fro.

'I can't see this, Sessendris. Whatever should Queen Fornis have against me? *I've* nothing against *her*! I've never even put myself forward—'

'You're young, you're very beautiful and you're a public heroine; the people used to worship her, and now they worship you. That's what she'll have against you, and she'll be watching Kembri like a hawk to see whether he favours you or not. He might feel himself forced to, you see, by sheer weight of public feeling. "Maia for Sacred Queen!" And then—'

'I'll go away—I'll leave Bekla—'

'That would be quite fatal, dear. Everyone would be wondering what you might be up to behind their backs. Remember Enka-Mordet. No, it's not that bad, Maia. By all means stay here and enjoy all you've earned. All I'm saying is, take the greatest care. Don't give anyone the remotest grounds for thinking you might be aiming higher, and don't listen to anyone who may suggest to you that you should. And now I'm off; I've stayed too long as it is. Good-night, golden Maia, and may Lespa guard you! Tell Ogma and the porter to forget I came here. No one else saw me.'

When Sessendris was gone and Ogma had brought in the lamps, Maia asked her to bring her needlework and sit with her for company. Yet although Ogma (who had never in her life been five miles from Bekla) did her best, talking of this and that and from time to time asking Maia to thread her needle—for her sight was poor—Maia herself was but indifferent company, preoccupied as she was with all that Sessendris had said. At last Ogma, perceiving that her mistress was not herself, but attributing it merely to fatigue and her state of health, suggested bed; and for some reason this homely proposal at last drew from Maia what was really in her heart.

'Ogma, what's become of Occula? Have you heard anything about her?'

Ogma, limping across the room with her work over her arm, stopped and turned.

'No, not once, Miss Maia. Not since—well, not since that last evening, when you both went to the gardens with the High Counsellor. But then they took her away to the temple, didn't they?'

'Yes, but is she with the Sacred Queen now, 's far 's you know?'

'With the Sacred *Queen*, miss?' Ogma was visibly surprised and agitated. 'Oh, Cran! If she went to the Sacred Queen anything could have happened to her.'

Maia stared at her, frowning.

'You didn't know, miss? The queen's got a terrible reputation that way.'

'I always thought there was some as was devoted to her,' said Maia, remembering Ashaktis.

'Maybe her own Palteshis,' said Ogma, 'and any as might just happen to suit her, like. But there's others as she's—well—got rid of, so they say.'

The realization that she had been several days in Bekla without making any enquiry about Occula showed Maia more plainly than anything else how weak and shocked she must really have been. She had been sleeping badly, troubled with pain as well as with anxiety about her scars (for she had four or five gashes altogether, though none so grievous as that on her thigh). Again and again she had woken from nightmares of fire in the dark, of roaring water and the boy Sphelthon crying on the blood-drenched ground. Protean they were, these fantasies, casting themselves like amorphous nets round her distressed mind; tormentors continually emerging in new and unexpected guises. The fire would dance before her, its flames murmuring 'Shagreh, shagreh', as they refused to cook her food. The water would become an insubstantial ladder on which she dared not set foot. Or she would be placidly swimming when the wretched boy, a weeping horror, would rise up out of deep water and fasten his bloody mouth on her flinching body. One night of full moon, having lain for two hours afraid to fall asleep again, she had resorted to her old solace, gone down to the Barb and, plunging in near the outfall of the Monju brook, swum half a mile to the Pool of Light, stepping out naked into the gardens before a gaping sentry of the Lapanese regiment. (Ogma had returned his cloak next morning, and this latest story of the Serrelinda lost nothing in the telling.)

But yet another preoccupation she had, besides her own health and recovery. Incessantly she dwelt on the memory of Zen-Kurel, recalling over and over each moment of their brief hours together, from the king's supper table to the daggers lying discarded on the floor and the running footsteps receding into the moonlight. She longed for him; she missed him every hour. Where was he? What had happened to him in the fighting? *Had* she saved his life? Surely she must have! To have known for certain that she had saved his life would have meant more to her than the knowledge of having saved the army and the Tonildan detachment. Karnat's force had suffered no very heavy casualties in the fighting: Sendekar had told her as much before she left Rallur. The king himself, she knew, was not among the dead, and Zen-Kurel had been one of his personal aides. She imagined him wading into the water, helping to pull the king ashore as the last rope was cut, translating to the king the answers of the few Beklan prisoners who had been taken back into Suba; then, perhaps, sent back across the Zhairgen with despatches for Keril-Katria. Of course he would have distinguished himself. He would no doubt be promoted— though she knew nothing about such things or what he might realistically expect. One thing, however, she was sure of. Whatever his adventures, he would not have forgotten her, any more than she had forgotten him.

The glaring inconsistency of her situation in regard to Zen-Kurel, which would naturally have been the first thing to occur to (for instance) Occula or Nennaunir if they had learned her whole story, did not strike Maia at all. It never once crossed her mind that her exploit must, of course, have come to the ears of all Suba, Katria and Terekenalt, or that Zen-Kurel—if he were still with King Karnat—had good cause not only to curse her very name and his own disclosure to her, but also, if he valued his life, to utter no word of their love to a living soul. Still more extraordinarily, if anyone (such as Occula) had pointed this out, Maia, while she would have been deeply grieved, would nevertheless have remained in no doubt that Zen-Kurel still loved her and had not renounced her in his own mind.

She, for her part, was scarcely ever free from the thought of him. She knew herself to have remained deeply in love with him. How could this be? A man whom she had known and with whom she had made love for perhaps four hours altogether: and she a girl who had, to use her own words, been in and out of bed with half a dozen men, both in the upper and the lower city. Yet she herself knew why. Alone of them all, Zen-Kurel had sincerely respected her womanhood—yes, where even Elvair-ka-Virrion had not, for all his fine words and elegant ways. And then, she had not come to him as a slave-girl, but as the magic Suban princess of the golden lilies. 'He asked me to marry him—he meant it—to marry him—' she whispered, swimming down the moonlit Barb.

Yet it was not even this sincere asking that lay at the heart of the matter. Others, no doubt, given the opportunity, might well have asked as much. It was that she herself could, she knew, create so much by loving a man like Zen-Kurel. In the midst of all the danger, uncertainty and squalor of Suba, he had had the power to carry her with him to a little island of security where they had dwelt together—for just how long was no matter. And thence had flowed into her a joy, a power and confidence which had enabled her to save thousands of lives. This, amazingly, was Maia's own, personal view of what had happened. Within herself she seemed to carry the seed of a great tree only waiting to grow and flourish, which now could not spring up for lack of soil—his presence. And this was frustration and torment.

There had lain the promise—there for the picking up, like a jewel lying on the ground. For a few hours she had held it in her hand. And by her own deed—the deed that had made her fortune—she had cast it away from her, as she had thrown her clothes into the Valderra. 'It's only the beginning, Maia—we'll meet again in Bekla.' He had meant that. If she had chosen, she need have done nothing but await their reunion—whenever and wherever it might have taken place.

Why had she, then, by her own deed, made it impossible? Not for luxury, wealth and fame; that much she knew. She would gladly forgo all that to lie once more in his arms in flea-bitten Suba. No, she had done what she did out of her own womanliness—because of Gehta and her dad, because of Sphelthon at the ford, because of the Tonildans downstream of Rallur. Yes, and for Zenka's own sake, too—poor, feather-brained boy, boasting that he'd kill twenty Beklans for her sake! She'd saved *his* life as surely as anyone else's in the whole silly, nasty business. He might be a bit disappointed now, but if only she could have him to herself for an hour or two she'd soon make him see it different; for a week or two; for a year or two: well, say a lifetime. She could do something, *make* something out of life with a lad like that, as she knew she never could with a showy gallant like Elvair-ka-Virrion.

When Shend-Lador and his friends had come to see her, she had asked them what news they could give her about the Terekenalt prisoners taken in the fighting. They knew no more, however, than Sendekar had already told her; namely, that there were something like seventy prisoners altogether, Subans, Katrians and Terekenalters, foremost among whom was the traitor Bayub-Otal. All had been sent under guard to the fortress at Dari-Paltesh, where they were to remain until the Lord General could spare time to consider what was to be done with them.

'Some of them are bound to have ransom value, you see, Maia,' explained Shend-Lador. 'And anyway they've all got hostage and exchange value against our men who got collared and taken into Suba. The Lord General will sort it out as soon as he's finished off Erketlis.'

'But Anda-No—I mean, Bayub-Otal's a son of the High Baron of Urtah. Haven't the Urtans said anything about him?' she asked.

Shend-Lador laughed. 'Not much they *can* say, is there? He was taken red-handed fighting for Karnat against the empire. Oh, no, Maia, you needn't worry: *his* number's up if anyone's is—public execution in the Caravan Market, I should think. Soon as there's time to spare for it, that is.'

He knew the names of no other prisoners, and neither did Sarget or Nennaunir. Durakkon, of course, she had not presumed to question. Nor, lacking Occula, had she disclosed to anyone the true nature of her interest.

During these days of her convalescence, her principal source of information was Ogma, who talked to hawkers at the door and brought back gossip with her shopping from the lower city. One day she returned so eager to talk that she came straight into the parlour and, clumping her way across the room with her basket still on her arm, came to a stop beside the couch on which Maia had been resting in the sunshine.

'Oh, miss, I was buying some vegetables—only we're right out of brillions as well as beans, and they had some nice fruit, all sorts, so I thought well, as you'd given me the money and we're not short nowadays, are we? any more than we were at the High Counsellor's, I might as well get some while they were there. And while I was buying them there was this woman come in as I know to talk to—I've met her two or three times in the shops, see—and she's married to a Tonildan, a man from east of Thettit, only they've been living here for quite a few years now, and she began telling me—'

Maia got up and half-lowered the slatted blind against the mid-day sun.

An air of inattention, she had found, often worked in bringing Ogma to the point.

'Well, this man has friends down Thettit way, miss, and they sometimes come up here on business—buying glass, only that's what he makes and there's none at Thettit, you see—and these men said to this woman, that's to say my friend in the shop as I was talking to, they asked her did she know why Lord Erketlis had declared against Bekla and started fighting?'

'Why, has there been any fighting?' asked Maia. 'I thought Lord Erketlis was lying low in Chalcon. He hasn't got all that many men, has he?'

'Oh, well, that's right, miss—at least, I think so—but I mean the real reason why he's started making trouble and declaring against the Leopards an' that.'

Maia waited.

'It only shows, miss, doesn't it, as there's justice above?' pronounced Ogma sententiously. 'I mean, there's some as brings down judgement on their own heads. That wicked man—of course I know you and Miss Occula *had* to do what you did; you hadn't got no choice—well, we none of us had, had we? And Miss Dyphna—'

'Ogma,' said Maia, 'what are you trying to tell me?'

Ogma leant forward, round-eyed. 'Miss Milvushina!'

'Milvushina? What about her?'

'Well, we all knew, didn't we, miss, why the High Counsellor was at the trouble of getting Miss Milvushina for himself? Because she was what she was—a lady—that's why. And he persuaded the Lord General—it's my belief he did—to send those soldiers to kill her father and mother just so he could have her for—well, for his horrible ways and that. Only I was there in the house all that night when you and Miss Occula was at Lord Elvair-ka-Virrion's party—the night when the soldiers first brought Miss Milvushina; and even the tryzatt, he was that disgusted by what he'd been made to do, like, and Terebinthia told me I wasn't to say a word outside and if I did she'd have me whipped and sold—'

'Ogma, what *is* it you want to tell me?'

'That was his own *death*, miss,' whispered Ogma, stabbing with her fore-finger, 'what he done then, the High Counsellor. This friend of mine in the market had it all from her husband's friends down in Thettit. Miss Milvushina, see, she was promised in marriage to Lord Santil-kè-Erketlis—'

'Great Cran!' said Maia, startled at last into full attention. 'Ogma, are you sure? She never said a word about it to me or Occula.'

'Well, no, miss, likely not,' said Ogma. 'I mean, Miss Milvushina wasn't never one for telling a great deal at all, was she, if you know what I mean?

547

But now it seems as Lord Santil's made a proclamation down in Chalcon and Tonilda, telling everyone what he's doing and why, and all such things as that: and the chief of it is, he says that it was all arranged between him and Lord Enka-Mordet that he was to marry his daughter, and it was going to be a public thing as soon as the rains ended, only for what happened to poor Lord Enka-Mordet. And he says—that's to say, in the proclamation he says—that *he* was the one as had the High Counsellor murdered, and that he'll never rest until he's revenged Lord Enka-Mordet and the dishonour that's been done to himself by Miss Milvushina being taken away.'

Maia, sitting in the sun-dappled window-seat, considered this in silent wonder.

'It only shows, miss, doesn't it,' resumed Ogma, 'as the gods above—'

'Where *is* Milvushina?' interrupted Maia. 'I remember now—that's to say I heard—that after the murder Lord Elvair-ka-Virrion took her into his own household, although by law she ought to have gone to the temple. The Sacred Queen was very angry about it.'

'She's still with Lord Elvair-ka-Virrion,' said Ogma. 'He's said as he won't give her up. But that's not all, miss, either.' She paused for effect.

'Well?' asked Maia.

'They say—that's to say, there's them as are saying, miss—that the Sacred Queen was for sending her back to Chalcon,' said Ogma. 'The rumour is that the Sacred Queen told General Kembri that Bekla had enough troubles as it was and to send the girl back and good riddance. But it seems Miss Milvushina said as she didn't want to go, and when the queen said she was temple property and to be disposed of as such, Lord Elvair-ka-Virrion said no, because she shouldn't never have been enslaved in the first place, so by rights she wasn't a slave at all. So then Queen Fornis got very angry, but when she told General Kembri to see to it, he said he was too busy and anyway it wouldn't make any difference, because Lord Santil wouldn't want her back now she's been—you know. So that's it, you see, miss, and it only goes to show, doesn't it—'

'Then you mean Milvushina's living with Lord Elvair-ka-Virrion now?'

'Oh, yes, miss,' said Ogma, 'and what's more, they say he's going to command a special band of soliders they're raising, to go to Chalcon and put down Lord Erketlis; that's as soon as they're ready. And Miss Milvushina, she's said all along that he's been that good to her in her trouble that she means to stay with him here in Bekla.'

And what did all this matter to herself? thought Maia, dismissing Ogma to go and set about cooking dinner. Once, there had been a time when she would have been wild with jealousy and full of resentment against Elvair-ka-Virrion. 'You're the most beautiful girl I've ever seen.' 'Thank you for my pleasure. It was much the best I've ever had.' This was not disillusion on her part, however: it was sheer lack of interest. With her new understanding, her opened eyes, she knew that Elvair-ka-Virrion was no man for her. He had once bedded her; she had enjoyed it; it had been a step up. He was the son and heir of the Lord General, while she was now the most celebrated, acclaimed woman in the empire. And that was all—that was the size of it. What could she and Elvair-ka-Virrion possibly create together, apart from mere physical pleasure? Milvushina was welcome to him. She did not want him. She wanted her Zenka.

She was in a situation of success and wealth such as she could never have dreamed of, and she had been warned that she had powerful enemies—potential enemies, at all events. She had betrayed the confidence of the man she loved, and by doing so had saved thousands of lives. She was revenged on Bayub-Otal as thoroughly as she or anyone could possibly have desired; yet now she only regretted it and pitied him. What a tangle of contradictions!

Ah! she thought, if only I could go and tell it all to that old Nasada! She could see him so clearly in her mind's eye—his fish-skin robe, his bushy eyebrows, his kindly, penetrating stare, his way of really listening to what you told him and then answering something you'd never have thought of for yourself.

'Oh, if *only* I could talk to Nasada!' she said aloud. 'He'd make sense out of all this: *he'd* help me to know myself. Only I shall never see him again, that's for sure. And Zenka? Never see Zenka again? Oh, *no!*'

She burst into tears; but, as is so often the way, having given rein for a time she felt better, and was able to enjoy entertaining Nennaunir to dinner and showing off her new furniture and other possessions.

Nennaunir's news was all of the forthcoming Chalcon expedition.

'There won't be anyone left here, you know, to go to bed with,' she said, shaking her head with mock concern and smiling mischievously at Maia across the table. 'You've saved the city and ruined the shearnas, Maia. Soon everyone'll be off to stick spears into Santil instead of zards into us.'

'But no one's got to go as doesn't want, surely?' asked Maia. 'Not from the upper city, anyway?'

'Well, the thing is,' answered Nennaunir, 'that Kembri's doing all he can to make them feel they ought to. As a matter of fact,' she went on, dropping her voice and looking over her shoulder for a moment to make sure Ogma was not in the room, 'I believe he's more worried than he cares to let people know. Galatalis—you don't know her, do you? A sweet girl, and so pretty; you'd like her, Maia—she was with him a few days ago and she told me he really didn't seem himself at all.'

'But he was going to lead the army on the Valderra, surely?' said Maia. 'Isn't he going to now, then?'

'Not if I know anything about it,' replied Nennaunir. 'Before the murder, oh, yes, he meant to take the army into Suba and attack Karnat on his own ground. A nice, offensive summer, my dear, with plenty of honour and glory for whoever was in command. But that's all changed now, you see. What with the trouble in Chalcon and all the unrest growing in the provinces since the murder, Kembri hasn't got the men to spare for attacking Karnat in Suba. He's had to give up that idea and leave the Valderra to Sendekar, with just enough men to hold it defensively. That's my guess, anyway.'

Maia told her what she had heard from Ogma about Milvushina and the proclamation of Santil-kè-Erketlis.

'So Sencho signed his own death warrant when he decided to help himself to a baron's daughter for fun?' said Nennaunir. 'Good! I've never been more glad to hear of anyone's death. But Santil—he's a danger to all of us, you know, Maia.'

'How's that, then?' asked Maia. 'He hasn't got the men to make all that much trouble, surely?'

'No, but don't you see, he's openly in arms against the Leopards. No one else in the empire has got as far as that before, not since they've been in power. And as long as they can't put him out of business, they can't afford to ignore him. There he is, offering at least a full belly to anyone who'll join him. As I see it, the longer he can keep going, the longer he's likely to. Men on the run will go to him instead of to Zeray. Anyone who's got on the wrong side of the Leopards will know where to head for, and there's quite a few of them, I should think, wouldn't you? Elleroth, for one; and Elleroth's the sort of man people *will* follow.'

'Who is this Elleroth?' asked Maia. 'I remember, now, the Urtans were talking about him.'

'He's the son and heir of the Ban of Sarkid,' answered Nennaunir. 'I met him once, a year or two back, when he came up here; a very amusing, dashing sort of lad, from all I saw of him. Sarkid's never had slavery, you know, and when the Leopards came into power the Sarkidians made it clear that they were quite ready to quarrel about that if they had to. The House of Sarkid claims to be descended from a legendary hero called Deparioth, who was a slave until he became Ban himself and set all the slaves free. That was hundreds of years ago, of course, but they've always stuck to it like glue. I suppose Sencho and Kembri must have decided that as long as they didn't try to spread their ideas outside Sarkid, it wasn't worth fighting about. But now Elleroth's taken a bunch of his lads to join Santil, and you can bet those diamonds you're wearing, dear—aren't they marvellous? I've never seen bigger, not even the Sacred Queen's—did the city give them to you?'

'Yes. Lord Durakkon gave them to me himself,' said Maia, 'when he come here to thank me. Made me cry, tell you the truth.'

'I don't wonder. Well, we know that's one Leopard who's not going to want anything from you in return, don't we? Where was I? Oh, yes, you can bet your diamonds that Kembri's got a headache about *that*. He must have decided he can't afford to leave the city himself, what with not having caught Sencho's killers and wondering where the next bit of provincial trouble's going to start. But he's sending Elvair—that's what I heard—with a specially raised force—Lapanese, Ortelgans, Belishbans, all sorts—to rout Santil out and finish him off. The Leopards must be desperate to stop the revolt spreading, I should think, wouldn't you?'

'Then why don't they send Milvushina back?' asked Maia. 'I mean, whatever she says, they could *make* her go, surely?'

'Wouldn't make any difference now,' said Nennaunir. 'Heldril aren't called heldril for nothing, you know: "old-fashioned people". As far as Santil's concerned, she's damaged goods and no wife for him any more. No, it's the insult to his honour that he's angry about. He was betrothed to a baron's daughter and the Leopards enslaved her and took her virginity, when by rights she belonged to him. As far as Santil's concerned, that's that, but he's in honour bound to revenge it. Sencho can't have known she was betrothed to Santil, or even he'd have thought twice, I imagine.'

'But if it can't make any difference, Nan, why's Fornis so keen to send her back? Only I was told she regular fell out with Kembri over it.'

'Ah!' Nennaunir put a finger to her lips. 'Well, I'll tell you what I *think* I know, Maia, because you're who you are and I've always liked you. But for Cran and Airtha's sake don't go repeating it; I never said anything, did I?'

Maia shook her head.

'Where's your servant?' asked Nennaunir, looking round into the room behind them.

'In the kitchen; asleep, too, if I know anything about her.'

'She can't possibly hear us?'

Maia shook her head.

Nennaunir leant forward where she was sitting. 'It's my belief that Fornis is almost at her wits' end,' she said, dropping her voice. 'She's had nearly two reigns as Sacred Queen, and that's something that's never been known before. Her second acclamation was all a put-up job, you know. There were plenty of people who shook their heads—secretly, of course, or they'd have found they'd shaken them off, I dare say—when she got the Leopards to agree to a second reign. Now *that's* due to end next Melekril,

551

and what does she mean to do next? No one knows. But she'll try to stay where she is, that's my guess. And any girl in the upper city she thinks might be a rival, she'll put her out of the way if she can. Milvushina's a baron's daughter. Elvair-ka-Virrion's made her his consort and apparently Kembri's supporting him. I bet the two of them have decided Fornis is no more use to them—the people would never agree to a third reign—and they're looking for someone to succeed her as the next Sacred Queen. And if I know anything about it, that someone's Milvushina.

'But that's not the whole size of it, not by a long way. You're in danger yourself, Maia. Yes, you are! I don't want to frighten you, but with a standing and a following like you've got now, I'm certain Fornis must have her eye on you. If I were you I should take great care: don't give her the slightest grounds for thinking you're ambitious.'

'I shan't,' said Maia. 'Sessendris has told me the same already.'

Nennaunir nodded. 'She's nice; you can trust her. Did she tell you they've just made another lot of arrests in Tonilda? No one important, though—all little people. They're bringing them up to Bekla now.'

She was silent for a time, but then suddenly burst out 'Fornis! Oh, Cran, she really frightens me! I'm lucky to be here myself; did you know that?'

'No, I never,' said Maia. 'How could I?'

'Well, I just wondered whether Sednil might have told you anything: about how he came to be doing five years as a branded man, I mean. Poor lad, he's doing it for me, that's the plain truth. But what could I do? I had no choice, else I'd be dead.'

'How ever was that, then?' asked Maia.

'It was all along of that Randronoth, the governor of Lapan,' said Nennaunir. 'He's well-known to have a fancy for very young girls: did you know?'

Maia laughed. 'I ought to: I had to spend the night with him once, when he was staying at Sencho's. Sencho offered him his choice and I was the one he picked. He didn't half have a go at me an' all!'

'Ah, yes: Randronoth wouldn't miss the chance of a girl like you. Well, then, you may perhaps know as well, do you, that the Leopards have had their doubts about him for some time? He's not entirely trusted, only they've never been able to prove anything. He really only held on to his governorship this last year or so by keeping in with Sencho. What'll happen to him now is anybody's guess.

'But I was going to tell you about Queen Fornis and Sednil, wasn't I? It happened more than two years ago, when I was still living in the lower city. I'd had a lover for some time before—an officer—but he'd been killed in battle, and after that I had quite a struggle for a bit. For some reason no one rich or powerful seemed to fancy me. In fact I was seriously thinking of selling myself to Lalloc, if only he'd promise to place me in some wealthy household up here. And it was during that bad time that I took up with Sednil. He's a Palteshi, you know, like me, and we'd first met in Fornis's army, when we were just banzis. He was working for a jewel-merchant in the lower city, but he used to make a bit extra by—well, by helping to get people interested in me—traders coming up to Bekla and so on. We lived together. Sednil was always very good about money; almost *too* good, really. He'd take money direct from men for introducing them to me—he regarded that as payment for work he'd done himself, you see—but he'd never take a meld of mine. He was terribly proud that way; he used to say he'd rather starve. Still, there was no danger of that, because what with the jewel-merchant and the tips from my visitors he was doing reasonably well.

'He was a lot of comfort in those days, was Sednil, and he was no fool. Saw things straight, you know, and often gave me good advice.'

'Ah, he gave me some, too,' replied Maia. 'What you'd call down-to-earth.'

Nennaunir nodded. 'Well, one time Randronoth had come up from Lapan to see Fornis and the Leopards on state business, and the next evening he was drinking with some of his own men down in "The Serpent". He's always been very free-and-easy among his own men, has Randronoth. And it was while he was there that Sednil fell in with him and managed to get him interested in me. Of course I fairly jumped at it; it was much the best opportunity I'd ever had in my life. Well, you know how it is, don't you? Sometimes it works, sometimes it doesn't. This did: I gave him a simply marvellous time; he really wondered which way the moon was going round. Actually, that was when I turned the corner, because later, when I'd got too old to suit his taste, he recommended me to several people in the upper city. But that isn't what I was going to tell you. That night, when he was feeling really contented and satisfied—and still a bit tipsy, too—he gave me a huge great ring he had—for a present, you know. I tried to refuse it, because I was afraid he'd only regret it later and that'd cost me more than the ring could possibly be worth; but he was very insistent and in the end I decided the easiest thing would be to take it.

'It wasn't a girl's ring at all: only a man could possibly have worn it. It was made like a coiled silver dragon with a great ruby in its mouth half as big as your little finger-nail. So I thought, "Well, if ever he asks for it back he can have it—always the honest shearna, that's me—and if he doesn't, I'll hang on to it for a year or so and then sell it." So next morning, off he goes as happy as a stag in autumn and I slept for the rest of the day. I'd left the ring lying on my dressing-table.

'Well, early that afternoon Master Sednil came in—he had a key, of course—and the first thing he saw was the ring. He'd never have taken it to sell—not without asking me—but it struck him as absolutely marvellous, and he couldn't resist putting it on and wearing it when he went back to the jewel-merchant's a bit later. He was going to show it off to him, you see. I never woke up until after he'd gone, and even then I didn't miss the ring. I had no idea at all what he'd done.

'Well, he was crossing the Caravan Market when as luck would have it he ran right into that woman of Queen Fornis's—you know, Ashaktis. Apparently the ring—and no one could possibly have mistaken it for any other—had originally been given to Randronoth by Fornis herself; and Ashaktis recognized it. And before Sednil knew what was happening she'd called two of the market officers—they all knew her, of course—and had him arrested and dragged up in front of Fornis.

'Fornis never even asked him what he had to say for himself. She just sent for Randronoth and asked *him*. Well, naturally, he wasn't going to say he'd given away the Sacred Queen's present to a shearna in the lower city. He said he'd lost it: must have dropped it in the street.

'Sednil was frightened to death, of course. He simply told the queen the truth about where he'd found the ring and asked for me as a witness. But meanwhile Randronoth had got to me first, and I won't tell you how much he gave me to swear I knew nothing whatever about it. I took it, and I've never looked back. But before you think too badly of me, Maia, let me tell you I *wouldn't* have kept quiet if the Sacred Queen had sentenced Sednil to hang, or to the Gelt mines. I thought he might even be let off altogether—after all, Randronoth had got the ring back—but Fornis was cruel as a cat. You could see she was enjoying it. She had him branded in the hand then and there, and she stayed herself to watch it done; and then she gave him five years' forced service—more than any city magistrate would have given him. And from that day to this I've been doing everything I can, not just to make it easier for him, but to get him set free. Only I daren't try too hard. Fornis—oh, believe me, no girl's safe who risks displeasing Fornis! There've been several girls she's taken a dislike to who've simply vanished. That's why I'm saying, Maia, for Cran's sake be careful!'

'Nan,' broke in Maia, 'tell me, where's Occula?'

'Occula?' answered Nennaunir. 'They took her to the temple for questioning—oh, weeks ago now. That's all I know. She may be dead. But if she *is* dead, she certainly wasn't publicly executed. Either she's still alive in the temple, or else they killed her there.'

'No,' said Maia. 'No, Nan. I can't tell you how I know—I daren't— but I know for a fact that she was sent for out of the temple by the Sacred Queen.'

'Then all I can say is, Cran and Airtha help her!' replied Nennaunir.

Maia began to cry.

'WHERE IS OCCULA?'

'I haven't been able to find out anything at all, miss,' said Ogma.

It was three days later. Maia, during the night after Nennaunir's visit, had lain awake for several hours, fretting over Occula. Might she perhaps already have died in the hands of the temple authorities, before Ashaktis had brought the queen's message to the chief priest? That would account for no one having seen her or heard anything of her. It seemed more probable, though, that she *had* been sent to the queen: and if so, then either she was still with her, or else the queen, finding her not to her liking, had dismissed her as she had dismissed Maia. Either that, or else the queen had—what had been her own phrase?—'got rid of her'.

Maia forced herself to look at the matter calmly. She knew intuitively that she could not go to Fornis and enquire what had become of Occula. This—especially in the light of the warnings she had had from Sessendris and Nennaunir—would be not only useless but dangerous. Besides, Fornis herself had assured her that if ever she were to disclose one word of what had passed between them, she should hang. The idea of alluding to it, even obliquely and in private, to this ruthless, cruel woman—and in the dark there rose before her inward sight the mane of glowing, red hair and the dominating, ice-green eyes—frightened her very much: for though Maia knew that she had all Bekla at her feet, she also knew very well that she lacked sophistication and experience, and was not at all sure how far she could safely go in asserting herself. She had been strongly advised to avoid doing anything likely to bring herself to the queen's notice; and with this advice all her own instincts accorded.

Occula, of course, had had many admirers among the young Leopards. Before the murder of the High Counsellor she had been—with Terebinthia's connivance—much in demand. But (and this again was Maia's instinctive guess) since the murder and her arrest and disappearance, things had changed. Neither Shend-Lador and his friends, when they had come to see her, nor Sarget, had made any reference to Occula, though none of them could possibly have forgotten that she and Maia had been together in Sencho's household. The plain inference was that it was no longer felt to be entirely wise to recall Occula or show any interest in her. Wryly, Maia remembered one of Occula's own favourite maxims. 'Never get ill, banzi, and never get into trouble: before you know where you are the water's up to your venda and the bastards are all runnin' like rats.'

Besides, if—as she surely would—the queen were to learn that she had been enquiring about Occula in the upper city, notwithstanding that she knew very well whither she had last been summoned, this would be as ill-received and therefore as risky as knocking on the queen's front door.

Early next morning she had taken the only practicable step she could think of. Calling Ogma in before the time at which she herself was usually woken, she took her into her confidence, omitting mention only of her own relationship with the queen. She told her of her anxiety for Occula's life, of her virtual certainty that Fornis had taken her from the temple to her own house; of the warnings she had received to keep herself out of the queen's eye; and of the consequent impossibility of pursuing enquiries on her own account.

'Ogma, dear, do you think *you* could try to find out something? I mean, do you know any of the queen's servants, or perhaps someone who does?'

'No, that I don't, miss, I'm afraid. I was hardly ever out of the High Counsellor's house, you see, and in those days I never went into the lower city. That's why it makes all the difference bein' here with you, only now I—'

'Where's Terebinthia, do you know?' interrupted Maia.

'Oh, she cut and run, miss. Didn't you know? Lord Elvair-ka-Virrion helped her to get out of Bekla quick—he'd paid her a lot, you see, for letting him take Miss Milvushina away with him before she could be sent down to the temple with the rest of us. Yes, the temple people were too late to catch the säiyett. When they asked about her, she'd already gone. I seem to remember she said something about she meant to go south—down Belishba way: that's where she came from, you know. They still want her for letting Miss Milvushina go, only they don't know where she is. Ah, well, but Terebinthia, she was always that artful, wasn't she, miss?'

Nicely set up with all our lygols, thought Maia, letting Ogma run on for a while. And she's one person who probably *could* have helped me—specially if I'd made it worth her while. *She'd* have known some girl in Fornis's household—or if she hadn't, she could probably have found me one without exciting suspicion. But Ogma? Looking at the ill-favoured, half-crippled girl, not particularly intelligent, clean or tidy; one of the countless army of decent, stupid drudges content to look to their betters for a little security in return for scrubbing the world's floors all their lives, she realized the total impracticability of sending her off to make a friend among Fornis's servants and then discreetly ask about Occula. The very idea was absurd. She tried to imagine Ogma going about to delude Ashaktis. It recalled to her one of old Drigga's most hilarious and delightful stories, in which the ox, while intending to deceive the monkey, unwittingly reveals to that perspicacious animal everything which he supposes he is keeping cleverly concealed.

'Something amuse you, miss?' asked Ogma, with an air of resentment against she could not tell what. Like most people of her sort, the notion that others might be laughing at her was never very far from poor Ogma's mind.

'Oh, I was only just thinking of old Terebinthia,' replied Maia. 'That time when the High Counsellor told her to—' and hurriedly invented the rest of the episode, to the delight of Ogma, who, naturally, had hated the säiyett—a domestic tyrant if ever there was one.

'Well, Ogma, dear, when you're out shopping, just ask around the market and so on, as if you were gossiping about the murder, but don't let on to anyone as it was me as wanted you to, d'you see? I know you were nearly as fond of Occula as what I was, and you must want to find out what's happened to her as much as I do. But just make it look like natural curiosity—don't go trying to get hold of anyone in the queen's house or anything o' that. Only we could both land up in trouble then.'

Perhaps these last words of hers had frightened poor Ogma a little too effectively, thought Maia now, listening to the total blank which was all she had to report after three days among the shops and stalls. She might not have been trying particularly hard. Yet the more sinister explanation would not leave Maia's mind: that Occula might have died weeks ago, her body disposed of in some way no doubt well-established between Fornis and Ashaktis, her name no longer spoken, any mark she had made on Bekla obliterated—another item from the High Counsellor's liquidated household.

'I haven't been able to find out anything at all.' And there was something about the way Ogma spoke which seemed to Maia to carry the meaning 'And don't ask me to try any more.' Yes, for sure she'd frightened her too much with her talk of the queen; but no more than she'd frightened herself. Fair's fair, she thought: I can't blame her.

But I'll be damned if I'll give it up myself. My Occula! My darling Occula, who saved me from that bastard Genshed and gave me back something to live for, and taught me all I've learned and even took care to send me out of the way before Sencho was killed, although she was half-crazy with fear on her own account! Occula, the only one who ever really loved me; except for—oh, how I wish I could tell her about Zenka! If she's alive, does she know—has she heard—about me? She can't not have. Then why hasn't she tried to send me some message? And thus once again the all-too-likely explanation returned upon poor Maia.

'Ogma, will you tell Jarvil, please, to ask for my soldiers to come this afternoon, as soon as it begins to get cool? I'm going to the temple to see the chief priest, tell them.'

Maia took this committal decision as unreflectingly as she had plunged into the Valderra. It was like mucking out the cows: the thing had got to be done and that was all there was to it. The thought that she could still desist, and the implication of what she was going to do—these notions crossed her mind only momentarily, to be brushed aside. How closely Fornis might be in the chief priest's confidence was something that it hardly occurred to her to consider, just as on the river bank she had given herself no time to think.

Having arrived at the temple precinct and been deferentially handed down from her jekzha by Brero, one of her soldiers, she climbed the broad steps to the portico watched by a small crowd, some of whom had followed her from the Caravan Market. The Tamarrik water-clock was just upon four hours after noon and even as she alighted, the purple-lacquered kynat released its silver ball to roll down the spiral and be caught in his cup by the divine child. Once she would have stopped to watch. Nowadays her public status required an air of more detachment and composure. Without turning her head, she passed between the two centre columns and, as the acolyte seated at the bronze doors rose and bowed, gave him her most gracious smile (he was no eunuch, she sensed) and asked to see the chief priest.

Nothing could have been more courteous than her reception. A senior priest escorted her up a staircase to a pleasant, cool room on the south side of the temple, sent a slave for serrardoes, thrilsa and Yeldashay, and sat down to converse with her until the chief priest should appear. Maia, who not unnaturally felt herself to have gained a good deal in poise and self-confidence since the days of Sencho, replied to him with what she hoped was restraint and assurance about her own health, the water-ways of Suba, the iniquities of the Chalcon rebels and the certainty of their early defeat by Elvair-ka-Virrion. At length the bead curtains at the doorway clashed lightly (reminding her on the instant of Terebinthia: she nearly found herself springing to her feet) and the chief priest entered, followed by an attendant, who remained standing by the door. The other priest bowed and left them.

Apart from Durakkon, this was Maia's first encounter, since her return, with any leading representative of the Leopard régime. There was no least trace of hostility, but nevertheless she began almost at once to sense that certain atmosphere of which Nennaunir had warned her. Last year she had been just a little girl for the basting, no one's enemy, a nobody whom there was no reason to harm. Now, the chief priest—who had last seen her trembling, dishevelled and filthy from days of imprisonment—was plainly wondering, behind his careful air of being honoured by a visit from the city's beautiful heroine, what she wanted from him and what her real

558

purpose might be. Quite early on in the conversation he contrived to stress the salutary and beneficial detachment of the temple from imperial politics and the value to the city of a priestly order of integrity which served Cran first and the secular rulers second. Maia could not help wondering whether, if he really supposed that she had wanted to sound out his view about herself as a possible successor to the Sacred Queen, she would have been quite such a fool as to come and do it face-to-face in a formal interview of this kind.

'My Guardian,' she said, using the correct and formal style of address to the chief priest by ordinary citizens, 'it's only a small matter I've come to ask you about. You'll no doubt remember the black girl, Occula, who was brought here the day before I came myself to be—er—prepared for my journey to Suba. You know, I expect, that she and I were close friends: we were in the High Counsellor's household together. Now that I've recovered my health, naturally I want to take up with my friends again. May I ask you whether Occula's still here in the temple, and if not, where she is?'

'Well,' he replied slowly. 'Well—what do you think yourself—don't you think—while these difficult times last—that's something of a matter— isn't it—which ought to remain, perhaps, between the temple and the Lord General? As you know, the girl—your companion, you tell me—was involved in the murder of the High Counsellor, wasn't she?'

'It's not for me to contradict you, my Guardian, but I reckon otherwise. In any case, I beg you to take pity on my anxiety about a dear friend to whom I owe more 'n what I can say. At least please tell me whether you positively know her to be dead—that is, whether she died here in the temple during the time I was gone from the city.'

He made no reply, only looking down at the table, patting it with his fingers in a gentle rhythm.

'If she is dead, my Guardian, surely it can do no possible harm to tell me? It seems—well, a small thing to ask, like.'

He evidently thought so, too. She could discern in him a certain feeling of anti-climax. This public idol and acclaimed beauty, this new, unassessed and still uncommitted personality in the upper city's endless currents of power-manoeuvre, had sought him out for a talk. Yet now it transpired that apparently all she wanted to know was the whereabouts of a black concubine.

For an instant she saw him almost imperceptibly shake his head in perplexity. Then he looked up, smiling.

'If I positively knew her to be dead, Serrelinda, I would tell you as much: I hope that helps you.'

'Then she is not?'

'I'm afraid I can't tell you any more.'

'Where is she? Is she——?' But here she checked herself. She dared not even imply that she knew about Fornis.

He smiled again and spread his hands, as though embarrassed by a question that she should really have known better than to ask.

She covered her lapse, speaking of other things, and a few minutes later thanked him and took her leave, the chief priest courteously wishing her all prosperity and summoning yet another priest to escort her from the temple.

'One more—oh, very trifling thing, my Guardian,' she said.

He turned at the door.

'There is a young man here, serving a sentence. His name is Sednil. He used to be a friend of someone—well, of someone I know.'

He smiled patiently. 'I believe—I can't really be certain—that we have three or four men here—of that kind. My officer of the household would know, of course, and I'm sure he'd be very ready to talk with you. It would—er—be most pleasant for him, I'm sure.'

He was gone, leaving her, thus put out of countenance, to cover her embarrassment by conversing with the priest. They returned along the corridors and down the staircase.

Arrived in the principal interior court below, where numerous suppliants, priests and servants were coming and going about their business, she had just contrived some remark about the swallows flitting in and out under the cornice when suddenly she caught sight of Sednil emerging—in a furtive manner, or so it seemed—from a doorway opposite. He was stooping under a great pannier strapped to his back, which appeared to be full of masons' rubble or something of the sort. It was, in fact, a few moments before she recognized him, but in those moments he had nevertheless already attracted her attention by reason of being easily the dirtiest and most wretched-looking person in the whole court. Indeed, it was rather startling to come upon such an object even casually present in a beautiful and imposing place designed and used expressly to confer credit on the city.

Maia, inclining graciously towards the priest as an indication of thanks and farewell, walked swiftly across the court and touched Sednil on the shoulder. Starting and jerking up his head, he plainly did not remember her for a moment. Then, uncertainly, and plainly not in the least knowing what he might have to expect, he said, 'Maia! Well—of course I'd heard——' but on the instant broke off, turning away. She had the impression that if it had not been for the heavy basket he would have shrugged his shoulders.

'Sednil, listen; I want to help you——'

'O Cran!' he said. 'Don't *you* start, too——'

'I mean it—'

'—Like Nan and all the rest. Why can't you let me alone?' Yet he made no further move to go.

As she hesitated he said, 'I can't stop about here. You'll get me into—'

'Sednil, I must know; where's Occula? Tell me, quickly. Is she still here or not?'

'What's it to you?'

'Oh, Sednil! You want money? Aren't I your friend—'

He gave a quick, bitter laugh and seemed about to reply, but she cut him short.

'At least tell me if you know she's dead. Please!'

'I don't know she's dead.'

'Then do you know she's alive?'

As though finally maddened by her insistence—for she had him by the arm, and under the weight of the basket he could not break free—he burst out, 'She was taken away by the queen's woman—the Palteshi woman. Now will you—'

'When? The same day as I was brought here?'

'No, the day after: the chief priest didn't want—'

At this moment a burly, scowling man in a sacking apron came hurrying out of the doorway near which they were standing, caught sight of Sednil and immediately dealt him a swinging buffet on the side of the head.

'What the hell d'you think you're doing? You know damned well you're not supposed to carry that stuff across this court, don't you? You lot go round the back, where you can't be seen. Just because that's heavy—next time I'll have you whipped—'

Maia, who had never been in a position of authority in her life, had in the first instant felt more cowed and caught in the wrong than Sednil, who looked about as startled as an ox by the all-too-familiar blows of its peasant master. Now, however, like someone suddenly remembering that she has unaccustomed money in her purse and therefore need no longer stand hungry outside the cookshop, she sprang into action. Looking the overseer—or whatever he was—straight in the eye, she said firmly, 'It was me as called the man: I wanted to speak to him.'

The overseer looked at her in surprise. The intervention of a priest or a noble being within his comprehension, he would have known his proper response, but girls who looked like demi-goddesses, clad in authority and diamonds, had not come his way before. After a few seconds he opened his mouth to reply, but had got no further than 'Säiyett—' when Maia stayed him with an uplifted hand. 'Please don't trouble yourself further; I shan't keep him a moment. You may leave us now.'

She turned back to Sednil. 'Then you think she's still with the queen?'

'Yes. Without she's dead she is.'

There was a cough at her elbow: she turned to see the priest who had accompanied her down the staircase.

'Er—säiyett—I wonder whether I may perhaps—'

'Well,' said Maia to Sednil, 'that's what Nennaunir asked me to tell you. And to give you this, with her love.'

Thereupon, very deliberately and taking her time, she took out a hundred-meld piece, pressed it into Sednil's hand, put her arms round his neck, kissed both his dirty cheeks and then walked slowly out of the temple.

'Oh, it makes me that *wild*!' she exclaimed to her soldier, Brero: but when he asked her what, she merely replied 'Don't matter,' and said no more.

It was during this return journey from the temple that she encountered Selperron and received his gift of flowers. When he first stopped her jekzha she thought, for a split second, that he was an assassin. She recovered herself instantly, but did not altogether forget the moment.

: 56 :

A SECRET VISIT

Lying awake before the birds began to sing, listening to the tiny sounds of darkness and feeling the now-familiar throbbing along her half-healed thigh, Maia considered her next step. Obviously, the chief priest must by now have learned that she had spoken with Sednil and what about. No doubt they had had the hundred meld off him too: that would not surprise her in the least.

The unnatural complexity and imponderable danger of her situation enraged as much as it frightened her. Why should she be frustrated in a matter which was entirely innocent and natural? Surely to Cran it ought to be understandable—acceptable at face value—that she should want to know the whereabouts of her greatest friend? Yet evidently it was not; and she had now given the suspicious priests something to fasten on and wonder about. Why exactly might the Tonildan girl be so anxious to get in touch with Sencho's black concubine? Simply because she had been fond of her—well, that might perhaps be all there was to it, and then again it might not. Maia, they knew, had herself spent a night with the queen— after which the queen had immediately sent for Occula. She had no idea of the relations between Fornis and the chief priest. To what extent did they confide in each other? Were they united in distrust of Kembri, or did they fear each other? Did the chief priest know anything about Fornis's private pleasures? Would he tell Fornis that she had been enquiring about Occula? If so, what would Fornis do? These inconclusive reflections, in the half-darkness and solitude before dawn, were enough to frighten any girl.

But if she gave up searching for Occula, what self-respect could she have left? It was not only that she herself needed Occula and could not bear the thought of continuing her life without at least finding out what had happened to her. Occula, if she was still alive, might quite possibly stand in need of her help. At the very least she had a duty to the gods and to all the sacred obligations of friendship to discover whether Occula was still alive. But how?

Suddenly there came into her head the recollection of Zuno, bowing at the doorway of the queen's supper-room and finding himself confronted by the girl whom he had compelled to trudge seven miles from Naksh in the heat of the day. Zuno owed his present position to Occula, and if anyone in all Bekla had reason to know that the two of them were bosom friends, it was surely he. 'You never know when he might not be able to do us a bit of good,' Occula had said. It was like one of old Drigga's tales, she thought. All those weeks ago, in Sencho's house, Occula had, in effect, given her a key to keep and told her that one day she would come upon the door it would open. But Occula—why, yes, *just* like a tale!—had had no idea that it would turn out to be a door behind which she herself was imprisoned.

Maia, like virtually everyone in the Beklan Empire, thought naturally and unconsciously of the world as a kind of divine machine (rather like the Tamarrik Gate) working in conformity with fixed, recurring accordances, correlations and principles. Some of these were, of course, self-evident—as that unusually large flocks of crows presaged ill-fortune, or that conception was more likely when love was made under the full moon. Others, however, were riddling and enigmatic, their homeopathic connections hard to discern; in some cases impossible without personal revelation through the favour of a god. In the old tales—and they, of course, were plainly the revealed truth of the gods, or why else would they have held good age after age?—no deed or occurrence, however apparently casual or improbable of consequence, was without its unforeseen fruition, good or bad. These, old Drigga had explained, were often ironic jokes on the part of the gods at the expense of mortals who had not the common sense or humility to keep their eyes and ears open to divine tidings. Here, obviously, was a clear instance. The real reason why Occula had been prompted to get Zuno his place was that the gods had known that one day the deed would yield advantage. It followed that Occula must still be alive and that she, Maia, was fated to find her. Greatly comforted by her intelligent arrival at this perception, Maia fell asleep again; and later that morning, after breakfast and a bath, sent Jarvil down to the lower city with a message to the slave-dealer Lalloc that she wished to see him on business as soon as possible. Whether or not Lalloc was in the city she had no idea. For all she knew, he might be anywhere from Herl to Kabin, buying stock or engaging fresh agents. Logically, however—that was, in accordance with the supernatural design perceived by her—he was bound to be on hand; and so it proved. The slave-dealer, dressed and be-jewelled in the florid style she remembered but now, many eventful months later, saw plainly (as she had not before) to be so tawdry and garish as to proclaim him the cheapest of imitation Leopards, presented himself in her parlour early that evening.

Maia, simply dressed in a grey Yeldashay metlan with crimson sandals and a gold chain at her neck, received him smilingly and with a careful avoidance of any condescension or superiority. The evening being warm and cloudless, she took him out to sit on the miniature terrace overlooking the Barb, where Ogma brought sweet wine, honey cakes and the little, sticky jellies called *prions*, which came up from Ikat. She had reckoned this sort of thing would probably be to Lalloc's taste and so it evidently proved, for he partook copiously, while giving every sign of feeling that much of the credit for her new standing was attributable to himself.

'Well,' he said, after admiring the house and enquiring about her health in a manner so superficial and perfunctory that from any person of breeding it would have been insulting, 'so you don't minding doing business, eh, with the man who once soll you?'

'Not in the least, U-Lalloc,' answered Maia. 'You've never done me any harm as I know of.'

'Well, well,' said Lalloc, rubbing his hands together so that the rings clicked on his fingers, 'I novver harm any of my girls, thot's it. Novver treat anyone bad. Where's the sense; 'cos you novver know where they going to fonnish up, eh? Now you fonnish up queen of Bekla and we're still good friends, isn't it?'

'I'm not the queen of Bekla, U-Lalloc,' said Maia quickly. 'I'll thank you to remember that, and not use that kind of talk where I'm concerned, either here or anywhere else. I don't reckon as Queen Fornis'd like it, do you?'

'No, no, of course, jost my joke,' replied the slave-dealer, putting his feet up on a stool and helping himself to another handful of prions. 'But oll the same, now you're big, important lady—most important ovver come from me, I toll you—'

Maia cut him short. 'U-Lalloc, I need another good, reliable girl in the house—someone strong, but young enough to be ready to do what Ogma tells her; and I need a man as can help the porter, too.'

'Ah, no trobble, säiyett. There's plonty coming in jost now, this time of year. Perhaps you like to comming down tomorrow, see as monny what you like. Or I bring one or two up here—whatever you like. How moch you want to spend, säiyett? Woll, I jost bring up the best, thot's it, eh?'

They talked on for a time, Maia half-serious and asking such questions as occurred to her; for after all, she might in all earnest enlarge her establishment—she could well afford it.

'Well, that's quite satisfactory, U-Lalloc,' she said at length, standing up and leaning over the balustrade. 'I'll think it over—what you've told me— and let you know. I'm obliged to you for coming up here so promptly. By the way, how's that young man of yours as brought me and my friend up from Hirdo last year? Is he still with you?'

It would be better, she had decided, not to reveal to Lalloc that she knew what had become of Zuno. The less that people—especially people like him—thought she knew about Fornis's household the better.

Lalloc began telling her effusively—again, one would have supposed that it reflected credit upon himself—about Zuno's advancement to the post of personal steward to the Sacred Queen, contriving to suggest that the position was that of a state official rather than a servant. Having let him talk on for a time she said, 'Well, I'm sorry he's left your service, U-Lalloc, 'cause now things are going so well with me, I'd have liked to meet him again. He was—' it cost her an effort, but she got it out—'he was good to us on the way up to Bekla, and I'd have liked to give him a little token of esteem.'

'Well, that's kind of dofficult, säiyett,' replied Lalloc. 'The Sacred Queen—she keep her personal household very private, yoss, yoss.'

'Still, I suppose you might sometimes have occasion to go there, U-Lalloc, on business—'

'Ollways when I'm going it's at night, säiyett—'

Yes, thought Maia, with those poor little boys, I'll bet. I wonder how many she's got through in seven years? She said casually, 'Well, I s'pose at that rate you can go there without anyone being all that much surprised to see you. So I could just go along with you and see Zuno, couldn't I? No one else need know it's me, of course, 'ceptin' Zuno himself.'

Before he could answer she went on, 'I'll have to leave you now, U-Lalloc, just for a minute or two: I'll be back directly. While I'm gone you can be having a look at this pretty little carved box. You'll appreciate the workmanship. It's from Sarkid, or so I was told.'

She had put eight hundred meld in the box. Probably twice as much as she need have, she thought irritably, taking care to make plenty of noise over going upstairs and calling to Ogma. But hadn't Occula herself once advised, 'Always bribe too much, banzi: the gaols are full of people who've offered too little.'

The moment she came back to the terrace and before he could speak, she said 'Please keep the box, U-Lalloc, as a gift from me. As to the other matter we were talking about, I'll meet you on the shore—just down there, see?—tomorrow night, about an hour after sunset. No one will be able to recognize me, don't worry. I'm sorry I can't stay any longer now.' And with this, turning away, she called, 'Ogma, will you please show U-Lalloc to the gate and tell Jarvil to get him a jekzha?'

Cran and Airtha! she thought; what have I done? The chief priest knows I've been questioning Sednil; and now this man can say I bribed him to get into the queen's house and see Zuno. What if it all gets back to the queen? Ah, no, but it's fated, else the gods wouldn't have put Zuno there in the first place. Come to think of it, it'd probably be a deal more dangerous to *disregard* a favour like that from the gods.

There was no moon and only the lightest of breezes stirred the surface of the Barb lapping against its grassy banks in the dark. The night was so still that Maia, pacing back and forth among the flowering shrubs and clumps of lilies, could hear the faint plashing of the Monju outfall, almost a furlong away beyond the trees. Already—or so it seemed—she had been waiting much longer than she had expected. Perhaps something had happened to prevent the slave-dealer from keeping their appointment? Well, but in that case would he not at least have let Ogma know as much?

The stars were clear, yet Maia, in the solitude, was suddenly overcome by foreboding and dread. Not far away shone the lamps of other houses; the houses of the wealthy, the powerful—yes, and the cunning and ruthless. There came back to her the memory of how once, when she was a little girl delirious with fever, she had lain and watched the walls of the hut ripple, melt and dissolve into smiles—expanses of horrible, silent smiles, merging and reopening until she could bear it no longer and started up in screaming terror. 'The heroine of the empire' Durakkon had called her, himself placing round her neck those diamonds, worth more than all the money her father and mother had ever made in their lives. And the retinue of courtiers and officers attending him—oh, how they had smiled and smiled!

Zenka, she thought; Zenka who had made her laugh with delight like a child at a fair, who had taken her with him—the only man who ever had—into a world of joyous, mutual understanding, his love-making the natural expression of his feeling, his delight in her company and his longing to please and protect her. What would she not give to have him standing beside her now and to feel his arm round her waist? O Lespa! she thought, if only I knew Occula was safe, I'd set out barefoot for the Valderra tomorrow and find him, wherever he is. And Nasada—if only I could just find that good old, straight-talking Nasada, he'd know what to do! Ah, to have to go all the way to the Suban marshes to find a man you can trust to tell you the truth!

She heard the sound of a cough, and turned quickly to recognize the bulky outline of the slave-dealer in the dark.

'U-Lalloc?'

'Oh, yoss, little säiyett, you think I'm not comming? No, I wouldn't let onnything going wrong, you don't hov to worry!'

His voice held a kind of jocular, conspiratorial familiarity which she found unpleasant. This was the kind of company, she thought bitterly, which she was now compelled to seek, simply to gain the innocent end of finding her Occula. She wondered how often he arranged clandestine matters of one kind or another in return for money. What grimy tunnel was this along which she was being obliged to creep towards her friend; and to what extent had she put herself in this man's power? Well, either I'll soon have an old head on young shoulders, she thought, or else no head at all.

She still had little idea whereabouts, among the lawns and gardens of the upper city, the Sacred Queen's house might lie. She had last come to it in a state of sleepless exhaustion, and when leaving next day had been in no mood to look about her. She was surprised, therefore, after they had been walking for what seemed less than a quarter of an hour—during which they had met very few passers-by—when the slave-dealer, stopping at the corner of a walled lane, turned to her.

'You put this cloak on now—pull up the hood, yoss, thot's right. You're a girl I'm bringing to soll—no one to see, I'm saying only Zuno ask I bring you for the queen, all right? Then later you're not there, the rest jost think you don't suit, thot's it.'

After a minute or two, as she walked on beside him up the lane, he suddenly said, 'Genshed; this man in Puhra; he treat you bad?'

Maia stiffened. To her the night when she had cowered from Genshed's knife, to be rescued by Occula in the nick of time, was like something from a vanished world—a world which, thankfully, she would never know again. She had no least wish to make Lalloc a confidant of that memory.

The slave-dealer, however, apparently had his own reasons for persisting. 'Occula say he treat you bad. She toll Zuno now she's good friends with the queen, she's gotting him killed.'

'So she *is* alive? She's *alive*? U-Lalloc, Occula's alive? That's what you're saying? She's alive?'

'Well, you toll her I sond Genshed away. I don't like what he did to you, it's right against all the rules. Still, I don't like he's killed, because thot maybe makes it harder gotting other men for the work, you know? But you toll her he's gone all right: he's gone so he don't be gotting killed.'

She plucked his sleeve. 'So she *is* alive?'

But now they were coming under an arch at the far end of the lane, into a courtyard surrounded by doorways and lit by three or four smoky torches stuck in brackets round the walls. A rotten-sweet smell of garbage, pebbly cobbles underfoot, a distant clatter of dishes, a puff of steam from an open window, a woman's sudden, impatient cry broken short. Yes, this must be their destination all right; the back-quarters of a wealthy house; and little enough it seemed to have in common with the palace to which Ashaktis had brought her that morning in early spring.

Lalloc stopped again. 'Now; you jost simple country girl. You don't know onnything what's hoppening. You put the hood round your face, look down at the ground, thot's right.'

He went over to one of the doors and knocked. She followed, eyes on the ground. The grinding of a key in the lock, the rattle of a bolt. 'You toll Zuno I come like he's saying. Confidential business.'

Still looking down, she let herself be led through the door, up three or four steps and into a small, stone-floored room smelling of oil, corn and sacking. They waited in silence, and she could once more hear from a distance the sounds of the kitchen and scullery. Then the door opened and Zuno's voice said, 'U-Lalloc! A most pleasant—ah—surprise. I don't remember that we had any arrangement tonight, but if I can be of any help to you, sir—'

Overcome by a sudden determination to get on with it and be damned, Maia flung back the hood and raised her head to face Zuno. Elegant as ever, not a hair out of place, his livery gleaming in the lamplight, he looked at her blankly for a moment before his eyes widened with surprise.

'Maia!'

She lost no time. 'Zuno, I've come to see Occula. I've come because she's my dearest friend and for no other reason at all. Will you help me?'

She had expected him to prevaricate, to demur, perhaps to need bribing, but to her surprise he showed no least hesitation.

'What you're asking is dangerous, not only for you and Occula but for me too. But I will do it. Fortunately the queen is at Lord Durakkon's tonight. Half an hour, säiyett, and no more, you understand? Come with me.'

Hooded once more, she followed him through the door, up a flight of stairs, along a corridor, up another flight. Suddenly she knew where they were. This was the upper gallery where she had walked with Fornis, had taken her in her arms and kissed her. And this—ah, this was the door of the very room in which she had woken and whence Ashaktis had taken her to the bath.

They entered. The room was unchanged, quiet and luxurious, its spacious length dim in the lamplight. A moth which had flown into one of the lamps lay struggling and crawling on the floor.

Occula, dressed in a long, dark-red robe embroidered with gold flowers, was lying on the bed. Her eyes were closed, their silvered lids, which matched the lacquer on her finger- and toe-nails, glittering faintly in the soft light. As Zuno tapped gently on the tiles with his staff she opened her eyes, sat up quickly and looked round at them.

'Banzi!'

Falling on her knees beside the bed, Maia flung her arms round Occula and pressed her face against her shoulder. For long moments she was aware only of Occula's flesh against her cheek; the singular, just-perceptibly granular quality, as of some fine fabric; the remembered smell, sharp and light, like clean coal. As though she were an infant or an animal, these sensations filled her entirely, mindlessly; self-sufficient, comforting and reassuring. Occula, too, was clearly beyond speaking, only rocking her gently to and fro and uttering soft, wordless murmurs of endearment. When at length they released each other, Zuno had gone and the door was closed.

'Is he—he won't—you trust him?' faltered Maia, her fear and anxiety returning once more, inescapable as flies.

Occula only nodded abstractedly, holding her at arm's length by the shoulders and looking at her as though hardly believing in her real presence. Then, with a quick smile, she said 'Doan' worry; he's a better lad than you might suppose, banzi. We hold each other up. Oh, Kantza-Merada be thanked for the sight of you! I tried to send you a message—oh, weeks ago. Did you ever get it?'

Maia shook her head.

'Bastards!' said Occula. 'Anyway, you're here now. Come on, take that cloak off; lie down and make yourself comfortable. Cran and Airtha, look at your thigh! What was that? The Valderra?'

'Ah.'

'Tell me everythin': I've only heard what they've all been sayin'. I doan' even know how you got into Suba. I suppose Kembri fixed it somehow, did he? But then how the hell did you—'

Maia interrupted her. 'No, no, all that'll have to wait, darling. There's so little time. You don't have to worry about me: *I'm* the one as has to worry 'bout *you*. Are you safe here, Occula? Only I know I'm the one as got you here: I spoke to the queen, see, 'cos I knew I had to get you out of the temple somehow. Only I've been wondering ever since—'

She stopped, for Occula was staring at her open-mouthed.

'So it was *you*, banzi! *You* did it! The rotten bitch, why didn' she ever tell me! And why to Cran didn' I ever think of it for myself? Oh, my precious banzi—'

Only once or twice before had Maia seen her so much softened, so stripped by emotion of her normal air of tough self-possession.

'But how did you get the chance, banzi! Who did you speak to?'

Maia told her of her first sight of Fornis on the night of the murder, of the queen's caprice which had briefly taken her out of Kembri's hands, and of what had followed.

'So you didn' fancy it?' asked the black girl, when she had finished.

'No, I *didn't*,' answered Maia. 'Nor I couldn't do it, neither—what she wanted. She soon enough got that all right.'

'I doan' blame you,' said her friend. Suddenly she threw back her head and laughed like the old, undauntable Occula, the canny girl on the way up. 'But you reckoned I *could*, did you?'

Maia hesitated, then laughed too. 'Well, I s'pose I reckoned you was a bit more professional, like.'

For a moment Occula ground her teeth and her lip curled. 'Oh, banzi, how right you were! Yes, I can do it all right. I give every bastin' satisfaction! This year's great success, you might say. My only problem is not to get a little too enthusiastic, you know? That'd be one way to finish my dirty work, wouldn' it? The most expensive way, and you might say what's expense, when it's for the peace of Zai's soul and the honour of our family? But banzi, I mean to get what I want cheaper than that, believe you me. I'm going to walk up out of the underworld on my two feet, like Kantza-Merada, you wait and see if I doan'.'

As Maia, only half-comprehending, looked into the familiar, dark, slightly bloodshot eyes under their silvered lids, she added, 'Of course you know everythin' now, doan' you? Pretty well everythin', anyway.'

'You mean, what you did—that night—Sencho—'

'Of course.'

'Yes, I think so. But Occula, was it planned—well, right from the start? From the Lily Pool?'

'Never you mind about the Lily Pool, banzi. That's neither here nor there. Less you know, less risk you run, right?'

'But you couldn't have known we were going to be sold to Sencho—'

'No, I didn',' replied Occula. 'Unless there's somethin' I doan' know about, that was just a bit of luck. Lalloc's no heldro, you can be sure of that: he sold us to Sencho in the way of business. Still—' she grinned—'it wasn' entirely unlikely, was it? Couple of nice girls like us, and old Piggy's well-known tastes.'

'But you knew about Zirek, the pedlar?'

'Not a thing, until he started talkin' about Cat Colonna. But after that, of course, and once word had got back where we'd landed up, banzi—'

'Got back? To whom?'

'Why, to Santil, of course.'

Maia, lying in her friend's arms, was silent, reflecting. A great many things were becoming clear in retrospect. At last she said, 'So it *was* Meris with Zirek that day, by the Peacock Gate.'

She felt Occula nod, and went on, 'Where's the two of them got to now, then?'

'I doan' know,' said the black girl grimly. 'I only hope they're better off than I am, that's all. But I've got another job to do, banzi, you see, before Zai's soul'll be at peace. Why d'you think I stayed in the boat when I could have bunked with them? I've not finished yet—not finished the goddess's work.'

The next instant she had burst out laughing, rolling over on her back and tugging at Maia's dress. 'Come on, sweetheart, let's have a look at you! That Ashaktis woman told me you'd been ripped from head to foot in the Valderra. Were you?' She pulled the dress over Maia's head, followed by her shift. 'Oh, Shakkarn, not a bit of it! Just one or two nice, honourable scars, enough to make a few jolly lads want to kiss 'em better, eh? That's my banzi! What you goin' to be, now you're back? Remember what we used to say at old Piggy's—thousand meld a bounce?'

'I know: but somehow I just don't fancy it, Occula. Anyway I don't need money—not at the moment, any road.'

'Doan' talk so wet-headed, banzi. A girl can always do with twice the money she's got: firs' law of the universe. Think of your old age.'

'Well, 'tain't just exactly that—' Maia, half-way through dressing again, hesitated. She longed to pour out to Occula the whole story of Suba, to tell her of Zen-Kurel and ask her advice. But was there time? Soon Zuno would return: soon she must be gone.

'No, why the hell should you?' said Occula unexpectedly. 'You saved the city, didn' you? Why not stick to your dancin'—for a bit, anyway? You can well afford to.'

'But Occula, dearest, how can *you* be so pleased that I saved the city? If only Karnat had got here—'

'Karnat, banzi? No, 'course we doan' want Karnat takin' Bekla. *Santil's* goin' to take Bekla—Santil and no one else.'

'But what's it to you either way? You're not Beklan.'

'No, no. But you know me, banzi; girl on the make—always was. Karnat—I doan' know Karnat an' he doesn' know me. But Santil—I'm one of his most successful agents, aren' I? If only I'm still alive when Santil takes Bekla, he might give me a nice, big piece of thrilsa for helpin' him, doan' you think? A bigger piece than ever Karnat would. Or a pottery cat, even. Pottery cat? Oh, Cran, I almost forgot! Banzi, can you do somethin'; without fail? I was goin' to try and do it some other way, but now you're here it seems providential. Tell me, d'you often go into the lower city?'

'No, not often, but I can do.'

'Do you remember the old woman in the sweet-shop, that day you were with Eud-Ecachlon? Well, go down there and tell her to clear out; now, at once! Tell her *I* said to get out like shit from a goose, right? This last lot of arrests in Tonilda—oh, never mind. But you *must* do it tomorrow, banzi! Promise me!'

'But the people, Occula! They always crowd me so. Couldn't I send Ogma? She's with me in my house now, you know.'

'Ogma's not the girl to let in on a thing like this: it wouldn' be safe. But if it's not done before this time tomorrow, it'll be too late. It was only the purest stroke of luck I found out myself. Fornis doesn' always keep her mouth shut, thank Cran: 'specially when she's enjoyin' the prospect of a little cruelty. It's not just *her* life—the old woman's, I mean—it's a hell of a lot of other people's, too, believe me.'

'I'll do it, darling,' said Maia.

There was a tap at the door and Zuno returned.

'Precious banzi,' said Occula, embracing her, 'come again if you can— it's like a drink of water in the desert—but be very careful. Zuno'll let you know when it's safe—' she turned to him—'woan' you?'

'Yes, I will,' he said. 'But now she must go, and quickly too. The queen's due back any minute.'

They reached the foot of the stairs—Maia once more wrapped in the hooded cloak—to find Lalloc chatting with a grey-haired, elderly woman in the stone-floored storeroom.

'You may take this—ah—young woman back with you, U-Lalloc,' said Zuno. 'I've talked with her, and I'm afraid she wouldn't do for the Sacred Queen.'

'Some people don't know when they're lucky,' said the old woman drily. She stood up, selected a key from her belt and unlocked the door into the courtyard.

MILVUSHINA TRANSFORMED

In her delight and relief at being with Occula once more, the change in her friend had not at once struck Maia. It did so later, however—and forcefully—as she lay awake in her great, soft bed, hearing the scarcely-audible lapping of the Barb and the intermittent calling of plovers from the slopes of Crandor beyond. It was now, in darkness and solitude, that she realized that, more than the warnings of Sessendris and Nennaunir, more than the urbane dissimulation of the chief priest, Occula's air of strain and urgency, of having little time to spare in a taut conflict against odds, had stirred in herself a true sense of impending danger. If Occula was afraid, then indeed there must be something to be afraid of. Maia found herself recalling the mysterious, hypnotic ascendancy which the black girl had exercised over Sencho during the last weeks of his life, at one and the same time inducing apathy and soothing petulance, bringing him step by step to a state of dependency on herself in which he had all but connived at his own death. She recalled, too, with an understanding denied to her then, what it had cost Occula spiritually to exert this influence, to exploit Sencho's cunning, vicious temperament so subtly that he had indulged himself in her ministrations without once coming to suspect what awaited him. She remembered the night when, for all the world like some highly-strung hinnarist driven to desperation by an intricate passage, Occula had given way to hysteria in the belief that she had lost her power to prevail upon the High Counsellor and incline him to her will.

How much more discerning and deadly an antagonist must be the Sacred Queen! And if Occula was up to the hilt in nothing less than the planned overthrow of the Leopard régime by the heldril, then she, Maia, must even now be standing on the lip of the same abyss. She had supposed—the kindly Sendekar had assured her—that she was returning to fame and fortune, the darling of the city, of all girls in the empire the most to be envied. To the recent warnings of her friends her reply had been, in effect, that she would take good care to sing small and keep out of harm's way. Yet now, at Occula's behest, she had promised to take a step—if only a small one—which, if ever it were to come to light, would condemn her outright as an agent of Santil-kè-Erketlis.

It was all very well for Occula to stress the vital importance of warning the old woman at once. Occula had never seen for herself the sort of thing that happened when Maia went into the lower city. And if, following her visit, the old woman and her son immediately fled, was not some conclusion sure to be drawn? She fell asleep at last resolved upon only one thing. Having given her word to Occula, she would not fail her.

Next morning, as is often the way, the simplest and most practical course entered her head at once. She would go down to the lower city incognito. She need not take her own jekzha; she could travel veiled—many older women did, especially in the dusty streets of summer—while to the guards at the Peacock Gate it would, surely, seem quite natural if she were to explain that she had grown weary of the crowds pressing about her and wished for once to be able to visit a friend in peace and quiet.

After breakfast she was already beginning her preparations—for the thing would be best over and done as quickly as possible—when she heard the unknown voice of some servant talking to Jarvil at the door. A minute later Ogma came hobbling up the stairs at her best speed, beginning to speak even before she was in the room.

'Oh, Miss Maia, whatever do you think? It's Miss Milvushina—oh, she's down below this minute, miss, and looking so beautiful, oh, you'd never think it was the same girl as was always crying her eyes out at the High Counsellor's, such a change for the better, oh, do you remember, Miss Maia—'

'Quiet, Ogma!' said Maia sharply. 'She'll hear you. Is she alone?'

'Yes, miss. Only just her maid came with her. And you'd never believe—'

'Then take her in some wine and nuts and tell her I'll be down directly. Then please come back and help me finish dressing. Show the maid into the kitchen.'

And what might this portend? she wondered. To be sure, she and Milvushina had never quarrelled and she had often done her best—inadequate as she had always felt it—to comfort the Chalcon girl in a misery and loss so terrible as to lie beyond normal comprehension. Yet for all that, she now realized, her present surprise arose because she had never expected Milvushina to seek her out or particularly want to see her again. They had had little or nothing in common and Milvushina, on account partly of her youthful immaturity and partly of the lonely wretchedness which had made her desperate to hold on to her own identity, had never been very successful in concealing her innate sense of superiority to the Tonildan peasant lass.

And then again, Maia had once or twice been an involuntary witness of obscene humiliations inflicted by Sencho on the aristocratic Milvushina—humiliations best forgotten. No, indeed, what possible reason had Milvushina to want to renew acquaintance with herself? Well, presumably she was about to discover. She had better put on her best front, go downstairs and see.

Wearing her diamonds and a robe of dark-blue silk with a train of jet beads trailing at the hem, Maia entered her parlour to find Milvushina no less splendidly turned out. Her green dress of finely-knitted wool was shot with silver threads which matched the chain binding her black hair, while round her neck was a collar of emeralds with a single ruby in the centre. Her big, dark eyes were emphasized at the outer edges with touches of a lighter green, and at her shoulder was a gold, enamelled brooch in the form of a crouching leopard. Immediately upon Maia's entry she sprang up, smiling and stretching out open arms.

Maia's first impression was the same as Ogma's. This was a transformed Milvushina; so much so that for one confused instant she actually wondered whether it could really be the same girl—a measure of the difference which self-respect and happiness (or the lack of them) can make to almost any human face and demeanour. The change lay principally in Milvushina's startling, hitherto-unseen air of animation, energy and alertness, compared with which her bearing at Sencho's was now revealed as uncharacteristic, a mere façade of taut moral courage, a keeping-up of appearances. Maia found herself thinking (her unaided imagination could not have run to it before) that this, no doubt, was the girl for whose hand Santil-kè-Erketlis had lost no time in making an offer; the girl who had not been seen since that morning in the rains when the Beklan soldiers had come down upon her father's house. She, Maia, would probably have to start making her acquaintance all over again—or something precious close to that, anyway.

While she was still upstairs, she had decided that she would be hanged if she was going to let Milvushina condescend to her or get under her skin. Now, however, with her own swift way of responding to the mood of the moment, she felt that she was going to have no need of such defensiveness. Milvushina might have the air of a princess and unconsciously effuse the authority of a baron's daughter, but nevertheless her present feelings towards Maia were evidently as warm as Maia felt her own becoming towards her.

She began, naturally, by praising Maia's heroism, saying that she had felt she could not rest content without coming to add her own thanks to those of the entire city. Yet she contrived to express this in words which to Maia—who ever since Rallur had been the recipient of so much praise—seemed not only spontaneous and sincere, but original too. When she had responded appropriately and they were beginning to talk of other things, something else struck Maia, inwardly, as extremely amusing; the more so as the joke was against herself. Although Milvushina's manner, which formerly had all-too-often seemed one of condescension and restraint in the presence of an inferior, was not essentially changed, it now appeared to her simply that of a lady by implication sharing with another lady a proper sense of their common superiority. Well, it's all according, I s'pose, thought Maia, with a wry admission to herself that as usual Occula had been right. Anyone's manner's just how it happens to strike someone else from where they're placed. She's changed all right, but I suppose I must have changed even more.

Not all the emeralds and silver in Bekla, however, could have quenched Maia's rustic curiosity or changed her conversational style to one of dignified restraint and elegant composure. Soon she was taking the lead in quizzing Milvushina about clothes and jewels, about her servants and what kind of hospitality she gave and received in the upper city. To all this Milvushina replied smilingly, cordially and without constraint. It was not long before the two girls (whose combined ages were less than thirty-four) had gone chattering upstairs to look through Maia's wardrobe.

After a while Milvushina, spreading across her lap a transparent, mauve robe embroidered with light and dark butterflies, which she had been admiring, sat down on the end of the bed and looked out across the Barb.

'This must sometimes remind you of Serrelind, I suppose,' she said. 'Do you ever miss Tonilda?'

'Precious little,' answered Maia. ''Twasn't as if we was exactly in clover, you know. To say the least,' she added.

Milvushina, looking up from the enormous eyes, nodded. 'I know: but has it ever struck you that at least what you remember's still there? I can understand you not wanting to go back—that wasn't really what I meant when I asked whether you ever missed it. At least it's still there, behind you, like the foot of a staircase—it still exists. Mine doesn't. It's vanished off the face of the earth.'

Maia, having considered briefly what reply to make to this rather unexpected remark, took refuge in tossing it back again.

'Does that make you miss it more, d'you think? Don't know as I'd much care if our old hut was gone—nor my mother neither, if you really want me to be honest. But then it's different for you, isn't it?' She sat down beside Milvushina and took her hand. 'I heard tell as—well, as there was those who wanted you to go back to Santil-kè-Erketlis; but you didn't want. Well, and I heard, too, that—well, that things wouldn't have been the same if you had. But suppose they *could* have been—' She stopped, and then resumed, 'Santil—that *was* what you wanted in the first place, was it? Before—before—you know?'

'Well, yes,' answered Milvushina. 'It was what my father wanted, you see, and it would have been a very honourable marriage, to a man who's still young and the foremost baron in Chalcon. But now I've done what you and Occula both did. Since everything's changed and can't be altered, I've made the best of it and changed myself too.'

'Are you all that much changed, then?' asked Maia. ''Course, we didn't know each other a year ago, but just strikes me as now you may have got back to more what you used to be, like.'

Two red-and-grey gaze-finches alighted on the window-sill and began pecking at the millet-seed which Maia had sprinkled. To her, feeding the birds was a luxury almost as pleasurable as hiring a hinnarist. Once, there would have been no millet to spare for the likes of her to be feeding to birds.

Milvushina's glance turned quickly towards the finches, then back to Maia with a smile.

'That night—you know—the night of—*his*—murder—there were two friends of my family up here for the festival.'

'Oh, ah,' said Maia. 'I 'member now; I met them in the gardens with Elvair-ka-Virrion; a brother and sister?'

'That's right. Seld-T'maa and his sister Varriah. Their parents used to be old friends of my father. Did you know that they came to—to the house that night, to see me?'

'Well, funny thing you should ask that, 'cos it so happens Elvair asked whether I thought Terebinthia would let them see you, and I said yes, I reckoned she would.'

'She did. They were actually with me—we were talking together—when news came of the murder. You can just imagine, can't you? The whole place was in utter confusion: Terebinthia went straight to the gardens. And that was when T'maa said he'd get me out of Bekla. He felt certain he could get me out through the Peacock Gate with himself and Varriah and we'd be off to his father's in northern Yelda.'

'Whatever went wrong, then?' asked Maia.

Milvushina laughed. 'I refused: or should I say I declined?'

Maia caught her breath. 'You never!'

'Well, you see, Elvair and I already understood each other. The night of Sarget's party—that night when you danced; oh, and weren't you good, Maia? I'll never forget it—we—well, we came to an understanding as early as that, really. And as things turned out, the day after the murder he simply came and took me away. Terebinthia—he bribed her an enormous amount to let me go: I was on the temple's inventory of the household, you see. But as it was, that very afternoon I was in Elvair's rooms at the Lord General's house. Terebinthia took the money and got out as quick as she could. I believe the temple are still trying to find out where she's gone.'

They both laughed, and Maia shook her head wonderingly. 'Well, there's a tale! Who'd ever have thought! When T'maa asked you, you weren't in two minds at all, then?'

'Not for a moment. You see, there wasn't anything for me to go back to. Oh, I don't mean I'd have been poor. I never really thought about that one way or the other. No, it's just that people in Chalcon don't think about things the way they do here. Never been there, have you?'

Maia smiled. 'No, but I've been in Suba. Reckon it can't be all that much different.'

'I'm a spoiled bargain, my dear. That's all they'd have seen in me, even though they'd have treated me kindly for my father's sake. Shop-soiled in Bekla.' She tossed her head and stamped her foot; at which the finches flew away. 'But not to Elvair. I'm not damaged goods to *him*. And he's all the world to *me*.'

This showed the free-and-easy Elvair-ka-Virrion in something of a new light, thought Maia: yet it sounded genuine enough—he might very well have fallen sincerely in love with this beautiful, high-born girl in her distress, and determined to save her from degradation and slavery. And for her sake he had gone the length of openly defying the temple authorities. Presumably he—or at any rate his father—could have afforded thirteen or fourteen thousand meld for Milvushina. But to have bought her would have been to accept the contention that she was legally a slave. Yes, and to have people saying, too, that his consort had once been a slave.

'So he really loves you?' she said. 'Well, I'm that glad! I am truly.'

'He's made life worth living again,' said Milvushina. 'That's what it comes to. Apart from everything else, he's given me standing and position here in Bekla, and I suppose I wouldn't be human not to like that.' She paused. 'It's all so strange, though.'

'Strange?' asked Maia. 'But you're a baron's daughter—?'

Milvushina laughed—the same happy sound which had so much startled Maia at Sarget's party.

'Bekla isn't Chalcon, dear. The kind of standing a Chalcon baron's daughter has is quite different from a Leopard's wife. I've had just as much to learn as ever you can have had, Maia, believe me.'

'D'you see much of the Lord General?' asked Maia.

'He's been very kind to me,' replied Milvushina. 'You know the Sacred Queen tried to make trouble about me and Elvair? She told Elvair to send me back to Chalcon, and when he refused she told Kembri to make me go. But Kembri wouldn't.' She picked up a carved onyx rabbit which one of Shend-Lador's friends had given to Maia, and began stroking it. 'He says I'm the luck of the empire!'

'Did he say that to Fornis?'

'I don't know,' said Milvushina. Then, suddenly, 'Maia, are you afraid of her?'

'Yes, I am,' said Maia, 'and I'll tell you straight, I wouldn't want anyone telling her *I'm* the luck of the empire, that I wouldn't.'

'Well, you are, aren't you? Oh, but Elvair wouldn't let anything happen to me! It's only that—oh, Maia, I do feel so frightened sometimes! I wish Elvair hadn't upset the chief priest and the Sacred Queen, even though I know it was for my honour. He told them straight out that I'd *never* been a slave—well, and that's true—and he wasn't going to pay a meld for me. But now, quite soon, he's got to go away, you know, to fight in Chalcon—'

'To fight Erketlis, isn't it? You don't mind that, then?'

'I only met Santil twice in my whole life,' answered Milvushina. 'And even then it wasn't the two of us alone. That's how things are done in Chalcon, you know. He was very charming, but, oh—it's not like Elvair. How could it be? When Elvair's made his name as a commander—as he surely will—and come back to Bekla, *then* I'll let myself feel safe and happy. I don't trust Fornis, Maia; not an inch. I have all my food tasted before I eat it. Do you?'

Before Maia could answer, Milvushina suddenly stood up, swaying on her feet, put her hands up to her face and took a few tottering steps across to the window.

'Oh, Maia! I'm so sorry, I think I'm going to be sick!'

She leaned over the sill, retching. Maia, thoroughly frightened by this sudden crisis following immediately upon her talk of the poisoning, jumped up and threw an arm round her shoulders.

'What can I do, dear? Shall I send for a doctor? Ogma! Ogma!' she called hysterically.

'No, no, it's all right, Maia,' answered Milvushina quickly. 'There's nothing wrong; don't worry. In fact the doctor says it's a good sign. Means everything's going on well.' She sat down again. 'It's all right. It's passed off.' She wiped her sweating forehead and looked up at Maia smiling, one hand on her belly.

Maia stared. 'You mean—Elvair's baby?'

Milvushina nodded happily. 'No one else's, that's for sure. If you'll stay with me I'll lie down for a little while and then I'd best be getting home.' She flung her arms round Maia's neck. 'Home! Yes, *really* home—something I thought I'd lost for ever! Oh, I'll make him *such* a home before I've done, you see if I don't!'

And now at last Maia did feel real envy, but not on account of Elvair-ka-Virrion. Why should she have her man, she thought, and not me mine? It was only for an instant. The next, she was once more mistress of herself and sat down beside the bed, holding Milvushina's hand and sending Ogma for cold water, a towel and some fresh fruit-juice.

'I'm so glad, dear,' she said. 'Just think—that night when Occula and me came back and found you alone—who'd ever have guessed it'd all turn out so well?'

: 58 :
A NEW SACRED QUEEN?

Durakkon was walking with Kembri and Elvair-ka-Virrion on the western ramparts—one place where they could be in the open air with no personal bodyguard and without fear of being overheard. The sun was setting, and below them, on their left, the Beklan plain stretched away fifty miles to the hills of Paltesh, now blackly outlined against a red evening sky. Here and there, in the hollows of its gentle undulations, villages showed as patches canopied with drifts of smoke in the windless air. From below came up the hum of the lower city, the countless, distant noises that comprised it merging into a general, evening greyness of sound, like reflections on a distant lake. A few hundred yards in front of them the Tower of Sel-Dolad rose high above the ramparts, the facets of its topmost balcony—a lofty bloom raised on a slender stem—catching the sunset light and momentarily gleaming here and there in their eyes as they strolled on, absorbed in talk. Each sentinel, as they passed, faced about from looking out over the plain and saluted, extending his right forearm across his chest.

'Well, I don't care,' said Durakkon, deliberately looking away from Kembri and letting his gaze rest on the distant, square bulk of the Gate of Lilies below and ahead. 'I'm glad the filthy brute's dead. How can it possibly have been in the public interest for a man like that to exercise power? Associating with him was too high a price to pay for anything he did for us. We're better off without him.'

'Oh, come, sir,' replied the Lord General. 'You must admit he was very successful in what he set out to do. He had a great flair for the work, you know. It's not just anyone who can succeed at that sort of work—picking the right men, knowing where to send them, being able to sift the information that comes in, tell what's important and what isn't and so on. We're going to have a job to replace him, I'm afraid. The great pity is that he kept nearly all he knew in his own head. After more than three months our intelligence is still going limping.'

'Well—' Durakkon gestured impatiently. 'Have you had any important information recently from the provinces?'

'The most important piece of news we've received,' replied Kembri, 'is that Karnat himself's gone back across the Zhairgen into Katria. Apparently he's got some trouble over in western Terekenalt which he thinks requires his personal attention. According to my information it's likely to keep him occupied for the rest of the summer. He's left troops in Suba, of course, but his personal departure means that there won't be any further attempts to cross the Valderra for the time being. That's all to the good. We can leave Sendekar to watch the Valderra, keep a regiment or two in Bekla in case of trouble elsewhere and use the rest against Santil-kè-Erketlis in Chalcon.'

'What do you mean—trouble elsewhere?' asked Durakkon. 'Why should there be any trouble elsewhere?'

'I'm not entirely happy about Urtah,' said Kembri. 'You'd have thought this last attempt of Karnat's would have taught them a lesson, wouldn't you—made them realize who their friends are? But according to the reports I'm getting, half of them are sorry Karnat didn't succeed. I don't know how Sendekar sees it, but I certainly wouldn't want to make an attack into Suba with the Urtans behind me in their present state of mind.'

'But the old High Baron—he's reliable enough, surely? He always has been.'

'Yes, sir. He wouldn't want rebellion and of course he's out to stop Urtah provoking us too far. But all the same, he signed the letter they've just sent us about Bayub-Otal. He and Eud-Ecachlon; both of them signed it.'

'What does it say?' asked Durakkon. (It should, he felt inwardly, have been sent to him personally.)

'It asks for the release of Bayub-Otal on their guarantee that he'll give no further trouble; or failing that, that we should spare his life while they come and talk to us about it.'

'It's quite understandable that the old High Baron should send a letter like that,' said Durakkon. 'Bayub-Otal's his son by the only woman he ever loved.'

'Oh, I know *that*,' replied Kembri, impatience and disrespect once more creeping into his tone, as it always did after a short time with Durakkon. 'But to ask that of us he must be going senile. Bayub-Otal's as guilty as he can be of deliberate, premeditated treason against Bekla. If we don't execute *him* we can never execute anyone again.'

'Then why haven't you executed him already?' asked Durakkon.

'Because I've stood the thing on its head to turn it to our advantage,' answered Kembri. 'I've had a reply prepared for you to sign, sir, which says that we'll spare his life for the moment—keeping him in Dari-Paltesh, of course—just as long as we can feel sure of the loyalty of Urtah. So there he'll stay until further notice—unless, indeed, we decide to bring him up to Bekla. He's our best hostage as long as the old man's alive. Whether Eud-Ecachlon'll feel the same when he succeeds his father is another matter.'

They had drawn almost level with the Tower of Sel-Dolad, and Durak-kon stopped for a moment, looking down towards a low, extensive, flat-roofed building lying just south of the tower and abutting the ramparts themselves.

'What's that place?' he asked. 'Do you know?'

'It's a depôt for hides and leather, sir,' replied Elvair-ka-Virrion. 'I was there myself with my quartermaster yesterday, picking up a bit more stuff for our trip to Chalcon. A man called N'Kasit rents it from the temple.'

'There's access to the ramparts from there, at a pinch, isn't there?' said Durakkon. 'Anyone who climbed up would only have to go a short way along these walls to get into the upper city.'

'I know,' replied Kembri. 'It's the only place like that in the whole of Bekla, though. I've sometimes thought of having it pulled down, but it's uncommonly solid, and it makes an excellent depôt; we wouldn't find another half so good. I've talked it over, actually, with the castellan, and we agreed that the best thing would be to keep a sentry here all the time and leave it at that. Anyway,' he resumed, turning away to continue their walk, 'so much for Urtah and Bayub-Otal. At least if they're no help I doubt they'll be any hindrance to us for the time being.'

To be told that something had already been considered and a decision reached was usually enough for Durakkon, who when it came to detail was as mentally lazy as many other idealistic people with high principles. He asserted himself by standing still, waiting for Kembri and Elvair-ka-Virrion to come back to him, and then raising a fresh subject.

'Chalcon,' he said to Elvair-ka-Virrion. 'You mean to lead the expeditionary force there yourself, in person?'

'Yes, sir,' replied Elvair-ka-Virrion. 'In fact, I'm as good as ready to leave.'

'It won't be an easy task,' said Durakkon, 'not in that kind of country; and of course Erketlis and his people know it inside out.'

'Oh, I've already thought of that, sir,' said Elvair-ka-Virrion. 'I've drafted half-a-dozen reliable men from Chalcon into the force. They know the country every bit as well as Erketlis himself.'

'You're confident, then?' asked Durakkon, with a smiling, rather avuncular manner. He did not altogether dislike Elvair-ka-Virrion, partly on account of his good looks and style, and partly on account of the confident energy and youthful exuberance he brought to whatever he took in hand, from giving a banquet to raising a regiment. 'Dear me, I wish I could still run upstairs like that!' he had said to him one day, after Elvair-ka-Virrion, returning from a hunting expedition, had dashed two steps at a time up the main staircase of the Barons' Palace to greet him.

'I've got the finest body of men in the empire, sir,' replied Elvair-ka-Virrion. 'I'd lead them into the Streels of Urtah!'

'Quiet!' said Kembri quickly. 'Don't talk like that, Elvair: I don't care to hear that sort of thing.' Durakkon, with pursed lips, looked away as though nothing had been said; and after a few moments Elvair-ka-Virrion, abashed at his unfortunate lapse but recovering himself, continued, 'I'm quite sure, sir, that with the quality of men I've got, we'll be able to drive right through Chalcon and make it impossible for Erketlis to maintain any sort of armed force there: and he won't be able to get away to Ikat or Sarkid. Somewhere or other we'll be bound to encounter him and destroy him. I don't know whether *he'll* be looking for a battle, but *I* certainly shall.'

Durakkon smiled indulgently but encouragingly. 'Well, it all sounds excellent, young man. You don't think perhaps he ought to have someone a little more experienced with him?' he said, turning to Kembri.

'I think he'll do very well on his own, sir,' answered Kembri.

For the Lord General's purposes it was important that his son should return to Bekla a successful leader in his own right—if possible a public hero. His plans for the future required not only followers whom he could control and trust absolutely, but also that they should command popular support. Elvair-ka-Virrion was well-liked in Bekla, but in the eyes of the people he was still no more than a young hopeful who had yet to make a name for himself. The time and opportunity were now at hand.

'When do you leave?' asked Durakkon at length. 'Is that decided?'

'The day after tomorrow, sir,' said Elvair-ka-Virrion. 'We ought to reach Thettit in three-and-a-half days quite comfortably. A day's rest, and then straight into Chalcon. Back in two months,' he added, looking round at the High Baron with a light-hearted grin.

'That will be,' said Kembri pausingly, 'that will be a little time before— or should I say in good time for?—the acclamation of the new Sacred Queen.' As Durakkon said nothing he went on, 'That's going to be—well, an important business, isn't it? I'm sure you're as anxious as I am, sir—as we all are—to see it turn out—er—in the right way.'

The sun had dropped behind the hills and dusk was rapidly falling. Already lamps were beginning to shine out in the city below. Durakkon turned about and they began pacing back along the wall, now seeing before them the majestic front of the Barons' Palace crowning the Leopard Hill with its ranks of slender spires.

Durakkon walked on in silence, as though awaiting something more. At length, however, as the Lord General did not continue, he said, 'I think you'd better tell me straight out, Kembri, what it is you have in mind.'

'I, sir?' answered the Lord General. 'I've nothing whatever in mind but

583

what's right and traditional: the choosing of a new Sacred Queen by popular acclaim. I merely said I hoped it would turn out well.'

'Don't try to make a fool of me!' retorted Durakkon angrily. 'I want to know whether you mean to try to have Fornis acclaimed for a third reign and if not, whether you've got any other woman in mind.'

'Well, do *you* think Fornis is likely to be acclaimed for a third reign, sir?' asked Kembri.

'No, I don't,' replied Durakkon. 'A woman well over thirty. Even a second reign's something that's never been known before: to try to bring about a third reign would be disastrous—utter folly. The people have some genuine religious faith left, if you haven't, and they'd see it as virtually provoking the gods to lay waste the city.'

'I agree, sir,' said Kembri. 'So who'd be best? Not to mince words, we need a Sacred Queen we can rely on.'

'One you can control, you mean, Kembri?'

'I didn't say that, sir. I said one we can rely on, in these difficult times, not to start going her own way or getting up to anything behind our backs. The girl must be beautiful, of course—the people regard that as no more than what's due to the god—and ideally she ought to be someone who already commands wide popularity in the lower city as well as the upper.'

'I suppose you're thinking of the Tonildan child, are you? The one they call the Serrelinda?'

'Well, she'd certainly be one possible choice,' replied Kembri non-committally.

'I liked her when I met her,' said Durakkon. 'She's—well, she struck me as typical of the sort of ordinary, decent people I wanted to help when I became High Baron.'

Kembri was silent.

'But frankly, I'd be almost sorry to see her pushed up into a position like that,' went on Durakkon. 'Because it'll be dangerous, Kembri; you know it will. Fornis isn't going to—'

'There is another possibility, of course,' said Kembri, interrupting him. 'And I'd certainly like to meet your wishes, sir, if we can: about not supporting the Tonildan, I mean.'

It was almost too dark, now, for him to see Durakkon's face, but nevertheless he turned and looked at him, halting a moment on the rough, uneven stones of the rampart-walk.

'I'm thinking of another girl. Sencho wasn't popular, of course: in fact he was hated. And what he got for himself out of the killing of Enka-Mordet—well, of course it didn't come out for some time, but when it did, a lot of people were so angry that I sometimes wonder whether he could have continued to get away with it if he'd lived. He'd have had to let the girl go.'

'But what's this got to do with—' began Durakkon.

'So naturally there's been a great deal of public sympathy for his wretched victim,' went on Kembri. 'Especially when my son told the temple authorities that she'd never legally been a slave at all, and that he was ready to defy both them and Fornis on her account. A very beautiful girl, Milvushina; and, of course, one whose acclamation as Sacred Queen would have an excellent effect in pacifying Chalcon and bringing a lot of the heldril there round to our side.'

'But her association with your son?' said Durakkon.

'Well, precisely, sir: I think that would be likely to go down very well with the people. The victorious young commander and his beautiful Sacred Queen: it would be just the sort of thing they'd like. But anyway, there you are; two excellent candidates from the Leopard point of view. Either would suit us, though on balance I think Milvushina would be the better choice.'

'I—well, I suppose so,' replied Durakkon rather uncertainly.

There was renewed silence as they walked on, reaching at length the steps leading down from the ramparts about three hundred yards west of the palace. Here Kembri halted, looked round to make sure the sentinel was not in hearing, and murmured, 'So you'll—er—speak to—'

'Speak?' answered Durakkon. 'What do you mean?'

'Well, sir, someone's going to have to tell Fornis that a third reign as Sacred Queen is out of the question. And there's no one who can perform that task with authority except the High Baron of Bekla.'

There was a long pause. At length, 'She has no legal power, sir,' ventured Elvair-ka-Virrion, in a tone which was meant to be encouraging yet sounded anything but.

'No; she has her own power, though,' answered Durakkon dolefully. Then, recovering his dignity as though with an effort, he said, 'Well, Lord General, I'll think it over, and let you know how and when I mean to go about it. You may both leave me now.'

The Lord General and his son bowed and descended the steps. Durakkon, turning away from them, remained alone, gazing out from the walls at Lespa's stars now twinkling more brightly above the darkening plain.

THE PRISONERS

Two hours before this, Maia had set about her task of taking Occula's message to the old woman in the sweet-shop.

In the event it proved easier than she had dared to hope. Nonetheless, she took a little while to find the shop; and the jekzha-man (who did not know who she was) had to be placated with extra money for all his stumbling up and down. Finally she made him go as far as Eud-Ecachlon's old lodgings, near the Tower of the Orphans—she could remember that all right, recalling the afternoon when she had acquitted herself so well—and then retrace his steps as though returning to the upper city.

Ah yes! and there, sure enough, *was* the sweet-shop, on the opposite side of the street, just before it came out into the Sheldad. Today, in fine summer weather, it had a different look, as revisited places often do; yet there was no doubt about it. Maia stopped the jekzha, crossed the street and went in.

The old woman was sitting behind her scales, and her lad could be heard clumping about somewhere in the back. A big, portly man, who looked like an upper servant, was making a great to-do over buying all manner of sweetmeats—no doubt for some supper-party of his master's—and it was plain that the old woman meant to take her time over obliging so good a customer. Maia waited. After a minute or two the lad appeared and came up to her, but she only shook her head, pointing and murmuring something about 'your mother.'

At last the self-important butler was done and strutted out, pocketing his list and giving an address in the upper city to which the stuff was to be delivered that day without fail. Maia went up to the old woman while she was still bowing and smiling behind him in the doorway.

'Good evening, mother,' she said in a low voice, 'and may Colonna and Bakris bless you. Last time we met, you told me I shouldn't never have come, so I'll be a bit quicker today. Occula—the black girl who was arrested when the High Counsellor was killed—she's still alive and sends you greetings. She says you're to get out now, at once, without stopping for anything.'

'I've been expecting it,' replied the old woman. 'Did she say where?'

Maia, shaking her head, produced a ten-meld piece. 'How about Urtah? Now sell me some sweets—anything you like—for the jekzha-man to see when I come out, and I'll be gone.'

Two minutes later she was back in her jekzha, out in the Sheldad and turning left towards the Caravan Market. After a few moments, however, she realized that they were not making any progress. Something ahead had halted the traffic and everybody seemed to be being pressed back against the shop-fronts on either side of the street. Her jekzha-man, jostled by four or five cursing porters, staggered a moment against another, righted himself, slewed round on the axis of one wheel and halted, wiping his face with his sleeve.

'Can't you go on?' she said impatiently. 'I want to get home.'

'Got to wait a bit, säiyett, I'm afraid. Here's the soldiers coming now, see 'em?'

She looked up the highway. Two files of soldiers were approaching, one on either side of the road; but very oddly, for they were side-stepping, facing outwards and pressing the people back against the walls with their spears held sideways. From further up, in the direction of the Caravan Market, there could now be heard a raucous clamour—ugly and malign, it sounded—coming gradually nearer, until one could distinguish individual, strident voices, like nails sticking out of the head of a cudgel.

'Oh, whatever is it?' she asked, frightened. The man did not answer and she rapped sharply on the rail. 'What is it? Tell me!'

'Won't be more'n a minute or two, I dare say, säiyett,' he answered. 'I reckon they're bringing in the prisoners from Tonilda—them heldro spies. I heard tell as they'd be here today.'

Even as he spoke she saw, across the heads in front of her, a tryzatt appear from the left, walking slowly yet somehow tensely and impatiently up the centre of the paved thoroughfare. Behind him came perhaps a dozen soldiers, spaced out on either side and carrying not spears, but leather whips coiled in their hands. They looked harassed and stretched to the limit, as men might look after hours spent in policing a plague-stricken town or struggling to bring home a leaking boat in bad weather. Their dust-grimed faces were streaked with sweat. They glanced continually this way and that and from moment to moment one or another would fling out his arm, pointing quickly, or call a hasty warning to a companion.

Yet it was not at the tryzatt nor yet the soldiers that Maia stared aghast, but at those walking between them—if walking it could be called. Singly—in twos and threes—in huddling, flinching groups like driven animals—little by little there came into view a dreadful procession. No wounded of a defeated army, stumbling from the battlefield, could have presented so terrible a sight. All were ragged, grey-faced, hollow-cheeked, staring about them either in deadly fear or else in a glazed, unseeing stupor of despair worse than any fear. Among them were a few women, one or two of whom might once have been attractive; and these, with their filthy faces, matted hair and look of exhausted misery, filled Maia with unspeakable anguish, so that she began to tremble and her head swam; so much worse they seemed than the rest, so much more a distorted travesty of what they must once have been. One man, tall and bony in his tatters, seemed to be attempting bravado, swaggering along alone and apparently trying to sing. As he came closer, however, it became plain that he was mad and virtually oblivious of his surroundings. Two more, as they limped forward, were supporting a woman between them and staggering from side to side. A fourth, with wrists chained together, was holding his hands in front of him and elbows to his sides, swaying in a kind of grotesque rhythm like a cripple trying to dance. Among them all—how many? Forty, fifty?—there was not one whom children would not have been terrified to see coming up a village street.

As they came on down the Sheldad, with its multi-coloured shops and ornate, stylish buildings, the crowd on either side broke into jeering and brutal laughter. A tradesman, lifting the pole which he used for raising and lowering the pent-shutter of his shop, jabbed with it, over the shoulders of the soldiers, at the man who was trying to sing. Missiles showered upon the prisoners—garbage, broken pieces of wood, a stone or two, an old shoe, a dead rat. One who tripped and fell was pelted until the nearest soldier, with a kind of rough sympathy, pulled him to his feet and supported him for a few yards, so that his tormentors were obliged to desist. Over all the hubbub carried the sharp, intermittent voice of the tryzatt, looking over his shoulder and continually urging his men to keep the prisoners closed up and moving.

Maia, cowering in the jekzha, felt as though trapped in a nightmare. It was all she could do not to get out and run away. This kind of cruelty was entirely foreign to anything in her nature. The whipping of Meris had been altogether different—for one thing, those whom she considered her superiors had been in deliberate control of it—from this unforeseen, frenetic, all-enveloping savagery. Intuitively she knew that these people were going to die. One had only to look at them: they could never come back from the place where they were. Some might well be close to death now: they looked it. Animals could not have suffered like this, for their owners, if only out of consideration for their own gain, would never have allowed animals to be treated half so badly.

And then, suddenly, she caught her breath; mouth open, hands pressed either side of her chin, rigid with incredulous, unspeakable horror; with a shock even beyond screaming. For it was Tharrin out there in the road: Tharrin lurching, tottering, wild-eyed, a long streak of blood down one side of his face, dragging his feet in broken sandals, suddenly flinging up one arm and ducking away from nothing, from an anticipated missile that he had only imagined. For one long moment—as though to put her in no doubt—he turned his head and stared full at her, but with no more recognition than a crazed cat looking down from a burning roof. Never in her life had she seen so appalling a look on any human face. Even if it had not been Tharrin's, it would have been enough to put her beside herself.

After a while—how long?—they were gone, followed by a rag-tag of urchins running behind, shouting with glee. The crowd broke up, the jekzha moved on. They were turning into the Caravan Market before the jekzha-man realized that Maia was sobbing hysterically.

'Yer, nasty business, säiyett, ain't it?' he remarked paternally over his shoulder. 'I don't go a lot on it meself. But you've no need to take on that way, y'know. They're all villains, the 'ole lot of 'em, else they wouldn't be there.'

'Where—where are they going?' she faltered, digging her nails into her palm and forcing herself to speak with something approaching self-control.

'Oh, it'll be the Old Gaol,' he answered. 'The one down in the Shilth.'

'Where's that?'

'The Shilth? That's the butchers' quarter, säiyett, about half-way between here and the Sel-Dolad Tower. Roughish kind of neighb'r'ood, that is, 'specially at night.'

'Take me there, please.'

'What's that, säiyett? Did you say take you there?'

'Yes, please.'

He stopped, looking back at her puzzled.

'Now, you mean?'

'Yes, please.'

He hesitated. 'Säiyett, it's none of my business, but—'

'Please do as I ask: or if you prefer, get me someone else. I realize I've kept you rather a long time already.'

She passed him down ten meld, at which he nodded, shrugged and turned back into the Sheldad.

During the next twenty minutes the façade which presented to the city the buoyant, resourceful and heroic Serrelinda crumbled, exposing a shocked and panic-stricken girl of sixteen, as devoid of worldly-wisdom as of dissimulation. Yet though she sat trembling and weeping in the jekzha, never for a moment did it occur to Maia to go home and concern herself no further with the condemned wreck who had once been her lover. On the contrary, by the time they had turned off the Sheldad and begun picking their way uphill through the foetid, fly-buzzing lanes of the Shilth, Maia had in effect been stripped of every coherent thought save her determination first to see Tharrin and then to do everything in her power to save him.

Outside the walls of the gaol—a dirty, ill-repaired but nonetheless very solid group of buildings, once a shambles, enlarged and converted some years before to meet the Leopards' need for another prison—she paid off the jekzha-man and told the gatekeeper that she wished to see the governor. The gatekeeper, an ageing man with conjunctive, mucous eyes, did not trouble himself to look directly at her while telling her that it was out of the question. She repeated her request peremptorily.

'Come on, now, lovey, run away,' he said, scratching himself and breathing garlic over her. 'It's no good, you know—you'd never be able to pin it on him, anyway. Do you know how many girls have come here trying, eh?'

Maia lowered her veil and threw back the hood of her cloak.

'I've no time to waste, and I'll be damned if I'm going to bribe you a meld! I'm Maia Serrelinda, from the upper city, and if you don't take me to the governor at once, I'll see to it that the Lord General himself learns that you refused to do as I asked.'

He stared at her, a stupid man taken aback, resentful but slow to react.

'You say you're the Serrelinda—her as swum the river?'

'Yes, I am. And don't have the impertinence to ask me why I'm here: that's no business of yours. Are you going to do as I say, or not?'

'Well,' he muttered. 'Well. Just that it's awkward, that's all.' He seemed to be trying to weigh up which would be worse for him—to refuse her or to risk the governor's displeasure. At all events this was what his next question suggested.

'You can't—well—tell me what it's about, säiyett?'

'Certainly. I wish to see a prisoner.'

His face cleared. 'Oh, you didn't say. If it's n'more'n that—' She waited. 'Only he's busy with the prisoners himself, säiyett, y'see. Don't know what he'll say. Still, I'll take you—' He turned away and she, following, stepped through the postern door to one side of the barred gate, which was promptly closed behind her.

He was striding ahead across the yard, swinging a stick in one hand, but she—to some extent brought to herself by her annoyance—retained enough self-possession not to hurry after him, so that after a little he was obliged to wait until she came up with him at her own pace.

The governor was a big, fleshy man with silver earrings and a beard dyed chesnut. He, too, evidently supposed at first that her errand must lie at his own door, for he began 'Well, my dear, but you shouldn't have come here, you know.' He drew up a rickety bench for her beside the table in a little, bare room looking out on an equally bare and dismal courtyard. It was twilight now and turning slightly chilly. Seeing him grope and fumble once or twice to close the window, she realized that his sight must be poor.

Yet really so poor, she wondered, that he could not tell whether or not he had ever seen her before?

'We have never met,' she said coldly. 'I am Maia Serrelinda, a personal friend of the Lord General Kembri B'sai.'

Instantly he had taken his cue, bowing and leering.

'Friend of the Lord General? Oh, friend of the city, säiyett, friend of the empire! And let me assure you, you have a friend in me, too, if I'm not presuming. To what—er—to what do I owe the honour of this visit?'

Maia, not unnaturally, could tell a lecher when she saw one, and realized with a touch of relief that this part of her task at least was going to be relatively easy.

'Sir, I want to see—'

'Oh—Pokada, säiyett, Pokada's my name; that's if you care to use it, of course.'

'U-Pokada, I need to talk to one of the prisoners who were brought in from Tonilda a little while ago.'

His face fell. 'Oh. I see. Well, naturally, säiyett, I'd always prefer to oblige a beautiful lady like yourself if I could. If only it had been someone who's here for theft or fraud—that sort of thing, you know. But political prisoners: no one's ever allowed to see political prisoners. That's a strict rule.'

She got up and stood beside him, pretending to be weighing her words, letting her body's scent steal over him and slowly drawing through her fingers the silk kerchief she carried at her wrist. After a little she murmured, 'Well, I suppose—I suppose no one need know, U-Pokada. I mean, only you and me; I shan't tell anyone.'

He hesitated. 'Well, säiyett—'

In a few minutes he had talked himself into promising that he would see what he could do tomorrow.

'No, it must be now, U-Pokada: I want to see him now, and then I'll go away and no one else will know at all.'

It was getting dark in the room. He went to the door and called for lamps, continuing to look down the passage until they were brought by a dishevelled old woman whose head jerked with a continual tic. When she had gone he came back and laid a hand on Maia's wrist, slightly clenching his fingers as he did so.

'Säiyett, it's risky. I oughtn't to do this; but you know—well, "Beauty's a key to unlock every door".' He hummed a moment, delighted with himself for having hit on so apt a phrase. The line came from a popular tavern song of the day.

'Is it a man?' She nodded. 'His name?'

'Tharrin. From near Meerzat, in Tonilda.'

'*Your* friend? A lucky—oh, well' (he laughed) 'he *would* be a lucky man if only he wasn't here, eh? But you've made *me* a lucky man, säiyett. Oh, yes, indeed!'

At the door he stopped. 'I have to ask: you haven't brought him poison?'

She looked up in amazement, wondering whether she had heard aright. 'Poison?'

He nodded.

'Brought him *poison*? Why ever should you think that?'

'Well, sometimes, you know, säiyett, prisoners—especially political prisoners—want to die quickly, and their friends want to help them. I have to see that doesn't happen.'

She had heard tell of such things, but to find herself dealing with them in all earnest made her feel still more strange and bemused. She tried to collect her thoughts. The man needed convincing: the most convincing thing, it seemed to her, would be the truth.

'U-Pokada, I mean to get this man released. I have influence. That won't harm you, will it?'

'Harm *me*? Oh—no, säiyett, not in the least.' He paused, apparently searching for something more emphatic. 'No, no, I should be *glad*! Whatever would please *you* would please me. Wait here, I beg you, and be patient. I don't know the man, you understand, but I'll find him.'

Alone, she waited in the empty room for what seemed a long time. It grew quite dark outside. She thought of Luma, sitting lethargic for hour after hour on the kilyett as it drifted down the Nordesh. She herself could not sit still, now pacing up and down, now opening the window and leaning out to pick fragments off the grimy creeper below the sill. Surely by now the man had had long enough to find anyone in the prison? Could he have betrayed her— sent a messenger, perhaps, to the chief priest? Should she go now, quickly? Yet if he had in fact betrayed her, to run away would avail her nothing.

The door opened behind her and she turned, but could not see clearly across the bright patch of light from the two lamps standing on the table between. As she came back to the bench the door closed and then she heard the lock click. Tharrin was standing before her, shivering in the stuffy room, not raising his eyes from the floor.

She had forethought that he was bound to look bad at close quarters; but not that he would smell worse than any animal (animals groom themselves), that the rims of his eyes would be crusted, his beard matted with old crumbs and dried spittle and that he would mutter and shake ceaselessly, cringing and wringing his hands like an old beggar.

'Tharrin,' she said timidly—for it seemed almost as though she were interrupting some horrible dialogue between unseen beings—'Tharrin, it's Maia.'

He made no answer and she put a hand on his wrist. 'It's Maia, Tharrin.'

Now he looked up, peering with half-closed eyes, as though through some kind of haze or distance between them.

'Maia? Oh—I remember.' He seemed about to say more, but then suddenly began to cry, or rather to whimper, dry-eyed and cowering, shaking his head and hunching his shoulders as though standing out in heavy rain.

'Tharrin—oh, poor Tharrin—listen to me! You *must* listen to me, you *must* trust me! I'm going to help you; believe me, I'm going to get you out of here, Tharrin. But I can't do it unless you'll talk to me. There's things I've got to know. Come on, sit down here and talk to me.'

As she pulled him gently by the arm he suddenly screamed, but so weak and puny a sound that it would scarcely have startled a bird. Drawing him down beside her on the bench, she could feel his ribs and backbone under his tattered robe. She recognized the robe. It was the one he had been wearing when they parted on the quay at Meerzat.

'Tharrin, dear, listen to me. I know just how you feel, because I've been through it, too. But I *can* help you: I've got money and influence: I'm a friend of powerful people; I'll save you. But to do that, I've got to know what's happened. Tell me what they say you've done.'

'Sencho,' he muttered after some moments. 'Sencho was too clever for us, wasn't he?'

'Sencho's dead, dear: weeks and weeks ago.' She wondered whether Pokada might be eavesdropping.

'Yes, of course,' he said. He looked up at her piteously. 'They're going to torture us, Maia: you can't know what it's like to wake and sleep day after day with the thought of that. People—people went mad coming up from Thettit. Made no difference: they're here just the same. Every day you wake up you remember—' He rocked himself backwards and forwards on the bench. She could see the lice crawling in his hair.

'Listen, Tharrin. Do you realize that I've become famous and rich? If I ask to talk to the Lord General, he'll see me; very likely the High Baron himself would see me. Do you know that?'

He nodded listlessly. 'Oh, yes, I'd—I'd heard. "Maia swam the river." I knew it must be you.' Then, with no change of tone, 'The bread's all green and mouldy, you know.'

She realized that after many days of ill-treatment and fear he had in all actuality become incapable of sustained thought—that his mind must spend all its waking time in virtually ceaseless flight from what it could not endure to apprehend. She wondered what his dreams could be like. Yet she would not allow herself to weep: this was no time for weeping.

'You were working secretly for the heldril in Tonilda, weren't you? Isn't that right?'

A nod. She took his hand in hers.

'That's where all that money used to come from? The money you used to give Morca? The money you spent on me?'

Another nod. 'I never thought—' he whispered.

'You took messages to Thettit? And to Enka-Mordet and people like that? And you brought messages back, did you?'

'Money for us at home. More money than I could have got any other way.' He paused. Then, 'Can't you kill me, Maia? Haven't you got a knife or something?'

'No, dear, no such thing. I'm going to get you out of here safe, I promise you.' She forced herself to kiss his cheek. 'I *promise*! Now listen to me, Tharrin, because this is very important. I'm going to speak to some of my powerful friends, and p'raps they'll want to see you; I don't know. If we're going to save you—and we are—you've got to pull yourself together and get ready to put on a good appearance. Now I'm going to call in that head gaoler or whatever he calls himself, and pay him to see you get everything you need. A bath and some clean clothes and proper food, and a comfortable bed. I'll bet he can fix all that if he wants to, and I'm going to see to it as he *does* want to. But you've got to *trust* me, Tharrin. You've got to be your own best friend. Come on, now, it's not too late to pull yourself together. This is Maia, your golden fish in the net; remember?'

'Yes, I remember. But I—I let you go. The slave-traders; I never even tried—'

'Never mind, dear. No need to talk about that now. You just stand up and try to look as manly and strong as you can, because I'm going to call him in and tell him what we need. You cheer up, now. Everything's going to be all right.'

She had about three hundred meld with her. It was not a very great deal, but it would do for a start and she could promise more. She went to the door, rapped firmly on it and called 'U-Pokada!'

: 60 :

PILLAR TO POST

It was not easy, even for the Serrelinda, to get hold of the Lord General at so busy and troublous a time. He was not at his house the following morning, though she arrived there so early that the steward—as she could perceive—was embarrassed, his slaves being still at work in the reception rooms and the place not yet ready to receive callers and petitioners. Both the Lord General, he told her, and the young Lord Elvair-ka-Virrion were already gone to the Barons' Palace; he understood that later in the morning they meant to go down to the lower city to review the troops leaving for Thettit tomorrow. The lady Milvushina, however, was upstairs in Lord Elvair-ka-Virrion's rooms. Should he tell her the säiyett had come?

It had not previously crossed Maia's mind to tell Milvushina of her trouble. Thinking quickly—the man in his scarlet uniform standing deferentially before her—she realized that she had no great wish to do so. No great wish? She hesitated. What did she mean in thus replying to herself?

Milvushina had gone out of her way to show herself a friend; to speak of herself and her situation without reserve; to make common cause with Maia, warn her, talk of her own anxieties and expectations. If Maia were to tell her now of Tharrin she would—oh, yes, certainly she would—show every sympathy and probably even promise to put in a word. She would be all benevolence. Yet in her mind would arise, unexpressed, a picture of the grubby little peasant girl tumbled on the shore by her mother's fancy man. In a word, it wasn't what Milvushina would say, but what she *wouldn't* say, which made Maia reluctant to tell her her trouble or ask for her advice. Often, although we may not be ashamed in our own hearts—may even be proud or glad—of something we have done, because by our own standards it was genuinely good—good, if you like, to ourselves and to the gods, who understand everything—yet nevertheless we still feel troubled by the idea of it becoming known to someone else whom we feel to be inflexibly different in outlook from ourselves. 'Oh—*she* just wouldn't understand.' 'So you're ashamed?' asks an inward voice. No, no, inward voice; don't be so simplistic. Do you think there is only one colour in the spectrum; or that some animal is universally 'unclean' because one out of the world's countless religions has always maintained so? It is, rather, just that her values are not ours; that's all.

Maia, somewhat to her own surprise, heard herself asking to see Sessendris. The man raised his eyebrows slightly, bowed and requested her to be so good as to accompany him.

Sessendris was dressed in a long white apron, making bread, her beautiful arms covered with flour to the elbow.

'Maia!' she said, looking up with a smile and tossing back her hair. 'How nice! You must wonder what in Cran's name the Lord General's säiyett thinks she's doing in the bakery. The truth is I enjoy it, and no one else in this whole house can make bread as well as I do. So you've caught me out, my dear. Now don't you go telling the whole upper city that the Lord General's säiyett's a baker, or you'll probably have me hanging upside-down!'

This unintentionally grisly pleasantry brought the tears to poor Maia's eyes. Apart from her initial collapse in the jekzha the previous afternoon, she had until now stood up pretty well to the shock and strain of the past fifteen hours; perhaps the better because the squalor, vulgarity and sordid ugliness, which to someone like Milvushina would have been almost the worst of it, were things she had grown up with. Now, however, she wept, standing unreplying in front of Sessendris with the tears running down her cheeks. Sessendris, nodding to the kitchen-maid to leave them, sat down beside her on the flour-sprinkled table.

'It's nasty,' said the säiyett, when she had heard it all. 'The truth is, the *world's* nasty, Maia Serrelinda. Haven't you learnt that yet? You ought to, I should have thought, after a few months with Sencho.'

'I'm—I'm getting to know, I reckon.'

'And you want to try to alter it, do you?'

'But Sessendris, surely they'll pardon him, won't they? I mean, if *I* ask them? They're always saying as I saved the city, and if—'

'Why d'you want him pardoned?' interrupted Sessendris. 'Do you still love him?'

'No,' replied Maia, so instantly and emphatically that the säiyett, nodding, was drawn to say, 'I see: you love someone else, do you? Well, never mind about that for now. But in that case why *do* you want him pardoned? From what you've told me, he's as guilty as he can be, and he never lifted a finger to try to help you when you'd been sold as a slave: and he *could* have, couldn't he?'

'How could he?' asked Maia.

'Why, at the very least he could have gone to one of his heldro masters and asked him to follow you up. That's what happened with Missy upstairs, as I dare say you know; but by that time she didn't want it. Anyway, suppose you *were* to get him handed over to you, what would you do with him?'

'I haven't thought yet. Send him home, I suppose.'

'To get into more trouble? He's been in and out of scrapes all his life, by what you've told me. He'll never change. You must know that, Maia, if you're honest. I just can't understand—well, what your idea is.'

'To save him from suffering,' said Maia.

'You're such a sweet, kind girl,' said Sessendris. 'D'you know, I used to be like you, believe it or not? You haven't grasped as much as I thought you had. Now you listen to me. You've gone up in the world. I've gone up in the world too: not like you—*you've* had a shower of stars poured into your lap—but still, I'm a long way above where I started. And when that sort of thing happens to you, you simply can't afford to be the person you once were. You can't be *two* people. You've become a new person and you've got to *be* her. To the upper city you're as good as a princess. Suppose you start begging for the life of this five-meld wastrel, the Leopards

596

aren't going to think any the better of you, are they? They'll just think you can't tell shit from pudding.'

'I'll go down into the lower city! I'll appeal to the people—' Maia was angry now as well as tearful.

'My dear, the people—they'd like it even less. Surely you can see that? The very *last* thing they want to think is that you're one of themselves. You're the magic Serrelinda, the girl who fooled King Karnat and swam the river. No one's good enough for you! And there you'd be, pleading for a—well, never mind. But you're living in the real world, Maia—the only one there is—and the world's been good to you. You've got to learn to accept it as it is.' Sessendris stood up and once more began tossing the flour. 'I'm sorry my advice is nasty medicine. But drink it! It'll do you good. The other won't, believe you me.'

At the Barons' Palace she was obliged to wait for some time. Officers— some of whom she knew, others she had never seen before—were coming and going and there was an atmosphere of males intent upon male matters, in which she felt unhappily intrusive and out of place. She was touched when the Tonildan captain—the very one who had come to thank her in Rallur—catching sight of her alone and obviously ill-at-ease, excused himself to three or four companions with whom he was about to leave and kept her in countenance by sitting down and conversing with her—as best he could, for he was none too ready of tongue—until a smooth and courtly Beklan equerry not much older than herself came up and begged her to accompany him to the Lord General.

In the Beklan Empire, maps—insofar as the term is appropriate—took the form of rough models, more-or-less to scale, built up, from local knowledge and eye-witness reports, either on trestles and boards or simply on the ground, with clay, twigs, pebbles and the like. Kembri and Elvair-ka-Virrion were standing at a plank table laid out to represent Chalcon, the Lord General pointing here and there as he talked. Elvair-ka-Virrion, dressed in a Gelt breastplate over a purple leather jerkin, looked up and smiled at Maia as warmly and gallantly as on that far-off afternoon when he had seen her for the first time in the Khalkoornil.

'Maia! Are you here to join up? Come to Chalcon and help us beat Erketlis! Then we'll make you queen of Tonilda and give you a crown of leopards' teeth. How about it?'

She smiled, raising a palm to her forehead. 'Happen I'd be less help than hindrance, my lord. All the same, there *is* something you can give me; cost you a lot less trouble an' all.' Seeing Kembri also smiling, she added, 'Reckon you must know as I've come to ask for something. Hadn't, I wouldn't be here.'

This was the first time that Maia had met with the Lord General since the day when she had been released from arrest by the intervention of the Sacred Queen. He looked strained and tired, but his manner, as he put down the stick he had been using as a pointer and took her hands in greeting, at first seemed friendly and well-wishing enough. She could not help thinking that Nennaunir had been rather hard on him. While it would certainly have been nice if he had come to visit her together with the High Baron, he must have had lots more important things to do. (Maia was of course vague about military matters, but tended to think of them as necessarily occupying soldiers from morning till night and often longer than that.)

'I haven't had any chance before, Maia,' said Kembri, 'to thank you for what you did in Suba. I thank you now. You'll remember I always told you that you might very well become free sooner than you could imagine.'

Somehow, as women can, she could tell that his words lacked real warmth and sincerity. For some reason, her success and fame were *not* particularly congenial to him. She felt mortified. There was no time to bother about that now, however. 'If you really are grateful, my lord,' she said, 'please do something for me. It's not a lot to ask. There's a prisoner among those as came in last night—'

She had had opportunity, since leaving Sessendris, to take thought and prepare her story along less ingenuous lines. Tharrin was her dear step-father. He had been the family's sole prop and mainstay in their poverty on the Tonildan Waste. She owed so much to him. When she had been enslaved he had sought her in vain—she had learned as much last night—and for her part she believed him innocent. If only his life were spared, she would see to it that he went home to those who desperately needed him and never fell foul of authority again.

When at length she had finished there was a pause. 'But if this man was such a good father to you all, Maia,' asked Elvair-ka-Virrion at length, 'how was it that you came to be enslaved?'

''Twas poverty, my lord—sheer hard times,' answered Maia. 'We was nigh on starving, see—'

'So he made ready money by acting as a rebels' courier,' broke in Kembri. 'Well, *you* may believe him innocent, Maia, but I can tell you that we *know*—Sencho knew—that every one of those prisoners is guilty twenty times over.'

Maia said nothing, and after a few moments he went on, 'Do you remember the day when we first talked about Bayub-Otal; the day you told me about the High Counsellor and Milvushina?'

'Yes, my lord; I remember very well.'

'So you won't have forgotten our talking about adventurers and their need to see clearly and not deceive themselves into thinking that just because they happen to have struck lucky, they can get away with anything.'

'I'm not deceiving myself, my lord. It's only that I can't bear the thought of my step-father being—being tortured and put to death.'

'Tortured? Put to death?' said Elvair-ka-Virrion. 'Whatever do you mean?'

'Why, he told me himself, my lord—I saw him in the gaol last night—as he knew he was to be tortured—'

'The man's a fool, then,' said Kembri shortly, 'or more likely the soldiers have been amusing themselves by telling him tales.' He picked up his stick and turned back to the map.

'Oh, don't be sharp with her, father,' said Elvair-ka-Virrion. 'A girl like her deserves better. Maia, let me explain. You ought to know—who better?—that human bodies are worth money. We only execute people if they're worth nothing—or if they've become so infamous that they have to be made a public example. These prisoners—they've got value as slaves. Provided these people answer our questions and tell us everything we need to know, they've got nothing to fear beyond being sold as slaves. You can probably buy your step-father if you want to. In fact, I think the prisoners have already been apportioned. There's a roll somewhere, father, isn't there?'

'Over there.' Kembri nodded towards another table.

'Apportioned?' asked Maia. 'What's that, then?'

'Why, when a batch of prisoners like this comes in,' said Elvair-ka-Virrion, 'strictly speaking their lives are all forfeit. But any Leopard who wants can put in a bid for so many at a price, and then they belong to him and he has the disposal of them. They can be sold, or given away, or just kept as slaves in his household—whatever he decides. Ah, yes, here's the roll. What did you say your step-father's name was?'

'Tharrin, of Meerzat.'

'I see. Yes, here he is. Oh!' Elvair-ka-Virrion, whose manner had seemed full of reassurance, suddenly stopped short and put the roll back on the table. After a few moments he said, 'Well, if I were you, Maia, I should try to forget about this.'

'Why, what do you mean, my lord? Who—who's got Tharrin, then?'

'The Sacred Queen,' replied Elvair-ka-Virrion. 'He's one of eight prisoners marked for her personal disposal. I'm sorry, Maia. When the Sacred Queen has the disposal of prisoners, you see, that's usually—well, rather different, I'm afraid.'

'But—but I could still buy Tharrin, my lord, couldn't I? From the queen?'

'You could try, certainly,' said Kembri, 'but if I were you I shouldn't.' He went to the door and summoned the young staff officer. 'Bahrat, the Serrelinda's leaving now. Show her to the door, will you? and then come back yourself.'

Two porters opened the double gates and her soldiers drew the Serrelinda's jekzha into the garden court of the Sacred Queen's house. Dew was still lying on the lawn, the western side of which sparkled in the sun now well risen above the opposite rooftop. A green-and-white-plumaged *memmezah*, red-billed and red-legged, was running here and there, foraging over the grass and now and then breaking into short, low flights. In one corner stood a little grove of purple-flowering *larn* bushes—somewhere between shrubs and trees—and among these four or five small, grey-green monkeys were leaping here and there, suddenly chasing one another and as suddenly breaking off. Bees droned among the flowerbeds. A peacock, trailing its tail, wandered pausingly across a narrow, stone-paved path and disappeared behind a low wall on its further side. There was a scent of lilies and of moist greenery and from time to time, from somewhere beyond the light pattering of the fountain, a blue-finch repeated its little, falling song.

Maia walked in the garden while her soldier Brero went to make enquiries. After a little she paused in the shade, leaning against a blossoming cherry tree. Looking up at the side of the palace facing her, she could recognize the gallery, with its trellised arcading, where she had embraced the Sacred Queen in the moonlight. Suddenly, as she stood gazing, a girl's scream sounded from above. It seemed like a cry of pain rather than of fear, and was quickly cut short, as though whoever uttered it had either been silenced in some way or had controlled herself. Maia wondered whether the girl—whoever she might be—had burned herself or dropped something heavy on her foot. At any rate it wasn't Occula—she could tell that. She fingered her diamonds nervously; chewed a blade of grass and picked at the cherry bark. Then, hearing the sound of a footstep on the path, she turned to see Brero coming towards her.

Somewhat to her surprise, the man told her that he had been given to understand that the queen would see her immediately. She followed him round the lawn and past the monkeys' grove to a stone doorway above which, in a recess, a little statue of Frella-Tiltheh the Inscrutable stood pointing downward at the sprouting tamarrik seed. Inside was a long, cool hall, elegantly tiled in red and white, where slim, fluted columns rose to a coffered ceiling. Scented shrubs were standing here and there in leaden troughs, and at the far end rose a staircase.

Zuno, waiting at the foot of these stairs, bowed to Maia without speaking and motioned to her to ascend. Arrived at the stairhead, she at once recognized the corridor where Fornis had tackled the guard-hound with her bare hands. Passing the actual spot, she noticed several scratches still remaining on the polished boards. Then they were climbing to the second storey.

Zuno stopped outside the queen's bedroom and knocked. After a few moments the door was opened by a woman—an obvious Palteshi—whom Maia had not seen before. She gave her name and the woman nodded to her to enter.

Fornis, half-naked in a pale-green dressing-robe embroidered with waves and fishes in silver, was seated at a dressing-table of inlaid sestuaga-wood. Open before her was a kind of cabinet full of jars of ointment, boxes of creams and unguents and bottles of lotion and perfume. Her shoulders and bosom were lightly sprinkled with an adhesive, golden powder which glittered where it caught the light. In one hand she held the heavy, carved comb with which she had combed Maia's hair in the bathroom, while with the fingertips of the other she was lightly rubbing an orange-tinted rouge into the skin round her cheekbones. As Maia raised her palm to her forehead, the queen turned her head and looked up at her over her shoulder.

Once again Maia saw, with that tremor which often comes upon us in the moment that we realize that we had forgotten the precise appearance of someone remembered with deep emotion—love, hatred or fear—the blazing hair, the ice-green eyes, the creamy skin, the buxom body at one and the same time opulent yet lithe and agile as an athlete's. Again she sensed the latent energy like a coiled spring, and the domineering, rapacious vitality which, striking upward through the leaves like a physical force, had literally thrown her off balance as she stood poised above the Barb.

Looking into those eyes, Maia knew that she was afraid. This was not Folda, the woman with whom she had eaten and drunk and whom she had failed to gratify. This was the legendary Queen Fornis, who carried within her the power to confront warriors, to outface monarchs and barons, subdue the priesthood and set at nought—with impunity, as it seemed— the very gods themselves. Princess of Paltesh she might have been born, and Sacred Queen of Airtha she might have become; yet ultimately her power stemmed not from these titles, but from some inscrutable, trans- cendental source compared with which mere human attributes were trifles; a source whose servants, once sent into the world, were authorized to stick at nothing. This power—so it appeared to Maia now—must have grown in Fornis like a tree. She had not always been thus; yet the seed had been born with her. Now it was full-grown. Ah; so tall that men—and women, too—could hang upside-down from the branches.

'Good morning, Maia,' said the Sacred Queen, somehow contriving, by her near-nakedness and casual pursuance of her cosmetic activities, to reduce to vain, pretentious triviality Maia's silk dress and diamond necklace. 'I trust you've been enjoying yourself since your return to Bekla.'

'Yes, thank you, esta-säiyett,' replied Maia, by the queen's tone put beyond doubt that there was to be no sort of renewal of a friendly relationship between them.

She was about to go on to enquire after the queen's health and well-being when she became aware of a kind of struggling commotion taking place further down the room. Looking over Fornis's shoulder, she now saw Ashaktis seated astride a bench, beside which was standing a dark, hirsute young man in a leather jerkin.

It was not at either of these, however, that Maia looked for more than a moment, but at the figure between them; a dark-haired, big-built girl, stripped to the waist, who was kneeling on the floor. Ashaktis, leaning forward and gripping her wrists, was holding her prone along the length of the bench. The girl's back was criss-crossed with bloody weals; and in the moment that Maia took in the scene, the young man struck her again with a thin, pliant stick on which blood was glistening. At this the girl flung back her head, showing a plain, rustic face contorted with pain, and Maia saw that she had a marked cast in one eye. She recognized her then, in spite of the distortion caused by the gag in her mouth. It was Chia, the Urtan girl with whom she and Occula had fought and then made friends in Lalloc's slave-hall.

'Oh, esta-säiyett, please!' Maia, who from the first had felt all embarrassment at standing beside the queen lolling in undress, now fell on her knees at her feet.

'What*ever's* the matter?' Fornis, peering in the mirror while with one finger she rubbed the rouge in just below her eye, spoke with an air of slightly irritated surprise.

'I beg you—please spare that girl, esta-säiyett, as—as a favour to me. I don't know what she's done, but—'

'My dear Maia, neither do I: I haven't the faintest idea. That's a kitchen-maid, or something of the kind, I believe.'

'But I knew her once, esta-säiyett: that's why I'm asking.'

'*Knew* her?' Fornis, frowning, looked perplexed to the point of annoyance, as though Maia had used some inappropriate or unintelligible word.

'Yes, esta-säiyett; when I was a slave, I knew her.'

'Oh, when you were a *slave*. I *see*!' She raised her voice slightly. 'Shakti, Maia wants you to let that girl go; apparently she used to know her when she was a *slave*. Just send her back wherever she came from, will you?'

At that moment Maia felt certain that either Ashaktis or Fornis herself had known—probably the poor girl had boasted about it in the kitchens—of her own acquaintance with Chia, and that the beating had been deliberately arranged as soon as Fornis had learned that Maia was downstairs and asking to see her.

As Ashaktis pulled the girl to her feet, threw her clothes round her and nodded to the young man to drag her out of the room, Fornis turned back to the dressing-table and began polishing her nails with a strip of bone bound in soft leather. Maia waited for her to speak, but she said nothing and after a minute or two laid the bone aside, stood up, opened a wardrobe and began looking through the gowns hanging there.

I'm the Serrelinda, thought Maia: I'm the Serrelinda. If I could swim the Valderra— Yet in her heart she knew that such thoughts had no real validity. If Fornis wanted the Valderra swum, she would simply order two people to go and do it; and if they drowned, two more.

'Esta-säiyett,' she said, 'I've come to ask you—to talk to you, if you'll very kindly hear me, about a man called Tharrin.'

'A man called *Tharrin?*' said Fornis, looking up sharply as though Maia had discourteously interrupted her. She paused. 'I think you mean a man called Sednil, don't you?'

Maia, momentarily startled and discomposed, hesitated. The green eyes rested upon her with a cool yet expectant stare.

'No, esta-säiyett,' said Maia, keeping her voice steady with an effort. 'Tharrin's a Tonildan political prisoner, and I'm told by the Lord General as he's one that's your property. He happens to be my step-father—my mother's husband—and I've come to beg you to be so good as to—to enter into my natural feelings, like, and let me buy him from you. You'd be doing me and my mother and sisters the greatest kindness.'

'Did you have a pleasant talk with the chief priest the other day?' asked Fornis rather absently, taking a gown out of the closet and holding it up against her body as Ashaktis came back into the room.

'Yes, thank you, esta-säiyett.' She did not know what else to say.

'You've been quick enough to come here this morning. It didn't occur to you before to come and ask *me* about your friend Occula, rather than the chief priest?'

'No, esta-säiyett: well, only I didn't feel it would be right to presume on our earlier acquaintance in that way. I reckoned as you might not like it.'

'I see. But you don't feel that now, over this—this—Tharrin?'

'Yes, I do feel it, esta-säiyett, very much. I've been afraid to come, 'cos I didn't want to displease you. Only he's my step-father, see, and I owe him a lot, and the Lord General told me as there wasn't any other way 'ceptin' to ask you.'

Fornis beckoned to Ashaktis to help her on with the gown. Maia stood unspeaking. After a time the Sacred Queen shook out her skirt and then sat down for Ashaktis, kneeling before her, to put on her sandals.

'I suppose you know, don't you,' she said, without looking at Maia; 'perhaps your friend Sednil, or somebody like that, will have told you, what sort of prisoners are normally allocated to the Sacred Queen and why?'

'No, esta-säiyett.' Her voice came in a frightened whisper.

'Those who are known to have been so basely treacherous and criminal that they can't decently be sold into slavery are allotted to the temple for sacrifice. There are eight such prisoners in the group brought in yesterday—seven men and a woman. Naturally I don't know their names, but with your wide acquaintance among those sort of people I expect you do.'

'No, esta-säiyett. All I know is as the Lord General told me that Tharrin was—was out of his hands, 'cos he belonged to you.'

There was another long pause while Fornis took off the sandals, tried on another pair and then began washing her hands in a basin held by Ashaktis.

'What extraordinary company you seem to keep, Maia,' she said at length. 'Kitchen-slaves, lower city shearna's pimps—I don't know. But of course if your step-father's a criminal and a traitor, I dare say that accounts for it.'

In spite of her terror, it occurred to Maia that she might very well have replied that the queen herself was among those who had sought her company. She said nothing.

'Well, so you want to buy this—person,' said Fornis. 'However, it's from the temple, not from me, that you'll have to buy him, as I've explained. And we don't drive bargains with the Lord Cran, do we?'

'I'm only asking to pay a fair price, esta-säiyett. I'm not suggesting bargaining.'

'I see. And what would be a fair price, do you think?'

'I don't know, esta-säiyett.'

'Neither do I, for no one has ever had the temerity to make such a request before. I shall have to think it over carefully: you may come back in three hours' time.'

Maia knew that the queen was hoping she would lose her self-possession and plead for an immediate reply—perhaps weep. She raised her palm to her forehead and left the room.

Zuno was standing at the foot of the lower staircase. As they were crossing the hall side by side he murmured almost inaudibly, 'What is it that you came to ask her?'

She hesitated, and he added, 'You can trust me, I assure you.'

'My step-father—from Tonilda—he's a prisoner—one of the lot that's to die, so she said. I came to ask her to let me buy him.'

They were close to a little alcove at the further end of the hall, near the door by which she had entered. Zuno, looking quickly round, drew her into it and stood facing her.

'What did she answer?'

His manner startled her. This was a new Zuno, his customary air of supercilious detachment set aside, a man dealing with her directly and speaking to a fellow-being.

'She says she'll think it over. I'm to come back in three hours.'

'You couldn't—er—forget about it, I suppose?'

She shook her head. 'Couldn' do that, no.'

'You owe your step-father a lot?'

'Whatever he's done, I can't just stand by and let that happen to him.'

Zuno was silent for some moments, gazing out into the garden. At length he said, 'And how did she treat you?'

'Bad. I'm afraid of her. I mean, she could have said yes or no straight out; but she's cruel, isn't she? It's—I don't know—it's not so much what she does as what she *is* that frightens me. I don't understand it—I've never done her no harm!'

'You'd better understand several things, Maia, before you decide to go any further with this business. Before you went to Suba, she and Kembri were still on good terms. She believed he meant to see that she was acclaimed Sacred Queen for a third reign: Ashaktis told me as much. But when he allowed his son to help himself to Milvushina and then refused point-blank to send her back to Chalcon, Fornis guessed at once—she's very quick and shrewd—that he must have the idea of getting Milvushina acclaimed Sacred Queen instead.'

He stopped, listening, and then looked quickly out of the alcove for a moment.

'Well, what of it?' asked Maia, made fearful by his tension and anxious, now, only to end this conversation and leave the house.

'When she sent you back to the temple to go to Suba,' said Zuno, 'that was by way of obliging Kembri. Her idea was that he could have you back and make use of you on the understanding that Milvushina would either be returned to Chalcon or else—well, put out of the way. She thought *you'd* probably die anyway, you see. But what happened was that Kembri refused to part with Milvushina and then you came back as—well, what you are now. She knows, now, that Kembri must intend to supersede her. Actually, he has no alternative: the people would never acclaim her for a third reign. Oh, she knows how to keep up appearances, but secretly she must be desperate. And she knows, too, who are her rivals. Kembri would prefer Milvushina: but left to themselves the people would undoubtedly prefer you.'

Maia nodded. 'I'd been warned already, come to that, only I never just 'zactly seen it quite so clear as what you've put it now.'

Zuno gazed in silence over her head as though what she had said did not really call for a reply. In memory she saw again the aloof young dandy whose fastidious hauteur had outfaced the brigands on the highway. She took his hand and smiled.

'But *you're* not afraid of her, are you, U-Zuno?'

'I? Oh, I find her most tedious. The truth is, she's reached a state of mind in which she's the deadly enemy of virtually any young woman in the upper city who commands popularity. If I could help you, Maia, I would. But now you tell me you're actually soliciting *favours* from her.' He shrugged his shoulders. 'That's playing into her hands. I can only advise you that *I* wouldn't want to offer myself as a plaything for her ingenuity. If I were you, I should desist. I say that as a friend.'

Two slaves, carrying brooms and pails of water, were approaching down the hall. Zuno, nodding and murmuring 'Certainly, säiyett, I quite understand,' bowed and held open the door.

: 61 :

THE QUEEN'S PRICE

It was from this hour that Maia began more and more frequently to imagine Zen-Kurel present at her side. Crossing the lawn to her jekzha and smiling, with a pretence of unconcern, to her soldiers as they scrambled up from the shade under the wall, she found herself making believe, child-like, that he and she were together, heads close as they talked, his arm round her waist. Brave, warm, a shade rash, a shade immature, infinitely likeable, himself somewhat, perhaps, in need of a loyal friend with a cool head, Zenka was admonishing her, in his eager, confident voice, not to be afraid of the Sacred Queen or her spiteful capers (yes, that was his phrase, 'spiteful capers'), because *he* would protect her and see that she came to no harm. 'And you don't mind that I'm doing this for Tharrin?' she asked him, as he sat with her in the jekzha, one hand gently caressing her scarred thigh. 'Of course not! I certainly wouldn't think much of you if you *didn't*.' 'And what's to become of him when we've set him free?' 'Why, he's to go home and keep out of trouble, what else? Once we're married—' 'Oh, Zenka, we're to be *married*?' 'Yes, of course. What's the point of waiting any longer?' 'Oh, Zenka—' 'And I'm proud of you, Maia. I'm really proud that you weren't afraid of the Sacred Queen.'

Walking by the Barb—for she could find no appetite for the meal poor Ogma had prepared—a fresh thought occurred to her, affording a curious, paradoxical comfort. She realized, now, that the reason why she had been excited by the punishment of Meris was that, unconsciously, she had been jealous of her—oh, Lespa! only to think of it now!—as Sencho's favourite. Yes, envious of that, and also of her experience, competence and brassy sophistication. Meris was tough. Of her own accord she had chosen to lead a life of crime and violence—she'd derived satisfaction and amusement from using her looks to lure men to disaster. If anyone could stand a good smacking, it was Meris. And had she not had her revenge on Sencho— literally pressed down and running over, one might say? Besides, she herself—Maia—had changed much since Suba: she would not feel now as she had then. The Maia who had attended Sencho at the Rains banquet had been a mere child. Yet that child, too, would have been horrified by the prisoners in the Sheldad and by coming upon poor Chia as she had that morning. 'You're not even cruel, are you?' Fornis had said to her. No, she wasn't.

There was, clearly, very little that did not reach the ears of Fornis. Was it not highly probable that she might have heard something from Sencho— or even, perhaps, from Terebinthia—about her, Maia's reaction to Meris's whipping which had misled her into thinking that Maia was just the girl to suit her? Once Sencho was dead she had certainly wasted little or no time. Yet it had taken her even less time to realize that she had been mistaken. 'You're naturally pure; one day it'll catch up with you—if you live that long.' 'I'll live, Zenka,' she said aloud. 'Oh, I'll live! And I'll find you again, believe me.' For nowhere in all her imaginings was there a particle of doubt that he had no more forgotten her than she him.

It was time to return to Fornis's house. She walked back along the edge of the reed-beds, beyond which a grebe, black-crested and ochre-necked, was swimming with its chicks on its back. One day I'll swim the Zhairgen to Katria, she thought, and Zenka'll be waiting for me on the bank.

The Sacred Queen, she was informed, was down at the archery butts behind the house; and thither Ashaktis conducted her. She said little or nothing on the way and Maia, for her part, offered no more than the few words necessary to ensure that Ashaktis could not say that she had behaved discourteously. The mown field, flanked on one side with pinnate-leaved, white-umbelled *brygon* trees, stretched away to the Peacock Wall, under which stood the targets—life-sized effigies of Katrian soldiers, their arms stiff as scarecrows' in the sunshine.

Fornis, now dressed, as though for hunting, in a green jerkin and leather breeches, paused briefly as she saw Maia approaching and then, having spent a few moments in adjusting the leather guard on her left wrist and forearm, fitted an arrow, drew and loosed at a target. The arrow hit its mark precisely. Maia stood waiting while the queen shot six more with equal precision. Then, leaning on her bow, she unstrung it and laid it down beside the remaining arrows on the trestle table beside her.

'You've come to speak to me?'

'No, esta-säiyett, for I've nothing more to say,' replied the invisible Zenka through Maia's lips. 'I've simply come as you asked me, to hear your decision.'

'About your brother, is it?'

'My step-father, esta-säiyett.'

'Ah, yes. I couldn't remember, I'm afraid. Well, you must know this man, I suppose. What do you think he's worth?'

At this Maia's heart leapt. Apparently the queen was at least ready to sell Tharrin on some kind of terms.

'I can't say, esta-säiyett: I've no experience, I'm afraid.'

'The man's life's dedicated to Cran,' said the queen, as though deliberating. 'But of course we must try to oblige you, Maia, if possible.'

'Thank you very much, esta-säiyett: I'm most grateful, and so will he be.'

'I've gone so far as to discuss the matter with the chief priest' (I wonder whether she really has? thought Maia) 'and we feel that, remembering your valuable services to the city, the god would probably be content to forgo this sacrifice in return for—shall we say?—ten thousand meld.'

She turned aside and began examining the fletching of one of the arrows.

So the game had entered another stage; and the silly mouse had afforded sport by showing, for a moment, that it had really supposed it was going to escape. Little or no experience as Maia had, she knew enough to be certain that Tharrin—an unskilled man in poor condition and over forty years old—was not worth a fifth of the sum the queen had named. She herself, as an outstandingly beautiful and almost untouched girl of fifteen, had been sold for fifteen thousand. Ogma, if she had not been given to the Serrelinda as a gift, might have been expected to fetch about eight hundred.

Yet the queen's game was far more ingenious than a mere promise followed by deprivation: that would have lacked subtlety. She had weighed to a nicety Maia's innate warmth of heart and genuine determination to save Tharrin if she could. With the special circumstance that Tharrin was temple property, a kind of deodand, it was possible publicly to justify the enormous sum demanded. But cleverer still, it would be just within Maia's power to raise it, provided she was ready to sacrifice most of what she possessed—her jewels, her silver and so on. However, there was an alternative way to get the money, as Occula would undoubtedly have reminded her; and this, she thought, she would certainly pursue.

608

'Very well, esta-säiyett. I'll buy him from the temple for that sum.'

'There's only one condition,' said the queen, smiling, 'which is un-avoidable, I'm afraid, remembering that the executions are due to take place tomorrow morning. I shall need to receive the whole sum from you in coin by this time tomorrow at the latest.'

Clearly, it had occurred to the queen no less readily than to Maia herself that, given time, and as the most adulated and desired woman in the city, she could have procured the money by the same means as Nen-naunir would have procured it; though this would have been a somewhat lengthy undertaking. To advance her such a sum at twenty-four hours' notice, however, would be beyond the means of any friends she possessed; beyond the means, indeed, of virtually anyone in the upper city.

A little distance away, a cat had appeared on top of the wall bordering one side of the field. Fornis, picking up her bow again, strung it and then, almost without aiming as it seemed, shot an arrow which passed between the top of the wall and the cat's belly. As the cat leapt out of sight she tossed the bow to Ashaktis, clicking her tongue with annoyance.

'That's enough for today, Shakti,' she said. 'My wrist's getting tired. Tell Occula to get the bath ready and call the little boys.'

With this she and Ashaktis turned away, leaving Maia alone in the field.

Having returned along the quiet, sunny avenues flanked by flowering trees, stone walls and trim gardens, Maia, as she entered her house, was met by Ogma with the news that Lord Elvair-ka-Virrion was waiting to see her.

As she came into the sunny parlour overlooking the Barb he sprang up from the window-seat and took both her hands in his own so eagerly that he almost seemed about to swing her off her feet.

'Maia! I was determined to wait until you came back! What a charming house this is they've given you! I do hope you're happy here, and getting well over your injuries—your honourable wounds, I ought to say. I only wish *I* had a few like yours to boast about—you're ahead of me there, I'm afraid—for the time being, anyway. But you're looking marvellous! More beautiful than ever.'

He had changed out of his military gear and was now dressed with all his usual flamboyance, plumed and blazoned like a kynat. She showed him over the house and the little garden, strolled with him down to the shore and back and then poured him wine as he sat once more by the window. She wondered what his reason might be for coming to see her. A few months ago she would have been in no doubt; but that, of course, was before Milvushina had joined his household. Milvushina—another enemy of the Sacred Queen: what subtle trap might be in preparation for her? Yet she, at least, had powerful protectors. The thought of her own insecurity was beginning to frighten her.

'Don't you think so, Maia?' asked Elvair-ka-Virrion.

She recollected herself with a blush. 'I'm sorry, my lord: please forgive me. I'm afraid I'd just let my mind wander for a moment, kind of. What were you saying?'

He paused, looking at her over his wine-cup with an air of the most sincere concern and commiseration, so that she found herself for a moment remembering old Nasada. At length he said, 'Maia, I don't know how you think of me, but I've always felt for you very sincerely, and not just since you became the Serrelinda, either. I'd like to think you feel I'm your friend. Anyway, I can tell when you're not yourself. You're still worrying, aren't you, about your step-father—that business you came to talk about in the palace this morning? What's happened? You don't want to drop it, but you're frightened of the queen; is that it?'

She looked up at him with brimming eyes.

'I'm *not* afraid of the queen. I'm *not*!'

'Don't be silly. Everyone is. Durakkon is, even my father—everyone.'

Slowly, and with hesitation—for she felt keenly not only her power-lessness to help Tharrin except at the cost of almost all she had gained, but also that the queen had succeeded only too well in making a fool and a dupe of her—she began to tell him what had happened since she had left the Lord General. When she spoke of how she had returned to the queen at noon Elvair-ka-Virrion whistled.

'You mean you went back there a second time and held her to her word?'

'Well, yes: s'pose you could sort of put it like that.'

'You realize there's probably not a man in my entire regiment who would have dared to do that? She might have put an arrow through you or just had you thrown down a well: oh, yes, she might, Maia, believe me.'

'Reckon she must 'a been savin' up, then, for something a bit more entertaining, like,' said Maia bitterly. She finished her story, this time telling frankly about her seduction by Tharrin. 'Poor Tharrin's nothing to me any more and never will be, but I can't just stand by and do nothing. Nor I can't see as it'd do the Leopards any harm to let him go. He's had that much of a fright, he'd never do nothing like that n'more; you can count on it.' She paused. Then, 'Do you know anyone as'd buy this house today for ten thousand meld down?'

'You really are that serious?'

'Yes, I am.'

He paused, reflecting. At length he said, 'You know I'm leaving tomor-row to lead the campaign in Chalcon? I'm giving the usual party—a

610

barrarz—tonight. All my officers will be there, of course—including Shend-Lador—and a lot of other people you know; Sarget for one; oh, and Randronoth, the governor of Lapan—you know him, don't you?'

'I ought to: I had to bed with him once at Sencho's.'

'Oh, he'd have liked that, Randronoth would. Well, Milvushina will be there, of course, and Otavis and Nennaunir. Your friend Fordil's bringing his drums and hinnaris along, and everyone's hoping you'll dance. That was what I came for—to ask you particularly. But in the light of what you've been telling me, I've just had another idea that may appeal to you. I think it'll work, provided we can get everyone in the right mood. I'm ready to do everything I can to help you in this business, Maia, I promise you.'

She gazed back at him, half-smiling in response to his smile, uncertain, puzzled but intrigued.

'Let's just have another stroll down that pretty garden of yours,' said Elvair-ka-Virrion, draining off his goblet and picking up his plumed hat from the table, 'and I'll tell you what it is I've got in mind. Cheer up: I think we may beat Fornis yet.'

: 62 :

THARRIN'S DISCLOSURE

She had sent Ogma down to the prison to say she was coming, and this time was received with the respect appropriate to the Serrelinda. Seen in the bright afternoon sunshine, from the window of Pokada's stuffy little room, the courtyard, like that of a barracks, and the ugly blocks seemed more arid and dismal than ever. Not a bush or bloom, not a blade of grass; even the creeper below the window-sill, she now realized, was dead. The sun, shining from a clear sky into this squalid, bare place served—so it seemed—only to stress its isolation and lack of all natural beauty—tree, flower or bird-song. Nowhere, in the still heat, was there a trace of any animate thing. Why, 'tis like being struck deaf, she thought. Everything's here, 'ceptin' for something missing that's enough to drive you mad.

Pokada, with a singular lack of tact, had asked her, in preliminary conversation, whether she was acquainted with Lalloc; to which she replied merely with a cold stare. This, however, had not been sufficient to discourage the gaoler from running garrulously on about his own association with the slave-dealer. After a minute or two it dawned on Maia that he was actually proud of it, and was boasting of his acquaintance with someone who in his world figured as an illustrious citizen. Lalloc, it appeared, was a not infrequent visitor on business at the gaol and had often shown himself most affable. 'Oh, yes, säiyett; oh, yes,' went on Pokada, 'we're not without our distinguished connections here, you know. Why, one day last year the Sacred Queen herself honoured us with a visit.'

'What she want to come here for, then?' Maia was momentarily startled out of her assumed composure.

'Oh, to select a man, you know, säiyett; a prisoner—for some purpose connected with the sacred office, she told me. Very conscientious, the Sacred Queen, I've always understood. No, no, you mustn't think of us here as just a bunch of old turnkeys, you know. "Why, you're quite a civic functionary, Pokada," U-Lalloc was kind enough to say to me once. Yes, a civic functionary—'

Maia, not without a certain bitter amusement, deliberately copied the detached manner which (not least because of its effectiveness) had so often irritated her in Milvushina; so that after a little more one-sided chat the gaoler took the hint and left her. Sitting on the bench, her arms before her on the table, she let her head droop and fell into a reverie from which she was roused by the opening of the door.

Tharrin was already looking better. For a start he was clean—or as clean, thought the new Maia, as people like him ever were. His hair was combed and she thought it quite probable that it might even be free of lice. He still looked gaunt and ravaged, a man who had undergone a dreadful ordeal, but the eyes that met hers now contained some self-possession— even expectancy—and after a moment he actually contrived a sort of half-smile as well. He was wearing presentable, if rough and mended, clothes and his nails had been trimmed and were no longer black. As soon as he perceived—which he did as quickly as a dog—that her mind was free of calamity, his manner began to assume a faint, residual hint of the former strolling rascal—ah, there's no real harm in him, to be sure—the tom-cat renowned for always falling on his feet. Oh, of course, it had been the very devil of a scrape, don't you know; worst he'd ever been in, matter of fact; there'd been times when he'd thought it was all up with him, honest. But girls had their uses, and somehow something always seemed to turn up lucky for a lad like him. Wouldn't you just know it?

Maia saw all this as clearly as Occula would have seen it. She knew that she would never want Tharrin again in a hundred years: yet she had hazarded her standing and risked her safety on his account, and was determined to go on doing so as long as necessary. Why? She knew why. He was an integral part of herself—of where she had come from and what she was—he was part of the furniture of her life. 'No, I'm just not *going* to get rid of that there old bench. It belonged to my mum and I like it, so there. More you goes on about it, more I'll stick.'

She smiled, and motioned him to sit down opposite her.

'Tharrin, I'm as certain as I can be that this time tomorrow you'll be free.'

She wasn't, of course: she only hoped to Cran she was right. But there was no point in 'perhaps' and 'maybe' and 'if only I can.' What he desperately needed was confidence and peace of mind. For him, uncertainty would be almost as bad as hopelessness, sitting in this place with nothing to do all day, waiting and thinking.

Across the table, he grasped her hand in both his own, smiling almost jauntily.

'Maia! I knew you could do it! You're the most wonderful girl! I'll never, never forget what you've done for me. My beautiful, golden fish!'

You bastard, she thought. You came home and found I'd been carted off to Bekla and you never lifted a finger even just to find out what had become of me. Beautiful, golden fish my venda! And yet I can't—how funny—help feeling a sort of affection mixed up with contempt.

But now it was time to get down to business and no messing.

'Tharrin, what do you mean to do once you're free? Will you go back to mother and the girls and take up where you left off, or do you want to take them away and start somewhere else?'

He paused. Well, her question certainly must have come a bit sudden, of course; but unless she was very much mistaken, his mind hadn't been altogether free from the notion that he might just baste off and try his luck somewhere else.

'You do *mean* to go back to mother, don't you?'

'Oh, yes, yes, Maia, of course! Oh yes, naturally. Have to look after them, yes; oh, always do that.'

'You see,' she said, smiling and stroking his hand, 'you'll be sort of on parole, Tharrin. If you—well, you know, if you was to get into any more trouble—I know you won't—but they'd take you in again, and I wouldn't be able to help you a second time. You do understand, don't you?'

He understood all right: she was pretty sure of that. What an extraordinary fellow he was, she thought. Talk about volatile! Just escaped from death by torture and in a wink he was almost sprightly, and then within the minute he was disappointed at being foiled in a little dodge to go off on the loose. Ah, to the rebels in Chalcon, very like. She'd bet anything that that had already occurred to him. Yet for the life of her she couldn't entirely dislike him. He'd got—well, humanity, kind of.

'Dearest,' she said, still holding his hand '—and I must call you that, even though we're not lovers any more—you've got to realize I've got a fair old bit of influence now.'

He laughed. He even slapped his thigh—at which his threadbare breeches gave off a puff of dust.

'I know! "Maia swam the river: Maia saved the city." I wonder what they said down at "The Safe Moorings", don't you? I haven't been there for weeks, so I can't tell.' He paused. 'In some ways it's a pity you did save the city, golden Maia. If you hadn't, Karnat would have been in Bekla by now.'

'Don't you give me that!' she flashed at him. 'If I hadn't, three hundred Tonildan boys'd be laying dead and done in Paltesh, and that'd have been just for a start! Anyway, Tharrin, don't you try and act up to me as you've got political principles about heldril and Leopards, nor none of that old moonshine. What you did was done for money, and you basting well know it. Not but what you weren't always generous with it,' she added, relenting a little. 'I'll give you that.'

'Kept a roof over our heads,' he muttered, his eyes on the floor.

'Well, just you see as you go on doing that, else I'll know the reason why.'

At that he looked up at her, straight and serious.

'Maia, I can't see why you should be bothering yourself so much about Morca; that I can't. She sold you into slavery, didn't she? A real dirty trick that was.'

The picture this called into Maia's mind—namely, of Morca as she had last seen her—prompted her next question.

'Is she all right? What was the baby—a boy?'

'No, another girl. Yes, she's all right as far as I know. Was when I left for Thettit, anyway. I was arrested in Thettit, you know. All the same, it's bound to have been rough on them with me gone. I dare say Kelsi and Nala—'

'Oh, I blame myself, that I do! I'll give you some money to take back, Tharrin. And just you mind it gets there, too, d'you see? Well, I *know* mum sold me, and that was cruel, I don't deny; but I can't say as she hadn't had that to make her, in a manner of speaking; and besides, her condition at the time and all. She was that upset, she did a lot more to me than what she need have; but all the same, look where it's got me—and when all's said and done she *is* my mother.'

Tharrin, getting up, walked across to the bright glare of the window and stood dark against the light. After a pause he said, 'I don't know what *she'd* say, Maia, but I reckon it's high time you were told.'

'Told? Told what?'

'That she's *not* your mother. You didn't know that, did you?'

'Not my *mother*?' Maia was at a complete loss. Had his sufferings turned his wits, or what? Tharrin said no more, and at length she asked, 'Whatever do you mean?'

'I'll tell you.' He came back and sat down. 'I'll tell you all about it, just

614

as she told it to me. Listen, Maia. Do you know how long ago your—well, your father and mother; I'll call them that for now—were married?'

' 'Bout twenty year now, isn't it? But Tharrin, I want to know, what d'you mean—'

'Listen! Yes, your father and Morca were married about twenty years ago. And there were no children. A farmer needs children, doesn't he? He needs labour. A farmer without children's an unfortunate man. But there were no children; and two years went by, three years, four and never a sign. Morca felt bad, even though your father never spoke a harsh word. It was a bad time—bad as could be, she said. It got to prey on her mind. No children—that's a bitter misfortune to bear, by all accounts.

'But I'll go on. One night in the rains it was pitch-dark and nothing but mud everywhere—well, you know how it is along Serrelind. The two of them had had supper and were just going to bed when suddenly they heard a noise outside—something quite big, stumbling about. They thought it must be a beast got loose.

'Your father went out with a lamp, but he couldn't see what it was and then the rain put the lamp out. And at that moment, in the dark, someone clutched his legs and there was a woman on the ground, crying and begging for help. He just picked her up and carried her indoors, all wet through as she was and all her clothes and her hair just one mass of mud, Morca said. They pulled the sodden clothes off her and washed her and put her into bed.

'She was only a young lass. I don't know how old—Morca didn't say— but not much older than you are now, I suppose. It was much as ever they could understand her, 'cos she was a Suban—a marsh-frog. Ah, but she was a regular pretty girl for all that, Morca said. Or she would have been, only she was in such a state; and she was pregnant. She was more than that; she was going to drop it any minute, she was going into labour. Oh, they were in a right taking, I'll tell you.

'Morca said she never asked her to account for herself. It was no time for that. But then the girl began talking of her own accord. She said her elder sister had been murdered in Suba—murdered by the wife of the High Baron of Urtah, she said: house burned in the night with her in it and her young son too. She said her sister had been some famous dancer and the High Baron had been her lover. That was why the wife had murdered her. And she herself had only learned of this that very morning, while she was out of her own house, gone down the village—I don't know, gone to buy salt or something, I think Morca said. She and her husband were living in eastern Urtah, not far from the highway between Gelt and Bekla. She never said where she first met him or how they came to be living there. Anyway, the girl had no sooner heard this than someone else came running

615

up and told her her own husband was dead—can you imagine it? They'd come upon him—some more of the High Baron's wife's men had—in his own home and killed him, just because he was the husband of the younger sister of this What's-her-name, this dancer in Suba. And now the men were going through the village, looking for her.

'Well, of course she was terrified out of her life, this poor girl. And she was all the more terrified because there wasn't anyone she felt she could trust. Well, I mean, a Suban girl, a marsh-frog come to eastern Urtah; you can just picture it, can't you? She'd be a real fish out of water, wouldn't she? Anyway, she panicked. She ran out of the village just as she was and went east across the Plain. She wasn't making for anywhere in particular. Once she got to the highway, of course, she ought to have tried to get to Bekla, but she didn't. I suppose she must have thought these men might follow down the highway looking for her. She just kept on east across the Tonildan Waste.

'Well, I've reckoned it since as she must have done twenty-five miles across the Waste, poor girl, and her in that state! Anyway, at last, in the dark and the rain, she collapsed outside your father's door.

'They went and got Drigga from up the lane and she and Morca did everything they could. And at one point they thought they'd pulled her through, Morca said. You'd been born—'

'Me?'

'Yes, you'd been born and everything seemed all right: but then she just bled and bled until she died, Morca said. But *you* were as bonny as could be.'

Maia was crying.

'Well, your father—I'll go on calling him that—he thought that after what the girl had told them, the less got out the better, or there might be some more of these Urtan men—these murderers—coming to look for *you*, d'you see? That queen—baroness—whatever she was—she meant business, that was clear enough. And old Drigga, she agreed. So what happened was, they buried the poor girl and no one the wiser—she's down by that big ash-tree beside the lake—'

'Oh, Tharrin! That ash-tree? *My* tree?'

'Yes, she is. And they gave it out—and old Drigga backed them up, said as she'd been in the know all along—that the baby was Morca's. Well, quite believable; I mean, it doesn't always show all that much with the first baby, does it? And Morca was ready with some story about having sworn a vow to Shakkarn that if only he'd take away her trouble, she wouldn't tell a soul until everything had gone off all right.

'So the long and short of it was they brought you up as their own daughter. But they never told you, because you'd have let on, wouldn't you?—children always talk—and they were still afraid of this woman and

616

what might happen. But apparently she died herself quite soon after you were born, so they needn't have worried; but they never knew that, you see. You don't get to hear all that much in country places, do you? and I suppose it never occurred to them to make enquiries. Anyway, that's the truth for you at last. Morca's not your mother.'

Maia was weeping so intensely that for a little while she could not speak. At last she said, 'I always wo-wondered why Drigga was so good to me. She was always—well, sort of specially kind. Oh dear, oh dear!'

Tharrin made no reply and she, at length getting her feelings a little more under control, went on, 'So—at that rate, then—I'm sister's daughter to this famous No—this famous Suban dancer?'

'Yes. Whoever she may have been: for it's all a long time ago now, isn't it? Anyway, you did Morca some good, didn't you? Four children she's borne since then and healthy as anybody's, even if they *are* all girls.'

Maia stood up. She must be alone to think.

'Thank you for telling me. Have you got everything you need, Tharrin? Are they good to you? Here's a hundred meld. Is there anything else you want? Tell me.'

'No, nothing. I'll be fine till you come back. Cran bless you, Maia! How can I ever thank you?'

'Well, I'll be back before noon tomorrow, and then you'll be free! You can count on that, so sleep well.' She kissed him warmly, feeling her tears wet against his face. 'Good-bye for now.'

On the way out, neither Pokada nor anyone else remarked on her weeping. This was a place where people often wept and after all, she had not told any of them that Tharrin was going to be released.

: 63 :

THE BARRARZ

What—even though it may involve neither pain nor danger—is more bewildering and agitating than to learn something of the greatest importance about oneself—something entirely unsuspected and highly extraordinary; verging on the unique: to find oneself in a situation which very few indeed (and none available to talk to) can have been called upon to face? Some there be who have found themselves heirs to kingdoms; others the sudden possessors of some hitherto undreamt-of knowledge or truth. Others again have stumbled, all unawares, upon some huge discovery, daunting, of incalculable import. Visions have been vouchsafed to simpletons, landfalls made by the lost and desperate, revelations bestowed upon purblind stumblers in the dark. My very self is changed for ever; I am not and can never again be the person I was. Why me, God, why me? My dazzled, peering eyes cannot make out the import, the perspective: a fly on the window-pane or a far-off mountain? But first and foremost, God, am I beneficiary or victim?

Maia sat in her garden above the Barb. From time to time she beat with the flat of her hand upon the seat-slats beside her, staring out unseeingly across the water. Again, she sprang up and began pacing back and forth over the grass; then gripped the rail of the fence with both hands and rocked herself backwards and forwards. To Ogma, peeping from an up-stairs window, it was plain that her mistress must have learned something to upset her: no doubt an affair of the heart, she thought with sluggish, lukewarm envy (for such things lay so far beyond Ogma's horizon that she had little real idea of them), yet for the life of her she could not imagine who it might be. Well, she knew that Maia was to attend Elvair-ka-Virrion's barrarz that night. No doubt more would become clear later, for to give her her due Miss Maia had never been one to make herself out better than anybody else, to act stand-offish or keep secrets.

In Maia's heart there was a kind of fighting. Part was enflamed with excitement by what Tharrin had told her, part full of trepidation, exposed and fearful as a fledgling just flown from the nest. She was, in fact, in a state of shock. Again and again she called before her mind's eye that grim, long-ago night which Tharrin had described to her—the exhausted girl, in mortal terror, stumbling on through the mud and rain she knew not whither, her belly big with—with herself! *She*, too had taken part in that dreadful journey towards death—and life! She saw her dear father—Ah, no! Now her father no longer—striding in out of the darkness with the lass in his arms: Morca staring in bewilderment and consternation: the dim-lit vigil over the sweating, babbling girl: Drigga heating water, making up the fire, comforting, reassuring. Then her thoughts leapt to the ash-tree by the lake—her own tree, from which she had so often dropped blissfully down into the water, to swim away, to escape from her drudgery and chores. Where exactly could the grave be? She called the surrounding ground before her mind's eye. There was nothing to see, no mound—well, no, they'd have made sure of that. Could it be that bit over by—But then she began to cry again and couldn't think straight any more.

Her father was not her father. And Kelsi and Nala and little Lirrit—oh, she'd been so fond of Lirrit, she'd been the one she really loved best—they weren't her sisters at all! And Morca? Well, at least that made what she'd done a bit more understandable. They mustn't be left alone, they mustn't go in want. She'd send them money. And Tharrin—she'd need to keep an eye on Tharrin: send one of her soldiers back to Serrelind with him: ah, make sure he got there and all, and the money too.

And she herself? She was a Suban—a marsh-frog! Well, half, for sure, anyway. But her real father—had *he* been a Suban? No, not if they'd been living in eastern Urtah: he'd have been an Urtan. Where exactly was the village? It shouldn't be difficult to find out—they'd not have forgotten the murder after as little as sixteen and a half years. There'd be people there who'd known her father and mother.

Nokomis! She was sister's daughter, then, to the fabulous, legendary Nokomis! Well, that explained a whole basting lot, as Occula would no doubt have remarked. And more than that, she and Bayub-Otal were cousins! And before the implications of this, poor Maia fetched up literally at a standstill and all of a shake, like a boat in the eye of the wind. 'Oh, it's all too much at one go, that it is!' she said aloud, as though declaring to the gods that she was just not going to play any more. She sat down on the grass and began chewing daisies; and a few minutes later Ogma came to tell her that dinner was ready.

Today she could eat all right. Both horror and uncertainty had left her. She knew what she meant to do, and her confidence was only slightly less than her determination. After the meal, telling Jarvil to admit no one, she lay down on her bed, escaping into sleep with the relief of a slave pitching a heavy load off his back and not caring which way up it landed, either.

When she woke, Ogma was rattling pails in the bathroom and a beaker of milk, its top covered with muslin, was standing on the table beside her bed. The sun was setting and the swifts were darting and screaming high up in the cooling air. A passer-by called to someone in the quiet road outside. A scent of planella drifted in from the garden. Suddenly it seemed to Maia that some god was revealing to her a truth—that the world was not, in fact, transfixed upon a few sharp, pyramidal points of great matters. Rather, it was supported easily upon countless passing moments, a myriad diurnal trivia, like the host of befriending butterflies in old Drigga's story, who carried the wandering princess up and over the ice mountain.

She drank the milk and stretched luxuriously, smelling the planella, admiring again the workmanship of the onyx rabbit and listening to the sound of water pouring into the bath. 'I'm not cold or hungry or ill,' she thought, 'and I've got me.' Somewhere outside, the blue-finch sang his little phrase, 'Never never never never *let*-you-fear.' It was the only one he knew. She laughed, sat up and swung her feet to the floor. She'd show them!

She would wear the cherry-coloured robe with the bodice of crystals— one of four or five which they had given her on her return to the city (for the authorities, having taken over Sencho's great mass of possessions and effects, had been weeks in disposing of them, and she had returned in time to be offered her pick of the wardrobe). The cherry dress had been lucky on the night of the senguela: it would be lucky now. For the rest, her diamonds and a spray of planella in her hair (which she would comb out loose over her shoulders) would do very well. Sixteen-year-old Maia had no need to wonder what Fornis might keep in her cabinet of unguents.

Coming downstairs in the rose-and-saffron half-light reflected from the Barb, over which the bats were already flittering, she found her two soldiers—summoned by Ogma—waiting to take her to the Lord General's house. She gave them ten meld apiece and told them to go and drink it. 'Half a mile up the Trepsis Avenue, on an evening like this? I'm walking!' At this their eyes opened wide, for in the upper city the only women who walked in public were slaves. But the Serrelinda—well, for the matter of that she might have been going to swim it (oh, yes, they'd heard that story all right) and no one would have had a word to say.

'But when shall we come to the Lord General's to bring you home, then, säiyett?' asked Brero. 'You needn't,' she said. 'I'll send you a message tomorrow morning.' At which he clapped his hand over his mouth to suppress an appreciative guffaw. She didn't mess about, did she, the little säiyett? Someone or other wasn't half going to be lucky.

The avenue seemed as full of scents as a flowerbed of summer bees, stirring and mingling, here and gone. Roses, lake water and planella, wood-smoke and dew, clipped grass and a sharp, resinous smell from where someone was sawing logs. She, the Serrelinda, was floating to her destination on the fragrance of the world, like the butterfly princess on her magic quest. She was on her way to save poor old Tharrin from the Sacred Queen. Ah, and after that she'd have to start thinking about Bayub-Otal and all. Shakkarn alive! He, the rightful Ban of Suba, was not only her liege lord but her own kith and kin! And anyway, even setting all that aside, she'd begun to think rather differently of him since Suba and since Nasada. Funny, she thought, how you get to altering your ideas about people as you find out a bit more about them. Like Milvushina.

Am I beautiful, Zenka? Zenka, am I the girl you can feel proud of? You never had the chance to show me off, Zenka, did you; to feel proud of your sweetheart in public, among other Katrians? 'You're the most beautiful girl in the world,' he answered. 'I'm always with you, all the time: I'll *never* leave you.' She broke off a spray of yellow *claris* trailing over a wall beside her. 'Take this, my darling,' he said, 'and wear it for me: if I knew of anything more beautiful to give you, I would. Well, we're on active service now, you know. Have to grab what we can get.' Oh, thank you, Zenka! I love you so much! Oh, do you remember how we chose a dagger? And you said—

From behind her sounded the soft flit-flat, flit-flat of a jekzha-man's feet in the dust and then a girl's voice, 'Maia! What in the *world* are you doing here?'

It was Nennaunir, wrapped in a gossamer-thin, azure cloak, a crystal-and-gold ring on one finger of the hand that held the rail as she leant towards Maia, her high-piled hair set now not with one but apparently about five garnet combs.

Maia laughed. 'Walking to Elvair's party.'

'Walking? You're out of your mind! Where are your soldiers, for Cran's sake?'

'I sent them off to get drunk.'

'Whatever for?'

' 'Cos I wanted to walk.'

Nennaunir shook her head and looked serious. 'It won't do you any good, Maia—not in the long run it won't—doing eccentric things like going about on foot in the upper city. I mean that as a friend. You've got a position to keep up, my lass. You can't just take it into your head to go strolling up the Trepsis Avenue in the twilight, loaded with diamonds. People may even start thinking you're a human being. Get in here with me, come on.'

Meekly Maia obeyed, settling herself comfortably beside Nennaunir as the man went on. The shearna seemed drenched in kepris—in the confined space of the jekzha it was quite overpowering—and this reminded Maia that she herself had forgotten to put on any scent. Never mind, she thought. There's sure to be some flowers; I can always pick up a jasmine wreath or something.

'I called round for you, as a matter of fact,' said Nennaunir, 'and Ogma told me what you'd done, so I was looking out for you. That girl, by the way,' she went on after a few moments, 'I don't think she's quite what you need, Maia, to be honest. Please don't take this the wrong way, but a girl as young as you are needs someone sharper and—well, knowledgeable about people and affairs and what's going on. It's a great pity you couldn't have kept that woman Terebinthia to look after you. I'm sure she'd have been delighted, if only it had been put to her.'

'*She* might have been, but I shouldn't.'

'Why, was she a bitch?'

'Hard as nails and mean with it. The house-slaves all hated her; always sniffing about. I used to feel she was like water round a boat: you always had to be taking care to keep her outside, kind of. Oh, no, Nan, I couldn't never have done with her—not after I'd had to obey her at Sencho's and do what she told me. Surely you can see that?'

'Well, p'raps. But all the same, Maia, just you and that poor little club-footed ninny together in that house—I'm not happy about it. Oh, I'm sure she's first-rate in the market; and she cooks a nice meal, I don't say she doesn't. But the upper city's a tricky place, and she's not at *all* the right sort to be personal slave to a young and inexperienced girl shot up into a big public position. I warned you only the other day: there's all kinds of unscrupulous people who'd like to make use of you; to say nothing of possible enemies. You ought to get yourself someone older and shrewder, someone who can see what's what and keep you straight. I wish *I* had, years ago; I'll tell you that.'

'I'll think about it, Nan: really I will.' Maia, like most of us when some more experienced friend criticizes arrangements which we had thought suitable enough but now begin to have sneaking doubts about, felt resentful, but had no wish to fall out with a good friend like Nennaunir.

'For instance,' went on Nennaunir, turning her sleek, shining head and looking Maia over appraisingly, 'Terebinthia would never have let you go to a barrarz dressed like that. Whose idea was that—yours or Ogma's?'

'Mine. Whatever's wrong with it? I wore this at Sarget's party in the Barons' Palace and—'

'I know, darling. I was there—remember? But it's not right for a barrarz.'

'What *is* a barrarz? Elvair was on saying that—"a barrarz"—'

Nennaunir silently drove one fist twice into the other palm, like a girl tried close to the point of outburst.

'So Ogma didn't know about a barrarz? Honestly—'

'Don't be cross, Nan: just tell me. There's a first time for everything, you know.'

'First time?' replied the shearna. 'I'm worried about you, that's all. There can be situations where a girl only has to be wrong once, you know.'

'But is a barrarz one of them?'

Nennaunir burst into soft, happy laughter.

'No, fortunately not. Of course you'll do very well as you are, Maia dear. I didn't mean to be a cat, truly. You're very lucky—you'll always look marvellous; for quite a few years, anyway. I heard you met King Karnat dressed in nothing but your shift and a bunch of golden lilies. Is that true?'

Maia stared. 'How on earth did you know that? I never told a soul!'

'Oh, news travels, dear; news travels.' Then, before Maia could question her further, she went on, 'Anyway, a barrarz: Cran help me, I should know! I've been to enough of them. It's the custom in Bekla—and elsewhere, for that matter—the night before soldiers are leaving on active service, for the commander to give a party for his officers—and some of the tryzatts too, sometimes. Well, it's apt to become a pretty rowdy affair, as you can imagine. They boast and shout and sing and drink themselves silly and naturally they generally get to basting the girls as well. The thing is, they're usually in a mood to be pretty open-handed—you know, ready to spend what they've got before they go. Many a good lygol I've had at a barrarz, though I admit I generally earned it right enough. I lost my virginity at a barrarz, actually—the one Kembri and Han-Glat gave in Dari-Paltesh before they marched on Bekla seven years ago.'

'So how do you dress for a barrarz, then?'

'Like a soldier's doxy, dear. At an upper city barrarz as classy as this one's going to be, it's fancy dress, really; but my job's to amuse people, after all.'

Leaning back in the jekzha, she opened the azure cloak. The flimsy, pale-green robe she was wearing beneath it was not only transparent, but in some curious way seemed less to cover than to display and intensify the smooth whiteness of her body. Crowning each of her breasts was a slightly convex silver figure, about two inches high, representing a laughing cherub. At their groins the craftsman had left holes in the silver, and through these Nennaunir had drawn her nipples. At her waist, beneath and not outside the robe, was a silver girdle, its clasp fashioned in the likeness of a naked nymph leaning backwards, half-reclining on her elbows. The aperture between her lustrous, up-drawn thighs was superimposed upon Nennaunir's navel.

'Clever workmanship, isn't it?' said the shearna, drawing Maia's fore-finger down to feel the smooth, weighty quality of the silver.

'But will all the girls be got up this kind of style?' asked Maia.

'Oh, no, I shouldn't think so,' replied Nennaunir. 'I just thought it'd be fun to wear these tonight: I got them in Ikat about two years ago. But here I've been chattering away and giving you all sorts of bad advice, and I nearly forgot what I really wanted to talk about—why I came round for you. Listen—this is terribly important. I believe a real chance has come up to get Sednil out of the temple; that is, for *you* to, if only you'll give it a try. Will you, dearest Maia? It would mean everything to me, and I'll always do you a good turn if ever I can.'

'*Me* get him out?' said Maia. 'How?'

Nennaunir paused for a few moments, gazing across the road at a wide, sloping bank of scented tigris, over which the moths were darting and hovering like tiny humming-birds. At length she said, 'You told me you once spent the night with Randronoth, when you were still at Sencho's.'

'Yes, I did,' said Maia. 'What about it?'

'Tell me, how did you get on with him?'

'Well, I don't just rightly know how to answer that,' said Maia. 'He didn't half enjoy himself, and he said as much, both to me and to old Sencho; but then men like that generally do enjoy theirselves, don't they, whether *you* do or not? I mean, they don't bother much about any give-an'-take. Far as I was concerned, it was all just part of what we had to do, like.'

'Well, whatever you may have thought at the time, it seems you really blew his ears apart for him that night,' said Nennaunir. 'Of course, Randronoth's a notorious baby-snatching goat—*I'm* too old for him, now; he usually likes them about fourteen—but apparently even he'd never known anything like *you* in all his basting life.'

'Very nice of him, I'm sure,' said Maia. 'Can't remember doin' anything as I thought such a great lot of myself.'

'No, of course not; how could you? But can you remember anything else about Randronoth?'

Maia, reflecting, frowned. 'Well, I don't just exactly know what you're on about, Nan, but I do remember one thing as struck me. He was very much taken with the clothes and jewels as I was wearing, and he asked me whether I had any idea what they might have cost: he reckoned it must 'a been all of seven thousand meld, he said. So I says, "Well, what you got in your arms now cost more 'n twice that"—which was true enough an' all. Only that seemed to get him going more than anything else. Seemed as if just the very idea of what I'd cost and what the clothes had cost and what the jewels had cost was enough to drive him wild.'

'Yes, well, I'm not surprised, because to tell you the truth Randronoth's already given me his own version of this; I mean, without exactly knowing what he was saying; just while he was telling me how marvellous you were. That man's got a kind of obsession about extravagance, though I don't believe he's ever realized it—not consciously. Randronoth loves to feel that there's any amount of wealth and expense tied up with his basting—it gets him excited. Give him some little banzi behind the hedge at a village festival and he wouldn't want her—probably couldn't do it. But Lalloc could doll the same girl up in a gold net and jewels and offer her for far too much, and Randronoth's zard would be splitting his breeches. It's a funny world, isn't it? That was what really led to all that trouble over poor Sednil, you see. I didn't want Randronoth's damned ring: as I told you, it wasn't a girl's ring at all. But it was the most valuable thing he happened to have with him, so he had to give it to me: it was part of the thrill; and to do him justice he never seems to regret these little larks afterwards. Even his bribe to keep me quiet was far more than it need have been.'

'But what about Sednil, then?' asked Maia.

'Well, now we come to it, pet; and if you don't like it, just say so; I shan't mind. Randronoth's up here again. He comes up every summer, you know, like all the provincial governors, to hand over his tax money. That's why he's brought so many soldiers with him. I hear they've drunk "The Serpent" dry already and now they're starting on "The Green Grove". Anyway, he came round to see me and all he could talk about was you.'

She paused, but Maia said nothing.

'He said he wanted you more than anything he'd ever wanted in the world,' continued Nennaunir. ' "The lovely, inaccessible Serrelinda." He knew you weren't a shearna, so could I help him—would I speak to you?'

'But—but why ever didn't he come and ask me himself, at that rate?' asked Maia.

'It seems he did,' replied Nennaunir. 'He went to your house this afternoon, but your porter sent him packing—said you weren't to be disturbed on any account. More or less told him to go and jump in the Barb, I gather.'

'I was asleep. I'd said as I didn' want to see anyone.'

'Oh—well, apparently Randronoth took it to mean you didn't want to see *him*.'

'Well, that's quite right,' said Maia. 'I don't feel inclined for anybody nowadays; not just at present.'

Nennaunir was no less swift than Sessendris had been. 'Someone you fancy, is there? Someone who's not here?'

'Well, maybe—I don't know, really, Nan. Only I just don't feel like becoming a shearna for the present, that's all.'

'Well, that's sensible enough. Who'd work if she hadn't got to? But listen—I asked Randronoth whether he'd be ready to do something out of the ordinary if only he could go to bed with you, and of course he said oh yes, he'd drink the Zhairgen dry and walk backwards to Zeray and half a dozen other stupid things. So then I reminded him about Sednil and said did he think that if he put his mind to it he could get him out of the temple; and he said he was pretty sure he could.'

'How?' asked Maia.

'Well, you see, he's got quite a few branded men working for him in Lapan; all the provincial governors have. And if he were to have a word with the household officer of the temple, who's in charge of the labour there—and slip him a few hundred meld, I dare say—he could probably fix up an exchange. A body for a body—why should anyone else care? Then once Sednil's been down in Lapan for a bit, Randronoth could probably arrange to have him discharged. Anyway, that's what he said and I think he'd keep his word—he's always been straight enough with me—if *only* he can get what he wants. And what he wants is you.'

Before Maia could answer they had arrived at the terrace flanking the door of the Lord General's house, where a group of girls and young officers were standing together in the sunset, drinking and talking as they waited for supper to be announced. Their arrival was the signal for Shend-Lador and a half a dozen others (among whom Maia recognized the big, bearded man whose breeches she had pulled about his knees in the Barb) to come crowding round their jekzha, shouting greetings and compliments and holding out willing hands to help them down.

'We'll talk about it later, Nan,' whispered Maia quickly. 'I'll try and help if I can, honest. Just let me think it over.'

Nennaunir nodded and at once, with the air of having never a care in the world, leapt headlong from the jekzha as lightly as a hare, to be caught by the bearded man, whom she immediately kissed and allowed to carry her up to the terrace with her arms round his neck.

Maia followed somewhat more sedately. Elvair-ka-Virrion himself came forward to hand her down and Milvushina—who, Maia noticed with relief, was dressed as demurely as herself—embraced her and led her over to where several porous, earthenware pitchers of wine, beaded with moisture, were standing in the shade under the terrace wall.

'Elvair's told me about your plan,' she murmured. 'I hope you'll succeed, Maia, with all my heart. You ought to: you seem to grow more beautiful every day. Being a public heroine obviously suits you.'

Maia enquired about the baby.

'Oh, I'm fine,' answered Milvushina. 'Sick as a cat every morning, and back-ache to go with it. The doctor says they're all good signs: the worse you feel, the more it shows he's getting all he needs.'

'It's a he, then?' smiled Maia.

'Elvair's been sacrificing to Airtha every third morning for a month,' said Milvushina. 'He dedicated his sword today, and swore to make over all his Chalcon spoils to her; prisoners, too. I never said anything, but I don't really want to see Santil become a temple slave: he's a very honourable, upright man, you know. Everyone in Chalcon admires him. I don't think he ought to be humiliated.'

'You're in no doubt he'll be captured, then?' asked Maia.

'Elvair's certain it'll all be over in two months,' replied Milvushina.

As they talked on, Maia gradually became aware that at this, the first party she had attended since her return to the city, she was plainly regarded as virtually a different girl from the Tonildan who had been one of Sencho's concubines. Nennaunir, a goblet in one hand, was already surrounded by young officers, among whom she was laughing and chattering with all her customary animation. A little further along the terrace stood the composed, elegant figure of Dyphna, talking gravely with Fordil and Sarget. They were evidently conferring about music, for every now and then Fordil, nodding or questioning as he did so, would beat a rhythm with one hand upon the table beside them. She glimpsed Otavis, too; still as startlingly beautiful as at the Rains banquet, but now dressed, for the barrarz, in a kind of provocative imitation of traditional Deelguy dress, with loose, gauzy breeches, two gold hoops round her neck and her hair in thick plaits fastened below each shoulder to cover her otherwise bare breasts. Several other shearnas were present—she recognized the black-eyed, merry little girl whom she had seen snubbed at the Rains banquet by Kembri's steward—and more were arriving, as well as several ladies who, like Milvushina, were evidently wives or sweethearts. There must, Maia thought, now be over a hundred men gathered on and near the terrace, yet none— as would undoubtedly have been the case last year—had come up to her of his own accord. Once she caught, from a little distance, a low voice, '*That's* the Serrelinda, look—the girl in red.' It seemed as though the entire company were filled with a kind of constraining awe of the girl who had saved them all from Karnat of Terekenalt.

A moment later, however, a man's voice behind them greeted first Milvushina and then herself. Turning, she saw Randronoth of Lapan. Plainly, here was one man who was neither daunted by the Serrelinda nor too respectful to look her up and down with the air of a boy scarcely able to contain himself before a bowl of strawberries.

'We met last year, Maia, at the High Counsellor's: I hope you haven't forgotten.' His eyes gazed into hers with a confident directness which said, '*I* certainly haven't: and I don't believe you will have, either.'

She paused, smiling, yet uncertain how to reply. She had no wish—as much for Milvushina's sake as her own—for him to begin talking of Sencho's household. But before she could speak he went on, 'The death of the High Counsellor was a terrible shock to me. When the news reached us in Lapan I could scarcely believe it at first.'

The three of them had conversed for no more than a short time when suddenly, bowing to Milvushina and asking her, somewhat perfunctorily, to excuse him, he took Maia's arm, led her some yards along the terrace and, halting beside the wall, turned to face her.

'Maia! Listen to me, Serrelinda! There's nothing I've ever wanted in my life so much as—'

But at this moment she felt her arm taken yet again: Elvair-ka-Virrion was beside them.

'Lord Randronoth, I'm sorry to interrupt, but I'm afraid I must take Maia away from you—for a little while, at any rate. My Ortelgan officers are very anxious to meet her, and—well, you know a commander's responsibilities—such a bore—but this *is* a barrarz and I have to consider my combatants first, as I'm sure you'll understand.'

It was said jokingly, yet Maia could nevertheless sense a slight taunt in his tone of voice, even as she saw the look, quickly quenched, of disappointment and chagrin on Randronoth's face. Next moment she was walking beside Elvair-ka-Virrion across the terrace, among the general concourse now going in to supper.

The barrarz was evidently not to be held in the panelled hall on the second storey, where the Rains banquet had taken place. The guests were being conducted to a less ornate, stone-floored room on the ground floor. It occurred to Maia, in the light of what Nennaunir had told her about the boisterousness to be expected on these occasions, that the Lord General had probably had in mind the risk of damage to his property. There was, for instance, no statuary in this hall and no display of such ornamentation as vases or carved lamp-stands. The chairs, tables and benches were strong and plain and the unfringed cushions of the couches were all made of the same stout, green cloth. Nonetheless, there was no cause for anyone to feel that Elvair-ka-Virrion was stinting his hospitality. Great quantities of cold meat, together with bread, fruit, nuts, cheeses, peeled eggs, cucumbers, gherkins and the like were already spread across the tables, and as the slaves hurried in and out, smells of roasting drifted into the hall from the adjacent kitchens. Maia had never seen such a display of wine-jars. Also—and this, as always, delighted her—there were flowers everywhere, sprays, garlands and bouquets, filling the place with colour and perfume. As a background to the guests' entry, Fordil and his men, already established on a low platform to one side, had struck up a repetitive, plaintive strain which, after a few moments, she recognized through the babble and hum of talk as an old Tonildan air, 'The Island of Kisses'. She had forgotten it—hadn't heard it for many a long day—not since leaving home, in fact. To encounter it unexpectedly here—found, as it were, in an old drawer of the heart— filled her with pleasure and a sense of propitious luck.

'Did you really mean it about the Ortelgans?' she asked Elvair-ka-Virrion, looking back at him as she reached across the table for some sprays of jasmine to take the place of the scent she had forgotten. 'I didn't know they was soldiers at all: didn't know there was an Ortelgan regiment, even.'

'Well, you're quite right; they're not regulars,' he answered, helping her to trim the jasmine and fasten it in her hair. 'But you see, their High Baron, Bel-ka-Trazet, wants to feel he can count on our help against the Deelguy if ever they should need it, so he's sent me five hundred Ortelgans under a young man called Ta-Kominion—a baron's son. I gather he had a bit of a job persuading some of his barons to go along with the idea—not all of them love us, you know—but Ta-Kominion himself seems a good lad. He's very young, it's true, but he's a good leader and a regular fire-eater; he can't wait to get to Chalcon.'

He took her arm again as they threaded their way among the benches and couches, where stewards were seating the guests, towards the upper part of the hall.

'The Ortelgans'll feel enormously flattered to have the Serrelinda seated with them for supper, and that'll be all to the good from my point of view. But I was thinking of you, too, Maia—' he smiled, and gave her a quick kiss on the shoulder—'I really was. Ta-Kominion's a very impulsive, susceptible sort of lad, and I know his father's rich enough. There's one of their barons here, too, though he's not part of the Chalcon contingent; a man called Ged-la-Dan, who's made a fortune out of eshcarz and ziltate from the Telthearna. His men dive for it, you know. It just crossed my mind that the Ortelgans'll probably be able to bid quite a lot if they want to.'

'It's very good of you, Elvair, to be at all this trouble on my account.'

He laughed. 'Feeling nervous?'

She shook her head. 'Never. Oh, no, there's nothing as I—'

Suddenly she stopped, staring in front of her and as quickly turning her head away in revulsion. Some thirty feet off, beyond a group of young Beklan officers and their girls, was sitting the same hideously disfigured man whom she had last seen in the gardens of the Barb on the night of the High Counsellor's murder. This, she now recalled Occula telling her, was Bel-ka-Trazet, the High Baron of Ortelga. She forced herself to look at him again. In this clearer light his face appeared even more ghastly, the left eye askew and pulled horribly down the cheek, half-lost beneath a great, seamed ridge of flesh running from nose to throat. As he spoke to the two men beside him his lips twisted crookedly, and she saw him pause for a moment and collect himself, grimacing as though the very act of utterance were a trial.

'Oh, Elvair,' she said, 'that Bel-ka-Trazet—oh, I don't mean to—only it's enough to make anyone take on bad. You surely don't mean that *he*— that you want me to—'

'No, don't worry, Maia,' answered Elvair-ka-Virrion. 'You can take it from me that Bel-ka-Trazet won't be putting himself forward as far as you're concerned. He's very proud, you know—severe and harsh even with himself. They say he never makes advances to women, because he'd rather not think they might be pitying him. Would it upset you to help a cow to calve?'

'No, 'course not.'

'Well, it would a lot of girls. But then you're used to it, you see. This is much the same. It won't bother you to be in his company after a little while. I like the man, myself. Grim he may be, but he's always been honest with us; and incidentally he's one of the best hunters in the whole empire.'

He led her across to the Ortelgans, and as he began speaking to Bel-ka-Trazet she glanced aside to see the other two men staring at her in the way to which she had become accustomed. The High Baron bowed, taking her hands in his own, and she forced herself to look directly at him and smile as naturally as she could.

'I'm honoured to meet you, säiyett,' he said, speaking with a peculiar, grating ring in his voice, so that she guessed that his throat, too, must have been injured. 'There's no one in Ortelga who hasn't heard of what you did for the empire in Suba. Perhaps, a little later, if you haven't grown tired of telling the story, my friends and I might be privileged to hear it.'

There were murmurs of agreement from his two companions. The older man, Ged-la-Dan, struck her unfavourably; a typical Ortelgan, unsmiling, dark and thick-set, looking less like a nobleman, she thought, than a butcher or a drover; however, there was nothing servile about his manner and he was dressed as richly as anyone in the room, with an elaborately-pleated, purple veltron and four or five strings of polished ziltate and penapa encircling his bull neck. By contrast, Ta-Kominion seemed a mere boy—barely eighteen, she guessed—fair-haired and very tall, with an eager, restless look, a ready smile and something compelling and persuasive in his manner which conveyed the impression that he placed unbounded confidence both in himself and in whomever he was speaking to. It was as though his eyes were saying, 'I know I can rely on you: I know you're my friend, and I'm heartily glad of it.' She felt a kind of generous warmth in him which made the prospect of supper with the Ortelgans more agreeable than it had seemed a few minutes before. Within her, the invisible Zen-Kurel instantly approved, assuring her that had things been different he and this man might have become good friends and comrades-in-arms. I can see why they've sent him to go with Elvair, she thought. Reckon I'd follow him all right if I was a soldier.

She now saw that there was a girl with them; but whether wife, mistress or shearna it was hard to tell. She, too, was dark; slightly built and quick-moving; pretty enough, with an intense, wide-eyed look—nervous, perhaps, thought Maia, of so many strangers and of the unusual surroundings. (It did not occur to her that she might also be nervous of the Serrelinda.) She smiled, but in response the girl merely gazed at her for a moment before dropping her eyes.

As Elvair-ka-Virrion, after speaking a few more words to Bel-ka-Trazet and the others, left her with the Ortelgans, she turned enquiringly towards Ta-Kominion. 'Your friend?'

'Yes, this is Berialtis,' he answered, putting the girl's hand into Maia's.

'She's a very wise girl. She can tell you all about the Ledges, if you like.'

'I don't want to talk about the Ledges,' said the girl quickly.

'The Ledges?' Maia was mystified.

'Berialtis grew up on Quiso,' said Ta-Kominion, 'but she didn't fancy becoming a priestess—sensible lass—so she went back to Ortelga. She's come along to look after me while we help Elvair to tidy up in Chalcon.'

'You'll be a bit of a traveller time you're done, then; same as me,' said Maia to the girl.

Herself feeling amiable enough, she was nevertheless aware that for some reason the girl did not like her. Could this be merely resentment—envy—she wondered; or did Berialtis perhaps suppose that she might have designs on Ta-Kominion? Somehow, she felt intuitively, neither of these explanations quite fitted. There was something else about the girl—a kind of general detachment and preoccupation, hard to define exactly, but as though she were not, for some reason or other, heart-and-soul in the occasion. Yet she was evidently a free woman and no slave. She was expensively, if rather quietly, dressed, in a plain blue robe and matching sandals which must have cost a good deal, and she had just spoken to Ta-Kominion as no slave-girl would. But if she was a shearna, why this inappropriate aloofness and lack of warmth, the very reverse of Nennaunir or of any competent professional? Perhaps this was the best Ortelga could put up in the way of a shearna? Probably it wasn't so very different there from Suba. This girl was just a variant of Luma, only she happened to be pretty. (But *I'm* a Suban, she thought yet again: O Shakkarn, *I'm* a Suban!)

As they seated themselves and the slaves began serving food and drink, Maia entered upon her task of making herself agreeable to Bel-ka-Trazet. She soon perceived what Elvair-ka-Virrion had meant. This must once have been a warm-spirited, accomplished young nobleman, full of ardour and enjoyment of his own ability and of the promise before him. He felt his disfigurement bitterly—however could it have happened? she wondered. Elvair-ka-Virrion had spoken of his skill as a hunter: a wild beast, then, perhaps?—but he'd be damned if anyone was going to be given the slightest cause either to pity or reject him because of it. Authority, self-possession, restraint, formidability, irreproachable correctness; these were the weapons with which he compelled the respect of his own people—no doubt a rough, superstitious lot who, unless he could make them fear, trust and admire him, would probably regard him as a man accursed. These were his harsh comforters, the tutelary demons who companioned him and gave meaning and purpose to his ravaged, deprived life. He lived with eyes in the back of his head. 'Look at Trazet trying to exploit his affliction.' 'Look at Trazet making up to that shearna. Wonder how *she's* feeling, poor girl?' No one was going to be given any least opportunity even to think things like this, let alone to utter them. What was it that Elvair-ka-Virrion had said—he was turning his island into a fortress? He's turned himself into a fortress an' all, she thought.

The High Baron's face was incapable of adopting the normal expressions which commonly complement speech, yet soon she began to find his conversation full of interest and his company absorbing. Her beauty—which, she knew, constrained so many men because of their self-conscious sense of their own desire for her—plainly caused him no more of a tremor than Fordil's hinnari would bring to a man tone-deaf. Yet he was neither detached nor incurious; and this was flattering. He quickly set about establishing to his own satisfaction that peasant or no, she was no fool. And this discovery once made, he showed his respect for her by talking more freely and making his conversation more demanding. They spoke of Terekenalt and Katria, of King Karnat (with whom, he told her, he had hunted leopards) and the water-ways of Suba. He asked her for opinions, and seemed to weigh them as seriously as he might those of his own barons. She found herself talking to him of Meerzat and Serrelind, and then even of her life in Sencho's house; for here, she felt, was a man without contempt for another's misfortune; one who, on the contrary, actually admired suffering and loss which had not been allowed to defeat the sufferer. To him, as to no one else she had met—unless indeed it was Nasada—all human beings, men or women, slave or free, evidently came alike. That was to say, he had slight regard for their rank or station, but treated them in accordance with his own estimation of their capacities. Unlike Nasada, however, he had little use for compassion. She recalled that he was widely renowned as a hunter. Perhaps, she thought, he saw men and women as he might see a quarry. The courageous, resourceful and adroit—these he respected and felt to be worth contending with. The timorous or slow were merely tedious and a waste of time.

Now and then Ged-la-Dan, by contrast uncouth and insensitive, put in a few words, sometimes complimenting her on something which did not deserve a compliment or again, asking her some question which unconsciously revealed a half-envious and half-contemptuous notion of her life in Bekla as a kind of stream of luxurious and extravagant frivolity, and of herself as a girl available to anyone who could pay. Her response to this was a blend of Occula and Nennaunir—part worldly-wise banter, part simulated warmth. Yet Ta-Kominion, she sensed, could perceive very well that she was thus employing the courtesan's skills to humour a boor. He, for his part—a young man in the company of his elders—said little, but his eyes seldom left her, so that she found herself feeling an altogether unshearna-like sympathy for Berialtis. True, she herself had come with a motive, and to this end she spared no pains to arouse the two Ortelgans. Yet she wished that, in accordance with the usual way of things, there could have been a third girl in the company. Perhaps Bel-ka-Trazet disdained such concessions to convention: no one need bother themselves to provide a girl for him. Or perhaps Elvair-ka-Virrion had been over-zealous to leave her a free hand. Still, it was becoming clear that conventions were going to matter less and less as the barrarz got under way. Several of the guests were fairly drunk already, and she had seen Nennaunir and another girl whose name she did not know openly walking here and there among the tables, graceful, pausing and predatory as herons in a stream.

As the feasting began to draw to an end and she got up to fetch the Ortelgans a tray-full of sweet things from the central table already filled by the slaves, there suddenly broke out a roar of acclaim and elation, and some ten or twelve young officers wearing the wolf cognizance of Belishba sprang up and made their way purposefully to the centre of the hall, not far from where she was standing. By no means sure what they might be up to, she made haste to get out of their way.

Having pushed the central table to one side and rather blusteringly persuaded several people near-by to move their benches and couches to make an open space, the young men formed up in a line. Then, linking arms and taking their time from the tallest of their number, whose bare chest was tattooed with two fighting leopards in red and blue (he could have done with some soap, thought Maia, wrinkling her nose as she made her way back to the Ortelgans), they began to sway and intone all together, gesturing as they did so with uniform, rhythmic motions.

Happening to meet Nennaunir—who had thrown off her cloak to display her transparent robe and silver ornaments to full advantage—she smiled and raised her eyebrows enquiringly.

'Oh, it's an old Belishban custom, dear,' said the shearna. 'A kind of wild warriors' dance: they call it a *straka*. In the old days they always used to do it before a battle: I thought somehow we wouldn't get off without one.'

The leader had begun a series of what seemed to be chanted adjurations to his followers, though these were in no language even remotely known to Maia.

'Kee-a, kee-a, kee-a! U-ay kee-a, u-ay kee-a!'

'*Ah*, hi *ha*!' responded his comrades, side-stepping as one.

'Bana, bana, bana! *Hi*-po lana, *hi*-po lana!'

'*Bah*, way *ma*!'

They sniffed at the air like hounds, baring their teeth and tossing their heads as they stamped and turned, grimacing fiercely, clapping their hands and brandishing imaginary spears.

Gradually the ferocity and pace of the dance increased. Their wide-stretched eyes glittered, they stooped their shoulders and bent their heads towards the floor, growling and snarling as they uttered the responses. They turned about with upstretched arms, then paired off and made believe to stab and savage one another. At times the leader's utterances would cease and then, after a moment's silence, they would burst all together into a kind of demonic chorus, as inarticulate yet plain in meaning as the baying of wolves.

The unhesitating unanimity with which they pounded the floor, clapped, suddenly paused to thrust out their tongues or slap their buttocks before resuming their ritual clamour, was hypnotic and infectious, stirring the onlookers until the hall was filled with battle-cries, yells of approbation and the hammering of knives and goblets on the tables. The Belishbans, leaving the centre of the room, began to prance and stamp their way in a line among the tables, making believe to stab the men and drag the girls away as they maintained their chanting. At length, nearing the door that led out onto the terrace, the leader, suddenly introducing a quicker, pattering chant—'Willa-*wa*, willa-*wa*, willa-*wa*'—snatched the beautiful Otavis—who happened to be the girl nearest to hand—almost out of the arms of Shend-Lador and tossed her bodily to his followers. As two of them caught and held her, the others closed about her in a group, where-upon the whole crowd, setting up a kind of quivering motion with their shoulders, formed a rotating circle about her as she was carried out of the room in their midst.

Maia, who had watched the whole extraordinary act with the breathless absorption always aroused in her by any dance—she would have liked to join in, or at least to have had the chance to learn it—turned to her companions to see Ta-Kominion grinning with excitement and obviously as much affected as herself.

'Oh, that was just about something! I've never seen the like of that before,' she said. 'Have you?'

'Only once, and that was at Herl, when I was no more than about nine.'

'Can *you* do it?'

He shook his head. 'Oh, no; it's not half as easy as it looks. You have to be a Belishban to be able to do it properly. It's the desert blood in them, they say. They used to do it out in the Harridan desert, where the sound carries for miles, to let the enemy know they were coming.'

'What enemy?'

'Oh, any old enemy,' answered Ta-Kominion, fondling her shoulders. 'I'm glad we're going to have them with us: I don't think Erketlis is going to care for them at all, do you? What do you think of them, my lord?' he asked, turning to Bel-ka-Trazet. 'Fierce enough for you?'

The High Baron paused, laying aside his unfinished apricots in sweet wine with an air of having made a sufficient concession to the practice of eating such rubbish.

'Why don't you tell that young Elvair to take along a herd of bulls to drive at the enemy?'

'Oh, you do them an injustice, my lord, I'm sure. There's a lot more to them than that.'

'I'd be glad to think so,' replied Bel-ka-Trazet. Ta-Kominion waited respectfully, and after a few moments the High Baron went on, 'What happened at Clenderzard, Ta-Kominion; do you remember?'

'The Deelguy thought they'd beaten us, my lord, but we made fools of them.'

'Do you remember me forbidding your father to attack them?'

Ta-Kominion roared with delighted laughter and at once turned to Maia as though she were the perfect companion with whom to share the joke.

'My father had us all lined up in a wood, Maia, and we were just going to dash out to meet the Deelguy when the High Baron here came up through the trees. "You'll do no such thing—no such thing!" My father said, "Why, my lord, we'll all be taken for cowards." "No such thing! No such thing!"'

Even Ged-la-Dan was grinning. It had evidently become a legend on Ortelga. 'So what happened then?' asked Maia politely, since it seemed to be expected of her.

'Why, so then the Deelguy came rushing in among the trees, but they couldn't get to grips with us. They couldn't see properly after the bright light outside, you see. Besides, they're plains people; they're not used to woodland at all and they got confused. We broke them up into groups and made a horrible mess of them. Oh, but I'll never forget my father's face, my lord! "No such thing! No such thing!"' Still laughing, he reached across the table and refilled Maia's goblet.

'When you get to Chalcon you'll do well to remember my advice to your father.'

Bel-ka-Trazet's low, hoarse voice rasped like a hoof on dry stones. 'I asked you, didn't I, whether you wanted to lead this expedition, and I gave you a fair and honourable chance to refuse?'

'You did, my lord; but I didn't refuse, did I?'

'We have to keep in with Bekla,' said Bel-ka-Trazet, 'so we've agreed to send five hundred men against Erketlis. Either you'll gain experience, Ta-Kominion, or you'll be no great loss to Ortelga.'

'Thank you, my lord,' replied Ta-Kominion happily. He seemed, Maia thought, quite used to this sort of thing from the High Baron.

Bel-ka-Trazet leant forward and gripped his wrist so hard that he winced. 'You're a reasonably good leader, Ta-Kominion—the men trust you—but you're very young. See your men come back alive, that's all: not everything's to be achieved by rushing head-down at the enemy. Remember the wood at Clenderzard. And if you *should* have to get them out on your own—'

'Get them *out*, my lord?'

'If you *have* to get them out on your own, which wouldn't surprise me at all,' said Bel-ka-Trazet, 'get out through Lapan. It's further, but you'll be safer than if you try to get out through Tonilda. In Tonilda they hate the Leopards.'

Ta-Kominion was about to reply when there was a further distraction. The Belishbans had come back into the hall, carrying Otavis shoulder-high in their midst. It was plain that she had made a hit among them while they had been out on the terrace. Excited and full of self-assertion among strangers, they felt that they had won a prize and meant to show it.

'Give her back!' yelled Shend-Lador, playing up to them, clenching his fists and squaring up in mock rage.

'Not on your life!' answered the tattooed leader. 'She's a soldier now, this girl! She's too good for you! She's joining up with us!'

'We'll have to initiate her,' cried another of them, 'if she's to be a Belishban officer. Isn't that right, boys?'

There was a general outburst of agreement, above which the leader shouted, 'What's it to be?'

'Toss her in a blanket!' bellowed a voice.

'Yes! Yes!' they cried. 'Get a blanket! Send her up to Lespa!'

Shend-Lador and two or three of his friends began protesting and were obviously ready to quarrel in earnest; but Otavis, sitting on high among the Belishbans, only shook her head, laughing. 'No, let me alone, Shenda! Don't be a spoilsport! You don't think I'm afraid, do you? What's the bounty?' she called down to one of the Belishbans.

'What bounty, sweetheart?'

'When you join up as a Belishban officer, of course! How much d'you get?'

'Oh, I see. Five hundred meld we get when we join.'

'Right!' said the beauty, taking off her earrings and necklace and passing them down to him. 'Just look after those for me, then. Five hundred meld, and don't forget it, any of you!'

After a few more unavailing protests from the young Leopards, two slaves were sent out and returned with a woven coverlet taken from some bedroom near-by. The Belishbans spread it on the floor and Otavis, as lightly and readily as though she were going to make love, lay down on her back, folding her arms under her breasts.

636

As eight of the Belishbans, four on each side, stooped to grasp the edges of the coverlet, hiding Otavis from view, Maia turned to Ta-Kominion.

'It's crazy! She'll be hurt for certain! Can't you go and ask Elvair to stop it?'

He shook his head. 'If she'd said she didn't want to do it, I would; but she's a clever girl. She's after her five hundred meld, isn't she? And a bit more than that, if I know anything about it.'

Before Maia could answer there broke out among the Belishbans a quick, shanty-like chanting. As it culminated, Otavis suddenly appeared flying upward, her gauzy Deelguy breeches billowing, one of her plaits come adrift to expose the breast beneath. She seemed entirely in command of herself and showed no least sign of fear as she went up about ten feet and then, her body tilting a little to one side, fell back into the taut coverlet among yells of delight.

'Higher this time!' shouted one of the Belishbans. 'Come on, get some zip into it, boys!'

Again Otavis shot up, this time with so much force that she actually half-vanished for a moment into the vaulted dimness above the lamplight. As, flushed and dishevelled, she fell back into the coverlet without having uttered a sound, cheers and applause broke out all over the hall, and Elvair-ka-Virrion called 'That'll do!'

'No, no!' shouted the big Belishban leader, holding up his hand as though exercising the authority of the frissoor (which he never asked for, thought Maia). 'Three times! Three times it's got to be, before she's an officer! Let her go, boys!'

'The beam! Mind the beam, you fools!' yelled Elvair-ka-Virrion suddenly. But Otavis had already been heaved out of the coverlet, this time in a kind of half-crouching posture which suggested that she had not been entirely ready.

The vault of the hall was spanned, at a height of about fifteen feet, by tie-beams, and straight towards one of these the shearna (Cran, she must weigh next to nothing! thought Maia) was sailing up as lightly as a squirrel. At Elvair-ka-Virrion's cry she turned her head, instantly saw her danger and flung out her hands. Then, as deftly as if she had intended it from the outset, she caught the beam, let her body swing down until she was hanging vertically, paused a second and then dropped back into the out-spread coverlet. A moment later she had climbed out and was standing among the Belishbans, smiling as she deliberately wiped her grimy hands on the leader's cheeks.

A perfect tumult of acclaim broke out, lasting for almost a minute. Elvair-ka-Virrion, striding forward, embraced Otavis and kissed her.

'Right, that's it! Now—where's her lygol?' he shouted, turning to the surrounding Belishbans. 'This is going to cost you all forty meld apiece, and I never saw it better earned in my life!'

'Ay, it damned well was, too!' answered one of them, slamming down four ten-meld pieces on the table. Drawing his knife, he offered it hilt-first to Otavis and knelt at her feet. 'Give me a ringlet, säiyett! Cut me off a curl to take to Chalcon and I'll wear it every day till I come back!'

'Why, at that rate she'll have none left!' cried the leader, also falling on his knees. But Otavis, smilingly raising them to their feet and returning the knife, merely strolled across to the table, called to a slave to bring some warm water and stood rinsing her hands while the Belishbans, one after another, put down their money.

'You've lost her, Shend-Lador,' said Elvair-ka-Virrion. 'They'll never let her go now!' The shearna, however, shook her head and, having beckoned to Shend-Lador to come and pick up the money for her, kissed her hand to the Belishbans and led him out of the hall at a run.

'Good lass! She knows what she wants after that little lark!' said Ta-Kominion approvingly.

Ged-la-Dan grunted and drained his goblet. 'So do I.' Reaching out a hand, he grasped Maia's ankle where she sat curled up on the couch. 'Listen, my girl, I don't know how much—'

Before he could say more, however, Elvair-ka-Virrion was beside them, cooling his flushed face with a painted fan and bowing to Bel-ka-Trazet.

'I've come to borrow Maia, my lord. It won't be a real barrarz, you know, unless she dances for us.'

Maia, glad of the opportunity to be elsewhere, got up readily enough, excused herself to the Ortelgans and went across to where Fordil and his men were sitting cross-legged among their outspread battery of leks, zhuas and plangent strings. As the master-musician rose to meet her, smiling with obviously sincere pleasure, she found herself thinking that she could have lived happily enough as a professional dancer, devoted from dawn till dusk to the service of the gods, falling asleep each night tired out with the worship of holy movement; wind and stream, fire and cloud; Lespa's contented slave. Might her aunt Nokomis even now, perhaps, be pausing a moment, in some celestial dance among the stars, to look down on her niece and bless her?

'Not the senguela tonight, U-Fordil,' she said, stooping to kiss his brown, wrinkled hands and grey-stubbled cheeks. 'It's got to be something simpler and shorter, that they can all follow. I'm sure most of them know precious little about dancing.'

'But they know about beautiful girls, don't they, säiyett?' he answered. 'What was that old Tonildan tale you danced for me in your house, the day I came up to play to you? I could follow that easily enough, even

638

though I'd never seen it before. Didn't you tell me you made it up yourself?'

'Oh, "Tiva"? Yes, I made that up, U-Fordil. That's to say, I heard the
story when I was little from an old woman at home, and I just made up the
dance for fun.'

'Well, anyone could enjoy that, sáiyett, the way you did it for me. And if
we just keep one of those Tonildan dance-rhythms going on the drums and
I follow you with the hinnari, this lot aren't going to find fault, are they?—
not in this mood and not with someone like you to look at.'

She had first begun to devise the dance in Sencho's house during Melekril
last year, at the time when Occula had been encouraging and teaching her.
It had been rudimentary enough then, but the idea had stayed with her and
grown in her imagination, so that since returning from Suba she had
rounded it out and turned it into something at least approaching a finished
dance. It was old Drigga's tale of Tiva, the fisher-girl of Serrelind; how, at
his desperate plea, she had spared the life of a great fish she had caught
one day in her nets; and of what had ensued. Certainly, she thought,
anyone ought to be able to follow it, and it should go down well enough.
Smiling and nodding to Fordil, she walked back to the middle of the hall,
where at Elvair-ka-Virrion's order the slaves were already beginning to
move the tables for her. She waved them away. She had already decided
how she was going to present this, and it wouldn't need all that much
space.

As soon as she had received the frissoor from Elvair-ka-Virrion, she
took up her position standing on a couch on the dais and picked up the
embroidered coverlet in which Otavis had been tossed—for it had been
left lying on the floor. She tried its weight. It was a shade heavy, certainly,
but not more than she could manage gracefully. The lamps would do as
they were. She signalled to Fordil, and as the zhuas began their rolling
imitation of a long swell on Lake Serrelind the hinnari took up again, very
quietly, 'The Island of Kisses.'

Maia stood aloft on the couch, one hand shading her eyes, the other
behind her on the tiller. She was Tiva, the girl from Meerzat who, when
her fisherman father died, had rejected all suitors, determined to carry on
his business on her own account. Again and again she flung out the
coverlet into the surrounding water, and each time she hauled it in, the
pattering leks reflected her excitement in the catch, which she sorted and
slung either overboard or into the well of the boat. As she worked she
swayed, feet apart to keep her balance on the tilting planks, and constantly
flung back her hair in the sharp wind.

At first there had been a certain amount of chatter and inattention
among the audience, many of whom were still full of Otavis. But as Fordil,

most skilled and responsive of accompanists, gradually began to play louder, and the beat of the zhuas, becoming slower and heavier, suggested Tiva's arrival above deep water, the interruptions gradually died away. While she was throwing out the anchors fore and aft and then setting her weighted ledger-lines on either side of the boat, Maia could sense that she had them entirely with her.

Then followed the sudden running out of the line, the startled realization that she had hooked something really big (the drummers' efforts here were masterly), the prolonged struggle of playing the fish and finally her incredulous, staring wonder as at last it broke surface some distance from the boat.

At this point one of Shend-Lador's friends, who had clearly had a good deal to drink and was equally clearly longing to be caught by the Serrelinda, jumped up and took it upon himself to become the fish. Maia, secretly irritated—for he was a clumsy lad, without presence or grace—nevertheless went along with this, playing the big fish as it ran among the couches and dived headlong for refuge beneath the great rock of a table. At last, bringing it gasping alongside, she whispered to the young man to be so good as to leave it at that; and covered his departure by a convincing struggle to get the real, imaginary fish into the coverlet-net and haul it aboard.

Then followed the fish's agonized plea for his life, Tiva's pity for him and her final agreement to spare him and plunge with him to his palace in the depths of the lake to receive her reward. Maia simulated the struggles of the fish by jerking movements of her own arm as she held him down, and convincingly suggested his difficult speech by bending her head, ear close to the table-top, frowning as she tried to comprehend the sibilant, fishy whispering.

The plunge overside in a pellucid, splashing glissando from the hinnari, the slow, groping descent into the green depths and the arrival at the bottom of the lake—these Maia executed with the style of a swimmer as well as of a dancer. Then she was weaving among the weedy couches and rocky benches, in and out, following the great fish through the under-water twilight. She had been half-expecting one or other of the young men to grab at her or otherwise to intrude on and spoil what she was trying to express, but on the contrary the hall was now completely silent, save for the deep beat of a single zhua and a sudden patter from the leks as a shoal of little, silver fishes darted past her in the gloom.

The fish king's gift of the magic, restorative stone, the regaining of her boat and its return to land—all this Maia enacted more simply and directly than she would have done if she had been dancing merely for her own pleasure, for she knew that this audience would become restive if she were to make it too long.

Then Fordil himself, having realized that there was no other way, spontaneously came forward to enact the king's herald, crying silently through cupped hands to this side of the hall and that, proclaiming with mounting anxiety and desperation the news of the king's mortal illness. He was just about to depart in despair when Maia came forward, humbly offering to do all in her power to cure the king. The herald at first rejected her, but she persisted with gentle confidence, and at last was escorted to the royal palace.

The lack of a king defeated even Maia's ingenuity. However, it mattered little. Holding the unseen magic stone aloft before her in her cupped hands and thereby contriving to suggest that it was both heavy and a thing of awe-inspiring and miraculous power, she vanished slowly, step by step, into the twilight beyond the lamps—the shadowy recesses of what she hoped her audience would perceive to be the royal bed-chamber. Then, after a pregnant pause, during which the zhuas, first suggesting the slow, laboured breathing of the sick king, gradually quickened to become his restored, healthy heart-beat, Fordil's men, at a cry of triumph from Tiva off-stage, burst into cries of joy. Thereupon Maia reappeared, crowned with flowers, to perform a whirling dance of elation and triumph, which she brought to an end by kneeling in tranquil adoration over the dark waters of the lake, head bent and arms outstretched in homage and thanks to the great Lord Fish.

The music ceased and Elvair-ka-Virrion came forward to take her hand and lead her back to her couch. Everyone was applauding, everyone seemed eager to touch her for luck and to call out praise and congratulations. Yet suddenly she found herself, with a quick flutter of dread, remembering Tharrin, hunched in his cell in the lower city, awaiting her return and placing all his hopes on her. The night's real venture was still to come. 'Forgive me, Zenka,' she whispered. 'And great Shakkarn, blow your divine breath into their loins: make them *burn* for me!'

Ta-Kominion received her rapturously and insisted on accompanying her back across the hall to thank Fordil and give him his lygol. When he saw Maia hand over four hundred meld the young Ortelgan's eyes widened, yet he said nothing. Maia, for her part, felt that she had never given away anything with a gladder heart. Her gratitude to Fordil knew no bounds.

A sudden thought struck her. 'U-Fordil, did you ever see Nokomis?'

'Nokomis?' He nodded. 'Once, säiyett. It's—oh, nearly thirty years ago now: I was still an apprentice. My master and I spent ten days in Kendron-Urtah.'

'What was she like?'

He shrugged, spreading his hands. 'What can I say? I suppose since then not a single day's gone by without my remembering her. At least it's freed me from the miseries other people seem to carry about with them.'

'Funny old fellow, isn't he?' said Ta-Kominion as they returned. 'He may *look* like an old beggar who's been tidied up and made presentable, but I'll bet he's got plenty salted away from all that twangling he does.'

Nennaunir would have let it go: the Serrelinda was young enough to feel indignant.

'He's a great artist, my lord! He's in the service of the gods!'

'Ah! And you too?' Ta-Kominion's smile was friendly but mischievous.

'Well, of course I'm not in the Thlela, no. I never had the chance, and anyhow I'm not that good. But I'd *like* to dance for the gods—'

'*What* gods?' It was Berialtis who had spoken, and Maia, turning towards her, saw her dark eyes, wide and unsmiling, fixed on her with an expression somewhere between condescension and contempt.

'What sort of a question's that, then?' flared Maia. 'Am I s'posed to answer it?'

'*Your* gods!' cried Berialtis. 'Your gods don't exist! Their worship's nonsense! And as for your Sacred Queen—'

'Berialtis!' The file-like rasp of Bel-ka-Trazet's voice frightened Maia. It had no effect, however, upon the Ortelgan girl, who seemed not even to have heard the High Baron as she continued to speak in an utterance almost trance-like and no longer directed specifically at Maia.

'God's truth flows from the Ledges of Quiso. There's healing there for the sick, comfort and wisdom for the wretched and lost. Bekla possessed that wisdom once, until greed and corruption destroyed it. A Sacred Queen whose business is whoring with a brazen image—'

The girl's voice had risen. People near-by were turning to stare.

'Berialtis,' said Bel-ka-Trazet, 'if you want to go home alive, be quiet!'

'But Lord Shardik will return to his faithful people,' continued Berialtis, speaking now in a kind of sibylline monotone, 'on that good night the children are taught to pray for. The Power of God will shatter the idolatrous baubles of the Tamarrik Gate, and once again his priest-king will walk through the streets of Bekla. God will reveal his truth through Lord Shardik and the Chosen Vessels—'

'Ta-Kominion!' said Bel-ka-Trazet, in a tone as minatory and unnerving as anything Maia had heard in her life, 'you brought this girl with you. If you value your life and hers, get her out of here before I have to speak again!'

Ta-Kominion had been staring at Berialtis with a kind of rapt attention, apparently oblivious to all else and hanging on her every word. Even Maia, though she had only the vaguest idea what the girl was talking about, could not help thinking that this divinatory passion—or whatever it was—was very becoming to her dark, intense style of beauty. Might that, perhaps, be the real reason behind this carry-on? The High Baron's voice, however, would have penetrated the trance of a sleep-walker.

'My lord,' muttered Ta-Kominion as though against his will, 'the girl's only speaking the truth—'

'And this is no time for it!' hissed Bel-ka-Trazet, rising to his feet and standing over Ta-Kominion like some ghoul of nightmare. 'If you do not—'

What might have happened next Maia was never to know, for at this moment Elvair-ka-Virrion appeared once more beside them. She had not felt so much relieved to see anyone since the night when she had recovered consciousness among the soldiers on the bank of the Valderra.

'Maia,' said Elvair-ka-Virrion, smoothly ignoring the altercation, of which he could hardly have failed to be aware, 'I think I'd be inclined not to wait any longer before starting our little venture. Otherwise they'll all be too drunk and a lot of them may have made—well, other arrangements, you know. What do you say?'

'I'd be glad to, my lord.'

For the second time she jumped up, smoothing down the skirt of the cherry-coloured robe. Ta-Kominion and the High Baron seemed too much preoccupied with each other to notice her, and she was about to leave without more ado when suddenly Ged-la-Dan grabbed her by the wrist.

'Where are you going this time, girl?'

She gave him her most dazzling smile. 'You'll see in a moment, my lord.'

'I want you here. You just understand, now, I'm not a poor man. I can—'

Elvair-ka-Virrion interrupted him.

'Well, Ged-la-Dan, if you've taken such a fancy to Maia, that may turn out to be very fortunate for you, as you'll see in a minute. But first of all I've got to take her with me—for the best of reasons. Sorry!'

Thereupon he took her arm and led her back towards the centre of the room, leaving Ged-la-Dan with some spluttering protest dying on his lips.

The barrarz was momently becoming more disorderly and rowdy. A group of Palteshi officers, linked arm-in-arm and swaying back and forth, were singing a bawdy song in chorus, with Nennaunir and the little, dark-eyed shearna in their midst. One of them grabbed at Maia as she passed.

'A girl of renown, from the top of the town:
Dari town, Dari town, that's where we laid her down—'

Elvair-ka-Virrion, seizing his arm, bent it back to make him let go and whisked Maia away, passing Shend-Lador and his friends, one of whom was doing his best to drink a goblet of wine standing on his head.

Elvair-ka-Virrion leapt onto a table, kicked a space among the knives and dishes and then, beckoning to the chief steward, took his staff of office and hammered on the table for silence. As soon as the babble and clamour had partly subsided he shouted, 'Listen! I've just this moment been told of a magnificent surprise for all of you! Something you weren't expecting! This is *really* going to make you glad you came!'

'We're glad now!' bawled Shend-Lador; at which there were shouts of assent.

'Well, then, you listen to me!' repeated Elvair-ka-Virrion, once again pounding with the staff. 'There are going to be a lot of surprises in the next month or so—but *they're* all going to be unpleasant ones for Santil-kè-Erketlis. This is a *pleasant* one—for all of *you*!'

He had their attention now. He's clever, thought Maia, putting it as he's only just heard of a surprise: say that, always makes anyone want to know what it is.

'We've had one victory this year already,' went on Elvair-ka-Virrion, 'when we saw Karnat off at Rallur. He got his feet wet in the Valderra and had to go back to Suba to dry them.' (Laughter and cheers.) 'And we all know, don't we, who we owe that to? Sendekar!'

At this there was more cheering, broken after a few moments by a shout from the far end of the hall.

'What the hell d'you mean—Sendekar? *He* didn't swim the Valderra!'

'*Maia's* victory!' cried a girl's voice. (That's Otavis, thought Maia: good for her!)

'Yes! Maia's victory!' replied Elvair-ka-Virrion. 'Of course it was Maia's victory! Sendekar's not here tonight, more's the pity, but Maia is, and she's got something for Bekla that even Sendekar hasn't!'

At this there was more laughter. Someone called out 'Whatever can *that* be?' while someone else miaowed like a cat.

'Expeditions like this cost money, believe it or not!' went on Elvair-ka-Virrion. 'All your arrows and shields and spears have to be paid for, and we can't squeeze *all* the money out of the wretched peasants.'

'You've got all old Sencho's money, haven't you?' shouted Ta-Kominion.

'Yes, but not his belly,' replied Elvair-ka-Virrion. 'It burst, and made a mess from here to Chalcon: that's what we've got to go and clear up. Now will you all *listen*? As you know, we've none of us been able to see a great deal—not nearly as much as we'd like—of Maia Serrelinda since she came back from the Valderra. She's been recovering from her honourable wounds and enjoying a well-earned rest. But as you've all seen, she's here tonight. And she's come on purpose to help Bekla! Maia, come up here, beside me!' He stretched out his hands. 'Here she is! The bravest and most beautiful girl in the empire!'

Maia, having taken his hands, was jumped up onto the table. Elvair-ka-Virrion stood her in the brightest patch of lamplight.

'Maia isn't a shearna, although there must be hundreds of people who wish she was. She doesn't *need* to be a shearna, because the Council have voted her the income she deserves for saving us all!'

At this the cheering broke out in an even more heartfelt tone. Maia's dance had already delighted everyone, but now that they had been reminded of her heroism and saw her, as it were, displayed before them as a living epitome of the beauty and desirability of womanhood, it was as though fresh admiration came gushing spontaneously from depths of feeling hitherto unplumbed.

'So!' shouted Elvair-ka-Virrion above the uproar. 'So—you must all have thought that this beautiful girl was as far beyond you as Lespa. *But,* entirely out of her love and devotion to the city, she herself has decided otherwise.'

Now there was silence; or the nearest thing to silence with which he had been heard so far. One or two people even called impatiently to others to stop talking, and a slave who was clattering some dishes was hustled out of the hall by the steward.

'I'm not saying the Council's stinted us for money,' said Elvair-ka-Virrion. 'They haven't. And I'm certainly not saying that this expedition of ours is ill-found. It's not. But any little jaunt of this kind can always do with more money, if only to provide for emergencies. And that's what's coming our way now, thanks to this splendid girl.

'We're all soldiers here, so I'll be plain; and that'll save time, for which some lucky devil's going to be grateful, as you'll realize in a minute. Maia's told me that she'll spend the night—and she's particularly asked me to say that she'll spend it warmly and generously—with whichever one of you puts up the most money for our expedition. In other words, the favours of Maia Serrelinda—which will probably never be available to any of you again, since she's not a shearna and isn't planning to become one—are up for auction tonight, and tonight only; and she's assured me that she's not going to keep one meld of it for herself.'

Taking Maia's hand, he raised her arm over her head. Then, above the fresh outburst of excitement spreading through the hall, he called out, 'Come on, then! Where's my first bid?'

This was the moment which Maia had been awaiting with some misgiving. From the first she had wondered whether Elvair-ka-Virrion's plan would work, and only her determination to save Tharrin at all costs had induced her to agree to it. It was not that she doubted the effect of her own beauty. This she had now come to accept, just as a champion athlete or wrestler must, if his daily life and dealings with other people are to make any sort of sense, realize and acknowledge that in this respect he is above the rest and that from the public point of view that is his *raison d'être*. When necessary she could—at all events to friends like Milvushina or Nennaunir—speak of it without self-consciousness; and she had learned to handle gracefully unexpected incidents like the homage of Selperron. But she also knew that men mostly prefer to admit to and pursue their desires privately, or at any rate only among their friends. If Elvair-ka-Virrion had negotiated an assignation for her she would have felt no qualms, and this was what she had in fact suggested while they were walking by the Barb that afternoon. He, however, had objected that it would be impossible at the very large sum she was trying to raise. Besides he, a prince of Bekla, could hardly tout and pander on her behalf. If, however, the thing could be put across as a kind of game, played in the libertine surroundings of a barrarz, that would be another matter. This proposal she had accepted gratefully. Yet would they really, she had wondered, even at a barrarz, and even for the Serrelinda, be ready to put their lust on display and openly bid against one another for her embraces?

She need not have worried. She had under-estimated either their concupiscence or her own allure, or both. Instantly, as Elvair-ka-Virrion asked his question, Ta-Kominion sprang to his feet.

'A thousand meld!'

This—about four months' wages for a farm-hand or a labourer—coming from so young a man, plainly struck the company as a flamboyant flourish rather than a serious offer. There was more laughter, mixed with ironic cheering, and someone, imitating a drill tryzatt on parade, shouted, 'Quicker than that, my man! Quicker than that!'

Before anyone else could speak Elvair-ka-Virrion called out, 'You'd better all realize that although this may be a barrarz, we're completely in earnest. Anyone who makes a bid will be held to it; and there's one other thing I forgot to say. The money's to be paid tonight, either in coin or else in something of indisputable value, like jewels or gold.'

'I said a thousand meld and I damned well meant it!' cried Ta-Kominion. 'I'll say it again—a thousand meld!'

At this moment Maia noticed that four or five slaves were extinguishing the lamps round the outer edges of the hall, while others were removing those on the tables near-by. It must have occurred to Elvair-ka-Virrion that his potential customers would feel more unconstrained in a dim light.

'*Two* thousand meld!'

That rough voice, she knew, was Ged-la-Dan's. The thought of having to spend the night with this sweaty, boorish Ortelgan, who had pulled her by the ankle and called her 'My girl' within an hour of meeting her, filled her with revulsion. O Cran, she thought, I'd rather be back with old

Sencho! At least he used to have baths. O Lord Shakkarn, don't let it be him!

There was no more laughter or cheering now. It had suddenly come home to the company that this had at least the makings of a highly dramatic matter. Just as a crowd, gathered round to banter and laugh at two men quarrelling, cease their raillery when the first actual blow is struck, so these roisterers had become vigilant and attentive upon hearing Ged-la-Dan's counter-bid. Although most of them were youngsters lacking anything approaching the means to take part, this only made it all the more exciting. To watch wealthy people competing seriously for a rich prize, which only one of them can attain, to the chagrin of the rest—this has aroused and attracted onlookers for thousands of years, and always will.

Maia, glancing sideways, saw Nennaunir bite her underlip and turn her head towards the man beside her with a quick, wide-eyed look of excitement. Directly beneath the table on which she was standing, a broad-shouldered tryzatt who looked like a Yeldashay was staring up, never taking his eyes off her as he tapped and tapped unconsciously with one hand on the table-top beside him.

'Three thousand meld!' shouted Ta-Kominion.

'Be quiet, boy!' snarled Ged-la-Dan.

The lighting round the edge of the hall had now become so dim that Maia could not see clearly, but it appeared as though some sort of scuffle had broken out. A dish clattered on the floor: then Ta-Kominion's voice, quick and gasping, said 'By the Ledges, if you don't—'

'Silence!' This was unmistakably Bel-ka-Trazet, who after a short pause came composedly forward into the brighter light, grasping Ta-Kominion's arm firmly in his own. A pretty, brown-haired girl in a yellow robe gave a little cry and sprang away at the sight of his face, whereupon the High Baron of Ortelga calmly sat down where she had been reclining, motioning to Ta-Kominion to sit beside him.

'You'll excuse us, my lord,' he said to Elvair-ka-Virrion in his strained, rasping voice. 'My friend here said three thousand meld and he's perfectly serious. Pray continue.'

'Three thousand meld!' echoed Elvair-ka-Virrion. 'Three thousand meld for the favours of the most beautiful girl in the world! Come now, gentlemen, haven't you got blood in your veins?'

'Yes, but not gold!' shouted one of the Belishbans.

They seemed to be conferring among themselves. Their dialect was unfamiliar to most Beklans, but to Maia, who had lived and worked with Meris, it was plain enough.

'—and then we'll draw lots.'

647

'Well, no wrangling afterwards, then.'

'You game, Yerdo? Two hundred each?'

After some more muttering the big leader, breaking away from the group, took a step towards Elvair-ka-Virrion and called out 'Four thousand meld!'

At this there were cries of disbelief and protest, but he added quickly, 'My lord, my friends and I are making this bid between us. Then we'll draw lots among ourselves to see who's the lucky man.'

Suddenly Maia realized that the business had become one of local pride—just as Elvair-ka-Virrion had foreseen that it might. The Belishbans were determined to secure her for themselves if they could; when they returned to Herl, at least one of them must be able to boast that he had made love with the one and only Serrelinda—he and he alone of all those under Elvair's command. It was certain that there was no other girl throughout the empire, however beautiful, who could have had this sort of effect upon her admirers, be they never so ardent. As she grasped this she blushed down to her neck and for all she could do the tears started to her eyes. In her mind's eye she could see the green-and-white stretch of the Serrelind waterfall, the scarlet trepsis-bloom and the long-stalked lilies in the shadows.

'You dazzle me—reckon I'll dazzle you!

> ' "Why was I born? Ah, tell me, tell me, Lord Cran!
> Isthar, isthal a steer—" '

'Speak to them, Maia,' whispered Elvair-ka-Virrion. 'They'll all go crazy now, if only you can make them.'

Stretching out open arms, she looked from one flushed, eager face to another; yet not a word could she say. Laughing, and quickly dashing the tears from her eyes, she pulled the sprays of jasmine from her hair and tossed them down among the Belishbans. Still she said nothing: but the mere sight of her, tongue-tied and overcome by their adulation, the tears wet on her glowing cheeks, was enough to accomplish Elvair-ka-Virrion's purpose. All round the hall could be heard mutterings and whispers as little groups of men began consulting among themselves—Beklans and Palteshis, Tonildans, Lapanese, Urtans and Yeldashay.

'She's too good for Belishba!' shouted a grey-haired man with the look of a veteran and a golden fountain embroidered across his robe. 'Kabin shall have her! Four thousand five hundred!'

'Six!' answered one of the Belishbans immediately.

'Four thousand seven hundred!'

It was at this instant that Maia, in the act of bending forward to accept a goblet which one of the young men was holding up to her, became once more aware of Randronoth. The governor of Lapan was seated on the end of a near-by couch, elbow on knee and chin on hand, gazing at her as though there were no one else in the hall. A slave who was going round with a full wine-jar, stopping beside him, spoke to him twice, but Randronoth appeared neither to see nor hear him. There was no companion or girl with him, and this isolation emphasized and heightened the intensity with which he was regarding her. After a moment, with no movement or alteration of his gaze, he said quietly, 'Five thousand meld.'

No sooner had he spoken than Maia felt certain that she had been continually in his thoughts ever since the night which he had spent with her; and that if that encounter were to have taken place now—many long months, several men and much garnered insight and experience later—she would certainly have recognized it for what it was; the inception of nothing less than an all-absorbing physical obsession. He was a man whose thoughts ran continually upon coupling, dominated by an inward concept not of ideal womanhood, of companionship or even of a girl able to amuse him or do him credit in public, but simply of a certain visual semblance and certain physical characteristics which excited him beyond all measure. And to this fantasy she—and in all his experience she alone—conformed entirely. This she could now perceive as plainly as if he had told her in so many words. What had haunted him since that night had been simply his physical recollections of her—visual, tactile; possibly even olfactory, too, for the matter of that. And despite—or perhaps because of—his ready opportunities for pleasure elsewhere, these had set up in him a relentless craving which her subsequent renown and exaltation had only served to enflame, for they had made him suppose the chance of actually basting her again to be gone for ever. Yet tonight, at the barrarz, it had suddenly reappeared, like a hunter's quarry given up for lost but now come wandering randomly, unexpectedly back out of the forest. At whatever cost, he was not going to let it go again.

He would be a procurer's dream, she thought: a man utterly in the grip of a specific and compulsive desire. There were no lengths to which he might not go.

Ah, but was there anyone else, any competitor to push him as far as she was hoping? His bid seemed to have altered the entire tone of the proceedings. The laughter and ribald gaiety had now drained away entirely, as though Randronoth had cracked a fountain-basin. Plainly many of those present—the provincial soldiers if not the Beklan girls—were feeling a shade uneasily that things had gone beyond anything they were used to or had ever experienced. Five thousand meld for a night with a girl—even the Serrelinda! Well, they'd heard tell of the extravagances of the Leopards and the vices of the upper city. Here they were, in all reality. And what, pray, might be going to happen next?

'Five—thousand—meld,' said Elvair-ka-Virrion slowly and deliberately. 'Well, of course that's not a trug more than Maia's worth, ladies and gentlemen—she's as far beyond value as the Tamarrik Gate—but at the same time it's a good deal by the standards of simple human beings like you and me. So from now on I shall be taking bids in thousands. As you know, that's the custom in Bekla when bidding reaches this sort of level, whether for jewels or gold or anything else. Now, who'll offer—'

He was interrupted by the crash of an overturned bench and a sudden commotion from the dimness beyond the lamplight. A cry of protest was followed by a snarling reply; 'Well, get out of the way, then!' and a moment later Ged-la-Dan came striding forward, his hand clenched on his goblet. Raising it towards Maia, he drank off the contents, wiped his mouth with the back of his hand and, looking directly at Randronoth, said, 'Six thousand meld!' as though striking a blow.

Randronoth, who had never once taken his eyes off Maia, did not even turn his head. Outwardly he appeared entirely calm, his hands lightly clasped between his open knees as he remained seated on the end of the couch, tapping one foot to the rhythm of the barely-audible hinnaris. Turning her head to meet his gaze, Maia suddenly felt as though, after looking out across the glittering surface of a lake, she had leaned over the gunwale to stare directly down into the depths below; a place of predatory silence, its nature utterly distinct from the windy, sunny world of the Belishbans and of Ta-Kominion. To this man there was no passion so serious as lust.

Randronoth took his time—partly, perhaps, with the intention of riposting to Ged-la-Dan's outburst with a pose of deliberate nonchalance. Yet also, Maia felt, he was savouring the moment inwardly and enjoying it for its own sake. She was in no doubt at all that he would continue to bid. Now that he had taken the vital step; had surrendered all prudence, jumped into the raging cataract of his own desire and left all else behind him on the bank, he had become like a man lost in music or prayer. To himself his surroundings were as nothing. He had, of course, heard Ged-la-Dan, but felt him as a stimulus rather than an obstacle.

Looking enquiringly at him, Elvair-ka-Virrion waited. A deeper silence fell. At length Randronoth, as though deliberately dropping a pebble into a pool, said quietly, 'Seven thousand,' and fell to examining his fingernails.

In the same instant Maia felt Elvair-ka-Virrion's hand on her shoulder. Before she could guess his intention he had loosed and pulled the cord at her neck. The cherry-coloured robe slid to her waist and then to her ankles, dropping as smoothly and readily as on the night when she had danced the senguela. She was standing in her diamonds, her shift of transparent muslin and a pair of silver sandals.

If there was one girl in Bekla able to take this kind of surprise in her stride it was Maia. Nennaunir—even Occula—would probably have felt impelled to respond provocatively, or perhaps to simulate embarrassment as a trick to tantalize her audience still further. Maia appeared not even to notice that the robe had fallen. Her hands did not move, nor did she turn her head to look at Elvair-ka-Virrion standing behind her. Only, she shrugged slightly and then smiled, as though on balance amused and relieved to find herself disencumbered of the robe, which seemed to have fallen from her as naturally as autumn leaves from a tree, disclosing more clearly its essential, pliant grace.

Serene and natural indeed she looked. Yet human desire is also natural, and Maia, standing as good as naked before two hundred men, could no more have failed to disturb them yet further than the smell of approaching thunder can fail to make uneasy the beasts of the wild. The young soldiers, unmindful of their own girls, pressed forward, jostling and staring, some in their excitement stumbling over benches or into one another. Maia, still smiling, gazed calmly down upon the throng of upturned faces bobbing and dodging hither and thither below her as men moved sideways or stood on tiptoe, instinctive and self-forgotten as children in their eagerness to see her more closely.

Randronoth, however, neither moved nor altered his expression. One might almost have supposed that he had been expecting the robe to fall. Either he was in no haste to gaze at her nakedness, so clearly was its recollection fixed upon his mind, or else—and more probably, thought Maia—to him, the sight was one not to be diluted by being shared with others. He could not stop this display, yet he would have no part of it. He meant to feast alone, in his own good time. Although she felt no desire or affection for him, she could not but be moved by so consuming an infatuation. If she were not much mistaken, he was ready to ruin himself for her. A more hardened girl might have felt contempt, but what Maia felt was something akin to fear. To be the possessor of such power was frightening; and the man's obsession, too, was frightening in itself. This isn't like the others, she thought—Kembri, Sencho, Elvair. They were just enjoying themselves; but this man'll stop at nothing, nothing at all. 'Tain't natural. Might it not even, in some way or other, prove downright dangerous to let him have what he wanted?

Only for a moment did she think thus. Then she recalled Tharrin, weeping with terror in Pokada's stuffy little room; and the cruel eyes of the Sacred Queen staring contemptuously into her own. As she turned her head away from Randronoth to assume once more her rôle of the transcendent yet tormentingly flesh-and-blood paragon of desire, a girl's voice—Nennaunir's—suddenly called 'Maia, look out!'

The shearna, who, together with four or five young Beklan officers, had pressed forward almost to the foot of the table on which Maia was standing, had been the first to see her danger. Ged-la-Dan, glaring with rage, the sweat standing on his forehead, had snatched up a knife which some slave had overlooked in clearing away and was lurching forward, his thick-set bulk sending four or five men stumbling this way and that. Reaching the table, he grabbed and pulled at it, so that Maia would have fallen if Elvair-ka-Virrion had not flung his arm round her. The Ortelgan, glaring upward, leaned forward for a moment as though to clutch her round the legs. Then, straightening up, he turned on Randronoth, still seated impassively on his couch, took a step towards him and roared, 'Eight thousand! Eight thousand! And let that do, damn you, unless you want—'

Elvair-ka-Virrion hit him across the back of the neck with the steward's staff, and he flung up his hands, his voice cut short. One of his penapa necklaces broke, and the big, rosy-pink stones (like a lot of half-sucked sweets, thought Maia) were scattered over the floor.

A girl screamed, and there were cries of anger and contempt. The Belishban captain grabbed another knife and rushed at Ged-la-Dan, shouting something incomprehensible and getting close enough to spit in his face before two of his comrades dragged him back.

'Damned Ortelgans!' called a voice from somewhere beyond the lamps. 'Why don't you go home and jump in the Telthearna?'

It was at this moment, while Maia hung trembling in Elvair-ka-Virrion's arms and Ged-la-Dan still stood facing Randronoth (who looked alertly up at him but made no move) that Bel-ka-Trazet came forward. As calmly as though breaking a dead stick from a tree, he took the knife from Ged-la-Dan's hand, whispered something in his ear and then turned to Elvair-ka-Virrion.

'I must beg your pardon, my lord, on behalf of my companions and of Ortelga.' He paused, and for a moment his horrific face appeared yet more distorted as he struggled with his feelings. 'You'll realize that this is no easier for me to say than it would be for' (he swept the room with a gesture) 'for anyone else. Please accept my apology. Let us now forget this incident and proceed.'

His self-control and resolute air of propriety was in such marked contrast to what had gone before as to have an immediate effect. Most of those present, angry and contemptuous though Ged-la-Dan's behaviour had made them, could still appreciate what this must be costing him and feel themselves in favour of sparing his feelings. An intensely proud man, he was doing what had to be done, and hating every moment of it.

As he broke off Nennaunir, looking, in her erotic trinkets, the very epitome of a wanton, tripped demurely forward, flung her arms round his neck and kissed him on his slashed, twisted lips.

'Of course we understand, my lord, and all of us gladly accept your apology. I know I'm speaking for everyone here.'

She *is* a clever girl, thought Maia: she really is. They'll remember that; the girl who embraced Bel-ka-Trazet of her own accord and kissed him.

But now Nennaunir was speaking to her. 'All right, Maia darling? Going on? We're all enjoying it if you are.'

Even though she was well aware that this was four-fifths the adroitly acted self-advancement of an experienced courtesan, Maia could not help feeling grateful. No doubt the shearna would have been only too delighted to be standing where she herself was standing now, but if this were so, any envy she might be feeling was under full professional control. Ever since her own return to Bekla, Maia reflected, Nennaunir had never said a spiteful word to her, either in public or in private, and had always been ready with friendly advice.

She smiled. 'I'm fine, Nan, thanks.'

Thereupon she nodded to Elvair-ka-Virrion, who kissed her cheek before releasing her and turning back to Bel-ka-Trazet.

'And your friend's bid, my lord: shall we forget that, too?'

'By no means,' replied Bel-ka-Trazet. 'It was made, and I will accept personal responsibility for it.'

'Well, then,' continued Elvair-ka-Virrion smoothly, turning to Randronoth, 'I have eight thousand offered, it seems, and that's against you, my lord.'

The governor of Lapan nodded in acknowledgement, but said nothing. Suddenly Maia was filled with dismay. The enormous sum reached had apparently daunted even Randronoth. He was not going on; and who could blame him? And she—O dear Lespa! she would have to spend the night either with Ged-la-Dan or with Bel-ka-Trazet. Biting her lip, she struggled with a rising nausea. She began to salivate, and quickly emptied her mouth under pretence of drinking again from her empty goblet. O Shakkarn! she prayed silently, Shakkarn, only save me! I can't face it!

Once again Elvair-ka-Virrion addressed Randronoth.

'Would you like a little time to consider, my lord? Shall we have a short interval now?'

Immediately Randronoth rose to his feet. For one agonizing instant Maia thought that he was about to walk out of the hall. For several moments he paused, as though to relish the last morsel of the occasion (the most extravagant, surely, in which even he could ever have participated, thought Maia). At length he answered, 'No, thank you. It's for everyone else, not for me, to take time—to regret what they've let slip.' Then, with Elvair-ka-Virrion looking enquiringly at him, as though for formal confirmation of what he had just implied, he added almost casually, 'Nine thousand meld.'

A long murmur, as of completion or fulfilment, ran through the hall. Maia, whispering, put her hand quickly on Elvair-ka-Virrion's arm. 'For Cran's sake stop now, Elvair! I can't take no more! I'd rather find the other thousand myself!'

'Sure?' asked Elvair-ka-Virrion.

'Yes, my lord! I just can't stand n' more, not now I can't.'

Elvair-ka-Virrion nodded, smiled and turned towards the guests as though to address them again. However, he had no need. It was clear that the legendary auction of the Serrelinda—for legendary it became in Bekla, and indeed throughout the whole empire—was concluded. Friends and sycophants were gathering round the governor of Lapan, addressing him with the half-congratulatory and half-envious admiration usually shown by people towards a man who has done something which, though they may consider it reckless and foolhardy, they cannot help wishing they had had the gall to do themselves.

Randronoth, however, plainly wanted none of this. It was not for show or notoriety but for that incomparable body (mounted by Sednil for nothing in a dusty attic of the temple) that he had bid nine thousand meld. As a slave handed him his cloak he raised his hand unsmilingly to those around him, walked over to where Maia was still standing beside Elvair-ka-Virrion on the table and, climbing up beside them, put the cloak round Maia's shoulders. Having stooped and picked up the cherry-coloured robe, he was about to help her down when Elvair-ka-Virrion stayed him.

'The money, my lord? A mere detail, of course, but we need to know—'

'She shall have every last meld in coin by dawn tomorrow,' answered Randronoth. 'Where would you like it brought, säiyett?'

'To my house, please,' replied Maia.

Now that the horrible prospect of Ged-la-Dan had been lifted from her, she felt light as a summer cloud. She'd done it! Fornis was defeated, Tharrin was saved! All that remained was to spend the night with Randronoth. Weary though she now felt, his craving, she knew, was such that little more than acquiescence would suffice. Smiling in her relief, she kissed him warmly and lingeringly, cheek and lip. 'Let's go there now—*now*—shall we?' And then, with a sudden rush of spontaneous ardour, 'Oh, thank you, my lord, for—for winning! I'm that glad as 'twas you!'

Yet during the hours that followed—those hours during which Randronoth seemed almost demented, so that even after his desire had spent itself once, twice and again he could not let be, but must still be caressing and touching her with hands, lips, tongue; embracing and fondling as though the gratification of his lust had been a mere preliminary to the more serious business of satisfying some even deeper need—she could not help wondering, as it would never have occurred to her to wonder last year in Sencho's house, what it was that he supposed he had bought. *Her* feelings were in no way engaged: her heart was far away; she was indulging him like a child, and this not because she had any particular wish to hold back or give him short weight, but because that was all she had it in her to do. Such as she had to give she was giving him—and little enough to her it seemed. Yet of this shortcoming—a mantled sun, a clouded sky—he was plainly unaware. He knew no better. The strings were not in tune, but this he could not perceive. Once, dropping off to sleep, she dreamed vividly that Zen-Kurel had come into the room and was standing silently beside their bed. She started up with an anguished cry, but Randronoth only laughed, took her by the shoulders and fell to kissing her breasts. Yet hadn't her distress been obvious? she thought, once more acquiescing. Well, if it had not, perhaps that was all for the best.

Throughout the whole night, though he was unfailingly courteous and also showed himself considerate and adept enough, she was roused no more than once, and that at the outset; and this impersonal, animal want once met, fell back upon the kind of pretence that Occula had taught her to employ with the High Counsellor. It was not difficult: she remained sincerely amiable and compliant, for the thought of Tharrin saved burned like a bright lamp in her heart, filling it full of tolerance—pity, even—for this poor, besotted man, who could see yet not reach her, his heart like a moth on a lighted window-pane.

: 64 :

THE MORROW MORN

Maia, who had slept again for an hour, woke soon after first light to see Randronoth, at her dressing-table, wetting his fingers to quench the smoking lamp-wick he had just blown out. As soon as she spoke he crossed the room, knelt at the foot of the bed, took one of her feet between his hands and began kissing it. She stroked his cheek with the other.

'You're up early.'

'I'm happy,' he answered.

How early, she was wondering, could she practicably expect to gain access to Fornis to ask for Tharrin's order of release? Well, she would simply go to the house as soon as she could, and if that was too early, she'd sit and wait.

He looked up at her, smiling. 'I can't do any more—more's the pity. Once I could have.'

'Forty-one's no age, Randro.' Then, fearing that he might suppose that she had known men of his age more virile, she added, 'You've shown me that already. It's silly to try and force yourself, after we've had such a nice time.' She patted the still-warm place beside her. 'Come back and lie down. There's something I want to ask you; something that's very important to a great friend of mine.'

'Which friend?'

'Nennaunir. You knew her very well at one time, didn't you? You saw her yesterday and talked about me?'

'Oh, she told you, did she?' For the first time he seemed displeased. 'You've only to tell a girl something, and it goes buzzing about the city like a bluebottle.'

'But darling, don't be silly; of course she told me. It was to *help* you! She told me you'd said you wanted me terribly, and would she speak to me about it? That was why I arranged for the auction at the barrarz, so that you *could* have me.' (He'd believe this, she felt sure; and anyway it was near enough true.) 'I'm not touching a meld of the money, you know.'

Lying down once more beside her, he made no reply, only looking at her with an expression of disbelief.

'It's true, Randro. The money, that's between you and the Leopards— or the army—or the temple. One of them, anyway: how should I know? But it's not for me at all.'

'Well, I heard Elvair say that, but I didn't believe him.'

'Well, you can. All *I'm* asking for, on my own account, is the same as Nan asked you for—to get poor Sednil exchanged out of the temple: to take him down to Lapan and see if you can't discharge him early.'

He frowned. 'Sednil? What's Sednil to you? Why do you so particularly want me to take all this trouble over Sednil?'

At this she burst out at him. 'Cran and Airtha, Randro, it's easy enough to see *you've* never been in trouble, let alone a slave! Can you imagine what it's like to be someone else's property? To possess nothing of your own, to have no rights at all, no say in where you go or what you do or even whether you live or die? That boy's as innocent as you and me' (and a damned sight more than you, she thought) 'and if it hadn't been for that stupid ring of yours, as you gave to Nan, he'd be free today. He's Nan's friend and he's my friend. People like us, who've been down on our luck and seen bad times, we try to help each other. Is that so very hard to understand?'

'Oh, I love to see you get angry!' he said. 'You really drive me crazy,

Maia! All right, I'll get the boy exchanged, I promise you, and I'll have him discharged within three months. I was wrong: put your arms round me. No, you stay on top. Oh, gods! Ah!'

Later he said, 'You know I have to go back to Lapan today? Why don't you come with me? I'll make you—'

Gravely, she shook her head. 'No, dear, that's impossible. Don't press me.'

'I don't know how I'm going to live without you, Maia. It could easily drive me to desperation, d'you know that?'

'You say that now, Randro; but there's others. You can't pretend otherwise.'

'Not like you. I've never known anyone like you, Maia. I'll find some reason to come back soon. But if I *do* get Sednil released—and you can give Nennaunir my word for that—will you spend another night with me as soon as I can get back to Bekla? I shall be eating my heart out until then.'

In spite of all she knew of him, she could not help feeling touched. The truth was that Maia had never quite been able to accept the effect of her beauty as something for which she bore no responsibility. (This was why she had behaved so generously and warmly to Selperron in the Caravan Market.) She knew that when Randronoth said that his longing made him feel desperate, he was speaking no more than the truth, and she felt not only sorry for him, but sorry also to have been the cause of it. In a way, she felt that she had wounded him for her own ends and ought perhaps to make some restitution. After all, she had quite deliberately set out to exploit his infatuation, and it had cost him enough.

'Well—'

He gripped her hand. 'Yes?'

A promise with no date for fulfilment is always perilously easy to grant, especially for the young. Maia's mind was running with excitement and pleasure on the release of Tharrin. She felt full of the elation of success. It had been a desperate venture and she had pulled it off. But she owed this to Randronoth—to his obsession and his reckless extravagance. Besides, to refuse would only upset him—just when everything had gone off so well. Nennaunir was going to be delighted, and she herself—well, she felt more than rich enough in spirit to give him a kind answer.

'Yes, darling, of course I will: only you *must* keep quiet about it. This auction was one thing, but if it gets round that you're counting on going to bed with me next time you come to Bekla, that'll be—well, I mean—I'd be—'

He smiled. 'Compromised?'

'Something o' that. Any road, I wouldn't want everyone knowing: so just you remember.'

Suddenly she sat up in alarm, listening. 'Whatever's that downstairs?'

What she had heard was heavy knocking at the outer door. There followed Jarvil's voice and another male voice answering. Randronoth, also listening, nodded unperturbed.

'That'll be two of my men, bringing your money. I sent them orders last night, before we left the barrarz.'

'You mean it's really down there? Nine thousand meld, in coin? Oh, Randro! Thank you! Thank you!'

She kissed him more warmly than she had throughout the entire night. 'Oh, I *must* go down and see it!' Jumping out of bed, she flung her robe round her. Then, turning back to him with shining eyes, 'Of course it's not that I don't trust you! You know that. It's just that—oh, I'm so glad! I'm so happy about it!'

He frowned, puzzled. 'But you just said you weren't going to get any of it for yourself. Maia, what's all this about? Has it got you out of a mess or something?'

She kissed him quickly. 'I'll answer that if you'll answer me another. Nine thousand meld—in ready money. Where did it come from?'

That had stopped him in his tracks all right; she could see that. He paused.

'Never ask me, Maia; you leave that to me. I'm hopelessly in love with you: I had to have you. That's enough for you—and best for you, too, believe me. Come on, I'll go downstairs with you and make sure it's all there. Then we'll have breakfast—I need it—and after that I'll have to go. I wonder whether you'll ever realize how much *you've* given *me!*'

She had *given* him nothing, she thought. He had sought pleasure, he had found pleasure, but she had not bestowed it. How strange that he should be in no doubt that he had acquired something which she had not conferred; and more, that he should be so much dominated by this unreality! Just so, old Drigga had once told her, might two people be together and one see a ghost while the other could not.

The Sacred Queen's garden was no less fresh and morning-scented than on the day before. The peacock was busy among a handful of corn-seed which a gardener's boy was scattering on the sunny lawn, while from somewhere out of sight, behind the purple larn bushes, sounded the clicking of a pair of shears.

Maia, without waiting to announce her arrival, made her way round to the stone doorway. Direct prayers were never offered to Frella-Tiltheh—the unknown and unknowable—but for a full minute or more she stood silently, with bowed head and outstretched palms, beneath the niche containing the cowled figure of the goddess; so long, indeed, that at length

Brero, waiting behind her, put down the box containing the money and turned aside to watch a squirrel in a near-by tree.

When at length she knocked, Zuno opened the door almost immediately. Pausing only a moment to glance towards the soldier in attendance behind her, he led the way across the red-and-white tiled hall and up the staircase. Plainly, she thought, her arrival had been expected; no doubt the events of the night were already known to the Sacred Queen.

At the top of the stairs he turned and said, 'You're to go straight in. She's due at the temple soon, you see, and she won't—' He hesitated. 'She certainly doesn't mean to be late.'

The bedroom door was standing open. Maia stopped in the entrance, looking in. Fornis was bustling about the room, moving hastily from one place to another, yet to all appearances doing nothing in particular. She seemed both excited and preoccupied. As Maia watched, she spread out her hands in front of her, examining first one side and then the other. Next moment she picked up her comb and looked in the mirror, but almost at once put it down, went across to the window and stood tapping her fingers on the sill. She was wearing a deep-purple robe embroidered with gold thread and her hair, piled high, was enclosed within the sacred crown of Airtha. Now, at close quarters, Maia recognized the great emerald which Occula, in the temple, had known for her father's. Of Ashaktis there was no sign: the Sacred Queen was alone.

Maia coughed and made a slight movement. Fornis, turning, for an instant, looked slightly startled, actually seeming not to recall who she was. Next moment, however, smiling cordially and graciously, she had come forward and taken the hand which Maia had raised to her forehead. Her own hand felt hot and sweating, and before speaking she passed her tongue once or twice across her dry lips.

'Maia! How delightful to see you again! I'm glad you've managed to come early: I should have been most disappointed to miss you; only I have to go out very soon, you see. Never mind: do sit down for a moment and make yourself comfortable. What a beautiful morning, isn't it?'

Her completely unexpected air of geniality and warmth left Maia—for some moments, at all events—speechless. Faced with any other woman who might have had the effrontery to adopt such a manner, following upon what had passed between them the day before, she would have found sufficient self-confidence to answer her as she deserved. But this was the Sacred Queen: nor was it only consciousness of her power and authority which threw Maia into confusion. There emanated from this extraordinary woman an almost hypnotic dominance and self-possession, so that quite possibly, if she had pointed to the moon and said, 'Oh, look at the sun!' a hearer's first reaction might well have been to wonder whether there was something wrong with his own eyes or even with his own mind. Just so Maia, for a fleeting instant, found herself wondering whether yesterday's encounter in the archery field had really taken place, and then—since it had—whether perhaps it might have been with someone else and not with the queen. Then, and only then, did it occur to her that the queen was entertaining herself. It amused her to treat people—particularly those who were helpless before her—with flagrant inconsistency, and to see how they responded while trying to keep themselves in countenance.

'Esta-säiyett,' she began, 'since you're in a hurry I won't keep you any longer 'n what I need to. I've brought—'

'Oh, come now, there's not all *that* much of a rush, Maia,' replied Fornis, motioning her towards one of the big, carved chairs and patting her forearm reassuringly. 'Do you know, I feel quite full of curiosity about you? Do tell me—' and at this she leant forward with every show of interest—'did you go to Elvair-ka-Virrion's barrarz for the Chalcon expedition?'

Did I—? But she must know every last thing about it, thought Maia.

'Yes, esta-säiyett, I was there for a time.'

'And I suppose it was great fun, was it? Lots of young men from all over the empire? I expect you danced, didn't you? I've heard about your dancing.'

'Yes, esta-säiyett: Lord Elvair-ka-Virrion asked me to dance.'

'What did you dance?'

She wants to see me lose control. She wants to see me break off short and start in about Tharrin and the money before she does.

'I danced an old Tonildan tale, esta-säiyett, about Lake Serrelind.'

'How charming! And the Ortelgan baron—er—what *is* his name, now?—he enjoyed it?'

'Lord Bel-ka-Trazet, esta-säiyett?' (That was one to her, she thought: obviously Fornis had meant Ged-la-Dan.) 'He didn't actually say as much, but I believe he may have.'

'But *Randronoth* did?'

'I'm sure he did, esta-säiyett.'

'Yes.' She smiled. 'I'm *sure* he did. Well, of course, that's one of the delightful things about Randronoth. As Sencho once remarked to me, he's always extraordinarily easy to please. He's perfectly happy with almost anything. Wouldn't you agree?'

'Yes, esta-säiyett.' She might have replied more, but meeting the cold, green stare above the smiling mouth, fell silent for very dread. Fornis was like the Valderra: it had not occurred to her till now that she might not get out alive.

There followed a short silence. 'Well,' said Fornis suddenly, 'I expect you'd like to talk about your step-father and the money, wouldn't you?'

'Thank you, esta-säiyett. I've got the money outside: ten thousand meld. Shall I ask my man to bring it in to you here?'

Fornis, still gazing at her with every appearance of sympathetic concern, nodded. Then she stood up briskly.

'No, no, I'll see to it; don't trouble yourself, Maia.'

She went out of the open door and Maia heard her walk down the corridor and call to Zuno. Her own pulse, she now realized, was beating very fast and she felt breathless. She wondered whether this had been apparent to the queen. Together with her fear of Fornis there had come upon her a vague but none the less disquieting presentiment—sprung no doubt from Fornis's cat-and-mouse affability—that some trick was about to be played on her. She tried to think what it could be. Fornis might say the money was short: she might take the money and refuse her the reprieve: or she—she might give her the reprieve and then have her murdered before she left the house. In sudden panic, Maia stood up and ran to the window. Perhaps she could climb down and get away before Fornis returned.

At this moment Brero came into the room—burly, familiar, smiling, the very embodiment of reassurance. In her unreasoning fear—the kind of fear Fornis so readily engendered—she had not considered what his presence here implied. Even Fornis could not hope to get away with the murder of a veteran of the Beklan regiment—or with cheating her before his eyes. True, he did not know the ins and outs of the business, but nevertheless he was—he could be—a witness.

'Brero,' she said quickly, leaving the window and crossing the room to where he was standing, 'I want you to stay close beside me, please, until we go. Don't leave me on any account, do you see?'

He looked surprised, aggrieved: probably he took it for a reproach. 'Well, of course, säiyett; if that's what you say. I only stayed outside 'cause it was the Sacred Queen's bedroom, like. I mean to say—' He broke off, but then resumed, 'Reason I come in now, säiyett, she told me to say would you please just step outside and join her?'

She nodded and smiled, and he followed her into the corridor.

Fornis was seated at a narrow table beneath one of the windows over-looking the garden, while Zuno, kneeling at her feet beside the open box, was counting the money. As Maia approached he closed the box and stood up, nodding corroboratively.

The Sacred Queen, who had beside her sealing-wax and a lighted candle, forthwith set about affixing her seal to a small sheet of parchment lying on the table. Maia, who had never seen this done before, watched intently as Fornis, with practised ease, melted the wax at the flame, dropped a round patch at the foot of the written parchment, wetted the seal with her tongue and pressed it down. The impress, precisely formed, depicted Airtha leaning over the sleeping Cran.

Fornis picked up the parchment, shook it back and forth a few times to cool the wax and then handed it to Maia with a smile and a benign inclination of her head.

'There you are, my dear: and now I expect you'll want to be off, won't you? I certainly must be: you'll excuse me, I'm sure.'

Getting up, she faced Maia for a moment, graceful, elegant and majestic. Though not an exceptionally tall woman, to Maia she seemed to rise above her like a tree, multifold, instinct with a quality of pliant, tense motion. She felt the Sacred Queen kiss her cheek and then saw her walking away with quick, agitated steps towards the stair-head.

The parchment felt cool, smooth and slightly greasy. Its very unfamiliarity seemed to confer upon it a magical, talismanic quality. Nevertheless she looked at it doubtfully, for not one word—not a brush-stroke—of what was on it could she read. Yet this alone—this thing of power—comprised all that she had sought and gained from her long night's work. Unless there was some trick, this was the actual instrument that would save Tharrin's life.

The queen was gone. Maia turned to Zuno, still standing beside her.

'Zuno, please tell me: is this really and truly an order of release for Tharrin, and is it—well, is it all right?'

He took it from her and read it through deliberately. There were no more than five or six lines in all.

'What is the prison governor's name, do you know?'

'Pokada.'

'Then it's entirely correct. It's addressed to him, it says "Tharrin" and the seal's her own and no one else's. You've only to take it down there.'

'Oh, Zuno, I can't believe it! Somehow or other I thought she'd—oh, I'm *so* glad! Oh, thank you, Zuno, thank you! Give my fondest love to Occula, won't you, and say I'm sorry I didn't see her?'

With this she turned and, closely followed by Brero, hurried down the corridor, down the stairs, across the hall and out into the garden, the parchment still clutched in her hand.

At the Peacock Gate she dismissed Brero and his mate, put on her veil and took the first jekzha she saw. To be sure, there would not be a great many idlers about the streets of the lower city this morning. Almost everyone who could would have gathered at or near the Blue Gate to watch Elvair-ka-Virrion and his men set out for Chalcon, but nevertheless she did not want to run any risk of being hindered on her way to the prison.

What would it be best to do, she wondered, once Tharrin had been handed over to her? Presumably he would simply be released to walk out through the prison gate: then she would have him entirely on her own hands. She couldn't take him back to her house in the upper city; that would never do. On the other hand, if she were to put him up at 'The Green Grove' or 'The Serpent' while she arranged for his return to Serrelind, there was always the risk—and no use pretending there wasn't—that he might skedaddle. Thinking it over, she decided the best thing would be to pay Lalloc to look after him for a day or two. He wouldn't be able to bunk from Lalloc's. Not very dignified, certainly, but really and truly he had no claim to expect more.

And she'd see him right. She'd see them *all* right; even Morca! Only, Tharrin was damned well going to do his fair share of getting the family back on an even keel again. She'd send a reasonable amount of money every month—ah! paid through some reliable person in Meerzat an' all—always provided he remained with the family, stayed out of trouble and did his fair share of keeping the place up together. Yes, that was the sort of thing to arrange. She might, perhaps, be able to manage something through the father of that poor lad Sphelthon killed at the ford. She'd done right by him even before she'd returned to Bekla, borrowing from Sendekar enough to pay a messenger to go to Meerzat and tell his parents; and in reply had received an unexpectedly dignified and touching letter from the father (Sendekar had read it to her) who had turned out to be a clerk in the provincial government and obviously a most respectable man.

There did not seem to be many butchers or meat-merchants at work as her jekzha came up through the Shilth; though she had to wait some minutes—her jekzha-man taking care to keep well back—while a herd of bullocks were driven past on their way to the shambles. Getting down at the gate of the gaol, she gave the man ten meld and told him to wait, saying that she did not expect to be more than a few minutes.

The mucous-eyed gatekeeper looked her over as listlessly as before.

'The governor, säiyett? Can't say, I'm sure. Only it's an execution morning, see? and that always means extra—'

She felt too light-hearted to be angry. Smiling, she gave him five meld.

'We've had all this before, haven't we? Just take me to U-Pokada's room, and then go and tell him as I want to see him very urgently.'

In the little, bare room she sat down and waited, impatient for nothing, fretting for nothing, as content with the present moment as someone who has just completed a long journey or finished reaping a field. She held the parchment in her hands, turning it this way and that and admiring the clear impress of the seal. Well, Cran and Airtha had been good to her, she thought. Perhaps, after all, even the Sacred Queen might not be without her good side. Nine thousand meld! Had any girl ever gone for as much, she wondered, in all the yesterdays of Bekla?

When Pokada came in she almost ran forward to take his hands before recalling the proper dignity of the Serrelinda. He had halted just inside the doorway, staring at her unsmilingly, his mouth drawn down in a startled, grotesque expression of dismay. He was roughly dressed—as roughly as any labourer—in an old, stained leather jerkin, sacking breeches and a torn woollen cap. His arms were bare to the elbow and down one forearm ran a long scratch, still bleeding, which he kept wiping with a dirty cloth.

'Säiyett—you must understand—I can't—not now—'

She held up one hand to silence him. Then, bowing triumphantly—making a little pantomime of it—she gave him the sheet of parchment.

'Read that, U-Pokada, please. Oblige me, U-Pokada, by reading that!'

Peering, he held it up to the light, saw the seal and started. Maia watched as his eyes travelled back and forth, slowly making out the few lines. Like enough, she thought, he wasn't much more used to reading than what she was. When he had finished he said nothing, only laying the parchment down on the table and staring at the floor without moving.

'Well, come on, U-Pokada,' said Maia at length. 'It's plain enough, surely? Only I got a jekzha waiting, see?'

'Säiyett,' said Pokada, still avoiding her eyes, 'the man is dead.'

'*What?*' cried Maia. 'What the hell do you mean, dead?'

'He hanged himself in his cell this morning.'

'I don't believe you! This is some trick to try to get money out of me or something! You just take me to him, now, and hurry up about it!'

As he said no more, she ran to him and beat her fists on his chest. 'It's not true! Not true! Come on, say it!'

'I think you'd better come and see for yourself, säiyett. I'm sorry.'

Bewildered, still disbelieving him because she was unable to take it in rather than because she thought he was lying, Maia followed the governor out of the room and then walked beside him down a stone-walled passage of which she noticed little or nothing. They came to a heavy, iron-bound door, and this he opened with a key at his belt. Beyond was a dimmer light, doors with grilles and an all-pervading, foul smell. A man appeared and spoke to Pokada, jerking his thumb over his shoulder.

'U-Pokada, this Urtan woman—'

'Not now,' answered Pokada, brushing him aside. 'Ask Tortil or someone; I'm busy.'

At the end of the passage they reached a row of eight or nine doors, all standing open. An old man was sweeping with a broom. As Pokada came up he moved aside and stood respectfully against the wall.

'Have they all gone?' asked Pokada.

'Yes, U-Pokada. Oh, yes, some time ago now: I'm just getting straight. That one who went for you, we had to break his—'

'All right, never mind,' replied Pokada. 'Go and get on with something else: I'll tell you when to come back. Well, go on!' he said, as the old man hesitated. He pointed to one of the open doors. 'He's still there, is he?'

'Well, that's it, U-Pokada, yes. Only there hasn't been time, you see—'

'Never mind. Do as I say: go on up the other end.'

In the doorway of the cell Pokada faced about, momentarily preventing Maia from entering.

'Säiyett, this isn't a pretty sight. All my men have had their hands full this morning, getting the queen's prisoners out to the temple. There's been no time to do more than take him down and lay him on the bed.'

She answered nothing. She believed him now; her mouth was dry; she felt sick. A moment later he had stepped inside the cell and she followed him.

Tharrin's body was lying on a narrow plank bed in the further corner. The clothes were those she had seen the day before and he still looked, as he had then, tidy and clean. Yet in the horror of recognition she noticed nothing of this. His head was twisted to one side, the neck distorted and encircled by a livid ring of bruised flesh. In places blood, now darkly clotted, had oozed from the chafed skin. The tongue protruded and the eyes were wide and fixed. One or two flies were walking on the face, which had already assumed a rigid, waxen quality. One arm hung down, the backs of the clenched fingers touching the floor. As she looked away, moaning and holding her hands to her mouth, Maia noticed a length of rope, one end of which was knotted round a bar of the high window. The lower end was still tied in a running noose.

Half-fainting, she fell on her knees beside the bed, took the cold hand in her own and tried to lay it across the body; but the arm was stiff and resistant.

She began to cry, stroking his other hand and kissing the mutilated neck and bared shoulders. He was cool and smooth as the parchment and stiff as a frosted branch. As the reality came flooding more deeply into her she wept passionately, on and on because it was easier than stopping, because she was afraid to think what would happen when she stopped. She felt consumed with pity for poor, shiftless Tharrin and the ugly squalor of his end. As she remembered his arms around her in pleasure, his easy laughter and the game of the golden fish in the net, her grief burst out yet more intensely, prostrating her so that she laid her head on his chest, grasping his shoulders and crying as though to sob the breath out of her body.

At last Pokada, putting his hands under her armpits, pulled her, still weeping, to her feet. As he made to wipe her face with the cloth at his belt she flung away from him, setting her back against the wall of the cell and glaring at him from reddened eyes that still poured tears.

'You killed him! *You* killed him! I'll see you hang upside-down for this!'

She was shouting hysterically, and he took a step towards her.

'Don't think you can kill me too! There's them as knows I'm here!'

'Säiyett, I give you my word I didn't kill him and nor did any of my men. He killed himself.'

'But he *knew* I was coming! He knew I was coming today to get him out! He *couldn't* have killed himself!'

Pokada hesitated. After a few moments he said, 'Säiyett, you'd better come back to my room. This is no place for us to talk.'

'Talk? You think I want to *talk* to you? I want to see you dead and damned, you bastard, and I will, if it's the last thing I do!'

Now he suddenly assumed a kind of stilted, homespun dignity and authority, like that of a gate-porter or a domestic steward. Perhaps, after all, he had not been made governor of the prison for nothing.

'Säiyett, little as you may wish it, I must request you to come back to my room, for I have something to say to you of a private nature. I regret to inform you that you have no choice, for the gates are locked and I can't let you leave until you've heard me. I've no wish to hurry you, however. You can either come with me now or stay here and come as soon as you feel ready.'

'Very well,' she said, 'I'll come. But before I do—' She pointed to Tharrin. 'Bring someone now—*now!*—to close his eyes and lay him out properly. And then see that he's treated decently and burned as he should be. I'll pay for everything. Will you promise me that?'

'Yes, säiyett: in fact I'll go and see to it at once.' He went out, and she heard him call a name: there were footsteps and muttered instructions, too low for her to catch the words.

They walked back together in silence. Once Maia stopped short, clutching the governor's arm as from somewhere not far off sounded a scream. He only grasped her wrist and led her on, through the iron-bound door and back down the passage to his room. Here she was overcome by a fresh seizure of grief; but now, from very exhaustion, she wept almost silently, sitting at the table, her head on her arms. At length, regaining some degree of composure, she said in a voice of cold accusation, 'U-Pokada, when I first came here, the day before yesterday, you asked me whether I'd brought poison, and told me as you had to make sure prisoners didn't kill themselves.'

He nodded, looking at her with pursed lips, like a man with something on his mind and unsure whether to tell it or not.

'Tharrin had no reason to hang himself. So if one of your men didn't hang him, who did, and why? And how did he get a rope?'

Still he said nothing, and she burst out, 'I warn you, U-Pokada, I'm going to make a public matter of it. I'm going to see you ruined for this.' She snatched up the parchment, which was still lying where he had left it on the table. 'Here's a pardon, sealed by the Sacred Queen herself, for a man who was in your charge—'

He was trembling now, the big, fleshy hulk of a man, fear written all over him, even his silver earrings shaking in his head.

'Säiyett—säiyett—'

'Yes?' But he said no more. 'Well, what?'

'Säiyett, I tell you—what I'm going to tell you—it—it puts my life in your hands. I tell you, and perhaps you get me hanged upside-down—if I tell you—'

'You mean you *did* murder him?'

'No, säiyett, no! I didn't murder him, no! I'll tell you the truth, I'll trust my life to you because I believe what everybody says, that you're a kind-hearted, good lady. Once you know the truth, then you're not going to be angry any more, you're not going to ruin me, because you're just and fair—'

She stamped her foot. 'Stop this stupid nonsense! Say what you have to say and get on with it!'

Pokada, having shut and locked the door, went over to the window, which he closed after peering outside. Then he sat down on the bench beside the table.

'Säiyett,' he whispered, 'do you know a Palteshi woman in the upper city? A woman close to the Sacred Queen?'

'Ashaktis, do you mean? A dark, middle-aged woman, with a Palteshi accent?'

'Sh! Säiyett, sh! We've got to whisper—'

Still angry, but nevertheless affected by his fear, she lowered her voice. 'Well? What about Ashaktis, then?'

'Säiyett, it was very early this morning: it was only just light. I was up, with two of my men, preparing for the executions. Only there are things we have to see to—the priests come—well, I don't need to tell you about that. But then Elindir, the man on the gate, he comes and beckons me to one side, so no one else can hear, and he says there's a woman come; and then he gives me a note with the queen's seal which says I'm to see her at once. But Elindir says she won't come further than the gate.'

He stopped, as though expecting Maia to reply. She said nothing and after a few moments he resumed.

'I went to the gate-house and there was the woman all muffled up—her face, too—nothing I could know her by again except her voice, her Palteshi accent. She said no one was to know that she'd gone into the prison. She hid behind a curtain while I called Elindir and told him she'd left. She told me to do that, and then to send him away again on some errand.

'Then she showed me another note from the queen, saying that I was to take her to the prisoner Tharrin in his cell. No one was to see her on the way. So I sent away the two men who were waiting for the priests, and took her to Tharrin myself. He was sleeping, säiyett, and when I woke him he smiled and said "Is it Maia come?"

'The woman told me to go away and wait up the passage, by the far door. And then after—oh, not very long, säiyett—five minutes, I suppose— she came back up the passage and she said "Now give me back both those notes." So then she had both the notes herself, you see, and I took her back to the gate and let her out. And the last thing she said, säiyett, she said "If the queen gets to hear one word from any living soul about my coming here, you'll hang upside-down, do you understand?"

'And then, not ten minutes later, we found Tharrin dead, just like you saw. Seven years, säiyett, seven years I've been governor here and not one condemned man has ever been able to kill himself before.'

Still Maia said nothing. 'Säiyett, I've told you because you said you'd see me ruined. But now you know the truth, you won't want to do that, will you? If the Sacred Queen gets to hear—'

'No, I won't say anything, U-Pokada,' replied Maia listlessly. She stood up. 'I'll go now. Come to the gate with me, please.'

'Säiyett,' he said, 'there's one thing you can comfort yourself with. At least you saved him from worse: he didn't have to go to the temple. And you and I, we're no worse off, are we, as long as we both say nothing?'

Her jekzha was gone, and rather than wait while another was fetched she put up her veil and walked away, down through the reeking lanes of the Shilth towards the Sheldad. Whether anyone spoke to her or tried to accost her she had no idea. In the Sheldad she found a jekzha and returned to the upper city.

: 65 :

A GLIMPSE DOWN THE PIT

The knife-blade was strong—too strong to bend or break on bone—and its point was very sharp. When she had told him that she would only need it for an hour, Brero had lent it to her without asking any questions. It was belted on her left side and her cloak hid it completely.

She had put her diamonds in their box and buried it in the garden. She would have liked to give them away—to Occula or even to Nennaunir—but that would have meant explanations and anyway there was no time. Delay was the last thing endurable now.

Nevertheless she set out on foot, partly because she did not want her soldiers to be accused, later, of having known where she was going, but principally because she wanted to feel herself alone with her purpose, deliberate and silent, pacing down the avenues and flower-bordered walks of the upper city. Behind her the Barb glinted in the mid-morning sunshine and the grey-green shadows on Crandor deepened as the sun moved southward above the summit.

I was born dirt-poor, she thought. I was sold for a slave; and I shall have died mistress of my own house in the upper city. Nothing's going to alter that.

This time she did not make her way to the garden of the queen's house, but straight to the further gate, where the porter, recognizing the Serrelinda as readily as would any other servant in the upper city, was prompt to accept both her five meld and her telling him that she had an appointment to see U-Zuno.

Slowly, as though in a dream, she walked across the courtyard towards the wide, stone front—the way she had come with Ashaktis on the morning when the Sacred Queen had taken her from Kembri. She met no one, but this did not surprise her. If, as she believed, the gods had appointed her their agent, then the gods would ensure that she was not hindered.

Climbing the broad steps, she paused a few moments before raising and letting fall the heavy, bronze knocker. It was bigger than her own hand, made to represent a crouching leopard. The sound, plangent and resonant, pleased her. Just so should the arrival be announced of an emissary of retribution.

Yet it was not Zuno but a very ordinary servant who opened the door; a middle-aged, stooping, grey-bearded man; some house-slave, it would seem, who had merely happened to be working near-by, for he was wearing a sacking apron, in the front of which he had stuck his duster and hearth-brush.

'Her Sacred Majesty's—' he began, before she had spoken.

'Are *you* the servant whose duty it is to answer this door?' she asked, staring at him coldly and haughtily.

At this the poor wretch clearly felt himself—and whatever authority he might have tried to exercise—at a disadvantage.

'Well, no, not exactly, säiyett. But you see, it's early for anyone to be calling, and what with the doings at the temple and that, they weren't expecting—that's to say, the doorkeeper—'

—Had slipped away for a drink and a chat, she thought. It might have been fore-ordained. She gave the man two meld, at which he stared and bobbed his head.

'It doesn't matter: I shan't be more than a few minutes. I wish to speak with Her Sacred Majesty's personal steward. I know where to find him, so you can get back to your work.'

She made her way along the jade-green colonnade, from the central ceiling of which hung the huge, winged figure she dimly recalled from the morning of her first arrival. It was, she now saw, an image of Canathron of Lapan, that vindictive dragon-god with serpent's head and condor's wings, flying inviolate through the midst of his nimbus of flames—fire being his natural element. Canathron was not worshipped in Bekla, except by such immigrant merchants and craftsmen as had come there from Lapan, and Maia could only guess that this must be an old treasure of the house; a gift, perhaps, or relic of some reign of a former Sacred Queen who had been Lapanese. She walked beneath it with mistrust and apprehension. She knew nothing of Canathron, except that he was reputed to be pitiless to his enemies. Might he in some way, perhaps, be a tutelary guardian of the house? Yet not even Canathron—no god or goddess whatever—would condone the unspeakable treachery and wickedness which she had come to avenge at the cost of her own life. At this thought she raised her eyes boldly to his jewelled ones staring down, held his gaze a moment and then passed on to the foot of the staircase.

Climbing the two flights to the gallery at the top of the house, still she met no one. She had been half-afraid of coming upon the lad with the great hound, but all was quiet as could be. Knowing her way, she went along the corridor to the door of the queen's bedroom, laid her hand on the hilt of her knife and strode in without knock or call.

Occula was lying on the bed, playing with a white kitten: she was alone in the room. As Maia entered she started, and the kitten, taking fright, jumped down and ran away.

'Banzi! What the hell are you doin' here?'

'Where is she?' asked Maia.

'Banzi, have you gone out of your mind? Who let you in? Tell me what you're doin' here.'

'Where is she?'

'D'you mean Fornis?' All in a moment Occula had leapt up, seized Maia by the shoulders, pulled open her cloak and disclosed the knife in its sheath. As she tried to take it from her Maia resisted fiercely, biting at her wrists. For fully a quarter of a minute the two girls struggled silently. Finally Occula stood back, panting.

'Banzi, just you give me that bastin' knife and get out of here! D'you realize she'll be back any minute and if she finds you here with that thing she'll have the perfect reason to see you put to death!'

'That's one thing she'll never see,' answered Maia, 'because I'm going to kill her first.'

'Oh, for Cran's sake!' cried the black girl. 'You never used to be such a damn' fool! Who let you in? Who knows you're here?'

'Don't matter. Once she's dead they can all do what they like. Or I will first.'

Occula buried her face in her hands and moaned.

'O Kantza-Merada! I can't *make* you go if you woan'—not without bringin' the whole place round us. Will you come with me to another room?'

Maia shook her head.

'But what's put you out of your senses like this, banzi? At least tell me that.' She moaned again. 'D'you realize every minute you stay here— Banzi, my own dear little banzi, for the sake of everythin' there's ever been between us, tell me what's happened, only be quick about it!'

Maia told her of all she had done to save Tharrin, of her visit to the prison that morning and of what Pokada had told her about the earlier, clandestine visit of Ashaktis. As she spoke of seeing Tharrin's body in the cell she began to cry again but then, dashing away the tears and clenching her fists, she ended, 'And now the gods have appointed me to kill her: that's for sure. Otherwise, how did I get in here so easy?'

'Banzi,' said Occula, taking her hands, 'you're wrong; and I'll tell you for why. *I'm* the one that's goin' to kill her; same as I killed Sencho. *I'm* the one the gods have appointed to put an end to these wicked people. I'm goin' to do it in my own way and my own good time; and when I'm done I'll walk out alive—you wait and see if I doan'. But it's a tricky business—for anyone that wants to stay alive, that is. The difference between you and me is, I know what I'm doin' and you doan'; not a bastin' thing. You'd just be throwin' your life away for nothin', because *I'm* goin' to get Miss Folda, *and* that damned Shakti woman, too. And I'm half-way there, banzi; I'm half-way there now! Doan', *doan'* go and throw your life away just because of poor Tharrin. She's guilty of far, far more than killin' Tharrin. She's guilty of every wickedness under the sun; murder, and treachery, and fraud—'

'Fraud!' cried Maia. 'Poor Tharrin put that clean out of my head! Ten thousand meld!'

'You're better off without that lot, banzi, believe me. There's certain to be trouble, but at least you'll be able to say you never touched a meld of it. Now answer me: do you want to die horribly and quite unnecessarily for ten thousand meld and a poor man you can't help any more?'

Maia was silent. The telling of her bitter story to her dearest and most trusted friend had done much to set things in proportion and to bring home to her impulsive heart the grim reality of the price she had thought herself ready to pay for revenge on the Sacred Queen. To die by torture or to stab herself to the heart: neither would bring poor Tharrin back to life; and as for Randronoth's nine thousand meld, well, it had never been hers and she had never reckoned it would be. Anger and humiliation at being hoodwinked and tricked by Fornis—were these, perhaps, as much a part of her motive as her grief for Tharrin? Her resolution began to waver.

'Banzi, love,' said Occula, 'there's no time to lose. She'll be back any minute, and if I know anythin' about it she'll be like a goat on the loose. You doan' know what she's like after these little sprees down at the temple. I can hardly stand it myself, an' that's sayin' somethin'. If she finds you—Banzi, give me that knife, and then I'll call Zuno to get you out of here. I suppose the knife's your soldier's, is it? I'll get it sent back later, somehow or other.'

Maia was about to give Occula the knife when the black girl, who had gone over to the open door, suddenly turned, facing back towards her with an expression of utter terror and dismay.

'Banzi! She's back! She's only just along the corridor! O Cran save us, she'll be here in a minute!' She looked frantically round the room. 'Get in there, quick! Get in that closet and doan' make a sound!'

Maia, with no feelings now but panic and desperation, slipped into the closet and lay down as Occula pushed the door shut. A few moments later the Sacred Queen entered the room.

It was clear that Fornis was wrought-up and in some kind of abnormal state. Her eyes were wide and her lips glistening and parted. She was panting and flushed and her hands trembled. As the black girl turned away from the closet and took a step towards her she mouthed 'Occula! Yes!' in a kind of swift gasp, and then stood waiting, apparently for some attention there was no need to specify.

Occula at once went to the door and closed and locked it. Returning, she faced the queen and in a contemptuous tone, as though rebuking a slave, said 'You're dirty! There's blood on your arms, you bitch!'

'Lick it off!' replied Fornis quickly. 'Lick it off, Occula, lick it off!'

Occula complied, the queen holding out her arms, staring before her and standing still as a post while she did so.

The closet door had swung slightly ajar, but Maia, though terrified of discovery, did not dare to pull it to, for the queen was only two or three yards away from her. Fornis, however, seemed in no frame of mind to notice anything. As Occula finished what she had been told to do, she sank to her knees on the floor, wiping her wet arms on her face and salivating down her chin.

'Well, and did you *enjoy* yourself down at the temple?' asked Occula in the same insolent tone, standing over her with her hands on her hips.

'Oh!—Two of them I did myself—how they screamed!' The queen clasped Occula round the waist. 'Get on with it, Occula! Hurry up!'

Occula spat in her face, pulled off the crown of Airtha, walked across to the mirror and adjusted it on her own head. Coming back, she ran her hands through the queen's elaborately-dressed hair, dishevelling it until it hung round her shoulders in an unkempt tangle, and then, stooping, gripped the hem of the purple robe and tugged it roughly over her head.

Fornis, her lips twisted in an unnatural grimace, remained kneeling on the floor. Occula, opening a drawer, took out a coarse, sacking smock— the kind of garment commonly worn by kitchen-slaves too mean ever to appear except among their own kind—a floor-cloth and a hearth-brush. She was closing the drawer when Fornis, with a kind of moaning excitement, prompted her. 'My shift, Occula, my shift!'

The black girl, crossing the room in two strides, seized the top of her embroidered silk shift between her hands, ripped it from hem to shoulder and tossed it into a corner. Then, flinging the smock and implements on the floor, she went over to the dressing-table, sat down with her back turned and began polishing her nails.

Eagerly and hastily the queen put on the sacking smock, which was stained, ragged, and so rank that Maia could smell it from where she was crouching in the closet. Beggars in the lower city smelt less disgusting. Dragging over an earthenware jar of water standing in the far corner of the room, Fornis began washing the floor on her hands and knees.

After about a minute Occula stood up in a leisurely manner, stretched her arms above her head, yawned and began to stroll towards the door. Reaching the queen she stopped, paused a moment to watch her and then kicked her in the stomach.

'You filthy slut! What the menstrual hell are *you* supposed to be doin'?'

'I've been told to wash the floor, please, säiyett,' replied Fornis in a low voice, without raising her eyes. 'I hope my noble lady won't—'

'Wash the floor, you turd!' cried Occula, kicking her again. 'You're not fit to wash a pig's venda! Haven' I told you I woan' have the floor washed like that? *Haven'* I? You zard-faced lump of dung!'

Paddling her bare feet in the film of water on the floor, she deliberately wiped one of them across the queen's face and then, putting it under her chin, pushed her roughly backwards, so that she measured her length in the grimy mess.

Fornis lay prostrate, shuddering with excitement. 'Oh, säiyett, säiyett!

Please forgive me—I meant no harm—I'll do it all again—don't whip me, säiyett!'

'How dare you speak to me in that insolent way!' shouted Occula, kicking over the jar and stamping her foot so that dirty water was splashed into the queen's face. 'I told you what would happen if you spoke to me like that again!' With this she picked up the sopping floor-cloth, wrung it out over the queen's shoulders, seized her by the hair, jerked her head back and stuffed it into her mouth. Then, pulling up her own skirt, she drew her hand between her legs and slapped the queen across the face.

As Fornis turned on her back, convulsing ecstatically, Occula plucked out the cloth, drew to one side and left her to her own devices. At length, her spasm of luxury subsiding, the queen once again rolled over in the morass on the floor, clasping the black girl by the ankles and whispering, 'More! More, Occula! More! Oh, you're marvellous! No one's ever been able to do it like you!'

'Like *me*, you disgustin', vile whore? You foul cow!' yelled Occula, trampling on her back. 'I'll teach you to lie there like a sow in shit, askin' for more! *I* saw you the other day, bastin' with the garbage-slave behind the midden! You thought no one could see you, but *I* saw you there, wrigglin' about in the muck on your hands and knees! You're not fit to live with ordinary, decent people! I'm going to chain you up to a kennel in the yard, with "Please shit on me!" written over the top!'

'Oh, säiyett! Oh, säiyett!'

'I'll "säiyett" you, you pig!'

Thereupon Occula, pulling up the smock round the queen's waist, beat her six or seven times with the flat of her hand across her bare buttocks, until she shrieked with pain.

'Now turn over, you nasty trollop! *Right* over, on your back! I want to look at you! No, do it properly, damn you!' shouted Occula, kicking and spitting on her again. 'Get those fat thighs apart, miss, before I have them well whipped!' Then, as the queen obeyed her, she seized the hearth-brush and thrust the handle between her legs until it disappeared.

Fornis screamed, squirming. 'Oh, be careful, Occula! Be careful! You'll injure me! You're hurting me!'

'Hurtin' you?' cried Occula, kneeling down beside her, pulling out her breasts and biting her nipples. '*Hurtin'* you? If I have any more insolence I'll stuff a nutmeg-grater up you and work it in and out. You beastly, stinkin' animal! I'd sell you for ten meld, but no one would buy you! You're not a human bein' at all; why, you wouldn' even make a decent piss-pot!'

And with this she straddled over Fornis, squatted down and urinated in her face, the queen babbling incoherently as she did so.

'Now clean me up! No, not with the cloth, you ape! Do what the apes do, and hurry up about it! I want to feel your—'

But at this Fornis once again discarded every vestige of control, losing all ability to sustain any longer her part in the revolting game and writhing on the floor in a perfect transport of voluptuous pleasure. From this second ecstasy she returned only very gradually, twitching where she lay and drawing long, shuddering breaths, as though she had run a race and was now utterly spent.

'Had enough?' asked the black girl, as the queen at length opened her eyes, drew out the hearth-brush and feebly tossed it to one side.

'Oh, Occula! Yes, enough now! Oh, that was wonderful! O Cran, but you really *must* be more careful! You've hurt me—'

'If I was more careful, you wouldn' enjoy it, would you?' replied Occula composedly. Fetching a bowl of clean water and a towel, she once more knelt beside the queen and wiped her face.

'Oh, yes, yes, that's true! You know, don't you? O Cran, I needed that! Oh, if only you'd been at the temple—'

'Let me get this thing off you now,' said Occula, biting her lip.

'I won't have it washed!' said Fornis quickly. 'That's the one that—'

'No, all right; but *you'll* need a bath, Folda. I told them to have it ready: Shakti'll be there now. You go along while I get cleaned up here. Sure you've had enough, now?'

'Oh, my black savage!' whispered Fornis, embracing her. 'Who sent you to me? D'you realize no one else in the whole empire would *dare* to treat the Sacred Queen to a quarter of that! That stupid little Maia—*she* was no good! Not even after six months of Sencho! Oh, I've played a nice game on *her*, the little nitwit! I'll tell you all about that later. Oh, Occula, what a good day it was for me when I got you out of the temple! You really enjoy it, don't you?'

Occula smiled. 'Yes, in my own way, Folda, I do enjoy it.'

'In your own filthy, dirty, black way. I love you! You're evil! You're a witch, aren't you?'

Occula, staring back at her, nodded gravely.

'You made that Urtan boy stab himself with a knife that wasn't there. I wish I'd seen that.'

'I wish you had.'

'You're frightening—you're splendid, Occula! You really understand about cruelty, don't you? Aaah!' The queen stretched luxuriously. 'I'm quite tired! Bath now, and then I'm going to have a nice sleep. What a delightful day!'

She stood up, slipped on the robe Occula was holding up for her, kissed her and ran out of the room. For some moments the black girl stood looking after her, then came back and pulled the closet door wide.

It was clear enough that she had been affected by what she had had to do. As Maia scrambled out, she shut her eyes for a few moments, leaning her sweating forehead on her forearm and retching; then, recovering herself, turned to Maia with a finger on her lips.

'Now get *out* of here, banzi,' she whispered. 'Doan' stop for anythin'! The knife you can leave to me. Zuno's at the top of the stairs; I've just seen him. He'll get you out by the back. Go on now—move!'

Dazed and speechless, Maia ran. Zuno guided her downstairs and as far as the gate behind the palace, but outside, in that same back lane along which she had walked by night with Lalloc, she suddenly came over faint, sank down and vomited. She felt feverish and hardly knew where she was going. Her own madness—Randronoth's—the queen's—all seemed blazing and burning in her head like meteors in a demented void. She was glad to accept the help of a kindly passer-by—some elderly house-slave returning from an errand—who, asking no questions and not even recognizing her, gave her his arm as far as the thoroughfare and saw her into a jekzha.

: 66 :

AND ANOTHER

'—I'm sincerely sorry. I'm sorry in many ways. But of course, your position in the empire will always remain a most honourable one; I hope you won't think anything else for a moment. We're very grateful to you; we always shall be.'

Durakkon, looking out of the window of the queen's reception room and picking with his finger-nail at the skin down one side of his thumb, paused for a reply. Fornis, however, said nothing and after some moments the High Baron reluctantly turned to meet her eyes. To all appearances she was waiting for him to continue. He had no more to say—indeed, in his tension and embarrassment he had already repeated himself, regretting and extenuating to an extent consistent, perhaps, with the manners of a nobleman but scarcely with the authority of the High Baron of Bekla. So potent and disconcerting, however, was the Sacred Queen's silent self-possession and air of not, as yet, having heard anything worth the time she had had to spend in listening, that Durakkon—actually against his own better judgement—found himself speaking again.

'You've done a great deal for the empire, esta-säiyett. There can be no one who's not fully aware of that. I know you'll understand that it wouldn't be possible—that the people themselves wouldn't accept—a Sacred Queen of—er—well, of the degree of maturity—' He broke off. 'Of course, you'll realize that Sacred Queen is one thing and Säiyett Fornis, ruler of Paltesh, is another. One's no more than an appointment—almost nominal—just for a fixed term. The other's what you actually are and always will be. There's no reason whatever for you to feel—er—well, in any way dispossessed.'

Still Fornis made no reply. They were both standing by the window and her eyes—though she was directly facing the late afternoon sunlight—looked steadily and unblinkingly into his own.

'Well, that's all I have to say, esta-säiyett, and I must say I'm glad to have finished saying it.' He laughed self-consciously. 'It's not always easy for me to—well, to carry out the duties of the High Baron. You've heard me very patiently. Thank you. If I can help you in any way at the end of this year—'

The Sacred Queen laid her hand on his arm. 'You suppose that *you* will depose *me*.'

From her inflexion, it might or might not have been a question. Durakkon found himself answering it.

'I've explained to you, esta-säiyett, that there's no question of deposition—'

He broke off, but spoke again as a thought occurred to him. 'Perhaps you would like to hear the Lord General and the Council—'

At this Fornis burst into a peal of laughter. 'Perhaps *you* would like to hear the Council, would you? What they think of you?'

Suddenly she was grave once more. 'Master Durakkon—may I call you Firebug, since everyone else does and we have known each other so long?— I am the Sacred Queen of Airtha, the intermediary of the gods. It is for *me* to say what will happen to *you* at the end of this year—to you and those of your fellow-conspirators who may still be left. Sencho, of course, is no longer a problem.'

'Conspirators? And pray, esta-säiyett, were you not also a conspirator, since that's the word you've chosen?'

'Did you come here to waste my time playing stupid games with words?' answered the queen. 'Well, I'm not altogether surprised: that's about all you've ever been fit for these past seven or eight years. Still, it's as well you *did* come, since it enables me to tell you what's going to be done and what part you'll play. At the end of this year, you will abdicate as High Baron—'

Durakkon bowed coldly. 'I'll leave you, esta-säiyett: you're plainly not yourself. Kindly think over what I've said and let me know when you're ready to talk with me again. For the time being—'

Suddenly Fornis took a step towards him, so that they were nearly touching each other. Durakkon almost threw up a hand to defend himself. When she spoke, it was in a hissing whisper.

677

'If regard is not paid to what I say, innocent people are going to suffer.'

'Esta-säiyett,' said Durakkon, with all the force at his command, '*I* rule here. I am sorry to be obliged to remind you of it.'

'And you know, of course, that half the Council want to get rid of you?' she asked. Turning on her heel, she walked away from him towards a cabinet on the opposite side of the room. 'You can hardly blame them, after all. The empire's full of disaffection as things are, and it hardly helps when the High Baron's universally known to be an ineffective dupe who commands no respect whatever.'

'It will do *you* no good to talk in this way, esta-säiyett,' said Durakkon. 'Remember, too, that if you compel me to take action against you, it will be in neither your interest nor the public interest.'

'The public interest?' cried Fornis, her eyes for the first time bright with anger. 'Oh, yes, *you've* always had the public interest so much at heart, haven't you? *You* were going to do so much for the empire, weren't you? So much for the common people!' She fixed on him a look of such evil malevolence that he stared back at her appalled. 'You really make me laugh! Why, the peasants—yes, the very beggars, too—they curse your name! You want proof? Do you seriously believe you'd be safe in any province of the empire without a guard? And as for the lower city, why don't you try walking by yourself as far as the Tower of Leaves one nice, dark evening? Do you really think you'd get there and back alive?'

'Silence, esta-säiyett!' cried Durakkon. But she had touched him on the raw, and the very fact that he spoke again showed it. 'I have more support as High Baron than you as Sacred Queen, and that I may have to prove to you.'

'Oh!' she answered. 'Oh, I see! Yes, really, what a lot they all think of the High Baron and his wonderful family! You did say "Silence", didn't you? That will be quite convenient, since I've something to show you, and I can keep quiet while you read it instead of talking nonsense to me.'

She unlocked a drawer in the cabinet and, without the least hesitation or searching, took out a sheet of written parchment, which she put into his hand.

'Of course, that's only a copy,' she said, 'but I'm sure the Lord General will show you the original if you ask him.'

'What is this, esta-säiyett?' said Durakkon. 'I don't wish—'

'Well, if you read it you'll know, won't you?' she said, and sat down in the window-seat.

He was about to give it back to her when his eye caught, written on the sheet, the name of his younger son. Startled, he read on.

'—embarrassing and extremely awkward if we were obliged to tell the High Baron in so many words that this young man is a grave liability as an officer. Yet he—' Here Durakkon came to the foot of the page. He hesitated a moment, then turned it and read on: Fornis watched him as he did so.

'Yet he has twice, now, shown himself unfit for action and you will understand that merely in the interests of discipline—to say nothing of the safety of others—I cannot retain him in his present command. I suggest that in the circumstances perhaps the most advisable and discreet course would be a transfer, with promotion, to the fortress at Dari-Paltesh—'

The letter, being a copy, was unsealed, but Durakkon could feel no doubt that it was authentic and that the writer was Sendekar. Naturally, he remembered very well his son's promotion and appointment to the staff of the fortress about eighteen months earlier. Kembri had congratulated him on the lad having been selected for so honourable a post. 'Now he's proved himself in the field, we feel he's exactly the sort of young man we need at Dari. It's a responsible position—'

How many people knew this shameful truth? Was it common knowledge throughout the army? How many other lies had been told to him? He could hardly keep tears from his eyes, for he had always greatly loved his younger son—a gentle, kindly young man—and felt proud of him. Clutching the parchment between trembling fingers, he looked up at the woman who had thus deliberately wounded him to the heart and now sat enjoying his misery.

'This document, esta-säiyett; it—it's no business of yours. It doesn't concern you in any way. How did you—?'

'Oh, do keep it,' she said lightly. 'You're welcome: I don't particularly want it. I'm sure it's of more use to you than to me.'

She was still sitting by the window. Silently, he laid the parchment beside her and was about to go when she spoke again.

'Would you care to see a note which your wife wrote to Spelta-Narthè?'

'Spelta-Narthè?' he said. 'Who is Spelta-Narthè?'

'Oh, no one at all. He's a slave: Elvair-ka-Virrion's huntsman. But he's very—er, accomplished and well-liked by a number of ladies, I understand. It's rather surprising that he can read, don't you think?—or perhaps not, all things considered.'

Without another word Durakkon left the room. Outside, one of the queen's waiting-women—dark and middle-aged, with the high colouring of a Palteshi—raised her palm to her forehead. After a moment he realized that she must have asked him some question.

'What?' said Durakkon. 'What did you say?'

'Your escort, my lord. Are you leaving her Sacred Majesty now? Do you wish me to summon your escort?'

'Oh—thank you,' answered Durakkon abstractedly. However, it had slipped his mind that he had already dismissed his escort some time ago, since before arriving he had accepted an invitation to supper with the Sacred Queen. He waited nearly half an hour alone in an ante-room while a runner was sent to recall them.

SUPPER WITH MILVUSHINA

The summer advanced. Pink water-lilies and beds of tiny-flowered, yellow *meleda* came into bloom along the shallows of the Barb, while the flocks of cranes which frequented it every spring departed in their thousands for the north, leaving the lake to ibis, egret and heron. Dragonflies, bronze and green, hovered in the sunny gardens and the bullocks grazing on Crandor's lower slopes could often be seen tossing their heads or suddenly leaping, tormented by gnats and clegs. In the middle of the day the only birds to be heard were the blue-finch and the little *damazin*, whose monotonous 'Treachree, treachree, treachree!', from his high song-post among the zoans, seemed the very sound of the still, hot sunlight. The bright flowers of the melikon tree—'False Lasses', as the peasants called it—shed their petals and began to turn to the glinting, golden berries which, though they looked so fine, were of no use to man or beast.

To and from the upper city, rich men came and went on profitable journeys—to their farm-lands in the provinces, to the timber forests of Tonilda, the silk and jewel markets of Ikat Yeldashay or the iron foundries of Gelt. Shearnas entertained and made money. Wealthy wives, alone with time on their hands, spent their days gossiping and over-eating, spending long hours in the cool bath or naked on the massage-couch, fancying themselves in love with others' husbands, or covertly visiting supposedly secret places of assignation well-known to every winking slave in their households. The Monju brook shrunk in its bed. Daily, messengers brought news from the frontiers and the Council deliberated in the Barons' Palace on the Leopard Hill.

In the lower city, droves of cattle and of slaves arrived in dusty clouds, both by way of the Gate of Lilies and the Blue Gate: wounded soldiers returned from the fronts and companies of recruits marched out under veteran tryzatts. Fleitil and his men put the last, finishing touches to the great statue of Airtha in the temple precinct. The beggars and cripples sat scratching themselves in the shade, ragged children pilfered from the stalls and the pilgrims murmured their prayers and made their offerings before the Tamarrik Gate. Lalloc, who had replaced Zuno with Megdon from the Puhra depôt, ordered him to sort out the prettiest girls from among the provincial consignments and prepare them for private sale in the upper city. In reply to his enquiries as to the present whereabouts of Genshed— for Occula had been insistent to learn what might have become of him following his flight—Megdon could tell nothing except that he had said he meant to clear out of the empire altogether and try his luck in Terekenalt. The old woman's sweet-shop was in new hands, repainted and smartened up. The gold and silversmiths were enjoying an excellent season, while the Street of the Armourers had more business up and down its steep length than the oldest could recall. No traveller from a distant land could have discerned that this was the heart of a realm where rebellion and civil war lay germinating behind the façade of mercantile prosperity.

Maia, still unable in her heart to feel any inclination for a lover, was nevertheless finding refusal even harder than before. The story of her auction had spread through the provinces, and although most, perhaps, of the wealthy visitors to the upper city were content—or at any rate appeased—merely to see the fabled Serrelinda, there were always some who (especially after they had caught a glimpse of her: for she was hanged if she was going to live the life of an anchorite) could not resist trying their luck.

There were many callers at her house by the Barb, and although no one offered her nine thousand meld (no one having nine thousand meld to offer), several men, sending passionate letters through Ogma or Jarvil, promised large sums in return for no more than an hour of her time. One young Belishban nobleman, who had been most persistent, at last stabbed himself one night outside her gate, but fortunately was picked up by his friends and taken home to recover. Gifts and flowers Maia accepted, although, remembering Milvushina's warning, she never ate sweetmeats or anything which had not been bought and prepared by Ogma. Letters she ignored and money her servants had orders to refuse. After a few weeks her attendant soldiers, at her own request, were increased to three, the third being necessary to protect her from spontaneous demonstrations like that of Selperron, some of which were of a less acceptable nature.

She began to go about more and accepted a number of invitations, mostly to small supper-parties and the like given by Nennaunir, Otavis, Dyphna and other reputable shearnas eager to show themselves her friends. Yet on such occasions she always asked her hostess to make it clear beforehand to the male guests that her favours were not available and that in this respect she would be displeased not to be taken at her word.

The upper city, of course, was sadly denuded of young men by the wars. Sarget the wine-merchant, however, at whose party in the Barons' Palace she had danced the senguela, became a good friend, perceiving and appreciating as he did her sincere love of music. On several evenings Maia found herself one of no more than four or five guests whom this quiet, unassuming man had invited to listen to Fordil and his players until a late hour. In this way she learned much, for Sarget would ask Fordil not only to play but to talk about his art, or perhaps to explain the intricacies of some composition—his own or another's. She never danced, however, at these supper-parties—only at her shearna friends'—for as often as not Sarget would have invited one or two members of the Thlela, and she knew well enough the difference between such natural grace and vivacity as she possessed and the life-long discipline and skill of dedicated professionals.

Yet with all these distractions, the recollection of Zen-Kurel never left her. That is to say, the conviction that Zen-Kurel was her lover refused to be relegated to the past. She could not think of him as gone, as nothing but a memory. Often she recalled what Occula had said to her in Sencho's house about work and pleasure. Poor Maia! she thought one day, in one of her rare indulgences of self-pity: reckon there's been a lot more on the work side than what there has on t'other. To only two men had she ever given her heart together with her body, and one of those had been no more than a green girl's introduction. To have loved Tharrin was hardly matter for poignant reminiscence: left to herself at home she'd have grown out of him—oh, yes—soon enough. Ah, that was just nature, she thought: any girl begins by feeling herself in love with the man who takes her virginity. That was why she still wept for him, why he still visited her dreams with his livid throat and his poor, staring eyes. But of course there had never been—never could have been—any notion of partnership or marriage between herself and Tharrin.

But her tears flowed also when she dwelt upon the brief hours which she and Zen-Kurel had spent together. She had fallen into a habit of recalling, of dwelling upon every least detail—things of no moment whatever; how in explanation she had tapped out a dance-rhythm with her fingers on his chest; how she had dropped one of the daggers and he had picked it up; the healed scar on his forearm which she had meant to ask him about and then forgotten—for all the world like some old man, with little left now to occupy his time, continually handling the petty treasures and souvenirs hoarded in his room. Yet this preoccupation was not of her own wish—or not entirely. There were plenty of times when she reminded herself of everything which common sense so cogently suggested. Why not forget? She was a public figure in a realm hostile to Katria. Zen-Kurel might already have put her out of his thoughts. And even setting that aside, on grounds of sheer probability it seemed all the world to nothing that she and he would never meet again. He might even be dead. Wasn't she as lucky as she could well be, the Serrelinda? It was open to her to pick and choose where she would. She could marry a powerful Beklan noble and live secure for the rest of her life.

And yet—and yet, she could not tell why, but she felt certain that Zen-Kurel was *not* dead. And with Maia, who no more weighed rational probabilities or assessed likelihood than any other girl in the half-civilized and superstition-dominated empire, intuitive certainty differed little from informed knowledge. And she was equally sure that he had not forgotten her, for if she knew how *she* felt, then she knew how he felt. 'And *I'm* no enemy of Katria, nor yet of Terekenalt,' she used to say to herself. 'I'm a Suban marsh-frog!' This, of course, was pure quibbling, for originally Suba had been bitterly hostile to annexation by King Karnat. But after the initial shock of what poor Tharrin had revealed to her Maia had first absorbed, then accepted and finally come to cherish as a delicious secret her exotic origins in that remote marshland whither she had actually been and hardly anyone else in Bekla had. Naturally, she also cherished the thought of Nokomis, just as anyone throughout the entire human race feels proud of a famous and distinguished forebear. No, she was no Tonildan and no Beklan either; and therefore no enemy of Katria.

Reason as she would, she remained convinced that she and Zen-Kurel were fated to meet again, though when and where she could not imagine. So persistently did this notion haunt her that one bright noonday, when the city walls seemed wavering in the heat and most of its people dozing in the shade, she went down to the temple and asked—as did many on occasion—for a seer to read the omens for her.

The man to whom she was conducted was a handsome young priest—no eunuch, but on the contrary possessed of a warm, reassuring manner; so that she found herself liking and (rather to her surprise) trusting him. He began by asking her to tell him, in confidence and without reservation, the entire matter on her mind, but this she felt unable to do.

'There's someone I hope to meet again,' she said. 'I believe I shall, but I want to know when and how.'

'A man or a woman?' he asked, smiling.

'Well—a man.'

'Where is he?'

She shrugged. 'I wish I knew. Far away.'

'So is there no ordinary, day-to-day likelihood of your paths crossing?'

She paused, troubled by the question. Yet there could be only one answer. 'No.'

'Do you believe that he will seek you out?'

'He would, but it's not in his power. He won't have forgotten me, I know that.'

683

'Säiyett, if the god and I are to help you, you must make the effort to be frank. Do you love this man? Who is he?'

She shook her head. 'I can't tell you no more. Here's the money. If you can help me, I shall be grateful: else we'll have to leave it.'

He nodded equably, accepting her at her word, and proceeded to the ·usual astrological questions about her age and the approximate dates of her first menstruation and loss of virginity. This done, he asked her to throw a handful of brightly-coloured sticks—red, blue and green—into a basin of sand; then to look at a sheet of gnarled bark and tell him what likenesses she perceived on its surface. At length he left her, retreating into a little alcove where he stood for several minutes in silence.

'This is all the god vouchsafes,' he said at last, returning to where she sat waiting. 'It's little enough, but then you have told me so little, säiyett. You will meet this man again if you yourself seek him; and else not. Also the god says, "Opportunity is all."'

'"Opportunity is all"?' she repeated, looking up at him in perplexity.

He bowed. 'I wish you well, säiyett. Believe me, I have done my best for you.'

Anyone might have said as much, she thought, going over it in her mind while Ogma prepared a cool bath and laid out for her two or three robes from which to choose for the evening. She had been invited to supper by Milvushina and, since she had been expressly told that no one else would be there, was naturally curious to know what she was to hear—or to be asked.

Anyone might have said as much. Still, that was nothing unusual. After all, doctors frequently advised, 'Go to bed until you feel better' and lawyers (or so she had heard) often said, 'You have a weak case and might as well not proceed'; and took their fees for saying those things. Well, to hear from a professional nothing more than the obvious at least clarified your mind and stopped you thinking in circles. 'If you seek him . . .' Yet how was she to do that? 'Opportunity is all.' Was she to make it, then?

'Zenka,' she asked silently, 'won't you tell me, darling?' But for once he made no reply in her heart, only smiling as he had smiled in the lamplight at Melvda when he had promised that he would always love her and begged her never to forget him.

Rather abstractedly, she selected a plain robe of very pale grey and a contrasting necklace of tawny ziltate beads from the Telthearna; a present from some admirer. No doubt, she thought, their price had lined some Ortelgan pocket; perhaps Ged-la-Dan's.

Milvushina received her warmly and affectionately. The old reserves which had at one time constrained their relationship had entirely vanished, due—or so Maia felt—not only to their closer acquaintance and happier fortunes, but also to a certain mutual dependence which each felt without actually saying as much. Milvushina, an aristocrat to her finger-tips but nevertheless a girl from the back of beyond, her man gone to the wars and her servants all Beklan, often found herself, even now, somewhat out of her depth. From Maia she could seek advice without breach of confidence or loss of dignity. Maia, for her part, was more than glad of a friend who, unlike the shearnas, was not for ever concerned with men, basting and the material advantages to be gained therefrom. Nennaunir and Otavis were warm-hearted, unenvious and the most easy-going and tolerant company imaginable, yet she not infrequently felt—to her own surprise and self-annoyance—that there were things about which she could not speak to them. Nennaunir, who admired her success, was plainly ready to stand by her anywhere; would have lent her money if she had needed it, lied for her or spoken up in her defence against anyone. Yet she could not have talked to Nennaunir about Zen-Kurel.

Milvushina was another matter. Although Maia had not as yet spoken to her of Zen-Kurel, she had come to feel that one day, when she was ready, she would probably find sympathy and understanding. What she felt to be their common bond was a sense of deep personal integrity transcending superficial contamination. Whatever had befallen Milvushina, whatever had been done to her, she plainly regarded as past and over, and her true self as remaining intact despite it. Her devotion to Elvair-ka-Virrion was no matter of expediency or eye-to-the-main-chance. In her own eyes she had neither come down in the world nor (like Nennaunir) up in it: she was Elvair-ka-Virrion's consort and the willing mother of his unborn child. With all this Maia felt herself entirely in sympathy.

Milvushina received her wearing a dark-blue, loose-bodied gown of Yeldashay silk on which was embroidered in gold thread a likeness of Airtha the mother almost identical to that which Maia had seen last year in the long gallery of this very house. Smiling, she put her hands behind her back and drew it close for a moment, to show Maia the swell of her belly beneath.

'Enjoying it?' asked Maia, passing an admiring hand over the curve.

Milvushina nodded happily, poured wine for them both and led her into the cool, flower-scented supper-room.

Maia, naturally, asked first about the latest news from Elvair-ka-Virrion and the Chalcon expedition, and of this Milvushina spoke with every appearance of cheerfulness, giving—very convincingly—the impression of having heard nothing which she could not mention in the hearing of the slaves.

'In the last letter I had—that was three days ago—he said they were a good thirty miles or more into Chalcon and sending out patrols to find

Santil's main force. It's very difficult country, he says—' Milvushina laughed—'well, *I* could have told him that—and it's not always easy to get supplies through. Apparently at least one baggage-train's been ambushed.'

'What d'you reckon's going to be the rights of it, then?' asked Maia.

'Well, if you really want to know, I think it'll all come to little or nothing,' answered Milvushina. 'I told Elvair as much myself. In those hills Santil can keep out of the way for as long as he likes—I should imagine—and then of course he's got the people on his side. I felt quite sure Elvair *would* have trouble feeding an army that size once they really got any distance into Chalcon. If you ask me, they'll be back before the end of the summer and no one much hurt on either side. But they'll have lots of rip-roaring stories to tell, won't they? Men always do.'

They talked of other things. After supper, however, when the sun had set, the slaves had brought in the lamps and left them together and she was sitting at her embroidery frame, Milvushina came back to the war in a rather different vein.

'I didn't want to say this before,' she said. 'I know slaves get to hear everything anyway, but I don't want them saying they heard it from me. I can't help worrying, Maia. Elvair says the whole country's bitterly hostile, even though he's had it proclaimed everywhere that they've no quarrel with anyone except Santil. I told him how it would be. My father was very well-liked, you see; and besides—well, I think they're angry about me, too.'

''Tain't all that surprising,' said Maia.

'Elvair says arrows come flying out of the trees, bridges get broken, sentries are found strangled—all that sort of thing—and never an enemy to be seen. But what in Cran's name did he expect?'

'Has he told Kembri all this, or just you?' asked Maia.

'I don't know what he's told Kembri,' said Milvushina. She paused, holding up two contrasting strands of yellow to the lamp. 'It's so hard to tell in this light, isn't it? Which one would go better with the green, d'you think?' And then, as Maia pointed to one of them, 'But I know what Kembri told *me*, only this morning. Not about Chalcon—about Urtah.'

'*Urtah?*' said Maia. 'What about Urtah, then? You mean as there's trouble there, too?'

'So Kembri was saying,' answered Milvushina. 'You know, of course, don't you, that the Urtans have been pressing for Bayub-Otal to be pardoned and released? Kembri's still holding him in Dari-Paltesh, to make sure his father keeps the province quiet; I don't know for certain, but it's my belief he's told the old man secretly that he *will* release Bayub-Otal as soon as things have quietened down and people have begun to forget about what happened in Suba.'

She refilled Maia's goblet. 'But the High Baron of Urtah's one thing, you know, and the Urtans themselves are another. There are a lot of people there who hate the Leopards and aren't content to wait. There's been trouble; no actual rebellion yet, but the next thing to it, and naturally Kembri's worried. There's unrest in Belishba, too. Apparently the governor's written to Kembri that there's so much heldro opposition to the slave quotas there that unless they're reduced he can't undertake to go on keeping law and order. It's the open fighting in Chalcon that's sparked all this off; I'm certain of that. I only wish to Cran the Leopards had left Santil alone and Elvair was safe back in Bekla. To tell you the truth, Maia, the whole thing's troubling me very much.'

She was silent for a time, and Maia was silent too, listening to the distant cry of the watchman on the Peacock Wall and the thin 'twink, twink' of bats hunting above the dark garden outside.

At length Milvushina resumed. 'But actually, none of this is really what I wanted to talk to you about, Maia dear. There's something else; something nearer home that concerns you as much as me.'

'Oh, ah?' Maia waited with some little apprehension.

'Do you remember,' went on Milvushina, 'one day when we were at your house, I told you I was afraid of Fornis?'

'Ah; on account of Elvair'd taken you away from old Sencho's,' said Maia. 'Nor he wouldn't send you back to Chalcon when she told him.'

'Well, it's worse now,' said Milvushina. 'Durakkon's told Fornis officially that at the end of this year she'll have to cease to be Sacred Queen.'

'Don't see as he could have done anything else,' replied Maia. 'I mean, her time's up anyway; more than up, isn't it?'

'Yes, but you can guess how much *she* likes the idea. And meanwhile everyone's begun talking about who's to succeed her.'

She gazed questioningly at Maia.

'Well, come to that, Sessendris was on about this to me—oh, weeks ago now,' said Maia.

'What did she say?'

'She said there was plenty of people in the lower city as'd like to see me acclaimed Sacred Queen, and I said that was silly. So then she said some of the Leopards would be ready to try it on if they thought it would be to their own advantage, like, and go down well with the people.'

Milvushina nodded. 'And Kembri himself wants it to be *me*.'

'Yes, Nennaunir told me that Kembri and Elvair would likely have the same idea about you, but I didn't know whether to believe her or not. Do you *want* to be Sacred Queen? 'Cos I don't, I'll tell you that much.'

Milvushina shook her head. 'No, I don't. Before Fornis it wouldn't have mattered all that much. But you see, Maia, during the last eight years

Fornis has given the Sacred Queen so much real power that the whole thing's become absolutely vital to anyone who wants to rule Bekla.'

'Well, far's I'm concerned, you can have it,' said Maia, smiling.

'Oh, you *still* don't see, do you?' replied Milvushina almost frantically. 'It doesn't *matter* what Durakkon said to Fornis: she *won't* go unless she's actually forced to, and she's as cunning and cruel as a whole army of devils! You and I—we're both in danger—in real danger—from her; but you most, because Kembri's protecting me. Oh, Maia, I'm so afraid she's thinking up some horrible plan to put you out of the way!'

At this Maia, weeping, poured out the whole story of Tharrin's death, omitting nothing. Milvushina listened without interrupting, her needle laid aside. As Maia ended she said, 'I knew your real reason for the auction at the barrarz, because Elvair told me. But I didn't know the rest. The cruel woman! How vile and wicked!'

'What d'you reckon Ashaktis told Tharrin, then?' asked Maia.

'That you were dead—that you weren't coming—that you'd deserted him—whatever would make him despair. And of course *she* brought the rope.'

'Milva, couldn't we say—I mean, sort of both announce publicly—as we don't neither of us want to be Sacred Queen?'

'Oh, no; that would only look ridiculous—I mean, before either of us has actually been put forward. All we can do is wait, and be terribly careful.' She hesitated; then suddenly said, 'Oh, Maia, *don't* go home tonight! Stay and sleep here!'

For the life of her Maia could not share such desperate and immediate anxiety as this. 'But—well, but I mean, I'll have to go home some time, Milva. I can't stay here for ever, can I?'

'Never mind; just stay tonight. I'd feel happier if you did. We'll sleep together, like last year when you used to comfort me.' She embraced Maia. 'You can comfort me again: I need it, I can tell you.'

Maia could only accept, and send Brero back with a message to Ogma.

The following morning the two girls were awakened by Milvushina's Beklan maid, a competent, handsome woman named Lokris. Bringing in a tray of milk, fruit, butter and fresh-baked bread, she asked Milvushina, 'Have you heard the news, säiyett?'

'From Chalcon, do you mean?' asked Milvushina apprehensively. 'What's happened, Lokris?'

'No, not from Chalcon, säiyett. I only asked because I thought you might not have heard last night. It seems the Sacred Queen's left Bekla for Paltesh. She went yesterday evening, but the Lord General wasn't informed until several hours after she'd gone. Her chamberlain, Zuno, came here with a message very late. Apparently he'd had orders not to deliver it earlier. She said she wanted to be among her own people for a while.'

'How did you come to hear this, Lokris?' asked Milvushina.

'Well, säiyett, we get to hear things, of course, but as you know, I don't go chattering as a rule. Only I thought—well, I thought this was something you might like to know about quickly.'

: 68 :

MAIA COMMISSIONS A SEARCH

The news that Fornis had left Bekla for Paltesh filled both the upper and lower cities, from the poor to their rulers, with speculation. The interest was of that unquiet kind which people feel when they suspect that a public occurrence is likely to affect their personal lives. One thing above all that the Sacred Queen was known for was a woman of decision; of action, energy and vigour. (It was common knowledge, for example, that an entire night without sleep was nothing to the Sacred Queen.) It was also known that she often did the unexpected, devising moves that could hardly have been anticipated. Finally, she was a great confronter and outfacer, always ready and more than ready to beard anyone at all and overcome them by sheer force of spirit and power of rejoinder. Both Kembri and Durakkon had good cause to know this, to say nothing of the chief priest, various provincial governors and countless smaller fry down to the wretched dog-boy.

If Fornis had left Bekla for Paltesh, therefore, it would certainly not be out of a nostalgic desire for a quiet holiday among her own countrymen. She must have some purpose, and as to what it might be there was much talk and guessing among the common people, to whom she remained what she had always been—a magical figure, intrepid, dazzling and numinous, her known cruelty rather adding to her goddess-like standing (for are not the gods cruellest of all?) than otherwise. (It is a curious fact that lack of pity is often condoned in people admired for their personal courage.) At the same time, the impossibility of her continuing as Sacred Queen was not disputed. Such a thing would be impious and accordingly most unpropitious, inviting the anger of the gods. Fornis herself must know this, and therefore presumably (thought the people) had no wish to incur divine retribution. Most in the lower city had hitherto supposed that she would either return to Dari to rule Paltesh, or else that she would accept some honourable religious appointment conferred by the High Baron, such as controller of sacred statues, images and mural paintings throughout the empire. Everyone, of course, remembered her march upon the city nearly eight years before, but this she could not be expected to repeat.

Both Durakkon and Kembri, however, would have been glad to feel sure of this. They were among those—that is to say, virtually everyone—to whom it had never occurred that Fornis would leave the city. Now that she had, the very fact was reason for disquiet. Fornis could be up to anything, and that she was up to something was certain. The lower city, who saw her only from a distance and, as it were, on her own terms, had scarcely any notion of the extraordinary blend of shrewd cunning and violent passion given to all extremes which made up her character. 'That woman,' Kembri had once said to Durakkon, 'would be capable of plotting to ruin herself and the world, as long as it destroyed her enemies and sated her pride.' Now, with the queen gone, Durakkon, still aghast and wretched from his glimpse of some of the grisly weapons in her secret armoury, could only await the outcome with misgiving. To command her return would be futile, for the secular power could claim no ultimate authority over the comings and goings of the Sacred Queen. Indeed, the only possible effect would be to prolong her absence. But then again, that? Might that in fact be relatively the safer course? (There could be no such thing as *absolute* safety for any enemy of Fornis.)

Maia, however, shared none of this disquiet; for her there was only the simple, delightful knowledge that the queen was gone. She had not realized how badly she had been afraid of Fornis, or in how many respects her fear had been affecting her life. She had in fact been afraid whenever she made new friends, afraid to entertain in her own house, to go freely about the upper city, to enjoy to the full her public popularity. Now, like an animal venturing little by little out of concealment, she began gradually to do all these things. She gave a party for thirty guests (the limit, she reckoned, for her house, and of course she had to hire extra servants for the occasion). Among those who came were one or two of the first wounded officers back from Chalcon, and little good it was that they had to tell. Guided by Nennaunir and Otavis as to who would be suitable, she began to invite a few of her better-connected admirers to call on her for wine and talk. Maia, of course, was no brilliant conversationalist, but she was a good listener, lively and quick to both sympathy and laughter, and with these qualities added to great beauty no girl has ever been able to go far wrong. By listening, too, she learned a good deal about affairs in the provinces, and began to understand what Kembri had meant by saying that men were apt to speak more freely and indiscreetly in the company of a beautiful girl whom they wished to impress. Indeed, she heard one or two things which she guessed that the Lord General would have been most interested to learn. However, she had not seen him since the morning when she had gone to the Barons' Palace to plead for Tharrin, and anyway she no longer regarded herself as his agent. As far as she was concerned, that had come to an end on the banks of the Valderra. She no longer had any need to better herself by bearing tales. Also, she felt intuitively that she had fallen out of favour with Kembri, and this she attributed to his having decided upon Milvushina and not herself for Sacred Queen. That, however, troubled her little, for she did not believe that he would go the length of seeking her life or her ruin.

So she fared abroad, and bought fine clothes, and slept till noon when she chose, and dined or supped with Sarget, and with Bodrin the Gelt iron-master, and such Leopard lords as her friends approved; and shed tears of rapture as Fordil's fingers called forth from the hinnari a divine sorrow in which all her own—and the world's—was dissolved. In the moment of awakening, and before ever her sleepy mind had fastened upon the actualities of the coming day, it would be filled with a delightful assurance that all was well. All, indeed, until she thought of Tharrin's ashes blowing on the easterly wind—ah! whither? Towards that remote west—Suba, Katria, Terekenalt—which somewhere in its immensity contained her own Zen-Kurel. She, the Serrelinda, who had saved the city, had been made a victim of the Sacred Queen's cruelty, wronged and cheated beyond anything that any honest heart should brook unavenged. And incomparably fortunate though she might be, she yet lacked the simple luck of thousands of peasant lasses whose lot lay far beneath her own; namely, to laugh and chide and bed and wake with her rightful man.

'Zenka! Zenka!'

'Did you call, miss?' said Ogma, coming into the steamy, perfumed bathroom where she lay naked as a bride and lonely as a widow.

'Oh, don't mind me, Ogma,' answered Maia, stretching for a towel to wipe her wet face. 'I'm all upside-down this morning! Dreams—star-gazing—never mind.' She broke off. 'Oh, but listen—I want to go down to the silk market later, will you tell Brero? There's a new trader up from the south: Otavis thought we ought to take the opportunity.'

'Opportunity, miss? Strikes me you're not taking all what you might.' For Ogma had been completely bowled over by Randronoth and the dawn delivery of the nine thousand meld (which she supposed to have been safely stowed somewhere or other) and had continually in her mind the prospect of a whole succession of lustful governors, councillors, merchants and what-not, whose tips to the Serrelinda's lady's maid (for Randronoth had been liberal) would carry her as far beyond her wildest dreams as ever Maia had been carried beyond hers. Nor, perhaps, could she—who had so often seen Maia return tousled from the couch of Sencho—altogether be blamed for wondering why on earth her mistress seemed too fastidious either to make three times as much money as any shearna in Bekla, or (if that was not to her fancy) at least to set about achieving a noble and wealthy marriage. There could be only one explanation.

'Miss?'

'Yes, Ogma?' Maia stepped out of the bath, flinging back her head and shoulders as she towelled her back. Then, as Ogma hesitated, 'Well, what?'

'D'you reckon they're going to make you Sacred Queen at the end of this year?'

In the freezing silence that followed her question, the wretched girl stammered, 'Well, miss, I—I only just—only people keep saying—I mean, there's them as—'

'Get *out*!' cried Maia, hurling the towel at her. 'Get out! And if ever you dare to talk to me like that again I'll have you sent to Zeray, d'you understand? *Zeray!*'

As Ogma, flabbergasted—for Maia was almost always the most easy-going and conversable of mistresses—stumbled out of the room, Maia flung herself across the massage-couch, sobbing, beating her clenched fists in the cushions and swearing as fluently as Occula herself.

'Opportunity!' whispered Zen-Kurel in her mind's ear. 'Aren't you the girl who had the wit to dress herself in golden lilies to meet the king? D'you suppose I've forgotten; d'you suppose I could *ever* forget my princess of opportunity? Only find the opportunity, Maia!'

After a time she dried her eyes, dressed and went pensively down to breakfast in the sunny garden. Half an hour later, the silk trader temporarily forgotten, she was lying in a low-slung hammock with one foot on the grass when Nennaunir, all diaphanous gauze and perfume, burst into the garden with a fervour like that of a hound welcoming a returning master. Before she rightly knew what was happening, Maia found herself embraced and so smothered with kisses that she could hardly find breath to greet the shearna or ask what it was all about.

At length Nennaunir rose from her knees beside the hammock and stood looking down at her with a smile that broke into the outright laughter of pure joy.

'You—you miracle-worker!' said the shearna, wiping tears from her eyes. 'You conjuress! How d'you do it—m'm?'

Maia, feeling good-humoured enough but a shade impatient of this unexplained transport, was visited by a touch of the Occulas.

'Well, on my back, mostly, but sometimes I—'

Nennaunir, grasping her two hands in her own, swung her to and fro in the hammock.

'Oh, Maia, *thank* you! Thank you from the bottom of my heart! What more—what more can I say?'

Maia looked up at her frowning, and shook her head.

'You mean to say you don't *know?*' asked Nennaunir.

'That's 'zackly what I do mean to say. What you on about?'

'It's Sednil! Sednil! He's back, he's back in Bekla! He's *free!* Randronoth's given him a release token! And now the Queen's gone, he's got nothing to be afraid of! I suppose you didn't arrange that too, by any chance, did you?'

Maia jumped up.

'Sednil; free? Oh, Nan, I'm so glad! Well, good old Randronoth—I never guessed he'd be that quick! I reckon he's a lot better than what he's given credit for; some ways, anyhow. What happened, then? Tell me! When did Sednil get back? Did he come straight to see you or what?'

'No, dear; *I* went to see *him*. Well, he couldn't possibly hope to get admission to the upper city, could he? He reached Bekla early yesterday morning. He'd been three days walking from Lapan. He was in rags—good as—and he had two meld on him. And then by sheer luck he overheard someone in the market saying look, that was the Serrelinda's servant-girl over there buying vegetables, so he went up to her and gave her his two meld to come and tell me. So it was your Ogma who brought me the news. That was why I was so surprised you hadn't heard.'

'So'm I. 'N then what?'

'Well, I went straight down, of course, and there he was, waiting by the Scales in the Caravan Market. My dear, we've hardly been out of bed for the last twenty-four hours! But I've got him some reasonable lodgings down near the Tower of the Orphans, and given him enough money to buy some decent clothes. He's started looking for work already.' For a moment Nennaunir looked troubled. 'I only hope he'll find something, and not get into any more trouble.'

'But surely, now, you can keep him going as long as ever he needs, can't you?' asked Maia.

'Yes, of course I could,' replied Nennaunir, 'if only he'd have it. But I told you before, didn't I? He's a very funny lad that way, is Sednil. That's partly why I'm so fond of him, I suppose. He won't take money from anyone unless he reckons he's earned it himself. D'you know he's actually tallied up everything I've paid out for him? As far as he's concerned it's a loan and he means to pay it back, every last meld. That's what's worrying me: I don't think he's going to find it all that easy. I'm never sure how much you know, Maia dear, about Beklan ways; but it's usually rather difficult for branded men to get respectable work. Silly, I call it, because often, of course, it only drives them back to crime.'

Ogma came into the garden to clear away the plates.

'Ogma,' said Maia, 'Miss Nennaunir tells me you saw her friend Sednil in the market yesterday, just after he'd got back from Lapan.'

Ogma looked startled and somewhat confused. 'Why, yes, that's right, miss: he came up and spoke to me.'

'It didn't cross your mind that *I* might be interested to know he was back?'

'Why, no, miss; I can't say as that occurred to me at *all*,' replied Ogma, in a tone of defensive indignation. 'Why, I didn't even know as you knew him!' Then, as Maia remained silent, she added, 'I hope you're not thinking as I acted wrong, miss, in not telling you? It never even entered my head. He didn't look—well, to tell you the plain truth, miss, and I don't want to speak out of turn, but he didn't look at all like someone as *you'd*—that's to say—' Conscious of Nennaunir's eyes on her, she became even more disconcerted. 'I'm sure I'm very sorry, säiyett, if I—'

Maia laid a hand on her arm. 'No, it's all right, Ogma. You weren't to know I knew him, and nobody's cross. Just forget all about it. I think Miss Nennaunir's staying to dinner' (Nennaunir nodded, smiling) 'so we'll have those pigeons U-Sarget sent, shall we? That's if you think they've hung long enough? How do you think they ought to be cooked? You tell me.'

'You know,' said Nennaunir, when Ogma had been sufficiently flattered, soothed and sent about her business, 'she was right, of course. Strictly speaking she wasn't to know. But all the same, a girl who's looking after someone like you really ought to have her ear a bit closer to the ground and be able to put two and two together better than that. It's part of her job—or it ought to be. Terebinthia, Sessendris: why don't you get yourself someone like that? You could easily afford it, and it might make all the difference one of these days.'

'No, I won't get rid of Ogma,' said Maia. 'She was with us at Sencho's and she knows my ways.'

'I'm not suggesting you should get *rid* of her,' replied Nennaunir. 'But why not get yourself a proper säiyett as well, someone a bit sharper—'

'Well, I'll think it over, Nan, honest; and I'll think it over 'bout Sednil, too, and help if I can.'

The truth was that sixteen-year-old Maia had no wish for an older, more experienced woman to tell her her own business. Club-footed, dull, dependent Ogma suited her very well and she had no intention of looking for someone like Sessendris, who had advised her against trying to help Tharrin and been proved abundantly right.

'Brero,' said Maia, 'd'you reckon you might be able to find me a particular man in the lower city, and get him up here without anyone taking any particular notice of it?'

It was two days after Nennaunir's visit. Maia, having taken what was for her a considerable time to reflect on an idea which had first occurred to her before the shearna had left, was now (with a certain amount of inward trepidation) putting it into effect.

Brero frowned, scratched his head and seemed about to reply, but Maia forestalled him.

'I'll tell you as much as I know. His name's Sednil and I suppose he's about twenty-one.' She went on to describe him as she remembered him. 'He's in lodgings somewhere near the Tower of the Orphans. He's been out and about looking for work, so likely he's been talking to people round there who'll remember him. And he's a branded man, Brero: crossed spears on the back of his hand. But he's finished his sentence: he's free now.'

'A *branded* man, säiyett?'

'Well, but he's got a release token. Anyway, he hadn't really done anything.'

'Oh, none the more for that, säiyett: that's nothing to me. Only you said you didn't want anyone taking any notice, and it won't be possible to take a branded man through the Peacock Gate without the guards wanting to know who he is and where he's going.'

'And yet I've got to see this man, Brero; and secretly, too. I've had instructions.'

'I understand, säiyett.' It did not surprise Brero to learn that Maia had had instructions. After all, she had had instructions to cross the Valderra, hadn't she?

'Well, for a start let's see whether you can find him, Brero. And if you do, don't say anything about me, understand? Give him this box—there's some money in it—and say it's an advance for a special job of work as'll be well-paid, and that if he's interested there's someone as wants to talk to him about it.'

'He wouldn't take the money, säiyett,' said Brero, 'but he says he's ready to talk about the work.'

It had taken him less than a day to find Sednil. The area along the banks of the Monju brook, between the two great thoroughfares of the Sheldad and the Kharjiz, was a comparatively quiet and respectable district; quite unlike, for example, the teeming alleys and warrens further west, between the Khalkoornil and the Tower of Sel-Dolad; and enquiries among its taverns and lodging-houses had soon put Brero on the right track.

'How did he act, like?' asked Maia. 'Did he seem surprised?'

'Well, more kind of suspicious, säiyett, really,' replied Brero. 'First of all he made me swear black and blue that 'twasn't anything to do with the Sacred Queen. He seemed real frightened of her.'

'Isn't everyone?' asked Maia.

'Well, yes, I suppose so, säiyett, in a manner of speaking. Only it didn't seem to make sense, like, her having gone to Paltesh, as everyone knows, and why *should* he suppose it might have anything to do with her?'

'Oh, he's got his reasons, Brero,' said Maia. 'Well, now what?'

'Well, what I was thinking, säiyett, if you're agreeable, we might make a little arrangement like this, seeing as you have to see the man secretly. I'll go down tomorrow night after sunset, and meet him by arrangement. We'll wait together in a jekzha wherever it suits you: perhaps the Monju bridge in the Sheldad would be a convenient place. Then I'd suggest that you follow in another jekzha about half an hour later—veiled, of course, säiyett. When you come to the bridge, you simply get into the other jekzha with this young man. He needn't show himself at all. Then the two of you can ride up and down the Sheldad—or anywhere—while you talk as long as you want. I'll keep your jekzha by the bridge, and as soon as you're ready you can simply come back, change over again and go home. It just struck me that that might be better than meeting in a house. I mean, in a house there's always bound to be someone who sees you come and go, isn't there?'

'Brero, they ought to make you a tryzatt, that they ought.'

'Well, one day, perhaps, säiyett. But I hope you won't go recommending me, for I'm in no hurry to change this job just now. Why, they might send me to Chalcon or the Valderra, mightn't they?'

'Oh, great Cran!' said Sednil. 'It's you!'

Maia laughed and lowered her veil again. 'Who'd you reckon it'd be, then?'

He was looking far better, she thought, than ever he had in the temple. Indeed, she would hardly have known him. Darkness had almost fallen, but there was enough light from the lamps and flaring torches of the shops and booths still open along the Sheldad to show her a spruce, alert-looking young man with a trim, black beard, dressed in a new veltron and leather breeches. More striking than his actual appearance, however, was the entire alteration in his manner, and the figure he cut in her female eyes. Before, it had always seemed to her as though his whole demeanour—his facial expression, his talk, his gait, his gestures—had been as it were dyed, soaked through and through with resentment and dejection, so that it had been impossible for him to speak or act without expressing these things, as involuntarily as a priest expressed solemnity or a clown the absurd. In short, he had been the very embodiment of a convicted prisoner. Now, all this—as near as she could perceive in the flickering half-light and street hubbub through which they were moving on—had disappeared, or very nearly so. She had always been puzzled by Nennaunir's devotion to Sednil. Now, she thought, she was seeing something like the young man whom Nennaunir had first known; before he, like herself, had fallen victim to the cruelty of the Sacred Queen.

'Well, it just never entered my head it'd be you,' he answered. 'But I suppose that was the idea, was it? Nowadays you have to be careful going about, I know that. I hope you've come so that I can thank you. Nan's told me what you did. The governor told me, too, come to that, when he gave me my release token. He gave me a letter for you as well: I meant to give it to Nan, but I forgot. It's back in my room now.'

'You can give it to Brero later.'

Now he set about thanking her in earnest, and that with an articulate warmth and fervour of which she would never have believed him capable. His sincerity went to her heart. Just as in the temple, on that morning of the festival when they had first met, she felt him to be someone like herself, someone whom she understood. Palteshi he might be, but she could tell without asking that he, like herself, had been born in a hut and known what it was to be glad of a lump of black bread. She was really delighted, now, to think that she had helped him; and relieved, too (for of this she had been doubtful before), to feel convinced that he was to be trusted with her secret.

'—And anything I can ever do for you—' he was saying, when she put a hand on his arm and, again raising her veil, bent forward and kissed his cheek.

'There is: but it's a very big thing, and I don't want you to think as you've got to do it because you're under any obligation to me. It's not a favour, it's a job. It might be dangerous and I'm paying according. There's no one else I can possibly entrust with it, Sednil. If you don't want to take it on, I shall have to leave it.'

Now he was once again the old, canny, worldly-wise Sednil.

'You'd better tell me a bit more about it, Maia.'

Suddenly a girl flower-seller jumped up onto the step of the jekzha, jolting it and causing the jekzha-man to turn and swear at her.

'Lovely roses, säiyett! Lilies, look, sir, and this purple cresset, real cheap!'

She held up her basket so that the sweet, fresh scents filled the dark interior of the jekzha. Behind her array of blooms she herself looked pinched and tired. Maia slipped a five-meld piece into her hand.

'I'll take this rose. Keep the money, dear. Good-night, now.'

The girl was beginning, 'Oh, bless you, säiyett——' when the jekzha-man slapped her arm. She rounded on him, cursing, dropped off the step and was gone into the dusky commotion of the Sheldad.

Maia smelt the rose, tapping it pensively against her upper lip.

'Sednil, what would you say if I was to tell you—if I told you that I'm— in love—with a Katrian—an officer in Karnat's army?'

He did not laugh, or say 'What?' or even come out with any sort of oath or exclamation. She could see that he believed her at once and took her seriously. For a little while he was silent; and she was silent too, waiting for him to answer her. And answer he did.

'*If* you said that to me, the first thing I'd ask is "Where is he now?"'

'I don't know. And that's what it's all about, Sednil.'

Slowly, and more than once with a catch in her voice, she told him how King Karnat had received her like a princess at Melvda-Rain; of the supper that evening, and of how Zen-Kurel had come to her house. As she went on to speak of their love and his promises, she began to weep in good earnest; yet he made no attempt to calm or pacify her, only waiting and listening as she faltered out the end of her tale—Zen-Kurel's disclosure to her of the king's plan, the night-march of the army to the river and her own desperate resolve.

When she had finished he remained silent while she dried her eyes and composed herself. At length he said, 'But I don't understand. If you loved this fellow—and you say you still love him—why ever did you risk your life to make sure Karnat's plan failed?'

She was astonished. 'Why, Sednil, to *save* them all; to stop the bloodshed, of course! Dear Lespa, if only you'd seen what I've seen! Listen, and I'll tell you—if I can.'

She told him of the night-crossing of the Valderra ford, of the slaughter of the patrol and how she had knelt over the dying Sphelthon. Then, for good measure, she added what the farm-girl Gehta had said to her about her terror of invasion; and lastly she spoke of the Tonildan detachment downstream of Rallur, which the Terekenalt army would have destroyed to a man.

'So if it hadn't 'a been for me, there'd have been another three hundred Tonildan fellows like that poor boy Sphelthon, and Cran only knows how many more besides. You must see that, Sednil, surely?'

'Oh, *I* can see it all right,' said he, 'and I admire you as much as anyone in the city. But what d'you suppose *he* thinks—your Katrian officer chap?'

'What *he* thinks?'

'Well, people in Terekenalt know what you did, same as people in Bekla. But on top of that, there's one thing your Zen-Kurel will know which no one else knows—that's if he's still alive and if he's had the sense to keep quiet. *He* knows how you learnt about the plan, doesn't he?'

For the first time—for it must be remembered that in addition to her youth and immaturity she had hitherto been entirely land-locked, as it were, in her own memories and dreams of Zen-Kurel, and had never discussed her love with anyone—there began to dawn upon the ingenuous Maia some idea of what Zen-Kurel must have felt upon hearing how the garrison at Rallur had been warned in time. Like a child to whom an adult points out something serious and unwelcome which till now has lain beyond the restricted field of personal experience, she sensed, vaguely yet dismally, that this was a matter she was not going to be able to disregard or ignore; and began by trying to do just that.

'I don't reckon he'd be angry—not if I could talk to him, like—explain—tell him the rights of it—how I felt an' that.'

'*Don't* you?'

'I *would* 'a done just that—told him how I felt—if only there'd been time: I *would* have! Fact I was starting to, only soon as he heard that trumpet blowing for the muster he was up and off—oh! that was so dreadful, Sednil! When I realized he was going to the fighting—' Her tears began to fall again.

'And you think he'd have listened to you, do you?'

'He loves me. We could have gone away together: we could have gone to his father's in Katria—'

'And him one of the king's personal aides? I thought you had more sense, Maia.'

'Are you jealous of him? Is that it?' She knew this was nothing to the purpose, but anything was better than accepting the truth.

'Well, I might be, but that's not the point. What I'm asking is, do you really suppose this fellow feels the same about you—that is, if he's still alive—knowing what he can't help knowing now? 'Cos if I was him I'd want to cut you up into fifty bits, that's what.'

As a last resort the Serrelinda fell back on her dignity. 'Since you're so keen on what's the point, that's not the point either, U-Sednil. The only point as far as *you're* concerned is that I happen to want to know where Zen-Kurel is now. That's the job I'm talking about; just that and nothing more. He's an enemy of Bekla, fighting for King Karnat, so I've got to be careful how I go about it, haven't I? No one's to know. I'm offering you four thousand meld to go and find out for me, and that's what I came here to say tonight. Never mind what you think Zen-Kurel thinks: that's none of your business. Do you want the job or not?'

'Four thousand meld?' He was clearly startled.

The jekzha had gone the length of the Sheldad and they had now reached the place, not far from the western clock tower, where it broke up into the narrower streets and lanes of the poorer quarter of the city. The jekzha-man stopped and turned his head.

'Where to now, sir?'

Maia gave him fifteen meld. 'Just turn round and go back. You needn't hurry.'

He shrugged his shoulders, pocketed the money and made the turn, pushing his way through a crowd of roisterers outside a tavern. As they got clear, a snatch of tipsy song came up from behind.

'—So then she jumped right out of Karnat's winder:
No one could hinder
The Serrelinda—'

Maia could not suppress a chuckle. 'Never heard that one before.'

'Nor me. They don't tell you, then, when they make them up?'

'Just as well they don't, some of 'em.'

At least it had blown away the ill-feeling between them.

'I'm sorry, Maia: you're the last person in the world I'd want to fall out with. Yes, I *will* do this for you—for *you*, and because I need the money. Four thousand meld! D'you really mean it? Cran, I could start a business with that!'

'That's if you come back, Sednil. Trying to get information about a Katrian—you'll be running a risk, you know. You can get to Urtah all right, I suppose?'

'That's no trouble: I could be looking for work, couldn't I? But how about the money?' asked Sednil. 'When d'you—'

'Half now and half when you get back. That's fair, isn't it? I brought it with me: two thousand. Here it is.'

'You trust me that much, then? Two thousand—I could be off with that, you know.'

'No, I trust you.'

'It's just that I've got out of the way of being trusted, that's all.' He paused. Then, 'Yes, Maia, of course I'm jealous of this Katrian.'

'Nennaunir loves you.'

It was his turn to flare up. 'Yes, so much that she wouldn't even speak up for me about that basting ring! She could have saved me—'

'Sednil, you couldn't expect it; you really couldn't. She would have, if the queen had sentenced you to the mines or to hang. She did all she could to get you out, and what's more she's succeeded—'

'*You* succeeded.'

'She still loves you, Sednil. She's told me as much. And now she's rich and successful you'd be a fool to leave her.'

'Well, that's my business. But I shan't tell Nan about this: I'll simply tell her that I'm leaving Bekla to look for work, and I'll be back as soon as I can.'

'You could go so far as to tell her you're going to Urtah. See, it's only that I don't like deceiving Nan any more 'n what we have to. She's been a good friend to me.'

'I shall go to Dari first, Maia. For one thing, it's less likely to attract attention than if I were to go straight to Urtah from Bekla; but besides that, my old mother's still living in Dari—or she was—and I'd like to give her some of this money. And won't she be happy and proud to see her son with a branded hand and a release token?' added Sednil bitterly.

'But can't you tell her as 'twasn't none of your fault?' said Maia. 'She ought to believe you—her own son.'

'Oh, yes, and then she can just explain to all the neighbours, can't she, and to everyone else who gets to hear? Poor old woman, she'll be glad of the money, though. But I won't waste any time in getting on with your job, Maia, I promise. I don't see why I shouldn't be back in under two months. You say this Zen-Kurel was brought up in Dari: well, I could have known him when we were banzis, couldn't I, and be wondering what had become of him? That's where I'll start asking around, and then perhaps move up into Urtah, or even cross the Zhairgen. I may not have to go to Suba at all.'

'How will you let me know when you get back?'

'I'll watch out for your lame girl in the market and tell her.'

'Here we are back at the bridge. Good luck, Sednil, and I'll pray for you. Don't forget to give Randronoth's letter to Brero, will you?'

: 69 :

AN UNEXPECTED VISIT

Randronoth's letter—which bore the Canathron seal of Lapan—was short and so simple that Maia was able—though with effort and a certain amount of inference here and there—to read it for herself. That, she supposed, was probably what he had intended.

'Beloved, beautiful Maia,

'I think of you always. I long to be with you again. I am sending you a present. Entertain and hear the messenger. He is my friend. He will tell you—' (The next bit was beyond her. Well, she thought rather impatiently, if he's going to tell me, don't matter, do it?) 'He is to be trusted. Sednil is free, as you asked. Your devoted lover, Randronoth.'

She put it aside without reflection. The memory of the Randronoth episode was most bitter to her, not through any fault of his, but on account of its horrible and humiliating outcome. She simply wanted to forget it, and to forget him too. She felt nothing for him, and his feeling for her both alarmed and vexed her. Like most outstandingly beautiful girls, Maia had no objection to being desired where she did not desire—it was unavoidable, anyway—provided the admirer's behaviour remained within reasonable bounds. But for a man in a high position to be virtually un-balanced—what she herself called 'touched'—on her account was worry-ing, simply because one never knew whether he might not do something embarrassing or even downright dangerous. The present, being from a provincial governor, would have to be accepted, of course. She only hoped it wouldn't prove to be one which would make it more difficult to refuse him what he wanted—for to refuse him she was determined.

Unless—she suddenly thought: unless—and try as she would, her sharp little peasant mind refused to drop it—unless Sednil were actually to find Zenka. Suppose Zenka were to say 'Yes, come' (for she still did not believe that his love could have altered: I was there and Sednil wasn't, she thought), then she was going to need all the ready money she could lay her hands on.

Quite apart from that, however, she was in a fair old bit of money difficulty anyway. She was two thousand meld out of pocket to Sednil, to say nothing of the thousand she had lost along with Randronoth's nine thousand to Fornis. And then when Sednil got back (as of course he would) there would be another two thousand to find. No doubt about it, she was running short—or she was going to run short. If she were to accept Randronoth again but no one else, it would be certain to get out. Everyone would assume that they were lovers. But suppose she were to accept three or four men—Randronoth among them, perhaps—just once apiece, just to get solvent once more? It went against the grain, certainly; it was clean contrary to her resolve that no one else should ever drink from that bright cup which she and Zenka had drained together. Yet what else could she do? And anyway she would be doing it only so that she could be ready at any moment to join him again—a swift and secret journey, involving instant down-payments and, no doubt, bribes. What sort of journey? Whither? Ah! this she could not envisage. But when the time came, Lespa would surely point the way.

It was early one evening—getting on for supper-time and the air cooling pleasantly—when Ogma came smilingly upstairs to tell her that a stranger was below and asking to see her. 'He says he's from Lord Randronoth, miss,' she said with obvious approbation, 'and to show you this.' It was yet another imprint of Randronoth's Canathron seal.

After taking her time over changing into a fresh robe and having Ogma brush and arrange her hair, Maia came leisurely down the staircase, paused for a minute in the hall to give Jarvil a few unnecessary instructions and then strolled into the parlour.

The man, who was sitting near the window gazing out across the Barb, stood up as she entered. He was unexpectedly young—only a year or two older than herself; tall, with black hair falling below his shoulders, and eyes of so deep a brown as hardly to be distinguishable from the pupils. He was elegantly—almost foppishly—dressed in a slashed, crimson veltron and yellow silk breeches, and wore at his belt a pouch or scrip of fine, tooled leather embossed with the Canathron emblem.

'Good evening, säiyett,' he said, crossing the room and taking her hands. 'My name is Count Seekron, of Lapan, and I come from Lord Randronoth. He sends you this gift and begs that you will graciously permit me to talk with you for a short time.'

The unsmiling intensity of his manner somewhat disconcerted her. He gave the impression of being taut—indeed, one might have said strung-up, nervous. His hands, she noticed, as he picked up the gift—which he had left on a near-by table—were trembling slightly. She felt no particular wish to put him at his ease, yet from mere wonted good nature she smiled as she motioned him to sit down again and took the gift from him.

It was a miniature cabinet, about three inches long and perhaps two inches wide and deep. The hinged doors, fastened together by a gold latchet, opened upon three tiny drawers, each lined with darkly-lustrous, gold-speckled lacquer. The top and sides, as well as the doors, consisted of panels of fine, white bone. Upon each the craftsman had carved in relief the likenesses of different fishes—twelve in all—and these, with their scales, fins, gills and eyes all perfectly represented, were stained and shaded in their natural colours. Eight tripartite corner-pieces of silver bound the seven panels together and the doors had flat, undulated hinges about an inch long. It was a miracle of skill and patient craftsmanship—and quite simply a rich woman's toy.

Maia had never before seen anything at all like this, and for some time kept turning it over in her hands, examining it with the same kind of incredulity and delight that the early Victorians must have felt upon first seeing photographs. She opened the perfectly-hung doors, pulled out the drawers and rubbed her fore-finger wonderingly over the slightly raised simulacra of the fishes, for she could not at first believe that they were not fixed or applied, but actually formed part of the surfaces of the panels themselves. Artistry of this order was something entirely new to her. She could never have imagined it and needed a little time to take it in.

Randronoth was shrewd, she thought. No one—no one, that was to say, with the least spark of sensitivity—could resist such a present. It was not a question of courtesy to the giver, or even of money value (although the piece must be worth at least two thousand meld and very likely more). It was the thing itself. Simply to see it would be enough to make anyone want to possess it. It was the very exemplar of a rarity and of exquisite, gratuitous luxury: and it was hers.

How cunningly it had been chosen to appeal to her! Oh, that did not escape her! Gold, jewels, robes—any ordinary kind of opulence—she could have declined. But this marvellous, unique plaything—whatever could you keep in it, she wondered; pins, rings, spools of silk?—how perfectly it was calculated to suit and to be irresistible to her in particular! Occula, perhaps, might just possibly have been proof against it: no one else that she knew. Any obligation involved in acceptance appeared negligible as she turned it this way and that, continually perceiving fresh details of skill and beauty. The piece was not only faultless; it was almost immoderate in the delicacy and quality of its workmanship.

'This—this is very kind of Lord Randronoth,' she murmured at last, latching the doors and placing the cabinet back on the table. 'Will you please thank him very much and tell him that I'm grateful and delighted?'

'Then *he* will be, säiyett,' replied the young man, smiling for the first time; yet rather formally and a little unnaturally, she thought—as though he were not really interested in the cabinet, but had something else on his mind.

'I've never seen work like this,' she went on, herself growing more relaxed in her pleasure over the gift. 'Do you happen to know where it came from?'

'That I can't tell you, säiyett,' he answered. 'It's old, I know that much, and I rather believe Lord Randronoth's family's possessed it for some time; possibly it may have been his grandfather who acquired it, for I know he once travelled a long way to the south, beyond Ikat Yeldashay. He—'

But with this he suddenly and rather oddly broke off, once more getting up and walking over to her where she still stood beside the table.

'Säiyett,' he said quietly, 'I would like to—that is—er—Lord Randronoth wishes me to talk to you privately.'

She frowned, startled. 'Well, isn't this private enough for you?'

'I would prefer it if we could walk in the garden, säiyett.'

She was on the point of refusing, for his peculiar, tense manner and lack of warmth (Maia was unaccustomed to detachment from men, particularly young ones) had not made her particularly like or want to oblige him. However, it would hardly do to accept Randronoth's present and then send his messenger packing unheard.

'I'll have some wine brought out on the terrace,' she said.

'Or we might, perhaps, walk down as far as the edge of the lake, säiyett.'

She stared at him, as though at an impertinent servant; but he only stared back at her unwaveringly, his pupils expanded, like a cat's, in the fading light. 'This is a serious matter, not primarily one of courtesy,' those eyes seemed to be saying. 'Surely you realize that?'

Still intent on showing that she and not he was in control, she called Ogma to bring her light cloak and a jug of wine. She filled a goblet for herself and one for him. He sipped it, again with his blank smile; but when they had descended the steps and begun strolling side by side between the shrubs and flower-beds towards the shore, she noticed that he had left it behind in the parlour.

He seemed hesitant to begin, and this annoyed her still more.

'Well, I s'pose no one's going to hear us here,' she remarked at length, 'without it's an owl.'

'Säiyett,' he said, still speaking very quietly, 'Lord Randronoth says that you will recall that at the end of this year the present Sacred Queen's reign comes to an end.'

Instantly she felt afraid. All that Milvushina had said came flooding back into her mind. Yet now she realized that she had taken Milvushina's warning only partly seriously. That is, she had believed her, but had not envisaged the dangerous thing actually happening or how she was going to meet it if and when it did happen. She had certainly not expected it to come from this quarter.

'Well, what of it?' she answered sharply.

'Her successor will be chosen by acclamation of the people.'

'But I suppose—' she turned aside for a moment, stooped and pulled off a dead head from a clump of flowering pinks—'that what'll really happen is that the Council will decide.'

'The Council may be divided, säiyett, but the people are not: that is what Lord Randronoth asked me to stress to you.'

Her knees were trembling and her bowels felt loose. There was a marble seat near-by, half-enclosed by trailing boughs, and here she sat down, laying one arm along the cool arm-rest. After a moment he also sat down, turning his head so that he was almost whispering in her ear.

'Fornis may make some desperate attempt to remain Sacred Queen, but this is bound to fail, because the people will not accept her. Already she has tried the patience of the gods too long.'

Seekron paused, but Maia said nothing, only staring ahead across the darkening Barb.

'One might have expected the Lord General to choose as Sacred Queen some lady commanding universal fame and approval. He has said nothing publicly, but it is known that in fact he favours the lady Milvushina, the daughter of the murdered Chalcon lord, Enka-Mordet; she who is now the consort of his son. He thinks that her election would do much to reconcile Chalcon to Bekla and diminish heldro opposition to the Leopards; and that when Elvair-ka-Virrion returns victorious from Chalcon, his popularity with the city will be so great that they will be ready to acclaim Milvushina as Sacred Queen.'

'She is with child,' said Maia shortly.

She meant no more than that Milvushina should be spared the stress, but Seekron evidently misunderstood her. 'Exactly, säiyett: most inappropriate. But even setting that aside, the lady Milvushina, while she is liked well enough by the people, is not the lady whom they love and honour most. It was not she who swam the Valderra and saved the empire.'

'Count Seekron,' said Maia with a quick gasp, 'I don't want to hear n' more of this. You just go home now and tell Lord Randronoth as I won't have nothing to do—'

'Säiyett,' he interrupted quickly, 'have you reflected? They say—that is, I know that you have more than once said—that you swam the Valderra not to advance yourself, but to prevent bloodshed and save lives.'

'Well, what of it?' she said. 'What's that got to do with this?'

'Säiyett, there is only one lady in all the empire so famous, so beautiful and so much loved and honoured by the people that they would be unanimous in acclaiming her as Sacred Queen. If you refuse, inevitably there will be civil strife and butchery. Before all's done, there will be six Sacred Queens and a thousand corpses for each. But if you accept, there will be unanimity and concord. Everyone believes that you, more than any woman in Bekla, possess the luck and favour of the gods.'

Here was a new slant on the business and no mistake! Maia sat silent, trying to take it in. Her immediate feeling was of being assailed. The quiet evening garden, with the moths flitting over the planella; her own, pretty little house, from whose windows Ogma's lamps were beginning to shine— something menacing, ghostly, a tall, vaporous figure, seemed stalking nearby, half-glimpsed among the dusky trees. So vivid was this fancy that she gave a quick, cut-short whimper, drawing her cloak closer about her and peering this way and that. Again Seekron misunderstood her. Plainly nervous, he stood up and also looked about them.

'Did you see someone, säiyett? Where?'

'No,' she said. 'You needn't worry. There's no one here 'ceptin' us.' Then, 'I don't want to be Sacred Queen. I want to stay 's I am.'

'But the gods want it, säiyett! You must recall that in the past there have been many whom the gods have called to perform their work on earth, who at first could not credit the vocation, because they felt themselves to be nothing but the most ordinary people; because in their humility they knew themselves to be but flesh-and-blood. Remember Deparioth, an orphan and a slave, who—'

'Oh, give over!' she cried. 'Let me be!' She sprang up and began pacing rapidly back and forth across the grass. 'U-Seekron, leave me! Go back to the house and wait! I need to think: I'll join you in a few minutes.'

She walked down to the lakeside. The stars were out now, brighter moment by moment as the last of the daylight ebbed away in the west beyond the Barons' Palace. As she turned her back on the lapping water and looked up the garden, she suddenly noticed something strange in the northern sky. Low down it was, an unusual patch of brightness, a kind of misty glow on the horizon; but whether man-made or natural she could not tell. Either seemed equally questionable. Yet there it was, a subdued luminosity, something like that preceding moonrise, though affecting a rather smaller area of the sky. For perhaps half a minute she stared at it, but was too much preoccupied with her own thoughts to concentrate upon it for longer. Whatever it might be, it was nothing to do with what had come upon her.

After a little it occurred to her that as yet she could not have heard the main part of whatever it was that Seekron had come to tell. Occula would undoubtedly have shown more self-possession. Occula would have heard him out and then either given him an answer or else—or else—(and here Maia grinned, feeling a little better) or else told him to damn' well baste off to Lapan without one. The least she could do was to hear the young man out, but on her own terms and—if only she could rise to it—with some air of authority.

Stooping, she wetted her hands in the lake and cooled her burning cheeks. Then she walked back to the parlour, taking care, as before, to enter unhurriedly.

'You must forgive me, U-Seekron,' she said, 'for not being quite myself just now. I'm sure you'll understand it came as a bit of a shock, like.' He was about to reply, but she went on quickly, 'Now, listen. I've taken in what you said, and I don't want to hear n'more by way of persuasion, d'you understand? You just tell me straight out and plain, now, what Lord Randronoth's message is, and then I'll see what I reckon to it.'

'But, säiyett,' he replied, 'you must swear to say nothing to anyone.'

'I won't say nothing to anyone,' she answered. 'There you are: that's plain enough; never mind 'bout swearing. And you can tell me in here, too.' And thereupon she refilled her goblet and sat down.

He had either to accept this or reject it. After a moment he decided to accept it.

'Säiyett,' he said, again almost whispering, 'Lord Randronoth has the whole of Lapan ready to declare for you as Sacred Queen. He believes that Bekla will acclaim you too. It may very well never come to conflict at all. Our immediate difficulty, however, is the Lord General's preference for the Lady Milvushina. As you know, many, though not all, of the Leopard Council support the Lord General, and besides, when Elvair-ka-Virrion returns victorious from Chalcon—' He shrugged his shoulders.

'Well, go on,' she said.

'Lord Randronoth thinks we ought to prepare while Elvair-ka-Virrion is still away. He himself has already made sure of General Sendekar. You won't be surprised to hear that General Sendekar has told Lord Randronoth that he would be ready to go through fire and water for your sake. Without him, perhaps, we could not have hoped for so much. But as you know, a large part of the army will follow Sendekar.'

Again he stopped and waited. Maia only trusted that she did not show the agitation she felt. Randronoth was one thing. Sendekar—unexcitable, rugged, kindly, decent Sendekar—was quite another. O Cran! she thought, don't say *he's* in love with me, too! That'd be a right old—

'Will you please go on, U-Seekron?' she said coldly.

'Säiyett, here are the names of seven men, either councillors or senior officers in Bekla now, whom Lord Randronoth either knows or has strong reason to believe will support him and support you. I am to ask you to— well, to make friends with these men—some you may know already, I dare say—entertain them, invite them to your house and so forth, but separately and at all costs without exciting the Lord General's suspicion. You need not yourself say anything to them about Lord Randronoth's scheme: in fact, better not. They will tell *you* what is afoot, when the time is ripe and according to the way in which matters develop.'

Suddenly she could contain herself no longer. She broke out, 'I want to know whether all this is because Lord Randronoth believes himself in love with me? Because if it is—'

'Oh, no, säiyett.' He smiled condescendingly and indulgently, evidently feeling this to be a naïve, over-youthful reaction. Why on earth, she thought, couldn't Randronoth have sent some older, more considerate man; someone a bit more relaxed and sympathetic?

'Lord Randronoth thinks that when you are acclaimed Sacred Queen, both the city and the empire will fall at your feet, and that those of your friends who have helped you, among whom he is proud to count himself one, will benefit accordingly.'

'Well, you tell him from me—'

'One thing more, säiyett. Lord Randronoth is well aware that to entertain well, to give presents and to make reliable friends costs money. He's sent you some, to use as you think fit for the advancement of your cause— *our* cause.'

'Money?' she said. 'What do you mean, money? How much?'

'Forty thousand meld; later, of course, there can be more, if it's needed.'

'Forty thousand meld, U-Seekron? You can't be serious!'

'Säiyett, I have it here.' He touched the Canathron scrip at his belt.

'Oh, great Shakkarn!'

Forty thousand meld! she thought: and apparently, from what Seekron had said, this represented only part of Randronoth's total efforts so far in various quarters. He must be throwing virtually the entire resources of the Lapan treasury into the plot. She had no idea how provincial governors settled accounts with the Beklan Council, but obviously there must be some sort of day of reckoning, and Randronoth would not be able to meet it. So unless there was something she did not know about, he was at this very moment past recall as a rebel against Kembri.

Well, but it might not come to rebellion. After all, merely to support a girl as a candidate to become Sacred Queen did not in itself constitute rebellion—though pretty obviously there was more at the back of this lot than just her becoming Sacred Queen. But anything could happen. Meanwhile, and immediately, a fraction of the huge sum she was being offered— a mere eight or nine thousand meld—would be enough to put her straight and get her out of her money difficulties. Yes, *and* to send a nice little bit to Morca and the family, too; for they had been much on her conscience since Tharrin died. Anyway, girls who had grown up in hovels on the Tonildan Waste didn't refuse enormous sums of ready money. Trouble next month? Next month's a long time off, she thought.

'Would Lord Randronoth expect me to render him accounts?' she asked.

'He said nothing to that effect, säiyett, but I hardly think so. After all—' he smiled again—'the expenditure might be rather difficult to itemize, don't you think?'

Forty thousand meld! Once she had learned from Sednil where Zen-Kurel was, she would be able to go to him like an arrow; go to him, too, with a dowry more than fit for a baron's daughter. And once out of the empire—

'I see,' she said. 'Well, you'd best come with me, U-Seekron. I've got a strong-box under the floor in the cellar. Give me the names: and you may tell Lord Randronoth that I'll do all I can to help him.'

THE COMET AND THE SCALES

Two nights later, after supper, Maia was giving instructions about the money to be sent to Morca. It was a right old lot, too; more than Morca would have seen in her whole life, Maia felt sure of that. Sarget, whom she had consulted (though without mentioning Tharrin), had recommended one of his agents, a steady, middle-aged man who regularly travelled the fifty miles to Thettit-Tonilda with consignments of wine. The journey usually took three to four days or even longer—loaded ox-carts being slower than an unencumbered man on foot—but Sarget thought it feasible enough for his agent to break off from the convoy at Hirdo and visit Lake Serrelind. A day should be quite enough for the business, and he could easily overtake the oxen before they reached Thettit. It was understood, of course, that Maia would make the détour worth his while.

Since Morca (like Maia herself) could more or less read simple words if she put her mind to it (her husband had taught them both as much as he himself knew of the tricky business) Maia had engaged a professional scribe to write a letter to be handed over with the money. When she came down to it, however, she could not find a great deal to say. Assuming that the family had already given Tharrin up for dead, she simply assured Morca that she knew he had died quickly and painlessly (why say more?) and that she herself had paid for his rites. She forgave Morca for what she had done and assured her that she bore no grudge. She sent her love to Kelsi, Nala and Lirrit and her blessing to the baby girl she had never seen. Then, on impulse, she added at the end, 'Tharrin told me about my real mother, so now I understand you—and everything—better.'

She had just handed over this letter to the man, together with the money, explained to him for the second time how to find Morca's hut and begged him to be sure to bring back word of how the girls were looking, when Ogma came running into the parlour, plainly frightened.

'Oh, miss!' she cried, not only interrupting Maia in mid-sentence but almost throwing herself into her arms as well, 'Oh, miss, have you seen it? Have you seen it? Oh, Cran, what's to become of us all, what's to—?'

'Ogma!' said Maia sharply. She felt thoroughly put out by the interruption. Ogma, for all her limitations, knew perfectly well the importance of keeping her place in front of visitors and strangers. 'Pull yourself together! I don't know what you're on about, but whatever it is, just tell me sensibly.'

'In the sky, miss!' whimpered Ogma.

'*What?*' cried Maia, now really angry. 'Have you gone off your head?'

Disconcertingly, Ogma fell on her knees at Maia's feet.

'Oh, Miss Maia, don't be angry! It isn't only me! Everyone's that scared—everyone! I went up on the roof—only I'd forgotten I'd left the clothes there to dry—and there it was! They're all out in the streets—everyone—'

This certainly sounded like trouble of some sort. What could it be—a riot? Bad news from one of the battle-fronts? She listened, but there was nothing to be heard. She turned to the man, shrugged her shoulders and asked him to be so good as to accompany her. Together they went upstairs and then up the flight of outside steps onto the flat roof.

The previous two nights had been, for once in a way, cloudy—at all events to the north and west—but tonight the sky was as clear as usual at midsummer. The sight that met their eyes caused Maia to start back with a cry, clutching at the parapet.

In the northern sky, fairly low though well clear of the horizon, hung a brilliant luminescence. 'Star' it could scarcely be called, first because it was far brighter than any star, but secondly because its refulgence had an undemarcated, gaseous quality, like an incandescent vapour, dimming at the periphery to become a kind of glowing fog as it spread into the surrounding void. From its lower edge tapered a streamer of filmy, powdery light, slightly inclined to the left, giving the whole phenomenon the likeness of a sword poised above the distant Gelt mountains. It appeared perfectly still and (unlike stars, which look like bright studs fixed into the sky and left there), as though invisibly but intentionally displayed by some supernatural agency.

Maia, oblivious of the man beside her, stared at it in dread. After a time (she did not know how long), like someone in a disaster or a wreck vaguely recalling the appointed procedure, she tried to stand unaided and extend her arms in the customary posture of prayer; but her knees gave way and she turned and clung once more to the parapet.

Faintly, in the lower city below, she could discern that the roofs were covered with people. There were all manner of sounds—calls and crying, ululations of prayer, what sounded like some soldiers raggedly singing a marching song—rising together in a cacophonous tumult, like that of a herd of frightened beasts, out of the obscure dimness. Yes, she thought; that was one thing the noises had in common; they all expressed fear. Yet the light itself was calm and silent as a seraph.

At this moment Sarget's man touched her arm.

'Säiyett, you're afraid: I'm afraid, too. This is a portent. Lespa's displeased, and who can tell why? But whatever it may foretell, the star itself won't do anything; nor we shan't alter anything, you and I, by standing here and letting it terrify us. Whatever's going to happen won't happen tonight.'

Maia hardly heard him. The terrible thing, she thought, about the enigmatic light was its inescapability. You could not fly from it, you could not shut it out. If you were to run from Bekla to Zeray, it would still be there above you.

The man spoke again. 'Säiyett, I'm just someone who works for U-Sarget, and you're a great lady of the upper city; I know that. But there are times—there are things—well, I've got two married daughters older than you. We're all men and women, säiyett—to Lespa we are. May I advise you?'

She nodded abstractedly.

'You swam the river, säiyett. That lot down there—you're their heroine. Whatever's coming, we can all try to keep our dignity, wouldn't you agree? Set them an example, you know.'

Maia was highly suggestible and, as we know, it seldom took her long to make up her mind. 'Yes, I *would* agree,' she said, 'and all I can say is "Thank you"—'ceptin' I reckon as your daughters got the best father anyone could have. Ogma!' she called. 'Bring me my cloak, please—the one with the embroidered stars. I'm going out!'

It is, on the whole, easier to appear brave when you already have a reputation that way and feel that courage is expected of you. Maia's third soldier was nowhere to be found, but this did not bother her now. Within twenty minutes the Serrelinda, dressed to kill, unveiled and seated in her golden jekzha, was entering the lower city through the Peacock Gate.

There was light enough for her to be recognized; and recognized she was, before she had gone two hundred yards down the Street of the Armourers. A big, brawny man—plainly one of the smiths—broke away from a crowd of his mates and ran across to the jekzha.

'Yes, it *is* the Serrelinda!' he called back over his shoulder. Then, standing squarely in the way and looking up at her, 'What's up, lass? Are you leaving the city, or what?'

'Leaving? Of course I'm not leaving!' she answered. There were seven or eight of them clustered round her now. 'What on earth would I be leaving for?'

Their answers came all at once, like a handful of gravel thrown at her. 'The star—' 'Unlucky—' 'What's it mean?' '—unlucky—' 'Where *are* you going, then?' '—quarrels among the gods, that's it—' '—we'll have to pay for it—' 'What d'you make of it?' 'Unlucky—'

'It *isn't* unlucky!' she cried, raising her two fists. 'It isn't! *That's* where I'm going—' she pointed ahead, downhill—'to tell them not to be afraid! There's nothing to be afraid of! It *isn't* bad luck, it's *good* luck!'

'How d'you know that, eh?' asked the big fellow. 'A bit of a girl like you—'

'Ah, and a pretty one an' all,' said someone else.

'Because Lespa told me in a dream!' shouted Maia at the top of her voice.

'A dream, eh?' said a red-haired man in a short, sacking smock, who reminded Maia horribly of the Sacred Queen attired for her pleasure. 'What's dreams?—just a lot of rubbish—'

'Then I s'pose you reckon it was all rubbish when Lespa told me King Karnat's battle-plan in a dream, do you?' said Maia.

This came out with the greatest conviction. In the moment that she was saying it she believed it herself. 'And I s'pose you'll say next that it wasn't Lespa who brought me safe across the river? D'you want to make her angry, talking like that? I tell you—this star's the sword of Bekla, come to destroy her enemies!'

'Is that the rights of it, säiyett?' asked the big man. 'Honest?'

'Of course it is!' answered Maia. 'Give me patience! Lespa sends you the best sign for a thousand years, and you stand there wondering whether it's good or bad—'

It was not only her beauty—that clear and patent sign of the favour of the gods—but her whole manner, her air of joyous confidence in the midst of their anxiety, which they found more convincing than any words.

'*I* believe her!' shouted an older man. 'Well, stands to reason, don't it? If the goddess was going to tell anyone, it'd be the Serrelinda she'd tell. Hasn't she had the goddess's favour all along?—and damned lucky for all of us, too! She's right, the star's good!'

By this time a considerable crowd had gathered round the jekzha, and Brero and his mate were fidgeting uneasily in the shafts.

'Where d'you want to go, then, säiyett?' asked the big smith. 'You want to go down the Market and tell the lot of them, is that it?'

'Yes, Baltis, yes!' cried Maia; at which there was a roar of laughter, while someone called out 'She even knows his name!' Smiths throughout the empire were generically called Baltis, but evidently this had been a rather luckier shot than that.

They opened up the way for her, calling out 'Maia! Maia!' and striding along beside the jekzha as the soldiers pulled it down the hill and into the sandy expanse of the Caravan Market. Here all manner of people—slaves, stall-keepers, shearnas, beggars, merchants, tradesmen and their wives—were gathered in groups, gazing northward at the comet and talking together; some among themselves in low voices, others loudly and excitedly, arguing and gesticulating. A few booths were open and one or two hawkers were also seizing the opportunity for business. In the half-darkness it was difficult to tell how many people might be there altogether, but Maia guessed perhaps a thousand.

713

'Are you going to the Scales, then, säiyett, or where?' asked Brero over his shoulder.

When Maia, prompted by the words of Sarget's man, had first set out, she had simply had it in mind to go down to the lower city, walk about among the people and show them that at any rate she, a popular public figure, was not afraid. As so often, she had acted on impulse and without any clear idea of what she thought was likely to ensue. In the Street of the Armourers she had answered spontaneously. Now—or so it appeared—she seemed expected to make some kind of speech. Yet she had no idea what to say.

The plinth of Fleitil's bronze Scales—those same onto which Selperron had climbed to get a look at the Serrelinda—was not infrequently used as a rostrum, both by official and unofficial public speakers. Possibly the smiths and armourers had not thought of the Scales until Brero spoke, but they did now all right.

' 'Course she is, soldier!' shouted Baltis. 'Why don't you pull her up the ramp? Then she needn't even get down.'

At one end of the plinth was a long, gently-inclined ramp, and up this (in the absence of any instruction to the contrary from the dazed Maia) the soldiers now drew the jekzha. Seconds later she found herself some six or seven feet above the sandy market-place, looking down on bobbing heads, flaring torches and everywhere faces, young and old, male and female, all unconsciously revealing their common anxiety and disquiet.

They had something else in common, however; they all knew her. She was their Serrelinda, their swimmer, the girl who had raised nine thousand meld in twenty minutes and given the lot (so they supposed) to the Chalcon expedition. She'd come for some purpose or other—that much was plain. They crowded round the Scales expectantly.

Maia was filled with a dismaying sense of her own lack of confidence and authority. If she had been going to dance, or even just stand up to be admired, she would have felt fine, but now—oh, Cran, it was like a dream!—she'd got herself into a situation where they were all waiting for her, not to dance but to speak. Looking round helplessly she saw yet again, hanging above the roof-tops to one side of the dark, slender column of the Tower of the Orphans, the silent presence of the comet. This was what they were all afraid of. So was she, but not in the same way that they were. They feared it, in ignorance, as a threat and a herald of disaster. She feared it as any true, loving worshipper fears and holds in awe the manifest revelation of the deity. Lespa was her guardian, her friend; what hadn't Lespa done for her? But awesome indeed, now, was this hitherto-unimagined majesty and glory of the astral Lady of Dreams.

She could only pray for help. Climbing down from her jekzha, she faced

714

the sword of light and raised her arms. Her prayer was unspoken yet passionate.

'Lespa, bestower of dreams and truth, mistress of order—of stars and seasons, moon and menstrual blood—you brought me here from the Tonildan Waste. I've always honoured you, dear goddess! Grant to me now that self-abandon and humility which you showed in your sacred union with Shakkarn.'

There was no time for more. Turning back towards the people below, she stepped forward to the edge of the plinth, hearing in her heart as she did so the cool voice of Occula, 'A pretty girl, banzi, starts a yard ahead. What happens after that's up to you, but often the yard can make all the difference.'

'Good people,' she cried, 'I've come to tell you that Lespa's spoken to me in a dream! Just as she spoke to me in Suba and brought me back safe, so now she's sent me here tonight.'

She stopped. Her mouth felt dry. She could not see their faces so clearly as she would have liked, but at least no one had interrupted. Yet she could find no more words.

'Her message, säiyett?' called a voice.

That was better; she could at least answer a question. 'The star!' she said, pointing. 'It means good and not harm to the city! There's no reason to be afraid! That's Lespa's message!'

'Tell us your dream, then, little säiyett,' shouted someone else; and there were murmurs of agreement.

'That I mustn't do,' she replied, spreading her hands and shaking her head. 'If you don't want to believe me, I can't help it. But I've come because Lespa sent me, to say she means us good and not harm. The star's sent for a blessing! That's why I'm not afraid, and nor should you be.'

At this there was some cheering, yet somehow it lacked conviction. So distrustful and canny is the human heart that, faced with the unknown, the strange and imponderable, it is always less ready to impute good than ill, and often, even when misgivings have been disproved on clear evidence, will obstinately cling to them, as though reluctant to be deprived of the opportunity to feel hapless and accursed.

'She's right!' shouted Baltis. 'Hasn't she been right all along?'

'Right for old Sencho, you mean,' called out someone, with a sneering laugh. 'You been listening to them big blue eyes and deldas, mate, that's your trouble.'

'I been listening to her as swum the river, damn you!' answered Baltis angrily. 'Are you telling me—'

Maia began to realize that if the matter were to come to contention, she had already exhausted whatever powers of persuasion she had ever possessed. Circumstances had not allowed her to go about the business as she had originally intended. Still, she had done her best and said what she had to say: it would go round the city. The thing to do now—if only she could manage it—was to make her departure with dignity.

Standing on the plinth above the bickering roughs—their oaths in her ears, their sweat in her nostrils—she now became aware of some new entry taking place on her left, from Storks Hill on the far side of the market-place. The torchlight was too patchy and intermittent to enable her to make out exactly what was happening, but she could see two files of soldiers—oh, Cran, yes! there must be twenty at least just gone across the lighted front of that stall—and hear authoritative cries of 'Back, there; back! Make way!'

What could it be? Something important from Chalcon? Could they have taken Santil-kè-Erketlis prisoner, or perhaps one of his captains? Suddenly the horrible thought came to her that Fornis might have returned. She thought of the cat on the wall. Fornis couldn't miss her, stuck up here on the plinth. Well, yes, but Fornis could hardly shoot her here, in the full public gaze. (Oh, couldn't she just? whispered an inner voice: that's all you know.)

Whoever it was, they were coming straight towards her, the soldiers in their two files carrying spears and torches alternately. People were scattering left and right. No, it could hardly be anything from Chalcon, for there were no sounds of cheering or acclaim. Nor could it be the Sacred Queen, or there would have been attendant women. Suddenly she recognized the chief priest, dressed in full regalia and carrying his staff of office. No sooner had he crossed the patch of light in which she had glimpsed him than he was immediately followed by the hulking figure of Kembri.

The soldiers—presumably in response to an order, though she had heard none—halted about forty yards from the Scales. She could see them clearly enough now. Her armourers and their disputants had fallen silent and were no longer looking at her.

The Lord General walked slowly and deliberately forward until he was a yard or two below her. There he stood still and looked up without speaking.

Kembri, though lacking the warmth and sociability ever to have become, like his son, a popular figure with the mob, was nevertheless held in respect as a strong, resolute man, a firm ruler and an able general. To most he represented security and his imposing presence, stern and tenebrous, never failed in its public effect. Yet now, as they stood face to face, the strikingly beautiful girl looking down upon the grim, black-bearded soldier, it seemed as though each possessed—and of this the watchers

716

undoubtedly had an intuitive sense—a counter-balancing, complementary authority; bestowed, as it were, by different (and perhaps emulous) deities. If the Lord General was someone to be reckoned with, then so too, in her way, was the Serrelinda.

Kembri himself must have felt something of this; or perhaps, more prosaically, he merely apprehended, surrounding Maia like a kind of invisible nimbus, the devotion of the people; for though his bearing suggested anything but amity, he still said nothing, his intention being perhaps to agitate Maia into speaking first. She too, however, remained silent, standing outlined against the light of the comet behind her shoulder.

At length the Lord General, speaking so quietly that he was heard by no more than those immediately about them, said, 'What are you doing here, Maia?'

'Speaking to the people, my lord.'

'About what?'

'About the star.'

'Why?'

'My lord, there was that many as seemed frightened and didn't know what to make of it, and I reckoned I might be able to reassure them, like.'

'Why?'

'Because I'm not afraid of it, my lord: I know it's for good and not for harm.'

'And do you think it's your business to interpret the stars; or the priests'?'

Maia hesitated. 'Well, I'm sure I never meant no harm, my lord, not to the priests nor to anyone else. I was just speaking as I felt, like, and I didn't see as it could do any damage.'

By now all in the market-place—and to Maia there seemed to be more every minute—had come crowding about the Scales and were listening to as much of the talk as they could catch.

For perhaps a quarter of a minute the Lord General stood silent with as much composure as if he had not been surrounded by an uncertain-minded crowd of a thousand or more. Then he strode across to the end of the ramp and began to climb it, no one saying a word as he did so.

Maia was conscious only that Kembri, while stopping short (probably in his own best interests) of actually having her thrown down or otherwise publicly disgraced, had plainly indicated that she had overstepped the mark. Faced with this situation, all her peasant stubbornness was aroused. She feared the Lord General as the peasant fears the landlord—because he had power. But although she now realized that she might have appeared to be anticipating the professional astrology of the priests, she also felt that in voicing her personal feelings about the comet she had uttered no more than anyone else up and down the city. She'd done no wrong and she didn't see why she should shift. Anyway there was nowhere to shift to, stuck up here.

Arrived on the plinth, however, Kembri simply ignored her, turning to the people below. Having a deep, resonant voice—always a great advantage in a commander—he hardly needed to raise it, so that he gave no least impression of self-consciousness or of straining to convince the crowd by rhetoric.

'I have been at the temple of Cran, conferring with the chief priest and his experienced astrologers about the meaning of this star. The chief priest is with me now, and we are returning together to the upper city to consult with the council. Tomorrow the heralds will announce the results of our deliberations.' He paused. 'To arrive at the truth, reliably and responsibly, is like making a good sword or choosing a good wife. It takes time. That is what your priests and rulers are doing for you now, and I shall leave you in order to go and get on with it.'

With this he walked back down the ramp, rejoined the chief priest and immediately set off across the market in the direction of the Street of the Armourers, the tryzatt superior hastily calling his men to order and overtaking him with something of a scramble.

'What about that, then, missy, eh?' called out the man who had spoken of Sencho.

'I didn't come here to argue,' answered Maia hotly, 'or to disagree with the priests; and you needn't think it. I simply came to say what the goddess told me. I don't stand to get anything out of this at all—'

'Except to make yourself look important,' said the man.

'How can she make herself look any more important than what she is now, you damn' fool?' shouted Baltis. 'Why don't you shut your blasted mouth?' And thereupon there was something of a concerted movement towards the man on the part of Maia's little group of armourers, which made him hastily follow Baltis's suggestion.

'Anyway, I'm going home now,' called out Maia. 'Thank you all for listening to me! Baltis!'—and, as he turned and looked up at her—'Catch!'

Normally she wouldn't have risked it, but she was chagrined, provoked and overwrought by what had happened, and in no mood to care a curse. Without giving Baltis a second's pause to grasp what she meant to do, she leapt off the plinth, flinging herself at him where he stood below. It took him entirely by surprise and he was only just in time to catch her. As it was, she hit her forehead rather painfully against his cheekbone and had to save herself by throwing her arms round his neck. Kissing him quickly on both cheeks, she slid to the ground.

'Stars alive, lass, you want to be a bit more careful! You very near—'

She held up her arms, smiling on those about her. 'Thank you—all of you! Good-night!' And with this she tripped across to the foot of the ramp and climbed back into her jekzha.

At least there was no doubt about the continuance of her popularity. She was cheered out of the Market, while a dozen young fellows contended with one another to give her soldiers a hand up the Street of the Armourers.

All the same, she couldn't help covertly shedding a few tears, and once back at home wept in earnest; partly from nervous exhaustion, but mainly from resentment. She'd only meant to reassure the people, and that despite the fact that she'd begun by being afraid herself. She'd never meant to go up on the Scales. How in Cran's name was she to know that Kembri and the chief priest would be coming back from the temple? Somehow it had all gone wrong.

However, once she had had a leisurely bath, got into bed and had Ogma bring her a good strong posset mixed with djebbah, she began to feel better, and soon fell asleep without the least trouble.

She was yet to learn exactly how wrong it had gone.

: 71 :
A VISIT FROM KEMBRI

Next morning Kembri, having apparently come on foot and alone, found Maia in the company of Nennaunir and Otavis, whom he immediately asked, not discourteously but nevertheless without apology, to leave. He refused wine and, Ogma having characteristically left the parlour door ajar, told Maia to shut it.

'Now, Maia, perhaps you'll tell me a little more about how you came to be on the Scales last night and exactly what you thought you were doing.'

Haltingly, and with several pauses (for what had happened was not entirely what she was saying had happened: for example, she had no wish to involve Sarget's man, who should by now be well on his way to Serrelind), Maia spoke of how she had seen the comet, how she had heard and felt the general dismay in the lower city and decided to set out with the idea of raising public confidence by showing herself unafraid.

'The truth is, my lord, when I first saw the star I was as much afraid as the rest, but then I got to thinking that as they all knew me and liked me, p'raps I could cheer them up a bit—that was about the size of it.'

'I see. But I'm told that you said, publicly, that you'd had a dream—that Lespa had spoken to you about the star.'

719

'That's right, my lord.' (There could be no denying this now.)

'What was the dream?'

'Why, my lord, I simply saw the goddess. She was—well, she was walking in a wood, like in the Shakkarn story, only it was night, and she—er—pointed up at the stars and said "Don't be afraid: it's good and not bad." That was all.' (It was the best she could do, anyway.)

'When did you have this dream?'

'Night before last, my lord.'

'And yet you say that when you saw the star last night you *were* afraid?'

'Yes, my lord, I was. See, I only remembered the dream after a minute or two; then it all come back to me, like.'

'But if you thought the dream was so important, why didn't you take it to the proper place; to the temple?'

''Cos I never thought of it, my lord.'

'I see. But I'm also told that you said, before you got up on the Scales, that you'd had a dream in Suba and that that was how you got to know about Karnat's plan. If that's true, it's more than you ever said to Sendekar or to me. To the best of my knowledge you've never spoken of how you came to learn Karnat's plan, and as you evidently didn't wish to tell us, I respected your wish and refrained from asking you. Yet now you've been out telling workmen and labourers in the lower city that you dreamt it. Are you setting up to be a visionary, or what?'

'No, my lord: 'twas nothing o' that sort, really. I just got a bit carried away, that's all. It was all along of arguing, like, with some of those armourer chaps. Truth is, I never meant to get up on the Scales at all. I only meant to go down to the lower city and let people see as *I* wasn't afraid, whoever else might be. I meant to do good, my lord, and I can't for the life of me see as I've done any harm.'

'*Can't* you?' And as he said this the Lord General looked so dire and baleful that poor Maia felt positively appalled.

'My lord, if you're angry, then all I got to say is I don't deserve it! It was you as sent me to Suba with Bayub-Otal, and that very near cost me my life. I done everything you wanted and more. I've got nothing against you nor anyone in the city. I only want to be let to live in peace and quiet.'

'I should like to feel sure of that, Maia.' He had been sitting in a high-backed, carved chair—a gift to the Serrelinda from the citizens of Thettit—but now he stood up and began pacing slowly up and down the room. 'I know, of course, that at the barrarz you sold yourself for nine thousand meld, which my son gave out was to go towards the cost of the expedition.'

'I never kept a meld of it, my lord.'

'Then where *did* it go, Maia? For it won't surprise you that I happen to know it never reached the army.'

'It went to the Sacred Queen, my lord. I thought Lord Elvair-ka-Virrion would have told you.'

'Why were you getting money for Fornis under a lying pretence of helping the expedition?'

She reminded him of how she had come to him to plead for Tharrin, only to be referred to the Sacred Queen; and then, restraining her tears as best she could, went on to recount how Elvair-ka-Virrion had suggested the auction and how she had found Tharrin dead next morning; only omitting, for Pokada's sake, what he had told her of Ashaktis's visit to the gaol.

'I see,' he said yet again. She was expecting him at least to express some pity for Tharrin and sympathy for herself, but he was evidently preoccupied with more important considerations.

'Well, that explains a certain amount. But I'm still wondering, Maia, what your real purpose may have been in going down to the lower city last night and speaking from the Scales.'

'It was like I've said, my lord; that and nothing else. I wish you'd tell me straight out what's on your mind.'

'I will, then. In a few months' time the Sacred Queen's four-year reign is due to end. It's the wish of Lord Durakkon, as well as of the Council and the army, that she should be succeeded by the lady Milvushina. They have excellent reasons, with which I entirely agree.'

'Well, I c'n promise you, my lord, I don't wish it no different, that I don't.'

He continued as if she had not spoken. 'But the Sacred Queen, by ancient custom, is chosen by acclamation of the people of Bekla. Now, Maia, if the people were called upon tomorrow, whom do you think they'd acclaim?'

She was silent.

'And if that girl goes about the lower city telling tales about Lespa revealing Karnat's plans to her in dreams, and claiming to know the meaning of the star before the priests have had time to utter a word, what am I and the Council to think?'

'My lord, I never give it a thought! 'Tweren't *like* that, not a bit! Honest, I give you my word I don't *want* to be Sacred Queen!'

'No? Then I'm puzzled, Maia. The night of the barrarz you spent with Randronoth, didn't you?'

'Yes, my lord. And as for why, I've just told you.'

'I can understand you not particularly wanting to become a shearna— you've got money enough without—but I find it puzzling that apparently—

I say *apparently*—you've taken no lover since you came back from Suba. I'm not the only person to think that strange.'

Yet even he could never guess about Zen-Kurel, she felt sure. She need only decline to offer any explanation.

'Well, after all, that's my own affair, my lord, if I just don't feel inclined. It's of no importance to anyone else as I can see.'

'I'm afraid that's where you're wrong, Maia. If you were a nobody, it would be different; but you're not, as you're perfectly well aware yourself. I want to know—is Randronoth your lover?'

'No, he's *not*, my lord! I only ever went to bed with Lord Randronoth the twice: once was last year, when I was still a slave at the High Counsellor's and he told me to, and the other was at the barrarz, because he was the one as bid the most.'

The Lord General sat down again and faced her. 'Yet not long ago he sent one of his young noblemen from Lapan—a man called Count Seekron—to visit you here, didn't he?'

Maia coloured, and saw that this was not lost upon Kembri. He had taken her unawares. After a few moments, however, it dawned on her that Randronoth had forethought that Kembri would be bound to learn of Seekron's visit and had already put her in the clear.

'Yes, certainly, my lord. He came to bring me a present from Lord Randronoth. P'raps you'd like to see it: here it is.'

Kembri examined the carved miniature cabinet carefully, opening and shutting it and turning it over in his huge hands.

'Very pretty. Very valuable, too, I should imagine. Hardly the kind of present a man gives a girl for a casual night's pleasure, do you think?'

'My lord, men send me presents from all over—men I've never even seen, some of them. The house is full of presents.'

'Hardly of this quality, perhaps. Was there a letter with it?'

'Yes, my lord; but I get dozens of letters no different. I never answer them; I throw them away. Lord Randronoth may fancy himself in love, but that's nothing to me, I can assure you.'

There was a long silence. Maia began to be filled with a certain sense of having kept the water out. It occurred to her, however, that many people buried valuables under their cellar floors and that she would not put it entirely past Kembri to have hers dug up. She had better find somewhere else: quickly, too.

At length the Lord General stood up, took a step forward and put his hand on her shoulder.

'Maia, you won't have forgotten the day when we talked about adventurers. There's only one touchstone an adventurer's judged by: success or failure. I'll be frank with you. I respect you because you've been

extraordinarily successful. I have two reasons for not doing away with
you—'

'Doing *away* with me, my lord?' She stared at him aghast.

'Just that. Pull yourself together: this is the real world, Maia. One
reason's personal and the other's—well, public. First, even a man like me's
not entirely devoid of human feelings. I admire what you achieved in Suba
and I feel as grateful to you as anyone else in Bekla. But just supposing,
Maia, that there was someone in Bekla who didn't feel in the least grateful
to you, who hated you and wanted to do away with you, they'd still find
that very difficult and even dangerous, because of your enormous popularity. There are many people in the lower city who believe you're more-
or-less divine. It's no exaggeration to say that if you were thought to have
been murdered, it would probably be very hard to keep the people under
control. That's the real reason why you haven't been. By Fornis, I mean,'
he added, as she remained looking incredulously up at him.

She answered never a word. His talk of murder—and her realization
that he was speaking of it as matter-of-factly as he might have spoken of
repairing a highway or collecting a provincial tax—had numbed her.

'So you're the people's pretty mascot. There's no real harm in that,
unless—*unless*, Maia, you let yourself become an implement in the hands
of unscrupulous people who try to make use of you for subversive ends.
Are you quite sure that you didn't go down to the Scales last night with the
idea of increasing your personal influence in the city?'

This, at least, she could answer with truth and conviction. 'Absolutely
certain, my lord.'

'Well, take care you're not misunderstood again, Maia, that's all. I'll
say this much: I believe you when you say you don't want to be Sacred
Queen. I don't see you as—' he paused, then shrugged—'ambitious.
There are people to whom the possession of real and actual power's
worth more than anything else—more than money, health, friends, peace
of mind. To certain people nothing outweighs the possession of power.
Fornis is that sort of person. So was that black girl-friend of yours, in
her own way. That's why I still believe she probably had some sort of
hand in Sencho's murder: she was the sort of person who would. You're
not.' For the first time he smiled, though somewhat constrainedly. 'But
people who *don't* live for power, Maia, are usually people who want to
lead normal lives and gratify normal appetites and desires. If you don't
want to be misunderstood and fall under suspicion, why don't you find
yourself a rich, noble husband and settle down to the sort of life and
position most girls would give their eyes for? You could have virtually
anyone you like; you must know that. I strongly suggest you get on with
it, do you see?'

She could not answer him. Nor could such a conversation, now clearly ended, be convincingly followed by any polite small talk.

'I'll think over your lordship's advice very carefully,' she said.

Ten minutes later, having walked with him as far as her gate, she was down in the cellar, removing Randronoth's money to a less conjecturable hiding-place.

: 72 :

FRIENDS IN SECRET

She was walking in the big, smooth-grazed meadow with Gehta, the girl who had befriended her at the farm on the journey to Urtah.

'Why don't you find yourself a rich, noble husband?' said Gehta. 'It means good and not harm.'

She was carrying Randronoth's carved cabinet of the fishes in one hand. She opened it and showed Gehta a sheet of parchment, sealed at the foot.

'That's an order of release,' she said. 'It's entirely correct; I've only to take it down there. Then Zenka and I can be married.'

'Ah,' said Gehta, 'but dad's farm's slap in the way.'

Then she was running with Zenka—her own, dear Zenka—his staff officer's badges on his shoulders and a dagger in his hand.

'Fornis—I'm going to kill *her* first,' he said. 'I'm utterly in love with you, Maia. I'll always love you. We'll meet again in Bekla and I'll marry you, if only you'll have me.'

'Oh, Zenka,' she cried in an agony, 'don't go! Don't go! You'll be killed, I know it!'

'What kind of talk's that, Miss Maia?' And with this he began to fade and disappear before her eyes, like morning mist on Crandor. 'What kind of talk's that, Miss Maia, Miss Maia?' And she was pitching in the Valderra, rolling hither and thither, struggling for her life.

'Miss Maia, Miss Maia! Oh, Cran and Airtha, you *are* a hard one to wake sometimes and no mistake!'

She was in her great, soft bed, with Ogma standing beside her. 'Oh, miss, I been calling and shaking you very near to pieces, that I have! I was going to let you sleep on, see, only there's a girl downstairs with a message. She says it's important and she's been told she's to give it you herself.'

Maia rubbed her eyes, yawning, and blinking at the sunshine.

'Do you know her, Ogma?'

'No, miss, but I done like you said and made sure she hadn't got no knife nor nothing of that.'

'Where's she from?'

'From the Sacred Queen's palace, miss. She says her name's Chia and you know her.'

'Chia? A big, dark girl with a squint and an Urtan accent?'

'That's her, miss. She seemed upset you wasn't awake. Said she couldn't stay all that long. That's why I come and woke you.'

'Send her up here now.'

A minute later Chia came hesitantly into the big, sunny, white-painted bedroom, gazing about her as though in fear. Her cropped hair was tousled and dirty: she was wearing a dirty sacking smock and had a shrinking, cringing manner, different indeed from the blustering, hefty lass in Lalloc's hall who had stuffed her apple core down Maia's neck. She looked under-fed, too, and it was easy enough to guess that she was no stranger to ill-treatment. Seeing Maia sitting on the edge of the bed, she stood stock-still and raised her palm to her forehead with downcast eyes.

'For Cran's sake, Chia,' said Maia, jumping up and taking her hands, '*don't* do that! How are you?'

'Oh, säiyett—'

'And don't call me säiyett, without you want to make me feel a total fool. Come and sit down. Would you like some breakfast?'

Chia nodded speechlessly and Maia called down to Ogma to double everything she was getting ready to bring upstairs.

It proved difficult to draw Chia out, but after she had wolfed down two or three eggs, half a loaf of bread and butter, most of a honeycomb, a pint of milk and some fruit, she began to gain confidence. Maia, sitting beside her in the window-seat, begged her not to hurry away. 'I'll see as you don't get into trouble,' she said. 'That's to say, long as you haven't run away?'

Chia shook her head. 'No; it's a message.'

'From the queen?' Maia, fearful, looked at her tensely. 'Has she come back?'

'No, she's still in Paltesh, far's I know. It's from Zuno.'

'Well, then, it can wait. Tell me what's been happening to you since we left Lalloc's.'

Chia's story would have drawn tears from a basilisk. Not long after Maia and Occula had left for the upper city to be sold to Sencho for fifteen thousand meld apiece, she had found herself on the block in the Slave Market, one of a job lot of six or seven unattractive but strong girls suitable for domestic work. She had not understood the bidding and had no idea how much they had been sold for; but she knew—and had good reason to know—who had bought them: the Sacred Queen's household bailiff. Since that day, the only occasion on which she had left the kitchen quarters at the palace had been when she was taken upstairs to be beaten in front of Maia. Upon her first arrival in the queen's house she had had a recurrence of the illness about which she had told Maia at Lalloc's; and had nearly died of it, since no one had paid her the least attention, except to drag her to her feet and set her to work as soon as she was sufficiently recovered to show fear of punishment. She had been ill-fed, worked from morning till night and never allowed further than the yard. Once—and at this point in her account she did break down—a letter had come for her, brought by a carrier from northern Urtah who had actually taken the trouble to go to Lalloc's and find out where she was. Herself unable to read, she had asked for help from the housekeeper, who, having taken it from her and read it, had torn it up and told her to get back to work.

Naturally the kitchen-slaves, like everyone else in Bekla, had heard how Maia swam the river, and Chia had let it be known that the two of them had been together at Lalloc's. One morning, many weeks later, Zuno had come down to the kitchens with a message that the Sacred Queen wished to know whether any of the slaves had ever been friendly with Maia. Chia, of course, had had no least idea what would follow. While being beaten she had been in such agony that she had not even realized that Maia had come into the room or had interceded for her. She had never known that Maia had been there at all, and had understood nothing about the business until now.

All this made Maia so angry that she was past caring what she did.

'You say Zuno sent you here this morning?'

'Yes, säi—I mean, Maia. He came downstairs and told the housekeeper it was me as was to go.'

'I see: so you've got every business to be here. That's all I need to know.'

Having told Ogma to get a bath ready for Chia, Maia sent Jarvil out to fetch a professional scribe. When Chia came downstairs an hour later, dressed in one of Maia's second-best robes (which was rather too small for her), Maia kissed her and said, 'Well, now *I'm* going to read you *two* letters, so just sit down and listen.

'"To the Sacred Queen's Household Bailiff. Sir, I write to inform you that I am purchasing your slave, Chia of Urtah, for the sum of two thousand meld, a price which I imagine you will not be disposed to regard as inadequate. The money is with the bearer of this letter, which you should receipt and return to me by his hand. Chia I have already sent to northern Urtah on personal business of my own. Maia Serrelinda."

'"To Surdad, elder of"—you'll have to tell me the name of the village, Chia—"greetings. The bearer of this letter is Chia, a girl whom you will recall that you selected for your Beklan slave quota last summer. She has been my slave, but on account of her excellent conduct I have freed her and sent her home. Please assure me by return that she will never be included in any future slave quota. Maia Serrelinda.'''

Chia was so much overcome by this that she could not really pay attention to Maia's despatch of Jarvil to the palace with the first letter and the money. It was not until Brero was being asked whether he would oblige by accompanying her down to the market and handing over the necessary payment for her to join the next caravan for north-eastern Urtah, Gelt and Ortelga, that either of the girls remembered that in the first place Chia had come with a message. They both burst out laughing, as much from high spirits as anything else.

'Well, what *is* the message?' asked Maia. 'From Zuno, you said?'

'He said your friend hoped you'd come—'

'My friend? Which friend?'

'That's all he said, Maia; "your friend."'

After a moment Maia guessed that Occula's very existence in the queen's private entourage was probably kept so secret that the ordinary household slaves were unaware of it. For the matter of that Kembri, from the way he had talked, apparently supposed that Occula was dead.

'I see. Well?'

'Your friend hoped you'd come tonight, once it was dark, and if possible bring—what was the name? Oh, yes, Milvushina. It's important, but come the back way and try not to be noticed, Zuno said.'

As soon as Chia, in tears of gratitude and sufficient funds for her journey, had left with Brero, Maia sent Ogma to Kembri's house with a pressing invitation to Milvushina to come to supper that evening. She herself could not help feeling rather apprehensive. She had hitherto supposed that Occula must have left Bekla with the Sacred Queen: evidently she had not. Why? If Occula had something on her mind which had made her risk sending for them both, it must be important.

There was no moon and despite the great comet, still burning if anything brighter in the north, the night was dark for summer. Brero, whom Maia had asked to say nothing about the visit, accompanied the two girls, veiled and on foot, as far as the walled lane leading to the kitchen courtyard. Here, unexpectedly, they came upon Zuno, who had apparently been waiting for them. Maia gave Brero ten meld to drink and asked him to meet them in two hours' time. Zuno, using his own key, let them into the palace and they climbed the two flights to the queen's panelled supper-hall without seeing anyone.

They had hardly slipped off their cloaks when Occula came in. Maia was touched to see that she was wearing an orange-coloured metlan not unlike the one she had brought with her from Thettit. (That must have been ruined long ago, thought Maia, for she remembered how Occula had

727

worn it to the gardens on the night of their arrest.) Having kissed them both, she held Maia at arm's length and looked her up and down.

'Precious little wrong with you, banzi, 's far as I can see.'

She herself looked drawn and wan, with a kind of greyness in her face which Maia had never seen before, but guessed to be the equivalent of pallor. The two girls had already had supper while waiting for the summer darkness to fall. Zuno brought wine, fruit and serrardoes, served them himself and then, nursing his white cat, sat down near Occula.

'You can trust me, säiyett,' he said to Milvushina (whom he had, of course, never previously met). 'Occula and I have sworn to get each other out of here by one means or another.'

'It's like bein' a monkey in a bastin' cage,' said Occula, draining her goblet straight down. 'I wasn' born for this, banzi—shut up all day and night and no use for me except—what you saw.'

'Why didn't she take you to Paltesh, then?' asked Maia.

'I doan' know for sure,' answered the black girl, 'but I think she decided I might be one too many. She took Ashaktis, you see. Whatever it is she's up to, she can' manage without Ashaktis to do her dirty work. Ashaktis and I have never really got on, and Fornis knows that. Ashaktis would get rid of me if she could, but she's too smart to try it on as long as she knows I'm what Fornis still wants. That might be it, or it might just be that she didn' want to be tempted to indulge in any little games while she's engaged on serious business—whatever it is. 'Cos believe you me, banzi, that bitch has got her back to the wall. She's desperate—doesn' care what she does; or who she kills, either. That's partly why I took the risk of sendin' for you both here—to warn you of that, face to face.'

'She frightens me,' said Milvushina. 'I'd never try to pretend she didn't. What's she planning, d'you suppose?'

'Cran alone knows,' replied Occula. 'But let's come back to that in a minute. I've got so much to ask you both that I scarcely know where to begin. Are you happy sittin' there, Milva, with that belly on you, or would you rather lie down?'

Milvushina smiled and shook her head. It was plain that her pregnancy gave her the greatest happiness.

'Rather you than me,' said Occula. 'No accountin' for tastes, is there? Yowlin' one end and shit the other. Still, never mind: we've got to be serious; there are things I need to know. The war, Milva—what's the latest news? I know what's put out by the heralds—everythin' everywhere's as jolly as a bull on a cow—but if us lot are goin' to stay alive I've got to know the real truth. Do *you* know it?'

Milvushina nodded, compressing her lips. 'Kembri doesn't tell me

728

everything. But of course I get letters from Elvair, and I quite often have the chance to listen to the staff officers or even just the soldiers.'

She hesitated; then asked, 'Which side are you on, Occula, anyway?'

'Reckon I ought to be askin' *you* that,' answered the black girl. 'Obviously you doan' want Elvair smashed up; but d'you want him to smash up Santil or what?'

'What I used to hope was that Santil would come to terms,' said Milvushina. 'I used to hope that Elvair's army just going into Chalcon might end the trouble.'

'Why, doan' you any more?'

'You haven't heard anything, then?'

'Well, of *course* I haven' heard anythin',' said Occula irritably, 'shut up here like a pig in a damn' sty. Not about Chalcon, anyway. Has Santil had a defeat or what?'

'Anything but. Elvair's falling back towards Ikat Yeldashay. He wrote to me—I've got it here—' she fumbled a moment in her robe and drew out a soiled, torn paper. '"We've been up and down this wilderness until the men are worn out, but the enemy are never where we expect to find them. They've driven away all the beasts and burned the farms. The only soldiers of ours to see any fighting are those who convoy the supplies. Things can't go on like this. The army's half-starved. Believe me, my darling, no one can know what it's like who hasn't wandered for days on end through these woods and hills and found nothing but the bodies of our stragglers. There's no help for it—we shall have to fall back on Ikat and try to work out some new plan. It will be better not to let my father know I've told you this."'

'Oh, men! Men!' cried Milvushina. 'Always fighting! "I'm braver than you are"; like a lot of little boys! If only Elvair was safe back and the whole thing forgotten! I *told* him what would happen—I *told* him! I know that country and *he'd* never been there before in his life. Chalcon's like a spider's web: they'll be lucky to get out at all, that's what I think now.'

'D'you think Bekla's goin' to fall, then?' asked Occula coolly.

'Bekla?' Zuno and Maia spoke together in astonishment.

'To Santil, you mean? Oh, never, surely?' said Milvushina. 'I mean, harvest's coming on, for one thing. Once Elvair's out of Chalcon, Santil's men'll want to get back to their homes.'

'Well, I wouldn' be too sure of that, if I were you,' answered the black girl. 'I expect you know there's trouble in Urtah and in Belishba, too. I heard that it's quite a serious slave revolt in Belishba, and Sendekar's had to bring men south from the Valderra to deal with it. You can bet your deldas—in fact you can bet Maia's—Karnat woan' have missed that.'

'But *Bekla*? *Fall*?' Milvushina knitted her brows. 'I haven't heard Kembri or any of the Leopards speaking about that as a serious possibility.'

'Well, personally I doan' give a fart if it does fall,' said Occula. 'But I've got to be thinkin' about my own plans. Sooner or later, you see, Fornis is goin' to come back, and if Bekla falls she's quite capable of sellin' herself to the other side. In fact that's almost certainly what she *will* do. She could twist anyone, that woman: yes, even Santil, I believe. "Oh, it wasn' really me, it was all those horrible Leopards! *Now* I can help you!" That'll be her line. She's as cunnin' as forty foxes. In fact she may very well be plottin' the fall of the city at this very moment.'

Occula, clenching her fists, jumped up and began walking up and down the little hall. 'Why the bastin' blue brothels d'you think she went to Paltesh? To be safe from Kembri, of course, and raise support among her own people, that's why! Kembri'd kill her if he could. Even Durakkon would kill her. But they're not goin' to rob *me*, either of them. *I'm* the one that's goin' to kill her, an' doan' you make any mistake about that!'

She stopped, gazing out at the pendent, misty fire of the comet where it hung above the Gelt mountains. Maia, looking up at her, was reminded of a silent, dark stream sliding between its banks. The stream flowed where it must: no telling the depth; no stopping it and never a sound. Ah! but *this* water would bear her up—friendly water, however dark and deep.

'Occula,' she asked, 'why don't you kill her in one of those horrible sprees of hers? You could do it easy and pass it off as an accident: say she brought it on herself.'

Zuno shook his head. 'No, no, banzi,' said Occula. 'What—a slave-girl bring about the death of the Sacred Queen? And one already more than suspected of helpin' to murder Sencho, at that? I'd hang upside-down quicker than a goat can get stiff. Besides, when I do it, she's goin' to know who I am and why it's bein' done. It'll be no bastin' accident, believe me. But the right moment'll be everythin'. That's why I've got to know as much as possible about what's happenin' and what's goin' to happen.'

'I'll tell you something else,' put in Milvushina. 'Kembri's afraid of her: he's as good as told me so. He told me that when they first seized Bekla nearly eight years ago, he and Sencho were just out to make use of her— you know, her magnetism and popularity with the people. He said he never realized then that before she'd finished she'd turn out to be more than they could handle.'

'Either she'll maintain herself in power,' said Zuno, 'or else, if she can't, she'll pull the city down round her own ears and everyone else's.'

'Well, never *mind*!' cried Occula impatiently, as though Zuno had uttered something completely trivial. 'That's enough about that green-eyed cow. You listen to me, banzi. First of all, what have you done with Chia?'

Maia told her.

Occula nodded. 'I hoped you might. That's why I asked Zuno to send her. H'm! Northern Urtah; that might prove quite useful, I doan' know.'

'How d'you mean?' asked Maia.

'Well, by all accounts they're a very funny lot up there, where she comes from,' answered Occula enigmatically. 'And of course she'll tell them what she owes Fornis, woan' she? And that might—Well, never mind. There's somethin' else I want to hear about. What's all this about you gettin' up on the Scales and talkin' about the star, as if you were Lespa or somethin'?'

'The star? Well, it just come into my head to see 'f I couldn't go down there and cheer a few of 'em up. I never meant to go on the Scales at all—'twas the armourers an' the rest as done that.'

'You and that Ogma, you're not safe, the two of you left alone together,' said Occula. '*She* might have thought to stop you goin' out, even if you couldn' see it for yourself. That girl's a fool an' so are you, banzi. Far as I can make out, you did the very thing everyone's been warnin' you not to do. It never crossed your mind, I suppose, that Kembri'd think you were puttin' yourself forward for Sacred Queen?'

'No, it never,' retorted Maia hotly, 'and n'more I was, an' so I told Kembri to his face when he come round yesterday.'

'The thing you must never forget, banzi, about Kembri, is that he's every bit as much a conspirator and a murderer as Sencho and Fornis. He was in on this Leopard business from the very beginnin', like them. He's completely ruthless. He's decided that Milva's the girl the Leopards need for Sacred Queen. That's why he didn' stop Elvair goin' round and takin' her the very day after Sencho was done in, even though he knew it'd make Fornis his enemy from that moment. Do you realize that if good old Sendekar hadn't made it impossible, by tellin' the whole army about you swimmin' the river before Kembri could stop him, Kembri'd almost certainly have had you killed by now, just to get you out of the way as a rival to Milva?'

'Ah, he told me as much yesterday,' said Maia.

'Cran, I'd almost rather be back at Piggy's,' said Occula, 'wouldn' you? Three nice bed-girls from the High Counsellor's, and here we are up to the neck in what's goin' to be the biggest shine for a thousand years, you mark my words. And there's no gett'n' out of it that I can see. Doesn' it frighten you?'

'Yes, it frightens me sick,' answered Maia. Yet still she said nothing of Randronoth's forty thousand meld.

'What really makes me sure these damn' Leopards are bound to go down in the end,' said Occula, 'is the filthy, blasphemous use they've made

731

of this whole Sacred Queen business. Come right down to it and they've spat in the gods' faces, that's what. They're not my gods, but never mind 'bout that. The whole point of the Sacred Queen always used to be that she was the gods' choice and not men's. She was supposed to be the gods' makeweight for man's imperfection. Men in power made the rulers—the generals and councillors and so on—but the Sacred Queen was honestly acclaimed by the people, and no hanky-panky. That's to say, the gods put it into the people's hearts whom to acclaim, and that was their own choice; not the rulers'. But Fornis, Sencho, Kembri—they changed all that, and Durakkon was the fool who went along with it. The gods'll have their blood for that in the long run, you see if they doan'.'

'You're the lucky one, aren't you?' said Milvushina to Zuno. '*You'll* be all right.'

'I may and I may not, säiyett; it all depends. I have no wish to stand or fall with the Sacred Queen, yet what else can I do? In practice I'm not free to leave her, and in any case I have no particular prospects elsewhere.'

'No, *you're* the lucky one, Milva, that's the truth of it,' said Occula. 'At least you've got Kembri and Elvair to protect you, and even if the city *were* to fall, they'd probably get you out alive. *You've* got no enemies, unless you call Santil an enemy. No, banzi, you're the one I'm worried about: there can' be any goin' back for you, you see. And yet you can' go on as you are. Kembri may not be prepared to go the length of killin' you, but Fornis will be when she comes back—as I'm sure she means to. And even if you were to cut and run, where could you go? Suba—Katria—Terekenalt—they'd tear you to pieces, after what you've done! And I can' see you in sanctuary on Quiso for the rest of your life. No; there's only two things you can possibly do, and I reckon I know which one'd be best.'

Maia would have liked Occula to take her in her arms and whisper in her ear, as in the old days in bed at Sencho's. The talk of killing had frightened her badly. Yet she did her best to make a joke of it.

'Well, come on, then! Reckon Terebinthia won't be eavesdropping just now.'

Occula, sitting down beside her, took her hand in her own. 'You could put your trust in the gods, banzi, and believe that they *mean* you to be Sacred Queen. That's one thing you could do; for there's hardly a doubt that if you're still alive and in Bekla at the end of this year, the people will acclaim you, Kembri or no Kembri. But it's my belief that if you stay here just as you are now, either Kembri or Fornis will get rid of you somehow.'

She paused. 'And the other?' asked Maia.

'The other,' said Occula deliberately, 'is to marry the richest and most powerful man you can find; preferably one with an estate in the provinces, where you can go and live in safety. You're not cut out for a life of high intrigue, banzi. You're too nice. A girl like you needs a protector—someone to belong to. And the long and short of it is, you can either choose the gods' protection, or a man's. I know damn' well which I'd choose—and if I doan' love you no one does.'

A silence fell. It was as though all four of them, sitting in the elegant, luxurious hall high above the teeming city, felt themselves isolated as though besieged; or surrounded by a flood lapping the base of their precarious tower with invisible waters of malevolence and peril. Suddenly Maia had the horrible fancy that the sunken rectangle of the central floor, enclosed within its honey-coloured walls and broad step of banded slate, was like a well down which her dead body could be pitched and vanish untraced. Setting down her goblet, she jumped up and almost ran across to the north-facing window.

The comet was low, its drooping tail partly obscured behind the jagged, barely-discernible line of the mountain peaks. The comet, she knew, had been sent by Lespa—Lespa who had saved her again and again. Yet why had she sent it? What did it mean? It was like the danger she was in, she thought. It made no sound, uttered no threat. It simply abode; whenever you looked up, there it was, undeviant and unchanged.

'Oh, Lespa,' she prayed silently, 'help me! I'm more afraid than ever I've been!'

For now, with Occula's words, her very real and immediate danger had at last become plain to her; the danger which, though in all conscience told clearly enough, had not been brought fully home by Sessendris, by Nennaunir, by Milvushina or even entirely by Kembri. It now seemed to her that she—she who had knelt beside the dying Sphelthon, who had swum the Valderra by night—had in fact never, in all her life, possessed any real power to distinguish between semblance and reality.

The sudden recognition of a lack in oneself of normal perception, of the ability to see in its true colours what has been plain as day to everyone else; the realization that in some important respect one has hitherto been like a child, not clearly differentiating actuality from fantasy, security from peril, truth from fallacy, can take place at any time in life, even to outwardly-seeming experienced people, and when it does is always mortifying. When it involves the apprehension of danger, the shock often comes with a kind of freezing effect, dream-like, momentarily cutting off awareness of companions and surroundings.

Still no one spoke. Maia stood still, supporting herself with one hand on the embrasure. Her hope of finding Zen-Kurel, of fulfilling their mutual promise to marry and live in Katria; it was as though a glaring, hard light had suddenly been turned upon this secret room in her heart, revealing—what? Flimsy walls, frail beams, a brittle door that any ruffian could kick

733

in. True, it was also revealed as no less beautiful than she had always known it to be—but utterly insecure. In this room, whatever its beauty, there lay no safety. Her love for Zen-Kurel would not save her, and she had been deceiving herself in thinking that it would. Yet if safety was what she must have, if safety was what she valued above all else, then no doubt about it, she must quit this beautiful, forlorn, memory-filled room for some stronger one. Her love for Zenka—her love of one night, which she nevertheless knew in her own heart to be entire and sincere—how much, in cold, sober fact, was that love worth to her? That, though Occula did not know it, had been the implication of her words to the hearer. Was she, Maia, ready to risk death—no fancy, no game, but the real, bowel-clutching prospect of being murdered—not in return for the certainty of finding and marrying her Zenka in the end, but in return for the mere chance that she might?

I must wait for Sednil, she thought. At the very least I must wait for Sednil and whatever news he brings. And that's a matter of time. But how much time will I have?

And now, suddenly, she knew the meaning of the great star: not the city's meaning—for the star, like a dream or an old tale, no doubt had many different meanings implanted in it by Lespa, for comprehension by various people—but her own meaning, the individual meaning Lespa had intended *her* to perceive. It was plain: there couldn't be a doubt of it! She herself was the star! This new-come presence, this gentle brilliance in the sky, with its streaming, golden hair, was the equivalent of herself in Bekla. It followed clearly that as long as *it* lasted, *she* would remain immune, the protected of the goddess. But when it departed she, too, if she had not by then found what she was seeking, would be fated to depart, either to death or to that dreary, marital refuge—death in life, as it appeared to her young heart—of which Occula had spoken. So much time, then, she had: so much time and opportunity the goddess was vouchsafing her.

She had the message. She longed, now, for some relief from her tension and anxiety; for some respite, however brief and illusory, from the strain of dwelling on love and danger. It's strange, she thought: all your life you hear the tales of the great deeds, the dangers and sufferings of the heroes and the gods and goddesses, but you never understand what they must really have felt until it's brought home to you through your own experience and your own heart.

She turned, came back from the window, put her arms round Occula and kissed her as they had been used to kiss in their first days of slavery, the days of her innocence and her wretchedness.

'I've taken in all you say,' she said, smiling. 'Don't worry, dearest, I'll survive. We all shall—all four of us; I know it.'

'Then you know a damn' sight more than I do, banzi.'

'Never mind for now. Occula, tell us one of your stories—like you used to. Like you did at Lalloc's that night—remember?'

'I remember: that was about Lespa, wasn't it?'

'Yes, tell us another about Lespa! The one about Shakkarn and how Lespa became a goddess: the story of the senguela.'

Occula looked round at the others. Milvushina smiled and nodded. Zuno refilled the goblets. Occula took another long pull, settled herself in the cushions and began.

: 73 :

THE APOTHEOSIS OF LESPA

'After young Baltis the smith had first made love to Lespa in the temple of Shakkarn—that day before the autumn festival, you remember, when she was supposed to be mending the altar cloth—they became lovers as dear to each other as good deeds are to the gods. They thought of nothin' else. Each of them used to lie awake at night, wishin' to be in another bed. For things were still no easier for them, you see, just because they'd succeeded for once in gettin' what they both wanted. Lespa's father still reckoned the family was a good cut above young Baltis, a mere smith's apprentice with nothin' beyond his pay and perks. And worse than that, realizin' he had such a pretty daughter—for Lespa was the talk of the place for miles around, so that people on journeys used to make a point of stoppin' by on some excuse or other, jus' to see her goin' to the well in the evenin' along o' the other girls—he'd begun gettin' grand ideas of marryin' her to some wealthy lord or maybe even a baron. I dare say there might have been three or four of that sort who passed that way not so very seldom, what with boats and so on goin' by on the Zhairgen or the Valderra. For as you know, I've always held out for it that sweet Lespa came from lower Suba. But I dare say you two want to have it that she came from somewhere in Chalcon or Tonilda, doan' you?'

'Suba!' said Maia instantly. ''Course it was Suba!'

'Oh, was it, now?' replied Occula, looking at her quizzically over the rim of her goblet. 'Travel broadens the mind, eh? Well, I expect Suba's a wonderful place for—er—'

'Frogs?' asked Maia, smiling. She had already slipped off her sandals: now she stretched out her legs, parted her toes and wriggled them, looking down at them and shaking her head.

'Webbed feet? Neither had Lespa,' said Occula. 'Her feet were so pretty the boys used to kiss the grass where she'd walked by. But I'll get on. Sometimes she and Baltis were able to steal a meetin'—it might be in the woods when she was gatherin' sticks, or p'raps it might be that young Baltis would be comin' back from some job he'd been sent out to do on a bull's stall or some bolts for a door, and he'd stop by at the back of the wood-pile and whistle like a blue-finch, and then Lespa would suddenly remember she had to go down the garden for parsley or some such little thing. But you know how it is, makin' love in a hurry—for a girl, anyway, and even for a few men, though not half enough of them—a bit of this and that and not long enough, as the stag-hound bitch said when the lapdog tried to mount her.

'Well, but sweet Lespa was a fine, spirited girl with a heart and mind of her own, and one way and another she managed to see to it that she and Baltis did sometimes meet together at night and no one else the wiser in the mornin'. And besides that, she managed to contrive that her father's ideas didn' get much further than his own head. If you're unlucky enough to be a girl—'

'I'm not unlucky,' interrupted Milvushina, smiling.

'Wouldn' change that belly of yours for old Sencho's, eh?' returned Occula. 'Well, you can stuff 'em from one end or you can stuff 'em from the other, I suppose: they seem to get bigger just the same. But I'll oblige you, Milva, and alter what I said. If you're *lucky* enough to be a girl, all the same you can' refuse to see guests who come to the house: but how much you say to them when they're there—that's quite another matter. I suppose Lespa's father could have ordered her to do this, that or the other, but somehow he didn'. I dare say she'd already got, even then, some of those qualities which people have been worshippin' these hundreds of years.

'Well, she loved Baltis as girls have always loved the first man who takes them. And for a mortal girl she could have done worse, no doubt, if only the immortal gods—whatever names we give them up and down the world—hadn' had other plans for her destiny. For he was a right enough young lad, and a servant of the gods himself in a manner of speakin', 'cos he was a smith; and as you know, the skill of forgin' metal's a gift from the gods, a divine secret which men could never have thought up on their own account, any more than they could have thought up music. Anyway, now Baltis and Lespa had this other divine gift between them as well, and that sort of pleasure's a plant that thrives on hoein' and waterin', so they say. They practised their music and they got pretty good at it.

'But then came the cruel wars. What wars they were I doan' know, and maybe it doan' matter all that much. All wars are the same to women,

736

aren' they? You lie in a cold bed and weep for what's gone, and those that doan' have to weep for ever are the lucky ones. No, doan' you go takin' on, Milva: he's the commander-in-chief, isn' he? *He'll* be back, you see if he woan'.

'Whatever wars they were, it seems that after a time the baron of those parts found himself hard-pressed for soldiers, and the need was so desperate that in the end all the village elders up and down the province agreed to a levy; and so in due time the baron's men came to Lespa's village to take their quota from among the young men. All the grown lads of the village—hunters, smiths, fishermen, farm-hands; no matter what they were, didn' make no difference—they had to stand forth, as the sayin' goes, to be looked over, and some right old weepin' and wailin' there was among the mothers and sweethearts and wives, I dare say.

'I doan' know how many they took from Lespa's village. But if the blasted quota had been no more than two, Baltis would have been one of them all right, for he had a pair of shoulders like barn doors: he must have been the likeliest-lookin' young chap they'd come upon in weeks. So, poor lad, he had to pack up his bits in a bag and belt on his sword (which he'd forged for himself, to make sure it was a good one, from a nice piece of Gelt iron he'd had marked down for a ploughshare) and away he went for a soldier, with Lespa hangin' on his arm two miles up the lane, cryin' her eyes out and not carin' now who saw her, either.

'After Baltis had gone, she felt just about as lonely and discarded as an old bucket thrown in a hedge. It wasn' even so much that he wasn' actually with her, for of course she'd already had to put up with a deal of that: it was the havin' nothin' to look forward to, nothin' to liven up the day with plannin' a bit of funny business: no more hope of slippin' down the garden for a handful of—er—parsley. And after a bit it got to downright, blasted starvation. 'Cos you know how it is: once you've had it and taken pleasure in it—well, you miss it, doan' you, just for itself? Anyway, Lespa did.' Suddenly Occula raised her voice. 'And she's not the only one, either!' She bit her finger for a moment and was silent.

At length she continued. 'And the attentions of the lads left behind didn' afford her any consolation, either. I dare say they seemed a poor lot after Baltis, and anyway Lespa wasn' a girl to throw away her self-respect and have people winkin' behind her back and sayin' she was the kind of lass who thought half a loaf was better than no bread. She wanted to think that wherever the wars had carried Baltis, he was stayin' true to her, and she reckoned the best way to be sure of that was to be true to him. She used to—banzi, what on earth's the matter? You're never cryin', are you? What the hell for? I haven't said anythin' funny yet.'

'You let me alone,' faltered Maia, wiping her eyes. 'I'm enjoying myself.

You just get on with the story, now. You ain't sat there to ask questions, you're sat there to tell the tale.'

'She used to go down the village and ask passin' travellers for news of the wars,' resumed Occula. 'But no one ever seemed to know anythin' about Baltis, and come to think of it, 'twasn' likely they would, him bein' just an ordinary soldier-boy among hundreds and thousands marchin' and batterin' up and down the land.

'Now after a time it got to be winter and then it was spring and still pretty Lespa was sufferin' in her heart and dodgin' all her father's schemes and goin' her own way alone as far as the lads were concerned. And there were one or two—there always are, aren' there?—that she'd sent packin', even though she did it nicely (for Lespa was never hard-spoken to anyone, though I dare say she might have been more or less forced to be a bit firm now and then—you know what some fellows can be like)—there were one or two who began sayin' there must be somethin' queer about her; pretty or not, she couldn' be a natural girl, or else she thought herself too good for anybody; and all such things as that. So she wasn' very happy, not even when the warm weather came, to hear the kynat callin' and see the brooks full of yellow spear-buds under the banks.

'Now one mornin'—one perfect spring mornin', that's how the story has it—with all the trees in new leaf, wild cherry and zoan and scented poplar an' I doan' know what-all—Lespa was told by her mother to go up to the wood and bring back a good, big faggot of sticks and maybe a log as well if she could manage it. So off she went, with the grass cool at her feet and all the daisies in bloom. But still she had thoughts for nothin' but Baltis gone to the wars. Yes, she was a girl forlorn and sad in springtime. So she wasn' in much of a hurry to get on with the business of gatherin' the sticks. She was in a mood for everythin' to seem a waste of time. She sat down by the brook for a bit and pulled some watercress; and then she just lay on the bank while the birds sang and the frogs sat on the lily leaves in the sunshine. But after a while she supposed she'd better get on with it, so she got up and climbed over the fence and went her way into the wood.

'But she still felt lazy; and worse than that, she felt inclined to mope and not at all in the mood for puttin' up a faggot and goin' home bent double under it. It was partly the spring weather and partly her own thoughts—'nough to put anyone in two minds, kind of style. It was quiet in the wood and the mornin' got hotter and hotter and still she hadn't really done any work—just a stick or two.

'After a bit she came on a pool among the trees. It was one of those nice, clear, brown pools you sometimes find: water tricklin' in one end and out the other, and no mud or dead leaves to speak of—just a clean, gravel bottom a few feet deep. She dabbled her toes in it and it didn' seem too

738

cold at all. In fact it seemed very invitin', and in a couple of minutes Lespa had stripped off and plunged in. Well, you know how it is: you seem to leave all your cares behind when you jump into the water. She was soon feelin' in better heart, splashin' about and as happy as a thrush in the rain.

'Now as I told you, didn' I, it was the sort of spring mornin'—never a better one since the world began—that brings the gods down to earth. For to begin with, you know, the gods created the earth as a pleasure-garden for themselves; and so it still is—in places, anyway: and the gods may still come around here and there, for all I know. But be that as it may, on this particular mornin', all those long years ago, the god Shakkarn—him as was a god before even Cran and Airtha; the god of rough, country places and honest, simple folk—he'd come down to earth to enjoy the spring and the scented leaves and the bees buzzin' about in the flowers.

'Now as you know—or even if you doan', for the matter of that—when the gods take bodily shape they assume whatever form best suits their immortal truth. That's to say, whatever truth they're manifestin' at that particular time. A god or a goddess is like bread, you know: you can dip bread into wine, or gravy, or custard, or honey, or any damn' thing you like, and that's what it'll taste of, and of course it'll improve the bread as well. And I've even heard tell that with the gods, it's not a matter of choice—no, not even for them. I've heard tell that there's a power that causes a god or goddess to assume the most fittin' form; accordin', I suppose, to such things as the time of year, the place they're visitin', the people they're manifested to and the gifts of blessin's they come to bring. A goddess might appear as a dragonfly or a moonbeam, and a god as a serpent or a leopard or an old pilgrim. It all depends. But *when* it happens, there's always some who feel the presence of the god and sometimes even recognize him, while others—the thick ones—see nothin' at all; and they just sneer at the clear-sighted ones and say they're conceited or mad, and give them a hard time; and now and then they even persecute or kill them. That's the sort of world this is.

'Anyway, divine Shakkarn was wanderin' through the summer wood-land in the incarnate form of a great, white goat: such a goat as has never been seen, I dare say, from that day to this. His coat was like white silk, his eyes shone brighter than jacinths, his hooves were like bronze and his two horns like the frame of a gold lyre. Goats break loose and stray sometimes, as you know, and very likely any dull-witted clodhopper catchin' sight of Shakkarn in the distance would just think it was someone else's strayin' goat and why the hell should he be bothered? and go on with his work. But anyone with the truth in them would feel and know the form of Shakkarn that day for the form of truth.

'Now as Shakkarn was wanderin' down among the trees in the woodland, he heard a sound of splashin' and a girl's voice singin' a little snatch of song; and a very pretty voice it was. So he thought he might as well have a look, and he came rather cautiously closer in the direction of the pool, not to startle whoever might be there. He went into the stream higher up and from there he looked down through the leafy branches. When he saw Lespa in the pool, that was a sight that made him stare and tremble, even though he was a god. He came very quietly out of the bed of the stream and then, just as though he might be strayin' aimlessly and nibblin' at the leaves and grass as he went along, he came down the bank and approached Lespa more or less at random.

'Lespa, standin' in the pool, gazed in wonder as this marvellous beast drew gradually nearer. For Lespa, you know—well, the last thing she was, was unfeelin' or slow in the uptake, and all she could think of was that she'd never seen such a beautiful creature in all her life. Almost timidly— or so it seemed to her—he approached to drink. She wasn' frightened, for the way he was goin' on, it wasn' a question of being afraid of him, but rather of being careful not to frighten him away. Slowly, step by step, she waded across the pool, stretched out a wet hand and touched him. He made no move and she began to stroke his back and scratch his ears. Then, just as she was, she drew herself out of the water and sat beside him in the sunshine, and as he still stood docile she put her arms round him and began rubbin' her cheek against his neck.

'Now the true title and style of the goddess, as you know, is "Lespa of the Inmost Heart", or sometimes "Lespa of Acceptance". Of all the gods and goddesses, she's the one who's entrusted with the divine task of re- vealin'—or at any rate of offerin'—to us the truth lyin' within ourselves; and each person's truth is different and unique. She reveals the truth, rather as a noble and generous lady might toss a piece of gold on the ground for a beggar to pick up. Yet amazin'ly, there are many who never bother to notice the gold where it falls, or even more amazin'ly, take it for rubbish and disregard it. They may even refuse it, and swear blind that they'll have nothin' to do with it and it's no part of them. Yes, they stop their ears against the goddess, because she tries to tell them somethin' about themselves that they doan' want to hear, you see. But be all that as it may, she's not called "Lespa of the Inmost Heart" for nothin', and we can take it as certain sure that the reason why that pretty village girl became the goddess of the Inmost Heart was because she herself, even as a mortal, was able to put into practice what she now requires of *us*—the humility and honesty to recognize the truth.

'As she sat there upon the bank of the pool, with her arms round the divine animal beside her, Lespa could sense the cravin' and burnin' of his desire. And this was nothin' less than the raw, unrefined need and longin' which rampages through the world and will no more be choked off than the lightnin' or the rain. This was animal nature; and as she recognized it, she knew also that she shared it. This, whether she liked it or not, was a part of herself made manifest.

'It was a hell of a shock. Ah, yes! Even to Lespa—and as yet she was just a mortal girl, doan' forget, and unacquainted with the mighty gods—it was such a shock as filled her with dread and even with horror and a flood of hot shame. She—she, a human girl, was an animal, and shared, at any rate in part, the nature of other animals. She was a female animal, subject to appetite, and to heat and instinct.

'All this came rushin' upon her with the vividness and force of a dream. 'Cos as you know, you can' control a dream and they can sometimes be frightenin'. She jumped up from where she was sittin' and ran a little way—as if *that* would enable her to leave behind what she'd just discovered!—her mouth open and her cheeks burnin'. Yet the god made no move to pursue her, though now she could plainly see for herself how strongly he was inclined to that. He was able to bear with her fear and frailty as she herself was not.

'Now some people will tell you that Lespa knew then and there that this was Shakkarn and that she was loved by a god. But I've known others who will have it that her humility and self-acceptance were much greater than that—that she simply accepted in all simplicity that she wanted to be basted by a goat. But myself, I doan' believe she thought anythin'—not consciously—at all. She simply surrendered herself to the inmost heart, like a bird that knows when it's time to fly south. And yet that's not altogether right either, for the birds can't resist—they just *have* to fly south—and Lespa—oh, yes, she *could* have resisted and run away from herself and from the god. There's thousands do—and by Kantza-Merada! can' you tell them when you have to do with them, too? This is the whole secret of the beginnin' of Lespa's divinity—that at the first she was afraid, shocked—probably even disgusted to be confronted with her own animal nature—but she knew—she had the courage to know—what to accept, just the same as she'd known what to reject after Baltis had been taken away.

'Falterin'ly, she came back to Shakkarn on the brink of the pool; and then she herself welcomed him, and she herself began what they were to do between them. There's one thing you can be quite sure of, banzi, as I've told you again and again; that whatever virtues you attribute to the gods, decency and shame are not among them. Shakkarn's more sublime and no more respectable than a thunderstorm or a flood.

'Now I've heard this story misused and profaned more times than I can tell you. In the Lily Pool at Thettit they had a whole room decorated with pictures of Lespa and the goat, and fellows used to pay extra to go and do it there. You simply can' get the truth across to some people: it's like blowin' a trumpet in the ear of a stone-deaf man. These stories are no good unless you find them and feel them for yourself. The whole point is that two completely different and contradictory things can be true at one and the same time. Sweet, bonny Lespa, who wouldn' have hurt a fly, as they say, was doin' somethin' everyone else would call filthy and abominable, which she herself knew to be the world's truth and a divine gift which she simply wasn't prepared to go on livin' without, whatever it might cost her.

'And *that*,' cried Occula, jumping up, refilling her goblet and slamming down the wine-jug so that the knives jumped on the table, '*that's* what makes the ruddy world go round—for those who doan' prefer to keep it standin' still. It takes courage!

'Now the way some people tell it, after that day Shakkarn and Lespa became lovers and used to meet in the wood, until someone or other in the village noticed and began to wonder where it was she used to go and what she was up to. But others say that everythin' happened that very same morning. It dun't really matter, and I'll go on with what does.

'There was an old woman out gatherin' sticks, same as sweet Lespa, and as she came up through the wood she heard somethin' that people doan' mistake for anythin' else, do they? the cryin' and babblin' of a girl in pleasure. Now any honest person with any sort of heart at all, if they find they've happened to stumble on somethin' like that, they go off the other way, doan' they? and take care not to make any noise into the bargain—'

'We never tell: you won't?' murmured Maia.

'What say, banzi?'

'Nothing. I was only just on remembering something, that's all.'

'Uh-huh. Well, this pokin', nasty-minded old woman wasn't one to tell shit from puddin', let alone a goat from a god. Oho! she thinks: some dirty wench is enjoyin' herself havin' it off in the wood and I'm not. I'll just look into this, I will, for the sake of village decency, and see what's goin' on! She might just as well have said "*Watch* what's goin' on", but she didn'. And so she came creepin' up among the trees and she saw for herself the claspin' and the mastery.

'Oh, wasn't there just a screamin' and a scrunchin' when she came runnin' back into the village? I dare say you could have heard her at Kabin from Zeray, if only she'd been there. Pity she wasn'. She didn' think of goin' and havin' a word with Lespa's mother on the quiet, as any right-minded person would 'a done. "Oh! Oh!" she screams at the top of her voice, so they all come runnin' out to see if she was on fire. "Oh! Oh! Do you know what I've seen? Do you know what I've just seen?" (Makin' the most of it, see?) "That filthy, dirty hussy Lespa—her as wouldn' look at any boy up and down the village this twelvemonth gone and now we know why, doan' we? That horrible, unnatural trollop—"

' "What?" they all cried. "Oh, what, oh, what?"

' "Up in the wood! Bastin'—with a goat! A goat, quite big, a big goat! Wait till I tell you all the details!"

' "We'll burn her!" shouted someone. "That's witchcraft, that is! Couplin' with a familiar! Sorcery! Necromancy! In our village!"

' "And what's more, she was *enjoyin*' it!" shouted the old woman.

' "That's the worst of all!" they cried.

'So then they all came out as against a thief, with swords and staves, and they were all sayin' what they were going to do to her and inventin' things as they went along. And they reached the wood and came burstin' in among the trees.

'Lespa and Shakkarn were lyin' easy beside the pool. Or maybe they weren' lyin' easy—how would I know? They must have heard the villagers comin', of course, from a little way off, but Shakkarn was a god, wasn' he? and he wasn' goin' to stop doin' anythin' he had a mind to just because of a bunch of ten-meld mortals—or any other mortals, come to that. And beautiful Lespa, she loved and trusted Shakkarn, and anyway she knew now who he was and although she must have felt troubled and—well—annoyed, I s'pose, and prob'ly frightened at bein' interrupted at such a time, she wasn' goin' to back down or run away. She was the beloved of a god, and anyway Lespa always had the heart of a queen.

'Well, up they all came, and of course they didn' even think of talkin' to Shakkarn, 'cos he was just a dirty, nasty goat, wasn' he? They began screamin' and shoutin' at Lespa, all shakin' their fists, and her standin' there without a stitch on, but no one thought to throw her a cloak or turn aside while she put on her clothes. And then someone threw a stone at her and hit her on the shoulder so that she cried out, and she was bleedin'.

'Then Shakkarn got up and stood in front of her and fixed his great, golden eyes on the rabble as they pressed forward. There was one man—a tailor, he was—who had a bean-pole with a sharp point in his hand, and he made a poke with it at Lespa's arm. And with that the whole lot screamed with shock and fear, for in that very moment each one of them felt that point jabbin' into their own arms, just as if it had been them. They didn' need any more after that. They turned and ran, helter-skelter, and in half a minute there wasn' a soul in the wood but Lespa and the lyre-horned god.

'And then Lespa found that in some way she'd become lighter than the summer mornin' air. She was floatin' with Shakkarn up through the trees and then higher than that. She wasn' cold and she wasn' bleedin' and "naked" was a word that had no meanin' as far as she was concerned, any more than it might have for a dragonfly or a swallow. And Shakkarn—he'd reassumed his true, divine form, though what that may be how can I or any other mortal tell? You and I would have been struck blind to look at him, but not his consort, upon whom he'd conferred his divinity. From morn to noon they rose, from noon to dewy eve, a summer's day, and with the settin' sun came to the zenith and the palace prepared for Lespa among the stars. And there she took up the work of the goddess that she'd become; 'cause if you think the gods doan' work, let me tell you they work a damn' sight harder than anyone else, except that it's not drudgery, but more like the work of some great musician or sculptor, so I've always understood.

'Lespa, doan' you see, she'd attained what all women seek, and that's completion; that completion whose very heart lies in its imperfection. And this is what she offers night by night to anyone with the courage and the patience to attempt it as she did. She sends dreams out of the darkness and the stars, and she asks you riddles and sets you puzzles and she stirs up the whole boilin' pot of Shakkarn to send fumes into your sleepin' head. Lespa of the Inmost Heart: shall I tell you what she's like? Back home—oh, back home—'

'Who's crying now?' asked Maia.

'Shut up!' cried the black girl passionately. 'Back home, in Silver Tedzhek, where I was born, there was a great, tessellated courtyard in front of the temple of Kantza-Merada, all green and gold. The tiles were glazed and hard as rock. One day, when I was still just a banzi, I was playin' there, waitin' for Zai—my father—an' I saw the green shoot of a plant stickin' up through the pavement. It was a nettle, no stronger than a bit of cloth. It had split the tile. I left it alone. If the goddess wanted to split her tiles—she's always doin' it—that was her business.'

There was a silence. Then Maia said, 'You're a nettle, too, aren't you?'

'You attend to your business and I'll attend to mine,' replied Occula. 'But I'll tell you this, banzi: it takes courage to puzzle out what Lespa's sayin'. She never tells you what to do: she tells you where you are. After that you're on your own.'

Through the northern window shone for a few moments the lights of the lower city clocks telling the hour.

'Still, you woan' want to go home on your own, will you?' said Occula. 'D'you think your soldier's come back by now?'

EUD-ECACHLON ASKS A QUESTION

Night by night the great comet poured out its hazy brightness into the northern sky, and throughout the city anxiety and wonder gradually diminished as still nothing happened and the prodigy became a thing accustomed. The priests, shrewdly no doubt, avoided committing themselves beyond affirming that the gods had given assurance (none knew how) that the apparition portended no harm. One day a crowd of orderly and respectful suppliants succeeded in confronting the chief priest as he was entering the Temple of Cran by the front portico, when to avoid or ignore them would have appeared undignified and perhaps even weak. He replied to their questions with grave self-possession and suavity.

'Consider,' said he, 'that many thousands of years ago the moon must have appeared in the sky for the first time. Can you imagine how astonished and bewildered the people of those days must have been to see it? What rumination and presentiment they must have suffered—yes, suffered, for of course they were only poor, ignorant folk in those days, without the benefits of modern knowledge and of all this' (waving his hand towards the spacious precinct and the Tamarrik Gate). 'To this day, how inexplicable, even if predictable, remain her phases, her waxings and wanings! Yet the moon is a blessing and no one now would dream of attributing ill-omen to the moon.'

'Is the great star here to stay, then, my Guardian?' asked someone in the crowd.

'How do we know?' he replied. 'Yet since you ask me, I would say not. All I am explaining to you is, that not every sign among the stars need or should be taken as the forerunner of some great change, let alone of disaster.'

'So the Serrelinda was right?' called out someone else.

'Not having heard her speak, I cannot say,' he answered with a sedate and condescending smile. 'Our astrologers, of course, have spent many years of study in learning their expert skills. I entertain nothing against the Serrelinda—'

'Better not!' muttered someone.

'She has served the city superbly in *her* way. *We* have to serve it in ours.' He spread his arms wide and raised his voice. 'I will pray to Cran and Airtha to bless you all for honest and true-hearted Beklans, whom the gods surely love.'

His scarlet-bordered robes swished on the pavement as he turned and ascended the steps into the noon-shadowed portico.

At about the same time Maia, who had begun—and to her credit was sticking to—a couple of hours' work a day on improving her reading and (which she found a good deal harder, since it had never really existed) her writing, was lying in the hammock in her garden, wrestling with a romance lent to her by Sarget, about the deeds of the hero Deparioth. Like nearly all people of relatively young civilizations—and certainly like virtually everyone in the Beklan empire at this time—Maia found it natural to read to herself aloud, and her soft, rather pretty voice, stumbling and hesitating over the more difficult words, mingled with the lapping of the Barb and the intermittent piping of a damazin among the trees.

'Give back the—the miry—miry—solitude,
'The thorns and briars—out—er—outstretched to bless.
'There lay my—*kingdom*, I reckon that is—past compare:
'This court's the desert—something wild—wilderness.'

She knew the story well. This was Deparioth's lament for the loss of the mysterious girl they called the Silver Flower, who, having saved his life in the terrible Blue Forest, had then vanished for ever. She read it through again.

'Give back the miry solitude,
The thorns and briars outstretched to bless.
There lay my kingdom, past compare.
This court's the desert wilderness.'

The Blue Forest she knew by repute for a wild and savage place in northern Katria, beyond the borders of the empire; somewhere near where, so she'd heard, the Zhairgen ran into the Telthearna. She began to muse, the scroll laid aside. If she were really to put her mind to it, could she get to Katria? Might she be able to reach the Zhairgen quickly and secretly, and then somehow cross it before she was missed? How far was it to the Zhairgen, anyway? It was, she knew, generally reckoned a good four or five days' journey to Dari-Paltesh; and the Zhairgen lay beyond that.

Oh, she thought, if only things could just be back as they were that night in Suba; the night he brought the daggers! We knew our own hearts then, and that was all we needed to know. 'Give back the miry solitude—'

Suddenly her melancholy thoughts were interrupted by a cry of 'Maia! Where are you?' It was a man's voice—one that she remembered well enough but could not instantly put a name to. She stood up, and as she did so caught sight of someone approaching from the direction of the house. As the voice called again, she realized why she had felt so much startled. It was an Urtan accent. Yet it was not—no, it was not Anda-Nokomis. For a moment she had thought it was, and now she felt disappointed that it wasn't. Fancy that! she thought. A moment later Eud-Ecachlon came running down the grassy path to the hammock and took her hands.

746

To Maia Eud-Ecachlon, a man in his mid-thirties, had always seemed old—certainly much older than any of his friends in Bekla. Though he associated with Elvair-ka-Virrion and other young Leopards on equal terms, she had always thought of him as a man nearer to the generation of Kembri, Sendekar or Sarget—as indeed he was. She recalled his rather slow, stolid ways, his diffidence and the contempt with which Occula had once referred to him as 'a one-balled Urtan goat'. Yet she well remembered, too, the last time they had been together—how long ago it seemed! during that afternoon in Melekril last year, when, standing in for Occula, she had given him the time of his life. That had been great fun and she had enjoyed it herself—at least to the extent of feeling that she had done a good job and a bit more besides. She recalled, too, how warmly she had spoken of their meeting again on his next return to Bekla from Urtah; for she had been quite carried away by her own skill and success that afternoon. No, she thought, she had never disliked Eud-Ecachlon.

To her eyes he was looking, if anything, even older. There was more grey in his beard and somehow his thick-set body had about it an impalpable air of bearing a burden. Yet here he was, greeting her with warmth and cordiality—no trace of constraint or self-consciousness now—and obviously delighted to see her again.

She was pleased enough to see him, too; invited him to stay to dinner and felt glad when he accepted. He spoke, naturally, of the Valderra and of her celebrity in the empire. 'Urtah would die for you,' he said. 'Do you know that? If Karnat had over-run Urtah—' And she, of course, let pass the awkward topic of Urtah's present loyalty to Bekla and thanked him graciously, wondering how much he was not telling her about the dissidents who were doing their best to stir up trouble in the province.

They spoke, too, of the murder of the High Counsellor and the strangely unsuccessful search for the killers. Eud-Ecachlon enquired after Occula and seemed distressed when Maia replied that she could not tell what might have become of her after the arrests.

'Poor girl!' he said. 'I suppose they must have done away with her. What a shame! She had such style, hadn't she? I don't mind telling you, that night when she made Ka-Roton stab himself I was terrified; but I must admit he *had* asked for it. Got a bit more than he bargained for, didn't he?'

Later, when dinner was over, she showed him Randronoth's miniature, carved cabinet; for she remained continually delighted by it and could not resist showing it off, though she said nothing about where it had come from. Eud-Ecachlon took it in his hands and admired it politely, though without any very close examination, so that she perceived what she could have guessed—that such things did not mean much to him and were rather beyond his powers of appreciation. Well, but all the same, they'd come her way a lot less than his, she thought. Although she'd not been brought up among beautiful things, she could nevertheless feel naturally thrilled by something as rare and marvellous as this. She thought of the Thlela and their dance of the Telthearna on the night of the Rains banquet in Kembri's house. She had never before seen the Thlela, yet she had needed no teaching that night.

It was while Eud-Ecachlon was still holding the cabinet in his hands and at any rate giving the appearance of examining it that he remarked, with no particular alteration of expression or manner, 'My father's ill, you know.'

'The High Baron, Euda? I'm very sorry to hear it. I hope it's not serious?'

He closed the little doors and latched them. 'Well, he's old, you know: I'm afraid he may not recover. Everyone in Urtah thinks the same, really.'

'I know you both love him—you and Bayub-Otal. And you're the heir, of course. It must be a worrying time for you, as well as a sad one.' And then, in her way of often coming straight out with anything that entered her mind, 'What's brought you back to Bekla, then, at such a time as this? I s'pose you have to see Kembri and the Council, do you, on behalf of your father?'

'Yes, well—that, I suppose.' He put the cabinet back in its place and sat down. 'Urtah's not an easy province to govern, you know.'

'Well, you can't very well try another one, can you?'

He looked up with a puzzled expression, as though taking what she had said seriously and considering it. He'd always been a bit slow, she recalled. 'I was only teasing, Euda. I'm sorry you've got all these problems, honest I am. I cert'nly wouldn't like to have to govern a province—any province.'

'Oh—wouldn't you? Wouldn't you really?' He looked up at her earnestly, with a kind of concern in his voice. He really was a funny old chap, she thought.

'Well, that's one thing I'm not likely to find myself doing, so I needn't worry, need I? Euda, tell me, Anda-Nokomis—that's to say, Bayub-Otal—will they let him out, do you think? Is that what you came to talk to me about? Could I help? I mean, if your poor old father's dying, like you say—'

'Well, that's one thing, that's part of it, yes.' He paused. 'Yes, of course, I came to see Kembri. Urtah's a divided province and that's its trouble, I suppose; and it's the Leopards' trouble too—they can't rely on it as they'd like to. Suba—it was Kembri and Fornis who sold it to Karnat, you know. Then my brother tried to get it back for himself—and the price was

748

helping Karnat to take Bekla.' (But he must know I know all this, she thought.) 'And he'd have succeeded, too, if you hadn't stopped him. What that would have meant for Urtah nobody knows, do they, since it didn't happen?'

As Ogma came in to clear away the dinner, Maia led Eud-Ecachlon back into the garden.

'But all most people in Urtah want is a quiet life,' he continued, as they strolled down towards the Barb. 'Like most people anywhere, I suppose. You see, it's eight or nine years now since Suba was given to Karnat, and what's Suba to an Urtan farmer with his beasts to feed and his harvest to get in? But then, on the other hand, there's my poor old father. He loves Bayub-Otal, and ever since the fight at Rallur he's been breaking his heart to think of him shut up in that fortress at Dari-Paltesh. I believe that's what's killing him—the uncertainty. We've been entreating Kembri for months to pardon Bayub-Otal, simply so that the old man can die in peace. But Kembri doesn't trust us, it seems. He doesn't trust Urtah not to try to regain Suba, not to use Bayub-Otal against Bekla.'

'And you want *me* to try to persuade him: is that it?'

'Oh, no, Maia. No, no, that isn't why I came at all.' Eud-Ecachlon came to a kind of indeterminate stop in his walk, looking down and kicking with one foot at the grass. 'They all think the world of you in Urtah, you know. Oh, yes, everybody does, I assure you.'

'Well, I must say you do surprise me, Euda, saying that. I'd have thought—well, you know—the girl who put paid to poor Anda-Nokomis—'

'Oh, no, Maia, no; the girl who stopped the bloodshed and saved Urtah from Karnat. That was what you did it for, wasn't it? That's what I was told you've always said, anyway; that you did it to stop the bloodshed.'

'So I did. I've nothing against Anda-Nokomis—leastways, not any more. I'd be real glad to hear as he'd been let out. Time 'twas all forgot, I reckon.'

They had almost reached the shore, and she turned aside to that same marble seat where she had sat to listen to Randronoth's emissary Seekron.

'Of course,' said Eud-Ecachlon, looking out across the water, 'I've never been married, you know. I was betrothed to Fornis once—did you know that? It was—oh, long ago now, when we were both young; before her father died, and before the Leopards came to power. I was in love with her. Can you believe that? I thought she was wonderful—a girl like a goddess. Her father, Kephialtar of Paltesh—he wanted the marriage, but she didn't. She took her father's boat on the Zhairgen and sailed it two hundred miles to Quiso. You've heard the story, I expect.'

'I've—yes, well, I've heard something about it, Euda, of course. But

749

'twas all before I was born, you know. Want my opinion, though, I reckon you were lucky. Married to Fornis? Doesn't bear thinking about, does it?'

He gave a short laugh. 'You're right, Maia, of course. But somehow that business knocked the stuffing out of me. You know—to be made a fool of, publicly, by someone you love, when you're young and—well, ardent, I suppose you'd say. Somehow I never could face the idea of marriage after that. Of course it's always disappointed my father; worried him, too. The succession, you know.'

Maia, while not unsympathetic, was now beginning to wonder how she could tactfully bring about his departure, for she had half-promised Mil-vushina a visit that afternoon. She had been afraid that after dinner he might make advances to her, perhaps reminding her how she had once been all fervour, speaking of his return and crying 'Soon, soon, soon!' However, he hadn't, which saved a lot of trouble. Perhaps now was the time to ask him to be sure to join her supper-party the evening after tomorrow and bid him good-bye until then. She began 'Euda—'

But he was still speaking. 'I've always known I haven't really got what anyone would call great powers of leadership—not for a ruler, that is. People don't actually dislike me, but they don't fall down and offer to die for me, either; not like the Terekenalters for Karnat, or even the Subans for Bayub-Otal, come to that. But with a girl like you—well, they'd only have to see you, wouldn't they?'

She was still preoccupied with what she had been about to say. 'I'm sorry, Euda, I'm afraid I wasn't just exactly following you.'

He turned beside her on the seat and took her hand.

'My father would rest in peace. And you—you've got dangerous enemies here—it's common knowledge. You'd have none, would you? And it would do more than anything else to reconcile Urtah to Bekla.'

She started up from beside him. 'What are you saying, Euda?'

'And I've already put it to Kembri that as part of the arrangement—as a sign of the Leopards' approval and goodwill—he should release Bayub-Otal on a firm promise that he'll give no more trouble. Kembri said he felt sure you'd be delighted. You'd realize, he said, that the arrangement would solve all manner of problems, for you and for Bekla. But apart from that, to be the first lady in the land—'

'Euda, are you asking me to marry you?'

'I'm asking you to marry me and to become High Baroness of Urtah: for the sake of my people and myself. *That's* why I came to Bekla. And I assure you it's with my father's full approval.'

Moaning, she sank down on the grass, her face buried in her hands. 'O Cran! O Cran and Airtha!'

He stroked her hair. 'What's the matter? It's a shock, Maia, is that it? I suppose I've done it clumsily. I'm afraid I'm not stylish and dashing, like Elvair-ka-Virrion—I know that. I'm just a heldro; I don't know how you go about these things in Bekla—'

'No, no; 'tain't that. Oh, I dunno what to say! You can't want *me*—a girl from Sencho's—'

'Don't talk like that! That's all past and over! I'm speaking to the renowned, heroic beauty Maia Serrelinda.' Then, as she said no more, her face still in her hands, he went on, 'Are you afraid of it? You shouldn't be. Do you know what they think of you in Urtah? Let me tell you something. Only the other day, on my way here, I was talking to one of my principal tenants, a prosperous farmer down towards the south-west of the province. It seems his daughter knows you—a girl called Gehta. She met you when you were with Bayub-Otal on the way to Suba. "She saved us all," he said. "I'd give her half my farm if she asked me for it. Why, if once those Terekenalters had got across—"'

With a dazed air, Maia, who could scarcely take in what he was saying, rose to her feet. 'I—can I think it over, my lord? I need time—'

'Does it need thinking over? To be High Baroness of Urtah?'

'I—oh, don't think as I don't feel all the honour you're doing me, Euda. No, it's—'

'I'm old, is that it? The upper city's smart and gay—'

'Oh, don't talk like that, my lord! It's not right for a high baron's heir to be talking like that—'

'Perhaps it's not. No, you're right, of course. Well, you'd be able to change me a good deal, I expect; a girl like you. If ever there was a girl who was obviously favoured by the gods—'

Maia, realizing that with this rather awkward, insensitive man their talk could hardly come to an end unless she were to bring it about herself, made a supreme effort to regain her composure.

'You'll understand, my lord—Euda—that this is all a surprise to me; unexpected, like. I feel sort of confused. I can't talk any more just now. Would you mind leaving me?'

'But what shall I tell Kembri?' he asked.

At this she could flare up, her tongue loosened naturally and spontaneously.

'Kembri? What in Lespa's name has Kembri got to do with it? This is between you and me, isn't it?'

He took it without a retort. 'I'm sorry. When shall I see you again?'

'I'll send you a message. You in the same lodgings—down by the Tower of the Orphans?'

'No; but do you know, I went back there this morning—just to see the room where we were so happy together that afternoon last Melekril? You won't have forgotten?' She shook her head. 'I'm staying in Kembri's house this time.'

'Are you? I see.' But still she couldn't feel for him the contempt which would have risen up in Occula.

She kissed him on both cheeks. 'Good-bye. I'll send my soldier, like I said.'

He raised his palm to his forehead, did the heir of Urtah, and walked away through the garden, leaving the Serrelinda pacing back and forth on the grassy shore.

: 75 :

AND GETS AN ANSWER

She could not sleep. The silence and the clear, bright moonlight seemed as though enclosing and holding her fixed, immobile—like a stone in the jam, she thought wryly. Every now and then would sound faintly the voice of the watchman on the Peacock Wall. Once she heard swans' wings overhead, and once a quick, harsh clamour as something alarmed the duck on the Barb. Whatever shall I do? she thought. What shall I do?

She had said nothing to Milvushina. She had not the least doubt that if she were to tell her about Zen-Kurel, Milvushina would be sympathetic and her secret would remain safe. No, it wasn't that. It was, rather, that she could not bear the highly probable prospect of Milvushina advising her to forget Zen-Kurel—advice which anyone would give, or so it seemed to her. That was beyond question, she thought, the advice she would get from Occula. She writhed to imagine Occula's generous, unselfish delight at the news of Eud-Ecachlon's proposal. 'High Baroness of Urtah, banzi? You're jokin'!' Yes, High Baroness of Urtah—a sixteen-year-old peasant girl from the Tonildan Waste. And not only on account of her beauty— not this time. She remembered how she had told Zenka, that night in Melvda-Rain, of her resentment that everything seemed to happen to her on account of her beauty, and how easily and confidently he had taken it in his stride and set it aside. 'You wouldn't like it much if I said you weren't beautiful.' And then—oh, how her tears fell at the memory!—he'd made love to her again—like a hero, like a god, like an overflowing fountain of joy and sincerity and—yes, regard—the like of which she hadn't known existed. 'When it comes, my girl,' old Drigga had said to her once, 'you won't have to worry about whether it's real or not. True love's like lightning—there's no doubt about it.' No, she thought wretchedly, *no* doubt about it. What am I to do? O Lespa, what am I to do?

Kembri had been clever, she thought: he was an adroit politician. And—yes—in his own grim way he was being kind to her—as kind as he was capable of being to anybody. She was as sure as she could well be that the idea had originated with him and not with Eud-Ecachlon. The very way Eud-Ecachlon had put it was enough to tell her that. And to do Kembri justice, he'd given her clear warning. Besides, to himself it must seem that he was treating her generously indeed. The marriage offered the solution to several problems, a most shrewd stroke of policy from every angle, public and private; to say nothing of the confidence he must feel in her as suitable for such a position from Bekla's point of view. By implication it was a bigger compliment than she could ever have expected to be paid to her. And Eud-Ecachlon—that decent, dull, not-too-sure-of-himself man, fated but not gifted to be a High Baron, burdened with the memory of an unhappy, ludicrous failure in love which had clouded him for years—he stood to get a bride whom thousands throughout the empire would give their eyes for.

So much for the protagonists. But politically, Kembri would have disposed, smoothly and irreproachably, of his greatest stumbling-block to Milvushina as Sacred Queen. He would have no need, now, to run the risk of killing a girl whose murder, even if only suspected, would bring the whole city about his ears; while from the point of view of the Leopards the Serrelinda ought to prove just the thing for Urtah. The Urtans would be delighted and flattered to get her. She would attract their loyalty and strengthen Eud-Ecachlon's position as High Baron. She might even, in some unforeseen way or other (if Karnat were to die, say, and the power of Terekenalt weaken), prove contributory to bringing about a peaceful re-unification of Suba with Urtah. There would be plenty of older people in Kendron-Urtah who remembered Nokomis. Kembri could not, of course, be aware of her, Maia's, actual blood-relationship to Nokomis, but the odds were that he had already learned of the striking physical resemblance. Yet the blood-relationship, if she were to reveal it, would constitute no bar to her marriage with Eud-Ecachlon. They were cousins. His father had been her aunt's lover; nothing more than that. Indeed, bearing in mind Nokomis's enormous celebrity, this would enhance, not detract from her status in Urtah.

Whereas if she were to refuse Eud-Ecachlon, there could be only one possible conclusion drawn by Kembri, the Council and the entire Leopard faction—that she had set her heart on becoming Sacred Queen at all hazards and reckoned she could achieve it by relying on the support of the people even against the Lord General. Well, she thought, maybe she could, at that, if she'd been cast in the mould of Fornis. Yet beloved of Lespa or not, she knew very well that she entertained no least desire to be Sacred Queen.

Now, for the first time, as she lay tossing restlessly, with the moonlight creeping across the floor, there came into her heart glimmerings of doubt: not of her love for Zen-Kurel—no, nor of his for her—but of its ultimate attainability. The fear of death—the fear of death as an imminent and actual probability—is a terrible thing, twisting and forcing the inward eye like a kind of distorting lens. In face of the fear of death, an alternative which would otherwise have seemed beyond bearing becomes at least endurable, while what was once felt as merely tedious or irksome appears positively attractive. Poor Maia had little doubt what would become of her, one way or another, if she were to refuse Eud-Ecachlon.

If only she had known anything at all of Zen-Kurel—simply his whereabouts! If she could have been sure of nothing more than that he was alive, then, she thought, she would also have known her answer. But to know nothing—nothing—

'What?' said the Fear of Death, squatting, hands clasped round bony knees, in the shadow under the window across the room. 'A Katrian boy you were with for—how long? Three hours? You must understand, Maia, that I've nothing whatever against you; but for a girl of your origins to be asked in all earnest to become High Baroness of Urtah, and reject it for the ridiculous, out-of-the-question possibility of somehow regaining a foreign lad who made love to you and was gone almost at once! Who may be anywhere, who may be dead: well, to be frank I thought you had more sense. I couldn't protect you, you know—'

'But I haven't any heart for it!' she cried out to the horrible shadow. 'High Baroness? What's Urtah to me, or a man who couldn't even see anything particularly beautiful about my cabinet of the fishes? And do you realize he never even said he loved me? Were you there? Do you remember what he called it? He called it "the arrangement"! Yes, "the arrangement"! Three hours—three days—what's it matter? What matters is the actual, physical memory of my Zenka—the things he said to me, the sound of his voice, the feel of his hands, what it was like to be with him, what it was like to know we understood and loved and respected each other! And I know what it would be like to *live* with him, too. I'd never have to be pretending to be something I'm not—not with him I wouldn't!'

'And then, you see, there's Fornis,' went on the Fear of Death, clicking slightly in moving to a more comfortable position against the wall. 'I'm sure you haven't forgotten Fornis, have you? *Kembri* as an enemy—well, I suppose at a pinch you could try going on your knees to Kembri. But Fornis, my dear! I mean, won't she be *delighted* to hear that you rejected Eud-Ecachlon in order to try to supplant her as Sacred Queen? For of course that's what she *will* think, no danger. Oh, I know it's the middle of the night and all that, but really I've only got your good at heart. I mean, you do remember, do you, those bodies hanging by the road when you and Occula were coming up to Bekla last year? And you remember Fornis getting back from the temple, do you, with the blood all over her arms yum yum? And you're completely defenceless, you see. Oh, yes, of course, I know about the comet; not quite so bright tonight, by the way, have you noticed—?'

'O Cran, let me alone!' she screamed silently. 'I'll do it! I'll do it! I'll tell them tomorrow! O Zenka! Zenka! If only I knew where you were! If only you were here to save me and take me away! But how can I die—yes, *die*!—for nothing but a memory?'

In spite of her near-hysterical fear, Maia did not lack awareness of the enormous consequence to herself of the decision she was now taking. She realized very well that she had been subdued by terror to conclude that, while she could and would have risked all for a realistic hope of recovering her flesh-and-blood Zenka, she was not equal to facing virtually certain death by murder for the sake of a love with no discernible hope or future. This was retreat; abandonment; surrender. She had a sensation of stepping down from some high, bright place into twilight, into a listless, sluggish world like that of oxen, a world where she did not want to be and had nowhere to go. She knew clearly enough that she was relinquishing the hope which had upheld her and prompted her actions ever since that night in Melvda-Rain. For months past she had known what she longed for, and now she had turned away from it.

And there were no compensations. If she had been five or six years older she might, perhaps, have comforted herself with the prospect of becoming the greatest lady in Urtah, a figure of power and consequence in the empire and one probably well able, with experience and the exercise of tact and discretion, to control and give guidance to a husband who would be only too glad to receive it. But what could all that mean to sixteen-year-old Maia, even had she been able to envisage it?

She fell asleep at last, just as first light was breaking and the mynahs and starlings were beginning to murmur along the ledges outside. She dreamt of the river and the soldiers who had carried her to Sendekar, but when she woke could find little meaning or comfort in the dream. Poor Maia was young enough to feel ashamed of what she was going to do; nor did it occur to her that this shame was creditable.

Brero, like the good fellow he was, could sense that something was wrong. He stood fidgeting on the little terrace as Maia, who had summoned him, at first remained silent, hesitating for the last time before sending her irreclaimable message. There were three possible ways of doing it. (Ah, rope, knife or poison, she thought bitterly; these being the options traditionally offered in the empire to someone compelled to commit suicide.) Either she could send Eud-Ecachlon a letter of acceptance, or she could herself go to Kembri's house and tell him; or else she could invite him to come and see her again. Not having much confidence for writing a letter (and not, of course, wishing to employ a scribe) and having no particular desire to encounter Kembri, she had decided on the last, and accordingly had packed Ogma off to the markets of the lower city for the makings of a slap-up dinner. It really was like being executed, she thought. If it had to happen, then it ought to be endured with style and courage. Yet now, with Brero waiting uneasily before her, she hung back, looked at the ground, drummed her fingers on her knee, began to speak and then broke off.

'Brero, I want you—I want you to—'

'Yes, säiyett?'

These were the last moments of her youth, she thought. She had only to speak, now, and her life would cease to be her own, for ever. Her tongue was like a knife, about to cut away all that was past, which would there-upon float away and disappear behind her. There'd be no delay, either; she felt sure of that. Kembri would not lose any time in making the news of the betrothal public throughout the city.

She stood up and turned aside, filled with an uncontrollable anguish. In the act of trying to speak her lips trembled and for a few moments her sight actually clouded over. She realized that Brero had taken her arm and led her the few steps back to the bench.

'Very awkward times, these, säiyett; very awkward for everyone.'

She looked up into his rugged, kindly face, not sure whether he meant something specific or was only trying as best he could to express a vague sympathy.

'I don't know whether you've heard the news, säiyett, but what they're saying in our mess is that Santil-kè-Erketlis has actually defeated Lord Elvair-ka-Virrion somewhere in Yelda, and our lads are falling back into Lapan. You wouldn't happen to know, I suppose, whether that's true?'

What's that to me? she thought. 'No, I haven't heard anything, Brero. If I do I'll pass it on to you.'

He hesitated. 'Säiyett, I can see you're a bit upset, like; and that's none of my business, of course. But for what it's worth, I'd like to warn you—though I hope you won't tell anyone it came from me—that I'm not the only fellow in our mob as reckons there's going to be a whole lot of trouble, and 'fore very much longer too.'

He paused, but she was too much preoccupied to prompt him.

'Only we sometimes get to hear things, säiyett, before they're given out by the heralds, you see; and sometimes, come to that, things that never *are* given out at all. Just, lads come back from the front and tell their mates. Well, you see, it's only that I'm hoping they'll let me go on being one of them as looks after you. I'm no coward—I've seen plenty of action since I first joined up—but it's a good soldier who knows how to look after himself, as they say. If you could use your influence—that's if you're satisfied, säiyett, as I hope you are—I'm sure I'll be very grateful.'

Recalled to her self-possession by this harmless and understandable bit of self-seeking, she smiled.

'Of course I will, Brero; don't worry. Now could you please be so kind as to go to the Lord General's house, ask for Lord Eud-Ecachlon of Urtah and tell him I'll be honoured if he'll come to dinner with me a little after noon today?'

'But whatever kept you so long, Ogma? Oh, yes, I'm sure you must have taken great care to get all the best you could find. I know you always do—those brillions look lovely, and so do the trout—only now it's so late in the morning. Lord Eud-Ecachlon will be here quite soon and you'll need all of an hour to get dinner ready. Do make a start as quick as you can, there's a dear.'

'Well, I *would* have been back a lot sooner, Miss Maia,' said Ogma, her voice taking on the querulous, defensive tone with which Maia had become familiar, 'if only it hadn't been for being bothered and pestered and—and followed all up the street and made to look that much of a fool until I didn't know if I was coming or going. And when you're a slave there's nothing you can do about it and—and 'tisn't likely, miss, that anyone's going to interfere to help the likes of *me*,' ended poor Ogma, who was obviously on the point of tears. 'It's all right for some, as has soldiers to pull them about in jekzhas—'

'Now, Ogma,' said Maia quickly, though inwardly she was fuming at this additional waste of time; it *would* have to happen now, she thought. 'Just try to calm yourself! It's all over now. Were they street louts, or what? You tell me who it was and I promise you I'll see they get something to remember. Did you tell them who you were and that you work for me?'

'Why, he knows very well as I work for you, miss. 'Course he does! That's why he was on pestering me and wouldn't go away. I had to call out to the guards on the Peacock Gate, else I couldn't have got away from him or got back here at all.'

Who the hell could this be? thought Maia. Not Randronoth—no, nor anyone else she could think of: presumably some boorish stranger from one of the outer provinces, besotted by having got a sight of the Serrelinda and ready to try anything. Well, there'd be an end to all that soon enough now.

757

'You say he knows you work for me?'

'Well, 'course he does, miss. That's why he wouldn't go away. "You take me through the gate with you," he says. "They know who you are and they'll let me through if you tell them the Serrelinda wants to see me urgently." So I says, "No," I says. "The Serrelinda's got a dinner party today," I says, "and you've made me late as it is. What I'll do, I'll tell her you're here," I says, " 'cos last time she said I ought to have let her know that much, but if you think I'm going to take a branded man through the gate into the upper city," I says—'

'Ogma! A *branded* man?'

'Yes, that there Sednil, miss, of course! He—'

'Sednil? You mean to say he's back here—already?'

'I don't know nothing about back already, miss, but that's who it was.'

'Ogma, never mind about the dinner! Just put all those things in the kitchen, quickly: then come back here. I'll write you a note for the guards on the gate. You're to go back at once, find Sednil and bring him here as quick as you can, understand? No, don't say any more; just do as I tell you!'

Snatching up her brush and ink, she sat down and began with laborious care, 'The barer of this worront is Sednil of Dari . . .'

'But Sednil, what brought you back so soon? I wasn't expecting you for—oh, for weeks! You've never been to Urtah, surely?'

'No,' he replied. 'No, I didn't go to Urtah; I just went to Dari.'

They were sitting side-by-side on the roof. Shortly after the flustered and thoroughly disgruntled Ogma had left on her errand, Brero had returned from the Lord General's house with the message that Eud-Ecachlon would certainly come as soon as possible, but regretted that he might be delayed by an important council meeting about to be held at the Barons' Palace. He had not yet appeared, and Maia had taken Sednil up to the roof, partly because it was the most secluded place in her small house and partly in order to make sure of giving a convincing impression that she was not at home for the moment, having had to go out for a short time—which was what Ogma had been told to say.

'But why? Oh, Sednil, you mean you've come back without finding anything out? After I'd given you all that money—'

'No, no,' he answered. 'I didn't need to go to Urtah, Maia: I found out all there is to be found out in Dari.'

His manner, grave and unsmiling, roused in her a quick trepidation. 'You mean—you mean Zen-Kurel's dead? You've found out that he's *dead*?'

'No, he's not dead. He's a prisoner in the fortress at Dari. There were quite a few, you know—Terekenalters, Katrians, Subans as well—taken in the fight at Rallur. Bayub-Otal was one of them, as everybody knows. Well, your Zen-Kurel was another. Apparently he was fighting like a perfect devil when he slipped and went down in the mud. Someone noticed from his badges that he was a staff officer and reckoned he might be worth a ransom, so they jumped on him and took him prisoner.'

'How did you find this out?'

'Well, when I told my old mother what I was up to—she sends you her blessings, by the way. She was more than grateful for the money—she said she knew there were some Katrian prisoners in the fortress and why didn't I check on them for a start, before I went to Urtah. I couldn't see there was any danger in asking straight out, so I went there and asked to see one of the captains of the fortress. The man I saw was Durakkon's younger son. He's no sort of a soldier at all, but he's a very decent, kind-hearted sort of fellow. Just as well—a real dyed-in-the-wool officer would probably have thrown me out. I told him my story about having known this Zen-Kurel when we'd both been banzis in Dari, and he told me at once—well, what I've already told you. Zen-Kurel's reasonably well, as far as I can make out—as well as anyone can be in that place—and Bayub-Otal too.'

'Then—then surely they'll all be let out, won't they, as soon as things have quietened down? I could send him a letter, couldn't I, 'specially if you say this son of Durakkon's is so nice? Or—oh, Sednil, I could ransom him myself, surely?'

'You might have tried, perhaps.' He gazed at her sombrely.

'What d'you mean?'

He took her hand. 'Maia, there's something more, and this is the bad bit, I'm afraid. Fornis is in Dari.'

'Fornis? Well, I know she is. What about it?'

'She's got the whole of Paltesh under her control, and it's rumoured that Han-Glat, who's in command of the fortress, has become her lover. That's what she intended all along, I dare say: Han-Glat's about the one man who *could* stand up to Kembri, you see.'

'Her *lover?*'

'Well, whether he is or not, no one's in any doubt that he's ready to do anything she wants him to. She's got Paltesh, she's got the fortress and she's got the prisoners. No one knows for certain what she's planning, but when I left, people were saying that she was in touch with some of the runaway slave bands in Belishba.'

Maia shook her head uncomprehendingly.

'Well, you probably know more about Fornis than I do, Maia: I only know she's a woman who's ready to stick at nothing; and very bold and cunning, too. I think what she may really be trying to do is to make

759

Kembri so nervous that he'll tell Durakkon to invite her to come back and confirm her as Sacred Queen again. And if he won't, she's perfectly capable of seceding from the empire and putting Paltesh at Karnat's disposal. At the least that would worry the Leopards very badly, but at the best—from her point of view, that is—she could hope to return to Bekla with Karnat and his army. That's to say, she could *give* him the empire!'

'Oh, damn the empire!' said Maia. 'The prisoners! The prisoners, Sednil—'

'Why, the prisoners are one of her strongest bargaining counters, don't you see? She's got Bayub-Otal and something like sixty or seventy Katrians and Terekenalters, including two or three of Karnat's best officers. She means to sell herself and them—and Paltesh—to her own best advantage, that's certain.'

Maia, white-faced, fists clenched, stood up, staring out over the parapet of the roof across the lower city. 'I don't care! I don't care for basting Fornis, or Han-Glat or the whole damned lot of them. Now I know Zenka's alive I'm going to get him out if it's the last thing I do!'

There was a long pause. 'Maia,' said Sednil at last, standing up and coming over to her side, 'would you think about marrying me? I've loved you, you know, ever since—ever since that morning in the temple. Do think about it seriously. A man of your own sort—someone you understand and who understands you. We could get down into Chalcon together before anyone missed you, and you'd be safe there. I know we might have a bit of a struggle to begin with, but I'd look after you and keep you safe—'

Turning, she laid a finger on his lips.

'I'm sorry, Sednil! I really am, because I like you and respect you. But it's not—well, it's just not what the gods say in my heart, that's all. Anyway, I told you before—Nennaunir loves you sincerely and you couldn't do better.' She paused. 'I must go downstairs now. Do you see—oh, careful! He might look up!—do you see that man waiting down there in the garden? I'm going to refuse *him*, too, even if it costs me my life; and I reckon—I reckon it probably will. Can you please wait up here until Ogma comes for you?' Embracing him, she kissed him warmly on the lips. 'Dear Sednil, thank you for helping me: I'll never forget it. I know what I'm going to do now: I didn't before; I only thought I did. So that takes care of everything between us—except for this.' And she handed him a small, plain wooden box.

'What's that, then?' he asked, in the dulled, heedless tone of someone upset and preoccupied.

'The other two thousand meld. Had you forgotten?'

*

760

Eud-Ecachlon's air certainly did not much resemble the conventional notion of a man in love. As Maia came up to him in the garden he smiled and took her hands; yet there was nothing particularly happy or eager in his manner, which seemed, indeed, abstracted; nor did he compliment her on her appearance or her dress. She knew him, of course, for an impassive man, not readily stirred—and anyway, she thought, 'twasn't as though she was going to say anything likely to make him start turning cartwheels. Yet all the same it nettled her—it affronted her sense of what was fitting—that he should to all appearances be so little on tenterhooks for her answer. She had left Sednil in tears, poor lad. From the look of things, she didn't reckon there were going to be many more shed round here. Well, that'd certainly make it easier; but all the same it annoyed her.

He drank down his first goblet almost at once, like a man who needed it. She smiled, making a little pantomime of looking in and finding it empty. As she picked up the wine-jug to re-fill it, he asked her 'Have you got any djebbah, Maia?'

'Djebbah? Yes, of course, if you want it. I'll call Ogma.'

He drained his first tot of djebbah, too; and then sat down, looking rather more relaxed.

'I'm afraid you must have had a bit of a bad old morning, Euda. Everything all right?'

'Anything but, Maia; though I wouldn't say it to anyone except you.'

'You mean the council didn't go well?'

'How could it? The news is about as bad as it could well be.'

'Why, what's wrong with the news, then?' asked Maia rather carelessly, as though the news were some sort of dish which Eud-Ecachlon had found not altogether to his liking.

He paused, seeming embarrassed, leaning forward as he tossed a handful of serrardoes one by one to a duck which had wandered up from the lakeside.

'Elvair-ka-Virrion,' he said at length. 'He's a friend of yours, isn't he?'

'Well, he's always been very nice to me. Yes, I'd say he *was* a friend.'

'What would you say if I told you he was a coward?'

'Well, if you really want to know, Euda, I dunno as I'd be so very much bothered. Men are always going on about fighting and cowards and victory and courage and—oh, all that stuff. Elvair's got nice manners and a kind heart—I know that much. Why; *are* you calling him a coward?'

'Well, it certainly looks that way, I'm afraid. And you may find that you've *got* to be bothered before long, whether you like it or not.'

She could have hit him. 'Well, my lord, seeing as you don't seem to have anything better to talk about, p'raps you'd better tell me.'

But even this, to all appearances, went over his head. 'Well, the news from Yelda is very bad. In fact, they're not going to give it out in the lower city at all. It seems that Elvair-ka-Virrion, after entirely failing to come to any sort of grips with Erketlis in Chalcon, decided to fall back on Ikat Yeldashay for supplies and a general re-fit. He thought—and I think Kembri thought, too, though he hasn't said so—that once he was clear out of Chalcon, Erketlis would leave it at that and go home. But he didn't.'

'Oh, didn't he?' asked Maia politely, since it seemed to be expected of her.

'No. He must be a very remarkable leader, that man,' said Eud-Ecachlon. 'He kept almost all his army together—apparently only a few went home— and made a forced march—something like fifty miles—through absolutely desperate country in less than two days. They got across the Thettit–Ikat road south of Elvair-ka-Virrion, so that he had to attack them.'

'But I thought that was what Elvair wanted all along?' asked Maia.

'Well, so did he, but by that time his men were in pretty poor heart. Anyhow, the long and the short of it is that he was beaten.' He hesitated, and then went on, 'But according to the officer who brought the news, he needn't have been. This man—Gel-Ethlin, his name is—made his report at the meeting this morning. He was so angry and upset that he couldn't contain himself—couldn't stick to what he'd been told to say. He couldn't even hold himself in on account of Kembri being there.'

'Why, what did he say, then?' asked Maia.

'Well, what it amounted to was that Elvair-ka-Virrion had made a complete mess of the whole battle. Gel-Ethlin said he gave no leadership at all and—well, more or less ran away, as far as I can make out. And then he broke off the action, even though his captains wanted to go on. Gel-Ethlin said to Kembri, "I'm very sorry, my lord, to have to report this, and believe me I wouldn't say it if I didn't feel I had to. If one word of it's proved a lie, you can hang me in the Caravan Market." '

Even Maia was startled by this. 'What did Kembri say?'

'Nothing. He thanked Gel-Ethlin as though he'd been reporting a fire or a broken bridge, and then he sent an immediate order to Randronoth to call up every available man in Lapan and go to Elvair's relief. But after what I've heard this morning, I very much doubt whether Elvair will be able to retain the command. I think his own people may very likely depose him in the field.'

'But Randronoth, you said?'

'Well, you see, even what I've told you's not the worst of it. It seems that after the battle Elvair-ka-Virrion, with the choice of falling back on Thettit or Bekla, chose Bekla, and his force is retreating now through eastern Lapan. But Erketlis has given out that what *he* intends, in the light of this victory, is nothing less than to take Bekla and destroy the Leopards—the slave-traders, as he calls them. He's had it proclaimed every-where from Ikat to Herl.'

Ogma appeared to announce dinner, and Maia, taking her guest's arm, led him back up the garden.

'What it comes to, Maia, I'm afraid, is that the whole empire's riddled with disaffection against the Leopards. Erketlis is the most serious, of course, but there's a slave rising half out of control in Belishba—or that's what it sounds like. Fornis has taken over Paltesh to play her own game—whatever it may be—and that damned Lenkrit's sneaking up and down in western Urtah, making all the trouble he can.'

He slit his trout, took out the tail, backbone and head and put them on the plate Ogma was holding ready.

'I'll tell you, I honestly wonder whether Durakkon and Kembri will be able to keep a roof over their heads in this storm. I say this to you, Maia, though I wouldn't say it to anyone else. I believe all the provinces are hanging back, waiting to see which way it's going to go. If Erketlis isn't beaten soon—' He shrugged his shoulders.

Could she herself make any use of this? thought Maia. If it were really the beginning of what Occula had called 'the biggest shine for a thousand years', did it offer her any practical hope of getting to Dari—to the for-tress—and then—? Perhaps someone—perhaps even Durakkon's son, if he had such a kind heart—could be cajoled or bribed? Yet she felt, desperately, the limitations of her youth and inexperience. Might Occula be persuaded to take the risk and escape with her? After all, Occula's chances of killing the Sacred Queen might very well be as good in Dari as in Bekla. Oh, ah, she thought, and as deadly dangerous too. Occula's wits, Occula's experi-ence, Occula's help—the price to be paid for these, like enough, would be a share in the appalling venture to which Occula had devoted herself. Well, so be it. Now that she knew he was alive, she was ready to go to any lengths for Zenka.

She realized that Eud-Ecachlon had apparently asked her some question. He was looking at her enquiringly and seemed a little put out.

'I said "I wonder what you think": or weren't you listening?'

'Oh, I'm sorry, Euda, I'm afraid my thoughts *had* wandered a bit, just for a moment. But after all, it's understandable, isn't it? You've told me enough this morning to worry anybody.'

It would have been nice, she thought, if he had tried to give her some reassurance; spoken a few comforting words—yes, even if they'd been so much moonshine—something like 'he was sure everything was going to turn out all right; she mustn't worry'—the sort of thing men usually said to girls when things were looking bad. However, he didn't.

'I was saying I thought it would all depend on the response Kembri gets from the various provinces. He's summoned every provincial governor except Randronoth—Randronoth's got his orders already, of course—to come to Bekla and renew their oath of allegiance to Durakkon. They've been told to be ready to tell him how many men they can send. What I asked was whether you had any idea how many Tonilda might be able to send. You come from down that way, don't you?'

'Yes, but—well, my lord, I mean, I wouldn't know about a thing like that; not someone like me.'

'Paltesh won't help, of course—not now Fornis is there. But Bel-ka-Trazet's already on his way from Ortelga, so I've heard; and believe it or not, there's someone coming from Suba.'

'From *Suba*, my lord? Why, how can that be? Suba still belongs to King Karnat, doesn't it? You don't mean to say as he's allowing someone to come to Bekla to talk about helping the Leopards?'

'Well, I don't know any more than I've told you,' answered Eud-Ecachlon, as Ogma took away the remains of his fish plate and put in front of him a dish of pork, with shallots and spiced brillions. 'The man who's coming—Kembri told us this morning—he isn't a baron or a governor at all, and he certainly hasn't been sent by Karnat. He's some sort of old medicine-man, or something. But apparently he commands such enormous respect all over Suba that when he said on his own account that he wanted to come to Bekla and talk to Durakkon, Karnat wasn't prepared to go the length of stopping him.'

'An old—*medicine*-man?' asked Maia, staring. 'Euda, what's his name, do you know?'

'Yes, I did hear it—wait a minute—yes; Nasada, that's it. Someone said that the Subans—why, what's the matter, Maia? Do you know him, or something?'

'Yes. Yes, I do!' She collected herself. 'Well, it's only just that when I was there I was taken bad, sort of, and he put me right, that's all.'

'Well, it's a small world, isn't it?' said Eud-Ecachlon. 'Did you like him? Is he really anything out of the ordinary or not?'

'If he's coming to Bekla I wouldn't—oh, no, I wouldn't want to miss the chance of meeting him again. Yes, I liked him very much.'

'Well, that won't be difficult,' replied Eud-Ecachlon. 'Our betrothal will have been announced, so of course you'll be able to meet any of the provincial governors and delegates you wish. In fact, I'm sure *they'll* all be very anxious to meet *you*. We ought to give a banquet, really. I'll mention it to Kembri—'

'Just a moment. Ogma, would you leave us, please, and shut the door behind you? What did you say, my lord?'

'I said I'd mention it to Kembri—'

'No, before that.'

'I said our betrothal will have been announced—'

'I'm afraid not, my lord. You never asked me for my answer, did you? I'm sorry if you took it for granted. I very much appreciate the honour you've done me, but I'm afraid my answer is no.'

He stared at her incredulously, looking completely nonplussed. '*What,* Maia?'

'I'm sorry, but I don't feel able to accept your offer, my lord.'

'You mean—you mean you're seriously rejecting the prospect—the certainty, that is—of becoming High Baroness of Urtah?'

'I'd really rather not discuss it or argue about it, my lord, if you don't mind. And I hope you won't ask me for reasons. I've thought about it very carefully and I don't feel able to become your wife.'

'Maia—I'd like to say "dear Maia"—you're very beautiful; and everyone knows that you're very brave, too. But you're also very young and—I hope you won't mind my saying this—not at all experienced. Have you talked this over with anyone and taken advice?'

'Forgive me, my lord; I don't have to answer that.'

'No, you don't *have* to: but I'm sure any sensible friend and well-wisher would tell you that you'd be going very much against your own best interests to refuse an offer—a future—like this.'

'Then I'm going against my own best interests, my lord. Don't let your pork get cold. Be a shame to waste it.'

'Maia, believe me, if you insist on this you'll be wasting a lot more. I don't want to frighten you, but it could prove a fatal mistake.'

'Fear would be a very bad reason for marriage, my lord.'

'Oh, Maia, I didn't mean that! But you're so young and you see everything—well, so black and white. This marriage would be much the best thing for you—and for me, too. You realize, don't you, that if you were an ordinary girl living in Bekla with her parents, they could tell you whom you were to marry and you'd be obliged to obey them?'

'Maybe, my lord; but as things are that doesn't happen to be the case.'

'Kembri might order you to marry, though.'

She paused a few moments, looking straight back at him. 'If you was to take me that way, my lord, I'm afraid I wouldn't reckon such a great lot to it; or to you, either.'

He was silent, toying with his pair of knives, first one and then the other. She got up and herself served him cheese and fruit, then went out to the kitchen and brought back the tray of little sweet dishes with which a Beklan dinner customarily ended. As she came in and closed the door he said, 'Maia, I must ask you this seriously. Is your real reason that you intend to become Sacred Queen? Because if it is—'

She answered him instantly and firmly. 'No, my lord, it's not.'

'But if you're still living here now, in this same way, at the end of this year, there's not the slightest doubt that the people will acclaim you, whether you wish it or otherwise. Have you thought of that?'

'My lord, you keep telling me I'm very young; and I haven't given you the back-answer as I could have. But yes, I *have* thought of it, and I'm afraid you must leave me to order my own affairs. I can only tell you again that I'm not planning to become Sacred Queen.'

'Then what *is* your idea of the future? Maia, I'm only thinking of your safety and welfare, believe me.'

The succession of grave, insensitive questions from a man old enough to be her father, whom she could hardly tell to go to hell, was beginning to have its effect. She clenched her hands and her voice rose.

'I've *told* you, my lord, as I don't want to talk about it n'*more*! Please let's stop now!'

'Well, if you say so, Maia, I must. But these are troubled times and I don't think you realize—I don't think you've got the slightest idea—what unscrupulous, ruthless people you'll be—er—disobliging. I thought you'd be *glad* to come and help me rule Urtah; to win the hearts of the people and restore unity there. Everyone would love you and honour you. A girl like you—well, from a poor home, if you don't mind my saying so—to become next thing to a queen—an important, influential figure in the empire—and you just say no—I don't understand it.' Then, suddenly, he broke out, 'Oh, damnation! And they'll all say *I* made a mess of it! I know that's what they'll say—'

'Who will, my lord?'

'Why, Kembri; and the Council—'

'Oh, I see. So it was Kembri as started all this, was it?'

'Yes. He told me he thought it would be an excellent thing both from your point of view and mine, and I absolutely agreed with him. It would solve all manner of problems—'

'I see. Well now, my lord, the banzi slave-girl's going to tell the middle-aged baron something he apparently doesn't know. Next time you're thinking of getting married, start by choosing a girl for yourself. And when you come to ask her, start by telling her you love her.'

'I really can't see that you've got anything to be so angry about, Maia—'

'There seems to be a lot you can't see, my lord.'

He sprang to his feet. 'Be careful how you make *me* angry—'

'*Me* make *you* angry? Lespa and Shakkarn! My lord, I wouldn't want either of us to lose our dignity. I've got a headache. Please finish your dinner: call the servant for anything you want. I'm going to lie down.'

NASADA GIVES ADVICE

At this season of the year the upstairs room adjacent to the Bramba Tower in the Barons' Palace—that same room in which Durakkon had been persuaded by Kembri and Sencho to consent to the killing of Enka-Mordet—was scarcely large or airy enough for ten men to confer together in comfort during the heat of the afternoon. Yet here they had been for half an hour already. The air had grown stale and heavy, for despite the height above the city there seemed to be no breeze. Durakkon, sweating under his robes of state, sat with one hand over his left eye, which had begun to hurt neuralgically. At the moment there was silence, for the Lord General, seated next to him, had just ceased speaking and was making notes and calculations with a stick of charcoal on a board.

The delegates were not seated formally, but here and there about the room. The governors of Kabin, Tonilda and Belishba sat side by side on the couch where Sencho had been accustomed to sprawl. Bel-ka-Trazet, his hands clasped about his drawn-up knees, was sitting in one of the window embrasures looking (thought Durakkon) like some ravaged kobold waiting sardonically for propitiation. Gel-Ethlin, in the undress uniform of the Beklan regiment, was at the other end of the table, next to Donnered, the representative of Sarkid (for Sarkid, like Urtah, was a province where Bekla maintained no governor). Eud-Ecachlon, who throughout the meeting had given the impression of being preoccupied and ill-at-ease, stood leaning against the door.

Despite Kembri's request, no representative had appeared on behalf of Gelt. None had been summoned from Paltesh; nor yet from Yelda, since the latter had effectively fallen to Santil-kè-Erketlis.

From time to time one man or another would glance towards the tenth person in the room; the oldest present, shock-haired, grizzled and silent, his sunken eyes gazing intently from his deeply-lined, brown face. He also, with his short, squat build, rather suggested to Durakkon some sort of goblin creature; yet—unlike Bel-ka-Trazet—one at the same time benign and magisterial, as though, while attending the meeting but not entirely of it, he was listening and even adjudicating from some detached, forbearing standpoint of his own. So far he had spoken only at the outset, when Durakkon had asked him to swear by Frella-Tiltheh the Inscrutable that he came in peace and would impart to Karnat nothing that he might hear about the forces, dispositions and intentions of Bekla. With this request he had at once complied in a manner which carried conviction to all present. This was Nasada, the renowned physician of Suba. Evidently the Lord

General had concluded that it would look better to grant than to refuse his request to attend.

'Captain Gel-Ethlin,' said Durakkon, at length breaking silence upon a nod from the Lord General, 'you've given us a very clear account of the difficulties our force met with in Chalcon, and I suppose we must also accept your account of what happened in the engagement with Erketlis on the Thettit–Ikat road. No!' he interjected quickly, as Gel-Ethlin seemed about to speak, 'I'm not suggesting that there was anything wrong or inaccurate in what you've told us, though I hope for your own sake that what you insisted upon saying about Lord Elvair-ka-Virrion won't turn out to have been malicious or exaggerated.'

'Men's lives, my lord—'

'Yes, yes; well, I know the Lord General has something to say in a moment about the future command. But first of all, I think you'd better go on to tell us what's known—that is, what the assessment was when you left—of Erketlis's present strength and intentions.'

'Well, my lord, we think that Erketlis's intentions have altered with his fortunes. He's a shrewd man and he knows how to seize an opportunity. We believe that at the beginning he probably intended nothing more than to defend Chalcon. But he seems to be very well informed about matters elsewhere. And also, of course, he was joined quite early on by young Elleroth of Sarkid, who brought him about five hundred irregulars—volunteers. No doubt it's Elleroth who's influenced him to go further.'

'Well, Elleroth's already a proscribed traitor, of course,' said Durakkon. 'He'll hang upside-down, Ban's son or no. You're not going to dispute that, I trust, Donnered?'

'I've no instruction from the Ban to do so, my lord,' replied the Sarkidian.

'We think,' continued Gel-Ethlin, 'that while Erketlis was following up our retreat from Chalcon, he realized he had a chance of making gains that would actually be worth more to him and his men than any harvest. Chalcon's not much of a corn-growing place, of course; but anyway, they didn't disband and obviously he must have persuaded them to attempt this dash for the Ikat road. They can't have slept for the best part of two days; and immediately after that we brought them to battle. And we could have beaten them, my lord,' cried Gel-Ethlin, 'if only—'

'Yes,' broke in Kembri gruffly, 'so you've said. But what's the position now?'

'The position now, my lord, is that Erketlis has taken Ikat Yeldashay—with all its resources, of course—and given out that he intends nothing less than the conquest of Bekla. He's pinning his hopes of popular support on his proclamation that he means to abolish slavery throughout the empire, except for prisoners taken in war. I haven't actually seen a copy of the proclamation, but I've talked to prisoners who have. What it boils down to, really, is the old heldro grievance. It starts by saying that taxation of the peasants in favour of the merchants is unjustly high, and then goes on that kidnapping and breeding for slavery have become an abuse and a danger—villages living in fear and so on, partly from the demands for slave-quotas and partly from gangs of runaway slaves turned bandit. Then it—'

'Yes, well,' said Kembri, 'we've heard all this, too. How does Erketlis stand, as you see it?'

'We've had refugee slave-dealers coming in from Ikat,' replied Gel-Ethlin. 'He's declared all slaves in Yelda free and offered enlistment to any who are ready to join him. Not only that, but immediately after the battle Elleroth led his own men about twenty miles into Tonilda, burnt the slave-farm at Orthid and brought most of the stock back with him. Apparently they actually carried the younger children on their shoulders. Their real purpose, I think, was probably to convince people that they're in earnest.

'Well, all this means, my lord, of course, that Erketlis has got a dangerously sizeable army down there now, even though half of them are untrained. He's training them as fast as he can and he's said in so many words that it's to take Bekla.'

'And Lord Elvair-ka-Virrion's force?' asked Durakkon.

'—Is moving westwards into Lapan, my lord, to put itself between Ikat and Bekla.'

'Had they received any Lapanese reinforcements from Lord Randronoth when you left?'

'None, my lord.'

'No doubt they will have by now: but in the light of what you tell us, that may not be enough to make sure of defeating Erketlis. That's what the Lord General's going to discuss now. Thank you, Captain Gel-Ethlin.'

'The first thing I want to settle,' said Kembri, 'is the command of the force in Lapan. I shall take it over myself as soon as possible, but meanwhile we need someone new, who wasn't in the defeat; someone who knows how to act quickly and ruthlessly.' He looked round the room. 'I don't think anyone's going to disagree about the choice. Lord Bel-ka-Trazet, I want you to go to Lapan at once and take over.'

It was always impossible to perceive any change of expression in the features of the High Baron of Ortelga. As everyone turned towards him, he swung his legs down from the window embrasure, pulled his veltron straight with a quick tug and for a few moments faced the Lord General without speaking.

'My lord,' he said at length, in his impaired, creaking voice. 'I'll waste no time in thanking you for the honour you do me. I don't wish to take the command for two reasons. First, I think Ortelga has already contributed enough. We sent you young Ta-Kominion and his men, and whatever may have happened I don't believe *they've* disgraced themselves or that they're likely to. But secondly, have you thought about the Deelguy? They know very well what's happening and I feel sure Erketlis is in touch with them. Ortelga has always been Bekla's main defence against the Deelguy and if you don't want them taking this chance to come pouring across the Telthearna, I think you'd do better to leave me in Ortelga.'

'Why shouldn't Ged-la-Dan command in Ortelga till you get back?' asked Durakkon.

'My lord, do you know why Ortelga remains loyal to Bekla? Because *I* do, principally. I was loyal to Senda-na-Say and I've been loyal to you. I personally believe that loyalty to be in Ortelga's best interests. But there are those who don't; those who dwell on the past, who pray for the return of Shardik the Bear, the power of God, and all manner of such-like nonsense. We're simple souls in Ortelga. I honestly believe you'd be taking me away from there at your peril.'

Kembri tugged at his beard, reflecting. 'Well, you may be right. I'd hoped to make this very well worth your while, but if you don't want the command you'd better not have it. I think you and I will have to consider this further in private, my lord,' he said to Durakkon, 'and confer the appointment tomorrow.' Then, without waiting for the High Baron's reply he went on, addressing the rest, 'Now, I want to make sure of the reinforcements that each of you has undertaken to raise. Kabin, five hundred. Tonilda, a thousand and a half. Urtah, two thousand. Lapan I've already put at something short of two thousand. What about Belishba?' he said, looking up under his brows at the governor sitting on the couch. 'One of the biggest provinces—the whole area west of the Zhairgen. You didn't tell me this morning. I need to know now. What can you promise?'

'My lord,' replied the governor—an elderly, stern-looking man, with the air of one who, while he might not march out to move mountains, would be hard to dislodge from any position he had taken up—'I'm sorry to tell you this, but the truth is that law and order in the province have declined very gravely. In fact, I was lucky to get here and whether I shall be able to return is another matter.'

'But the men?' pursued Kembri harshly.

The governor folded his hands before him. 'I must make three things clear, my lord. First, heldro sympathies west of the Zhairgen are, I would imagine, probably stronger than anywhere else in the empire. Karnat himself, in fact, has a certain influence among the minor barons and landowners. It's not easy, you see, to prevent a certain amount of intercourse with Terekenalt, even though we maintain a closed frontier across the Harridan Neck, and a boom across the Zhairgen. Secondly, as you know, I have been contending all this year with bands of runaway slaves turned outlaw. General Sendekar has given me valuable help—without that we would have gone under and no doubt about it—but as things are at the moment there can be no question of impressing able-bodied, law-abiding men away from their homes. They would simply resist; and to be frank with you, my lord, I don't know that I should greatly blame them. It's easy to sit here in Bekla and talk of levying provincial troops. Do you realize that in Belishba every village maintains an all-night guard, and that men work in the fields with their arms to hand, ready to assemble at the sound of a trumpeter on continual watch?'

Kembri seemed about to speak, but before he could do so the governor went on, 'And now comes the proclamation of this man, Santil-kè-Erketlis, that he will reduce peasant taxation—we're a ploughman's province, my lord, stuck out on the edge of the Harridan—and do away with slavery apart from men taken in war. I have obeyed your summons to come here. You appointed me and I thought it my duty to come. But I'm afraid—and if this angers you I can only express my regret—that I can't undertake to send men to Lapan.'

Kembri, head bent forward, spoke over a clenched fist laid before him on the table. 'Do you mean that you'll send only a *few* men, or not *one* man? Think carefully before you answer.'

'I believe, my lord, rightly or wrongly, that my first duty is to the province. I have indeed thought very carefully, as you may suppose. I'm afraid my answer is, not one man.'

Instantly, Kembri had drawn his dagger, crossed the room in two strides and thrust the point against the governor's throat. 'Not one man?'

The governors of Kabin and Tonilda, at either end of the couch, sprang apart in consternation. Neither Gel-Ethlin nor Bel-ka-Trazet made any movement, but Eud-Ecachlon clutched Donnered by the arm as if for reassurance.

'Not one man?' repeated Kembri deliberately.

The governor, slowly lifting his hands to the back of his neck, drew over his head the official chain, from which depended his seal of office, and hung it on the dagger pressed to his throat, so that it was left dangling.

'I was expecting this. There's a letter to my wife in my pocket.'

As every man in the room waited for the great spurt of blood from the jugular vein, Nasada got up from his stool and hobbled forward. With a kind of unreflective, self-possessed authority, rather like that of an adult who, though not given to interference, nevertheless thinks it time to part two children before someone gets seriously hurt, he gently drew the point of the Lord General's dagger to one side, took off the chain, which he dropped into the governor's lap and then, looking directly at Kembri with an air of apology, said, 'I wonder, my lord, whether you'd be so kind as to call a servant to bring me some wine—or some water, for that matter. If you can allow me, there are one or two things about Belishba that I'd rather like to say before you all reach a decision. Only it's become so hot and stuffy in here, don't you think?'

While speaking, he had somehow managed to interpose himself between the governor and the Lord General, who drew back a pace, glowering. For an instant it seemed as though he would strike Nasada. The old man continued to peer up at him with an unaltered expression of polite solicitation. Kembri laid a hand on his shoulder as though to push him out of the way, but this he seemed not to notice. At this moment his very helplessness and frailty became instruments of great—indeed, of insurmountable—power. If Kembri were to use violence on him now, he would injure himself far more than Nasada: and on this account, by the same token he could not practicably use violence on the governor.

After staring at him for a few seconds Kembri said, 'Very well, U-Nasada. We'll hear you,' and returned his dagger to its sheath.

'Thank you, my lord,' replied Nasada. 'I greatly appreciate your courtesy.'

Kembri nodded to Gel-Ethlin, who went to the door and sent one of the sentries for wine, serrardoes and thrilsa. Meanwhile Nasada, drawing up his stool to the couch, began conversing with the governor, in an unraised but clearly audible voice, about the navigability of the upper Zhairgen where it divided Sarkid from Belishba.

'I've always wanted to visit Sarkid, you know,' he said. 'Only it's as difficult to find time in Suba as it is here, believe it or not. Donnered, do you think I could get up there by water from Suba in—what? Five or six days? It would be much the easiest way, at my time of life.'

Before the wine had been brought he had become the centre of a group of four or five men discussing, relaxedly and almost with animation, the entirely unexceptionable subject of travel by river throughout the empire.

'Only it's of interest to me, you see,' he said, turning to Kembri with a slight suggestion of self-depreciation. 'In Suba we seldom travel in any other way. I often wonder why I haven't become rheumatic: but it's possible, I suppose, that marsh frogs are immune to rheumatics.'

Kembri was obliged either to smile or else to appear churlish, and a minute later himself handed Nasada his wine. The old man drank it slowly, and at a halt in the conversation got up and went over to sit beside Bel-ka-Trazet, with whom he was evidently acquainted. At length, as it became clear that the fear and tension had subsided and the mood of the room had cooled to something at least approaching composure, he returned to his stool and sat down as before, silent but alert.

'Well, Nasada,' said Kembri, 'let's hear, now, what you have to say.'

'My lord,' replied the old man, speaking slowly and appearing from time to time to pause to choose his words (Bel-ka-Trazet was not the only man to suspect that his real purpose might be to add weight to what he said and compel the attention of his hearers), 'I told you that I wished to speak about Belishba. We each of us see things in the light of our own particular trade, don't we? You see with the eyes of a warrior. To a merchant the thing—whatever it is—appears different, and a farmer sees it in yet another light. I'm a physician—insofar as anyone can be, for the truth is that we really know very little about disease and cure, though one day that may change, I suppose. But, Lord General, being a physician I see your empire as if it were sick, and I don't think anyone could deny that at the moment it is, though we may differ about the cause.'

He stopped, looking down at the floor and frowning. 'Well, I mustn't stretch the comparison too far. I'm not a general or a statesman, so I'm not an empire-doctor—only a people's doctor. But nonetheless, I'm going to risk telling you something which may seem like impudence. If you'll—er— allow me to imagine for a moment that the empire *is* a human body, then the place where its illness shows most clearly is Belishba. Not Chalcon, but Belishba.'

He seemed now to be waiting to see whether the High Baron or anyone else would interrupt him, but none did. After a few moments he looked up at Kembri, who merely nodded.

'I wonder,' he went on almost gropingly, 'that's to say—I'm not sure— whether you already know—all of you—what the one thing is which makes people ill more than anything else. You'll tell me the gods inflict illness for their own best reasons, and you're quite right; so they do. They visit illness on people who for one reason or another are thwarting or crossing their divine purposes. I expect you think I mean you, Lord General, but I don't. Not in the least.'

By this time he had caught the interest of everyone in the room, and there was silence as he refilled his goblet, took a few sips and cleared his throat.

'What I've learned, after years of experience of sick people, is that the one thing that makes them most likely to get ill—that holds the door open, you might say, for illness to come in—is hopeless frustration. The gods want people, don't they, to be human beings—to work and play and eat and mate and love and hate and all the rest of it? What's called living a natural life. They'll struggle for that. That's to say, when they haven't got what they want they'll struggle for it, because it's the will of the gods that they should. That struggle's healthy—quite often they thrive on it. But when they can't struggle—when struggle's not possible, so that they have to resign themselves and to give in, do without wives or children or money or cows or whatever it is—then they often get ill and in some cases they may even become deranged in one way or another. In other words the chief single cause of illness, in my experience, is hopelessness.

'People will go to almost any lengths to avoid hopelessness, and that's not really surprising, since the gods are telling them to—inwardly, I mean—and threatening them with illness or madness if they won't. I don't know whether you know this, but slaves get ill more than anybody else—much more than free people, even poor ones. The gods make them ill for not being what they want human beings to be; for existing for other people's benefit and not for their own. I'm not talking about slaves like bed girls, who sometimes quite enjoy it and usually have the hope of buying themselves free. I'm talking about working slaves all over the empire. Their frustration's not so much a question of not getting paid. Quite a lot of free peasants hardly use money, come to that; in Suba it's almost unknown. No, their difficulty is that they're not free to come and go, not free to get married, to leave work or a master they don't like and so on. And that's where Belishba comes in.

'The governor here said just now that Belishba's a ploughman's province. So it is; but also, Lord General, as I'm sure you know, it's the principal province where wealthy Leopards work estates with slave labour. The slave quotas taken from local villages are high, too, and there are two slave-farms where children are being bred for slavery. The gods are continually telling these people in their hearts that if they accept that they have no hope of living naturally they'll become either ill or mad. So of course a lot of them have tried to prevent that by desperate measures. You've got a province full of desperadoes there, terrorizing villages. But Belishba's no more than the biggest abscess. The poison's all through your empire to some extent, I'm afraid.'

He stopped, bending his head forward, scratching the back of his scrawny neck and screwing up his face as he did so. The effect was grotesque, but no one laughed. At last he said, 'I think that's what this man Erketlis has in mind, really. Abolishing slavery—he doesn't think it's going to make anyone more prosperous. But it *will* mean that people can keep their own children, feel safer in their beds and journey about without having to choose between risking their lives or paying bribes to bandits.'

'Isn't it more likely,' interposed Durakkon, 'that he's just a small baron who's suddenly seen a chance to become powerful and has hit on this idea as a way of gaining support?'

'I wonder, my lord,' answered Nasada, 'whether you'd forgive me if I leave you for a minute or two?' He smiled wryly at Durakkon. 'Old men have to pass water rather more often, I'm afraid.' As he stood up Donnered handed him his stick and Eud-Ecachlon opened the door for him.

When he came back he said, 'I suppose, my lord, that the time's come for me to admit—and if you don't like it I can only say I'm sorry—that in a way, I'm here as a sort of envoy or emissary or something like that, although it's entirely on my own account, I assure you. Erketlis hasn't sent me and neither has Karnat. I'm just an old Suban medicine-man. They both know I'm here—at least I think they do—but neither of them's told me what to say.'

'Then what is it you want?' asked Kembri brusquely. 'We've been waiting long enough to hear it.'

'Well, I think, to avert bloodshed, really,' answered Nasada mildly. 'Like Maia, who swam the river, you know; though I don't look much like her, do I? But I am a doctor, after all, and that's my only excuse. I must admit it's gratifying that my reputation's apparently respectable enough to have got me in here: I never really thought it would. I feel rather out of place and I'm quite ready to go if you want me to.'

'But you have some suggestion to make?' asked Durakkon.

'Yes; at least, I think I have,' said he. 'You see, the trouble is that this woman Fornis is back in Dari-Paltesh, and a good many people in Suba think that if you, my lord, get mixed up in a lot of fighting with Erketlis in Yelda and Lapan, she's quite likely to seize the opportunity to march on Bekla. If she and Han-Glat were to do that, Sendekar couldn't possibly stop them, you know—not with the troops he's got now; to say nothing of the state Belishba's in.'

'For a country doctor, you seem to know a lot about the empire's problems,' said Kembri sardonically.

'If you'll allow me to say so, my lord, I think he does,' put in Bel-ka-Trazet from his seat in the window. 'But what's to be done about them's another matter.'

Durakkon inclined his head towards Nasada.

'What *is* to be done?' he asked.

'Well, since you ask me, my lord,' replied Nasada, 'and I assure you it's *only* because you ask me—I'd say, give Erketlis reliable pledges that you'll abolish the slave-farms and slave quotas step by step during—well, say the next six or seven years; reduce the burden of taxation on the peasants and small landowners, and then invite him to join you in getting Belishba under control and perhaps in superseding Fornis.'

'And you're seriously suggesting he'd agree to that, are you?' said Kembri.

'I happen to know it,' said Nasada quietly. 'I'm not saying anything about the possible long-term consequences for Suba, because I'm really here on Karnat's sufferance; but naturally I'm not unmindful of them.'

Before Durakkon could speak again, Kembri had stood up and, gently enough, raised the old man to his feet with an arm under his shoulders. 'Well, you won't be expecting an answer to all that this afternoon,' he said. 'You'd better leave us to think about it. I'll call my aide to escort you to your quarters.'

: 77 :

NEWS OF FORNIS

'D'you know you've fair took my breath away?' said Maia. 'I reckoned you'd jump down my throat and call me all manner of fool, that I did.'

'Well, of course it's lunatic,' answered Occula, 'and damn' dangerous, too. But how can I tell you to drop it when it's no crazier than what I'm tryin' to do myself? If you love this Katrian boy, then you love him and that's all there is to it. Anyway, by all I ever heard of Katrians he might do you a lot better than any of these miserable Beklans—that's if you ever get him back, and if he's still of the same mind, which doesn' seem very likely, does it? No, I'm not really worried about you fallin' in love with a Katrian—or a Suban, or a bastin' Deelguy if you want to. What's worryin' me is whether you can survive this mess you've got yourself into. You'd say I'm tough and cunnin', wouldn' you? No one could say I'm not, actually. And even I nearly came unstuck over Sencho. In fact I *would* have come unstuck—dead and gone by now—if you hadn' saved me and got me in here. But *you*? Well, you're not silly, banzi, I know, but you're no match for Fornis, are you? What the bastin' hell d'you think *your* chances are of reachin' Dari-Paltesh and gettin' this man out? The whole place is in the hands of Fornis, for a start, and doesn' she just about love you?'

They were sitting in the cool air on the roof of the Sacred Queen's house. It was nearly two hours after sunset and the lower city, spread out below the Peacock Wall, was everywhere dotted with points of lamplight. The half-mile length of the Sheldad, where it ran from the Caravan Market to the western quarter, showed as a bright line, while beyond lay the similar but longer, more irregular line formed by Masons Street, the Kharjiz and the Khalkoornil. The five towers stood black against the deep blue of the night sky, and above all shone the cool, still radiance of the comet.

Vigilant it seemed to Maia, like a silent, heedful judge presiding over the contention of a court-room. Suddenly the imposing, stone-built city appeared to her as nothing more than an anthill of scurrying midgets, meanly self-absorbed and pitifully unconscious of their own triviality, the brief duration of their lives and the committed watchfulness of the supernal powers. They would all die: they were all answerable. She, too: for her life, for her love. Reaching out, she caught Occula's hand in her own.

'Sorry, banzi,' said the black girl, returning squeeze for squeeze, 'have I put the wind up you? Well, could be all for the best—'

'No, 'twasn't you, dear,' replied Maia. 'Well, I mean, yes, 'course I'm scared, but I feel I've just got to go on and that's all there is to it: else there's no sense in anything.'

'But how the hell are you goin' to set about it, banzi? Have you really thought seriously? I doan' like it one little bit—not on your own. You'll come unstuck for sure.'

'Well, I was hoping as you might come with me, Occula. If we could only get to Paltesh together, I might help you to kill Fornis and you could help me to get Zenka out.'

A flock of wild duck flew over the roof in their usual arrow-head formation, calling together as they disappeared into the darkness.

'Be all right if we could pop down to Paltesh like that, wouldn' it?' said Occula. 'Peck her bastin' green eyes out and back for breakfast. No, I'm sorry, banzi, it woan' do: I only wish it would. You see, everythin' in my little game depends on keepin' Fornis's favour and confidence. If I went to Paltesh, I'd have disobeyed her—anyway, I'm a slave, remember?—and I'd almost certainly have given the game away, too.'

Maia was about to answer when suddenly the black girl burst out, 'Cran and Airtha, you doan' know the half of it! My life's hangin' on a thread—the thread of her whims and her filthy, beastly wants! You realize, doan' you, that that's all that saved you and me after old Piggy was done in? Shall I tell you somethin' else? What you saw—she does that because she *prefers* it. She doesn' *want* men; she wants that! All that stuff about never havin' a lover because she knew she was the Sacred Queen and the bride of Cran—that's all my venda! And another thing; do you know she's more than once had girls put to death when she'd lost interest in them?'

'Ah, she told me that herself,' said Maia.

'Ashaktis told *me*, to try and frighten me: and I woan' say she didn', either, but I wasn' goin' to show it. You may have noticed that the little boys aren' here any more.'

'I thought she must have taken them with her,' said Maia.

'Oh, no,' said Occula. 'Just get some more when she comes back.'

'You mean they've been sold off?'

'No; *not* sold off,' said Occula. 'Children talk, you know. But those ones woan'.' She paused. 'I sometimes think I'll go mad! She's the most cruel, wicked woman in the world. But I'll get her, doan' you worry. When the time comes, Kantza-Merada will tell me what to do. But I'm sorry, banzi, I'm afraid it woan' be at Paltesh.'

For a time neither girl said more. The big summer stars moved slowly on the sky—Clypsil, Pildinakis and the constellation of the Otter, which Maia remembered old Drigga teaching her how to recognize when she was still a little girl. From the two clock towers the lamps shone out for the hour. A tryzatt carrying a torch came along the wall, changed the sentries and returned the way he had come.

'If you must go, why doan' you take Nennaunir and young Sednil?' asked Occula suddenly. 'I know you couldn' pay Nennaunir a fraction of what she's makin' here in Bekla, but you did her such a good turn by gettin' Sednil freed that she probably wouldn' mind—that's to say, long as it didn' take more than a few weeks. They're both Palteshis, aren' they? That could be a big help.'

'It might have been a good idea,' answered Maia.

'But—?'

'There's only one thing wrong with it—'

'Oh, Cran! Doan' tell me!' said Occula instantly. 'You mean somethin' about seven inches long, pointin' in the wrong direction?'

'Well, yes.'

'Bloody, bastin' men!' said Occula angrily. 'Always spoilin' everythin' with their stupid—'

'Oh, Occula, that's nothing!' interrupted Maia. 'I haven't told you yet about Eud-Ecachlon. And this really *is* frightening me. You remember I told you how Kembri came to my house while Nan and Otavis were there, and how he sent them away; and then he said that if I didn't want to be misunderstood I ought to find myself a rich, noble husband—'

'Yes, of course I remember. Go on.' Occula spoke in a tone of tension and alarm. 'What about it?'

'Well, soon after that Eud-Ecachlon came to see me, and asked me to marry him. He said his father was near to die and he'd soon be High Baron of Urtah.'

'What did you say?'

'I asked him to give me time to think it over, and that night I got so frightened I decided the next day I'd tell him yes: but then Sednil came back that very morning and told me Zenka was a prisoner at Dari.'

'So what happened then?'

'Eud-Ecachlon came back and I refused him.'

'Banzi, do you realize— Who's that?' Occula turned quickly towards the stair-head on the opposite side of the flat roof.

778

'It's I,' replied Zuno's smooth, controlled voice. 'Occula, I've just learned some news which I think you ought to hear at once: Maia too.'

He groped his way across the roof-top, his eyes not yet adapted to the darkness.

'Lalloc learned this an hour ago by a messenger from one of his overseers near Dari. I happened to be down at Lalloc's when the man came in. Apparently Fornis has gone through a ceremony of marriage with Han-Glat. They've raised a force—the man couldn't say how large, but the nucleus, of course, is Palteshi. However, it seems they've been joined by a sizeable group of escaped slaves from Belishba, and the whole lot have already set out for Bekla. Sendekar tried to put some sort of opposition in their way, but he's hopelessly over-extended, of course, and they brushed it aside quite easily. This man said Fornis had given out that since Elvair-ka-Virrion had shown himself incapable of defending Bekla against Erketlis, she meant to do it herself.'

'Let her come!' said Occula. 'I'm ready! But banzi, listen to me. In all seriousness, and as the best friend you've got, I honestly think that the only place for you now is Quiso. You can claim the sacred sanctuary for six months, you know—if only you can get there.'

Maia seemed hardly to have heard her. While Zuno was speaking she had listened to him intently. Now she asked 'The prisoners—the prisoners in the fortress—what's happened to them? Did Lalloc's man say?'

'Yes, he did,' replied Zuno. 'Fornis and Han-Glat have got all the officers and some of the tryzatts with them as hostages, to make sure that they're not attacked by Karnat in the rear. What's more, it seems that when Durakkon's younger son, who was second-in-command at the fortress, tried to stop them, they took him as a hostage, too. It's well-known, of course, how fond Durakkon's always been of the boy.'

'So Zenka's in the hands of Fornis!' said Maia. 'Quiso be damned! I'm staying here till she comes.'

Walking away to the further end of the roof, she stood gazing at the comet, arms raised and palms outward. They could hear her sobbing as she prayed.

'Whether Bel-ka-Trazet's right or wrong about Ortelga and the Deel-guy,' said Kembri, '—and he may very well be right—one thing's certain: we can't *compel* him to take command of an army.'

'I wonder he didn't accept it, though,' said Eud-Ecachlon (well aware that it was not going to be offered to himself). 'Defeat Erketlis? He'd be celebrated throughout the empire and I suppose he'd come by a fortune as well, wouldn't he?'

'Certainly; *if* he beat him,' answered Kembri, 'but he doesn't want to run the risk, that's the size of it. I wonder what he knows that we don't. He said he was loyal to Bekla and so he is, I've never doubted—to *Bekla*. But the truth is, it doesn't make much difference to him or to Ortelga who actually rules here. He's High Baron of that lump of mud in the Telthearna, and he means to hold on to what he can feel sure of. Which is more than we may be able to do, my lord, I dare say,' he said, turning to Durakkon, 'as things are going at the moment.'

Durakkon had been staring out of the window. The face he now turned towards the Lord General resembled that of some weary, ageing vagabond overtaken by storm and nightfall. It was not apparent whether he had heard what Kembri had said. He nodded, looking at him vacantly for a few moments; then said 'Yes, yes, of course,' and for a moment buried his face in his hands.

The three were alone together. The High Baron was dressed in a plain grey robe, with no adornment except the Leopard cognizance on a gold chain round his neck. During the last day or two, after learning the news of Fornis's advance with the hostages from Dari, he seemed to have aged ten years. Since the meeting at which Nasada had spoken he had made, in effect, no contribution to public business. To the provincial governors he had spoken no more than courtesy required, and that listlessly and with an air of indifference to their replies. Despite the personal grief and anxiety which they had in common Kembri, who was naturally courageous and stimulated to action by danger and adversity, had found his patience with the High Baron wearing even thinner than usual. Now, by way of emphasis and of rousing him from his dismal preoccupation, he let his fist fall on the table.

'The *vital* thing,' he said, 'which we've got to do as quickly as possible, is to defeat Erketlis before he can raise the whole of the south against us. Everything else is secondary—even Bekla itself. For that reason, my lord, I'm going to Lapan at once, to take over the command of the army in person. I shall come back, of course, as soon as possible; that's to say, as soon as Erketlis is dead or no longer a threat.'

Durakkon nodded, and Kembri turned back to Eud-Ecachlon.

'There'll be a temptation—' (he did not say to whom) 'there'll be a strong temptation, as you'll realize, to retain here the reinforcements coming in from the various provinces, and use them against Fornis. I'm giving you the task of assembling and arming those reinforcements as soon as they arrive, and getting them down to Lapan as fast as possible. Do it efficiently, Eud-Ecachlon, and you won't be a loser by it, I promise you.'

'But—er—Fornis?' asked Eud-Ecachlon.

'Fornis and Han-Glat; yes. Now understand this. It's only necessary to hold Fornis up long enough to allow our reinforcements from the provinces to be sent down to me in Lapan. But those four thousand men I've got to have, do you understand?'

Eud-Ecachlon nodded. 'But then, what about Bekla?'

'I'm leaving enough regular troops—not many, but they should be enough—to hold Fornis up for about two weeks.'

'And after that?'

'You'll occupy the citadel and hold it against Fornis when she takes the city. Once Erketlis is out of the way I shall return immediately and deal with her. She'll be hopelessly outnumbered; she won't have a chance. Anyone but a power-crazy woman would have seen that from the beginning.'

Durakkon, who had been tracing patterns with his finger on the table, looked up, unexpectedly alert for a moment.

'Lord General, who have you in mind to command this remnant force which is to delay Fornis?'

'If the plans I've explained have your approval, my lord, as I hope they have, I think it important that you should command it yourself. It'll make all the difference if the men know that the High Baron is leading them in person. I certainly wouldn't ask you to undertake a full campaign at your time of life, but as things are you won't be long in the field: two weeks at the most. Then you'll fall back on the citadel.'

'I would prefer not, Lord General.'

'My lord, there is no one else of sufficient prestige and standing to put heart into the men.'

Durakkon raised his grey, haggard face and stared at Kembri. He had seen less desperate looks, thought the Lord General, on scaffolds.

'You had better understand me, Lord General. I have no objection either to fighting our enemies or to dying in battle. But among those in the hands of that evil woman is my son—'

The Lord General sprang to his feet so violently that the bench on which he had been sitting overturned with a crash. His massive figure, as he bent forward over the table, seemed to obscure the light.

'*Your* son? *Your* son, my lord? Do you think you're the only man whose son—'

He was bellowing. Eud-Ecachlon could hear a murmur and stir in the next room, where the senior officers were waiting. He laid a restraining hand on Kembri's arm. The Lord General controlled himself. When next he spoke his voice was almost a whisper.

'I would rather that *my* son was where your son is now.'

Saluting Durakkon, he turned and strode out into the corridor, followed by Eud-Ecachlon. They walked in silence the length of the Barons' Palace and so out into the northern portico overlooking the Leopard Hill's tiered terraces. Here Kembri, with the air of one wishing to convey, by speaking of some relatively slight matter, that he has recovered his self-possession, asked, 'By the way, there's been so much to attend to that I forgot to ask what arrangement you've come to with Maia.'

Eud-Ecachlon made no reply, and after a moment the Lord General stopped in his walk and looked round at him with a lift of his heavy eyebrows.

'She—refused me.'

The eyebrows came down like a portcullis. '*Refused* you? Gods! What reason did she give?'

'None, really. She just said she didn't want to do it. I feel angry and—well—humiliated, I suppose. She'd have done very well for Urtah, and I entirely agree with all you said when you first put the idea to me.'

'That child's been her own worst enemy ever since she came back from Suba,' said Kembri. 'It's a great pity, for in a way I've always rather liked her. Still, as things have turned out she'll have no time to think better of it. Once Erketlis has been checked and Fornis has been defeated, we can't let *her* stand in the way of our plans.'

'You mean, your plan that Milvushina should be acclaimed?'

Kembri nodded. 'That's vital—more than ever, now. Don't you see, if a Chalcon baron's daughter's reigning as Sacred Queen—with our blessing—that'll make it virtually impossible for Erketlis to attack Bekla? She could denounce it in the name of Airtha and his whole position would become extremely difficult, to say the very least.'

'So Maia—you'll kill her?'

Kembri hesitated. 'Well, she'll have to die, certainly; and soon, too—before the acclamation of the new Sacred Queen. The difficulty is that the least suspicion of murder would make for more trouble than we could handle. Frankly, I've got no time to think it out at the moment: it *will* become important later, though.'

'But Fornis will be in Bekla before long, won't she?' said Eud-Ecachlon. 'Why not leave it to Fornis to kill her? I should think we can rely on that, wouldn't you?'

The Lord General paused, almost as though reluctant to reply. Then he said, 'Well—perhaps that may prove to be the answer. Let's wait and see.'

78

SUPPER WITH NASADA

Nasada sat facing Maia in the soft lamplight. She could smell the light, honey-like bouquet of the Yeldashay in the goblet at his elbow. She had given him a supper fit for the High Baron and he had obviously enjoyed it. She would have given him her jewels, her house, herself if he had wanted them. Whatever Ogma's limitations in other directions, thought Maia, thank Cran she could at least cook when she put her mind to it.

She had threaded her hair with more than fifty gold beads and coiled it in plaits round her head (it had taken over an hour), and was wearing her diamonds and a plain, quite unrevealing robe of white and pale-pink silk with a pleated skirt, and white leather slippers with a gold leopard on each toe. Against all reason and probability she felt elated and full of confidence. There was that in the mere presence of Nasada which banished anxiety. Looking at him—gnarled and grey-headed, yet robust and infinitely reassuring—she was reminded of some huge-branched old tree of magic properties; such as had been revered time out of mind by Tonildan villagers, on which women hung dolls for fertility and bunches of herbs and flowers for the recovery of the sick. You could hang your troubles on him all right: he wouldn't break.

She had refused Eud-Ecachlon: she was probably going to die. (Often, the young face this prospect with more courage and acceptance than the old, for they have more vigour to do it with, little empty time to reflect and less of the past to lose.) Well, let it come. Meanwhile, for the present it fairly warmed her heart to be able at last to show her gratitude to old Nasada and let him see her, just for this once at least, as the Serrelinda, the idol of Bekla and the heroine of the empire. But then again, looking at him, she found her mood changing to one of illogical conviction that of course her troubles would come right, somehow or other. His very existence was like an assurance to this effect.

He broke the silence. 'It's nice, isn't it, to see something made by men which is as beautiful as something made by the gods, and with no more harm in it than a flower or a bird?'

He was holding Randronoth's cabinet of the fishes between his hands, turning it this way and that in the lamplight, admiring it by touch as well as by sight. That was what she used to do herself—she delighted in the feel of it, its smoothness and squared, panelled symmetry—and he had needed no suggestion from her to discover the same pleasure.

'I've often wondered, U-Nasada,' she said, 'why they chose to carve it with fish particularly. I mean, you know, the one who made it and them as it was made for.'

'Perhaps because it's made of fish.'

'Made of fish? You're teasing me!'

'I'm not: I meant the bones of a fish.'

'You've picked on the wrong girl, U-Nasada. I'm from Serrelind, remember? I know about fish and fish-bones. A fish would have to be the size of this room before you could cut panels like that.'

'Oh, yes, at least; possibly bigger. I've never seen them myself, but I know they exist; a thousand miles from here, in waters far bigger than Serrelind. Some of these carved fish are strange to us, too, you see. But obviously they must exist.'

Anyone else she would have told to go and jump in the Barb. Being Nasada, she felt that what he said, or something like it, must be true. Anyway, she didn't care: it was enough to be in his company. He evidently believed it and she knew he wasn't making fun of her, even though she'd started by saying he was.

He put the cabinet back in its place. 'Beautiful things seem even better when they come from far away, don't you think? They're like the stars, then: we don't know how they began, but we do know they're beautiful and do no harm.'

'But isn't Bekla beautiful, too?'

'Yes; and that's just the difference. It *is* beautiful, but it's like a poisoned well with lilies growing round it. It's become a death-trap. What used to be natural has been—' He paused, then shrugged. 'Made evil.'

She waited for him to go on. 'Oh, yes,' he said at length. 'I know the people in Suba are ignorant and dirty and stupid. They get ill from the climate, too, and most of them don't live as long as people here; at least, I shouldn't think they do. But they don't cheat and rob and murder one another. Do you know that Suba—I still can't help thinking of it as part of the empire—is about the one place left where people can travel in safety and don't have to go armed, and lock everything up? And you know why I've come here, too, don't you? To try and stop even more blood being spilt. We've got that much in common, you and I.' He sighed. 'But you succeeded in your attempt and I haven't in mine, I'm afraid.'

She was eager to speak of something else. Indeed, she had been determined to.

'U-Nasada, I want to tell you something as I haven't told to anyone else in the, world.'

He looked up quickly, as though already half-guessing what it was that she was going to say.

'*I'm* Suban! What d'you think of that? Nokomis was my mother's sister.'

Then she related all that Tharrin had told her about her father's murder, her mother's flight and her own birth. He listened in silence, but she could see tears in his eyes and, remembering how he had once spoken to her of Nokomis, could feel how deeply he must be moved.

When she had finished he did not at once reply, seeming to be weighing all that she had told him and considering how to answer. At last he said, 'I'll say something you may not like to hear. You're the most beautiful woman in the empire, the most admired and the most—well, prized, I suppose. A sort of princess, really. But even so, and setting aside all question of your safety, I myself believe that you'd be *happier*—that's to say, more fulfilled and more likely to live naturally and well—in Suba.'

She gazed out of the window at the gentle, scented night, the moonlit sky, the rippling Barb and the slopes of Crandor beyond: then round at her elegant, luxurious room.

'Do you think they'd accept me, U-Nasada, after what happened at Melvda?'

'Well, the short answer's yes, although the details might need a little working out. I don't mean that you'd live a life entirely without troubles and problems, you know.'

She nodded. 'I know.'

Suddenly she was kneeling at his feet, her head in his lap, sobbing her heart out.

'Oh, Nasada, if only you knew how I long for peace and for an end to being afraid all the time! People as you can't trust and you wonder what's in their minds and what they're on about behind your back—'

He stroked her hair and took her hands between his own.

'Has someone been offering you marriage?'

How incredibly startling and instant his penetration was, she thought; just as it had been in Suba. It was disconcerting; yet such swift, outspoken understanding was very comforting, too. With him, talk never went in circles, nor yet stayed in one place. That was the nature of his truth: he never wasted time making kindly noises. He was like the seeker of the hidden treasure in old Drigga's story, whose tongue, enchanted, had the power of a sharp sword.

'Yes: Eud-Ecachlon of Urtah. He said his father's dying, and I'd be High Baroness when he succeeded. I refused him.'

'Do you want to tell me why?'

She hesitated, and at once he said, 'You don't have to. I said "Do you want to?" and that's all I meant.'

'I want to.'

So then it all came pouring out—Zen-Kurel and the daggers; their passionate exchange of promises at Melvda: her determination to forestall the whole business of the night attack, to save Zenka's life and the lives of the Tonildans: her ignorance of what had become of Zenka, her longing

785

for him, her sense of loneliness and loss in the midst of Bekla's adulation. Her avoidance of accepting a lover, Kembri's false suspicion of her motives for doing so, the priest's cryptic words at the temple, the death of Tharrin, Randronoth and the money, Sednil's mission and what he had found out. She wept herself into exhaustion, ending at last, 'And I don't care if Kembri kills me or Fornis kills me or *what* they do, the whole damned lot of them—I won't, I *won't* run away and leave Zenka in that woman's hands. Either I'll save him or else I'll die trying.'

There was another silence, and again she knew that he had entered into all she was suffering.

'I—was wrong,' he said after a time, 'I see that, now—about something I said earlier.' She waited. 'I said I thought beautiful things were better when they came from far away, and then I said Bekla was a place where what used to be naturally beautiful had been spoilt. Some of it hasn't.'

With *his* admiration behind her, she felt, she could attempt anything. Even if she failed, her integrity would have earned his respect—an incomparable honour.

'So what are you going to do?' he asked, suddenly and briskly, with a complete change of manner. Once more he was pressing ahead. That her love for Zen-Kurel and her (most would say) hopeless purpose were right and unquestionable—with him, all that went without saying. Now, as naturally as though they had been engaged upon some matter such as a journey or a purchase, he was down to considering ways and means.

'I don't know, U-Nasada: I don't know *what* to do. I've thought of going out by myself to meet the Palteshi army and offering to ransom Zenka.'

'With anyone but Fornis that might have worked. But once bitten, twice shy, don't you think? If I were you I shouldn't go paying any more ransoms to the likes of her.'

'Then what?'

He bent and kissed her cheek, raised her to her feet and himself remained standing until she had sat down once more in her own chair.

'For the time being it all depends on the fighting, doesn't it? I don't know what Kembri's plans are, of course, but obviously he'll have to send some sort of troops against her, and I think you can only wait for the outcome.'

'But the priest said, "You'll find him if you seek him yourself" and then he said, "Opportunity's everything."'

'But that works both ways, you know—like a lot of things those sort of people say to you. It could mean "*Wait* for the opportunity", couldn't it? And as things stand just at this moment, I don't think you've got one. You're young—eager—brave—you find inaction hard to bear—you want to feel you're doing something—anything. I know that feeling. But I think you *must* wait and see what comes of the fighting.'

'But by then it could be too late, U-Nasada!'

'No, I don't think so. Your Zen-Kurel's a Katrian hostage: that's to say, he's being held by Fornis to ensure that Karnat won't attack Paltesh. People are usually reluctant to kill hostages, you know. It's not like spending money or using soldiers: it's very much a last resort. Once you've killed a hostage, that's that: you've antagonized the other side and got nothing for it. So I'd say, wait here and Zen-Kurel will probably come to *you*, one way or the other: and *that'll* be where your opportunity begins. Waiting can be the hardest work in the world, you know. You *are* doing something for Zen-Kurel, simply by waiting here.'

She forced a smile. 'Shagreh.'

'Shagreh.'

'What *does* it mean, U-Nasada? Every time I thought I knew, next time it seemed to mean something different.'

He laughed. 'It can mean almost anything you like, including "Yes" and "No", and "I don't know." But as you're Suban, at least you'd better learn to pronounce it properly. It's not "Shagreh": it's "Shagreh".'

'Shagreh.'

'No! "Shagreh".'

'I said "Shagreh".'

'I know you did. You're still saying it. It's "Shagreh".'

'Oh, Nasada, what's the Suban for "I love you: you cheer me up"?'

'No Suban would phrase it like that. Let me see—'

For the next three-quarters of an hour Maia tied her voice into knots of Suban articulation and inflexion, laughing delightedly at Nasada's comic pretences of impatience and inventing more and more absurd or outrageous phrases for him to teach her. He entered into the game as gaily as though he had been the same age as herself, so that she wondered with admiration and even with regret what he could have been like when he was. After her soldiers had left to take him, in her jekzha, the short distance back to his quarters, she went to bed feeling more hopeful and encouraged than for many days past.

79

FAREWELLS

'I'm sorry, Brero,' said Maia.

She was most anxious that he should believe her. She would have hated him to think that she did not feel sincere regard for him—for all three of them, but him in particular. 'I've done everything I can, honest I have.'

It was true; she had. She had even steeled herself to go and see Eud-Ecachlon, whom Kembri, she was told at the Barons' Palace, had left in charge of the musters. She had waited an hour and been treated exactly as she had expected—with chilly correctness and a firm assertion that as matters stood no single available soldier could be dispensed with. 'You know, of course,' Eud-Ecachlon had said coldly, 'that if it were possible I would certainly make an exception in favour of *you*.' Maia had coloured, raised her palm to her forehead and left him without another word: so she had deprived herself of discussing any question of substitutes, or of how she was expected to get about without her soldiers.

Now, Brero and his mates were standing before her, equipped for active service—swords on left hips, daggers on right, Gelt breastplates, hard leather helmets and leggings; lacking only their shields, which they had left outside. They had come to say good-bye, and as far as they were concerned it was plainly a keen disappointment, not lacking the bitter ingredient of a feeling that she had let them down. After all, the Serrelinda—if she couldn't get anything done as she had a mind to, who could? Probably they'd already been boasting to their comrades that the thing was as good as fixed.

So they stood fidgeting and ill-at-ease, these strapping fellows, on the polished floor of her parlour, perhaps secretly wondering whether even now, maybe, if only one of them could manage to say the right thing—

'I'm sorry, Brero. I went to see Lord Eud-Ecachlon myself: I'd have seen the High Baron if I'd thought it'd have made any difference.'

'Yes, of course, säiyett.'

'Surely it won't be very long, will it? One Beklan's worth six o' those rotten old Palteshis any time. I tell you what, Brero: you bring me back that woman's head and I'll give you five thousand meld for it, I swear I will. Oh, I'm sure you'll be back soon: why, it might be no more than a week!'

'Well, we'd all like to think so, säiyett, of course. A lot can happen in a week, can't it, one way or the other? But you'll be safe enough; don't worry, we'll see to that.'

Suddenly she was on her feet, taking his hands, taking the others' hands in turn, looking into their eyes with the most earnest desire to convince them.

'Oh, Brero, I really did do everything I could to keep you with me, honest! I'm not as powerful as you think, and that's the truth. I've got enemies, you know, and I'm not sure they aren't worse than yours, 'cos you can see yours.'

He was embarrassed. 'You mustn't take on this way, säiyett. You've always done the right thing by us; and we've enjoyed lookin' after you.' (Murmurs of corroboration.) 'D'you remember that young chap that day in the Caravan Market, him as bought all the flowers and soaked you wet through? And how I had to pull the wheel over his foot to get rid of him! Ah! we had some good times, didn't we?'

She gave them two hundred and fifty meld each. She had had it ready. They'd been expecting something, of course, but not as much as that: it was equivalent to about six months' pay. She gave each of them a keepsake, too—or perhaps it was a talisman for good luck and safety, was it? After all, she'd touched them, hadn't she, and if the Serrelinda wasn't lucky, who was? For Brero, a little onyx bull no bigger than his thumb; and for the other two, an Airtha in malachite and a silver Canathron to be worn as a charm (for the third fellow was Lapanese). No meanest curmudgeon could have argued that all this wasn't generous, and as they thanked her she felt that at least she had convinced them that she was not indifferent to their fortunes and welfare.

'We'll have to be going now, säiyett,' said Brero a minute or two later. 'The muster's at noon, you see. You did say, didn't you, that you'd be needing your jekzha?'

She nodded. 'That's right. The wise man—the doctor from Suba—he's going north to Quiso, you know, and there's a caravan leaving this morning: I'm taking him down to join it.'

'You do know, säiyett, don't you, that the caravans have to assemble at the Blue Gate today—outside it, I believe—because the muster's in the market? Anyway, I've hired two porters to pull you down there. They're waiting now.' He grinned. 'They won't be like us, of course, but I dare say you'll get there, one way or another.'

When they had gone, she went outside and stood for a little while on the terrace, watching the shadow of the gnomon just perceptibly moving on her bronze sundial. The sundial had been a gift from Bodrin, the wealthy metal-master of Gelt, who had had it set up with precision by two of his own craftsmen. Although she enjoyed possessing such a marvel—there were very few in Bekla, and it always impressed even the most aristocratic visitors—she had never really understood it, and had once made Sarget burst out laughing—no common occurrence—by enquiring whether it worked equally well by moonlight. There were three lines of verse carved round the base, and these at least she had mastered—'Time is a flower, In Tiltheh's power: Pluck thou the hour.' She read them now, and they gave her little comfort. Reckon I'd alter that, she thought. 'Waiting's a task, The gods do ask. Wear then thy mask.' Still, that wouldn't mean much, would it, not to anyone 'ceptin' me?

The hired porters were ageing men in torn, dirty clothes. One had a limp and the other a white, sightless eye. She guessed they were the best that Brero had been able to drum up for her. Kembri's muster officers, she knew, had been thorough and ruthless with all who could not bribe them enough. Probably almost every able-bodied man in the city, unless he were a craftsman of more use to the Leopards if left alone, had been impressed either as a soldier or as some sort of auxiliary. She wished she could have had a more thorough look round for herself, or at least have had a chance to put these men into respectable clothes.

Once through the Peacock Gate, however, with Nasada, cloaked and booted for his journey, hunched beside her, she found the Street of the Armourers plunged into such turmoil that there was hardly anyone to notice even the Serrelinda. A number of people seemed to have decided to leave Bekla on their own account and were piling handcarts with their possessions. Many of the shops were shut, but this had done nothing to diminish the universal agitation. Men, some more-or-less armed and others not armed at all, were on their way to the muster, some singly, others in groups. A number of these were clearly strangers to Bekla, levied from the provinces. Once, a little distance off, she saw a party who looked very like Tonildans being shepherded along by a Beklan tryzatt. She called out to them and waved, but could not attract their attention over the heads of the crowd.

It was clear enough that there would be no getting across the Caravan Market and probably no getting down Storks Hill either, and Maia told the men—who were already dawdling, and muttering to each other—to pull off to the left, cross over one of the little bridges spanning the Monju brook and so come down into the Sheldad.

The Sheldad, however, was if anything worse than the Street of the Armourers, seeming as it did to be full of wailing women either parting from sweethearts or husbands or else accompanying them to the Caravan Market. Maia told the men to get straight across it and go down by the Tower of the Orphans; an easy landmark, yet still they objected, grumbling over their shoulders above the surrounding tumult that it was too far and they didn't know the way. It so happened that at this moment Maia caught sight of a passing officer whom she knew—an honourably disabled man, now employed on staff duties, whom she had met at one of Sarget's supper-parties. Climbing down, she ran across to him, explained her difficulty and begged him to put the fear of Cran into her surly hirelings. This he at once did very effectively and Maia, knowing the district well enough, thereupon directed them out of the Sheldad and on towards the Kharjiz.

'Do you know,' she remarked conversationally to Nasada, pointing to the house as they passed it, 'I was once sent there to go to bed with Eud-Ecachlon?'

'Well,' he replied, 'that's one thing you won't have to do any more, isn't it? Whatever happens, I'm sure you're well out of marriage with an Urtan. They're proud people, rather humourless and terribly quick to resentment. Anda-Nokomis has got a lot of Urtan in him, you know: always talking about his honour, and never a joke or a laugh. Have you ever seen Anda-Nokomis really laugh? You've refused Eud-Ecachlon, and you were perfectly entitled to; but he won't forget it. Stay here and save your Zen-Kurel; I'm one who honestly believes you will. But after that get straight out of Bekla. It's a devils' playground, Maia.'

They passed the Temple of Cran and the Tamarrik Gate, and so came at last to the Blue Gate and the walled precinct outside. Here there was barely time for Maia's tearful thanks and farewells, and the bestowing on her of Nasada's blessing, before the captain of the caravan—a well-known mercenary employed by the merchants' guild of Kabin—came forward personally to conduct the wise man from Suba to his place in the leading ox-cart (in those further back, road dust was apt to be troublesome, especially at this time of year), after which he was prompt to obey his orders from Eud-Ecachlon to get off punctually and leave the city approaches clear for the military.

Maia returned past that same guard-room where once the soldiers had taken pity on her and Occula. Then, on impulse, she told the men to turn left, up Leather-Workers Street and so into the Caravan Market. Her officer friend had certainly done wonders for their frame of mind, for they obeyed her without a murmur.

All the efforts of the municipal slaves to keep sprinkling the sandy expanse of the Caravan Market had not succeeded in keeping down a thin haze of glittering dust, through which the impressed men were moving half-heartedly to their various rallying points. Here they stood coughing, many with rags or cloths held over their faces. There was a general atmosphere of uncertainty and irresolution; less, perhaps, of unwilling or faint-hearted men than of men at a loss, genuinely ignorant of what was required of them. Maia had not gone half-way along the colonnade bordering the north side of the market before it became clear enough to her that half these conscripts were peasant villagers who had almost certainly never been ten miles from their homes in their lives. Many looked nervous and a few actually frightened, simply of their imposing surroundings. Some were joking and sky-larking to keep up their spirits, others sitting on the ground as glum and silent as beasts in market-pens; cowed by homesickness, by fear of the future and the uncertainty of everything around. Among them, contrasting sharply, walked brisk, uniformed tryzatts of the Beklan regiment, who had evidently been given the task of organizing them into squads. This they had apparently decided to set about by dividing them into spearmen, swordsmen, bowmen and so on, irrespective of where they had come from. Maia watched with pity—indeed, she came within an ace of intervening—as a tryzatt almost forcibly separated a simple-looking lad with a sword from another—obviously his mate and probably the only person in the whole crowd whom he knew—carrying a spear, and led him away across the market to join a group of strangers. She could see the boy, as he looked back over his shoulder, trembling and almost weeping. A little farther on, an officer had succeeded in forming thirty or forty men into a ragged line. Having looked them over, he called out three, seemingly more or less at random, and, conferring upon them then and there the rank of sub-tryzatt, told them that they were now in charge of the rest and would be answerable for them. At every egress from the market a regular soldier had been posted to discourage the inclinations of anyone who might be so lacking in public spirit as to be tempted to melt away.

Even Maia could see that these were not what anyone in his senses could call a likely lot. She wondered what kind of men Santil-kè-Erketlis had, and in what spirit they had carried out their forced march and fought their battle at the end of it. Obviously they must have had every confidence in their leader and believed that what they were being required to do would turn out to their own advantage. Had any of these men around her, she wondered, any real idea of what they were being compelled to fight for? They comprised, between them, a very fair sample of the sort of bumpkins the Leopards had oppressed by restricting the selling prices of cattle, corn and timber. Who ought to know if not she?

The jekzha had just come opposite 'The Green Grove' (which was shut, no doubt on Eud-Ecachlon's orders) when in the colonnade Maia recognized Milvushina's maid Lokris. Lokris had set her back against one of the square columns and was doing her best to ward off two rough-looking men who were plainly pestering her—more for their amusement, it seemed, than with any real expectation of obtaining her favours. As she attempted a cuff at one of them, he dodged to one side, sniggering, while the other pulled at the shoulder of her robe.

Maia got down and went across to them.

'Do you know who I am?' she said coldly, looking from one to the other.

Plainly they did not know what to make of her youth, her Tonildan accent, the richness of her clothes and the authority and confidence of her manner. They stood looking back at her with stupid, hesitant grins of mingled bravado and uncertainty.

'Where do you come from?' she asked one of them sharply.

'Kabin—if it's any business of yours, dearie.'

Neither was armed, but they could only, she thought, be part of the levy. She called to a passing tryzatt, who at once came over and saluted her.

'You know me, don't you?'

'Yes, of course, säiyett.'

'These two men have been molesting my servant.'

The tryzatt instantly felled one of the men with a blow to the stomach, spun the other round by his jerkin and slapped his face.

'Just leave them to me, säiyett: I'm sorry you've had the bother. Kabin's sent us up some right ones this time, and that's a fact.'

Maia took Lokris by the arm, led her back to her jekzha, helped her in and told the men to go on.

After a few words of sympathy from her and thanks from Lokris, she asked, 'But how do you come to be down here, Lokris? Whatever brought you into the market, anyway, at a time like this?'

Lokris explained that she had been fetching a fresh supply of medicine for Milvushina.

'The doctor says she has to take it regularly, säiyett, but what with one thing and another I never noticed until last night that we were clean out. Of course I came straight down this morning, but the 'pothecary who's always made it up for her, his shop's shut and I couldn't make anyone hear. So I came on to this other man I know in the colonnade and simply went on knocking until he let me in.'

'Well done!' said Maia. 'Did you get it?'

'Oh, yes, thank you, säiyett. I'm very glad indeed for your help and for the lift back, too. To tell you the truth, I think the sooner I'm back the better.'

'Nothing wrong, I hope?' asked Maia quickly.

Lokris lowered her voice, while at the same time her manner underwent a subtle change from that of a servant speaking to a lady to that of a woman speaking to a woman.

'Lord Elvair-ka-Virrion's back,' she said. 'Did you know?'

'No, I didn't,' answered Maia. 'When?'

'Yesterday morning,' said Lokris. 'There was another officer with him, Captain Shend-Lador, and his own soldier-servant, and that was all. Seems they'd left the army in Lapan and been travelling four days, just the three of them. They came in by the Red Gate.'

'The Red Gate?' asked Maia in amazement.

The Red Gate into the citadel, on the summit of Mount Crandor, was a low arch in the south wall of the city, through the whole width of which flowed a swift brook, the Daulis. The bed had been artificially deepened, making it impassable except to those who knew the subaqueous windings of a narrow causeway of living rock left standing about two feet below the surface. Shend-Lador, of course, as the son of the citadel commander, would be familiar with these.

'He didn't want—or else he didn't dare—to come through the city, you see,' said Lokris. 'His servant went round by the Peacock Gate and told the Lord General that he was waiting up by the falls—the White Girls. So then a message was sent up to the citadel to open the Vent for them.'

'How is Lord Elvair-ka-Virrion?' asked Maia.

Lokris looked round at her quickly, as though astonished to be asked and not immediately knowing how to reply. After a moment she took refuge in a return to formality.

'What can I tell you, säiyett? He's taking it very badly, but of course that's no more than one would expect.'

'Taking it badly?'

Lokris perceived that in certain respects the Serrelinda was still ingenuous.

'Säiyett, I don't know, of course, how much you've heard, but the truth is that Lord Elvair-ka-Virrion is as good as ruined. People are saying that he mismanaged the campaign in Chalcon so badly that a great many lives were lost that needn't have been. If it's true, that's bad, of course, but it's not the worst of it for his reputation. The battle they lost—everyone says he actually ran away, and him supposed to be commander-in-chief. The captains deposed him and sent him home. And no one would even go along with him—only Captain Shend-Lador.'

'Is the Lord General very much upset?' asked Maia.

'The Lord General refused to see him,' answered Lokris. 'He left to take over the command in Lapan this morning, and I heard that he meant to tell the army that Lord Elvair-ka-Virrion was no longer his son and he was going to disinherit him.'

Maia's immediate feelings, as she recalled Elvair-ka-Virrion's invariable courtesy to the slave-girl she had once been and his kindness and help over the auction at the barrarz, were of indignation.

'I don't see as they've any call—' she was beginning, when their conversation was interrupted.

The jekzha-men had succeeded, with a good deal of difficulty, in getting round the north and part of the west side of the market-place. Near the

Bronze Scales the Beklan regiment were drawn up, their ordered ranks and uniform breastplates forming an island of trim regularity in the surrounding commotion. The officers were standing together at one side, and Maia recognized three or four, including the commander, Kerith-a-Thrain, a soldier of exceptional prestige and distinction. They were all looking in one direction and, following their gaze, she saw the High Baron Durakkon himself, fully accoutred and accompanied by two or three aides, approaching from the Street of the Armourers. This, of course, was the direction in which she herself was going. The crowd had fallen back on either side, but after a moment's consideration Maia thought it best simply to tell her jekzha-men to halt where they were until the High Baron had passed.

As he drew level with the jekzha, however, Durakkon suddenly stopped and turned towards her. For an instant she thought that he was going to rebuke her. Then she saw that he was smiling. A moment later he strode across the intervening space between them, his aides following a yard or so behind.

'Maia!' he said, seeming as oblivious of their surroundings as though Ogma had just shown him into her parlour. 'I'm very glad to see you here! Have you come to watch us march out?'

Blushing, she scrambled down, raised her palm to her forehead and was about to fall on one knee when he took her hands in his own. He said no more, however, apparently waiting for her to answer his question.

'I've just come back from taking U-Nasada down to the Blue Gate, my lord. He's going to Quiso—to see the Tuginda.'

'You're lucky to have a friend like that,' replied Durakkon. 'He's a wise man; and a good man, too. I only wish we'd—' He broke off. 'Have you still got your diamonds?'

'Why, yes, my lord, of course. Ask me in fifty years, I'll still be saying yes to that!'

'Well, I may not have the chance: but I'm glad you like them. You deserved them.'

How sad he looked, she thought: how old and gaunt and wretched! Yet it wasn't because he was afraid; she could tell that. He had, rather, an air of deep grief and resignation. It had never before occurred to her that the High Baron might have troubles like everyone else.

'I wish you luck, my lord, and the favour of the gods. Are you going to fight Santil-kè-Erketlis?'

He smiled. 'No, General Kembri's doing that. We have to fight Queen Fornis, I'm afraid. A pity, isn't it?'

He was talking down to her, but she didn't mind. To her, now, he seemed just a nice old man. He'd taken a fancy to her—people often did—

and, being a great lord, was indulging that fancy for a few minutes before setting out on his dismal business.

'My lord! Oh, I know how much you must have to think about just now, but can I—can I make a request of you, seeing as you've been so kind as to stop and speak to me?'

'What is it?'

'It's about—it's about the hostages, my lord. Them as Queen Fornis has got, I mean.'

'The hostages?' His manner became suddenly grave and tense. 'What about the hostages?'

'One of the Katrian officers, my lord; his name's Zen-Kurel. He was—he was kind to me while I was in Suba. If—if you can only save him—'

'Maia, we're going to save every one of the hostages if we can. No one's got better reason than I have, I assure you.'

As her brimming eyes met his, she felt sure that he had guessed her secret. Yet intuitively she knew that he didn't regard her as a traitor for falling in love with an enemy of Bekla. In some strange way the two of them were accomplices: in his heart also there lay something—whatever it might be—which meant far more to him than the Leopards and his public position.

'I must be going now, Maia. Zen-Kurel of Katria; I'll remember that name. But will you grant *me* a request, too?' He was smiling again. Was this a joke? How should she answer?

'Why, yes, my lord; of course.'

'They call you "the luck of the city", you know. The gods love you; everyone knows that. Perhaps you'll be so gracious as to give me a keepsake, for luck. I rather think we may be going to need all the luck we can get.'

Cran alive! Whatever had she got with her that was fit to give to the High Baron? To accompany Nasada she had dressed very simply, without jewels, for he was always so plainly dressed himself. She felt at a complete loss. Then, suddenly, she remembered King Karnat and the golden lilies: that had worked all right.

'I'll be honoured, my lord.'

Deliberately, the Serrelinda stepped forward, drew the High Baron of Bekla's dagger from its sheath and with it cut off a thick curl from the golden mass round her shoulders. She replaced the dagger, knelt to kiss his hand and at the same time closed it on the curl. Then she stood up, raised her palm and climbed back into her jekzha. Thus was born another of the legends told of her long afterwards.

Lokris was already gone: presumably, not knowing how long the Serrelinda and the High Baron might stay talking, she had decided that she might get back quicker on foot. Maia remained where she was, watching until the Beklan regiment had formed column and left the market-place.

For longer than fifty years, in the event, she remembered how she had seen the High Baron march out to die. She must have been the last woman he ever spoke to—except for one.

: 80 :
SHEND-LADOR'S STORY

'—And that was the most shameful thing I've ever seen,' said Shend-Lador.

It was the third night after the departure of Durakkon to westward and of the levies to Kembri in Lapan. Bekla seemed dulled and muted. Trade had declined, and all the lower city bustle that went with it. Hospitality and entertainment had dwindled too. Maia had scarcely been out, except to visit Nennaunir, whom she found in low spirits because Sednil had not been able to escape the levy.

It was strange to see the Peacock Wall sentinelled by old watchmen instead of soldiers; and strange, too, to see relays of porters filing up to the citadel laden with provisions. It was as though the city were holding its breath, listening and waiting; and this tension was heightened by the heat of late summer.

'This is no season for campaigning, you know, säiyett,' Jarvil—an old soldier—had remarked to Maia. 'No good'll come of it, you see.'

'But it's the same for both sides,' she answered.

'Oh, maybe, säiyett, maybe; but all the same, no good'll come of it, either way. It's not the right thing for men to be out campaigning, not at harvest-time.'

Unnatural, she thought; unpropitious, unlucky. Yet still the comet burned: she was still safe. If only there had been a friend to talk to, confide in! If only there were some news!

Shend-Lador, therefore, when he came, she had received most gladly. When Ogma entered to announce him, she had been struggling once again with 'The Deeds of Deparioth'. She laid the scroll aside and jumped up eagerly.

He was leaner and browner, and his clothes were more carelessly worn than in the old days. Yet he was the sort of uncomplicated young man who, without particularly considering the matter, holds it virtually a point of honour always to behave in a light-hearted, cheerful manner. He would have been ashamed for anyone ever to see him looking gloomy, except perhaps at a funeral or some similar occasion. No doubt he had joked his way through the whole Chalcon campaign and done his best to keep his men's spirits up through everything.

'I hope you're as glad to see me, Maia, as I am to see you,' he said, as soon as they had sat down. 'Well, let's say almost as glad, since you've got all the advantages.'

'I couldn't have hoped to see anyone better,' she answered.

'No swimming in the Barb tonight, then?' he asked, jerking his thumb over his shoulder. 'Too shallow for high diving now, is it?'

'I will if you will,' she answered mischievously, pouring his wine.

'Why,' said he, 'you don't think I'd put you to the trouble of saving my life twice, surely? It wasn't worth saving once, you know. All the same, I'm glad you did it. Otherwise I wouldn't be sitting here now, would I, drinking Yeldashay with the Serrelinda?'

He had a charming aptitude for paying compliments with every appearance of sincerity and conviction. He admired her dress, praised the wine, was enchanted by the cabinet of fishes and insisted on Ogma accepting ten meld. He told a bawdy joke which was really funny, making Maia roar with laughter and slap his hand in mock reproof. For some time longer they talked of trivial things, both aware that they were circling a whirlpool whose centre they could not, ultimately, avoid.

It was when he got up and crossed the room to fetch a box of nut thrilsa which he had brought as a present, that she first noticed that he was limping.

'What is it?' she asked, pointing. 'Have you been wounded?'

'Oh, it's nothing,' he answered, grinning. 'I was running much too fast to collect anything serious, believe me. It'll be all right in a week or two.'

'But did you walk back with Elvair from Lapan like that?'

'Well, someone had to come with him,' said Shend-Lador.

'Shenda,' she asked, 'what happened? What *really* happened? All I've heard is rumours and tales from people who weren't there. If you're really grateful that I saved you, tell me the truth.'

'No getting out of that, is there?' he said, sitting down again and picking up his goblet. He paused. 'You really want to hear everything, do you? Only—'

'Yes, I do. I've always liked Elvair: he's been very kind to me. If he's in trouble I'm sorry.'

'Well, all I can honestly say, Maia, is that it's a pity for a lot of good lads that he couldn't just have stayed here and gone on being kind to you.'

She said nothing, waiting.

'It wasn't too bad at the start,' began Shend-Lador after a little. 'The men were all in good heart and we went into Chalcon as keen as a pack of hounds on the scent. But before long we found we couldn't seem to come to grips with the enemy; and then we had to face the fact that it wasn't safe even to send out patrols to try and discover where he was, because they simply got cut up. It's appalling country—thick woodland, a lot of it, where you can't see further than a few yards, with torrents coming down out of the mountains every mile or so; not particularly wide, but swift, and very nasty to ford.

'What we wanted, of course, was a battle, but that wasn't Erketlis's idea at all. And the plain truth was that Elvair didn't really know anything about generalship or campaigning. Nor did I, come to that, but we had experienced officers who did. There was a regular officer, Kapparah, who struck me as particularly useful—a crafty professional survivor if ever I saw one. But Elvair wouldn't hear a word from him.

'"You know the mistake, don't you?" this Kapparah said to me one night when we were by ourselves. "The mistake is obliging Erketlis by charging up and down this Cran-forsaken wilderness. What we ought to have done was pitch camp somewhere not too far into Chalcon, somewhere where we could be sure of our supplies; burned some villages, taken a few hostages and waited. If you're dealing with one of these proud-hearted, feudal heldril like Erketlis, sooner or later his people are going to start telling him it's a matter of honour to attack; 'Drive the hated invader from our native soil' and all that. Then we could have fought him where we wanted, in a spot of our own choosing. As it is, we're looking about as ridiculous as a man chasing an untrained puppy. Just what the puppy wants, of course."

'Up and down, round and round we went, and nothing to show for it, until the men were tired out and began to lose heart and confidence. And Elvair—he didn't really give any leadership: he didn't even set the men an example of courage and endurance. He didn't see enough of them, for a start. And he didn't seem to have a plan. I've known him for years, of course, and I could tell he was jittery—he was bothered by the solitude and the casualties.

'And then at last, one night, we got what we'd really been needing all along: a bit of reliable information from a deserter—a Beklan. Kapparah actually recognized him—a fellow who'd been enslaved five years ago. This man came and told us where Erketlis was—about five miles away—and said he'd lead us there. He was perfectly genuine—there wasn't any doubt about that at all.

'"Well," I said to Elvair, "my men'll be ready in twenty minutes—less, if I've got anything to do with it. I'll get straight back to them now." And do you know, Maia, he looked up at me—he was sitting at a trestle table in his tent—and he said "I think this needs careful planning, don't you? We'll have an officers' meeting first thing in the morning."

'"For holy Cran's sake!" I said. "How long d'you think it's going to take Erketlis to realize this man's missing, and where he must have gone? Every blasted minute's precious!" I said. "Why, he may be off already!"

'"Oh, no, I don't think so," says Elvair. "We'll sleep on it, that'll be best."

'I knew then, Maia: I realized—well, I don't know any other way of putting it—I realized he was no good. He'd been offered Erketlis's head on a plate and he'd convinced himself—he really had, as far as I could see—that he was acting responsibly and doing the right thing. I tried to reason with him: I tried all I knew and at last he said, "I'm sorry, Shenda, this is my decision, not yours, and I'm afraid I'll have to give you an order. Don't discuss it any more."

'The next day we went after Erketlis and of course he'd gone: and I'm as good as certain that in his own mind Elvair was relieved.

'Well, you've heard—at least, I suppose you have, haven't you? In the end we fell back on to the Thettit-Ikat road, after losing something like a hundred and eighty men. And then at last we found that Erketlis was doing what we'd been praying for all along. He was offering a battle—yes, after a forced march through country which had worn *us* to shreds. He'd got south of us and was blocking the road; waiting for us on open ground.

'It must have been about a couple of hours after noon, I suppose. We weren't harassed at all as we approached. We deployed about half a mile away and came forward in line. They had their centre right across the highway. There was a bit of a slope in their favour and they obviously had a few more men, but that was all. You could see Erketlis—there was no mistaking him—talking to his men and giving encouragement, and they were all shouting back and banging on their shields.

'Kapparah was in command on our right and there was no holding him. He went straight into them without waiting for orders, even. I was in the centre, with Elvair, and we must have been about two hundred—well, say three hundred—yards from the enemy when I saw that we were being attacked from behind on the left. It was Elleroth of Sarkid, with his band of home-made freebooters—volunteers—whatever he calls them. They'd lain down in a hollow, behind some bales of straw, until we'd passed them. Well, they took us a bit by surprise and drove in our left more than I really cared about, but it wasn't a patch on Kapparah. He'd beaten his lot all to blazes—you could see them actually running away—almost the whole of the enemy's left wing.

'Elvair had halted the centre and was just standing there, watching. I said "Go on, Elvair! Go on! We've got them!"

'"Oh," he said, "our left—our left's not secure. I think it's a bit risky, don't you?"

'"For basting Shakkarn's sake!" I said (sorry, Maia). "If we don't pile in now we'll lose our best chance! *Their* left's collapsed! Lead the men in—or tell Ta-Kominion to lead them in—or *I'll* do it—anything! Only we *must* get on with it!"

'So then he went out in front of the men and gave the order to charge. We were running towards them side by side, he and I, with everyone yelling behind us, keen as knives. And we must have been about—oh—thirty yards from the enemy, I suppose, when suddenly Elvair stopped dead in his tracks. And then—well, Maia, I'm afraid I can't put it any other way—he simply turned round and ran back through our own front rank.

'Everyone saw it, and of course everyone wondered what on earth could have happened. A moment later we closed with the enemy and there was some pretty nasty fighting for a bit and I got this, incidentally' (he touched his leg), 'but the real sting had gone out of our attack because the men were completely bewildered—no one knew, now, what the hell was supposed to be going on. Kapparah was cutting his way in towards us and he actually got through and joined up with us, but by that time our attack had just fizzled out for want of leadership. Erketlis had lost quite a few men—especially on the left—but so had we; and of course the trouble was that he was still there, where he'd been to begin with, blocking the road. We hadn't shifted him.

'The officers all wanted to go in again, but once an attack like that's failed, you know, it's very difficult to get the men to renew it. And it couldn't have been more conspicuous, you see, what Elvair'd done. You couldn't disguise it, you *couldn't* gloss it over. We went back about a quarter of a mile and hung about and argued. The enemy never moved: I reckon they must have been too tired for Erketlis to risk a counter-attack. Kapparah was crazy to have another go, but Elvair'd got nothing to say to it and there was no one else who had any recognized authority or standing, you see. And then the Tonildans started muttering and saying it was only forty miles to Thettit and what were they waiting for—oh, Maia, to tell you the truth I'd rather not go on! In the end we just sort of drifted off the field. And that was the most shameful thing I've ever seen.'

'Well, all I can say is—' began Maia; but Shend-Lador had not done.

'We retreated a few miles and camped for the night. They didn't pursue us. Erketlis had got what he wanted; Ikat; because we hadn't stopped him. And yet we'd had him as good as beat! He'd taken a risk and it wouldn't have come off, if only—' Shend-Lador drove his fist into his palm.

'The captains met next day and deposed Elvair. There'd have been no holding the men otherwise. I said I'd go back to Bekla with him—I was no use with this leg anyway, you see. The army fell back into Lapan and

Kapparah took over the command. He'll have handed over to Kembri by now.'

He helped himself to a lump of thrilsa. After a moment, nibbling, he smiled and winked at Maia. 'Never mind; they say Lespa dreams it all, don't they? Poor girl must be just about tossing and turning in her sleep by now, I should think. I wish she'd wake up for a piss: I've had about enough of this particular dream, and that's a fact.'

'Oh, quiet, Shenda!' cried Maia, who was superstitiously frightened by impiety—especially where Lespa was concerned. 'But I don't understand! I was told as Randronoth was supposed to be going to join to you with every man he had. When did you and Elvair leave? Didn't you see Randronoth at all?'

'Well, that's the mysterious thing,' replied Shend-Lador. 'No one's seen hide nor hair of Randronoth or any of his men, either. When I left with Elvair, they'd already sent two messengers to ask where the hell he was and what he meant to do.'

'So it'll be all right now, will it?' asked Maia. 'I mean, that ought to be enough to keep Erketlis from getting anywhere near Bekla?'

'I wish I felt sure of that,' said Shend-Lador. 'Kembri's a good general, but what he's got there is a demoralized army to which I gather they've just added a bunch of untrained, reluctant conscripts. As for Randronoth, if I were Kembri I'd believe him when I saw him.'

'Why, where d'you reckon he's got to, then?' asked Maia.

'Well, I think he's like the rest of them—hanging back and waiting to see how things turn out. The provinces have all got enough troubles of their own, you know, Maia. There are half-a-dozen heldro scraps going on in as many different provinces, and no governor's got men to spare. I heard that most of the men they sent up to Bekla for Kembri were just about the bottom of the barrel: they'd even let 'em out of the gaols, some of them.'

'Ah!' said Maia, 'That just accounts for something as I saw t'other day, down the Market. I'd say you were just about right.'

'Well, I might find myself catching it in the neck yet, I suppose,' said Shend-Lador, rather in the tone of voice in which he might have said he was expecting to be badgered by creditors. Looking down at the gold Leopard emblem round his neck, he pretended to tug at it. 'It won't come off, you see. But *you'll* be all right, Maia. You're going to be Sacred Queen, aren't you? That'll mean—'

'No!' she cried, stamping her foot. 'No! I'm *not*, and I'm sick and tired of bein' told as I am! I—'

'Well, that's only what everybody's saying,' he answered. 'But whether or not, no one's going to be in a hurry to chop up a lass like you. It isn't even as if you'd been a Leopards' shearna or any particular Leopard's girl, is it? I think you've handled things very cleverly from that point of view.'

'First time anyone's said that, I'll tell you, Shenda. Far's I can see, most of 'em reckons I'm just about suicidal not t'ave taken up with some big Leopard to protect me by now.'

But his thoughts had apparently run on. 'I wouldn't like to be Milvushina, though, would you? If Erketlis *does* get to Bekla—' He shook his head. 'And then, Elvair's little lapse: whatever happens—even if we were to win hands down—I don't see what they're going to be able to do with him after this. Ambassador to Deelguy'll be about the size of it, I suppose: something like that.'

'How's Milva taken it?' asked Maia.

'I haven't seen her. I'm afraid she may be regretting she didn't take Fornis's tip and go back to Chalcon like a good girl.'

'I'm damned sure she isn't!' cried Maia. 'Want my opinion, all you men make a lot too much of this fighting carry-on. There's Elvair, as nice a fellow as ever—'

'I *personally* don't make much of it,' replied Shend-Lador. 'Only I *do* think it's bad luck, don't you, when ordinary, rough-and-ready fellows entrust their lives to people who've always lived in luxury and had the best of everything, and then those people lead them badly and let them down in the pinch? That's all I'm saying. I mean, take that lame slave-girl of yours—would *you* run away if someone else was going to knock her about?'

Maia made no reply.

It was not in Shend-Lador's nature, however, to rub anything in until it hurt. '*I'm* sorry for Elvair,' he said, 'and I've told him as much. I'd help him if I could, but how's anyone to help him? He's ruined himself, that's about the size of it.'

'You could let yourself be seen about with him,' said Maia.

'Well, so I will, if ever we get back to any sort of ordinary life,' answered Shend-Lador.

Suddenly he fell on one knee before her. 'Maia, you're beautiful; you're lovely! I adore you! That's what I really came to say, only you made me waste such a lot of time talking about the war. Won't you go to bed with me?' He slapped his pockets. 'I believe I've got fifty meld left somewhere, so I won't charge you!'

She could not help laughing, and did not resist even when he kissed her and ran his hands for a moment over her deldas under their smooth, close-fitting silk bodice. But still she shook her head as he released her.

'Why,' said he, 'this is worse than Chalcon—to keep looking at the jam-pot and get no jam.'

'There's no one else gets any, honest,' she answered, smiling.
'Randronoth?'

'Yes, once—for nine thousand meld—and I never touched a trug of it. But he'll never get it again.'

'It was for the Chalcon expedition, wasn't it?' said Shend-Lador. 'What a waste! I'll bet it was all Lapanese taxes, too.'

'It was a waste all right,' said Maia. 'You can take that from me, Shenda. I'll tell you what wouldn't be, though. If you really meant what you just said, go and see Elvair. Go and see him *now*, and have a drink with him.' At random she picked up a silver filigree box from a side-table. 'Give him that from me and tell him I'm his friend. It'll give you an excuse to go.'

He kissed her again and this time she returned his kiss. They walked together to the outer door, where Jarvil gave him his belt and sword.

'"No one could *hin*der, The Serre*lin*da!" My lads used to sing that in Chalcon, you know. By the way, have you noticed, the big star doesn't seem so bright tonight? May be gone soon, I suppose.'

Maia looked up into the nortern sky. It was even as Shend-Lador had said.

: 81 :

RANDRONOTH

She woke with a start. Ogma was bending over her with a lamp, her familiar, ugly face all shadow one side and wavering, yellow brightness the other. Maia sat up quickly.

'What is it, Ogma? Is the house on fire?'

'No, miss, it's—'

'Is there fighting or something?' She swung her legs out of bed.

'No, miss; it's Lord Randronoth.'

'What d'you mean, Lord Randronoth? Where? You mean he's been killed or what?'

'No, miss; he's downstairs.'

'Downstairs? Ogma, have you gone crazy? He can't be downstairs; he's in Lapan and it's the middle of the night! Go back to bed.'

'Säiyett—Miss Maia—it's not my fault! Lord Randronoth was knocking and he woke Jarvil: and Jarvil looked out and saw it was Lord Randronoth and he just had two soldiers with him, no one else. So then Lord Randronoth said he had to see you at once—it was very important. And Jarvil came and woke me and said what should he do? So of course I said yes, let them in—'

804

'But Ogma, whatever for?'

'What, Lord *Randronoth*, miss?' said Ogma in a puzzled tone, as though Maia's question were quite inexplicable. 'Well, of *course* I let him in!'

The sweaty smell of her, stooping over Maia in her night-dress, came strong. It had always been a job to get Ogma to wash. Maia, now really angry, felt ready to box her ears. She was perfectly entitled to hit Ogma, of course, only she never had as yet.

'Well, now you just go down and tell him to go away again. Go on!'

'I don't reckon he'd do it, miss. Well, not for my saying so, that is. He seemed kind of—well, I don't know—kind of beside himself, like: not what you'd call normal, he isn't.'

'Well, then, what the bloody basting hell did you let him in for?' stormed Maia. 'Great Cran, Ogma, I often wonder why I don't sell you, I really do! No, all right—' holding up her hand—'you needn't start in. I suppose you'd better give him some wine and tell him I'll be down in a few minutes. Now light me some lamps and then get out of here!'

Randronoth! she thought. Randronoth—here, in the middle of the night; when he ought to be at the front in Lapan. Did Eud-Ecachlon know he'd come to Bekla? Probably not.

No doubt about what he's here for. What else could he be here for? And thereupon Occula took over. The bloody crazy damned basting menstrual tairth-struck bastard! And it's completely compromising! It leaves me wide open! Oh, Cran! and with Eud-Ecachlon, of all people, left in command of the city! I've *got* to get him out of here somehow!

She was hurrying into her clothes, yet even in this crisis stopped to wash her face and comb her hair. Middle of the night or no middle of the night, she'd be damned if she was going to let Randronoth or anyone else see her all in a flurry and looking like—what was it Occula used to say?—a pig's venda in a thunderstorm. Becoming a little more composed as she looked at herself in the mirror, she put on her diamonds and the jewelled Leopard emblem with which the Council had presented her. Then, with all the outrage, authority and dignity of which she was capable, the Serrelinda made herself walk slowly down the stairs and into the parlour.

Randronoth was standing in the middle of the room. Under his long cloak he was fully armed—sword, dagger and breastplate. He had taken off his leather helmet and cleared a space for it on one of her side-tables. As she entered he held out his arms, smiling with an apparently sincere and perfectly spontaneous expression of joy and triumph.

'My love! My queen!'

'Lord Randronoth,' she said sharply, 'have you gone out of your mind? Do you know what time it is? Please leave my house immediately!'

'Oh, I can well understand it's a shock,' he replied. As he spoke he unbuckled and cast aside his sword-belt, flung back his cloak and sat down. 'But it's the finest shock you'll ever have had in your life, my love, believe me! Listen and I'll explain.'

'I'll listen to nothing! Get out of my house; now, at once! If you don't, I'll send the porter for the night-watch, and believe me I mean it! I don't care if you're the governor of Lapan or anywhere else. I will not be subjected to this sort of behaviour in the middle of the night! If you really have anything to say to me—and I'd imagine the first thing you ought to explain is why you're not with the army in Lapan—you can come back tomorrow morning. Now if you're worth calling a nobleman, get out!'

'Not so fast, Maia,' he said. 'If we're to take Bekla, you and I, you've got to help me. And if you find yourself giving up no more than half a night's sleep before we're done, you'll be lucky.'

'Take Bekla! Whatever are you talking about?'

He laughed. 'Taking Bekla.'

Maia felt herself close to tears of desperation. If she could, she would have thrown him out by force. For a moment she turned away to hide her feelings. Zenka! Zenka, tell me what to do! Come and help me!

'Stop arguing with him,' replied the invisible Zenka. 'He's obviously not here for the reason you thought. Make him tell you what he's up to!'

'Randro,' she said, pulling up a stool, 'you must realize that this is a great shock to me. You'd better tell me what it's all about. You owe me that at least.'

'As if you knew nothing?'

'As if I knew nothing.'

'Very well: since you seem to want to act the simpleton, Maia, I'll go back to the night of the barrarz. You remember we made love, I suppose? You've not forgotten *that*?'

She compressed her lips with annoyance. Her head was beginning to ache.

'And you may possibly recall that you promised me that if I got Sendil freed, you'd spend another night with me next time I was in Bekla?'

'Well, if that's all you want, why can't we get on—'

'Wait a minute! Of course it is—I never stop thinking about you—but just now there are more important things to be done. You'll remember, too, that Seekron came to see you. I know, of course, what he told you. I'll remind you, shall I? He told you that the whole of Lapan was ready to declare for you as Sacred Queen. He gave you the names of several Leopard councillors who were ready to join us; and he gave you forty thousand meld.' Randronoth paused a moment and then repeated it. 'Forty thousand meld. Didn't he?'

'Yes,' she whispered.

'And you took it, and you sent me back word that you'd do all you could to help me?'

The reckoning day, she thought. Oh Cran, the reckoning day!

'Randro, I'll give you back the money—half of it now, this very minute! If only you'll let me alone—'

He held up his hand.

'Oh, Randro, you can go to bed with me all you want! Only please, please leave me out of—'

'Well, as it's turned out, you see, events have moved rather faster than we expected. In this life one has to be able to seize opportunities.'

Opportunity is all, she thought. Opportunity is all. O Lespa, save me!

'The long and short of it is that the Leopards are ripe for destruction. Sencho's dead, Durakkon's a puppet. Kembri's no more than a murderous ruffian and his son's a proved coward. As for Fornis—'

She burst out, 'So you're working for Santil—?'

'For Erketlis?' he said. 'Never in a hundred years, my love! I'm working for myself—and for you! *I'm* the man, not Kembri, that's going to save Bekla from Santil-kè-Erketlis.'

'You must be out of your mind, Randro! Have you thought about this, really and truly? You'll only be throwing your life away; oh, and mine too, Randro! Please—'

'Indeed I've thought about it,' he answered. 'Listen and I'll tell you. Erketlis has defeated—shamefully defeated—the force the Leopards sent against him; and I can tell you that that force are in very poor heart now. Kembri's reinforcements, I'm told, are just about the sorriest bunch between here and Zeray. If I'd joined *them* I'd have been a raving lunatic. Meanwhile Durakkon's been sent out against Fornis with orders to try to hold her up until Kembri gets back. But Kembri never will get back. The plain truth is that Bekla's lying here under Mount Crandor like a dropped purse. Who's going to grab it first, Santil or Fornis? Neither; *I* am!'

'You mean you've got enough men—'

'Yes; Bekla will be in my hands by tomorrow evening; by *this* evening, I ought to say, since it's getting on for morning. When I got Kembri's order to call up every man in Lapan, I obeyed it, with his full authority behind me. But we didn't go anywhere near Elvair-ka-Virrion's lot; no fear! I've got four thousand men, under Seekron, marching up to Bekla now. That's not a great many, but it'll be enough.'

'But Randro—'

'The plain truth is, there's no one here to stop us; only Eud-Ecachlon and a handful of second-rate troops. Seekron will be here by this afternoon. We shall simply take the place over.'

'Well, just you leave me out of it! I don't care what I said—'

807

He ignored her interruption. 'But it's not enough just to *take* a city, Maia. It's got to be *held*, too. If you've ever fed those ducks out there' (he jerked his thumb towards the Barb) 'you'll know what happens when one of them manages to grab a big bit. The inhabitants—we're going to need their support and goodwill if we're to hold the place.' He laughed. 'Of course the best thing for us would be if Santil and Kembri were to destroy each other and Fornis and Durakkon were to do the same. But something tells me that won't happen—things are never so simple. One or other of them will be coming against us; perhaps more than one. That's why I'm here tonight; to talk to you. The people of Bekla are going to be united behind their new Sacred Queen; the Serrelinda.'

She flung herself at his feet, clasping his ankles.

'No, Randro, no! Oh, *please* don't try to make me! I won't do it!'

He raised her to her feet with an air of genuine bewilderment.

'But Maia, my darling, you *said* you would! You told Seekron. You took the money, too.'

'Oh, I didn't realize, Randro! I never thought it would come to this! I didn't mean it—'

'Well, there's four thousand men marching on Bekla now who are quite sure you did, and they're not going to be all that pleased if you back down, I tell you.'

He took her face between his hands, tilting it up and gazing down into her eyes.

'You're essential to us, Maia! My men know me, but the people of Bekla don't. You they *do* know—to say the least.'

'But you can't *make* me do it against my will! You *can't!*'

'This is the first inkling I've had that you weren't entirely with us, Maia. What's happened to make you start jibbing now? Are you a coward—like your friend Elvair-ka-Virrion?'

''Tain't a question of being a coward; though I don't mind telling you I'd be scared stiff—if I was going to do it. But I won't do it! I'll give you back the money!'

'Haven't you used any of it as I said?'

She shook her head. 'I'll be honest. Some I've spent, but most of it I've still got. I'll give it back to you, and the rest as soon as ever I can.'

He was silent, sitting bent forward, elbows on parted knees, tapping his scabbard on the floor between his feet. At length she said, 'Will you please leave now, Randro? I want to go back to bed.'

'The comet's waning,' he said. 'Have you noticed? That's a sign the gods mean the Leopards to fall.'

'Will you only *go*?'

He looked up sharply. 'I'm sorry, Maia,' he replied, 'but the answer's no. Seekron has orders to report to me here as soon as he enters the city.'

'Randro! *Here?*'

'So I'm afraid I can't let you leave this house until Seekron comes: until we've taken the city, in fact. Then I shall have you proclaimed queen, publicly, from the Scales. And no one's going to like it very much, Maia, if you're taken up on the Scales crying and making a fuss, in front of the whole city. Can you imagine it? What it comes to is, I'd say you haven't much choice.'

At this she leapt up and was already at the door when he said, 'There are two of my soldiers out there, with orders to stop anyone leaving the house. Better keep your dignity, Maia!'

'This is insufferable, Randronoth! In my own house?'

'As insufferable as taking forty thousand meld and doing nothing in return? I'm sorry, Maia: I thought we were friends. Yes, and I thought we were lovers, too: it was you who made me think so. But I'll tell you, I'm not going to be thwarted now. Things have gone too far. If you didn't want to play this game you should have told Seekron in the first place.'

'You're holding me a prisoner, then?'

'I wouldn't call it that, Maia. Let's hope we can reach a better understanding during the next few hours. I love you, and in that I'm perfectly sincere.'

'Can I go back to bed now?'

'You can; but I'm afraid I shall have to join you. Your bedroom window isn't very high and I wouldn't put it past a girl like you to jump out or climb down.'

'If I promise not to?'

'Promise? You promised to do all you could to help us.'

Once upstairs, however, he made no attempt to make love to her, but merely dozed in a chair. She lay in her bed, at first feigning sleep, yet falling asleep at last from sheer weariness and nervous exhaustion.

When she woke it was daylight. For some time she lay unmoving, with closed eyes, reflecting on her plight. For the moment, clearly, there was nothing to be done. Later, perhaps, there might be a chance to escape. Meanwhile, the most prudent course seemed to be not to fall out any more with Randronoth, but to try to smooth things over and pretend to assent to his plans: in that way she might even be able to create an opportunity. Still without moving, she prayed long and earnestly to Lespa and at last felt in her heart some stirrings of comfort and reassurance. If I die, she thought, I shall have died for Zenka's sake. I could have gone to Quiso with Nasada: there was nothing to stop me. I'm here, and that must be Lespa's will. Surely she'll protect me.

She murmured, opened her eyes and sat up. Randronoth was awake, seated in the chair and looking at her. She jumped out of bed, ran over and kissed him on both cheeks.

'I'm sorry I was angry,' she said. 'I was that tired and frightened and it was such a shock. I'll do my best to help you, Randro: only it's enough to scare anyone, you must surely see that.'

He nodded, holding her hands and kissing them. 'I want your servants to think there's nothing out of the ordinary—for the moment, anyway. I'm here as your lover—your porter thinks so and your slave-girl too. I've told my soldiers to say nothing to the contrary. The girl—what's her name, Ogma?—do you generally send her to the market?'

She nodded.

'Let her go. It can't do any harm. I've already given her money and told her to say nothing outside about my being here. We'll have breakfast now.'

During the morning Maia did all she could to give the impression of having recovered her calm. For a time she worked on a piece of embroidery, then read for an hour and practised her writing. She was hoping that Nennaunir or Otavis might come to the house, but there were no visitors. The city, when she went up on the roof towards noon, seemed more than usually still and unstirring in the heat: the markets looked almost deserted.

'The caravans aren't coming in,' said Randronoth when she remarked on it. 'There's nothing arriving now from Ikat, you see, or Herl—or from Dari, for that matter. But I dare say stuff will still be coming from the north, unless trouble's broken out there, too.'

She offered an inward prayer for the safety of Nasada, but said no more.

During the early afternoon Randronoth became increasingly restive, making Maia accompany him while he returned several times to the roof to look out to the southward.

'Seekron should have been here by now,' he said. 'I hope nothing's gone wrong.'

'Why, how could it?' asked Maia, hoping with all her heart that it had.

'Well, before I left Lapan I'd found out all I needed to know about the whereabouts of Erketlis; and of the Beklans—the Chalcon force, I mean. But Elleroth—that's another matter entirely.'

'I've heard of this Elleroth before,' answered Maia. 'Who is he? I thought he was with Erketlis?'

'He's the eldest son of the Ban of Sarkid; and as to what he is, he's a very active young fellow spoiling for trouble, that's about it. He's popular in Sarkid, he's a good leader and he's never made any secret of his heldro sympathies. As soon as Erketlis took up arms, Elleroth got together a bunch of volunteers and went off to join him in Chalcon. But after the battle, when Erketlis went south to take Ikat, Elleroth lit out on his own to break up the slave-farm at Orthid in Tonilda. And where he may have got to now I've no idea. That bunch of his can move very fast when they want to, and I wouldn't put it altogether past him to be giving Seekron some trouble.'

'But how would he know about Seekron?' asked Maia. 'My friend Shend-Lador was here only yesterday and he had no idea what you were up to.'

'Well, it's simply that I don't trust Elleroth not to be anywhere, that's all,' said Randronoth, and relapsed into a moody silence.

About an hour later Maia, dozing on her bed, was roused by knocking on the outer door. Looking out of the window, with Randronoth at her elbow, she was startled to see none other than Brero, dishevelled and covered with sweat and dust, gesticulating and talking earnestly with old Jarvil and Randronoth's two soldiers.

Randronoth drew her back into the room. 'Who's that?'

'It's Brero!' she answered, staring. 'My soldier as used to look after me. He was one of those as went off with Durakkon three days ago—'

'With *Durakkon*?'

'Yes; against Fornis. Randro, something bad must have happened!'

Randronoth reflected a moment, staring down at the floor. Then he said, 'Let him in,' and led the way downstairs.

: 82 :

BRERO'S RETURN

Brero, when he came into the parlour, was obviously close to exhaustion. His eyes were bloodshot and his sweat had left long, grimy streaks in the dust clinging to his face. He seemed scarcely able to stand as he saluted them with a dirty, bound-up hand across his chest.

Maia pointed to a chair. 'Sit down, Brero. Ogma!' (for the girl, sensing bad news, was peering in at the door) 'bring some wine!'

'Water for me, säiyett, if it's all the same to you,' said Brero, coughing. 'I—I'll pull myself together in a minute. I'm right done up and that's the truth.'

When the water was brought he drank almost a pint without stopping, drew breath for a few seconds and then drank again.

'You've hurt your hand,' said Maia.

'It's nothing. I'm sorry, säiyett; my feet are that dirty—your floor.'

'Oh, never mind about that. You'd better have a bath, Brero, and we'll find you some fresh clothes.'

'Thank you, säiyett: but first of all I think you'd best hear what I've got to say—you and this gentleman—'

'This is Lord Randronoth, governor of Lapan.'

'I'm sorry, my lord.' He tried to rise to his feet: Randronoth motioned to him to sit down again. 'You'd better hear it at once. The High Baron's dead. Queen Fornis—'

'Durakkon—dead?' cried Randronoth. 'Are you sure?'

'I saw it with my own eyes, my lord. I'll tell you the way of it.'

'Yes, quickly,' said Randronoth.

'I'll be as quick as I can, my lord, for tell you the truth, I believe the Serrelinda may be in danger.'

'Go on,' said Randronoth. He shut the door.

'As you know, my lord, we left here three days ago. I saw the High Baron more than once during the march. He didn't strike any of us as acting like himself; not like a man in his normal senses, so to speak. Seemed like he was in a kind of a daze. Well, once, for instance, when we were crossing some roughish ground on the plain, he tripped and fell; and if you'll believe me, säiyett, he never tried to get up on his own account; just lay there until two of the officers helped him back to his feet. There was some of the lads was saying in so many words that he must 'a been bewitched. And yet at night—both nights—when we'd pitched camp, he come round and spoke to everyone as kind and pleasant as you please. Of course, he was always very well-liked, you know, säiyett, was the High Baron—'

'Get on with it!' said Randronoth. 'What *happened*?'

'Yes, of course, my lord; I'm sorry. Excuse me, I'm that dry.' He drank copiously once more and then continued.

'It was yesterday morning, still fairly early—maybe three hours after sunrise—when one of our patrols came back to say that the Palteshis were only two or three miles off. We were marching in four columns, side by side, it being very open country, like, out on the plain, as you'll know, my lord, and it just so happened that I was quite close to Lord Kerith-a-Thrain and the High Baron when the patrol came in, so I could hear what they were saying. "Within an hour, I'd guess, my lord," the officer said. "They're in no sort of order—strung out all over the place—but I'd say they might be about twice as many as what we are."

'"But what about their quality?" asks Lord Kerith-a-Thrain. "How did they strike you?"

'"No sort of quality at all, my lord, most of 'em," says the patrol captain. "There's a few look all right, but half of them's no more soldiers than what they're musicians."

'So with that Lord Kerith-a-Thrain gives the order to halt and form line, with our two wings sloping back. That's what's generally done for a defensive fight, you see, säiyett, if there's a risk of outflanking—'

'Will you get on and come to the point?' said Randronoth.

'I'm sorry, my lord. So after a little we saw their dust and then they came in sight. Well, you've told me to be quick, so I won't say more than that the patrol captain was right. There certainly were a lot of them, but just louts for the most part: just an armed mob. They was all yelling and shouting and no sort of order to them. They stopped about a quarter of a mile away from us, just as they were, in their different crowds and companies, all over the place. I could see Queen Fornis; there was no mistaking her. She was right in the centre, with a crowd of Palteshi officers, and she was armed just the same as they were.

'And then, before Lord Kerith-a-Thrain had had time to speak to him, the High Baron—I heard him very plain—he said "Keep the men here, Kerith, I'm going out to talk to her about my son. I shan't need to take anyone with me."

'Well, then, Lord Kerith, he tried to argue, my lord, but I won't waste your time with that. In the end the High Baron walked out between the two armies all by himself, and we saw him go up to the queen, and the two of them was talking and then they disappeared together—back through the enemy's line, I mean.

'Well, we was stood there a goodish time and then at last the High Baron came out and walked back to us: and he said to Lord Kerith-a-Thrain, "She's promised to release my son. She's asked that we divide into two parts, as a sign of good faith—one here and one over there." So Lord Kerith-a-Thrain said, "I don't like that, my lord," but the High Baron said, "I want my son out of her hands: she's sworn by Frella-Tiltheh to do us no harm. Do as I say."

'Well, so then he went back, my lord, and Lord Kerith-a-Thrain broke us into two lines, facing inwards, I suppose about three or four hundred yards apart. And we stood watching while the queen and her Palteshi officers led their army forward between us. The High Baron was walking beside her, and a young man as must have been his son, I suppose.

'And then, my lord, when they'd got fairly in between our two lines, the queen suddenly called out, and the men who were with her—four or five of them—they turned and set upon the High Baron and the young man and cut them down, and the queen stood and watched them do it.

'When Lord Kerith-a-Thrain saw that, he called out to attack them and so we did. But there weren't enough of us, you see. I'm certain we could have held off any sort of attack they might have made on us, but we simply hadn't got the numbers to make an attack ourselves—specially split in two like we were. There wasn't the co-ordination, like, you see, and most of the lads were that shaken by what they'd seen—well, there was something uncanny about it, my lord; hundreds standing watching and the High Baron going along that quiet and trusting—almost like he was a kind of sacrifice, as you might say. I can see it now, and the queen standing over his body on the ground. We was going in all anyhow and—and—well, it didn't work out, my lord, that's all.

'I never seen the end of it, because Lord Kerith-a-Thrain told one of our tryzatts to send two men back to Bekla at once with the news. So me and a mate of mine, Crevin, was told to get back here as quick as we could. I won't say I was sorry to be picked, either. Tell you the truth, I was glad to get out of it. We've never stopped, Crevin and me, for well over twenty-four hours. I'm all in and that's a fact.'

'Where's Crevin now?' asked Randronoth sharply.

'Gone to the Barons' Palace, my lord, to report to Lord Eud-Ecachlon.'

Randronoth turned to Maia. 'This may turn out all to the good: Fornis is bound to have had losses. You've done well,' he said to Brero. 'Here's twenty meld. You'd better go and get yourself something to eat and drink.'

'Why can't he bath and eat here?' asked Maia.

Randronoth shook his head. 'No, not here.'

She felt angry. 'Why not?'

'That's all right, säiyett,' said Brero, before she could remonstrate further. 'I'll just be getting back to quarters now. I expect we'll meet again when things are quieter. I hope so, I'm sure.'

He saluted, turned on his heel and left the house.

And now what? wondered Maia. But she could not think clearly, could not dispel the dreadful picture in her mind's eye—the brown, dusty plain in the fierce heat, the divided, inward-facing ranks of the Beklans watching uneasily; and between them the grey, stooping figure of Durakkon, with his son, pacing beside the Sacred Queen—yes, in all truth as though ensorcelled, she thought. Who else but Fornis could have exercised this power to make a man hand himself over to his own destruction; and then devised so stylish a public ceremony of treachery and murder? What pleasure and satisfaction it must have given her! Far more than the relatively paltry affair of Tharrin.

And what now? What now? Assuming that Fornis's Palteshis had succeeded in beating off the Beklan attack and getting between Bekla and Kerith-a-Thrain, they would probably reach the city some time tomorrow; certainly no later than the day after. Yet before then Randronoth's men would have arrived. What would Eud-Ecachlon do? He would presumably be forced to make common cause with Randronoth: he would have no choice. And he would probably have been safe enough in doing so, too, thought Maia, had his enemy been anyone but Fornis. For Maia, who had thought she knew the Sacred Queen, was now beginning—as had others in the past—to descry in her undreamt-of, far horizons of cunning and cruelty, and attribute to her insuperable powers. If Fornis intended to take Bekla, no doubt she possessed the demonic means to do so.

Randronoth was speaking. 'What did you say?' she asked him dully.

'I said, "I'm going up to the roof to watch for Seekron. Will you please come with me?"'

'I want to lie down,' she said. 'I feel bad.'

'Tell your slave to bring a mattress up, then.'

There was an awning over one corner of the roof, and here she lay in the hot, windless shade, hands pressed over her throbbing eyes. The Sacred Queen was coming: Zenka was in her power. And not only Zenka, but Anda-Nokomis, towards whom her feelings were now utterly changed. She was a Suban by blood; he was not only her cousin but her rightful lord, to whom accordingly she owed a sacred duty of service and loyalty. Yet how could she hope to help either of them now?

Her very thoughts had become hysterical. She was obsessed by the figure of the approaching queen; the queen never at a loss for some vile, unforeseeable stratagem.

To her the queen no longer seemed a human opponent, but a kind of inanimate doom: a black pit; or rather, perhaps, a flexible, sticky web, in which the more one struggled the more one became enmeshed, until at length the victim hung inert—whether dead or dying was of no consequence, though the latter would afford the queen more enjoyment. So terrible now to Maia was this access of helplessness and despair that had it not been for Randronoth's enforced restraint she might, despite her love for Zen-Kurel, have fled from the city—yes, alone and on foot—anywhere, so long as it was away from Fornis. She did not believe that the combined forces of Randronoth and Eud-Ecachlon—she did not believe that any power on earth—could prevent Fornis from entering Bekla and putting her to death.

Once more—after how long she could not tell, though opening her eyes she saw that the sun was westering—she was roused from her desolation by the sound of knocking below. She would have got up and looked over the parapet, but Randronoth, gripping her arm, held her where she was, himself kneeling beside her and waiting. After less than a minute they heard Ogma calling from below.

'Can't I go down?' she said.

'No: tell her to come up here.'

Before Ogma had uttered a word it was plain that her news was bad. She stared from one of them to the other as though afraid to speak. Maia, catching her fear, started forward.

'What's happened? Who is it, Ogma?'

'It's—it's Lokris, Miss Maia,' stammered Ogma, but said no more, as though to remain silent might somehow prevent the news from being true.

'Lokris? From Milvushina?'

'Oh, Miss Maia, she's been taken bad! She's in labour before her time! Lokris says the midwives are there and the doctor too, and they're afraid for her. She's in a bad way, Lokris says: and she's asked for you to go to her as quick as you can.'

'Milvushina!' cried Maia. 'Oh, why didn't I think of it before? I might 'a guessed!'

'Seems as 'twas all the upset and worry, Miss Maia; Lord Elvair-ka-Virrion coming back the way he did—'

'Yes, of course—'

'Lokris says ever since he got back, miss, he's shut himself up alone in the Barons' Palace. He wouldn't go to the Lord General's house. So in the end Miss Milvushina took Lokris with her and went to the Palace herself, but he wouldn't see even her; and that's where she was took bad. That's where she is now.'

'Oh, my lord—Randro—' Maia collected herself. 'Ogma, go down and tell Lokris to go back and say I'm coming at once.'

As soon as the girl had gone she turned back to Randronoth. 'Randro, I promise you—I swear by Frella-Tiltheh I'll say nothing to Eud-Ecachlon or to anyone else. I *swear* I'll come straight back here—oh, within the hour if you say so—only please let me go to Milvushina!'

He shook his head. 'This is war, Maia: Seekron will be here before sunset. Eud-Ecachlon—Elvair-ka-Virrion—they're the enemy. I can't let you go anywhere where you might talk to them.'

'But if I don't go it'll look more suspicious! Surely you can see that?'

He shrugged his shoulders. 'By tonight the city will be in my hands. Until then you must stay here. Anyway, what good could you do?'

'She's my friend and she's in bad trouble! Oh, Randro, you said you loved me!'

'This is no time to argue, Maia.'

Suddenly, in the midst of her frenzied fear for Milvushina, an idea came into her mind; one so simple that she could only wonder that it should not have occurred to her before. This was Randronoth that she was dealing with—Randronoth who had paid nine thousand meld.

She sat down and dried her eyes. After a little—he was still looking out southward—she said, 'Well, I can see your point of view, Randro. It *is* war, and I know you've got to think of your men first. I'm sorry you reckon you can't trust me, but there it is: I must just try and accept it, mustn't I? Shall we go down, now, and have a drink in the garden? I could do with it, I know that. One of your soldiers could watch for half an hour, couldn't he?'

After a moment's thought he replied, 'Very well,' and put out his hand to help her down the stairs.

While he was instructing the soldier she called Ogma into the parlour.

'Ogma, don't argue with me or act anything out of the ordinary, d'you see? Just bring some wine and nuts and that out into the garden, and do it quickly!'

As soon as he had joined her she led him into the garden, poured the wine, handed him his goblet and drank deeply herself.

'Ah! That's better! I'm feeling a lot better now,' she said. 'Give me your arm, Randro; let's have a little stroll. There's something I want to show you, down by the shore. Did I ever tell you about the golden lilies I picked for King Karnat in Suba? No? Well, 'twas like this, see—'

Talking on, she drew his arm through hers, leading him gently and leisurely on among the shrubs and flowerbeds, fragrant in the cooling air of evening. The western sky was reddening and there was no least breath of wind.

'Do you know something, Randro?' she said. 'I've longed for you so often since that night of the barrarz. You were wonderful! We had so much pleasure, didn't we? Do you remember in the morning, when you thought you were finished and then you found you weren't?'

'Yes, I do,' he replied. 'I wouldn't be likely to forget that, would I?'

'We can't make love now, though,' she said, and drew his hand from her waist up to her bosom. 'What a pity! For there'll be no chance later tonight, will there? Not once Seekron gets here. You'll have far too much to do.'

'I thought you didn't want to make love,' he answered.

'Why, when did I say that? You never asked me, did you?'

They had reached the marble bench near the Barb.

'You've seemed so angry and upset all day. Naturally, I thought—'

'Sometimes being upset brings a girl on all the harder; didn't you know that?' She kissed his ear, nibbling the lobe. 'It's all the strain and excitement and that.'

'Maia, are you serious? Do you really want to make love?'

For answer she flung her arms round his neck, kissing him passionately and pressing herself against him. He responded, panting, and caressing her with trembling hands.

'Let's go back to the house, then. Come on!'

'Oh, no, Randro! I couldn't! I mean, I couldn't let myself go; not with the soldiers there and everyone knowing. No, I'm afraid we'll just have to leave it for now.' She pressed herself to him still more ardently, putting one hand on his thigh. 'It's a shame, isn't it?'

'No one can see us here.'

'Oh!' She stood back, wide-eyed, holding her hand over her open mouth. 'Oh, Randro, *no*! How *can* you—'

He smiled delightedly. 'You're Lespa; I'm Shakkarn. Why not?'

'Oh, no!' But his fingers had already begun to unfasten her robe at the neck, drawing it down and drawing down her shift to bare her deldas, which he stooped to kiss.

'Well—well—I don't know. Oh, Randro, it's so nice!' She kicked off her sandals, let her clothes fall and stood naked before him. 'You, too! You, too! Only just turn round a moment, darling: I want to make water and I can't do it with you watching.'

'Can't you?' He gave her a playful smack on the buttocks. 'All right.' Turning his back, he began pulling his leather jerkin over his head.

Now! she thought. Now! And she ran, ran, bounding through the grass to the water, her deldas leaping, her hair flying behind her. Splash! Splash! Hopping ankle-deep, wading knee-deep, deeper, two or three agonizingly slow, pushing, thigh-deep steps. Then she had plunged forward and struck out into the Barb. Behind her she could hear Randronoth calling 'Maia, come back!' And then, 'Maia, this will cost you your life! I warn you, come back!'

On she swam, never once looking round. The water was smooth—far smoother than Serrelind as she had known it a many a time. Yet in her haste and desperation, she realized, she was swimming too fast: at this rate she would be exhausted before ever she could reach the western end of the Barb. Besides, there was a slight but steady current against her, for she was in the line of flow between the infall and outfall of the Monju brook. She must settle down, for she had more than half a mile to go. Would Randronoth try to follow her round by the bank? No, almost certainly not, for he would realize that if she saw him waiting for her on the bank she would simply stay in the water, while he would be bound to draw attention to himself and disclose his presence in the upper city.

: 83 :
AT THE BARONS' PALACE

Maia's swim down the Barb took her over half an hour. Although, naturally, the thought of Milvushina was never entirely absent from her mind, the necessity of swimming distracted her, eased her tension and afforded her the comfort of exercising a familiar skill at which she was adept. It was satisfying, too, to think that this skill had enabled her to get the better of Randronoth.

Once she scattered a flock of black swans, the great birds, with their red beaks, all rising together from the water, circling wide to her left and re-alighting near the infall of the Monju behind her. As she rounded the peninsula, swimming more slowly now and from time to time turning on her back to rest, there came into sight the gardens where Sencho had died, the tree from which she had dived and the inshore pool where she had saved Shend-Lador. They looked different now, she thought, and in a way unfamiliar. The difference, she realized after a few moments, lay in her-self—in the eyes with which she saw. *They* were the same, but she was no longer the slave-girl who had accompanied Occula and the High Counsellor on that fatal evening. There returned to her mind the unsolved mystery of Zirek and Meris. What could have happened to them after they had fulfilled their task? Were they dead? But if so, where were their unfound bodies? Might they, after all, have escaped? Did Occula know? Herself and Occula—were they the only people left in the city who knew who had killed Sencho?

Before her rose the grassy terraces of the Leopard Hill, and above them the Palace, its twenty round towers clustering darkly, like a bed of gigantic reed-maces, against the sunset sky. At this sheltered, western end the water, reflecting the reddened clouds, was glass-still; so still that her approach sent long, undulant ripples shorewards. She could see no one—no sentry by the waterside, not a soul looking down from the verdant slopes. It might have been the enchanted castle in one of old Drigga's tales—the stronghold of Canathron, who returned to it each night. And if, she thought, Canathron were even now to come flying home out of the flames of the sunset, would he spread his healing wings and save Milvushina? But she had never prayed to Canathron; and this seemed no time to start, when she had just hoodwinked and outwitted the governor of Lapan.

About a hundred yards out, she found herself in her depth; but being still far from spent, swam gently on—it was easier than wading—until, coming to rest at length on the gravelly sand inshore, she stood up, sluicing her body with cupped handfuls of water.

Milva, she thought: Milva. What could *she* do to help her? Although she could recall the birth of each of the girls she had once believed to be her sisters, none had involved any complication or danger: Morca had always given birth almost as easily as slipping off her pattens. Whatever was wrong, it would be beyond any knowledge or experience which she pos-sessed. She knew Lokris for a sensible, level-headed woman: it would be most unlike Lokris to say that Milvushina was in a bad way unless it were true. Deep—atavistically, indeed—in every woman lies the fear of this occu-pational danger, just as in every man there lies the fear of death by conflict or violence. As she stepped onto the bank Maia had no thought for anything else. She had even forgotten her own nakedness; or rather—as with the wounded or the grievously ill—in her present circumstances nakedness was a matter of no particular consequence. She hadn't time now to be bothering about such trivialities, the unimportance of which must surely be as plain to anyone else as to herself.

Zig-zag she climbed the Leopard Hill, up the narrow paths between the low stone walls and little, secluded arbours designed for meditation, confidential talks and lovers' meetings. There were no lovers there now; no friends disputing about music or sculpture, no circumspect councillors seeking a quiet word in private. Though Maia did not know it, Eud-Ecachlon, as soon as he had heard Crevin's report, had alerted everyone of consequence in the upper city and sent runners to warn the lower city marshal to close and double-guard all gates, including the Peacock Gate. Shock and panic were already spreading across the whole of Bekla. The High Baron, lord of the empire, betrayed and cut down by—of all people—the Sacred Queen, in full view of thousands! In all the city's history such a deed had never been imagined, never dreamt of. What might be fated to follow an event so unthinkable? The legends, the annals, the lore of the priests were alike silent. The dead—might they now rise from their graves and walk the streets; the earth quake, the rocks be rent, the Temple of Cran fall? Not for nothing, then, after all, had Lespa set her great light to burn in the northern sky.

As the sunset—a brilliant, glowing chiaroscuro of saffron, crimson and green—faded and dusk darkened the terraces below, the two sentinels at the eastern door of the palace, new-levied peasant strangers to Bekla, their nerves already shredded by rumour and speculation, but most of all by the unconcealed alarm and dismay of their superiors, were suddenly stricken aghast to see the shadowy form of the goddess Lespa walking intently towards them in the failing light. There could be no mistaking the apparition. Very beautiful she was, with a more than earthly beauty, a matchless young girl immune to age or death; quite naked but, goddess-like, without the least air of self-consciousness or shame. Her superb body was glistening with drops of water from the clouds through which she must have descended, while her long hair, also damp, fell in a golden drift about her shoulders. Her bare feet made no sound. Despite its marvellous beauty her face—and what else would you expect?—was very sorrowful, grave and absorbed, yet with a purposeful look, as though she well knew her divine intention, whatever it might be.

Letting fall their spears, the sentries fled into the palace.

Maia, having entered under the portico, looked about for someone to guide her. There was no one to be seen, however, and she climbed the first staircase she came to, which brought her out on an open landing hung with tapestries. Yet here, too, all was deserted.

In this shady, eastward-facing place she felt, for the first time since setting out, a touch of cold. She had not seen the sentries run, but now it occurred to her that her nakedness might hinder her mission. Eud-Ecachlon, who was presumably somewhere in the palace, might have her apprehended, or perhaps some rougher man, a soldier or servant, might molest her. As she stood in perplexity she remembered the night of the senguela, when she had pulled down one of Sarget's wall-hangings to dress up as the prying old woman. Opposite her was a window, with curtains of green and blue silk. Scrambling up into the embrasure, she found that she could lift down the pole and slide them off. One would be enough. As a Tonildan peasant girl she had learned two or three different ways of draping and knotting a rectangle of woven cloth into a garment. Those who possessed such things had been lucky: most wore sacking or home-spun. In less than two minutes Maia was at least presentably clothed and making her way down the upper corridor.

Rounding the next corner she saw coming towards her a girl carrying a bundle of clothes.

'The lady Milvushina,' she said. 'Where can I find her?'

'The lady Milvushina, säiyett?' answered the girl. 'They say she's very ill—'

'I know that!' said Maia. 'Just tell me where she is.'

Turning, the girl guided her down the corridor, climbed a staircase and in silence pointed to a closed door a few yards further on. Maia thanked her with a nod, tapped on the door and entered.

Four women, one of whom was Lokris, were gathered about a bed on the opposite side of the big, luxurious room. With them was an elderly, grey-bearded man, his bare arms streaked with blood. All five looked round at her and the old man, staring severely, seemed about to speak.

'I'm Maia Serrelinda, doctor,' she said, before he could do so. 'I've come because I was sent for.'

Silently, he laid one hand on hers and, looking into her eyes, shook his head. One of the women was silently weeping. Suddenly, Maia caught her breath in an involuntary spasm of fear and horror. That smell—that terrible smell—when had it last overcome her, where had she known it before? Next moment she knew. She was back in the darkness and firelight on the banks of the Valderra, kneeling beside Sphelthon, the dying Tonil-dan boy. For a moment she actually seemed to hear his voice. Then the doctor's hand was gripping her wrist and she was turning with him towards the bed.

Milvushina, very pale, her forehead and chin beaded with sweat, lay covered only with a sweat-damp, crumpled sheet. Her long, black hair was tumbled about her. One bare arm was stretched across the bed. Her breathing was laboured and uneven. Her mouth was open, as were her great, dark eyes, yet it seemed as though she saw nothing, for they were staring fixedly upward toward the ceiling. Maia's immediate impression was of a being isolated beyond reach of anyone around her. She looked partly like an animal caught in a trap and partly like someone compelled to expend, upon some immense labour, nothing less than every scrap of energy at her command.

Maia took her hand.

'Milva,' she said. 'Milva? It's Maia: I'm here.'

Slowly, Milvushina seemed to return from a great distance. Her head rolled, her eyes found Maia's and she gave the faintest trace of a smile.

'Maia,' she whispered.

'Yes. You must rest, darling,' answered Maia. 'I won't leave you. It'll be all right, you'll see.'

Very slightly, as though even this was an effort, Milvushina shook her head. 'I'm dying.'

'No, you're not, dearest.'

Milvushina's hand clenched weakly on Maia's. After a few seconds, having gathered strength to speak again, she murmured, 'Don't—don't—I need you—' She broke off, shutting her eyes and biting her lower lip, apparently seized once more with pain.

Maia bent her head to her ear.

'I won't go away.'

It seemed doubtful whether Milvushina had heard her. Her hand lost its grip and she began once more her heavy, intermittent panting.

Maia stood back from the bed. 'What's happened?' she asked Lokris. 'What's gone wrong?'

'It was the news, säiyett,' answered Lokris, 'and then Lord Elvair-ka-Virrion refusing to see her or speak to her. She went into premature labour this morning, but she's only bled ever since and we can't get the baby born.'

'Can't you cut her?' asked Maia, turning to the doctor.

'I have cut her, säiyett. I'm very sorry. Believe me, I've done all I can—all anyone could. These cases are always dangerous. No doctor can ever be sure—'

'You mean she's dying?'

'Säiyett, the loss of blood—'

'There's no hope?'

He shook his head. 'The internal bleeding can't be staunched, you see. I've given her a drug for the pain. There's nothing more I can do.'

Maia, falling on her knees beside the bed, laid her cheek against Milvushina's shoulder. She did not move as the women drew off the sheet and once more began changing the blood-drenched dressings. When they had finished the room seemed very silent and dim. Later, Maia became vaguely aware that someone had brought more lamps. Later still, Milvushina stirred, moaned and spoke without opening her eyes.

'Maia?'

'Yes, dear; I'm here.'

'Tell Elvair—tell—'

'Yes, Milva?'

'I love him. I—don't—blame—' Suddenly, startlingly, her utterance became clear and lucid. 'He's being silly. No blame. I love him, say.'

'I'll tell him.'

'Promise?'

'Yes, Milva: I promise.'

Milvushina's hand pressed hers once more. She seemed to be trying to say something, but no words came.

Someone brought a stool and Maia sat on and on beside the bed, holding Milvushina's hand and watching in the lamplight the slight movements of her lips and eyelids. They ceased. After a long time—as though, having resisted to the last, she had finally been compelled, against every spark of her will, to acquiesce—she knew that Milvushina was dead.

She stood up, gazing down at the body. Milvushina looked unbelievably young—about twelve—a child with enormous eyes that stared and stared unblinkingly, as though in accusation. It was the eyes that were staring, not Milvushina. She had gone, leaving this sorry likeness behind.

Maia realized that she was very thirsty. She turned to Lokris. 'Bring me some water, Lokris, please.'

'You mean, to drink, säiyett?'

When Maia had drunk the water she said, 'You say Lord Elvair-ka-Virrion's here in the palace?'

'Yes, säiyett.'

'Take me to him, please.'

Another woman might perhaps have asked questions or argued, but it had no doubt occurred to Lokris that she could not be blamed for doing as she was told and also that in the circumstances that would be the least troublesome thing to do as far as she herself was concerned. Picking up a lamp, she walked half-way to the door and turned, waiting for Maia to join her.

The doctor touched Maia's arm. 'I trust you won't lay blame on me, säiyett. I assure you I did all that was possible.'

'No,' she replied, shaking her head. 'No, you needn't worry.'

Making their way down the passage, neither she nor Lokris spoke. Maia had little awareness of their surroundings. Once a middle-aged woman—

823

seemingly some kind of upper servant—coming out of a doorway, stopped short and cried in a low voice, 'Oh, Lokris, what's happened?' Lokris caught her eye, shook her head and walked on.

On the landing where Maia had taken down the curtains a lamp was now burning. Lokris picked it up and handed it to Maia.

'I think you may need this, säiyett.'

'Shall I? Why?'

But Lokris only nodded, leading her up the staircase to the second storey. Maia could hear a murmur of voices behind a door, but this they passed, entering a colonnade like the one in Kembri's house where she had attended the Rains banquet. At its far end they came to another closed door, ornately carved, with recessed panels and a great latch of bronze, the stop cast to resemble a hound and the fall-bar a bone clenched in its jaws. Here Lokris stood to one side, inclining her head.

'Lord Elvair-ka-Virrion, säiyett.'

In the terrible distress and grief consuming her, Maia's self-possession was like a frail raft on a swirling flood. In imminent danger of being overwhelmed, it still remained afloat, though barely.

'But I must see him alone, Lokris. Are you sure there's no one with him?'

'Yes, säiyett.'

'How can you be sure?'

'I am sure, säiyett.'

'Well, then, will you please go in and tell him as I'm here?'

For a moment Lokris hesitated. Then she said, 'Säiyett, I think it'll be better if you simply go in yourself; and take the lamp with you.'

Maia stared, but Lokris merely averted her eyes, looking down. After a moment Maia raised the latch, putting her shoulder to the heavy door. It yielded and she stepped inside.

The room was not quite in darkness, for it faced west and was still faintly twilit. One would not have expected to find anyone in it, however, unless they were either asleep or making love. Yet this was not a bedroom. No; this, with its profusion of stools and small tables, its sideboard covered with silver dishes and goblets and its trophies hung on the walls, had the appearance of some kind of ante-room, perhaps adjoining a hall next door. Holding up her lamp, she looked round her in perplexity.

'Elvair?' she said timidly; but there was no reply.

She turned this way and that, looking round the big, shadowy room in apprehension, and was just going to hurry out again when she realized that someone—a motionless figure—was sitting on a tall, armless chair by the window. The back of the chair was towards her and its occupant seemed gazing out towards the darkling west. Maia, carrying her lamp, crossed the room and stood beside the chair. The figure was, indeed, Elvair-ka-Virrion.

He looked as a man might who had spent days in prison. He was hollow-cheeked, pallid and unwashed and his hair and beard were unkempt. She could smell his stale sweat. His torn, travel-stained clothes must be those in which he had come back from Lapan. One of his bootstraps was broken and trailing on the floor. Beside him stood a tray on which were plates and the remains of untouched food. She saw mouse-droppings and a fretted, nibbled crust.

He did not move as she touched his shoulder.

'Elvair? Elvair, it's Maia.'

He looked up for a moment. 'Maia. Oh, yes.' Dropping his chin on his hands, he resumed his abstracted staring towards the west.

She knelt beside his chair and put her hand on his wrist.

'Elvair, I'm so sorry—I'm very sorry that I've only come to add to your troubles. I wouldn't do it if I hadn't got to, honest.'

It would be easier, she thought, if only he would ask her what her news was and she could answer him. But as she waited he put aside her hand, stood up, took two or three steps across to the window and continued gazing out into the near-darkness.

Maia, still kneeling on the floor, began to cry—for Milvushina, for Tharrin, for Sphelthon, for her own terror of death, for the loss of Zenka, the fallen darkness and the hopelessness of the entire world.

He seemed unaware of her weeping; but she was weeping from the heart, and for some little time continued without any attempt to control herself or to speak again; while he stood silently, his back turned, both of them as it were isolated in separate cells of suffering. At last Maia recalled that she had come in fulfilment of the promise she had made to Milvushina.

'Elvair? Elvair, I've brought bad news; but you must hear it.'

For all the response he made he might not have heard her. In a sudden passion she jumped up and ran across to him, tugging at his arm and beating her fist on his chest.

'She's *dead*, Elvair; Milva's dead! She told me I was to come and tell you she loved you and she didn't blame you for anything. She didn't blame you for anything!' As he still said nothing she stood in front of him, put her two hands on his shoulders and cried, 'Do you hear me? Milva's dead, I tell you! The baby's dead and Milva's dead!'

For a moment he looked coldly into her eyes, much as he might have looked at a servant who had had the temerity to interrupt him while absorbed in some complicated matter. Then, once more staring over her shoulder, he muttered just audibly, 'I don't care. Go away.'

As though he had struck her, Maia started back. As though he had struck her she drew in her breath and raised one hand to her cheek. Then, like one suddenly perceiving in the room the presence of something monstrous and appalling, she snatched up the lamp and ran stumblingly to the door.

Lokris was seated on a bench about twenty yards up the colonnade. As Maia came out she stood up, but if she had not caught her arm Maia would have run past her.

'Let me help you, säiyett: these corridors can be a little treacherous after dark. I wouldn't want you to fall. Please take my arm.'

They walked on together, Maia with the one lamp held in her left hand, Lokris with the other in her right. As they reached the landing on the first floor Lokris asked, 'Will you wish to leave the palace now, säiyett?'

'Yes,' she answered. 'Yes, I'll go now, Lokris. Only I shall need some shoes—sandals—anything will do.'

'Take mine, säiyett: I think they'll fit you well enough.'

Lokris took off her sandals, knelt and strapped them on for her.

'Will you be needing anything else, säiyett? A jekzha?'

Maia had, of course, no money with her, and in her shocked and broken state of mind could not face the embarrassment of asking Lokris to go and get her some and waiting while she did so.

'No, Lokris, thank you: I'll walk on the terrace for a little while.'

Lokris accompanied her as far as the north door of the palace, and here they parted without having spoken of what had taken place.

: 84 :

MAIA GOES HOME

It did not matter where she went, she thought. It didn't matter what happened. The gods, who had done this to Milva, could now do whatever they liked with her. She would go home, and Randronoth could kill her if he wanted. Go home—yes, that would surprise the gods. The gods would not be expecting that.

Slowly she descended the road down the Leopard Hill into the upper city. Although many people passed her, hurrying in both directions, it did not really strike home to her that any upheaval was taking place. The barracks of the upper city—a square, gloomy building—lay about a quarter of a mile ahead, and here she could see torches and hear noise and commotion. But she merely walked on, stumbling once or twice in Lokris's sandals, which were not in fact a very good fit.

She thought of the handsome, dashing young man who had spoken so charmingly to Occula and herself in the Khalkoornil on that first afternoon in Bekla, when they were being taken to Lalloc's. She remembered the sound of Milvushina's weeping on the night when she and Occula had returned from Sarget's party—that same night when she had cursed Bayub-Otal and vowed to harm him if she could. She thought of the good-natured, sympathetic Elvair-ka-Virrion, who had made love with her and later had been so ready to help her with his notion of the auction at the barrarz; and again, of Milvushina smiling as she sat on the couch in the Sacred Queen's supper-room. Behind all sounded old Nasada's thin, dry voice, 'Get out of Bekla. It's a devils' playground.'

Once or twice, as she made her half-shuffling, ungainly way along the road in the elf-light of moonrise, men spoke to her; but she did not even hear them, passing on in a trance of wretchedness which communicated itself without the need for any reply on her part.

It was a night, however, when few in the upper city were of a mind to be accosting girls. So far as property owners and their servants were concerned (and most dwellers in the upper city were either one or the other) all thoughts were centred upon Santil-kè-Erketlis and the defeated Leopard force in the south. If Erketlis and his heldril were indeed to take the city, as he had said he intended, what was the prospect for merchants—and especially for slave-traders? And beyond these material fears lay the deep, superstitious anxiety engendered by the news of Durakkon's death at the hands of Fornis. There was a general, intuitive feeling that that business was neither conclusive nor concluded; it must inevitably have some further outcome; and though no one could guess what that might be, the prospect gave rise to uncertainty and dread.

About the streets people were hastening hither and thither, nearly all, so it seemed, concerned in one way or another with the safety of their property. There were not many to take more than momentary notice of a distraught girl in tears, obviously intent on some destination. No doubt she had received bad news. Many had.

Yet all of a sudden Maia, now well past the barracks and less than three furlongs from her own house, found her way blocked by a man standing squarely in front of her. Moving to one side, she tried to walk past him; but he spread his arms, and rather than have him grab hold of her, as he seemed about to do, she stepped backward, looking down at the ground and ignoring him in the hope of being left alone.

'Ah!' he cried. 'A shadow will cover the city! A shadow!'

She recognized him then, with the weary resentment of one who, though deep in affliction, understands that nevertheless there is to be no escape from the tedium and vexation of having to deal with an intrusive eccentric.

Jejjereth, as he was commonly known (the name had a slightly obscene meaning in Beklan), was a familiar figure in the streets and markets of the lower city; one of those grotesque, half-crazy declaimers and self-styled prophets who always knock about large cities; fantastically clad, of no fixed abode, part laughing-stock and part accorded, by the common people, a kind of rough recognition for having shown themselves to possess at least a crude form of moral courage and sincerity; who stand in public places orating disjointed nonsense about imminent wrath and judgement to such as have nothing better to do than listen until they weary of it, while wags shout ribald questions over their heads. 'A shadow will cover the city' was notorious as one of Jejjereth's favourite utterances. Maia could recall having once seen him in the Caravan Market, his rags fluttering as he was dragged off the Scales and sent packing by two of the municipal slaves. Sometimes he would stand at one or other of the lower city gates, haranguing visiting pilgrims and other passers-by until the sentries, having decided that he had had his fair turn, moved him on. To come upon him in the upper city was all but incredible. At any other time she would have wondered how he could possibly have got in. Now, she merely hoped he would let her alone and go away.

'A shadow!' he cried. 'A shadow to enshroud the evil—the gluttons and their trulls, the liars, the murderers and men of blood!' He made a wide, sweeping gesture, spreading his grimy cloak before her like the wing of some huge, tattered bird.

'The whores! The murderers' whores shall hang upside-down, with their legs apart to let in the blowflies!'

'Jejjereth,' she said quietly, as he still blocked her way, 'please let me pass. I've never done you any harm and I want to go home.'

Now he peered at her more closely. 'Maia! Maia swam the river!'

'Yes, yes,' she replied soothingly (she was only humouring a zany by completing a catch-phrase), 'Maia saved the city. Please let me go by.'

'Saved the city!' he shouted. 'Yes, Maia saved the city for the cruel to commit more murders, for the wicked to enjoy more lust and greed! But a shadow will cover the city—'

By this time several people had stopped—household slaves and the like, to whom the sight of him in the lower city was familiar enough.

'What in Cran's name are you doing up here, old fellow?' said a night-watchman, taking him by the arm. 'Who let you in, eh?'

Jejjereth, having turned to face him, spoke behind his hand in a voice which everyone could hear. '*She* let me in,' he said. '*She* let me in—to call down vengeance on corruption! Yes, to go even to the Barons' Palace! Jejjereth's not afraid to strike, no, no—'

'What, this girl here? Don't tell me *she* let you in—'

'No! No! Not her! It was the Leopardess—the swift one, with the green— ah! She let me in, to bring judgement—'

'Which Leopardess, old boy?' asked someone else. 'Come up here to baste a few expensive ones for a change, have you?'

'A shadow will cover the city—'

'Yeah, and a bull will cover a cow an' all. And you've been covering a Leopardess, is that it?'

'Perhaps that *is* it,' put in the night-watchman. 'Some of these rich women in the upper city've got peculiar tastes, y'know. Now come on, old lad,' he said, gripping Jejjereth more firmly. 'Never mind about Leopardesses an' that; you just hop it to the Peacock Gate, else you'll know all about it, see?'

Suddenly and frighteningly, Jejjereth drew a long, sharp-pointed knife from under his cloak. '*She* gave me this,' he said, grinning round at them. '*She* gave me this: she said, "Take this *folda*, go to the Barons' Palace and strike down the wicked—"'

'Here, you'd better just give that to me,' said the watchman, startled. 'That's dangerous, that is. Might hurt someone.'

Maia, glad to have avoided further unwelcome attention, left them at it and continued on her way.

Ten minutes later she was walking up to the door of her own house. Although she could almost find it in her heart to hope that he might, she did not believe that Randronoth would kill her. It was more likely that he would still want to do what he had been tricked out of doing. Oh, she thought, if only her ashes were blowing over Serrelind, and Kelsi and old Drigga weeping for her! If only it could all be over!

Suddenly she saw that the door of her house was standing wide open. Lamplight shone from within. She stopped—she was about forty yards away—but there was nothing to be heard. As she stared, puzzled, at the open doorway, she began to make out beyond it signs of confusion and disorder. A big, painted vase which had had its place in the porch was fallen and smashed to fragments, and a long, white splinter was projecting from the woodwork of the inner door. Near it, on the floor, she could glimpse something which looked like a bundle of old clothes tossed down all anyhow.

What could this mean? Robbers? Some violence between Randronoth and Eud-Ecachlon, informed of his presence in her house? She approached the door cautiously, but there was nothing more to be seen, and still she could not hear a sound.

Suddenly, at the very foot of the steps, she stopped short with a scream. What had looked like old clothes on the floor of the porch was in fact the dead body of Jarvil. His eyes were fixed, his teeth clenched and the hilt of a knife, which one of his hands was clutching, protruded from his chest.

To Maia's enormous credit her first thought was for Ogma. Sickened and terrified though she was, she did not run away, and hesitated for no more than a moment as she listened once more for any sound from within the house. There was none. As quietly as she could she entered the porch, stepped over the body and opened the inner door into the entrance hall.

Here, as was customary of an evening, three or four lamps were burning. She looked about her in the silence, wondering whether or not to call out to Ogma. Jarvil, she remembered, used to keep a club in his lodge by the door. She went and got it, and with this in one hand stole up to the open door of the parlour.

The room was frighteningly devastated. One of the silken wall-hangings had been ripped down. Both the small tables lay overturned and broken, and the ornaments and artifacts from them were scattered over the floor. A jug and two goblets were lying in a pool of spilt wine. The silver mirror, too, had fallen from the wall: as she moved, it caught the lamplight, flashing a moment in her eyes. Two of the cushions on the big couch had burst open, and their flock stuffing was strewn across the room.

Maia, however, noticed little or nothing of this in detail, for there was worse to be seen. On the far side of the room, in the shadow beyond the lamplight, were stretched the bodies of Randronoth's two soldiers. A dark, glistening expanse of blood, half-dried, covered the tiles around them. One had had time to draw his sword, which lay beside him—a typical Gelt short-sword, the broad blade tapering to a point. The other must simply have been trying to escape: he was stretched prone, one arm extended, the hand apparently dragged or fallen from the latch of the door leading into the garden. His dead face was turned towards her.

She ran out quickly into the hall but then, turning faint, stood leaning dizzily against the newel-post at the foot of the staircase.

Now, after some moments, she could indeed hear a noise—a kind of low, suppressed whimpering and moaning from upstairs. The voice was Ogma's. She listened intently, but could hear no one else. She called out, 'Ogma! It's Maia!'

The whimpering stopped on the instant, but there was no reply. She called again, 'Can you hear me?' This time, after a pause, Ogma's voice answered faintly, 'Miss Maia?'

'I'm in the hall: can you come down?'

'I'm—I'm hurt, miss,' replied Ogma in a weak, tremulous voice.

Maia ran upstairs. Lamplight was shining from her bedroom and she went in. The first thing she saw was the body of Randronoth, dressed in nothing but a pair of breeches, lying across her bed. It was the most appalling sight imaginable. His throat had been cut—the head, indeed, almost severed—while across his chest and stomach were three or more ragged, gaping stab-wounds. Coverlet, sheets, pillows—all were drenched in blood.

Ogma was half-lying near the door, her back against the wall. She was bleeding from eight or nine cuts, each about two inches long, in her shoulders and upper arms. In one hand she held a blood-stained towel, with which she was weakly dabbing at these wounds.

'Oh, Miss Maia,' she cried faintly, 'I'm that bad!'

Maia knelt, raised the girl to her feet and then, herself desperate to get out of the room and away from the horror on the bed, supported her to the bathroom. Here she set about washing her cuts and binding them up. Although scarcely capable of coherent thought, the wounds nonetheless struck her as odd; all were of more or less the same length and depth—almost like surgical incisions—as though inflicted deliberately and, as it were, at leisure. Little as she knew about wounds, these seemed hardly of a kind likely to be inflicted by violent men in an attack.

The cold water made Ogma flinch and cry out, but after a while, when Maia had bandaged her as best she could, she began to recover herself a little.

'There isn't—there isn't anyone else in the house now, miss, is there?' she faltered.

'Poor Jarvil's dead,' replied Maia. 'And so are the two soldiers.'

'Then they must have gone, miss.' Ogma stood up hesitantly, clutching Maia's arm.

'You'd be the better for some djebbah,' said Maia. 'Come downstairs with me.' It was clear to her now that Ogma, though badly shocked, was able to walk and in no danger of bleeding to death.

Together they went down to the kitchen. The fire was still in: Maia put on more wood. It did not occur to either of them to leave the house or run away. Maia, indeed, was beyond all deliberation and hardly knew what she was doing. She searched through two or three cupboards for the djebbah before catching sight of it in full view on an open shelf. The bite of the liquor cleared her head and partly pulled her round. She poured some for Ogma and made her sip it until it was all gone. The girl still sobbed and whimpered, fingering her bound-up cuts. Once, when a wood-knot exploded in the fire, she leapt up with a cry of fear.

Maia fetched a stool, sat down facing her and took her hands.

'Now; tell me what happened, Ogma.' There was no pause in the girl's weeping and Maia shook her gently. 'Come on, dear, pull yourself together! You *must* tell me!'

'Oh, Miss Maia—Lord Randronoth—' She stopped.

831

'What about him? Come on, Ogma, *tell* me!'

'Well, I'd just lit the lamps, miss, and put them round the house like I always do, when he came in from the garden, dressed just in his breeches. He seemed—oh, ever so angry and put out, like. So I asked him were you coming in to supper now, but he never answered me: he just went up to your bedroom and shut the door. So then I didn't know what to do, miss, and I went down the garden to look for you, but I couldn't find you: just your clothes, like, laying on the ground. I didn't know what to think. I was frightened.'

Ogma stopped as though she had no more to say. She was clearly still in a state of shock, ready to retreat into stupor from her own recollections. Maia shook her again.

'Ogma! You can't go to sleep now! Go on!'

Ogma rubbed her eyes with her knuckles. 'When I came back—when I came back into the house, miss, the soldiers—the soldiers asked where you were and I said I didn't know. So then they said as Lord Randronoth had told them to watch from the roof and wake him when the soldiers came—'

'The Lapanese soldiers, you mean? Count Seekron?'

'I don't know, miss. They didn't say—just "the soldiers". But then they said, "We'll have a drink first. Bring us some wine in the parlour," they said. Well, I knew that was wrong, Miss Maia, but I was frightened of them, you see, and I didn't know where you were or when you was coming back, like, so I did what they told me. I'm sorry, miss—'

'That doesn't matter now. Just go on.'

'Well, I brought the wine, miss—only not the best, it wasn't: I thought for the likes of them—'

'Oh, never mind that! What *happened*, for Cran's sake?'

'Well, miss, they got to drinking, see, in the parlour, and then there come a knock, and I don't know why, I reckoned it might be you, though why you'd be knocking on your own door, but I wasn't really thinking, see—'

'So then?'

'Well, then I went to the door, miss, and Jarvil had opened the panel, see, to look who it was, and then he shut it and he turns round to me and he says, "I don't know what to do," he says. "It's the Sacred Queen."'

'The Sacred Queen!' cried Maia incredulously. 'That's not possible! She's miles away, out on the plain, this very minute.'

'No, miss: I looked out and it was the Sacred Queen there; her and a big, rough-looking man dressed like an officer, miss, and the queen was sort of dressed up like a soldier, too, and they was all covered with dust, like they'd come a long way; and the queen, she calls out, very angry-like, "How much longer am I to be kept waiting?" she says. "Are you going to open this door or do you want to hang upside-down?" she says. Oh, and when I looked out through the panel, the way she looked back at me, miss, it frightened me that much, you can't imagine—'

'Oh, yes, I can! Well, so what happened then?'

'I opened the door, miss, and—'

'You *opened* the door?'

'Yes, miss. Well, you weren't there to ask, see, and she was that angry, I didn't know what else to do—'

'Ogma, did you know that she hates me and wants to kill me? That she has done for weeks?'

'No, I didn't know, miss: I'd no idea. Leastways, not then I hadn't—'

Maia could scarcely believe her ears. Bitterly, she recalled the advice of Nennaunir and her other friends about engaging a shrewd, quick-witted woman to run her household.

'Well, go on.'

'Well, the moment I opened the door, miss, they both pushed past me and the big man put his hand over Jarvil's mouth and stabbed him with his knife. And then the queen, she grabbed me and pulled my head back and she had a knife, too, and she says, "You make a sound," she says, "and I'll cut your throat." But then after a moment she said, "Now, you tell me where Randronoth and Maia are," and she was holding this knife against my throat, miss, and she said, "Are they upstairs?" and I said, "Yes! Yes!" Only I was that frightened I hardly knew what I was saying, you see.

'So then she said, "You come with me and show me," she said. She twisted my arm up behind me, miss, and she put her hand over my mouth and we went upstairs like that. And the big man, he'd drawn his sword and he went into the parlour. But I never heard no more of that, see, because when we got upstairs she never asked me which door nor nothing, she just threw open your bedroom door and there was Lord Randronoth laying on the bed, kind of half-awake, like. So then she gave me a great push against the wall as fair winded me, and she ran straight across and began stabbing at Lord Randronoth—oh, it was that dreadful, miss, I can't tell you no more, really I can't—'

'If I can hear it, you can tell it. Go on, Ogma!'

'Oh, the blood! The blood everywhere, miss, and the queen, she was— she was shouting and laughing, and she kept stabbing him again and again, and then she sort of rubbed all her hands and her arms and face, miss, with the blood, and then she sat down beside him on the bed and she very near cut his head off—I never seen—I never dreamt—laughing all the time—'

Ogma became hysterical. When at length Maia had been able to restore her to something faintly resembling self-possession she went on,

'So then the queen come back to me, miss; only I was standing against the wall, you see, and I was screaming. And she says, "Stop that," she says, "or I'll stop it for you." And then the big man, he come up the stairs and his sword all covered with blood, and he says to her, "I've finished; have you?" And she says, "No, not yet. I'm only half-done," she says.

'She was holding me by the hair, miss, and she says, "Where's Maia?" And I said, "I don't know." So then she cut me with her knife and she says again, "Where's Maia?" and I says, "I don't know!" So she was cutting me, and every time I said, "I don't know! I don't know!" she cut me, miss, and she—well, it was like she'd been drinking or something o' that; she was—she was kind of staring and excited and—oh, I can't rightly tell. So then at last she said, "Would you like me to put your nasty little eyes out?" she said: and I screamed out, "I don't *know*, säiyett; I *swear* I don't know! I only know she's not here."

'So then the big man, he says, "Oh, come on, Fornis. It's obvious she doesn't know: we're only wasting time. You can kill Maia later: we've got to be going."

'So then the queen said to me, "Shall I kill *you*? No, you're not worth killing, are you? You'll be able to tell dear Maia all about it, won't you?" Or—or 'twas something like that, miss, as she said, but tell you the truth I don't just rightly remember. So then they went away—I remember that— but I don't remember anything else until I heard you downstairs. I must 'a just gone off, like.'

While Ogma was speaking, Maia's sense of unreality and nightmare had intensified. She sat staring before her, trying to get her thoughts into frame. How *could* Fornis be in Bekla? Obviously she must be, yet it seemed impossible. Did Eud-Ecachlon know? And she herself—what was she to do now? Where could she go for safety?

At this moment she heard light, hurried footsteps coming through the porch and into the hall. For a few moments she sat petrified. Then Occula's voice called, 'Banzi! Banzi, are you here?'

Maia jumped up and ran out into the hall. Occula, dressed in a leather tunic and breeches, with a knife at her belt, was standing in the parlour doorway, staring at what lay within. Hearing Maia, she drew the knife and spun round quickly, then ran forward and took her in her arms.

'Oh, banzi, thank the gods! I thought—oh, never mind—'

'What is it, Occula? What's happened?'

'Never mind that, either! There's no time to talk! Banzi, you've got to get out fast! Get out *now*! Understand? Now!'

'But where to, Occula?'

'There are people who'll help you. Listen to me carefully.'

'But Occula—'

Ogma had come into the hall; a pitiful sight, crying and wringing her hands, her arms bound with strips of bloody towelling. Occula stamped her foot with impatience.

'I've no time, banzi, for Cran's bastin' sake! Your life's in deadly danger! Shut up and listen! Have you got any money?'

'Yes, plenty. But—'

'Then take it all with you. Now understand this. You're not to go by the Peacock Gate or you'll be killed, d'you see? Fornis has got men there. Go across, quick as you can, to the western walls. If you meet a sentry, bribe him. They're all old watchmen, anyway: there's very few soldiers left in the place, except Fornis's—'

'But is Fornis really here, Occula? Ogma said, but I can't hardly believe it—'

'Yes, banzi! Yes, she *is*, and she's lookin' for you to *kill* you! After she'd killed Durakkon and beaten Kerith-a-Thrain, that woman and Han-Glat got here two hours ago, with five hundred men. They were goin' all last night and all today. And to see her you'd think she'd jus' got out of bed. I believe she could do it again if she wanted to.'

'But—they let her through the gates?'

'Of *course* they did: who'd stop *her*? They'd let her through the gates of hell, wouldn' they? And they will one day, too, if I've got anythin' to do with it.'

'But what's happened to the hostages, Occula? Has she killed them?'

'Bayub-Otal and the other officers she brought with her. They're down in the gaol. Now banzi, will you do as I say and get *out*, damn you?'

'Yes, I will. The western wall, you said. Then what?'

'Go along the wall and then scramble down onto the roof of a big stone warehouse you'll see below you, just this side of the Tower of Sel-Dolad. Ask for a man called N'Kasit and say Cat Colonna and all that—you know. He'll help you to get out of Bekla. And now I'm goin' myself—fast! Bless you, my dearest banzi! Thanks for everythin'! Kantza-Merada, what a bastin' farewell after all you and I've been through together! But we'll meet again one day, you see if we doan'!'

'But what about Ogma here? I can't leave her, Occula.'

'O Cran! I'll take her with me and get her to Nennaunir or someone. Doan' worry, Fornis woan' bother lookin' for her, once she finds you're gone.'

And with this Occula grabbed Ogma by the wrist and dragged her out of the house.

Left alone, Maia was overcome by a terrible seizure of horror—the mental paralysis of extreme fear and distress. Crouching in the privy as her bowels emptied in an agonizing flux, she gasped and retched, while the sweat poured off her. At length her head cleared, and as she began to recover herself the full force of Occula's warning came home to her. She had to fly for her life—now, instantly.

But there could be no avoiding what had to be done by way of preparation. Trembling, she returned to the bedroom and there, averting her eyes from the bed, put on those same travelling clothes in which she had returned from Rallur. The jerkin had capacious inside pockets, and into these she stuffed not only all that was left of the money Seekron had given her—a good twenty thousand meld and more—but also her diamonds. Over the jerkin she buckled a belt with a sheathed knife. Half-way down the stairs, it occurred to her that she ought to take a cloak. Although to return to the bedroom yet again was almost more than she could bring herself to do, once there she not only took care to pick out her stoutest and most serviceable cloak, but before leaving spread another over poor Randronoth's face and chest. Back downstairs, on a final impulse she went quickly into the parlour, snatched up the cabinet of fishes and thrust it into one of her pockets. Then she ran through the hall, past Jarvil's body and out into the darkness.

: 85 :
AT N'KASIT'S

To cross the upper city to the western walls took about twenty minutes. By now Occula's words—and Occula's fear—had sunk in to such an extent that she was afraid to go by the main thoroughfare leading past the barracks towards the Leopard Hill. The byways nearer the Peacock Wall would take her closer to the queen's house, yet nevertheless she felt that this would involve less chance of being molested or recognized.

The confusion and clamour throughout the city had increased and at the gates of many houses armed servants were standing on guard; yet none challenged or tried to stop her. Once she hid behind a clump of trees while six or seven ruffian-looking men with cudgels approached and passed, talking together in some language unknown to her. Yet otherwise she met with no adventures, and went so quickly that she was surprised when at length she saw the western walls looming in front of her, a dark, level line in the moonlight.

Nor, surprisingly, did anyone try to stop her climbing the stone stairs where the road ended below the walls. She stepped out onto the height of the ramparts and looked about her. To her right, the lower city fell away to the Gate of Lilies and the open square of the Slave Market. There, too, she could hear tumult and see an unusual number of lights—both lamps in the houses and torches in the streets. There was a light in the high, square crow's nest of the Tower of Sel-Dolad, not three hundred yards away. She wondered who could be up there at this hour: watchmen, no doubt, looking out for the approach of Fornis's army from the west.

Turning in the direction of the tower, she began walking along the ramparts. She was obliged to go slowly, for the paving was uneven and once or twice she stumbled over projecting stones. Ahead, where the Peacock Wall joined the ramparts, she could see a sentry gazing out over the plain below. As she approached he turned, levelled his spear and challenged her.

She stood still, looking at his face under the leather helmet. Just as Occula had said, this was an oldish man for a soldier—forty-five at least—with a grizzled beard, bushy eyebrows and lips sunk in upon a toothless mouth above a sharp-nosed, canny face. He did not look like a Beklan. She smiled at him, throwing back her hood.

'Can you let me pass?' she asked.

He shook his head. 'No one's to pass. You didn't ought to be up here at all: you must know that.'

This man, if she was any judge, was from Kabin. Probably Eud-Ecachlon had held a few back from the draft. Anyway, he had not recognized her and clearly didn't know who she was.

'No one's seen me; only you. You can't get into trouble letting me pass.' She paused. 'I've got money.'

He shook his head again. 'You shouldn't offer money: you just go back, now, go on.'

'Ah, but all depends how much, doesn't it? I've no time to bargain, dad. I'll give you all I've got—a thousand meld.'

In the moonlight she saw the surprise on his cunning, peasant face. That had got to him all right.

'A thousand meld? Don't try it on, my girl: you haven't got that much.'

'Oh, yes, I have. Only you be straight with me, just. I'm in danger: I've got enemies and I've got to get out quick. You know as well as I do everything's upside-down. No one'll ever get to hear.'

Far away, on the other side of the city, a sudden clamour broke out. They both started, turning to stare in the direction of the Blue Gate a full mile away below.

'What's that?' said the man. 'That's never the Palteshis, comin' that way!'

'No,' answered Maia. 'The Lapanese have got here first.'

'The Lapanese?' He stared at her.

'Those will be Lord Randronoth's men. Anything can happen now. If I were you, I'd take this thousand meld and make myself scarce. Either that or go and join them, dad.'

He paused, his crafty eyes sizing her up—her good clothes, her beautiful face, her soft, well-kept hands. Even at such a time as this he must be bargaining: to the likes of him it was second nature.

'Well, but it's a big risk, now, missie, isn't it?' He shook his head. 'Couldn't take a risk like that for less than fifteen hundred.'

'All right,' she said. 'Only for Cran's sake leave it at that. Here comes your tryzatt, I reckon, to see what that noise is about.'

Indeed, they could both see the silhouetted figure of the tryzatt, about two hundred yards off along the rampart, staring eastwards. Maia offered the money, which the man at once grabbed and stuffed into his jerkin.

'Go on, then, missie, quick, 'fore he sees you.'

Maia darted past him and was gone.

She had run hardly any distance, however, before she saw below her what could only be the warehouse of which Occula had spoken: a flat-roofed, sprawling place, too big for any private dwelling. There was a dim light in one window, but no other sign that anyone was there.

She looked round for a way down, but as far ahead as she could see there were no steps. The drop from the walls to the abutting roof was all of nineteen or twenty feet: she could never hang and let go without risking injury.

She hurried back. The sentry was still where she had left him and the tryzatt had come no nearer.

She called in a low voice, 'Sentry!'

Agonizingly slowly, he came up to her. 'What you want now, then?'

'I got to get down onto that roof; only it's too far to jump. I could just about do it holding onto your spear, though.'

She had expected him to ask for more money, but to her surprise, after a moment he said, 'All right, then; only quick,' and went back with her along the wall. Above the warehouse roof he lay down, holding his spear vertically over the edge of the wall to the full extent of his arms.

'You'd best be quick, missie: only I can't hold your weight more 'n a few seconds, see?'

It was still a long enough drop to frighten her, but once she was at the end of the spear, arms outstretched, there was no help for it. She let go and fell about eight feet onto the roof.

She landed with a harsh jolt, and doubled up painfully on her knees. She had scratched one arm and torn her cloak. She looked upward, but the soldier had gone. Scrambling to her feet, she leant for a minute or two against the wall, then began to limp across the roof. Somewhere there must be a way down.

838

After searching in the dark for some minutes, during which she could hear the uproar on the other side of the city increasing, she came upon a flight of steps, ramshackle and with no outer handrail, and started nervously groping her way down, one foot and then the other, leaning inward against the wall. As she neared the bottom a man's voice from the shadows below said sharply, 'Who's that? Stay where y'are!'

This pulled her together. Maia—with good reason—possessed confidence in her ability to conciliate strangers. Besides, Occula had told her whom to ask for.

'I'm looking for N'Kasit,' she answered.

After a few moments the voice said, 'A woman, eh? Are y'alone?'

'Yes.'

'Who are you? What were you doing on the roof?'

'I've come along the ramparts from the upper city. I'll explain everything if only you'll take me to N'Kasit.'

'He expecting you?'

'I was told to come here and ask for him,' answered Maia.

At this moment there was the sound of a door opening, and a flicker of light revealed, just ahead of her, the black, vertical line of the corner of the building. Another voice said, 'What is it, Malendik?'

'A woman, sir, asking for you.'

'What's your name?' said the other voice.

'Maia Serrelinda.'

There was a whistle of surprise. 'The Serrelinda? Are you telling the truth?'

This annoyed Maia. It was months since anyone had spoken to her like this and she had become unused to it.

'Yes, I damn' well am; and what's more, I'm getting tired of standing up here. If you're N'Kasit—'

'You'd better come down.'

Maia fumbled and clutched her way down the last of the steps. Two figures, one disconcertingly huge, the other—who was holding the lamp—small, compact and intent, stood outlined in an open doorway.

'Come on in quick!' said the smaller figure, himself turning to lead the way.

Maia, following them through the door, found herself in an immense, cavernous, echoing building, everywhere divided by walls and partitions. There was an all-pervading smell of leather and hides, together with a sour, acrid odour—perhaps some sort of fluid used in treating them. The lamp, bobbing on ahead of her, threw great, jumping shadows into the invisible roof.

The men, without looking round to see whether she was following or not, were walking briskly along a sanded pathway running between the bays. She had almost to run to avoid losing them. At length they turned aside into a kind of shed constructed against one corner of the warehouse; a lean-to hut, with two wooden walls, two stone walls and a ceiling of sagging planks laid atop. There was a rickety table, on which were some tallies, a few papers and an abacus; two or three benches, some clay bowls and cups on a shelf and in one corner a narrow, untidy bed on which a big, square-headed tabby cat lay dozing. This was evidently both the warehouse office and the cubby-hole of anyone who had to sleep on the premises.

As she followed them in, the two stood regarding Maia. The big man, she could now perceive, was obviously some sort of workman or hired hand of the other. He was not only tall but plainly immensely strong, with shoulders and arms that looked as though they could lift an ox. He was dressed in sacking and his hands were rough and dirt-engrained—the hands of a labourer.

N'Kasit himself looked about thirty-five; quick-glancing, yet with a shrewd, prudent, unexcitable air; a typical merchant, she thought, both circumspect and enterprising. She could imagine everything in his life, including his marriage, his friends and his amusements, being subordinated to an over-riding ambition for gain: yet not only, perhaps, material gain; this was a man who might well be aspiring to social—even political— advancement as well. He seemed a younger, more mundane version of Sarget, and had no doubt a similar, though as yet unfulfilled, desire to reach the upper city. Could *he*, of all people, really be a secret agent of the heldril? If so, he had certainly contrived a most convincing front. Anyone would have thought him a mercantile Leopard of Leopards.

'You'd better sit down, säiyett,' he said, pushing forward an old chair with two dirty cushions—the only one in the room. 'I'm sure it's not what you're used to, but come to that, we don't often have visitors like you, either.'

She sat down wearily and gratefully. And good cause she had to be weary, she thought. Yet for the first time that day she felt secure: these men, she felt intuitively, were not going to betray or harm her.

N'Kasit poured wine. It was rough, bitter stuff, but she was glad of it and drank off her cup almost at once. Having refilled it, he offered her bread and cheese, but this she declined. All she wanted now was to get on. How quickly could she reach the gaol? If she was to save Zenka and Anda-Nokomis every minute might be vital.

'I suppose you need quite a few cats in a place like this,' she said, nodding towards the tabby on the bed. 'I'm fond of cats myself; I've got a beauty at home. She's called Colonna, like the one in the old story, you know.'

'I remember,' answered N'Kasit, 'but I always thought the one in the story was called Bakris.'

'Will you help me to get out of Bekla, then?' she asked him, smiling.

He did not smile back, however, only continuing to regard her steadily and gravely, as he might when considering some business proposition and taking care to display no reaction. She glanced across at Malendik, but he, his wine-cup buried in his great hands, was gazing down impassively at the dusty floor.

'I think it's rather a case of whether *you'll* be of any help to *us*, isn't it?' said N'Kasit at length. 'They're going to try tonight. With all this confusion, they'll never have a better opportunity. Where do *you* come in?'

She shook her head. 'I don't understand.'

'Didn't Occula tell you? It was Occula sent you, I suppose?'

'She hadn't time to tell me anything, U-N'Kasit, except as my life was in danger from Fornis and I must get out at once.'

She went on to speak of Randronoth, of the death of Milvushina, the murders at her house and finally of Occula's frantic warning.

'Fornis is in Bekla *now*?' he asked, when she had finished.

'Yes. I couldn't hardly believe it myself.'

He sat frowning. 'I'm sorry for all you've been through,' he said at length, though in a level, unemotional tone. 'Poor young Milvushina! That's a great pity. I remember her father well; he came to see me once at Kabin. He was the one who suggested I should come here, and then Erketlis sent me the money to do it. I've never met *him*, though—not yet. It was one of his agents, a man called Tharrin, who brought the money. He's dead now; but he never told them anything. He must have been a brave man.' He paused. 'What do you mean to do, then—get to Santil in Yelda? Is that your idea?'

'I don't know yet,' she said. 'I haven't thought.'

'Occula didn't tell you about the others?'

'Well, there wasn't time, see? She just said to come here and you'd help me.' She looked up at him appealingly. 'You will, won't you?'

But the level-headed man of business still seemed concerned less with the beautiful Serrelinda than with the problem she presented.

'If things were normal and you'd been able to leave the city publicly— the Serrelinda on a trip to Tonilda or something like that—we might have been able to send them with you disguised as servants, but as it is I can't see that you're any use to us at all. In fact, with Fornis after your blood you're a liability, aren't you?'

'I don't reckon Occula was thinking that way. She just wanted to save me.'

'Do you want to hide here for a day or two, then, to see which way things go? I'd risk that much; for Occula I would.'

She shook her head decisively. 'No, I must get out tonight, whatever happens. Soon as possible, too, U-N'Kasit. There's—well—important reasons why I can't afford to wait.'

He shrugged. 'Well, at that rate I can only leave it to them to say whether or not they'll take you along.'

He turned to Malendik. 'You'd better bring them in here: then they can see her for themselves and make up their own minds.'

Malendik gone, they sat in silence. Maia was thinking, 'Whoever they are, they're not going to stop me going to the gaol.'

She began imagining what she would say to Pokada, what he might reply and how she would set about prevailing upon him.

The blanket across the entrance was drawn aside and two people sidled in; a woman followed by a man. In the lamplight, Maia looked blankly for a moment at their pinched, bedraggled forms: then she uttered a startled cry.

'Meris!'

'Maia!'

The two girls stared at each other. Behind Meris stood a gaunt figure—none other than the Tonildan pedlar, Zirek. He was pale as a plant kept long in the dark, hollow-cheeked and sunken-eyed as any dungeon inmate, yet still with a faint touch of his old, vagabond swagger. Indeed, he was less changed than Meris, that one-time exquisite paragon of hard-bitten, worldly sensuality. She had all the look of a girl who, having endured months of anxiety, was now close to collapse. Her dark hair hung about her shoulders lank as rope. Her lips twitched continually and she could not keep her hands still. After a few moments, without another word, she sat down unsteadily on one of the benches.

Zirek stepped forward and took Maia's hands.

'There's no hard feelings as far as I'm concerned, Maia.'

'Hard feelings, Zirek? Why should there be?'

'Well, you saved the damned Leopards all right, didn't you, swimming the river? But just speaking personally, I wouldn't have cared to see the empire fall to Karnat: I'd rather see it fall to Santil. Perhaps it will now, if only the gods are kind. Besides, you helped us kill Sencho, didn't you, even if you didn't know it at the time? So I say, no hard feelings.'

Magnanimity sat strangely on him, she thought. In his rags and pallor he looked squalid as any beggar. But he was clean—life in the upper city had made her sensitive and fastidious on this score—and there was something about him which suggested that in spite of everything he had retained both humour and self-respect.

'I knew all along as it must 'a been you and Meris,' she said. ''Cos d'you know, I saw you, that same morning in the crowd at the Peacock Gate?

But what beats me is, however did you get away? I reckoned you must be dead for sure.'

'It was the tryzatt on the western wall that night,' he answered. 'He was a Tonildan, you see, who'd been a servant of Senda-na-Say. It was all arranged beforehand: he got us out along the rampart. He was never suspected, and for all I know he's still in the service.'

'And you've been hiding here ever since? All these months?'

'Yes, and I'm basting near mad with it!' broke in Meris. 'I wish to Cran I'd never said I'd do it! Oh, Maia, you can't imagine—'

'Steady, love,' said Zirek. 'It's over now, good as. We're going to get out tonight, remember? We owe everything to N'Kasit here,' he went on, turning back to Maia. 'He's hidden us all this time, and he didn't stand to get anything out of it. Once we'd done the job, you see, we were no further use to the heldril.'

'Well, even I'm not quite as canny as that,' said N'Kasit, with the trace of a smile. 'All the same,' he said to Maia, 'it was touch and go more than once. It's not easy to search a place like this, of course—full of holes and corners piled up with stuff—but Kembri's lot were very thorough and they came back more than once. Luckily, I've got a good reputation. The Leopards think I'm a loyal, reliable army contractor.'

'And what the hell are *you* doing here, Maia?' asked Meris, in none too friendly a tone.

'I want to get out of Bekla with you,' replied Maia.

Meris stared, blinking and twitching. N'Kasit broke in, 'She's got good reason. Fornis reached Bekla this afternoon; her and Han-Glat—'

'Fornis?' cried Zirek. 'Never!'

'Yes; so the Serrelinda's just told me. I know it seems incredible, but isn't everything about that woman incredible? She' (he pointed to Maia) 'got home this evening to find Randronoth of Lapan and her own porter murdered and her house turned upside-down. And she was lucky, at that: they missed her. Occula sent her here to us.'

'Occula? That girl's got more courage than all the rest of us put together,' said Zirek. 'But you say you want to come with us, Maia? That's a shade awkward, is that.'

'But I can't go on my own, Zirek. Please—'

'Well, the trouble is, everyone knows you by sight, don't they? And Fornis is sure to have left orders at the gates. They'll obey *her* all right, you can be sure of that. Eud-Ecachlon'll be no match for her; he may even be dead already.'

'Seekron might be a match for her, though.'

'Seekron? Who's he?'

843

Maia told them of Randronoth's plan to seize the city and what she had already seen from the western ramparts.

'Cran alive! That alters things!' said Zirek. 'Couldn't be better for us, N'Kasit, could it? Eud-Ecachlon, Fornis and Seekron all at each other's throats. The whole place'll be—'

'There's another thing, Zirek,' broke in Maia. 'I've got money with me—a fair old bit, too—reckon you'd find it come in useful.' She smiled. 'I suppose you could have it off me and then go by yourselves, but I hope you won't.'

'Cran and Airtha, what d'you take me for?' he replied with a touch of asperity. Then he grinned, recalling the jaunty lad who had come to sell his gew-gaws to Sencho's concubines. 'The money'll come in handy, I dare say, but it's the pleasure of your company that makes such a delightful prospect, m'dear. You never know, we might even need a swimmer, too, 'fore we're done. How soon do we start, N'Kasit?'

'Soon as you like,' replied N'Kasit. 'But remember, Zirek, it was your own decision to take the Serrelinda. I didn't force it on you, and I don't want anyone saying later that I did.'

'You must be the only man in Bekla who's ever thought of *her* company as being forced on anyone,' replied Zirek. 'You cold old fish! I hope you make your fortune! You deserve to. When Santil gets here, he'll cart you off to the upper city and make you a baron, I expect.' He took the merchant's hands in his own. 'Thanks for all you've done. May the gods bless you! What more can I say? I hope we meet again one of these days. Can you give us some good, stout shoes, and perhaps a bite of food to take along with us?'

'Shoes—you're in the right place for those, and cloaks too,' said N'Kasit. 'They can come out of stock. The food'll have to be bread and cheese—what there is of it.'

Twenty minutes later, Malendik having been sent out to look up and down the street, Maia, Meris and Zirek slipped unobtrusively out of a side door and set off downhill towards the alleys of the Shilth.

: 86 :

'OPPORTUNITY IS ALL'

It was no more than three hundred yards to the gate of the gaol. As they reached it Maia stopped and turned to Zirek.

'I'm going in here, Zirek. It won't take long.'

'Why, what the hell d'you mean, Maia? This is the gaol, for Airtha's sake!'

'I know; that's 'zackly why I'm going in. The Ban of Suba's in there. Fornis brought him up here as a hostage, but he's coming out with us now.'

'Maia, have you gone stark, raving mad? It can't be done! What makes you think they'll hand him over to you?'

'Money,' she answered. 'Come on, quick; let's get it over with.'

'You didn't say anything about this to N'Kasit, did you?'

'No; but I'm going in all the same. You can either come with me or wait out here.'

'But—but it doesn't make sense, Maia! If it wasn't for what you did at the river, he'd never have been taken prisoner at all, would he?'

'Maybe,' she said, 'but sometimes things change. Are you coming or not?'

It was Meris who replied. 'No, we're not: you'll never come out of there alive, Maia. You might as well go and give yourself up to Fornis straight away.'

Maia looked at Zirek, but he only nodded in corroboration. Without another word she turned and left them, walking resolutely across the road and up to the gate of the gaol without once looking back.

The mucous-eyed, listless gatekeeper was on duty in his lodge. She gave him twenty meld. Once, she thought, it was nothing at all: then it was five. You pay your own fear.

'I have to see U-Pokada at once: I'll wait in his room.'

The stuffy little room was in darkness and she made the man leave her his lamp. She could not sit still, but paced up and down—five steps this way, five that—praying passionately to Lespa, yet hardly knowing what she was saying in her tension and anxiety.

At length the door opened and Pokada appeared with a second lamp, wiping his dyed beard with the back of his hand. Evidently she had interrupted his supper. His manner suggested none of his former obsequiousness. He shut the door behind him, bowed and stood waiting without a word.

'I hope I find you well, U-Pokada,' she said.

'I am well, thank you, säiyett; but busy. How can I help you?'

'U-Pokada, I'm in haste too, so I'll tell you straight out. I'll give you ten thousand meld, money down, to hand two prisoners over to me immediately.'

'Ten thousand meld, säiyett? That's a lot of money.' He paused, then repeated unsmilingly, 'Yes, that's a lot of money, ten thousand meld.'

'Well,' she said, 'it's no less than I'll pay, I assure you.'

He seemed to be deliberating. 'Which two would those be, säiyett, I wonder?'

'Lord Bayub-Otal, the Urtan, and a Katrian officer named Captain Zen-Kurel.'

845

'Ah. Yes. Well, säiyett, if you'll excuse me, I'll just go and look at my lists. I take it those are two of the prisoners who came in this afternoon, with the Sacred Queen?'

'Yes, they are.'

He went out. The silence returned. How lifeless this dismal place seemed always to be! she thought. Every least, intermittent noise was like a stone thrown into a pool. Someone went quickly by outside. A dog barked. A door banged. There was a sound of running feet dying away in the distance.

She stood looking out of the north-facing window. The comet had become so dim that anyone not having seen it before would hardly, she supposed, have spared it a glance. A mere glow in the sky it seemed, no longer the radiant emissary of Lespa. Filled with sudden misgiving, she shivered and turned away.

Pokada returned. 'Yes, I have these two men in my charge, säiyett.'

'And you'll release them to me for that sum?'

He made no reply, so that at length she repeated it.

He shook his head. 'It's not possible, säiyett, for that money; no, nor for any money, I'm afraid. I'm answerable for them to the Sacred Queen, you see.'

'The whole city's upside-down,' she said. 'You could always say they escaped.'

'No one escapes from here: I'd be the one upside-down, säiyett, believe me.'

'I'll pay you generously. Perhaps I could just manage a little more than ten thousand meld.'

He sat down. 'Well, shall we talk about it, säiyett? I don't mind talking about it, you know. Yes, let's discuss it for a little while.'

But there was a kind of temporizing in his manner, a lack of conviction, which puzzled and disturbed her.

'You mean, talk about how much?'

'Well, yes; and about what you'll do with them—where they go and so on.'

'But I can't see that that's anything to do with you, U-Pokada. Why should you want to know that?'

'Well, you see, säiyett—you see—Have you ever been to Ikat Yelda-shay?'

'No, never. But what's that got to do with it? U-Pokada, please—'

'Well, I was there once, you know. Yes, I was there once. Oh, some years ago, now. A nice city. Yes. But now it's in the hands of Santil-kè-Erketlis, they say. That's not good, is it? But of course General Kembri will beat him. No doubt of that—'

'U-Pokada, what's all this got to do with the prisoners?'

'Well, you see, säiyett, if you were going to Ikat Yeldashay, now—'

'U-Pokada, I don't want to appear rude, and I know as I can't afford to offend you, but I'm in great haste. If we're going to come to an agreement, for Cran's sake can we do it quickly, because—'

The door was flung open and two soldiers came into the room, their swords drawn in their hands. Maia, jumping up from where she was sitting, started back against the wall. Pokada also rose, but he showed no surprise, merely standing with folded arms as one of the two soldiers looked from him to herself.

'Is this the girl?' asked the soldier, and Pokada replied, 'Yes.'

Staring at them in the lamplight, Maia wondered what it was that seemed unfamiliar. The older was a tryzatt, the younger a common soldier. Both had an outlandish appearance, and their uniform, too, was unusual. Then, with an even worse access of fear, she saw that both were wearing the Fortress cognizance of Paltesh. These men were Palteshis.

The tryzatt seized her arm. 'Are you Maia Serrelinda?'

She struggled, and he gripped her tighter. 'Yes, yes, she is!' said Pokada, rubbing his hands. 'You came quick. You came quick. That's good! That's very good!'

'Who are you?' she whispered.

'Guard commander at the Gate of Lilies: I'm arresting you on the Sacred Queen's instructions.'

'What for?'

'She'll tell you that when she sees you.'

In dread worse than ever she had known she stood, her legs almost giving way under her, while they tied her hands behind her back. Then the tryzatt, nodding curtly to Pokada, followed the soldier as he pushed her out into the yard.

'Will you—will you let me go for ten thousand meld?' she asked, as they approached the gate.

'Not for twenty, neither,' answered the tryzatt in his grating, Palteshi accent. 'You're going to Queen Fornis, that's where you're going.'

Suddenly both soldiers stopped, peering ahead of them towards the gate of the gaol. There was a flurry of tossing torches, their resinous, smoky smell drifting across the yard. Together with this came a sound of voices, stamping boots and the clink of arms and accoutrements. Evidently a considerable body of men had just entered the gate.

The two Palteshis stood irresolute. However, they did not have to wait long. Four torches detached themselves from the mass and came quickly towards them. Within a minute they were surrounded by a group of ten or twelve soldiers, led by a heavily-built man wearing the insignia of a captain.

'You belong to General Han-Glat?' asked the captain brusquely.

'We serve him and the Sacred Queen, sir. Tryzatt Nethik, acting on orders from—'

'Save your breath and you might even save your life, if you're lucky. Hand over your arms.'

The tryzatt hesitated. 'May I respectfully ask, sir—'

'Who I am? Captain Mendel-el-Ekna of Lapan, that's who I am. In case you didn't know, Bekla's now under command of Lord Randronoth.'

'Sir, with all due respect—'

'Respect my venda.' He drew his sword. 'Hand over your arms, or you won't even have the chance to wish you had.'

The two Palteshis, having no alternative, obeyed.

'Right,' said the captain. 'Now, I've taken over this gaol; have you got that? Are there any more of you Palteshis here?'

'No, sir.'

'If that turns out to be a lie you'll be killed. Where's the prison governor?'

The tryzatt pointed across the yard.

'Who's this girl? What were you going to do with her?'

'The Sacred Queen gave orders that she was to be arrested wherever she might be found, sir. I was appointed guard commander at the Gate of Lilies this evening, and I received a message from the governor of the gaol, that she was here. 'Cordingly I came and arrested her.'

'Why are you wanted by Queen Fornis, then?' asked the captain, turning to Maia. 'Untie her hands,' he added to one of his own men.

'I'm Maia Serrelinda,' she answered. 'Queen Fornis—'

'Maia Serrelinda, the friend of Lord Randronoth?'

She hesitated no more than a moment. 'Yes.'

Disconcertingly, the captain dropped on one knee and proffered the hilt of his sword. Smiling, she laid one hand on it and he stood up.

'And what can we have the honour of doing for you, säiyett?'

'I came here to ask the governor for the release of two prisoners—my friends; victims of the queen—but he kept me talking in his room so that he could betray me to these Palteshis.'

'*Did* he?' replied Mendel-el-Ekna. 'Fearon,' he said to his own tryzatt, 'go back and take over at the gate. The rest of you, come with me.'

When they thrust their way into his room Pokada—for he was still there—sprang up and cowered against the wall, grasping quickly enough that these were no friends. Mendel-el-Ekna was about to run him through when Maia caught his arm.

'Don't, captain! Spare him, for my sake!'

'But you say this is the man who betrayed you to the Palteshis?'

'Yes, but I can't bear to see anyone else killed. I've seen—oh, I've seen that many today, I'm half mad with it! Please spare him!'

'You dirty bastard!' said the captain, hitting Pokada across the face. 'Think yourself lucky! Now go and fetch the säiyett the men she asked you for, and basting quickly, too! You three go with him, and if he tries any nonsense, kill him!'

They waited, eight or nine of them crammed into the little room. The smell of unwashed, sweating men was overpowering. Her wrists smarted where the cord had chafed them. I can't stand much more, she thought. Reckon I'll faint in a minute.

'Stuffy in here,' remarked Mendel-el-Ekna suddenly. He pulled open the wooden shutters, wrenched them off the hinges and threw them out into the yard. 'That's better.' One of his men caught Maia's eye and winked.

'Will you be needing an escort?' went on the captain. 'You and your friends—where are you going?'

'I just want to get them out of Bekla,' she answered. 'Anywhere'll do for now.'

He frowned, puzzled. 'Were you going to return to Lord Randronoth alone, then, across the city?'

'There was a man with me before I was arrested by the Palteshis—a man and another girl—only in all the confusion we got separated, see?'

'So you came in here by yourself? That must have taken some courage.'

'She's the Serrelinda, sir, ain't she?' said one of the men.

'We'll escort you as far as the Blue Gate,' said the captain. 'I've got to go back there, anyway.'

Before she could reply the door opened and two of the three soldiers returned. With them were Bayub-Otal and—and—O Cran!—her heart missed a beat and she actually staggered, clutching at the captain's arm for support. Yes, it was indeed Zen-Kurel.

If the sight of Zirek had caught her unprepared, the sight of Zen-Kurel utterly overwhelmed her. She stood crushed and shattered by the recognition, tears streaming from her eyes.

Not infrequently it happens that a person—or even a place—deeply loved and lost, becomes in memory more an idea in the heart than a precise visual recollection. It is as though what has been clung to and valued were not the outward semblance, the visible form—that is only the shell of a nut—but rather what it signifies. Thus, the memory of home is less the actual look of the place than the recollection of security and of being cherished. To a girl, the memory of her lover may well transcend his bodily and facial appearance—left far below, as it were—to signify rather the delight of love-making and of being understood and esteemed more deeply than she had ever believed possible. Actually to set eyes on him once more in the flesh often has an unexpected impact, for in absence the mind had retained only vaguely the details of features; yet now these, which during separation were confined in some shadowy kennel of the memory, come bounding forth, pell mell, like released dogs jumping on a homecoming master and stopping him in his tracks.

Yet Maia's case, though of this nature, was in addition grievous and horrifying beyond expression. What she felt was like the infliction of a wound. Her first, spontaneous association was of a ballad that old Drigga used to sing—a ballad which, when she had been a little girl, had more than once frightened her to tears. It was the chilling tale of Terembrô, the dead lad who returned to visit his former love by night. The very words came back to her; she could hear them, sung in old Drigga's quavering voice.

> 'O my dear heart, my dearest lover,
> Where's that colour you'd some time ago?'
> 'O the grave has worn me and the clay has torn me;
> I'm but the ghost of your Terembrô.'

Bayub-Otal, tall and raw-boned as he had always been, looked more or less as she remembered, though plainly suffering from cruel privation. But Zen-Kurel; her beautiful Zenka, the handsome, light-hearted, devil-may-care young officer who had made her laugh for joy at nothing, had teased her out of absurdity and then teased her back into it, in whose secure arms she had lain in tears of happiness! Ah! gods! nothing in her life had ever remotely approached what she underwent in the moment that she recognized this groping, helpless wreck of her former lover. It was not possible, she thought, to suffer like this. It was beyond the frame of the world and the order of things appointed: the gods must surely intervene to stop it. Yet they did not.

Zen-Kurel was hollow-faced and very pale, skeletal in appearance, breathing in gasps and shivering continually. His eyes were half-closed, his cracked lips dry and his mouth fallen open. The soldiers had each drawn one of his arms round their necks and were gripping his wrists; otherwise he would have fallen. His knees were bent and his head hung forward on his chest. He did not look up as he was brought into the room, and seemed unaware of his surroundings.

The sight shocked everyone present. One soldier uttered an exclamation of horror, cut quickly short. After a few moments Mendel-el-Ekna said to Maia, 'You say you mean to take them out of the city—both these men?'

With a great effort she controlled herself. 'Yes; I must.'

'Well, it's for you to say, säiyett: I'm at your orders. But that man—he's a Katrian, isn't he?—do you think he can do it? He's very bad indeed: anyone can see that.'

850

'If only we can get them both away—just a few miles, captain—I'll be able to look after them. I'd be more than glad of your help.'

'Very well; you shall have it.' He turned to one of his men. 'That damned swine of a governor—go and make him give you a stretcher. We'll get them as far as the Blue Gate for a start.'

The stretcher, made of poles and sacking, was stained with what looked like dried blood. Maia recoiled from the thought of its probable use in the routine of the prison.

Zen-Kurel had shown no sign of recognizing her, but for the matter of that she doubted whether he had any idea at all of where he was or of anyone around him. Bayub-Otal, however, took her hand, looking at her gravely.

'We owe this release to you, Maia?'

'Yes, Anda-Nokomis.'

'Strange! You say you're going to take us out of Bekla?'

'Ah, that's if we can; only it's risky, see?'

'I believe you. Who are these men?'

'Lapanese.'

'Lapanese? Where's Kembri, then?'

'Gone south to fight Erketlis. The Lapanese are in revolt—they mean to take the city before Fornis can.'

'Then I suppose we may—But Zen-Kurel's in a very bad way, Maia: I only hope he can survive.'

'We must get him out of here,' she answered. 'Away from Fornis, that's the first thing. Look, they're ready to go.'

Mendel-el-Ekna himself accompanied them, with eight men. It was not until they came out from the Shilth into the western end of the Sheldad that Maia grasped the full extent of the chaos. Far and near, the entire city was full of flame and clamour. Frighteningly close, in the half-darkness, a running fight was going on between two bands of soldiers; yet she was quite unable to tell which side was which. All around them rose shouting and the clash of arms. Dead bodies sprawled in the road and wounded men were crying out and cursing. The captain remained entirely unmoved.

'Nothing to worry about, säiyett: our people have got things well in hand. Whatever you do, just keep going.'

As they stumbled on, it became clear that the whole length of the Sheldad was taken up with the fighting. Soon they were forced to a halt. Gangs of rogues and beggars, more dangerous than wild animals, were dodging among the soldiers, robbing whom they could and looting booths and shops. In doorways Maia could see grim-faced men with cudgels in their hands, plainly ready to defend their premises against all comers. From upper windows screaming women were pelting raiders trying to break in below. In several places fires had started, and above the all-pervading din rose sounds of crackling flames, falling beams and the intermittent crash of collapsing roofs. A lurid glow blotted out the stars.

'Do you know your way through this damned place?' shouted the captain in her ear.

'Best go down to the Slave Market, I reckon,' she answered, 'and then try to get up the Kharjiz and past the temple.'

Once out of the Sheldad they met with less trouble. What isolated fighting they came upon they were able to avoid, while almost all the looters and footpads who saw them sidled off, daunted by the sight of their breastplates and weapons. They had one brief skirmish, however, with an armed gang too drunk to realize they had met their match. Mendel-el-Ekna went for them with grim relish, dropping two in the gutter before the rest took to their heels. Twenty hectic minutes later they reached the Blue Gate.

Here a noisy, milling crowd were being held in check by a line of Lapanese soldiers standing shoulder to shoulder, spears extended and swords stuck ready to hand into the timbers at their backs. The captain's men, with some difficulty, forced a way through for Zen-Kurel's stretcher. The tryzatt in command of the spearmen, sweating and helmetless, saluted Mendel-el-Ekna with a look of relief.

'Any chance you can give us a hand, sir? Count Seekron's orders, to let no one through the gate, but they're all in a panic to get out of the city and I don't know how much longer we can hold them.'

'Where *is* Count Seekron?' asked Mendel-el-Ekna.

'Gone to the upper city, sir, to find Lord Randronoth. No one knows where he can have got to.'

A stone from somewhere in the crowd splintered the woodwork of the gate, narrowly missing Maia where she stood beside the stretcher. 'Give the men bows, tryzatt,' said the captain. 'Order these bastards to disperse and threaten to shoot if they don't. Be quick, too!'

Suddenly, from near the front of the crowd, a voice shouted, 'Maia! Maia!' Turning, she saw Zirek and Meris trying to push their way towards her. She gripped Mendel-el-Ekna's arm, pointing.

'Captain, that's the man and the girl I told you about; the ones who were with me. Please get them over here if you can!'

'Bring them into the guard-room!' shouted the captain to two of his men. 'And *you'd* better get in there, too, before you get hurt,' he added to Maia. 'Go on; I'll see to your friends!'

Thus, after the lapse of a year—and hardly in better case—Maia entered once more the guard-room where she and Occula had been befriended by the soldiers on that sweltering afternoon when they had trudged into Bekla behind Zuno's jekzha.

Two minutes later she was joined by Zirek and Meris. Meris had a swollen lip and a cut on one arm.

'Right; now we've got to get you out,' said Mendel-el-Ekna. 'Can you walk?' he asked Bayub-Otal.

The Ban of Suba shrugged. 'When I can't, I'll stop.'

'Then the quicker you're all gone the better. Serrelinda, I can spare you two men to carry the stretcher. But get him to some sort of shelter as soon as you can, do you see? Otherwise he'll die. And then send my men straight back; I need them.'

She kissed his hands and thanked him with tears in her eyes, but he made light of it.

'Oh, I'd do more than that for you, Serrelinda. Don't worry, I'll tell Lord Randronoth we got you and your friends away all right. See you when you get back.'

The tryzatt opened the postern and in the flickering darkness they slipped through behind the line of spearmen. Immediately the door shut to behind them. In front, on either side, stretched the high, backward-tilting walls of the outer precinct, leading down to the caravan roads below.

'Which way?' asked Bayub-Otal as they reached it. He spoke gaspingly, through clenched teeth.

'That's for you to say, my lord,' she replied.

'I'd say south, my lord,' said Zirek. 'But it might be best to get off the road soon. I reckon the less we're seen the better.'

'Then south it is,' said Bayub-Otal.

Ten minutes later Maia looked back. The eastern walls of the city showed as a black line, beyond which the glow of flames shone luridly on the base of a canopy of smoke. The hubbub, diminished by distance, had become an ugly, throbbing din, like that of some swarm of gigantic insects roused to anger.

'A devils' playground,' she whispered, gazing.

'What?' asked Zirek, ahead of her. 'What did you say, lass?'

'Nothing,' she answered, turning to catch up with him. 'Only something as somebody once said to me. Still got the bread and cheese all right, have you?'

She never saw Bekla again.

: PART IV :
THE SUBAN

WHAT MAIA OVERHEARD

Maia had been milking the cows. She had not lost the knack—or at all events it had come back quickly enough—but her soft, white fingers and pampered, upper city wrists were aching, and now the yoke seemed pressing hard on her shoulders. All the same it was reassuring—the feel of wooden pattens on bare feet and the well-remembered sensation of treading on cracked, summer-baked mud and powdery dust. The dark cowshed was heartening, too, with bright spots of light showing through the knotholes of its planks; likewise the stamping and kloofing of the cows and the smells of cow-dung and of evening water from the brook outside. Her mind might prompt her as often as it liked that she was not out of danger, but in her heart these familiar things spoke of security. It is always satisfying to show oneself unexpectedly capable in some chance-encountered situation where one's companions are all at sixes and sevens. Meris was a shocking bad hand about the place, and even Zirek, though willing enough, knew next to nothing and was continually having to be instructed.

Doing her damnedest to look as though she didn't find the pails heavy, Maia carried them across the yard, through the stone-flagged kitchen and into the little, narrow dairy beyond. Here she set them down, ducked out of the yoke and then, lifting first one pail and then the other, emptied them into the big clay vessels on the shelf above the churn.

Even the dairy was not properly cool this weather. The milk would have to be used quickly. A little would be sold round about, but most would go to themselves—drunk fresh or made into butter, cheese or whey. This was hardly more than a subsistence farm, a bit better than Morca's patch on the Tonildan Waste, but still a long way behind the kind of place where Maia had met Gehta. The farmer, Kerkol, his wife Clystis and her fourteen-year-old brother lived almost entirely on what they produced. Still, at least there was plenty of black bread, cheese, brillions and tendrionas. The strangers weren't eating them out of house and home and Kerkol was glad enough of their money, to say nothing of the extra help.

Coming back into the kitchen, Maia stepped out of her pattens and rinsed her hands in the wooden tub opposite the door. The water was getting greasy, she noticed: she'd tip it out after supper and refill the tub from the brook. She gave her face a quick rub with her wet hands and was just drying it on a bit of sacking when Clystis came in.

Clystis was a big, healthy girl, happy in her youth and strength—in being equal to life—and in her first baby, a boy not quite a year old. She had a quick mind and from the first had struck them all as more forthcoming and go-ahead than her husband, a slow, rather taciturn fellow who always seemed happiest out working. It was undoubtedly Clystis who had convinced Kerkol that they stood to gain from letting the strangers stay. He himself, like most peasants, tended to be dubious of anything unfamiliar.

Clystis smiled at Maia, showing a row of sound, white teeth. 'Cows done, then?'

'Ah.' Maia smiled back. 'Gettin' a bit quicker now, see?'

'Didn't take you long, did it? How many days is it you been here now?'

'Ten.' Maia looked round towards the passage. 'How is he this evening?'

'The poor lad? I reckon he's a lot better. The young chap's with him.'

They had never been asked where they came from, nor their names; and Clystis never used any except Maia's. Bayub-Otal was 'the gentleman', Zen-Kurel 'the poor lad', Zirek 'the young chap', while Meris was 'your friend' or 'the other girl'. They were fugitives from the fighting beyond; a 'beyond' known only vaguely to Kerkol and Clystis, neither of whom had ever been to Bekla.

During the night of her flight from the city and all the following morning, Maia had been in a state of almost trance-like shock. If she had not been young and in perfect health she would have collapsed. Zirek and Meris, after their months of hiding, were weak and not rightly themselves: nervous, unsteady, starting at everything and incapable—or so it seemed—of normal talk or thought. Only Bayub-Otal, though clearly almost at the end of his tether from fatigue and lack of sleep, had remained comparatively self-possessed, limping on beside Zen-Kurel's stretcher, leaning on a long stick cut with Maia's knife and now and then exchanging a word with the soldiers. Long afterwards, Maia still remembered that night as the worst of her life.

Some time after moonset they stopped in a thicket. Maia, who alone knew how large a sum of money she was carrying, and remembering the footpads on the way up from Puhra the year before, was so much afraid that she could not bring herself to rest. At the near-by call of an owl she leapt up and would have run if Bayub-Otal had not restrained her. They had been there no more than five minutes before she asked him whether they could not go on.

'But where to, Maia?' he replied in a dry whisper. 'We may just as likely be going into danger as away from it.'

'Where you making for, then, sir?' asked one of the soldiers who had been carrying the stretcher. 'Only we didn't reckon to come this far: the captain's expecting us back.'

Maia gave them twenty meld apiece. 'I'll write something to your captain,' said Bayub-Otal. 'It won't be much further, but if we don't get this young man into shelter he's going to die.'

The second soldier nodded. 'Looks bad enough now. Should I try to give him some water, do you think, säiyett?'

She shook her head. 'He couldn't swallow it.'

She herself now believed that Zen-Kurel would die. Since she had first seen him in Pokada's room he had not spoken a word, though once or twice he had muttered unintelligibly and moaned as though in pain. To add to her misery and the nightmare-like nature of all she was feeling, it now seemed to her that she would have done better to leave him in the care of the Lapanese. But—Fornis? She doubted whether, with Randronoth dead, the Lapanese could hold the city. Before long either Kembri or Fornis would recapture it. So in that respect they had been right to escape; yet if only they had stayed, Zen-Kurel would have had a chance of recovery.

She was kneeling beside him when Bayub-Otal, taking her hand, drew her to one side.

'Maia,' he said, 'I'm too exhausted to think clearly, but can I ask you this? Have you any destination—any plan?'

She shook her head. 'No, Anda-Nokomis. All I ever had in mind was to get the four of you out of Bekla.'

'*You?*' He looked at her in perplexity, apparently wondering whether his hardships might not have brought about some breakdown in his rational powers. 'But—er—*why?*'

She shrugged. 'Well, I did, anyway. What d'you reckon we ought to do now?'

'You aren't counting on help from anyone else?'

'No.'

'Have you got any money?'

She gave a wry little laugh. 'Much as you like.'

'Then we ought to try to find some sort of shelter: a farm; somewhere like that. The lonelier the better: pay them to take us in. Otherwise Zenka'll die. These soldiers, too—we can't keep them. They're impatient now: they want to be back with their friends, looting Bekla.'

'I'll pay them to go on, Anda-Nokomis, until we find somewhere.'

So in the morning, an hour or two after sunrise, they had come, a hobbling, staggering little bunch of exhausted vagrants, to Kerkol's farmstead—a house and some acres of rough fields about three miles west of the Ikat road. Kerkol and the lad, Blarda, were in the fields, getting in the last of harvest, and Maia had gone in alone and spoken with Clystis in the dairy. They had taken to each other. Besides, the sight of Zen-Kurel would have wrung pity from anyone with the least spark of humanity, and Maia was offering good money. She had assured the girl that his illness was no pestilence. They were fugitives, victims of the hated Leopards. They wanted to stay only until Zen-Kurel was better, and would move on as soon as they could. Kerkol, when he came in at mid-day, had found three of them sound asleep on straw in the barn, with Maia watching by Zen-Kurel, whom Clystis had told the soldiers to put into Blarda's bed. Inclined to be surly at first, he had gradually warmed to the pretty girl so obviously in distress; and being (as they later came to perceive) a man who secretly knew his wife sharper than himself, he was finally persuaded that there was more to be gained from letting them stay than from sending them packing. In any case, with the soldiers already gone, to compel them to leave would certainly have meant Zen-Kurel's death.

By the following day everyone except Zen-Kurel was in better shape. Zirek and Meris, naturally, were only too glad to get out of doors and try to give some help about the place. Zirek made fun of his own ignorance and clumsiness, and sometimes made even Kerkol laugh with his clowning. Maia had forgotten the stormy streak in Meris; or perhaps, she thought, their former circumstances had prevented her from seeing it in its true colours. In Sencho's house, where they had all been slaves and all afraid of Terebinthia, her continual foul language and swiftness to anger might almost be said to have expressed a common feeling. Now, seeing her tense, glittering-eyed manner among ordinary, decent folk and blushing before Clystis to hear her cursing over the butter-churn, she began to understand why Terebinthia had been so anxious to get rid of her. Meris might be all very well for a concubine, but she was precious little use for anything else. She was a natural trouble-maker, not really capable of steady work, short-tempered as a bear and as prone to outburst. One evening, tripping over Blarda's whip in the dusky passage, she snatched it up, swearing, and snapped it across her knee. Maia, apologizing to Clystis, did her best to make out that Meris had had a very bad time and was not herself.

This sort of thing was worrying enough, but in addition Maia had had once or twice seen Meris glancing at the fourteen-year-old Blarda with a look which she herself understood if no one else did. A baste in the barn, she thought, even with an innocent, might be neither here nor there, but she doubted whether Meris would rest content with that. Before she was satisfied, someone would have to suffer. She was a girl getting her own back on the world, and the innocuous and simple were her natural prey. Even with nothing else to worry about, Meris would have been a nuisance, but with Zenka on her hands Maia simply had no energy or attention to spare.

Next to Zen-Kurel, Bayub-Otal was the worst affected. There could be no question, for the time being, of him helping on the farm. He was worn out and half-starved, and for several days could eat only whey, eggs in milk and such other slops as the kindly Clystis prepared. His feet were in such a terrible state that Maia could not imagine how he had walked from Bekla. She had learned, of course, on the journey to Suba, that he was an exceptionally unflinching, determined man, but she had not hitherto realized how much he was capable of enduring.

Resting by day in the shade of the sestuaga trees on one side of the yard, he told her, at odd times and little by little, all that had befallen him since the fight near Rallur. The prisoners, as she knew, had been sent to the fortress at Dari-Paltesh. Here they had been in the charge of Durakkon's younger son, a humane but very ineffectual young man who, it was generally known, had been promoted out of harm's way before he could discredit himself further in the field. Plotho ('the rabbit'), as he was nicknamed, had done what little he could to make their lives bearable, forbidding the soldiers to ill-treat them and ensuring that their wounds received attention. Despite his kindness, however, several had died.

'You were locked up all that time, then?' asked Maia, trying to imagine it.

'No,' replied Bayub-Otal. 'It's not like that at Dari-Paltesh. There are no dungeons. The lowest floor lies below the level of the moat like the bottom of a great, drained well. We were free to wander about. We looked after each other as best we could. We lost count of time. The food was very bad and there was never enough, and although we'd made everyone swear to divide it fairly there were always quarrels. One man was killed in his sleep—'

'How?' asked Maia.

'Sharp stick driven through his throat. We never found out who'd done it. I keep dreaming I'm back there, though I suppose it'll stop after a time.'

In telling her all this Bayub-Otal never uttered any word of reproach against Maia. He might have been talking to someone who had had no more to do with his capture than had Clystis. Nor was there in his manner any suggestion that he particularly wanted to arouse remorse in her. Most of what he told her, indeed, was vouchsafed with his habitual restraint, briefly and bit by bit, in reply to her own questions.

A day or two later he went on to tell her how Han-Glat and Fornis had given orders to bring out the officers and tryzatts—some nineteen or twenty altogether—to join the march from Paltesh to Bekla. These were supposed to be hostages against the risk of an attack across the Zhairgen by Karnat, but it soon became plain that although that might be a principal reason for their presence, there was another. During the march the Sacred

Queen had devised various ways of amusing herself. She had begun by compelling the hostages to beg on their knees for their rations, or else go hungry; but after a day or two had become more ingenious, requiring them to perform various things to their own degradation—things of a nature which Maia recognized as being in accordance with what she herself had seen in Fornis's bedroom on the morning when Occula had hidden her in the closet.

Bayub-Otal had held out against this cruelty, and accordingly he had starved; or rather, he had half-starved, for it so chanced that one of the Palteshi guards, who had a Suban wife in Dari, knew him to be none other than Anda-Nokomis. This man, moved to pity, had risked giving him scraps when no one was looking: otherwise he would have died.

He told Maia how, very soon after the murder of Durakkon and his son, Fornis, as soon as it was clear that Kerith-a-Thrain lacked numbers to destroy her army, had persuaded Han-Glat to join her in a forced march to take Bekla by surprise.

'She knew that Kembri had gone south to fight Santil-kè-Erketlis and that Eud-Ecachlon had no troops worth the name. But she knew, too, that he could still close the gates against her, and she meant to get there before he'd even learned of Durakkon's death.

'There wasn't a single man in that company of Han-Glat's with more speed and endurance than Fornis. I'd never have believed it possible. She led them for twenty-four hours without sleep and with scarcely a halt. They ate as they marched. Half of them were barely on their feet, but only one man tried to drop out. It was in the early morning, just after first light. He said he'd twisted his ankle. She called him out and asked him whether he was married, and he answered yes. So then she said she'd spare him the shame of going home and telling his wife that a woman had more guts than he had. She had a spear in her hand—she was carrying everything the men were carrying—and before he'd had time to say another word she'd run him through. "Now we'll get on!" she said. "We've wasted enough time already." No one else could have done a thing like that and not been faced with mutiny. The men simply left him lying there and followed her like dogs.'

'But Zenka—on the march from Dari—was he—forced to—you know—?'

'Zen-Kurel? He held out for quite a time. But that was part of the sport for Fornis, of course, to see how long some people would hold out. It was I who advised him to forget his pride and take his food. I told him that if we ever got out alive it would all be forgotten anyway. But he still got far too little, because for a full ration she used to make people do—well—things to each other, and that Zen-Kurel always refused.'

'Did she bring all the hostages on this dash for Bekla, then?'

'No, only about a dozen, I think, but I'm afraid I wasn't even counting very well by then. How she picked them I can't tell. I doubt she knew herself: she's mad, really, you know. Not raving mad, but—well— deranged. I think she just couldn't deny herself the pleasure of keeping a few with her. Three of us fell down on the way and she speared them, too. To tell you the truth, I remember very little about the last part of the march. But you'll understand now why Zenka's so ill.'

'And you walked here with us—the night after that?'

'To save my life, yes. What was the alternative?'

'You could have stayed with the Lapanese in Bekla.'

'They'll never be able to hold the city. Eud-Ecachlon's got the citadel, you told me, and once the rest of Han-Glat's troops reach Bekla the Lapanese'll have no chance. Besides, you say Randronoth's dead?'

She nodded. Their talk had tired him—he was still very weak—and after a little she left him to rest while she went to milk the cows. Alone in the shed, she wept to think of her own part in all this misery. 'But what else could I have done?' she whispered aloud. 'Dear Lespa, what else could I have done? I never wished Karnat's men any harm.'

She had as yet told Bayub-Otal nothing of Tharrin's story or of whom she had discovered herself to be. Intuitively, she felt that the time had not yet come.

Yet this was not the only cause for weeping which afflicted her during these days. Indeed, she was thankful for the relief and distraction of work-ing on the place, for whenever she was unoccupied, and always when she lay down to sleep, her thoughts were so wretched that in all reality she would rather have had to endure again the pain and illness she had suffered after swimming the Valderra. Worst—obsessive, indeed—was the memory of Milvushina; that futile death which made nonsense of any notion of the gods as kindly patrons of mankind. Many times, recalling the cruelty which Milvushina had endured, the dignity and courage she had maintained in the face of it, her brief span of happiness as the lover of Elvair-ka-Virrion and the selfless generosity she had shown at her pitiful end, Maia would begin sobbing, and steal away to some lonely place where no one could see her. How poignantly, now, did she recall Occula's reproof for her childish, unimaginative resentment of Milvushina's aristocratic reserve and brave show of detachment in Sencho's house!

In actual fact, of course, Maia had finally achieved a deep affinity and friendship with Milvushina, and had come both to love and respect her. Yet that only served, now, to heighten her sorrow, and she mourned for her friend with an intensity which, while it was upon her, blotted out all else. This was poor Maia's first experience of true, grievous bereavement.

The death of Sphelthon, a stranger, had frightened and horrified her. The death of Tharrin had angered and humiliated more than it had actually afflicted her—except with pity. But the death of Milvushina, a girl of her own age, whom she had comforted in affliction, her companion both in misery and good fortune, she many times wished, and wished sincerely, that she could have taken upon herself. Whatever the future might hold, never again would she see the world through the eyes with which she had seen it before Milvushina died. This was her real loss of innocence; far sharper and deeper than that conventionally-termed 'loss' which she had so gaily experienced in the fishing-net.

Coupled with this grief was a bitter sense of reappraisal and disillusion, flowing from the memory of her last sight of Elvair-ka-Virrion and of what he had said. To her, he now stood for the whole upper city and almost everyone in it.

At other times she was troubled by the fear of pursuit and murder. They had heard no news, either of Bekla, or of Kembri and Erketlis to the east; and Kerkol—never talkative anyway—seemed oddly reluctant to try to get hold of any. Seekron must have discovered, of course—perhaps even before she had left Bekla—that Randronoth had died by violence. Might she herself be suspected of his death? (It did not occur to her that Ogma, given the chance, could testify to the contrary.) But perhaps Fornis and Han-Glat had already overcome the Lapanese? If Fornis were now mistress of Bekla, one of the first things she would certainly apply herself to was hunting down the Serrelinda: and one man unlikely to put any obstacle in her way was Eud-Ecachlon. But again, was it possible that Santil-kè-Erketlis might have defeated Kembri? This, she realized bitterly, was the best hope for herself—for all five of them. In other words Bekla, the Leopards and the whole upper city—not entirely excluding that happy, golden innocent known as the Serrelinda—stood revealed as so much glittering dross, internecine and treacherous, as Nasada had said. For it seemed to her now that she could not excuse herself from the general indictment. She, Maia, had done with them; but had they done with her?

Later, the reason for Kerkol's uncommunicative disposition became reasonably conjecturable. Somehow or other he had managed to dodge being taken for a soldier, and he was not unnaturally afraid that it might catch up with him. As Maia knew, it was in fact unlikely to do so now, when whatever authority might be left in Bekla could hardly have tentacles to spare for probing after odd peasants in lonely places. But Kerkol was not to know this, and his anxiety explained his unfriendliness on their arrival; for though slow and dour he was not, as they gradually learned, an ill-natured man. Although it was harvest-time, he had even taken a turn or two in watching beside Zen-Kurel at night. Everyone, indeed, except Bayub-Otal, had a share in this, for Zen-Kurel was never left alone.

During the first few days they had all felt almost certain that he could not recover. He seemed to have no vitality to combat the ceaseless, restive discomfort under which his mind and body appeared to be crumbling away. At first he could keep down no food at all, and although unconscious of where he was or who was with him, seemed never truly to sleep. He tossed and turned continually, muttering unintelligibly and giving himself no rest. Yet when they spoke to him he neither replied nor gave any sign that he had understood.

Maia's grief was extreme, and the worse for having no one to whom she could unburden herself. She could not make a confidante of Meris, while Zirek she felt she hardly knew. Clystis, of whom, on account of her kind heart and honest, decent goodness, she had become genuinely fond, she already felt she knew well. But it would have been quite beyond Clystis to comprehend her dealings with Kembri and Karnat or her secret mission to Suba: and if she had tried to explain, it would only have seemed, to a simple woman like Clystis, as though she were boasting about her grand, exciting life in high places.

There was no one to whom she could have spoken freely except Bayub-Otal; and he, even when answering her questions, always maintained that same unsmiling reserve and detachment which had galled her in the old days, when her pride had been so bitterly hurt by his indifference to what she now thought of as her stupid, childish advances. She perceived that he meant to maintain between them that indeterminate yet apparently impassable distance which had always been part of their relationship. She, of course, had never, before now, had any chance to speak to him of what had passed between herself and Zen-Kurel at Melvda-Rain. Yet surely he must know? He and Zen-Kurel had spent months together in the fortress. Besides, what motive could he suppose her to have had for risking her life in Bekla to effect Zen-Kurel's release?

Always, however, his manner, as he sat in the shade or walked slowly back and forth on the path beside the brook, rather resembled that of some Beklan dignitary or provincial delegate such as she had now and then met at supper-parties in the upper city: polite and courteous, yet offering no crack through which she could thrust any real confidentiality, let alone any plea for comfort.

All five of them, she often felt, were in ignorance and uncertainty about one another, their perception obscured by troubles past and present as though by clouded, muddy water. Well, if he preferred to wait for the mud to settle, she had no choice but to do the same. Zenka's recovery was more important than any ease of mind she might have been able to derive from pouring out her feelings to Bayub-Otal.

And now, at last, he *was* recovering. They had finally allowed themselves to feel sure that he would not die. He had been taking food, had had long spells of tranquil sleep and was beginning to look less haggard and famished. Yet still he did not recognize even Bayub-Otal, and had not conversed intelligibly with anyone. It had now become Maia's chief anxiety that his mind might not recover. If that were the will of the gods, she believed she could accept it. (So generous-hearted in love are the young, so eager to give all, so heedless of long years ahead and of all that is truly involved in an act of self-sacrifice.) Certainly, when she had fallen in love with Zen-Kurel at Melvda-Rain, a great part of it had been that he was so plainly a likely lad. Nonetheless, it had not come deliberately, from her mind, but spontaneously, from her heart. She had loved him for himself and as he was, not primarily for any material expectations. Besides, through her care and devotion he might in time recover, which would be matter for great pride. Yet inwardly she shrank from such a prospect, and prayed with all her heart that it might not have to be. Of all the afflictions that oppress mankind, insanity is the hardest for friends to accept and the hardest to reconcile with any faith in divine order.

'How is he this evening?'

'The poor lad? I reckon he's a lot better. The young chap's with him.'

Clystis went across to the fire, over which, on a heavy chain, hung a bronze cauldron. She was understandably proud of this, for there were not many to be seen in farm kitchens in the empire. Into it, of course, went practically everything edible. During harvest, Kerkol and Blarda had been lucky enough to kill two hares in the corn. These had been duly hung, skinned and quartered, and had gone into the pot that morning. This, as Maia well knew, was luxury.

Clystis added more water, stirred the pot with a wooden ladle and sipped.

'M'm, that's a nice broth! I'll put in a few brillions. I reckon he might manage some of it for supper, don't you?'

'Ah!' answered Maia. 'I'll take it along, if you like.'

'He's been talking to the young chap, you know,' remarked Clystis casually.

'*What?*' Maia turned, staring as if unable to believe her ears. 'Talking sense, d'you mean?'

'Young chap said so. Said he seemed ever so much better.'

'Oh, Clystis!' Maia came over to the fire. 'You couldn't have told me anything better!'

'Reckoned you'd be pleased.'

Clystis had never said a word to suggest that she had perceived Maia's feelings about Zen-Kurel but, as Maia was well aware, not to have done so she would have to have been a lot stupider than she was.

Ladling out the broth, she gave Maia the bowl and a spoon. Across the steam and the savoury smell the two girls met each other's eyes and smiled complicitly. Then Maia, holding the bowl carefully in both hands, made her way down the short, dark passage-way towards Zen-Kurel's room.

The door was just ajar. She had not yet reached it when her ear caught the sound of two voices—Zirek's and Zenka's. She felt so happy that she could scarcely contain herself. It was she who should be talking to him, of course, not Zirek. Nevertheless, it occurred to her that in her present state of emotion it might perhaps be better not to burst in upon them. He still needed to be kept free from excitement. She paused to compose herself, and as she did so caught the tail-end of what Zirek had been saying.

'No, no, Fornis isn't here. You'll probably never see her again.'

There was a pause, and then Zen-Kurel's own voice, the voice she remembered, restoring on the instant, as might a smell or a song, the entire feel of that night in Melvda-Rain, replied, 'I don't—understand. Is she dead?'

From where Maia was standing his utterance was barely audible, thin as a stream shrunken by drought.

'Not that we know,' answered Zirek. 'She's in Bekla.'

Zen-Kurel seemed, as best he could, to be weighing this. At length he said, 'And we're not. Is that right?'

Zirek must have nodded, for after a moment he went on, 'Then—where?'

'You're safe,' said Zirek, 'with friends. Nothing to worry about, sir. But you've been very ill. Why don't you just try to rest now?'

This time there was a still longer pause, almost as though Zen-Kurel had decided to follow this advice. Maia tiptoed forward and had just reached the threshold when he spoke again.

'Where's Anda-Nokomis, then? Is he dead?'

'Who?'

'Suban leader—withered hand—'

'Oh, he's here too; he's all right—more or less.'

'Where—are we, then—with Erketlis?'

'No, but we're safe. Why don't you just rest now, sir?'

Zen-Kurel's next words, though still weak, were spoken in a tone of authority.

'I shall be able to rest better if you'll tell me a little more, please. What is this place?'

'A farm; a good way outside Bekla, quite lonely. We brought you here. We all escaped from Bekla together, you see, sir.'

'Why—why did *you* need to escape, then?'

'Well, it was me as killed Sencho, you see—me and a girl. She's here too.'

'*You* killed Sencho? You your*self*?'

'You lie down, now!' said Zirek sharply. 'You've been very ill, sir, and if you don't keep quiet you may be ill again, and that won't help anybody. These questions'll keep. I can't tell you everything all at once. Anyway, either Clystis or Maia'll be bringing your supper in a minute.'

For a few moments Zen-Kurel made no reply. Then, in a tone of puzzled uncertainty, he asked, 'Maia? Who's Maia?'

Zirek did not answer at once and he went on more urgently, 'You don't mean—not the girl who swam the Valderra?'

'Yes, she's here with us,' said Zirek.

'Maia? But—but why don't you kill her, then?'

'Kill her? What you talking about? Why, it was her as got you and your friend out of prison in Bekla. Near as a touch got killed herself doing it.'

Maia, holding her breath behind the door, stood still as moss.

'Then,' said Zen-Kurel, 'it can only have been for some vile, mean purpose. That bitch—' She heard Zirek try to answer, but he ran on, his voice rising, 'She's the most treacherous, rotten whore in the world! Oh, yes, she fooled me all right! She betrayed us all and she'll betray you, too, if you don't kill her! I know what I'm talking about! Go and kill her now, before it's too late! Tell Anda-Nokomis I want to see him—get him in here—'

Maia heard no more. Still clutching the bowl of broth, she stumbled back up the passage and into the kitchen. Clystis, busy at the table, looked up in surprise.

'Wouldn't he have it, then?'

Maia, not answering and almost upsetting the bowl in putting it down, went across to the door that led into the yard.

'Maia, you all right?'

'Yes; I'll—I'll be back in a minute.'

Out she ran, across the yard to the belt of trees. He wasn't there and she pushed through them, down the slope beyond to the bank of the stream.

'Anda-Nokomis?' she called.

He stood up. He had been sitting in a kind of little arbour about a hundred yards downstream, where a tangle of scarlet trepsis trailed over the bushes. She ran along the bank, but just as she reached him tripped and measured her length at his feet. He bent to help her up, but she only lay sobbing, face down, her head on her arms.

He knelt beside her. 'What's happened, Maia? What's the matter?'

'Zenka! Zen-Kurel, Anda-Nokomis—'

'O gods! Has he taken a turn for the worse?'

'No, no! He's able to talk now. He told Zirek—I heard him, I was in the passage—he said I was the rottenest—woman in the world; he said why didn't you *kill* me—' Her weeping became passionate and uncontrollable.

Bayub-Otal waited in silence. At length, in a cold, expressionless tone, he asked, 'Are you so very much surprised?'

'*What*, Anda-Nokomis?' She knelt up and looked at him, her face swollen and tear-wet. After a moment, like a child driven to desperation by someone else's inexplicable failure to understand the obvious, she shouted, 'Well, '*course* I am! What d'you think—'

He took her hand and she allowed him to lead her the few steps into the arbour. Here there was a big log, from which a segment had been cut, making a flat seat. They sat side by side. The stream below was a mere trickle, almost lost among clumps of water-plants and dried beds of weed. A pair of green dragonflies were hovering and darting here and there.

'There's a lot I'm extremely puzzled about,' he said, 'and obviously if we're to go on at all it's got to be sorted out. Do you want to talk, or shall I?'

She was still weeping, but he made no attempt to check or comfort her. After a little he went on, 'One thing's plain: you evidently don't see what's happened in the same light as I do or as Zen-Kurel does. If you did, you wouldn't be here.'

She did not answer, but he had caught her attention and she was waiting to hear what he was going to say next.

'I'll start from the beginning. Last Melekril, in Bekla, I—well, I thought that perhaps I'd found a friend; a young slave-girl. I never made friends easily in Bekla, of course, being a suspect and dispossessed man with no prospects. But I liked this girl and felt sorry for her. Anyone with the least decency would have felt sorry for her. She was very young and inexperienced and she belonged to the most evil, disgusting brute in the upper city. She was being sent from one bed to another for money and even seemed to be taking to it. It was obvious that in a year or two she'd be corrupted and that in a few years after that she'd probably be on the scrap-heap—that's if she hadn't been brought to some horrible end first. I thought she deserved better.

'One night, soon after the murder of her master, I received a warning to leave Bekla at once. Within the same hour the girl came to my lodgings in terror—or so you'd have thought. She said she'd escaped from the temple—from torture—and implored me to help her.

'I got her out of Bekla and took her with me to Suba. I told both Lenkrit and King Karnat that she was a girl to be trusted. I pointed out that she'd be valuable to us because of her extraordinary resemblance to my mother,

Nokomis. She was treated honourably and gave the most convincing appearance of being entirely on our side.'

For a moment Bayub-Otal's voice quavered. He bent down, picked up a stick and began breaking it into pieces and tossing them into the stream.

'That same night, however, she quite deliberately seduced one of Karnat's staff officers, a young man who knew—and she must have known that he knew—the plan of attack. He told it to her. He was much to blame, of course, but then he trusted her, you see; just as I did. She'd been very cunning in convincing him that she'd fallen in love with him.

'In fact, she achieved all that the Leopards could possibly have hoped for. She made her fortune that night. She became a demi-goddess, almost; her fame spread throughout the empire and beyond. It spread to Suba; and to Katria and Terekenalt. It even spread to Dari-Paltesh, where some of the men she'd betrayed—the ones who weren't dead, I mean, or who hadn't managed to get back to Suba—were shut up in squalor and misery. I remember one man actually cursing her with his last breath.'

The light was fading. The dragonflies had vanished. In an isolated pool a little way downstream, some tiny fish suddenly skittered across the surface, here and gone, like the margets in Suba. A flock of starlings flickered over on their way to roost.

'But then, quite suddenly, when this same young staff officer's at death's door himself, after suffering the most revolting cruelty and degradation at the hands of Queen Fornis, he's taken out of prison in Bekla and carried away delirious. Some days later he recovers his senses and almost the first thing he hears is that among those with him is this same girl—the girl he trusted, the girl who betrayed him. This makes him feel angry and per-plexed—afraid, even, perhaps.'

As though he were now going back to the farmhouse, Bayub-Otal stood up and stepped out onto the bank. Then, without looking round, he said, 'He's not the only one. Perhaps that girl *might*, in fact, be better out of the way. There's no telling what she might get up to next, you see.'

He had gone some yards when he found Maia beside him.

'Anda-Nokomis!'

As though at any rate unwilling to fail in propriety he halted, but did not look at her.

'Here's one thing there's no catch in it, and you'd better just know it! I'm your cousin! My mother was Nokomis's sister.'

The tone in which she spoke carried immediate conviction. He looked at her, startled. After some moments he said, 'We'd better sit down again, and you can tell me what makes you think that.'

Thereupon he himself returned and sat down, but she was so much agitated that she could not keep still, pacing back and forth on the bank as she talked.

'Earlier this summer, while you was still in that prison, the Leopards arrested a bunch of heldro agents in Tonilda. One of them was my step-father, Tharrin; the man as took up with my mother—or her I always thought was my mother. He'd been a secret messenger for Erketlis. Tharrin was the first man as I ever went with. That's how I come to be sold for a slave; only Morca, her I thought was my mother, she found out, see? And she tricked me and sold me while Tharrin was away.'

'Go on,' said Bayub-Otal.

'I talked to Tharrin in prison before he died, and it was then as he told me—'

She went on to speak of the assassins sent from Kendron-Urtah and of her true mother's desperate flight and pathetic death. When she had ended Bayub-Otal remained silent, gazing down at the brook. 'Do you believe me?' she asked at length.

'Yes, of course,' he answered. He nodded slowly. 'You couldn't be lying about *that*.' She winced at the emphasis. 'In fact, it explains a great deal.' He looked directly up at her and for the first time she could see that he was moved.

'I can tell you your mother's name. Her name was Sheldis. I remember her in Suba when I was a child, but I never knew what became of her. Children don't think much about anyone who isn't there, of course. When I grew older, I learned that she'd married an Urtan and tried to settle down quietly, but they'd both been murdered on the orders of my father's wife. I suppose when the murderers got back to Kendron-Urtah they'd naturally have reported that they'd been entirely successful. After all, Sheldis, not her husband, was the one she really wanted dead.' After a pause, he added, 'The village is Kryle, in eastern Urtah. I'm afraid I can't remember her husband's name—your father—but you could easily find out.'

While he was talking she had sensed a barely-perceptible softening of his earlier hostility; yet not enough to make her want to try to explain to him the truth, *her* truth, about what had passed between herself and Zenka at Melvda-Rain and the true reason why she had swum the Valderra. He had as good as threatened her life. That life—her life as the Serrelinda—had conferred on her a dignity and courage of which the Tonildan peasant girl would not have been capable. She would be damned if she was going to beg for it—or even to seem to be doing so—by offering unsought explanations. If he was so keen to kill a defenceless girl, let him. She was, of course, too young for it to occur to her that he himself might, beneath his harsh manner, feel grieved and sorrowful. In telling him of her mother, she had been concerned simply to let him know who it was he would be killing—a girl as well derived as himself, or nearly; his kinswoman, one whose resemblance to the legendary Nokomis was no mere coincidence.

After an even longer silence he said, 'I talked to you without mincing words because I think you ought to realize how much misery and suffering you've caused with your treachery and your cold-hearted deceit of that Katrian lad. You broke his heart—do you know that? *I* had plenty of time in Dari-Paltesh to get to know it. He couldn't believe you'd done that to him: yet there it was, beyond doubt or argument. While you were living in luxury in the upper city, he was keeping half-alive on filthy scraps, with nothing to think about but the false words you'd said and the promises you'd broken.'

She answered nothing, only looking him in the eye and waiting.

'Do you want to say anything?' he asked.

'No, thank you.'

'Well, there are one or two things puzzling me, so perhaps I'll go on to ask you some questions. First, was it on orders from Kembri that you went with me to Suba?'

'Yes.'

'But I suppose—I want to be fair to you, Maia—you had no alternative?'

'Not really. Only I hated you then, see. By the time we'd reached Suba I didn't hate you any more.'

This seemed to take him aback; he hesitated, thrown out of his customary, bleak composure. After a pause he went on, 'Then I suppose that it was just a matter of your own self-interest being too strong, was it? Here was this golden opportunity to make your fortune and you took it?'

Of all that she had been accused of that evening, the thing—naturally— which had cut her to the heart had been the unquestioning assumption that she had deliberately deceived Zen-Kurel, that she had felt no sincerity and had gone about to seduce him for her own gain. She could not, would not speak of it.

'You can suppose what you like, Anda-Nokomis.'

'Very well. Now there's something else: something that struck me as odd while we were coming here. Those Lapanese soldiers who were with us—they knew you'd swum the river, of course, but they told me that no one had ever learned how you discovered Karnat's plan: it was commonly believed that Karnat himself must have told you.'

'Anybody wants to think it was Karnat, that's their business.'

'You never told Kembri or Sendekar what actually happened?'

'No, nor any of the Leopards.'

'Then may I ask, lastly, why you went to the trouble and risk of releasing us and getting us out of Bekla?'

She shook her head.

'I suppose you're working for Erketlis now, are you? He pays better, or he's going to win and there's still time to change, is that it?'

Once again, it did not occur to her that the mordancy and scorn in his manner might flow from his own pride and pain; from his sense of disillusion with someone for whom he had allowed himself the rare luxury of feeling affection. Nor did it occur to her that he might want her—might almost be begging her—to tell him he was wrong, to give him an explanation which would somehow or other clear things up. All she knew was that apparently neither he nor Zenka had been able to see all that was plain as noonday; Gehta and her dad's farm, poor Sphelthon at the ford, the detachment of three hundred Tonildans downstream of Rallur, the horrible risk of death to which she had twice exposed herself in order to save—amongst others—two people she loved and who, whatever they might have suffered, were now indisputably alive. She felt ready to weep with chagrin. Mercifully, Occula came boiling up.

'You dirty, rotten, basting venda!'

'Ah, unmistakably one of Sencho's young ladies! Perhaps—'

But before he could say more, his name was being called from up by the sestuagas and a few moments later Zirek came running along the bank.

'Sorry to interrupt you, Anda-Nokomis, sir—you too, Maia—but there's wonderful news! Captain Zen-Kurel's taken a great turn for the better! He's in his right mind and he's been talking to me. I've told him to stay quiet, of course: but he's made a good supper and he seems comfortable. He asked me to say would you go and see him, Anda-Nokomis.'

'Thank you,' said Bayub-Otal. 'I'll go at once.'

He walked away towards the house.

Zirek clapped Maia on the shoulder. 'I'm a pedlar, remember? I sell anything—good news an' all! It's cheap to pretty girls like you, too—only a kiss.'

Absently, she put one arm round his neck and kissed his cheek. He raised a hand to his face.

'Tears, eh? Well, it's natural, I suppose. You love him, don't you?'

Of course, she thought, he did not know that she had overheard what Zen-Kurel had said. Himself a good-natured, easy-going fellow, he had probably discounted it, anyway, as the petulance of a sick man who had had a bad time.

After a moment he laughed.

'Come on, Maia! You can't fool the demon pedlar of Tonilda! D'you think I can't see what's plain before my eyes?'

'There's some can and some can't,' she said, and wandered away along the bank, where the bats had begun hunting for moths in the dusk.

*

'Kill her?' said Bayub-Otal, with an air of indifference, moving the candle to where it no longer shone into Zen-Kurel's eyes. 'Well, from all that Zirek fellow's told me, I'm sure Fornis would be happy enough to do that for you.'

'Before she kills us, I mean,' said Zen-Kurel. 'Otherwise how can we feel safe? We know what she's capable of, don't we?'

'Well, you certainly make it sound very convincing. Would *you* care to do it, perhaps?'

'How can I do it while I'm like this, Anda-Nokomis?'

'Oh, well, it might wait a day or two, I suppose. But I was only thinking, Zenka, if she really *is* working for Erketlis now, might it perhaps be a little unrealistic to kill her? I mean, in that case it would be for revenge, really, wouldn't it, and not for our safety? If she's really gone over to the heldro side, she won't be likely to harm us any more.'

'There's no telling which side she's on, is there? Do you mean to say—'

'Now, you mustn't get excited, Zenka. Just lie back and go on drinking that milk. Where was I? Oh, yes, it did occur to me that we're supposed to be noblemen, you and I, though I admit no one would have thought so in Dari-Paltesh. So perhaps personal resentment wouldn't really be a very appropriate motive for killing this peasant girl—'

'But Cran and Airtha! doesn't she deserve it? Think of the—'

'Oh, no doubt. But at that rate, surely, the correct thing would be to have her properly indicted, as soon as we get anywhere where we're among heldro people and there's any sort of law and order. After all, Erketlis must know what she did. Everyone does.'

'Yes, everyone does! So it's not only a case of how much she harmed us. She's made me look the biggest fool—'

'You know, Zenka, it's very odd, but she hasn't.'

'She *hasn't*?'

'No. She's consistently kept it a complete secret, how she found out that plan of Karnat's. Plotho told me, when we were in Dari-Paltesh, that no one had any idea how she'd found it out: and those Lapanese soldiers who carried you here told me exactly the same. Everyone supposes Karnat himself must have told her, and apparently she's let them go on thinking that. She's assured me that she never even told Kembri or Sendekar—she didn't need to, of course; the thing itself was enough for them—and I personally believe she's speaking the truth. These farm people too, you see; *they* know what she did, but they *don't* know how she found out the plan. I asked them.'

'Perhaps there are some things that even she's ashamed of.'

'Perhaps. But anyway, I've just thought of two rather more down-to-earth reasons for not killing her. First, we haven't any weapons—I only wish to Cran we had; and I'm sure these farm people wouldn't like it if we hanged her. But secondly, she's got money and we haven't any at all. Whatever we decide to attempt, money's going to be important. I don't really care for the idea of killing her and then taking her money, do you? Sencho might, I suppose. That would be quite in his line, but hardly in ours.'

'All right, Anda-Nokomis, you've convinced me: so what *are* we going to do with her? Leave her here?'

'Difficult, isn't it?' said Bayub-Otal. 'I mean, we can't get away from the fact that she very nearly got herself killed getting us out of Bekla—'

'Without her, Karnat would have taken it months ago.'

'I know: but we've got our reputations to bear in mind. We both hope, don't we, that the Leopards are going to be defeated, that Santil's going to take Bekla and make peace with Karnat, and that you're going to get back to Katria and I'm going to get back to Suba.'

'Have you ordered the wings for the pigs?'

'Well, but seriously, Zenka, we don't want some sort of half-and-half rumour following us for years, that we abandoned this girl—possibly left her to the mercy of Fornis—after she'd got us out of Bekla at the risk of her own life.'

'Well, what, then?'

'I think that all depends on what we decide to do ourselves as soon as you're better. What do you want to do; make for Erketlis at Ikat Yeldashay?'

'No, be damned to that!' said Zen-Kurel. 'You talk about our reputations. Karnat's still at war with Bekla. I'm one of his officers and I've escaped from the enemy. My duty's to report back as soon as I can, not to go buggering about with irregulars at the other end of nowhere.'

'Well, I'll go along with that, Zenka. If it comes to that, I want to get back to Suba. The only question is how?'

'The left foot, the right foot. What's to stop us?'

'Be sensible: it's more difficult than that. We're completely ignorant about our enemies. We can't go back to Bekla, obviously. If we go directly west, it'll take us into Paltesh—Fornis's province. And I repeat, we haven't got any weapons, in a country swarming with bandits and escaped slaves; though we might try to buy some later, I suppose, with Maia's money.'

'Well, what's your idea, then, Anda-Nokomis?'

'We won't discuss it tonight. It's high time, now, that I left you to sleep. But it did just cross my mind that we can't be too far from the upper Zhairgen. If only we could reach it and get hold of a boat, that might be the answer.'

Clystis came in, clicking her tongue.

'It's not my place to say it, sir, but you shouldn't keep the poor young man talking any more. We don't want him bad again, do we, just when he's begun doing so well?'

'You're quite right and very kind, Clystis,' replied Bayub-Otal. 'I'm just going. Boats cost money, you know, Zenka. But put it out of your mind now and go to sleep.'

: 88 :

MERIS IS MISTAKEN

A week passed. Zen-Kurel steadily regained his health. He was a difficult invalid, with all the impatient restiveness of a young man not used to restraint on his bold, forceful character. He fretted to be up and about. Zirek remarked one day to Maia that he could not imagine how he had survived imprisonment at Dari-Paltesh. 'You'd wonder he hadn't knocked those damn' walls down, wouldn't you?'

These days were among the most unhappy Maia had ever known. She had, of course, foreseen—had not Sednil stressed it plainly enough in Bekla?—that Zenka was bound to be angry over what she had done. But in her youth and inexperience, and in the ardour of her love for him, she had entirely under-estimated that anger. She had supposed that she would be able to explain matters. It is a common error of the young and sincere, when they know that they have at least an arguably valid point of view and have acted from honest and justifiable motives, to feel that others will surely understand if only there is a fair chance to make everything clear. The discovery that even friends and loved ones can misconceive, can remain deaf to explanations; or worse still, receive them with frigid courtesy and a humiliating assurance that to be sure they quite understand— this is perhaps the most painful of all steps on the road to maturity. Ever since Melvda-Rain there had never been far from Maia's mind the memory of the passionate, heartfelt promises which she and Zenka had exchanged. He had made them as ardently as she. In *her* heart, nothing had superseded those promises—not her new-found wealth, the city's adulation, the advances of any number of rich admirers or Eud-Ecachlon's offer of an outstanding marriage. The only man who had bedded her since parting from Zenka was Randronoth, whom she had accepted solely in order to save poor Tharrin's life. By her reckoning, she had sacrificed enough to her love for Zenka to convince anyone of her sincerity. Hadn't she lived, for his sake, in almost daily danger of being put out of the way by Kembri or Fornis? And finally, hadn't she unhesitatingly entered the very doorway of death to release him and Anda-Nokomis, her liege lord, from prison in Bekla?

Of *course* he would come to realize that she had swum the river only to stop the bloodshed and save the Tonildans! Nasada had grasped it. So, obviously, would Zenka, in whose arms she had known herself entirely understood and fulfilled.

What—in the light of her own memories—had never once occurred to her, was that he would have concluded that all the promises, all the joy, the choosing of the daggers and every other happy delight, had been nothing but deliberate, cold-hearted deception—that he had been the dupe of the Leopards' cleverest agent. As often as she thought of that, tears of mortified disappointment sprang to her eyes.

It had also not occurred to her—and it hurt her very much that his memory should (so she felt) be at fault in this respect, since she herself remembered every whisper, every touch, every kiss and look—that he would believe that she had gone about to worm Karnat's plan out of him. Why, he himself had begun the talk of it, and insisted on telling it to her— or anyway, that was how it appeared to her in recollection. Nor did she for one moment regret—and she wasn't going to say she did—what she had done to prevent the whole silly, nasty business of the fighting. Given, of course, that he thought she had acted cold-heartedly from the outset, it didn't make much difference what he thought about that particular detail. Yet it added still further to her grief.

Furthermore, she thought—remembering her talk with Bayub-Otal on the bank—she had unimaginatively under-rated how dreadfully Zenka had suffered. The months of foetid twilight, anxiety, bad food and near-madness, with the deaths of his comrades and his own self-reproach gnawing at him night and day—all this, in his mind, was attributable to her alone. He was only too well aware of the dreadful things *he* had suffered on *her* account. He did not know, and there was no one to tell him—least of all herself—what she had suffered on his.

For there was no approaching him. The day after their talk she was feeding the hens when Bayub-Otal, ever punctilious, took the opportunity to speak to her while no one else was near. It was important, he said, that at present Zen-Kurel should not be upset or over-excited. He was sure she would understand that for that reason it would be better if she were to keep out of his way for the time being. She had responded with two words of acquiescence, followed by a correct, cold and formal apology for having, being a Suban, sworn at her liege lord; and this he had accepted with a silent bow.

Yet even had things been otherwise, her womanhood was firm that it

877

was beneath her to take the first step. If he should later want to talk to her, she was ready. Meanwhile, though her heart might break, she felt, as any woman would feel, that she was not going to initiate explanations.

And yet, far below her unhappiness, at some profound level within her, there shone out intermittently a kind of here-and-gone glimmer—like the *taulapa*, that phenomenon of the Pacific, the phosphorescent streaks appearing at depth which, because they are always aligned towards the nearest land, were once invaluable in darkness to Polynesian navigators of days gone by. The mind of a man is like a ruled kingdom: it may often be badly ruled, or partly or wholly in anarchy, but nevertheless a ruled kingdom is what it is supposed and trying to be. Women are microcosms, in which the mind, instinctive as the great migrations of terns, is subject to all manner of age-old, God-given stimuli comparable to seasons, stars and winds. Maia understood more of Zen-Kurel than she knew, or than he knew himself. Deep below the unnavigable tempest of his anger there still flashed, involuntary and unregarded, his former desire; and not only desire, but also the memory of that world-changing affinity which at Melvda-Rain had cried aloud to his heart that here at last was a girl whose capacity and abilities were at least equal and certainly complementary to his own; a girl whom to love was a privilege and not an indulgence; the girl the gods had intended to stand up beside him so that one plus one would total more than two. The very excessiveness of his antipathy—his refusal to let her come near him—was indicatory. What was it he unconsciously feared in himself, from which he had to take such strenuous steps to keep her apart? All this Maia sometimes glimpsed as dimly and fitfully as a weather-beaten, exhausted migrant, its wings sodden with rain, might for an instant perceive, behind scudding clouds, the shape of Orion or the Southern Cross.

It was not, of course, lost upon Clystis that the two of them were on bad terms and that Maia was unhappy. Yet she asked no questions, only letting Maia see that she felt sympathetic. Insofar as her own feelings could be inferred, they appeared to be that the quicker Zen-Kurel recovered his health, the quicker the trouble was likely to blow over (she could, of course, have no idea of its gravity) and to this end she applied herself with natural, unselfish kindliness.

After four or five days he was up and about, and almost at once began to show his natural force of character and those qualities of initiative and resourcefulness which had gained him his place on Karnat's staff. At first, while still not allowed to do much, he busied himself in shaping three rough but serviceable bows and then in cutting and fletching arrows. There was, of course, no metal for the tips, but he sharpened and fire-hardened the points so skilfully that they felt strong enough to penetrate not only flesh but any clothing lighter than leather. He then set to work to make three wooden spears.

'They'll be a lot better than nothing, Anda-Nokomis,' he said, offering Bayub-Otal his choice, 'and we may be able to come by some knives later on.'

There was no dissuading him, a day or two later, from going out to reconnoitre beyond the bounds of the farm. He took Zirek, but would not let Bayub-Otal accompany them. 'Three's really no better than two, Anda-Nokomis,' he said. 'Not on a job like this. One of us ought to stay behind, and the Ban of Suba's more valuable than me.'

Bayub-Otal smiled and gave in, only begging him not to exhaust himself. Maia, who had overheard their conversation while hanging out the washing, drew the conclusion that Bayub-Otal was not going to be able to stop Zen-Kurel from doing anything he had decided upon.

He returned that evening. Maia was at her needle, helping Clystis to patch and darn. Naturally, it was beneath her dignity to get up and leave, and she sat working silently while he and Zirek ate supper and talked to Bayub-Otal.

'You were right about the upper Zhairgen,' he said. 'We're only about eleven or twelve miles from it here.'

'You didn't go that far today, I hope?' said Bayub-Otal.

'I would have,' replied Zen-Kurel, 'but it's not so easy as I've made it sound. Two or three miles from here you come to a forest stretching all the way down to the north bank. Eight or nine miles of deep forest, Anda-Nokomis—Purn, they call it—dividing Bekla province from Lapan.'

'I don't see any point in making for the Zhairgen unless there's some hope of getting hold of a boat,' said Bayub-Otal. 'How far does the forest extend along the river; did anyone tell you that?'

'I was told it goes as far as the Ikat road one way and the Herl–Belishba road the other,' answered Zen-Kurel, 'but I don't think we ought to risk being found on either of those roads, do you?'

'I agree about the Ikat road,' said Bayub-Otal. 'Kembri's army will almost certainly be somewhere near there. Anyhow, that's not the way we want to go. But the Herl road—'

'We could very well get into just as much trouble on that,' said Zen-Kurel decisively. 'What d'you think, Zirek?'

'Well, I doubt we could get there, sir, anyway,' answered Zirek. 'It must be nearly twenty miles, I'd guess, across dangerous country—robbers and that, I mean—to say nothing of the river.'

'What river?' asked Bayub-Otal. 'You don't mean the Zhairgen?'

'No, he means the one they call the Daulis,' said Zen-Kurel. 'It rises on Mount Crandor, you know, Anda-Nokomis—actually inside the citadel, so I'm told—and then comes down in a chain of falls they call the White Girls. Down here it's not all that wide—we went and had a look at it today—but it's deep. There aren't any fords and I don't believe we could get across. I think,' he added with a certain emphasis, 'I think only an *expert* could hope to do that.'

Maia gave no sign of having heard him. Zirek drew in his breath involuntarily, and it almost seemed as though Zen-Kurel himself half-regretted what he had said, for he went on rather hurriedly,

'But going into the forest may be a bit risky—there seem to be no tracks at all, and apparently hardly anyone ever goes in.'

'Ah, that's right,' put in Clystis. 'You don't want to get wandering about in there, sir, not in Purn you don't. Lose your way easy—there's them as has—an' you'd be lucky to get out again. 'Sides which there's all manner of wild beasts an' that—'

'But I think we *are* going in, all the same,' continued Zen-Kurel, smiling at her. 'You see, Anda-Nokomis,' he resumed, 'no one from Bekla's going to find us in there, are they? And once we've reached the Zhairgen, we'll be able to follow the bank down to some sort of town or village and then get hold of a boat. I was told today that there's a town about twenty miles below where the Daulis runs into the Zhairgen.'

'Do you know anything about that, Clystis?' asked Bayub-Otal.

'Well, I've cert'nly heard tell of a town,' she replied. 'Nybril, they call it, but none of us has ever bin that far. It's—oh, right away beyond the other side of Purn, see.' Looking up at Zen-Kurel in the candlelight, she shook her head. 'There's no one goes into Purn, sir. You'd really best not try that, honest.'

'Well, but we can't stay here for ever, Clystis,' he said, 'kind as you are.'

'You're very welcome to stay as long as you like,' she answered. 'That's if you don't mind—'

Suddenly the door into the yard was flung open so violently that it crashed against the wall behind, and Meris came into the room. Her dress was torn at the shoulder, exposing one breast, her hair was dishevelled and she was bleeding from a graze on her arm. Without a word she went across to the tub and began to rinse her face and arms. Then, turning to Clystis, she said sharply, 'Perhaps I could use your needle and thread, could I?'

'Why, whatever's happened?' asked Clystis, staring.

Meris went over to her and plucked the needle from between her fingers.

'Oh, nothing but what you're quite used to *here*, I dare say,' she replied; and thereupon sat down and began stitching up her ripped bodice.

At this moment Blarda entered. Everyone turned to look at him. The

880

boy was plainly not himself. He had a hang-dog look, faltering and apprehensive, and his eyes wandered from one person to another. In the middle of the room he stopped uncertainly, as though awaiting he could not tell what.

'But what's *happened*?' asked Clystis, with more urgency.

Meris laid down the needle, put her hands in her lap in such a way that the bleeding graze showed more plainly in the candlelight, and gazed at Blarda with compressed lips.

'It's not my fault!' blurted Blarda. No one said anything and his voice rose hysterically. 'It's not *my* fault, sis! I never done anything, honest!'

Meris, tapping the fingers of one hand on the opposite wrist, let out her breath and cast her eyes up to the ceiling. Clystis, her cheeks flaming, stood up and advanced on Blarda, who backed away, whimpering.

'Are you going to tell me what's *happened*?' she said in a whisper like a passing arrow.

'I—I—that's to say—well, she got angry all on a sudden, like, didn't she?' said Blarda, now almost in tears.

'*Why* did she?' said Clystis. 'What are you talking about?'

'It's not fair!' burst out Blarda. 'The other day she says to me—she says "Let's go in the hay"—'

For two minutes he babbled on with the inability, typical of a youngster in trouble and under pressure, to do anything but come out with all the banal and embarrassing truth.

'But what's happened *now*?' interrupted Clystis at length. 'Are you or aren't you going to tell me why she's—'

'She was in the shed, wasn't she?' muttered Blarda. 'Up by the hay. So I says to her, "Come on, then," and I went to—to do like we done before, see. But then suddenly she comes over angry. She says "Go away!" So I says "No," 'cos I thought she was only playing around. And I had my hand down inside the front of her clothes and she pulls away and then she says, "Now look what you done," she says, and I tried to stop her but she went off quick. Honest, sis, I never done anything 'ceptin' what—well, what—'

To an elder sibling, the emergent sexuality of the younger is often shaky ground; sometimes a matter of sensitivity to the point of anger; a cryptic variant of the discomposure not uncommonly felt by parents. Clystis, like most country folk, spoke and behaved to people according to her own personal opinion of them. Respectful towards Bayub-Otal and Zen-Kurel, she had already sized up Meris accurately enough. She now turned and faced her, hands on hips.

'Perhaps *you* can tell me some more about what the lad's bin saying, can you?'

'Perhaps I can,' replied Meris coolly. 'What would you like to hear? He's coming on very well, really. He'll be ready to clear out of this place soon, I wouldn't wonder.'

'What the devil d'you mean, coming on very well?' shouted Clystis. 'Are you sayin'—'

'Yes, I am,' answered Meris. 'He *is* coming on very well. He just got a bit over-excited, that's all.' She dabbed ostentatiously at the bleeding scratch. 'He's much better than your husband already. Well, I dare say you *do* know about *him*. Anyway, I do if you don't.'

'*What* did you say?' cried Clystis, staring.

'Not my fault,' said Meris composedly. 'Poor man, I feel sorry for him. I was just obliging him, really.'

'You liar!' screamed Clystis, bursting into tears and stamping her foot. 'You're lying, lying—'

'Lying?' said Meris, standing up and facing her. 'How funny, then, isn't it, that I should know that Kerkol's got a mole at the bottom of his zard, just a bit on the right side? And how funny that I should know he's got a white scar on the other side, just at the top of his left thigh! In fact I'll tell you some more while I'm about it, if you like. He—'

'No, you won't,' interjected Zen-Kurel suddenly. Hitherto none of the three men in the room had spoken, as though each felt that to try to intervene in an unhappy family affair of this kind would avail little and possibly even do more harm than good. Now, however, Zen-Kurel's manner was unhesitant and authoritative. He stood up and crossed the room, interposing himself between the two women.

'Go outside, Meris, please,' he said.

'Outside? Where?' answered Meris insolently.

'I don't mind where,' replied Zen-Kurel in the same quiet, controlled tone, 'but don't come back until I send for you.'

As Meris hesitated he gently raised his hand, as though if neccesary to take her by the arm. Meris tossed her head, flung down the bone needle on the flags and went quickly out of the door. After a moment Zirek followed her.

Clystis, sitting at the table with her face sunk on her arms, was weeping unrestrainedly. Maia put a hand on her shoulder.

'Look, dear, you mustn't take on like this. It's not the end of the world. There's lots of worse things—'

'You let me be!' cried Clystis. 'You'll have to go now—tomorrow—all of you. You can't stay here after this!'

Maia, concerned only to comfort her, felt at a loss. It had never entered her head that Meris, in indulging her taste for mischief, would make such a cruelly thorough job of it. In effect, thought Maia, she had inflicted a wound which would go on hurting Clystis for years, perhaps for life. She racked her brains for some sort of comfort.

'Listen, she's not worth crying about, Clystis—'

'It's *Kerkol* I'm crying about,' sobbed the girl. 'Oh, I never did Meris any harm—'

'Meris is a bad, spiteful girl,' said Maia, 'and that's no more than the truth.'

At this moment Zen-Kurel spoke again. 'Well, I'm fairly certain, myself, of something that *is* the truth. Clystis, will you try to listen to me, please, because I think this is very important?'

His voice had a compelling quality and a quiet confidence which reinforced his request so effectively that Clystis raised her head, looking at him in silence. He, however, was looking not at her but at Blarda, standing over by the far wall with a look of utter dismay, as though he had opened a door at random and found he had let out a wolf.

'Blarda,' said Zen-Kurel, 'can you come over here, please? There's nothing at all to be afraid of. I'm not going to hurt you; I just want to ask you a question, that's all.'

Rather nervously, Blarda complied.

'Well,' said Zen-Kurel, smiling and taking his hand, 'so you and Meris have been amusing yourselves in the barn; and I'm sure no one's going to blame you for that. A handy young fellow like you—why on earth wouldn't you? As far as I'm concerned you can go with all the girls between here and Bekla—probably will, I dare say.'

This produced from Blarda the ghost of a smile.

'Now look,' went on Zen-Kurel, 'answer me this like a good lad and don't be ashamed, because I'll tell you now, I've done the same kind of thing myself, and that's no more than the truth. When you've been with Meris—you know, afterwards, when you were talking and so on—did you ever tell her what Kerkol looks like with no clothes on? You know what I mean, don't you?'

'Yes,' whispered Blarda. 'Yes, sir, I did.'

Zen-Kurel nodded. 'But that was only because she asked you, wasn't it?'

'Yes, sir.'

'Do you think Kerkol could ever have done the same with Meris as you did?'

Blarda shook his head. 'I'm quite sure he couldn't, sir.'

'Why?'

''Cos he don't like her. He's said so to me—oh, three four times.'

'Thank you,' said Zen-Kurel. 'I'm very glad, Blarda, that you had the guts and honesty to tell me that. Now would you please go and ask Meris to come back in here?'

Meris returned almost at once, shut the door, put her back against it and stood waiting with a look of sulky disdain.

'Meris,' said Zen-Kurel, 'we're leaving here tomorrow. I'm afraid you'll have to stay behind, but I thought you'd probably want to know all the same.'

'Stay behind?' said Meris, visibly startled.

Zen-Kurel said nothing.

'Stay behind?' cried Meris. 'What the basting hell do you mean? Why?'

'Because Lord Anda-Nokomis and I have decided that that would be best,' replied Zen-Kurel. 'Besides, since you have this attachment to Kerkol—'

'Kerkol?' said Meris. 'I've no more had anything to do with Kerkol than Maia there!'

'How very strange!' said Zen-Kurel. 'Well, then, it must all be a mistake, but Clystis very unfortunately got the idea from somewhere that you had. I'm afraid you may quite accidentally have upset her. So I'm sure you'll want to reassure her and beg her pardon.'

'Sorry!' snapped Meris, as though she were spitting in the gutter.

'Oh, in proper words and a proper voice,' said Zen-Kurel a shade more sharply. 'But if you prefer, you can leave it over until the rest of us have gone tomorrow.'

There was a pause. Zen-Kurel picked up the bone needle from the floor and began idly examining it in the candlelight.

Suddenly Meris, pushing herself forward with a thrust of her shoulders against the door, went quickly over to Clystis.

'The truth is I've never had anything at all to do with Kerkol,' she said. 'I'm very sorry and I beg your pardon.'

'Why did you try to make me think you had, then?' asked Clystis.

'I don't know. Like I say, I'm sorry.'

'And you found out those things by asking Blarda?'

'Yes.'

'He didn't tell you first: you asked him?'

'Yes.'

'But *why*?'

'I don't know.'

'She—er—she *did* kill Sencho,' murmured Bayub-Otal. He had not spoken since Meris's first entry, and Blarda and the three girls all looked round at him.

'Yes, she *did* kill Sencho,' replied Zen-Kurel, not taking his eyes off Meris, 'and that shows how courageous and useful she can be when she likes. Well, do you want to come with us tomorrow, Meris, or not?'

'Yes, please,' said Meris, like a child. Suddenly she snatched up Clystis's two hands and kissed them. 'I'm sorry! I'm really sorry! Oh, if only—'

The door from the yard opened again and Kerkol came in, followed by Zirek.

'Sorry I'm late in, lass,' he said to Clystis. 'Had a bit of trouble with two goats got out down the bottom. I was on gettin' 'em back and then I had to mend the gap they'd bin through, see?'

He stooped to rinse his head and shoulders in the tub.

'I'm afraid we've got to leave you tomorrow, Kerkol,' said Zen-Kurel. 'It's a pity, but there it is. I'm fit enough now, you see, and we've got important business elsewhere. We're going to miss you all, and that's a fact.'

Kerkol nodded stolidly, dried his face and sat down at the table.

'Ah, well, that's it, then.' He paused. 'Place won't seem the same, will it, lass?' Then, to Bayub-Otal, 'Reckon we'd best have a bit of a drink on it, sir, while she's gett'n' us some supper. Fetch a drop of djebbah up, Blarda lad, so's we c'n drink good luck to 'en all.'

: 89 :
INTO THE FOREST

Later Bayub-Otal asked Maia, Meris and Zirek to accompany him down to the stream. The night was clear and star-lit, with a faint breeze from the east and a scent of planella from Clystis's little patch of garden. Of the comet there was no longer the least trace. Maia, who ever since her childhood had been alive to the progress of the seasons with an apprehension almost as unconscious as that of birds, felt sure that it could not now be much longer until the rains.

Bayub-Otal sat down on the ground, looking from one to another as he spoke.

'What we have to get clear now, I think, is where we're making for: I mean, where each of us wants to go. As you know, Zen-Kurel wants to get back to Terekenalt and I mean to return to Suba. What about you, Zirek? You're a Tonildan, aren't you?'

'Well, I don't know as that really comes into it, sir,' he answered. 'Specially just at present, when no one knows what's going to come out of all the fighting. I'll take my chance with you; as far as Lapan anyway. Then if Lord Santil's still in business, I'll go and join him—that's if you agree. Only I've got a notion he might be quite pleased to see them as killed Sencho; he's got a reputation, you know, for not being mean to people who've done him a good turn.'

'Yes, he has,' said Bayub-Otal, 'and after all you've risked and suffered, both you and Meris are fully entitled to whatever he'll give you. Well, that's clear, then.'

With a certain air of embarrassment he continued, 'And have *you* thought, Maia, about where you're going?'

She had indeed. She wanted and intended to go wherever Zen-Kurel went; and if she could not, she did not care what became of her.

'It's all one to me, Anda-Nokomis,' she said. 'Perhaps I may think of something later.'

'But do you want to try to reach the Zhairgen with us?' He was just perceptibly impatient.

'That'll do as well as anything else. Will you excuse me if I go to bed now? I'm very tired.' And she turned away without waiting for a reply.

When they came to set out the following morning, it was clear that Zen-Kurel must have been giving thought to the importance of maintaining at least a civil working relationship with the two girls. He greeted both of them courteously if rather distantly, and went on to say that he thought they could hope to reach the Zhairgen that evening.

'Of course it won't be like twelve miles in open country,' he said. 'It'll be rough going in the forest, I dare say, but we can make sure of keeping our direction by following the Daulis downstream. Even if we do have to spend a night in the forest, we shall be able to manage all right. A fire's the great thing. I was once three nights in the Blue Forest in Katria, and that was quite bearable.'

They had become his soldiers, thought Maia, with secret, fond amusement. He felt it his responsibility to look after them, to show no favourites, to set an example and raise everyone's confidence. In some respects she felt so much older than he. Probably it was as well that for now things should remain as they were; impersonal and matter-of-fact. Anyway, he should have all the loyalty and help he would permit her to give him. She would act her part of the dutiful follower, even though she suspected that in his courage and ardour he might very well be leading them all into grave danger. Reckon I've caught love like I was ill, she thought. I couldn't stop loving him whatever happened, whatever he did. I've got to suffer it, but I'll be damned if I'm going to show it.

Bayub-Otal was his usual chilly, composed self. His great virtue, thought Maia—one more likely to appeal to men than women—was his consistency. He could always be relied upon to be much the same, whether in good fortune or bad, in danger or out of it. She could well imagine that he must have been a tower of strength to his friends in the prison at Dari-Paltesh.

Meris seemed subdued—even anxious to please. That was the pathetic thing about Meris, thought Maia. It was as though she really couldn't help the things she did. So then someone hit her or humiliated her and she became quite a nice girl—for a while. She wondered how deeply Zirek felt about her. Despite all they had undergone, she was still very beautiful; and obviously, as Zen-Kurel had conceded, indisputably possessed of courage and endurance.

Zirek himself struck Maia as being in a mood of well-masked apprehension. When Zen-Kurel's back was turned he winked at her and mimed the action of tossing a coin, catching it in his palm and turning it over on the back of the other hand. Then, pretending to uncover and look at it, he stared up at her with an expression of comical dismay.

Their farewells were brief but sincere. Kerkol and Blarda wished them luck and Clystis gave them what food she could spare. Maia gave her an extra hundred meld, embraced her and wished her the perpetual favour of the gods. Then they set off across the pasture in the direction of the river.

They reached it about two hours later, just as the day was growing hot. The bank, though rough and lonely, was fairly open. The river was about twenty yards wide and certainly deep. Despite the time of year, there was no bottom to be seen. There was indeed a good, steady current, but nothing so swift as Zen-Kurel's account had led Maia to expect.

'No crossing that, you see, Anda-Nokomis,' said Zen-Kurel in a conclusive tone.

'And no point, either,' replied Bayub-Otal, 'if we can reach the Zhairgen without.'

They turned downstream, picking their way through gradually thickening scrub and now seeing ahead of them the outskirts of the forest, dark against the growing glare of the southern sky. 'It'll be cooler once we get in there,' said Zen-Kurel, slashing at the flies with a broken-off branch.

The approach to the forest consisted of fairly close brush and, beside the river, wide patches of dried-up reeds and cracked mud, which at any other time of year would have been impassable. These they pressed through, putting up great clouds of gnats which tormented them, following them about in front, as Zirek put it, and settling on their necks and arms. Once Meris startled a bright-green snake, which whipped between her and Maia and was gone before either of them had time to feel afraid—of that particular one.

Emerging at length from the further side of this marshland, they found themselves at the foot of a long, gradual slope, so thickly overgrown that they could not really see how high it might be. To the right of this the river wound away among tangles of undergrowth until it was lost to sight.

'We mustn't lose touch with the river, Anda-Nokomis, if we can help it,' said Zen-Kurel, 'but the best thing will be to get up this ridge and then go down and pick up the bank again. We'll be able to see more of the lie of the land from the top.'

They began to climb. Maia, who had started a menstrual period the previous morning and now had a headache, was beginning to feel thoroughly out of patience. Damn these fools who couldn't swim! There—just there—was the river—safe, smooth, cool and free from flies. She could easily have been three or four miles down it in an hour.

'Are you all right, Maia?' asked Bayub-Otal, turning back to give her his hand over a fallen tree-trunk. She nodded curtly, smacked a gnat on her arm and pushed on uphill.

An hour later, having at last topped the ridge, they found themselves gazing down on the forest proper. The prospect was formidable and worse. Maia, surveying it with something close to terror, could only suppose that either Clystis must have thought that Zen-Kurel possessed magic powers or else that she had been too nervous of him to speak out more strongly.

Ahead of and below them lay a vast, shallow dip, something like two or three miles across. In every direction, as far as the eye could see, it was compact with trees, unbroken and even as a roof in the still heat. So uniform, so featureless was this prospect that they might have been looking out across a smoothly undulant, green lake. No tree seemed taller than another and none, one would suppose, could have moved even in a wind, so close together were they crowded. Looking at that forest, no one could tell in what millenium he might be living. The god of that place, thought Maia, was not hostile to mankind; no, he was simply indifferent, distinguishing not at all between men, beasts and the insects darting among the leaves. Once in there, their lives would have no more value than those of ants; and they themselves would be as helpless.

On the farther side of this great bowl the horizon was closed by a line of the same trees; and one could imagine the forest continuing unchanged beyond. Away to their right, below the ridge on which they were standing, they could catch, here and there, glimpses of the river.

'Jumping Cran!' muttered Zirek, staring. 'It can't be done, sir!'

'Nobody has to do it who doesn't want to,' replied Zen-Kurel with (so it seemed to Maia) a somewhat forced air of confidence. 'Personally, I'm going to Terekenalt and that's the way. But let's have a rest and eat now, shall we?'

'I was just thinking about the eating,' said Bayub-Otal. 'I think it may take us quite a long time to reach the Zhairgen through that; certainly two days. We ought to be rather sparing, I think, of what food we've got.'

'We might be able to kill something,' said Zen-Kurel. 'I'd like a chance to try these arrows.'

Having eaten, they descended the ridge, making once more for the river, and now entered in earnest the forest depth. Within half an hour Maia was almost as frightened as though Fornis herself, innumerably multiplied, were lying in wait behind every tree. There was no true light; only a murky, green gloom filtering down from far above, so dim that neither they themselves nor the trees cast shadows. They could not see more than twenty or thirty yards ahead, partly for the gloom and partly for the undergrowth all around. The humidity was like damp felt clinging to skin and clothes; a thick, resistant film which they seemed to thrust apart with their bodies in pushing on. There were weird, disturbing noises—sudden cries and chatterings, and sometimes the squawking of alarmed birds in the confined stillness—but the creatures making them remained unseen. She felt diminished, shrunken as though by an evil spell, a minute creature walking between the legs of a giant. And the giant was vigilant. He, she now knew, was the god: a god unknown to man; nameless—what were names?—infinitely remote and old. He was watching them as he watched everything in the forest, yet their fate was nothing to him. Nor would propitiation be of the least avail. He was lord of a world in which prayer had no meaning and death itself very little; a world in which the frog sat impassively as the snake approached closer to devour it.

After a time they had lost all sense of direction. There was, of course, no telling where the sun might be. Zen-Kurel, using Maia's knife—the only one they had—tried to maintain a line by marking successive tree-trunks, but the undergrowth, in many places so impenetrable as to force them to turn this way and that, rendered the scheme futile. After a long time they came upon a tree already marked and realized that they must have returned to it. Of the river there was neither sight nor sound.

Zen-Kurel, however, remained outwardly calm. The river, he insisted, could not be far away, but when Zirek asked him how he could be sure that they were not going away from it, he could only reply that he expected before long to come on some tributary brook which they would be able to follow. As the afternoon wore on, Maia began to entertain first the possibility, then the likelihood and finally the conviction that they might very well wander until they died. When, like a spectre, the idea first glimmered in her mind, she dismissed it as a morbid fancy. But with growing thirst and fatigue adding to the discomfort of her menstruation, it was all she could do—and, as we have seen, Maia did not lack courage—not to give way openly to her fear. If ever they *did* find the basting river, she thought, she would plunge in and be damned to the lot of them, so she would. Meanwhile, Meris was showing no alarm whatever. Meris, as well she knew, had seen unspeakable things, and survived them. She, Maia, was not going to be put to shame by Meris. Well, not yet, anyway.

At last they happened to come out into a clearing—an acre or two of relatively open ground which none of them could remember seeing from the ridge. Here there must have been, or so it seemed, some local disease of the trees, for a great many were dead; several leaning against those still living, others lying their huge length along the open ground. There was a little pool of water, too, in a rock-hollow, from which they drank. Although this was apparently fed by a spring, it flowed nowhere, the overflow merely seeping away into the surrounding, parched ground.

Now at last they could see the sun. It was low, reddening to evening, and lay on their right. Looking back, they could catch sight, far off above the trees, of the ridge which they had descended.

'Well, at least we've been going more or less in the right direction, Anda-Nokomis,' said Zen-Kurel, 'though I'm afraid we must have gone something like two miles for every one that's been any good to us. And now we know where the river must be, too.'

'I don't think we'd better try to reach it tonight,' said Bayub-Otal. 'Everyone's tired out. Wherever we are, we're going to need a fire, and there's plenty of dead wood here. I suggest we camp.'

'How much further d'you reckon it is to the Zhairgen, then, sir?' asked Zirek. 'We've got very little food, and the girls can't be expected to stand up to much more of this.'

'We must just hope for the best, mustn't we?' replied Bayub-Otal expressionlessly. He turned away and began gathering sticks with his one hand.

'We shall get there tomorrow,' said Zen-Kurel. 'Why not, once we reach the river bank?'

A few hours later, as night fell with only the briefest of twilight, Maia realized that in the forest, darkness called forth another world. Here, human order was reversed. Daylight was the time appointed by the god for concealment, inaction and sleep. In daylight he was sole, a presence absorbing his creatures into himself, sheltering them from the intrusion of that upstart, the sun. At nightfall he became manifold, breathing into them his fell, rapacious spirit, so that they became as he, indifferent to fear, suffering and death, intent only upon obeying his will. They must kill and eat, for with the renewal of day it was decreed that they should return once more into the single essence of their master. Kill—be killed: eat—be eaten: which, mattered little. This was their pursuit and calling, and they were impelled to it without power of decision.

Zirek still had his pedlar's fire-making tools—quartz, iron and sulphur— and had little trouble in transferring the flame to a heap of dry grass. Soon their sticks were burning well, and Maia and Meris joined the men in dragging up fallen branches and logs. Having no axe, they set the logs to burn at one end, pushing them forward into the blaze as they were consumed. Neither Bayub-Otal nor Zen-Kurel said anything about turns on watch, and Maia guessed that the three men had already come to some arrangement among themselves.

When she had eaten the few mouthfuls that were her share of supper, she wrapped herself in her cloak and lay down to sleep. Yet tired out as she was, sleep would not come. She was hungry; her head ached; her belly hurt. Her flux had come on strongly and there was nothing clean or dry to put between her legs. But these discomforts were as nothing compared with her terror of the forest and the thought of the morrow. I can't go on, she thought. Even if no one'll come with me, I'll go back to the farm alone. Yet she knew very well that she could not attempt it.

The active night was full of wild, disturbing cries. From somewhere far off sounded a many-voiced clamour which must, she thought, be the howling of wolves. As she lay listening to this and trying to guess how distant it might be, there came from close by a deep, mewling cough, repeated several times. She turned faint with fear. At supper-parties in the upper city she had once or twice listened to Beklan hunters' stories of the great cats. An armed man, someone had told her, stood no least chance against one of these creatures, and hunters invariably left them alone in their wild, forest territories, which, he had added, it was their nature to defend fiercely against intruders.

Looking out into the darkness she could see, here and there, eyes reflecting the firelight—some glowing red, others white or green. There seemed a continual coming and going of eyes between the trees. They were being watched. How could these watchers be anything but hostile? And they themselves—what could they do against them? Nothing; and this was the worst of her fear. Danger is far harder to bear when one can neither retaliate nor fly.

Meris was sleeping as soundly as a child. How strangely contradictory people often were, thought Maia. Meris, the agent of so much pointless, destructive trouble, had been composed and co-operative all day; unsmiling, but also uncomplaining and performing promptly whatever was asked of her. Probably the men felt less encumbered by Meris than by herself.

Zirek was on watch, pacing slowly up and down on the opposite side of the fire as he looked out into the darkness. In one hand he was carrying his bow and an arrow, but seemed not so much tense as simply wary. On impulse she got up and walked round to him, conscious of the fouled cloth chafing between her legs. He nodded and smiled but said nothing.

'Zirek,' she whispered, 'how are we going to get out of this?'

He raised his eyebrows, feigning surprise.

'Why, your chap's going to get us out, isn't he?'

'My chap?' She was vexed. She did not want teasing.

'Well, the man you love, then. But he *has* been your lover, even if he isn't now.'

'Oh, don't be silly, Zirek! It really makes me angry to hear you go on like that. Why, he *hates* me! He thinks I tricked him and deceived him.'

'Maybe he does: but he's still in love with you, even if he wishes he wasn't.'

'How do you know that? He's never told you so, I'm sure.'

'No, but I can tell. A man can tell, you know.'

'How?'

'I don't know, but you can.' He paused. 'Well, for a start, the way you treated each other at the farm.'

'But Anda-Nokomis—he's just as angry with me for swimming the river.'

'I know, but *he* hasn't been your lover. He's just in love with you: that's different.'

'*What*? Zirek, whatever do you mean? I never heard such nonsense!'

'Funny, isn't it, how men can see things women can't? And sometimes the other way round. But I'd bet all I've got; which isn't much, unless we ever get to Santil. If only we *can* get to Santil, though, I reckon I'll be made for life. He might even give me some sort of estate, I dare say.'

'Will you marry Meris, then?'

He looked at her sidelong and winked. 'Pretty girl, isn't she?' Then, briskly, 'But we were talking about you, Maia, not about me. Your Katrian, he's a good lad. *I* trust him, anyway. He's got plenty of guts and he's no fool. I'm sure he *will* get us through this damned place, somehow or other.' He shoved the heaviest log a couple of feet further into the fire with his foot and added some sticks to make a brighter blaze. 'Besides, he's still in love with you, so he's bound to.'

Suddenly, about eighty yards away among the trees, something squealed in agony. It was the death-cry of some fairly large animal—monkey, or *jivda*, perhaps, or creeping *hakkukar*. They both waited unspeaking, but nothing followed—only the resumption of the swarming babble all about them.

'And that's why I personally believe he *is* going to get us out of it,' said Zirek. 'Or you are, or someone is. Because that's what the gods intend, you see. They've put it into our hearts. We shan't die. We've all of us got much too much motive for staying alive.'

'Even Meris?'

'Meris? She's got more motive than all the rest of us put together.'

'What's that, then?'

'To be basted by more men than any girl yet. Do you know, she even managed to have a few while we were hiding in the warehouse? Malendik, of course; and even N'Kasit, now and again. But others, too. I was always terrified she was going to get us caught, only somehow she never quite did.'

He looked up at the scatter of stars visible above the clearing. Then, turning aside and making as though to rake the fire with his wooden spear, he asked, 'Did you know it was me that gave the information about Tharrin?'

'About Tharrin? To Sencho, you mean?'

'Well, Tharrin was—he meant something to you once, didn't he?'

'How did you know?'

'Oh, pedlars hear everything, you know; and people in Meerzat are no blinder than anywhere else. I've often felt very bad about Tharrin. But you see, I had to give some sort of worthwhile information to Sencho if I was going to keep him convinced that I really was a Leopard agent. And anyway, the plain truth was that Tharrin had as good as done for himself before ever I spoke a word.'

'It doesn't matter now,' she said. 'Not any more it doesn't.'

'I'd warned him to get out,' went on Zirek, 'but he was always such a fool. Tharrin—he never really understood what he'd taken on, you know. It was all just a matter of easy money—kind of a game—to him; until the day he found it wasn't, I suppose. "Oh, I'm a master of cunning!" he said to me once. Cran! That was about the last damn' thing he was! Santil had already come to see him as a liability—he could never keep his mouth shut, you see. All the same, I've been very sorry, Maia. I wanted to tell you and get it off my chest.'

'It doesn't matter now—not any more,' she said again. 'Tharrin—if he hadn't 'a done for himself one way he'd 'a done it another; I c'n see that now. But Bekla—Sencho—the Leopards—it's all so far away now, isn't it?'

'Not for Occula it isn't. She's pledged herself to her goddess, you know, to revenge her father; to revenge him or die. I was there, in Thettit, when she did it. I believe she'll succeed, too.'

'I pray for Occula night and morning,' she answered. He nodded; then raised her hand to his lips for a moment.

'I reckon my watch is finished and more than finished. The demon pedlar's given good value, as usual: I'm going to wake the young master. Why don't you get some sleep now, Maia? It's a short enough night and you'll need it all tomorrow. There isn't really anything to be afraid of, you know. None of those bastards out there's going to come any nearer, and we've plenty of wood to last till morning.'

She gave him a quick kiss on each cheek and went back to her place. Her head still ached, but she felt in better spirits for their talk. Yet how strange—what he had said of Zen-Kurel and Anda-Nokomis! She couldn't tell what to make of it. Both the forest clamour and the eyes were still as present as ever, yet now she was so tired that she was past all caring. They can eat me in my sleep, she thought; I wouldn't even bother to wake. Soon she was sleeping as soundly as any healthy sixteen-year-old in the world.

: 90 :

DOWN THE DAULIS

When Maia awoke, in daylight, the first sight that met her eyes was Zen-Kurel standing a few yards away and looking intently down at her. Somehow she had the feeling that he had been doing so for a little while. His expression was certainly not one of dislike. It was difficult to feel sure exactly how it struck her; it suggested at one and the same time both aloofness—well, distance, say—and a kind of wistful admiration; rather as a man might look while standing beside a lake and watching a graceful boat passing off-shore. However, it was only there for a second, for she had hardly met his gaze before he had glanced away.

She looked around her. There was no one else in sight. Uncertain and alarmed, she addressed him directly for the first time since Suba.

'Where are the others?'

'They've gone hunting.'

But *he* hadn't, she thought. Why not? If they were going hunting, the obvious person to leave behind would have been Anda-Nokomis.

He said no more, and she began to feel tense and embarrassed. After a little she rubbed the sleep out of her eyes, got up and went into the undergrowth to pass water and get cleaned up as best she could.

She remained there until she heard the others coming back.

The only person who had had any success was Meris, who had shot a fair-sized monkey. Zirek had missed a parrot and lost the arrow. It was clear, however, that both he and Bayub-Otal were in better spirits, while Meris, when Maia congratulated her, came close to smiling.

'I always could shoot,' she said. 'Latto used to say I had a natural eye. You never know what's going to come in useful.'

'Oh, I don't know; sometimes you do,' said Zirek, looking at her with his head on one side. Maia had to turn away to conceal her amusement. Yet all the same, she thought, perhaps there had once been a time when Meris's ways had had power to give him pain.

Zen-Kurel gutted, skinned and quartered the monkey with Maia's knife and they roasted it over the glowing ashes. It tasted better than she had expected; especially the kidneys, which they shared between them. Wiping her knife and sheathing it at her belt, she recalled what Zirek had said about the gods intending them to survive. Well, it wouldn't hurt to believe it: he himself evidently did. She only wished that she, like him, had the assurance of gaining everything she desired in the world.

Setting off westwards into the forest, they soon found themselves lost in the same dim maze as before. Indeed, thought Maia, one might suppose it to be the very ground they had covered yesterday. In this place there were no landmarks, no localities, no distinctive features at all. The thought of the identical miles of jungle extending round them began to fill her with despair.

She was plodding behind Zirek, thinking wretchedly of her house in Bekla and wondering what might have happened to Occula, when Zen-Kurel, who was in front, turned quickly round, a finger to his lips, and gestured to them to remain still. For a moment she felt afraid, until she saw that he was not. The next instant he had crouched down, pointing towards a place a little way ahead where the undergrowth and bushes appeared to have been trodden almost flat.

As they waited silently, her ear caught a sound familiar enough from days gone by—the grunting of pigs. A moment later the leaders came in sight between the trees; two big boars, tusked and bristle-backed, making their way along what must for them be an accustomed track. They were followed by about a dozen sows and as many piglets.

Zen-Kurel whispered first to Bayub-Otal and Meris. Then, having crept silently over to Zirek and herself, he murmured barely audibly, 'They'll be making for the water. We'll follow them.'

It was an eerie business—proper job for a ghost, she thought—this stealing through the gloom in the wake of the unhurrying sounder. Zen-Kurel led the way, flitting from one tree-trunk to another and often, without looking round, motioning to them to stay where they were.

At last, after what she judged to have been well over two hours, Maia found herself peering cautiously down into a shallow dell of bare earth. Here the pigs were gathered; several, on the far side, wading and rolling in a muddy, shallow morass. Beyond lay the river, overhung with trees and flowing smoothly from right to left.

Meris touched Zen-Kurel's arm. 'Can't we kill one? Choose a piglet: all shoot together.'

The nearest piglet was hardly more than twenty yards away below them. Zen-Kurel, Zirek and Meris crept back among the trees, strung their bows and laid arrows on the strings. Then they stood up together, came quickly forward and loosed within a second of one another.

Zirek missed, but the other two arrows pierced the piglet's flank. It squealed shrilly and on the instant the whole sounder, heaving themselves up from the mud, went blundering away through the undergrowth. As the wretched piglet tried to follow, Meris hit it with a second arrow and it fell to the ground, jerking and kicking. Zen-Kurel, leaping down, transfixed it with his stake.

'Eat it now, sir?' asked Zirek, following with Maia and pulling his arrow out of the ground. Zen-Kurel nodded and Zirek at once set about making a fire.

About an hour later, as they were quenching the ashes and Zirek was getting together what little remained of the meat to carry with them, Maia finally gathered courage to speak.

'Captain Zen-Kurel, I want to make a suggestion. I hope you'll listen to it fair and square, 'cos I reckon it might make a lot of difference.'

They all stopped what they were doing and looked at her with some surprise, for not once in their hearing had she addressed him directly before. Zen-Kurel, too, was obviously startled.

'Naturally I'll listen,' he answered after a few moments; his manner suggesting that while he did not particularly wish to, he had no alternative, 'if you've got something to suggest which you think's important.'

She forced herself to look him in the eye and assume an air of detachment.

'Trying to walk down the bank of this river's going to be next to impossible. I don't reckon it can be done, not with all the undergrowth an' that.' She waited to see whether he would interrupt her, but he said nothing. 'What we ought to do is use the river. I don't mean swim; even without tools we can make a raft as'll be plenty good enough. Three or four logs, that's all, lashed together down their length. You don't sit on it: you just hold on to it and it'll take us down.'

He was looking at her uncertainly and frowning slightly. She hurried on, 'I wouldn't have said anything, only I reckon it might very well make all the difference 'tween being dead and staying alive.'

It was Bayub-Otal who broke the pause. 'I think she's probably right, Zenka, but before we make up our minds I'd like to get a clearer idea of this raft and how we're to make it.'

'I've helped to make them on Lake Serrelind 'fore now,' she said. 'Of course we had proper cord for binding then, but I reckon creeper'll do near enough, long as we use plenty, right down the length. 'Sides, we can use some of our clothes as well.'

As they discussed the idea, it was clear that Zen-Kurel was anxious to avoid giving any impression that he might be prejudiced against Maia. He sat silently, looking from one to another and listening intently. It struck her that he had probably realized, as had she, that in fact the practicability of her plan depended on whether the rest of them decided in favour of attempting it.

'Maia,' asked Meris, 'are you sure there's nothing in the river that might attack us?'

She shook her head. 'River's safer than the forest. All we'd have to look out for would be sunken branches an' that under water, might go into you, but 'tain't very likely. 'Course, we don't even have to make a raft. If everyone had a log it would be enough to keep afloat. Only we could put our stuff on a raft, see.'

Having said this much, she kept quiet. To be too insistent would only spoil everything. Anyway it could, she felt, only be a matter of waiting until they had accustomed themselves to the idea. After all, the only alternative was the forest, and surely to Cran they must have had enough of that by now?

'But this raft—it can only be a very rough sort of job, Maia, can't it?' asked Zirek. 'What happens if it hits something in the river and falls to pieces?'

'We'd still be able to get to shore holding on to the logs,' she said. 'I taught myself to swim holding on to a log, when I wasn't no more 'n five or six years old.'

'Years and years ago,' said Zirek solemnly. Even Zen-Kurel smiled.

Anda-Nokomis was with her, she knew; the least fit for it of them all. Even as she realized this, Zirek put it to him point-blank.

'Do you want to try it, sir?'

'Y-es,' he replied pausingly. 'Yes, on the whole I think I do. Even if we don't get very far, you see, we'll still be no worse off.'

'I think we must try it,' said Zen-Kurel. 'I admit I had no idea the forest would be as bad as this. If we're to get through at all it's the river or nothing.'

They toiled for three or four hours, and with every hour Maia's standing gained. Though she was, of course, careful to avoid any suggestion of it, they were dependent on her. Zen-Kurel, obliged from time to time to confer with her as the work went on, spoke to her with detachment, his manner suggesting that their joint need made it necessary, for the moment at all events, simply to concentrate on what had to be done.

Finding suitable logs took longer than Maia had expected. When she had first put forward her suggestion, she had had in mind the idea of a raft about five feet long and three feet wide, made of no more than four logs. They were lucky enough to find two good ones almost at once. One was already smooth along its entire length, while the other had a few out-growths and small branches which they were able more or less to trim with her knife. After this, however, they hunted in vain for the best part of an hour. Finally Maia decided that they would have to be content with two smaller rafts.

For the second raft they made do with three thinner logs of unequal length. One was more crooked than she really cared about—there would not be a snug fit along the length—but as long as there was enough lashing she judged that it would probably serve at a pinch.

There was no lack of creepers, but the difficulty was to disentangle them from the branches and one another. Maia, knowing that possible collisions, prolonged immersion and the force of the current were bound to soften and slacken them, insisted on their using a great many—up and down the whole length of the logs, like a weave. When this task was at last finished, they strengthened the bindings with their tunics, knotted together by the sleeves. The creepers might break up, thought Maia, but at least these would not. Her own tunic, however, with the money in it, she kept on, reckoning that it would not be too heavy for her to swim in. Both rafts were far from perfect, but it was now well after noon and if they wanted to escape a second night in the forest they must get on.

In the event, two rafts proved better than one would have been. In the first place they were, of course, lighter and therefore easily carried out through the inshore mud. As Bayub-Otal said, they could hardly have hoisted anything bigger. And once in the water they were more manoeuvrable and easily controlled.

All but Maia, as soon as they found themselves out of their depth, drifting with the current and entirely dependent on the support of the logs, were hard put to it not to give way to fear. To them, this was an altogether strange and hazardous experience. Even Zen-Kurel was tense, biting his lip and clutching tightly as the raft he was sharing with Meris began to bob and gather the full speed of the current.

The river, running strongly between dense trees and half-dried swamps, was for the most part narrower than Maia had expected; and therefore deeper, too, she thought with relief. The last thing she wanted was for someone to become entangled in weed or ripped by a submerged branch, and then perhaps to panic and lose hold. Any quick, unexpected tilt would be unfortunate, too, for their few belongings—their bows, arrows and spears, their shoes and what little food was left, together with three cloaks (Zen-Kurel and Bayub-Otal had none), were stacked on the rafts; lashed down, of course; but they would be better dry than wet.

As soon as Maia had shown Meris how to trim her raft by pressing down on it more strongly than Zen-Kurel, she left them, swam across to the other and held it back until the first had floated past, so that the two were in line instead of side by side. In this way both could drift on the midstream current without risk of fouling each other.

For the first quarter of an hour and more she remained hard at work, continually swimming back and forth between the rafts to right them as they drifted one way and another and above all to keep an anxious eye on the lashings. However, they seemed to grow none the looser for being soaked and after a time she decided that they would probably hold up well enough, unless either raft were to get snagged or rammed.

She could not help feeling, now, that she was lucky in her companions. Meris, agile, and hard as nails, had never been one to ask or expect indulgence from anybody. Things might have been very different, thought Maia, if it had happened to be Nennaunir or Otavis. As for Bayub-Otal and Zen-Kurel, both had soon fought down their initial nervousness and begun to steer their rafts by using their free hands. Only Zirek—to his own chagrin and annoyance—remained tense and clumsy, so that for a while Maia stayed beside him, patiently demonstrating again and again what she wanted him to learn.

After they had been drifting for nearly half an hour there came into sight, about two hundred yards ahead, what she had been dreading—a fallen tree spanning almost the entire stream. A quick look showed her that under the right bank, where the base and the torn-up roots were lying, there was probably just room for the rafts to pass below the trunk where it slanted down to the water. From midstream to the left bank extended a hopeless tangle of branches and trapped flotsam.

It was not going to be possible to guide both rafts across to the right bank in time.

'Anda-Nokomis,' she said, 'try to do all you can to stop your raft ramming the tree hard, 'cos that might break it up. I'll be back as quick as I can.'

With this depressing advice—all she had time for—she left him, swam ahead to the other raft, gripped it with both hands and succeeded in swinging it over to the right, just upstream of the overhanging trunk, where she let it go. The raft slipped away from her, passed under the trunk and continued on its way.

Meanwhile Bayub-Otal and Zirek had drifted into the branchy tangle in midstream. To free them proved beyond her powers. For several minutes she struggled, sawing at the sodden branches with her knife and trying as best she could to pull the raft backwards and sideways. At last she was obliged to tell Zirek and Bayub-Otal to scramble up onto the transverse tree-trunk and crawl along it as far as the right bank, thus lightening the raft sufficiently for her to drag it across to the gap and hold it while they slid back into the water on either side. A moment later they were through.

Meanwhile, however, Meris and Zen-Kurel had drifted alarmingly far ahead. It took Maia twenty minutes or more to overtake them and then to halt their raft inshore until the other had closed the distance. She felt exhausted and was glad enough to hold on beside Meris until she had recovered herself.

For three hours and more they drifted on with the stream. The river made many bends, and towards the end of the afternoon she realized that they must have travelled a considerably greater distance than the breadth of the forest. Never once had there been any break in the gloomy tangle of trees and creepers, and she supposed that after all there was no remedy but they would have to pass another night in Purn. At that rate it was time to be looking out for a place to come to shore and get a fire going before sunset.

Just as she was about to put this to her companions, Meris laid a hand on her arm.

'Maia, listen! What's that noise?'

Maia pinched her nose and blew her ears. The sound, still distant but clearly audible between the trees, called to mind instantly her childhood; then, hard upon, a swift rush of fear. Who should recognize that sound if not she? It was the pouring of a fairly heavy waterfall.

: 91 :

THE SARKIDIAN CAMP

There was no time to be lost. Already she could feel the current growing swifter and, looking ahead, see the banks narrowing. In one way this was an advantage, for she could hope to get the rafts inshore more quickly. Which bank? she wondered. The left; yes, it must be the left, for they were a little nearer that side and even seconds might be vital. It looked nasty, though. At this time of year, with the river at its lowest, the bank was steep and high; four or five feet of dried-up earth and stones falling more-or-less sheer to the water, and nothing that she could see—no overhanging bushes or branches—to catch hold of. That seemed strange: why weren't there any? Throughout the afternoon they had come down many reaches with similarly steep banks, but all, as far as she could remember, had been to some extent overgrown.

Anyway, there was no time to be thinking about it. The lip of the falls was only about a hundred yards away now, and since she couldn't see the river beyond, they must be high enough to be dangerous. She called back to Bayub-Otal.

'Anda-Nokomis, I'm going to drag this other raft over to the bank. Try to come in to the left. I'll only be a minute!'

In fact it took her something less than a minute to push Zen-Kurel and Meris into the slacker water under the bank, but already the second raft had drifted past her.

'I'll have to leave you!' she cried to Zen-Kurel. 'Find something to hold on to—anything!'

He nodded with assumed unconcern. 'We'll be all right: you get on.'

Now she was swimming in a frenzy, desperately trying to overtake Zirek and Anda-Nokomis as they were swept on towards the lip of the falls. She could see the mist of spray and hear from the further side the ceaseless, plunging boom. The current had grown headlong: she felt as though she were falling. Gasping, she reached the stern of the raft, clutched it and swung it over to the left. As she did so she saw that the lashings at the forward end had at last worked loose. The raft was not responding as a single whole. Any strain and it would come to pieces.

If I was to swim for the bank on my own now, she thought, I'd get there in time. If I was to swim for the basting bank—

She swam to the front of the raft, pressed the logs together as hard as she could and then, turning on her back, began pulling it inshore behind her.

Everything was tumult, everything was spray and thunder and an appalling sensation of swift, uncontrollable gliding. The eyes of Anda-Nokomis and Zirek were staring into hers as she still struggled, throwing all her weight sideways against the current. She went under, swallowed water, came up and kicked out once more.

Something jabbed her right shoulder: she was pivoting on it, pivoting to the left; something bending, pliant and rough, not so thick as her arm. She snatched at it, clutching, holding on.

'Grab it, Zirek!'

The stern of the raft was rotating. Her left arm was round Anda-Nokomis's neck and shoulder. She was looking down into seething water and white spume fifteen feet below. What was it she'd got hold of? She looked round and back at her right hand: something grey and gnarled, like a stiffened rope. It was the exposed root of a tree projecting from the earth of the bank; bending with their weight, yet enough to hold them as long as she herself could hold on. Then the raft broke up and spun away, turned back into two logs that hung a moment on the lip of the falls and toppled, gone, lost in the roaring smother below.

Anda-Nokomis was shouting in her ear. 'It's too much for you! Let go!'

'No!'

'Yes! Never mind me! Let go!'

'No!'

'—'bove you!'

Was it "'bove you!' he had said? She could see almost nothing now. Her ears and nostrils were blocked with spray. She was hanging in a howling, spray-clouded trance. Her arm—her arm was giving way. She couldn't hold on any longer. Tharrin, Sphelthon, Randronoth—she could hear their voices, men's voices, calling, shouting to her, the dead.

Rough, dry hands caught her under the arms, heaving her upward.

'Let go of him, lass! Let *go*! We've got him!'

Her left arm was strengthless, numb. She let go of Anda-Nokomis. She was being dragged upward, earth and stones grating against her sodden tunic, pulled backward, heels slithering over grass, coming to rest on her back, looking up at leaves and the sky.

After a few moments of choking bewilderment she struggled to her knees. 'Anda-Nokomis!'

'I'm here,' his voice answered.

She looked about her. She was on the bank of the river, immediately above the falls. Anda-Nokomis, water streaming from his hair, shoulders and arms, was standing near-by. Further off, to her right, Zirek, on his hands and knees, was vomiting water. Something out in the stream caught her eye. It was the second raft, floating past and over the brink.

There were men all round her: forty, fifty, it looked like. She stared at them in amazement. Had Lespa sent them, or what? Some were armed. Others had axes, saws, scythes, heavy hacking knives. One of them spat on the ground. They were human, then: she was alive.

These were soldiers; they had pulled her and Zirek and Anda-Nokomis out of the river. And—and—? Quickly she looked upstream. Meris and Zen-Kurel, also surrounded by soldiers, were limping towards her along the bank.

One of the men had spoken to her. She realized he had spoken, but had not caught what he said. She turned and looked at him.

He was perhaps twenty-five, of middle height, with a shock of short, brown hair and bushy eyebrows. His grey eyes were rather small, his nose rather broad, and he had a strong chin. He looked a rugged, practical sort of man; resourceful if not clever; one not to be trifled with or turned aside. He was holding a drawn sword, and as he spoke again he leaned forward, pointing it upstream to emphasize his words.

'Who's up there? How many?'

'What? I don't—'

'Come on, no time to waste, that's it! Who's up there? How far off?'

Another, younger man laid a hand on his arm. 'Steady, captain. We've only just got the poor lass out of the water, for Cran's sake!'

'No time to waste, Tolis,' retorted the captain. He laid one hand on Maia's shoulder. 'Come on now, you tell me—'

A gasping voice said 'Just a moment.' It was Zen-Kurel, with Meris hanging on his arm. He looked badly shaken, trying not to show it but unable to help himself. He hesitated a moment, closing his eyes and clenching one hand impatiently as he pulled himself together. Then he said, 'Thank you for saving us. Lucky you were here. May I ask who you are?'

'No, you answer me,' replied the shock-headed man peremptorily. 'I've no time to waste.'

'If you'd just listen to me for a moment—' began Zen-Kurel.

'There are more of us than you, that's it,' said the captain. 'So you just sit down and answer my questions.'

Zen-Kurel shrugged his shoulders and sat down. Maia sat beside him. His sacking smock was ripped across and beneath it she saw a bleeding gash along his right thigh. She pointed to it.

'That ought to be seen to.'

Zen-Kurel looked at it with surprise. 'I never even felt it!'

'You wouldn't,' she said. 'It's the water—softens your flesh. You can get badly cut in warm water and never feel it at all. That ought to be seen to!' she said to the captain.

He made an impatient gesture to one of his men, who went away, came back with a cloth and began binding up the wound with intent detachment, like a servant waiting at table.

'Where have you come from and who's upstream?' said the captain. 'How many?'

'I'll answer you,' replied Zen-Kurel firmly, 'when you've told me who you are. Are you for Erketlis or the Leopards, or neither?'

'Look, if necessary we can torture you—'

'I know that. But you say you're in a hurry, so it'll be quicker to answer me. Are you for Erketlis or Kembri?'

'Why, they're from Sarkid!' said Meris suddenly. 'Look at their corn-sheaves!' She pointed.

The soldiers' clothes were rough, torn and anything but uniform. Several, however, were wearing the corn-sheaves emblem of Sarkid.

'We're with Elleroth of Sarkid,' said the captain shortly. 'Will that satisfy you?'

'Indeed it will,' said Bayub-Otal, speaking for the first time. 'In that case, you will be glad to know that my name is—'

'I'm not interested in your names,' interrupted the captain. 'I want to know who's upstream? How many and how close?'

'There's no armed force at all upstream,' replied Zen-Kurel. 'The forest's empty and as far as I know there's nothing between you and Bekla.'

This plainly had a considerable effect on the soldiers standing round.

There was a buzz of talk and some of the men began calling to others further off.

'Well, at that rate what were you trying to get away from? Must've been something pretty bad to make you risk *that*.' He jerked his thumb towards the falls.

'I was about to tell you who I *am*.' Bayub-Otal spoke with icy dignity. 'I am Anda-Nokomis, son of the High Baron of Urtah, and Ban of Suba.'

'Anda-Nokomis? Are you sure?'

Maia could not restrain a slightly hysterical gurgle of laughter. The captain looked round at her angrily, then turned back to Bayub-Otal.

'I heard you were dead.'

'Then you heard wrong.'

By this time both Bayub-Otal and Zen-Kurel, soaking wet and dressed in torn sacking, had evidently begun to strike the captain as people of rather more weight than he had originally supposed.

'Well, I'm sorry, my lord; only the times are every which way just now, that's it, and you must admit you don't look like the Ban of Suba, now do you? Put yourself in my position. We're the pioneer group of Lord Elleroth's company, across the Zhairgen on our own. We don't know the first thing about the forest ahead, the whereabouts of the Leopard army or anything else. We're just clearing the bank when suddenly *you* come floating down like a lot of blasted turtles. What am I supposed to do—guess who you are or just salute you on sight?'

Maia laughed again. She was beginning to like this man.

'For all I know *you* could be reconnoitring, couldn't you?'

'Do people generally go reconnoitring unarmed,' said Zen-Kurel, 'and take a couple of girls with them?'

'Leopards? They never go anywhere without girls, I'm told. Shearnas on the blasted battlefield, that's it—'

'We're *not* Leopards, curse you!' cried Zirek suddenly. 'I'm the chap as killed Sencho—me and this girl here. Santil knows me well enough.'

At this there was another buzz of excitement among the soldiers. They were crowding round so closely now that Maia, still sitting on the ground at their feet, was beginning to feel shut in and oppressed.

'Captain,' she said, 'could we go somewhere less crowded? This is making me feel bad.'

He stared at her, apparently surprised at a girl speaking up for herself at all. After a moment he looked at Bayub-Otal, who nodded.

'Everyone back to work!' shouted the captain. 'Go and get on with what you were doing! You'd better stay here with us,' he added to Tolis.

The men dispersed. Maia now saw that what they were engaged in doing was felling the saplings and undergrowth along the bank. Downstream of the falls a narrow, recently-cleared track wound away out of sight.

'You were lucky,' said the captain to Bayub-Otal. 'If you'd come down an hour earlier you wouldn't have found us above the falls.'

'But how is it we didn't see your men on the bank?' he asked.

'The men were taking a break under the trees. We heard you shouting. Now look,' he went on, 'Elleroth will certainly want to see you and I shall have to make a report to him. Tell me how you come to be here.'

Bayub-Otal proceeded to do so. Mollo and Tolis listened attentively.

'Well, you'd better take them back to camp, Tolis,' said Mollo at length. 'Tell Elleroth I'll be back myself before sunset.' And thereupon he walked away to where the men had resumed work.

'Is it far?' asked Maia apprehensively, as Tolis began conducting them downstream. She felt almost too tired to take a step.

He shook his head. 'Less than a mile: just across the Zhairgen. We've got a raft on ropes. It'll carry away in the rains, of course, but it's all right for now.'

The path Mollo's men had cleared was narrow, but the job had been done very thoroughly and it was easy walking. As they went on in single file, the sound of the falls gradually receding behind them, Tolis asked over his shoulder, 'Have any of you met Elleroth before?' As no one answered, he said 'No?'

'What's he like, then?' asked Zirek.

'Well, obviously *we* all like him,' answered Tolis, 'or we wouldn't be here. But he may not be quite what you're expecting.' He laughed. 'You'll be all right, though.'

With this enigmatic remark he continued on their way.

Maia noticed a flask attached to his belt. She touched his shoulder.

'Can I ask you what's in that?'

'Djebbah,' he answered. 'D'you want some?'

'No, but that cut on Captain Zen-Kurel's leg ought to be cleaned. Could turn nasty else.'

Zen-Kurel tried to demur, but Bayub-Otal was emphatic in supporting Maia. 'Of course it must be cleaned. River water at this time of year. *Any* Suban could tell you that.'

It was not lost upon Maia that that included her—and that he must have meant it to.

Tolis gave her the flask. Taking out the stopper, she turned to Zen-Kurel.

'It'll sting.'

He nodded indifferently. She gripped his thigh with one hand, untied the cloth and began cleaning the wound with one corner, remembering as she did so the last time she had touched his body. Looking up, she met his eye for an instant and felt herself colouring. Was he thinking the same?

'I'm going to tie it a little tighter.'

'Thank you. That feels much more comfortable.'

They went on. Evening was beginning to fall, but in the forest the air remained humid and close. After a little she smelt wood-smoke and could hear through the trees a distant, multiform hum and murmur. A few minutes later they came out on the north bank of the Zhairgen at its confluence with the Daulis. Now, at low water before the rains, the two rivers mingled with scarcely a ripple, shrunken between their banks; the Zhairgen, perhaps forty yards wide, flowing darkly here under the trees, but on the opposite side—the open bank beyond the forest—tinged with the light of the westering sun.

It was at this open bank that Maia stared. She remembered the soldiers' camps at Melvda-Rain. What she was looking at now appeared less like a camp than a sort of village. She could see women tending fires, girls carrying water-jars and children running about shouting and playing. Over an area of perhaps three or four acres the scrub bordering the bank had been cut down and the ground cleared. Shelters of poles and straw thatch stood in neat rows. Stacks of wood had been piled at intervals and near these, away from the huts, cooking fires were burning under pots hung over dug-out trenches. From a tall mast in the centre of the camp a banner—three corn-sheaves on a blue ground—hung drooping in the still air.

The others, like Maia, stopped short, gazing at the scene in surprise.

'You say the *Leopards* never go anywhere without women?' said Zirek at length.

Tolis laughed. 'Captain Mollo said that; I didn't. Those are the women and children we brought from the slave-farm at Orthid.'

'What are you going to do with them?' asked Maia.

'I've no idea; you'd better ask Lord Elleroth. Most of them'll be coming with us to Bekla, I dare say.'

'But do you seriously mean to march to Bekla through the forest?' asked Zen-Kurel.

'Oh, we'll march to Zeray if we have to. You don't know Elleroth.'

The raft ran on a rope fixed to stout posts driven into either bank. It looked solid and well-constructed, and Zen-Kurel admired it.

'Oh, we're first-class pioneers all right,' said Tolis. 'By Shakkarn! we ought to be by now, too, the work we've put in these last few weeks. We cleared the ground for those huts, and now we're chopping down Purn!'

'Well, if you're going to take those women and children through the forest,' said Zirek, 'all I can say is I hope the rains don't start while you're still at it.'

'I'm with you there,' said Tolis, as they stepped out on the further bank. 'I'll take you straight up to Elleroth now. You don't mind waiting, do you, while I go in and tell him who you are? I'm sure he won't keep you hanging about long.'

He led the way to a larger hut in the centre of the camp. No one they passed paid them any particular attention and Maia guessed that among this motley community on the move the sight of strangers had not the same effect as in an ordinary village. Probably no one thought in terms of strangers at all.

There were no guards outside the hut. Tolis left them and went in. They were glad enough to sit on the ground in the evening sunshine. To Maia it was a conscious pleasure simply to be still, to close her eyes and know that they were not going to spend the night in the forest. She hoped this Elleroth would give them a good meal. Beyond that and sleep she had not the least wish to think for the moment.

She was roused by a child's voice beside her.

'You're new, aren't you? Have you just come?'

She raised her head. A little girl, perhaps six or seven years old, was standing on the grass near-by, looking them over with a self-possessed air. She herself certainly merited a glance. She was slim, dark-eyed and dark-haired, with a long, straight, intelligent nose and something strikingly graceful and vivacious in her manner, as though, like a warbler in the spring trees, she could not keep still, but must be constantly moving in response to everything round her. She was bare-footed and dressed in a makeshift, grey tunic, on the skirt of which some coloured beads had been stitched—by herself, it looked like. She was carrying a length of old cord and, in the few moments while she waited for Maia to answer her, swung it two or three times, skipping first on one foot and then the other. Indeed, she seemed so full of vitality that Maia half-expected her to go bouncing away without waiting for a reply. As suddenly as she had begun, however, she stopped skipping and stood looking down with a pert air which suggested that she thought it was about time she was answered.

Maia laughed. 'Yes, we're new. What's your name?'

'Melathys,' said the child. She skipped again. 'My name's Melathys. I knew you were new, knew you were new!' She was plainly gratified to find herself right. 'You weren't at Orthid, were you?'

'Where's Orthid?'

'Where we were before the soldiers came.' She sat down beside Maia. 'The soldiers killed Snekkeron, and then they took us all away.'

'Who was Snekkeron?'

'The dog-man—the top man at Orthid. He used to walk about with a big, white dog. Then anyone did anything he didn't like, he used to tell the dog to bite them.'

'Did the soldiers kill the dog, too?'

'I don't know,' said Melathys. 'What's *your* name?'

'Maia.'

'And where are *you* going?'

'I don't know.'

'Oh, haven't they told you yet? When are they going to?'

'How d'you mean?' asked Maia.

'Well, we're all going to different places. But you see—' and here the little girl, bending forward, looked at Maia bright-eyed, with the obvious self-satisfaction of one about to impart something which will establish her as superior and enviable. This must have been why she had raised the subject. 'I'm going to a *special* place—a *holy* place. They *chose* me to go!'

'How marvellous for you!' said Maia. 'Where is it?'

'It's called Quiso,' replied Melathys. 'Quiso of the Ledges. So I shall be a Ledge myself when I'm grown up.'

'You mean a priestess, don't you?'

'Bria's going too,' said Melathys quickly (to avoid accepting the correction, or so it seemed to Maia). 'We're going with Captain Muzarkalleen. He was hurt in the fighting, but they'll make him better at Quiso, you see.'

She looked at Zen-Kurel, lying supine on the grass near-by.

'You belong to him, don't you?' she asked.

'No,' answered Maia. To her annoyance she felt herself colouring once more.

'To him, then?' asked the child, looking at Bayub-Otal.

'No.'

Melathys looked puzzled. 'She *does* belong to you, doesn't she?' she asked Zen-Kurel. 'She's pretending, isn't she?'

'Here,' said Maia desperately, 'I'll teach you a new game if you like.'

Standing up, she took the little girl in her arms and as best she could—for she was quite a weight—began tossing her up and down.

> '*Bring* me my *dagger* and *bring* me my *sword.*
> *Melathys* the *lady* to *go* by my *side.*
> *I'm* off to *Bekla* to *meet* the great *lord*—'

But at this point, as once before, she was interrupted. Tolis had come out of the hut and the others were on their feet. She kissed Melathys and put her down.

'I'll have to go now. Good-bye: I hope you'll be very happy at Quiso.'

The little girl ran off through the sunset light. Maia, looking back as she went towards the door of the hut, saw her turn and wave before she disappeared round one of the shelters.

: 92 :

ELLEROTH EXPRESSES AN OPINION

Immediately inside the hut was a kind of miniature ante-room or lobby, its walls made of thin, wooden partitions. Here weapons, shields, cloaks, boots, belts and every kind of military gear were hanging on nails or laid out on the floor. It was all neatly disposed, however; the floor was sanded and clean and the general impression was of preparedness rather than disorder. On the far side of this improvised antechamber was another entrance, covered with a curtain made of old cloaks stitched together. This had been half drawn aside by a tall young man, who was standing in the aperture and regarding them intently, though with a cordial smile.

This personage immediately made a strong impression on Maia. Since she was at the rear of their little group and he was not for the moment directing his attention to her, she was able to look at him closely. He was tall—slightly taller, indeed, than Anda-Nokomis—and clean-shaven (which was unusual in the Beklan Empire at this time). His fair hair was cut rather shorter than was fashionable in the upper city. He had blue eyes, a short—indeed, rather a stubby—nose and very even, white teeth, which made his smile attractive. He was wearing a very well-fitting, spotlessly clean, grey veltron and over this a blue robe elaborately embroidered—weeks of work, thought Maia—in gold thread. Round his neck was a fine chain, from which hung a corn-sheaves emblem in wrought silver. Not only his dress but his manner was strikingly elegant, reminding her a little of Elvair-ka-Virrion; yet for all his youth he had an experienced, seasoned, responsible look which—as she could now appreciate—Elvair-ka-Virrion had never possessed. Despite this, however, he struck her as a man with whom humour and amusement were prevalent, so that even his elegance seemed a kind of joke, an act deliberately put on the better to deal with the world and keep it in a good temper.

Elleroth—for it was he—stepped forward and took Bayub-Otal's hands.

'Are you really Anda-Nokomis of Suba? Do you know, I can only just manage to believe that you've really appeared out of the forest like a benevolent wood-spirit? Still, fortunately that's belief enough. This is an honour and a great pleasure. Santil-kè-Erketlis told me he thought you were dead, you see. It's rather refreshing, don't you think, to find that even he can be wrong from time to time? I mean, it restores one's faith in universal human fallibility. I'm very glad to welcome you and your friends. Come inside and have some wine for a few minutes before you go to your quarters, so that I needn't wait to begin enjoying your company. They're heating some water for you now and I've told them to find you all some fresh clothes. You'll be tolerant of our emergency wardrobe, won't you? We've all been running about a good deal just recently, you know.'

As he talked he was conducting them through the inner entrance into the main body of the hut beyond. It was rough-and-ready enough—three trestle tables, four or five benches and a kind of dresser or sideboard which the camp carpenter must have knocked together from such materials as he had been able to come by. On this stood a few dishes and goblets of bronze and a good many more of wood and horn, together with some knives and two or three wooden trenchers containing fruit and black bread. A group of four or five young officers stood up as the strangers entered, their eyes moving immediately to Maia and Meris.

Elleroth himself poured and served the wine, handing it round from a tray carried behind him by a soldier servant.

'We ought to have a nice, popular toast, don't you think, that everyone can drink with unbridled enthusiasm?'

'To heldro victory?' suggested Zen-Kurel, smiling and raising his cup.

'Heldro victory!' echoed Elleroth. 'And no heeltaps!'

They drank the toast. Maia was startled by the quality of the wine. During the past year she had, of course, learned a great deal about wine; and to be perfectly honest, she thought, she could not remember to have tasted better, even at Sencho's. Just as she was thinking this, Zirek corroborated it.

'By Shakkarn, sir, that's a drop of the real stuff, all right! That ought to make victory certain enough for anyone, I'd say!'

'It comes up from Ikat,' said Elleroth. 'The vintner follows us about at enormous risk; to make his fortune, you know. He's caused more casualties than the enemy so far. Perhaps we should all have some more; what do you think?'

No one refused. Maia, silent, had the impression that Elleroth, under cover of this urbane drollery, was weighing them up and forming his conclusions. After a few moments he went on, 'Anda-Nokomis, of course I know very well where *you* fit into our wicked schemes. In fact, I've already taken the liberty of sending a messenger to Santil to tell him you're with me.' (For a moment Maia wondered how he could feel so certain, until she recalled that of course he would know about the withered hand.) 'But tell me, now, about your friends.' He looked genially from one to another.

'Tolis says that apparently two of you are really and truly the hero and heroine who killed Sencho. You ought to be rewarded with a kingdom: two kingdoms. You, was it?' he said to Zirek. 'And you, säiyett? May I have the honour of embracing you both?'

Maia thought it highly probable that this was the first time in her life that Meris had been addressed as 'säiyett'. It must also surely have been the first time that she had blushed, which she did as Elleroth embraced her and kissed her on both cheeks.

The admiration of the young officers was warm. They began eagerly asking Zirek and Meris how they had contrived the killing and about their escape. After a little, however, and before Elleroth had had time to enquire about Zen-Kurel or Maia, Bayub-Otal interposed, 'U-Elleroth, what I would like to suggest, if I may, is that we should go to our quarters now and make ourselves presentable; and then, after we've had something to eat—if that's not hoping for too much—I'll tell you how we all come to be here.'

'Well, then, you must be sure to break off at the most exciting point,' replied Elleroth, 'and I'll be delighted to provide you with a bowl for people to put their melds in before you go on. But come along, let me show you the way. The water must be hot by now.'

As she followed them out, Maia heard Bayub-Otal saying to Elleroth in a low voice, '. . . in private, really . . . few things need to be explained.'

'Of course,' answered Elleroth. 'No questions until you're ready, then.'

Outside, a woman of about thirty, with black hair and a missing front tooth, was waiting, evidently to take charge of Meris and herself. The excellent wine, on an empty stomach, had rather gone to Maia's head and she felt quite content to be shepherded along in a not unpleasant haze of evening air, failing light, wood-smoke and the shouts and calls of children, until they came to the shelter prepared for them.

'My name's Tekordis,' said the woman chattily. 'I was two years at Orthid, but now I've taken up with a tryzatt on the general's headquarters. How do *you* come to be here?'

'Oh, we're refugees from the Leopards,' answered Maia, happy to be stripped off and sitting rather muzzily in a tub of warm water. 'We were coming through the forest and had the good luck to run into Captain Mollo.'

The woman, who was obviously impressed at their having been received personally by Elleroth, asked no more direct questions, but was plainly hoping to learn more if she could. Both girls, however, felt that it might be more prudent not to oblige her. Maia, changing into the rough but clean clothes she was given, nevertheless took care to retain her travel-stained tunic, with the money and valuables in its pockets. Tekordis having found

911

them a comb (which they were obliged to use for their nails as well as their hair), they felt they had done as much as they could by way of preparing for supper.

Walking back towards Elleroth's headquarters, they passed a group of soldiers throwing dice on the grass, who, as they went by, made their approval plain enough. Maia, well accustomed to this sort of thing, acknowledged them with a smile and a wave.

'Maia,' asked Meris a few moments later, 'have you got any money?'

Maia, never one to cavil at a little stretching of the strict truth in a good cause, shrugged her shoulders.

'Lend you ten meld if you like.'

'We could make a damned sight more than that in a place like this,' said Meris. 'Or I could, anyway.'

''Tain't for me to tell you what's what, Meris, but we're supposed to be guests of this Elleroth, and anyway Anda-Nokomis wouldn't—'

'Oh, balls!' said Meris. 'You're a fine one to talk, Säiyett Serrelinda, aren't you? D'you think I don't remember you tickling up old Sencho and enjoying every minute of it? Give me that shit—'

'Shut up!' cried Maia angrily. 'Haven't you made enough trouble already, without going looking for more here? Great Cran, 's far as I can make out you've only to hang on till you get to Erketlis to be set up for the rest of your life, and now you want to start working this place on your back! Anyway, here's that young Tolis coming to meet us. Elleroth's sent him to hurry us up, I s'pose.'

Elleroth was as good as his word to Bayub-Otal. During the meal (too many damned flies! thought Maia: in the upper city, she'd forgotten how bad they could be at this time of year) he asked no questions, but talked instead of the Chalcon campaign, Santil's victory on the Thettit–Ikat road and the dash he had made afterwards to take the Orthid slave-camp.

'Dear me, we did proceed rapidly,' he remarked, stabbing with his knife at a lump of cheese. 'I sincerely trust I'll never be required to do anything so energetic as that again.'

'But did Santil order it, or did you dream it up by yourself?' asked Zen-Kurel.

'Well, he—er—he may have mentioned it to me in passing as a sporting possibility,' replied Elleroth. 'I honestly find it difficult to have any very clear recollection: that march—I began to fear that creation would expire before we got there. I was praying ardently to be struck down with sunstroke, but I confess with no very lively hope of success. And the dried meat and bad water kept on making me sick. Digestion is the great secret of life, after all. Do have some more cheese; then you can at least console yourselves by eating while I talk. That may not only comfort you a little for the quality of the conversation but also increase our mutual confidence.'

'You're sure of that, are you?' said Zen-Kurel, smiling and helping himself to the cheese.

'So sure that I'll be delighted to offer you an appointment as a captain in this band of ragamuffins, if you like,' answered Elleroth. 'We're a trifle short of officers at the moment. They *will* keep on doing such foolish things—'

'Not for lack of example, sir,' put in one of his captains.

'I do set a bad example, I know,' sighed Elleroth, nodding dolefully. 'We don't actually *pay* anyone for participating in this rabble, you know,' he went on, turning back to Zen-Kurel, 'but if you'd care to take part in the loot of Bekla—'

'It's been looted already, sir, I rather think, both by the Palteshis and the Lapanese,' replied Zen-Kurel.

'Yet you yourself succeeded in bringing away some—er—swag of this exceptional quality?' asked Elleroth, smiling towards Maia.

It was said as lightly and charmingly as any compliment ever paid, yet an awkward silence fell. Maia bit her lip and looked down at the table. Elleroth, perceiving that he had unwittingly said something unfortunate, hesitated, clearly hoping that someone would come to his rescue. It was Zen-Kurel himself who answered him.

'No, in point of fact it was *she* who brought *us* away: otherwise we'd still be there; or else dead. We're all greatly in her debt. But tell me, Lord Elleroth, if I'm not asking you to betray any secrets, what's your strategy in trying to reach Bekla through Purn? You've set yourselves an even harder job than Orthid this time, haven't you?'

'I'm sadly afraid we may have,' replied Elleroth, taking his cue gratefully, 'but if anyone can get us through that forest, Mollo will. We're lucky to have a pioneer commander like him. As for the strategy—well, that's supposed to be a little surprise for Kembri, really. You see, he knows where Santil is, but at the moment he doesn't know where *we* are: at least, I don't think he does. He must think his right flank's completely secure, resting on Purn. So I thought, well, supposing we were to go up through the forest, and then pop out—pop out, you know, just nip across and cut the Ikat–Bekla road behind him, that might make him feel slightly uncomfortable. What d'you think?' It was clear that he respected Zen-Kurel and was genuinely seeking his opinion.

Zen-Kurel paused, reflecting. 'If you can *do* it, yes; but the forest's very bad, you know. And it can't be long now until the rains, either. Besides, we don't know, do we?—Kembri may already be falling back on Bekla.'

As their military talk continued, Maia began to feel so tired and drowsy that she could hardly keep her eyes open. Snatches of the conversation reached her meaninglessly through a daze. The discomfort of her period, the anxiety of the previous night in the forest, the long swim ending in the terror and near-disaster of the waterfall—all these had by now exhausted even her youthful vitality. Looking across at Meris, she could see that she was in little better case.

The young officers, delighted by the unexpected surprise of having two such girls as guests in the middle of a hard campaign, would hardly have noticed if she had made no response at all to their sallies and tall stories. They were perfectly happy just to look at her; to speak to her and merely to enjoy her presence. They were not going to let her go for as long as they could keep her. She realized that if she did not extricate herself, no one was going to do it for her.

She turned to Elleroth. 'My lord, if you won't mind, I'm really that worn out I'd like to go to bed now. We've had a very hard day and I'm almost asleep as 'tis: I reckon Meris feels the same. Would you be so kind as to excuse us?'

Elleroth, as might have been expected, was immediately all courtesy, begging the girls' pardon for his lack of consideration and asking whether they needed anything else which he could provide. He was about to call a servant to accompany them back to their quarters when Zirek also begged to be excused, saying that he too felt very tired. One of the officers thereupon suggested that by way of an end to the evening they should all escort the girls to their shelter and sing them a song. This was enthusiastic-ally received. Maia, only too glad that she was really going to be allowed to go to sleep, consented as gracefully as anyone could have wished; and thereupon she and Meris, amid much laughter and cheering, were carried shoulder-high into the sultry, brilliantly starred night and—after a little tipsy altercation about the right way—back to their shelter, leaving Elleroth alone with Bayub-Otal and Zen-Kurel.

'Through the forest? Well, apart from anything else, you see,' said Elleroth, refilling the wine-cups himself (he had dismissed the servants), 'we have to stay on the move if we're to keep ourselves in supplies. There aren't a lot of us, it's true—rather less than five hundred, now—and since we got back here we've been able to get stuff sent up from Sarkid. But I can't go on drawing on Sarkid for more than another few days. Then there's the whole question of reward—loot, boodle, plunder and spoil. My men are all volunteers and I haven't paid one of them a meld as yet. They've fought and marched splendidly, but all they've got out of it so far is women. You know that old story, "Oh, gods, not rape again!" Now that they've blooded themselves on that Elvair-ka-Virrion fellow, what we need is a really impressive exploit, leading to a dramatic victory. Not to mince words, I'd like to be the first heldro into Bekla and send a runner to Santil with the news. You see, *he's* still got Kembri between him and Bekla, but I've only got Purn. Santil will be taking on Kembri and I shan't be there. So I really ought to have a go at Purn, if only to justify my existence, don't you think? And, of course, cut off Kembri's retreat, if we can.'

Bayub-Otal nodded. 'Yes, I follow all that. It's only that Zenka and I have had a taste of that forest, and we wouldn't like you to come to any harm.'

'Well, I'll have to be the judge of that, won't I?' replied Elleroth a shade brusquely. 'I confess I could do with a little more sheer manpower to cut our way through. Still, never mind; that's enough of that. Anda-Nokomis, I really can't wait any longer to learn why you're not dead, and what exactly happened at Rallur.'

Bayub-Otal's account lasted some time, though he omitted any reference to what had passed between Zen-Kurel and Maia. Elleroth listened intently and asked several questions. At last he said to Zen-Kurel, 'Yes; well, I see now why my little sally about your swag fell even flatter than most of my efforts. Most unfortunate. No one ever invites me twice, you know. But it certainly *is* rather mysterious, isn't it? This Serrelinda girl—and now that one's seen her one has to admit she really is all they say: if she can look like that after two days in the forest, Cran knows what she must have looked like in the upper city—first she makes her fortune by betraying you all to Sendekar on the Valderra, and the next thing you know she nearly loses her life getting the two of you out of prison and out of Bekla. If I hadn't actually met her, I'd be the first to say she'd realized that Fornis was out to kill her and was trying to change sides in time to save her own skin.'

'You mean you *don't* think that?' asked Zen-Kurel.

'Well, somehow it doesn't quite square with the impression I've formed of her, though I can't say exactly why. Tell me, has she herself raised the matter with you at all?'

'No, not at all: not once.'

'I mean, she hasn't suggested that since she's saved your lives you might now save hers by writing a nice, cheery letter to Santil, or anything like that?'

'No, nothing like that,' replied Zen-Kurel.

'And how has she made out on your little journey? Has she been useful at all since you left Bekla?'

'Well, the plain truth is that without her we wouldn't be here.'

'It never occurred to you to slice her into little bits for what she'd done in Suba?'

'It occurred to Zenka,' broke in Bayub-Otal, 'but to tell you the truth I dissuaded him.'

'Why?'

Bayub-Otal paused. Elleroth, perceiving that his hesitation proceeded not from ignorance or uncertainty, but from doubt over whether to speak or to remain silent, was beginning, 'If you'd rather not—' when suddenly Bayub-Otal said, 'This will have to come out some time or other, so it may as well be now. That night at the farm, Zenka, when you and I talked about Maia, there was something I didn't tell you.'

'You mean you and she had already come to some sort of understanding?' Zen-Kurel spoke so sharply that both his hearers were startled.

'No,' replied Bayub-Otal, 'no, nothing like that. I haven't any—understanding with her. It was something she told me.' They waited and he continued, 'She'd told me that she and I are kinsfolk; in fact, we're first cousins.'

'She *told* you that?'

'Yes. That evening, at the farm.'

'And you believed her?'

'Oh, yes,' said Bayub-Otal, 'there's no doubt about it at all. She's my mother's sister's daughter, and what she said explains a great deal. I'll tell you how.'

He did so, ending, 'I can't see how this poor man Tharrin could possibly have made up that story—or why he'd want to. Besides, it explains not only her extraordinary resemblance to my mother, but also why the Tonildan woman she *thought* was her mother should have felt able to sell her as a slave.'

'It might explain something else, too,' said Elleroth. 'I hasten to say I'm only trying to make the best case I can for a girl who's struck me, quite frankly, as being rather honest and likeable. From all you've told me she's certainly not short on courage.'

'What does it explain?' asked Zen-Kurel.

'I only remarked that it *might*. You said this girl didn't find out that she was your cousin—that her mother was Suban—until some considerable time *after* her exploit on the Valderra. But mightn't that discovery have altered her whole outlook very much?'

'Then why hasn't she said so?'

'My dear man, actions speak louder than words. She *has* as good as said so, or so it seems to me. Presumably the poor girl has her pride. You don't expect her, do you, to go down on her knees and say, "I've discovered I'm a Suban, so please will you forget all about the Valderra and spare my life?" She's told you who she is and left the rest up to you: I call that dignified.'

'So—that might mean—you're saying, are you, that that might mean—'

Zen-Kurel came to a stop, but Elleroth said nothing to help him to a conclusion, only gazing at his shadowed face in the candlelight and waiting. 'She could have had a perfectly creditable motive—' he stopped again— 'for taking the enormous risk of going into that prison to release us?'

'Well, as I see it, having learned that she was first cousin to the rightful and imprisoned Ban of Suba, she was simply fulfilling her duty to her liege lord with the utmost courage. That's if you want my personal opinion.'

After a long pause, Zen-Kurel said, 'I suppose—well, I suppose that might be the truth of it.'

'And what's more, you *hope* it is, don't you?' said Elleroth. 'Seeing through brick walls is rather a speciality of mine, you know. The clairvoyant freebooter—'

There was a tap on the doorpost outside: Elleroth's personal tryzatt drew aside the curtain, entered and saluted.

'Excuse me for interrupting you, Lord Elleroth, sir, but there's an urgent message from the guard commander. One of our patrols has reported a large force bivouacked about a mile away to the east. The patrol commander says they evidently don't know anything about us yet. He took good care not to be seen or heard, but he got close enough to hear some of them talking, and he's more or less certain they're Ortelgans.'

: 93 :

MAIA'S NIGHT ADVENTURE

Maia woke in the dark. The air was close and heavy. She was sweating but her headache had gone. She could not tell how long she had been asleep, but it felt like not very long—perhaps only an hour or two. Everything seemed quiet outside and she had no idea what might have woken her. The bed was comfortable enough; better than she'd expected, in fact. She'd drop off again in a few minutes.

She wondered whether whatever it had been might have woken Meris too. She murmured 'Meris?' but there was no reply.

'Meris?' Suddenly she felt more or less sure that there was no one there: the realization jolted her wide awake.

She slid out of her bed, reached across and felt the other one in the dark. Yes, it was empty; but in this heat there was no telling how long Meris might have been gone—an hour or only a few minutes. Well, but perhaps she was with Zirek.

And perhaps she wasn't, reflected Maia. The thought of the trouble that

Meris was capable of causing made her feel quite sick with apprehension. Elleroth, of course, was obviously no kill-joy. If Meris wanted a bit of fun with one of his men, whether officer or soldier, that would no doubt be all one to him. Or even if Meris was plying for hire; though in a guest of the commander that would look pretty disreputable. Knowing Meris, however, there was always the likelihood that she would not rest content with that. What Meris enjoyed was using her sexuality to make trouble. She recalled their interrupted quarrel earlier that evening. She wouldn't put it past Meris to devise some way of involving her, Maia, simply out of spite. Since the affair at the farm she had probably felt a grudge against Zenka, too. She might even—oh, no!

Yet why not? This camp was full of all manner of people who scarcely knew one another. Would Meris be capable of—might she have gone to— to hurt Zenka, or discredit him by means of one of her tricks? Zirek had told her how it had been when they killed Sencho. 'She seemed to go completely crazy—she went on stabbing and stabbing in a kind of—well, I don't know, a kind of rapture—I had to drag her away.'

This recollection was enough for Maia. Quickly she got dressed and went outside. The shelter allotted to Bayub-Otal, Zenka and Zirek was not far off, but in the dim starlight and this unfamiliar place it was difficult to recall exactly which one it was. She set off in the general direction, hoping that something might turn up to help her.

She could tell now, by the stars, that it was not very late in the night. Perhaps Meris had waited no longer than it had taken herself to fall asleep. Suddenly she caught sight of a sentinel, javelin over his shoulder and shield on the other arm, pacing slowly between the huts. She ran towards him. He stopped, raised his javelin and called sharply, 'Stay where you are! Else I'll throw!'

Accustomed to the ways of the upper city, she had not taken into account that these were men who had just undergone a hard campaign. She stood stock-still as the man came up to her.

'You're breaking curfew. Why?'

'What curfew?'

'There's a curfew on women from two hours after sunset. You've no business to be out of your hut: I can take you in charge for this. What are you doing?'

'I'm sorry: I'm a stranger. I only came tonight. I'm worried about my friend—the girl who's sharing my shelter. I woke up and found her gone and now I'm looking for her. But she may be with a man—I don't know— in one of these huts here.'

The sentry remained unsympathetic. 'Well, there's a man who was sleeping on his own in there—that one.'

He pointed. She was about to leave when he put a hand on her shoulder. 'I'll come with you.'

As they went towards the shelter he added, 'If you've just come here, you'd better understand once and for all that women aren't allowed to go wandering about the camp at night. That's been a strict rule since Orthid. Place'd be like a damn' cat-house else, some of the women we took out of there.'

'Well, that's as may be,' retorted Maia briskly. 'All I want is to find my friend. Neither of *us* came out of Orthid: we're personal guests of Lord Elleroth.'

There were three beds in the hut. Two were empty: Zirek was sound asleep on the one farthest from the entrance. Maia shook him awake with some difficulty.

'Zirek, it's Maia! I woke and found Meris gone. Have you seen her?'

'Oh, Cran and Airtha! That blasted girl! No, I haven't! Who cares, anyway? Let me alone, lass; I want to sleep!'

'Where's Anda-Nokomis and Zenka, then?'

'Aren't they here? Well, then, as far as I know, they can't have come back from Elleroth, that's all.'

At this moment all three of them became aware of a kind of muffled commotion somewhere in the distance—voices both of men and women, together with the piping cries of children and the occasional wail of a baby. As they listened it seemed to be coming nearer.

'What's that, then?' said the sentry.

'If you don't know, I'm sure I don't,' replied Maia. Her first thought was that it could only be something to do with Meris.

They went back outside, followed a few moments later by Zirek. In the starlight they could make out a considerable crowd approaching between the shelters. It consisted mainly of women, dishevelled and obviously frightened, many leading children or carrying babies. On either side were soldiers, whom Maia could hear giving encouragement and reassurance in low voices.

'Come along, now, m'dear.' 'Won't be for long; you'll soon be back.' 'Only for the kids' safety, you know, that's all.' 'Sorry, missus, not now, strict orders.' 'Yes, General's coming directly to tell you all about it himself.' 'Get in that hut there, Liftil, wake 'em up, get 'em out!' 'Keep that kid quiet, lass! Much for your good as everyone else's!' 'Come on now, keep moving! Keep moving!'

It was a strange sight in the starlight—the shadowy, ever-growing crowd shuffling along, the women and children stumbling out of the huts by twos and threes, the soldiers hastening hither and thither, the continual, low-voiced injunctions, the quickly-stifled whimpers of the babies, the rustling and soft padding of feet through the dry grass and over the bare-trodden ground.

Suddenly there were low calls of 'Wait! Wait there!' and a tryzatt, holding out a spear, butt foremost, ran quickly to the head of the straggling procession. The women stopped, looking about them uncertainly in the gloom and plainly apprehensive. Then Elleroth was among them, smiling and greeting individuals here and there, putting a hand on this shoulder and that, distributing reassurance and encouragement as he made his way to the head of the crowd and then turned to speak to them.

'I've just had word of a band of strangers a little way off, over there.' He pointed. 'They're camped, but apparently they don't know about us yet. If they don't attack us we're certainly not going to attack *them*, so don't worry. They may even be friends—we simply don't know: we have to find out. And while we're doing that we mean to make sure you're all safe—even if it means you have a sleepless night, my dear.' He smiled at a woman standing near-by.

'So we want you to go across the river, please. There'll be soldiers to look after you and you'll be in no danger from wild animals or anything like that. You'll probably all be back by morning; but meanwhile, will you all help me and my soldiers by making as little noise as you possibly can? As soon as I know any more myself I'll make sure you're told. So don't worry, and just make yourselves as comfortable as you can.'

In the gloom, Maia had made out the unmistakable figure of Bayub-Otal, standing against the wall of a shelter. As the women and children began shuffling on once more towards the river, she went across to him.

'Anda-Nokomis!'

He looked round. She could perceive that in the moment that he recognized her his spontaneous reaction was one of pleasure and relief. 'Anda-Nokomis, do you know any more about this? Who are these strangers?'

He hesitated, and she pressed him. 'Anda-Nokomis, please tell me as much as you know.'

'It's very little, Maia. A patrol's reported that there's a sizeable force camped about a mile away over there, upstream. They weren't there yesterday, so presumably they're on the march. That's all we know as yet.'

'How many, Anda-Nokomis?'

'I tell you, Maia, we don't know. We've got to find out. It could possibly be Kembri and his whole army. That seems unlikely to me, but we can't rule out that possibility.'

'Where's Zen-Kurel?'

'Gone to get hold of some weapons: and so must I.'

'What sort of men were these the patrol came on?'

'We think Ortelgans.'

'*Ortelgans?*'

'Maia, I can't stay talking any longer: it's possible we may be attacked, you see. You and Meris must go across the river with the other women. I'll see you tomorrow; and if not, thank you for all you've done for us since Bekla.' He paused, and then added, 'Er—I think I may have been—er—too hard on you that evening at the farm. I should be very glad to think so—cousin.'

He stooped quickly, kissed her cheek and was gone into the gloom, leaving Maia staring after him.

Behind her someone coughed, and she turned to see a man wearing tryzatt's insignia on either side of his corn-sheaves emblem. Before he could speak she said, 'I'm a personal guest of Lord Elleroth. I'm waiting to speak to him before I cross the river.'

He looked at her uncertainly, but the Serrelinda—even deprived of her upper city splendour—had acquired a certain authority which carried its own weight. After a moment or two he replied, 'Very well, säiyett. But please try not to be too long,' saluted and left her.

It was during the course of this night that Maia carried out what was, perhaps, when all is said and done, the most remarkable exploit of the legendary Serrelinda; less dramatic, possibly, and to outward appearances less suicidally heroic than the swimming of the Valderra, but nevertheless a deed stamping her quite clearly as a woman no less exceptional (to say nothing of being considerably less nasty) than Queen Fornis. In retrospect, no one was to feel more surprised than herself. Yet she was not surprised at the time, for with Maia impulse was everything.

Often, throughout these past months of the summer, both awake and in dreams, it had seemed to her that the ghost of the wretched Sphelthon had been attendant near her, silently reproachful, wistfully jealous of her youth and beauty on behalf of all those—of all in the world—who had died young. In the dreams he said never a word, merely gazing at her sorrowfully—sometimes a strong lad in his prime, sometimes the poor, blood-battered victim who was all she had seen in reality—and in some strange way making her feel guilty that he should have lost his life while she retained hers to enjoy. Sometimes he came gliding after her down a long corridor which turned into the watery, overhung channel of the Nordesh. Sometimes she was dancing the senguela and, crossing the floor to speak to Fordil, would meet instead his eyes looking up at her above the leks and zhuas. Why she should feel guilty on account of his death she could not tell. Indeed, with her reason she knew that of course no tribunal, whether of gods or men, could conceivably indict her for it. And yet he haunted her, as it were entreating her to perform some deed which would give rest to his ghost, atone for his desolate ruin. In Tharrin's cell she had felt his

921

presence, at Milvushina's bedside and in the room where Randronoth lay slaughtered. Sometimes it had even seemed to her that her own life would be a small price to pay for the placation of this pathetic visitant. Yet he did not come, she knew, simply to make her suffer. No; he had some undisclosed, unspoken purpose. Nor could she pray for release from him, since he came, she was instinctively aware, not by the will of Cran or Airtha, of Lespa or Shakkarn, but from Frella-Tiltheh the Inscrutable, she who has no eyes to see us; no ears to hear us; no being, indeed, that we can comprehend; she who, while infinitely remote and inaccessible, is yet within ourselves, both each and everyone.

If there were indeed Ortelgans out there in the wasteland beyond the camp, then surely they could only be those whom Ta-Kominion had led to Chalcon as part of Elvair-ka-Virrion's force. Five hundred Ortelgans; she recalled Bel-ka-Trazet saying so at the barrarz. She remembered, too, how he had also said that their assignment was largely a matter of policy. 'We have to keep in with Bekla. But see your men come back alive, that's all. And if you have to get out, get out through Lapan.'

Could it really be the whole of Kembri's army out there, with the Ortelgans nearest? Or had Ta-Kominion, perhaps, after the defeat on the highway and the deposition of Elvair-ka-Virrion, decided not to wait for Kembri, but to save his men and make the best of his way home rather than face destruction with the Leopards?

Maia stood abstracted, musing in the darkness, while all around the soldiers made a final search of the shelters, here and there coming across some bewildered woman or terrified, deserted child and guiding them down to the river.

She had liked Ta-Kominion and he had liked her. It was he who had opened the bidding at the barrarz; he had gone to three thousand meld, she recalled—probably most of what he had in the world—before being obliged to drop out.

It would be no use trying to talk to Elleroth: no use trying to talk to Anda-Nokomis. As responsible soldiers they could not discount the possibility that it might be Kembri out there; or even if it was not, that whoever it was might strike first and ask questions afterwards. They would tell her to leave their own business to them and join the other women across the river.

But if she herself could only get to Ta-Kominion and tell him that these Sarkidians had no more wish to fight than he had, then any amount of misunderstanding and bloodshed might be prevented. It would be no use waiting until the morning. Once blood had been shed, injury sustained, pride aroused, these men would be at each other like cocks in a pit.

Yet if it *was* Kembri's whole army? He would most probably put her to death, if only for having been with Elleroth. He desired her death, as she knew. For long minutes she stood irresolute, feeling Sphelthon's invisible presence, his gaze upon her in the darkness. She raised her eyes to the glowing stars.

'O Lespa! Send me a sign! Only send your servant a sign!'

At this moment, from somewhere in the camp, there came faintly to her ears the cry of a lost child. 'Mother! Mother!' The voice was Tonildan.

Maia began to run. Bending low and peering this way and that, she dodged between the huts, came to a dry watercourse, dropped silently into it and began making her way along it in the opposite direction from the river. After going about two hundred yards she climbed out on the further side, lay prone until she was sure there was no one near and then set off eastward through the dried-up bushes and scattered clumps of trees.

She went cautiously, dodging from one thicket to the next and stopping continually to look ahead of her and listen. At all costs she must avoid running into one of Elleroth's patrols and being brought ignominiously back to the camp, for in that case it would certainly be supposed that she had been deserting—or perhaps even worse.

Once she thought she heard voices at a distance, but after waiting for some time decided that it could only have been her own frightened fancy. The scrub was open enough for her to keep direction by the stars, and this she took for a sign of Lespa's favour. Any road, she thought, there's no Valderra here. Whatever happens, I shan't drown.

None the less, she was never for a moment free from apprehension and the fear of death. The solitude, utterly still, seemed menacing. There was not an owl, not a bat to be heard. The very silence of this wilderness seemed unnatural. Twice she almost turned back; and twice glimpsed Sphelthon glimmering among the trees, a wraith that vanished even in the instant that she perceived it. Her tears were falling, but whether for him or for herself she could not have told.

For perhaps half an hour she wandered on through the empty wasteland, a prey to every kind of misgiving. Perhaps it had all been a false alarm and there were no soldiers at all? Or perhaps, whoever they were, they had already gone. Perhaps she had taken the wrong direction and already left them somewhere behind her. If they really existed, perhaps they were not Ortelgans at all, but runaway slaves like those with whom Meris had lived in Belishba. Even if they were Ortelgans, nevertheless Ta-Kominion might not be with them. He might be dead; or they might have mutinied against him. If he *was* with them, it now seemed to her unlikely that she would be allowed to speak with him at all. Or even if she were, why should he believe her, why should he trust *her*? What proof could he have that she was not a decoy sent by Elleroth?

Yet still she went on. The only possible thing to do, she thought, was to act on the assumption that the Ortelgans were there, that they were alone and that Ta-Kominion was with them.

She was picking her way through a thick grove of scrub willow when she once more heard voices. This time there was no doubt about it: they were low but distinct. As she stopped, holding her breath, she realized with a shock that they were very close—no more than twenty or thirty yards away among the trees.

She stood listening intently.

'. . . should've stayed where we were, if you ask me.'

'All depends, though, don't it? Who's to tell?'

Silence returned. She wondered whether the men had moved away; yet she had heard nothing. After what seemed a long time she heard a cough. Then the first voice, still speaking low, said, 'The basting rains, though; how's he think we're going to get back once *they* start?'

'Well, I reckon soon as he's sure which way it's gone he'll go over, that's his notion.'

'What, to Erketlis, you mean?'

'Ah. Quickest way home, see?'

This was enough for Maia. The men were speaking so quietly that she could not be sure of their dialect, but what she had been able to hear had convinced her that they must be Ortelgans speaking of Ta-Kominion. Well, she thought, reckon this is what I come for. If I'm going to die I'd best just get on with it. She called in a low voice, 'Can I talk to you?'

There was a sound of startled movement, and then one of the men replied, 'Who's there? Who are you?'

'I'm a woman, and I'm alone. Can I come and talk to you?'

'What you want, then?'

'I'm a personal friend of Lord Ta-Kominion. I've got an urgent message for him.'

She could hear the men muttering. Then the same voice said, 'Who's it from, then? And who *are* you?'

'I'll tell that to Lord Ta-Kominion.'

At this moment a new, authoritative voice said, 'What the hell's all this basting row? Weren't you told to keep quiet, eh?'

'It's some woman, tryzatt, off in those trees,' said the second man.

'What the hell d'you mean, a woman?'

'Says she knows the commander; wants to see him. Knew his name an' all. Got a message, she says.'

'I'm alone, tryzatt,' called Maia. 'Can I come and talk to you?'

The tryzatt was evidently a man of fairly quick mind. 'Where did you meet the commander?'

'In Bekla, at the barrarz in the upper city, with Lord Bel-ka-Trazet and Lord Ged-la-Dan.'

'What's his woman's name, then?'

'Berialtis: brought up on Quiso.'

There was a pause.

'Come out steady,' said the tryzatt at length, 'hands on your head.'

Maia did so. The three men confronting her were typical Ortelgans, stocky and dark, the tryzatt, who had a raw, barely-healed scar across his forehead, considerably older than the two soldiers.

'A place like this—how do you come to be here?' he asked, looking her up and down.

'I've no time to explain,' answered Maia, with as much authority as she could muster. 'My message is urgent, see, and it could very well save your lives. You got to take me to Lord Ta-Kominion at once.' As he hesitated, she added more vehemently, 'For Cran's sake, what harm do you think *I* can do? Why else would I be here alone, in the middle of the night—'

'Well, that's what I'd like to know,' replied the tryzatt. But as he spoke he gripped her arm, turned and led her away with him.

They went fast through the trees and bushes. Soon Maia became aware that the tryzatt was picking their way among men lying on the bare ground. From what little she could see they were tattered and dirty, with a general look of ill-being. All were fully clothed, with their arms lying ready to hand. Most seemed asleep, but here and there a few, lifting their heads or propping themselves on their elbows, stared as she and the tryzatt went past. None spoke, however, and Maia guessed that their orders about silence were strict. Perhaps, indeed, orders were unnecessary: no doubt Chalcon had been a hard school.

They came to a rough shelter made of branches laid either side of a pole on two forked sticks; hardly more than a kennel, its ridge perhaps three feet from the ground. A sentry was standing beside it. The tryzatt addressed him in a whisper.

'This woman says she's got a message for the commander. Seems genuine enough.'

'You're asking me to wake him?'

'That's for you to say.'

'Well, be fair,' replied the man. 'You're the tryzatt, not me.'

'You're his orderly, not me.'

The man was beginning, 'I'd best go and ask Captain Dy-Karn—' when from inside the shelter Ta-Kominion's voice said, 'What is it, Klethu?'

'This is Maia Serrelinda here, my lord,' said Maia quickly. 'I need to speak to you urgently: for your sake, not for mine.'

'*Maia?*' he replied in a tone of astonishment. Then, with a quick note of alarm in his voice, 'Who's with you? What's happened?'

'There's nothing wrong, my lord, but—'

'Where have you come from? Who's sent you?'

'I've got some very important news for you.'

'Wait, then.'

After a few moments Ta-Kominion came elbowing his way feet first out of the shelter and stood up. He was wearing a ragged shirt and breeches and looked, as she could see even in the dim starlight, like a man utterly worn out; a very different figure from the high-spirited youth who had opened the bidding at the barrarz. Her expression, as she took his hands in greeting, must have revealed her feelings, for before she could speak he said, 'You needn't waste your sympathy on me: we've plenty worse. But Maia, how in Cran's name do *you* come to be wandering about alone in a place like this? Are you on the run or something?'

'You could call it that. But now *you* must tell *me* something, my lord, 'cos I've got to know this if I'm to help you. Is this Kembri's whole army, or are you here on your own?'

He took her arm and led her away among the trees. Like the tryzatt, he spoke in whispers.

'Why do you ask me that? Why have you come?'

'Answer my question and I'll explain. It can't hurt to tell me: I can't leave here without you let me, can I?'

As he hesitated she took his hands once more, looking up into his bloodshot, hollow eyes.

'Honest, my lord, I only want to help you: and I've risked my life to come here.'

'Everyone's life's at risk here,' replied he. 'I wouldn't give much for our chances now and that's the truth. We left Kembri's army the night before last and we've been going ever since. The men are on their last legs. We've got no food left, either. But I'll get some of them back to Ortelga yet, you see if I don't.'

'Listen to me, my lord. There's a way to put the whole thing right, if you'll only do as I say.'

'But who's *sent* you?' he asked again, impatiently.

'Just listen, my lord, please! Sit down and listen to me.'

Ta-Kominion sat down on the ground, his arms round his updrawn knees, looking up at her with an expression suggesting that although he would like to believe her, he felt that to do so would be foolish.

'About a mile away over there,' said Maia, pointing, 'is Lord Elleroth of Sarkid. He's on his own like you, and I should guess he's got about the same number of men.'

Ta-Kominion seemed about to spring to his feet, but Maia restrained him.

'They know you're here, but they don't know yet whether it's only you or Kembri's whole army. What I'm trying to tell you is that they're as much afraid of you as what you are of them.'

Ta-Kominion buried his face in his hands. 'Oh, Shardik, that's about all we needed! Pinned against the river, too! That's basted everything!'

'No, it hasn't, my lord. Don't you see, if you're not fighting for the Leopards any more, Elleroth's got no quarrel with you? You ought to *join* him—he needs men—it'd be as big a weight off his mind as what it'd be off your'n. Why don't you come back with me now and talk to him?'

'It's a trick! A Beklan trick!' In the half-darkness the girl Berialtis had come up silently and was standing beside them, clutching a soldier's cloak round her. She was shivering in the hot night and looked no less wretched than everyone else whom Maia had seen. 'Don't go, Komo! She's lying!'

Her dark eyes glared at Maia—the eyes of a fanatic, intensified by fear and privation.

Maia stood up and faced her. 'All right, that's it, then; I done my best. My lord, I hope you'll have the kindness to let me go back where I come from.'

'Be quiet, Berialtis,' said Ta-Kominion. 'I'm commanding here, not you. Maia, how can I be sure of this man Elleroth—heir of Sarkid, isn't he? How can I be sure I can trust him?'

'My lord, I'll be honest with you. Like I said, no one's sent me: I just thought this lot up on my own. Lord Elleroth doesn't even know I've come—'

'You're not his woman, then?'

'Oh, Cran, no! I just don't want to see the two of you tear each other to bits, that's all; 'cos that won't be no good to you nor nobody.'

'Berialtis, go and wake Dy-Karn and bring him here. Don't argue; just do as I tell you for once.'

'You let yourself be taken in by this Beklan bitch; an unbeliever! *I* haven't forgotten that filthy barrarz, if you have—'

'Neither have I,' said Ta-Kominion, getting up. 'I'll go myself: you'd better come with me, Maia.'

Reaching his shelter, they found a group of four or five young men whispering together.

'These are all the officers we've got left,' said Ta-Kominion. 'Captain Dy-Karn, my second-in-command: Maia Serrelinda.'

There were murmurs of surprise. 'You'd better tell them, Maia, what you've just told me,' said Ta-Kominion.

Maia did so.

'But this Elleroth's an out-and-out heldro, isn't he?' asked Dy-Karn.

'Why else would he be with Erketlis? If you trust us all to him, Komo—'

'All I can say is I've met him,' said Maia, 'and I don't reckon as he's one to take unfair advantage. I can't say n'more, 'ceptin' they're all as scared of you as what you are of them.' As they hesitated, she added, 'You don't have to surrender to them nor any o' that. Just offer to join them. Any road, what else you going to do?'

'By the Ledges, and I reckon she's about right there!' said another of the officers. 'No food, men worn out, couldn't fight if they had to—'

'When we left Kembri, you see,' said Ta-Kominion to Maia, 'no one else knew what we were going to do, naturally. We reckon his lot can't last even until the rains. Erketlis'll destroy them; and we weren't going to wait for that. We were reckoning on crossing the Zhairgen by the Ikat high road, but we found the bridge held by Beklans—too many for us: so we had to come on downstream. I've been hoping we might get across somehow at Nybril, but obviously we can't get to Nybril if Elleroth's in the way.'

'Elleroth's got a raft on ropes across the Zhairgen,' said Maia. 'He's cutting his way through Purn, but he needs more men to make sure of it before the rains. If you was to join him, I reckon he could probably feed you an' all. How many you got?'

'Only about three hundred and fifty now. We lost a lot in Chalcon.'

'The girl's right, my lord,' said Dy-Karn. 'After all, we can always tell this Elleroth that if he won't have us, we'll sell our lives very dear. I'll come with you if you want.'

In the event three Ortelgans set out with Maia; Ta-Kominion, Dy-Karn and an older officer named Selta-Quaid, who limped on a stick and appeared to have been wounded in half a dozen places from head to foot. The men had been woken and were standing to arms. Word had, of course, got round of what was toward. As they passed through the different groups there were murmurs of 'Good luck, sir!' 'Tell 'em we're not beat yet, general!' 'Bring us back a few sheep, sir!' and the like. It was plain that Ta-Kominion still retained their loyalty and confidence.

The short summer night was drawing to an end and the sky behind them paling. The wilderness seemed as empty and almost as silent as before, save for the first pipings of awakening birds. She herself felt ready to drop. She had been tired enough the night before, and had had only an hour or two of sleep.

But Sphelthon: ah! *he* was asleep now; deeply and peacefully. She could feel it in her heart, his peace, gleaming like dew on a meadow. He was gone, but had left his blessing upon her. She had poured out on his poor, far-away grave the offering of her night's fear and resolution, and it had been sufficient even for Frella-Tiltheh.

She was startled from these thoughts by her name being called from a distance. All four of them stopped in their tracks, listening. The sound was coming from some way off among the broken woodland. There was, to say the least, nothing furtive about it. It was like the crying of wares by a street-trader. 'Maia! Maia!' Whoever was calling plainly did not care who heard him. After the long hours of stealth and whispering, the concealment and silence of the tense night wanderings, the effect seemed almost preternatural, a shattering of normality sharp as lightning or the sudden falling of a tree.

After a few moments Maia (who had recognized the voice) replied, 'Here I am!' There was strenuous movement in the bushes some way off, a sound of running footsteps and next moment Zen-Kurel, armed, burst out of the undergrowth and halted a moment at the sight of the Ortelgans. Then he drew his sword.

Maia's companions instantly drew also, but she ran forward, stopping midway between them and Zen-Kurel.

'What's happened, captain? What's brought you here?'

He looked at her, opened his mouth to speak and then looked away, seeming out of countenance.

'I—er—well, I came to look for you, that's all. You've been missed.' Then, as it were assuming a harsher note to cover his embarrassment, he asked abruptly, 'Who are these men?'

'They're Ortelgan officers,' she answered no less coldly, 'come to talk with Lord Elleroth. I think you'd better put up your sword, captain. I'm acting as their surety.'

Zen-Kurel, frowning perplexedly, did as she had suggested.

'What do they want with Lord Elleroth?'

'I reckon that's between him and them,' she said; 'in the first place, anyway.' Then, as the three Ortelgans came up, 'This is Lord Ta-Kominion of Ortelga: Captain Zen-Kurel of Katria.'

Ta-Kominion bowed, concealing his surprise. 'Has King Karnat seconded officers to Erketlis, then? I didn't know that.'

'No,' replied Zen-Kurel, 'I'm here by an accident of war. I was a prisoner of the Leopards in Bekla, but I managed—that's to say, Maia—she—er—she contrived my escape.'

'*Did* she?' answered Ta-Kominion. 'At that rate, it seems we all owe her a debt in common.'

It was full daylight now, the clear sky already blue, the grasshoppers beginning to chirp in the brown, dry grass. Pushing through a belt of trees near the river, they found themselves within fifty yards of eight or nine Sarkidian soldiers. They had thrown a plank across the dried-up watercourse which Maia had crossed the night before, and set up an outpost on the nearer bank.

Maia again went forward, and addressed the tryzatt.

'Tryzatt, these Ortelgan officers have come in peace to talk with Lord Elleroth. Can you please conduct them to him at once?'

She had already turned away by herself when Zen-Kurel overtook her. 'Where are you going, Maia?'

'Across the river,' she said, 'to join the other women and go to sleep; I'm very tired. Thank you for coming to look for me.'

: 94 :

MERIS'S LAST ESCAPADE

As the servants removed the Ortelgans' knives and plates and cleared the table Elleroth, who had briefly left them, returned and drew up a bench. With him were Mollo, Tolis and two or three more of his officers, as well as Bayub-Otal and Zen-Kurel.

'I've sent all the food we can spare over to your camp,' he said to Ta-Kominion. 'I'm afraid it's rather penitential stuff, but perhaps your sybaritic connoisseurs will make allowances. Have you many sick and wounded?'

'Too many,' replied Ta-Kominion. 'We had our own surgeon with us, but he died in Chalcon, poor fellow. The High Baron's not going to be pleased about that: he was a good doctor—trained on Quiso.'

'Well, that's the place, no doubt of it,' said Elleroth. 'I'm sending Muzarkalleen, one of my officers, to be treated by the Tuginda, if only we can get him there. He got badly cut up at that little affair on the highway.'

'So did we, sir,' said Dy-Karn. 'Lost seventy-six men, though some of them may have been able to get themselves back to Ortelga, I hope.'

'I'll send our doctor over to your camp,' said Elleroth. 'Could you see to it, Tolis, please? But that reminds me, Ta-Kominion; I'd like your advice. We have these slave children to find homes for, you know, and it's not easy. I'm determined they shall go to good homes, not to places where they'll remain slaves in everything but name. I had a notion to send two of the girls to Quiso with Muzarkalleen, as a sort of offering. You never know, they might make priestesses one day. What do you think?'

'Are they clever?' asked Ta-Kominion.

'One of them—Melathys—struck me as a particularly sharp child,' answered Elleroth. 'That's why I picked her.'

'Well,' said Ta-Kominion, 'I imagine that if they're clever they'll be welcome. A little non-Ortelgan blood among the priestesses might be all to the good. They'll be well treated, anyway; you can be sure of that.'

'Well, it's a small matter,' said Elleroth, 'but I'm glad to hear you approve. Still, we'd better get down to business, hadn't we? You say Kembri's in a bad way?'

'We all think his position's hopeless: that's why we're here, of course. You see, the army was badly demoralized in Chalcon and the reinforcements from Bekla—well, they've turned out worse than nothing, really. And then on top of that we heard that Randronoth had defected—'

'So it occurred to you to tiptoe away on fairy feet, in darkness and clandestine order, did it?'

'Well, you have to put yourself in Ortelga's position,' replied Ta-Kominion. 'Bel-ka-Trazet's policy has always been to keep in with Bekla, so that we can count on help against the Deelguy when it's needed.'

'Dear me, yes; those dashing, vagabond laddies—'

'This isn't the first time Ortelga's had to choose the right moment to run up a tilting plank to the other end,' put in Dy-Karn. 'It was the same when the Leopards deposed Senda-na-Say.'

'Kembri was very insistent that we should send men to join Elvair-ka-Virrion,' said Ta-Kominion. 'Bel-ka-Trazet didn't really care for the idea, but he couldn't very well get out of it. So he picked on me.' He gave a short, sardonic laugh. 'Oh, I admit I was keen enough: I reckoned we'd all do very well out of it; but that was more than Bel-ka-Trazet ever thought, if I know anything about him. Why, even at the barrarz in Bekla he was warning me to get out quick if we had to. I didn't think much about it at the time, but after the battle I felt it would be best to bring what was left of the men back as soon as I could.'

'Yes, indeed,' said Elleroth, 'and perhaps a short billet-doux to Santil wouldn't come amiss, either: but that's for you to decide. Well, let us consider the ins and outs of this jolly log-roll, shall we? As a matter of fact, it will be literally that, as Captain Mollo will now explain.'

'Got to get up through Purn before the rains, that's it. Need more men—got to get on faster.'

'Northward through Purn: one might almost call that a step in the right direction as far as you're concerned, might one not?' asked Elleroth. 'Have you a few meaty lads capable of swinging an axe?'

'Yes, but no axes.'

'I have some more axes coming up from Sarkid, but swords are good enough for undergrowth and that sort of thing. Well then, when we get out on the other side of Purn I have a fancy to turn east and cut the Bekla–Ikat road behind Kembri. He'll really love that, if he hasn't already fallen back on Bekla. Would you care to join us in a little spree of that nature?'

'Well, if that's your price,' replied Ta-Kominion, 'we'll have to pay it—'

931

'Think of the novelty; the wonderful excitement—'

'—but from what I've seen, Kembri may very well collapse before he can fall back anywhere, if Erketlis attacks him.'

'We don't know what's happening in Bekla, though, do we?' said Elleroth, dropping his bantering manner and speaking more seriously. 'Who's got it? Fornis, Eud-Ecachlon or the Lapanese?'

'I suppose Erketlis *means* to have it, doesn't he?' said Dy-Karn.

'Certainly; and before the rains, if he can. I've no quarrel with Eud-Ecachlon; but that evil woman mustn't be allowed time to make herself stronger in Bekla. I'll admit I *am* afraid of her. She's a sorceress: she can bewitch people out of their right minds; and she'd destroy the empire before she'd relinquish power—call in the Deelguy or something like that.'

Ta-Kominion nodded. 'That's what I think, too. Well, let's agree on this much. As soon as my men have had a day's food and rest and got back some spirit, we'll help you through the forest. Then let's talk again in the light of what we find out when we get to the other side. That's meant to be honest and no more than I'm ready to stand to. Will you accept it?'

'Yes, I will,' said Elleroth. He gave Ta-Kominion his hand. 'I'm sure Maia will be delighted to hear about this little bargain of ours.'

'By the Ledges, that's a girl, sir!' said Dy-Karn. 'I couldn't believe it last night, when she said she'd come across to us of her own accord.'

'Oh, really? Now I could, you know,' answered Elleroth. 'As a matter of fact, that was why I recalled our patrols. When I was told she was missing, I had a sort of notion that she might be paying you a call; and I didn't want anything to spoil it—no little animosity in the tenebrosity, you know, or anything like that.'

'You mean you'd already thought we might join you?'

'I mean nothing so vainglorious. I had no idea—none of us had—whether you might not be Kembri in full fig. As a military commander I could hardly do anything very amicable, could I, until I knew that? Awkward chap, Kembri; might have been rather stuffy, don't you know. But that splendid girl—she took the whole risk on herself and saved us all any amount of trouble, to say the very least.'

'You might have let me know earlier that she was gone, sir,' said Zen-Kurel. 'I didn't learn it till just before dawn.'

'Oh, might I, now?' replied Elleroth, gravely returning his glance. 'Do you know, I'm afraid that never really occurred to me? I thought you'd said earlier on—'

'If we'd only known,' broke in Bayub-Otal, 'I think we'd *both* have gone out after her a great deal earlier.'

'Well, I thought it would be a shame to wake you,' replied Elleroth suavely, 'after the hard day you'd had. However, next time she does anything like that, I assure you I'll—'

Suddenly Tolis burst in, wide-eyed. As everyone looked up Elleroth broke off, laying a hand on his arm.

'I infer that something untoward has occurred, Tolis,' he said composedly. 'I wonder what. Not Kembri, I hope?'

'No, sir,' said Tolis. 'There's been a murder in camp, sir: a woman!'

'O gods!' said Elleroth, getting up. 'How boring! I knew it would happen sooner or later. Who is it?'

'It's the girl who came last night, sir,' said Tolis, 'with these officers—'

'Not Maia?' cried Zen-Kurel. Bayub-Otal, white to the lips, sprang to his feet, gripping the edge of the table.

'No, sir,' answered Tolis. 'The other girl, the Belishban girl; she's dead, sir!'

'Do we know how?' asked Elleroth, taking his sword-belt from the orderly.

'Yes, sir. There's two men being held under guard. They reported the girl's death themselves. They admit having caused it.'

'Who are they?' said Elleroth.

'Lortil and Dectaron, sir. Captain Mollo's company.'

'But great Cran, those are two damned good men, that's it! Never been in any sort of trouble! What the—'

'Calm yourself, Mollo! Obviously we must look into this at once. Where have they put the poor girl?' Elleroth turned to Tolis.

'In one of the shelters, sir, up the lines.'

Elleroth looked round at the officers present. 'Mollo and Tolis, you'd better come with me; and of course you'll wish to come, too, won't you?' he said to Bayub-Otal and Zen-Kurel. 'Perhaps the rest of you won't mind waiting here for the time being—unless, of course,' he added to Ta-Kominion, 'you'd prefer to go back to your camp and start making arrangements in the light of what we've just agreed. We'll meet again later.'

Having taken Ta-Kominion's hands for a moment in farewell, he ducked out under the curtain which the orderly was holding aside.

The body of Meris, covered with a blanket, was lying in the further corner of the shelter to which Tolis led the way. A soldier on guard saluted as the commander entered. Gently, Elleroth drew back the blanket from the head. The girl's face was contorted, the teeth clenched, the lips drawn back so far that the cheeks were ridged under the open eyes.

'Where's the wound?' asked Elleroth.

'Her neck's broken, sir,' answered Tolis.

One of Meris's arms was protruding stiffly from under the blanket.

933

Elleroth took the cold hand in his own, stooped and touched it with his lips. He turned to Bayub-Otal and Zen-Kurel.

'I'm more sorry than I can tell you. My guest—your friend—I feel to blame.'

As Bayub-Otal murmured some conventional words of demurral, Zirek entered in tears and fell on his knees beside the bed.

'Someone must put some clothes on the body and lay her out decently,' said Elleroth to the soldier.

'Yes, sir,' he answered. 'There's some women waiting. Only tryzatt Miarn said not to alter anything until you'd seen her, sir, and said what was to be done, like.'

'Perfectly correct,' said Elleroth. 'Tell the tryzatt to let the women come in. And say a pyre's to be prepared for this evening.'

'Sir.'

Elleroth was turning to go when Zirek touched his hand.

'I'd like to—to stay here and pray for a minute or two, sir, if I may, before the women come. I won't be long.'

'Of course,' replied Elleroth. He turned to the soldier. 'Wait outside, please, Hospa, until U-Zirek has finished.'

'Sir.'

'Where are the two men under guard?'

'With the tryzatt, sir. They're not making no trouble, sir; only they've asked if they can see Captain Mollo.'

Elleroth nodded. 'Well, Captain Mollo, will you go and talk to them, and then bring them to me under guard as soon as you're ready? Shall we say in about half an hour?'

The officers went out, followed by the soldier. Zirek, left alone, stood for some time praying with raised, outstretched arms. Then, bending forward, he drew the blanket entirely away from the body, so that Meris lay naked before him as she had so often lain in life—the firm, smooth thighs, the gentle curve of the belly with its deep, hollow navel, the big circles round the nipples like dark-hued lilies on rose-pink water—a reversal of nature. Even now, against wish and will—so that he felt ashamed, and once more covered the body—her stricken, cold beauty had the power to kindle desire. He knelt and kissed her feet, one and then the other.

'I'm sorry, lass,' he said aloud. 'Cran knows I'm sorry. I'd have loved you and kept you safe, if only you'd let me. I always said you'd do it once too often, but you wouldn't listen, would you? At least it'll leave you in peace now.'

The sentry, who had retired to a decent distance, returned at the sound of his voice. 'I'm sorry, sir, did you speak to me? I'm afraid I didn't catch what you said.'

'No, that's all right, lad,' said Zirek. 'I'm done now, thanks. Let the women come in.'

Elleroth and Mollo looked up at the two soldiers standing before them. Both were conspicuously scratched and had bled about the face and neck. On either side of them stood their own tryzatt and another. Bayub-Otal, Zen-Kurel and Zirek were standing behind and to the left of Elleroth. The hut was close and stuffy, and all nine men were sweating.

'Now,' said Elleroth, looking from one prisoner to the other as he addressed them, 'you had better both understand at once that this is a very serious matter indeed. A young woman has come to a violent end. She was a secret agent of General Erketlis, who had carried out a very important and dangerous exploit in Bekla with the greatest heroism. She had escaped and was on her way to General Erketlis to be honoured and rewarded. She was a personal friend of the gentlemen you see here, and she was my guest and therefore under my protection. Now have you understood that, Dectaron?'

'Yes, sir.'

'And you, Lortil?'

'Yes, sir.'

'Am I to understand that you admit having caused this woman's death?'

'Yes, sir.'

'Both of you?'

'Yes, sir.'

'I want to be perfectly plain with you. You realize that this is a hanging matter?'

'Yes, sir.'

'I understand that you both came to tryzatt Miarn of your own accord and reported that you'd killed the woman. Is that correct?'

'Yes, sir.'

'Well, Dectaron, you're the older man. You'd better tell me what happened.'

'Beg your pardon, sir; might we have permission to sit down, sir? Not meaning any disrespect—'

'I think everybody had better sit down,' said Elleroth. 'Tryzatt, please set some more benches. Thank you. Now, Dectaron, how did this come about?'

'Well, sir, it was like this, sir. Last night I was on guard duty, sir, and we enforced curfew on the women and children at the usual time, in accordance with standing orders. It must have been about two hours after that, sir, as I was going round the far end of the camp on my beat, that I happened to be passing close to my own shelter, as I share with another man, Olfane, only he was on the guard too. There was no one about at all, when suddenly I sees this young woman coming towards me quite openly, sir. So I challenged her and asked her what she thought she was doing out at that hour. And she come up to me, sir, and put her arms round my neck and asked me if I'd like to go with her. "For forty meld," she says, "you can do with me whatever you like."'

Dectaron stopped, met Elleroth's eyes for a moment and looked down at the earth floor, hesitating.

'Go on,' said Elleroth, grimly.

'She was—well, sir, she was very pressing, sir, sort of; she'd got her robe open and her deldas bare and—well, the long and short of it was, sir, I'm afraid it was too much for me, and I agreed with her for thirty meld, which was all I'd got.'

'Even though you were supposed to be on guard?' asked Mollo.

'Yes, sir, I'm afraid so, sir. So I took her into my shelter, which was empty and just close by, as I've explained. And we were—we were there together, sir, for some time, like.'

'And did you give her thirty meld?' asked Mollo.

'Yes, sir.'

'Did you find that money on her, tryzatt?' asked Elleroth.

'In her clothes, sir, yes: that and a little more, actually.'

'Go on, Dectaron.'

'Well, sir, after a while I said, "You realize I'm supposed to be on guard duty?" Naturally I was afraid of being missed, sir, you see. And she said that was nothing to her, so I says, "Well, it is to me," I says, "and I'll have to be getting back quick." So then she asked could she stay where she was, and I told her I thought it would be best if she did, right up until the morning, rather than start running about the camp again and getting into more trouble—'

'But she hadn't *been* in any trouble up till then, had she, soldier?' said Mollo. 'And who's to blame for that, eh?'

'I am, sir.' Neither Elleroth nor Mollo said more and after a short silence the wretched man, who was clearly very much afraid, went on.

'Well, so I left her there, sir, in my bed, and went back on guard duty: I hadn't been missed and I spent the rest of the night on and off sentry-go in the usual way.'

'Excuse me, sir,' broke in Lortil, 'but I'm just as much to blame, sir, and if it's in order, I reckon I ought to go on now.'

'Very well,' replied Elleroth.

'Well, sir, I was one of those detailed to go across the river with the women and children. Some stayed over there all night, but the lot I was with were ordered back to camp very late, and then we were dismissed.

And I was coming back to my shelter, sir, next to Dectaron's, when this girl came out. She was naked, sir, and she came up to me and began—well, sir, she began making up to me and asking me to come into Dectaron's shelter with her.'

'For money?'

'Yes, sir. I only had twelve meld and so I told her, but she said that would be all right. Like Dectaron told you, sir, she was very pressing, like.'

'And you *weren't*, I suppose?' asked Mollo. 'Is that it?'

'No, sir: I can't deny as I was willing enough. I spent the rest of the night with her and early this morning we were both asleep when Dectaron came back off guard.'

'And what happened then?' said Mollo sardonically to Dectaron. 'You were delighted, I suppose?'

'Well, sir, as soon as I come in I realized what must have happened—that's to say, that she'd taken on another man to make herself some more money. But I wasn't angry, like I might have been if it had been some man as I didn't know. Only you see, sir, Lortil and me, we've been together all through the campaign, ever since we joined up—'

'I know,' said Mollo. 'Share and share alike, eh? You seem to have stuck to that very thoroughly. Well, go on.'

'Well, sir, I woke the both of 'em up, and told the girl it was high time for her to be going before the tryzatt come round. I didn't want anyone finding her in my shelter, you see.'

'Didn't you really? Well, so what did she say to that?'

'Well, sir, this was when all the trouble began, and I'm sure I'm very sorry for it—we both are—but we didn't go to start it, sir, and that's as true as I'm here. First of all the girl set out to try and make us jealous of each other. Anyone could see she hoped we were going to get angry—start fighting an' that. Only of course that didn't work, for the reasons as I've explained. So when she saw that was no good, sir, she got up off the bed, just as she was—with nothing on, I mean—and she says, "Oh," she says, "I want another hundred meld before I'm going out of here." So I told her I hadn't got any more money to give her even if I'd a mind to, which I hadn't, and Lortil told her the same. So then she said, "Well, you'd better go out and get some, then—borrow it or something o' that, because I'm not going else, and if you try to make me I'll kick up such a shine as'll bring your tryzatt and officers here as fast as hounds," she says.

'Well, at that, sir, we both of us did get angry, I'll admit. So Lortil, he says, "Don't you try that stuff with us," he says. "Come on," he says to me, "if she won't put her clothes on, we'll just have to put 'em on for her, won't we?" So he goes to grab her and stuff a cloth in her mouth, sir; keep her quiet, see, while we was getting her clothes on. But she was too much for us, sir, and that's the plain truth. She bit my finger very near through, and then she flew at Lortil, sir, scratching and biting, and at the same time she'd begun screaming at the top of her voice, just like she'd said she would. So I thought, well, this has got to be stopped quick, I thought. She had her arms right round Lortil, sir—only he still had nothing on, you see—and she was biting and scratching at his shoulders and his neck. So I tried to pull her away from him, only I couldn't—she was locked against him that tight there was nothing I could get a hold of. Well, I wasn't thinking too clearly, sir: I mean, the girl was carrying on like a wild animal, really, and we were both just about frantic. She had her teeth sunk in Lortil's shoulder, and I took her by the head and jerked it back—well, it *was* hard, I don't deny it was—only I felt I had to get her off him at all costs, you see. And then all of a sudden she just went limp and fell on the ground, and Lortil, he says, "Oh, Cran almighty," he says, "I reckon her neck's broke!" And so it was, sir; she was dead as a rat. There was nothing we could do. So as soon as we realized that, Lortil says, "Well, there's no help for it," he says. "Only thing to do is make a clean breast of the whole business." So we went straight off and reported to tryzatt Miarn. And that's the truth, sir, every word. We're both very sorry this should have come about, only there *was* provocation, like.'

'Do you want to ask these men any questions, Captain Mollo?' said Elleroth.

'We've only got your word for all this, haven't we?' said Mollo. 'You've no other evidence to put forward?'

'No, sir, 'ceptin' for the bites and scratches, and we had no reason to want to kill the girl, sir. Neither of us had had any drink—it was early morning, like I said: and as soon as we realized what we'd done we come straight forward, sir.'

'Do you want to ask any questions?' said Elleroth, turning to Bayub-Otal, Zen-Kurel and Zirek. They shook their heads.

'Is the guard outside?' asked Elleroth.

'Yes, sir,' answered the second tryzatt.

'Take them outside and keep them somewhere near-by,' said Elleroth. 'Tryzatt Miarn, will you stay behind, please?'

When the two soldiers had gone he said, 'Now, I want your personal opinion of these men, Miarn.'

'They're both good men, sir. Done well in Chalcon, sir, and in the battle, too.'

'Do you believe they're telling the truth?'

'Seeing what you said about the dead young woman, sir, I'm very sorry to have to say it, but yes, sir, I think they are.'

'How much money did you find in her clothes?' asked Elleroth.

'Forty-two meld, sir; all in one-meld pieces.'

'Thank you, tryzatt; that's all.'

The tryzatt saluted and went out. Elleroth sat silent for almost a full minute. At length he said, 'I confess this defeats me. Here's this obviously very brave and charming girl, who went to Bekla and helped to kill Sencho—one of the most heroic exploits I've ever heard of in my life—and according to these men—and they *are* decent enough men in the normal way, as I know myself—wouldn't you agree, Mollo?—'

'Two of the best I've got. Can't expect soldiers to be basting saints, that's it, 'specially after a campaign like this—'

'Excuse me, sir,' said Zirek. 'I'm afraid the truth is that what seems so strange to you is perfectly understandable to me. I knew Meris very well: I believe every word the soldiers said and I can tell you why.'

The others listened as he told them all he knew of Meris, from Belishba to Lapan.

'Poor girl!' said Elleroth, when he had finished. 'Well, she's not the first and she won't be the last. Thank you, Zirek: that makes everything very clear. So you'd agree, Mollo, that she really brought it on herself?'

Mollo nodded morosely. 'But they can't be let off altogether.'

'Oh, no. They're both guilty of condoning a woman in breaking curfew and whoring round the camp; and on top of that, Dectaron's guilty of leaving his duty while on guard, and that's a serious offence. What do you think?'

'I'd offer them their choice between dishonourable discharge and a flogging.'

'But—er—wouldn't that just mean that you'd lose two good soldiers?'

'Not a bit of it! The men are all convinced they're going to be looting Bekla in two weeks from now. That's what they've marched and fought all the summer for—to line their pockets. Offer Dectaron twenty lashes and Lortil twelve. They'll take them; you'll see. And it'll be very good for morale, Elleroth, believe me, when word gets round that you and I evidently think discharge now would be a punishment as bad as a flogging. The men'll all be sure that you must know for certain we're on the point of taking Bekla, that's it.'

'Very well: I agree,' said Elleroth. He became pensive once more. 'Poor Meris! You've told us, Zirek, that she enjoyed making trouble. She certainly managed it this time, but it was rather expensive for her, wasn't it? And to think she only had to wait a little while to be rich and secure for the rest of her life! Human nature's a strange thing.' He stood up. 'Well, we'd better go and finish our job, I suppose—which I don't relish.'

'Nor I ours,' murmured Zirek. Elleroth looked up at him enquiringly, and he said, 'Someone's got to tell Maia.'

Bayub-Otal and Zen-Kurel exchanged a glance. There was a short silence.

'I suggest all three of us go together,' said Zen-Kurel.

Meris burned at nightfall, her pyre surrounded by hundreds of pitying onlookers, for the women and children had been brought back from the other side of the river and many of the Ortelgans, more than content with Ta-Kominion's news of his negotiations with Elleroth, had already come over to the Sarkidian camp to fraternize. Untimely death, of course, was nothing out of the ordinary either to the soldiers or the ex-slaves, but throughout the camp there had been much talk of the beautiful girl, a guest of the commander, who had succeeded in a desperate exploit for the heldril and been on her way to Santil-kè-Erketlis to receive her reward. Fanned by hearsay, indignation had spread against the men responsible for her death, until Mollo obtained Elleroth's consent to assemble his own company—the culprits' comrades—and tell them the rights of the matter before having the punishment inflicted (for, as he had guessed, both declined discharge and even accepted the alternative with some relief, since the possibility of being hanged for murder had been doing nothing for their peace of mind).

As the ceremony of the burning began—four soldiers, each with a resinous torch, standing to the corners of the pyre to set light to it simultaneously—Zirek moved quietly away from the group round Elleroth and stood apart, gazing intently as the blaze spread inward. Maia, overcome with grief and by the majesty and solemnity of the occasion, did not notice that he had left her side. It was only later, after Elleroth had stepped forward to throw the appointed grain, salt and wine upon the embers; after the people had begun to disperse and Bayub-Otal and Zen-Kurel had taken their places on either side of the commander as part of his recessional escort, that she caught sight of him standing solitary, with bowed head and folded arms.

She made her way to him and stood unspeaking by his side. They were alone, for Elleroth's officers, in accordance with custom, had formed two files behind him as he made his departure.

After a little Zirek said, 'She had more courage than anyone I've ever known—except for Occula. She never flinched that night, never hesitated, never showed any fear either before or after. I couldn't have done it without her, you know.'

'And I couldn't have done what she did: I know that.'

'Killing Sencho—that was vital, you see. The Leopards' whole intelligence system fell to pieces. I wonder whether anyone in years to come will remember her name and what she did.'

'The gods will remember.'

'The gods? You'd wonder sometimes, wouldn't you? She's forfeited everything; and who—what—drove her to that but the gods?'

'You know, Zirek, somehow I feel Meris would have undone herself one way or another, even if she'd been given a fortune.'

'Maybe; but there she is now. Forty-two meld and a bonfire. Not even a *tarpli*—not from these strangers.'

'I never thought of the tarpli,' said Maia. 'Do they have them in Belishba same as we do in Tonilda?'

'Of course.'

The tarpli, though not universal throughout the Beklan empire, was a tribute of obsequy rendered throughout Tonilda and certain other provinces. A poem or verse mourning the dead person and recalling his or her life and character would be composed by some relative or friend and sung or declaimed as the pyre burned low. Often, among simple people in the country villages, it would be rough doggerel enough, but nevertheless might well have taken the maker a deal of trouble and be offered with sincere feeling. Maia had composed one in her own mind for Tharrin, though only Lespa had been permitted to hear it.

'I made one up for her,' said Zirek, 'but no one said anything about a tarpli and I didn't care to put myself forward among these officers with their fine ways.'

She took him by the hand and led him up to the edge of the pyre, until the heat forced them to a halt.

'Now sing it.'

He hesitated. 'It's not like a real tarpli—not like they generally are. But—I don't know—some god put it into my mind.'

'Then he must have done it for Meris. Give it to her, go on. I'm stood here: I won't let anyone stop you.'

Zirek, raising his arms as in prayer, began to sing. His voice was true and sure and after the first line or two rang out with a confidence which carried its own authority. Before the close many of the dispersing onlookers had turned back to listen and he, perceiving this, repeated his threnody from the beginning.

> 'The swift, black river withers in its banks,
> Buried in gaunt trees, blind to the sun.
> Only a deep chattering of stones
> Tells where the cold fingers of current run.
>
> And faint ghosts of bones that lie in the wood
> Flicker and cackle together among the branches.

Two green eyes move silently to drink,
Crouching on huge, imagined haunches.

A noise of running, and startled birds fly up
In the distance. What was that, that suddenly cried?
Footsteps . . . Only the river pouring down
And the dumb, warlock forest stretched beside.
Now I remember how, in that still town,
They told of a girl wandering till she died.'

In the succeeding silence, Maia stood for some moments as unstirring as
though it had indeed been a god who had devised the words. Then,
turning to Zirek, she flung her arms round his neck, clinging to him and
weeping. This strange, oblique lament had pierced her as no conventional
elegy for Meris could have done. He stood quietly, suffering her thus to
reciprocate what he had offered. The people went away once more and
they were left alone.

At length, looking up, she saw Anda-Nokomis beside them. He took
Zirek's hand in his own.

'The tarpli, was it?'

'Yes, sir.'

'That's well done. I'm to blame: I overlooked it. But you didn't, so all's
as it should be.'

He waited without impatience while Maia recovered herself and dried
her eyes. Then he said, 'Elleroth wants to see the four of us. There's no
hurry; whenever you're ready.'

'I'm ready, Anda-Nokomis,' said Maia.

: 95 :

DESTINATIONS

Elleroth, having nodded to the servant to leave them, looked up at his four
guests.

'The dead are at peace,' he said. 'We have to believe that.' No one spoke
and he went on, 'I can't imagine the gods being very hard on that poor girl,
can you? It's been a miserable business; I hope that at least you're able to
feel that everything's been done decently and properly.'

'Yes,' replied Bayub-Otal. 'We're all well satisfied as far as that goes. It
was most good of you, with so much else on your hands.'

'No, we're the people who feel under an obligation,' said Elleroth, 'and as far as we're concerned it's not discharged yet. I need to know what you want to do now, so that we can help you to do it. But before we come to that, may I ask you, Serrelinda, to do me the honour of accepting this little keepsake on behalf of me and my men?'

It was his own neck-chain, with the silver corn-sheaves emblem.

Maia's lips trembled. Yet as one might have expected, the Serrelinda, who had been presented to King Karnat dressed in golden lilies and given a tress of her own hair to Durakkon in the Caravan Market, was equal to this moment also. Having returned the Sarkid commander's smiling gaze for a moment, she bowed her head in a silent gesture of recognition and gratitude as demure as any virgin acolyte of the Thlela. As she did so he bent forward, placed the chain round her neck and centred the emblem at her bosom.

'He knew neither his father nor his mother,' murmured Elleroth.
'Among strangers he laboured as a slave,
An exile in a country not his own,
The Lord Deparioth, God's appointed sword.'

This was part of the traditional lament for the hero Deparioth, known as 'The Tears of Sarkid'. Maia could only guess that Anda-Nokomis must have told him her story.

She raised her head. 'Thank you, my lord.' Running her fingers down the chain, she closed her hand on the corn-sheaves emblem. 'It's just over my heart: I reckon that's the right place for it, don't you?'

They all laughed delightedly, and as she sat down Zirek stooped and kissed her shoulder.

'Well,' said Elleroth briskly, 'as I've said, you shall have every help from us. U-Zirek, let's take you first, shall we; for I rather think there's not much doubt about you, is there? You'd like a safe-conduct to Santil, wouldn't you?'

'Thank you very much, my lord,' replied Zirek. 'Yes, that would take care of everything as far as I'm concerned.'

'It's not thirty miles to my father's estate in Sarkid,' said Elleroth. 'You've only to get there in one piece to be treated to all you deserve— he'll be more than delighted when he learns who you are—and from there you should easily be able to reach Santil in two days.'

'Well, I'll make so bold as to tell your father, my lord, what I think of his son.'

'I fear that *he* may tell *you*,' said Elleroth, 'what he thinks of an heir who goes off freebooting with Santil without asking either consent or blessing—which he knew he wouldn't get, of course. But that won't affect my father's hospitality, I can assure you. Give him my dutiful greetings and tell him to expect me back when Bekla's fallen. And now, Lord Anda-Nokomis, what are *your* plans?'

'The Ban of Suba,' he replied, 'has a duty to get back there as quickly as he can.'

'That's what I thought you'd say, and I can only applaud. However, has it occurred to you that under present conditions, the most feasible route may unavoidably be circuitous—not to say ambagious, periphrastic and anfractuous? In a word, have you considered going back to Suba via Bekla? We'd be only too delighted for you to join us.'

'I'm honoured, Elleroth, and thank you. My own people will follow a one-handed man because they owe allegiance to his legendary mother's son, but I don't think I could reasonably expect the same of your men.'

'Anda-Nokomis, I could do with a really knowledgeable, competent chief of staff. Can't I tempt you?'

'I'm sorry, Elleroth, to disappoint you, but I've thought about this very carefully, and I'm certain that my best chance of getting back to Suba is to make for Nybril and try to come by a boat.'

Elleroth nodded. 'You're right, I dare say. An epitaph, on my behalf—no chief of staff. So be it. But Captain Zen-Kurel, surely I can tempt *you*, can't I? We really do stand in need of another experienced, able company commander. Since Chalcon we've lost two or three senior officers we could very ill spare. Won't you come with us and help to cut Kembri to pieces?'

'It's tempting,' he answered, 'and like Anda-Nokomis, I'm flattered. But the hard fact is that I'm still an officer of King Karnat's staff. That appointment's never been terminated, as far as I know. So I'm afraid it follows that I've got to do all I can to get back.'

'Ah, well: easy come, easy go. But now, Maia! Maia Serrelinda! *You'll* come to Bekla with us, won't you? Or would you rather go with Zirek, to be rewarded by Santil? I'll be more than happy to give you a letter telling him what you've done for us, and I've no doubt Ta-Kominion would be glad to as well.'

As Elleroth waited for her reply, Maia looked up to see all four of them regarding her intently. She coloured; yet her answer came without hesitation.

'My lord, a little while back you said something as made me think you may already know that I'm Suban.'

'Well, I've—er—heard something to that effect, yes.'

'I want to go to Suba.'

'You mean, to *live* there?'

Returning his gaze, she remained silent.

'But why, Maia?'

'Because I'm Suban, my lord.'

'But mightn't that be rather—er—difficult for you?'

She stood up. 'And I think Lord Anda-Nokomis is quite right. Going to Nybril will be our best way, my lord. I wonder whether you'd be so good as to excuse me now? It's been a long day and I'm that done up: I'll be back for supper, of course.' Taking his hands, she smiled at him no less dazzlingly than she had once smiled at Selperron from her golden jekzha. 'I'm very much looking forward to it.'

She went out. After a few moments Elleroth crossed to the sideboard, picked up the wine-jug and refilled the cups.

'Well, dear lads, that's certainly put me in my place, hasn't it? And it's rather put paid to the turncoat theory as well, don't you think? Suba: h'm! There's really no accounting for tastes, is there? No offence, Anda-Nokomis, I assure you, but I imagine there's bound to be a certain change in her life-style, to say the least. Er—is all well with you, my dear Katrian comrade?'

Zen-Kurel was staring before him with an expression of agitated and baffled amazement.

'Suba? The girl must have gone out of her mind! They'll tear her limb from limb!'

'Not if I have anything to do with it,' said Bayub-Otal.

'Not if you *do*,' said Elleroth. He looked quizzically for a moment from one of them to the other. 'Well, now I must be off: there are a few things to be seen to in the camp before we meet again for supper. Do make yourselves comfortable. There's hot water whenever you want it. Just tell one of the orderlies.'

He went out, singing to himself just audibly,

> 'As I roved out—one early-y mor-orning,
> To view the forest and to take the air,
> I there did meet with a fair pretty mai-aiden—'

His voice, receding, died away as the servants came in to tidy the room and lay the table for supper.

A NIGHT ENCOUNTER

The next morning was again clear-skied and as hot as ever. Almost every available man, including many of the Ortelgans, had been sent across the river to continue cutting the forest-track under Mollo's direction, and there were not a great many, apart from Elleroth himself, Zirek and Ta-Kominion, to wish god-speed to Maia and her two companions. Their escort—none other than Tolis and tryzatt Miarn, with twenty men—assembled outside Maia's shelter to accompany her to Elleroth's headquarters. They had brought a litter for her, but she smilingly declined it.

'I'd rather walk, and that's no more 'n the plain truth,' she said to Tolis. 'After all, 'tain't as if it was all that far to Nybril. Tell you what, though; if I get tired, I'll jump in the river and swim.'

At this there was a general laugh, for naturally her fame as a swimmer was well-known to everyone. It was not more than twenty miles down river to Nybril, but in view of the heat and his wish to be as considerate as possible to his guests, Elleroth had begged them to take two days over it.

'Why don't we make a raft and just float down?' Maia had asked him at supper the night before.

'A raft for twenty-six people?'

'No, just the three of us.'

'You're having an escort because of the very real risk of bandits and cut-throats,' he answered. 'We can't rule out the possibility of some sort of robbers with boats on the river. That's the sort of thing the Leopards have reduced the empire to. Cran only knows how long it's going to take to restore law and order when we've taken Bekla.'

They had given her new shoes and a brand-new cloak and tunic. (She couldn't help wondering where they had come from. The truth was that Elleroth had sent to Sarkid for them, about twelve miles each way.) Her Beklan cloak and tunic had been ruined in the forest and the river, but fortunately the new tunic, like the old one, had pockets capacious enough to hold her money and valuables.

She felt in good shape and ready for anything. The most substantial reason for this—even stronger than the idolization of the soldiers and Elleroth's unconcealed regard—was the complete change in Anda-Noko-mis's manner towards her. Often, during those days at the farm, she had felt wretchedly certain that nothing could ever alter his aversion and contempt—no, not if she were to call down Lespa to carry him to Melvda-Rain and crown him with stars. Her deed in Suba, with its terrible (and

946

unintended) consequences, had put her beyond the pale, and all she had done since or ever could do was doomed to be regarded as worthless.

Yet at supper last night she had realized that this had changed. Anything that ordinary people would regard as warmth or cordiality was not really, of course, within Anda-Nokomis's capacity; yet she, who knew him so well, could perceive clearly the alteration of his feelings. She could only suppose that he must have been reconsidering one thing with another—the escape from Bekla, the raft, the waterfall and her night excursion to the Ortelgan camp—and had at last decided to forgive her. She was not to know that in fact it was none of these things which had tipped the scale in that proud, obsessed mind. Maia's disclosure that she was his cousin had brought about in him a turmoil of perplexity. For some days he had been quite unable to decide whether it could or should alter his view of her—whether it ought to make any difference to his condemnation of her unspeakable treachery. Yet nevertheless, within the hour and while he was still very much confused, it had been the real though undivulged cause of his persuading Zen-Kurel against killing her. Only much later did he realize the full significance of the fact that when she had betrayed him to Sendekar she had not herself known either that she was Suban or that they were cousins. If she had known that she was Suban, would she have done it? He had concluded not.

And then, following upon her saving of his life at the waterfall—and beyond all question that had been a brave, loyal deed, for no one could have blamed her if she had judged it impossible to attempt—had come Elleroth's very cogent suggestion that from the moment she had discovered that they were kindred—that she was a Suban and he her liege lord—she could hardly have risked more or shown greater courage on his behalf.

Yet even all this had not been enough for a man like Bayub-Otal. What had taken him completely by surprise and finally overcome his last reservations, had been Maia's instant and unhesitating reply to Elleroth that she was a Suban and wanted to go back to Suba. And when Elleroth had hinted at what she must already have realized—that this could not but involve her in grave difficulty and danger—she had politely snubbed him and put paid to any further discussion of the matter. Until that moment it had never occurred to Bayub-Otal that when it came to the point Maia, Suban or no, would decline reward and honour from Santil-kè-Erketlis in favour of a hazardous journey to return to Suba and live there. Neither at that time nor throughout the evening had he said one word to express his astonishment; yet he had hardly been able to sleep for its effect. And it was this effect, evidenced by all manner of minute changes in that diffident, haughty man, which Maia was well able to sense and appreciate. Anda-Nokomis, she felt, was now

947

more truly her friend than he had ever been. Might she dare hope to recover yet another friend?

Alas! she was soon made sure that there was little enough prospect of that. Zen-Kurel remained all courtesy and detachment. She was still his responsibility: just that. And that, she felt sure, was the only reason why he had gone out to look for her yesterday, when he had learned that she had set out for the Ortelgan camp. He had regarded it as no more than his duty.

It is perfectly possible—indeed it is common—to be delighted and gratified at one level of the spirit while remaining deeply unhappy at another; and so it was now with Maia. Naturally, the acclaim of the soldiers and the change in Anda-Nokomis had pleased her—she would scarcely have been human if they had not—yet she would gladly have given all in exchange for the longing of her heart.

In truth, she thought dismally, it boiled down to something very simple. It was nothing to do with what she had merited in the past or whatever she might merit now. It was nothing to do with the fortress at Dari-Paltesh or the escape from Pokada's prison; with the rafts or the waterfall or the Ortelgan camp. The plain truth was simply that Zen-Kurel was no longer in love with her. Once he had been and now he wasn't. She loved him but he did not love her.

In such a situation both merit and reason are alike immaterial.

Where love cannot fulfil itself through reciprocity, it can do so only through sacrifice. And this, of course, was the real reason why she had instantly told Elleroth that she was going to Suba and then evaded any discussion either of her motives or of the danger. If it was the last thing she did, she was going to play her part in Zen-Kurel's return to Katria. It might very well be the vital part, too, for a boat would cost money. Besides, did either of them know how to handle a boat? She doubted it. She alone had the money to buy a boat and the skill to sail it down the Zhairgen to Katria. What was going to become of her after that was immaterial. This was high truth. The low truth would keep till later.

This was her melancholy solace as Zen-Kurel politely greeted her that morning. Yet solace it was, sure enough, to see his obvious hopefulness and the eager spirit with which he discussed the final arrangements with Tolis as they prepared to set out.

She kissed Zirek good-bye with tears.

'I only hope you're doing the right thing, lass,' said he. 'I suppose you know best; but it's not too late to change your mind even now, you know.'

She shook her head, her eyes brimming.

'No, I can't do that. But I'll miss you, Zirek, very much I will. Don't forget me, will you?'

'That's not likely,' answered he. 'When I'm a rich man, with my own estate, I'll send for you to come and be my guest; you and your husband, eh?'

'Oh, Zirek—'

'Look, they're starting,' he said quickly. 'Don't get left behind, my pretty girl: that wouldn't do, would it? Might never get to Kat—I mean to Suba.'

He grinned, putting a hand on her shoulder. 'It's true what I said in the forest that night, you know. He *is* still in love with you. You wait and see if I'm not right. Only we never really seemed to get any time to talk, did we, you and me?'

He kissed her once more; then turned aside as Elleroth came up to wish her well. A minute or two later they were on their way.

Two of the soldiers were familiar with the country between the camp and Nybril; a half-wild, little-frequented district, the indeterminate borderland between Sarkid and Lapan. With these as guides they made their way unhurriedly downstream. All that morning they met no one, save for three young fellows out hawking and, later, an old man gathering sticks. This seemed encouraging. Local people, at least, were apparently ready to venture out on their normal business. Tolis asked the old man whether he was not afraid of robbers. The old man shrugged.

'One's always afraid. These are rough times. But you have to live, and I haven't much that any robber would want. I scratch a living and trust in the gods. What else can you do?' Maia gave him ten meld and they left him staring after them, shading his eyes with his hand.

After some six hours the guides were sure that they were now at least half-way to Nybril, and Tolis and Zen-Kurel began looking for a place to camp for the night.

Maia, having persuaded one of the soldiers to come with her to carry back her clothes, strolled half a mile upstream and swam down to cool off. Like the Urtans at the Olmen, the lad was disconcerted at her stripping naked, and she could not prevail upon him to walk back along the bank beside her. It was the same when she waded ashore: everyone was busy elsewhere. Yet in her absence they had done enough and more to show her what they felt for her. Camp had been pitched upon the edge of a little grove, and in the centre of this they had erected for her an arbour with which Lespa herself might not have been displeased. Leafy boughs had been bent, interlaced and tied down to form a kind of hedge round a central patch of turf, and here they had made her a bed of pliant branches and a mattress of grass covered with cloaks. At its head, strands of scarlet trepsis had been entwined on the hedge-wall to read 'Serrelinda'.

Later that evening she danced for them: 'Astiguata' and 'The Long

Reeds', two dances of Tonilda which she'd known from a child; artless stuff—hardly the thing to set the upper city alight. But then she had no Fordil—only their rhythmic clapping and a man who sang 'Diddle diddle di-do'. Yet she enjoyed it, while to the men it was like water in a desert. After supper enough wood was collected to keep a fire going all night, sentries were posted and most of the men were soon asleep.

Maia lay wakeful. A few stars twinkled through the branches and she could just make out the gentle, continuous lapping of the river fifty yards away. Nearer by sounded the minute rustlings of the thicket in the sultry dark. They had given her a personal sentry—more as a mark of esteem than from any real need she might have to be guarded—and from time to time she could hear the man quietly moving or clearing his throat a little way off among the trees.

It seemed to her now, in that state of half-dreamlike imagination often induced by silence, night and fatigue, that she herself had been gliding away—yes, a year and longer now—upon a river fully as grim as that which Zirek had evoked in his tarpli for Meris. She thought of all those she had encountered, good and evil, who had gone under in that river—Sencho, Sphelthon, Tharrin, Durakkon, Milvushina, Jarvil, Randronoth, Meris. She thought, too, of those whom likely enough she would never meet again—the three girls she still thought of as her sisters; Sednil, Ogma, Nennaunir, Otavis and above all, Occula. 'O Lespa!' she prayed. 'Sweet Lespa, that's preserved me through so much, preserve Occula too. Don't suffer that cruel woman to kill her; and let the two of us meet again one day. Let it be part of your dream.'

She herself was still adrift on that river which had killed so many. Towards what falls was she drifting now and where would she come ashore? Danger, she thought, always danger, danger. I live in danger like a fish in water. Never a safe bed and a strong, loving arm round me, same as any girl back in Meerzat.

Suddenly she sat up quickly, startled by sounds of movement just outside the entrance to her bower. The sentry was making some slight but deliberate noise to attract her attention. After a moment, his voice said, 'Säiyett?'

'What is it?' she said sharply.

'There's one of the gentlemen wants to speak to you, but he says only if you're not too tired.'

'Who is it?'

'It's the Suban lord, säiyett: Anda-Nokomis.'

Anda-Nokomis, that chilly exemplar of propriety, the last man in the empire to make his way to a girl's bed at night! Her curiosity was aroused. Whatever he might want, it could not be her body: and whatever it was he wished to say, he was giving her the option of refusal. But then he would, wouldn't he?

What could conceivably be at the back of this? She really could not refrain from finding out.

'Very well,' she answered. Drawing her cloak around her, she propped herself on her elbows and waited.

After a few moments Bayub-Otal, cloaked like herself, came quietly through the opening and sat down on the ground beside her. She could tell at once that he was agitated.

'Maia,' he said, speaking just above a whisper, 'thank you for letting me come. I haven't sent the sentry away, so you needn't worry about appearing compromised. I need to talk to you alone, and there seemed no other opportunity.'

'Not tomorrow, in Nybril?' She shrugged, putting on a little act of not being particularly interested but nevertheless bearing with his whim, however incorrect.

'I felt—I felt I ought to speak to you before we reach Nybril.'

'*Ought?* Why, what have I—'

'No, no! I only meant—'

He stopped. She had never seen him so hesitant and unsure of himself. This was not the haughty, frigid lord of Suba whom she had come to know so well.

'I—' Then, suddenly, 'Maia, what I want to say to you is that I've done you wrong. I've done a very grave wrong to your honour and integrity as a Suban, and I'm extremely sorry for it. May I ask your forgiveness?'

'Why, how's that, then, my lord?' This was disconcerting—embarrassing, too.

'Please don't call me that. Use my name.'

'Well, then, Anda-Nokomis, there's nothing to forgive.'

'Oh, yes, there is. If you had treated *my* honour as a Suban as I've treated yours, I believe it would have driven me to—'

She put her hand on his. 'Ah, well, but that's different, in't it? I'm not the Ban of Suba, am I?'

'I've slighted and insulted you on account of what you did before ever you knew yourself to be Suban. I've altogether failed to realize the depth of your loyalty to me or your feeling for Suba.'

I can't disabuse him, she thought. What good would it do? It'll be better for both of us if he goes on thinking I've been acting on account of being Suban. Zirek could see the truth, but not Anda-Nokomis, thank the gods.

'Well, dun't matter, Anda-Nokomis, honest. You needn't get so worked up; you're making me feel that awkward. Let's just say n'more about it.

951

Reckon I'd 'a felt the same as you if I'd bin shut up all that time in that old fortress.'

'If only you'd learned earlier that you were Suban—'

'Ah, well, but I didn't, did I? What's gone's gone; and now's now.'

'Yes,' he said agitatedly, 'now's certainly now; very much so. That's the rest of what I felt I had to say.'

She waited—truth to tell, with some little apprehension, for she knew her man, and this loss of self-possession was so much unlike him as to be disturbing. He seemed to need time to choose his words; hanging his head, plucking at the grass and once or twice looking up as though making a false start. Finally he said, 'To decide to go back to Suba: that shows exceptional courage, too.'

Another silence. 'You see, there'll be those who don't know what you and I know. They'll only know about the—about the Valderra.'

'Doesn't matter,' she answered listlessly, her thoughts already straying.

'It would matter to *me* if they killed you; it would matter very much, Maia.'

But not to me. O Lespa, I believe my heart's breaking! Why do I have to undergo all this talk of Suba and what's going to happen when Zenka's gone? Can't I find some way to get this man to go away?

Just as she was about to thank him for his kindness and ask him to leave her to sleep, he spoke again.

'Your loyalty to Suba—your loyalty to me, too—they do you more credit than I can express, Maia. I've come to realize that you're like me—you're not a person who asks for favours, are you? You prefer to let deeds speak for themselves. But I can't believe that it hadn't already crossed your mind that in choosing to go back to Suba you'd be in danger.'

Why can't he go? she thought.

'I felt sure it must have been worrying you, even though you're too courageous to talk about it or let anyone see it. That's why I came to speak to you tonight; to spare you any further worry as quickly as I could.'

As she shook her head uncomprehendingly, he took her hand in his.

'Maia, I love you. I've come to admire you and love you more than any woman I've known since my mother died. I've come to ask you to marry me—to be my wife in Suba. You'll be safe then; and happy, too, I sincerely hope and intend.'

She was taken so utterly by surprise that she could only stare at him. The idea of Anda-Nokomis as a lover—as any woman's lover—now seemed so incongruous, so anomalous as to seem totally out of character. It was as though he had said that he had decided to sell himself into slavery or become a priest of Cran. She realized now that she had never—no, not even at the time when Kembri had first put her in his way—thought of

952

Anda-Nokomis as a sexual being; as someone naturally capable of feeling desire. Yet she felt no impulse to laugh, as Nennaunir might have. Whatever else he might or might not be, Anda-Nokomis was a man of the most dutiful responsibility, a man of his word, who never spoke more than he felt, or intended to perform. If *he* said he loved her, what he meant was that he had formed the purpose of committing himself to being her loyal husband for the rest of his life: and also, as he had made clear, that he had considered the position she was bound to find herself in if she returned to Suba, and was ready to identify himself with it and make it his own personal concern.

The next thought that occurred to her was that, unlike Eud-Ecachlon, he did not stand to gain anything at all from marrying her, apart from herself. From the point of view of his public position she would, initially at all events, be the gravest possible liability. It was an enormous—an over-whelming—compliment; by far the greatest ever paid to her in her life. What he intended was nothing less than to invoke on her behalf the full weight of his authority as Ban of Suba, to reinstate and vindicate her in the eyes of those who would otherwise kill her. Yes, and to put that authority at risk, too, for it would take a fair old bit of carrying off, would that. They might not be so keen on him when he turned up with her and made it clear that he meant it. She could imagine the reaction of Lenkrit, for example, upon learning the news. But if she knew Anda-Nokomis, he had already thought about this. He said he loved her and he meant just that. She had in all actuality won his heart. Well (she couldn't help adding), what there was of it. For his, as she well knew, was a heart incapable either of glowing with warmth or sparkling with humour.

What a lot of strange and different things men meant when they said 'love', she thought: Tharrin, Elvair-ka-Virrion, Randronoth, Anda-Noko-mis. Pity they can't boil them all down together—sport, pleasure, generos-ity, desire, respect. If I had any sense I'd accept this offer from a high-born, honest man who means what he says and won't ever change. But I *haven't* any sense—either that or else too much. I don't love him—I can't feel anything for him—so what can it matter to me? Once, in Melvda-Rain, Maia, you had a gold crown, studded with diamonds: but it's gone, gone; so what would you prefer now—bronze, lead or copper? What do I care?

She began to cry from sheer mortification, seeing in her mind's eye Zen-Kurel, the way he walked, the curl of his hair, his trick of opening and closing his hand when he was considering a problem. Oh, don't go through it again! *Don't* start going through it all again, what the two of us said to each other that night in Melvda-Rain! Don't!

Anda-Nokomis was speaking. 'Oh, Maia, I'm sorry to have upset you. I only meant to relieve you of anxiety by speaking as soon as possible.'

953

She was trying to imagine herself as his wife. She could not—even though she respected him, even though it might make all the difference between safety and a death not so very different from Meris's. Such was her distress and confusion that she could only cling to him, sobbing.

'Maia—'

'I can't say anything, Anda-Nokomis. Not now. Leave me, please! Just leave me!'

At this moment, while the poor, perplexed man, who plainly did not know what to make of it, was still holding her silently in his arms, there were sudden sounds of alarm and commotion outside the grove. A voice shouted, 'Stand to!' followed by other voices, running footsteps and the clattering of arms hastily snatched up. Then came actual sounds of fighting, angry cries and the clang of weapon on weapon. These, however, ceased quickly, as though a scuffle had broken off short. Tolis's voice called, 'Tryzatt Miarn, get everyone on their feet!'

Bayub-Otal, without haste or the least sign of disquiet, gently released Maia and stood up. Having listened for a few moments, he said calmly, 'I suppose I'd better go and see what's happening,' went over to the gap by which he had entered and stepped outside.

'What is it, sentry?'

'Robbers, sir—something o' that. Tried to rush us, I reckon, but looks like the lads have seen them off.'

Bayub-Otal returned. 'I'll have to go. I'm sorry to leave you, Maia, but at least I know you're equal to it. I'll come back as quickly as I can.'

Left alone, Maia did not take long to decide against remaining where she was. Wrapping her cloak round her, she got up and went outside. Her sentry was standing with his back to her, looking out through the trees. Beyond, she could make out hurrying figures and firelight. She pushed quickly through the bushes as far as the sentry, who checked her with a movement of his arm.

'I wouldn't go out there, säiyett. Don't let them see you. Might just set 'em off again, like.'

'Don't worry, I won't show myself,' she answered. 'I only want to find out what's happening. You can come with me if you like.'

They went cautiously forward to the edge of the grove. In the light of the setting half-moon she could see Tolis standing to one side and in front of his men, who were drawn up in extended line. On the ground immediately in front of them lay two bodies: they were without armour and did not look like soldiers. From beyond, out in the dim scrub and fern, came intermittent taunts and cries of defiance.

'Go on, be off with you!' shouted Tolis. His voice, though clear and confident, was somewhat high in tone, and a mocking falsetto echoed, 'Be off with you!' followed by jeering laughter.

'You'll get nothing here,' cried Tolis again, 'unless a few more of you fancy being killed.'

At this the hubbub died down, and then a voice shouted, 'All right, then; give us food and we'll go.'

Tolis made no reply. A few stones came flying out of the darkness, together with a clumsily-made arrow which one of the soldiers turned aside with his shield.

'Kind of an awkward situation, sir,' said the tryzatt.

'You'd better get the men back,' said Tolis. 'They're too exposed. The only reason I put them out there was because I hoped it might frighten the bastards away.'

As the men, still maintaining line, came backing in among the trees, the same voice out of the darkness shouted, 'If you won't give us food we'll have to come and get it. We've had nothing for two days.'

'That's not our fault,' called back one of the men. 'Think we're going to waste our food on a pack of thieving swine like you?'

'We're not thieving swine,' answered the voice. 'We're respectable men, give us a chance. We're starving, that's what.'

It was the soldiers' turn to jeer in reply to this; but suddenly above the clamour rose a new voice. 'Where are you from?'

Maia started. It was Zen-Kurel, somewhere over to her left. Getting no answer, he repeated, 'I asked where have you come from?'

After a short pause someone in the dark answered 'Belishba.'

'Why?' asked Zen-Kurel.

'You'd bin there you wouldn' ask why.' Another voice added, 'They're free men in Sarkid, aren't they?'

'Runaway slaves,' said Tolis to the tryzatt. 'I thought as much. I dare say they *are* desperate, poor bleeders.'

'You say you're respectable men,' called Zen-Kurel. 'Well, now's your chance to show it, because I'm going to take you at your word.'

Next moment he had stepped out from among the trees and was walking purposefully out into the dark scrubland. Anda-Nokomis's voice called, 'Zenka, come back!'

Zen-Kurel turned for a moment and waved his hand; then he continued on his way.

'Silly basting bastard!' muttered one of the soldiers to his mate, a few yards away from Maia. 'What's he reckon to do, then?'

She sprang forward, startling the two men, who had not known she was there. 'No! No! Zenka, come back!'

She was running, shouting hysterically, when a soldier caught her round the waist and held her fast. She struggled, beating at him with her fists, then dropped her head on her chest, weeping. When Tolis and the tryzatt came up she had fainted and was lying on the ground with the soldier bending over her.

They splashed water in her face. After about half a minute she came to herself to find Tolis holding her by the shoulders.

'I beg you, säiyett, don't make a scene. The men are jumpy enough already.'

'O Lespa!' she moaned. 'Tolis, can't you stop him? Go and *stop* him!'

'Too late for that now, säiyett, I'm afraid. He didn't give me the chance. Get back, Dellior!' he called sharply to a man who had left the line, apparently to relieve himself. 'No one said anything about standing down!'

There was silence all along the line now, and silence from out in the scrubland also. Maia felt as though she had become a string about to snap. This tension was unendurable, this mute waiting in the yellow elf-light of the setting moon; nothing to be heard but the frogs in the half-dry river pools; nothing to be seen but the stillness of the arid fern. Once she allowed a low whimper to escape her. Tolis, on one knee close by, looked quickly round and shook his head.

She could not have told how long it was since Zen-Kurel had gone; only that the moon was lower and the suspense worse. She could hear the men whispering to one another, but caught no words.

'Should we give him a shout, sir?' asked Miarn.

'Not yet,' answered Tolis.

She realized that Anda-Nokomis was standing behind them, hunched and watchful as a heron in shallows. After a time he murmured almost inaudibly, 'Perhaps they've gone.'

'With him?' said Tolis.

'Or without him: no telling.'

Maia stood up. 'I'm going to—'

'Säiyett, please don't compel me to stop you.'

Just as she was wondering whether to draw her knife and make a dash for it, she caught sight of something moving out in the grey-yellow dimness. A shape—one person or more—was approaching. In a low voice Tolis said, 'Keep still! No one to speak!'

Within half a minute they could see that in fact three men were coming towards them.

'Is he there?' asked Tolis.

Maia passed her tongue over her dry lips. 'Yes.'

The men stopped some forty or fifty yards from the edge of the copse. Then Zen-Kurel's voice called, 'Tolis, can you hear me?'

Tolis answered and was about to go forward to join them when Zen-

956

Kurel spoke again. 'They don't want you to come any closer. I've just come to tell you what we're going to do.'

'Cran's zard!' muttered one of the soldiers. 'Basting man don't want to live!'

'These men aren't criminals,' said Zen-Kurel. 'They've escaped from slavery in Belishba and they've had a very bad time. They're quite ready to join Elleroth and I've assured them he'll be happy to take them on. So I'm going to guide them as far as the camp and act as surety for them. I expect to be back here by a couple of hours after dawn, but if I'm later than that, just go on to Nybril—don't wait for me.'

It was plain that none of this was to Tolis's liking. He appeared not only at a loss but flustered. 'What the hell are we going to do?' he asked the tryzatt. 'Damned Katrian! We're responsible to Elleroth for him!'

'Can't do nothing, sir,' replied Miarn. 'They've got him out there with them, haven't they?'

'Yes, but when Elleroth—' But before Tolis could say more, Bayub-Otal called out, 'Zenka, can I come with you?'

There was a pause, apparently while Zen-Kurel conferred with his companions. Then he answered, 'No, they say not.'

'Very well,' replied Bayub-Otal. 'We'll keep you some breakfast.'

'Elleroth's going to be glad a bunch of men like these weren't wasted,' called Zen-Kurel.

With this he and the other two turned and disappeared once more into the gloom. The frog-croaking silence returned.

'Stand 'em down, sir?' asked Miarn after two or three minutes.

'Oh, yes, any damned thing you like!' replied Tolis petulantly. 'You'd wonder who was in command here, wouldn't you?'

'D'you reckon he'll be back, sir?'

'Of course he won't!' said Tolis. 'Men like that? They'll cut his throat as sure as the rains are coming! These blasted Katrians—they're all the same—throw their lives away and call it soldiering! Karnat's wildcats! I believe they'd set themselves on fire just to try and show they were braver than anyone else! Why the hell couldn't he do it some time when we weren't responsible for him? Lord Elleroth's going to play hell! "Why did we let it happen?" As if *we* could have had any idea what he was going to do!'

'Going to wait for him, then, sir, or not?'

'I haven't decided yet,' said Tolis. 'I'll tell you tomorrow.'

He was walking away when Maia followed him.

'Can I speak to you?'

Tolis turned to her with the air of a young and harassed man retaining his self-control with difficulty.

957

'Säiyett, you're the last person to whom I'd want to be discourteous, but I've simply had enough for one night. Please go back to bed. We'll talk in the morning.'

Within the hour Maia had become so much demented with fear that she could no longer keep up appearances or conceal her distress. Her thoughts—if thoughts they could be called, that succession of visions and sensations overwhelming her mind like some evil dream—were plunged into a kind of vortex, a vicious circle from which there was no escape save hysteria. It was as though she were running in terror from one room to another, only to find herself fleeing at last back into the first. This first was a sense of panic horror, much like the shock felt by one who suddenly finds herself falling from a height, or wakes to realize that the house is burning. Then followed the images—apprehensions, vivid as flashes of lightning: Zenka surrounded and fighting for his life, Zenka tortured by the fugitive slaves, Zenka's body flung into the river, Zenka bleeding, Zenka murdered. And flying from these she ran full-tilt, as against a wall, into her awareness—like that of one hearing herself sentenced to death—that this was no dream, but reality; and taking place not in the past or the future, but in that present from which there is no escape. Thence to the weeping, the entreaties to the gods for reassurance—to the gods who could not give it. And so back to the panic and the horror. The Serrelinda, who had made her way into Pokada's prison and into the Ortelgan camp by night, was not equal to this unremitting torment of inaction.

A common, general misery, such as a flood or some civic calamity, has at least the effect of bringing people together and uniting them in fortitude and mutual succour: 'I mustn't let the others down.' Perhaps the worst of a private affliction is its effect of isolation. Personal grief, like deafness or a glass prison, sequesters the sufferer and separates her from others, who cannot by the nature of things enter into her agony. Even so may one see a maimed animal limping on among the indifferent herd.

The near-by soldiers were far away, in a world where people talked together, kept watch, slept or rolled dice by the fire: they were close—as close as sane men standing by the bedside of one who knows he has gone mad.

Maia was aware that Anda-Nokomis was sitting beside her, since from time to time he spoke to her or touched her hand. Yet it was little he said, seeming as he did to find her affliction almost as grievous as she herself; though his recourse, characteristically, was to silence and to that lonely patience which had so long been habitual with him.

She knew that most, if not all, of the soldiers felt sure that Zen-Kurel had thrown his life away for nothing and that they thought him a fool for doing it. If anything they despised him, since his valuation of the risk he had taken was beyond their comprehension, much as the incentive of an explorer seems foolish to those who wonder why he could not have stayed safely at home.

She made no attempt to talk to Anda-Nokomis, simply keeping her lonely suffering, as it were, alight for a lamp which might somehow guide Zenka back. Yet even this flickered and died at last as she fell asleep from exhaustion.

Her sleep was full of dreams; or rather of visitations, without visual images or even any illusion of sequence in time; dreads and forebodings, by their very universality and formlessness more intense and veritable than any to be suffered in real, waking life: like huge, hazy masses driven before a great wind—transcendental sorrow made manifest—towering over and dwarfing all emotion of which mere humanity was capable. She stifled in clouds of anguish, lay buried under mountains of regret, struggled and drowned in cataracts of loss. And she, who had been unable to sleep—she could not wake.

At last, contracting, as it were, in order to enter the finite, visible world, the cloud-dreams crystallized into figments she could apprehend and seem to see—persons, time, even a situation. It seemed that Zenka—her own Zenka, her lover as he had once been—had indeed returned and was standing beside her bed in Melvda-Rain. He was weary and travel-worn, yet full of pride and fulfilment; at which she felt no surprise, for it was once more the night when they had become lovers. Yet now Anda-Nokomis was there also; a strangely two-minded Anda-Nokomis, at one and the same time glad and despite himself sorry to see Zenka back.

Zenka spoke to him. She seemed to hear his very words. 'It was well worth the risk. Good men, some of them—thousand pities if they'd been killed in a pointless scrap.'

'Why,' she cried gladly, 'that's just how *I* felt, too, that night in Melvda! You understand then, don't you? We understand each other now, Zenka, my darling—'

As she seemed to say this, an enormous relief and happiness filled her, a certainty that now everything would be all right. Yet he appeared not to hear, even though he was looking down at her as Anda-Nokomis laid a hand on his shoulder in congratulation.

'She was very nearly your only casualty,' he said. 'I've really been afraid for her reason. She's been in a terrible state.'

She tried to move, to stretch out her hands, tried to speak again, but it had become one of those dreams in which you couldn't. And now Zenka—it seemed to be his turn to appear two-minded. He frowned, looking down and tapping with one foot on the ground.

'Then all I can say is, it's been *her* turn to know what it feels like.'

King Karnat's trumpet was sounding for the muster. Zenka went away and she knew she had to go and swim the Valderra again. The soldiers had pulled her out and were bending over her.

She opened her eyes. It was Anda-Nokomis. Slowly, she remembered where they were and what had happened last night. Had she then been dreaming or awake—or both?

It was broad daylight. She sat up, looking round at the interlaced branches, the drooping, withered trepsis bloom spelling 'Serrelinda' and at Anda-Nokomis beside her.

He smiled his restrained, distant smile. 'Our friend's back.'

'He's back?'

'He was here just now, while you were still asleep. He got those men to the camp quite successfully and handed them over to Elleroth. I don't think he was gone nine hours altogether.' He paused. 'Twenty miles and a sleepless night; but more peaceful than some people's, I think, all the same.'

Relief surged over her as over an exhausted castaway washed up on a beach. She wanted nothing: the immediate moment was enough. She lay back, content merely to remain where she was and know that Zenka was alive. So fully did this feeling possess her that for some time she did not even mind that in this woken, real state they were not reconciled and that of course he could not have heard what she had said to him in her dream. No matter. She would still be able to help him to get to Katria; still be able to make her sacrifice. That was enough, for she had thought herself deprived of it and now she had it back, the bitter solace of her integrity.

: 97 :
NYBRIL

They brought her some food, and Tolis sent to enquire whether she still wanted to talk to him. Yes, she said, and when he came thanked him graciously and sincerely for looking after her when she'd lost her head the night before; so that he hardly knew what to reply. Well, he'd acted as he thought best: he hoped she didn't mind: decisions weren't always easy: sometimes these things had to be done. Neither of them mentioned Zen-Kurel.

Maia, little though she knew of soldiering, could not help being impressed by the practised ease with which the Sarkidians cleaned up and cleared the camp site. Having no axes for a pyre or spades for burial, they could only commit the two dead men to the river. Both were young and not ill-looking, though sadly gaunt and famished. One, so Maia thought, a little resembled Sednil. She felt full of pity for them. At her request (she doubted whether it would have been done otherwise), the tryzatt brought her some grain, salt and wine to fling after them into the river. She picked an armful of flowers, too—thydis and marjoram, bartsia and planella—sprinkled them on the current and as they drifted away offered a prayer that the young men might meet with Sphelthon and share his peace.

'You didn't feel in any danger?' she asked Zen-Kurel as they were setting out. She felt able, now, to address him directly, though still avoiding any suggestion of warmth or particularly friendly feeling. He, for his part, seemed to have come to regard their relationship as one between two people working with mutual respect towards a common end, without seeking or expecting more.

'No one need have felt in any danger,' he replied. 'It should never have been allowed to come to blows at all.' Then, as Tolis came up, he shrugged and broke off with the air of one refraining from criticism of colleagues, however well justified.

It was no more than nine or ten miles to Nybril, which they reached about noon. Unconsciously, Maia had entertained in her mind a picture of a place something like Meerzat—a little, riparian town, with regular trade and boats coming and going as on Lake Serrelind. The reality was dis-appointingly—indeed, dauntingly—different. Nybril Point, the rocky bluff rising above the confluence of the Flere and the Zhairgen, possessed no harbour remotely resembling Meerzat's sheltered, south-facing bay. Almost the sole advantage of the place lay in its virtual impregnability, a narrow triangle of which two sides were rivers. Long ago, some baron had built a castle there, but for many years past no baron had wished to live in so uninviting a spot, whose only mercantile value was as a stopping-off point for wool- and timber-laden rafts coming down the Flere from Yelda. (There was a depôt on the upper Flere about ten miles south of Ikat.) In years to come Sarkid was to develop Nybril, constructing a mole and introducing ferries to either shore, but at this period of the empire's history it was still little more than a windy rock where a largely hereditary com-munity of about two thousand souls were content to eke out a living in the knowledge that they were at least secure from pillage. Strangers, apart from the raft-men and occasional pedlars, were rare and not particularly welcome, since their reasons for coming were suspect.

The arrival of Tolis and his men, whose approach had of course been observed and reported an hour earlier, was watched by a fair-sized crowd from the walls on either side of the gates. His authority from Elleroth having been duly accepted, he was accorded a reserved welcome by the

Elder, who nevertheless unbent slightly upon being told that the soldiers were to leave before nightfall.

A man appointed to act as guide escorted Maia, Zen-Kurel and Anda-Nokomis half-way down the steep, western slope of the headland to 'The White Roses', one of the two or three inns in the town, which was also a fishing-tackle store and a corn chandler's. It hardly measured up to 'The Safe Moorings', and although Maia had never had any great opinion of Frarnli, she was in no doubt that Frarnli would have been able to keep the place a deal cleaner, tackle store or no. She had not sat down for long on the little upstairs balcony before the warmth of her body brought a swarm of ticks out of the woodwork of her chair.

They were eating fish broth with black bread when Tolis came in to tell them, with aloof but self-conscious correctness, that he was now leaving. If he had been expecting any sort of protest he was disappointed. Zen-Kurel, having ordered up a bottle of wine to drink to Elleroth's fortunes and a speedy heldro victory (which Tolis could hardly decline) thanked him most courteously for all he had done for them and then insisted on accompanying him to the town gates to bid farewell to tryzatt Miarn and the men.

Anda-Nokomis went too but Maia, who felt angry, stayed behind. Having slept until the cool of the evening, she washed in a pail of tepid river water and then went out onto the balcony, taking with her a stool which she hoped would prove to be without inhabitants.

She had a spacious view of the confluence, and for the best part of an hour, with the slowly-setting sun full in her eyes, sat contemplating the scene below her, the converging rivers and the comings and goings on land and water. To her left the Flere, boundary between Sarkid and Belishba, came flowing down from a blue distance of woods interspersed with cultivated, plain-like country. Far off, she could make out grazing flocks and smoke-crowned villages. A peaceful, fertile country it looked—Sarkid of the Sheaves, the hero Deparioth's land. On her right the upper Zhairgen came swirling round the base of the rocky promontory which cut off her view of the wilder country through which they had just come. She recalled how someone, at a party in Bekla, had once described Nybril to her as being like the stone in a cherry.

Yet it was the water below her—the water and what was on it—which most closely engaged her attention. As we know, Maia was knowledgeable about water, and what principally struck her was its unpleasant choppiness and general look of nasty, unmanageable turbulence. Where the two main-streams met there was a clearly visible seam and an extensive area of broken water, in which she could see logs, large branches and other flotsam tossing and tumbling. Maia, like everyone else in the empire, was accustomed almost unconsciously to animate impressive places and natural phenomena, just as she had animated the forest of Purn. Under that water, she felt unreflectingly, dwelt a spirit—demi-god or demon—harshly jealous of his realm, who brooked human beings thereon with an ill grace and hard sufferance.

Nybril, as she could now appreciate, was suitable for a river port only to the extent that from it, during the summer, merchandise could be sent downstream on rough, expendable rafts. The town had not grown up as a port but as a stronghold. The current was too strong for the place to be readily accessible except from upstream. It could never enjoy Meerzat's regular, easy comings and goings of boats. To be sure, there were a few small ones tied up along the little front below, but they did not look at all strongly built or fit for rough water, and she supposed that they were used only for fishing under the lee of the promontory and perhaps for direct crossings into Belishba at seasons, such as this, when the water was low and the current slack enough to permit of it.

The sinking sun turned the whole, receding expanse of the river—the broadest she had ever seen—to a dull crimson, glittering with quick streaks and flashes of gold. By contrast, the great cracks in the dried mud exposed along the banks showed pitch-black—deep, jagged crevices as broad as a man's hand. Even up here, high above the meeting-point of the two rivers, there seemed to be no breeze. The big, palmate leaves on the trees below her hung still as though waxen and nothing stirred the white dust that covered the steep zig-zag of the lane descending to the quay. I ought to feel at peace, she thought: there's no danger and there's a bed for the night. And yet I feel—well, I dunno: it's not right, somehow; it's not what I expected. I'll be glad when we've been able to get fixed up to go.

Hearing a movement behind her, she turned to see Anda-Nokomis standing in the entrance to the balcony. She smiled and gestured to him to join her, but though he came forward to sit beside her he did not smile in reply.

'Soldiers gone?' she asked.

'Oh, yes; some time ago now.'

'I ought to have gone to thank them myself. Wish I had, now.'

'You can't be blamed,' he answered. 'That young Tolis fellow should never have taken them away. He did it out of pure ill-humour. They very nearly mutinied: they'd been looking forward to a night on the town—such as it is.'

'You mean he resented what Zenka did last night?'

'I do.'

'I wish I was still—well, what I used to be,' she said. 'I'd 'a seen as he heard some more about it 'fore I'd done.'

'But if you were, it would never have happened, would it?'

She laughed, but once again he did not.

'You never laugh, Anda-Nokomis. I could make a beggar laugh easier 'n what I can you.'

'I *am* a beggar, actually. I don't particularly like coming to ask you for money, but I've no alternative. The man insists on a down payment to-night. I don't know where he thinks we might disappear to, I'm sure. I nearly refused, but it would have been more trouble than it's worth.'

'How much, Anda-Nokomis?'

'Three hundred meld.'

'You'd best take three thousand, and give some of it to Zenka. Then you needn't either of you go short or be caught without. Come on, now—' as he hesitated—'that'll be best for all of us. You don't want to look silly or short of money in front of these people.'

'But will that leave you with enough?'

'Did ought!'

'Are you sure?'

'I'll count it out in front of you if you like, Anda-Nokomis.'

This time he did smile as he shook his head. She gave him the money and they were silent for a little while, watching the glow fade from the breadth of the river below.

'Did *you* resent—well, anything that happened last night?'

She looked round at him quickly. 'Oh, no, Anda-Nokomis, never!'

Yet evidently he was expecting her—waiting for her—to say more. She sought for something—anything—to smooth over the situation. He deserved all the kindness of which she was capable. 'How *could* I resent it?'

'Why, as I said, because I've treated you badly and insulted you. I misjudged you, Maia.'

'And *I* said, didn' I, as that was all over? No, Anda-Nokomis, of course I didn't resent you asking me to marry you. And I believe you when you say you love me. I reckon we both understand each other better now than what we ever have, don't you?'

'And yet—I don't have to ask for my answer, do I? If I'd known earlier how you feel, I might not have spoken. But you'd succeeded in keeping your feelings very well concealed until the moment when you actually thought Zenka had gone to his death last night. I had no idea.'

Would he ever make a ruler, she wondered; a man capable of perceiving so little?

'But Anda-Nokomis, at that rate why ever did you think I got him out of the gaol in Bekla?'

'Why, you could have had several reasons: because you'd learned he'd been my closest friend in Dari-Paltesh, because you knew it would please Santil-kè-Erketlis, or simply because you weren't going to leave a man like that to the mercy of Fornis.'

That was the trouble about Anda-Nokomis, she thought. To himself he made perfectly good sense and you couldn't really argue with it. And it was all rubbish; it missed the only real point. Her feelings had been plain both to Zirek and to Clystis: probably to Meris, too. Fortunately, however, she didn't have to say this. While she was still wondering what she *could* say, he spoke again.

'But Maia, I'm afraid that at that rate it must be very disappointing for you.'

'Unless,' she said suddenly, as the idea came into her head '—I've only just thought—unless I *wasn't* altogether dreaming.'

'Dreaming? When?'

'When he said about it being my turn to know what it felt like.'

He frowned. 'I'm sorry, I'm afraid I don't—'

She dropped on her knees beside him, put her arms round his neck and kissed him—the first time she had ever done so.

'My lord—my cousin—my dear friend: I'll tell you one thing, anyway— I've never been paid a greater compliment in my life, and I'm sure I never shall be again. I mean that with all my heart!'

'There's nothing more to be said, then?' he replied.

'There can't be: I'm so sorry.'

'But Suba, Maia—your safety—'

She threw back her head and laughed as gaily as once she had in the fishing-net. 'Occula used to say "Stuff it!" Look, Anda-Nokomis, we're here, the three of us, something like eighty miles from Katria and Suba, and no real idea yet how we're going to get there. You said—and don't think I don't feel it very kindly—that you wanted to relieve my anxiety. Surely the best way to relieve *everybody's* anxiety is to put all this by just for now, and stick to the job of getting ourselves down-river. 'Cos tell you the truth, I reckon 'tain't going to be all that easy. If you really want to do something for me, do that.'

He was silent for what seemed a long time. 'Perhaps you're right,' he said at last. 'We'll do as you say.'

He stood up. 'Where's Zenka, do you know?'

'No; I thought you did.'

'Let's go and find him—have a drink—order a good supper—anything you like. And then tomorrow we'll see about getting a boat.'

AN UNEXPECTED MEETING

When Maia woke the following morning—not quite so badly bitten as she had expected—it was to the certainty that the rains were imminent. Since 'The White Roses' lay half-way down the western slope of Nybril, there was no view to the east even from its roof, but nevertheless she could sense the oppression, the piling-up of the clouds far away beyond Tonilda, beyond Yelda and Chalcon. Soon the wind would begin and the white mist would come rolling. Everyone would be glad of the rains, glad of the relief, the release; everyone but themselves, stranded on this rock in the Zhairgen. What if they were forced to spend Melekril here?

She said nothing of her apprehensions, however, either to Anda-Nokomis or to Zenka. It was plain that they had not seen the place and its limitations so clearly as she. They thought they were going to go out, much as they might go to a market, buy a boat and go down the river. Well, possibly they would: she wasn't going to start discouraging them or letting them think she was trying to show how clever she was. She'd come along and see what happened.

After breakfast they set out together, down the steep lane winding between hovels, stone walls and hedges of grey-leaved keffa-kolma—the only thing that'll grow here, I suppose, thought Maia: back home we used to pull it up and burn it.

At length they emerged on to the quay-side. A few boats were out fishing. As she had expected, they were all anchored—or perhaps foul-anchored—well within the area of calmer water above the meeting-point of the two streams. One or two had masts, but not a sail was hoisted in the still air. None had either deck or cabin or was what you'd call, she thought, a travelling craft.

Anda-Nokomis, seeing a little group of men busy with tackle a short distance away, went up to them and, having greeted them politely, said he wanted to buy a boat stout enough to travel down the river. This, as Maia could have told him, was a mistake. She herself, if she'd been a man, would have passed the time of day, talked about the coming of the rains, asked a few questions about the fishing, repeated a rumour or two of the fighting in Lapan and said nothing at all about boats until someone— either that time or next time—got as far as asking what might have brought her to Nybril.

Oh, ah, they said. A boat? Well. One asked another to chuck him that length of line over there. Did he reckon it could do with a bit more grease rubbed in? Anda-Nokomis, interrupting, asked them whether they knew of anyone who would sell a boat. A boat? Well, now, they couldn't say. There wasn't all that many boats sold, really, not without a man was to die, and not always then. Boats—well, they nearly always got passed on, didn't they?

But might not someone sell one exceptionally, Anda-Nokomis persisted. Well, they hadn't just exactly heard of anything like that; not just lately they hadn't. Every man had his own, you see. Needed it for his living, didn't he?

What was the river like further down, enquired Zen-Kurel. They shook their heads. They didn't really know. None of them had ever been all that far down. It was the getting back, you see, wasn't it? Strong current—well, yes, everyone knew that. Very dangerous for a lot of the year, specially in the rains. Oh, yes, desperate in the rains. Well, and after all, what would anyone be wanting to go down there for? Quickest way to get yourself drowned. Someone else sucked on a hollow tooth, spat in the water and nodded in corroboration.

With them and with others Anda-Nokomis spent nearly a couple of hours pursuing enquiries. No one was uncivil, though one or two seemed sullen; but always he found himself helpless in the face of that reticent, non-committal evasiveness which is the reaction of most remote-dwelling people the world over to a brisk, direct approach from a stranger. Maia, who had grown up among such people, understood their feelings very well, though she could not have explained them in words. These people depended for a sense of security on doing what they and their fathers had always done in the only place they had ever known. That much they could feel sure of. Anything new or unusual probably had a catch in it. They were prone to a kind of cryptic envy, too. This stranger, this gentleman was eager for a boat; they had only to do nothing in order to frustrate him. (And indeed after a time, although he retained his courtesy and self-possession, Anda-Nokomis's frustration began to show fairly clearly.) Towards the end of the morning and at about the tenth enquiry, Maia was left in little doubt that their fame was travelling before them.

Once Zen-Kurel, falling into conversation with a couple of youths who were playing *wari* with coloured pebbles in the shade of a tavern wall, and finding them comparatively forthcoming in response to a few jokes and a little banter, asked whether it might not be possible to obtain a passage on one of the rafts coming down the Flere from Yelda. Why, yes, they answered. People often travelled down on the rafts, though usually from higher upstream. There wasn't all that many started from Nybril, though. Yes, it was the Flere pretty well all the rafts came down: very few down the upper Zhairgen. Lapan and Tonilda didn't go for the same markets downstream—or so they'd always understood. But very likely the gentle-man would know more about that than what they did.

But there wouldn't be any more rafts coming down the Flere now. It was the rains, you see, as'd be starting any day. Oh, yes, both the rivers got fair desperate during Melekril. They'd break any raft to bits like you'd break an egg in a pan. 'Twas like the wrath of Cran to see the water going past the rock. You couldn't sleep in your bed at night for the roaring.

By this time Maia was beginning to feel embarrassed and ill-at-ease. She had grasped the situation clearly enough and disliked looking conspicuous and—she suspected—silly. She could imagine how she herself and Kelsi, only a year or two back, would have stood giggling to watch Anda-Nokomis striding up and down like a pair of shears. Want the truth, this just wasn't a place where boats were to be bought. Any man who made a boat made it for himself; and any family who owned a boat used it and needed it. If anyone was to buy a boat in Nybril, it would be an altogether exceptional transaction, involving probably a few days of preliminary drinking and talk to get a man out of his shell, followed by suggestion, negotiation and bargaining. Zenka, with a little coaching, might be the man for it, but Anda-Nokomis certainly wasn't.

Acting on impulse—well, what the hell, she said to herself, if *she* didn't need a drink who did and anyway she was past caring about convention—she unobtrusively left Zen-Kurel (Anda-Nokomis was about two hundred yards away, pursuing some line of his own) and went quickly round the corner to the door of the tavern. Now that she was able to view it up and down, it looked a good deal more inviting than one would have expected. It was called 'The Butt Inn' and had a sign depicting, on one side, a goat impelling a customer through the door. On the other side, inevitably, were Shakkarn and Lespa, though portrayed quite decently and even rather attractively, considering that this was Nybril. Both the door, which was standing open, and the shutters had plainly been re-painted quite recently and there were boxes of flowers on the window-sills. One or two people were sitting outside on benches. She couldn't hear anything in the way of rowdy noise or low company from inside, and as she paused in the doorway all she could smell was clean sand and baking bread. Nice surprise, she thought: well, here goes.

Maia, of course, was more than used to being stared at. Upon her entry—oops! one step down—she could see very little, her eyes not having adapted from the sunny glare outside. She could sense, however, that a few people were looking at her. At the same time—and this, which was rather puzzling, she perceived distinctly as soon as her sight began to return—they didn't seem particularly bothered or surprised. In the Beklan empire women seldom went into taverns alone, and if they did were usually either frowned upon or else asked if they would care to step into the back room. Maia had been expecting the latter. On the contrary, however, the atmosphere seemed positively friendly. Two rather prosperous-looking men drinking at a side table smiled and nodded to her, while a big fellow with untidy hair, a slight limp and a clean sacking apron, who was filling a jug from a barrel in the far corner of the room, put it down, came over and asked her politely what he could have the pleasure of getting for her.

Maia's opinion of Nybril began to improve. This was almost up to Beklan standards—lower city, anyway. Why couldn't they have put up here, she wondered, instead of that mouldy old 'White Roses'? She ordered a bowl of serrardoes and a good, big jug of Yeldashay. She'd just have a quick cupful herself and then go out and call the others in to join her.

'A big one, säiyett?' said the potman. 'Expectin' comp'ny, eh?'

'Why, yes,' she smiled. 'How did you guess?'

'Oh, I've got second sight,' he answered, chuckling in a rather familiar way which slightly annoyed her. 'Won't keep you a moment, säiyett. Just let me know if you want any—er—help, won't you?'

The serrardoes were crisp and fresh and the Yeldashay was at any rate passable. She drank half a cupful and leaned back in her chair, feeling distinctly better. At this moment, looking up, her eye met that of another girl, perhaps two or three years older than herself, who was sitting by herself under the window on the far side of the room. She was a pretty girl, with a good complexion and fair hair, neatly if rather flashily dressed, and she was looking at Maia with a not unfriendly but rather puzzled expression.

Maia, not unnaturally, could tell a shearna when she saw one. That explained everything, of course. The Butt Inn, though obviously not a brothel, must be a place of resort for shearnas, who no doubt paid a commission to the house. Naturally, she had heard of such places, but had never actually been in one before. Plainly the first thing to do was to reassure the girl that she was not going to try to move in on her territory.

She refilled her cup, stood up and strolled across to the window. She was just about to speak when the girl spoke first.

'She didn't tell me anything about you.'

'Who?' asked Maia.

'Well, Almynis, of course. Still, never mind; why don't you come and sit here, with me? Shirgo!' she called to the potman, pointing across to Maia's wine-jug and serrardoes. 'Can you bring—' she turned back to Maia—'What's your name?'

'Maia.'

'Oh, yes, everyone calls themselves Maia now, don't they, since the Valderra? What's your real name?'

Maia laughed. 'It really is Maia.'

The potman brought over her wine-jug and serrardoes and she topped up the girl's cup. She was beginning to have quite a reassuring feeling of old times. Perhaps Nennaunir and Otavis would be dropping by in a minute.

'I suppose Almynis forgot. Or did you only meet her this morning or something?'

'Look,' said Maia, 'I'll be straight with you. I'm not working here at all, not for Almynis or anyone else. I only got to Nybril last night and I just happened to drop in here for a drink, that's all.'

'In *here*! By your*self*?'

'Well, like I said, I'm strange to Nybril: I've had a rather trying morning and I just fancied a drink.'

The girl nodded towards her jug. 'What, that lot?'

'Well, you see, I'm with a couple of fellows, and they're still doing a bit of business outside. They'll be here in a minute or two. What's *your* name?'

'Mesca, I'm called.' They both smiled. 'Mesca' was not a recognized girl's name. It meant 'Twilight', a typical shearna's sobriquet.

'Have you been long with this Almynis?' asked Maia.

'Well, nobody has, actually. We're still building up the business, you see—or she is, anyway. She only came here herself about eight or nine months ago; I'm not sure where from, tell you the truth. I was one of her first girls. I've been married, actually, but poor Lindulel—my husband— he was drowned a couple of years back, and by the time I met Almynis last spring I'd had enough of trying to make ends meet on half of nothing.'

Maia nodded sympathetically. 'Better 'n mucking out the cows, in't it?'

'Oh, you *have* done a bit, then?'

'Well, yes; back where I come from; only like I said, I'm not doing anything just now. Tell me how Almynis works—or how you work for her.'

Mesca looked at her genially but shrewdly. 'Well, great thing about Almynis is, she came here with quite a bit of money. She told me she'd heard about this house being up for sale on the edge of town—you know, usual thing, old man died and the next of kin in Ikat reckoned they'd rather have the money than the house. Anyway, Almynis bought it and I tell you, she's really turned it into something. She must have spent a packet on it. There's about half a dozen of us working for her now. She drives a damned hard bargain, but by Cran! she doesn't half know the job. Must have had a lot of experience somewhere. She gets more out of the fellows than ever the likes of you and me could working on our own, and a fair old bit gets passed on, you see, so I reckon it's worth it. 'Sides, she's got a lot of style. Makes you feel better, working in a nice place. Oh, I do just about hate anything squalid, don't you?'

Maia agreed. 'But is there really that much—you know—business in a place like Nybril?'

'More than you'd think,' answered Mesca. 'You see, all summer there's the rafts coming down the Flere, and Almynis's house is right on the water. Those raft fellows are all out on their own, money to spend, and Almynis makes damned sure they've nowhere better to spend it. What she offers is a good supper, a girl all night and breakfast in the morning— that's for those that can afford it. And they pay all right, believe you me. But there's quite a bit of local business too—you'd be surprised. You see, like I said, Almynis knows how to get a bit of style and glamour into it. There's a really nice garden going down to the water, and one or two smart little boats an' that—'

'Boats? Did you say boats?'

Mesca laughed. 'There's some fellows like doing it out of doors, and some seem to like doing it in a boat, for some reason. Well, that old High Counsellor in Bekla, he was doing it in a boat when they killed him, wasn't he? You must know about that, surely?'

Maia admitted to having heard something about it. 'But then,' she went on, 'if you work at this place of Almynis's, what are you doing here now?'

'Ah! I'm what Almynis calls a flesh-and-blood proclamation; cheese in the mousetrap, dear. Obviously she can't make proclamations through the town crier, so she makes them through displaying us where we can be seen. Only like I was telling you, we're building up the business. It's off-season now for the rafts, you see, so we're up for a bit more local custom, if we can get it interested.'

She was about to go on when they looked up to find themselves confronted by the men who had smiled at Maia when she came in. Or to be more accurate, they were confronted by Shirgo, the potman, who asked Mesca whether he might have the pleasure of introducing her and her friend to two very pleasant gentlemen. (Maia noticed him pocketing their ten meld.)

At this moment Maia would have found an excuse to leave, if it had not been for what Mesca had said about Almynis's establishment, which had interested her considerably. She smiled at the men, poured them each a drink from her jug and settled back in her chair as they began the sort of conversation usually pursued in situations of this nature.

After the four of them had been talking and drinking together for no more than a few minutes, one of the men, obviously eager to get in ahead of his companion, asked Maia point-blank how much she wanted for her favours. It was like 'The Bow and Quiver' at Khasik over again, only this time there was no Zuno—and no Occula.

There was no timid little Tonildan peasant-girl, either. The Serrelinda, of course, was fully up to handling a contingency of this sort, and was about to do so when Mesca, obviously with the kindly intention of sparing a younger girl embarrassment, weighed in on her behalf. She repeated the joke about being a flesh-and-blood proclamation, and then explained to the men that while there were no facilities on the premises, she was the living proof that if they cared to go a little way upstream to Almynis's house on the riverside they could, at a most reasonable price, have more pleasure than they had ever imagined possible. Thereupon, the first man immediately asked Maia whether she personally would be there.

Maia had no wish to upset Mesca, to whom she had taken rather a liking, or to spoil business for an honest if somewhat rustic shearna. She smiled and said well, she might, she wasn't sure. You see, there was a gentleman as had particularly asked her to visit him that afternoon—she couldn't tell quite how long she'd be. It really was very nice at Almynis's, though, she could assure them.

After a few more minutes the men, having grasped that this was a case of somewhere else and later on, took themselves off, assuring Mesca that she was a fine girl and they'd be seeing her later, and her pretty friend too. As they went out into the sun-glare, Mesca raised her head and pouted her lips at Maia in a mock kiss.

'Thanks, Maia. That was nice of you and I won't forget it. But now, do tell me why you've come here and what you're doing in Nybril. *Two* fellows, you said? Lucky old you!'

Maia thought quickly. 'Well, yes and no. Funny thing is, neither of them's mine, believe it or not. We—well, we're survivors, really. The fighting's been bad, you know, up in Lapan. We lost everything and a lot of people got killed. I've seen that I couldn't tell you! All same, the three of us got away and managed to get down here.'

Mesca gave her another shrewd glance. 'Deserters?'

Maia shrugged.

'D'you need money, Maia?'

She shrugged again. 'Who doesn't?'

'Have you thought of working for Almynis? You could make a nice little bit—well, just part-time if you wanted—see you through Melekril, wouldn't it? Only like I said, we're out to expand a bit if we can.'

'Tell me again where it is,' replied Maia. 'If I can get away, I'll come out and see your Almynis. P'raps 's afternoon.'

'Shall I tell her to expect you, then?'

'Yes. Yes, all right, Mesca! But if it's all the same to you, I'll be slipping along now. It's just that I'd rather not let these fellows of mine know—not just for the moment, anyway.' She kissed Mesca quickly on the cheek. 'You c'n finish what's left in my jug, can't you? Ought I to leave something for Shirgo? Only, I mean, he doesn't know, does he, but what I——?'

'Don't worry; I'll see to that,' answered Mesca.

Emerging into the sunshine, Maia almost collided with Anda-Nokomis in the doorway.

'Why, Maia, we've been looking everywhere for you! We couldn't think where you'd got to.'

'I only went for a drink, Anda-Nokomis.'

'By yourself? In a place like this?'

'Believe me, Anda-Nokomis, it's a lot less dangerous than the upper city. Let's go back to dinner, shall we? P'raps we'll have some better luck later on.'

Pleading fatigue and the heat, she had gone to lie down until Zenka and Anda-Nokomis were safely out of the way, still pursuing their search. She was worrying about what to do with her money and valuables while she went to Almynis's house. Funny, she thought, lying on her bed in the still heat of the afternoon and looking round the bare little room; when she'd set off for the Ortelgan camp by night, she'd carried the lot and never given the matter a thought; and here she was, bothering herself about what to do with them while she paid a visit to a small-town pleasure-house. Well, she could only suppose that that night the greater danger had driven the lesser one out of her head. That night, she'd reckoned on being killed. She wasn't supposing that she'd be killed at Almynis's, but she did think it was within the bounds of possibility that she might be robbed.

What would Occula do? She pondered, and suddenly it occurred to her what Occula probably *would* do. Having found a couple of inches of unstitched seam along the edge of the mattress, she thrust well into the flock everything except a thousand meld. Three hundred of this she put back into her tunic pocket; the rest, tied up in a towel, she carried downstairs.

The landlord was dozing on a bench. She roused him.

'I'd be very grateful for your help: two things, really.'

As usual, it was an advantage to be a pretty girl. He smiled broadly.

'Of course, säiyett.'

'When I was up north, I was asked to deliver a letter to a lady in Nybril called Almynis. Do you happen to know where she lives?'

He chuckled. 'Oh, ah, yes, säiyett, of course. Very nice lady. Rich lady, too. It's not so far from here, her house. Shall I tell the boy to take the letter for you?'

'No, thank you. I have to talk to her myself. But I'd be grateful if the boy could come along to show me the way.'

'Of course, säiyett: I'll call him.'

'The other thing: I've—er—got rather a large sum of money here: I'd rather not go out with it on me. I was wondering if you'd very kindly look after it until I come back?'

'Certainly, säiyett: but I hope you don't want any of that there writing, saying how much an' that. Only there's no one in this house can write.'

'Oh, I know I can trust you,' she smiled. 'It's only that it *is* rather a lot— all I've got, actually.'

'How much, säiyett?'

'Well—seven hundred meld.' And she looked at him wide-eyed.

'Oh, yes: that'll be all right, säiyett. It'll be perfectly safe with me.'

She counted it into his hand and two minutes later was on her way, escorted by the pot-boy. It was not very likely now, she felt, that her room would be searched.

The lad's dialect was so thick that she could barely understand him. He was happy enough, however, for she had given him five meld for himself— more than he saw in a week, very like. As they reached the top of the hill and came over the crest she could see, sure enough, the cloud-banks out to the east, more than a hundred miles away. To her left, below her and beyond the walls, lay the river bank along which they had come with Tolis. On the right, along the nearer bank of the Flere, extended what was evidently the wealthy neighbourhood of the little town. There were several stone-built houses; not large by Beklan standards, but trim and quite well-maintained. One, with what seemed from this distance a very pretty, neat little garden extending down to the river, reminded her poignantly of her own house in the upper city. I wonder who's living there now, she thought; and the tears pricked her eyes, for she had loved it dearly, her house.

She pointed. 'Is *that* Almynis's?'

'Naw, säiyett. Fu'r 'long: artside o' warls.'

It did not take long to reach the walls. They were obviously very old, not mortared, built of rocks and stones piled on a base of natural crags and all of five feet thick. Those who raised them, thought Maia, all those years ago, must have heaved and dragged and carried every rock for miles around. There were no steps, as there were leading up onto the Beklan walls. The boy, like one doing an accustomed thing and seeming to need no permission, disappeared into a near-by shed and came out with a ladder which he set up and climbed. Maia having scrambled after him, he pulled it up and then lowered it for them to descend on the other side.

A track ran parallel with the walls, towards the gates in one direction and down to the Flere in the other. The boy left the ladder lying under the wall and they set off towards the river.

The grasshoppers zipped in the short grass. The heat was intense. There

974

was no one else on the track, but some oxen were gathered in a shady place, watched by a little, ragged girl who begged from the lady as she passed. Maia gave her a quarter-meld: she took it and ran back to her beasts without a word.

The boy stood still, pointing. 'Therr!'

About two hundred feet below them lay a square, white dwelling. It was larger than her house in Bekla, very smooth and clean-looking in the glaring sunshine. On the flat roof bay-trees and laurels were standing in big, terra-cotta pots. She could not see a single stain or crack in the wall facing her. The pale-grey, louvred shutters, like closed eyelids across the windows, suggested the very acme of shadowy coolness and seclusion within. On this nearer side, a lower stone wall projected at right angles from the town walls, then itself turned at a right angle and so ran down to the shore. Within this enclosure lay the garden, entirely surrounding the house. It was profuse with arbours, little groves and bright flower-beds. A green lawn extended down to the river, where she could see a stone jetty and a small boat-house.

From the baking hillside above, where the stones, flickering in the sun, were too hot to touch, the place looked a veritable sanctuary of verdurous ease. Maia could see two men trudging back and forth from the river, each carrying two buckets on a yoke. Clearly, their job must be to water the garden almost continuously throughout the day. Nothing less could possibly keep it looking like that. It shone and glittered, vibrant in contrast to the still, dried-up scrubland. As she stood gazing, a faint scent of lilies came drifting upward.

'Arright, säiyett?' asked the boy. She nodded rather abstractedly. In the light of her twenty-four hours' experience of Nybril she had not been expecting anything quite like this. To say the least, she thought, Mesca had not been guilty of exaggeration. This Almynis obviously had money and knew how to make good use of it, too. Occula ought to come and have a look at this; it might cool her off a bit about the Lily Pool.

Dismissing the boy, she walked on down the hill. Since she could see no gate in the garden wall facing her, she rounded the right angle and followed it down its length to the shore. Still there was no gate, but the wall came to an end some yards short of the water's edge, and she walked round it onto the lawn. Not far off was one of the water-carriers, white-bearded, stooping and gnarled, with a wide, flat straw hat on his head.

'I've come to see the säiyett Almynis. Will it be all right to go up to the house?'

He squinnied up at her, old eyes peering out of a crumbling dwelling— as it were from far away—at youth and beauty which once, perhaps, he might have hoped to attain. Not any more. Not now.

975

'Why not?'

She gave him five meld, at which the poor old fellow uttered an exclamation, touched it to his forehead and called down a blessing on her. She went on between the trees and shrubs with their smell of moist greenery. Glittering gnats were darting among them and butterflies fanned their wings on the stones. The double doors giving on the garden were louvred like the shutters, made of sestuaga wood, very light and delicate and fastened with a bronze chain. She was about to knock when she saw, standing on a little, round table beside the door, a copper hand-bell. It was made in the form of four naked girls facing outwards and arching their bodies, hands raised above their heads to meet round the handle—an erect zard carved in some dark, smooth wood. Wouldn't Nennaunir just about fancy one of those? she thought; and forthwith picked it up and rang it. Like a sheep-bell it was not resonant, but gave off a hollow, cloppering sound, which somehow went with the hot afternoon. She held it up and looked inside, expecting the tongue to be another zard: however, it turned out to be a boy and girl clasped in each other's arms. She had just replaced it on the table when the chain was drawn and the doors opened by an enormous man—the biggest she had ever seen in her life, except for King Karnat. The chucker-out, she thought: these places always employed a strong fellow.

He certainly was an intimidating sight, bare-armed, bare-footed and muscled like an ogre. She only just restrained herself from raising her palm to her forehead.

'I've come to see the säiyett Almynis,' she said.

'She's expocting you?' He spoke like Lalloc—like a Deelguy.

'A girl called Mesca told Almynis I was coming.'

'You com in.' He stood aside.

She stepped into a big, cool room. There were couches covered with bright rugs and cushions, a long dining-table with benches on either side and a central pool with a fountain; but the fountain was still. All the windows were shuttered against the sun, except for one, a dazzling rectangle on the far side of a couple of steps leading up into a little colonnade at the other end of the room.

'You waiting here. I toll her.'

She began wandering about the room, admiring the fittings and furniture, most of which looked new. One wall was decorated with a series of licentious pictures, another with a charming painting of swans alighting on a lake.

All of a sudden Maia stopped short. On a small, lacquered table against the wall stood a little cluster of ornaments and pretty artifacts—a pair of candle-snuffers made like a silver dragon, the corn-sheaves of Sarkid carved in Ortelgan ziltate, a golden filigree sweet-box and so on. Among these was a little carving, in greenstone, of two goats mating. One exactly like it, she remembered, had had its place on the edge of the fountain in Sencho's dining-hall. She had once asked where it came from and been told from some foreign land beyond Yelda.

She would never have imagined there could be two such. She stepped forward and was just going to pick it up when she realized that the huge bodyguard had returned and was standing at her elbow. Without speaking he gestured towards the unshuttered window behind her.

She looked across the room. The dark shape of a woman, looking out of the window, was outlined against the light. She must have entered without a sound from somewhere along the colonnade. Maia crossed the room, went up the steps and raised her palm to her forehead.

'Säiyett Almynis, thank you very much for letting me—'

The woman turned. 'Hallo, Maia.'

For a moment Maia stared; then, with a cry, she recoiled, clutching with one hand at the painted column behind her.

'Terebinthia!'

: 99 :

A HARD BARGAIN

Maia's fear upon recognizing Terebinthia was, of course, instantaneous and irrational. During her months in Sencho's house it had been second nature to all the girls to regard Terebinthia, even in her moods of relative amiability, as the very embodiment of ruthless cunning, a woman out for her own interests and nothing else. What happened to girls who did not suit those interests had been exemplified by Meris. Occula, maturing her secret, desperate design day after day, had feared Terebinthia as she had never feared Sencho. Terebinthia's lack of all kindness, warmth or humour, her self-contained vigilance, her minacious domination over the household, the impossibility of ever hearing her coming or of guessing how much she really knew—all these had created an atmosphere which would certainly not have obtained if the säiyett had been someone like Sessendris. Maia had not, of course, seen Terebinthia since the evening when she and Occula had set out with Sencho for the party by the Barb. Small wonder, then, that in the first moment that she recognized her, it did not immediately occur to her that a great deal had happened since they had last been together. The most frightening thing about Terebinthia had always been that you never knew where she would be next; and of that there could scarcely have been a more startling instance than now.

977

As Maia stood breathing hard, one hand against the column at her back, Terebinthia, all serenity, took two steps forward and, smiling, embraced her. Then she gestured towards a curtained opening a little way up the corridor—the one through which she must have entered.

'We'll go to my room. I hope this is as pleasant a surprise for you, Maia, as it is for me. Somehow, when Mesca told me, I had an idea it might be you.'

If Maia could have fled from the house she would have done so; but somehow it was still not in her power to resist the smooth domination which Terebinthia had always exercised. Having recovered a little from her initial shock, she was doing her best to tell herself that she no longer had any reason to be afraid of Terebinthia. On the contrary, she had cause—yes, of course she had cause—to be glad that the woman she had come to see had turned out to be an old acquaintance with every reason to feel well-disposed towards her. Lespa's stars! Enough of the money she'd made had found its way into Terebinthia's pocket: and she'd always been obedient and co-operative and never done Terebinthia any harm.

And yet she *was* afraid. The Terebinthia she had known had never been kind or generous to anyone. Always in dealing with her there had been apprehension, an atmosphere of cat-and-mouse; and it had not evaporated—not as far as Maia was concerned. But she's no longer got the power! thought Maia desperately. She hasn't got the power like she used to. She's no more säiyett now than what I am. Yet even as she tried to impress this on herself her misgiving grew. This acquaintance she had rediscovered was no friend, had never been a friend.

'Well, I certainly never could have guessed that Almynis would turn out to be *you*,' she replied, in a tone as light and genial as she could manage. 'Never even entered my head! You've certainly got a nice place here. Gave me a surprise: I mean, in Nybril—well, it's rather out of the way, isn't it?'

'Perhaps,' agreed Terebinthia, 'but that has its advantages for me, as I'm sure you must realize.'

Opening a door on their left, she gestured to Maia to enter. Maia found herself in a small sitting-room, pleasantly cool, with a floor of pale-green tiles, two couches, a table with benches and a wide window, west-facing and shuttered. The tiles were dappled by sunlight through the louvres.

'Sit down, Maia,' said Terebinthia. 'You must have had a hot walk from Nybril. We'll have some wine and you can relax a little.'

She had seldom felt less relaxed, thought Maia. Terebinthia went to the door and called. Maia (who had not sat down, but remained standing tensely in the middle of the room) heard a girl's voice responding. Returning, Terebinthia looked at Maia with an air of mild surprise, paused a moment and then, with a slight shrug of her shoulders, sat down herself.

'You're looking well, Maia. Renown evidently suits you. You've done very well for yourself, haven't you? Or ought I perhaps to say you *were* doing well for yourself? I wonder what may have brought you here?'

Her broad, sleepy-eyed, dark-complexioned face regarded Maia intently, very like a cat indeed, and she leaned back, spreading her arms along the top of the couch as she waited for Maia's answer.

To Maia there seemed no point in beating about the bush.

'I left Bekla because Queen Fornis tried to murder me.'

Terebinthia nodded, rather as though Maia had told her that she had decided to travel for her health.

'Are you alone here, then?'

'No: I'm with Bayub-Otal of Urtah and a Katrian officer of King Karnat.'

Terebinthia raised her eyebrows. 'A *Katrian* officer? And Bayub-Otal, you say? I thought he'd been killed in the fighting at Rallur.'

'No: they were both prisoners in Bekla, but the three of us were able to get away.'

There was a tap at the door and a fair, slight girl, who looked no more than eleven, dressed in tawdry finery like Mesca, came in with a tray—a wine-flask and cups, serrardoes and a plate of prions. Terebinthia remained silent while she set down the tray and left them. Maia, whom the child had rather reminded of Kelsi, was unable altogether to contain her feelings.

'Isn't she rather young for—for the work here?'

'She *is* young, of course,' replied Terebinthia smoothly, 'but she's shaping well, I'm glad to say, and learning quickly.'

She poured the wine and handed Maia her cup. Suddenly, Maia was overcome with a terrible conviction that the wine must be poisoned. Don't be silly, she thought; why should she poison you? Well, to please Fornis and reinstate herself. For envy. For what she can get.

'Bayub-Otal knows I've come here today, of course,' she said.

'Of course,' replied Terebinthia; and drank. Maia sipped too, staring down into the cup. It looked like ordinary wine—she could see no discolouration—and there was no unusual taste. She helped herself to a prion and nibbled it. Her hand was trembling, but perhaps Terebinthia had not noticed.

'And how's dear Occula?' asked Terebinthia suddenly, putting down her cup.

'Occula? Oh—oh, she's fine,' answered Maia. 'That's to say, she was when I come away.'

Terebinthia waited enquiringly, allowing it to be clear that she knew that Maia must know that this was not an adequate reply.

'She was arrested after the High Counsellor's murder, of course—'

'You *both* were, weren't you?' said Terebinthia.

'—only Queen Fornis took a fancy to her, see, and she's been with her ever since.'

'Queen Fornis? And yet you say she tried to kill *you*?'

'Well, thing was, she thought I was out to be Sacred Queen, see; but I wasn't.'

'No, of course not; because you and Occula were working for the heldril all along, weren't you? You contrived the murder of the High Counsellor between you.'

There was no disguising, now, the malice in Terebinthia's eyes. The Serrelinda, however—now that it was out in the open—was equal to looking steadily back at her.

'I had nothing whatever to do with it, Terebinthia. I didn't know anything about it until it happened.'

'Well, of course I must take your word for that, mustn't I?'

'You can. I'll be perfectly frank with you: I'm not sorry he died, but I had nothing to do with it.'

'And Occula?'

'I've no idea.'

'Come, come, Maia. You and she were inseparable. You're telling me she told you nothing?'

'She'd nothing to tell, Terebinthia, that's why. Had, she'd 'a told me; I agree with you that far.'

'It's important to me, you see,' went on Terebinthia. 'I've got a lot to thank them for, those who killed Sencho. I was under suspicion of having had to do with it myself; I knew that. As if *I* could have had any motive for wanting him dead! He was worth a fortune to me. But I wasn't going to wait to be condemned by the Council. So I had to forfeit everything and leave Bekla at once.'

'Is *that* why you left?'

'Of course. But I could never have succeeded if Elvair-ka-Virrion hadn't paid me very generously in return for letting him take Milvushina away the day after the murder. He got me out of the upper city in disguise, with everything valuable I could carry. Why else do you think I'm here with a false name in a place like this, instead of Ikat or Herl-Belishba? So you see I've very little reason indeed to feel friendly towards those who killed Sencho.'

Maia, who was now beginning to feel really frightened, gazed back at her silently.

'And now *you* know, don't you, where I am? You could tell anyone you wanted to. I confess that worries me rather, Maia.'

Had there been something in the wine? Maia's head was swimming. The room seemed like a little box, over which was brooding an enormous presence; the forest-giant of Purn, the gigantic doorman—they were one and the same. She wiped the sweat from her forehead. She must retain an outward appearance of self-possession.

'Poor Milvushina's dead, you know.'

'Milvushina? How?'

Maia told her, restraining her tears with some difficulty.

'I see,' said Terebinthia. 'I heard about Durakkon; and I knew about the battle, of course. News comes down the river with the rafts. But I didn't know about Milvushina. And so Queen Fornis has taken Bekla, has she?'

'That's more than I can tell you, Terebinthia. When we got away, her Palteshis were still fighting it out with the Lapanese.'

'So now—you're here,' continued Terebinthia ponderingly, 'and looking for work, so Mesca said. You need money, Maia, do you?'

'No, I *didn't* come here for money, actually.'

But clearly Terebinthia did not mean to permit any interruption to the delicious moment of springing the mousetrap.

'I'm not at all sure—' she stood up, walked slowly across to the window and made some minute adjustment to the louvres '—really—' she returned and sat down again '—whether I ought to allow you to leave this house alive.'

'Why ever would that be then, säiyett?' Involuntarily, Maia's voice had risen. 'I told you, you've no reason to be revenged on me.'

'Perhaps not; but then you know now, don't you, where I'm to be found? And the Leopards would like to learn that.'

She wants me to plead for my life. She wants me to go about to convince her there'd be no point in killing me. Reckon I'll have to, an' all.

'But Terebinthia, I'm not going back to Bekla—ever.'

'So you say now; but one never knows. And people can still talk, even though they may not actually be in Bekla; and news can travel.'

'But everyone reckons Erketlis is sure to beat Kembri and take Bekla.'

'Perhaps, Maia, perhaps. And do you think Erketlis is any more likely than Fornis to feel kindly disposed towards Sencho's former säiyett?'

'If you was to kill me, säiyett, that'd be proper bad for you. Bayub-Otal and Zen-Kurel, they both know I'm here, and so do the folks at "The White Roses". But what's more, I'm under the protection of Lord Elleroth of Sarkid. I did him a good turn, see, and only day before yesterday he give us an officer and twenty soldiers to escort us here.'

'Oh, it will be an accident, Maia, of course: a most unfortunate accident. You fell in the river. You slipped on the stairs. There'll be witnesses. We shall all be heart-broken.' She smiled. 'That's why your wine isn't poisoned. You thought it might be, didn't you?'

Somehow, somewhere, Maia could sense the existence of a loophole. A loophole. Terebinthia had some purpose. There was something, something that she was waiting for, hoping to hear. At this moment her threat was half real and half a cruel game. It was up to her victim to tip it one way or the other. She had to come up with some good reason why the balance of advantage for Terebinthia lay in not stopping her mouth.

'Säiyett' (she couldn't help it now) 'there's one thing you're wrong about. I didn't come here to ask you for work, and I don't need your money.'

'Really, Maia?' That had caught her attention all right.

'No. My friends and I want to reach Katria by going down the river. That's why we came to Nybril—to buy a boat. But tell you the truth, it's not turning out all that easy.'

'Well?'

'Well, Mesca said as you had boats. I come to see whether I could buy one off you.'

It was plain that this was something new and unexpected: it had taken Terebinthia by surprise. So Maia was not penniless? There was more to be gained here than the satisfaction of killing her? Terebinthia had always been a great one for money. That was what she lived for.

Her next remark came pat as an echo. 'You have money, then?'

'Well, not all that much, but enough to pay a fair price for a boat, I reckon. I haven't got it here, though. It's with my friends in Nybril.'

'And what makes you think I'd be likely to part with a boat?'

'The rains are coming, säiyett. I reckon whatever your clients do during Melekril, they don't baste in boats. Turn one of your boats back into money, use that money to make more and get another boat run down from Yelda in the spring. I'd be doing you a good turn.'

'You always were a shrewd little thing, Maia. I had hopes of you once. It's a pity those days are gone.'

She was silent, meditating. 'You say you're making for Katria?'

'Yes.'

'And staying there for good?'

'I'm not coming back, Terebinthia. And I shan't tell anyone that Almynis of Nybril used to be Sencho's säiyett. Why should I? What good would it do me?'

'Well.' Terebinthia drummed her fingers lightly on the table. 'Well.' For the second time she stood up. 'We'll go down and look at the boats, Maia, if you like.'

The boat-house had a green, watery smell and was full of echoing knocks and wooden scrapings, of the *slock* of water and bright, elastic reflections shimmering on the under-side of the roof. Maia had not expected so many boats. There were five in all: two rowing boats; a long, rectangular, flat-bottomed affair like a Suban kilyett and two larger, single-masted boats, the masts unstepped and sails furled. The bigger of these was about twenty feet long and had a tiny cabin amidships, most of which was taken up by a big, comfortable-looking feather mattress. The rudder, rowlocks and oars—two pairs—were shipped aboard. There were two bailers, and anchors fore and aft. All in all, thought Maia, as likely a boat as one could well hope to find. She was careful to maintain a straight face and speculative air, but while she was doing so Terebinthia broke in on her pose of deliberation.

'You can take it from me, Maia, that nothing smaller than that boat is going to be any good to you on the lower Zhairgen. It's either that or drown. Once the rains have set in you'll probably drown anyway, but that's your affair.'

Maia was looking into the well of the boat. There was almost no bilge. She was evidently sound enough. She was jammed up against the other boats, of course, but as far as Maia could tell she had no noticeable list. How well she would answer and steer was another matter.

'You needn't stand there poking it about,' said Terebinthia. 'You can take it out for a few minutes if you want: there's very little current inshore on this side. I'll call the Deelguy to go with you. You'll find there's nothing wrong with it. If you want it, you can have it for sixteen thousand meld.'

Maia looked at her in amazement. 'But—but a *brand-new* boat like that wouldn't cost *eight* thousand on Serrelind! Anyway, I haven't got sixteen thousand—'

'Take it or leave it,' said Terebinthia sharply. 'It strikes me you're in no position to bargain, Maia. The rains are coming. It might cost you more to spend Melekril in Nybril, the three of you.'

'But I haven't got it, säiyett.'

Terebinthia walked out of the boat-house and called to the gardener to come and lock it. As Maia came out, the man threaded in the chain and began putting the bow of the heavy Gelt lock through the links.

'All right, Terebinthia,' said Maia. 'I'll take it out and try it.'

MIST AND RAIN

The mist lay everywhere, far and near; filling the savage, desolate miles of the forest of Purn; obliterating the wasteland where Elleroth's camp now stood empty; lying thick upon the two rivers, blotting out rocks and rapids, reed-beds and the silent backwaters where flotsam circled for hour after hour in the rotating eddies. It covered the Nybril confluence, changing it to a seemingly illimitable expanse of featureless, deserted water, whence even the fowl had stolen away to shelter (for water will not run off a duck's back for ever and saturated feathers are fatal).

Nybril lay beneath the mist as though submerged. The whole promontory had disappeared under the silent, grey mass rolling over walls and housetops, creeping down the steep streets until each corner and crevice of the town had been penetrated, as a cavity is filled with putty pressed home. By nightfall those few still on the streets were hurrying either to their own houses or else to some equally welcome destination— for the taverns were doing brisk business as people drank and made merry over the commencement of Melekril and the coming of the rains.

The mist penetrated every room where a fire was not burning, hanging in the air, surrounding each lamp-flame with a dull, foggy nimbus. By its very nature it seemed to cast a blight, so that honest warmth became thick and close, and shelter constrictive: yet to this the merry-makers paid no heed.

Out of the mist, slowly, grew the rain: at first no more than a moisture suspended in the air, sinking onto roofs, copings and leaves until everything was damp to the touch; then droplets, minute particles like a powder of water, felt by the hurrying home-goers on foreheads, ears and the backs of hands; and at last as a fine mizzle, drifting out of the east on the gentle but ceaseless wind rolling the mist onward into Belishba and beyond to Katria and Terekenalt.

In Maia's upstairs room at 'The White Roses', where Anda-Nokomis, Zen-Kurel and she were preparing to leave, the rain, as darkness fell, had become just heavy enough to be heard on the roof above. They had eaten a meal, paid their score and bought from the landlord enough food—mainly bread, cheese and dried fruit—to last for about two days.

'That going to be enough, you reckon?' asked Maia when Anda-Nokomis brought it upstairs and divided it to be stowed in the packs which Zen-Kurel had persuaded Tolis to leave with them upon his departure.

'I don't know,' he replied. 'I can only tell you what the landlord said. By the way, here are the seven hundred meld you left with him: I *have* counted them. According to him, it's about seventy miles down the Zhairgen to the southern border of Katria. During summer the rafts usually take three days over it, stopping off at night. But he says that now the rains have begun we ought not to attempt it at all. He tried to dissuade me, but when he saw that was no good, he said our only hope was to keep going night and day. He said if we didn't do it in a day and a half at the most we'd have no chance, because after only a few hours the river floods and becomes completely unnavigable. No boat can live in it, he said.'

He paused, listening as the light rain pattered overhead and dripped down outside the windows. 'The eastern provinces have already had this for hours, of course: their rain's coming down both rivers now.'

'Why don't you stay here in Nybril, Maia?' asked Zen-Kurel. 'I think both Anda-Nokomis and I would rather feel you were safe.'

She smiled, and he half-returned it, as though despite himself. 'If that boat's to get to Katria I reckon you're going to need me.'

Zen-Kurel seemed about to reply, but she cut him short. 'Anda-Nokomis, we ought to be going. The man downstairs is right; sooner the better, else we'll have no chance.'

'You want actually to take the boat out tonight?'

'Once the rain's really settled in the mist lifts; you know that. There'll be a bit of a moon most of the night. Even behind clouds that'll give enough light for us to drift a fair old way by morning, long 's we keep a good look-out and stay offshore. We'll have to take it steady, of course, but it might make all the difference.'

'Mightn't we run aground or hit something in the dark?'

'Well, that'll be all according,' she answered, 'but if that landlord was right about one thing, it's that every hour's one less and there aren't all that many.'

Bayub-Otal was silent, considering. Standing thus, gawky and pondering, in the middle of the room, he looked so characteristic, so comically typical of the Anda-Nokomis she had come to know and feel affection for, that she burst out laughing, jumped up and took his hands.

'You afraid, Anda-Nokomis? 'Cos *I* am, tell you that! Come on, let's be going.'

He glanced at Zen-Kurel, who shrugged and picked up his pack.

The big room downstairs was crowded and full of babble and laughter. Two groups of drinkers were bellowing different songs, taunting their rivals and trying to drown each other. Maia and her companions edged their way through the crush, reaching the door unhindered. Anda-Nokomis already had his hand on the latch when a big, fair-bearded man with a broken nose caught Maia by the shoulder.

'Don' want be going out there, lass! Pissing down! Whyn't stay here 'n have nice drink with me?'

'All right,' she smiled. 'Tomorrow night I will.'

'No good t'morrow night: place'll be drunk dry!'

'Then here's your health!' she answered; took his half-empty wine-cup out of his hand, quickly drained it and tossed it into the air above his head. Then, as he made a clumsy grab to catch it, she slipped past him, through the opened door and out into the misty darkness.

The rain was falling more heavily now and the mist, as she had foreseen, was growing gradually less dense. Drawing their cloaks round them and raising the hoods, they climbed the rocky lane, crossed the market-place and came to the town gates. When Bayub-Otal put his head round the door of their lodge the watchmen were sitting snug by the fire with a jug of mulled wine, playing some game on a board marked out in charcoal on the table. One of them, grumbling, got up and reached for the keys hanging on the wall.

'Off to Almynis, I suppose, are yer, like the rest of 'em? Won't be home till morning if I know anything about it. All right for them as can afford it, eh? Stuffin' good money up some painted shearna's tairth.'

Anda-Nokomis made no reply as the man went stumping outside. Stooping over the chain of the gate, he looked back at them over his shoulder. 'Come on, then, let's have it! 'Zact money, too: none of your ten-meld pieces; I can't change 'em.'

'Have what?' asked Zen-Kurel brusquely.

The man clicked his tongue with impatience. 'Two meld each after dark: you know that as well as I do.'

'I certainly don't—' Zen-Kurel was beginning, when Maia broke in.

'Here *is* ten meld, but we don't want any change. Have a drink with us, just to start off Melekril.'

'Well, there's a good-hearted lass!' he said, pocketing the coin and drawing the chain. But as she passed him he drew her on one side and muttered, 'I'm sorry to see you off to Almynis, a young girl like you: I've a daughter no older. Why don't you find yourself a good husband and forget these tricks? She's hard as stone, that one. You mark my words, she'll cheat you and you'll only wish you'd never seen her.'

She would have liked to reassure him, to tell him he needn't worry on her account; but there was not time. Taking his rough hand in both of hers, she bent and kissed it quickly; then turned away and rejoined the others. She never knew whether the man had been within his rights in demanding the money.

The moon gave no more than the dimmest, suffused light from behind the clouds, and they had to pick their way slowly along the track running parallel with the walls. The baked, high-summer earth was slippery with the rain which had not yet turned it to mud, and patches of mist were still hanging on the high ground between the gates and the steep descent towards the Flere. Once they came over the top, however, and within sight of Terebinthia's house below, the going grew a little easier. The place was blazing with light, which glittered among the veils of rain drifting across the hillside. They could hear the music and laughter half a mile off.

Maia, knowing no other way, led them along the wall, on to the now-soggy lawn beside the river and so up the garden to the door. When she rang the bell the huge Deelguy opened at once. Looking past him she caught a glimpse of the big room crowded with men, some with girls on their knees, all gazing at something out of sight beyond; probably a kura, she supposed. The giant bowed, spreading his hands.

'You comming in, yoss?'

'No!' she replied firmly. 'Tell your säiyett that Maia Serrelinda is here. Say I've brought the money and we want to go straight to the boat.'

He was back almost at once. 'She say you govving the money, then I take you.'

'No!' she said. 'Tell her we'll pay the money when we've got the boat.'

This time the Deelguy returned with Terebinthia, who was wearing a very low-cut, sleeveless, scarlet dress and a heavy necklace of penapa stones. 'Don't be silly, Maia. Come in and have a drink.'

'I'm sorry, säiyett, but the river's rising and we're in a hurry. If you'll come down to the boat-house with us—or send your man, I don't mind which—I'll hand over the money once we've got the boat and seen as she's all she should be.'

'Then you can go without, you little cow,' said Terebinthia.

'That *would* be a pity, säiyett. I've got all your money here and what's more, I've got two armed men to defend me. So I'd have to go away, wouldn't I? and do all that talking as you were so anxious about this afternoon. I wouldn't want that, would you?'

For fully ten seconds Terebinthia glared at Maia, who returned her stare unwaveringly. Then she snapped, 'Very well. Braishdil, fetch my cloak and a pair of clogs. Come with us yourself and bring a torch.'

The boat, as far as Maia could see, was as she had been that afternoon. Having checked the oars and all the other equipment, she nodded to her friends to climb in. Then, carefully turning her back on them, she paid out the money on a bench, the Deelguy holding the smoky, flaring torch as Terebinthia counted it, biting each coin.

'You're going to your death, you know, Maia,' said Terebinthia finally, having dropped the last hundred-meld piece into her scrip. 'That's your own affair, of course, but in many ways I wish you weren't. You'd much better stay here. You'd soon make a lot more than ever you did at Sencho's, you know.'

'I'm sorry, säiyett. We just see things different, that's all.'

'Evidently,' replied Terebinthia. 'But I'm afraid the truth is that you won't be seeing anything at all soon, Maia. I've been perfectly straight with you: that's a good boat. But if it was twice as strong, it wouldn't get to Katria in the rains. So just remember, I told you to think better of it and you wouldn't. Braishdil, push it out.'

She watched silently as the great, lumbering fellow dragged the boat free from those against it as easily as he might have pulled a piece of firewood out of a pile, drew it forward and pushed it out into the dark water along the verge. As soon as it was clear of the bank she called, 'That'll do!' The man left them and followed her out through the side door of the boat-house. They heard the chain fastened and then saw the torch bobbing back up the garden until it was lost to view. They were alone in the darkness, the river and the falling rain.

Their thick, soldiers' cloaks were drenched. Maia could feel hers wet against her shoulders and the upper part of her back.

'What do you want us to do now, Maia?' asked Anda-Nokomis from the bow.

'We've got to get across to the other bank, without drifting down no more 'n what we can help. If we get into that stew out in the middle below the town, we're finished.'

'How's it to be done?'

'Row across as quick as we can and hope the current in the centre doesn't turn us downstream too hard.'

'I'm afraid rowing isn't my strong point, Maia.'

O Lespa! she thought. She'd forgotten that; his hand! Of course she could row, but if they weren't to be swept down in midstream the steering was going to be important and she'd rather have had the doing of that herself. Still, there were no two ways about it, and no sense, either, in making him feel worse than he must already. She got up and went forward to the rowing-seats amidships.

'Zenka,' she said—it had slipped out before she'd thought about it— 'give me one of those oars and take the other yourself. You go that side, 'cos you'll pull stronger 'n me, and that'll help to keep her head from turning downstream. Anda-Nokomis, you take the tiller and keep her pointing half-upstream as steady as you can.'

'The trouble is,' he said, having stumbled to his seat in the stern, 'I can't see anything out there.'

'You'll just have to go best you can, by the light from the house behind. But you'll be able to tell when we've got across, near enough, 'cos the current'll slacken. Anyway, you ought to be able to make out the bank, just about, before we get to it. Here, wait, Zenka! Careful! Let me put that rowlock in for you! If that was to fall overboard we'd really be in trouble. Right; now you pull how you like, only hard: I'll work in with you, don't worry.'

It was a heavy boat to get under way, but Zen-Kurel handled his oar better than she'd dared to hope. Pulling her own, she kept her eyes on the light from Terebinthia's house and within half a minute saw it swing over to her right. Good; the bow was heading upstream.

'Fine, Anda-Nokomis!' she panted. 'Keep it like that!'

Even as she spoke the port bow began to meet the midstream current. The lights swung back again until they were once more astern; then until they were almost directly on her left. The water gurgled and knocked against the side, racing down in the dark. They were being swept downstream fast.

'Right, Anda-Nokomis, right!' she cried. 'Hard over to your right!'

It was very frightening. She had never imagined they would go down so fast. At this rate they would be well below Nybril in a matter of minutes and into the central boil of the confluence. She could see the speckled lights of the town rushing past on her left. The rain was blowing straight into her face from astern.

'Harder, Zenka!' She herself had never pulled so hard. As she well knew, she was pulling for her life.

Ah, but they *were* gradually forcing their way across the current! She could feel it; and besides, the lights, even as they fell so fast behind, were gradually moving over towards her right until at length she was looking straight at them. Then, slowly—very slowly it seemed—the current began to slacken and the chattering of the water against the side below her grew less until it had almost died away. They were still drifting down, but far more gently and in smooth water.

She slumped over her oar, drawing deep, shuddering breaths. The sweat was pouring off her and her heart was thumping. She retched, but nothing came. Zenka had stopped rowing too, and seemed to be waiting to be told what to do. She wiped the rain out of her eyes and sat up straight.

'Anda-Nokomis, can you—can you see the bank?'

'I'm not sure,' he answered, 'but there's something ahead; rushes, perhaps.'

They took a few more cautious strokes.

'At least it's answering now,' said Anda-Nokomis. 'It didn't, out there.'

'It did, only you couldn't feel it; hadn't, we wouldn't be here.'

She thrust her oar straight down into the water and at the full extent of her arm touched bottom. At the same moment the low moon, breaking for a moment through a rift in the clouds, showed them the left bank about twenty yards away. Turning to look astern before the moon disappeared again, she could see—or thought she could see—that they were about four or five hundred yards below Nybril, with the confluence, already become a terrifying, foaming cauldron, lying between. Now that she was no longer rowing, she could hear the noise of it; a deep, sullen thunder, not loud but continuous, like the rolling of a great drum.

'I'm sorry,' she said, 'but I got to rest for a bit: I'm tot'lly all in. Anda-Nokomis, try to keep her drifting gently close to the bank. And Zenka, you go up in the bow with that oar and just keep on feeling ahead for rocks or shoals an' that. There's anchors fore and aft: keep them ready to throw out. Give a shout if you want me. I won't be very long, honest.'

And with this poor Maia crawled into the cubby-hole and lay down, utterly spent. But the big, soft mattress, on which so many jolly jinks must have been enacted, afforded her little solace. Already the rain, blowing in from astern, had soaked it. Miserably, she crawled as far forward as she could and curled up, knees to chin. It made little difference. She could almost have wrung out her cloak, while her sopping tunic and shift clung round her like warm slime. She could feel the shape of her diamonds and of Randronoth's casket pressing against her body. After an unavailing wriggle or two she tugged off her tunic and, having felt carefully round the seams of the pockets to make sure they were still holding, dumped it beside her and drew up her wet cloak for a blanket.

She had one consolation, however. They were moving smoothly, without listing or checking. Terebinthia had charged her somewhere between two and three times its value, but at least she had spoken no more than the truth when she had told her the boat was a good one.

Now and then, without distinguishing what was said, she could catch Zenka's voice speaking to Anda-Nokomis and feel the boat slightly changing course. But there were no sudden thuds or alarms and after a while her tension—for she had been fully expecting them to hit something or other in the dark—gradually diminished. She had not meant to sleep, yet soon, lacking all power to resist, she was dead to the world; and for some three or four hours the exhausted girl remained unstirring.

Meanwhile their progress was slow, for both Bayub-Otal and Zen-Kurel were only too well aware of their own lack of skill and experience. Offshore, to their right, the current was swifter—they could hear it and could just make out, too, the froth of broken water in midstream—but they were unwilling either to disturb Maia or to run any risks which they might not be able to handle themselves. The inshore water seemed blessedly free of obstacles and for this they were content to settle. The need for continuous vigilance was strain enough in itself.

At some uncertain time during the long night Bayub-Otal dropped the stern anchor, went forward to Zen-Kurel and suggested a rest and a bite.

Having lowered the bow anchor as well, they sat down side by side, legs stretched out, backs against the forward wall of the cubby—little shelter from the relentless rain—and ate a few mouthfuls of bread and cheese.

'How long till morning, do you suppose?' asked Zen-Kurel in a whisper.

'Three hours, perhaps.'

'Is Maia still asleep?'

'I think so.'

'She deserves it: we ought to let her sleep as long as she can.'

For a time they were silent. Bayub-Otal pulled out his flask and they each took a mouthful of djebbah. At length he said, 'She's saved us again and again since Bekla. Without her we'd have died in the forest.'

'That or been killed by the Ortelgans.'

'We wouldn't have this boat, either. And that brothel woman—Maia had to overpay her; I'm certain of that—they took so long over it. First and last, she's spared herself nothing whatever on our account, that's about what it comes to.'

'It's like Deparioth and the Silver Flower,' said Zen-Kurel.

'Oh, do they know that in Katria, too?'

'Oh, yes, naturally. Well, it was in the Blue Forest that the traitors abandoned Deparioth, of course—left him to die—and the magic girl came to save him. I kept thinking about that while we were in Purn.'

'But Zenka, you said you hated her. You wanted to kill her.'

For some time Zen-Kurel made no reply. At last he replied, 'What I know now is that I've never really stopped loving her: I only thought I had. Oh, yes, I *wanted* to stop loving her; of course I've hated her for what she did in Suba. I still don't understand it, but now I don't think any more that it was just deliberate, cold-hearted deceit and treachery. There was something—something behind it that I don't understand. O Cran, how I've hated her! But what I've discovered is that you can hate someone like poison and still not be able to stop being in love with them.'

Bayub-Otal said nothing and after a few moments Zen-Kurel went on, 'Her beauty—her courage—what she *is*—they're too strong for my hatred, I suppose, if you like to put it that way. I've never known a girl like her— never dreamt there could be one. Whatever she thought she was doing that night in Suba, there must have been some good reason. It's like the gods, really: in my mind, I mean.'

'Like the *gods*? What do you mean?'

'Well, the gods often inflict terrible, even shameful suffering on us, don't they? And there's no accounting for it. But people still go on worshipping them because of things like sunsets and music. She's like that: or I am, whichever way you like to put it. I couldn't stop loving her—I mean, admiring and longing for her—not if she were to cut my throat.'

'She still—she still loves *you*, you know,' said Bayub-Otal rather falter-ingly, after a pause.

'Why, did she say so? I can't believe that.'

'No, but the night you took those men back to Elleroth I thought she was going to go out of her mind; and it was entirely on your account. In fact I told you as much when you got back; you remember?'

'But that might not necessarily—' He stopped. 'Well, but even if—I mean, how can I—after all that's happened—'

Suddenly they both sprang to their feet, Zen-Kurel nearly falling his length on the drenched, slippery planking. The boat was swinging round in the current, rotating by the bow.

For the next few moments they were at a total loss, with no idea what could have happened or what to do. Then the boat, having turned stem to stern, fetched up with a jerk in the running flood as the bow anchor rope went taut and held.

Maia woke instantly. The first thing of which she was conscious was the wet. She was wet through from head to foot—hair, ears, eyelids, hands, sandals. She was lying in a soaking wet hollow the shape of her body. For some reason, however, the rain no longer seemed to be blowing in upon her, though she could hear it beating on the planking above her head.

Something was wrong. That jerk; she'd felt that all right—that was what had woken her. But they were not aground; they were at the full extent of a rope, as she could feel by the wavering of the boat. What in Cran's name was going on?

Without stopping to put on her tunic or cloak, she elbowed her way out into the little well astern and stood up, facing forward. Immediately she felt the rain full in her face. So they must be pointing upstream.

'Anda-Nokomis, what's happened?'

'We'd stopped for a rest, Maia. We had both anchors down, and I think the stern one must have pulled out.'

Quickly she turned, found the stern anchor rope in the dark and pulled on it. At least the anchor had not carried away. It was still on the other end, though not touching bottom.

'How long have I been asleep?'

'I can't say: three or four hours, perhaps.'

'And the river's been rising all the time,' she said. 'That's why the anchor came adrift: likely it never had a proper grip of the bottom to start with. We must raise the other one and then turn her downstream again.'

Yet try as they would, they could not pull up the bow anchor. All three of them hauled until they had actually dragged the heavy boat two or three feet upstream against the current, but still the anchor would not budge.

At length Zen-Kurel stood back, panting, and at once the boat drifted back downstream and fetched up at the full extent of the rope.

'We'll have to cut it, Maia.'

'No!' she said. 'Not till I've been down to have a go at freeing it.'

Zen-Kurel took her by the wrist. 'Maia, I won't allow it.'

She turned on him with icy anger. 'Will you please let me go?' He did so. 'Thank you. Now listen. If I know anything about it, it's probably hooked itself under a log or something o' that. If I do manage to clear it, you'll feel the jerk as the boat lifts, 'cos she's down by the bow now: that's on account of the river rising. Then she'll start to drift, and you'll have to pull me back. Not too sharp, though, or you'll catch me with the anchor like a fish on a hook.'

'Shouldn't we drop the other anchor first?' asked Anda-Nokomis.

'No,' answered Maia decisively. 'We're not risking this happening twice. You shouldn't have anchored at all, Anda-Nokomis: not in this current, with the river rising. You should've tied up to the bank.'

Without another word she slipped off her sandals, leaned well out over the bow, gripped the taut rope with both hands, took a deep breath and went overside.

At once she felt the strength of the current. It fairly jerked at her arms. Her hair streamed backwards and she could feel the flow over her shoulders and along the length of her back. Lose the rope and you're done for! Hand over hand, down and down. Eyes shut, free hand feeling ahead. Pain across the forehead and under the eyes. I'll get the basting thing up if it kills me! She found the shank of the anchor and felt soft, water-soaked twigs brushing against her face and shoulders like a swarm of long-legged insects. Then—ah! just as she'd supposed—a thick branch; absolutely unyielding, yes, and therefore sticking out from a sunken tree-trunk, probably, but no need to find out about that. One fluke of the anchor neatly under it, snug as fingers round the handle of a basket. Hadn't even pierced the wood. O Cran, I can't hold my breath any longer! I can't! Push it down by the shank, turn it away from you—I'm drowning, drowning, I can't hold my breath: let it out then, girl, but once you do there's no more—it's clear, it's free!

She almost lost hold of the rope as the anchor leapt upward, jerked by the buoyancy of the released boat above. With the last remnant of her consciousness she got both hands to it and felt them pulling her up. Give me air, O Cran, just give me some air and I'll never ask for any least thing else, ever again!

Her head and shoulders came clear of the surface and she drew in her breath. It was over. She could breathe.

They gripped her under the arms and dragged her aboard. For a good half minute she lay prone on the planking, vomiting water and drawing one breath after another.

At length she stood up.

'What's happening? Who's got the tiller?'

'I have,' answered Bayub-Otal from the stern. 'I've turned us downstream and I'm keeping as near in to the bank as I can.'

'You're too brave for your own good, Maia,' said Zen-Kurel. 'Please don't try anything else like that.'

She was about to answer when she became unthinkingly aware that something was still amiss. The boat, though now free, was lower in the water and moving very sluggishly. She made her way aft. She could hear the bilge slopping in the dark. Gods! she thought. No wonder the damned mattress was sodden to pulp!

The well of the boat, astern of the cubby-hole, was awash with the rain. She put one foot into it. It was over her ankle and half-way up her shin.

'Zenka!' she called. 'Come and help me bail!'

He was beside her in moments. She felt so angry and harassed by all that had been allowed to go wrong that she simply put one of the wooden bailers into his hand and herself took up the other without a word.

Can't take your eye off them for a minute. Silly bastards sit there for hours in this rain and never even think of bailing! Why the hell did I ever come? They deserve to drown.

The rain was falling yet more heavily now, pouring over them, rattling on the boat and hissing on the water. Every time she turned to empty the bailer overside it stung her ear and cheek, so that at length she could stand it no longer and asked Zen-Kurel to change places: but soon it felt as bad on the other cheek.

There seemed no end to the bailing. In all seriousness—for there was still very little to be seen—she began to wonder whether the rain could actually be gaining on them and filling the boat. Her right arm grew so tired that she had to change the bailer to her left hand and work that much more clumsily. She knew her pace was slackening, but there was no pause in the steady rhythm with which Zen-Kurel bent and flung.

'Here, let me take over, Maia,' said Bayub-Otal from behind her. 'You go and steer for a bit.'

At that moment the bow struck full tilt against something hard and unyielding. There was a shuddering thump of wood against wood.

Zen-Kurel, first to collect himself, stood up and went forward.

'We've hit the bank!'

'But that's impossible! The bank's here on my left,' called back Bayub-Otal.

'I can't help it. It can only be the bank. It's revetted with wooden stakes.'

Maia felt herself giving way to bewilderment and near-desperation. The darkness and rain were like a curse, destroying whatever they tried to do. The bilge water was inexhaustible. She was aching in every muscle. Now, to crown it all, the bank had apparently become bewitched and altered its position in the dark. Another knock like that would probably stave in the bow. I must keep my head and think straight, else we're going to drown and that bitch Terebinthia'll have been proved right.

'Zenka!' she called. 'Is there soft ground behind the stakes?'

'Too soft! It's all mud.'

'Hook the anchor in behind the stakes, then, and hitch the rope as short as you can. We'll just have to wait for daylight. We can't risk another bang like that.'

Zen-Kurel did as she had said. Once more the boat pivoted, the stern swung over to fetch up against the bank and sure enough Maia found at her left hand a line of thick, wooden stakes, driven side by side into the bed of the river. Their tops were only an inch or two clear of the surface. She plumbed again with the oar, but this time could find no bottom. So the stakes—which were stout and firm—must be something like ten or twelve feet long at least. Each one was nearly as broad across the top as the width of her hand: a stout structure, whatever it might be.

This was something altogether outside Maia's experience. She could only suppose that they must have run into some sort of mole or jetty projecting into the stream. But why would there be such a thing in this solitude, with no lights, no voices, no signs of a village or even a house? At a loss, she felt afraid. Yet she was still more afraid of her own fear. Once I lose my head we're finished! Having dug in the stern anchor in the same way that she had told Zenka to secure the other, she went back to bailing, helped by Bayub-Otal.

'Maia,' said Zen-Kurel, 'I'm going to find out what sort of place this is.'

'No, don't, Zenka!' she cried. 'You'll never find your way back and anyway, what good can it do when all we want's to get away as soon as we can?'

But as usual there was no stopping Zen-Kurel. Clambering over the side, he vanished into the dark. After a few minutes she shouted, 'Zenka! Can you hear me?'

'I'm here,' he replied, so close that she jumped. The beating of the rain had prevented them from hearing him returning. A moment later he was back on board and had taken the bailer from her.

'This is an island,' he said, 'and as far as I can make out, it's no more than eight or nine yards across. There's nothing on it at all, and yet it's revetted right the way round with these stakes.'

'I can't believe it!' she said. 'We'll wake up in a minute and find ourselves back in—Anda-Nokomis, where would you like to find yourself back in?'

'Melvda-Rain,' he answered, still bailing.

He'd never had any basting tact, she thought. Not that this was much of a time or place for it. She said no more.

Little by little, half-light began to creep into the cloud-thick eastern sky, disclosing as dreary a prospect as could well have been found in all the world, and immediate surroundings as strange as any to be imagined.

: 101 :

DOWN THE ZHAIRGEN

At this relatively early period in its history, there were throughout the empire very few bridges; none of wide span and only one of any real solidity—that eighteen miles south of Bekla, which carried the Ikat highway. (This was the bridge which the seceding Ta-Kominion had found too strongly held against him.) To transport the stone from Crandor and construct it, some seventy years before, had been an immense labour in which, needless to say, the great Fleitil had been instrumental. There were two wooden bridges across the Serrelind, a relatively small river; one south of Kabin and one north of Thettit; and a similar bridge across a narrow reach of the upper Flere, between Ikat and Herl. The Herl–Dari highway, however (where Meris had been so active), was dependent upon a ferry across the Zhairgen.

Had it not been for a most singular exception to this primitive absence of bridges, Belishba could not have formed part of the empire at all, for it could have had neither direct trade communication with Bekla nor any reliance on Beklan military protection against Terekenalt and Katria. At the point equidistant between Bekla and Herl-Belishba, the River Zhairgen was a good hundred and fifty yards wide and all of twelve to fourteen feet deep, with a fairly strong midstream current even in summer. Here, however, lay the phenomenon known as the Narboi, a scattering of islets varying in diameter from a few feet to about ten yards, between which the river ran in channels differing in width to about the same extent.

An irregular, zig-zag chain of these islets had been strengthened and made firm against erosion by stakes driven into the river bed round their circumference. The Renda-Narboi—the Bridge of Islands—consisted of horizontal, traversing lengths of beams and stout planking, some seven or eight feet wide, extending from one islet across to the next. There were thirteen of these in all, so solidly constructed that each could bear the weight of an ox-cart. They were kept in repair and renewed as often as necessary, but each year, before the onset of the rains, were raised by means of block and tackle—no light undertaking—and brought in to the banks, to prevent them being smashed or carried away by the flooded river.

It was the staked side of one of the larger Narboi—that nearest to the left bank—which the boat had rammed in the dark. The slow coming of light revealed the bow dented and splintered, though not dangerously. All around lay a scene to strike dejection into the stoutest heart. The river, beneath the rain pouring from the mass of low cloud overhead, was turbulent and already very high. One or two of the islets had by this time vanished under the spate, while others were only partly visible, covered by a dirty, ochreous foam that lapped about their bushes and long grass. The central current, checked by the islets filling about a third of the total breadth of the river, funnelled at the gaps in midstream, gushing through with the speed of a mill-race. On either bank, as far as eye could see, extended a dismal, flat plain, across which wound the deserted stone-and-mud line of the highway. About a mile away on the southern, Belishban side, the huts of a village were just visible.

There were wooden huts at each end of the bridge also: in summer these were occupied by the toll-collectors, but now they were empty. Downstream the river, extending still wider, flowed away through a countryside already streaked in the lower ground with broad flashes and seasonal lakes of flood water, their surfaces mottled by the rain.

Maia sat tugging at her soaking tunic, which she had managed with some difficulty to put back on and button. Her long hair clung to her back like weed to a wet rock. She was feeling chilled through and slightly feverish. She had managed to eat some food, but would have given a hundred meld for a hot drink.

'Maia,' said Bayub-Otal, 'surely this is where we have to decide, isn't it, whether to go on or not? We could leave the boat here and make for Herl, though whether that would be any safer there's no telling. The country's known to be full of fugitives and outlaws.'

'Suppose we're right in thinking it's a matter of fifty or sixty miles down to the Katrian border,' said Zen-Kurel, 'how long will that take, Maia?'

'Well,' she answered, 'if the boat'll stand up to it and nothing goes wrong, we might get there by tonight, I suppose, in a current like this. We've got all of twelve hours and more. Just be a matter of staying afloat and keeping going.'

'But is it safe?' asked Bayub-Otal, staring out across the seething flood-stream. 'It looks—'

'Oh, don't be so damn' silly, Anda-Nokomis,' she answered angrily. 'Of *course* it's not safe! Honest, I sometimes wonder whether—'

997

'I really meant, is it possible?'

'Y-es, I think it just about might be,' she said, 'but only if we get on now, 'fore the river gets much worse. I can steer the boat all right, and as long as we keep in midstream and nothing hits us, I reckon we ought to stay afloat. How we come to shore'll be another matter, though, Anda-Nokomis. Have to think about that when we get there.'

'What do you *want* to do, Maia?' asked Zen-Kurel.

'If *you* still want to go back to Katria, I'll do what I can to get you there,' she said.

'I believe you can and will,' replied Zen-Kurel. 'The gods are with you. They've been with you all the way from Bekla.'

Before she could reply there came the sound of a voice hailing them from some way off.

'You, there! You in the boat!'

They looked up. Four men were approaching from the direction of the distant village. One, walking by himself slightly ahead, seemed to have a certain air of authority. The others, wearing cloaks and leather helmets and carrying javelins, were evidently soldiers.

The strangers reached the bank of the river about eight yards away from the islet to which the boat was secured. The leader, looking from Bayub-Otal to Zen-Kurel with an unfriendly expression, said sharply, 'What are you doing here?'

Bayub-Otal stared haughtily back at the man. He was of average height, sharp-faced and rather slightly built, with the look of a steward or some similar minor official. His manner suggested a kind of energetic, unthinking obstinacy, rather like a good dog which nothing is going to stop doing what it has been told.

'I said, "What are you doing here?" ' repeated this personage impatiently.

'I heard you,' replied Bayub-Otal.

'If it comes to that,' asked Zen-Kurel, 'what are *you* doing here?'

'I'm the supervisor of this bridge,' replied the man, 'come to check the river level since last night. That's what I'm doing here. Now will you *answer* me? Who are you?'

'What's that to you?'

'Well, you've badly damaged three of those stakes, for a start. But what I want to know is why you're trying to take that boat down the river in these conditions. You must be up to no good or you wouldn't be doing it. Either you're fugitive criminals or you've got stolen goods on board— both, very likely. You'll just bring that boat over here to be searched, and give me an account of yourselves.'

'Do you know who I am?' asked Bayub-Otal in freezing tones. 'I am the Ban of Suba.'

'I don't care who you say you are,' replied the man. He gestured towards the soldiers standing behind him. 'Are you going to do as I tell you or not?'

As he snapped his fingers all three of the men raised their javelins.

Bayub-Otal made no least move. 'I've no doubt you're only trying to do what you believe to be your duty, my good man, but I must tell you—'

'And *I* must tell you to damn' well baste off, you interfering bastard!' cried Zen-Kurel. 'Go on, that's the way; over there!'

Maia had never heard him swear before. Evidently the man's manner, following upon the danger and strain of the long, sleepless night, had proved too much for him.

At this one of the soldiers, without waiting for orders, flung his javelin at Zen-Kurel. He swayed aside just in time. It grazed the right side of his neck, drawing an immediate spurt of blood, and stuck in one of the stakes lining the bank behind him. On the instant he turned, pulled it out and hurled it back. It hit the man full in the chest, piercing through his sodden cloak. He fell to the ground, clutching at the protruding shaft and scream-ing horribly. Zen-Kurel grabbed up his sword-belt from the deck, drew his sword and brandished it above his head.

There was no reason why the other two men should not have flung their javelins and killed him on the spot, but they did not. Probably neither they nor their master had ever before seen someone badly wounded in anger: it is a notoriously demoralizing experience, particularly if the victim is noisy in his agony. As the wretched man continued to writhe and scream in the mud—which was turning bloody round him—they took to their heels, followed a moment after by the supervisor.

'We'd better go across, I suppose,' said Zen-Kurel coolly, 'and see whether there's anything to be done.' The wound in his neck was bleeding freely, though the rain was washing the blood away as fast as it flowed.

He pulled out the forward anchor from behind the stakes of the islet and then, before the current could take the boat, threw it across to catch in the bank as a grapnel. It held, and as Maia released the stern anchor also the two men hauled the boat across the narrow gap.

The soldier, however, was dead: the javelin had pierced his heart. Zen-Kurel drew it out and dropped it in the mud beside him.

'I'm sorry,' he said to Bayub-Otal, 'but you must admit he asked for it.'

'Well, at least that resolves any remaining doubts we may have had,' replied Bayub-Otal. 'Obviously we can't stay here now.'

They cast off. Maia allowed the boat to drift stern forward through the channel between the shore and the islet and then ported the helm to turn the bow and take them out into midstream.

The swift, turbid current was undulant, suggesting an uneven bed below. Certainly, she thought, in such a flood as this the bed itself might be no danger, but could there be rocks? If they struck anything at this speed there would be no hope for them. Standing precariously up, she scanned the river ahead. She could see no breaking water or any other signs of rocks or shoals. Probably every fixed obstacle was many feet under by now.

Having explained to her companions what to look out for, she left them to take turn and turn about in the bow, equipped with an oar to fend off floating timber or any other heavy débris they might encounter.

The task of steering grew increasingly harrowing; the worst strain she'd ever known, she began at last to feel, for she could never relax or let her attention wander for a moment. The boat veered and yawed continually, thrown this way and that by the current, and she was for ever having to alter course to turn the head back downstream. There was no least abatement of the undulant, rocking swell; and the irregular swoop and pitch of the boat, which jolted every time it fell, began to make her feel giddy and sick.

The rain filled her eyes, her ears and nostrils. She seemed to be breathing as much rain as air. But whereas the rain desired only their suffering, she thought, the river desired their death. Both the men seemed to be feeling the strain hardly less than herself. Not surprising, she thought: they'd had no sleep all night. Bailing had to be kept up continuously. All morning the unending scoop and fling, scoop and fling went on in front of her as she sat hugging the tiller between arm and body and clenching her teeth to stop them chattering.

They passed many inflowing tributaries. All were in spate, chattering like apes or roaring like wild beasts. The noise in itself was frightening, but some, entering the river directly at right angles, took and spun the boat uncontrollably, so that she sat terrified, fully expecting it to fill and founder as it rolled and tossed like a dead cat in a weir.

And yet it did not. Terebinthia had been honest that far. It was as sound a boat as ever she'd known. Again and again it righted itself, answered the tiller and resumed its headlong course downstream.

It's the speed, she thought: I'm not used to this rocking speed. Who could be? Usually in a boat, if you see something ahead there's time to think what you're going to do: but this is more like falling. Dear Lespa, I'll never keep it up! If only I could have a rest! But there's nowhere we can hope to pull in and stop. Anyway, we've *got* to get down to Katria 'fore nightfall, else we're done for.

The sun, of course, was invisible. She wondered whether it was yet afternoon. She had no idea how far they might have come; twenty miles? Thirty miles? The flooded, featureless landscape, the unremitting rain beating from astern, and above all the grey solitude, had a stupefying effect. No landmarks, no people, no birds, no sun in the sky. It was like a ghost world from one of old Drigga's tales.

No time, she thought, there's no time in the ghosts' world. Ghosts got nothing to look forward to, that's why. *Stop* it, Maia! You're going to get Zenka to Katria, remember? They're relying on you, they mustn't see you feeling down.

I don't mind about my house in the upper city—not really. Or all the people cheering, or the clothes and presents an' that. But I do wish I could sit and listen to old Fordil just once more. I never knew anything could be so beautiful.

A poignant, falling phrase from one of Fordil's Yeldashay *teviasalas* came into her head, expressing an infinity of sorrow, the whole world's beauty dying like a sunset. For all she could do, her tears began to fall. Don't make no odds, she thought; won't be noticed in the rain.

But she was wrong. Zen-Kurel, a strip from his cloak bound round his wounded neck, looked up, bailer in hand.

'Maia, what's the matter?'

His voice was full of plainly sincere concern.

'I'm all right,' she said.

'Are you cold?'

'No; not really. Just don't feel quite myself, that's all; bit feverish. It'll pass off. Has your neck stopped bleeding?'

'It must have. That was hours ago.'

'Take that off, then, and give me Anda-Nokomis's flask there. I'll clean it up.'

'Your hand's trembling,' he said after a few moments.

'It's the steering,' she answered. 'You know, the going on and on.' Even as she spoke she realized that they had yawed off course yet again, and put the helm over just as Bayub-Otal called a warning from the bow.

'Why not let me take over for a bit?'

'If it was Lake Serrelind or the Barb I would, but this is too dangerous. You've got to know what you're doing and be able to act quick.'

'But we must be sensible, Maia. You've been steering now for hours, and even you can't go on for ever. You'll collapse or faint, and then we'll all be finished. You'd better teach me: come on.'

'But the bailing—'

'I know: but once I've got the idea you can catch up with it, and then keep an eye on me while you bail.'

He sat down in the stern, took the tiller from her and grasped it as he had seen her do.

'You've got to keep thinking ahead, Zenka. Only the rate we're going, it all happens so quick: I'd best keep one hand on the helm myself for a bit, so's you can feel what I do. There's only so much I can tell you, see: the rest you've got to learn for yourself. Oh, Cran, look *out!*'

Talking, they had both failed to notice that they were approaching yet another tributary. As they came level with the confluence the bow slewed and the boat listed, the current lashing down the length of the starboard beam. Maia, thrown on top of Zen-Kurel, involuntarily flung her arms round his neck.

They had both lost hold of the helm. She grabbed it, pushed herself upright by pressing with her other hand against his shoulder and turned the bow downstream again. Zen-Kurel picked himself up.

'I must learn to do better than that. I only hope it isn't going to be too expensive. Come on, give it back to me and I'll try again.'

They sat side by side, swaying and pressing against each other with the unpredictable and often violent motion of the boat. Maia, tired out and feeling increasingly feverish, grew impatient and once or twice flared up with an exasperation of which she felt ashamed even as she spoke. Yet he accepted every reproof without retort. At length, satisfied that he had acquired a passable proficiency, she felt able, though rather hesitantly, to leave him and set about catching up with the bailing.

The continual danger and need for concentration and action gave them no chance to talk of anything else, yet nonetheless she could feel in his manner a new warmth and friendly solicitude. Since that terrible evening at Clystis's farm, when she had heard him curse her and demand her death, he had found himself compelled, in spite of everything, to respect her. She knew that much—had known it ever since Purn. But now, for the first time, he was speaking to her not merely as though he respected her but as though he liked her too. He wanted to help her and to lessen her anxiety and distress. Yet she wasn't just one of his soldiers any more, to be looked after as a responsibility. Whether or not he was aware of it, he was showing that he regarded her as an equal and a friend.

These thoughts, however, passed only very vaguely and indistinctly through her mind, for as the afternoon—it must surely be afternoon now—wore on and the rain continued to beat down until it was difficult to remember what things had been like before it began, before being wet through from head to foot had become the natural condition of life, she began to feel more and more despondent. As everyone knows, a continuous, unrelenting pain—toothache or earache—is hard to endure. So with this peril and instability. It was as though a carpenter's plane were gradually and steadily shaving away her courage and self-control. Always coming nearer was the inevitable moment when she would no longer be able to endure, would break down and become worse than useless. 'O Lespa,' she prayed, 'let me drown before that happens! Then at least they'll remember me kindly.'

By degrees there came stealing upon her that heightened yet distracted sensitivity which often accompanies the early stage of a feverish illness. While her touch and hearing seemed to have become more acute—so that, for example, the bailer in her hand felt grainy and rain-smooth with a palpability more intense than she had hitherto been aware of—her perception of their surroundings and her relationship to them had also changed, growing blurred and indistinct. It appeared now almost dream-like, this watery wasteland, not subject to normal laws of nature and causation. She would not have been altogether surprised to see it break up and crumble in the rain, start revolving like a wheel or simply vanish before her eyes.

She had not been expecting the trees. Although when she first saw them approaching she did not suppose she was imagining them, yet at the same time they did not seem entirely real. As a matter of fact, in her situation and her slightly delirious condition this was a perfectly reasonable—or at any rate understandable—reaction, for the trees—acres of them—seemed growing up through two lakes of brown water extending one on each side of the river. As they drew nearer, she could see this water actually winding among them, through and over the undergrowth, curling round the thicker trunks like streamers of fog round the towers of the Barons' Palace. She'd no sense of danger, though—not yet. It was like an illusion, a kind of cosmic dance of the trees and water; like the Thlela's dance of the Tel-thearna which had so much delighted her at the Rains banquet.

She caught his arm, pointing. 'Look, Zenka, look! The trees—the trees are dancing!'

He stared at them and seemed to be turning it over in his mind, as though she had said something requiring serious consideration. It was she, not he, who first grasped that she had spoken foolishly. With a sense half of pride and half of shame, she understood that he had become so much accustomed to her talking sense—or at any rate not talking nonsense—that he had been wondering what she might have meant by her metaphor.

'I'm sorry,' she said. 'Silly fancy. Afraid I'm feeling a bit light-headed. Only the trees—they just don't look real, somehow.'

'They're real enough,' he answered. 'I only hope we can get through them, that's all. Well, in one way it's all to the good, I suppose.'

'What is?'

'The forest.'

'Forest?' Muzzily, she was trying to remember what a forest was. 'Is it the Blue Forest?'

'No: that's up north of Keril. This can only be what they call the Border Forest, between Katria and Belishba. We got quite near the other side of it once, about three years ago, when I was first with the king. At the time he was thinking of attacking Belishba, but nothing came of that.'

'Are we in Katria, then, once we're in the forest?'

' 'Fraid not. Katria's not far to the north of the forest, though.'

'Then why did you—' She screwed up her eyes, blinking in the rain. Whatever had she been going to say? 'Why did you—oh, yes: why did you say it was good, then?'

'Well, we've come so fast—faster than ever I thought we would. It can't be all that much further to Katria now. We must make quite certain we're across the border, though, before we take the boat in to shore.'

'How can we?'

'I don't know. But most Belishbans hate Katrians, naturally, and the frontier's guarded even in the rains—or it always used to be.'

'You'd better go and tell Anda-Nokomis: I'll take the helm back.'

A minute later they were among the trees: but this was as different from their water-journey through Purn as a leopard from a cat. That, for Maia at all events, had been—or so it seemed now—a straightforward affair, in slack water and high summer heat. She had felt so strong and capable then, and the water, just as in old days on Serrelind, had been her friend. This flooded forest, with the river swirling among the trees, and the bushes struggling like drowning animals—oh, gods! and there was a real drowned animal, look, a wretched fox floating on the current—seemed not only malevolent but unnatural, too. Many a rainy season had she seen, yet never a land grotesquely awash as a courtyard where a fountain-basin has given way.

Still concentrating the shreds of her energy and vigilance on keeping the boat in midstream, she saw, as they were swept further into the forest, the water thick with débris—leaves, sticks, branches, lengths of creeper, fragments of roots and sodden tangles of grass. They were approaching a bend: on its edge, just where the point must once have been before the flood submerged it, the trunk of an ash-tree rose out of the river. It was like her own dear ash-tree on the shore of Serrelind, where she used to go to escape from Morca and the housework; from whose branches she had so often dropped down into the lake. Looking at it, she felt for a moment cheered and encouraged.

Ah! she thought, but her fever must be coming on worse, for before her rain-blurred eyes the tree seemed slowly moving. Now be sensible! It's just another stupid fancy; you're frightened and tired out! Just keep the boat pointing downstream.

But no; the tree really *was* leaning; listing, slowly tilting, for now she could see another tree behind it remaining upright and still. Then suddenly, shockingly, the tree was keeling over, first quicker and then all in a moment very fast, its tilt become a toppling downfall, as though it had been felled with an axe. The whole ramous structure of branches and drenched leaves was rushing downward. Fifty yards ahead, the surface of the river foamed and whelmed as the trunk hit it and disappeared. Waves tossed the boat, knocking and jouncing under the timbers, then abating, diminishing. Only a tangle of earth-covered roots remained sticking up out of the shallower water along the submerged bank.

Maia, putting the helm hard over and feeling the sluggish response of the bilge-heavy boat, knew with fear that they were already too close. They were not going to be able to round the fallen tree. The boat was turning to port, certainly, but not fast enough: they were going to be caught and enmeshed in the tangle of sunken branches.

Then, before her eyes, the tree began to move again. Just as a minute ago it had begun to move through the vertical, now it was slowly moving through a horizontal plane. Slowly at first and then faster, the topmost branches pivoted downstream with the current, while at the same time the tangle of roots twisted to face her. The boat, itself seeming to drift faster as it approached, came all in an instant abeam of the tree, scraping against one or two of the topmost branches even as the current drew them away to starboard. Before she had time to think, they were past: the tree was gone. Collecting herself as though awakening, she realized confusedly that they were now too close to the left bank, and brought the boat back into midstream.

Zenka had returned to her side. He was smiling—though largely for her benefit, she rather thought.

'I hope there aren't any more like that, don't you?'

Returning his smile, she took his hand for a moment in her own.

'Just as well you came along with us, isn't it?' he said. 'Otherwise we certainly shouldn't have got as far as this. Anda-Nokomis thinks there may be no more than three or four miles to go now.'

'He'd best be right,' she answered. 'Light's going, I reckon.'

It was hard to be sure among the trees, under the press of low cloud and heavy rain, but certainly the recesses of the forest seemed dimmer, evanescent in a distant twilight. Some distance behind them another root-dislodged tree subsided into the river. It was not at once dragged clear of the bank, but was still hanging in the current as they floated on and lost sight of it.

'Oh, we mustn't, we mustn't go wrong now!' she cried suddenly. 'Not now, not right at the end! Dear Lespa—' She raised her arms and tried to stand up, but he, laying a finger on her lips, drew her down beside him.

'Steady, Serrelinda! Why don't you go and take over from Anda-Nokomis for a bit? He's been up there long enough now. I'll carry on here.'

Anda-Nokomis was hanging intently over the bow, the oar gripped in his good hand, from time to time reaching out to push away logs or floating branches as they drifted alongside. When she touched his shoulder he looked round and gave her one of his rare smiles.

'You got us out of that all right, then? I confess I never thought you would. I should have known you better, Maia.'

'If you don't know me by now, Anda-Nokomis—Put the wind up you, did it?'

Still smiling, he shrugged. 'Possibly.'

'Well, it did me,' she said, 'tell you that much. Here's your flask: better have some, 'fore I drink the lot.'

He shook his head. 'We may be glad of it later.'

'We'll be in Katria tonight, Anda-Nokomis: think of that! Somebody'll take us in for sure: we've still got a bit of money left. Hot food, dry beds, a fire—oh, a fire, Anda-Nokomis!'

As she spoke they suddenly felt a heavy blow aft. There was a sound of splintering wood and a cry of alarm from Zen-Kurel. The boat turned sideways on to the stream and checked. During the few moments that it took Maia to hasten back astern, it turned yet further and then began drifting stern forward, wavering with every fluctuation of the current.

'Zenka, what's happened?'

Zen-Kurel was standing up, facing the stern and holding the tiller-bar in both hands.

'Rudder's smashed, Maia.'

'Smashed? How?'

'I was looking out ahead—I never thought of looking astern as well. We'd just come through that last fast patch into this pool when a log overtook the boat and rammed us from behind. It's still out there, look— see it?'

'Oh, Shakkarn!' she said. 'Here, get out of the way! Let's have a look, see how bad it is.'

It was as bad as could well have been feared. The log had split the rudder along a jagged line from top to bottom. Almost the whole blade had carried away. The stern-post, though splintered, was still in position, as were the rudder-head and tiller, but naturally, with the rudder-blade gone, these were useless.

Of course, she thought, it would not have occurred to Zenka (as it would unthinkingly to herself) that, having just come down a length of swift water full of heavy flotsam into a relatively still reach, he was in danger of being rammed astern. It was her own fault for having left him alone: she should have known better. One of Zenka's strongest characteristics, she had come to realize, was his unfailing assumption of confidence, which made people implicitly believe in and go along with him, usually without reflecting just how wise it might be to do so. Zenka—and this was no small part of why she had fallen in love with him, why she still loved him and could never love anyone else—believed in all honesty that any gap between what he knew to be possible and what he wanted to achieve could be bridged by sheer courage and determination. It was this buoyant, indomitable serenity in adversity which made him so attractive; ah! and so dangerously easy not to doubt, an' all. By implication he'd convinced her, at a time when she'd been too overwrought not to swallow it, that valour and resolution were enough to steer a boat in a timber-strewn flood-race. Well, it had probably done for them; there were still plenty of other things to hit, and now the boat was out of control.

'I'm sorry,' he said.

'Couldn't be helped,' she answered rather absently. She was trying to think what, if anything, could be done. 'Much my fault as yours.'

The boat was turning all ways at once now; sometimes stern foremost, then spinning in a cross-current only to veer away again on the instant. She felt more horribly in danger than at any time since they had set out.

'Zenka,' she said, trying to speak calmly, 'bring me an oar, quick as you can.'

There was no time to go looking for a length of rope. She hadn't seen any on board and wouldn't know where to start looking. The stern anchor rope would have to do. At least it was long enough and about the right thickness; and they'd still have the bow anchor.

As Zenka came back with the oar she drew her knife, cut the anchor rope and hitched it round the rudder-head.

'Now lash the oar to the rudder-head, Zenka,' she said. 'Like this, look; over and under and round and round. Only you'll do it better 'n me, 'cos it's got to be real tight, see. I'll support the oar while you lash it; mustn't lower it into the water till you're done.'

Despite the continual lurching of the boat he was deft and swift, pulling the lashing tight with his full strength at each turn, frapping it closely and finishing, as she showed him, with another hitch to hold all firm. She had never before used a stern oar for steering and was surprised, when they were done, to find how well it answered. She had not foreseen that oar and lashing together would pivot easily about the rudder-head without working loose: the oar could be turned as far as a right angle to the boat, to check and turn it almost instantly. Its only disadvantage was that its length, together with the force of the current, made the sheer effort of working it for any time more than she could manage.

'You'll have to help me, Zenka,' she panted, having righted the boat and recovered the midstream channel. 'This'll do fine as long as we're careful, only I just haven't got the strength. See if you can get us round this bend that's coming up.'

He could. He did. Or rather, she provided the judgement, leaning this way and that on the handle of the oar, but relying on his greater physical strength to reciprocate and carry out what she wanted. As the boat rounded the bend without mishap, they broke into simultaneous cries of excitement. The trees were less dense and no more than five hundred yards ahead, as near as she could judge in the failing light, lay open water—the further edge of the forest.

'Anda-Nokomis!' she called. 'We're through!'

: 102 :

THE FRONTIER

Anda-Nokomis, turning in the bow, raised his hand in the traditional Beklan gesture of acknowledgement to the winner of a contest. At this same moment, as they still stood side by side with the oar between them, Zen-Kurel, as naturally as a bird might alight on a branch, put his free arm round Maia, drew her to him and kissed her.

She clung to him, both arms round his neck, now laying her face against his soaking wet hair, now returning his kiss again and yet once more as the rain ran down their faces and mingled between their lips. At last, releasing him, she gasped, 'The boat, my darling! We've still got to get to Katria.'

'I know. But at least tell me one thing now. I want us to be as we were in Melvda-Rain. I want you to marry me. Will you?'

'Yes, of course! Further to starboard; hard over, quick!'

The river, as it emerged from the forest, was broader, though flowing no less swiftly, for here, as far as they could make out in the falling dusk, it had not yet burst the distant, stony dykes on either side. They were in less danger now, for the trees had gone, there seemed to be no obstacles ahead and for the moment at all events little or no heavy débris in the main channel. The boat, however, had filled with so much rain and grown so heavy that it was actually hanging in the current—moving, certainly, but Maia, looking overside, could see sticks and leaves passing them at twice their speed. They had very little freeboard, too.

'Darling, yes will have to do for now.'

'It'll do very well,' he answered. 'You'd better bail again, I suppose.'

'Anda-Nokomis,' she called. 'Come and help me!'

'Do you think it's safe to leave the bow?'

'Yes: we're moving so slow. Only we got to bail this water out, else we'll never get there 'fore dark.'

They both set about bailing, while Zen-Kurel remained at the steering-oar. Maia, in spite of the great flood of joy filling her heart, knew now that she was undoubtedly ill—ill enough to need to go to bed as soon as she could. Her head ached, her throat and ears were horribly painful and she was feeling even more light-headed than when they had entered the forest.

'D'you mind if I have a go at the djebbah, Anda-Nokomis?' she asked, shivering. ''Fraid I'm took bad: it's the wet and bein' s' tired out. I'll be better once we c'n get warm and dry.'

He nodded and passed her the flask, and she took a good, long pull. She could feel the fumes rising consolingly to dull her pain. Leaning forward, she kissed Anda-Nokomis on both cheeks. 'You've been the best of friends to me, Anda-Nokomis, that you have! When you're back in Melvda-Rain—when you really *are* Ban of Suba—can we come and be your guests, Zenka and me?'

'Yes,' he answered, 'you shall. And no one shall speak a word against you.'

Yet as he spoke he looked so downcast and low that she felt ashamed, and very sorry that in her happiness she had spoken with so little consideration for his feelings.

'Dear, dear Anda-Nokomis, I'm so sorry about—you know; honest I am! Oh, sometimes, I just about wish I could split myself in two!'

'It would have to be a thousand and two, I think, Serrelinda,' he answered with a smile. It was the only joke she ever heard him make.

'Anda-Nokomis,' she said (bail and fling, bail and fling, oh Cran! don't I feel bad?), 'do you know there was one time when I cursed you, and swore that if ever I could harm you I would? Doesn't seem possible now, does it? Live and learn, that's about it. Fools don't know who their friends are, I reckon.'

'When was that?'

'After you'd made me dance the senguela at Sarget's party in the Barons' Palace; that was when.'

'But—er—surely you made rather a success of it, didn't you, as far as I recall?'

(As far as I recall. Oh dear, oh dear!) 'I know. It was on account of—of something else.' The djebbah was really taking effect now: her head was fairly spinning.

'Well, but you *did* harm him, didn't you?' said Zenka, 'and me too, come to that. But it's all dead and done with now.'

'My love, I never went to harm you, nor Anda-Nokomis neither.'

'*What?*'

'No, I never! Oh, darling Zenka, I wanted to *save* you both! Oh, and so many more! Anda-Nokomis, do you remember Gehta at the farm?'

1009

'Gehta at the farm? What farm? Don't you mean Clystis?'

'No, *no*!' He looked blank. 'Then surely you remember Sphelthon at the ford? Poor boy, *he's* at peace now, anyway.'

'She's light-headed,' said Zenka sympathetically. 'It's not surprising. We must take care of her once we—'

'I'm *not* light-headed!' she cried. 'It's *men* that's light-headed! All of you, everywhere! If you'd only *seen* that poor boy at the ford.'

She began to cry. 'I never meant you to go to that horrible fortress, or be tormented by that wicked woman. I *never*! I never meant to betray you! I didn't do it for the Leopards! I didn't do it to be the Serrelinda! I just wanted to stop you all killing each other! I'd seen what fighting *did* to people! I wanted Sendekar to get to the river in time to stop your king getting across, only it just didn't work out like that.'

Anda-Nokomis put his arm round her.

'You'd better tell us everything, Maia—about Gehta and Sphelthon and all the rest. A great deal seems to have happened on our journey to Suba that I failed to see.'

By fits and feverish, tipsy starts, she told them everything—how Gehta had told her of her terror of an invasion of western Urtah; how she had knelt by Sphelthon at the ford; how she had been left alone in Melvda-Rain when the armies were assembling, to reflect on Karnat's plan and what it would mean for her own people.

'But I never let on to any of the Leopards, Zenka,' she ended. 'I never told Sendekar or Kembri or any of them as it was you that told me. I loved you then and I love you now and that was why I went to the gaol that night in Bekla and made them let out the both of you.'

Zen-Kurel, leaving the oar to trail in the current, dropped on his knees and kissed her.

'Whether you were right or wrong doesn't matter any more. What matters is that you didn't do it for yourself or to harm anyone. You did it out of pity, didn't you? I might have guessed that.'

'But if you'd known in Melvda-Rain that you were Suban—' Bayub-Otal was beginning, when all three of them looked up in surprise, hearing a long, ululating call in the distance. Zen-Kurel, gripping the oar once more, trimmed their course, while Bayub-Otal, helping Maia to her feet, stood looking out over the water.

'Who is it?' asked Zen-Kurel, peering from one bank to the other. 'Is it us he's calling to?'

After a moment Maia pointed. Perhaps two hundred yards off and a little astern, in the bare, flat fields stretching away behind the dyke, a man was waving to them and pointing downstream. He was clearly a shepherd, for with him were two dogs and a little group of three or four sheep huddled together. In all the rainswept desolation there was not another soul to be seen.

'Those'll be strays he's been out after,' said Anda-Nokomis.

'What's he saying, though?' said Zen-Kurel, cupping his hand to his ear. The man, as best he could, was running after them, plainly agitated. His voice reached them again.

'Boom! Boom!'

'What's he mean?' asked Zen-Kurel. 'That's nonsense—boom, boom!'

'I wish it was,' said Maia. 'He's warning us there's a boom across the river lower down.'

'I remember now,' said Bayub-Otal. 'Some Belishban once told me in Bekla: they keep a boom across the river at the frontier, to stop rafts and boats and make them pay duty. No doubt they stop fugitives, too,' he added grimly.

'A boom?' asked Zen-Kurel, 'across a river this breadth? What can it be made of, for Cran's sake?'

'There's only one thing it could be made of,' said Maia. 'Ortelgan rope: probably with bells, to give warning if a boat runs on it at night.'

'Can't we cut it, then?'

'They wouldn't have a boom if you could get past it that easy. It'll be nearly as thick as your arm, and winched up level with the surface. There'll be a frontier post with bowmen, for sure.'

'But if we stop they'll recognize us,' said Bayub-Otal. 'This hand of mine—everyone knows what I look like: you too, Maia, come to that. And they'll be Leopard soldiers, probably warned already to look out for us. Anyone in Bekla would guess that since we escaped I'd be trying to get to Suba. If we're brought ashore in Belishba we'll be seized and held; that's certain.'

'Perhaps I could bribe them,' said Maia.

Zen-Kurel shook his head. 'They all hate Katrians too much, my darling. They'd only take all you'd got and then send us back to Bekla; there or Dari.'

No one spoke for more than half a minute, while the boat, rain-heavy again now, drifted on in the dusk. The only sounds were the creak of the steering-oar and the rain on the timbers.

'Here's what we'll do,' said Maia suddenly, 'and you'd just better listen, the both of you, 'cos there's no time to think of anything else. There's the guard-houses now, look, only just down there. See the lights?'

Zen-Kurel looked where she was pointing. 'Gods! One each side! Who'd have thought it? And look, further down still there's a village; can you see? That must be in Katria!'

'Will you only *listen*?' she said again. 'It's ten to one there'll be no one actually outside in all this rain. That means we won't be spotted until we hit the boom. Then I reckon it'll go taut and ring a bell. Each of you get hold of an oar, now. I'll take the boat over towards the left bank and run her on the boom sideways on, best as I can. Then you'll both have to jump for it. The oars'll hold you up, near enough, to go down a hundred yards and get ashore.'

'But what about you?' asked Zen-Kurel.

'Soon as you've gone I'll dive in and swim under water far 's I can. I'll be there 'fore you, no danger. Might give you a hand out, even.' She gave each of them a quick kiss. 'Now grab your oars and get over that side, 'cos here it comes.'

She leant hard on the steering-oar, turning the boat to port as they drifted down towards the guard-huts facing each other on opposite sides of the river. The smoke from their chimneys hung low over the roofs and lamps were alight inside. She could hear male voices, but there was not a soul to be seen. Good!

On either side, sticking up out of the flood water between the huts and the river, were two stout posts. Their tops were cloven, and in these grooves ran, as she expected, a thick rope. Upon the river side of each hung a bell as big as her head. She couldn't see how the ends of the rope were secured; probably to iron rings, she supposed, but all she was looking at was the river between. About ten feet out on each side the rope, sagging, disappeared into the water. How far would it be under in the middle, then? Could she have hoped to sail over it? Hardly; they'd have thought of that. It wouldn't have been worth the risk to try: if it had turned out wrong her men would never have been able to reach the bank from mid-stream. Anyway, it was too late to change now.

Ahead she could see a regular undulation where the river flowed over the rope. With all her strength she shoved the handle of the oar over to starboard. The boat turned and checked broadside on to the stream: then the starboard beam drifted gently against the rope. The boat listed but the rope gave only slightly—less than she'd expected.

'Now!' she cried, and in the same moment heard both the bells ringing. Anda-Nokomis and Zenka, clutching their oars, flung themselves over the starboard side.

Maia remained standing in the tilted stern, clutching the steering-oar to keep her balance. This was the bit she hadn't told them about. She un-buttoned her tunic, letting it hang open, and ripped her shift to the waist.

A voice was shouting 'Turn out! Turn out!' Soldiers, one or two with torches, others stringing their bows, were pouring out of both guard-huts, peering into the rain as their eyes adjusted to the almost-gone light.

'Help!' she cried. 'Help me! Oh, Cran, I'll drown if you don't help me!'

'What the hell d'you think you're doing, girl?' shouted one of the men; the tryzatt, she supposed. 'Where've you come from?'

'I didn't know about the rope!' she shouted. 'Oh, please help me!'

'Well, you know now,' answered the tryzatt. 'You mean you're alone?'

'Yes: I took the boat to run away from home. Please help me!'

'My stars, just look at her!' shouted another of the soldiers.

'Can you swim?'

'A little, yes. Oh, but I'm so frightened!'

No one had spotted her men yet; she mustn't look in their direction for fear of drawing attention to them. By now they might have had almost long enough to get ashore and out of bowshot.

At this point the matter was taken out of her hands. A sudden, sharp impulse of the current tilted the boat yet further, though still it hung against the ropes. Water came pouring over the starboard side. It was going to sink.

Maia plunged forward and under water. Although she kept her eyes open, she could see nothing. The current was swift and full of frightening drags and counterflows in which she was tugged helplessly one way and another. Obviously she was going downstream, but in which direction—right or left—she had no idea. She swam on for as long as her breath would hold, then came up, turned her head and looked quickly behind her.

Her heart sank. She must have gone from side to side, for she was no more than thirty or forty yards down from the rope, if that. On either shore there seemed to be something like twenty men, all gazing intently downstream. At that very moment one of them saw her and pointed.

'There she is, look!'

'Come in to the bank, girl,' shouted the tryzatt, 'else we'll have to shoot, and I mean it!'

She dived again, trying, in the swirling mirk, to swim to her left. Her head seemed splitting, now, and she felt so feverish and ill that she hardly knew what she was doing. Yet when she came up once more she was much further downstream and closer in to the left bank, where the water was lying almost level with the top of the dyke.

'There she is!' came the cry again. She looked round. Two or three soldiers, their bows in their hands, had run along the bank from the guard-hut and were approaching her. She was utterly spent, yet she turned and swam on. She had not gone ten yards before a swift 'Whaup!' sounded close to her ear. A moment later she saw the arrow floating a foot or two ahead.

I can't do any more: I'm drowning: I'll have to come ashore. Lespa be praised, they haven't seen Zenka and Anda-Nokomis: they must have got away. I shan't even be able to try to escape: I'm as sick as ever I've been in my life. O Zenka, just when we'd found each other again! I'm so sorry, my darling!

With a few last, failing strokes she reached the dyke wall. The top was only a few inches above her. She put her hands on it, pushed feebly upward and got her chin on the coping, but she could do no more. Trying to pull herself up and out she sank back, sobbing with pain, with the grief of loss and the bitterness of defeat. And now, in her delirium, it seemed as though Queen Fornis herself was standing on the bank, her green eyes staring as once in the archery field. 'Two of them I did myself!' What cruelty would be devised for her?

Two soldiers were striding towards her through the nightfall. Their footsteps came crunching over the loose shingle and as they drew closer she could see the Leopard cognizances on their shoulders.

'Ah, my lass! Not so clever after all, were you?' said one. 'That's the end of that little game, then. Come on, now, up with you!' He stooped, gripped her wrists and dragged her roughly over the wall.

'It's not all that far back, Yellib,' said the other. 'We can carry her easy enough.' They had her between them now, holding her by the arms and legs.

'Stop!'

Both men started and looked round. Anda-Nokomis, soaking wet from head to foot and almost as tall as the splintered oar he was still carrying, was stalking towards them. As he strode up they stood rooted to the spot. Authority surged from every inch of him as menace from a crouching wolf.

'You are violating the frontier!' Without taking his eyes from them, he indicated Maia with a gesture like that of Frella-Tiltheh pointing to the tamarrik seed. 'You have no business here! Leave that girl instantly and get back where you belong!'

They obeyed him, laying her down on the soggy, granular shingle. As they straightened up, however, one of them found his voice.

' 'E's only one man, ain't he?'

'That's right,' said the other. Then, to Anda-Nokomis, 'Who are you, anyway?'

'How dare you question me?' thundered Anda-Nokomis. 'I am the Ban of Suba, and if you do not immediately take yourselves back over the frontier—'

In that moment an arrow, flying out of the half-dark, struck him with terrible force just where neck met shoulder, burying itself four inches deep. A great spout of blood gushed out. Anda-Nokomis staggered and fell to the ground as a third soldier came running up, triumphantly waving his bow.

But now, from a little distance away, came cries of anger and attack, running feet and threats uttered in a foreign tongue. The newcomer pulled at his comrades' arms.

'Come on, here's the basting Katrians! We'd best get the hell out of it, quick! Have to leave the girl, else they'll have us!'

And thereupon all three turned and disappeared upstream.

Maia dragged herself to her hands and knees. Specks of light were floating before her eyes and all manner of water sounds, real and unreal, coming and going in her ears. Slowly she gained her feet. Anda-Nokomis had fallen on one side. His blood was pouring over the gravelly shingle. She staggered across to where he lay, knelt beside him and took his head on her arm.

'Anda-Nokomis.'

He stared past her, and she laid one hand against his cheek.

'Anda-Nokomis, it's Maia! It's your Maia here!'

Suddenly his eyes saw her, he recognized her. His terrible, blood-slobbering mouth moved and seemed to smile. He was trying to speak. She bent her head and kissed him.

'Anda-Nokomis—'

He grasped her wrist. Quite clearly, he whispered, 'When Suba's free, you and I, we'll—' Then his hand dropped and his head fell sideways on her arm.

Someone was standing beside her. She looked up. It was Zenka. There were others all around—soldiers, some of them, and rough-looking villagers like those she'd seen in Suba, carrying clubs and mattocks, their hair and beards beaded with the rain.

'Maia! I brought them as quick as I could! Oh, gods, what's happened? Anda-Nokomis—'

She clutched him round the legs, sobbing hysterically. Then everything grew indistinct, and she fell unconscious across the blood-drenched body of the Ban of Suba.

They carried her up the slope from the river to the houses—Zhithlir, southernmost village of Katria. The women and children crowded at the doors, staring silently as they slipped and staggered along the mud-churned street towards the Elder's house. Zen-Kurel limped beside Maia, himself scarcely able to keep up with the soldiers.

'You'll give her a bed and look after her, won't you?'

'Don't worry, sir,' answered the Katrian tryzatt. 'She couldn't have struck luckier, as it happens. There's an army doctor here on his rounds of the frontier posts.'

'Lucky?' said Zen-Kurel. 'Yes, she's always been lucky, tryzatt, you know. The gods are with her, else I wouldn't be here now.' He turned and looked back at those carrying the body of Anda-Nokomis, the arrow still embedded above his collar-bone.

'*He* never had any luck, poor man. Not once.'

'Oh, really, sir? That's bad, now,' replied the tryzatt stolidly, not knowing what else to say.

Zen-Kurel looked round him at the pall of wood-smoke, the dripping thatch of the roofs and the muddy alleys channelled with rivulets. Every hut, he now saw, had fastened to its door a wreath of yew or of cypress. The soldiers were wearing black ribbons at their shoulders, and from the roof of the Elder's house, as they approached it, a black flag drooped like a great, dead crow hung on a post.

'What's this, tryzatt? That flag, the wreaths—'

The tryzatt turned to stare.

'You mean you haven't heard, sir?'

'Heard what?'

'The king, sir. King Karnat was killed in battle four days ago, over on the western border. They've brought the body back to Kenalt for burning tomorrow.'

Stunned, Zen-Kurel made no reply, halting a moment and then wandering on a few paces apart. Yet by the time they reached the Elder's house he had recovered himself sufficiently to be able to give an account of how the Ban of Suba and himself had escaped from Bekla, thanks to the heroic help of none other than Maia Serrelinda, who had brought them safely through Purn and then down the Zhairgen to the frontier.

They heated water for him, gave him wine and food and prepared him a bed. Throughout the night, however, he sat watching beside Maia. Towards morning she woke, still weak and feverish but clear-headed, spoke to him and wept bitterly for Anda-Nokomis. She told him, too, how in the misery of her heart she had reflected that if love could not express itself in fulfilment it could do so only in sacrifice. 'But it wasn't me,' she sobbed, 'it wasn't me, in the end, as made that sacrifice!'

At this Zen-Kurel wept too. 'He insisted on waiting for you on the shore. He said I was the one who must go for help, because they'd take more notice of a Katrian.'

'If he hadn't done what he did, they'd 'a come too late.'

Maia remained low and grief-stricken for several days. But she was a strong, healthy girl, the doctor said, and with rest and care would be right enough in a week or two.

REUNION IN KERIL

It was nearly two years later. The summer was proving prosperous, pasture and stock thriving and crops ripening towards harvest. There were some weeks to go until the dog days: trees, grass and flowers were still fresh and verdant, the breezes cool but the streams, even in northern Katria, delightfully warm for splashing and lazing. For a one-year-old it was perfect weather; weather for crawling about in the sunshine and getting into everything, picking things up and stuffing them in the mouth unless or until they were removed; standing up and taking a few triumphant steps before falling flat with a howl to be snatched up and comforted by the Suban nurse; for being bounced up and down by one's joyous mother in the shallows, with screwed-up face and vocal noises interpretable by the affectionate and indulgent (and what other kinds of people might inhabit the world, pray?) as intelligible speech. The gold-and-purple kynat had come, bringing warm days and the gods' blessing, filling fields, woods and the hearts of hearers with its fluting call, 'Kynat, Kynat will tell!' The blue-finches sang, black-and-white plovers tumbled headlong from sky to earth and of an evening the trout rose to the *gylon* fly.

Keril-Katria was a pleasant enough town, thought Maia, strolling in the cool of the late afternoon along the tree-lined thoroughfare now known as King Karnat Avenue. Of course it was not remotely comparable with Bekla. There was hardly a single stone building, though a few were of brick. Most, however, were like those in Melvda-Rain—long, one-storey houses of wood, painted outside in the bright colours as much favoured by Katrians as by Subans. However, it was reasonably clean and safe to walk about in, possessed a number of quite good shops and honest traders once you knew where to look for them, and could even offer a certain amount of entertainment—jugglers, acrobats and dancers—well, passable dancers, if you could contrive to forget what you remembered and do your best to appreciate the Katrian style. In fact it was a nice enough place for a little jaunt, a trip to town; with quite a generous bit of pin-money, too, a couple of serving-men from the estate for attendants and the Suban girl to look after little Zen-Otal (or Anda-Serrelinda, as most called him at home) and take him off her hands when she wanted a respite from the happy, arduous business of motherhood. It certainly afforded a pleasant break from fulfilling the duties of mistress of the household (to say nothing of those of the dutiful, affectionate daughter-in-law) throughout Melekril and spring on the remote estate. Things had gone well enough, though. In fact, they'd been very happy and enjoyable—better than the first Melekril and spring, the early months of her marriage.

It had not been easy to begin with. She had been heavily dependent upon Zen-Kurel's devotion to build up any true sense of security and confidence in her new country, her new people and surroundings. For a start, there had been the language. Katrian Chistol—to say nothing of the dialect spoken by most people on the estate—bore little resemblance to Beklan: it was in effect another tongue. Zenka had had to find her an interpreter—that same Suban girl who had now become Zen-Otal's nurse. After about a year, however, she could rub along fairly well in Chistol, though the woodmen and the laundry maids still floored her at times. Still, she could joke with them about it now: she'd come to know them all so well.

Then there were the difficulties inseparable from her position as Zenka's wife, and mistress of the estate. Maia had not been born to authority or brought up to expect to have any. The Serrelinda, of course, had had authority, but it had been of an unusual kind—that of a public darling, a talismanic beauty and heroine, with no functions to fulfil beyond those of existing and being seen; a golden meteor, trailing light. (And indeed only last year a far-ranging pedlar from the empire, complete with scarlet hat, green shirt and white-striped jerkin—he even looked a bit like Zirek: it had brought a tear to her eye—had told her that what people in Bekla now said of the comet was that it had presaged the passing of the Serrelinda.) In Bekla she had never had duties to perform or decisions to make on behalf of others. She had had to begin as a complete learner; but the housekeeper, the head cook, the baker, the *clarzil*—the old beldame who minded their infants for the women out working in the fields—they'd all backed her up loyally and pulled and pushed her here and there while she was getting the hang of things. She suspected that Zen-Kurel had told them to make sure they did, and let him not hear anything to the contrary. But in thinking this she failed to give herself credit for her own likeable nature and pleasant manner of dealing with people. Maia possessed natural charm and what are sometimes called 'pretty ways'. Men will work for advancement or wealth, for a principle or a common cause. Women, by and large, work best for people they like. Little by little Maia began to exercise authority because she came to realize that the others wanted her to. In any society, someone has to give the orders and decide what is going to be done; but most prefer someone else to do this on their behalf. Maia had first to learn that authority was expected of her and then, as it were, to put it on and wear it without tripping over the hem. It had been difficult, and more than once she had lain awake beside Zen-Kurel (with Anda-Serrelinda kicking her from within) having all sorts of second thoughts and hoping to Cran that what she had said was to be done tomorrow would turn out to be all right.

Then, of course, there had been the legend of the Valderra to be relegated. While she and Zenka had been travelling up to the estate in northern
Katria and when they had first arrived there, this had been a haunting
nightmare. She was half-expecting to be murdered or at the least persecuted
and victimized. But in fact, as she came to realize, these fears existed very
largely in her own mind and there alone. A remote community, almost
entirely self-supporting—a society of hunters, foresters and husbandmen—
concerned during nearly all the hours of daylight with the unchanging,
yearly round of subsistence; their art and recreation self-made, their topics
and news largely that of local birth and death, good luck and calamity—
they took her as they found her; and they found her pretty, sensible and
eager to please. There were, of course, a few ex-soldiers about the place,
two of whom had actually been in Katria with the king, and certainly,
when these men had had a skinful, some black remarks had been passed
down in the local tavern at one time and another—remarks about basting
treachery and Beklan trollops who'd found gold between their legs while
poor fellows died for it in Dari-Paltesh. But the short answer from most
had been that that was then and this was now, and wasn't she as nice a
lass as you'd hope to come across and anyway who'd suffered more, by all
accounts, than the young master and he seemed happy enough, didn't he?
Little by little the pot simmered down; but it is always hard to know how
to bear yourself when you have a fair notion that hard things are being
said behind your back; so this had been another problem.

With her widowed father-in-law relations had, of course, been still more
difficult at the outset. Zen-Bharsh-Kraill was an old adherent of King
Karnat and had been a famous warrior in his day. His other, younger son,
a brave officer, had been killed in the king's army (though not on the
Valderra), and his daughter was married to one of the king's most illustrious captains. As a nobleman, his knowledge and outlook went not only as
wide as Katria but as wide as Terekenalt itself. He knew Maia's past and
her fame well enough. From the outset Zen-Kurel had had to put his foot
down in no uncertain manner. There had been one terrible evening when
he had hurled his goblet across the room and said that at this rate he
would disclaim his inheritance, take his wife to Dari-Paltesh and set up on
his own account. Maia had cried herself to sleep and woken crying, protesting that she was nothing but a hindrance and a bad bargain to him—
until it came to her that she was only adding to his difficulties and transferring to him her share of the burden, since for days past he had been
doing all he could to mediate and to resolve their difficulty. His outburst
had been due to strain and entirely exceptional. What he needed was a
sane, cool contribution from a strong, balanced partner; not a resourceless,
weeping child. This was perhaps the moment when Maia made the dis-

covery that moral may sometimes be even harder to exert than physical courage. Zenka had taken her by the shoulders in the lamplight, kissed her and looked into her eyes. 'Been to any good Ortelgan camps lately?' She had laughed—Cran alive! This fuss, after all they'd been through together!—and hugged him; they had made love and next morning a most sedate, self-possessed Maia had sought out her father-in-law and successfully conducted a long talk ending in mutual, more friendly understanding. After all, his wife had been Beklan. He was secretly delighted that Zenka had come home alive and well to run the estate and was not ignorant, either, as to who was largely responsible for this. Nowadays, so it seemed to her, old Zen-Bharsh-Kraill was coming at last to like her and respect her ideas about things in general. Predictably, the birth of Zen-Otal had altered everything for the better. Grandchildren always do.

Her labour—surprisingly for such a well-built, healthy girl—had not been easy. During her pregnancy she had often felt poorly and run-down—a good sign, the doctor said, for the baby is a parasite on the mother and her malaise shows that the baby is getting all it should. It had been a strain. She was not in the best of spirits and was all-too-much inclined to dwell on Milvushina. As her time approached, Zen-Kurel had effected a masterly surprise. One day, without a trace of fore-warning, she had woken late to find Nasada sitting beside the bed. Actually struck dumb for a few seconds, she had wondered whether he could be real. Then she flung herself into his arms, crying with happiness and relief, already sure that now everything was going to be all right. The old man—still dressed like a Suban marsh-frog in his fish-skin smock and bone amulet—told her how Zen-Kurel had sent to Melvda-Rain and begged Lenkrit, now Ban of Suba, to ask him to come and attend his wife's lying-in. Lenkrit had readily put a kilyett and paddlers at his disposal.

'I hope you'll tell me,' he said, when she had recovered herself and they had had breakfast together, 'all about your adventures on the Zhairgen. Twenty minutes crossing it was quite enough for me.'

That evening, at supper, she had worn her diamonds and, later, shown him once again poor Randronoth's cabinet of the fishes. It had its place, now, on her dressing-table, and contained her brooches, ornamental pins and the like.

'U-Nasada, do you remember the night when we had supper in Bekla, and you told me as this was made from the bones of fishes bigger than my room?'

'I remember, Serrelinda.'

'Do you still think that?'

He laughed. 'I don't just think it, now: I know. I've learned a lot in my travels.'

1020

Well, let him tease, she thought. U-Nasada ought to be allowed a tall story or two. Just to see him once more sitting at her supper-table in the lamplight—a less luxurious and elegant supper-table these days, but plenty on it all the same—filled her with confidence and reassurance. Everything she'd done, she thought, had been right after all—the heart's commitment, the suffering, the danger—and now she could thank him for his part—no small one—in bringing about this happy outcome.

'Do you remember how you told me I'd do better in Suba than in Bekla?'

'Yes, I do. More truth, I said, didn't I? Something like that.'

'I know what you meant now. It just suits me here—I'm happier than I ever dreamt I could be—and it's not so very different from Suba, is it?'

'What a shame,' he replied, 'about Anda-Nokomis! They've put up a fine memorial to him, you know, at Melvda. It says he was the steadfast Ban of Suba, who died for his people.'

'Oh, he'd have liked that!' She paused. 'Might even have made him smile, poor old Anda-Nokomis.' Then, 'It was me he died for: I never forget it, and neither does Zenka.'

He confirmed to her what she had already heard by rumour and report, though it seemed of little importance to her now, in the midst of all the duties and preoccupations of her new life: namely, that Santil-kè-Erketlis had taken Bekla unopposed after a three days' march in the blinding rains; that the Leopards had been displaced and slavery ended in the empire. Kembri was dead, but when she asked about Elleroth Nasada knew little about him. Nor could he tell her anything of Elvair-ka-Virrion or of Fornis.

'No one in Suba knows,' said he, 'what's become of Fornis. She seems completely to have vanished. Very odd.'

'Nor they don't know in Paltesh, even?'

He shook his head. 'There's something strange about it. I wonder—?' He hesitated. 'Such an evil woman—' Then he seemed to check himself. 'Well, never mind. Perhaps we should just thank the gods she's no longer in Bekla and leave it at that. Surely we've got something better to talk about than Fornis.'

'Shagreh.'

'Great Shakkarn! You said it right!'

'Well, they say it here too, see. Comes in useful and all, U-Nasada; kind of a philosophy, like, in't it?'

'You look very well on it, anyway. You must be doing what you like.'

'I am.'

'That's the real secret of health, of course. I tried to tell Kembri that once, but he wouldn't have it.'

1021

Three days later she went into labour. It was a trying affair, lasting over thirty hours. She was not helped by her memories of Milvushina. Without Nasada, however, it would have been a great deal worse, for the midwife was an old body armed with snakeskins, a rabbit's paw, dirty hands and mumbled charms. Nasada was short with her. He remained completely calm and confident throughout, so that Maia, as she bore down again and again, felt strength pouring out of him into her racked, sweat-drenched body. He was like a glowing brazier at the centre of the house that was her labour, seeming to warm and encourage everyone—but particularly the heroine—by his mere presence. He had, his manner suggested, seen it all before and was in no doubt of the outcome. She found herself wondering whether he would have saved Milvushina. Very likely he would.

When at last she had been delivered and was putting Zen-Otal to her breast; when Zenka had come in, kissed his wife and son with tears and gone out to announce the news to the waiting household and then to everyone on the estate (wearing, in accordance with tradition, a wreath of planella; if it had been a girl, the wreath would have been of trepsis), she looked up and said, 'I wish I knew how to thank you, U-Nasada. Do you know, when I was still just a banzi on Lake Serrelind I saw you once in a dream? Before ever I was sold as a slave; before ever I'd had a man, even.'

He bent forward, stroking the baby's head.

'I hardly *could* know that, if you come to think of it. Tell me.'

She told him the dream—what a long time ago it seemed! How she had found herself the Queen of Bekla, scattering figs as she drove her goat-carriage through the crowds, only to come at last upon himself, in place of her own reflection, gazing up at her from the green depths of the lake.

'It's all plain enough now,' she ended, 'but of course I couldn't make head nor tail of it then. I went out and swam in the lake and gave the dream back to Lespa, 'cos I couldn't understand it.'

'Well, she's certainly sorted it out for you, hasn't she? I think you ought to thank her, not me.' But she could see how much pleasure it had given him to be told.

A day or two later he had returned to his water-ways and his devoted marsh-frogs.

That had been more than a year ago. She had followed his parting instructions to the letter and surely there had never been a finer baby than Zen-Otal.

As a matter of fact this was the reason why she was here now in Keril-Katria. Nasada had sent a message that he wanted to scratch the baby's arm against the fever, as he had (she might recall) for the young Suban Kram. Zen-Kurel, himself no Suban, had been inclined to make light of the matter; but on this occasion Maia, though she had lost nothing of her respect and admiration for her husband (indeed, it had rather grown, if anything, for while he had retained all his endearing cheerfulness and self-assurance he was maturing, becoming less youthfully precipitate), was determined to have her own way. If Nasada thought it ought to be done, then done it was going to be. However, the old man had said that he would prefer to avoid a second journey all the way to northern Katria. Could they, perhaps, meet in Keril? So here, of course, she had come, leaving Zenka to see to the business of the summer cattle-fair, where he expected to make a good profit.

Nasada had now left Keril, having duly scratched Zen-Otal, pronounced him as likely a child as ever he had seen in his life and advised her to wait a few days before returning home, as the scratching might bring on a touch of fever, though nothing to worry about. So here she was, strolling along King Karnat Avenue on a fine summer evening, perfectly happy to be a country girl on a visit to town, with nothing to do for a nice change and all of five hundred meld from a generous husband to lay out on herself.

A little way off was a small ornamental lake, where white cranes were feeding; nothing near so beautiful as the Barb and only about a quarter the size; still, perhaps she might walk there for a while before returning to her inn—'The Keg and Kynat', a respectable, not-too-expensive house—for supper. After that perhaps she'd ask one of her men to attend her to the dancing. (A lady in Katria was not expected to go about alone. She oughtn't really to be out alone now, but once a Beklan, she thought—well, perhaps not always a Beklan: but not a back-of-beyond provincial, either, to be subject to every hidebound convention while she was out on a bit of a spree.)

All of a sudden she became aware of some sort of stir further up the road. People were running forward in eager excitement. She could hear cries of enthusiasm and admiration—even a cheer or two. A voice was shouting, 'Make way! Make way there!' Surely that was a Beklan accent?

Married lady and mother or no married lady and mother, Maia, at eighteen, had not lost her capacity for girlish excitement. What could it be? She could glimpse, above the heads of the gathering people, a tall man in an ornate head-dress, carrying a wand of office. It was he who was shouting, 'Make way!', but for whose benefit she could not see. Could it perhaps be Lenkrit, or someone like that, on a state visit from Suba; or just possibly even the new King of Terekenalt? She had heard tell of nothing of the kind, but that was not surprising. Anyway, whatever it was, she wasn't going to miss it. It'd be something to tell Zenka and his father when she got home. 'Oh, and I saw the king. What d'you think of that?'

Her matronly dignity (such as it was) cast aside, Maia began to run like the others, her sandalled feet kicking up the soft dust of summer. She slipped sideways past two or three men in sacking smocks, bumped into and apologized to an old market-woman with a basket, managed to get another yard or two closer to the front, stood on tiptoe and looked over the shoulder of a lad with a hinnari on his shoulder.

The tall man in the head-dress was certainly Beklan: now that she could get a good look at him there was no doubt of that. Although he was wearing a silver-and-green uniform he was not a soldier, but evidently some sort of steward or major-domo. Still shouting, 'Make way! Make way!' and now and then pushing people back with his staff of office, he was nonetheless making slow progress, for the crowd was thickening. Behind him, dressed in the same uniform, came three equally smartly-dressed men, while behind these again came two youths pulling a flower-bedecked, red-and-yellow jekzha. Seated in this was the centre of attention—a young woman at whom everyone was pointing and staring. She was dressed in a gold-embroidered robe of scarlet silk and flaunting a great fan of peacock feathers, while round her neck, on a gold chain, hung an enormous emerald set in silver. From time to time she raised one hand to the people, showing her very white teeth in a flashing smile. It was not remarkable that they were all wonder-struck, for none of them could ever have seen a girl like this before. Not only was she resplendent in the prime of youth and health, radiant with prosperity and plainly enjoying every moment of the adulation; she was also alert as a leopard and not quite so black as its spots. She was Occula.

In the instant that Maia recognized her the jekzha had passed by. The major-domo having succeeded at last in clearing a way, the boys quickened their pace and entered the side-street opposite.

Maia, frantically pushing and thrusting, burst out of the crowd, tripped, fell, got up again and ran after them shouting, 'Occula! Occula!'

People were closing in behind the jekzha, blocking her way. Still shouting, she shoved and pulled them aside, so that several cried out angrily. She only ran on all the harder, calling and stumbling but gradually catching up. Another uniformed attendant, bringing up the rear, turned and stared at her as she came dashing towards him.

'Occula! Occula!'

'Get back, woman!' he cried. 'What do you think you're doing? Here!' he called to one of the others in front. 'This mad woman! Come and—' He stopped her, striking an ill-aimed blow which glanced off her shoulder. She bit his hand. 'Occula! Occula!'

They had her by the arms now, two of them. She was struggling. Then, all of a sudden, they were knocked aside by a swinging cuff apiece.

'You bastin' idiots, doan' you know who it is? Let her alone, damn you! Get over there and wait till I call you!'

The next moment she and Occula were clasped in each other's arms. There was a fragrance of kepris and beneath that the old smell, as of clean coal. The gold-embroidered robe scratched her face, but she hardly felt it.

'Banzi! Oh, banzi, banzi, I doan' be*lieve* it!'

They looked at each other with tears streaming down their cheeks. People were crowding round, chattering like starlings, the liveried servants doing their best to hold them back.

'I thought you were in Terekenalt! They said you'd married your officer fellow and gone to live in Terekenalt!'

'No, it's Katria.'

'Oh, Katria, is it? Hell, look at all these bastards! We can' talk here. Banzi, are you busy? Were you goin' somewhere?'

'Oh, Occula, how can you ask? No, of course I'm not!'

'Well, get in the damn' jekzha, then. Quick, too, before this bunch of bumpkins trample us both to buggery! Florro!' she shouted to the major-domo. 'You'd better try another street or somethin'! The Serrelinda and I want to get back as quick as we can.'

'Where are we going?' asked Maia as she climbed in.

'"The Green Parrot",' said Occula. 'Do you know it?'

It was the most luxurious and expensive hostelry in Keril. The idea of her staying there had not even occurred either to Zenka or herself.

'Well, sort of,' she said, 'but actually I haven't been to Keril all that often. It's quite a long way up north, see, where Zenka and me live.'

'What are you doin' here now?'

Maia explained. 'And you?'

'I'm with Shend-Lador. Remember him? He's on a diplomatic mission for Santil. What a bit of luck runnin' into you! We're only stayin' here tonight—off to Terekenalt tomorrow. Shenda's goin' to talk to the new king, you see.'

'What about?'

'Oh, banzi, doan' be a fathead! How the hell should I know what about? Some sort of trade agreement—frontiers—politics—that sort of bollocks.'

'You always used to be political enough.'

'I wasn'; I was the vengeance of the gods, for my own personal reasons. That's different; and anyway it's all over. I'm the bouncy girl; remember? Thousand meld a bounce? But I'm well beyond even that now. I'm the black Beklan knockout, dear. Shend-Lador's mistress, richer than forty shearnas on golden beds.'

'Oh, Occula, I'm so glad! You always said you would be.'

'Shenda's talkin' to the High Baron of Katria in private this evenin',' said Occula. 'So you can come and have supper with me, can' you? You say no and I'll have you knifed and thrown down a well, banzi; I swear I will.'

'My little boy—' she was beginning.

'Yes, where have you left him?'

'We're at "The Keg and Kynat". My Suban girl's looking after him.'

'I'll send Florro with the jekzha to bring them both round to the "Parrot". Then he can suck your deldas all the evenin' if he likes, same as old Piggy used to. What's his name?'

'Zen-Otal: they all call him Anda-Serrelinda.'

'Of course. Poor old Bayub-Otal's dead, though, isn' he?'

'Yes, nearly two years ago now. He died saving my life, Occula! I'll tell you all about it over supper. Oh, Cran, I'm so happy to see you! Who'd ever have expected it?'

'Well, here we are,' said the black girl, as they drew up in front of 'The Green Parrot'. 'Kantza-Merada, what a dump! Best you can hope for here, I s'pose. Still, at least we've got a set of private rooms; and you'll get a damn' good supper, banzi, I can promise you that; *and* a nice drop of Yeldashay. We brought some along with us, just to be on the safe side.'

: 104 :

AN ACCOUNT SETTLED

Perhaps it was not altogether surprising that Occula had put on weight, thought Maia, herself feeling rather like Sencho as she leaned back against the cushions. During the past two years she had forgotten about suppers like this. The Yeldashay had gone to her head, too, for she was no longer used to it. She felt splendid. They had eaten and drunk and chattered their heads off. At length Occula had dismissed the servants and Maia had recounted all her adventures from the night when her friend had come to her house in Bekla to warn her to get out of the city.

Zen-Otal was fast asleep on another pile of cushions in the corner of the room. Occula had admired him—her unparalleled boy—with polite praise, but was plainly not all that much enraptured. However, Maia had not really expected that she would be. She realized, now, that motherhood was one of the gods' great tidings to which Occula was simply deaf, and likely to remain so; just as, she remembered, good old Brero, who would never have dreamed of causing her a moment's vexation, had once remarked, 'I can tell you all about music, säiyett, in one word: no good.' There was no earthly point in letting things like this annoy you: you might as well expect a cat to eat hay. Yet she could remember the time when for her Occula had possessed the wisdom and infallibility of a demi-goddess. What a shame, she thought, that while Occula had been able to teach her so much, she herself would never be able to communicate to her the first thing about motherhood! She wasn't fool enough to start trying, either. And Occula, she felt sure, must even now be entertaining feelings not unlike her own—what a pity to see her banzi, the one-time Serrelinda, fallen a victim, like all the rest, to the absurd slavery of marriage and maternity!

'I didn' tell you, banzi, did I,' said Occula, refilling her goblet and putting her feet up on the supper-table, 'that I've got Ogma in my household—have had for over a year? I know she'd want to be remembered to you. I'll give her your love when I get back, shall I?'

'Oh, yes, do! Poor old Ogma—clump! clump! Well, I'll bet she's as happy with you as it's possible for her to be anywhere.'

'Of course, I've got more sense than to do what you did, banzi—put her in charge of the place. Nearly cost you your life, didn' it?'

'I suppose you've got some marvellous, charming säiyett, have you?' Maia felt much too replete and happy to take offence.

'Well, yes, I have; but Zuno's the one actually in charge. He'd never dream of leaving me. Well, you never know, of course, but I shouldn' *think* he would.'

'Then Fornis—Fornis didn't take him with her?'

Occula looked up quickly. 'Where d'you mean—where to?'

'Wherever she's gone.'

For several seconds Occula made no reply. Then, putting her feet down again, she said very quietly and directly, 'Banzi, you'd better tell me—how much do you know about—about where Fornis went?'

Maia frowned at her, puzzled. 'Well, nothing, I reckon. We're a bit out of the way here, see. Only old Nasada, that's my doctor from Suba—'

'Yes, I've heard a good deal about Nasada. What did *he* tell you?'

'Well, he said no one in Suba knew what had become of Fornis; and then he said it seemed strange.'

'I'm surprised he hasn' guessed—a man as knowledgeable as that. P'raps he has.' She fell silent again, twisting a great gold ring on her finger and apparently deliberating with herself.

'Banzi,' she said, looking up suddenly, 'if I tell you—everythin'—will you swear by Frella-Tiltheh never to breathe a word—even to your wonderful Katrian husband?'

'Well, of course, dearest, if you ask. But—'

'It's not because I'm afraid of—of anythin' that could come to me from—from livin' men. It's because some things are—well, simply not to be told. But I doan' believe Kantza-Merada would want me not to tell *you*: not after Tharrin, and not after all we've been through together. When you've heard me out you'll understand. Go on, banzi—swear by Frella-Tiltheh.'

'I swear by Frella-Tiltheh the Inscrutable, and by the divine tamarrik seed, never to repeat to anyone what you're going to tell me.'

'Good! Listen, then. And you'd better have some more of this Yeldashay, banzi, 'cos you're goin' to need it!'

She refilled Maia's goblet and her own, drank deeply, and began.

'The night you left Bekla, there was fightin' all over the city; the Lapanese, and Fornis's Palteshis. Remember?'

Maia nodded.

'It went on all that night and into the next day. But what finished it was when the Lapanese finally got it through their heads that Randronoth was dead. The news took hours to get round, you see: the fightin' was so confused, all over the place. But once his officers knew for a fact that Fornis and Han-Glat had murdered him, they lost heart. Two of his captains—young Seekron and another man called Mendel-el-Ekna—'

'Ah, he was the one as got us out that night!' said Maia.

'Was he? I'm not surprised: everyone spoke well of him in that business. Well, they got together what was left of the Lapanese and took them back south again. Still, never mind that for now. I'll come back to that: what I want to tell you about is my part.

'So Fornis had the city, and no one to dispute it except Eud-Ecachlon. He was supposed to be holdin' it for Kembri, but he was shit-scared, and I doan' blame him, because he hadn' enough men to hope to beat Fornis. Those he had he took and shut himself up in the citadel.

'So there was Fornis—and Zuno and Ashaktis and me along with her, of course—in the Barons' Palace, givin' out that she'd restored the rightful dominion of the Sacred Queen in accordance with the will of the gods. And what she meant to do about Kembri and Santil-kè-Erketlis I never knew. Perhaps *she* didn', either; 'cos matters were taken out of her hands. And who d'you think did that, banzi?'

'You?'

'No; you.'

'*Me?* Occula, whatever d'you mean?'

'I'll tell you. You remember we were talkin' just now about N'Kasit, the leather dealer I sent you to, in the big warehouse? He was one of the best agents the heldril had, you know. He was a heldro agent for five years and no one ever suspected him—not even Sencho. He had a few narrow squeaks after Sencho was killed, though. They searched his warehouse more than once.'

'I'm not surprised he wasn't suspected,' said Maia. 'I remember Zirek calling him a cold fish and that's how he struck me, too: what you'd call imperturbable, like.'

'Well, there *was* another side to him, I can assure you, banzi,' said Occula, 'as you're about to hear. It must have been next day—yes, it *was* the next day—after the Lapanese had left Bekla, that Fornis sent Ashaktis to tell the chief priest she was comin' down to the temple. I knew what that meant: she was goin' to set about frightenin' him into supportin' her for a third reign as Sacred Queen. I believe she'd have done it, too—she could do anythin', that woman—only it never got that far, you see.

'She set out from the Barons' Palace about an hour later, and she told me and Zuno to attend her. She'd helped herself to your golden jekzha, banzi, and I can tell you it didn' half make me grind my bastin' teeth, comin' along behind, to see her sittin' up in that. Still, it proved a mistake, as you'll hear.

'Soon as we got down to the bottom of the Street of the Armourers, we could see there was somethin' goin' on in the Caravan Market. Someone was up on the Scales, talkin' and wavin' his arms, and a whole crowd of people were listenin'; and you could see they were on his side, too, whatever it was all about.

'Well, as you know, Fornis was always a great one for confrontin' anyone or anybody. Give her a situation and an adversary and she'd always wade in. Most people prefer to avoid trouble if they can, doan' they? She knew that, and she knew how to make the most of it. She'd tackle anyone face to face.'

'I know,' said Maia. 'I remember her putting down Kembri and the chief priest and the governor of Tonilda, all in one go. I was in a terrible bad way when she came in, but I've never forgotten it. She took me away and they couldn't stop her, that was what it come down to. They couldn't stand up to her at all.'

'Only you couldn' do what she wanted, could you? Her funny little games? Well, I doan' blame you, banzi. I couldn' have done it myself if I hadn' had Kantza-Merada with me, and Zai's unavenged ghost as well.

'Anyway, that mornin', as soon as she saw the crowd round the Scales, Fornis told the Palteshis who were pullin' your jekzha to go straight over. And when we got closer, I saw it was N'Kasit who was up there, boomin' away like a cow after a calf. They were all listenin' to him, and no one— no soldiers nor anybody—tryin' to stop him.

'"So," he was declaimin' as we came up, "where *is* she? That's what *I'm* askin'. If she hasn' been murdered, where is she? The girl the gods sent to preserve the city—the girl who swam the Valderra! Where is she, the luck of the empire? Her house is empty, her servants are gone. If you doan' believe me, there's a man here from the upper city, and he's *seen* her empty house with his own eyes!"

'They were all hangin' on every word he said, and he was so wrapped up in it that he never noticed Fornis comin' up behind him.

'"I'll *tell* you where she is," he shouted. "She's been *murdered*, for envy of her beauty and her luck—the luck of the gods, which she passed on to all of you! Why are you all standin' there like a bunch of idiots, when you've been robbed of your sacred luck? Where's your Maia Serrelinda? Why doan' you go to the upper city and demand to know?"

'He was doin' it so convincin'ly that he had me badly worried. I was wonderin' whether you could ever have reached his warehouse that night, or if you had, whether you'd managed to get out of Bekla alive.

'Well, all of a sudden he looked round and there was Fornis starin' up at him without a word. He hadn' been expectin' that, of course, and he stopped dead in the middle of what he was sayin'.

'She took her time, lookin' him up and down. Everybody was watchin' and waitin' to see what would happen. And at last she said "Come here."

'Well, that put him fair and square on the spot, banzi, you see; because either he had to climb down off the Scales and go and stand in front of her, or else he had to refuse to obey the Sacred Queen—and he hadn' quite got himself up to that pitch yet.

'He hesitated for quite a few moments, and Fornis just sat there and waited. And then he climbed down off the Scales—yes, he did: she was incredible, that woman, wasn' she?—and he went and stood in front of her.

'"Now," she said, "what *is* all this that you've been talkin' about, may I ask?"

'You could see he was frightened, but he still did his best to stand up to her. "We're talkin' about Maia Serrelinda, esta-säiyett," he answered. "We want to know where she is. We believe you've done away with her."

'"Oh, really?" says Fornis, noddin' once or twice and fannin' herself— it was scorchin' hot that mornin'. "I see! Well then, you'd better learn differently, hadn' you? For as it happens I know who killed Maia."

'That fairly made my blood run cold, banzi, for I believed her. Everyone believed her. You could see it in their faces. They were all paralysed like rabbits by a stoat. And what she was goin' to say next I doan' know, but if she'd told them all to go up the Sheldad and jump in the Monju I believe they'd have done it.

'"I think you'd better come along with me to the temple," she said to N'Kasit, "so that we can sort this little matter out."

'And then, banzi, just for once she got a taste of her own medicine; the only person in the whole of Bekla, I suppose, who wasn' afraid of her. Well, you'd *have* to be mad, wouldn' you, not to be afraid of *her*?'

'Who?' asked Maia, leaning forward and gripping the edge of the table. 'Who, Occula? Who?'

'D'you remember old Jejjereth, the crazy prophet-man?' replied the black girl. 'It was him. All in a moment he'd leapt out of the crowd and there he was, dancin' and jabberin' like a great, stinkin' ape alongside your jekzha.

'"Ah!" he shouted. "A shadow! A shadow will cover the city! The evil woman who gave me a knife to kill Maia! But I wouldn' do it! And when you shall see a murderess sittin' on the sacred throne, then you shall know that the judgement of the gods is nigh at hand!" And he said a whole lot more like that, banzi. He was wavin' his arms about and hoppin' from one foot to the other, and then he tried to climb up into the jekzha.

'Fornis didn' hesitate a second. She drew her knife—she never went anywhere without a knife, you know—and stabbed him straight to the heart. He went down without another word; but he was kickin' and thrashin' about in the dust for quite a bit, and the blood was somethin' to see: I can see it now.

'"Right, let's get on," says Fornis to the jekzha-men. "We've wasted enough time here." And off they set.

'But N'Kasit wasn't followin' her as she'd told him to.

'"She's killed poor old Jejjereth!" he yelled to the people. As if they needed any tellin'! "Poor old Jejjereth, that never harmed anyone! And she's got Maia's jekzha, too!"

'And that was the last I saw, because Fornis jus' went straight on without takin' the slightest notice, and none of them dared to touch her.

'We didn' go to the temple, though. She'd changed her mind about stayin' down in the lower city. As soon as we got down to the bottom of Storks Hill she made them go round by the Slave Market and back to the Peacock Gate without goin' through the Caravan Market again at all.

'Well, that evenin' I was helpin' Ashaktis to wait on her at supper when Zuno came in and said there was an officer outside who wanted to speak to her.

'"What d'you mean, an officer?" says Fornis. "Who is it?"

'Well, before Zuno could answer the officer came in, and who d'you reckon it was?'

Maia shook her head.

'It was Shend-Lador,' said Occula. 'I'd heard he'd come back to Bekla with Elvair, but of course I hadn' actually seen him. He saluted Fornis and then he said, "Esta-säiyett, you must excuse this intrusion. Believe me, it may very well save your life and that's my only excuse."

'Well, you remember Shenda, doan' you? It'd be very difficult for anyone, even Fornis, to get angry with Shenda. He always had a sort of a way with him, didn' he?

'"You'd better tell me, then," she said.

'"It's the chief priest who's sent me, esta-säiyett," says he.

'"The chief priest?" answers Fornis. "Well, you go back and tell the chief priest that if he's got anythin' to say to me he can come up here and say it for himself."

'"Well, that's just it, esta-säiyett," said Shenda. "He can't."

'"What d'you mean, he can't?" she asked.

'"Well, esta-säiyett, it so happened I was down at the temple this evenin', havin' treatment for this wounded foot of mine from one of the priests. And while I was there, all of a sudden we heard this commotion outside. So the doctor and me, we went out to see what was up, and there was the chief priest and a lot of others; and down in the Tamarrik Court below there was this crowd—all sorts; women, too—and the chief priest was tryin' to calm them down; only he couldn' make himself heard. They just kept on shoutin' 'Serrelinda! Serrelinda!' and 'Murder! Murder!' and 'Jej-jereth!' and things like that.

'"Well, I'll cut it short, esta-säiyett," goes on Shenda. "What it comes to is that the chief priest's sent me to tell you that the whole lower city's in a state close on disorder and riot. He sent me because he thought that as a wounded officer I'd be able to get through the streets without bein' set upon. There's no priest dares put his face outside the temple, you see. What the people are sayin'—and I beg you to bear in mind, esta-säiyett, that I'm only reportin' what the chief priest told me to tell you—is that you've murdered Maia Serrelinda. To be perfectly blunt, esta-säiyett, they're demandin' your life. The chief priest thinks you should leave Bekla at once, and keep out of the way for some time. He hopes you'll send him word where you are, and he'll let you know as soon as things are better."

'And then, while Fornis was still chewin' on that, Shend-Lador added, "The chief priest particularly asked me to say, esta-säiyett, that if he can' assure the people that you've left the city, he woan' be answerable for anythin' that may happen."

'Well, the next few hours were like a bastin' madhouse, banzi: you can' imagine it. Fornis insistin' she'd go down to the lower city herself and give them a piece of her mind, and Han-Glat preventin' her more or less by force: and then there were two more frantic messages from the chief priest, one brought by a pedlar and the other by a shearna called Nyllista (and I wonder what *she* was doin' in the temple, doan' you?). No one else could get through the mob, you see. You never heard such a shine in your life.

'Well, at last, in the middle of the night, above five or six hours after Shend-Lador had first come, Han-Glat told Fornis in so many words that she'd have to get out. And he flatly refused to come with her. He'd got Bekla and he meant to hang onto it. She raged and stormed and cursed, but he wouldn' budge an inch. And at last it began to dawn on Miss Fornis that if she refused he might even go the length of killin' her himself—that or else hand her over to the mob. The riotin' had been goin' on all night and we were half-expectin' them to come over the Peacock Wall any moment. The Palteshis were there to stop them, of course, but even they were pretty badly shaken by this time.

'Fornis's plan, when at last she'd been forced to accept the idea of leavin', was to rejoin her army—the army she'd left on the plain after she'd murdered Durakkon. She couldn' make out why they hadn' turned up: she'd been expectin' them every hour. And then, in the middle of that very night, while we were packin' up and gettin' ready to go, a couple of Palteshi soldiers arrived with news that must have shaken even her.

'Sendekar—good old Sendekar, out on the Valderra—*he'd* heard the rumour that Fornis had murdered you. Well, of course, banzi, if ever you had a friend in the whole empire it was Sendekar. And since he'd found out that Karnat had gone off to western Terekenalt and any sort of attack across the Valderra was unlikely for the time bein', he'd turned half his lads round and gone east. He'd joined up with Kerith-a-Thrain and between them they'd attacked the Palteshis a second time and made quite a mess of them. Just how bad a mess we couldn' make out, but the two soldiers were quite clear that there was no longer any chance of the Palteshis reachin' Bekla. And by the same token Fornis couldn' hope to get to them.

'You had to admit she had courage, the bitch. She heard the messengers out without a tremor; and then she said to Han-Glat, as cool as you like, "Very well," she said, "since you're so anxious to see the back of me, you cowardly bastard, I'll go to Quiso, and Cran help you when I get back. I shan' need anythin' from you, except half a dozen soldiers. Here are the names of the particular men I want: go and get them yourself, now." And do you know, banzi, Han-Glat just took the list out of her hand and went off to fetch them? "And you, Shakti," she said, "get my clothes and stuff together, and hurry up about it. I'm takin' you and Zuno and Occula, that's all."

'So about an hour later, banzi, we were let down on a rope over the eastern wall of the upper city, hardly a quarter of a mile from your house. There was no other way out, you see: we couldn' go into the lower city, and as for the Red Gate, Eud-Ecachlon had the citadel and that was that.

'You'd have thought Fornis was off to a festival. Do you know, if I'd been some stranger who didn' know what a cruel, wicked woman she was, I believe I'd have found myself admirin' her that mornin'? You

1033

could see how she'd kept herself in power all those years. The Palteshis we had with us would have done anythin' for her, and she—well, she treated them exactly as if she was their officer—checkin' their weapons, givin' them nicknames and encouragin' them and makin' jokes and—well, all the rest of it. I got the notion that above all else she wanted to distract their minds from any idea that she was runnin' away. She spoke several times about "When we get back" and how they could all look forward to Melekril in Bekla, and a lot more stuff like that. She acted as if she was in the very best of spirits.

'"Are you reckonin' on walkin' the whole way to Quiso, Folda?" I asked her as we were startin' out.

'"How else?" she answered. "It'll do you all good—blow the cobwebs away. It's only a hundred miles: I could be there and back in ten days. Why? Doan' you fancy it?"

'"But the mountains, esta-säiyett?" asked Zuno. (He wasn' lookin' a bit happy: not his idea of fun at all, of course.)

'"Never been there?" said she. "Very beautiful, Zuno: you'll like them, though of course we shall have to hurry through rather, if we're to get to Quiso before the Rains. Step out, my lad! I've got a hundred meld on you to be the first man into Gelt!" They all laughed at that—except Zuno. I believe she really *was* enjoyin' herself. She felt quite certain—she had for years—that nothin' could really get the better of her in the long run.

'At firs' we went straight up the Gelt high road. But durin' that mornin' I began to have a very strange feelin'. At the time I thought it mus' be the heat. It was swelterin' hot—you've no idea. Some of the soldiers were close to droppin', and she was carryin' his pack for one of them, if you please. She was carryin' as much weight as any of the other nine of us, and more than some.

'The feelin' was that I had to get Fornis to leave the highway. And then I realized it was Kantza-Merada speakin' in my heart. She was tellin' me what to do. Only I wasn' to learn everythin', because if I had, I'd have got so frightened that I'd probably have made Fornis suspicious by actin' unnaturally. For that matter, you know, the gods have carried out their purposes through idiots and children before now. Their agents doan' have to understand what they're doin'—not for the purposes of the gods they doan'.

'About noon we spotted a village off to the west, in a patch of trees on the plain. It's very bare country, you know, north of Bekla, before you get up into Urtah. Just the plain one side and the Tonildan Waste the other and the road goin' on for mile after mile, up one slope and down the next. Any trees you see have usually been planted, to make a bit of shade and shelter—near a well, as a rule, for there aren' any rivers—not one.

'"How about a rest and a bite over there in the shade, Folda?" I said. "You can' expect everybody to have your kind of stayin' power."

'Well, at first she said no, but after a bit I managed to persuade her that there was no point in wearin' them all out on the first day; so we went about a mile off the road, down a track to the village, and had some sour wine and a meal in a dirty little tavern. She kept the hood of her cloak up and anyway there was hardly anyone there but us.

'From then on, banzi, I was puttin' everythin' I had into workin' on her the same as I worked on Sencho. I knew what I had to do. Oh, but it was far, far harder than with Sencho, and that was hard enough! And that knife business with the Urtan fellow at the party that night—that was child's play compared to this. A strong, cunnin', powerful woman, still in her prime! You see, I had nothin' to go on at all except what Kantza-Merada was tellin' me. I didn' know myself what my purpose was supposed to be. All she'd vouchsafed to me was that I *must* keep Fornis off the high road—away from other travellers—as we went on across the plain.

'When she was ready to go, I suggested that if we were to stay on the open plain there'd be more chance of a bit of sport with her bow. She was always a great one for that, you know. Well, so we went on by cattle-tracks to the next village and the one beyond that, arrows on strings all the time. She shot a couple of kites, both of them busy with carrion, and one of those wild dogs. We came on a pack that apparently didn' know enough to keep out of bowshot—not out of her bowshot, anyway.

'When we stopped for the night she was still in good heart. She'd been sayin' we were goin' to camp, but as things turned out we lodged in a little sort of hamlet—a very poor, pinched place, where they were only too glad to see the colour of our money. She made me sleep with her. She'd told the soldiers she kept me as a sort of personal bodyguard, and she sent Ashaktis off to sleep somewhere else. She enjoyed vexin' Ashaktis from time to time, you know: it was all part of the queer relationship they had with each other.

'Well, I needn' go into all the details, banzi, but by the next night I suppose we must have been thirty or thirty-five miles from Bekla, with about twenty miles to go to the Gelt foothills. And that was when the goddess began speakin' again, and when I began gettin' really frightened.

'I can' explain this, even to you: I couldn' explain it to anyone who didn' know it for themselves. I remember once, back in Silver Tedzhek, when I was no more than about eight, I heard Zai talkin' to an old priestess. An' I understood what they were talkin' about all right, even though I couldn' have explained it. She said "Great sufferin', unendin' longin' and continual prayer: when these trench and water the heart, the goddess will spring up in it at last."

'Well, she was springin' up now all right, and I hadn' been so frightened since I crossed the Govig—no, not even on the night when we killed Sencho—because what she told me—*all* she told me—was that we were gettin' closer and closer to a place of terrible dread and power. The dread was like a sort of invisible mist, thickenin' all the time we went on, because we were gettin' nearer and nearer to this place, whatever it might be. And I was the only person who could feel it, banzi; the only person out of all the ten of us. The soldiers were all cheerful enough, and Ashaktis seemed in better spirits than when we started. The only person who noticed the state I was in was Zuno: he couldn' imagine the reason, but at least he showed me a bit of consideration; and I was glad of it, I can tell you. I felt as though an invisible thunderstorm was comin' up, darker and closer all round me. Only this wasn' thunder; it was fear; fear in the very air I was breathin', in my lungs and my heart. And all the time Kantza-Merada was sayin' to me, "This furnace is bein' heated for you: it's *your* place that is comin', and *your* hour." Closer and closer and worse and worse, until I could hardly go on. Once, for about half an hour, I couldn' even breathe properly. My lungs sort of closed up and the air itself seemed thick as blankets: it was like drownin' on dry land. Fornis thought I was puttin' it on because I wanted to stop for a rest, and she began teasin' me. I let her go on thinkin' that. The breathless fit passed off after a time, but I was still afraid.

'That second night I couldn' sleep. Fornis had had me do what she wanted and she was sleepin' sound as a child, while I lay sweatin'. At last I slipped out of bed and went outside. It was a bright, clear night full of stars, but that didn' make me feel any better. I had a horrible fancy that the stars were like those studs they fix inside a guard hound's collar, so that you can control it by twistin'. I was the hound, and the goddess had me by the collar, pressin' the studs of the stars against my throat. I remember beggin' her for relief, but all she said in my heart was "Remember your father. That is why you have been brought here."

'I wandered down between the huts until I came to the far end of the village. I felt drenched in fear—you could have squeezed it out of me. I scarcely knew what I was doin'. I believe I was goin' to run away— anywhere, just as long as it was away. And then, suddenly, someone near me said, "Occula!"

'It was a girl's voice and I knew I'd heard it somewhere before. That was all—I was in such a state that I thought it must be a ghost. I looked all round in the starlight and again the voice said, "Occula" very quietly, sort of quick and low.

'And then I saw her, crouched down in the bushes. I went across to her. She was real all right. D'you know who it was? It was Chia, the girl you hit over the head with the fryin'-pan at Lalloc's: the girl you bought and sent home, remember?'

'Cran almighty!' said Maia. 'Of course I remember her! Yes, of course, she *was* Urtan, wasn't she?'

'She clutched my wrist. "Occula!" she said. "I saw when you came this evenin'. It's her, isn' it? It *is* her?"

'"Yes," I said. "It's her all right."

'"I knew it," she said. "I knew I couldn' be wrong. I've told them, Occula."

'"Told who?" I said.

'"Them. Tomorrow you go that way, look." She pointed across the plain in the dark, and it was exactly where the fear was comin' from. "It's only a mile or so," she said. "Not far at all."

'"But how did you know I was goin' to come out here?" I asked.

'"I knew," she said. "I was waitin' for you."

'"I'm half mad with fear now," I said. "Where are we goin', Chia? What is it I have to do?"

'And do you know what happened then, banzi? She stood up and put her arms round me and she whispered, "I'm afraid darlin' Shockula's in for a bit of an ock! But I'll pray for you, my dear."

'And then she was gone. But suddenly I didn' feel afraid any more. Oh, yes, the fear was still there. It was like a great, deep lake, stretchin' all round me, and I was still in it. But before, I hadn' been able to swim, and now I could. That's the only way I can put it.

'I went back to the hut and slept till mornin'.

'We were up about an hour after dawn and I felt as though I'd said good-bye to everythin' and everyone I'd ever known. The men cleared up and packed their kit. Ashaktis paid the Elder and Fornis told me to go and ask our best way. I went off and pretended to ask some of the village people, and then I came back.

'"They say that's best, Folda," I said, pointin' where Chia had. You could see now, by daylight, the ground slopin' up out of the village for about a mile; up to the top of a kind of ridge—quite easy goin'. She'd nothin' to say against it and we set out.

'I knew then that all I had to do was listen to the goddess and commit myself completely to obeyin' her, even to the point of layin' down my life. Lay down my life? Oh, that seemed easy, compared with the fear she'd taken away.'

Occula paused for a few moments, as though listening. Then she got up, went quietly over to the door and suddenly flung it open. There was no one outside. She shut it, came back, sat down beside Maia and continued in a lower voice.

1037

'We were in Urtah, now, of course. I doan' know how much you know about Urtah, banzi, but it's all grazin' country up there, green and well-watered—the valley of the Olmen. We'd crossed the Beklan plain and now we were comin' into the Urtan cattle country. When we got up to the top of that ridge we could see it all spread out below. The change, after the plain—well, I suppose it struck me all the harder because I hadn' been expectin' it. It was so green: in spite of the time of year it was scarcely dried up at all. It was like a sort of huge cattle-meadow goin' on for miles; an enormous saucer with low hills all round the edge. They've looked after it for generations, of course, and Cran only knows how much cattle-dung and stuff must have gone into it. We could see a good many villages, and I thought I could make out the Olmen—oh, must have been eight or nine miles away; but it was all mixed up with horizon haze, and smoke, too, from the villages on the skyline. And there were these great flocks—sheep as well as cattle—all over the grasslands, with dogs and little boys and girls herdin' them. I s'pose you've done it yourself, haven' you?'

'Well, sort of,' answered Maia. 'But 'course we never had all that many beasts, you see.'

'It certainly was a sight—talk about prosperous! That's what the soldiers thought, too, and Ashaktis and even Zuno. Only he was limpin' already. He'd already told me he didn' know how he was goin' to last out the day. I remember one of the soldiers shadin' his eyes and saying, "Shakkarn! There's a few thousand meld walkin' about down there!" And Fornis said, "Well, Taburn, when we get back I'll give you a farm, if you think you can live with the Urtans." And he said, "Ah, that's just it, esta-säiyett, isn' it? The bulls'd be all right, but what about the men?" "Kill them off," said Fornis. "Slaughter the men and keep the bulls." So they went on jokin' like that as we began comin' down off the ridge.

'I'd been doin' my best all along to keep up my act as the Sacred Queen's favourite, but now I could hardly manage it any more. The goddess had risen up erect in my heart, like a snake that's goin' to strike; and me—I was like a hinnari string—ready tuned, oh yes; but so taut I could have screamed.

'"You're very quiet this mornin', Occula," says Fornis. "Somethin' on your mind?"

'And it was just at that very moment, banzi, as she said that, that I saw—oh, how can I make you understand? Were you ever plagued by wasps in summer, until you went out to find the nest and destroy it? You know—you walk along the edges of the fields, and the banks and patches of trees, and then perhaps you see one or two wasps comin' and goin', and then more, and you get closer until at last you come on a hole or perhaps just a crack in a ditch, and then all of a sudden you realize there they are, crawlin' in and out in hundreds: the place your trouble's been comin' from. This was like that, only a million times worse.

'It wasn' far away—about half a mile below us. There were three very strange-looking rifts—sort of chasms—side by side on the open grassland. They were narrow, and the same distance between each; and they were all the same length, as if someone might actually have made them, a long time ago; only it would have to have been a god or a giant, because they were big—oh, I suppose three or four hundred yards long, each of them. You couldn' see how deep they were, because they were full of trees, and the branches stretched right across like a sort of carpet—they were as narrow as that. The grass and weeds were growin' tall all round them—you could see no flocks ever went there: and there were no paths leadin' to them; nothin'. And this was where the fear was comin' from—tens of thousands of ills and terrors and evils, creepin' out and flyin' off into the air. They were about their own business, and it wasn' men's business; and oh, banzi, I was the only one of us who could feel them or know they were there! I'm a dead girl, I thought: no human bein' can know that and go on livin'. Yet still I wasn' afraid, because it was *my* death. It was my own death, for Zai and for Kantza-Merada, and I was entirely ready for it.

'"Oh, no, Folda," I said—and I felt as though I was in a play, speakin' words through a mask—"No, I was just lookin' at those funny clefts down there and wonderin' what they could be: only I've never seen anythin' quite like them before, have you?"

'"Where?" she said, and then she caught sight of them for herself. "Why, no, I haven'," she said. "You're right; they *are* funny. Come on, we'll go down and have a look at them; it'll be a bit of sport. I wonder how deep they are."

'So she led the way down in the sunshine; and I was walkin' beside her while she talked away. And then all of a sudden she stopped and said, "Ah, here's someone comin' to meet us. He'll tell us, I expect."

'It was an old man who was comin'; a man who looked a bit like a priest, very grave and dignified, but roughly dressed and shabby-lookin' compared with the priests in Bekla. Although it was so hot, he was wrapped in a cloak and he was walkin' with a long staff; it had symbols cut on it and some sort of letters, too. There were two or three younger men with him—just ordinary herdsmen, they looked like. I didn' notice anythin' particular about them.

'The old man bowed to Fornis and greeted her very courteously and then he asked her whether we were strangers travellin' through.

'"Yes, that's right, my good man," she said, "but you needn' think you're goin' to get any sort of toll out of us, though I doan' mind givin' your men the price of a drink. But since you're here," she went on, before he'd had time to answer, "perhaps you can tell me somethin' about those queer-lookin' ravines. I want to go and have a closer look at them."

'"Can you tell me their name?" he asked her.

'"Oh," says she, "I thought *you* were goin' to tell *me* that. You live here, doan' you?"

'"I do, säiyett," he said; and now I could see—only she couldn'—that in some way I can' explain he'd taken charge of her, like a priest when an animal's taken to the temple. "I and my men will walk down there and show them to you, since you wish it."

'So then Queen Fornis stepped out in front with the old man, and Ashaktis and Zuno and me, we came behind with the herdsmen. But never a word we said to each other—not once. The men said nothin', you see, and it wasn' Ashaktis's way to waste words on people she despised. Zuno was frightened, because he was sure now he wouldn' be able to finish another day and he knew what Fornis had done to the soldier who'd foundered on her march to Bekla after she'd killed Durakkon. As for me, I felt as though I was walkin' to my own execution. I kept lookin' round at the sun and thinkin', "I'm seein' that for the last time." But even now I wasn' afraid. It was all a dream—a trance in the sun, with the grasshoppers zippin' and now and then one of those hollow, flat sheep-bells clopperin' from somewhere along the slope. There were a lot of ant-hills, I remember, and a smell of chamomile and tansy in the air.

'I could hear Fornis laughin' and talkin' to the old man, but he didn' laugh back. He jus' kept up with her, leanin' on his staff and every now and then noddin' as she spoke. I felt—well, I felt we'd become a kind of procession. There was somethin' grave and ceremonial about it, for all Fornis was so glib and so much taken up with the prospect of sport.

'We came to the tall grass surroundin' the ravines, and she led the way straight in, tramplin' it down as she went. We followed her in single file, now, because it was up to your waist and there were a lot of nettles and thistles too: but she didn' mind them; she was so eager to get there.

'So we came up to the lip of the middle ravine. It was very abrupt, like the edge of a cliff, but all overgrown, and the long grass actually tangled up with the leaves of the trees. The trees were growin' out of the sides of the ravine, you see, and their leaves and branches stretched almost right across, as I told you. But now that we were on the very edge, lookin' down, the leaves weren' an unbroken coverin', as they'd seemed when we were up on the ridge. You could see, now, down among the branches and through them. And below them, banzi, below the leaves, there was nothin'—nothin' at all: just bare, stony ground, almost sheer, slopin' down into darkness. Do you remember that day at Sencho's, when we put the two big silver mirrors opposite each other and took it in turns to look in; and you were so frightened? This was far worse. That place went down for ever. It was as though you were lookin' into the night sky from the other side. I tried to imagine it, goin' on and on, down and down, nothin' but stones and rock; not a beetle, not a fly, not a sound since the world began.

'I came back four or five steps from the edge. I felt faint; Zuno actually had to hold me up for a few moments. I knew now what the goddess required of me and why she hadn' told me before: it would have driven me mad and I'd never have got there. I'd thought she only required my death; but she was requirin' more than that. I remember once in Thettit seein' a condemned man brought out, and he was puttin' on one hell of a good act; until he actually saw the scaffold.

'Fornis had come back a few yards, too. "Well," she said—and she actually clapped the old man on the shoulder, as though they'd been in a tavern together—"this'll be a lark, woan' it? How deep is it, do you know?"

'"I can't tell you that, säiyett," he answered.

'"Well, then," she said, "we shall just have to find out, shan't we? Shakti, you'll come, woan' you? Remember the herons in Suba?"

'Ashaktis had looked in and she was white to the lips. "I'm sorry, säiyett," she said. "I'm afraid I'm a little too old for it now. I beg you to excuse me."

'"Oh, Cran's teeth!" said Fornis. "The whole damn' place seems to be full of cowards and weaklin's today, what with you and Zuno. I shall have to think what I'm goin' to do about it later, shan't I? Come on then, Occula! Apparently it's just you and me."

'"Yes, Folda," I said. "Just you and me."

'So then she went off into the bushes by herself. I suppose the truth was that it had loosened even *her* bowels, but it hadn' loosened mine. While she was gone I stood and prayed aloud. I didn' care who heard me—to tell you the truth, by this time I was hardly thinkin' about anyone else bein' there at all. I went through the litany of Kantza-Merada for the last time.

'At the word of the dark judges, that word which tortures the spirit,
Kantza-Merada, even the goddess, was turned to a dead body,
Defiled, polluted, a corpse hangin' from a stake.
"Most strangely, Kantza-Merada, are the laws of the dark world
  effected.
O Kantza-Merada, do not question the laws of the nether world."

The goddess from the great above descended to the great below.
To the nether world of darkness she descended.
The goddess abandoned heaven, abandoned earth,

Abandoned dominion, abandoned ladyship,
To the nether world of darkness she descended.'

Occula was sobbing. After a few moments she dug her nails into her palm, drew a deep breath and went on.

'I was just finishin' when I felt a hand on my shoulder. I stopped and looked round: it was the old priest. I knew now that he was a priest. He was a herdsman, but he was the priest of that place, too: whenever there was anythin' needed to be done, as you might say.

'He stared into my eyes for what seemed a long time. At last he said, "Those whom I serve have spoken in my heart and told me that you are the one appointed to carry this out. Am I right?"

'"Yes," I said.

'"But you have no weapon."

'"I'm the weapon," I answered.

'He stared into my eyes again and then he said, "Even here there is the frissoor. You have it. Do as you judge best. I will pray for you."

'And then Fornis came back, all stripped and ready. She patted Zuno on the cheek. "Cheer up, little chap," she said. "If I doan' forget, I'll stick a knife in you this afternoon, and then you'll have nothin' more to worry about, will you? Now come on, Occula, if you're ready."

'And with that, and without a moment's hesitation, she went over the brink of the ravine, and I went after her.

'Now I'll try to explain the way of it, banzi, as best I can. First, at the top, there were the trees. The side wasn' absolutely sheer—not to begin with: it was a steep, earthy slope, with the trees growin' out of it—small oaks and thorn and that sort of thing. They were growin' outwards from the face, so you could catch hold and slither down between them from one to another.

'We pushed through the first branches and leaves, and even there it felt uncanny and threatenin'. Those leaves seemed to be whisperin' all round us, and I had a horrible feelin' that they knew we'd come; or that somethin' did, anyway. The upper leaves were very thick and green—they had the air and light, of course—but then, almost at once, only a few feet down, they got fewer and yellower, as if they were sick or in prison. And then we were down among the trunks, with their gnarled, exposed roots, and the earth and stones. If you'd let go of whatever you were holdin' on to, you'd just have gone slidin' straight down.

'As my eyes began to get used to the light I made myself look down, and I could see that where the trees ended—they got fewer, you see, and more spindly, until there weren' any more—there was a kind of ledge—a shelf, not regular but more or less level; I suppose it might have been four or five feet wide, but only here and there. Fornis had got down there already, quick as a cat, and she was waitin' for me. I reached it about twenty yards away from where she was standin'. I stopped a moment to get my breath and then I went along towards her.

'I didn' say anythin': it wasn' time yet. I looked up and there was green light above, comin' through the leaves; it wasn' like the light in an honest, decent wood, but sort of thick and waverin', like light under deep water; and it was all criss-crossed by the branches, like the bars of a cage. We were in a cage—a cage with a ceilin' but no floor.

'Before I reached her I went to the edge and peered over. It was sheer from then on. Only there were projections here and there—spurs of rock and so on. It would be just possible to climb down, if you were crazy. What you'd be goin' down into was nothin'; empty darkness. And the goddess was tellin' me I had to go. There was only me, all alone, against the strength and power of that wicked woman. Oh, banzi—'

Occula was clasped in Maia's arms, shuddering and moaning like a child woken from nightmare. Maia stroked and kissed her, murmuring reassurance, and after a little the black girl went on.

'Fornis was standin' with her hands on her hips, smilin' and lookin' sort of exultant. You could see she was pleased with herself. She was always excited by danger—any sort of demandin' exploit. As I stepped back from the edge she called out "Occula—"

'And then even she was frozen with horror, and worse than horror: for the moment she spoke it was as if the whole place had been set on fire, leapin' with voices like flames. "Occula! Occula! Occula!" They weren' ordinary, decent echoes. In fact I doan' believe now that they were echoes at all; and if you'd heard them you'd feel the same. They were *voices*—of creatures, of bein's about whom we know nothin', through the mercy of the gods. How can I call them evil or mad, when words like goodness and sanity had no more meanin' in that place than they have out beyond the furthest star? Hell isn' people torturin' you, banzi: I know that now. Hell's nothin': hell's not-things takin' the place of things. Silence is a natural thing; and these voices were neither speech nor silence, and that's the only way I can put it. Just to hear them was an agony, and I mean a *real* agony, like burnin'. They seemed to tear through your head. I fell down, and for all the sense I had left I might have gone over the edge; but I didn'.

'Then Fornis put her hand on my shoulder and shook me; and she stooped and whispered in my ear, not to wake those voices again. She said, "Do you want to go on, or are you afraid?"

'And still it wasn' time. I wondered how much more the goddess expected I could suffer. I thought, "Does she want her weapon to break in her hand?"

1043

'I nodded, but Fornis seemed to be hesitatin', so I went to the edge again and looked down. I had to get her to go on: that was my first task. This time I was tryin' to pick a way of goin' down from one handhold and foothold to the next. As soon as I'd seen what I thought was a possible way—if you could call it that—I jus' caught her eye and then let myself over without a word.

'She was followin' me now: she had to if she was comin', for there was no other way down—not in either direction, as far as you could see. I knew the goddess had put it into her heart that she wasn' goin' to be beaten by me, so it was just a question of whether I could survive long enough. Banzi, I can'—I honestly can' describe to you the terror of climbin' down into that place. It was shiverin'ly cold, and not wet but very smooth, so that everythin' I touched felt slippery—dry and slippery, like a snake's skin. Once a stone I was holdin' pulled out of the sheer face, and I just managed to grab another in time. I needed bare feet. I kicked off my sandals and they fell away, but there was no sound from below to show when they'd reached bottom. And I'll tell you somethin' else. I'd cut my hand, and it was bleedin' green. That's the truth.

'As long as I doan' fall, I thought, it doesn' matter how far down we go: I shall never come back anyway. I was out of my mind by this time, and I felt full of a sort of mad elation, as if I'd drunk a flask full of djebbah. That's why I doan' remember any more. I can' even guess how deep we went: it may not really have been very far—I doan' know. It felt like a mile.

'At last, in a place where you could just see—only there was nothin' to be seen now; not even earth; only the rock—I came to a second ledge, a bit longer than the height of a man and only a foot or two wide. And there, in the rock face, I caught sight of an almost regular, zig-zag crack that looked a bit like the symbol for "Zai". So I knew this was the place, and I stood still and waited for Fornis.

'She was down about a minute later. One of her fore-arms was bleedin' green, too; and her hair was green. She'd been changed, ready for what I had to do. I gave her my hand onto the ledge and we stood there together while she got her breath. Then she whispered, "I think this is far enough, doan' you?"

'"Yes, this is far enough," I answered.

'I pulled her round by the arm to face me and looked into her eyes, and I knew she couldn' look away. But still she wasn' afraid—not yet.

'"Why are you lookin' at me like that?" she asked. She was angry.

'"I want to ask you a question," I said. "Where did you get the emeralds in the Sacred Queen's crown?"

'She didn' answer, but I could see now that she knew. My question had fallen into her heart as my sandals had dropped into the abyss.

'"Do you remember the black jewel-merchant who came to Bekla across the Harridan?" I asked her.

'*Now* she was frightened all right! You wouldn' think it possible, would you? Water could flow uphill: Queen Fornis was frightened.

'"Do you remember he had a little girl?" I said. "No, look at me! Do you remember?"

'She shrank back, but I had her by the arm. "You? I gave orders for your death!" she cried. She was past rememberin' the voices, and the whole frightful place rocked and rang in the dark, "Death! Death! Death!"

'But I'd been changed, too. Those voices were subject to the goddess, and now she'd possessed me entirely. I'd become like a rock in a flood.

'I was still lookin' steadily into Fornis's eyes. As I raised my right hand she did the same, and we stood opposite each other like that. I stepped forward and drew her knife from the sheath at her belt and she never moved. I offered it to her hilt first, and she stretched out her arm and took it. Yes, she took the knife from me, banzi, jus' like Ka-Roton that night in Kembri's hall; and then, as we still stood face to face, she turned the point round and drove it straight into her own heart.

'The green blood came spurtin' out, and as she sank down on her knees I pointed over the edge. "Your little boys are waitin'," I said, "and Dur-akkon, your friend!" And all the voices howled and clucked and cackled, "Friend—end—end—end!"

'And at that she fell all along, with her head and shoulders across the edge, and I put my foot against her body and pushed, and she screamed and went over, with her own knife still stickin' in her breast. And then I fainted, because the goddess had left me alone with the voices and the screamin'.

'I must have lain unconscious a long time: I doan' know how long. When I came to myself I was lyin' on the ledge with my arms soaked in Fornis's blood. It was only then I realized how narrow it was. It was barely wide enough to lie down. I doan' know why I hadn' fallen.

'The goddess was gone: I was by myself in the dark. I felt cold, and very hungry and thirsty.

'The reason I can' tell how long I was unconscious is because I doan' even know how long it took me to climb back. That was almost as hard as goin' down had been. I'd finished what the goddess required and she had no more use for me. If I could manage to get myself back, that was my business. She wasn' concerned one way or the other; and I certainly hadn' the gall to pray to her to save me. But as I groped and clutched and panted and clambered I felt Zai's peace in my heart, holdin' me up as often as I had to stop and hang on until enough strength came back into my arms to start pullin' up again.

1045

'The evil and the loneliness were worse than the danger; so bad that once or twice I nearly let go, just to bring it all to an end. I went so slowly: I seemed to be climbin' for hours; but I was climbin' towards the light, and that was what saved me. I could see that greenness filterin' down from above, comin' nearer, and after a long time I began to feel more confident of gettin' out.

'At last I pulled myself back up onto the first ledge again, with the stunted trees just above, and there I stood and prayed and gave thanks to the goddess, not for savin' me but for what was accomplished and ended. I stood prayin' until my heart was emptied of prayer, like drainin' a cup. I'd never prayed like that before.

'When I stepped out into the grass it was late afternoon by the sun and the day was coolin'. I waded out by a different way, and as I left the tall weeds and grass and sank down on the turf—oh, banzi, you can' imagine what that felt like! It wasn' just knowin' you were goin' to live; it was havin' left that place behind—I saw the old priest comin'. He stooped and pulled me to my feet as if I'd been a little girl, and then he took me in his arms without a word.

'I didn' say anythin', either—not for—oh, minutes, I suppose. At last I whispered, "It's done. Shall I go now?"

'At that he released me and stood back, shakin' his head. We sat down together on the short grass in the beautiful, calm evenin' smellin' of dew and tansy. Seemed as though I'd never seen evenin' before, and the swifts wheelin' and screamin' overhead like blessed spirits. I was cryin'. I said, "Where are the soldiers?"

'"Gone," he answered.

'"And Ashaktis?"

'"She is dead."

'I didn' ask him how. It was nice of him to have tidied up for me.

'"Zuno?"

'"He shall stay here with you until—"

'And at that, banzi, I interrupted him. It surprises me now: but I interrupted him because I was frightened. "You mean I'm to be kept here, sir?" I cried. "You mean to keep me here?"

'He took my hand again.

'"My child," he said very gently, "you have come alive from the Streels of Urtah, like the Lord Deparioth's own mother. In all the years I have served the Streels this has never happened—no, nor yet in my lifetime, so far as I know. Yet even so, if that were the whole of it, you might perhaps go your way, though I should be sorry, for you would die and you deserve better. But there is more. You have been the instrument of those nameless ones who bring retribution upon crimes beyond mercy or forgiveness:

1046

upon those whose lives, continuin', defile the very earth. My child, you are deodand. Where you have been and what you have performed have taken you beyond the circle of life."

'"I know that," I said.

'"If you want to come back; if you want your life to continue and not to be forfeit to the gods, you must undergo purification and the ritual of return. To have come alive from the Streels is to be a livin' phantom, until we have done what is needful for you."

'"But will my goddess accept your ritual?" I asked. "My gods are not yours."

'"All gods are the same here," he said. "I shall invoke her for you, and she will hear. You need have no fear on that score."

'"How long—?" I was beginnin', when he added, "The rains will begin soon. You are welcome to spend Melekril here with us—you and the young man too."

'And so I did, banzi. I woan' tell you about all the rites and ceremonies and prayers. I couldn', anyway. They're secret, and I've already told you far more than I ought. It was a long business and a lot of sufferin', for the shock had gone far deeper than ever I realized that evenin'. I stayed all through Melekril, and I found more kindness and peace in that place than anywhere in my life since I left Silver Tedzhek. But when the spring came back—the spring before last—I was as fresh and strong as the leaves, and as ready to return as the kynat.

'One fine mornin' we set out together, Zuno and I. We went east to the high road and travelled back to Bekla with one of the iron caravans comin' in from Gelt. It only took four days.'

: 105 :

MAIA ANSWERS A QUESTION

'Go on,' said Maia, as her friend fell silent. Occula's tale had affected her so deeply that she felt almost as though she herself had been carried into that other world of terror, and now also needed help to recover diurnal reality and mundane things. She wanted—she longed desperately—to hear and chat about living people and their affairs and fortunes. And Occula must need that, too. 'Tell me about Bekla. Tell me everything that's happened since I left with Zenka and Anda-Nokomis.'

Occula caressed and kissed her, smiling. Her happiness at being once more in Maia's company—at being able actually to see and touch her—was evident enough.

'Homesick, eh?' To all appearances she had resumed her old self, her terrible story cast aside like a black cloak from a brightly-coloured robe. But certainly Maia—who if not she?—could sense that this was partly acting; nevertheless it was acting which, given the right response, would soon become reality.

'P'raps. Little bit. Go on, Occula!'

'Well, what shall I tell you?' said the black girl, reaching across for the Yeldashay. 'When we got back we found a whole lot had happened. To begin with, Santil had taken Bekla—that was just after the rains began— and Kembri was dead. The way it all came about was like this. Elleroth was forcin' his way up through Purn, and he'd been joined by the Ortelgans—oh, yes, well, of course you know that: I ought to say you *did* that, oughtn' I? Apparently they only jus' managed to cut through Purn before the rains. What Elleroth wanted was to seize the bridge over the Zhairgen—the road to Ikat—if he could, and cut Kembri off from Bekla. Well, apart from the rains, which put a lot of his men down with fever—'

'Ah!' said Maia. 'A few hours of it was enough for me. I was took real bad.'

'I'm not surprised. Well, seems Elleroth and Ta-Kominion only had about four hundred men between them by the time they actually got to the road. But then they were joined by young Seekron and Mendel-el-Ekna, who were tryin' to get Randronoth's lads back to Lapan after failin' to take Bekla. And that lot, all together, were too much for the men Kembri had left at the bridge. They surrendered to Elleroth.

'Santil had marched north out of Ikat with the idea of attackin' Kembri in Lapan. When he started, he didn' feel there was really much hope of beatin' Kembri and gettin' to Bekla before the rains—he's told me as much himself, actually. Still, he thought he ought at least to try and attack the Chalcon army again as soon as possible, and not just sit around doin' nothin' while Kembri pulled them together. But what actually happened was that with Santil in front of them and Elleroth and the Lapanese behind, they mutinied. There was a commander called Kapparah.' Occula grinned. 'I've been to bed with him, actually. A real, hardened campaigner if ever there was one.'

'I remember Shenda talking about him,' said Maia. 'He was the one as did so well in the battle on the road, wasn't he?'

'That's the fellow. Well, he led the mutiny. He said that with half a dozen different factions fightin' all over the empire and the whole place in chaos we'd have King Karnat down on us any day—obviously he must know very well what was goin' on—and the time had come to put a stop to it. They killed Kembri, of course; cut him down outside his own tent and sent his head to Santil. I can' honestly say I felt sorry.

1048

'So then Santil joined them and took over the command, and they marched fifty miles to Bekla in the rains—leastways, the ones who got there did. Elleroth wasn' with them, though. Seems he'd got badly cut up in a skirmish. One of his officers, a man called Mollo, saved his life and took him home to Sarkid. D'you know, I've never met Elleroth to this day? I often wish I had. I fancy the sound of him. He's quite a lad, by all accounts.'

'Ah, he is that,' said Maia. 'I liked him very much. I don't think he'd be one to bounce you, though, somehow.'

'Oh, no?' said Occula. 'Want to bet? He might get the chance yet, you never know. Anyway, where was I? Oh, yes, Santil takin' Bekla. Well, there were plenty of high-up people in the upper city who managed to change sides quite successfully. Santil's a merciful man, you know. In fact, I'd say a very merciful man indeed, as I'll tell you in a minute. But the real genius behind the side-changin' lark was Shenda. It made his fortune—and mine too, I s'pose, really. For that's how I come to be here now, my dear, drinkin' this bowl of Yeldashay.'

'Shenda?' said Maia. 'But you were saying just now as Han-Glat was holding Bekla, after he'd got rid of Fornis.'

'Yes, well, but this was where Shenda came in. You remember, of course, that Shenda was wounded and stayed in Bekla after he'd come back with Elvair. I told you how he came up from the temple that night to give Fornis the chief priest's message. I've often thought it's wonderful how the most unexpected people sometimes rise to an occasion—especially when somethin' has to be done and there's no one else to do it. Those last few days before the rains, that boy really got busy. You could say he revealed a real flair for diplomacy. Well, but he's a likeable lad, isn' he? He talks straight and plain, he always seems cheerful and he's got a knack of makin' people think he's not as clever as they are but all the same he's honest; so they find themselves supposin' they've thought up all by themselves what he wanted them to think but never said in so many words. I've seen him do it again and again now.

'Anyway, Shenda told Han-Glat that he wanted to go up to the citadel to see his father (his father was the castellan, you remember), and Han-Glat said all right. So off goes Shenda like a dutiful son, but when he got there he talked to Eud-Ecachlon. He told him straight out that he thought tryin' to hold the place for Kembri had become a hopeless business. Shenda said why didn' he surrender to Han-Glat and accept a safe-conduct to go home to Kendron-Urtah and succeed his father as High Baron, which was what the gods had always meant him to do?

'Well, poor old Eud-Ecachlon never was very bright, was he? I reckon he could have asked fifty thousand meld for handin' over that citadel to

Han-Glat. *I* would have. I mean, it's quite impregnable, it was victualled for about a year and he could have held it against Santil and Han-Glat put together if he'd wanted. But anyway, he didn'. Probably he just wanted to get back home as soon as he could. Shenda got him to agree to come and talk to Han-Glat.

'Well, so then Shenda goes back to Han-Glat, if you please, and they talked for hours. Shenda pointed out that Sendekar was comin' from one direction and Santil from another and surely the best thing Han-Glat could do was to drive a bargain while he still had time—I mean, while he still had Bekla to bargain with. Han-Glat could see the sense of that all right. Apart from anythin' else, he had himself to bargain with, you see. Han-Glat's an engineerin' genius: there's no one to touch him in the whole empire. Bridges, roads, fortifications—you let him alone for those. That fortress at Dari—it's a bastin' miracle! I saw it for the first time a week ago. Any commander who passed up the chance of gettin' Han-Glat as an officer of works would be crazy.

'So the long and short of it was that Shenda made Han-Glat think that he himself had decided which side his bread was buttered; and he sent out envoys to Sendekar and Santil and said he'd hand over the city *and* the citadel in return for a high command for himself and no revenge or executions against the remainin' Leopards. Well, they both accepted that quick enough. I mean, the alternative was for Han-Glat to sit comfortably in Bekla through the rains, while they didn'. He's Santil's director of fortifications now: rich and powerful, and everybody's happy.

'So most people managed to sit the thing out quite comfortably. They always do, of course. Well, apart from anythin' else, a city like Bekla's got to be run by people who know it and know how to keep law and order. Santil just took them over, and he's rulin' very well. Everybody likes him. What Shenda's here for now—when he gets to Terekenalt, I mean—is to try to negotiate the return of Suba to the Beklan Empire. Lenkrit's joinin' us in Terekenalt to talk to the new king. I think it'll go well, myself.'

'But you were saying something about Santil being a very merciful man indeed,' said Maia. 'What was all that about, then?'

'Oh, yes, banzi; to be sure! Your friend Elvair-ka-Virrion—'

'Oh, what about him?' said Maia, with a quick shudder. She had not forgotten her last meeting with Elvair at the Barons' Palace.

'Well, of course, if there was one man Santil was in honour bound to destroy it was Elvair. As you remember, when Sencho was killed Elvair took poor Milvushina, who'd been betrothed to Santil, and refused to return her. It was common knowledge that he and Kembri meant to make her Sacred Queen if Elvair had beaten Santil. And they'd have done away with *you*, banzi, doan' you make any mistake about that. Oh, yes, they would!'

'I don't believe Elvair would ever have agreed to harm me,' said Maia hotly. 'I don't care what anyone says—'

'All right, all right, banzi! Calm down! Anyway, if you *were* his friend, one thing's certain: after you left Bekla he hadn' another left in the world, unless perhaps it was Shenda. He was disgraced and ruined beyond all hope of recovery, and he knew it. Well, he'd gone mad, good as, hadn' he? But d'you know who came forward and said she'd always loved him? Who was ready to put herself in danger and plead for him and stick by him? Have a guess!'

Maia pondered. 'I've no idea. Never Otavis, surely?'

'Oh, Cran, no! Otavis—she'd much better fish to fry. Give it up? Sessendris!'

'Sessendris?' said Maia, astonished. 'Well, who'd ever 'a thought it? What happened, then?'

'The way I see it's like this,' said the black girl. 'You remember Sessendris was Kembri's säiyett? Well, Kembri's household was gone, of course, and all he'd possessed was forfeit, wasn' it? Sessendris had to think what she was goin' to do. Mind you, I always liked her—a nice woman. I mean, if only we'd had her at old Sencho's instead of that bastin' Terebinthia, things'd have been very different, wouldn' they? I think she was speakin' no more than the truth when she said she'd always been very fond of Elvair. Anyway, she showed it now: either that or else she took a tremendous gamble to save somethin' for herself out of the wreck of Kembri's household. She went to Santil and begged for Elvair's life, and he actually agreed to spare him—I dare say he thought he was hardly worth killin', he was held in such contempt by everyone—provided she took him away somewhere, to the back of beyond.

'And so she did. They raised enough money between them to buy an estate somewhere up by Kabin, and there they are now, as far as I know.'

'Well, I hope they're happy, that's all I've got to say,' said Maia. 'I always liked Elvair. He was ever so nice to me, and just because he couldn't do that silly fighting—'

'And told everyone he could, and led hundreds of lads to their death,' said Occula. 'Still, we woan' argue about that, my precious banzi. I'll tell you about another man who's got a nice estate nowadays—Zirek. Santil gave him Enka-Mordet's estate in Chalcon.'

'He never!'

'He did. Well, there were no next-of-kin left to inherit, you see, and it needed someone to step in and take over before it all went to pieces. Zirek's married to a Chalcon girl and doin' very nicely, apparently. I can' quite see him runnin' an estate, somehow, can you? But apparently he's thrivin'. He sent me a message—by a pedlar, if you please—sayin' wouldn'

I go down there and stay with them? Well, p'raps I will one day, who knows?'

'But what happened when you got back to Bekla?' asked Maia. 'To yourself, I mean? Do tell me.'

'Oh, to me? Well, it was a bit like you comin' back from the Valderra, only not quite so spectacular, of course. No one knew exactly what had happened, you see. A few people know the name "Streels"—though it's very unlucky to utter it—but no one really knows what they are, or what happens there. That's why I made you swear, banzi; and I strongly advise you never to break that oath, for your own sake.'

'I shan't,' said Maia. 'Don't worry!'

'Well, anyway: they didn' know what had happened, but they knew I'd put paid to Fornis single-handed, because Zuno told them—that and no more. Santil sent for me and more or less offered me whatever I wanted, within reason. I said all I wanted were Zai's jewels that Fornis had stolen. The rest I'd do on my own. He gladly gave me all the jewels, every one of them'—Occula touched for a moment the great emerald at her throat—'and then he said that of course I must have a house of my own in the upper city. Well, when I got to thinkin' about it I didn' see why I shouldn'. After all, N'Kasit had got one—and very well-deserved, too, everybody said. Fordil, too, by the way.'

'Oh, I'm so glad!' cried Maia. 'He was the best of the lot, was old Fordil! If anyone ever deserved honour and glory it was him!'

'Oh, they come from all over everywhere these days, and pay him thousands to teach them; and he plays for the Thlela, of course. Anyway, Santil *did* give me a house, and whose d'you think it was? Whose?'

'Never *mine*?'

Occula nodded, smiling. Maia looked at her with tears in her eyes, but whether of joy or sorrow even she herself could not have told.

'You doan' mind, banzi, do you?' asked Occula, with a touch of anxiety.

Maia shook her head. 'Does the pantry door still stick? Ogma never could remember to get it fixed. Used to drive me wild, that it did.'

'Probably. But tell you the truth, I only lived there until the beginnin' of last Melekril. That was when I joined Shenda and gave up bein' a shearna. We'd both made fortunes, anyway, you see. We're livin' in what used to be Sencho's house: that's a laugh, isn' it? I've changed it completely, of course. You'd hardly recognize it if you went back.'

'Oh, do tell me! Every last thing!'

Occula did so, at length and in detail. 'Kantza-Merada was still in our old place under the floorboard in the bedroom where we hid her that night—the night of the killin'. Remember?'

Maia nodded. 'I'm so glad no one else found her!'

'And I've got Lokris as my säiyett, although, as I said, it's Zuno who really runs the place—specially when we're not there. Only Shenda's been travellin' all over the empire this summer, you see—wherever Santil wants any bargainin' or mediatin' done. I rather enjoy it.'

'I should just about think you would!' said Maia, recalling the triumphant figure riding through the streets that afternoon. 'But what about our friends the shearnas, Occula? Do give my love to Nennaunir, won't you? She was always such a good friend to me.'

''Course I will. She'll be delighted to hear I've seen you again. Well, *she's* given up bein' a shearna, too, 'cos she married Sednil, you know.'

'I always hoped she would. Are they all right?'

'Oh, rather! It was really all along of that four thousand meld you gave the boy for findin' out where your Zen-Kurel had got to. D'you know what he did? He bought himself a share in Sarget's wine business, and he's never looked back. He's prosperin'.'

'Oh, that's just about fine, isn't it? But you mean Sarget really took him—a branded man?'

'Nan told Sarget how unfairly he'd come by the brand: and Sarget said any friend of yours was a friend of his. So you see, banzi, you've gone on doin' good even in your absence. Oh, yes, and that reminds me! Sarget's married Dyphna! What d'you think of that?'

'Dyphna? But Sarget was quite old—all of forty and more, I reckon! I thought he'd never marry anyone.'

'Come right down to it, I think it was the music. Dyphna's got a real feelin' for that, of course. And besides, she's so accomplished and sort of—well, impressive, isn' she? She always put on such a stately sort of act—not like us bouncy girls—you and me, I mean. I think Sarget had come to feel he needed someone classy to match the style of his establishment and do the honours. And I must say she does it very well. Otavis is still in business, though. By Airtha, she's goin' to end up really rich, that girl! She seems to get more beautiful every day. They fairly fight for her.'

'I remember the Belishbans tossing her in a blanket at the barrarz. But Occula, do you know anything about dear old Brero, as used to pull my jekzha? He was always such a good friend.'

'You mean senior tryzatt Brero, of the Beklan regiment? Well, do you know, banzi, I never even knew he'd been one of yours! That's because I was shut up in Fornis's house all those months, of course. Never really knew what was goin' on at all; well, only bits here an' there. Everyone who ever made a friend of you ended up lucky, didn' they?'

Suddenly the door opened and Shend-Lador, magnificently dressed in a

1053

gold veltron with a scarlet cloak, came into the room, started to speak to Occula and stopped dead at the sight of Maia.

'Maia! Great Cran, wherever have *you* sprung from?'

They embraced, Shend-Lador laughing delightedly. He kissed Maia again and again, warmly admired the sleeping Zen-Otal and then enquired after Zen-Kurel (whom he had never met). When he had refilled the goblets and sat down, Maia was obliged to tell her story all over again.

'Poor Meris!' said Shend-Lador, when she had finished. 'But I'm not really surprised. And you say Terebinthia took sixteen thousand meld off you for the boat?'

'Yes, she did. After that I hardly had anything left, 'cept for my diamonds. But there's no point in getting her into trouble now, Shenda. It's all done and over with.'

'Oh, no, Santil wouldn't want to get her into trouble, certainly. But she always was a daylight robber robbing in daylight, and I think it would do her a world of good to have a taste of her own medicine and have to give you back the difference between that and a fair price. What would you say the boat was really worth?'

Maia considered.

'Well, it was a good boat, Shenda. Fact, I'd go so far as to say it was a very good boat. It saved our lives. But it wasn't worth more than eight thousand at the very outside.'

Shend-Lador nodded. 'Where *is* your estate—Zen-Kurel's estate? Somewhere up towards the Blue Forest, isn't it?'

Maia told him.

'I'll see you're sent eight thousand meld within the next two months. We won't do anything to Terebinthia, though, so don't worry.'

'Eight thousand meld! For me? Oh, Shenda, you *are* good! Thank you so much! I *am* grateful!' She kissed him again.

'Sounds as though you could do with it, banzi,' said Occula drily.

'Well, 'course I can! What d'you think?'

'What do I *think*? What do *I* think?' Occula looked Maia very straight in the eye. 'I think, "Banzi, why doan' you come back?"'

Maia started, looking quickly round at Shend-Lador, who nodded, smiling.

'Come back? Why, whatever d'you mean?'

Occula had risen to her feet and was standing with outspread arms. 'Bekla's not the same without you, that's what I mean. *I'm* not the same without you! Lucky, golden Maia! We *all* miss you; the gods' sweetheart! Your name's still a legend in Bekla and it always will be. They still drink to you and sing songs about you. The Thlela have created one of their sacred dances about your deeds and adventures: did you know that? The best thing that could happen to you and to Bekla would be for you to come back to the city you saved—the city you conquered—the city that's yours by right of the gods!'

Maia stared at her speechlessly. Tears were standing in Occula's eyes.

'Banzi, you doan' look all that well off. D'you think I can't price those clothes you're wearin'—the best clothes you've come up to Keril in? And you're obviously as happy as any steward's wife to be promised eight thousand meld—not that that isn' quite a slice, I'll admit. But the Serrelinda! The sacred luck of the city! A small baron's wife in up-country Katria! You'll end up dull as a cow in a field.'

'Why, someone else said that to me once!' said Maia: but she did not say who.

'Is that where you want to live out your life and grow old? Your hands—they look like they did when I first met you in the slave depôt at Puhra; when I beat up that bastard Genshed for you. You work along with your women, I'll bet, and more credit to you! But oh, banzi, what a waste! What a terrible waste!'

Still Maia said nothing.

'You could bring your baby, banzi. 'Course you could! And your husband—he was one of Karnat's personal officers, wasn' he? Santil would give him an honourable command and a house in the upper city. He'd be glad to have a man like that. Why doan' you come back?'

Maia took her hands. Every word had sunk into her heart. She recalled Selperron (whose name she had never known) filling her golden jekzha with flowers. She recalled the people cheering, the young armourers jostling for the privilege of helping to pull her up the hill to the Peacock Gate. She saw in her mind's eye the guests crowding forward at the barrarz, and heard again the sound of Fordil's leks and zhuas as she began the senguela in the Barons' Palace. She heard Elvair, yes and Randronoth, crying out in ecstasy in her arms. She saw the Barb glittering in the summer morning and heard the gongs of the clocks as Ogma prepared her scented bath. She saw, too, her timber manor house in Katria and heard the hands calling to one another in their guttural Chistol as they dispersed after the day's work and Zenka came in to supper.

She put her arms round Occula's neck and kissed her. 'Dearest, shall I tell you the truth—the real truth? I honestly and sincerely don't want to come back. It's not the baby, and it's not thinking what Zenka would want. It's truthfully what *I* want, for my own life. I want to stay as I am. I love it. But don't ask me to explain, 'cos I don't understand myself. Ask Lespa!'

She looked out of the window at the sky. 'It's late. I'll have to be getting back, dearest. Oh, I have enjoyed it so much! Dear, dear Occula! Cran bless and keep you both! I'll be round early tomorrow to see you again before you leave for Terekenalt.'

She picked up Zen-Otal, who stirred, whimpered a moment and then went back to sleep. Occula and Shend-Lador walked downstairs with her, chatting at the door while Florro had the jekzha brought round. In the spring night the town was very quiet. A dog barked, a watchman called from some way off. Maia, gazing up at the clear stars, was already thinking pleasurably of her return home, and of how Zen-Kurel was sure to be looking out for her and would run down to meet her in the lane beside the stream.

The Beklan Empire

WILD LAND

R. Telthearna

GELT MO

SUBA · Lukrait

The Nordesh

U R

Melvda-Rain

River Olmen

Keril ·

Rallur

Kendron

River Valderra

KATRIA

PALTESH

Dari

Bekla

Mt Crandor

The Harridan Neck

Purn Forest

R. Daulis

Border Forest

· Ferry

Fal

The Renda Narboi

Harridan

BELISHBA

· Nybril

SARKI

Desert

Herl

River-Fl